Harper und Brothers

Harper's Young People 1880

Harper und Brothers

Harper's Young People 1880

ISBN/EAN: 9783742802347

Manufactured in Europe, USA, Canada, Australia, Japa

Cover: Foto ©Andreas Hilbeck / pixelio.de

Manufactured and distributed by brebook publishing software (www.brebook.com)

Harper und Brothers

Harper's Young People 1880

HARPER'S

YOUNG PEOPLE

1880

NEW YORK
HARPER & BROTHERS, PUBLISHERS
FRANKLIN SQUARE

INDEX TO ILLUSTRATIONS.

GENERAL INDEX.

POETRY.

Vol. I.—No. 1. | Published by HARPER & BROTHERS, New York. | Price Four Cents.

Tuesday, November 4, 1879. | $1.50 per Year, in Advance.

THE BRAVE SWISS BOY.

I.—THE SWISS PEASANT AND HIS SON.

THE first beams of the morning sun were tipping with fire the jagged and icy peaks of the Wellhorn and Wetterhorn, those gigantic monarchs of the Bernese Oberland, when a slender youth came out to the door of a small herdsman's cottage near Meyringen, and looked up at the sky to note the weather.

"We shall have a splendid day, father," said he, after glancing all around for a few minutes. "There isn't a cloud to be seen, and the fir-trees sparkle like silver in the morning air."

"I am glad to hear it, Walter," replied a powerful voice from inside the cottage, "for I must cross the hill to Grindelwald to-day to see my cousin. It is a long journey, and much pleasanter in fine weather than in rain and fog. You can let out the goats, and look after the cow, for we must milk them before I go."

"Oh, Lieseli is not far off," was the rejoinder; "I see her coming along; she is passing Friedhardt's house now. She is a good cow, and always knows when it's milking-time. But what is that?" he exclaimed, after a short pause. "Friedhardt is driving her into his yard!—Eh, neighbor! what are you doing? Don't

"Yes, of course I do," replied the farmer, roughly. "But I've taken a fancy to the cow, and mean to keep her. You can tell your father that, if you like, and say that if he wants her he can come and fetch her."

"Father! father!" cried the boy, turning round. "Neighbor Friedhardt has taken our cow away. Come and get her back."

Obeying his son's call, Toni Hirzel hastened out of the cottage just in time to see his neighbor locking the byre upon Lieseli, the only cow he possessed.

"Oho, my friend," he exclaimed, "what is the meaning of this?"

"Don't you understand, Hirzel?" replied his neighbor, in a mocking and sarcastic tone. "Recollect what you promised me the other day. You have been owing me forty francs since last winter, and said you would pay me yesterday. But as you have forgotten it, I have taken your cow, and mean to keep her till I get the money back."

Toni Hirzel frowned and bit his lips. "You know very well," said he, "that I have not been able to pay my small debt. My poor wife's illness and funeral cost me a great deal of money; but you know quite well that I am an honest man, and that there is no need for you to behave in such an unkind and unfriendly way toward me. It is not neighborly, Friedhardt."

"Neighborly nonsense!" replied the farmer. "The cow belongs to me until you pay the money."

With these words he turned on his heel and went into his house, the size and general appearance of which be-

tion behind him; but as he was preparing to give a deadly stroke, the point of the sword accidentally struck her a violent blow, and she instantly expired at his feet. Upon seeing what had happened, he immediately surrendered himself, saying he did not wish to live, his earthly pleasure being gone. He was executed the next day, but we fail to perceive on what ground, either of justice or of humanity.

THE PREAY CHAMBER.

By an Old Boy.

BEFORE I had been long at Mr. Gray's boarding-school, to which I was sent when I was a very young boy, and which was very different from such schools as St. Paul's, I heard of a mysterious and horrible place called, as the boys said, the Preay Chamber. We supposed it to be a gloomy

pity my poor little self as I look back upon that moment. I advanced to the master's chair, and stood before him in the presence of the school, with my guilty right hand closed at my side. There was awful silence as the master said,

"Joe, what have you in your hand?"

"Nothing, Sir."

"Joe, hold out your right hand."

I held it out.

"Now, Joe, you say that there is nothing in your hand?"

"Yes, Sir."

"Open your hand, Joe."

I opened it, and the lump of sugar dropped to the floor.

It was the first lie I had ever told, and my terror and shame were such that the recollection has been a kind of good angel to me ever since. The master said a few solemn words, the justice of which my poor little heart could not deny, although he had exposed me to a cruel ordeal; and then,

this time, and for my sake, I hope that you may be let off from the Preay Chamber."

I went back, and with tears and catchings of the breath I repeated the message. Mr. Gray listened; and when I had done, he said:

"Joe, you are a very naughty boy; but as you say that you are sorry, and will try to mend, and as dear Mrs. Gray intercedes for you, you need not go this time to the Preay Chamber. But remember, it is only for this time."

I was like a victim suddenly released from the stake, and the narrow escape I had had from the mysterious chamber of doom made that dungeon still more awful. There were very few references to the chamber afterward, and gradually its name disappeared from our talk and from our fear. Now and then some boy asked, "What has become of the Preay Chamber?" But nobody answered. If an older boy asked Mr. or Mrs. Gray, they only smiled, and said nothing. The terror gradually died away, and the chamber of horrors

CHESTNUTTING.—Drawn by W. P. Snyder.

THE STORY OF A PARROT.

THE children were thinking of something very important. Anybody could see that. Papa and mamma wondered why they were so serious and silent at the breakfast table, and mamma was astonished when Carrie, and even little Hope, begged to walk part of the way to school with Louis, because they had never thought of doing such a thing before. Louis was a bright-faced, curly-headed boy of ten years, Carrie was eight, and little Hope was only six. Mamma was always very kind to her little folks, and as the morning was sunny, she said they might go if they would put on their heavy shoes and their cloaks and hoods, for there was a white crisp frost all over the grass. Mamma watched them with pride as they scampered down the garden path leading from the front piazza to the street, but had she heard their conversation she might have staid at home from the party she was going to that evening, and put a veto on their grand plan.

"Now, Louis," said Carrie, as soon as they were away from the house, "you know you promised to sit up with Hope and me to-night and listen, because nurse says at midnight all birds and beasts talk so children can understand every word; and papa and mamma are going to a party, and they won't come home until ever so late."

"Nonsense!" said Louis, who felt very much wiser than Carrie, she being to his mind "only a girl;" "I don't believe nurse's story. I can always understand what Fritz says, and I say he can not bow-wow any plainer than he did this morning when he bid me good-by."

"Yes, he can," persisted Carrie. "Nurse says so, and she knows, for her grandfather told her all about it when she was a little bit of a girl, and he was a real old, old man. If people believed it so many years ago, it must be true."

Louis's confidence in his own wisdom was somewhat weakened by the thought of nurse's grandfather, but, boy-like, he only began to sing tauntingly:

"Into woods where beasts can talk,

their lessons to mamma, and then went to play with Fritz, the big dog, Snow, the white kitty, Lorito, a large gray parrot, and the new canary which papa had bought only the day before.

When evening came papa and mamma went to the party, and nurse, who had forgotten all about her grandfather and the red and white cow, wondered why the children went to bed so willingly, for they were sometimes very willful, and made nurse a great deal of trouble when she undressed them. She was very glad they were good to-night, because, as "mamma" was away, she had made up her mind to go to a party herself, the house-maid having promised to run up to the nursery if she heard the children calling. There was little danger, however, that they would call for a drink of water or anything else that night, for as they were not in the least sure of nurse's sympathy in their midnight vigil, they had agreed to go to bed as quiet as mice and watch their chance of slipping unobserved to the library, where their pets spend the night. Long after nurse had gone down stairs, and when the house was very, very still, Carrie sat up in bed and gently called her brother, who slept in a little room of his own adjoining the nursery.

"Louis! Louis!" she said.

"Oh, don't bother," answered Louis. "It won't be midnight for ever so long."

"But if we stay in bed we shall go to sleep. Hope is half asleep now."

"No, I'm not sleepy," said little Hope, "and I'm going to get my kitty and go right down to the library this very minute." She rolled out of bed, and went to the basket in the corner where kitty was fast asleep, and bundled her up in her little fat arms.

The children all started to creep down stairs, but they shrank back a little from the dimly lighted hall below, which somehow did not look a bit as it did in the daytime. "Come on," said Louis, who felt very grand as the protector of his sisters; "I've brought my new bow and arrow, and if there is a villain there, you'll see how quick I'll lay him out. I'm not afraid, anyway, where Fritz is," he added, half to himself. They marched along very softly, their little bare feet sinking into the soft velvet carpet. Louis went boldly ahead with his bow and arrow, Carrie followed, her jet-black hair streaming down over her white night dress, and little Hope came close behind, hugging her white kitty, who winked in astonishment at this strange proceeding. When they reached the library, Fritz, who was stretched on the Turkish rug before the grate, in which a piece of English coal was burning slowly, rose to his

had his beak buried in his feathers and his eyes shut fast. He opened his eyes, however, when the children came near, and put down his head to be rubbed, but after a few sleepy grunts he said, "Poor Lorito, poor Lorito," and shut his eyes again. Evidently the children's pets had no inclination to be sociable just at present. Just then the French clock on the mantel-piece struck ten.

"We shall have to wait ever so long," said Louis, "because they won't talk till midnight. Let's lie down on the rug with Fritz."

So the three children cuddled close to the big dog and waited. Louis pulled mamma's blue and red afghan from the lounge, and after tucking it carefully over his little sisters, crawled under it himself, and—

"Bow-wow," said Fritz. "Who's got a story to tell, I wonder? I'm not going to tell one, that's very certain, for I scratched my throat this morning with a chicken bone."

"Mew-mew," said the white kitty. "I've done lots of work to-day. I unwound a big ball of green worsted for my little mistress, and I'm tired. Let somebody else do the talking."

"Peep," said the canary. "I'm a stranger; I only arrived yesterday, and I ought to be entertained. Some other time I will tell you all my adventures, but to-night I prefer to listen. I would like to hear from that gray-coated gentleman over there in the corner, for as he is a very distant relation of mine, both of us belonging to the great bird family, I would, I am sure, take great interest in his history."

"Lorito, you will have to do all the talking to-night," said Fritz and the white kitty both at once. "Tell our new friend Pique all the wonderful things you have seen, and all the strange adventures you have been through."

Thus entreated, the gray parrot, after flapping his wings several times, in a lazy manner, began to tell his history.

"I will begin my story," said the gray parrot, "with the good old times when my grandfather and grandmother lived in the hollow of a giant

THE BOY'S TELESCOPE.

THE parson's boys were very fond of astronomy. They knew the chief constellations, and kept the place of the planets as they moved along among the stars. When their father told them how splendidly the moon and the planets look through a telescope, they were sadly disappointed to learn that a telescope costs so much money that he could not think of buying even one of the smallest size. Happening to hint that perhaps one might be made at home at small expense which would show the moon in new light and bring Jupiter's moons to sight, they gave him no rest till he had agreed that he would "see about it."

A few days afterward he showed the boys two common tin tubes which the stove man had just made. One was

small tube, as it did through the glass alone. It did. "Now," said he, "*if you hold this tube up to Jupiter, at thirty-six inches from the glass there will be a very small image of him and his moons.* If we could only see that image or picture through a microscope, we might see the moons as plainly as we see Jupiter himself with the naked eye."

"Why won't our microscope do?" asked Walter.

The parson said we couldn't get the image and the microscope together rightly; but while he was explaining, he was also unrolling another paper, out of which came a big bulging glass almost as round as a boy's eye. The edges of this had been ground down so that it would go into the end of the small tube, and it was fastened in just as the other was, only the slide needed to be a little longer, because the glass was thicker. This was a one-inch eyeglass; that is, it must be an inch *from the object or image at which you are looking.* He then cut in a piece of paper a round hole about as big as a shirt button, and pasted this over the eyeglass, and covered the end of the tube around, so that no light could come in there except through this small opening in the paper, which was so put on that the eye must look through the middle of the glass. He also pasted some strips of brown paper around the other end of the telescope, jutting over the object-glass just enough to keep it from breaking, and to prevent any light from coming through the edges, but not letting the paper touch this glass, as it did the eyeglass. The object-glass wants all the light it can get.

The boys had the first look; but they could see nothing, though the woods to which the glass was turned were yet visible.

"What's the focus of the glasses?" asked the parson.

"Thirty-six inches and one inch," was the correct answer.

The boys marked where the thirty-six inches ended, measuring from the object-glass. They then brought the eyeglass up to within about an inch of that, and looked through it again.

"Oh-oh-oo!" exclaimed Frank; "I see the trees

hour in a little while. The instrument cost the person only forty cents for the tubes; the glasses were given, but ought not to cost more than a dollar or two. If a one-inch eyeglass can not be had, a two-inch eyeglass will answer quite well. The reason for having two tubes is that eyes differ, and that what is bought for a thirty-six inch glass may be an inch or two more or less than that, so that the smaller tube must be moved back and forth till the eye finds where the view is plainest. This instrument shows the moon beautifully. You read of the circular mountains and the extinct volcanoes; here you see them. It is especially delightful to see in the new moon the light breaking over the mountain-tops and through the notches while all the plain behind is yet in the dark. Though it is now a good while since the person made the telescope, he waits impatiently every month for the new moon to come again.

THE MAGIC BOTTLE.

THERE are few persons who have not been puzzled, when witnessing the exhibitions of conjurers and performers of feats of legerdemain, by the *magic bottle*, out of the neck of which the exhibitor can pour any one of quite a number of liquids at his will. It may interest the reader to see an explanation of the means by which the apparently magical effect is produced, especially as it involves an explanation of a certain philosophical principle which it is very useful for all to understand.

The pressure of the atmosphere all around us is so great that no liquid can issue against it from a close vessel, unless air is at the same time admitted to balance the external pressure by an internal one of the same amount. In the case of pouring water from a bottle the mouth of which is moderately large, the air passes in in large bubbles as the water comes out, producing the gurgling sound always heard in such a case.

Where the orifice is too small to allow of the admission of these bubbles of air, the liquid will only flow out as fast as the air is allowed to enter in some other way, as shown in the engraving, where the water will not issue from the lower end of the tube except when the finger is raised from the upper end so as to admit the air.

There are various ingenious contrivances by means of which curious effects are produced through the operation of this principle. One, called the magic funnel, is made double, with a space inclosed between the walls. There is an orifice communicating with this chamber at the top of the handle, which orifice is so situated that it can be opened or closed at pleasure by the thumb of the person holding it without attracting the attention of the spectator. Now if the body of the funnel is filled, or partly filled, with pure water, while the hidden chamber contains a liquid deeply colored—with cochineal, for example—the person holding it can cause pure water to flow from it by keeping the orifice in the handle closed by his thumb, or colored water by simply raising his thumb and allowing the liquid in the concealed chamber to flow out and mingle with the clear water as it issues from the tube below.

The magic bottle acts on the same principle, though presenting it in another form. The bottle is usually made of tin, though colored on the outer surface to represent glass. Within, it contains several different receptacles, as shown in Fig. 1, each communicating by a separate pipe with the mouth of the bottle. Each of these receptacles is also provided with another tube, by which air may be admitted so as to allow the liquid contained in it to flow. These air tubes open by orifices in the side of the bottle, as shown in Fig. 2, which are covered and concealed by the thumb and the ends of the fingers of the operator, and may be kept closed or may be slightly opened at pleasure.

FIG. 2.

By this means any one of five different liquids may be poured from the mouth of the bottle.

Of course it requires some dexterity to manipulate such an apparatus skillfully, in order to keep all the holes concealed from the spectators, and to open the right one, just enough to admit the air, and at the right time. The point of interest, however, for the general reader in the whole subject is the philosophical principle which is involved, namely, that the pressure of the atmosphere in every direction all around us is such that no liquid can issue from any orifice against the force of it acting *from without inward*, unless by the admission of air or the providing by some other means of an equal force to act *from within outward* as a counterpoise.

TWO WAYS OF PUTTING IT.

The Sultan awoke with a stifled scream;
His nerves were shocked by a fearful dream:

An omen of terrible import and doubt—
His teeth in one moment all fell out.

His wise men assembled at break of day,
And stood by the throne in solemn array.

And when the terrible dream was told,
Each felt a shudder, his blood ran cold,

And all stood silent, in fear and dread,
And wondering what was best to be said.

At length an old soothsayer, wrinkled and gray,
Cried, "Pardon, my lord, what I have to say;

"'Tis an omen of sorrow sent from on high:
Thou shalt see all thy kindred die."

But one of them, stepping before the throne,
Exclaimed, in a loud and joyous tone:

"Exult, O head of a happy state!
Rejoice, O heir of a glorious fate!

"For this is the favor that shall win,
O Sultan—to outlive all thy kin!"

Pleased was the Sultan, and called a slave,
And a hundred crowns to the wise man gave.

But the courtiers they nod, with grave, sly winks,
And each one whispers what each one thinks,

"Well can the Sultan reward and blame:
Didn't both of the wise men foretell the same?"

Quoth the crafty old Vizier, shaking his head,
"So much may depend on the way a thing's said!"

To our Young Friends:

As we can not expect to receive letters from you until you have been notified of the existence of our Post-office Box, we open the correspondence by writing to you, and asking you to think of us in the future. We should like to hear from you upon any subject which may interest you. If you have any questions to ask regarding your studies or your reading, we shall take great pleasure in advising you; or should you desire any information which you can not obtain from books within your reach, we will do our best to aid you. We shall also be glad to hear about your games, your pets, or about any curious thing in nature which may come under your observation.

You must bear in mind that your communications must be very brief, because there are so many of you that we can not give a great deal of space to any one. We will endeavor to be kind and attentive to each and all alike.

It is very easy in these times to send letters in Uncle Sam's big mail-bag; and when you write on your neat, delicate note-paper, and put the pretty postage-stamp on the right-hand corner of the envelope, perhaps you never think of the way your great-grandparents used to work when they wanted to send a letter. First they took a very large square sheet of coarse blue paper, or, if they were young ladies and fancy-minded, one with a bright tint of pink or yellow. As postage was high, when they had written the pages full, straight across, they would turn the sheet sideways, and write at right angles to the other lines, and then cornerwise, perhaps, with a different-colored ink. There were no envelopes in those days, and the sheets had to be ingeniously folded, so that no curious postmaster could pry into family secrets. There was always a portion of the last page left blank, to form the outside of the letter, which, after being folded and directed, was sealed with a big red wafer. It was then ready to be started off the next time the stage-coach came through the town, for there were no railroads in those days, and often the mail-bag was carried miles and miles on horseback through wild regions where now the steam-engine whirls along with its long train of cars.

It was not necessary in those days to prepay the postage, which was much dearer than it is now. There were no postage-stamps, and big figures were written or stamped on the outside of the letter to denote the cost of transportation. In those times it often took weeks to send a letter to places where now only a day is required.

Do any of you know the name of the man who first thought of the great benefit cheap postage would be to the world, and can you tell something about the great work he accomplished in that direction, and when and where he died?

Our Post-office Box is now open for your contributions, which we trust will be neatly and cor

THE ORPHANS.

A boy who is not fond of fun and frolic may possibly make a tolerable man, but he is an intolerable boy.

An Irish lover remarked that it is a great pleasure to be alone, "especially when your sweetheart is wid ye."

If a man's horses should lose their tails, why should he sell them wholesale?—Because he can't retail them.

"I'd just like to see you," said a blind man to a policeman, who told him he would lock him up if he didn't move on.

A little girl of four years was recently called as a witness in a police court, and in answer to the question what became of little girls who told lies, innocently replied that they were sent to bed.

When a certain King of England visited Scotland, many years ago, the following conversation took place between two countrymen:

SANDY. "Weel, Jock, hae ye seen the king?"

JOCK. "Oh ay, I hae seen the king; but I wadna gang the length o' the street to see him again. He's just made like ony ither man, an' they tell't me his arms were a lion an' a unicorn."

A QUANDARY.—If a boy should catch hold of your coat, and ask if he had the wrong pig by the ear, would you answer yes or no?

A REMARKABLE CASE OF SHYNESS.—A sensitive little boy, having been threatened with a whipping, immediately hung his head.

A little girl being asked by her grandfather where cream came from, replied, with the greatest simplicity, "In old grandfather's cow."

A man who lisped, having bought some pigs, asked a neighbor for the use of a pen for a few days. Said "I tell you again," exclaimed the man, angrily, "I mean not two thousand pigs, but two thows and two pigs!" "Oh, that is what you mean, eh? Well, the pen is at your service."

LETTER PUZZLE.

First is in long, but not in short;
Second in leap, but not in small;
Third is Ellen, also in Anna;
Fourth in wagon, not in van;
Fifth in fun, but not in sport;
Sixth in heart, but not in weight;
Seventh in ale, but not in cider;
Eighth in bow, but not in arrow;
Ninth in would, but not in could;
Tenth in water, but not in land.
In these rhymes there may be found
A living poet much renowned.

What is it that always has some hitch about it?—A harness.

Which is the most contemptuous bird?—The owl; he hoots at everything.

GYMNASTIC EXERCISES.

Pole-Leaping.—The pole which is used for this exercise should be of sound ash, rounded throughout its length, which should be in proportion to the height of the jumper and the space to be jumped over. It is advisable to practice this kind of jumping at first without a run. For this purpose he who is about to jump fixes the end of the pole in the ground in front of him, at a distance which may be gradually increased with the efforts of the jumper; then he seizes the pole with his two hands—the top one a little above his head, and the lower one a little above the level of his hips. He springs off equally with both feet, throwing most of his weight upon his arms, and pushing himself forward as far as possible by bearing on the pole, which he then slackens, and falls to the ground, trying to alight as softly as possible. If he fell on his heels, all the body receives a great shock; the brain strikes against the bones which surround it, which may often re- places himself at a certain distance from the space over which he is to leap, and after having seized the pole with his right hand a little above his head (the thumb in the air), and with his left hand a little above his thighs (the thumb downward), he starts forward, holding the lower end of the pole in front of him. Arrived at the edge of the ditch, or whatever it may be, over which he is to leap, he sticks the pole in the ground before him, then, by sudden and active effort, he raises his body, bearing his hands on the pole in such a manner as to turn it from the right-hand side to the left, and leaps the space, the body being nearly in a horizontal position; he then reaches the ground by bending the joints of the legs. He should at first practice at short distances.

Indian Clubs.—The exercises with the Indian clubs are of a more recent date than those with dumb-bells. They were introduced into Europe by a military officer, who had seen the Persians exercise with them. These exercises are performed alternately with the two hands, and sometimes simultaneously, with two instruments of a massive conical form, which in Persia are called *mels*, and in India *mugdurghs*. They are very useful for increasing the muscular power of the arms and shoulders, opening the chest, and strengthening the hands and wrists. They have also the advantage of rendering the player with them ambidextrous, or two-handed; that is to say, of making the left hand as able and vigorous as the right, and enabling him to use one as readily as the other. As instruments of exercise they are as fitted for women and girls as for men and boys. Gracefully used, they give a good carriage and deportment, not always obtained by other means. Dumb-bell practice should precede the use of the Indian clubs. In beginning with the latter, take off your coat and vest, loosen your braces and waistband, and put on a belt.

The most simple exercises with the Indian clubs consist in carrying them to the shoulder, sometimes with the right arm, sometimes with the left—in carrying the club before and behind, to the left and to the right. In the more difficult exercises you move the clubs alternately around the body, seizing them at first by the hand, and holding them parallel to the legs, the arms held down without stiffness, the clubs in a straight line with them. Then raise the right club, without the slightest jerk, in front and near to the body in the direction of the left shoulder, until the forearm passes the head, the club always remaining vertical. Then continue to pass the club behind the body, bringing it toward the right shoulder, and letting it gradually descend to the ground. The same movement is repeated with the left club, by commencing to raise it toward the right shoulder, and so on continually. Practice all the movements slowly; but when you have once familiarized yourself with the exercises you may execute them more quickly, always taking care that one club descends while the other ascends.

A NEW SERIAL
BY GEORGE MACDONALD.

A brilliant serial story by GEORGE MACDONALD, with illustrations by ALFRED FREDERICKS, will shortly be begun in HARPER'S YOUNG PEOPLE.

HARPER'S YOUNG PEOPLE.

HARPER'S YOUNG PEOPLE will be issued every Tuesday, and may be had at the following rates:

Four cents a number.

Single subscriptions for one year, $1 50; five subscriptions, one year, $7 00—payable in advance. Postage free.

Subscriptions may begin with any number. When no time is specified, it will be understood that the subscriber desires to commence with the number issued after the receipt of order.

Remittances should be made by Post-office Money Order, or Draft, to avoid risk of loss.

Published by HARPER & BROTHERS, New York.

Vol. I.—No. 2. Published by HARPER & BROTHERS, New York. Price Four Cents.

Tuesday, November 11, 1879. $1.50 per Year, in Advance.

[Begun in No. 1 of Harper's Young People, November 4.]

THE BRAVE SWISS BOY.

II.—A PERILOUS ADVENTURE.

IT was still early in the day when Walter left the cottage a second time. His heart was cheerful, and his movements light and rapid. Instead, however, of taking the road leading to the inn, he struck off in a zigzag path through the valley toward the Engelhorn, whose jagged and lofty peaks rose far up into the blue sky. After a short time he reached the large and splendid glacier that lies between the Engelhorn and Wellhorn, cast a hasty glance at the beautiful masses of ice burnished to prismatic brilliancy by the morning sun, and then turned to the left toward a steep and narrow path leading to the summit. As the road grew more difficult at every step, his progress became much slower, and he purposely reserved his strength, knowing well that it would be severely taxed before he gained the object of his journey. After a toilsome ascent of half an hour he reached the lofty crag called by the mountaineers the Warder of the Glacier, and sat down to recover his breath.

It was very necessary for him to take a little rest, for the way he had come, although long and tiring, was as child's play compared with the difficulties he had yet to overcome. He had to climb the steep and dizzy heights that towered above his head; and instead of walking along a narrow foot-path, he would have to clamber over rocks and loose stones, to pass close to the most dreadful precipices, and across foaming mountain streams, till he reached the height at which the refreshing green had disappeared, with nothing visible but huge masses of brown and gray rock; where no other sight met the eye but that of mountains called its love-song from the waving branch; where no sound was to be heard save the smothered thunder of the avalanche, the roaring of the cataracts which poured forth from the melting glaciers and made courses for themselves through heaps of rough stones; and now and again the harsh and discordant scream of a solitary vulture that with outspread wings circled slowly aloft, piercing into the valleys with its keen eye in search of prey. Into these wild and lonely regions Walter had to climb in order to reach the lofty crag whereon the vulture—the far-famed Lämmergeier of the Alps—had reared her eyrie.

But these difficulties had little terror for the cool-headed and brave-hearted mountain youth, who had from his earliest days been accustomed to roam on dizzy heights where the slightest false step would have been destruction. He was determined to finish what he had begun; and gratitude to the noble and generous stranger lent new courage to his soul, and strength and endurance to his frame.

After a short rest he jumped up again, and renewed the toilsome ascent, following slowly but steadily the dangerous track that led to the summit of the mountain. His feet often slipped on the bare and polished rock; sometimes he slid ten or twenty paces backward over loose pebbles, and again sank knee-deep in the snow which here and there filled the hollows; but nothing daunted him or caused him to swerve from his purpose. At last he reached a broad sheet of ice with innumerable crevices and chasms, on the further side of which a narrow ridge like the edge of a knife stretched above a wild and lonely valley, the base of which yawned two or three thousand feet below. At the extreme end of this ridge the nest he was in search of was built on a small point of rock, the sides of which descended precipitously into the depths below.

With his eye fixed on the distant crag, Walter commenced the passage of the ice-field. The utmost caution being necessary at every step, he felt carefully with his long staff to ascertain whether the snow that covered the icy mass was fit to bear his weight, or only formed a treacherous bridge over the numerous ravines which yawned beneath. Bending his way round the large chasms, he leaped easily over the smaller ones with the aid of his staff; and after avoiding all the more dangerous spots, he succeeded, by caution and presence of mind, in safely reaching the further side of the glacier, where the last but most perilous part of his journey was to begin.

As he stood there leaning on his alpenstock, out of breath with the exertion he had undergone,

My uncle has brought me a little alligator from Florida, and mamma says I may keep it if I can take care of it. It is in a big tin pan of water now, and every day it jumps out and hides in some corner. I have given it crumbs of bread and cake, but it does not eat them. Please tell me how I can keep it, and what it will eat.

WILLIE J. H.

A small aquarium would serve as a comfortable home for your alligator, only you must provide a board on to which he can crawl to dry himself, for he does not like to spend all his time in the water. To feed him, take very tiny pieces of raw beef, and hold them toward him. If he is lively, he will dart after them with wide-open mouth. If you are afraid he will nip your finger—if he is very young he can not bite you—put the bits of meat on the end of a wire. If you do not wish to have a hunt for him every morning, you must cover your aquarium with coarse wire netting, for young alligators are always eager to escape from confinement.

Are you going to give a work-box department for little girls? I and five others are going to have a fair to raise money to make a Christmas-tree for a little sick [illegible] whose mother is very poor, and we want to make everything for the fair ourselves. One of us has a lot of pretty cards with pressed sea-weed she arranged last summer, and we thought they would be prettier if we could make them into little books or baskets. Could you tell us how to do it?

LENA W.

We shall not give a special department to fancy-work, but we shall now and then have short papers, like the one on page 14, telling how to make pretty things. Meanwhile perhaps some at that port; the latter was a floating reformatory, while the former was established for the purpose of training American boys to officer and man our merchant ships. The course of instruction embraces a short review of arithmetic, grammar, and geography, a thorough drill in marline-spike-work, handling sails, boats, oars, etc.

When the *St. Mary's* leaves her dock for the annual cruise, the school routine is changed, the first-class boys having lessons in navigation, steering, heaving the log and lead, passing earrings, etc., while the second class are aloft "learning gear," *i.e.*, following up the different ropes which form a ship's machinery, and fixing in the mind their lead and use, and a sure method of finding them in the darkest night. This last is absolutely necessary, for if a squall should strike the ship, and the order, "Royal clew-lines, flying-jib down-haul—Smith, let go that royal-sheet!" were given, it would be very mortifying, as well as dangerous, if he had to answer, "I don't know where it is, Sir."

The boys, assisted by a few able seamen, form the crew of the ship. They stand watch, make, reef, and take in sail; do all the dirty work, tarring down, painting, scraping, and slushing. They stand watch and watch, keep at night a look-out on the cat-heads, gangways, quarters, and halliards, where they are required to "sing out" their stations every half hour, to be sure that they are awake. Many are the instances of boys falling asleep, and being awakened by a lurch of the ship, singing out at the wrong time, and once a sleepy look-out reported "Light, ho!" and to the officer's "Where away?" was obliged to answer, "It's the moon, Sir!"

Then there is the excitement of reefing top-sails. Your hammock seems especially comfortable as you drowsily feel the exaggerated pitching of the ship and the rattle of rain on deck, when the boatswain's shrill call rings through the ship, "All hands, reef topsails; tumble out, and up with you, everybody!" Under Egyptian darkness, driving rain, and

city—the queer little donkeys with very large loads of oranges, the queerer river craft, the windmills, and even the dress of the natives seem familiar as you recall the pictures in your primary geography. The return voyage home in the "trades" is delightful—a warm sun and a good steady breeze, not a brace touched for a week or more, a water-spout and a rain-squall to vary the monotony of the every-day routine. Then the colder weather as you near Hatteras, a glimpse of old Montauk through the fog, a sharp look-out for beacons and buoys, the song of the leadsman, the quick tramp of men clewing up sail, a heavy splash and the rattle of chain, and we are anchored fast in New London mud. "All hands furl sail," now; no noise, for the *Saratoga* lies right ahead, and on board of a man-of-war it is

J. J. WALL. B. C. FULLER. J. J. CRAWLEY.

GRADUATES OF THE "ST. MARY'S" SCHOOL-SHIP.—PHOTOGRAPHED BY PAGE.

FRIENDSHIPS OF ANIMALS.

A VERY sharp fox-terrier belonging to the writer never could be induced to regard a cat in any other light than that of an enemy. Having to go and live in a house where a cat was kept, the first thing the dog did was to turn the cat out. As mice, however, were troublesome, and as the terrier, even with the best intentions, could not banish them, another cat was considered necessary; so a kitten was secured, and in due time introduced to its future companion the fox-terrier.

The little cat put up its back and spat at the dog, which was at last made to understand that it was to leave the kitten alone. For some days the two animals regarded one another with suspicion; at length the cat came up and licked the dog's nose. From that hour their friendship was established. They became inseparable; then the kitten soon discovered that the dog's tail and ears made excellent play-things, and in the meekest and most submissive manner the dog allowed the kitten to pull it about as much as it pleased. Very often, however, the dog felt inclined to play; then for about five or ten minutes the two would rush round the room; but it generally ended in the cat retiring under part of the furniture, to escape being somewhat roughly upset by the impetuous rushes of its canine playmate. Sometimes, when the kitten wanted to play, nothing could induce the dog to get up, and at other times the kitten would take no notice of the dog's pressing offers of a romp.

When lying still and dozing, the two were generally to be found close together, and at night the cat invariably curled itself up on the dog's back, and so went to sleep; but curiously enough, although the dog made no objection to this arrangement, it would not on any account get up into its bed if the cat was there first. On one occasion, and one only, the two were seen in a very comical position. The dog was sitting up on the hearth-rug, solemnly gazing

The two stood looking at one another about ten yards apart, when the dog became aware of the presence of the stranger. Knowing a way up on to the wall, it immediately ascended, but when it got up, its companion was between it and the other cat. However, the dog crawled along the wall to get at the interloper, and as there was no room to pass, simply knocked its little friend over, and then made a great effort to catch the enemy.

It was curious to see a dog perpetually rushing at cats, and then returning from the chase to gambol about in the most friendly manner with another cat. The friendly intercourse with the one never had the slightest effect in changing its animosity to others. The dog's affection even went

sent some years ago to the *Naturalist*, on the authority of Mr. Donaldson. His gull was quite an epicure in its way, and fancied sparrows' flesh for dinner. But as it had to cater for its own luxuries, the question of catching the sparrows became an important one. However, the gull thought the matter over, and soon devised an excellent scheme for capturing the four or five sparrows which it required as a daily *bonne bouche*. It fraternized with a number of pigeons which were fed in the yard where the gull was kept. The crafty bird had made a note of the fact that several sparrows always came down at feeding-time to get some of the food spread for the pigeons. "By getting among the pigeons, and keeping my head down,"

ON GUARD.

Halt! Not a step farther! Don't move for your life!
 You're a very nice squirrel, I haven't a doubt
(Although you've forgotten, I see, to put on
 Your kilt and your jacket before you came out),
But where you are now you must stay for an hour
 Or two, and quite silent even while you must keep,
For a weary long way we have travelled to-day,
 And my dear little master lies there fast asleep.

Of course you don't know—you've grown up in the woods,
 With no one to teach you—how fine 'tis to be
Great artists as we are! You've heard but the birds,
 And seen only squirrels jump round in a tree.

ON GUARD.—Drawn by Sol. Eytinge, Jun.

THE LITTLE GENIUS.

LITTLE five-year-old Bertie was very fond of sitting at the study table with his brothers and sisters, especially when they were doing their drawing lessons. But he was not satisfied with watching them. He too wanted to draw and paint, and the older children, who were very fond of him, were always glad to indulge him by lending him their brushes, paints, and pencils. But they soon found that he was very wasteful of their materials, and would use up colors and paper faster than they could be supplied. At last they thought of a better plan. As Bertie was too young to draw nicely, they bought him some wonderful picture-books, all in outline, a box of cheap water-colors, and some brushes. Then Bertie was happy. He would sit for hours painting the pictures in *Jack the Giant-killer*, *Mother Goose*, and other story-books for little folks. When he had finished all his little books his mamma brought out some old papers which she had saved, and cutting out the nice pictures, gave them to him to paint. This he did very beautifully. Sometimes he would make funny mistakes, painting green on the horses, and blue on the little dogs and pussy-cats, but this did not happen often. In a little while he had so many nice things painted that his sisters made him a big scrap-book to keep them in, to look at when he grows up.

Bertie may not become a great artist, but his sisters evidently regard him as a lit-

THE LITTLE GENIUS.

e those I see in the
Wonldo's that he
climbed up on the
placed the pail on
cellar window.
ere so covered with
ittle of the blessed
own there could not
he broom, and care-
ed the spider-webs,
ished the four panes
the very next after-
t the geraniums, and
to greet it. When
shelf (holding a few
t it looked so dingy
ll she had scrubbed
re, but also scoured
e put them back in
it looked like new.

—"I wouldn't, if I were a flower. I think the flower that grew in a cellar the best and sweetest of you all."

All was silence when she ceased speaking, and from that day to this never has she heard lily or daisy, rose or geranium blossom, speak again.

GLOVE CASE.

THE holiday season is approaching, and little girls, who have generally more time than money, are employing their leisure moments in making pretty gifts for their papas and mammas, and brothers and sisters, which will give double pleasure as being the work of their own hands. Here is a pretty holiday gift, which our young friends can readily make with the help of the following description: Cut of Bordeaux velvet one

GLOVE CASE.

PAPA FIGHTS THE SERPENT.

[CONTINUED FROM No. 1, PAGE 6.]

THE STORY OF A PARROT.

A BABY parrot who has just burst forth from his shell is not pretty to look at; indeed, I dare say you would have thought me exceedingly ugly. Like my brother and sister, I had a big bald head and a tremendous beak, while my wrinkled body was very small. I seemed to be all head, beak, and claws. Yet I remember perfectly well hearing our parents say to the many friends who came flying from all parts to offer them congratulations that we were the three most beautiful children ever born. I believe parents always think their children beautiful, and of course no one is ever so impolite as to contradict them.

We were very hungry babies, and poor papa had very hard work to bring home enough food to fill our three big beaks, which we kept wide open from morning till night. Mamma was very particular that our food should be of the most delicate kind, and papa often had to make long journeys through the forest to gather seeds and berries. He was a very kind papa, and if, as sometimes happened, he complained that his wings ached from flying so much, and that we made so much noise he could not sleep, mamma had only to call his attention to our rapid growth, and the beauty of our soft gray feathers, to put him at once in the best of humor. "They are magnificent children," he would say at such times, "and when they grow up I shall do as well by them as my father has done by me." Little did he think in those happy days that I, his oldest son, would soon be lost to him forever.

Our life was indeed peaceful, although we were subject at times to some anxiety from the attacks of certain wicked creatures which haunted the shores of our beautiful river. I remember, as if it had taken place yesterday, what happened one beautiful morning while papa had gone out to find our breakfast. Mamma had nestled down with us, and had coaxed us into taking a little

She was naturally very brave, and I think, to protect her children, she would have flown in the face of a lion. She now rushed to the door of our nest, where she stood, her feathers bristling, ready to give fight to whatever might try to enter. As she filled the whole doorway with her spread wings, we could not peep out to see what was the danger, although we stood on tiptoe and tried with all our strength to push our heads through her feathers. She gave us some smart taps with her claw, and ordered us back to the interior of the nest; and when she at length told us in a frightened whisper that papa was fighting with a ferocious serpent, we huddled together as close as we could in the very bottom of our hole. We knew that serpents murdered young parrots and ate them, for only the day before we had heard a neighbor telling mamma that one of these monsters had eaten six little parrots, children of a dear friend of hers, for his breakfast. Although mamma had said, after she went away, that she was only a gossip, and said such things to frighten us, now we were sure it was the truth, and we expected to see the serpent's head thrust into our nest, his mouth open to devour us. My brother and sister were half dead with fright. I tried to cheer them, assuring them that papa was strong enough to drive away a whole army of monsters, and when mamma suddenly flew away from the door, I crept up cautiously and peeped out. What was my relief to see papa flying rapidly toward the river, with an enormous serpent hanging dead in his claws! I screamed the good news to my brother and sister, but they refused to be comforted. In vain I assured them that the danger was over, that the serpent was conquered—was dead, in fact—and that papa had thrown the loathsome body into the river, that we might not be frightened at the horrible sight. My brother and sister continued crying and trembling until papa and mamma returned.

When at last we heard their joyful cries as they approached the nest, all three of us crept up to the doorway to welcome them. I shall never forget the tenderness with which they regarded us. Papa, who was still trembling with excitement, kissed us gently, while my poor mamma exclaimed, "Saved! my darlings are saved!" and her eyes shone with pride at the courage of her husband.

My feathers grew so rapidly that papa, who was very proud of me, I being much larger than my brother, would often say, "Bravo, my boy! You will soon be strong enough to go out with me into the forest."

In our first attempts to fly we were guided by mamma, who assisted us to hop about on the branches near our nest. After several of these short trials of strength papa took my brother and myself to visit our grandparents, who lived in a noble tree not far away. Never shall I for-

We had already made several short excursions, when one day—the most sorrowful day of my life—a boat, which we had been watching anxiously as it came up the river, stopped at the very roots of our tree. There were two men in it. As I peeped from the door I saw one man leave the boat and begin to climb up the trunk toward our nest. Mamma had told us only that morning that robbers had been seen on the opposite shore of our river, and that they were searching for young parrots, whom they tore away from their parents, and sent far away to a foreign country to be sold. "At the least danger," mamma had said to us, "fly. Man is a more formidable enemy than the serpent."

The man climbed nearer and nearer to our nest. Our parents were both away from home, and upon me, as the strongest and oldest, fell the responsibility of saving the family. There was not a moment to be lost. Aided by my brother, I threw my little sister, who was half dead with fright, headlong from the nest, and had the satisfaction to see her fly safely into the neighboring thicket. She used her little wings with strength and courage which would have been impossible for her to show except under the excitement of such terrible circumstances.

When my sister was saved, I hurried my brother after her, and he too escaped. Faithful to my duty, I remained the last in the nest, and at the instant when I spread my wings to fly away, the cruel hand of the robber closed tight around me. At that dreadful moment I fainted, and I remember nothing more until I found myself in a large cage with a number of other parrots, prisoners like myself.

Of the continuous misery of the long sea-voyage that followed I can not even now endure to think. More than half my companions perished; and when at last we reached this great city, which I hear men call New York, I myself was nearly dead from confinement and sea-sickness.

[TO BE CONTINUED.]

BUNNY AND BOW-WOW.

1.

Hum, Bunny! Now for lots of fun;
Get down, and have a jolly run.
I've moped about the house all day with
The want of somebody to play with.

2.

How stupid on the floor you lie!
Come, jump about, and let's be spry.
What, can't you even lift a paw?—
The dullest beast I ever saw!

3.

I won't be patient any more,
But drag you all about the floor;
I'll make you run, I'll make you jump—
How do you like that?—bump, bump, bump.

4.

What, haven't yet a mind to play?
I'll quickly teach you to obey.
You needn't hope now to get clear off.
Look out there, or I'll bite your ear off!

5.

I'm certain nothing can be done
To make you join in any fun;
It does no good to shake or beat you,
So now I've half a mind to eat you.

6.

Well, there! you're done for now! Oh dear!
What makes me feel so very queer?
What were you good for, anyway,
Not fit to eat, and wouldn't play?

his gun, but the sparrow flew away. This vexed him extremely, and he said, "As long as I live I will not [illegible]

asked whether he had regained his appetite. "No, ma'am," said the boy, "not exactly; his appetite is very poor, but his drinkable is as good as ever."

There is one thing which a man with two eyes can never see with one of them, and that is the other one.

"I expected a good deal of panes at my work," as the glazier said to the window-sash.

Miss Jemima Wilkinson, whom her parents refuse to allow her to go to a ball, [illegible] a bawl at home.

The man who was lost in slumber found his way out on a nightmare.

A school-master asked one of his boys, on a cold winter morning, what was the Latin word for cold. The boy hesitated a little, when the master said, "What, sirrah, can't you tell?" "Yes, sir," said the boy, "I have it at my fingers-ends."

MATHEMATICAL PUZZLES.

No. I.

Two countrymen were going along the road, each driving sheep.

Said one, "Hi, neighbor, give me one of your sheep, and then I shall have twice as many as you will have."

"Nay, neighbor," replied the other, "give me one of your sheep, and then we shall both have the same number."

How many sheep did each have?

No. II.

An old man lived in a little hut by a bridge which crossed a deep river.

One day a wicked water-spirit appeared to him and said: "My friend, I know you are very poor. Now I will increase whatever money you may have twofold, asking only in return this small favor, that every time you cross the bridge you will throw twenty-four cents into the water, and at the same time the money you have left shall be doubled." The poor old man was delighted at what he thought a generous offer of the water-spirit, and faithfully fulfilled all the conditions; but, to his sorrow and astonishment, when he had three times thrown the tribute of twenty-four cents to the water-spirit, he found himself penniless.

How much money did he have when the water-spirit first appeared to him?

No. III.

A good mother went to buy eggs for her children, for the Easter season was approaching, and the eggs were to be colored red and blue. She bought from a grocer half of his entire stock and half an egg more. Then a second woman came, and she bought half of what the grocer had remaining and half an egg more. A third woman and a fourth woman did the same thing, and in the end the grocer had one egg left.

How many had he in the beginning?

No. IV.

A man had seven sons, and a property of $[illegible]. Now the younger sons were jealous because their father cared more for the elder brother than he did for them, and they entreated him to make his will in their favor. To satisfy their demands he made his will, and the younger sons were contented. This is the will: The eldest son to have $[illegible] and an eighth of what remained; the second son to have $[illegible] and an eighth of what remained; the third, $[illegible] and an eighth of what remained; the fourth, $[illegible] and an eighth of what remained; the fifth, $[illegible] and an eighth of what remained; the sixth, $[illegible] and an eighth of what remained; the seventh and youngest to have all that remained when the sixth had taken his share.

What share of the $[illegible] did each receive?

A NEW SERIAL

BY GEORGE MACDONALD.

A brilliant serial story by George MacDonald, with illustrations by Alfred Fredericks, will shortly be begun in Harper's Young People.

Harper's Young People.

Vol. I.—No. 3. | Published by HARPER & BROTHERS, New York. | Price Four Cents.

Tuesday, November 18, 1879. | Copyright, 1879, by Harper & Brothers. | $1.50 per Year, in Advance.

THE TOURNAMENT.—Drawn by James E. Kelly.

recover, so concluded that he must have dropped it after the deadly encounter.

"That doesn't matter much," said he to himself, as he looked at the size of the bird. "It is a good exchange; and if I give the stranger the old bird with the young ones, I dare say he will give me another knife. What a splendid creature! Fully four feet long, and the wings at least three yards across. How father will open his eyes when he sees the dead Lämmergeier—and the Scotch gentleman too!"

Tying the legs of the bird together with cord which he had fortunately brought, he slung it across his shoulder to balance the weight of the bag, and then started on his journey across the glacier, the foot of which he soon reached, and was then within hailing distance of the hotel where the stranger was residing.

It was a good thing that he had not been kept longer away, for the sun was beginning to set by the time he reached the valley, and only the highest peaks were lit up by its departing glory. Tired fight it out; and there's the end of it. I couldn't think of being ungrateful after so much kindness."

"Well, my lad, you have proved most clearly that you have a thankful heart and a cool and determined head," said Mr. Seymour, not without emotion. "Maintain those characteristics, and use them always for good and noble purposes, and I am sure you will find the end of every adventure as satisfactory as this has been to-day. I owe you a new knife and a suit of clothes; for the old vulture that has used you so badly was not in our bargain this morning. But we will talk about that another time. You had better go home now, for I think your father will begin to feel anxious about you, as it is getting late. I will come and see you in the morning."

Walter left the room in great glee. He stopped a few minutes in the court-yard to tell the impatient guides what he had gone through, and then hurried home as fast as he could, where he found his father waiting for him with some impatience. "Everything is settled, father!" he exclaimed, as he clasped him round the neck. "We shall get our cow back again now; for I've got the money, and Neighbor Friesbards can't keep her any longer. I've brought it back with me from the Engelhorn."

The peasant could scarce believe the hurried words of the excited boy, and was afraid his head was turned, until Walter opened the little cupboard where he had put the money, and laid the two bright gold pieces on the table. There was no longer any room for doubt; and the poor man's eyes sparkled with delight as he looked at the coin which was just sufficient to pay his debt and rescue the cow from the hands of his neighbor.

"But how did you come by all this money, Watty?" he inquired. "I hope you have got it fairly and honestly?"

"Yes, quite honestly, father," replied the boy, with an open and confident smile.

"Well, tell me— But no; I must go and get Lisel out of prison without a moment's delay. Come along with me to Neighbor Friesbards's, Watty."

Away went the happy pair to the neighboring farm-house; and although Friesbards looked sullen and displeased when Toni Hirzel laid the gold pieces on the table, it was no use for him to offer any resistance; so he went rather sulkily to the cow-house, and let out the captive animal, which was followed home by the peasant and his proud son, and got a capital supper in her old quarters.

and I prayed for help before I set out, and several times afterward."

"That was right, Watty, my son. Never forget God, and He will always be with you, and protect you all your life long. And now, good-night, dear boy."

"Good-night, father," replied Walter, heartily; and both retired to their humble beds, and were soon wrapped in deep and healthful slumber.

(TO BE CONTINUED.)

A GIGANTIC JELLY-FISH.

FEW excursions can be proposed more acceptable to young folks than going a-fishing, and perhaps the most delightful sort of fishing is to be had by accompanying some old fisherman out into the broad ocean.

There are many circumstances that contribute to make a day's sport of this kind more enjoyable than pond or river fishing, and not the least of these consists in the wonderful variety of the creatures to be caught.

In our inland streams and lakes in any given locality the kinds of fish to be caught are well known, and, comparatively speaking, there are not many different sorts; but in ocean fishing the oldest fishermen, and those most accustomed to the sorts of fish generally found in their fishing grounds, every once in a while happen upon creatures the likes of which have seldom, perhaps never, been seen before. Only a short time since a Nantucket fisherman, rowing slowly along, buried the prow of his boat in some partly yielding substance that brought him to a stand-still. Somewhat startled, he went forward, oar in hand, to find his little craft imbedded in the body of an enormous jelly-fish, the largest ever seen. The soft and yielding body of the creature offered so little resistance to his oar when he tried to push off, and he saw himself so hopelessly entangled in the mass of slime and tentacles, that, instead of attempting to free himself, he determined to tow it ashore, which he did by passing a sail-cloth under its body and rowing slowly homeward.

THE CAPTURE.

THE FIRST DROP OF BITTERNESS.

Come, little one, open your mouth!
  I know it is bitter to drink;
But if you'll stop squirming and squalling,
  You'll have it all down in a wink.
The poor little baby is sick,
  And this is to cure the bad pain;
So swallow the medicine, darling,
  And soon you can frolic again.
How glad should we be, who are older,
  And have bitter burdens to bear,
To find out some wonderful doctor
  With cures for each sorrow and care!

At the Bottom of a Mine.—Years ago some Welsh miners, in exploring an old pit that had been long closed, found the body of a young man dressed in a fashion long out of date. The peculiar action of the air of the mine had been such

THAT EARTHQUAKE!

DID you ever play in a cellar? I don't mean a cellar with a smooth floor, and coal-bins, and a big furnace, and shelves with jars of nice jam on them and glasses of jelly; I've been in that kind of a cellar too—I like quince jelly the best; it's first rate spread on bread and butter—but I'm talking of another kind of a cellar, one with the house all taken away, and only a big brick chimney left in the centre, with the top knocked off of that, and bricks and pieces of stone and chunks of mortar scattered all round; with berry bushes growing in one corner, and wild vines growing all around the edges.

There was just such a cellar as this where I used to live, and Kate and Teddy Ames, who lived in the next house, used to come over and play in the cellar with Billy and me.

Billy was my brother, eight years old, and the best fellow to play with you ever saw, because he

"man Friday" by turns. We walked about in the cellar pretending to look for the print of naked feet, Billy going in front carrying a rusty old broken musket we had found in the garret, and a piece of rubber hose (Billy always could find or make anything we wanted) for a telescope, which he used to look through to see if there were any savages in sight when he climbed up to the edge of the cellar.

The cellar was really an island, just like Robinson Crusoe's; for Billy and Teddy had digged a ditch all round it, and filled it with water; but it was a very trying sort of an ocean, 'cause we had to fill it up every morning.

Teddy, who could whittle nicely, made some little canoes, and when Billy was looking through the hose for savages, it was Teddy's part to poke the canoes with a long stick like a fish-pole, so they would float right in front of Billy's hose. Then Billy would scramble down the wall, and come running to us 'round behind the chimney,

THE FIRST DROP OF BITTERNESS.

BILLY WATCHING FOR SAVAGES.—Drawn by C. S. [illegible]

that blew;
brother Harry has promised (he's ever so kind, I'm sure)
end them his beautiful yacht when they sail on their wedding tour.
make believe it's the ocean, the lake in the Park, you know;
Charlie, the little sailor, is so delighted to go,
ay! he does look charming in his suit of navy blue.
member, my most particular friend, is little Nelly Drew.

h! they are coming, Mary. Oh, they are a lovely pair!
rlie, the black-eyed sailor, and Rose with her golden hair.
sn't she look like a fairy peeping out from a flowery cloud,
hat lovely dress and veil? But we mustn't talk out loud.
could just squeeze out a tear—I suppose it's the proper thing,
she is my only child—but indeed I would rather sing.
the sun is shining brightly, and everything seems gay,
to Charlie, the dear little sailor, my dolly is married to-day.

[Continued from No. 8, Page 15.]

THE STORY OF A PARROT.

o many months had passed since I was stolen from my beautiful home that I was already ird of considerable size. I was brought on re by a sailor, who took me to a dismal place a dirty, noisy street, where I found several dred other birds—parrots, canaries, Java sparrows, and many kinds I had never seen before, fined in small cages. The confusion of sounds dreadful, and I was sorry to hear that most the conversation was the most malicious gos. I was received with shouts of derision, and rue my appearance was as wretched as poss e. My feathers were soiled and broken, and as overcome with sadness. The air of the re was stifling and although the man who had

on whose banks it stood; I breathed the perfume of thousands of wild flowers; crowds of brilliant birds came hurrying to comfort me; I saw again my father, my mother, my brother, and my sister; I believed myself free once more. Alas! sorrowful was then waking from all those delights.

"Are you happy?" my master would say. "Have you eaten your breakfast, Lorito?" Yes, indeed, I had breakfasted. I did nothing but eat breakfast from morning till night. I grew very fat, and what was worse, I became so stupid that I repeated like an echo all my master's words. "Have you eaten your breakfast?" I would scream; and my master would laugh, and toss me a lump of sugar. That was my only recreation—to repeat my master's words and eat sugar. I was gradually losing all sense of honor and truth, and to be praised and get a lump of sugar I would rest my beak in my claw and say, with a languishing air, "My head aches; let me alone." My head did ache, too, sometimes, remembering the days when I knew only the language of my fathers, when the sweet voice of my mother waked me in the morning to pass a happy day playing with my brother and sister. Solitude and confinement had soured my character. The rings of my chain hurt my feet so that they were becoming swelled and inflamed. I

"TEARING OUT NAIL AFTER NAIL."

first I was more anxious than malicious, but, alas! I had scarcely started on my voyage of discovery when I perceived a small blue and gilt bowl standing upon the marble hearth. It contained the [illegible] ordered as a healing bath for my [illegible]. The fragrance was so enticing that, forgetting the good precepts my mother had taught me, I dipped my beak into the bowl and took a long drink, nor did I stop so long as a single drop remained.

No sooner had I swallowed the contents of the bowl than I felt a strange burning sensation in my head, which seemed on the point of dancing away from my body. I was possessed of an [illegible] desire to bite something, and I gazed eagerly around the room in the hope of finding some enemy with whom I could engage in mortal combat. I saw no moving thing in the whole apartment which I could attack, but unfortunately my eyes fell upon some shining brass nails, which served as ornaments round the edge of a table. To my heated imagination each nail seemed glaring directly at me, mocking me like the evil eye of a bird of prey. I climbed rapidly toward the table, and climbing up one of its legs, I seized a nail in my beak. To my great delight I found I could easily pull it out, which I immediately did, and threw it spitefully away. With yells of triumph I crept all around the table, clinging with my claws, and tearing out nail after nail as I went, until every one of those aggravating glaring eyes lay scattered over the carpet.

Although I was victorious in my [illegible] with the nails, my only

ing around for a new victim, I saw a bottle standing upon a table in the centre of the room. The old saying that he who drinks once will drink again is one of the truest of proverbs, and I can only [illegible] the bottle than I made all possible haste to reach it, hoping that it contained some wondrous elixir. To be sure, the liquid in the bottle was very dark colored, and had an unpleasant odor, but in my eagerness I paid little attention to these things. I tried to force it, but the mouth of the bottle was too small for my beak, and all my efforts were in vain. In my rage I vowed revenge, and, screaming loudly, I threw the tantalizing thing with violence to the floor.

Alas! my ill behavior was sadly punished. The bottle I had overturned was filled with ink, and I was spattered from head to foot with the vile black mixture. My beautiful plumage, of which I had been so proud, was defiled. I was both horrible and ridiculous. In this miserable and forlorn condition I climbed back upon my perch, and in a most wretched frame of mind waited to be discovered, and perhaps punished.

[TO BE CONTINUED.]

A Curious Incident.—Horses will form strong attachments for dogs, but it does not often happen that a horse derives any real benefit from having a canine friend. The following case will show that a dog may sometimes return a horse's affection in a very practical manner. A man living in the country had a horse which happened to be turned out just as his carrots were ready for pulling. He also had a dog that was on the best of terms with the horse. One day he noticed that his carrots were disappearing very fast, but he was almost certain that no one had gone in and stolen them. Still he determined to watch, and see who was robbing him. His vigilance was rewarded, for he caught the thief in the very act of pulling up the carrots. Then he cautiously followed him from the garden, and found that he went off in the direction of the field where the horse was. Arrived there, the owner of the carrots saw that the horse was the receiver of the stolen goods. The thief was his dog. In some way the dog had discovered that the horse had a partiality for carrots, and was unable to gratify its taste; but with a sagacity that is almost incredible the dog found the means of obtaining the [illegible] for his friend, and this he did without scruple or his master's consent. There was something more than instinct in this dog's head. But any one who takes real notice of the habits and curious doings of animals must inevitably come to the conclusion that the theory is not tenable which maintains that animals can not think and reason.

I was very glad [illegible] the first number of Young People [illegible] every week. [illegible]

MAMIE.

We do not know any proper English name for Edelweiss. The German name is composed of two words—edel, signifying noble, and weiss, white. If you are studying botany, perhaps you can determine to what family the flower belongs—that is, if you have any carefully pressed specimens.

Will you please tell me why the Bank of England is called "the Old Lady in Threadneedle Street," and who first called it so? I would like to know, too, when the Bank was founded, and when the building it now occupies was erected. [illegible]

Will not some of our "young people" send answers to "Jim's" questions?

The picture of Chestnutting in the first number of Young People puts me in mind of our beechnutting parties. On the hill where my papa's house stands there are a large number of beech-trees, and I and my two little brothers [illegible] a fine time gathering the queer three-sided little nuts. A beech forest is very beautiful in autumn, when the golden leaves are fluttering down to the ground, and the smooth straight gray trunks stand like silver-gray pillars. When we gathered the nuts we spread some old sheets and blankets under the tree, because the nuts are so very small that otherwise we might never have been able to find them among the heaps of dry leaves. They are nicest to roast [illegible], something like chestnuts, and are so abundant that sometimes we get a whole barrel from one tree. We like them better than chestnuts, and they keep all winter. My brothers and myself always take a pocketful to school to eat with our luncheons. We often find them in the spring among the heaps of last year's leaves, and after they have lain under the snow all winter, they begin to sprout when the first warm days come, and then they are very nice to eat.

I hope the Young People will tell us of some good [illegible] games, for we [illegible] know what to do [illegible] We always learn our

WIGGLES.

We were scattered about our sitting-room table; the early tea was just over, and a good long evening before us. (We're mamma, papa, Bob, Mamie, and Nelly. I am Nelly, and the eldest of the family—except papa, of course.)

Papa was reading the evening paper—something about stocks, I suppose; Bob had both elbows firmly planted within two inches of the student-lamp, handy for upsetting in case he moved; Mamie was looking as doleful as if she had lost her kitten; and I was gazing in the fire and dreaming.

"Wish I had something to do," yawned Bob.

"So do I," said Mamie.

"Play checkers," I suggested.

"No; only two can play that," objected Mamie. "Papa, don't you know something we can play?"

"Well," said papa, folding up his paper, "let me see. Bob, take yourself out of the lamp. Play 'Recondite Forms.'"

"What's recondite?" growled Bob.

"Recondite means *hidden*, *concealed*, and this game is called 'Recondite Forms' because— But you will understand it better after you have played it. I want pencils and some rather thin paper."

Bob and Mamie collected the pencils, I brought a supply of French note-paper from my desk, and we all drew our chairs about the table, ready for work.

Papa took a pencil, and made a kind of wiggle, like No. 1 in the picture; then he laid over that another sheet of paper, which was thin enough to allow the pencil mark to show through; this he carefully traced, so as to have an exact copy, and did the same with two other sheets; then gave us each one, and told us to see what kind of a picture we could make out of it; we might add to the line as much as we pleased, but we must not alter nor erase it.

"Oh," said Bob, "I don't know what to make!"

"Hush!" said Mamie; "I want to think."

Then silence reigned—at first puzzled, but afterward busy.

"I've got it!" shouted Bob, dropping his pencil.

"So've I," echoed Mamie.

"Now for a grand exhibition!" said papa, collecting the papers, and laying them in a row on the table.

Bob had made a parrot out of his "wiggle," papa a graceful floating figure, Mamie a high-heeled shoe, and I a fool with cap and bells.

"Now," said papa, "do you see why this is called 'Recondite Forms'? In this first line all the other figures were hidden, and it took only a few pencil strokes to bring them out."

"Yes, I see," said Bob. "Now let's try some more wiggles."

"Wiggles!" said papa; "I don't know but that's a better name than the other."

"So you; recon-dite is awful hard," said Mamie.

"Wiggles it is, then," said papa.

And "wiggles" it has been ever since. I will add, for the benefit of those outside my own small circle, that instead of French note-paper, the common white wrapping-paper, such as grocers use in tying up parcels of tea, is just as good for the purpose, and a great deal cheaper. With several sheets of this, and two or three lead-pencils, "wiggles" may be played for a whole evening.

In the picture No. 6 is a new "wiggle" for you to try your hand upon. See what you can make of it, and in the next number I will give you my idea.

Hats.—The felt hat is as old as Homer. The Greeks made them in skull-caps, conical, truncated, narrow, or broad-brimmed. The Phrygian bonnet was an elevated cap without a brim, the apex turned over in front. It is known as the cap of Liberty. An ancient figure of Liberty in the times of Antoninus Livius, A.D. 115, holds the cap in the right hand. The Persians wore soft caps; plumed hats were the head-dress of the Syrian corps of Xerxes; the broad-brim was worn by the Macedonian kings. Castor wore a blind-man-buff. The Armenian captive wore a plug hat. The merchants of the fourteenth century wore a Flanders beaver. Charles VII., in 1449, wore a felt hat lined with red, and plumed. The English men and women in 1510 wore close woollen or knitted caps; two centuries ago hats were worn in the house. Pepys, in his diary, wrote: "September, 1664, got a severe cold because he took off his hat at dinner;" and again, in January, 1665, he got another cold by sitting too long with his head bare, to allow his wife's maid to comb his hair and wash his ears; and Lord Clarendon, in his essay, speaking of the decay of respect due the aged, says "that in his younger days he never kept his hat on before those older than himself, except at dinner." In the thirteenth century Pope Innocent IV. allowed the cardinals the use of the scarlet cloth hat. The hats now in use are the chalk hat, leather hat, paper hat, silk hat, opera hat, spring-brim hat, and straw hat.

Sponges.—The coarse, soft, flat sponges, with large pores and great orifices in them, come from the Bahamas and Florida. The finer kinds, suitable for toilet use, are found in the Levant; the best on the coast of Northern Syria, near Tripoli, and secondary qualities among the Greek Isles. These are either globular or of a cup-like form, with fine pores, and are not easily torn. They are got by divers plunging from a boat, many fathoms down, with a heavy stone tied to a rope for sinking the same, who snatches the sponges, puts them into a net fastened to his waist, and is then hauled up. Some of the Greeks, instead of diving, throw short harpoons attached to a cord, having first spied their prey at the bottom through a tin tube with a glass bottom immersed below the surface water.

VOL. I.—NO. 4. | PUBLISHED BY HARPER & BROTHERS, NEW YORK. | PRICE FOUR CENTS.

Tuesday, November 25, 1879. | $1.00 per Year, in Advance.

[Begun in No. 1 of Harper's Young People, Nov. 4.]

THE BRAVE SWISS BOY.

III.—THE CHAMOIS-HUNTERS.

EARLY the next morning the door of the little mountain cottage grated on its hinges, and Mr. Seymour entered the small apartment, eagerly welcomed by Walter, who ran forward to meet him.

"What! you are up already, my boy, and as fresh and lively as if nothing had happened!" said he. "I fully expected to find you knocked up and ill after all the exertion and fatigue of yesterday; but I am glad to see that you are so much stronger than I gave you credit for. How is your back, though, Walter? Don't the wounds made by the vulture's claws pain you very much?"

"They were very sore last night, Sir," replied the boy; "but father bound them up nicely for me, and says they will be much better in a week."

"Delighted to hear it. But where is your father? I don't see him."

"He is outside, Sir, with Liesli, the cow that we recovered through your kindness," replied Walter, with a grateful look. "She is the best cow in the valley."

"Ah, here comes your father," said Mr. Seymour, with a smile, stepping forward to grasp the hand which Toni Hirzel held out toward him, while thanking him in hearty but simple words for the kindness he had shown to his boy.

"Don't mention it, my friend. What I gave to the boy was given very willingly, and he has richly earned not only that, but a few francs more, which I am still owing him. But we will square accounts now. Here, Walter; there is forty francs for the old vulture which you captured so bravely; and here is another sixty francs for the torn trousers and the knife you lost."

With these words Mr. Seymour counted out five bright gold pieces on the table, to the wonderment of Toni Hirzel and his son, neither of whom could utter a word.

"But, Sir," exclaimed Walter, finding his voice at last, "the vulture, the trousers, and the knife all put together are not worth twenty francs!"

"They are worth more to me," replied the gentleman, "and you must allow me to pay for them according to my opinion of their value. So make no more words about it, my boy, but put the money in your pocket. I hope it may prove useful to you."

Tears started into Walter's eyes. "Oh, father!" he exclaimed, "only look at all this money! We shall be able to buy another cow, and make twice as much cheese as we do now. We shan't have to borrow anything from Neighbor Fernhardt any more, and if everything goes on well, we shall soon be able to build a house as good as his. It will be a blessing for you to have a comfortable house in your old age."

But Toni Hirzel shook his head. "Don't talk so fast, my boy," said he, and before saying farewell, Walter asked and obtained leave to visit the friendly traveller soon; but when he went to Rosenlauibad three or four days afterward, he found that Mr. Seymour had received a letter from home, which had compelled him to take his immediate departure.

The summer passed away; autumn came, and stripped the leaves from the trees; the first flakes of snow fluttered in the air; the days were growing shorter, and the quiet and solitary valley took its turn in the changes of fortune which so frequently occur in the outer world. Although Toni Hirzel was sober and industrious, he could not escape the common lot of humanity. He sustained a heavy loss at the beginning of winter in the death of his favorite cow. Soon afterward the severity of the weather drove from the mountains the wolves, which broke into the stable during the night and killed two of his five goats.

These losses were serious to the poor man. The only property he possessed in addition to his ing the snow from the mountain-sides, and calling into life hundreds of sparkling streams. Waterfalls foamed and thundered; enormous masses of snow came crashing down from the mountain-peaks; while amid the noise and thunder of avalanches the sun exercised its silent but mighty influence, renewing the mountain greenery, converting the barren ground into a verdant carpet. The birds returned from their winter home, and again burst into joyous song; and again the budding trees proclaimed that winter was over and gone.

During the dreary winter-time the simple wants of the two mountaineers had been supplied by much toil and much privation, so that the return of the vernal season was hailed with joyful acclamation.

"It is time for us to be off now," said the hunter one morning to his boy; and day after day, whenever the weather was favorable, they might have been seen climbing the lofty mountain ranges in search of game, sometimes not returning to their little cottage for several days. At other times, however, after unspeakable trouble and danger, they would return home in great glee, the father bearing a large chamois slung across his shoulders, to be sold for a good price to the landlord of the inn.

Toni was looked upon by all the country round as the best hunter in the district, and he was determined to maintain his reputation. By the end of August, when the summer was approaching its end, he had shot thirty chamois, and the best of the season was still before him.

"Now, Watty," said he, "we must look out for the winter. We have got on famously through the fine weather, and have made a little money; but there's not enough yet for what we require, and we must work away for some time still before we get as much as will replenish our empty byre."

"I will do all I can to help you, father,"

WATTY AND HIS FATHER HUNTING.

"Yes; that will be the best, father," replied Walter. "I thought of that myself."

"Well, then, let it be so. We must be off before daybreak to-morrow morning."

Tom made the necessary preparations the same evening, and long before the first beams of Sol were visible on the following morning, he left the cottage with his son. After a toilsome ascent of half an hour, they separated. The father turned to the left toward the steep and craggy Engelhorn, after he had described the exact point toward which Walter was to drive the animal, while the boy ascended up the dangerous ridges of the Wellhorn, to find the chamois, and drive it to the place where his father was to lie in wait.

"Be very careful, Walter," said his father to him ere they parted; "don't be reckless or foolhardy."

The boy promised to be watchful, and they separated, each to his own share of the toilsome and perilous undertaking. Taking advantage of the rocks and stones which marked the path of a former glacier, Walter reached the summit of the Wellhorn without much difficulty, after an hour and a half's climb. Taking a small telescope from his pocket, he peered anxiously across the field of ice which separated him from the Engelhorn, and descried his father working his way cautiously along the edge of the glacier till he gained a part of the rocks that seemed to afford a possibility of climbing. He then had the satisfaction of seeing him sit down to rest.

"He has got just to the right spot," said he to himself. "He must have seen the track. It is just fifty feet from there that the chamois springs across a crack in the ice to get to the pasture higher up; and when he once gets sight of him, father won't let him escape. But, first and foremost, I must find the game, and start it across."

No sooner said than done. Clambering from rock to rock, always observant and watchful, the resolute youth pursued his way. Suddenly, however, he stood still, and threw himself flat on the ground.

"I thought so—there he is!" said he to himself. "I must work my way carefully round to the right, and then frighten him off with a shout."

Taking stealthy advantage of every rock that could screen him from observation, Walter raised his head now and then to make sure that the chamois had not taken fright and scurried from the spot. When he had thus reached the right position, he started to his feet and uttered a loud halloo! With a bound the chamois sprang down to the field of ice, which it crossed with light and rapid strides.

"The game is ours!" exclaimed Walter, with delight. But his joy was premature. Now began a chase, which lasted nearly an hour, until the animal approached the spot where Walter's father lay, when it suddenly stopped, gave a tremendous spring to the right, fled across the glacier with the speed of an arrow, and was out of sight in an instant.

"He must have seen father, or else scented him," said Walter to himself. "Our trouble is all in vain for to-day, so I must go acquaint father with the result."

A few minutes brought the lad to where his father was awaiting the appearance of the buck; but Walter saw at once that the elder sportsman was aware of what had happened. His father beckoned to him to be silent, and pointed to a small green spot above the steep sides of the Engelhorn. Turning his eyes in that direction, Walter recognized the chamois standing on the scrap of meadow.

"Now we've got him," whispered his father. "He can't take the steep sides of the mountain, and we've cut off his retreat; so come along, my boy, as fast as you can."

Moving hurriedly over the ice, they soon reached a point from which they could get a good view of the chamois. Unfortunately, however, a large chasm in the ice lay right before them, and stopped their progress. The chamois had cleared it, but it was quite beyond human strength and

SEA-CUCUMBERS.

Toward the end of October of every year there is a harvest of cucumbers in mid-ocean. These cucumbers, however, are not at all like those we see on our tables. In the first place, they are not vegetables, but animals, and, in the second place they grow upon the bottom of the sea. The general appearance of the creature can be seen in the accompanying cut. There are many species, but they all possess elongated worm-like bodies, with thick leathery skins, and a crown of feelers, or tentacles, about the forward extremity. All species, likewise, exercise the same astonishing method of revenging any liberties taken with their persons, by suddenly and unexpectedly ejecting their teeth, their stomach, their digestive apparatus—in fact all their insides, so to speak—in the face of the intruder, reducing themselves to a state of collapse, and

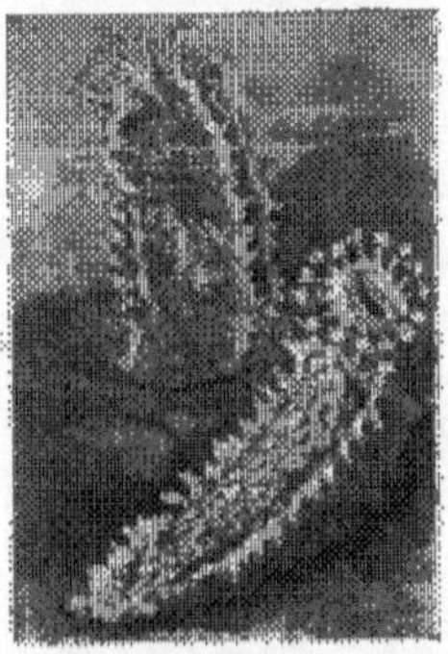

SEA-CUCUMBERS.

making of themselves mere empty bags, until such time as their wonderful recuperative powers enable them to replace the organs so summarily disposed of; for, wonderful as it may seem, teeth, stomach, digestive organs, and all soon grow again. Moreover, these stomachs have digestive powers that are not to be despised, far surpassing even those popularly ascribed to the ostrich, for the sea-cucumber actually seems to feed upon coral, and even granite has been found in its stomach.

Sea-cucumbers, as they are popularly called, are also known by the name of trepang and sea-slug. Scientific people call them *Holothuroidea*, but why, no one has ever been able to find out, since the name has no meaning. Sea-cucumbers are considered a great delicacy by the Chinese.

THE PROCESS OF SCALDING.

Thousands of Chinese vessels, called junks, are fitted out every year for these fisheries. Trepangs are caught in different ways. Sometimes the patient fishermen lie along the fore-part of vessels, and with long, slender bamboos, terminating in sharp hooks, gather in sea-cucumbers from the bottom of the sea, so practiced is hand and eye that the catch is never missed, and is discovered sometimes at thirty yards' distance. When the water is not more than four or five fathoms deep, divers are sent down to gather these culinary monsters, as seen in the illustration, the boat and junk remaining near to receive the harvest.

As soon as the trepangs are collected they are carried to the shore, where they are scalded by throwing them after that large iron pans set over little ovens built of stones. Here they are stirred about by means of a long pole resting upon a forked stick, as seen in the illustration. In these caldrons they remain a couple of minutes, when they are taken out, disemboweled with a sharp knife, if they haven't already thrown up their stomachs, and then taken to great bamboo sheds containing still larger boilers. In these latter is a new mixture with mimosa bark. A lively picture ensues; all is bustle, noise, and activity. The bubbling of the great caldrons, the incessant chatter of those engaged in the work, the dumping

BOILING AND CURING.

of fresh loads of sea-cucumbers into the vessels, and the removal of others to hang in clusters on the ropes above, or be deposited on hurdles to dry in the sun, make "confusion worse confounded," and give the spectator a new and realizing sense of the confusion of tongues at the Tower of Babel.

The sea-cucumbers having been smoked in the large caldrons (for the mimosa bark is consumed in the process), and then dried, are ready for the market, and, packed in bundles, are stowed away in the holds of the junks and borne off shore.

They are said to taste like lobsters; but if they look, as one traveller says they do, "like dried sausages rolled in mud and thrown up the chim-

BENJAMIN FRANKLIN.

BENJAMIN FRANKLIN, born in Boston in 1706, when a boy laid down certain rules of conduct which he always followed. He made up his mind to be temperate, orderly, frugal, and industrious. When ten years old, he cut wicks for candles, minded the shop, and ran errands for his father, who was a tallow-chandler. He did not, however, neglect his books, for he tells us, "I do not remember when I could not read." Though no boy ever worked harder, he was fond of manly sports, and was an expert swimmer. Not liking the tallow-chandlery business, his father apprenticed him to a printer. This was precisely the kind of work which suited Franklin. When hardly eighteen years old, he was sent to England to buy printing material, and to improve himself in his trade. As a printer in London, a very young man, entirely his own master, with no friends to control him, surrounded by temptations, those rules which he had fixed upon early in life were of singular benefit to him. Returning to America in 1726, in time he opened a modest printing-house in Philadelphia. Industry, honesty, and good work made him successful. He became member of the Assembly, Postmaster, and during the Revolution, while in France, induced that country to espouse our cause. If to-day the world has to thank Americans for making electricity their servant, Benjamin Franklin first discovered its most marked qualities. With a kite he brought down the spark from heaven to earth, and held it under control. Franklin died, honored by all his countrymen, in 1790.

When a lad, hungry and tired, he landed in Philadelphia with a dollar in his pocket, he bought some bread, and marched through the streets munching his crust. He happened to see a young lady, a Miss Read, at the door of her father's house. He made up his mind then and there that he would marry her; and so in time he did. Strangely enough, that exact part of New York from whence *Harper's Young People* is issued is called Franklin Square.

FRANKLIN AND HIS LOAF OF BREAD.

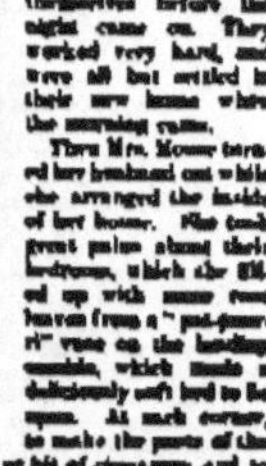

MR. AND MRS. MOUSE.

ONCE upon a time there lived a Mr. and Mrs.

till I have thoroughly examined the place to see if it will suit, for I am tired of having to change every week like this."

"Very well, dear," said his wife, "I quite agree with you. I am as tired of this moving as you can be. Do you know, I am getting quite thin from all this worry of dogs and cats. I feel quite home in my coat, and I feel so dreadfully nervous of traps every time I venture out at night into the kitchen."

"Poor little thing!" said Mr. Mouse; "but I think I know of a place that may suit us. The old lady that lives up stairs in her bedroom is a kind old woman, I have heard cook say. Don't you think we might look behind the wainscot of her room, and see if it would suit?"

So they agreed to go up stairs that very night and pay a visit to the old lady's room. The old

under the wardrobe, where nobody could possibly see them going in and out—just to her liking. With a little nibbling of the wood here and there inside the hole, she thought it would make the most delightful home anybody ever had. There were no nasty draughts to give her colds, and if they wanted a little amusement during the day, there was the whole length of the wardrobe to race along under; for, to tell the truth, Mr. and Mrs. Mouse were both quite young yet, and enjoyed a good scamper immensely. She also found that there had been no other mice for a very long time, if there ever had been. She was very glad of this, as she by no means approved of a lot of other mice being there to interfere with her and her husband. Mr. Mouse was equally pleased with what he found.

The old lady who lived in the room was constantly having all kinds of invalid messes, arrowroot, gruel, etc. There would have been quite enough to eat from what she left alone; but besides all her eatables, there was a large cage full of birds, that scattered their seed about in all directions, and Mr. and Mrs. Mouse were very fond of bird seed. Then there were always bread-crumbs about, and lumps of sugar; in fact, both Mr. and Mrs. Mouse agreed in thinking that there had never been a place so thoroughly fitted for them in every way. So, after examining the room in every corner, and being quite satisfied, they both scampered off down stairs again, and, avoiding the cat, got safely home.

Next day they set about moving, or rather next night, for they did nothing all day but pack up their trunks and rest themselves before the night came on. They worked very hard, and were all but settled in their new home when the morning came.

Then Mrs. Mouse turned her husband out while she arranged the inside of her house. She took great pains about their bedroom, which she filled up with some rose leaves from a "pot-pourri" vase on the landing outside, which made a deliciously soft bed to lie upon. At each corner, to make the posts of the bed, she stuck a clove or bit of cinnamon, and to make the curtains over the top and at the sides she rubbed a spider's web, which looked lovely. When she had finished all her arrangements she called Mr. Mouse in, and when she heard his little squeaks and screams of delight, she was fully sat-now live in peace. After living there some time they found out that the old lady was very fond of all kinds of animals, and the idea of anything being killed was dreadfully painful to her. She was not aware that a cat was kept below stairs, or she would not have allowed it, for she was very fond of mice. Mr. and Mrs. Mouse knew they were perfectly safe with her, but they were not at all as sure of her maid, who looked very cross and grumpy. So things went on for some time very happily, and Mrs. Mouse began to look about for a good place to put her babies in, for she had fifteen of them. She found a large bottle under the wardrobe at one end, and so she told her husband she would put them there. It was not very nice of Mr. Mouse, but he disliked those babies. He thought them hideous, nasty little things, without any hair at all on their bodies, and he thought them horrid for the perpetual squeaking they kept up. He also said that he thought Mrs. Mouse might very well have been satisfied with half the number; but he only said that once, for his wife fired up in a moment, and said he was

Vainly did Mr. and Mrs. Mouse say to their children, in the most solemn tones, "Don't go near that cage; I don't quite know what it is, but I'm sure it is dangerous." The young ones did not mind them. They thought they would only go and look at it, and then the toasted cheese smelled so very good, it could do no harm just to try and taste it; and so *five* of them were caught, and next morning were given to the cat.

All the other brothers and sisters went into deep mourning, and could be seen wiping their eyes with their tails a great many times during the following days. Then one or two of them thought change of air would be the best thing for them, so they went down stairs for a short time, and when they came back, to Mr. Mouse's disgust, they each brought back a wife or a husband.

Mr. Mouse was quite angry at such an addition to a family already too large, he thought; so that evening, instead of staying quietly at home, and watching the young ones run races, he was so disturbed in his mind that he went out for a walk.

The moonlight was coming in through the window

the old lady's night-cap tasted like. He nibbled and nibbled until he had made a large hole; and then, finding it so amusing and nice, he crept under the clothes, and ate several large round holes in her night-gown. But alas for poor Mr. Mouse! The old lady in her sleep happened to roll over on her side: there was a faint squeak, rather muffled by the bedclothes, and Mr. Mouse's days on this earth were over.

Next morning the old lady said to her maid, "Brown, I wish you would look at my cap; there was something tickling and pressing my head last night, and also my leg." Brown looked, and was horrified at the big hole she found on her mistress's cap; but she was speechless when on looking into the bed she found Mr. Mouse's dead body, and two more holes in her mistress's night-gown. She wanted to get a dog or a cat, and any amount of traps; but the old lady was so sorry for the mouse she had killed that she made the excuse that perhaps he was the only one left, and that they would wait a little longer and see. Brown gave in, as she could not help

TOO MUCH TURKEY—THE KEEPER'S DREAM.—Drawn by F. S. Church.

into the room with her. "Oh, grandmamma!" she cried, "you must put on your things and come out. I have brought the carriage for you; the sun is shining so brightly; the wind is from the south, and it is quite summery. It will do you so much good to get some fresh air."

"Oh, little one, I could not," said grandmamma; "I have not been out for months, and I don't know where my things are. I don't think I can go out to-day. It does me almost as much good to see your bright face."

"You must come out, grandmamma; it's no use making excuses," said the young lady; and so the old lady gave in, as everybody did to this sunshiny little woman.

As soon as the two young Mrs. Mice heard the doors of the wardrobe opened, they scampered away as fast as they could. The bonnet was taken out, and then the muff, and you can think what a scene there was when the nasty hairless little mice tumbled out, and they found how utterly destroyed both bonnet and muff were.

That was the last of the Mouse family. The old lady moved into another room the next day. Her old room was cleared of furniture, the mouse-holes stopped up, a cat put in at night, and a bull-terrier by day, and traps of all kinds. Every mouse was killed, and not a single one from any other part of the house had courage to go into that room after such a tragedy.

The Raven Stone.—In Germany a superstition prevails that if the eggs are taken from a raven's nest, boiled, and replaced, the old raven will bring a root or stone to the nest, which he fetches from the sea. This "raven stone" confers great fortune on its owner, and has the power of rendering him invisible when worn on the arm. The stone is said to make the nest itself invisible; it must be sought with the aid of a mirror. In Pomerania and Rügen the method is somewhat different. The parent birds must have attained the age of one hundred years, and the would-be possessor of the precious "stone" must climb up and kill one of the young ravens. Then the aggressor descends, taking careful note of the tree. The old raven immediately returns with the stone, which he puts in the dead bird's beak, and thereupon both tree and nest become invisible. The man, however, feels for the tree, and on reaching the nest, he carries off the stone in triumph. The Swabian peasantry maintain that young ravens are nourished solely by the dew from heaven during the first nine days of their existence. As they are naked, and of a light color, the old birds do not believe that they are their progeny, and consequently neglect to feed them; but they occasionally cast a glance at the nest, and when the young ones begin to show a little black down on their breasts, by the tenth day, the parents bring them the first carrion.

Good-Night and Good-Morning.

OUR POST-OFFICE BOX

LETTER FROM A LITTLE GIRL ABOUT "HARPER'S YOUNG PEOPLE."

NEWPORT, RHODE ISLAND, November 6, 1879.

MR. EDITOR,—I don't know who to put at the head of this letter, because I don't know your first name. I wonder if it is Uncle Jake.

Papa found me reading what he called a "trash paper" the other day, and he said he would take a good paper for me if I would not read any more of that kind of trash; and he said you was going to print a new paper for young folks, and this morning he brought one home—the very first number; but he said he was disappointed in the size of it, and that it was not quite half as big as an ordinary paper at four cents, and I am afraid he will not take it for me; but mamma says if I write to you perhaps you would give me some good reason for the paper being smaller than papa expected, so that he will keep his promise, for I like the paper very much, and I have read about the "Brave Italian Boy," and so has father; and he says it is better than the kind of paper they throw in the door—"to be continued." So please tell me why your paper is not as big as the "trash papers," as father calls them, and I will be very thankful.

LOUISA M. D.

There are several reasons why *Harper's Young People* is not as large as the journals which you call "trash" papers. In the first place, *Harper's Young People* is very carefully printed on extra fine paper, which makes the type and illustrations look so clear and beautiful. And then a very large price is paid to the artists who draw the pictures, to the engravers who reproduce them on wood, and to the authors who contribute the reading matter which you find so interesting. The picture of "The Tournament," for instance, on the first page of the preceding number, cost over one hundred and fifty dollars for drawing and engraving. Some of the pictures will cost even more than that. If *Young People* was a larger weekly paper, and just as good in every respect as it is now, the price would necessarily be larger; and then some of our young readers might be deprived of the pleasure of having it.

Harper's Young People comes out every Tuesday; and if you read all the stories, poems, etc., and make out the puzzles and enigmas, you will find that it will take all the time you ought to spare from study, play, and other callings. We mean to make *Young People* the very best weekly for children in the world, so that they will always be glad to see it, as they would welcome a visit from a pleasant companion.

The following letters have been received in reply to the question, in the first number of *Young People*, as to the originator of cheap postage.

NEW YORK CITY.

The founder of the system of prepaying postage by placing a small label on one corner of the letter was Sir Rowland Hill. It was first advocated by him in 1837, and stamps were first used by the British Post-office May 6, 1840. They were introduced in the United States in 1847. Sir Rowland was born at Kidderminster in 1795, and died at Hampstead August 27, 1879, at the age of eighty-four.

WARREN J. LEE.

BROOKLYN, NEW YORK.

In answer to your question in the first number of *Young People*, asking if any one knew the name of the man who first thought of cheap postage, I would say that it was Sir Rowland Hill, of England. He died a few months ago at Hampstead, near London, and was buried in Westminster Abbey.

The answer to your letter puzzle in the same number is "Longfellow."

F. E. HUME (11 years old).

Clara S. Gardiner, St. Louis, Missouri, sends a similar reply.

Correct answers to letter puzzle have also been received from Albert E. Hebert, New York city, and Annie B. Stephens, Elizabeth, New Jersey. Several correct answers to the mathematical puzzle have been sent in, and will be published as soon as other correspondents have had time to try their skill.

LOUIS H. PATERSON, Montclair, New Jersey.—If you will put a very little oil of cloves, or still better, a few drops of creosote, into your ink, it will

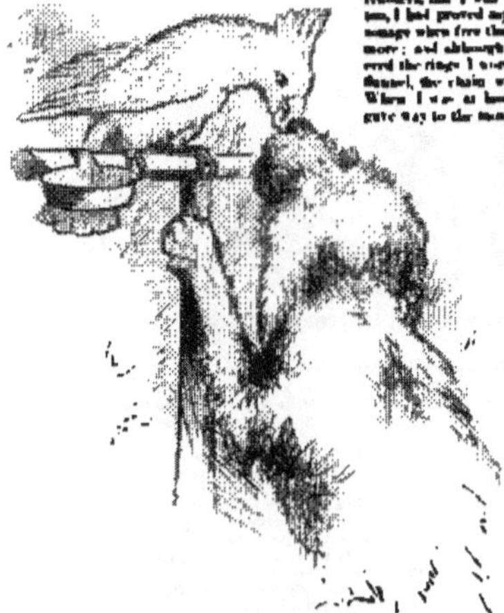

"FRITZ ADORED SUGAR."

(Continued from No. 3, Page 23.)

THE STORY OF A PARROT.

I SOON heard the sound of voices, and in a moment my mistress with the children entered the room. I greeted them with screams and laughter, while the whole party stopped in astonishment at the wrecked condition of the pretty sitting-room.

"Oh, Lorito, you bad, bad boy!" said Louis, shaking his finger at me.

"Bad boy! bad boy!" I screamed, to the great delight of the children, who forgot in an instant the mischief I had done, and began to laugh heartily. Seeing my advantage, I kept up a constant rattle of all the ridiculous nonsense I knew. The wine was still dancing in my head, and I made a very sorrowful exhibition of myself.

The children's mother soon discovered the empty bowl lying tipped over on the hearth.

"Poor Lorito is drunk," she said, laughing; "he has swallowed every drop of the wine. We must not blame him for his naughty actions. He is only a bird, and has not enough sense to let wine alone."

She then began to lament the loss of my beauty. I was indeed a frightful object; and when I heard my mistress declare that if I could not be cleaned I must be turned out of the house, my terror at the thought of losing what I had begun to realize was a comfortable home brought me to my sober senses at once. I hung my head and was silent. For the first time in my life I was mortified and ashamed of myself.

It was now decided to try water on my feathers, and Louis, perching me on his shoulder, carried me to the bath-room. I did feel the greatest inclination to bite his ear, but I contented myself by gently pulling his hair, which made him laugh.

It was a great luxury to get into the bath-tub, for no one had ever given me water to wet my feet for a very long time; and although parrots do not care to get in the tub every morning and flutter and sputter like canaries, still they like to wet their feet, and, above all things, they enjoy a gentle shower-bath, like a summer rain.

I can not say the bath the children gave me was what I would have chosen myself, for they rubbed me and scrubbed me and tumbled me feathers, but I was cold and miserable. Then, too, I had proved myself such a destructive personage when free that my feet were chained once more; and although my mistress had kindly covered the rings I wore round my ankles with soft flannel, the chain was still a dreadful burden. When I was at last left alone on my perch, I gave way to the most sorrowful meditations.

Still, all my present happiness dates from that troublesome time. The children were with me constantly, and their kind treatment completely cured me of my ugly, malicious temper. I then became acquainted with my dear friend Fritz, in whose company I have spent many happy hours. In order to talk with him I was compelled to learn his language, and soon I could bark so well that little Hope would clap her hands and say, "Our Rito makes a better doggie than Fritz himself."

Often when I sat on my perch Fritz would lie on the carpet near me, and we would hold long conversations together. He, too, had met with disappointments in life, and we consoled each other. We shared constantly the good things given us, and I soon discovered that Fritz adored sugar. As there were always some pieces in my feed dish, I kept them for him, and many a frolic we have had, for I never could help tantalizing him by holding the tempting morsel higher than he could jump.

I have had some nice friends in the garden, for in warm weather I was often carried out and placed on the branch of a tree, where I had the companionship of butterflies and bees and many kinds of birds. Although they were neither so large nor so beautiful in color as those I knew in my childhood on the banks of the Congo, still I found them excellent company. I would have been perfectly happy in the garden had it not been for the chain which fastened me to the branch; but experience had made me wiser than formerly, and I had learned not to expect perfect happiness, so I wore my chain patiently.

My feed dish was fastened at my side, and as it was always well filled with sugar, bird seed, and other dainties, I often offered some to my new friends; but so awed were they by my size and grand appearance that they feared to approach me, although they would sit on a neighboring branch and talk to me by the hour. Suddenly an idea occurred to me, which I at once put in practice. Springing from my branch, I hung in the air by my chain, which was not only healthy exercise, but left my feed dish free for my guests. They came in crowds, the sparrows of course, hundreds of them, and also robins and finches. So often was this repeated that, to the great surprise of the children, my feed dish was emptied several times every day.

"Mamma," I heard Carrie say once when they were all in the garden together, "Rito eats like an ogre. I am afraid he'll kill himself."

"The fresh air makes him hungry," said Louis, who always had a wise reason for everything the hay meadow, you eat like an ogre too. I heard grandma say so."

"Yes, I did eat all the jumbles in grandma's tin cake-box," said Carrie; "but that was only once, and every day nurse has to fill Rito's feed dish seven or eight times. He eats enough for ten Ritos."

"Oh, mamma, look at him!" screamed little Hope, who at that moment spied me indulging in my favorite exercise, swinging back and forth on my chain. The children and their mother ran toward me, while I, with one of my loud laughs (which I have heard some people say was a very wicked laugh: *I don't think so*), skillfully swung myself back to my branch, frightening as I did it a crowd of my feathered friends who were gathered about my feed dish. The children's mother saw them fly away. "Look," she cried; "there go the ogres. It is those thieving sparrows who eat so much, and not Lorito himself."

Now the sparrows may be too bold sometimes, but I do not think they are thieves, and it made me very angry to hear them called such a bad name. I screamed and struck my wings together so violently that I slipped from the branch, and was again swinging in the air by my chain.

"Mamma, Rito will break his legs, and then we shall have to kill him," screamed Louis, in alarm.

"Take off his chain, oh, mamma, do," said kind-hearted Carrie; while little Hope pleaded in her sweet voice: "Poor Rito will be good, mamma. He won't bite things any more."

You can not imagine how eagerly I listened to the discussion, for to be free from my chain was now my sole ambition. My heart was touched by the affection of the children, and when, to my intense delight, their mother yielded to their entreaties, I made a firm resolve that I would never bite and tear things again, unless by good luck I could find an old newspaper or a worthless stick, because I knew if I could not use my beak occasionally, it would ache as bad as Carrie's tooth does some nights when she goes crying to bed.

Since that time my life has been very peaceful.

I am free as air, my wings have recovered their strength, and I go wherever I please. Whenever my little master Louis whistles for me I answer him at once, for I have learned to whistle as well as he, and I always go as fast as I can to perch upon his hand.

When night comes, and it grows dark, I go into my cage myself, and my good friend Fritz always sleeps near me.

I have not forgotten my dear papa and mamma, nor my brother and sister, and I often wonder if they are still living in the beautiful hollow tree by the Congo; but I have learned to love new things, and to remember my childhood as a sweet dream instead of a lost and longed-for reality.

The gray parrot gave a little soft laugh, and was silent.

"I declare," said the canary, who had listened very attentively, "you have seen a lot of trouble. But why such a quiet, gentlemanly bird as you should have such a passion to bite and tear things, I can't imagine. Now my family—" But what the canary had to tell will always be a mystery, for at that moment the door opened and in came papa and mamma from the party.

"Oh, Fritz, you naughty dog!" said mamma, when she saw her pretty afghan lying in a heap on the floor. But when she lifted it to put it back on the lounge, she found Louis, still hugging his bow and arrow, Carrie, Hope, the white kitty, and Fritz, all curled up in a little warm bunch, sound asleep.

At that moment nurse, who had just returned from her party too, came running down stairs in great alarm.

"Sure, ma'am, the children ain't in their beds at all," she began, but stopped in astonishment when she saw her little charges sitting on the rug, rubbing their fists into their sleepy eyes.

"They did talk," said Louis, as soon as he was wide awake enough to speak. "Lorito told us all about his brother and sister and everybody."

"Yes, mamma, and he's so sorry he slipped over the tub," said Carrie.

"Good Kito loves me," said little Hope; "he wouldn't bite me for anything;" and she hugged her white kitty, and went fast asleep, with her little head on mamma's shoulder, while mamma laughed merrily at the children's wonderful dream.

The gray parrot did not say a word. He sat very quiet in his cage, his head buried in his feathers, and his eyes shut tight.

But if, as mamma said, the children had been dreaming, it was very funny indeed that they all three dreamed exactly the same thing.

THE END.

A GREEDY BOY'S THANKSGIVING DREAM.

Relative Age of Animals.—The average age of cats is 15 years; of squirrels and hares, 7 or 8 years; rabbits, 7; a bear rarely exceeds 20 years; a dog lives 20 years, a wolf 20, a fox 14 to 16; lions are long-lived, the one known by the name of Pompey living to the age of 70. Elephants have been known to live to the age of 400 years. When Alexander the Great had conquered Porus, King of India, he took a great elephant which had fought valiantly for the king, and named him Ajax, dedicated him to the sun, and let him go with this inscription, "Alexander, the son of Jupiter, dedicated Ajax to the sun." The elephant was found with this inscription 350 years after. Pigs have been known to live to the age of 30, and the rhinoceros to 20; a horse has been known to live to the age of 62, but they average 25 or 30; camels sometimes live to the age of 100; stags are very long-lived; sheep seldom exceed the age of 10; cows live about 15 years. Cuvier considers it probable that whales sometimes live 1000 years. The dolphin and porpoise attain the age of 30; an eagle died at Vienna at the age of 104; ravens have frequently reached the age of 100; swans have been known to live to the age of 300. Mr. Malerton has the skeleton of a swan that attained the age of 200 years. Pelicans are long-lived. A tortoise has been known to live to the age of 107 years.

WIGGLES.

THE thick black line in this picture is a fac-simile of the line No. 6 in our last Wiggles, which we submitted to our readers, on which to test their ingenuity.

We subjoin another Wiggle, and shall be happy to see what our young friends can do with it.

A NEW SERIAL
BY GEORGE MACDONALD.

A brilliant serial story by GEORGE MACDONALD, with illustrations by ALFRED FREDERICKS, will shortly be begun in HARPER'S YOUNG PEOPLE.

HARPER'S YOUNG PEOPLE.

HARPER'S YOUNG PEOPLE will be issued every Tuesday, and may be had at the following rates:

Four cents a number.
Single subscriptions for one year, $1 50; five subscriptions, one year, $7 00: payable in advance. Postage free.

Subscriptions may begin with any number. When no time is specified, it will be understood that the subscriber desires to commence with the number issued after the receipt of order.

Remittances should be made by Post-office Money Order, or Draft, to avoid risk of loss.

Published by HARPER & BROTHERS, New York.

A LIBERAL OFFER FOR 1880 ONLY.

☞ HARPER'S YOUNG PEOPLE and HARPER'S WEEKLY will be sent to any address for one year, commencing with the first number of HARPER'S WEEKLY for Janu-

Vol. I.—No. 5. Published by HARPER & BROTHERS, New York. Price Four Cents.

Tuesday, December 2, 1879. $1.50 per Year, in Advance.

THE TWINS.

YOUNG bears have always been great favorites as pets, being playful and affectionate when kindly treated. They can be trained to perform all kinds of amusing tricks; and their antics when playing together or with children are very laughable. They have been taught to execute difficult parts in theatrical displays, among other things, to ring bells, pretend to fall dead when shot at, beat the drum, and go through the manual exercise of the soldier with the musket.

But though playful and harmless when young, they can not be trusted when their teeth and claws are full grown. Then their good nature can not be counted on; and many instances have occurred in which they have repaid friendly confidence with sudden treachery. It must be said in their favor, however, that their wildness is often the result of bad treatment or thoughtless teasing. There is a story in point of a planter in Louisiana who once picked up a young cub that had either been abandoned by its mother, or had run away from the parental den. He carried it home and threw it down in the yard, where it was immediately adopted by the little negroes. It became a great favorite with them, sharing

grew large and stout, and learned to box and wrestle with the boys so well that visitors to the plantation were always entertained with these droll exhibitions.

But one day, in the spring, when he had been about a year in captivity, Billy was detected in making free with the young cabbages in the garden. A stout negro man picked up a branch of rose-bush, and gave the marauder a playful stroke. Filled with rage, Billy sprang upon the man, clasped him as if he had been a bundle of straw, and bit the poor fellow so severely that he died. Billy was at once shot. A pet that could not control his temper better than that was considered rather too dangerous to keep.

In a wild state, when in distress, young bears utter cries like those of a child in trouble. During an overflow of the Mississippi the inhabitants of a plantation were alarmed by the dreadful wailings, as was supposed, of some children in a swamp. After a careful search two little cubs were found in the hollow of an old tree, locked in each other's arms. The mother bear had been drowned or shot, and these funny little "babes in the woods" were crying with fright and hunger, and appeared to welcome the protection of man with real joy.

Bears are very fond of whiskey and other

[Begun in No. 1 of HARPER'S YOUNG PEOPLE, Nov. 4.]

THE BRAVE SWISS BOY.

IV.—A TERRIBLE FALL.

FOR a moment father and son stood silent on the brink of the crevasse, looking after the chamois.

"We can't get across here, father," said Walter, in a whisper; "let us try and find some other way."

"We can't find a better spot than this," replied his father, examining his gun.

"But what's the use of shooting him? What's the good of a dead chamois if we can't get him?"

"When he's once dead, boy, we'll soon find some means of getting at him," was the answer. "A board laid over the crevasse will be an easy way of recovering the venison."

"But we haven't got a board, father."

"That we'll see about. Just stand on one side, Watty."

The hunter cocked his gun, took aim for a moment, and was going to fire, when he turned suddenly pale, and dropped his arm.

"What's the matter, father? Do you feel ill?" inquired Walter, with anxiety.

"No," replied the huntsman; "but it seemed as if the ice was giving way just as I was going to fire. But it can't be," he continued, stamping his foot; "the ice is solid and firm enough."

"Let us go home, father," implored Walter. "I feel a presentiment that something will happen. Come home now, and we can try for the buck to-morrow."

But the old mountaineer had in the mean time become self-possessed again, and again raised his gun to fire. Just as he pulled the trigger, however, his foot slipped, and with an exclamation of horror, Walter saw him carried rapidly toward the rift in the ice, and suddenly disappear. With the recoil of the gun the hunter had lost his balance on the slippery ice, and at the same moment that his shot struck the chamois, he was hurled into the rift.

"*Father! father! father!*" screamed Walter, throwing himself on the ice, horror-stricken, and peering wildly down the crevasse. "Father, speak!"

All was silent. Only a slight trickling, as if from some subterranean stream, reached his ear.

For several minutes the youth lay at the edge of the chasm convulsed with terror. When he "Father!" he cried again into the abyss that yawned beneath him—"father, speak to me, for God's sake!"

A sudden thrill passed through his frame as a low murmur came up from the icy grave. He strained his ears to listen to the broken words.

"I am alive, Watty," was the reply of the unfortunate man; "but my ankle is out of joint, and one of my arms broken. I shall never see the light of day again."

A cry of mingled joy and agony burst from Walter's lips.

"Don't be afraid, father," he exclaimed. "You shall be rescued, with God's help. Have you got your bag with you?"

"Yes, but my bottle is broken."

"Well, then, take mine. I'll lower it down with a cord. Have you got it?"

"Yes," was feebly answered. "I can hold out now for a while, unless the cold strikes me."

"Courage, father, till I run down to the village, and get the neighbors and shepherds to come with ropes and poles. Try to hold out for a couple of hours, and with the help of God you with a godspeed Walter hurried off to rouse the neighbors to the rescue.

It was a dangerous journey that the brave boy undertook for his father's rescue; but courage, and the agility which is acquired by those who are accustomed to the mountains from childhood, enabled him to reach the valley in a wonderfully short time. Pale as death, with hands bleeding, and clothes torn to shreds, he rushed to the inn, which was the nearest spot where help could be found. His appearance naturally created consternation, and in answer to the numerous questions addressed to him he related in a few breathless words the dreadful accident which had befallen his father. A score of stalwart hands were instantly ready to rescue the unfortunate man from his dreadful position; the landlord of the inn ordered ropes, poles, and ladders to be got in readiness, and meanwhile pressed refreshment on the well-nigh exhausted youth. Moments were precious, but ere long the party reached the scene of the disaster, when Walter, leaning over the edge of the cleft, cried to his father, and was answered.

"Yes, I'm still alive," replied the mountaineer, in feeble tones; "but I am almost frozen to death, and in dreadful pain. Make haste and help me, if you can, for I'm losing my senses."

"Down with the rope!" shouted the landlord, who had himself come up with the party.—"Look out, Hirzel! Place the loop over your shoulders and under your arms, and try to draw it tight. There are plenty of strong arms here that will soon get you up."

The rope having been made fast to an iron stanchion driven into the ice, the looped end was lowered away into the chasm; but no sign was made by Hirzel that he had obeyed the directions, and fastened it round his body.

"Father, why don't you make haste?" exclaimed Walter in agony.

But there was no answer.

"He must have fainted at the last moment," said the landlord; "and if so, then may God have mercy upon him! for not a living creature could venture such a depth."

"*I* will venture it!" exclaimed Walter, seizing the rope. But twenty hands held him back. "Let me go!" he cried. "I must save my father!" and breaking loose with a sudden effort from the men who surrounded him, the courageous youth seized the rope and disappeared in sight of his horror-stricken companions.

A few terrible moments passed, when a shout

"LET ME GO!" HE CRIED. "I MUST SAVE MY FATHER!"

"Pull steadily, my men," cried the good landlord; "but pull as if your own lives depended on it. I can see them now!" exclaimed he, gazing into the gloomy abyss. "Hursel seems to have fainted, just as I thought, but Watty has fastened the rope round him securely. Pull away! they will be at the top in a few seconds."

Encouraged by success, the men redoubled their efforts, and had soon the satisfaction of landing father and son safely on the ice.

A rough kind of stretcher having been hastily made of poles and ropes, the wounded hunter was laid upon it and carried home; and as there was no lack of stout hearts and sure feet, the journey was accomplished without accident. After setting his broken limbs and binding up his wounds, the doctor, who had been speedily called in, expressed the hope that Hursel's life would be saved, but he doubted very much if he would ever be able to climb the mountains for chamois again. Walter was thankful to find that his father's life was in no danger, and had himself so far recovered his equanimity as to be able to relate how he had rescued him from his icy grave, and how he found that the rope, instead of having reached the wounded man, had actually rested on a ledge ten feet above the place where he lay. Walter, who felt devoutly thankful that his efforts had been so successful, was overwhelmed with praises for his heroism.

Nor was the chamois forgotten. The generous landlord had it brought down to the inn from the spot where it had fallen, and sent an ample equivalent to Hursel's cottage.

[TO BE CONTINUED.]

THE PROFESSOR ON TWINKLING.

JACK was delighted with the idea. Gus differed from him entirely. Joe and I, being girls, pronounced it—horrid.

"Papa wants us to, you know," said May, who always sets us straight.

Jack, who had recently joined one of the college societies, moved that the Professor be cordially supported. "His lecture last week was exceedingly entertaining," he argued. "That he should be so good as to come here and talk to us about his wonderful science in a pleasant familiar way, simply because he's papa's old friend, shows the interest he takes in the family."

"Do hush, Jack."

"My dear sister, I can not. What the Professor has to tell us about the heavenly bodies—"

"I hate the heavenly bodies," growls Gus.

"Is it jealousy, Augustus, because they are allowed to stay out late nights, while you are not?"

"Whatever it is, I agree with him," puts in Joe, who always stands by Gus. "I hate astronomy too."

"Feeling as I do, Josephine, that your knowledge in the science is confined to 'Twinkle, twinkle, little star,' and the fact that 'the moon is made of green cheese,' I am surprised at you."

"What makes them twinkle?" asked May.

The Professor heard this, for he was just coming up stairs.

"What makes them twinkle, May?" and the Professor seated himself in an easy-chair, as if ready to talk.

"I don't know, Sir. Won't you please tell us?" the word astronomers use is refracted. Now the stars are so far away from us that through the largest telescopes they are still only points of light. As the rays come down through space there is nothing to break or refract them, but when they reach our atmosphere, there is the tremulous agitation of the air and ascending vapors. By these the rays coming from the tiny points are at intervals turned aside from the narrow space of the pupil of the eye. When the eye is assisted with the wide opening of the object-glass of a telescope no such thing happens. So Jack is right; the stars don't twinkle. When viewed through a telescope, they are found to shine with a steady brightness, and hence the motion is only in appearance. Several astronomers have little to say about it; but it is due, doubtless, as Sir Isaac Newton explains in his celebrated *Principia*, to the ascending vapors and tremulous movements of the atmosphere. You have seen how the heated air or gas rising from a stove will sometimes make things behind it tremble and dance. Now if a small candle were burning on the other side of the ascending vapor, its flame, though really steady, would seem to flicker."

"Then, Sir, the stars, being so very far off, appear so very little, and the rays of light they send are disturbed by atmospheric vapor, and thus to the naked eye they twinkle."

"Yes," said the Professor. "The sun and moon, as you know, present broad disks, with lights radiating from every point—"

"Please, Professor," interrupted May, "tell us what a 'disk' is. Jack's big words are dreadful to understand; and this, although a little one, seems just as bad."

"I don't wonder it puzzled you, May. We use the word disk for the face or surface of a heavenly body which appears to have some size. You may always stop me when I use a word you don't understand; but when I have once told you, I shall want you to remember; for we can not know much about science unless we learn some of the hard words. I was saying that the sun and moon present broad disks, so that if some of the light is intercepted, the eye does not notice the loss. The same is true also of the planets, which appear large when they are magnified, but not of the stars, owing to their immense distances; and when the impurities in the atmosphere obscure or divert the narrow line of light they send to us, the eye perceives it at once. Some of the stars appear very brilliant through the large telescopes, but the light still seems to proceed from a single point. There are some four or five thousand stars that can be seen without a telescope."

"Why," interrupted Joe, "I thought it where a confused light comes from a sort of star-cloud, which has received the name of 'Milky Way.' But the stars that can be seen separately are very easily counted. Some persons can see rather more than others, on account of their eyesight being naturally better, or improved by use. A rough count of the number that could be seen through Herschel's famous telescope made it twenty thousand. The great telescopes more recently made would probably show as many as forty or fifty millions."

"I should think," said May, "that it would be awful nonsense to count so many things just alike, and that the man would often count the same one over and over without knowing it, and would never be sure that he had counted right."

"They are not all alike," said the Professor. "They differ greatly in brightness, and to some extent in color, and in other particulars. They have been divided according to their brilliancy into sixteen classes or magnitudes. The fifteen brightest stars are said to be of the first magnitude, the fifty next of the second, and so on to the sixth, which comprises the faintest stars visible to the unassisted eye. The brightest star of all visible in our latitude is the dogstar, which gives four times as much light as any other. In every age of the world there have been learned men interested enough in the stars to make catalogues of them, giving their magnitudes and their positions."

"I think they must have been very slow and stupid fellows," said Gus, "or they would have found something better to do."

At this the Professor laughed.

"I think, Gus, you are hungry, and have your mind on mutton-chops. I shall not talk to you any more this morning; but, after lunch, if you will look in one of the great books in papa's library, which he will point out, you will find pictures of all the great telescopes in the world. The best one in our own country is that at the United States National Observatory at Washington. Without the aid of these wonderful instruments we should never have learned much about the stars."

"ALL DAY HE BASKED IN THE FULL SPLENDOR OF THE SUN."

THE HISTORY OF PHOTOGEN AND NYCTERIS.

A Day and Night Mährchen.

By GEORGE MACDONALD.

III.—VESPER.

Behind the castle the hill rose abruptly; the northeastern tower, indeed, was in contact with the rock, and communicated with the interior of it. For in the rock was a series of chambers, known only to Watho and the one servant whom she trusted, called Falca. Some former owner had constructed these chambers after the tomb of an Egyptian king, and probably with the same design, for in the centre of one of them stood what could only be a sarcophagus, but that and others were walled off. The sides and roofs of them were carved in low relief, and curiously painted. Here the witch lodged the blind lady, whose name was Vesper. Her eyes were black, with long black lashes; her skin had a look of darkened silver, but was of purest tint and grain; her hair was black and fine and straight-flowing; her features were exquisitely formed, and if less beautiful, yet more lovely from sadness; she always looked as if she wanted to lie down and not rise again. She did not know she was lodged in a tomb, though now and then she wondered she never touched a window. There were many couches, covered with richest silk, and soft as her own cheek, for her to lie upon; and the carpets were so thick she might have cast herself down anywhere—as befitted a tomb. The place was dry and warm, and cunningly pierced for air, so that it was always fresh, and lacked only sunlight. There the witch fed her upon milk, and wine dark as a carbuncle, and pomegranates, and purple grapes, and birds that dwell in marshy places; and she played to her mournful tunes, and caused wailful violins to attend her, and told her sad tales, thus holding her ever in an atmosphere of sweet sorrow.

IV.—PHOTOGEN.

The witch at length had her desire, for witches often get what they want: a splendid boy was born to the fair Aurora. Just as the sun rose, he opened his eyes. Watho carried him immediately to a distant part of the castle, and persuaded the mother that he never cried but once, dying the moment he was born. Overcome with grief, Aurora left the castle as soon as she was able, and Watho never invited her again.

And now the witch's care was that the child should not know darkness. Persistently she trained him, until at last he never slept during the day, and never woke during the night. She never let him see anything black, and even kept all dull colors out of his way. Never, if she could help it, would she let a shadow fall upon him, watching against shadows as if they had been live things that would hurt him. All day passed into a world as unknown to her as this was to her child—who would have to be born yet again before she could see her mother.

Watho called her Nycteris, and she grew as like Vesper as possible—in all but one particular. She had the same dark skin, dark eyelashes and brows, dark hair, and gentle, sad look; but she had just the eyes of Aurora, the mother of Photogen, and if they grew darker as she grew older, it was only a darker blue. Watho, with the help of Falca, took the greatest possible care of her—in every way consistent with her plans, that is, the main point in which was that she should never see any light but what came from the lamp. Hence her optic nerves, and indeed her whole apparatus for seeing, grew both larger and more sensitive; her eyes, indeed, stopped short only of being too large. She was a sadly dainty little creature. No one in the world except those two was aware of the being of the little bat. Watho trained her to sleep during the day, and wake during the night. She taught her music, and taught her scarcely anything else.

VI.—HOW PHOTOGEN GREW.

The hollow in which the castle of Watho lay was a cleft in a plain rather than a valley among hills, for at the top of its steep sides, both north and south, was a table-land large and wide. It was covered with rich grass and flowers, with here and there a wood, the outlying colony of a great forest. These grassy plains were the finest hunting grounds in the world. The chief of Watho's huntsmen was a fine fellow, and when Photogen began to outgrow the training she could give him, she handed him over to Fargu. He with a will set about teaching him all he knew. He got him pony after pony, larger and larger as he grew, every one less manageable than that which had preceded it, and advanced him from pony to horse, and from horse to horse, until he was equal to anything in that kind which the country produced. In similar fashion he trained him to the use of bow and arrow, substituting every three months a stronger bow and longer arrows, and soon he became, even on horseback, a wonderful archer. Every day, almost as soon as the sun was up, he went out hunting, and would in general be out nearly the whole of the day. But Watho had laid upon Fargu just one commandment, namely, that Photogen should on no account, whatever the plea, be out until sundown, or so near it as to wake in him the desire of seeing what was going to happen; and this commandment Fargu was anxiously careful not to break; for although he would not have trembled had a whole herd of bulls come down upon him, charging at full speed across the level, and not an arrow left in his quiver, he was more than afraid of his mistress. So that, as Photogen grew older, Fargu began to tremble, for he found it steadily growing harder to restrain him. He did not know what fear was, and that not because he did not know danger; for he had had a severe laceration from the razor-like tusk of a boar—whose spine, however, he had severed with one blow of his hunting-knife before Fargu could reach him with defense.

When the boy was approaching his sixteenth year, Fargu ventured to beg of Watho that she would lay her commands upon the youth himself, and release him from responsibility for him. One might as soon hold a tawny-maned lion as Photogen, he said. Watho called the youth, laid her command upon him never to be out when the rim of the sun should touch the horizon, accompanying the prohibition with hints of consequences none the less awful that they were obscure. Photogen listened respectfully, but knowing neither the taste of fear nor the temptation of the night, her words were but sounds to him.

VII.—HOW NYCTERIS GREW.

The little education she intended Nycteris to have, Watho gave her by word of mouth. Not meaning she should have light enough to read by, she never put a book in her hands. Nycteris, however, saw so much better than Watho imagined, that the light she gave her was quite sufficient, and she managed to coax Falca into teaching her the letters, after which she taught herself to read, and Falca now and then brought her a child's book. But her chief pleasure was in her instrument. Her very fingers loved it, and would wander about over its keys like feeding sheep. She was not unhappy. She knew nothing of the world except the tomb in which she dwelt, and had some pleasure in everything she did. But she desired, nevertheless, something more or different. She did not know what it was, and the nearest she could come to expressing it to herself was—that she wanted more room. Watho and Falca would go from her beyond the shine of the lamp, and come again; therefore surely there must be more room somewhere. As often as she was left alone she would fall to poring over the colored bass-reliefs on the walls. These were intended to represent various of the powers of Nature under allegorical similitudes, and as nothing can be made that does not belong to the general scheme, she could not fail at least to imagine a flicker of relationship between some of them, and thus a shadow of the reality of things found its way to her.

There was one thing, however, which moved and taught her more than all the rest—the lamp, namely, that hung from the ceiling, which she always saw alight, though she never saw the flame, only the slight condensation toward the centre of the alabaster globe. And besides the operation of the light itself after its kind, the indefiniteness of the globe, and the softness of the light, giving her the feeling as if her eyes could go in and into its whiteness, were somehow also associated with the idea of space and room. She would sit for an hour together gazing up at the lamp, and her heart would swell as she gazed. She would wonder what had hurt her when she found her face wet with tears, and then would wonder how she could have been hurt without knowing it. She never looked thus at the lamp except when she was alone.

(TO BE CONTINUED.)

EMBROIDERED CANVAS RUG.

THE pretty glove-case published in No. 2, November 11, was warmly welcomed, and our young friends are eagerly clamoring for more holiday gifts that they can make readily and cheaply. In compliance with their wish we will occasionally furnish fancy articles that can be manufactured by little hands. One of the most tasteful and useful presents that we can suggest is a handsome canvas rug, which can be easily made with the help of the accompanying picture and description, and which is sure to prove a successful Christmas gift. The rug is made of écru linen Java canvas, which, with the border, can be bought cheaply in any large fancy store. The centre of the rug is twenty-eight inches long and nineteen inches wide, and is embroidered in loop stitch with claret-colored worsted. The border is four inches wide, and is worked in cross stitch with similar worsted. That useful periodical, *Harper's Bazar*, gives full directions for working these and many other stitches. Almost every little girl, however, knows how to make these simple stitches, or can find some one to show her. The rug is lined with gray drilling,

Fig. 1.—Rug.—[See Figs. 2-4.]

Fig. 2.—Reel for Rug, Fig. 1.

and edged with fringe, of which the illustration Fig. 4 shows a full-sized section.

To make the fringe first twist together threads of claret-colored worsted. For this purpose use a wooden reel, the middle rod of which forms a movable handle. One side of the reel is furnished with brass hooks on the ends. Lay a thread of claret-colored worsted on the upper hook as shown by Fig. 2, turn the reel quickly, holding the thread double with the left hand and the handle of the reel with the right hand until the thread has been twisted long enough to be wound on the reel, with the hands in the position as shown by Fig. 3. When the threads have been twisted of sufficient

Electric Ornaments.—Some curious trinkets, to which certain motions can be given at will by means of electricity, have recently been devised by an ingenious Frenchman, M. Trouvé. Two of these are scarf pins: one has a death's-head, gold or enamel, with diamond eyes and ivory articulated jaw; the other has a rabbit seated upright on a bar with a little bell before it, to be struck with two rods held in the animal's fore-paws. An invisible wire connects these objects with a small hermetically closed battery, the dimensions of which is about the size of a cigarette. It is kept in the waistcoat pocket, and acts only when turned horizontally or inverted. When a person looks at the pin, the owner, slipping a finger into his pocket, turns the battery, whereupon the death's-head rolls its eyes and grinds its teeth, or the little rabbit beats the bell with its rods (through electro-magnetic action). A third kind of ornament is a small bird set with diamonds, to be fixed in a lady's hair, and the wings of which can be set in motion electrically.

The Great Wall of China.—An American engineer engaged in the construction of a railway in China, gives the following account of this wonderful work. The wall is 1728 miles long, 18 feet high, and 15 feet thick at the top. The foundation throughout is of solid granite, the remainder of compact masonry. At intervals of between two hundred and three hundred yards towers rise up, twenty-five to thirty feet high, and twenty-four feet in diameter. On the top of the wall and on both sides of it are masonry parapets to enable the defenders to pass unseen from one tower to another. The wall is carried from point to point in a straight line, across valleys, plains, and hills, sometimes plunging down into deep abysses. Rivers are bridged over by the wall, while on both banks of large streams strong flanking towers are placed.

Fig. 3.—Reel for Rug, Fig. 1.

MARGOTTE'S STORY.

"I WILL tell you the story," said Margotte, pausing in her knitting, as we leaned together over the white palings of her little garden. "Yes, there is a story, madame—a story of a wolf; but you have got it wrong, madame, and I must set you right."

Picture a sunset in the Pyrenees, a glorious crimson sky tipping the distant peaks with pale pink, and deepening the purple shadows on the nearer mountains—the mountains that inclose and overtop Margotte Nerale's pretty house. I had come for a quiet month to this picturesque, secluded village, and though my month was over, I was tempted to linger day after day, for the sake of the sunshine and the mountains, and not least, perhaps, for the sake of these two peasant girls, with whom I lodged.

Margotte was the youngest of the two by fifteen years—the three boys who came between had died—and though it is very long since we leaned side by side over the white palings I can always call her to mind as she stood knitting there.

She was tall and strong, and finely made, with a clear white skin, and brown hair waving in heavy masses under her white starched cap. She had beautiful

dropping her knitting into her apron pocket: "I will tell you the story of the wolf, madame. Léontine is out, and it is a grand story—a story I should like you to hear."

"It was night," said Marguerite, "a cruel, cold winter night, such as we who live amongst the mountains have terrible cause to dread, for it means hunger and cold—sometimes absolute famine. It means the children crying for food when there is none to give them, and the wolves howling in the distance. Ah! those wolves, madame, how they make one shudder with their monotonous howls, that seem so near at first, and then die away into the far distance!

"Well, it was night, as I have said, and the baby was asleep, as it might be here, and Léontine was knitting on the hearth, and Marcelle, a friend of Léontine's, was chattering to her, kneeling on the stones, and the door was on the latch.

"That was the mischief, you see; but Léontine was young then, and Marcelle was a giddy, thoughtless chatterer, and she had run in with her shawl over her head for an hour's talk. Léontine has told me of it so often that I almost seem to see the two girls crouching by the fire that sent bright and flickering reflections on to the snow outside.

"Suddenly, as they talked, there came distinctly to them the howling of the wolves across the snow. Marcelle put her hands over her ears and shuddered. Léontine knelt up and stirred the fire.

"'Come closer, my friend,' she said; 'it is a dreary sound. Thank God, we are safe here!'

"'Are we safe, do you think?' asked Marcelle, with chattering teeth. 'I dare not go home to-night. Will your mother let me stay here, Léontine?'

"'Surely,' said Léontine.

"She was so brave, my sister, my dear, dear sister, madame, and so gentle! she took Marcelle's head upon her knee, and put her knitting aside to soothe her terror.

"'We are quite safe, Marcelle,' she said, 'and mother will soon be back. It is a dreary night.'

"It was a dreary night, dark and still and terribly cold; the white flakes were falling slowly to the earth, and covering the mother's footsteps on the path.

"Léontine walked over to the window and looked out; the firelight was dancing and flickering on the snow outside, and making a cheerful patch of ruddy light in the darkness, which would guide the mother's steps for her home-coming. Through the darkness the howling of the wolves seemed nearer.

"'Ah, they are coming closer,' said Marcelle, starting upright. 'Can you see them, Léontine? I am afraid!'

"Léontine was leaning close to the glass, pressing her face against it.

"'Yes, I see shadows,' she said; 'they are coming to the light, Marcelle. No! it is only one shadow, after all; we must not frighten each other.'

"She turned with a faint smile to Marcelle's shuddering face, and tried to draw the curtains with her trembling hands, but the shadow on the snow was very near.

"'Do not be afraid, my dear,' she said, kneeling down upon the hearth again, and drawing Marcelle's cold hands into her own strong ones. 'Be brave; we are quite safe, you know; the door is strong, and God is so good, Marcelle.'

and a terrible howl that seemed to shake the little cottage to its foundations. Then—oh! think of it, madame—the door—the door against which you lean—was burst open, and out of the darkness a great wolf came bounding in, and paused for a minute on the threshold.

"Léontine was upright in an instant, standing before the cradle. Even Marcelle rose also, and stood shrieking on the hearth.

"But the great, lean, hungry wolf came slinking on—and it passed Léontine, and took the little baby from the cradle.

"Léontine had stood as if rooted to the spot, with her burning eyes fascinated by the awful sight; but now she strode to the table, and took a knife. And yet she dared not throw it, because of the baby, madame.

"They seemed so helpless all of a sudden, those two girls, while the great beast crept past them again, trotting to the door. Marcelle had taken a fagot from the fire, and cast it at him, but he only shook it off, and growled savagely, bounding out into the snow.

"Ah, madame, it was terrible—terrible; and yet, as Léontine always says, God is good.

"For while Marcelle was crying by the empty cradle, and the snow was sweeping into the room and putting out the fire, Léontine had sprung to the door, and had flung herself to the ground, with her brave white face not two inches from the wolf's glaring eyes; she stretched out her hands and caught him by his shaggy coat, twisting her strong fingers into his matted hair. She still held her knife firmly, but she dared not use it.

"She succeeded in her wish, madame, however; the wolf was surprised and angry. With a low, fierce growl, that made Marcelle's heart beat to suffocation, he dropped the baby.

"Léontine has told me often that she never knows how she came living out of that terrible struggle; she says she remembers crying aloud to God to keep the baby safe, and to take the life she offered up so willingly instead. She remembers striking with her knife at the great body that fell upon her, bleeding and suffocating her; then there came to her ears a dim faint sound like music, and my crowing was the baby, you have guessed, madame—and then silence, such silence as Léontine says she thinks will be like the silence of death.

"But it was not death. Ah, no—there is Léontine, you see, coming up with her pitcher from the well; and the wolf, the last wolf killed in St. Priest, lies buried not a foot from where we stand; but Léontine will carry her trophy of victory to her dying day. Some people say that her face would be very beautiful but for the scar; but for me, madame, I think that it is the scar that makes her face so beautiful."

OUR POST-OFFICE BOX.

OUR young friends must not be impatient if their communications are not noticed immediately. Our space is limited, and we answer or print letters in the order in which they are re-

[illegible] story is very pretty, but we have no room to print it.

[illegible].—The full operations in figures should be sent with all answers to mathematical puzzles.

LYMAN C.—Your land-turtle will eat pieces of pear or sweet apple, bread, cake, and many other things. It will also live many months without eating at all. You can keep it in a box, and it will be happier if you give it a little earth to dig in. If the earth is deep enough, it will make a burrow and sleep in it until next spring. We know a little girl who received a present of two land-turtles, which she placed in the yard. In a few days she was unable to find them, and gave them up for lost. The next spring, six months afterward, she was digging in her flower beds, when, to her astonishment, she found her two lost pets, who opened their eyes on being disturbed, and crawled sluggishly out of their hole. They had been asleep all through the cold weather, for turtles are very long lived, and they can easily give a whole winter to a single nap. Rev. Mr. Wood, in a note to White's *Natural History of Selborne*, gives a very interesting account of a tame turtle which he allowed to crawl about his study. The turtle showed a great genius for climbing, and at one time actually succeeded in scrambling upon a footstool. He says: "Its food consisted of bread and milk, which it ate several times a day, drinking the milk by scooping up some of it in its lower jaw, and then by throwing its head back the milk ran down its throat."

YOUNG CHEMIST.—Spread on your paper first a solution of iodide of potassium, then a solution of nitrate of silver. Iodide of silver forms, and saturates the paper. The excess of nitrate of silver and the heavy yellow powder which forms are now washed off, and the paper is ready for the camera. The picture may be developed by a solution of gallic acid mixed with a very small quantity of an aqueous solution of acetic acid and nitrate of silver. The picture is fixed by washing with hyposulphite of soda. If you wish to derive any pleasure from photography, you would better drop the old-fashioned paper process, and turn your attention to ferrotypes, or negatives on glass, as with these good results are more easily obtained than with paper.

We acknowledge very pretty and neatly written letters from St. Clair Nichol, Listowel, Ontario, and Charles L. Benjamin (nine years old), Washington, D. C., both containing correct information respecting Sir Rowland Hill.

CLARENCE H. H.—Your answer to No. 4 of the mathematical puzzles is right. If you look carefully you will discover why the others are wrong.

G. A. Page sends correct answers to Nos. 1, 3, and 4 of the mathematical puzzles in our second number, also to numerical charade. Many thanks to "an instructor and lover of young people" for her kind note. We are sorry it is anonymous.

A correspondent sends answers to puzzles which we have not considered, as no signature accompanies them. Our young friends will please sign their full names to communications, which we will not print if so requested.

"Little Polly, will you go a-walking to-day?"
"Indeed, little Susan, I will, if I may."
"Little Polly, your mother has said you may go:
She was nice to say 'Yes;' she should never say 'No.'"

Six little people out for a walk;
They would let you know where, if they only could talk.

Three tabbies took out their cats to tea,
As well-behaved tabbies as well could be:
Each sat in the chair that each preferred,
They mewed for their milk, and they sipped and purred.
Now tell me this (as these cats you've seen them)—
How many lives had these cats between them?

Will you be my little wife,
If I ask you? Do!
I'll buy you such a Sunday frock,
A nice umbrella too.

And you shall have a little hat,
With such a long white feather,
A pair of gloves and sandal shoes,
The softest kind of leather.

And you shall have a tiny house,
A beehive full of bees,
A little cow, a largish cat,
And green sage cheese.

Yes, it is sad of them—
Shocking to me;
Bad—yes, it's bad of them—
Bad of all three.
Warnings they've had from me. Yet they will row about;

Poor Dicky's dead!—The bell we toll,
And lay him in the deep, dark hole.
The sun may shine, the clouds may rain,

Vol. I.—No. 6. | Published by HARPER & BROTHERS, New York. | Price Four Cents.

Tuesday, December 9, 1879. | $1.50 per Year, in Advance.

TWENTY MILES AN HOUR.

It was the 6th of January, that great holiday in Russia, when the river Neva is consecrated with pomp and ceremony, when soldiers parade and priests say mass, and the Emperor is visible, and the cannon roar. And it was a gloriously bright and beautiful day; but Ivan and Olga, looking out on the broad street and the glittering pinnacles of the palace chapel, watching the sledges fly by with people all muffled in furs, were two very discontented children. They had an English governess—for Russian children have to study English as Americans do French—and they had been so naughty, so impatient, and indifferent to lessons, that Miss Stanley had forbidden their going out to see the sights. This was hard indeed, but it was needful; that the children could not understand, and they walked from the great porcelain stove, which reached to the ceiling, over to the double windows, all packed with sand, and having curious little paper cornucopias of salt stuck in it to keep the frost from making pictures on the glass, to and fro, to and fro, in great unhappiness. Outside, the thermometer was away below zero, but inside, thanks to the stoves and the great copper heaters, it was as warm as toast.

"Now, Olga," said Ivan, after an hour or two of this tiresome way of spending time, "I am not going to stand this any longer; if I can not go to the Neva, I am

three. Every one was at church, and the dvornik, or porter who guarded the front door, was snoozing soundly, wrapped up in his sheep-skins, near the heater. They got their fur mittens and tippets and cloaks down from the pegs where they were hanging in the heated air, and put them on in silence. In silence, too, they lifted the huge bolts, and slipped out into the street. It was too cold to speak, for the air would have frozen on their lips, and they hurried to a corner where usually there were to be found sledges, whose drivers can endure any amount of cold, and who even sleep out at night at theatre and opera while waiting for their masters. Here Ivan found what he wanted, though the man's dull gaze seemed to ques-

ON THE ICE-HILL.

which is always holding and ready for use. Olga had scarcely time to think what she was about before she was seated behind Ivan, and away they flew down the side of the frozen mountain, all as hard as glass. But now it began to snow fast, thick, and furious, and the people could not keep it off the ice. Ivan was getting tired, too, and his hands were cold. This fun of going twenty miles an hour had filled him with glee; but Olga [illegible] her heavily, and he found it hard to guide his sled. Suddenly he made a swerve to the left, and, with a fearful jerk, over they went. It was a dreadful blow, and had it not been for the kindness of the people in charge, both might have been badly injured; but they were picked up and carried to the pavilion, rubbed with snow on their noses and ears, and finally packed in a sledge and driven home. How differently they looked at the glittering crowd, and watched the animated scene! They had gone out full of excitement and daring; resolved as Ivan was to resist authority, he now was full of shame that he had gotten himself into a scrape. His fingers ached, and Olga was crying and complaining of her ears. As they neared their home a troika drove up with ladies wrapped in sables, and their mother and Miss Stanley alighted.

"Ivan! Olga! where have you been? what have you been doing?"

They told their story when they got in-doors, and Ivan had begged some kopeks with which to pay the waiting isvoshchik—for his money had been exhausted; and it was settled that they had been sufficiently punished when it was discovered that Ivan's fingers and Olga's ears were frost-bitten.

Both were sent to bed for fear of further harm from the cold, which is considered by Russians the

BURIED TREASURE.

Once a time—I do not know
Exactly where, but long ago—
A man whose riches were untold,
Silver and precious stones and gold,
Within an Eastern city dwelt;
But not a moment's peace he felt,
For fear that thieves should force his door
And rob him of his treasured store.
In spite of armed slaves on guard,
And doors and windows locked and barred
His life was one continual fright;
He hardly slept a wink by night,
And had so little rest by day
That he grew prematurely gray.

At last he dug a monstrous pit
To hold his wealth, and buried it
By night, alone; then smoothed the ground
So that the spot could not be found.
But he gained nothing by his labor:
A curious, prying, envious neighbor,
Who marked the hiding, went and told
The Sultan where to find the gold.
A troop of soldiers came next day,
And bore the hoarded wealth away.

Some precious jewels still remained,
For which a goodly price he gained,
Then left the city, quite by stealth,
To save the remnant of his wealth;
But now, by hard experience taught,
A better way to keep it sought.
Broad lands he bought, and wisely tilled;
With fruits and grain his barns he filled;
He used his wealth with liberal hand;
His plenty flowed through all the land;
And, hid no longer under-ground,
Spread honest comfort all around.

Thus calm and prosperous pass the years
Till on a fated day he hears
The Sultan's mandate, short and dread,
"Present thyself, or lose thy head!"
Fearful and trembling, he obeys,
For Sultans have their little ways,
And wretches who offend their lord
Share bastinado, sack, or cord.

Before the dreaded throne he bowed
Where sat the Sultan, grim and proud,
And thought, "My head must surely fall,
And then my master will seize all
My wealth again." But from the throne
There came a calm and kindly tone:
"My son, well pleased am I to see
Thy dealings in prosperity;
May Allah keep thee in good health!

"But why need we be in such a hurry?" inquired Seppi.

"Because we've nothing more to stay for, and the longer we stay here, the more expense we shall cause to Mr. Friedhardt, and that would be very wrong."

The drover shrugged his shoulders, and after a long interval added, cautiously, "You must be very soft, Walter. If you were only a little more wide-awake, we might make a good thing for ourselves out of this affair, and no one be any the wiser."

"In what way?"

"Don't you see what I mean?" continued Seppi, with a cunning smile. "You've got about one-third more cash than Friedhardt expects. What is there to hinder us from dividing it between us? It would be a good thing for us, and nobody could ever find it out, because we should both keep it dark."

"I hope you are only joking," said Walter, with a serious look. "Do you think I am going to swindle my master because he has put so much confidence in me? You can't surely be in earnest, Seppi. You only want to test my honesty."

"Bother your honesty," returned Seppi. "Sharpness is better than honesty nowadays. You've got more than thirty thousand francs in that belt round your waist; we've only got to divide it between us, and then we could lead a glorious life in Paris. No one could ever find us out, for the city is so large that Friedhardt might search for weeks before getting on our track. Look at that, Walter! You'll perhaps never have such a splendid chance again as long as you live. What have you to lose at home? Nothing. You'll only be a poor half-starved fellow if you go back. Now's your time. Seize the opportunity at once, like a man."

Walter refused, with great indignation, to heed this infamous advice. His earnest words were followed by a loud burst of laughter from his companion. "Don't fly into a rage, comrade, and excite yourself that way," said Seppi. "You don't seem to know what a joke is. Just as if we could pocket all that money without the police being at our heels directly. Why, we

fall. I know a cheap and comfortable inn there; so the sooner we're off the better."

Much pleased that his companion should agree so readily to leave Paris, Walter felt sorry that he had entertained any doubts of his character, even for a moment. Their simple preparations were speedily made, and half an hour afterward they set out upon their return, and took the road to Belmy.

It was dark by the time they reached their destination; but as Seppi knew the village well, he had no difficulty in finding the inn, which was about ten minutes' walk from the high-road. The house was old and uncomfortable in its appearance, and produced a very unfavorable impression upon Walter; but the welcome they received from the landlord was so cordial that the impression was at once removed. An old married couple and a young and powerfully built fellow seemed to be the only occupants of the large building. At Seppi's order a bottle of wine was brought, and Walter, being somewhat fatigued with the journey, was easily persuaded to take more than

"HE UNBUCKLED THE MONEY-BELT."

anything he asks for; but keep an eye on him, for he is not right in his head, and must either have some one always with him, or be locked in his room. I can't take him with me in the morning, and so I have brought him here, where I know he will be in good hands. You will promise to attend to what I have told you, André?"

"Your instructions shall be attended to," replied the other, slipping the gold coin which Seppi tendered him into his pocket. "You shall have no reason to complain."

"That's well. When I come back you shall have another gold piece if I find everything right. And look here; only bolt the outer door to-night instead of locking it, or else leave the key in the lock, so that I can get away in the morning without waking anybody."

The man promised to attend to that also, and quitted the apartment. When he was gone, Seppi bolted the room door, and gazed at his unconscious companion with a malicious scowl.

"Fool!" said he, "I made you a fair offer when I proposed to go halves with the money; but as you were idiot enough to decline, so much the better for me. When you wake in the morning you'll be sorry you let the chance slip."

Then muttering to himself, he unbuckled the money-belt that was round the waist of the sleeping youth, and fastened it securely round his own. He then abstracted Walter's passport and the other papers that were in his pockets, without arousing him.

"He lies there like a dead dog," thought the drover; "and, with the dose I gave him, is not likely to trouble any one till morning."

Waiting impatiently for more than an hour, until every one was in bed and the house silent, Seppi quitted the room on tiptoe, locked the door on the outside, and crept noiselessly along the passage and down the stairs. André had not forgotten to leave the outer door unlocked, and pushing back the bolt with the greatest caution, the ruffian slipped out, and as soon as he had got clear of the village hurried away at the top of his speed.

The Swiss drover had shown great cunning in his scheme to get possession of the money from

GOLD-FISH.

SOME time during the seventeenth century, about two hundred years ago, Portuguese sailors saw swimming in the lakes and rivers of China and Japan a very beautiful variety of fish, which glistened like gold. They captured some specimens, and brought them to Portugal. The little fish found the lakes of Europe as pleasant to live in as the lakes of China, and they at once domesticated themselves, and raised their little families, until the European streams became well stocked with these beautiful creatures. They are also found in many brooks and streams in the United States.

The glistening gold-color of these fishes made them much sought for as household ornaments, and the demand for them became so general that establishments were opened for raising them for the market. One of the largest and most celebrated of these places for gold-fish breeding is in Oldenburg, Germany, where more than a hundred small ponds contain the fish in all stages of growth, from the tiniest baby to the big stout fellow eight and even ten inches long. The little ones are carefully kept apart from larger ones, for the gold-fish is a wicked cannibal, and devours its little brothers and sisters, and even its own children, whenever it has an opportunity. At the same time it is a great coward, and will hide away from fish much smaller than itself that have the spirit to attack it. A gentleman who possessed an aquarium in which were several large gold-fish, once placed a tiny "pumpkin-seed," or sunfish, about the size of a silver half dollar, in the water. Watching anxiously to see that the gold-fish did not injure it, what was his astonishment to see the "pumpkin-seed" dart furiously at the larger fish, which huddled themselves in a corner, or scurried hastily through the water to hide among the stones and minute grottoes of the aquarium! From that moment the

represents them, when moving, in a shifting and changeable variety of dimensions, shades, and colors, while the two mediums, assisted by the convex-concave shape of the vessel, magnify and distort them vastly." Still, the fish may be healthier if kept in an aquarium, as it allows more surface to the water, and consequently more air and ventilation. In any case, fresh water should be given the fish at least every other day, and if the globe or aquarium be ornamented with rocks and water-grasses, the fish should be carefully dipped out once a week, and the rock thoroughly cleansed from all impurities.

Although the fish draw nourishment from animalcules supplied by the water, and will live a long time without other food, it is advisable to feed them by throwing bread-crumbs, or flies and

STRANGE GOLD-FISHES.

[Begun in No. 5 of HARPER'S YOUNG PEOPLE, Dec. 2.]

THE HISTORY OF PHOTOGEN AND NYCTERIS.

A Day and Night Mährchen.

BY GEORGE MACDONALD.

VIII.—THE LAMP.

WATHO having given orders, took it for granted they were obeyed, and that Falca was all night long with Nycteris, whose day it was. But Falca could not get into the habit of sleeping through the day, and would often leave her alone half the night. Then it seemed to Nycteris that the white lamp was watching over her. As it was never permitted to go out—while she was awake at least—Nycteris, except by shutting her eyes, knew less about darkness than she did about light. Also, the lamp being fixed high overhead, and in the centre of everything, she did not know much about shadows either. The few there were fell almost entirely on the floor, or kept like mice about the foot of the walls.

Once, when she was thus alone, there came the noise of a far-off rumbling: she had never before heard a sound of which she did not know the origin, and here, therefore, was a new sign of something beyond these chambers. There came a trembling, then a shaking; the lamp dropped from the ceiling to the floor with a great crash, and she felt as if both her eyes were hard shut and both her hands over them. She concluded that it was the darkness that had made the rumbling and the shaking, and rushing into the room, had thrown down the lamp. She sat trembling. The noise and the shaking ceased, but the light did not return. The darkness had eaten it up!

Her lamp gone, the desire at once awoke to get out of her prison. She scarcely knew what out meant; out of one room into another, where there was not even a dividing door, only an

Nycteris could see better than any cat, but now her great eyes were not of the smallest use to her. As she went she trod upon a piece of the broken lamp. She had never worn shoes or stockings, and the fragment, though, being of soft alabaster, it did not cut, yet hurt her foot. She did not know what it was, but as it had not been there before the darkness came, she suspected that it had to do with the lamp. She knelt, therefore, and searched with her hands, and bringing two large pieces together, recognized the shape of the lamp. Therewith it flashed upon her that the lamp was dead, that this brokenness was the death of which she had read without understanding, that the darkness had killed the lamp. What, then, could Falca have meant when she spoke of the lamp *going out*? There was the lamp—dead, indeed, and so changed that she would never have taken it for a lamp but for the shape. No, it was not the lamp any more now it was dead, for all that made it a lamp was gone, namely, the bright shining of it. Then it must be the shine, the light, that had gone out! That must be what Falca meant—and it must be somewhere in the other place in the wall. She started afresh after it, and groped her way to the curtain.

Now she had never in her life tried to get out, and did not know how; but instinctively she began to move her hands about over one of the walls behind the curtain, half expecting them to go into it, as she supposed Watho and Falca did. But the wall repelled her with inexorable hardness, and she turned to the one opposite. In so doing she set her foot upon an ivory die, and as it met sharply the same spot the broken alabaster had already hurt, she fell forward with her outstretched hands against the wall. Something gave way, and she tumbled out of the cavern.

IX.—OUT.

But, alas! out was very much like in, for the same enemy, the darkness, was here also. The next moment, however, came a great gladness—a fire-fly, which had wandered in from the garden. She saw the tiny spark in the distance. With slow pulsing ebb and throb of light, it came pushing itself through the air, drawing nearer and nearer, with that motion which more resembles swimming than flying, and the light

fire-fly had gone on shining, Nycteris would have seen the stair turn, and would have gone up to Watho's bedroom; whereas now, feeling straight before her, she came to a latched door, which after a good deal of trying she managed to open—and stood in a maze of wondering perplexity, awe, and delight. What was it? Was it outside of her, or something taking place in her head? Before her was a very long and very narrow passage, broken up she could not tell how, and spreading out above and on all sides to an infinite height and breadth and distance—as if space itself were growing out of a trough. It was brighter than her rooms had ever been, brighter than if six alabaster lamps had been burning in them. There was a quantity of strange streaking and mottling about it, very different from the shapes on her walls. She was in a dream of pleasant perplexity, of delightful bewilderment. She could not tell whether she was upon her feet or drifting about like the fire-fly, driven by the pulses of an inward bliss. But she knew little as yet of her inheritance. Unconsciously she took one step forward from the threshold, and the girl who had been from her very birth a troglodyte stood in the ravishing glory of a Southern night, lit by a perfect moon—not the moon of our Northern clime, but a moon like silver glowing in a furnace—a moon one could see to be a globe—not far off, a mere flat disk on the face of the

astronomers might envy the rapture of such a first impression at the age of sixteen. Immeasurably imperfect it was, but false the impression could not be, for she saw with the eyes made for seeing, and saw indeed what many men are too wise to see.

As she knelt, something softly flapped her, embraced her, stroked her, fondled her. She rose to her feet, but saw nothing, did not know what it was. It was likest a woman's breath. For she knew nothing of the air even, had never breathed the still new-born freshness of the world. Her breath had come to her only through long passages and spirals in the rock. Still less did she know of the air alive with motion—of that thrice blessed thing, the wind of a summer night. It was like a spiritual wine, filling her whole being with an intoxication of purest joy. To breathe was a perfect existence. It seemed to her the light itself she drew into her lungs. Possessed by the power of the gorgeous night, she seemed at one and the same moment annihilated and glorified.

She was in the open passage or gallery that ran round the top of the garden walls, between the cleft battlements, but she did not once look down to see what lay beneath. Her soul was drawn to the vault above her, with its lamp and its endless room. At last she burst into tears, and her heart was relieved, as the night itself is relieved by its lightning and rain.

And now she grew thoughtful. She must hoard this splendor. What a little ignorance her jailers had made of her! Life was a mighty bliss, and they had scraped hers to the bare bone. They must not know that she knew. She must hide her knowledge—hide it even from her own eyes, keeping it close in her bosom, content to know that she had it, even when she could not brood on its presence, feasting her eyes with its glory. She turned from the vision, therefore, with a sigh of utter bliss, and with soft quiet steps and groping hands stole back into the darkness of the rock. What was darkness or the laziness of Time's feet to one who had seen what she had that night seen? She was lifted above all weariness, above all wrong.

When Falca entered, she uttered a cry of terror.

"NYCTERIS OPENED HER EYES AND LOOKED AFTER HER JUST IN TIME TO SEE HER VANISH THROUGH A PICTURE."

when she read of the day and the sun, she had the night and the moon in her mind; and when she read of the night and the moon, she thought only of the cave and the lamp that hung there.

X.—THE GREAT LAMP.

It was some time before she had a second opportunity of going out, for Falca, since the fall of the lamp, had been a little more careful, and seldom left her for long. But one night, having a little headache, Nycteris lay down upon her bed, and was lying with her eyes closed, when she heard Falca come to her, and felt she was bending over her. Disinclined to talk, she did not open her eyes, and lay quite still. Satisfied that she was asleep, Falca left her, moving so softly that her very caution made Nycteris open her eyes and look after her—just in time to see her vanish—through a picture, as it seemed, that hung on the wall a long way from the usual place of issue. She jumped up, her headache forgotten, and ran in the opposite direction; got out, groped her way to the stair, climbed, and reached the top of the wall.—Alas! the great room was not so light as the little one she had left. Why? Sorrow of sorrows! the great lamp was gone! Had its globe fallen? and its lovely light gone out upon great wings, a resplendent fire-fly, soaring itself through a yet grander and lovelier room? She looked down to see if it lay anywhere broken to pieces on the carpet below, but she could not even see the carpet. But surely nothing very dreadful could have happened—no rumbling or shaking, for there were all the little lamps shining brighter than before, not one of them looking as if any unusual matter had befallen. What if each of those little lamps was growing into a big lamp, and after being a big lamp for a while, had to go out and grow a bigger lamp still—out there, beyond this out?—Ah! here was the living thing that would not be seen, come to her again—bigger to-night!—with such loving kisses, and such liquid strokings of her cheeks and forehead, gently tossing her hair, and delicately toying with it! But it ceased, and all was still. Had it gone out? What would happen next? Perhaps the little lamps had not to grow great lamps, but to fall one by one and go out first?—With that came from below a sweet scent, then another, and another. Ah, how delicious! Perhaps they were all coming to her only on their way out after the great lamp!—Then came the music of the river, which she had been too absorbed in the sky to note the first time. What was it? Alas! alas! another sweet living thing on its way out. They were all marching slowly out in long lovely file, one after the other, each taking its leave of her as it passed! It must be so; here were more and more sweet sounds, following and fading! The whole of the Out was going out again; it was all going after the great lovely lamp! She would be left the only creature in the solitary day! Was there nobody to hang up a new lamp for the old one, and keep the creatures from going?—She crept back to her rock very sad. She tried to comfort herself by saying that anyhow there would be room out there; but as she said it she shuddered at the thought of empty room.

When next she succeeded in getting out, a half-moon hung in the east: a new lamp had come, she thought, and all would be well.

It would be endless to describe the phases of feeling through which Nycteris passed, more numerous and delicate than those of a thousand changing moons. A fresh bliss bloomed in her soul with every varying aspect of infinite nature. Ere long she began to suspect that the new moon was the old moon, gone out and come in again, like herself; also that, unlike herself, it wasted and grew again; that it was indeed a live thing, subject like herself to caverns, and keepers, and solitudes, escaping and shining when it could. Was it a prison like hers it was shut in? and did it grow dark when the lamp left it? Where could be the way into it?—With that, first she began to look below, as well as above and around her, and then first noted the tops of the trees between her and the floor. There were palms, with their red-fingered hands full of fruit; eucalyptus trees crowded with little boxes of powder-puffs; oleanders with their half-caste roses; and orange-trees with their clouds of young silver stars and their aged balls of gold. Her eyes could see colors invisible to ours in the moonlight, and all these she could distinguish well, though at first she took them for the shapes and colors of the carpet of the great room. She longed to get down among them, now she saw they were real creatures, but she did not know how. She went along the whole length of the wall to the end that crossed the river, but found no way of going down. Above the river she stopped to gaze with awe upon the rushing water. She knew nothing of water but from what she drank and what she bathed in; and as the moon shone on the dark, swift stream, singing lustily as it flowed, she did not doubt the river was alive, a swift rushing serpent of life, going—out?—whither? And then she wondered if what was brought into her rooms had been killed that she might drink it, and have her bath in it.

Once when she stepped out upon the wall, it was into the midst of a fierce wind. The trees were all roaring. Great clouds were rushing along the skies, and tumbling over the little lamps: the great lamp had not come yet. All was in tumult. The wind seized her garments and hair, and shook them as if it would tear them from her. What could she have done to make the gentle creature so angry? Or was this another creature altogether—of the same kind, but hugely bigger, and of a very different temper and behavior? But the whole place was angry! Or was it that the creatures dwelling in it, the wind, and the trees, and the clouds, and the river, had all quarrelled, each with all the rest? Would the whole come to confusion and disorder? But as she gazed, wondering and disquieted, the moon, larger than ever she had seen her, came lifting herself above the horizon to look, broad and red as if she too were swelled with anger that she had been roused from her rest by their noise, and compelled to hurry up to see what her children were about, thus rioting in her absence, lest they should rack the whole frame of things. And as she rose, the loud wind grew quieter, and scolded less fiercely, the trees grew stiller, and moaned with a lower complaint, and the clouds hunted and hurled themselves less wildly across the sky. And as if she were pleased that her children obeyed her very presence, the moon grew smaller as she ascended the heavenly stair; her puffed cheeks sank, her complexion grew clearer, and a sweet smile spread over her countenance, as peacefully she rose and rose. But there was treason and rebellion in her court; for ere she reached the top of her great stairs the clouds had assembled, forgetting their late wars, and very still they were as they laid their heads together and conspired. Then combining, and lying silently in wait until she came near, they threw themselves upon her, and swallowed her up. Down from the roof came spots of wet, faster and faster, and they wetted the cheeks of Nycteris; and what could they be but the tears of the moon, crying because her children were smothering her? Nycteris wept too, and not knowing what to think, stole back in dismay to her room.

The next time she came out in fear and trembling. There was the moon still! away in the west—poor, indeed, and old, and looking dreadfully worn, as if all the wild beasts in the sky had been gnawing at her; but there she was, alive still, and able to shine.

[TO BE CONTINUED.]

The Royal Fern.—A legend has been handed down from the time of the Danish invasions of Britain, explanatory of the generic name of Osmunda—an island, covered with large specimens of this fern, figuring prominently in the story. Osmund, the ferryman of Loch Tyne, had a beautiful child, who was the [illegible] of his life and the joy of his [illegible] Danes were making their terrible descents upon the coasts of Great Britain, slaughtering the peaceful inhabitants, and pillaging wherever they went, no man could say how long he would be free from molestation and outrage. But Osmund, throughout the troublous times, had lived quietly in his country home with his wife and beautiful daughter.

The peaceful calm of his life was, however, destined to be broken. One evening the ferryman was sitting, with his wife and child, on the margin of the lake, after his day's work. The setting sun was tingeing with roseate glory the fleecy banks of cloud, piled up against the horizon, silvering the surface of the rippling lake, and adding a richer hue to the golden locks of Osmund's darling child. Suddenly the sound of hurrying footsteps startled the quiet group. Men, women, and children came hastening from the neighboring village, and breathlessly, as they passed, they told the ferryman that the terrible Danes were coming. Quick as thought Osmund sprang to his feet, seized his wife and child, and hurried them into his ferry-boat. Away he rowed with them—pulling for very life—in the direction of a small island in the lake, densely covered with the tall and stately fronds of the royal fern. He quickly hid his precious charges amongst the clustering fronds, and then rowed rapidly back to his ferry place. He had rightly divined that the Danes needed his assistance, and would not hurt him.

For many hours of the ensuing night he worked with might and main to carry the fierce invaders across the ferry. When they had all disappeared on the opposite bank, Osmund returned to his trembling wife and child, and brought them safely back to his cottage. In commemoration, it is said, of this event, the fair daughter of Osmund gave the great island fern her father's name. Those who care not to accept this fanciful origin of the name Osmunda, will perhaps incline to another suggestion which has been made, that the generic name had been derived from an old Saxon word signifying strength, the specific name indicating its royal or stately habit of growth.

TRAVELLING BAG FOR PETS.

LITTLE girls who like to carry their pets with them on a journey will be glad to know how to make this pretty and convenient bag, by means of which Fido and Muff can travel like princes. The bag is made of black leather, and is closed on the side with a lock and key and clamps. The pocket for holding the dog is fifteen inches wide and nine inches and a half high. The front is cut out, leaving a margin on the edges an inch and a half wide, and the opening is filled with a wire screen, through which the little prisoner can see and breathe freely. For protection, the screen is covered by two leather flaps, fastened one at the bottom and one at the top of the bag, which overlap each other, and are secured by steel clasps.

We do not print all letters received, as some are too long, and others simply ask a question, to which we give an answer. Here is a pretty letter which needs no comments:

I am a little boy eleven years old, and have been living in South Carolina, but last summer I got hurt while playing with the boys, and have been sick ever since. I have not walked for five months. My parents have brought me to Salem, Massachusetts, where I could have good doctor's care. My cousin, who lives in New York, very kindly sends me *Harper's Young People*, and I want to tell you how much I enjoy it. I am very lonely lying still all the time, but the boys come to see me, and one of them has two rabbits for me when I am able to take care of them. I wish all the little boys and girls could have your paper, it is so nice.

Horace F. M[illegible].

"Fred," of Montclair, New Jersey, writes:

I have a handsome yellow cat named Goldy. My cousins Howard and Charlie have a cat named Sharky, and a dog named Jack. Papa reads me *Harper's Young People* every Sunday, and I like it very much.

Here are some very pleasant words from J. E. Woolbridge, Duluth, Minnesota:

I wish to tell you how I like your paper. I do really like it. I wish you would put boys' pieces in the paper for speaking in school. I live in Duluth, on the shore of a very big lake—the biggest in the world, I think. I am seven years old. I have a little yellow dog, and he grins when he is pleased.

Jacob Long.—The examinations for admission to the school-ship *St. Mary's* are easily passed by any school-boy of moderate ability, but it is indispensable that the applicant be physically sound, and of good moral character. Neither money nor influence is needed to gain admission, and the expense on entering is confined to the cost of outfit and uniform. You can make fuller inquiries of David S. Wetmore, Esq., chairman of the Committee on Nautical School, of the New York City Board of Education, or on board the *St. Mary's*, which is now in winter-quarters at the foot of East Twenty-third Street, New York city.

C. D. F.—The measurement of glasses for "Boy's Telescope" refers to the focus, not to the size of glass. Any reliable optician will supply you with the lenses.

Annie P.—Your answers to puzzles are correct. We do not know the address of Lulu W., but will print it if she will send it to us.

"Lorne," Dubuque.—Your account of Sir Rowland Hill is correct, and very neatly written, but as it is almost the same as those we have already printed, we do not give it.

"Max."—Your numerical charade is very good, but contains too many repetitions of the same letter to be perfect; therefore we do not print it.

Answers sent by R. Dunlop Foster, Chicago, to mathematical puzzles are correct, with the exception of No. 2, which is not carried back to the original amount possessed by the poor old man when the water-spirit made his first offer.

M. A. C., Rochester, writes: I have commenced taking your little paper, and I write now to tell you that I am delighted with it. I read it to my brothers and sisters, who are very much interested in the story of "The Brave Swiss Boy."

J. E. B., another bright little girl, gives us a scolding, which we hope she will retract before long.

R. A. T.—We can not give any puzzles not accompanied by full name and address of the sender, as well as the answers.

The following communication from a youthful reader in Washington, D. C., will be of interest to young bicyclists in other cities:

Here in the City of Magnificent Distances, where [illegible]

ing, the speed of the bicycle surpasses even that of the horse.

Many of the streets are "concrete," and a run over them is sure to be attended with boundless pleasure, and often a race.

There are about thirty bicyclists in the city, twenty of whom have formed a club. To see them, with their blue caps and leather leggings, six abreast, coming down the Avenue with their arms folded, causes many an equestrian to spur up his horse in vain.

Through the surrounding villages it is a common occurrence to see eight or ten bicyclists pass, especially on public holidays.

Many riders have a small bell attached to the handle, which is rung as an alarm to pedestrians, for the approach of the bicycle is as devoid of noise as that of the tiger. In the evening a lantern also is hung on the axle of the driving-wheel between the spokes, and the noiseless and rapid approach of such a red light might suggest to a stranger thoughts of the infernal regions.

In conclusion, I will say that bicycling is the most exhilarating and invigorating pastime for boys ever yet discovered.

N. L. C.

THE CAT SHOW.

A THANKSGIVING EPISODE.

By Mrs. W. J. Hays,

Author of "The Princess Idleways."

"YES, next month comes that old, everlasting Thanksgiving-day. I wonder why we have to spend more than half of it at the dinner table!"

"Suppose we don't? Let us strike out on a new lead."

"What can we do? Grandmother's pumpkin pies must be eaten, and grandfather's great turkey must be carved."

"Well, Charlie, I like originality."

"What is that, Sue?—anything in the candy shop?"

"You dreadful boy! You are just too—"

"Sweet for anything," put in Charlie.

Sue jumped up and tried to box his ears; but she chased him out into the hall, and tripped over the mats, and away he went up the stairs, and stood laughing at her as she gathered up her worsted-work.

"If *I* were a gentleman," said Sue, in her haughtiest manner, "I would assist my friends when misfortune overtook them."

"Hear! hear!" cried Charlie.

"I had the nicest little plan to propose," she went on.

"What was it, Sue?" said Charlie, whose curiosity was aroused.

"Not a word more to one so ungallant, so very rude."

"Ah, Sue dear," coaxed Charlie, coming down and putting his arm around her, "you are the nicest little sister in the world, if you did want to box my ears. Now tell us the plan, that's a darling."

"Well, it isn't much, after all; it is only that I want to make Thanksgiving a little more of a reality, and I thought—if we could do something for somebody, which would make him thankful, wouldn't it be nice."

"And who did you think of?"

"I thought of old black Betsey and her husband, they both are so old and so poor. Suppose we give them a dinner?"

"All by ourselves? Where would we get the money?"

"We will have an exhibition of cats. I will borrow Aunt May's old tabby, and John's big Tom, and Little Bell's five white kittens, and we have our own, and you can get others, and we will rig up a room in the barn, and put placards up, and I will tie bright ribbons on all their necks, and we'll charge ten cents for grown people and five cents for children, and—oh, I don't know what else."

"Splendid!"

The idea suited Charlie, and no time must be lost. Every day was valuable. Mother was consulted, and had no objections. Father gave permission to use the harness-room. The cats were borrowed: big cats and little cats, sleepy old pussies and lively young kits, gray cats, white cats, and "cherry-colored cats," as the placard read. "For one day only," was also on the placard. Charlie was door-keeper, and a busy time had Sue in keeping peace among the pussies. They screamed and scratched, and kept up a perfect *Pinafore* chorus, until the child wished she was deaf, or could give them all opiates; but the day wore on, and all the children of their acquaintance enjoyed the sport, and not a few of the elders looked in upon them. By evening Charlie was rejoicing in the possession of a full money-box, but his face grew long as he counted the proceeds. In reply to Sue's eager query of "How much?"

"Only two dollars and a half," was his dejected reply.

"Well, we can buy lots of things with that," said Sue, whose knowledge of marketing was limited.

"I am afraid it will take all for the turkey."

"Then we'll get chickens," said Sue.

"And how about cranberry jelly?"

"Mother will give us apples from her barrel."

"And celery, and sweet-potatoes, and all the other goodies?"

"We must make it all do. I will go to Mr. Scott, the grocer, and tell him we want everything at the very lowest price."

"Well, I leave it all to you," said Charlie, with masculine disdain of details, and scorn for so small a sum.

"That is right. You'll see how I will manage," said Sue, confidently.

ey leaves, [illegible] pounds of jasmine blossoms, and 20,000 pounds of tuberose blossoms, together with an immense quantity of other material used for perfume. Victoria, in New South Wales, is a good place for the production of perfume-yielding plants, because such plants as the mignonette, sweet verbena, jasmine, rose, lavender, acacia, heliotrope, rosemary, wall-flower, laurel, orange, and the sweet-scented geraniums grow there in greater perfection than in any other part of the world. South Australia, it is believed, would also be a good place for the growing of perfume-producing plants, though at several

stham. Such a form of painting possibly existed in ancient times in China—perhaps to distinguish fighting men.

ANSWERS TO MATHEMATICAL PUZZLES IN NUMBER 7.

No. 1.—The first man had 7 sheep; the second man had 5 sheep.

No. 2.—The old man had 21 [illegible] when the water-spirit first appeared to him.

No. 3.—The grocer had 31 eggs; the first woman bought 16, the second woman bought 8, the third 4, and the fourth 2.

No. 4.—Each son received $7000.

ANSWER TO M[illegible] CHARADE IN NUMBER 7.

[illegible]

HARPER'S YOUNG PEOPLE.

HARPER'S YOUNG PEOPLE will be issued every Tuesday, and may be had at the following rates:

Four cents a number.

Single subscriptions for one year, [illegible]; five subscriptions, one year, [illegible]—payable in advance. Postage free.

Subscriptions may begin with any number. When no time is specified, it will be understood that the subscriber desires to commence with the number issued after the receipt of order.

Remittances should be made by Post-office Money Order, or Draft, to avoid risk of loss.

Published by HARPER & BROTHERS, New York.

A LIBERAL OFFER FOR 1880 ONLY.

HARPER'S YOUNG PEOPLE and HARPER'S WEEKLY will be sent to any address for one year, commencing with the first number of HARPER'S WEEKLY for Janu-

Vol. I.—No. 7. | Published by HARPER & BROTHERS, New York. | Price Four Cents.
Tuesday, December 16, 1879. | Copyright, 1879, by Harper & Brothers. | $1.50 per Year, in Advance.

ONE TOUCH OF NATURE.

BY MRS. W. J. HAYS,

Author of "The Princess Idleways."

MRS. DOUGLAS was looking over her shopping list, and Lily Douglas was looking over her mother's shoulder. The Christmas Charity Fair was so soon to be held that Mrs. Douglas had a world of business to attend to, for of course her table must be full of pretty things suitable for the season. She was going out this morning to finish all her purchases, and Lily had been promised a corner of the carriage if she would be as quiet as she knew how to be, and not take cold. This was joyfully acceded to, for with all the glories of the shops to look at, could she not be still? and with her new velvet cloak and warm furs, how could she take cold?

So she bounced into the brougham after her mother, and curled herself into the smallest possible space, that there might be room for all the packages. Such smiling brown eyes under sweeping lashes looked up at the sky as she wished for snow, and so warm a little heart beat under the velvet and furs as the brougham rolled down the street, that more than one passer-by gave her smiles in return. They had not long been out when the snow came indeed, as if just to oblige the little maiden: first in a soft, slow way, then taking a start as if it were in earnest, down came the feathery flakes.

"Oh, mamma," she cried, "aren't you glad? Just look at the lovely

"Yes," said mamma, abstractedly, reading off her list; "one dozen decorated candles; three screens, gilt; six lace tidies; fifteen yards blue ribbon; dolls—oh, Lily, I have forgotten the dolls, and I must have them in time to dress them. Knock on the window, and tell Patrick to turn down town again; but I am afraid the snow will be deep before we can get home."

"So much the better, mamma," exclaimed Lily. "Oh, I am so glad it has come!"

Mamma smiled back at her little girl's radiant look, as she said, "What will all the little poor children do?"

"Do?" answered Lily; "why, they will sweep the walks—look! there they are now. What fun! I wish I had a broom, and a tin cup for pennies."

Mamma could have preached a little, but she refrained. She did not even venture to call to Lily's notice the pinched and blue noses and the chapped hands of the little army of sweepers which had so suddenly appeared.

The brougham stopped at her signal, and Mrs. Douglas went into an immense toy-shop, while Lily watched the movements of a little girl who had attracted her. The child was thin and pale; an old ragged sacque was her only outer garment, and the sleeves were so short that half her arms were exposed; on her head was an old untrimmed straw hat; on her feet shoes large enough for a woman; a faded bit of cotton cloth was twisted about her neck; in her hand was a broom, made of a bundle of sticks, such as street-sweepers use. She would make a hasty dash at the snow, and then, as if struggling between duty and pleasure, would rush from her sweeping to the shop window, and gaze with an eager and fascinated intentness at the toys within. Lily looked at her until she became tired: then

THE POCKET BLOW-PIPE.

BY WILLIAM BLAIKIE.

had passed, but while they were partaking of the refreshment that had been hastily prepared, he joined in the conversation.

"My dear Seymour," said he, "I think I know a better plan to get on the track of this swindler than if we had the help of all the policemen of Paris."

"Name it," returned his friend.

"Well, you know the St. Bernard dogs are the best in the world for following up a scent; and as Hector is a capital specimen of the breed, I think we can not do better than set him on the track."

"But the dog doesn't know him, so how can he trace him?"

"The fellow has perhaps left something behind him in his hurry; if so, then let Hector get his nose to it, and I'll wager anything that he'll follow him up even if he is fifty miles off."

"That's a capital idea," assented Mr. Seymour, delighted at the prospect of serving his young friend. "Hector knows that we're speaking about him. See how knowing he looks! Run, Walter, and see if your precious companion has left anything behind him."

Accompanied by André, who began to perceive that Sepp had cheated him, Walter sped up stairs to the room in which he had slept, and soon returned in triumph.

"He has left some of his clothes," exclaimed the now excited youth. "They are worthless things; and certainly no loss to him, after getting possession of all that money."

"Not so worthless after all," signified Mr. Seymour. "Who knows but we may find this bundle worth fifty thousand francs to you, Walter, or rather to Mr. Fritzberg? Lay it down here. Now then, Hector, take a good sniff."

The hound jumped from the carriage, smelled the bundle all round, then looked up at his master in an intelligent way, and gave a short deep bark.

"Hector will be on the track immediately," was the assurance given by Mr. Lafond. "Find—seek—find, my fine fellow!" he exclaimed.

The animal thoroughly understood its master's wish, and ran round the inn with its nose close to the ground. Suddenly it came to a stand, looked back, and gave another short bark, as if to say, "Here!"

"Bravo, Hector!" exclaimed both the gentlemen, in delight. "Come and smell again. Good dog!"

The dog sniffed the bundle once more, and after making a similar detour of the inn, stood still at the old spot.

"He has got the scent now, without a doubt," said the stranger. "Keep up your heart, young man, and we'll get the money out of this scoundrel's clutches just as certain as you got the birds from the Engelhorn for my friend. Jump into the carriage. Follow the dog, postillion. Off with you!"

The pursuit continued rapidly. The sharp-scented hound never showed the least doubt or wandering. On a few occasions it turned off into by-paths to the right or left, but always returned in a few seconds to the main road that led to Berne.

The horses were changed two or three times, but the dog seemed as fresh as when the pursuit commenced. It was growing late in the afternoon; but although Hector continued to hold on as before, Mr. Lafond shook his head, and began to doubt whether they were on the right track after all.

The two friends made a careful calculation of the time and distance, and Mr. Seymour also began to feel rather anxious. He stopped the carriage, called the dog back, and made him smell Sepp's bundle again, which they had taken care to bring with them. The dog gave the same short sharp bark as before, then turned round again, and continued the journey in the old direction.

"I haven't the least doubt now," said Mr. Seymour, cheerfully. "We must be on the right track. Go on, postillion!"

After the lapse of half an hour the dog stopped suddenly, threw its head up in the air, and sniffed all around in evident confusion; then, after making a slight detour with anxious speed, leaped across the ditch by the roadside. With a loud bark that seemed to express satisfaction, the intelligent creature made for a small clump of bushes at a little distance from the road, into which it dis-

appeared. In the course of a minute or two the barking was renewed, but this time in a threatening tone.

"We've got him!" exclaimed Mr. Seymour. "There's no doubt the fellow found he could get no farther, and has taken up his quarters in the cover yonder, to make up for the sleep he lost last night."

"Let us go over there, then," said his companion, leaping from the carriage and across the ditch. "Hector is calling us, and is sure to be right."

Mr. Seymour leaped the ditch, followed by Walter and one of the two postilions. Guided by the barking of the dog, they soon reached the thicket, and there found the man they were in quest of, pinned to the earth by the sagacious animal.

"Oh, Seppi! Seppi!" exclaimed Walter, in astonishment and sorrow, "how could you be guilty of such an act as this?"

The conscience-stricken man paled before the indignant youth.

"I will give you back everything, and beg your pardon for all I've done," whined the wretched drover. "If you will only release me from this savage brute that has nearly been the death of me."

At the call of his master the dog quitted his hold, and Seppi handed Walter the money-belt.

Walter counted the notes and gold, and was glad to find the contents untouched. Seppi rose to his feet meanwhile, but stood looking to the ground in shame and fear.

Walter, feeling compassion for him, begged that he might be let off; and Mr. Seymour consented.

Seppi was overjoyed at being let off so easily. He had not dared to expect that Walter would have taken his part, and felt truly thankful that his first great crime had not met with a severe and terrible punishment. With entreaties in his voice, he thanked his former companion, and with unaffected emotion assured him solemnly that he would never again stretch out his hand to that which did not be-

lies all in a little dead heap in his house, and Mike, the gardener, says the weasel has killed him. He saw it prowling round the barn last night, and why he didn't set a trap and catch it I don't see."

Mamma put aside her sewing, and went to comfort Harry, who began to cry bitterly for the loss of his pet.

"Poor Bunny!" said mamma; "he should not have been left out when Mr. Weasel was around. But we will buy another Bunny, two Bunnies, a white one and a black one, and they shall have a nice little house in the wood-shed, where no weasel can find them."

Harry brightened up at once at the prospect of having two Bunnies, while mamma said: "Now let us talk a little about the weasel. It is not so much to be blamed, after all, for killing Bunny, for it was born with the instinct to catch rabbits

still it seemed as if Nature and all her pretty minstrels were fast asleep. All at once I heard a hoarse voice, which seemed at my very feet. 'Chu-lunk, chu-lunk, chu-lunk,' it said. It must have been the chorister calling his frog chorus together for their evening song, for in a moment a multitude of voices were answering from the long grasses, the bushes, the water—indeed, the whole neighborhood, a moment before so quiet, was alive with little frog people. They evidently had some cause of complaint against a very wicked person, as my little Harry has just now, for I distinctly heard one say, 'Stole a rabbit, stole a rabbit;' while another answered, 'I saw him do it, I saw him do it.' Then the whole chorus burst out, 'We'll pull him in, we'll pull him in.' 'Plump, plump, plump,' added one voice more revengeful than all the rest. I sat very still, waiting to see who was to be pulled plump into the water. I did not have long to wait, but I fancy things took a turn contrary to the one desired by the frog people. There was a sudden rustling in the bushes, a sharp, quick sound like the springing of a cat. The chorus was still in an instant, but the entire shore of the little pond was covered with rushing, springing, jumping frogs. Pell-mell they tumbled over each other in headlong race for the water, to escape their cruel enemy, which now appeared, and showed himself to be a slender little weasel. He darted here and there among the helpless frogs, which made no attempts to 'pull him in,' but bent their whole efforts toward self-preservation. At length, seizing a fat frog in his mouth, the weasel turned and disappeared noiselessly among the bushes. Peace reigned once more, but the little frog people had all jumped into the water, and not a voice was heard protesting or uttering further threats."

"And did the weasel get more than one poor little frog, mamma?" asked Harry.

"No, he carried off only one frog," replied mamma; "but he killed several more, which he left lying dead in the grass. I dug a hole in the sand with a sharp stick and buried them, on

WEASEL AND FROGS—THE INTERRUPTED CONCERT.

killing the buffaloes. One morning, when he happened to be on the ground a little earlier than usual, and before his attendants, he caught sight of an animal unknown to him, stealing from a hollow into which the sun rays had not yet reached. Like a swift shadow it sped over the grass, slinking southward to the forest. He gave chase, noted the body of a buffalo it had half eaten, and pursued it the harder. But with great leaps and bounds the creature shot farther and farther ahead of him, and vanished. Turning, therefore, defeated, he met Fargu, who had been following him as fast as his horse could carry him.

"What animal was that, Fargu?" he asked. "How he did run!"

Fargu answered he might be a leopard, but he rather thought, from his pace and look, that he was a young lion.

"What a coward he must be!" said Photogen.

"Don't be too sure of that," rejoined Fargu. "He is one of the creatures the sun makes uncomfortable. As soon as the sun is down he will be brave enough."

He had scarcely said it when he repented; nor did he regret it the less when he found that Photogen made no reply. But, alas! said was said.

"Then," said Photogen to himself, "that contemptible beast is one of the terrors of sundown, of which Madam Watho spoke."

He hunted all day, but not with his usual spirit. He did not ride so hard, and did not kill one buffalo. Fargu, to his dismay, observed also that he took every pretext for moving farther south, nearer to the forest. But all at once, the sun now sinking in the west, he seemed to change his mind, for he turned his horse's head, and rode home so fast that the rest could not keep him in sight. When they arrived, they found his horse in the stable, and concluded that he had gone into the castle. But he had, in truth, set out again by the back of it. Crossing the river a good way up the valley, he reascended to the ground they had left, and just before sunset reached the skirts of the forest.

The level orb shone straight in between the bare stems, and saying to himself he could not fail to find the beast, he rushed into the wood. But even as he entered, he turned and looked to the west. The rim of the red sun was touching the horizon, all jagged with broken hills. "Now," said Photogen, "we shall see;" but he said it in the face of a darkness he had not proved. The moment the sun began to sink among the spikes and saw-edges, with a kind of sudden flap at his heart, a fear inexplicable laid hold of the youth; and as he had never felt anything of the kind before, the very fear itself terrified him. As the sun sank, it rose like the shadow of the world, and grew deeper and darker. He could not even think what it might be, so utterly did it enfeeble him. When the last flaming scimitar-edge of the sun went out like a lamp, his horror seemed to blossom into very madness. Like the closing lids of an eye—for there was no twilight, and this night no moon—the terror and the darkness rushed together, and he knew them for one. He was no longer the man he had known, or rather thought himself. The courage he had had was in no sense his own; he had only had courage, not been courageous; it had left him, and he could scarcely stand—certainly not stand straight, for not one of his joints could he make stiff or keep from trembling. He

changed," from the youth who had climbed the hill as the sun went down! A mere contempt of himself, the self that contemned was a coward with the self it contemned! There lay the shapeless black of a buffalo, humped upon the grass: he made a wide circuit, and swept on like a shadow driven in the wind. For the wind had arisen, and added to his terror: it blew from behind him. He reached the brow of the valley, and shot down the steep descent like a falling star. Instantly the whole upper country behind him arose and pursued him! The wind came howling after him, filled with screams, shrieks, yells, roars, laughter, and chattering, as if all the animals of the forest were careering with it. In his ears was a trampling rush, the thunder of the hoofs of the cattle, in career from every quarter of the wide plains to the brow of the hill above him! He fled straight for the castle, scarcely with breath enough to pant.

As he reached the bottom of the valley, the moon peered up over its edge. He had never seen the moon before—except in the daytime, when he had taken her for a thin bright cloud. She was a fresh terror to him—so ghostly! so ghastly! so gruesome!—so knowing as she looked over the top of her garden wall upon the world outside! That was the night itself! the darkness alive—and after him! the horror of horrors coming down the sky to curdle his blood, and turn his brain to a cinder! He gave a sob, and made straight for the river, where it ran between the two walls, at the bottom of the garden. He plunged in, struggled through, clambered up the bank, and fell senseless on the grass.

XII.—THE GARDEN.

Although Nycteris took care not to stay out long at a time, and used every precaution, she could hardly have escaped discovery so long, had it not been that the strange attacks to which Watho was subject had been more frequent of late, and had at last settled into an illness which kept her to her bed. But whether from an excess of caution, or from suspicion, Falca, having now to be much with her mistress both day and night, took it at length into her head to fasten the door as often as she went out by her usual place of exit; so that one night, when Nycteris pushed, she found, to her surprise and dismay, that the wall pushed her again, and would not let her through; nor with all her searching could she discover wherein lay the cause of the change. Then first she felt the pressure of her prison walls, and turning, half in despair, groped her way to the

was shining, and came to a door. She managed to open it, and, to her great joy, found herself in *the other place*, not on the top of the wall, however, but in the garden she had longed to enter. Noiseless as a fluffy moth she flitted away into the covert of the trees and shrubs, her bare feet welcomed by the softest of carpets, which, by the very touch, her feet knew to be alive, whence it came that it was so sweet and friendly to them. A soft little wind was out among the trees, running now here, now there, like a child that had got its will. She went dancing over the grass, looking behind her at her shadow as she went. At first she had taken it for a little black creature that made game of her, but when she perceived that it was only where she kept the moon away, and that every tree, however great and grand a creature, had also one of these strange attendants, she soon learned not to mind it, and by-and-by it became the source of as much amusement to her as to any kitten its tail. It was long before she was quite at home with the trees, however. At one time they seemed to disapprove of her; at another, not even to know she was there, and to be altogether taken up with their own business. Suddenly, as she went from one to another of them, looking up with awe at the murmuring mystery of their branches and leaves, she spied one a little way off which was very different from all the rest. It was white, and dark, and sparkling, and spread like a palm—a small slender palm, without much head; and it grew very fast, and sang as it grew. But it never grew any bigger, for just as fast as she could see it growing, it kept falling to pieces. When she got close to it, she discovered it was a water-tree—made of just such water as she washed with, only it was alive, of course, like the river—a different sort of water from that, doubtless, seeing the one crept swiftly along the floor, and the other shot straight up, and fell, and swallowed itself, and rose again. She put her feet into the marble basin, which was the flower-pot in which it grew. It was full of real water, living and cool—so nice, for the night was hot.

But the flowers! ah, the flowers! she was friends with them from the very first. What wonderful creatures they were!—and so kind and beautiful—always sending out such colors and such scents—red scent, and white scent, and yellow scent—for the other creatures! The one that was invisible and everywhere took such a quantity of their scents, and carried it away! yet they did not seem to mind. It was their talk, to show they were alive, and not painted like those on the walls of her rooms, and on the carpets.

She wandered along down the garden until she reached the river. Unable then to get any further—for she was a little afraid, and justly, of the swift watery serpent—she dropped on the grassy bank, dipped her feet in the water, and felt it running and pushing against them. For a long time she sat thus, and her bliss seemed complete, as she gazed at the river, and watched the broken picture of the great lamp overhead, moving up one side of the roof to go down the other.

XIII.—SOMETHING QUITE NEW.

A beautiful moth brushed across the great blue eyes of Nycteris. She sprang to her feet to follow it, not in the spirit of the hunter, but of the lover. Her heart—like every heart, if only its fallen skins were cleared away—was an inexhaustible fountain of love: she loved everything she saw. But as she followed the moth, she caught sight of something lying on the bank of the river, and not yet having learned to be afraid of anything, ran straight to see what it was. Reaching it, she stood amazed. Another girl like herself! But what a strange-looking girl!—so curiously dressed, too!—and not able to move! Was she dead? Filled suddenly with pity, she sat down, lifted Photogen's head, laid it on her lap, and began stroking his face. Her warm hands brought him to himself. He opened his black eyes, out of which had gone all the fire, and looked up with a strange sound of fear—half moan, half gasp. But when he saw her face he drew a deep breath, and lay motionless—gazing at her: those blue marvels above him, like a better sky, seemed to side with courage and assuage his terror. At length in a trem-

"Was it a dream, then?" resumed Photogen, rubbing his eyes. But with that his memory came clear, and he shuddered, and cried, "Oh, horrible! horrible! to be turned all at once into a coward!—a shameful, contemptible, disgraceful coward! I am ashamed—ashamed—and so frightened! It is all so frightful!"

[TO BE CONTINUED.]

IN LUCK.

BY MRS. ZADEL B. GUSTAFSON.

LILY DE KOVEN was in luck. Luck, you know, is a word which stands for that which comes to you without your having done anything to get it for yourself; and as she had never done

"BIDDY HELD IT OUT IN A KIND OF STUPEFIED DELIGHT."

eyes roll, drew off one of its tiny silk shoes and stockings, passed her hand over the lace train.

"I'll keep it," said Lily; "and now you bring me the whole family."

When all her dolls, little and big—all of them had been handsome in their day, but some of them were a little the worse for wear—were laid on the bed, she put the new one, with curling yellow hair almost exactly like her own, on the pillow beside her, and took up the others one by one.

"You can throw that one away," she said at last, holding out one which had a broken arm, and was looking crushed at the elbow; "I don't want but twelve children, anyway."

When her maid went out, Lily looked at her new doll, touched its hair and rich costume, but there was not any wonder in it for her; there had never been a time when she had not had as pretty dolls as money could buy; so Lily sighed and fell asleep almost immediately. Now Lily's maid left the disgraced doll on a chair in the kitchen, and there Mary the cook found it. It had on a pretty muslin dress and sash, and nice embroidered under-wear, just like any fashionable young lady. It was Christmas week, and Mary had bought a doll to give to her little niece on Christmas day, and seeing at once what a treasure this costume would be, she took it off, did it up as fresh as new, and made the doll she had bought look quite like a princess in it. So the old broken-armed doll had not a rag left of its former glory. But luck sometimes comes even to dolls.

Three days later, early in the cold morning, a little girl stood ankle-deep in the new-fallen snow in front of the grand house where Lily De Koven with her twelve waxen children lived.

This little girl was Biddy O'Dolan, and Biddy O'Dolan was in luck on this cold morning.

She had on nothing that you would call clothes; she had on duds. She had no parents and no home. She had some straw in a cellar, where other children who were duds slept at night on other bunches of straw. She was a rag-picker and an ash

particular, in a kind
all; even such a doll
her little cramped,
suddenly she tucked
finger-people around
it, and with a scared
lily's fine house, she

was like a little hum-
against the breast of
ad anything to love,
ad got this doll into
l it, and I think, she
and something which
ething. And as for
, it had never been
and cast out, it had
ad come, if it could
ent back of its whole

the whole story of
did for the doll, and
but to-day I want to
hing else, and if you
ead yours, and then
tory.
-dren have a way—
in the play-room—of
together in a circle
, just as our friends
a ring around us.
day. As she ran on
stantly thinking of
city thought of since
efore. It was then
a house and cart,
ne of the New York
she had been lov-
a great mystery to
thing she had naked
Christmas greens on
little cat and around
ling in this window,
to Biddy's house of
l as a whole summer

the meaning of these
noticed that the lit-
it all the boy, and
says "jolly." That
doll, the thought of
did not understand
there should be such
of little children, she
e lady and her little
n sorry for her. He
ng a finger on a whole
s pain spoken in the
four children of New
by the good luck of
easant things, that it
just one tenth of such
New York hospitals?
dle surprise there on
You know the best
a be like home with
But if you want to
ent like home to the
happy day, you can
over all your little
can part with. You
books that have been
d of odds and ends,
lighten the face of a
n a hospital cot. A
again. Then, too, you
things, so that before
s have the stories and
playthings that will—
on who can mind the
empty away into the
ce-time, and so, when
ngs you can gather
ace, these other chil-
an Christmas time of
a; for when you are
from your plenty
ns will like to think
ful hands and hearts
sunshine which you

OUR young correspondents ask us for so many things that it would be impossible to gratify them all at once. Their requests are carefully filed, however, and will not be forgotten.

Hattie V., Cincinnati, writes:

I have a little brother eight years old, who has a great wish to learn to play the violin. The other night he said to papa, "I wish I was a king." "Why?" asked papa. "Because a king has so much money, I would choose a large Cremona [illegible] to practice, when I played the fiddle." Papa gets Harper's Young People for him, and is going to have it bound.

Bessie B., of Wisconsin, says:

I am a constant reader of Young People, especially the "Post-Office." I think that game called "Wiggles" is splendid fun, for I like to draw.

The following is from Lilian, of Louisville:

My papa gets Harper's Young People for us, and we like it very much. My mamma looked for something nice for us to read, and she thinks this is the very thing. The page is so beautiful coming for the three little girls, and they are so glad to welcome it for us as the flower we looked for.

Answers to "Inquisitive Jim" are received from Charles W. L., and F. B. Reese (both aged eleven years), who give correct information concerning the establishment of the Bank of England, and from C. W. Gibbons, who writes a full description of this celebrated institution, which we are compelled to condense: "The Bank of England was first suggested by William Paterson, a London merchant, and was incorporated under its present name in 1694, during the reign of William and Mary. The business of the bank was conducted at Grocers' Hall until 1734, when the house and garden of Sir John Houblon, the first governor, were purchased as a site for the present building, which, although not imposing as a whole, contains some handsome architecture based on ancient models. The principal entrance of the bank is on Threadneedle Street, but why it is irreverently called "the Old Lady" I do not know. Can any one tell me?"

Edwin K.—"General" is the highest rank in the United States army. It was created in July, 1866, and bestowed upon General Grant, who had for two years previous held the position of Lieutenant-General. When General Grant resigned his position on being elected President of the United States, Sherman became General, and Sheridan Lieutenant-General.

"Reader Boy."—Cape Trafalgar derives its name from Taraf-al-ghar—signifying "promontory of the cave"—the appellation given it by the ancient Moors.

Robert N.—You will find the information you desire in the "Post-Office" of our sixth number.

Harry L. G.—"American Club Skates" are the most popular at present among boys, as they require neither straps nor heel plate, and fit very firmly to the foot.

Daisy Chase.—The directions for keeping gold-fish, given in Harper's Young People, No. 6, will apply to your "common fish."

Ralph.—General George Washington was born in a modest mansion near the Potomac, half way between Pope's and Bridge's creeks, Westmoreland County, Virginia. Of this mansion nothing now remains but a few scattered ruins. It was destroyed by fire while Washington was still very young, and his father removed to a country residence in Stafford County, near Fredericksburg.

Frankie H.—We would very gladly help you and your sister "in the information," but have not room enough in the "Post-Office" to describe some things. We refer your sister to directions and S. also to suggestions for Lulu W., in this column. You will say these are all for girls. Now boys can make many pretty things with a scroll saw, such as frames, brackets, and boxes, all suitable for Christmas.

Lulu W. can arrange her cards of pressed sea-weed prettily by taking two good-sized scallop shells, and fastening the shells and cards together with a bow of ribbon at the back. By using blank cards a pretty autograph album may be also made. It is easy to drill holes in the shells through which to pass the ribbon, and they may be ornamented with paintings or pictures pasted on. A. P.

Perforated paper case for Lulu W. Take a piece of perforated card-board about two inches and a half square, work an initial or any little figure on one side, on the other side "Stamps" in small letters. Line the pieces with bright-colored silk, and bind three sides together with ribbon. It can be made more ornamental by putting tiny bows at the corners. L. B.

B. W. and Amelia F.—Your suggestions to Susie D. C. are good, but not new enough to print. Thanks for your pleasant letters.

We acknowledge the receipt of a prettily written letter from Robert S., St. Johns, Michigan, and answers to puzzles from Gussie L., Robert N., Grace A. Mc., William C. K., Heywood C., F. H. Brown, Addie A. B., C. W. J., Edwin Van K., Joseph S. G., Martha W. D., Bessie McL., Charles E. L., and C. F. D.

THE SNOW-FLOWER.

IN California, the land of wonders, is found a wonderful plant. The traveller who is exploring the Yosemite region in June will find lingering patches of snow and ice amongst the cliffs, and there he may be fortunate enough to see this astonishing production rising fresh and superb beside its icy bed. It springs from the edges of the snow-banks, growing ten or fifteen inches high, and is called in common phrase the "snow-flower," from its location, not its coloring, for it is blood-red, of the richest crimson carmine, buds, flowers, stems, leaves, and sheathing bulb all of the same ensanguined hue. The flowers are thickish, something like the pyrola, and its manner of growth resembles the hyacinth, with bell-shaped flowers clustering along the upper part of the stem, and green, pointed leaves. This plant is mentioned by Mr. Hesse in his book on California, and specimens have been sent to the North, but they are generally in very poor condition when they arrive.

As the years slip by, no doubt many of the now quite youthful readers of this paper will find themselves wandering among the snow-crowned cliffs of the Yosemite, and to them, perhaps, the crimson blossom of the snow-flower will be welcomed. They may then like to remember that its botanical name is

SPOON-FACES.

When they're bright and shining
Like the summer moons,
Two queer faces look at you
From the silver spoons.
One is very long, and one
Broad as it can be,
And both of them are gruesome things,
As ever you did see.

Then careful be, young people,
And do not whine or frown,
Lest some day you discover
Your chin's a-growing down.
Nor must you giggle all the time
As though you were but loons;
We want no children's faces
Like those in silver spoons.

The Largest Tree in the World.—In San Francisco, encircled by a circus tent of ample dimensions, is a section of the largest tree in the world—exceeding the diameter of the largest tree of Calaveras by five feet. This monster of the vegetable kingdom was discovered in 1874, on Tule River, Tulare County, about seventy-five miles from Visalia. At some remote period its top had been broken off by the elements or some unknown force; yet when it was discovered it had an elevation of 240 feet. The trunk of the tree was 111 feet in circumference, with a diameter of 34 feet 4 inches. The section on exhibition is hollowed out, leaving about a foot of bark and several inches of the wood. The interior is 100 feet in circumference and 30 feet in diameter, and it has a seating capacity of about 200. It was cut off from the tree about 12 feet above the base, and required the labor of four men for nine days to chop it down. In the centre of the tree, and extending through its whole length, was a rotten core about two feet in diameter, partially filled with a soggy, decayed vegetation that had fallen into it from the top. In the centre of this cavity was found the trunk of a little tree of the same species, having perfect bark on it, and showing regular growth. It was of uniform diameter, an inch and a half all the way; and when the tree fell and split open, this curious stem was traced for nearly 100 feet. The rings in this monarch of the forest show its age to have been 4840 years.

Sweet Scents.—Perfumes were used in the early times of the Chinese Empire, when ladies had a habit of rubbing in their hands a round ball made of a mixture of amber, musk, and sweet-scented flowers. The Jews, who were also devoted to sweet scents, used them in their sacrifices, and also to anoint themselves before their repasts. The Scythian ladies went a step further, and after pounding on a stone cedar, cypress, and incense, made up the ingredients thus obtained into a thick paste, with which they smeared their faces and limbs. The composition exhaled for a long time a pleasing odor, and on the following day gave to the skin a soft and shining appearance. The Greeks carried sachets of scent in their dresses, and filled their dining-rooms with fumes and incense. Even their wines were often impregnated with decoctions of flowers. The Athenians perfumed pigeons with liquid perfumes, and let them fly about a room, scattering the drops over the

THE MOTHER SINGS SOFTLY TO HERSELF:

Play, baby, in thy cradle play—
Tick goes the clock, tick-tick, tick-tick;
And quick goes time, quick, quick!
Grow, baby, grow, with every day—
Tick goes the clock, tick-tick, tick-tick;
And babyhood will pass away,
For quick goes time, quick, quick!

Not long can mother watch thee so—
Tick goes the clock, tick-tick, tick-tick;
And quick goes time, quick, quick!
To pretty girlhood thou wilt grow—
Tick goes the clock, tick-tick, tick-tick;
To womanhood, before we know,
For quick goes time, quick, quick!

Play, baby, in thy cradle play—
Tick goes the clock, tick-tick, tick-tick;
And quick goes time, quick, quick!
And some brave lad will come some day—
Tick goes the clock, tick-tick, tick-tick;
And steal my baby's heart away!
Ah, quick goes time, quick, quick!

Charley Haags is a nice boy, but it was not right of him to take his big dog Towser to school when he heard the teacher was going to give him a flogging. And then to say he was afraid to send the dog home because it was so vicious, and might turn on him.

TO THE READERS OF

HARPER'S YOUNG PEOPLE.

A CHRISTMAS GREETING.

The publishers of Harper's Young People congratulate their readers on the approach of the merry holiday season, and take pleasure in announcing the enlargement of this journal to sixteen pages, beginning with the Christmas number, which will be published December 23.

This change will enable the publishers to give their young readers every week an increased variety of stories, poems, sketches, and other attractive reading, from the best writers that can be secured. The publishers will also avail themselves of this occasion to present Harper's Young People to their subscribers in new and enlarged type, which will greatly add to the beauty and attractiveness of its appearance.

No pains or expense will be spared to make Harper's Young People the most entertaining, interesting, high-toned, and popular weekly paper for the youthful readers of America.

Harper's Young People will be issued every Tuesday, and may be had at the following rates:

Single Copies	$0 04
ONE *Subscription, one year*	1 50
FIVE *Subscriptions* "	7 00

Payable in advance. Postage free.

Subscriptions may begin with any number. When no time is specified, it will be understood that the subscriber desires to commence with the current number.

Remittances should be made by POST-OFFICE MONEY ORDER or DRAFT, to avoid risk of loss.

Address HARPER & BROTHERS,
Franklin Square, New York.

A LIBERAL OFFER FOR 1880 ONLY.

Harper's Young People and Harper's Weekly will be sent to any address for one year, commencing with the first number of Harper's Weekly for

VOL. I.—NO. 8. PUBLISHED BY HARPER & BROTHERS, NEW YORK. PRICE FOUR CENTS.

[Begun in No. 1 of Harper's Young People, November 4.]

THE BRAVE SWISS BOY.

VII.—A GLIMPSE OF PARISIAN LIFE.

THE bright rays of the morning sun filled the room when Walter awoke from his long and refreshing sleep, to gaze in astonishment at the rich and beautiful furniture that adorned the apartment. Silk curtains, mirrors that reached to the ceiling, beautiful carpets, attractive pictures in gilt frames—all was new and dazzling to the unsophisticated mountain youth. He was still gazing in wonder at all these glories, when Mr. Seymour, who had slept in the next room, suddenly opened the door.

"Jump up, Walter," said he. "Breakfast is ready, and my friend wants to speak to you; so be as quick as you can."

"I shall be ready in a few minutes, sir," he replied, as, springing out of bed, he washed and dressed himself, and respectfully greeted the two gentlemen, who sat enjoying their coffee in an adjoining room.

At Mr. Seymour's invitation Walter helped himself to breakfast; and when he had finished his meal, looked up inquiringly at the stranger.

"Well, then, Walter," said he, in a kindly tone, "tell me in the first place what you intend to do, now that you have got your money back?"

"Oh, that is very readily answered, sir," replied Walter. "I shall buckle the belt round my waist again, and return home to-day."

"I thought that was your intention, Watty," said Mr. Seymour; "but it would be much safer and far easier to send the money through the post. You will then have no further risk of being robbed, and Mr. Frieshardt will be sure to get it in a day or two. As regards yourself—"

Mr. Seymour hesitated, and his friend took up the conversation. "Yes, Walter, you must stay here for the present," said he, "and not dream of leaving me—at least for a long time."

Walter was taken aback. What could the stranger mean? Unable to comprehend the motive of such a remark, he looked in confusion first at one, then at the other, and was greeted only with a hearty laugh.

"I am very much obliged to you for suggesting how I should send the money home," said the lad; "and it was certainly very strange that Mr. Frieshardt did not think of that, for it would have saved all this trouble with Seppi. But what, sir, am I to do here? What is there to prevent my returning home?"

"A proposal that my friend Mr. Lafond has to make to you," replied Mr. Seymour. "My friend is in want of an active and trustworthy servant, and thinks that you would suit him well. I think you should take the situation, Walter, for you will be looked upon rather as a confidential attendant than as a servant, and you will be well paid into the bargain. In a few years you will have earned money enough to provide comfortably for your father in his old age."

The last words decided Walter. If he could only relieve his father's declining years from care and anxiety, he was content to give up his home for a time, and therefore agreed to accept the proposal. The contract was soon arranged, and Walter entered upon his new duties the same day. He wrote a long letter to his father, explaining the reason of his remaining in Paris, and comforting him with the assurance that when he returned home he would bring plenty of money with him. By the same post he sent a bank draft to Farmer Frieshardt equivalent to the value of the cattle money; and a few days after removed into Mr. Lafond's splendidly furnished mansion. Mr. Seymour did not accompany his friend, having to leave Paris to continue his travels.

Thus Walter, who had suddenly risen from the position of a poor drover to that of the principal servant and favorite of a rich young Parisian, found no reason to regret the change that he had made. Mr. Lafond treated him in the kindest and most friendly way, so that he soon became thoroughly attached to him. But in the course of a few weeks he observed certain traits in the character of his new employer that occasioned him both sorrow and anxiety, and almost made him regret that he had not returned to his quiet but innocent home. Although a kind-hearted man, Mr. Lafond was weak-minded and changeable; and like many other wealthy young men without any occupation, he was addicted to pleasure and dissipation, and spent whole nights at the gaming table, to the ruin of both his health and morals. As he was of a delicate constitution, these excesses soon produced a very marked effect upon him, and did much to shatter his health.

Early one morning Mr. Lafond came home, after a night of gambling, looking pale and more exhausted than usual. Walter, who had been sitting up for him, was terribly alarmed at the appearance which he presented. "Oh, my dear sir," said he, with a deep sigh, as he gave him his hand out of the carriage, "how grieved I am for you!"

Mr. Lafond stared at Walter with his glassy eyes, and tried to speak, but could only utter a few disconnected words that were quite incomprehensible. Besides this, he was so unsteady on his feet that he was obliged to lean on Walter to prevent himself from falling. The faithful servant was terribly shocked to find his master so intoxicated as to be almost deprived of his senses, and lost no time in getting him to his room that his distressing and disgraceful condition might not become known to the rest of the household. After undressing him, which cost a great deal of trouble, Walter got his master to bed, and then sat down, and became lost in thought.

It was not until late in the day that Mr. Lafond woke from his troubled sleep, and was surprised to find Walter sitting by his bedside. "Poor fellow!" he said, in a good-natured tone, "I'm afraid I kept you waiting long for me last night. You are a faithful servant, and shall have your wages raised immediately."

"I am very much obliged to you, sir," said he; "but I can not take more of your money. I have only waited here to request my discharge from your service."

Mr. Lafond stared at the young man with surprise. "What!" he exclaimed; "you want to leave me! What has put that in your head? Has any one here done anything to make you uncomfortable?"

"No, sir, no one," was the quiet but firm reply. "I have met with nothing but kindness since I have been in your house, and you have been more than generous to me; but I can't bear to stay here and see you digging your own grave. It breaks my heart, sir; and I would rather wander barefoot back to my own mountains than witness it longer."

"Why, Walter, I'm afraid you're turning crazy," exclaimed his master, angrily. "Don't let me hear any more of this nonsense! What can it matter to you whether I die soon or not? At any rate you must stay with me, and give up such foolish notions."

Walter shook his head. "No, sir; I must go," he replied. "I can be of no use here. It makes me quite miserable to see how you waste your money in the gaming house, and ruin your health by overindulgence in wine. If my caring for you were not sincere, it would be a matter of no consequence to me whether you went to destruction or not; but," he added, while tears started to his eyes, "I trust, sir, you will pardon me for saying that I can not look on carelessly while you are ruining yourself; and so I hope you will let me go."

The reckless gamester was quite moved at the devotion and faithfulness of his servant. Springing from bed, he wrapped himself in his dressing-gown, and walked hastily to and fro in the apartment for a few minutes in silence. At last he paused before Walter and grasped his hand. "You are a straightforward, warm-hearted fellow," he exclaimed. "But the more I am convinced of that, the less disposed am I to part with you. Will you not stay with me?"

"No, my good master, I can not," answered Walter, firmly.

"Not even if I promise to turn over a new leaf, and neither to drink nor gamble any more from this day?"

Walter was in a measure re-assured by these words, and his eyes were lit up with a new hope. "Ah! if you really will do that, sir!" he exclaimed. "That alters everything; and I shall be as overjoyed to stay with you as I should have been sorry to leave you."

"Then that is settled," said his master, in a serious tone. "I am obliged to you for speaking so faithfully to me. I know that I have been living in a foolish way; but I will be different for the future. That you may rely upon."

Walter's joy was so great at hearing this unexpected resolution that he nearly burst into tears. Unhappily, however, he was soon to experience the disappointment of all his hopes.

For a fortnight Mr. Lafond kept his promise faithfully; but at the end of that time he again yielded to the old temptation, and after a night of revelry returned home in broad daylight in a state of complete helplessness. The servant renewed his entreaties and warnings; reminded his master that the physician had declared that his existence depended on his leading a sober life, and obtained from him a renewal of the broken promise. But alas! it proved as vain as before. In a few days all his hopes were again crushed, and his prayers and entreaties were only answered by his master with a shrug of the shoulders.

"You know nothing about it, Walter," said he. "The temptation is so strong, that one can't be always resisting it."

"But it is your duty to resist it, sir; and you can succeed if you will only make up your mind to do so."

"It's too late now," replied the other, with a faint smile. "I have fought and fought, and been beaten at last. I shall give up fighting now."

"Are you really in earnest?" cried Walter, anxiously.

"I am really in earnest," replied Mr. Lafond.

"Then I must indeed quit your service, sir. I will not stay here if I can not save you from rushing headlong to destruction."

"Silly fellow!" replied his master, testily. "What more would you have? It will be for your direct advantage to stay with me. Look at my condition. The doctor was quite right in saying that I couldn't live another year. Remain here for that short time, and you shall be well paid for your services. I will take care not to forget you in my will."

The young Switzer could not restrain his emotion at hearing his weak-minded but good-natured master talk in such a careless way about death. Unable to speak, he turned to leave the room, when Mr. Lafond called him back.

"Have you no reply to make to me?" he demanded, in an offended tone.

"Nothing more than this, sir—that your doctor assured me that you might live for ten, twenty, or even thirty years longer, if you could only be persuaded to live in a sober and reasonable way. Oh, my dear sir," he exclaimed, "do give up these habits that are ruining body and soul, and I will devote my whole life to you!"

"No use," was the gloomy reply. "If I were to make new resolutions, they would only be broken, as the others have been. The doctor is quite mistaken in his opinion. I suppose I must fulfill my destiny. So let the matter drop, Walter."

"Anything can be done if one is only determined," persisted the young man, with entreaty in his tone.

His master turned away and shook his head. "Too late, too late. I haven't the moral courage or determination."

"Then may God have mercy upon you!" replied the servant, solemnly. "This is no longer a place for me."

Swayed on the one hand by a sense of duty to himself, and on the other by pity for his terribly misled master, Walter sorrowfully quitted the apartment, and after packing a few things, returned to take his final leave. Mr. Lafond, however, would not bring himself to believe in the reality of such a sudden and determined resolution, and used every argument to induce the lad to change his mind. He even begged him as a personal favor to remain, but Walter persisted in his determination; nor could the most lavish offers of emolument induce him to stay and be a helpless spectator of the ruin of one whom he was unable to save.

"If I were only as determined as you are," sighed Mr. Lafond, "how much better it would be for me! But now it is too late. Farewell, then, Walter, if you have made up your mind to quit my service. But though you leave me, it is not necessary that you return to your mountain home. I received this letter from my uncle, General De Bougy, who lives in Rouen. The old gentleman is in want of a steady and trustworthy servant, and asks me to send him one, so I think the best thing you can do will be to go there for a twelvemonth. You will find him a better master than I have been; and if you are really determined to leave me, you might do worse than enter his service. I feel sure you will be comfortable."

Walter shook his head. "I shouldn't like to go into another house, sir, after the experience I have had in your service."

"But you will be serving me, Walter, if you go and assist my uncle in his old age. Recollect, I only ask you to go for a year. It is the last request I have to make. Surely you won't refuse?"

"Well, sir, I will go for a year, since you urge it so strongly," assented Walter, who could no longer resist his master's appeal. "When shall I start?"

"When you please. You will be welcome there at any time."

"Then I will set out at once, sir; the sooner our parting is over, the better."

"But if it is so painful to you, why go away at all? You know how glad I should be for you to stay."

"And you know, sir, why I am obliged to go," replied Walter, firmly. "Pardon me, dear sir, for speaking any more on the subject; but if you only had had the resolution to—"

"I'll make another trial, Walter," said Mr. Lafond, with a smile that contrasted strongly with his sunken and wasted features. "You shall hear from me in three months," he continued; "and perhaps— Well, we shall see. Good-by, and my best wishes go with you!"

Walter grasped the hand which his master extended, and kissed it fervently. "God bless and preserve you!" said he, with tears in his eyes. "If prayers, earnest prayers for you, can be of any help, you will be saved."

"Farewell, Walter. You have been a faithful servant," exclaimed Mr. Lafond, with painful emotion. "God be with you!—perhaps we shall never meet each other again."

So they parted. Walter went by the first conveyance to Rouen to the house of General De Bougy; and his former master sank into profound grief as he dwelt upon the affection and solicitude which the young Switzer had shown toward him. "Only a year sooner," he mused, with torturing anguish, "and I might have been a saved man! Now, alas! thou hast come too late, noble and generous heart!"

[TO BE CONTINUED.]

THE BEAUTIFUL CHRISTMAS GREEN.

ONE of the pleasantest pastimes of the whole year for country children is gathering Christmas green. This is done before the very cold weather begins, otherwise the beautiful club-mosses and ground-pines would be frozen solid in the damp soil of the swamps and woods, or the whole would be covered with a snow carpet, broken only by rabbit and squirrel tracks. The freshest green for Christmas trimming is found in damp meadows or on springy hill-sides, where it nestles in the moist earth, overshadowed by thickets of alders and birches. It grows in the forests too; not so much among pine-trees, as the dry carpet of fallen needles is less nutritious than the loam produced by the accumulations of dead leaves of oak, maple, and beech trees.

There are many kinds of ground evergreens, most of them members of the *Lycopodiaceæ*, or club-moss family. There is the creeping club-moss, the cord-like stem of which, sometimes yards long, hides among the dead leaves, and sends up at intervals graceful whorls of bright green. Tiny bunches of short white roots run down in the damp mould, where they find nutriment for the plant. If you work your finger under the stem, and pull gently, it is wonderful to see the long and beautiful wreath slowly disentangle itself from the forest floor, disturbing hundreds of little wood-beetles, which scurry away to hide again among the woodland rubbish. There are two kinds of creeping green very common in all moist wooded lands at the North—the kind with leaves rising in whorls, and that with a stem covered with bristle-like spikes. This last variety has leaves, not very abundant, which resemble a sprig of young fir, and is sometimes called "ground-fir." It is of a deep rich green color, but not so graceful for trimming as the other kind. Besides the creeping green, there are many varieties of what children call "tree-green," independent little plants rooted deep in the mould, which send up a single stalk about eight inches high. Some of these are such perfect little trees as to appear diminutive copies of the firs and pines towering far above them, and are called "fir club-moss." A pretty evergreen to mix with the more feathery varieties is the *Chimaphila umbellata*, or prince's-pine. It has bright shining dark green leaves, which have a very bitter taste, and is sometimes called bitter winter-green.

BRINGING HOME CHRISTMAS GREEN.—Drawn by J. O. Davidson.

As all these ground varieties need to be gathered before ice and snow begin, often weeks before Christmas, care must be taken to keep them from drying. They should be heaped up in some cool, damp place, where they will not freeze, and should be sprinkled plenteously every day. The boys make frames in the form of crosses, stars, wreaths, or letters, and the girls find a pretty pastime in tying on the greens. As fast as the designs are finished they must also be laid away and kept damp until Christmas. Woodland mosses, holly leaves and scarlet berries, and dried everlasting flowers are pretty to mix with the green. Branches of hemlock and young firs for Christmas trees are cut as near Christmas-time as possible. If a room is to be made into a bower of hemlock boughs, they should not be fastened up until the morning of Christmas-eve, as the heated air of the house loosens the flat, tooth-shaped leaves from the branch, and the least movement sends them in clouds to the floor. Any one who has tried to sweep them from the carpet after Christmas will prefer some other variety of green for trimming another year.

The immense amount of green brought into New York

city the week preceding Christmas can scarcely be estimated. Viewing the hundreds of young firs in the markets, and the enormous numbers of wreaths and other designs, it would seem as if the forests and swamps had been stripped to such an extent that nothing would be left for another year; but so prodigal is Nature of her beautiful club-mosses and her aromatic pines, that what is gathered for holiday trimming amounts to little more than a weeding out of superfluous growth. Many of the greens sold in the New York market come from New Jersey. Schooners bring them from all along the coast, freight-cars come loaded with the beauty of the inland hills, and huge market carts trundle their precious burden from the near-lying forests and damp meadows. Although it is prohibited by law to cut young trees from the barrens along the coast, as the growth of pines keeps the sand from drifting, many small coasting vessels drop into the bays and inlets around Sandy Hook and other parts of the Jersey shore a little before Christmas-time, and send their crews ashore by night to secure a cargo to bring to New York.

It would be interesting to follow this woodland treasure after its arrival in the great city; but one thing is certain—wherever it is, even if it be only a sprig in the hand of a sick child, faces are brighter, hearts are happier, and the sweet words, "Merry Christmas," have a deeper significance.

CHRISTMAS PUZZLE.

THE answer to this puzzle will form an appropriate motto for the card in the centre. This is the way to work it out: First find the names of the articles around the card, and write them all down in a row with the numbers below them. For example, one of the words is "EYE." Put it down thus:

E Y E
10 3 11

and all the rest in the same way. Each name will have just as many letters as there are figures, else you may know your guess is wrong, and you will have to try again. After you have made out all the pictures and written down the names, you will have thirty-nine letters. Out of these thirty-nine letters you are to make the eleven words that form the inscription. To do this, write on another sheet the numbers

1 2 3 4 5 6

7 8 9 10 11

widely apart, so as to leave room for all the words to be written under them. Then place each letter where it belongs under these numbers. Take the word "EYE." E is numbered 10, then put E under the figure 10; Y is numbered 3, put Y under 3; E is numbered 11, put E under 11. When you have placed all the letters, arrange those under each figure so as to make a word. The whole will be the inscription for the card.

A CHRISTMAS STORY.

BY MRS. W. J. HAYS,

AUTHOR OF "THE PRINCESS IDLEWAYS."

"NOW, Teddie, be a good boy, there's a darling, and, little Clover, don't tease Daisy. Please let mamma go away to church and know that you are all sweet and lovely and clean as new little pennies to-night."

Splash went one little body into the bath-tub, and splash went another, and again a third; and then, like so many roses after a shower, out they came, dripping, and laughing and screaming with glee. The little mother was kept busy enough, for it was Christmas-eve, and the carols and anthems were to be rehearsed for the last time, and Mrs. Morton's clear soprano voice could not be spared. Indeed, her voice was all that kept Teddie and Clover and Daisy in their neat little box of a house, for their father, a brave fireman, had been killed more than two years before at a fearful fire, and since then their mother had striven hard to maintain her little family by sewing, and singing, and doing whatever work her slender hands could accomplish which would bring in food and clothing for her children.

"Be dood, Teddie," repeated Daisy, after her mother, as she shook out her little wet curls at him, and Clover solemnly raised his finger at his bigger brother, with the warning,

"Remember, Santa Claus comes to-night."

"Yes, and the stockings must be

hung up," said Ted, who forthwith proceeded to attend to that important duty.

"There! how do they look?—one brown, that's mine; one blue, that's Clover's; and one red, that's Daisy's." They were pinned fast to the fender with many pins and much care.

"But, mamma," said Clover, "the stove's in the way. Santa Claus can't get down with that big black thing stopping the chimney."

"Oh, the fire will go out by-and-by, and then he may creep through the stove-pipe and out of the door."

"He'll be awful dirty, then," said Daisy.

"Well, 'he was dressed all in fur from his head to his foot, and his clothes were all tarnished with ashes and soot,' so that is to be expected. But really, dear children, you must jump into your beds, and let me tuck you up; it is time for me to go."

Very quickly the rosy little faces were nestling in the pillows, and Mrs. Morton, after kissing them, put out the lamp and left them to their slumbers. Hastily putting on her cloak and bonnet, she paused at the door of her sitting-room to see if the fire was safe. The room was dark but for the gleaming stove, the chairs and table were all in order, and in one corner, under a covering of paper, was the little tree she had decked in odd moments to delight the eyes of her children. She could not afford wax candles, so the morning was to bring the tree as well as the other gifts. Sure that all was in readiness, she tripped down the stairs, locked her door, and sped over the snow to the church, the two tall towers of which stood out against the starry sky.

As she entered the church, her mind full of her duties and her heart tender with thoughts of her children, she thought she saw a dusky little object crouching in the angle made by the towers; but she was already late, and had no time to linger. Up she went to the choir, which was full of light, but the body of the church was dark. Without any words, she took up her sheet of music and began to sing. Never had the carols and anthems seemed so sweet to her, and her voice rose clear and pure as a bird's. The organist paused to listen, and her companions turned satisfied glances upon her; but she went on unconsciously, as a bird does until the burden of its theme is finished, and its exultant strains are lost in silence. They went over the whole Church service, the glorious *Te Deum*, the *Benedictus*, and the anthem for the day, "Unto us a Child is born, unto us a Son is given," and every delicate chord and fugue had to be repeated until the desired perfection of harmony was attained. It was really a very long and arduous study; but of all days Christmas demands good music, and they were willing to do their best. At last all were satisfied, and somewhat tired; but the organist turned to Mrs. Morton, and asked her if she would sing one hymn for him alone, as he especially desired to hear her voice in this one tune. Of course she could not refuse, and to an exquisitely harmonious air she began,

"Calm on the listening ear of night
Come heaven's melodious strains,
Where wild Judea stretches far
Her silver-mantled plains.

"Light on thy hills, Jerusalem!
The Saviour now is born!
And bright on Bethlehem's joyous plains
Breaks the first Christmas morn."

Only the first and last verses of that exquisite hymn; but like "angels with their sparkling lyres," her voice seemed to have lost its earthliness, and soared, as if it were winged, up to the very gate of heaven. When she ceased singing, there was a hush upon all, as if they had been carried near to the celestial portals.

One by one they pressed her hand in quiet congratulation, and with a "Merry Christmas" bade her good-night. Mrs. Morton was a little excited with her unusual efforts, and while the old organist was locking up, thought she would run down and warm herself in the church. As she hastened toward the great heater, she tripped over something, which, to her great surprise and alarm, she perceived what appeared to be a great bundle was in reality a sleeping child.

Yes, a child, and a little one—a boy of not more than seven years, with elfish brown locks, and eyelashes which swept the olive tint of his cheek. All curled up in a heap, in clothes which a man might have worn, so big and shapeless were they, with one arm under his head for a pillow, and the other tightly grasping a violin. Far had he wandered in the cold wintry air, until, attracted by the light and warmth of the great church, he had stolen in for shelter, and then as his little ears drank in the melody of the rehearsing choir, and the warmth comforted him, he fell fast asleep. He was dreaming now of the warm sunny land of his birth; olive-trees and orchards, purple clusters of the vineyards, donkeys laden with oranges, and the blue sky of Naples shining over the blue bay. Then, in his dream, an angel came floating down out of the pure ether, wafting sweet perfumes on its white wings, and singing—oh! what heavenly strains!—till his little soul was filled with joy; for the angel seemed to be his mother who had died, and her kind voice again saluted him, and he answered, softly, "Madre mia!"

"Poor child!" said Mrs. Morton, softly, "it seems a pity to waken him, but we must do it; he can not stay here all night." The old organist touched him; but his sleep was too sound for a touch to arouse him, and Mrs. Morton had to again and again lift his head and stroke his little brown hand, before, with amazed and widely fearful looks, he answered them.

"Who are you, child, and what are you doing here?" asked the organist.

"I'm Toni, Toni," was the answer, and he began to cry. "Oh, please let me go; the Padrone will kill me."

"Why will he kill you, and why are you here?"

"He will kill me because I have no money. I have lost, also, my way."

"Have you no home, no mother?" asked Mrs. Morton, gently.

"No, signora, no, madame, no mother. We all live, Baptiste and Vincenzo and I, with the Padrone. We play the harp and the violin; but I was tired, and I could not keep with the others, and they scolded me, oh, so sharply! and I was weary and cold, and crept in here where the angels sing, and it was so beautiful I could not go away."

The organist muttered, "Police," at which the child again sobbed violently. "Yes, to the station-house, of course, he must go."

But Mrs. Morton remembered the three faces asleep on their pillows at home, and as she looked at this tear-stained, dirty little gypsy, she said to the organist, "I will take care of him to-night." So, under the stars, the Christmas stars, gleaming so brightly, she led the little wanderer home.

All was still and safe in the little house. "Not a creature was stirring, not even a mouse." The fire still gleamed in the kitchen and the sitting-room, and it was the work of only a few moments to divest the little musician of his uncouth garments, to pop him into the tub of hot suds, to scrub him well, until his lean little body shone like bronze, to slip him into a night-gown, to give him a slice of bread and butter, and then to tuck him up on the cozy lounge.

The children slept like tops, and the tired little mother was glad to say her prayers, and lie down beside them.

The stars were still shining when she awoke; for Christmas-day would be a busy one, and there were no moments to lose. Already the milkman was at the door, and the hands of the kitchen clock pointed to six.

Hark! what was that?

A long, low, sweet sound, like a voice calling her. She listened, and again it came. "Glory to God in the highest, and on earth peace, good-will toward men," so it seemed to breathe. Then it rose in a gay carol, a sweet gushing thanksgiving, and the children came tumbling down in their night-gowns; they rushed to the door of the sitting-room, and there beside his improvised bed stood the young musician, playing on his violin as if all the world were his audience. His brown eyes flashed now with light, and then grew dark and tender, as he drew the sweet sounds out. The children gazed in wonderment: where had this child come from? had he dropped from the stars? had an angel come among them? He played on and on, until, from sheer fatigue, he put his instrument down. Then Teddie and Clover and Daisy came about him; they touched his hands, his curly locks, his violin, to see if all were real. Then they whirled round the room in a mad dance of delight, for the mother had uncovered the tree, and it was really Christmas morning.

Ah, what a happy day for poor little Toni! How nice he looked in Teddie's clothes! how gentle he was with Daisy! how he frolicked with Clover! and when Mrs. Morton came from church, how softly he played all his pretty melodies for her! It was a day of feast and gladness; and when, to her surprise and pleasure, a committee of church people waited upon Mrs. Morton to give her a purse, through the meshes of which glittered gold pieces, she said then and there that Toni should never go to the harsh and cruel Padrone again.

Perhaps some time as you listen to a sweet voice singing to the accompaniment of a violin you may think of Mrs. Morton and Toni, and be glad that the world bestows its applause and its gifts upon them, and that the vision of his mother and her love which came to Toni on that Christmas-eve has been made to him a reality.

(Begun in No. 8 of Harper's Young People, December 2.)

THE HISTORY OF PHOTOGEN AND NYCTERIS.

A Day and Night Mährchen.

BY GEORGE MACDONALD.

XIV.—THE SUN.

THERE Nycteris sat, and there the youth lay, all night long, in the heart of the great cone-shadow of the earth, like two Pharaohs in one pyramid. Photogen slept, and slept; and Nycteris sat motionless lest she should waken him, and so betray him to his fear.

The moon rode high in the blue eternity; it was a very triumph of glorious Night; the river ran babble-murmuring in deep soft syllables; the fountain kept rushing moonward, and blossoming momently to a great silvery flower, whose petals were forever falling like snow, but with a continuous musical clash, into the bed of its exhaustion beneath; the wind woke, took a run among the trees, went to sleep, and woke again; the daisies slept on their feet at hers, but she did not know they slept; the roses might well seem awake, for their scent filled the air, but in truth they slept also, and the odor was that of their dreams; the oranges hung like gold lamps in the trees, and their silvery flowers were the souls of their yet unembodied children; the scent of the acacia blooms filled the air like the very odor of the moon herself.

At last, unused to the living air, and weary with sitting so still and so long, Nycteris grew drowsy. The air began to grow cool. It was getting near the time when she too was accustomed to sleep. She closed her eyes just a moment, and nodded—opened them suddenly wide, for she had promised to watch.

In that moment a change had come. The moon had got round, and was fronting her from the west, and she saw that her face was altered, that she had grown pale, as if she too were wan with fear, and from her lofty place espied a coming terror. The light seemed to be dissolving out of her; she was dying—she was going out! And yet everything around looked strangely clear—clearer than ever she had seen anything before: how could the lamp be shedding more light when she herself had less? Ah, that was just it! See how faint she looked! It was because the light was forsaking her, and spreading itself over the room, that she grew so thin and pale. She was melting away from the roof like a bit of sugar in water.

Nycteris was fast growing afraid, and sought refuge with the face upon her lap. How beautiful the creature was!—what to call it she could not think, for it had been angry when she called it what Watho called her. And, wonder upon wonder! now, even in the cold change that was passing upon the great room, the color as of a red rose was rising in the wan cheek. What beautiful yellow hair it was that spread over her lap! What great huge breaths the creature took! And what were those curious things it carried? She had seen them on her walls, she was sure.

Thus she talked to herself while the lamp grew paler and paler, and everything kept growing yet clearer. What could it mean? The lamp was dying—going out into the other place of which the creature in her lap had spoken, to be a sun! But why were the things growing clearer before it was yet a sun? That was the point. Was it her growing into a sun that did it? Yes! yes! it was coming death! She knew it, for it was coming upon her also! She felt it coming! What was she about to grow into? Something beautiful, like the creature in her lap? It might be! Anyhow, it must be death; for all her strength was going out of her, while all around her was growing so light she could not bear it!

Photogen woke, lifted his head from her lap, and sprang to his feet. His face was one radiant smile. His heart was full of daring. Nycteris gave a cry, covered her face with her hands, and pressed her eyelids close. Then blindly she stretched out her arms to Photogen, crying, "Oh, I am so frightened! What is this? It must be death! I don't wish to die yet. I love this room and the old lamp. I do not want the other place! This is terrible!"

"What is the matter with you, girl?" said Photogen. "There is no fear of anything now, child. It is day. The sun is all but up. Good-by. Thank you for my night's lodging. I'm off. Don't be a goose. If ever I can do anything for you—and all that, you know—"

"Don't leave me; oh, don't leave me!" cried Nycteris. "I am dying! I can not move. The light sucks all the strength out of me. And oh, I am so frightened!"

But already Photogen had splashed through the river, holding high his bow that it might not get wet. He rushed across the level, and strained up the opposing hill. Hearing no answer, Nycteris removed her hands. Photogen had reached the top, and the same moment the sun-rays alighted upon him: the glory of the king of day crowded blazing upon the golden-haired youth. Radiant as Apollo, he stood in mighty strength, a flashing shape in the midst of flame. He fitted a glowing arrow to a gleaming bow. The arrow parted with a keen musical twang of the bowstring, and Photogen darting after it, vanished with a shout. Up shot Apollo himself, and from his quiver scattered astonishment and exultation. But the brain of poor Nycteris was pierced through and through. She fell down in utter darkness. All around her was a flaming furnace. In despair and feebleness and agony she crept back, feeling her way with doubt and difficulty and enforced persistence to her cell. When at last the friendly darkness of her chamber folded her about with its cooling and consoling arms, she threw herself on her bed and fell fast asleep. And there she slept on, one alive in a tomb, while Photogen, above in the sun-glory, pursued the buffaloes on the lofty plain, thinking not once of her

the roof of her house—where baby could never have got—than in it, while if dear mamma came near her, with her long flounces, Fluffy was on them at once, and stuck there like a hairy burr. That was the sad thing about Fluffy, she was such a gad-about, being everywhere where you didn't expect her to be; and so tiny that even when you did expect her, nobody knew she was there.

She was lost about ten times a day, and found in the most astonishing places. Once in mamma's work-box, where she was looked for, but not seen, being taken for a ball of worsted; and once in papa's shooting-jacket pocket, who took her to his office with him, under the impression that she was his seal-skin tobacco pouch.

Moreover, a very fashionable lady called one day, and took Fluffy right away with her, the poor little dear having clung to her mantle, and been amalgamated with its fur trimmings.

To say that dear papa was "weak" about the fair Persian is to take a very favorable view of his devotion to her; but dear mamma said it was "quite ridiculous to make such a fuss about a kitten"—and never herself lost a chance of picking it up and fondling it in her arms. The rest of the family were described by their cousin Charley, who lived over the way, as "sunk in the Persian superstition," and even as "addicted to nigger worship"—an allusion to Fluff's sable hue.

And now comes the best part of the story, which is, of course, the "creepy-crawly" and horrible part.

Cousin Charley had a mastiff dog called Jumbo, ever so high and ever so huge, with great hanging chaps (which are pronounced chops, you know) on both sides of his jaws. If you never saw him open his mouth, I can scarcely give you any idea of it; but if you have seen pictures of Vesuvius during an eruption, think of the crater. It was said by his master that Jumbo would never hurt a fly, but that was not the point with those who were not flies, and all these stood in great fear of him. It is very little satisfaction to one who meets an elephant in his morning's walk, in a narrow way, to have read that that creature is the most gentle of mammals (or mammoths); and similarly there was no knowing what catastrophe might not take place from the presence of Jumbo, though he might not mean to bring it about. He was positively too tremendous for society; while, out-of-doors, I never knew a dog so respected—and avoided—by other dogs.

To see Jumbo and Fluff together was to behold the meeting of two extremes of the animal creation; the introduction of the King of Brobdingnag to the Princess of Lilliput, or of Chang, the Chinese giant, to Mrs. General Tom Thumb. Yet, if you will believe me, on Jumbo's first appearance on our drawing-room rug, Fluff scampered up to him (all on one side, as usual) and hung on to his tail! The moment was one of terrible suspense, not only to her, but to the spectators generally, except Charley, who said, "Oh, Jumbo won't mind," which might or might not have been the case; for it is my fixed conviction that that noble animal was totally unaware of what was taking place, so to speak, behind his back, and to this hour is ignorant of the indignity that was put upon him.

One Sunday morning, in midwinter, Jumbo called without his master, and walked into the back parlor without being announced; there was no living creature there except himself and Fluff, and when the family entered the room *there was only Jumbo*. They looked everywhere for his late (yes, his *late*) companion; but she had vanished. Whither? To this vital question it seemed to their horrified minds that there was but one reply; it was in vain for Jumbo to assume an indifferent air, as though he would say, "How should *I* know?" The accusation that trembled on every lip was, "The dog has swallowed her." He looked about the same size as usual, but that was nothing; fifty Fluffs would not have made any external difference. One of his chaps, indeed, seemed to hang a little lower than usual, but she was not there. He yawned—nobody believed in *that*; it was just what a dog would do, conscious of crime and assuming unconcern—and everybody shuddered. What might not that enormous throat have swallowed, and thought nothing of it! Messengers were dispatched at once for Charley, who came and cross-examined the animal; but he only shook his head and wagged his tail. These actions might have been proofs of his innocence if Fluff had still been with us, but as it was, it only showed his callousness—the callousness of cannibalism.

All sat round Jumbo in a circle, and listened in solemn silence. Even the tiniest mew of farewell would have been welcome, but it was not vouchsafed. Nothing was heard but the thumping of that wicked tail (to which they had once seen Fluffy cling) upon the bear-skin rug on which they had so often lost her. She was not there now, for they took it up and shook it. She was not in the envelope case upon the writing-table; nor in the coal-scuttle, for they took the coals out one by one, to be quite sure; nor in the work-box, for it was Sunday, and it was not there; nor up the curtains, for they examined them with "the steps"; nor up the chimney, for the fire was alight; nor in either of papa's boots, which were set on the fender to get warm. She was gone from their sight like a beautiful dream, though still, alas! in a manner, *present*.

Dear papa was the first to recover from the catastrophe. "Whatever has taken place, my dears," said he, "we must go to church; the last bell is already ringing."

Dear mamma sighed, and took the hands of the two youngest children, leaving her muff to hang from her neck by its ribbon. She felt that in that hour of trouble the clasp of her fingers would be a comfort to them.

The whole family walked together like a funeral procession, and they could see the neighbors draw long faces, under the impression that there had been some fatal domestic calamity to account for such looks of woe. Even Charley was affected, though he could hardly believe even yet in his favorite's guilt, while Jumbo came behind with his tail between his legs—either from the stings of conscience, or because he knew he would be left as usual at the church door.

I am afraid the thoughts of some of the little party wandered a little, during the first part of the service, in the supposed direction in which Fluff had gone; but the sermon riveted their attention. They wished sincerely Jumbo could have been there to hear it, for it was upon cruelty to animals. It had just begun, and dear mamma had for the first time got rid of her books and placed her hands in her muff, when she drew them sharply out again and turned very red. At the same time a piteous little mew pervaded the sanctuary. At home we could not have heard it a yard away, but the church, being built for sound, developed those delicate notes. At the same time all the people on the right hand of the aisle began to smile. Fluff's little black face had protruded itself at that end of the muff. Dear mamma hastened to close it up with her hand, and then all the people on the left hand of the aisle began to smile. Fluff's little black face had peered out at the other end. Then dear mamma, in desperation, put in both her hands, and then the imprisoned Fluff began to mew indeed. "How hard must that heart be," said the clergyman, going on with his subject, "who would ill use an innocent, helpless kitten!" "Like me, like me," said Fluff, or so it seemed to say, in its piteous way. The people in both aisles fixed their eyes on dear mamma, who in vain pretended to be rapt in the sermon; they knew very well by this time what was wrapped in her muff, and in the end dear mamma had to go. The denunciations of the clergyman against cruel people followed her down the aisle, and were supposed, no doubt, by those who didn't know her, to have a personal application, for Fluff was

"FLUFF'S LITTLE BLACK FACE PRESENTED ITSELF."—DRAWN BY A. B. FROST.

mewing all the way. It was altogether a most terrible business. What all the family felt, however, when they got home, was that an apology was, in the first place, due to Jumbo for the imputation on his character, and it was offered (on a plate of beef bones) in the amplest manner, and accepted in a similar spirit.

THEY GOT THE TURKEY.

BY MRS. MARGARET EYTINGE.

THE shop of Mr. Oncomander Golong looked, that 24th of December, like a bower. Two young cedar-trees stood one on each side of the doorway; long garlands of evergreen, sprinkled with bright berries, were festooned all over the walls; and every turkey there, and there were lots of them, hanging like some new kind of gigantic fruit from the mass of green that covered the ceiling, had a gay ribbon tied around its neck. And such a wonderful picture in the way of freshness and color as the big window presented to the passers-by! Bunches of crisp light green celery leaning up against heaps of brown, pink-eyed potatoes and honest red onions; fiery-looking peppers side by side with golden oranges and yellow lemons; hard, smooth, shining cranberries trying to look as though they were sweet; great fat pumpkins; piles of green and piles of rosy apples; bunches of fragrant thyme; and more turkeys, some with and some without their feathered coats, but all, as I said before, with gay ribbons around their necks. Dear me! if Santa Claus could have only looked into that window and peeped into that shop, how pleased he would have been, and how he would have laughed! And he certainly would have taken Mr. Oncomander Golong for a long-lost brother, for never before did mortal man so strongly resemble the children's old Christmas friend. Snow-white hair, long snow-white beard, twinkling blue eyes, round, fat, red, good-natured face, a fur cap on his head, bunches of holly berries pinned here and there on his shaggy jacket, and a laugh—good gracious! such a loud, hearty, mirth-provoking laugh, that the very people on the street, hearing it, began to smile, and feel that Christmas was here indeed. And I tell you Mr. Oncomander Golong was busy that day, and so were all the men and boys employed by him. Turkeys and other things that had been ordered the evening before, turkeys and other things that had been ordered early that morning, and turkeys and other things being ordered all the time, were to be packed away in huge baskets, and sent to their respective destinations. But he wasn't so busy but that he stopped a moment from his work to give a piece of meat to a poor dog that had trotted hopefully into the shop (having evidently translated the name "Golong" over the door into "Come in"), and was asking for it with his eyes. And as he rose from patting the dog, he saw two children standing before him, also asking for something with their eyes. They were poorly dressed children, but the girl had a sweet, bright face, and the boy was as jolly-looking a little fellow as you could find anywhere. His cheeks were as round, if not as red, as Mr. Golong's, and his merry black eyes actually danced in his head. Now if there was one place in Mr. Oncomander Golong's heart softer than the rest, it was the place he kept for children; and so when he saw these two looking up in his face—the boy with boyish boldness, and the girl with girlish shyness—he said, in the cheeriest, kindest manner, "Well, small people, what can I do for you?"

"We would like to tell you a story," answered the boy, in a frank, pleasant voice.

"Tell me a story!" repeated Mr. Golong, in a tone of great surprise.

"Yes, sir, please—a Christmas story," was the reply.

"Bless my heart! what a queer idea!" said Mr. Golong, and he laughed a silent laugh that half closed his eyes and wrinkled his nose in the funniest way.

"Wouldn't you like to hear one?" asked the girl, coaxingly.

"Of course I would—I'm very fond of stories—but I don't see how I can spare the time. We're so busy just now, and likely to be until night," said Mr. Golong.

"It's only a short one," said the boy.

"A very short one," added the girl.

"Well, go ahead," said the good-natured old fellow. And he sat down on a barrel of potatoes, and his young visitors placed themselves one on each side of him.

"One Christmas-time," the boy began, "there was a big tenement-house in this city, and ten families lived in it, and every one of these families 'cept one knew they were a-going to have turkey for their Christmas dinner. They knew it sure the day before Christmas, all 'cept this one. The family that wasn't sure the day before Christmas morning lived on the top floor, and it was —it was—"

"Mrs. Todd, Neal Todd, Hetty Todd, and Puppy Todd," prompted the girl.

"Yes, it was them," said the boy, and went on with his story again: "Mrs. Todd was Neal's and Hetty's mother—they hadn't any father; he died three years ago—and Puppy was their dog. Mrs. Todd is one of the best mothers ever lived, and she sews button-holes on boys' jackets for a big store; and Hetty cleans up the house, and gets the supper, and such things; and I—I mean Neal—runs errands for folks when he can get a chance after school. His mother wants him to go to school till he's fourteen anyhow, 'cause a boy that has some education can get along better than a boy that don't know anything. And this family, though they were very poor, had always managed to have a turkey dinner till the Christmas I'm telling about, and Mrs. Todd she loved turkey."

"Didn't Hetty and Neal?" asked Mr. Golong, closing his eyes and wrinkling his nose again; and he hurried away to wait on a stout lady, all covered with glittering jet ornaments and bugles, who must have been a very particular customer, she talked so loud and so much.

"Didn't Hetty and Neal?" he repeated, when he came back.

"Oh, my! I guess they did!" said the girl, her eyes sparkling.

"They'd 'a been funny fellows if they didn't," added the boy; "but, 'pon their words and honors, they wanted it more for their mother—she's such a good mother, and has so few good things to eat—than they did for themselves. And it made them feel awful bad when she came home and cried 'cause some wicked thief had stolen her pocket-book with half a week's earnings in it, and the two-dollar bill that the boss had given her to buy a Christmas dinner with besides. And so the boy Neal—he's kind of a nice chap, ain't he, Hetty?"

"Awful nice," replied Hetty, with a mischievous little giggle.

"And he says to his sister—she's awful nice, ain't she, Hetty?"

"Kind of nice," said Hetty, with another little giggle.

"He says to his sister," continued the boy, "'Don't say anything to mother, but put on your hat and bring a basket, and we'll make a try for a merry Christmas dinner—turkey and all.' And they went round the corner to a beautiful market, kept by a gentleman who looked exactly like Santa Claus—".

Mr. Onesander Golong laughed aloud this time, and flew to wait on another particular customer.

"So he looked like Santa Claus!" he said, with a chuckle, when he sat down on the barrel of potatoes again.

"The very image of him!" said the girl, with great emphasis.

"The boy," began the boy once more, "had run errands for him two or three times, and each time had got two apples or oranges besides the reg'lar pay; and he was good to cats and dogs. So this chap went to this gentleman—he took his sister along, 'cause he thought Mr. Golong would like to see her—and they told him their story. And the boy says, when it was done, 'If you would only trust us for a turk—I mean, a turkey, and a few other things, I'll work for you all holiday week, and another week too, after school. My name's Neal Todd, and my mother is a real nice woman, and I love her just as you used to love your mother when you was a little boy.' And the gentleman, says he, 'Being as it's Christmas-time, and I look so much like Santa Claus, I'll do it.' And he did. And that's all."

Mr. Onesander Golong burst out a-laughing, and oh! how he laughed! He laughed until the tears ran down his cheeks. He laughed until he nearly fell off the barrel. He laughed until everybody far and near who heard him laughed too, and the very roosters in the poultry shop over the way joined in, and crowed with all their might and main. And they got the turkey.

"AND THEY GOT THE TURKEY!"

BOOKS SUITABLE FOR HOLIDAY PRESENTS.

GIFT BOOKS FOR BOYS AND GIRLS.

The Boy Travellers in the Far East.

Adventures of Two Youths in a Journey to Japan and China. By Thomas W. Knox. Illustrated. 8vo, Cloth, $3 00.

An Involuntary Voyage.

A Book for Boys. By Lucien Biart. Illustrated. 12mo, Cloth, $1 25.

Stories of the Old Dominion.

By John Esten Cooke. Profusely Illustrated. 12mo, Illuminated Cloth, $1 50.

The Story of Liberty.

By Charles Carleton Coffin. Copiously Illustrated. 8vo, Cloth, $3 00.

The Boys of '76.

A History of the Battles of the Revolution. By Charles Carleton Coffin. Copiously Illustrated. 8vo, Cloth, $3 00.

The Fairy Books:

THE PRINCESS IDLEWAYS. By Mrs. W. J. Hays. Illustrated. 16mo, Cloth, 75 cents.

THE CATSKILL FAIRIES. By Virginia W. Johnson. 8vo, Illuminated Cloth, Gilt Edges, $3 00.

FAIRY BOOK ILLUSTRATED. 16mo, Cloth, $1 50.

PUSS-CAT MEW, and other New Fairy Stories for my Children. By E. H. Knatchbull-Hugessen, M.P. Illustrated. 12mo, Cloth, $1 25.

FAIRY BOOK. The Best Popular Fairy Stories selected and rendered anew. By the Author of "John Halifax." Illustrated. 12mo, Cloth, $1 25.

FAIRY TALES. By Jean Macé. Translated by Mary L. Booth. Illustrated. 12mo, Bevelled Edges, $1 75; Gilt Edges, $2 25.

FAIRY TALES OF ALL NATIONS. By E. Laboulaye. Translated by Mary L. Booth. Illustrated. 12mo, Cloth, Bevelled Edges, $2 00; Gilt Edges, $2 50.

THE LITTLE LAME PRINCE. By the Author of "John Halifax, Gentleman." Illustrated. Square 16mo, Cloth, $1 00.

FOLKS AND FAIRIES. Stories for Little Children. By Lucy Randall Comfort. Illustrated. Square 4to, Cloth, $1 00.

THE ADVENTURES OF A BROWNIE, as Told to my Child. By the Author of "John Halifax, Gentleman." Illustrated. Square 16mo, Cloth, 90 cents.

Songs of Our Youth.

By Miss Mulock. Set to Music. Square 4to, Cloth, Illuminated, $2 50.

Books for Girls.

Written or Edited by the Author of "John Halifax, Gentleman." Illustrated. 6 vols., 16mo, Cloth, in neat case, $5 40; the volumes separately, 90 cents each.

Little Sunshine's Holiday.—The Cousin from India.—Twenty Years Ago.—Is it True?—An Only Sister.—Miss Moore.

Pet; or, Pastimes and Penalties.

By Rev. H. R. Haweis, M.A. With 50 Illustrations. 12mo, Cloth, $1 50.

What Mr. Darwin Saw

In his Voyage Round the World in the Ship "Beagle." Adapted for Youthful Readers. Maps and Illustrations. 8vo, Ornamental Cloth, $3 00.

Our Children's Songs.

Illustrated. 8vo, Ornamental Cover, $1 00.

Smiles's Books for Young Men:

SELF-HELP.—CHARACTER.—THRIFT. 12mo, Cloth, $1 00 per volume.

Books for Young People.

By Paul B. Du Chaillu. Illustrated. 5 vols., 12mo, Cloth, $1 50 each.

Stories of the Gorilla Country. Wild Life under the Equator.
Lost in the Jungle. My Apingi Kingdom.
The Country of the Dwarfs.

Dogs and their Doings.

By Rev. F. O. Morris. Elegantly Illustrated. Square 4to, Ornamental Cloth, $1 75.

Abbotts' Histories.

Illustrated. 16mo, Cloth, $1 00 per volume; $32 00 per set.

Cyrus.—Darius.—Xerxes.—Alexander.—Romulus.—Hannibal.—Pyrrhus.—Julius Cæsar.—Cleopatra.—Nero.—Alfred.—William the Conqueror.—Richard I.—Richard II.—Richard III.—Mary Queen of Scots.—Queen Elizabeth.—Charles I.—Charles II.—Josephine.—Maria Antoinette.—Madame Roland.—Henry IV.—Margaret of Anjou.—Peter the Great.—Genghis Khan.—King Philip.—Hernando Cortez.—Joseph Bonaparte.—Queen Hortense.—Louis XIV.—Louis Philippe.

John G. Edgar's Juvenile Works.

Illustrated. 16mo, Cloth, $1 00 each.

The Boyhood of Great Men.—The Footprints of Famous Men.—History for Boys.—Sea-Kings and Naval Heroes.—The Wars of the Roses.

Henry Mayhew's Works.

Illustrated. 16mo, Cloth, $1 25 per volume.

The Boyhood of Martin Luther.—The Wonders of Science: Young Humphry Davy, the Cornish Apothecary's Boy.—The Young Benjamin Franklin.—The Peasant-Boy Philosopher: Founded on the Life of Ferguson, the Shepherd-Boy Astronomer.

Science for the Young.

By Jacob Abbott. Profusely Illustrated. 4 vols., 12mo, Cloth, $1 50 each. 1. Heat; 2. Light; 3. Water and Land; 4. Force.

Adventures of a Young Naturalist.

By Lucien Biart. Edited by Parker Gillmore. 117 Illustrations. 12mo, Cloth, $1 75.

How to Get Strong,

And How to Stay So. By William Blaikie. Illustrated. 16mo, Cloth, $1 00.

HARPER'S YOUNG PEOPLE.

Harper's Young People will be issued every Tuesday, and may be had at the following rates; *payable in advance—postage free:*

Single Copies................4 cts. | One Subscription, *one year*...$1 50 | Five Subscriptions, *one year*..$7 00

Subscriptions may begin with any number. When no time is specified, it will be understood that the subscriber desires to commence with the number issued after the receipt of order.

Remittances should be made by POST-OFFICE MONEY ORDER, or DRAFT, to avoid risk of loss.

Address HARPER & BROTHERS, Franklin Square, New York.

A LIBERAL OFFER FOR 1880 ONLY.

☞ Harper's Young People *and* Harper's Weekly *will be sent to any address for one year, commencing with the first number of* Harper's Weekly *for January,* 1880, *on receipt of* $5 00 *for the two Periodicals.*

WE give our correspondents a hearty Christmas greeting, and present them with an enlarged and handsome *Young People*, which we hope they will receive with the same kindness and appreciation they have already shown us. We shall give them weekly a great variety of stories, poems, and instructive reading, printed in large, clear type, on firm, handsome paper. The popularity of our Post-office Box is shown by the increasing weight of our daily mail-bag, which comes to us overflowing with pretty messages.

POTTSVILLE, PENNSYLVANIA.

Papa has brought us several numbers of *Young People*, and as you ask us little folks to write to you, I thought I would tell you how much we are pleased with the paper. The story of the "Brave Swiss Boy" is so interesting I can hardly wait for the next number to come. What a good, brave, and honest boy Walty was, and what a plucky fight he had with the vultures! The picture of the "Monkey on Guard" is very fine. I like stories of brave boys and pictures of smart monkeys. Papa is going to take *Young People* for me next year, and I am going to keep every one. The paper is just the right size to make into a book for Jamie and Maggie.

PAUL W. C.

BROOKLYN, NEW YORK.

I like your paper very much, and am always glad to get it. I have a nice old bachelor uncle in New York, who sends it to me every week. I should like very much to see this in print. If it is, I may try again. I have been very sick with diphtheria, and I don't like it a bit. I made 'most three dollars taking medicine, and I liked that very much. As you ask for short letters, I will stop.

CARRIE L. S.

DETROIT, MICHIGAN.

I have read *Young People*, and it is very nice indeed. My mother told me that you were going to publish a paper for children, and said I could take it. I have read all the "Story of a Parrot," and it made me laugh very much. I think *Young People* is better than anything that has been published for children, and I will read every number that is issued, and thank you kindly for such a nice paper.

WILLIAM B. K.

WATERTOWN, CONN.

As you kindly invited us all to write to you, I would like to tell you about a pet pigeon I had. I called it Lily, because it was so white. I got it when it was a little bit of a thing, and I did not keep it in a cage. I taught it to eat out of my hand, and when I came from school and called Lily, it would come flying from the barn-yard, where it was with the other pigeons, and light on my shoulder, and put its bill up to my mouth. One day I called Lily, and it did not come. I went to look for it in the barn-yard myself. It was there, but it would not come to me, and always after that it was wild. I think *Harper's Young People* is a very nice paper, and mamma thinks she will take it for me. My papa has taken *Harper's Weekly* and *Monthly* ever since they were in existence.

SARAH E. H.

YONKERS, NEW YORK.

I was very glad when papa came home with a little paper for me, and I took it from his hand and looked at it for about ten minutes, and then asked him if he would take it for me. When he found out that I read it all through, he asked which story I liked the best, and I told him, "The Story of a Parrot." Papa takes *Harper's Magazine*, but I would rather have *Young People*. I have read all about the "Brave Swiss Boy," and I hope he will become rich.

BELL H.

WASHINGTON, INDIANA.

Cousin Orie and I were delighted when Uncle Will (he is Orie's papa, and I live at his house) brought us *Young People*, and now we eagerly watch its coming every week. I think Wally Hiesel was a brave and noble boy to risk so much for his father.

A. H. A.

WAVERLY, NEW JERSEY.

Your nice paper comes with mamma's. We have had lots of fun with the "Wiggles." Won't you please answer this question: In our dining-room there is a big looking-glass. In front of the glass there is a table. When a lamp is set on the table, it looks as if there were two lamps. Please tell me whether the lamp on the table and the one reflected in the looking-glass will give as much light as two lamps.

KATIE S.

The lamp and its reflection will not give as much light as two lamps, and the intensity of light thrown from the mirror depends upon the distance of the lamp from its surface, and also upon the nature and thickness of the mirror itself.

MABEL E. F. S.—The first condition for admission to the *St. Mary's* is a residence in New York city. The remainder of your question is answered in the Post-office Box of our sixth number.

J. R. B.—We do not know how to prescribe for your poor sick rabbit.

NELLIE B.—All stars appear to twinkle except the planets. We can not tell the reason any plainer than it is already given by the "Professor."

VERY pleasant letters, and also answers to puzzles, are received from Henry C. L., Allie D., Frank S. M., Elsie P. D., Theodore F. L., Charles E. L., M. W. D., Lilian, "Subscriber," C. F. C., F. Coggswell, Claude C., Charles F. and George J. M., Victor E., J. G., M. R. E. S., Charlie G., and Anna B.

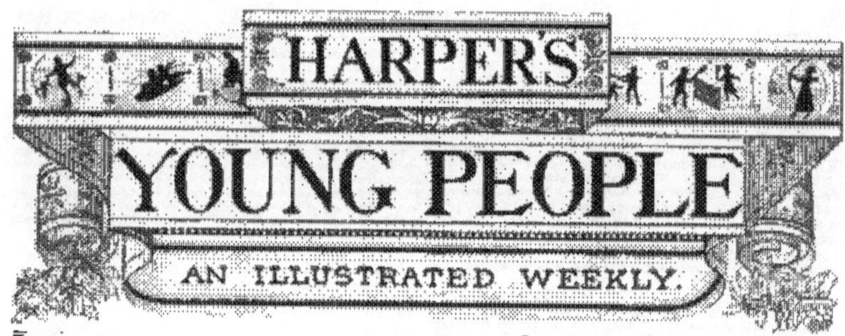

HARPER'S YOUNG PEOPLE

AN ILLUSTRATED WEEKLY.

VOL. I.—NO. 9. | PUBLISHED BY HARPER & BROTHERS, NEW YORK. | PRICE FOUR CENTS.

Tuesday, December 30, 1879. | $1.50 per Year, in Advance.

A COASTING SONG.

FROM the quaint old farm-house, nestling warmly
'Neath its overhanging thatch of snow,
Out into the moonlight troop the children,
Filling all the air with music as they go,
Gliding, sliding,
Down the hill,
Never minding
Cold nor chill,
O'er the silvered
Moon-lit snow,
Swift as arrow
From the bow,
With a rush
Of mad delight
Through the crisp air
Of the night,
Speeding far out
O'er the plain,
Trudging gayly
Up again
To where the fire-light's
Ruddy glow
Turns to gold
The silver snow.
Finer sport who can conceive
Than that of coasting New-Year's Eve?
Half the fun lies in the fire
That seems to brighter blaze and higher
Than any other of the year,
As though his dying hour to cheer,
And at the same time greeting give
To him who has a year to live.
'Tis built of logs of oak and pine,
Filled in with branches broken fine;
It roars and crackles merrily;
The children round it dance with glee;
They sing and shout and welcome in
The new year with a joyous din
That rings far out o'er hill and dale,
And warns the watchers in the vale
'Tis time the church bells to employ
To spread the universal joy.

Then the hill is left in silence
As the coasters homeward go,
And the crimson of the fire-light
Fades from off the trodden snow.

So the years glide by as swiftly
As the sleds rush down the hill,
And each new one as it cometh
Bringeth more of good than ill.

COASTING NEW-YEAR'S EVE.
Drawn by C. Graham.

THE FAIRY'S TOKEN.

Ethelreda, the Fairy of Northland,
  Was singing a song to herself,
As she swung from a wreath of soft snow-flakes,
  And smiled to another bright elf.

What token shall we send to our darling,
  Our name-child, fair Ethel, below
In the home which is down in the valley
  All covered and calm in the snow?

Shall we gather our glorious jewels,
  And wind them about her little form?
They would glitter and glance in the sunshine,
  And merrily gleam in the storm.

Shall we clothe her in whitest of ermine,
  And robe her as grand as a queen;
Weave her laces of ice and of frost-work,
  A mantle of glistening sheen?

She would shudder and cry at the clasping,
  She would moan aloud in her woe,
And think the gay robes had been fashioned
  By cruelest, bitterest foe.

I will none of these gifts for my darling,
  Neither jewels nor laces rare,
Neither diamonds nor pearls of cold anguish—
  My gift shall be tender and fair.

Early Ethel awoke Christmas morning,
  And found on her pillow that day
A bunch of bright little snow-drops,
  From kind Ethelreda, the Fay!

(Begun in No. 1 of Harper's Young People, November 4.)

THE BRAVE SWISS BOY.

VIII.—THE REWARD OF FIDELITY.

WALTER met with a friendly reception from General De Bongy—a brave old warrior who had served under Napoleon, and fought at Waterloo, where he had been severely wounded, and had lost his right foot by a cannon-ball. His hair was gray, and his countenance weather-beaten; but in spite of his age and infirmities he enjoyed tolerably good health, and was always in good humor. Having from long experience become a keen observer of those around him, it was not long before he recognized the merits of his new servant, to whom he soon became as much attached as his nephew had been.

Walter had been about three months in the general's service, and it seemed to all appearance as if he was likely to become a permanency there, when a letter arrived from Paris, the reading of which suddenly changed the customary gayety of the old man into the deepest gloom.

"This is a sad affair," said he to Walter, who happened to be in the room at the time. "My poor nephew!"

"Mr. Lafond? What is the matter with him?" inquired Walter, earnestly.

"He is ill, dangerously ill, poor fellow, so the doctor informs me," replied the general. "You can read the letter yourself. He seems to complain of being surrounded by strangers, with no one in the house that he can rely on. If I were not such an old cripple, I would go and help him to the best of my ability; for although he has led a thoughtless, reckless life, a more thorough-hearted gentleman does not live. Poor Adolphe!"

"I must go to him, sir," said Walter, suddenly, after hastily reading the letter, the perusal of which had driven all the color from his cheeks.

"You! Why, it is not long since you left him; and what do you want to go back for?" inquired the general, in surprise.

"Can you not guess, sir? I must go and nurse him. He must at least have one person near him to pay him some attention."

"If you care for him so," exclaimed the general, "why did you leave his service?"

This led Walter to explain to the old gentleman the reasons which had compelled him to give up his situation, and again to beg permission to act the part of nurse to his former master. A tear sparkled in the old man's eye as the youth declared the attachment he had always cherished for Mr. Lafond. "Go to him, then," said he. "I can not trust him to a more faithful attendant; and as soon as I can I will follow you, and take my place with you by his bedside. Poor Adolphe! Had he only possessed firmness of character, and avoided bad company, he might have been well and strong to-day. But his unhappy weakness has brought him to the grave before his time, in spite of all my warnings and entreaties. As he has sowed, so must he reap. Ah, Walter, his fate is a terrible proof of the consequences of evil habits. But all regrets are useless now. Let us lose no time in giving what little help we can."

Making all the necessary preparations for the journey without a moment's delay, Walter soon reached Paris. When he entered the chamber of Mr. Lafond he was shocked at the change which a few short months had made in his appearance. It was evident that the doctor had rather disguised than exaggerated the danger he was in. The sunken eyes and withered face showed only too plainly that the space of time allotted to him on earth was but short. Walter sank on his knees by the bedside, and taking the pale and wasted hand in his, breathed a prayer that God might see fit to deal mercifully with a life yet so young; while the invalid smiled faintly, and stroked the cheek of his faithful attendant.

"Dear Walter, how good of you to come back!" murmured the invalid. "I thought you would not leave me to die alone. I feared that your prediction would prove true, and therefore I did not wish you to go home. I wanted to have a true friend with me at the last moment, which I feel can not be far off now."

The faithful Switzer saw that Mr. Lafond too well knew the critical condition he was in to be deceived by any false hopes, and he therefore did everything in his power to make the last days of the dying man as free from pain and discomfort as possible. Who could tell what might be the effect, even at so late a period, of careful nursing and devoted attention? But all his thoughtful and loving care seemed in vain.

"The end is coming," said the invalid one evening, as the glowing rays of the evening sun streamed into his apartment. "I shall never more look upon yonder glorious sun, or hear the gay singing of the birds. I have something to say to you, Walter, before I go. Do you see that black cabinet in the corner? I bequeath it to you, with everything it contains, and hope with all my heart that it will help you on in the world as you deserve. Here is the key of my desk, in which you will find my will, which confirms you in the possession of the cabinet and all its contents. And now give me your hand, dear boy. Let me look once more upon your honest face. May Heaven bless you for all your kindness and devotion! Farewell!"

Walter bent over the face of the dying man, and looked at him with deep emotion. He smiled and closed his eyes; but after lying in a quiet slumber for about an hour, he awoke with a spasm; his head fell back, and the hapless victim died in the arms of his faithful servant.

The long hours of the night were passed by Walter in weeping and prayer beside the corpse of the master to whose kindness he had owed so much; but when morning dawned he roused himself from his grief, and gave the directions that were necessary under the melancholy circumstances. It was a great relief to him that General De Bongy arrived toward evening to pay the last honors to his deceased nephew. Two days afterward the funeral took place; and as the mortal remains were deposited in the family grave, Walter's tears flowed afresh as he thought of the many proofs of friendship he had received from his departed master.

A day or two afterward he was awakened from his sorrow by news from home. The letter was from Neighbor Frieshardt, who again thanked him for the money he had received for the sale of the cattle, praised him for the faithfulness and ability with which he had managed the business, and then went on to speak of Walter's father. "The old man," he wrote, "is in good health, but he feels lonely, and longs for you to come back. 'If Watty only were here, I should feel quite young again,' he has said to me a hundred times. He sends you his love; and Seppi, who is still with me, and is now a faithful servant, does the same. So good-by, Walter. I think you now know what you had better do."

Without any delay Walter hastened to the general, showed him the letter, and told him he had decided to leave Paris and return home.

The general used all his powers of persuasion, promised to regard the young mountaineer as his own son; but it was all of no use. Walter spoke so earnestly of his father's solitary home, and the desire he felt to see his native mountains once more, that the old gentleman had to reconcile himself to parting with him. "Go home, then," said he. "When the voice of Duty calls, it is sinful to resist. But before you go, we must open my nephew's will. It will surprise me very much if there is nothing in it of importance to you." Unlocking the desk, the will was found sealed up as it had been left by Mr. Lafond. After opening it, the general read the document carefully through, and laid it down on the table with an expression of disappointment. "Poor fellow!" he exclaimed. "Death must have surprised him too suddenly, Walter, or he would certainly have left you a larger legacy. This is all he says about you: 'To Walter Hirzel, my faithful and devoted servant, I bequeath the black cabinet in my bedroom, with all its contents, and thank him sincerely for all his attention to me.' That is the whole of it. But never mind, my young friend; the old general is still alive, and he will make good all that his nephew has forgotten."

Walter shook his head. "Thanks, a thousand times, dear sir, but indeed I wish for nothing. My feet will carry me to my native valley; and once I am there, I can easily earn my living. I dare say there will be some little keepsake in the cabinet that I can take in memory of my poor master, and I want nothing more."

"Then search the cabinet at once. Where is the key?"

"Here," said Walter, taking it from his pocket. "Mr. Lafond gave me the cabinet shortly before his death, and handed me the key at the same time."

"And have you never thought of opening it to see what it contained?"

"No," replied Walter. "It did not occur to me to do so. But I will go and see now." With these words he left the room, and went up to the apartment where the piece of furniture stood. In the various drawers were found the watch, rings, and jewelry his master had been accustomed to wear. As he viewed these tokens of regard, his eyes were bedewed with melancholy gratitude. Carefully placing the jewelry in a little box, he was about to close the cabinet again, when his eye fell upon a drawer which he had omitted to open. Here, to his infinite surprise, he found a packet with the inscription, in his late master's handwriting, "The Reward of Fidelity," which, on opening, he found to contain bank-notes for one hundred thousand francs.

"Well, what have you found?" inquired the general, eagerly, when the half-bewildered youth returned.

"This watch and jewelry, and a packet of bank-notes," replied Walter, laying them on the table.

"One hundred thousand francs!" exclaimed the old gentleman. "That is something worth having. Why, that will be a fortune to you; and I am now sorry that I did my nephew the injustice to think he had forgotten you. I wish you joy with all my heart!"

"For what do you wish me joy, sir?"

"For what? For the money," said the general, in surprise.

"But that is not for me," said the Switzer, shaking his head. "This watch and the jewelry I will keep as long as I live, in memory of my good master; but the money must have been left there by mistake, and I should feel like a thief if I were to take any of it."

The old general opened his eyes as wide as he could, and stared in astonishment at the simplicity of the youth. "I'm afraid you are out of your mind," said he. "The will says, 'The black cabinet, with all its contents.' The bank-notes were in it, and of course they are yours."

"And yet it must be a mistake."

"But I tell you it is no mistake," exclaimed the general, impatiently. "Look at the inscription, 'The Reward of Fidelity!' To whom should that apply but to you? Put the money in your pocket, Walter, and let us have no more absurd doubts about it."

But the young man persisted in his refusal, and pushed the packet away from him. "It is too much," said he; "I can not think of robbing you of such a large sum."

"Well, then," said the general, greatly touched by such singular unselfishness, "*I* must settle the business. If you won't take the money, I will take you. From this day, Walter, you are my son. Come to my heart. Old as it is, it beats warmly for fidelity and honesty. Thanks to God that He has given me such a son in my lonely old age!"

Walter stood as if rooted to the spot. But the old man drew him to his breast and embraced him warmly, till both found relief for their feelings in tears.

"But my father," stammered the young man at last. "My father is all alone at home."

"Oh, we will start off to him at once, bag and baggage," exclaimed the general. "I know your fatherland well, and shall very soon feel myself more at home there than I am in France, where there is not a creature left to care for me. Yes, Walter, we will go to the glorious Bernese Oberland, and buy ground, and build a house, within view of your noble mountains, and live there with your father. He shall have cattle and goats to cheer his heart in his old age, and we will lead a happy life together as long as God spares us."

Walter in his happiness could scarcely believe his ears, and thought the whole a splendid dream. But he soon found the reality. The general sold his property in France, and departed with his adopted son to Switzerland, where he carried out the intention he had so suddenly formed. Old Toni Hirzel renewed his youth when he had his son once more beside him, and he and the general soon became fast friends. A year had scarcely passed ere a beautiful house was built near Meyringen, and furnished with every comfort; while an ample garden, surrounded by meadows, in which cows and oxen fed, added to the beauty of the scene. Walter's dream had become a reality; and everything around him was so much better than he had ever dared to hope, that his heart overflowed with gratitude to God, and to the benefactor who had done so much for him.

Nor was this prosperity undeserved. Walter had not spent his time in idleness and sloth. He knew that the diligent hand maketh its owner rich, and he managed the land with so much energy and skill that he soon became renowned as one of the best farmers in the Oberland. The general and Toni assisted him with their counsel and help as far as they were able; and the old soldier soon experienced the beneficial influence of an active out-door life and the change of air and scene. His pale cheeks grew once more ruddy with health, and he soon grew so

"HE WRAPPED HIMSELF IN HIS DRESSING-GOWN, AND WALKED HASTILY TO AND FRO."

active that he even forgot that his right foot lay buried on the field of Waterloo.

Thus the little family lived in happiness, enjoying the good wishes of all their neighbors, and the gratitude of all who were in want; for they were always ready to relieve out of their abundance any who needed it. Mr. Seymour increased their happiness by visiting his friend Walter nearly every year, and rejoiced in the prosperity which God had bestowed upon him as a reward for his honesty and uprightness.

THE END.

AROUND THE WORLD IN A STEAM-YACHT.

THE beautiful steam-yacht *Henriette*, of which a picture is given on this page, has just left New York, bound on a pleasure voyage around the world. Her passengers are her owner, M. Henri Say, and his wife and child, and they will doubtless have a most pleasant voyage, and see many strange sights and countries before it is ended.

The general outline of the route to be pursued is from New York down the coast, touching at Baltimore and Washington, and possibly at some of the Southern ports, then to the West Indies, where several weeks will be spent in cruising among the beautiful islands. Some of the principal South American cities will be visited before stormy Cape Horn is doubled, and the *Henriette* enters the quieter waters of the Pacific. Then the plan of the voyage includes the Sandwich Islands, San Francisco, Japan, China, Australia, the East Indian islands, India, Arabia, the Red Sea, Egypt, the Suez Canal, Turkey, the many interesting countries bordering on the Mediterranean, and at last France, where M. Say's home is, and where the long voyage will end in the harbor of Nantes.

The *Henriette* was built at Newburgh, on the Hudson, last summer, at a cost of $50,000, and was originally named the *Shaughraun*, but she was sold, and her name changed, before she went on her first cruise. She is rigged as a topsail schooner, and under steam can make seventeen knots an hour, which is very fast travelling. She is 205 feet long over all, and is the largest steam-yacht but one ever built in this country. She is to be accompanied in her trip around the world by a smaller steam-yacht, or tender, named the

Foliet, in which will be carried quantities of choice provisions and extra supplies of all kinds. The crew of the *Henriette* numbers thirty men, all of whom are French, excepting her engineers, who are Americans, and the discipline maintained on board is that of a French man-of-war.

THE NEW YEAR'S ERRAND.

"WHAT are those children doing?" asked the clergyman of his wife a few days after Christmas.

"I really can not tell you, James," was the reply, as his wife peered anxiously over his shoulder, and out of the window. "All that I know about it is this: I was busy in the pantry, when Rob put his head in, and asked if he could have the Christmas tree, as nearly everything had been taken off of it; so I said 'Yes,' and there he goes with it, sure enough. I do hope the wax from the candles has not spotted the parlor carpet."

WHAT BECAME OF THE CHRISTMAS TREE.—DRAWN BY C. S. REINHART.

"Don't be anxious, wife; 'Christmas comes but once a year, and when it comes should bring good cheer.'"

"Yes," said the careful housewife, "I suppose I do worry. But there! it is snowing again, and Bertha perched up on that tree on Rob's sled, and she so subject to croup!"

"The more she is out in the pure air, the less likely she is to take cold; but where are they going?"

"I really do not know, James. Did you ever see a dog more devoted to any one than Jip is to Rob? There he goes, dancing beside him now; and I see Rob has tied on the scarf Bertha knit for him; that is done to please her. She did work so hard to get it finished in time before he came home for the holidays."

"She is very like her own dear little mother in kindness and care for others," was the reply.

The mother gave a bright smile and a kiss for the compliment, but a little wail from the nursery hurried her out of the room.

Christmas at the parsonage had been delightful, for, first of all, Rob's return from boarding-school was a pleasurable event; he always came home in such good spirits, was so full of his jokes and nonsense, and had so many funny things to tell about the boys. Then there was the dressing of the church with evergreens, and the decoration of the parlor with wreaths of holly or running pine, and the spicy smell of all the delicacies which were in course of preparation, for Sally was a famous cook, and would brook no interference when mince-pies and plum-pudding were to be concocted.

But the children thought the arrival of a certain box, which was always dispatched from town, the very best of all the Christmas delights. This box came from their rich aunts and uncles, who seemed to think that the little parsonage must be a dreary place in winter, and so, to make up to its inmates for losing all the brightness of a city winter, they sent everything they could think of in the way of beautiful pictures, gorgeous books, games, sugar-plums, and enough little glittering things for two or three trees. Of course the clergyman always laid aside some of these things for other occasions, lest the children should be surfeited.

And so Christmas had passed happily, as usual. The school-children had sung their carols and enjoyed their feast, the poor had been carefully looked after and made comfortable, and there had come the usual lull after a season of excitement. It was now the day before the first of the new year, and the parson was writing a sermon. He was telling people what a good time it was to try and turn over a new leaf; to be nobler, truer, braver, than they had ever been before; to let the old year carry away with it all selfishness, all anger, envy, and unloving thoughts;

and as he wrote, he looked out of the window at the falling snow, and wondered where Rob and Bertha could have gone.

Dinner-time came. Aunt Ellen, mamma, and the parson sat down alone. "Where are those children?" repeated mamma.

"I do not think you need be worried, Kate," said Aunt Ellen. "Rob is so thoughtful, he will take good care of Bertha. They have perhaps stopped in at a neighbor's, and been coaxed to stay."

"Very likely," said the parson. And then the baby came in, crowing and chuckling, and claiming his privileges, such as sitting in a high chair and feeding the cat, and mamma had enough to do to keep the merry fellow in order, or his fat little hands would have grasped all the silver, and pulled over the glasses.

After dinner, while the parson let the baby twist his whiskers or creep about his knees, mamma played some lovely German music, and Aunt Ellen crocheted. The short afternoon grew dusky. Baby went off to the nursery; the parson had lighted his cigar, and was going out for a walk, but mamma looked so anxious that he said,

"I will go look for the children, Kate."

"Really, I think you will have to give Rob a little scolding, my dear. He should have told us where he was going."

"Yes, I suppose so," said the parson; when just then there was a gleeful cry—a merry chorus made up of Rob's, Bertha's, and Jip's voices, and there they were, Bertha on the sled, and Rob was her horse.

"Where have you been, my son?" said the parson, trying to be severe. "You should not have gone off in this manner for the whole day without asking permission."

Rob's bright smile faded a little; but Bertha said, quickly, "Please, papa, don't scold Rob. If you only knew—"

"Hush, Bertha!" said Rob; and red as his cheeks were, they grew redder.

"I am sorry you are offended, sir. I did not mean to be so long. We were detained."

"What detained you?"

"And where did you get your dinner?" asked mamma.

"Oh, we had plenty to eat."

"But you don't intend us to know where you got it?"

"No, sir," said Rob, frankly.

"Now, papa, you *shall* not scold Rob," said Bertha, putting her hand in his. "Come into your study. Go away, Rob; go give Jip his supper. Come, mamma;" and Bertha dragged them both in to the fire, where, with sparkling eyes and cheeks like carnation, she began to talk: "Mamma, you remember that scrimmage Rob got into with the village boys last Fourth of July, and how hatefully they knocked him down, and how bruised his eye was for a long time?"

"Yes, I remember, and I always blamed Rob. He should never have had anything to do with those rowdies."

"I didn't blame him; I never blame Rob for anything, except when he won't do what I want him to do. Well, the worst one of all those horrid boys is Sim Jenkins—at least he was; I don't think he's quite so bad now. But he has been punished for all his badness, for he hurt his leg awfully, and has been laid up for months—so his mother says; and she is quite nice. She gave us our dinner today. Somehow or other, Rob heard that Sim was in bed, and had not had any Christmas things, and that his mother was poor; and she says all her money has gone for doctor's bills and medicine. And so it just came into his head that perhaps it would do Sim good to have a Christmas-tree on New-Year's Day; and he asked Mrs. Jenkins, and she was afraid it would make a muss, but Rob said he would be careful. And so he carried our tree over, and fixed it in a box, and covered the box with moss, and we have been as busy as bees trying to make it look pretty. And that is what has kept us so long, for Rob had to run down to the store and get things—nails and ribbons, and I don't know what all. And Sim is not to know anything about the tree until to-morrow. And please give us some of the pretty things which were in our box, for we could not get quite enough to fill all the branches. Rob spent so much of his pocket-money on a knife for Sim that he had none left for candy; for he said the tree would not give Sim so much pleasure unless there was something on it which he could always keep."

Here little Bertha stopped for want of breath, and looked into the faces of her listeners.

The parson put his arm around her as he said, "I hardly think we can scold Rob now, after special pleading so eloquent as this; what do you say, mamma?"

"I say that Rob is just like his father in doing this kindly deed, and I am glad to be the mother of a boy who can return good for evil."

The parson made a bow. "Now we are even, madam, in the matter of gracious speeches."

So Sim Jenkins woke up on New-Year's Day to see from his weary bed a vision of brightness—a little tree laden with its fruit of kindness, its flowers of a forgiving spirit; and as the parson preached his New-Year's sermon, and saw Rob's dark eyes looking up at him, he thought of the verse,

"In their young hearts, soft and tender,
Guide my hand good seed to sow,
That its blossoming may praise Thee
Wheresoe'er they go."

LAFAYETTE'S FIRST WOUND.

THE Marquis of Lafayette came to this country to give his aid in the struggle for liberty in 1777, and his first battle was that of the Brandywine. Washington was trying to stop the march of the British toward Philadelphia. There was some mistake in regard to the roads, and the American troops were badly beaten. Lafayette plunged into the heart of the fight, and just as the Americans gave way, he received a musket-ball in the thigh. This was the 11th of September. Writing to his wife the next day, he said:

"Our Americans held their ground firmly for quite a time, but were finally put to rout. In trying to rally them, Messieurs the English paid me the compliment of a gunshot, which wounded me slightly in the leg; but that's nothing, my dear heart; the bullet touched neither bone nor nerve, and it will cost nothing more than lying on my back some time, which puts me in bad humor."

But the wound of which the marquis wrote so lightly, in order to re-assure his beloved wife, kept him confined for more than six weeks. He was carried on a boat up to Bristol, and when the fugitive Congress left there, he was taken to the Moravian settlement at Bethlehem, where he was kindly cared for. On the 1st of October he wrote again to his wife:

"As General Howe, when he gives his royal master a high-flown account of his American exploits, must report me wounded, he may report me killed; it would cost nothing; but I hope you won't put any faith in such reports. As to the wound, the surgeons are astonished at the promptness of its healing. They fall into ecstasies whenever they dress it, and protest that it's the most beautiful thing in the world. As for me, I find it a very disgusting thing, wearisome and quite painful. That depends on tastes. But, after all, if a man wanted to wound himself for fun, he ought to come and see how much I enjoy it."

He was very grateful for the attention he received. "All the doctors in America," he writes, "are in motion for me. I have a friend who has spoken in such a way that I am well nursed—General Washington. This worthy man, whose talents and virtues I admire, whom I venerate more the more I know him, has kindly become my intimate friend . . . . I am established in his family; we live like two brothers closely united, in reciprocal intimacy and confidence. When he sent me his chief surgeon, he told him to care for me as if I were his son, for he loved me as such." This friendship between the great commander, in the prime of life, and the French boy of twenty, is one of the most touching incidents of our history.

The Rock of Gibraltar.—This great natural fortification, which among military men is regarded as the key to the Mediterranean Sea, abounds in caverns, many of which are natural, while others have been made by the explosion of gunpowder in the centre of the mountain, forming great vaults of such height and extent that in case of a siege they would contain the whole garrison. The caverns (the most considerable is the hall of St. George) communicate with the batteries established all along the mountain by a winding road, passable throughout on horseback.

The extreme singularity of the place has given rise to many superstitious stories, not only amongst the ancients, but even those of our own times. As it has been penetrated by the hardy and enterprising to a great distance (on one occasion by an American, who descended by ropes to a depth of 500 feet), a wild story is current that the cave communicates by a submarine passage with Africa. The sailors who had visited the rock, and seen the monkeys, which are seen in no other part of Europe, and are only there occasionally and at intervals, say that they pass at pleasure by means of the cave to their native land. The truth seems to be that they usually live in the inaccessible precipices of the eastern side of the rock, where there is a scanty store of monkey grass for their subsistence; but when an east wind sets in it drives them from their caves, and they take refuge among the western rocks, where they may be seen hopping from bush to bush, boxing each other's ears, and cutting the most extraordinary antics. If disturbed, they scamper off with great rapidity, the young ones jumping on the backs and putting their arms round the necks of the old, and as they are very harmless, strict orders have been received from the garrison for their especial protection.

Gibraltar derives its chief importance from its bay, which is about ten miles in length and eight in breadth, and being protected from the more dangerous winds, is a valuable naval station.

SANTA CLAUS VISITS THE VAN JOHNSONS.

SWING low, sweet chariot—
Goin' for to car' me home;
Swing low, sweet chariot—
Goin' for to car' me home.
Debbil tought he would spite me—
Goin' for to car' me home,
By cuttin' down my apple-tree—
Goin' for to car' me home;
But he didn't spite ah-me at all—
Goin' for to car' me home;
For I had apples all de fall—
Goin'—

"Oh, jess shut up wiff yo' ole apples, Chrisfer C'lumbus Van Johnson, an' listen at dat ar wat Miss Bowles done bin a-tellin' me," said Queen Victoria, suddenly making her appearance at the gate which opened out of Mrs. Bowles's back garden into the small yard where her brother sat with Primrose Ann in his arms.

The Van Johnsons were a colored family who lived in a Southern city in a small three-roomed wooden house on the lot in the rear of Mrs. Bowles's garden, and Mrs. Bowles was their landlady and very good friend. Indeed, I don't know what they would have done without her, for when she came from the North, and rented the big house, they were in the depths of poverty. The kind lady found them work, gave them bright smiles, words of encouragement, fruit, vegetables, and spelling lessons, and so won their simple, grateful hearts that they looked upon her as a miracle of patience, goodness, and wisdom. And as for Baby Bowles—the rosy-cheeked, sweet-voiced, sunshiny little thing—the whole family, from Primrose Ann up to Mr. Van Johnson, adored her, and Queen Victoria was "happy as a queen" when allowed to take care of and amuse her.

"Wat's dat ar yo's speakin' f" asked Christopher Columbus (so named, his father said, "'cause he war de fustest chile, de discoberer ob de family, as it war") as Queen Victoria hopped into the yard on one leg, and he stopped rocking—if you can call throwing yourself back on the hind-legs of a common wooden chair, and then coming down on the fore-legs with a bounce and a bang, rocking—the youngest Van Johnson with such a jerk that her eyes and mouth flew open, and out of the latter came a tremendous yell. "Dar now," said Christopher Columbus, "yo's done gone an' woked dis yere Primrose Ann, an' I's bin hours an' hours an' hours an' hours gittin her asleep. Girls am de wustest bodders I ebber see. I allus dishated girls."

"Ain't yo' 'shamed yo'seff, Chrisfer C'lumbus," said Queen Victoria, indignantly, "wen bofe yo' sisters am girls! But spect yo' don't want to listen at wat Miss Bowles done bin a-tellin' me. Hi! Washington Webster's a-comin', an' I'll jess tell him dat ar secret all by hisseff."

"No yo' won't; yo' goin' to tell me too," said her big brother. "An' yo' better stop a-rollin' yo' eyes—yo' got de sassiest eyes I ebber see since de day dat I war bohn—an' go on wiff yo' story."

"Story!" repeated Washington Webster, sauntering up to them, leading a big cat—dragging, perhaps, would be the better word, as poor puss was trying hard to get away—by a string.

"'Bout Mahser Zanty Claws," said Queen, opening her eyes so wide that they seemed to spread over half her face. "Miss Bowles says to-morrer's Chrismus, an' to-day's day befo' Chrismus, an' to-night Mahser Zanty Claws go 'bout"—lowering her voice almost to a whisper—"an' put tings in chillun's stockin's dat 'haved deirselfs."

"Am Mahser Zanty Claws any lashun to dat ar ole man wiff de allspice hoof?" asked Washington Webster, with a scared look.

"Allspice hoof! Listen at dat ar foolish young crow. *Clove* hoof, yo' means," said Queen Victoria. "Dat's anodder gemman 'tirely. Mahser Zanty Claws am good. He gits yo' dolls, an' candies, an' apples, an' nuts, an' books, an' drums, an' wissels, an' new clos."

"Golly! wish he'd frow some trowsus an' jackits an' sich like fruit 'roun' here," said Christopher Columbus.

"Trowsus wiff red 'spenders an' a pistil pockit," said Washington Webster, "an' a gole watch, an' a sled all yaller, wiff green stars on it, an'—"

"Yo' bofe talk 's if yo'd bin awful good," interrupted Queen Victoria. "Maybe Mahser Zanty Claws disagrees wiff yo'."

"Who dat ar done gone git her head cracked wiff de wooden spoon fur gobblin' all de hom'ny befo' de breakfuss war ready?" said Washington Webster, slyly.

"I 'most wish dar war no Washington Websters in de hull worle—I certainly do. Dey's too sassy to lib," said Queen Victoria. "An' *sich* busybodies—dey certainly is."

"But how am we to know wedder we's Mahser Zanty Claws's kine o' good chillun?" said Christopher Columbus. "We's might be good nuff fur ourseffs, an' not good nuff fur him. If I knowed he come yere certain sure, I git some green ornamunters from ole Pete Campout—he done gone got hunderds an' hunderds an' piles an' piles—to stick up on de walls, an' make de house look more despectable like."

"Let's go an' ax Miss Bowles," said Queen Victoria. "Baby Bowles am fass asleep, an' she's in de kitchen makin' pies, an' she know ebberyting—she certainly do."

And off they all trooped, Primrose Ann, cat, and all.

"Come in," called the pleasant voice of their landlady, when they rapped on her door; and in they tumbled, asking the same question all together in one breath: "Mahser Zanty Claws comin' to our house, Miss Bowles?" Christopher Columbus adding, "'Pears dough we mus ornamentem some if he do."

Mrs. Bowles crimped the edge of her last pie, and then sat down, the children standing in a row before her.

"Have you all been very good?" she said. "Suppose you tell me what good thing you have done since yesterday afternoon. Then I can guess about Santa Claus."

"Primrose Ann cried fur dat ar orange yo' gib me," said Queen Victoria, after a moment's thought, "an' I eat it up quick 's I could, an' didn't gib her none, 'cause I's 'fraid she git de stummick-ache."

"I car'd home de washin' fur mammy fur two cakes an' some candy," said Washington Webster.

"And you?" asked Mrs. Bowles, turning to Christopher Columbus.

"I run 'way from 'Dolphus Snow, an' wouldn't fight him, 'cause I 'fraid I hurt him," said Christopher, gravely.

Mrs. Bowles laughed merrily. "Go home and ornament," she said. "I am sure Santa Claus will pay you a visit."

And he did; for on Christmas morning, when the young Van Johnsons rushed pell-mell, helter-skelter, into the room prepared for his call, a new jacket hung on one chair, a new pair of trousers on the other; a doll's head peeped out of Queen Victoria's stocking; a new sled, gayly painted, announced itself in big letters "The Go Ahead"; lots of toys were waiting for Primrose Ann; and four papers of goodies reposed on the lowest shelf of the cupboard.

"'Pears dat ar Mahser Zanty Claws don't take unt measure fur boys' close," said Christopher Columbus, as he tried to struggle into the jacket. "Dis yere jackit's twicet too small."

"An' dis yere trowsaloons am twicet too big," said Washington Webster, as he drew them up to his armpits.

"Lor' bress you, honey-bugs!" called their mammy from the doorway, "yo' has got tings mixed. Dat ar jackit's fur de oldder boy, an' dem trowsis too." And they all burst out laughing as Christopher Columbus and Washington Webster exchanged Christmas gifts, and laughed so loud that Mrs. Bowles came over to see what was the matter, bringing Baby Bowles, who, seeing how jolly everybody was, began clapping her tiny hands and shouting, "Melly Kissmas! melly Kissmas!"

"LOR' BRESS YOU, HONEY-BUGS! YO' HAS GOT TINGS MIXED."—Drawn by J. E. Kelly.

ONE HUNDRED YEARS AGO.—Drawn by Kate Greenaway.

PET AND HER CAT.

Now, Pussy, I'm something to tell you:
  You know it is New-Year's Day;
The big folks are down in the parlor,
  And mamma is just gone away.

We are all alone in the nursery,
  And I want to talk to you, dear;
So you must come and sit by me,
  And make believe you hear.

You see, there's a new year coming—
  It only begins to-day.
Do you know I was often naughty
  In the year that is gone away?

You know I have some bad habits,
  I'll mention just one or two;
But there really is quite a number
  Of naughty things that I do.

You see, I don't learn my lessons,
  And oh! I do hate them so;
I doubt if I know any more to-day
  Than I did a year ago.

Perhaps I am awfully stupid;
  They say I'm a dreadful dunce.
How would you like to learn spelling?
  I wish you could try it once.

And don't you remember Christmas—
  'Twas naughty, I must confess—
But while I was eating my dinner
  I got two spots on my dress.

And they caught me stealing the sugar;
  But I only got two little bits,
When they found me there in the closet,
  And frightened me out of my wits.

And, Pussy, when people scold me,
  I'm always so sulky then;
If they only would tell me gently,
  I never would do it again.

Oh, Pussy! I know I am naughty,
  And often it makes me cry:
I think it would count for something,
  If they knew how hard I try.

But I'll try again in the new year,
  And oh! I shall be so glad
If I only can be a good little girl,
  And never do anything bad!

HOW SUNKEN SHIPS ARE RAISED.

When a ship sinks some distance from the shore in several fathoms of water, and the waves conceal her, it may seem impossible to some of our readers that she can ever be floated again; but if she rests upon a firm sandy bottom, without rocks, and the weather is fair enough for a time to give the wreckers an opportunity, it is even probable that she can be brought into port.

In Boston, New York, Philadelphia, Baltimore, Norfolk, and New Orleans, large firms are established whose special business it is to send assistance to distressed vessels, and to save the cargo if the vessels themselves can not be prevented from becoming total wrecks; and these firms are known as wreckers—a name which in the olden time was given to a class of heartless men dwelling on the coast who lured ships ashore by false lights for the sake of the spoils which the disaster brought them.

When a vessel is announced to be ashore or sunk, the owners usually apply to the wreckers, and make a bargain with them that they shall receive a certain proportion of her value if they save her, and the wreckers then proceed to the scene of the accident, taking with them powerful tug-boats, large pontoons, immense iron cables, and a massive derrick.

Perhaps only the topmasts of the wreck are visible when they reach it; but even though she is quite out of sight, she is not given up, if the sea is calm and the wind favorable. One of the men puts a diving dress over his suit of heavy flannels. The trousers and jacket are made of India rubber cloth, fitting close to the ankles, wrists, and across the chest, which is further protected by a breastplate. A copper helmet with a glass face is used for covering the head, and is screwed on to the breastplate. One end of a coil of strong rubber tubing is attached to the back of the helmet, to the outside of which a running cord is also attached, and continued down the side of the dress to the diver's right hand, where he can use it for signalling his assistants when he is beneath the surface. His boots have leaden soles weighing about twenty-eight pounds; and as this, with the helmet, is insufficient to allow his descent, four blocks of lead, weighing fifty pounds, are slung over his shoulders; and a water-proof bag containing a hammer, a chisel, and a dirk-knife is fastened over his breast.

He is transferred from the steamer that has brought him from the city to a small boat, which is rowed to a spot over the wreck, and a short iron ladder is put over the side, down which he steps; and when the last rung is reached, he lets go, and the water bubbles and sparkles over his head as he sinks deeper and deeper.

The immersion of the diver is more thrilling to a spectator than it is to him. The rubber coil attached to his helmet at one end is attached at the other to an air-pump, which sends him all the breath he needs, and if the supply is irregular, a pull at the cord by his right hand secures its adjustment. He is not timid, and he knows that the only thing he has to guard against is nervousness, by which he might lose his presence of mind. The fish dart away from him at a motion of his hand, and even a shark is terrified by the apparition of his strange globular helmet. He is careful not to approach the wreck too suddenly, as the tangled rigging and splinters might twist or break the air-pipe and signal line; when his feet touch the bottom, he looks behind, before, and above him before he advances an inch.

Looming up before him like a phantom in the foggy light is the ship; and now, perhaps, if any of the crew have gone down with her, the diver feels a momentary horror; but if no one has been lost, he sets about his work, and hums a cheerful tune.

It may be that the vessel has settled low in the sand, that she is broken in two, or that the hole in her bottom can not be repaired. But we will suppose that the circumstances are favorable, that the sand is firm, and the hull in an easy position.

The diver signals to be hauled up, makes his report, and in his next descent he is accompanied by several others, who help him to drag massive chains of iron underneath the ship, at the bow, at the stern, and in the middle. This is a tedious and exhausting operation, which sometimes takes many days; and when it is completed, the pontoons are towed into position at each side of the ship.

The pontoons, simply described, are hollow floats. They are oblong, built of wood, and possess great buoyancy. Some of them are over a hundred feet long, eighteen feet wide, and fourteen feet deep; but their size, and the number of them used, depend on the length of the vessel that is to be raised. Circular tubes, or wells, extend through them; and when the chains are secured underneath the ship, the ends are inserted in these wells by the divers, and drawn up through them by hydraulic power. The chains thus form a series of loops like the common swing of the playground, in which the ship rests; and as they are shortened in being drawn up through the wells, the ship lifts. The ship lifts if all be well—if the chains do not part, or some other accident occur; but the wreckers need great patience, and sometimes they see the labor of weeks undone in a minute.

We are presupposing success, however, and instead of sinking or capsizing, the ship appears above the bubbling water, and between the pontoons, which groan and tremble with her weight.

As soon as her decks are above water, so much of the cargo is removed as is necessary to enable the divers to reach the broken part of the hull, which they patch with boards and canvas if she is built of wood, or with iron plates if she is of iron. This is the most perilous part of the diver's work, as there are so many projections upon which his air-tube may catch; but he finds it almost as easy to ply his hammer and drill in making repairs under water as on shore.

The ship is next pumped out, and borne between the pontoons by powerful tugs to the nearest dry-dock, where all the damages are finally repaired, and in a month or two she is once more afloat, with nothing to indicate her narrow escape.

(Begun in No. 8 of Harper's Young People, December 2.)

THE HISTORY OF PHOTOGEN AND NYCTERIS.

A Day and Night Mährchen.

BY GEORGE MACDONALD.

XVI.—AN EVIL NURSE.

WATHO was herself ill, as I have said, and was the worse tempered; and, besides, it is a peculiarity of witches that what works in others to sympathy, works in them to repulsion. Also, Watho had a poor, helpless, rudimentary spleen of a conscience left, just enough to make her uncomfortable, and therefore more wicked. So when she heard that Photogen was ill she was angry. Ill, indeed! after all she had done to saturate him with the life of the system, with the solar might itself! He was a wretched failure, the boy! And because he was *her* failure, she was annoyed with him, began to dislike him, grew to hate him. She looked on him as a painter might upon a picture, or a poet upon a poem, which he had only succeeded in getting into an irrecoverable mess. In the hearts of witches love and hate lie close together, and often tumble over each other. And whether it was that her failure with Photogen foiled also her plans in regard to Nycteris, or that her illness made her yet more of a devil's wife, certainly Watho now got sick of the girl too, and hated to have her about the castle.

She was not too ill, however, to go to poor Photogen's room and torment him. She told him she hated him like a serpent, and hissed like one as she said it, looking very sharp in the nose and chin, and flat in the forehead. Photogen thought she meant to kill him, and hardly ventured to take anything brought him. She ordered every ray of light to be shut out of his room; but by means of this he got a little used to the darkness. She would take one of his arrows, and now tickle him with the feather end of it, now prick him with the point till the blood ran down. What she meant finally I can not tell, but she brought Photogen speedily to the determination of making his escape from the castle: what he should do then he would think afterward. Who could tell but he might find his mother somewhere beyond the forest! If it were not for the broad patches of darkness that divided day from day, he would fear nothing!

But now, as he lay helpless in the dark, ever and anon would come dawning through it the face of the lovely creature who on that first awful night nursed him so sweetly: was he never to see her again? If she was, as he had concluded, the nymph of the river, why had she not re-appeared? She might have taught him not to fear the night, for plainly she had no fear of it herself! But then, when the day came, she did seem frightened: why was that, seeing there was nothing to be afraid of then? Perhaps one so much at home in the darkness was correspondingly afraid of the light! Then his selfish joy at the rising of the sun, blinding him to her condition, had made him behave to her, in ill return for her kindness, as cruelly as Watho behaved to him! How sweet and dear and lovely she was! If there were wild beasts that came out only at night, and were afraid of the light, why should there not be girls too, made the same way—who could not endure the light, as he could not bear the darkness? If only he could find her again! Ah, now differently he would behave to her! But alas! perhaps the sun had killed her—melted her—burned her up!—dried her up: that was it, if she was the nymph of the river.

XVII.—WATHO'S WOLF.

From that dreadful morning Nycteris had never got to be herself again. The sudden light had been almost death to her; and now she lay in the dark with the memory of a terrific sharpness—a something she dared scarcely recall, lest the very thought of it should sting her beyond endurance. But this was as nothing to the pain which the recollection of the rudeness of the shining creature whom she had nursed through his fear caused her; for the moment his suffering passed over to her, and he was free, the first use he made of his returning strength had been to scorn her! She wondered and wondered; it was all beyond her comprehension.

Before long, Watho was plotting evil against her. The witch was like a sick child weary of his toy: she would pull her to pieces, and see how she liked it. She would set her in the sun, and see her die, like a jelly-fish from the salt ocean cast out on a hot rock. It would be a sight to soothe her wolf-pain. One day, therefore, a little before noon, while Nycteris was in her deepest sleep, she had a darkened litter brought to the door, and in that she made two of her men carry her to the plain above. There they took her out, laid her on the grass, and left her.

Watho watched it all from the top of her high tower, through her telescope; and scarcely was Nycteris left, when she saw her sit up, and the same moment cast herself down again with her face to the ground.

"She'll have a sun-stroke," said Watho, "and that 'll be the end of her."

Presently, tormented by a fly, a huge-humped buffalo, with great shaggy mane, came galloping along, straight for where she lay. At sight of the thing on the grass he started, swerved yards aside, stopped dead, and then came slowly up, looking malicious. Nycteris lay quite still, and never even saw the animal.

"Now she'll be trodden to death!" said Watho.

When the buffalo reached her, he sniffed at her all over, and went away; then came back and sniffed again, then all at once went off as if a demon had him by the tail.

Next came a gnu, then a gaunt wild boar. But no creature hurt her, and Watho was angry with the whole creation.

At length, in the shade of her hair, the blue eyes of Nycteris began to come to themselves a little, and the first thing they saw was a comfort. I have told already how she knew the night daisies, each a sharp-pointed little cone with a red tip, and once she had parted the rays of one of them, with trembling fingers, for she was afraid she was dreadfully rude, and perhaps was hurting it; but she did want, she said to herself, to see what secret it carried so carefully hidden; and she found its golden heart. But now, right under her eyes, inside the veil of her hair, in the sweet twilight of whose blackness she could see it perfectly, stood a daisy with its red tip opened wide into a carmine ring, displaying its heart of gold on a platter of silver. She did not at first recognize it as one of those cones come awake, but a moment's notice revealed what it was. Who, then, could have been so cruel to the lovely little creature as to force it open like that, and spread it heart-bare to the terrible death-lamp? Whoever it was, it must be the same that had thrown her out there to be burned to death in its fire! But she had her hair, and could hang her head, and make a small sweet night of her own about her! She tried to bend the daisy down and away from the sun, and to make its petals hang about it like her hair, but she could not. Alas! it was burned and dead already! She did not know that it could not yield to her gentle force because it was drinking life, with all the eagerness of life, from what she called the death-lamp. Oh, how the lamp burned her!

But she went on thinking—she did not know how; and by-and by began to reflect that, as there was no roof to the room except that in which the great fire went rolling about, the little Red-tip must have seen the lamp a thousand times, and must know it quite well! and it had not killed it! Nay, thinking about it farther, she began to ask the question whether this, in which she now saw it, might not be its more perfect condition. For now not only did the whole seem perfect, as indeed it did before, but every part showed its own individual perfection as well, which perfection made it capable of combining with the rest into the higher perfection of a whole. The flower was a lamp itself! The golden heart was the light, and the silver border was the alabaster globe skillfully broken and spread wide to let out the glory. Yes; the radiant shape was plainly its perfection! If, then, it was the lamp which had opened it into that shape, the lamp could not be unfriendly to it, but must be of its own kind, seeing it made it perfect! And again, when she thought of it, there was clearly no little resemblance between them. What if the flower, then, was the little great-grandchild of the lamp, and he was loving it all the time? And what if the lamp did not mean to hurt her, only could not help it? The red tips looked as if the flower had some time or other been hurt: what if the lamp was making the best it could of her—opening her out somehow like the flower? She would bear it patiently, and see. But how coarse the color of the grass was! Perhaps, however, her eyes not being made for the bright lamp, she did not see them as they were! Then she remembered how different were the eyes of the creature that was not a girl, and was afraid of the darkness! Ah, if the darkness would only come again, all arms, friendly and soft everywhere about her!

She lay so still that Watho thought she had fainted. She was pretty sure she would be dead before the night came to revive her.

XVIII.—REFUGE.

Fixing her telescope on the motionless form, that she might see it at once when the morning came, Watho went down from the tower to Photogen's room. He was much better by this time, and before she left him he had resolved to leave the castle that very night.

The darkness was terrible indeed, but Watho was worse than even the darkness, and he could not escape in the day. As soon, therefore, as the house seemed still, he tightened his belt, hung to it his hunting knife, put a flask of wine and some bread in his pocket, and took his bow and arrows. He got from the house, and made his way at once up to the plain. But what with his illness, the terrors of the night, and his dread of the wild beasts, when he got to the level he could not walk a step farther, and sat down, thinking it better to die than to live. In spite of his fears, however, sleep contrived to overcome him, and he fell at full length on the soft grass.

He had not slept long when he woke with such a strange sense of comfort and security that he thought the dawn at least must have arrived. But it was dark night about him. And the sky—no, it was not the sky, but the blue eyes of his naiad looking down upon him! Once more he lay with his head in her lap, and all was well, for plainly the girl feared the darkness as little as he the day.

"Thank you," he said. "You are like live armor to my heart; you keep the fear off me. I have been very ill since then. Did you come up out of the river when you saw me cross?"

"I don't live in the water," she answered. "I live under the pale lamp and I die under the bright one."

AN EMBARRASSMENT OF RICHES.—DRAWN BY J. E. KELLY.

"I would not have behaved as I did last time if I had understood; but I thought you were mocking me; and I am so made that I can not help being frightened at the dark too. I beg your pardon for leaving you as I did, for, as I say, I did not understand. Now I believe you were really frightened. Were you not?"

"I was, indeed," answered Nycteris, "and shall be again. But why you should be, I can not in the least understand. You must know how gentle and sweet the darkness is, how kind and friendly, how soft and velvety! It holds you to its bosom and loves you. A little while ago I lay faint and dying under your hot lamp. What is it you call it?"

"The sun," murmured Photogen; "how I wish he would make haste!"

"Ah! do not wish that. Do not, for my sake, hurry him. I can take care of you from the darkness, but I have no one to take care of me from the light.—As I was telling you, I lay dying in the sun. All at once I drew a deep breath. A cool wind came and ran over my face. I looked up. The torture was gone, for the death-lamp itself was gone. I hope he does not die and grow brighter yet. My terrible headache was all gone, and my sight was come back. I felt as if I were new made. But I did not get up at once, for I was tired still. The grass grew cool about me, and turned soft in color. Something wet came upon it, and it was now so pleasant to my feet that I rose and ran about. And when I had been running about a long time, all at once I found you lying, just as I had been lying a little while before. So I sat down beside you to take care of you, till your life—and my death—should come again."

"How good you are, you beautiful creature! Why, you forgave me before ever I asked you!" cried Photogen.

Thus they fell a-talking, and he told her what he knew of his history, and she told him what she knew of hers, and they agreed they must get away from Watho as far as ever they could.

"And we must set out at once," said Nycteris.

"The moment the morning comes," returned Photogen.

"We must not wait for the morning," said Nycteris, "for then I shall not be able to move, and what would you do the next night? Besides, Watho sees best in the day-time. Indeed, you must come now, Photogen. You must."

"I can not; I dare not," said Photogen. "I can not move. If I but lift my head from your lap, the very sickness of terror seizes me."

"I shall be with you," said Nycteris, soothingly. "I will take care of you till your dreadful sun comes, and then you may leave me, and go away as fast as you can. Only please put me in a dark place first, if there is one to be found."

"I will never leave you again, Nycteris," cried Photogen. "Only wait till the sun comes and brings me back my strength, and we will go away together, and never, never part any more."

"No, no," persisted Nycteris; "we must go now. And you must learn to be strong in the dark as well as in the day, else you will always be only half brave. I have begun already, not to fight your sun, but to try to get at peace with him, and understand what he really is, and what he means with me—whether to hurt me or to make the best of me. You must do the same with my darkness."

"But you don't know what mad animals there are away there toward the south," said Photogen. "They have huge green eyes, and they would eat you up like a bit of celery, you beautiful creature!"

"Come! come! you must," said Nycteris, "or I shall

have to pretend to leave you, to make you come. I have seen the green eyes you speak of, and I will take care of you from them."

"You! How can you do that? If it were day now, I could take care of you from the worst of them. But as it is, I can't even see them for this abominable darkness. I could not see your lovely eyes but for the light that is in them; that lets me see straight into heaven through them. They are windows into the very heaven beyond the sky. I believe they are the very place where the stars are made."

[TO BE CONTINUED.]

New Year's Gifts.—The custom of giving and receiving gifts at the new year dates from very early times indeed. The Druids used to cut down branches of their sacred mistletoe with a golden knife, and distribute them amongst the people as New-Year's gifts. As they cut it down they used to sing—

"Gather the mistletoe, the new year is at hand."

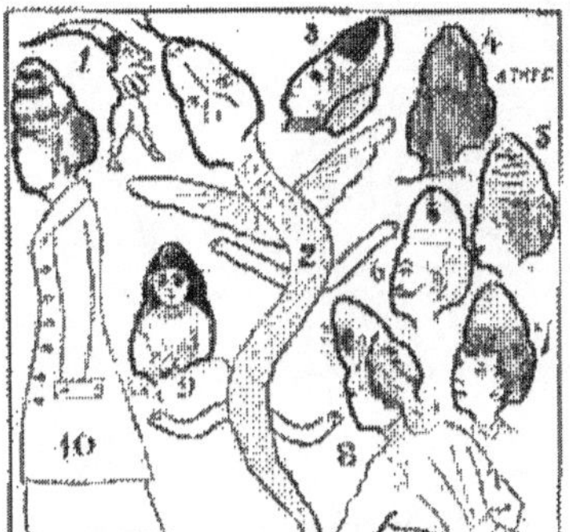

WIGGLES.

THESE are filled-in wiggles that several of our young correspondents have drawn from the outlines given in Nos. 3 and 4 of *Young People*. They are the contributions of H. W. K., Jessie Beal, J. A. Wells, H. W. P., J. M. W., Lil, A. B. Crane, K. M. W., Fred Hueston, and H. E. M. Wiggles similar to design were also received from Cyrus O., Virgie Cummings, W. G. Page, J. H. Grosart, Sadie Valtin, and others. Next week we shall show you what we make from wiggle No. 4, and at the same time give a new one.

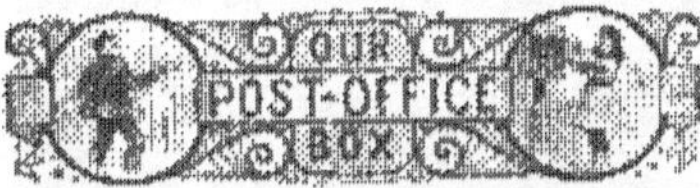

WE wish all our young readers and correspondents a very happy New-Year, success in their studies, and pleasant hours with teachers and school-mates. We hope our friendly intercourse will continue, with increasing interest to them and to us. At the beginning of a new year it is well to remember that the surest way to gain happiness for ourselves is by trying to make others happy.

Schenectady, New York.

I thought I would write and tell you that I love *Harper's Young People* very much. I am eight years old. I have a little brother who is 'most two years old, and I have a cat four years old. I have an aquarium with six fish in it, and a turtle. The turtle's name is Snap.

Florence E. B.

Port Jefferson, New York.

I want to write a note to tell you how I came to take *Young People*. One evening papa brought me the first two numbers, and I enjoyed the "Swiss Boy" and the other stories so much that I thought I would like to take it. So my papa, my mamma, my two brothers, and I myself gave something toward it, and I shall expect it with pleasure every week.

Nellie D.

Galena, Illinois.

I like *Harper's Young People* very much. The illustrations are beautiful, and the Post-office Box and all, and contribute this, my first newspaper correspondence, to that department. The picture "The Day Before Thanksgiving," on the first page of No. 4, is very comical, and reminds me of things I have seen myself. I am twelve years old.

Morna P.

South Evanston, Illinois.

I am so glad you have published this little paper. I think it is the best thing I have ever seen. Papa reads it too, and thinks it is real nice for little folks. I like the story of the "Brave Swiss Boy" very much.

Erma T.

Worcester, Massachusetts.

Dear "Young People,"—I like you very much, especially the story of the "Brave Swiss Boy." The way I came to take you was this: father saw an advertisement in a paper, so he let me go up to a news-room and get you.

Rosie D. C.

Henry F. B.—Electric ornaments are not easily obtained in this country, as but very few have been imported for sale.

Montague L.—It would occupy too much space to describe the game you require.

A. H. A.—There is no such class of people as you refer to. Exceptional cases may exist.

Kate S. (nine years).—Your puzzles are very neat for such a little girl to compose.

Martha W. D.—Your puzzle is good, but we are afraid our young readers would never make it out, as it requires an extraordinary amount of geographical knowledge.

"Enquirer," Madison.—A phonograph can be obtained of Thomas A. Edison, Menlo Park, New Jersey, from whom you can also obtain a price-list. You will find interesting information in a book entitled *The Telephone, the Microphone, and the Phonograph*, by Count Du Moncel, recently published by Messrs. Harper and Brothers.

Pleasant and welcome letters are acknowledged from Abraham L. M., Alie M. B., and Julian S. U.

F. B. H.—Thanks for your pretty operation in figures.

The following explanation of the name irreverently applied to the Bank of England is from Harry H. Bell, Louisville, Kentucky:

The Bank of England was founded in 1694. There is no bank equal to it in the management of national finances. It is located in Threadneedle Street. Cobbett called it "The Old Lady in Threadneedle Street," because, said he, the governors of the bank were, like old Mrs. Partington, an invented character of Sydney Smith's, trying with their brooms to keep back the Atlantic waves of progress in national affairs.

NEW YEAR'S CALLS.

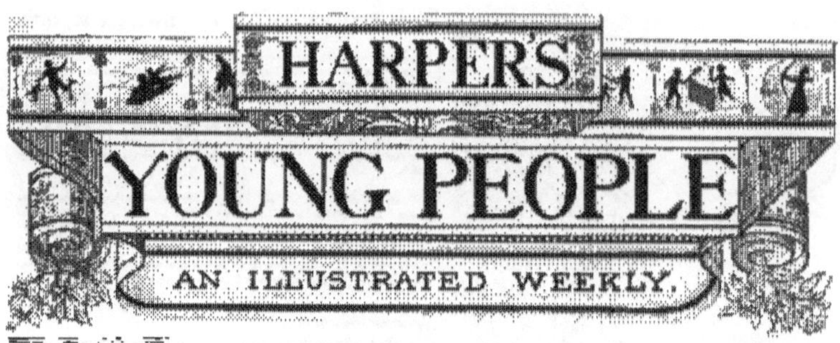

VOL. I.—NO. 10. PUBLISHED BY HARPER & BROTHERS, NEW YORK. PRICE FOUR CENTS.

Tuesday, January 6, 1880. $1.50 per Year, in Advance.

SQUIRRELS AND WILDCATS.

THE most graceful of all the little inhabitants of the forest is the squirrel. It is to be found in nearly every country, and is always the same merry, frisky little creature. The general name for the great squirrel family is *Sciurus*, a compound of two pretty Greek words signifying shadow and tail, the beautiful bushy tail being a universal family characteristic. Of the many varieties found in our Northern woods the most common of all is the little chipmunk, a beautiful creature of brownish-gray, with stripes of black and yellow on its back, and a snowy white throat. It is the only burrower of the family. Choosing some sheltered place under a stone wall or a clump of bushes, it digs a hole which often descends perpendicularly for a yard or more before branching off into the winding galleries and snug little apartments, some of which serve as store-houses where nuts, corn, and seeds of different kinds are hoarded away for its winter supplies. The little corner of the burrow used as a nest is carefully and warmly lined with dry leaves and grass, and here the tiny squirrel slumbers during the cold winter months. Chipmunks are very plentiful in the country, and may be seen any sunny day scampering along the stone walls, or up and down the trunks of nut trees, their little cheeks, if it is in the autumn, puffed out round with nuts, which they are carrying to their winter store-house.

A FAMILY IN DANGER.

The larger varieties of squirrels, which make their nest in trees, are the red squirrel, often found in pine woods, as it is very fond of the cones of pine and fir trees; the gray squirrel, a magnificent fellow, with such a voracious appetite that it is said one squirrel alone will strip a whole nut tree; and the black squirrel, a handsome, glossy creature, which is so hated by its gray brothers that both are never found together in the same nutting grounds. As the gray are the most numerous, at least in this part of the country, they generally succeed in driving away the black members of the family, so that they are not very often seen.

The little flying-squirrels, the dearest little creatures for pets, are natives of the Rocky Mountains, but are found in all parts of the United States. They are very lazy, and sleep nearly all day, coming out at twilight for a merry frolic, leaping, flying, or scampering at pleasure among the tree-tops. They generally make their nest in some hollow trunk, where it is very difficult to find them.

The nest of a gray or red squirrel is a wonderful piece of architecture. It is usually built in the crotch of some large branch, near or directly against the main trunk of the tree. The spherical-shaped exterior is a mass of interwoven twigs, so carefully placed as to afford ample protection against rain or snow; leaves and grasses are stuffed inside, while the little bed where the squirrel nestles and takes its nap is of the softest and driest moss. In this pretty snuggery five or six little squirrels are born early in the warm weather. The mother is very watchful and very affectionate. If any wicked boys disturb her, or a natural enemy, some beast or bird of prey, comes near, she takes her little ones in her mouth, like a cat with its kittens, and hastily carries them to a more secure hiding-place. The parent squirrels never go away from the nest, but play and jump about on the branches near by, until the little ones are strong enough to accompany them, when the whole family may be seen springing from tree to tree, or scampering up and down the tall trunks, waving their beautiful tails, and breaking the silence of the woods with their merry chattering. They are wonderful jumpers, and can spring from the highest branches to the ground without harm. They are not runners, but can jump so nimbly through the grass and dried leaves that it is impossible to catch them.

The favorite food of the squirrel is acorns, nuts, and seeds and grain of all kinds, and it will sometimes nibble leaf-buds and tender shoots of young trees in the spring. Its teeth are so sharp and strong that it will gnaw the hardest nutshell. Nothing is prettier than to see this graceful creature sitting upright, its beautiful tail curled over its back, gnawing at a nut which it skillfully holds in its fore-paws. As it is not afraid unless one approaches too near, when it whisks out of sight in a twinkling, its habits may be easily studied.

It is a very provident little animal, and lays up large stores of nuts for its winter food. As those which live in trees have no store-house like that of the chipmunk, they deposit their hoard in hollow trunks or under heaps of dried leaves. Nothing is more common than to find little stores of nuts in a snug corner in hickory woods, carefully packed together by these cunning creatures.

Squirrels make pretty pets, and when captured young can be tamed, and often become very affectionate. A young squirrel may be allowed to run about the room, and it will often be found curled up fast asleep in mamma's work-basket, or papa's pocket, or some other funny hiding-place. As it grows older it becomes more mischievous, and must be kept in a cage, or books, furniture, and everything in the room will bear the marks of its sharp little teeth. It belongs to the order *Rodentia*, or gnawing animals, and if kept in confinement, must be given a plenty of hard-shelled nuts to use its teeth on. Its cage should also be kept very clean, for the squirrel is the neatest little beast imaginable, and spends much time at its toilet.

It is sad to think that this innocent, playful denizen of the woodlands should have many and deadly enemies. Even in the forests of inhabited regions, from which wild beasts have been driven, hawks and owls are ever on the watch to pounce upon it; and in the wild woods, especially in cold countries, where the squirrels are most plentiful, there are many enemies—pine-martens, which climb trees and spring from branch to branch almost as nimbly as the poor little squirrel they persecute, and the terrible wild-cat, which seeks its unsuspecting prey by night, or in the twilight, when the squirrels are gambolling merrily among the leafy branches before cuddling to sleep in their little nests. With sly caution the wild-cat creeps noiselessly through the underbrush, and with one savage spring it destroys the peace of some poor little squirrel family.

Wild-cats, although they belong to the same great family as the quiet little pussy which likes to sleep on the hearth-rug, are considered by naturalists to be an entirely different species. They are much larger than the domestic cat, and have a short, stubbed, and very bushy tail. They are terrible enemies of birds and all the small inhabitants of the forest, and will often attack animals larger than themselves. They pass most of the day stretched out upon some large limb of a tree, sleeping, after the fashion of cats, with one glistening eye always on the watch for prey. At night they descend, and creep through the underbrush, searching for food. They are very skillful at fishing, and are often found near large ponds, where they watch not only for fish, but for all kinds of water-birds which haunt the surrounding marshes.

They seldom attack men unless enraged or brought to bay. Woe to the hunter who fires a careless shot, for the angry beast springs at him with great fury, and inflicts fearful and sometimes even fatal wounds with its sharp claws. It has no fear of dogs, and will pounce upon them, sometimes killing them before the hunter can come to the rescue. Tschudi, the Swiss naturalist, tells of a wounded wild-cat, which, lying on its back, fought successfully with three large dogs, holding one fast in its teeth, while with its claws it dealt powerful blows to the other two, with singular instinct aiming at their eyes, until the hunter, by a skillful shot, put an end to the conflict, killing the ferocious beast, and relieving the poor dogs, which were nearly exhausted.

(Begun in No. 1 of Harper's Young People, December 2.)

THE HISTORY OF PHOTOGEN AND NYCTERIS.

A Day and Night Mährchen.

BY GEORGE MACDONALD.

XVIII.—REFUGE.—(*Continued.*)

"YOU come, then, or I shall shut them," said Nycteris, "and you sha'n't see them any more till you are good. Come. If you can't see the wild beasts, I can."

"You can! and you ask me to come!" cried Photogen.

"Yes," answered Nycteris. "And more than that, I see them long before they can see me, so that I am able to take care of you."

"But how?" persisted Photogen. "You can't shoot with bow and arrow, or stab with a hunting knife."

"No, but I can keep out of the way of them all. Why, just when I found you, I was having a game with two or three of them at once. I see, and scent them too, long before they are near me—long before they can see or scent me."

"You don't see or scent any now, do you?" said Photogen, uneasily, rising on his elbow.

"No—none at present. I will look," replied Nycteris, and sprang to her feet.

"Oh! oh! do not leave me—not for a moment," cried Photogen, straining his eyes to keep her face in sight through the darkness.

"Be quiet, or they will hear you," she returned. "The wind is from the south, and they can not scent us. I have found out all about that. Ever since the dear dark came I have been amusing myself with them, getting every now and then just into the edge of the wind, and letting one have a sniff of me."

"Oh, horrible!" cried Photogen. "I hope you will not insist on doing so any more. What was the consequence?"

"Always, the very instant, he turned with flashing eyes, and bounded toward me—only he could not see me, you must remember. But my eyes being so much better than his, I could see him perfectly well, and would run away round him until I scented him, and then I knew he could not find me anyhow. If the wind were to turn, and run the other way now, there might be a whole army of them down upon us, leaving no room to keep out of their way. You had better come."

She took him by the hand. He yielded and rose, and she led him away. But his steps were feeble, and as the night went on, he seemed more and more ready to sink.

"Oh dear! I am so tired! and so frightened!" he would say.

"Lean on me," Nycteris would return, putting her arm round him, or patting his cheek. "Take a few steps more. Every step away from the castle is clear gain. Lean harder on me. I am quite strong and well now."

So they went on. The piercing night-eyes of Nycteris descried not a few pairs of green ones gleaming like holes in the darkness, and many a round she made to keep far out of their way; but she never said to Photogen she saw them. Carefully she kept him off the uneven places, and on the softest and smoothest of the grass, talking to him gently all the way as they went—of the lovely flowers and the stars—how comfortable the flowers looked, down in their green beds, and how happy the stars, up in their blue beds!

When the morning began to come he began to grow better, but was dreadfully tired with walking instead of sleeping, especially after being so long ill. Nycteris too, what with supporting him, what with growing fear of the light which was beginning to come out of the east, was very tired. At length, both equally exhausted, neither was able to help the other. As if by consent they stopped. Embracing each the other, they stood in the midst of the wide grassy land, neither of them able to move a step, each supported only by the leaning weakness of the other, each ready to fall if the other should move. But while the one grew weaker still, the other had begun to grow stronger. When the tide of the night began to ebb, the tide of the day began to flow; and now the sun was rushing to the horizon, borne upon its foaming billows. And even as he came, Photogen revived. At last the sun shot up into the air, like a bird from the hand of the Father of Lights. Nycteris gave a cry of pain, and hid her face in her hands.

"Oh me!" she sighed; "I am so frightened! The terrible light stings so!"

But the same instant, through her blindness, she heard Photogen give a low exultant laugh, and the next felt herself caught up: she who all night long had tended and protected him like a child, was now in his arms, borne along like a baby, with her head lying on his shoulder. But she was the greater, for, suffering more, she feared nothing.

XIX.—THE WERE-WOLF.

At the very moment when Photogen caught up Nycteris, the telescope of Watho was angrily sweeping the table-land. She swung it from her in rage, and running to her room, shut herself up. There she anointed herself from top to toe with a certain ointment; shook down her long red hair, and tied it round her waist; then began to dance, whirling round and round, faster and faster, growing angrier and angrier, until she was foaming at the mouth with fury. When Falca went looking for her, she could not find her anywhere.

As the sun rose, the wind slowly changed and went round, until it blew straight from the north. Photogen and Nycteris were drawing near the edge of the forest.

larger: it was coming across the grass with the speed of the wind. It came nearer and nearer. It looked long and low, but that might be because it was running at a great stretch. He set Nycteris down under a tree, in the black shadow of its bole, strung his bow, and picked out his heaviest, longest, sharpest arrow. Just as he set the notch on the string, he saw that the creature was a tremendous wolf, rushing straight at him. He loosened his knife in its sheath, drew another arrow half way from the quiver, lest the first should fail, and took his aim—at a good distance, to leave time for a second chance. He shot. The arrow rose, flew straight, descended, struck the beast, and started again into the air, doubled like a letter V. Quickly Photogen snatched the other, shot, cast his bow from him, and drew his knife. But the arrow was in the brute's chest, up to the feather; it tumbled heels over head, with a great thud of its back on the earth, gave a groan, made a struggle or two, and lay stretched out motionless.

"I've killed it, Nycteris," cried Photogen. "It is a great red wolf."

"Oh, thank you!" answered Nycteris, feebly, from behind the tree. "I was sure you would. I was not a bit afraid."

Photogen went up to the wolf. It was a monster! But he was vexed that his first arrow had behaved so badly, and was the less willing to lose the one that had done him such good service: with a long and a strong pull he drew it from the brute's chest. Could he believe his eyes? There lay—no wolf, but Watho, with her hair tied round her waist! The foolish witch had made herself invulnerable, as she supposed, but had forgotten that, to torment Photogen therewith, she had handled one of his arrows. He ran back to Nycteris and told her.

She shuddered and wept, but would not look.

XX.—ALL IS WELL.

There was now no occasion to fly a step farther. Neither of them feared any one but Watho. They left her there, and went back. A great cloud came over the sun, and rain began to fall heavily, and Nycteris was much refreshed, grew able to see a little, and with Photogen's help walked gently over the cool wet grass.

They had not gone far before they met Fargu and the other huntsmen. Photogen told them he had killed a great red wolf, and it was Madam Watho. The huntsmen looked grave, but gladness shone through.

"Then," said Fargu, "I will go and bury my mistress."

But when they reached the place, they found she was already buried—in the maws of sundry birds and beasts which had made their breakfast off her.

Then Fargu, overtaking them, would, very wisely, have Photogen go to the king, and tell him the whole story. But Photogen, yet wiser than Fargu, would not set out until he had married Nycteris; "for then," he said, "the king himself can't part us; and if ever two people couldn't do the one without the other, those two are Nycteris and I. She has got to teach me to be a brave man in the dark, and I have got to look after her until she can bear the heat of the sun, and he helps her to see, instead of blinding her."

They were married that very day. And the next day they went together to the king, and told him the whole story. But whom should they find at the court but the father and mother of Photogen, both in high favor with the king and queen. Aurora nearly died for joy, and told them all how Watho had lied, and made her believe

"IT TUMBLED HEELS OVER HEAD WITH A GREAT THUD."

Through Watho, the mothers, who had never seen each other, had changed eyes in their children.

The king gave them the castle and lands of Watho, and there they lived and taught each other for many years that were not long. But hardly one of them had passed before Nycteris had come to love the day best, because it was the clothing and crown of Photogen; and Photogen had come to love the night best, because it was the mother and home of Nycteris. Were they not both ripening, however, to bear the power of a brighter sun still, when the one should follow the other into a yet larger room?

THE END.

Carrier-Pigeons.—The speed of carrier-pigeons appears to depend as much on the clearness of their sight as on the strength of their wings. In an experiment recently made with some Berlin pigeons, on a clear day, a distance of over three hundred miles, from Cologne to Berlin, was accomplished in five hours and a half, or at the rate of nearly sixty miles an hour; while the most expeditious of a group let loose the next day—a day not of the same kind—took twelve hours to reach Berlin. Hence it would appear that in the latter case a good deal of the pigeons' time was taken up in exploring the country for landmarks. It is not by instinct, but by sight, that the carrier-pigeon guides its course.

PUTNAM'S NARROW ESCAPE.

BY BENSON J. LOSSING.

MANY years ago I was riding in a light carriage between Greenwich and Stamford, in Connecticut. After descending from high ground by a road cut through a steep declivity, I observed some rude stone steps upon the abrupt slope, which were half concealed by shrubs and brambles. An old man was standing at a door-yard gate near by, and I inquired of him the meaning of those steps.

"Before the Revolutionary war," he said, "the people from this way, when going to the church on the hill yonder, had to go nearly a mile around. To give those who were on foot a nearer cut, those steps were placed there. They are the rocks," he continued, "that people believed 'Old Put' went down when he escaped from the British dragoons at Horseneck. He didn't go down the steps at all, but went zigzag from the top to the bottom of the hill, very near them. I stood just here listening to the firing above, when I saw the general rushing down the hill like a madman, as he seemed, for you see it is very steep. As he flew past me on his powerful bay horse, all bespattered with mud, I heard him cursing the British, who had pursued him to the brow of the precipice, but dared not follow him further."

My informant was General Ebenezer Mead.

The whole story may be briefly told. Putnam and a few foot-soldiers were attacked near the church by some British dragoons on a warm morning in March, 1779. So much greater was the number of the assailants than the Americans, that the latter fled for safety to the swamps near by. Their leader, who was mounted, turned his face toward Stamford. Finding himself in danger of being caught, he wheeled suddenly, his horse at full speed, and descended the declivity as described. The dragoons dared not follow him in his perilous ride, but sent pistol-balls after him. Putnam escaped unharmed to Stamford, where he quickly gathered the militia, and rallied some of his scattered followers. Then he pursued the invaders in turn as they retreated toward New York, and making nearly forty of them prisoners, he recovered much of the plunder which they were carrying away with them. Those famous steps, associated with one of the perilous feats of a bold American soldier, may be seen at this day, not far to the right of the highway, as you go from Greenwich to Stamford.

"RUSHING DOWN THE HILL LIKE A MADMAN."

HARE AND HOUNDS.

I HAVE never taken part in "Hare and Hounds," but I feel as if I had, because, in the first place, I have read *Tom Brown*; and in the second place I have a brother who is devoted to athletics, and who has just returned from a "run" with his club. It is just like a real hunt, only all the animals are human beings; two boys are hares, and carry bags full of scraps of paper, which they scatter as they go; any number of boys are the hounds, and follow this paper scent; two boys are the whippers-in, who call the "pack" together with great tin horns; one boy is master of the hunt, and does nothing in particular, though he is supposed to arrange everything.

My brother got up at an unearthly hour on the morning of his hunt, in order to meet his fellow-dogs and their prey at the Grand Central Dépôt at nine o'clock. I am sure that he was over an hour before time, though he will not own to more than a quarter of it; I know that he had a jolly time, anyway. But I will give his report in his own words.

"Such fun! We ran twelve miles—*twelve miles!* Just think of it! Why, we got way up round Spuyten Duyvel—from High Bridge, you know; but first, you know, we all met at the dépôt; then when we got to High Bridge we went to the hotel and changed our things. We started from there. We only intended to run twelve miles, but the hares took us twenty; they meant to take us up to Yonkers, they said. Never mind; they got the worst of it—they had to run the fastest, you know. Didn't we tear through the country!—up hill and down dale, over stone walls and brambles and down swamps; one fellow got up to his knees in water. We lost the scent once, near a railroad track, and it took us about five minutes to find it.

"The hares had colored papers, pink, blue, white, and yellow, and they looked quite pretty scattered all over the ground.

"The people about the country seemed to take a great deal of interest in us; one or two told us which way the hares had gone; a policeman too, near High Bridge, told us. They seemed to understand all about it. I thought they'd think we were crazy—a whole lot of fellows in white caps tearing through the country in that way.

"Oh, that reminds me: two little boys asked one of our fellows what we were going after. 'Two men.' 'What have they done?' 'Stolen our watches;' and they stood staring after us with their eyes and mouths as wide open as—as—oh, anything.

"Oh, I must tell you: one time just as we were going along the road we heard a tremendous noise on the other side of the fence; we thought it was one of the whippers-in blowing the horn—it sounded exactly like it—and we turned round, and there we saw a little donkey coming hee-hawing over the hill after us—a pretty little gray donkey; then one of the whippers-in blew the horn, and the donkey was just delighted—tickled to death; he hee-hawed and capered about, and ran alongside of the fence, wanted to join us—had a fellow-feeling, I suppose. Just then a little girl came running out of a house, calling him; she was afraid we were going to hurt him, or something, I suppose; and when we looked back again he was standing still, just as quiet as could be, and the little girl had her arms around his neck. It made me think of Titania, in Shakespeare, you know.

"We did have a run, I can tell you. One of our fellows got hungry, and stopped at a farm-house, and got some bread and guess. I wish I'd thought of it too. Some of the country we went through was beautiful—up by the Hudson. We could see the river winding along, and catch glimpses of the Palisades—perfectly beautiful. We couldn't have had a better day, just cold enough, and not too cold.

"We were *awfully* tired, though, and *hungry*—you'd better believe it! Why, it was two o'clock when we got back to the hotel, and we had started at *ten*, you know—four hours. Didn't we go for that dinner just as soon as we'd changed our things!—they'd kept it waiting for us since twelve. Didn't we eat! Turkey, cranberry sauce, potatoes, cider, coffee, pumpkin pie, and I don't know what besides. We were almost too hungry to enjoy it at first, but we *did* eat. I had two plates of turkey and four cups of coffee; the coffee was pretty weak, but we made up for it by taking enough. I think we must have scared those hotel people. The man and his wife and daughter waited on us, and we did carry on so—firing things at each other, you know; and then after dinner we went up in the parlor and played and sung college songs, 'Upidee' and 'Co-cachalunk,' and all those things. Such a row as we made!

"But coming home in the Elevated was the worst. How those fellows did carry on! Just imagine—about twenty of us—my gracious! what a noise we did make! We kept the car in a roar. One fellow would go 'Ee-oh,' and then another fellow would go 'Oh-ah,' and then they'd all go together. One of the fellows put his head out of the window, and another fellow immediately dragged him in and began patting his hair down as if it was a wig, you know. We made puns on each other's names, and whistled and sang, and oh! carried on like sixty. One man with a black beard laughed at us ready to kill himself, and a brakeman on the back platform was grinning from ear to ear.

"Well, we did have a day of it, I can tell you—but won't we all be as stiff as bricks to-morrow!"

I will only add that I do wish I had been one of those boys; but—I am glad that I wasn't that hotel-keeper.

THE SCHOOL-CHILDREN'S WELCOME.

SATURDAY, December 20, was a splendid holiday for the school-children of Philadelphia. All through the week they had been reading of the receptions given to General Grant in honor of his return from his journey around the world, and now they were to take part in a welcome of their own.

There was, in the first place, a grand street procession of boys, to the number of nearly four thousand—quite an army, in fact—who marched in four great divisions, each headed by a band. The boys were well drilled, and stepped gayly to the music, with soldier-like bearing and precision. As the General rode between their lines he was greeted with enthusiastic cheers. No doubt he was as much gratified by this boyish welcome as by the grand military display that attended his entry into the city.

After reviewing the lads, General Grant was escorted to the Academy of Music, where almost as many school-girls as there were boys in the procession were assembled to give him a reception of a gentler kind. It must have been a pretty sight—more than three thousand lassies, all in their teens, and all in their best attire. As soon as he appeared, two thousand sweet voices joined in the grand melody of "Hail to the Chief!" which was sung with enthusiasm and fine effect. The General acknowledged the courtesy in a short address. Several other speeches were made, interspersed with patriotic songs.

Of all the festivities of the week, the one General Grant will probably remember with most pleasure will be the reception given him by the boys and girls of the public schools.

"OLD PROBABILITIES."

THE next time the Professor came, it was in a dense fog. The morning was so damp and disagreeable that we hardly expected to see him. He did not disappoint us, but seemed to have come almost before the sun was fairly up, it was so dark.

"What makes a fog?" asked Gus.

"I meant to have talked about something else, Gus," answered the Professor; "but you have chosen a subject for me. It is a very good one, too, and quite suitable to the occasion. Fogs are nothing more nor less than clouds. They usually float aloft, a mile or more high, but sometimes drift down to the ground and lie all around us. They are so light that they rise and fall from very slight causes, when there is no wind. A brisk breeze soon drives them off."

"But what are clouds made of?" inquires May, who has become such a favorite with the Professor that she never hesitates to stop him when she wants anything explained.

"Clouds, May, are made up of small particles of water or vapor slightly chilled. When vapor or steam is hot, it can not be seen, but is invisible like the air. You have noticed the steam from a tea-kettle. Near the spout it is hidden, but a little farther off, where it has got cooled by mixing with the air, it begins to look gray, like a cloud. If the kettle be allowed to boil a long while, so that a large quantity of steam is formed, it will collect on the walls and window-panes, where, becoming thoroughly chilled, it turns again to water, the same as it was when first poured into the kettle. So it is with the clouds out-of-doors; when the sun comes out bright and hot, it dries them up, as we say; that is, it heats them so much that they become invisible. Cool air mingling with them brings them into sight again; and, if cool enough, it condenses."

"Oh dear!"

The Professor laughs. "There can be no doubt about it, May, science is full of big words. We will say that the cool wind makes the clouds heavy by squeezing them together, and sends them down in drops of rain. This is called condensing."

May rewards the Professor for his simple explanation with such a bright glance that he proceeds with an illustration.

"You have made soap-bubbles, and seen how they will float around in the air, and sometimes be wafted clear up above the trees, until they get broken, when they come down drops of water. The particles of vapor that form clouds are little bubbles, or hollow spheres filled with air. When a cold wind crushes them, they become solid, unite with one another, and fall as rain-drops. Cold water is much heavier than air; but water made hot by fire or by the sun, and turned into vapor, is lighter. In time of a fog the vapor is just warm enough to have the same weight as the air, so that it neither rises nor falls, but remains quietly near the ground."

"Professor," remarked Joe, "did you not say that when the sun came out bright and hot, it dried up the fog? and is not the fog the very thing that keeps the sun from coming out?"

"Yes, my dear; but fogs usually gather at night, and when the sun rises in the morning, he goes to work at once to heat them up and make them disappear. But when he finds them very thick, and is hindered by cold air, he may be a good part of the day in working his way through, or he may even have to go down before he is able to show himself. Generally, however, he gets help from the wind, and then the fog goes off in a hurry."

"Is there no way," asked Gus, "of knowing when the wind will spring up, and give us some clear cold weather? Ted Wynant's cousin has an ice-boat, and we are all waiting for a ride on the river."

"There is Old Probabilities," said Jack; "but he can only tell a day or two ahead, and seems rather uncertain at that, and afraid to express a decided opinion. It is a little this or a little that, a little cloudy or a little cooler, and the wind is to blow a little in nearly every direction. Most people laugh when they talk about him, as if he was not of much account, or had grown stupid in his old age. If he would only foretell a hurricane or a deluge, and bring it around, why, then we would know what he is good for."

"Such a test would be rather costly," said the Professor, smiling. "It is better to give the old gentleman a little time to establish his reliableness; for in truth he is yet very young—a mere child of eight or ten years. And considering that he undertakes to forewarn our whole country as to the coming weather, so that everybody will have time to get ready for it, we must admit that he is doing all that his age warrants."

"Where does he live?" asked Gus.

"We have been talking somewhat absurdly," replied the Professor. "Instead of a single person, there is what is called the United States Signal Service, which has been in operation eight or ten years, and comprises some two hundred or more men, scattered all over the country, from Maine to California, and from the Gulf of Mexico away out to the Northwestern lakes. The men at these various stations watch the weather very closely, and at a particular time every day send word regarding it by telegraph to the main office at Washington, where the different reports are carefully studied, and an opinion formed as to what the weather is likely to be in different sections of the country during the next twenty-four hours or more, and the result is then published in the daily newspapers and at the numerous post-offices throughout the land. The matter is yet somewhat uncertain, and occasionally mistakes are made."

"But will they ever get so that they can tell exactly every time?"

"We hope so. The warnings given are usually right, and are becoming more and more reliable every year. In 1878 it was estimated that about seventy-seven out of a hundred of them were found to be correct; more recently they have been declared accurate about ninety times in a hundred. So, you see, good progress is being made; and the Signal Service system is becoming very useful to the nation, for property and life can often be saved from destruction when the approach of a severe storm is known.

"The New York *Herald* has encouraged the study of the weather for many years, and its managers now send word to England by the Atlantic cable when a storm is to be expected there. They have lately sent notice of so many ugly ones, which have promptly arrived, that our English cousins are complaining of the unfair treatment of the *Herald*."

"Are they really so absurd?" asked Jack.

"Yes," said the Professor; "they facetiously intimate that when Providence controlled the weather they fared well enough; but that since the *Herald* has undertaken to run that department they have been doomed to storms, fogs, and rain. To give an instance of the faith, Jack, that the English people put in our Signal Service, there is a story told of an English lady who last autumn desired to give a lawn party. The season was an unusually rainy one, and such entertainments had, in consequence, been given up. The lady, however, sent her invitations, and calmly announced that the day she had selected would be clear. When asked how she had dared to take such a risk, she replied, 'There was no risk whatever; I had telegraphed to the man in New York.'"

The children all laughed, and it was some time before the Professor could quiet them sufficiently to add the few words that concluded his little lecture.

"The most violent storms have been found generally to whirl in circles, and are called cyclones. In some parts of the world they are very disastrous. One occurred in India in 1864 that destroyed 45,000 lives in a single day. Ten years earlier, when the English and French were at war with Russia, a storm was observed to begin in France and to be moving eastward. Timely warning was sent to the allied fleet in the Black Sea. The storm came with such terrific violence that, had it not been expected, it would probably have destroyed one of the most splendid navies that ever rode the waters, and perhaps have changed the issue of the war."

TROUBLE IN THE PLAY-ROOM.

"I DON'T care—I'm just as mad as I can be. To keep me in just for a little rain! I won't be good—I won't play with my dolls. I'm going to whip every one of them, and put them to bed this very minute."

Such a little termagant as Bessie Hatch looked at that moment, with her black eyes flashing, her hands clinched, and her cheeks like two flaming poppies! Half irritated, half amused, Annie, the Irish nurse, regarded her for a moment.

"Indade, but it's a swate timper you have, Bessie Hatch; and I hope for your own sake it 'll be minded afore you grow up. It's not I will be lettin' you out, when your ma lift particular orders you wasn't to go if it rained. Just hear how the storm's batin' agin the windows. Your cousin won't expect you at all. Oh, bate your dolls as much as you like!" as Bessie made an angry rush toward them; "it won't hurt their feelin's much, I guess. There's Baby cryin'!" she added, suddenly, and hastened toward the room at the end of the hall.

Bessie meantime had snatched her largest doll from the chair where she was reposing, and belabored her soundly with a piece of whalebone that lay near at hand. Then, after shaking her heartily, she tossed her on to the bed, where she lay with her black eyes shut, as if overcome by her feelings. She was a very handsome wax doll, with chestnut hair done up like a lady's in puffs and curls. She had a somewhat haughty expression, carried her head a little to one side, and was dressed in the "latest style."

Grace, a porcelain-headed doll, dressed simply in a blue muslin and a white apron, received her punishment next, and was deposited by Miss Augusta's side.

But Winnie, dear Winnie, Bessie's favorite doll, could she have the heart to punish *her* this way?—Winnie, with her golden-brown curls and beautiful hazel eyes, and her dear little face rounded and moulded like a child's. How lovely was her smiling mouth! With what confiding affection she seemed to look up at Bessie, as the latter took her up in a hesitating way! But the recollection of her lost pleasure came back to her, and with it the spite and anger that had animated her a moment before. Winnie received her whipping like the rest; but instead of tossing her on the bed, Bessie set her back in her little chair, turning her face to the window that she might not see it.

Somehow her anger seemed to have spent itself with that last whipping, and a feeling of shame was creeping into her little heart. She had intended to go through her baby-house, chastising all its inmates, but instead she took a picture-book, and lay down on the lounge by the window.

How quiet everything seemed! Annie had carried Baby down stairs to feed him. She heard no sound but the murmur of the sewing-machine in the next room, where Jane Kennedy, the seamstress, was working. She felt drowsy and sleepy. Slowly her head sank down among the cushions of the lounge, and the drooping eyelids closed.

A rustling sound near her made her open them with a start, and in a minute more she was sitting bolt-upright, staring with all her eyes. For there stood a little figure no taller than Winnie, dressed in a white fleecy robe trailing on the ground. Her soft black hair reached to her feet, and over it she wore a wreath that sparkled like dew-drops in the sun.

Some fear mingled with Bessie's admiration as she gazed upon her. For a frown was on the fairy's brow, and the dark eyes she fixed upon the child were full of displeasure.

Tap, tap, tap, came the sound of little feet approaching. Bessie looked round, then shrank back, terror-stricken. Well she might, for her dolls Augusta and Grace had somehow found the use of their limbs, and were rapidly nearing the lounge. But they paused not far from the fairy, and reached out their little hands to her with a supplicating gesture.

"Kind fairy! good fairy!" they said, in shrill piping voices, "avenge the wrong done to us. That child, who calls herself our mother, has beaten us cruelly, just because she had nothing else to vent her spite upon; we had done no harm in any way. Punish her, good fairy; make her sorry for having treated us so."

"I will give her into your hands," said the fairy, gravely. "See that you punish her as she deserves."

Bessie, who lay trembling and burning with mingled fear and shame, now rallied her courage, and raised her head again. She could not help laughing at the idea of her own dolls punishing her.

"You foolish little fairy!" she said, laughing; "I could manage them both with one hand; and if—"

She stopped aghast, for the fairy raised her wand, and it flashed like a dazzling sunbeam full in the child's eyes. She covered them with her hands, glancing up just in time to see the fairy float away on her silver wings.

But how came she, Bessie, on the floor, and why did it seem like a great meadow stretching around her? The lounge had become a mountain, and the ceiling of the room looked nearly as broad as the sky.

It was the same room, the same familiar objects, only how monstrous everything had grown! Was that immense building in the corner her baby-house?

Bessie's little head swam; her heart beat tumultuously. A light mocking laugh near her made her glance quickly round.

Who was this tall figure in a trailing gray silk, looking down at her with severe triumph in her black eyes? That chestnut hair, that beautiful red and white complexion—could this be Augusta, her own doll?

With a scream of terror, Bessie was darting away, but waxen fingers seized her tender little arm, closing tightly upon it. Oh, how they hurt! She struggled and kicked, but could not get away.

"Let me go!" she cried out; "I'll pay you off well, Miss Augusta, if you don't. Remember, you're my doll—"

"Pay me off!" cried Augusta, with another shrill laugh. "You poor silly midget! don't you know how the fairy's wand has changed you? Why, you don't reach to my knee. No; I am going to pay you off, and handsomely too. Grace, bring that piece of whalebone directly."

"If you dare!" cried Bessie; but Grace clattered up toward her, her stolid countenance fairly beaming. Bessie tried to dodge behind Augusta, but she held her tightly by both arms.

"A FROWN WAS ON THE FAIRY'S BROW."

"Lay it well over her shoulders, Grace; make 'em tingle!" she cried; and thick and fast fell the blows, while poor Bessie writhed and protested and threatened in vain. When Grace's arm was tired, Augusta took her turn. After beating Bessie to her heart's content, she seized the child by her shoulders, and shook her till her head fairly turned round.

"There!" she said, tossing her on to the doll's bed in the corner; "lie there, miss, till Winnie comes. Poor thing! she's gone away to cry somewhere, but as soon as she comes back she shall have *her* chance. Come, Grace, we will go for a walk."

She walked haughtily away, followed by the admiring Grace. Poor Bessie lay sobbing and crying. Her shoulders and back were smarting, her little arms black and blue from the pressure of Augusta's fingers.

"I'll run away and hide somewhere," she said at last.

Creeping off the bed very cautiously, she was stealing away, when something seized her again. She gave a cry of despair, and looking up, saw Winnie's sweet face.

"Who are you?" she asked. "Are you a new doll?" holding her gently but firmly.

"Oh, Winnie!" said Bessie, and hid her face in shame. Augusta came mincing up with a triumphant air, and related the action of the fairy.

"Now it's your turn," she said, handing the whalebone to Winnie. But she tossed it indignantly aside.

"Strike her! Never! No; I would rather remember her kindness to me. Don't cry, little mother," she added, stooping to kiss her. "If the fairy comes again, I will ask her to change you back."

"No, no!" cried Augusta and Grace, in a terrible fright, but Bessie did not hear. She was sobbing with her face in Winnie's neck.

"Oh, Winnie! Winnie! how can you be so kind? I would rather you gave me a beating."

But Winnie wiped her eyes, and smiled so brightly on her that Bessie's heart began to revive a little. Ere long they were playing together, and it would have been rare sport for any child to see Winnie wheeling Bessie in a tiny tin cart no bigger than a match-box. Then they had a grand game of hide-and-seek in the stocking basket Annie had left on the floor. Grace soon joined them, while Augusta, quite gracious by this time, sat eying them complacently from her arm-chair.

"Bessie! Bessie! your mamma's come in, and wants to see you."

Bessie started up, rubbing her eyes. She looked in a dazed sort of way at Annie, then at the corner where she kept her dolls. There they sat, all three in a row as usual.

"Who put them there—my dolls? Did they really whip me?" she asked, confusedly. Then she blushed, and hung her little head.

"Who put them there? Why, I reckon they got tired of lying on the bed, and walked over to their chairs," said Annie, with a mischievous gleam in her eye.

"You put them there," said Bessie; but she wished she could feel quite sure. Catching up her darling Winnie, she walked off to her mother's room.

All the rest of that day Bessie treated Augusta and Grace with the utmost respect; and when she had undressed them and put them to bed, she lingered as if anxious to say something. At last she stooped down and whispered: "I don't believe it's true; but I'll never whip you or get into such a passion again. I didn't know how ugly it was till I saw you behave so yourselves. And please, if it is true, don't ask the fairy to make me little again, for I mean to be good now."

As for Winnie, darling Winnie, she lay all night in Bessie's arms, her head hugged close to her breast. And the piece of whalebone stood bolt-upright in Bessie's match-box, where she had stuck it that it might always remind her of the lesson of that day.

THE CHILDREN'S WELCOME TO GENERAL GRANT.—Drawn by A. B. Frost.—[See Page 98.]

HOW AUNT PAM BECAME A SMUGGLER

BY MRS. FRANK McCARTHY.

MY name is Tom Barnes, and I live on the other side of the river, just far enough from New York to go there once in a while with pa to a show. That's all the city's good for, anyway. We can't get up shows here very well; but when it comes to other fun, we can beat you city folks all hollow. You see, you haven't got the things to work with that we have—the woods and water and things. But I'll tell you about Aunt Pam—her name is Pamela, I think, but we call her Pam for short. She wasn't ever married, though I guess she's old enough. Somebody once said Aunt Pam was an old maid; but that can't be, for old maids are always cranky, and get out of bed backward every morning. Now Aunt Pam was never cranky in her life; and I know she gets out of bed like everybody else, for I've slept with her many a time. And nobody in their senses would call Aunt Pam old, and you'd better believe she's jolly. The house ain't anything without Aunt Pam.

My sisters are all girls, you see, and so taken up with worsted-work, and practicing, and one thing and the other, that I don't know what I'd do without Aunt Pam. I tell her everything; but I couldn't about the smugglers' cave, because the fellows wrote it all down in black and white, and we took a solemn promise to keep it a secret. We all live close to the water; and having everything handy, we made up our minds we'd make a smugglers' cave. We got to work lively; and while some of the fellows were digging out the bank, others chopped down small trees and bushes, and made a covered archway to crawl under, so that the opening of the cave couldn't be seen. We pulled the young twigs and vines down over the chopped ones, rolled logs inside for seats, and things began to look quite ship-shape.

It was no easy job, I can tell you. We worked like beavers to get the cave the way we wanted it; but when it was done, it was what you may call hunky-dory. Bill Drake's father had a flat-bottomed boat that we got into and rowed along shore. We rigged up a sail; but there was something the matter with it, and it kept flopping about, and wasn't much good, but anyhow it looked nice. We never went far from shore. We weren't afraid, but we didn't care to. Smugglers always kept along shore.

We all had blue shirts, and pulled our caps down over our eyes to look fierce. And Bill Drake kept an old pipe of his father's in his mouth; it hadn't any tobacco in it, but it was a real pipe, so we made Bill captain. The thing was to get lots of traps into the cave to look like smuggled goods. We fished up old bathing pieces and bits of broken bottles, and Bill brought down a red petticoat; but the best of all was Aunt Pam's shawl.

Now I'd scorn to do a mean or sneaking thing, especially to Aunt Pam, but she didn't seem to care a button for that shawl. I didn't think it was worth twopence. She used to wear it in all sorts of weather, and it looked to me as if it was patched up out of bits that she hadn't any other use for. I'm sure she'd worn it since she was a baby. I could remember seeing that shawl around as long as I could remember anything, and it was just the thing for our cave. It was kind of like a Turk's head turban as to color; and when it was fixed over Bill Bates's bathing suit, and one corner hung down over the rock, it made the cave look bully. I went into Aunt Pam's room one morning, and found it thrown over the foot of the bedstead, like an old blanket, and I carried it off to the cave.

When I came home from school, I saw Aunt Pam out walking with a worsted thing that one of my sisters made for her, and I thought it was enough sight handsomer in the way of a shawl. I went on down to the cave, and when I got home again there was a regular hullabulloo in the house.

The girls were ransacking the closets, Aunt Pam was flying around like a hen with its head cut off, and everybody was turning everything inside out. "Maybe Tom's seen it," said mamma. "Tom, have you seen your aunt Pam's shawl?"

"That old thing she used to wear around?" I said.

"Old thing!" they all shrieked together. "Why, it's a camel's-hair shawl; it's worth five hundred dollars."

"Oh no!" I said. "I beg your pardon; there wasn't the hair of a camel, or even a cat, in the shawl that I mean; it was just sewed together on the wrong side like a bed-quilt."

"That was it, you ridiculous boy," said my sisters. "Have you seen it?"

"Seen it!" said I; "I've only seen it every day since I was born, and yet I remember it well." I went whistling away, and they began to rush around again for that shawl.

I felt pale under my whistle. Five hundred dollars! who'd 'a thought it? Down in the smugglers' cave! Goodness gracious! No wonder it looked just the thing. No wonder we all cottoned to that shawl from the start.

"I always told you something would happen to it," said mamma to Aunt Pam. "You flung it around like an old rag."

"That was the comfort of it," said Aunt Pam. "It couldn't be hurt. It could be worn in all weathers—to a wedding or a funeral, to church or to a clam-bake. It was always in the fashion, and everybody knew what it was worth."

"Except me," I said, under my breath.

"Oh, my beautiful shawl!" said Aunt Pam, beginning all at once to feel the full shock of her loss. The tears rolled out of her dear old eyes, and my sisters began to snivel, as they always did.

Mamma said it must be looked into, and for a moment I was scared. I thought of the smugglers' cave.

"What must be looked into?" I said.

"Why, the loss of the shawl," said mamma. "It must have been stolen out of the house."

Our up-stairs girl was passing through the room when ma said that, and she turned red and pale.

"Did you notice Maggie?" mamma said, when the door was shut.

"Oh, mamma!" we all cried out, for we thought the world of Maggie. I couldn't help wondering how it was she was so red and flustered, while I was as cool as a cucumber. Aunt Pam declared she wouldn't have Maggie's feelings hurt for the world; and I said she was innocent, in a deep low solemn voice, but nobody paid any attention to me. Then I stopped to think before I went on. How could I betray my comrades and the whereabouts of the cave? I remembered the last piece I spoke in school, and how I hollered out the words,

> "O for a tongue to curse the slave
> Whose treason, like a deadly blight,
> Comes o'er the counsels of the brave,
> And blasts them in their hour of might!"

Could I be that traitor? No indeed—not much! Yet here was a dreadful row in the house, and the only way to mend matters was to get that shawl again as soon as possible. I resolved to get it that very night, and when I listened to an advertisement that Aunt Pam had written out for the paper, I saw my way clear. She said no questions would be asked if the article was promptly returned. That settled it. I went up to my room, and wrote out the following in a disguised hand:

"Secrit and kunfidenshal—the shawl's all right."

I waited till after supper, slipped it under Aunt Pam's door, and going out the back way I took a cross-cut down to the shore. Now pa won't let us go out at night to play, and I think that's a mistake, because we can't get used to the dark if we don't. The whole world looked queer somehow to me by starlight. The moon hadn't come up yet, and at first I could hardly see my hand before my face. I never saw such ugly shadows, and once I had to stop and get breath before I could make up my mind to pass a clump of old mulberry bushes. Once in a while I heard a crackle behind me like a footstep, but I didn't look back. I knew my only chance was to plod ahead, no matter how my heart thumped or my knees shook. I thought of everything I could to bolster me up—of dear old Aunt Pam and poor little Maggie. But the sound of the waves on the beach was awful! They roared like so many wild beasts. It was as black as ink on the water, and the twinkle of the light-house seemed a hundred miles away. It was so lonely and wild that my heart was in my throat. And suppose, thinks I, when I get in the cave, the waves come up and devour me! Suppose somebody has crawled in there to sleep, some tramp or something, and he should catch me by the leg! Or the bank should tumble in on top of me! All my spunk was gone, and I turned to run, when, bunk! I came into something behind me.

"Ow!" I screamed, and "Oh!" exclaimed somebody, and wasn't I glad to find it was dear old Aunt Pam. She scared me, though, for she was as white as any sheet, and grabbing me in her arms, she began to cry over me.

"Tell me all, Tom," she said. "I got your note, and I followed you. You bad, wicked, dear little wretch, tell me everything. If the shawl's got lost, never mind, Tom; I don't care; only tell me, and come back home."

Poor, dear Aunt Pam! she told me afterward she thought I had done something to the shawl, and ran away in my fright. We were both pretty well broke up, and I couldn't help crying a little bit myself. But of course I couldn't go home now without the shawl. I began to feel as brave as a lion now Aunt Pam was there. The thing was to get her out of the way while I went into the cave. It looked awful down there in the hollow, and the wind was getting up, the water swashed around, and I couldn't help thinking there might be a tramp in there. All at once a bright thought struck me. Aunt Pam wasn't afraid of tramps; she wasn't afraid of anything. And, after all, it was her shawl. If it was worth having, it was worth going after. But how about betraying the boys? Another bright thought struck me. I'd make Aunt Pam one of us. She could say the words over after me, and she could crawl in and get the shawl, while I kept guard outside: and if anybody says Aunt Pam is old after that, they must be crazy. She said all the words solemnly, one after another; then she crawled in, and dragged out every blessed thing she could lay her hands on. I put 'em all back the next morning, and the best of it all was that Aunt Pam never gave us away. She just told the folks she found the shawl herself, and she did, you know —didn't she?

MATHEMATICAL PUZZLES.

No. 5.

Two boys kept neighboring apple stands, and each had thirty apples to sell every day. One sold his at the rate of two for five cents, and received seventy-five cents, and the other at three for five cents, and received fifty cents, the total being one dollar and twenty-five cents. It happened one day that one of the boys was sick, and the other engaged to sell the whole stock of sixty apples at the same rate. "Two for five, and three for five, that's five for ten," said he, and five for ten he sold them. But to his astonishment, when he got through he had but one dollar and twenty cents instead of one dollar and twenty-five cents. Now how did he lose five cents?

No. 6.

"How old are your children?" asked a lady who was visiting a friend, the mother of three beautiful daughters. "My eldest daughter is just double the age of my youngest daughter," replied the mother, "and the age of my other child is that of her youngest sister and one-third more. Their three combined ages make exactly the sum of my age, and I shall be sixty-six one year from to-day." What was the age of each of the three daughters?

THE OLDEST ROSE-BUSH IN THE WORLD.

THEY say it is the oldest, and who knows that it is not? I will tell you the story as it was told to me, and you shall see what you think of it.

There is a funny old town in Germany called Hildesheim, a little out of the way of travellers, but full of curious and interesting things, and over its fine cathedral walls climbs a rose-bush so large and strong that it may well be a thousand years old, as they say it is.

"A thousand years ago," said the sacristan, "the country all about here was a forest."

If you have studied history, you will see the story may be true so far, for you know Charlemagne became Emperor of Germany in A.D. 800, and that Germany was little better than a wilderness then.

"One day," continued the sacristan, "Louis the Gentle, the son of Charlemagne, went hunting with all his retinue in this forest. They had with them a box of relics."

Relics, you must know, were pieces of the dress of martyrs and saints, or something that martyrs and saints had touched in their lifetime, or perhaps even the bones of martyrs and saints.

"When they encamped for dinner, the gentle Louis wished to put this box of relics away very carefully, and looking about, he saw a beautiful blooming rose-bush, which must have been quite large even then, as he concealed the box in its branches.

"Perhaps they hurried away in pursuit of game after dinner, or perhaps they ate too much, and, as often happens in such a case, they forgot to be as religious as they were before dinner. However it was, at all events they rode away without the relics, and never missed them till the next day.

"Then Louis was full of shame, and declared they must ride back again, and never give up searching till they found the box.

"So they rode for many a weary hour, searching the by-ways of the forest—for there were few roads—till at last they all suddenly stopped, full of awe and wonder.

"It was a beautiful June day, and the birds were singing, and the flowers were blooming; but, lo! just before them they saw a glade in the forest where the fresh white snow lay like a soft thick carpet over everything.

"And yet it did not cover everything either. For in the centre of the glade grew a lovely rose-bush, with hundreds of bright blossoms upon it, and this was the bush in which the box had been hidden. Louis hastened forward, and grasped the box; but, lo! here was another miracle: it had grown into the wood of the rose-bush so firmly that it could not be taken away.

"Then Louis fell on his knees, and said he would receive this as a sign, and he vowed to build a cathedral on the spot.

"They called the snow 'holy snow,' because it had hidden the ugly remnants of their feast with its purity, but had left the rose-bush free, and they named the cathedral and the town which sprang up about it Hildesheim, which in old, old German meant 'holy snow.'"

It is certainly an enormous rose-bush, and its roots grow wide under the cathedral. Over them, in the crypt, is an altar said to be of pure silver, and it looks as if it might be. On the altar are heaped great bunches of artificial roses, which they persuade the ignorant peasants are actual blossoms of the rose-bush itself, even when it is leafless and bare in the winter.

I can not say that all the sacristan's story is true, but I know that the rose-bush of Hildesheim is the largest one I ever saw, and that the town is a very old place. Indeed, a few years ago, some wonderful gold and silver vessels were dug up there, which must have been used by an almost forgotten race. If any of you live near Washington, you can see copies of them in the Smithsonian Institution.

CROCHET PURSE.

THIS pretty purse will make a nice gift for some of our young people. It is worked with red saddler's silk in open-work double crochet, and consists of an oblong bag pointed toward the bottom, and furnished with small slits at the top on both sides. The purse is closed with two metal bars, finished with knobs, and joined with a chain and ring. An ordinary steel slide may be substituted. A metal acorn finishes the bottom. Make a foundation of 96 st. (stitch), close these in a ring with 1 sl. (slip stitch), and crochet the 1st round.—4 ch. (chain stitch), the first 3 of which count as first dc. (double crochet), then always alternately 1 dc. on the second following st., 1 ch.; finally, 1 sl. on the third of the first 3 ch. in this round. 2d round.—1 sl. on the next st., 4 ch., the first 3 of which count as first dc., then always alternately 1 dc. on the next ch. in the preceding round, 1 ch.; finally, 1 sl. on the third of the first 3 ch. in this round. Next work 24 rounds like the preceding round, but in the last 10 rounds narrow at intervals, and instead of 1 dc. pass over 2 dc., so that in the last round only 8 dc. are worked. Run the working thread through the st. of the last round, draw it tight, and set on the acorn. Then finish the purse in two parts, working on the upper side of the foundation st. 3 rounds in the preceding design, going back and forth, and in the last round fasten in the bars as follows: * 7 ch., pass over 3 dc., lay on the bar from the wrong side, carry the ch. across the bar to the wrong side, 1 sc. on the next ch., 7 ch., carry them over the bar to the front, pass over 3 dc., 1 sc. on the next ch., and repeat from *.

"ONT DAYKUMBOA."

IN the parlor of a dear old-fashioned country house two elderly ladies are seated, one knitting, the other reading the report of yesterday's sermons, giving bits aloud now and then; on the carpet a little boy about three years of age is sprawling, apparently trying to swim on dry land.

The lady knitting is Miss Helena Oakstead, the lady reading is Miss Judith Oakstead, and the small boy is Master Ralph Oakstead, the eldest son of the youngest brother. If you go to the other side of the hall you will find the eldest brother (Master Ralph's uncle) in his study, writing an essay full of great big words. He is Professor Oakstead.

Master Ralph is spending the day with his relatives, and has gotten on with them very well so far, as his sister Daisy, two years his senior, whom he rules right royally, has acted as court interpreter; but she has just departed for a drive with a neighboring friend, and the aunts are left in sole charge of his Highness.

He is very gracious at first, looks over a picture-book with Miss Helena, and makes eager but unintelligible remarks respecting the "bow-wows" and "moos," to which Miss Helena answers, "Um, dear," as being the safest thing to say. But now he is silent, and has been so for at least ten minutes.

"How good Ralph is!" half whispers Miss Helena.

His Highness pricks up his ears.

"Yes, dear little fellow; and he has no one to play with, either."

His Highness sits up—he speaks.

"Ont daykumboa."

"What is it, dear?" says Miss Judith.

"Ont daykumboa," repeats Master Ralph.

"What does the child mean?" asks Miss Helena.

"I don't know. What do you want, Ralphie?"

Ralph, with a look of mingled contempt and pity at his stupid relatives, says, slowly but emphatically, "Ont daykumboa."

"Perhaps he is hungry. I'll go and get him a piece of cake," says Miss Helena.

The cake is brought, and promptly accepted; but it is evidently not the thing for which his soul longs, for after devouring half the slice he plaintively murmurs, "Ont daykumboa."

"Well, isn't that daykumboa?" says Miss Judith.

Ralph gives her a scornful look as sole answer, and finishes his cake in awful silence. As the last crumb disappears he sighs, "Ont daykumboa."

"What on earth and under the sun does the child want?" is the combined exclamation of the aunts.

"Perhaps Elijah can help us."

"Oh yes, he knows everything pretty nearly; but he may not like being disturbed now—he's writing, you know."

"Well, perhaps Victoria might be able to tell; she used to take care of children."

So Victoria is summoned from the kitchen. She is a tall majestic negress, who looks as if she had just stepped out of history. Her speech does not quite come up to her stately mien.

"Why, what's de matter wi' de chile?" she queries.

All of Ralph's reply is lost except "daykumboa."

"Well, come 'long wi' Victoria—she git you kumboa. What, ain't gwine to come! Oh laws! dat ain't bein' good bo'."

For Master Ralph has seated himself flatly on a footstool, and with his back against the wall, refuses in the dumbest of dumb-show to be entrapped into "gwine" anywhere.

Miss Helena suggests that they bring to him whatever they find that is at all likely to be "daykumboa."

So at the feet of his Royal Highness is laid such a queer collection of articles as never before appeared in that trim sitting-room: a *Child's History of England*, a bottle of mucilage, a pair of scissors, a coal shovel, a comb and brush, a bunch of flowers, a photograph album, a bottle of ink, and goodness knows what besides. Miss Helena

"ONT DAYKUMBOA."

ransacks her brains and her bureau, Miss Judith brings every portable in the room, and Victoria literally squanders the contents of her larder, but all to no purpose, and what is worse, his Highness, becoming alarmed at such unusual behavior, begins to moan "Ont daykumboa" in a way that draws tears to the eyes of his aunts.

"Judith," exclaims Miss Helena, "the case is getting desperate. We *must* send for Elijah, no matter if he does get angry.—Victoria, just go to the study, and tell the Professor that he *must* come here for a few minutes. Do you hear—*must!*"

Victoria, looking as scared as only a solemn-natured darky *can* look, departs, and returns speedily with the Professor.

"Is anything the matter with Alcibiades?" he asks. Alcibiades, be it known, is what the Professor always calls Ralph—"for short," he says.

"He is in a most peculiar condition, Elijah—persists in calling for *daykumbox*, and we can not understand what he means."

"What is it that you want, my boy?" inquires the Professor, bending his dignified back and knees, so as to bring his gray head on a level with Ralph's "curly pow."

Ralph turns to him with an expression of relief, as much as to say, "Well, here's a reasonable being at last," and explains, "Ont daykumbox."

"And what is daykumbox?" says the Professor.

"Daykumbox," repeats Ralph, with a lingering hope that perhaps he is going to get some satisfaction; but this creature is just as dull as the rest, and his Highness, with great want of dignity, begins to whimper.

"The child seems to be in pain," says the Professor, standing up, and regarding his nephew with concern. "Perhaps he has hurt himself."

"I never thought of that," cries Miss Judith.—"Have you hurt yourself, Ralphie?"

"Ont daykumbox," is the only response.

Little Birdie.

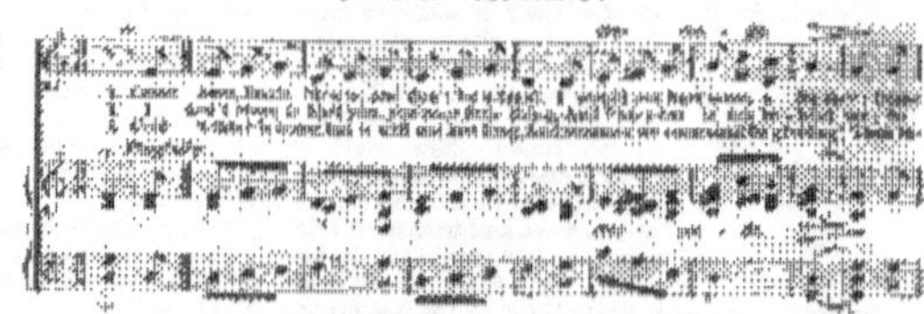

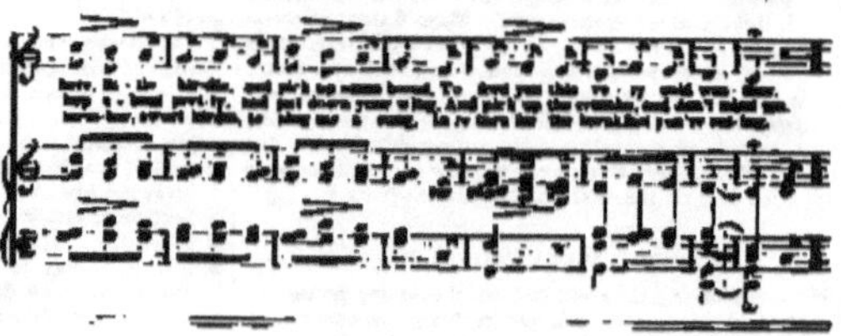

"Looks like he gwine to hab a fit. I gib de chile a good warm bath, if I's you," suggests Victoria.

Miss Helena eagerly catches at the straw.

"That's a good idea, Victoria. Just fill the little foot-tub with hot water, and bring it right in here."

Victoria hurries off to get the bath, and the Professor, seized with a new idea for the explanation of the mystery, goes to his study to search his dictionary for "daykumbox" in some dead or living language.

The foot-tub is brought, and the aunts proceed to undress his Highness, whereat he waxes wroth. They persist; there is a frightful howl, a struggle, and the tub of hot water is very vigorously overturned among the photographs, scissors, and eatables that strew the floor. The Professor, in alarm, comes tearing in, a book in each hand. At that moment a patter as of small feet is heard in the hall, and a little figure with flying golden locks darts into the room.

Ralph rushes into her arms in a kind of ecstasy, crying, "Oh, daykumbox! daykumbox!"

"What is it that Ralph is saying, Daisy?" eagerly asks Miss Helena, in the lull that follows. "He has been wanting daykumbox all the afternoon."

"He says, 'Daisy come back,'" answers the little girl. "That's what you wanted—wasn't it, Ralphie?"

"Es, me ont daykumbox," assents his Highness.

The Professor regards his niece with humble admiration not unmixed with awe, and retires to his study to lay his dictionaries by. Victoria rolls her eyes ceilingward, and says, "Well, I declar'!" then falls to work picking up the ruins of their various offerings, and the two ladies turn to help her after a little silent astonishment.

Ten minutes after, his Highness is seen in the garden pouring sand down his sister's neck, and sternly ordering her to "sit 'till," when she objects, in a tone that makes his aunts wonder if this can be the same boy who spent the greater part of two hours in wailing, "Ont daykumbox."

A SCARECROW NO SCARECROW.

An umbrella for a scarecrow
  Was in a corn field placed,
And with loud caws the sly old crows
  Around it gravely paced;
When suddenly a shower fell,
  And under it they went,
And staid until the rain had ceased,
  As in a little tent.
Then said they, as they all trooped out,
  "*That* man's a jolly feller;
Not only plants the corn for us,
  But lends us his umbreller!"

The Paradise of Insects.—None but those who have travelled on the Upper Amazons can have any idea of the number and voracity of the insect torments which work their wicked will on the bodies of the unfortunates exposed to their attacks. The "mucuins," or small sand-flies, form by far the most important section. In the villages, round which the forest is cleared away for some distance, the mucuins are generally pretty quiet during the day, except where darkness prevails; there they are ever busy, and are a perfect plague. The triumphant note of a mucuin which has made his way under your curtains is more annoying than even his bite; and should you have been careless in getting into bed, and been accompanied by two or three of these blood-suckers, we will defy you to sleep until you have exterminated them.

In the forest and on the river the mucuins are always busy. Men sometimes get into the vessel's tops, and there cover themselves with sacks, notwithstanding the heat, rather than remain below exposed to their attacks. Fortunately they can not stand a current of air, and so when under way the vessel is comparatively free from them, but when at anchor these pests are something awful. To get rid of them is next to impossible. Creosote will keep them off, but the remedy is as bad as the disease. Whitewash will drive them away, but when dry its power ceases; and the only thing to do is either to cover all exposed parts of the body with black pigment *à la mode Indienne*, or else to "grin and bear it."

Scarcely less troublesome than the mucuins are the mosquitoes, although they have the negative merit of biting only by day. They are minute creatures, not much larger than a pin's head; they prefer the backs of the hands to any other spot for their attacks. But, unlike the mucuin, which, when undisturbed, gorges himself until unable to fly, and becomes an easy prey to your avenging finger, the mosquito never seems to take too much to prevent his easy escape on the slightest appearance of danger, being evidently just as wide-awake when full as when empty.

Everywhere in long grass lurks the "moquim," a little red insect so small as to be almost imperceptible, but which fastens on the legs, causing the most intolerable itching.

There is a fly which burrows in the skin and deposits an egg, both in human beings and animals. This produces a maggot, similar in shape to that of the common blow-fly, but much larger, probably analogous to the Guinea-worm.

Then there are "chigos," which burrow mostly in the soles of the feet. You feel an intense itching, and on examination find a little thing like a pea just under the epidermis; this is the bag containing the young chigos, which must be carefully picked out with the point of a knife, and the cavity left filled with tobacco ash.

Huge spiders abound, whose very appearance inspires a wholesome dread of a nearer acquaintance, but which are harmless enough if let alone. In fact, on board the steamers, almost every cabin is tenanted by one large spider, whose presence is tolerated on account of its being a deadly foe to cockroaches, which abominable creatures swarm on board. Sometimes he is not visible for a fortnight or more at a time; but he leaves tokens of "having been there," in the shape of the empty husks of cockroaches, from which he has carefully abstracted the interior. These spiders have the power of springing upon their prey from a distance, and some of them are so large and powerful as to kill and devour small birds.

In passing through the narrow forest paths it is necessary to be on the look-out for the wood-ticks, which are very difficult to get rid of if once firmly attached; also for the large black ants, an inch and a half in length, with stings like a hornet's; and the saüba ant, without sting, but armed with nippers like a pair of surgical lance-forceps, which are running about everywhere. One may sometimes chance upon a column of the dreaded "fire-ants," marching in regular military order; and if he does, the only thing is to bolt at once, for neither man nor beast may withstand the fire-ant and live. When at length the traveller stops to rest, he must take care to examine the camping ground to see that neither centipede nor scorpion is there.

Frequently both centipedes and scorpions are found on the steamers, introduced, no doubt, in the wood used for fuel. One day, while the writer was watching the hands taking wood from canoes alongside, from one of the logs pitched on board was dislodged a scorpion, which fell on the naked left arm of a man keeping tally at the gangway. Astonished by his sudden flight through the air, the animal remained perfectly still. The man never moved a muscle, and quietly raising his right hand, flipped it away with his fingers and thumb. It was very neatly and coolly done; and he thus escaped a sting, which he no doubt would have received had he tried to brush it hastily away.

"A most enchanting story for boys."
PITTSBURGH TELEGRAPH.

AN INVOLUNTARY VOYAGE.

By LUCIEN BIART,

Author of "Adventures of a Young Naturalist."

TRANSLATED BY

Mrs. CASHEL HOEY and Mr. JOHN LILLIE.

ILLUSTRATED.

16mo, Cloth, $1 25.

A very charming book, brimming full of adventures, and has not an uninteresting page between its covers.—*Baltimore Gazette.*

A book that is at once novel and entertaining. * * * All the book is lively, and the voyagers have some adventures, the telling of which is as entertaining as any book of Jules Verne's, besides having nothing in them that is improbable or extravagant.—*Philadelphia Bulletin.*

A most enchanting story for boys. * * * It is a story of adventure, and also contains much interesting and useful information.—*Pittsburgh Telegraph.*

A narrative crowded with adventure, told in the lively and graphic style for which the French writers of books for boys are so noted.—*Cleveland Herald.*

One of the most attractive books of the season. * * * Spirited sketches of travel and adventure on the open wave, among the islands and on southern coasts, fill these chapters. But the main point which gives them their highest favor is the experience of naval warfare during our late civil conflict.—*Observer, N. Y.*

Published by HARPER & BROTHERS, N. Y.

☞ *Sent by mail, postage prepaid, to any part of the United States, on receipt of the price.*

A BOOK FOR EVERYBODY.

Ninth Edition now Ready.

HOW TO GET STRONG, AND HOW TO STAY SO. By WILLIAM BLAIKIE. With Illustrations. 16mo, Cloth, $1 00.

Your book is timely. Its large circulation cannot fail to be of great public benefit.—Rev. HENRY WARD BEECHER.

It is a book of extraordinary merit in matter and style, and does you great credit as a thinker and writer.—Hon. CALVIN E. PRATT, *of the New York Supreme Bench.*

A capital little treatise. It is the very book for ministers to study.—Rev. THEODORE L. CUYLER, D.D., *in New York Evangelist.*

It is unquestionably one of the most practical and useful books on this topic which have ever been published in this country.—*N. Y. Evening Express.*

We know of no man in America more capable of writing such a book, or who has a better right to do so.—*Portland Daily Herald and Globe.*

It will pay any person—whether a farmer or lawyer, laborer or idler, school-girl or house-wife—to buy and read it, and follow its teachings.—*Springfield Union.*

A veritable treasury of muscular common-sense.—*Charleston News and Courier.*

The Fairy Books.

THE PRINCESS IDLEWAYS. By Mrs. W. J. HAYS. Illustrated. 16mo, Cloth, 75 cents.

THE CATSKILL FAIRIES. By VIRGINIA W. JOHNSON. 8vo, Illuminated Cloth, Gilt Edges, $3 00.

FAIRY BOOK ILLUSTRATED. 16mo, Cloth, $1 50.

PUSS-CAT MEW, and other New Fairy Stories for my Children. By E. H. KNATCHBULL-HUGESSEN, M.P. Illustrated. 16mo, Cloth, $1 25.

FAIRY BOOK. The Best Popular Fairy Stories selected and rendered anew. By the Author of "John Halifax." Illustrated. 16mo, Cloth, $1 25.

FAIRY TALES. By JEAN MACÉ. Translated by MARY L. BOOTH. Illustrated. 16mo, Bevelled Edges, $1 75; Gilt Edges, $2 25.

FAIRY TALES OF ALL NATIONS. By É. LABOULAYE. Translated by MARY L. BOOTH. Illustrated. 12mo, Cloth, Bevelled Edges, $2 00; Gilt Edges, $2 50.

THE LITTLE LAME PRINCE. By the Author of "John Halifax, Gentleman." Illustrated. Square 16mo, Cloth, $1 00.

FOLKS AND FAIRIES. Stories for Little Children. By LUCY CECILIA LILLIE. Illustrated. Square 4to, Cloth, $1 00.

THE ADVENTURES OF A BROWNIE, as Told to my Child. By the Author of "John Halifax, Gentleman." Illustrated. Square 16mo, Cloth, 90 cents.

Published by HARPER & BROTHERS, New York.

☞ *Sent by mail, postage prepaid, to any part of the United States, on receipt of the price.*

WHAT MR. DARWIN SAW

In His Voyage Round the World in the Ship "Beagle."

ADAPTED FOR YOUTHFUL READERS.

Illustrated, 8vo, Cloth, $3 00.

A capital book on natural history for young readers.—*Hartford Courant.*

A superb volume filled with maps and pictures of beasts, birds, and fishes, as well as the faces of all sorts of men, and with all this a most delightful story of real travel round the world by a very famous naturalist.—*Christian Intelligencer, N. Y.*

To the intelligent boy or girl the book will be a perfect treasure. * * * Every statement it contains may be accepted as accurately true. * * * This book [illegible] truth is stranger than fiction.—*Philadelphia North American.*

It can scarcely be equaled anywhere [illegible] interest and instruction.—*N. Y. Times, Phila.*

MODEL WORKING
TOY ENGINES AND FIGURES.

We send Engine, Figures, Pulleys, &c., all complete as per cut, and in working order, by mail, for $1 50.

PECK & SNYDER,
124 and 126 Nassau Street, N. Y.

FRAGRANT
SOZODONT

is a composition of the purest and choicest ingredients of the vegetable kingdom. It cleanses, beautifies, and preserves the TEETH, hardens and invigorates the gums, and cools and refreshes the mouth. Every ingredient of this Balsamic dentifrice has a beneficial effect on the Teeth and Gums. Impure Breath, caused by neglected teeth, catarrh, tobacco, or spirits, is not only neutralized, but rendered fragrant, by the daily use of SOZODONT. It is as harmless as water, and has been indorsed by the most scientific men of the day. Sold by druggists.

"A book beyond the pale of criticism."
N. Y. DAILY GRAPHIC.

THE

Boy Travellers in the Far East.

ADVENTURES OF
TWO YOUTHS IN A JOURNEY
TO
JAPAN AND CHINA.

Illustrated, 8vo, Cloth, $3 00.

A more attractive book for boys and girls can scarcely be imagined.—*N. Y. Times.*

The best thing for a boy who cannot go to China and Japan is to get this book and read it.—*Philadelphia Ledger.*

Juvenile literature seems to have come to a climax in this book. In literary quality and in material form it is a decided improvement on anything of the kind ever before produced in America.—*N. Y. Journal of Commerce.*

One of the richest and most entertaining books for young people, both in text, illustrations, and binding, which has ever come to our table.—*Providence Press.*

Published by HARPER & BROTHERS, N. Y.

☞ *Sent by mail, postage prepaid, to any part of the United States, on receipt of the price.*

"A nice Gift for Children."
PITTSBURGH TELEGRAPH.

THE PRINCESS IDLEWAYS,

A FAIRY STORY.

Illustrated, 16mo, Cloth, 75 cents.

Written in a simple but charming manner, and illustrated by beautiful pictures, so that a youngster just past the first reading-book would appreciate every word.—*Christian Intelligencer, N. Y.*

The illustrations are worthy of special commendation. Any so airy, pretty, and full of grace, have rarely appeared in any American book for children.—*Hartford Courant.*

The language in which it is told is so pure and agreeable, that parents and good bachelor aunts will find it a pleasure to read it aloud to the little ones.—*Boston Courier.*

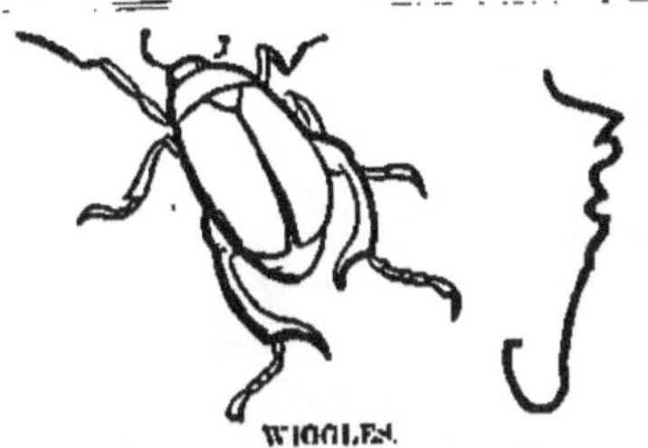

WIGGLES.

Of these two Wiggles, the first is what our artist makes of the outline given in No. 4 of *Harper's Young People*, and the second is a new Wiggle, in which we hope our young readers will take as much interest as they have in those already published.

During this new year we anticipate much pleasant intercourse with our young friends. We thank them heartily for the favors already received, which from their genuine childishness we know have come direct from their own little hearts and heads. Our paper is received by children who live in all parts of this country, in England, Germany, France, South America, Cuba, and Mexico; and we would like to offer them a few suggestions which, if faithfully carried out, will add interest to our Post-office Box, and give much valuable information.

In the first place, many of you have household pets—birds, squirrels, fishes, turtles, and other little live creatures. We are sure of this, because already some of you have asked us questions regarding the care of them. Now, if you watch your pets carefully, you will learn many pretty facts of natural history; and it would do you good, and please us, if you would write us about their habits, what food they like best, and how they behave. If your communications are brief enough, we shall gladly print them.

Then as spring comes on—and it will come very soon to some of you in the South—watch for the first spring flowers, the sweet trailing arbutus, the pretty violets and wind-flowers, the crocuses, and other early spring blossoms, and tell us when you find them, and in what pretty corner they were nestled in the woods, among bushes by the old stone wall, or in the open sunny field. Let us see what little girl or boy will find the first willow "pussies." And you will all be interested to learn how much earlier the spring blossoms come to you who live South and West than to you in Maine and Canada.

Then there will be the coming of the birds to watch for—the robins and blue-birds; some of you will see them all winter, and the dear little snow-birds, which sing and hop about so merrily on cold, biting mornings when your own little fingers are half frozen as you scamper to school over the snow crust. Watch all these beautiful things of nature, dear children, and write us whatever you find out from your own personal observation.

In that way our Post-office Box will become a delightful and instructive natural history exchange between the little folks of all sections of the country. Perhaps, also, the children in England and other lands beyond the sea will now and then favor us with bits of information about their own birds and flowers. You must excuse us for writing so much, leaving not room enough to print half of your own pretty communications.

"Earl" writes from Chicago: "I live on the West Side, and the ponds are frozen strong enough for skating. I have been skating twice at Jefferson Park." That does not look much like hunting for willow "pussies," does it? And perhaps you are laughing, because we remind you of spring now just when you are beginning to plan for skating parties. But willows grow all around the ponds where you skate, and you will never see the bare twigs without wondering how soon you can write and tell us the downy "pussies" have appeared.

I am six years old, and I live in Hastings, Nebraska. I like *Harper's Young People* very much. I have a duck, a chicken, a pig, and a little rat dog whose name is Jip. I would like to know how to teach him to catch rats. He by accident caught one the other day, fastened in the pig-pen fence, and killed it before it got loose.

ARTHUR R. N.

QUINCY, ILLINOIS.

My papa takes your paper for their folks, and I like it first rate. The stories in it are very good. It is hard for me to say which I like best. I wish you could see my pet chicken.

MARY E. H.

WILLIE J. M.—In gardens and hot-houses, where they are not liable to accident, toads have been known to attain the age of thirty-five and even forty years. The wonderful stories sometimes told of living toads being found imbedded in solid rock, where they must have been imprisoned for ages, or in the heart of ancient trees, are not well authenticated, and such cases have never come under the observation of scientific men.

NEW YORK CITY.

I am very much obliged to you for telling me how to feed and house my land turtle. I have also three water turtles, one bull-frog, two large toads, and twenty small toads. Please tell me how to feed them. I keep them in a large yard, and I never feed them, so I often wonder how they live. Your paper is getting better every week, and the story about "Phaeton and Nycteris" is about the best you have published.

LYMAN C.

Your toads have found plenty of insects for food in the yard where you keep them. They might be taught to eat sugar, but they prefer a diet of worms, ants, and small bugs. They will probably crawl under a stone or into some hole, and lie numb all winter. Bull-frogs also eat worms and insects, and very large ones are said to eat even small animals, such as mice and snakes. Water turtles eat the stems of water-weeds and small mollusks, but they can live a long time without food. They might eat bits of bread. You can try and see. Both they and your bull-frog would be grateful if you gave them a tank of water to swim in.

WELCOME letters are acknowledged from Mamie T., Orange, New Jersey; Althea B., Macon City, Missouri; F. Coggswell, Hudson, Wisconsin; H. W. Singer, Cincinnati, Ohio; Ernest B. C., Shelbyville, Tennessee; Willie E. H., Hartford, Connecticut; and Dorsey Cassie, Wabash, Indiana.

HOW TO MAKE A CHEAP SLED.

Procure a long, narrow boy, lay him on his back, and fasten ropes to his legs, and your sled is ready for use.

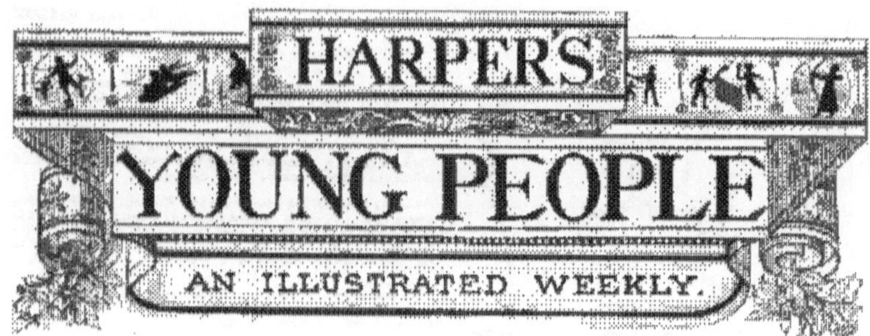

VOL. I.—NO. 11. | PUBLISHED BY HARPER & BROTHERS, NEW YORK. | PRICE FOUR CENTS.
Tuesday, January 13, 1880. | $1.50 per Year, in Advance.

JEANIE LOWRIE, THE YOUNG IMMIGRANT.

BY MISS F. E. FRYATT.

IT was early winter evening at Castle Garden, the scores of gas jets that light the vast rotunda dimly showing the great hall deserted by all the bustling throngs of the morning, save the few women and children clustered around the glowing stove, and closely watched by the keen-eyed officials who smoked and chatted within the railings near them.

Sitting apart from these, taking no notice of the gambols of the children, was a wee lassie of perhaps eight summers, her round, childish face drawn with trouble, and her great blue eyes brimful of tears. She was evidently expecting somebody, for her gaze was fixed on the door beyond, which seemed never to open.

It was little Jeanie Lowrie waiting for her grandfather's return. Old Sandy Lowrie, thinking to take advantage of their stay overnight in New York to visit his foster-son, who had left Scotland for America when a lad, had gone out in the afternoon into the great city, bidding Jeanie carefully guard their small luggage—a few treasures tied up in a silken kerchief, and Granny's precious umbrella, which was a sort of heirloom in the family.

JEANIE AND THE UMBRELLA.

While the great crowd surged to and fro, and the winter sunlight flooded the room, Jeanie had been content to watch and wait, half pleased and half frightened at the shouts and noises that fill the place on steamer day; but when the men, women, and children all went away, by twos and threes, save a few, and silence came with the increasing darkness, and the dim gas jets were lighted overhead, her heart, oppressed by a thousand fears, sank within her, and she fell to sobbing bitterly.

Now there were not wanting kind hearts in the little groups around the stove; for there was Mary Dennett, with her five laddies, going to join her husband at the mines in Maryland; and Janet Brown, her neighbor, with her three rosy lassies; and Jessie Lawson, with her wee Davie; and not one of these three would see a child suffering without offering consolation. Kind Janet soon had her folded in motherly arms in spite of the bundle and the great umbrella, which the lassie stoutly refused to part with for a moment; and Mary Dennett, crossing over to the counter on the far side of the room, bought her cakes and apples; while the children, not to be outdone, made shy endeavors to beguile her into their innocent play.

But to each and all of these Jeanie turned a deaf ear, moaning constantly: "I want my ain, ain gran'daddie; he has gaun awa', an' left me alane. Oh, gran'daddie, cam back to your Jeanie!"

The evening wore on into night, and still no Sandy came to comfort Jeanie; but there came that great consoler, sleep. Soon she slumbered in Janet's arms, and the kind soul, fearing to waken her, held her there till the beds for the little company were spread on the floor; then she laid Jeanie tenderly down, with her treasures still clasped in her arms, and covering her, stooped to print a warm kiss on the round tear-stained cheek, not forgetting to breathe a prayer for the missing Sandy's safe return.

The snow glistened on the walks and grass-plats of the park without; the wind roared down the streets and whistled among the bare branches of the trees, and rushing along, heaped up the waters in huge billows, dashing them against the great stone pier; men passed to and fro, but Sandy came not, for far off in the great city he had lost his way.

In vain he had asked every one to tell him where his foster-son Alec Deans lived. Meeting only laughter or rebuffs, he tried in the growing darkness to find his way back to Castle Garden, but could not. No one seemed to understand him, or cared to; so at last, worn out in mind and body, he sank down on the stone steps of a house, unable to proceed a step further.

Bright and early the next morning at Castle Garden the women were roused from their sleep, for the beds must be rolled up, and the place cleared for the business of the day, and all must be ready for the early train.

In the confusion of preparing the children for breakfast and the journey, the women had forgotten Jeanie for the time, till suddenly Janet, spying her, with her bundle and her umbrella, standing and casting troubled, wistful glances at the door, ran over and brought her to where the women and children were drinking coffee from great cups, and eating rolls of brown-bread and butter. Seating her in the midst of them, she said, "Eat a bit o' the bannock, dearie. Gran'daddie will cam back wi' a braw new bonnet for Jeanie, and then we'll a' gang awa' i' the train together."

"I dinna want a bonnet," cried Jeanie; "I on'y want gran'daddie."

"Dinna greet, bairnie; he'll no leave ye lang noo."

But the old man, contrary to their hopes, failed to appear, so there was a troubled consultation among the women regarding Jeanie. They had all lived neighbors to the Lowries, a mile or so beyond the dike which is a stone's-throw from the duke's palace, near Hamilton; the "gudemen" of their families, hearing great reports of the mines in America, and the times being hard for miners at home, had gone out to verify them, Angus Lowrie among the rest. All four had prospered, and now sent for their wives and bairnies. Young Lowrie, however, was doomed to the bitter sorrow of never more seeing the bonny wife he had left behind him, for a fever had carried her off in her prime; so that Jeanie, her bairn, was left to the sole care of her grandfather, who loved her tenderly, as the old are wont to love the young.

While the women were in the midst of their dilemma, half resolved to carry off the "lane bairnie" privately, lest the officers should interfere, the superintendent, seeing some trouble was afoot, came over and soon settled the matter, for there was a law on the subject that he was bound to obey.

But we are quite forgetting old Sandy all this time. Seeing that he was lost, and there was no help for it, that he should sit down in the particular spot he did was a peculiar stroke of good fortune, for it was the very house he had been seeking, and what was most wonderful, just at that moment the door above opened, and down came Alec Deans in time to hear Sandy's faint cry, "God help my puir Jeanie!"

Alec Deans had not heard the dear Scottish accent in many a year, so straightway that sound went to his very heart-strings, making them thrill and tingle with a joy that was as suddenly turned to pain, when, stooping down, he found the old man fallen back as one dead.

With little ado—for Sandy was small and thin—he lifted him bodily, carried him up the steps, and rang a peal which soon brought his wife to the door. Placing the old man on a sofa in the warm sitting-room where the light fell on his poor, pale face, Alec Deans in a moment recognized his foster-father, and set to work to restore him. The long stormy passage, and the trials incident to emigrant life on shipboard, added to the fatigue and fright of his night's wanderings, had so told on the old man's feeble frame, that after much effort on the part of Alec Deans to revive him, he could do no more than move restlessly, murmuring, "Puir Jeanie! Puir wee bairnie Jeanie!"

Before he could well tell his story, the most of it became known to his foster-son, for the Commissioners, finding he did not return to Castle Garden, sending Jeanie weeping away to the Refuge on Ward's Island, and notifying the police, advertised the missing man in the papers.

It was on the second day after Sandy's falling into such good hands that Alec, reading the morning paper at his breakfast table, saw the advertisement describing Sandy to the very Glengarry cap he wore on his head when missing.

In short order he made his way to the Rotunda at Castle Garden, told the old man's adventure, and obtained a permit to bring Jeanie away from the Refuge.

There was an hour to spare before the little steamboat *Fidelity* would start for Ward's Island, so Alec, being a thoughtful man, employed it in purchasing a pretty fur hat and tippet and some warm mittens, lest Jeanie should suffer from cold, for it was a bitter day to sail down the East River.

When Alec, arriving at his destination, was taken into the long school-room, and saw the sad pale-faced little creatures bending wearily over their lessons, stopping only to lift timid glances to his friendly face, as if they would gladly pour out their little hearts to him, he was filled with a great pity and a sharp regret that he could not take the wee things away with him, and give them each the shelter of as happy a home as that in which his own Phemie bloomed and flourished.

"Jeanie Lowrie, step this way; you are wanted," exclaimed a teacher.

Poor Jeanie, as she came reluctantly forward with downcast eyes, looked as if she feared some new disaster. Pale and dejected, could this be the blooming lassie who so short a time since parted with her grandfather!

"Jeanie," said Alec, softly, "I've come to take you to your gran'daddie. Here's some warm things; put them on, and get ready."

"Oh, sir, may I gang awa' frae here to see my ain, ain gran'daddie ance mair?" cried the lassie, the glow of a great joy dawning on her pale face and lighting her eyes.

"Yes, Jeanie," said Alec, brokenly, "home with my Phemie: he's there. There, do not cry; the trouble is all over," said Alec, soothingly, carrying her away in his arms, and trying to stay the sobs that convulsed her small body.

Arrived at Castle Garden, a new surprise awaited him and Jeanie, for who should be there, pacing up and down in his strong impatience to see the bairnie, but Angus Lowrie. He had left his Southern cottage, which was prepared for their arrival, and hastened on to know the fate of Sandy and Jeanie. And now he had his darling in his strong arms, and so great was his joy that he could do little but press her to his breast, then hold her off and look into her eyes again and again, seeing mirrored there the eyes of his girl-wife Elsie, whom he had loved with a love he would bear to his grave.

And now they must hasten to the dear old father who had braved the perils of the wintry deep that he might bring Elsie's one and only treasure to her husband, little recking that, far away from kith and kin, he should lay his old bones in a foreign land. If sorrow had had power to steal the roses from Jeanie's cheek, joy planted new and fairer ones there; and never did a brighter light dance in the blue eyes than when, a little later, with a soft sound of rapture, she flung her arms around Sandy's neck, crying, "My ain, ain gran'daddie, ye s'all never, never leave me ony mair!" Jeanie's presence did more to set old Sandy on his feet again than all the physic in the world; so in a few days the happy trio were whirling off to the mining village in Maryland, where they are living and prospering to-day.

LADY PRIMROSE.

BY FLETCHER READE.

CHAPTER I.

"As it fell upon a day
In the merry month of May."

IT was a long, long time ago that it happened—so long, in fact, that most people have forgotten all about it—but once upon a time, as the old, old stories tell, there lived in the village of Hollowbush an old woman and a little girl.

And other people lived there too; but that does not concern us. The old woman, plain and brown and wrinkled though she was, was the wisest and kindest old lady anywhere to be found, which is reason enough for her being in the story; and as for the little girl, you have already guessed that she is Lady Primrose; but how she came to be Lady Primrose is what makes the story.

The village of Hollowbush was as pretty a place as you would care to see—a quiet, quaint little town, where the grass ran up and down the streets in a wild, free way it had, to which no one thought of objecting; but as year after year went by, and the little girl who lived there grew older without, unfortunately, growing wiser, she became so tired of Hollowbush and its grass-grown streets that she was almost ready to run away.

"If I were only rich," she was constantly saying to herself, "then I might go where I chose."

Now it came to pass that one day in the merry spring-time, when the world is so sweet and fragrant that you can hardly put your nose out-of-doors without feeling as if you had tumbled head-foremost into a huge bouquet, this little girl sat by the open window, wishing and wishing with all her might that she were rich.

"For then," she said to herself, "I could have a diamond necklace; and perhaps," she added, aloud, "I might have a jewelled coronet, like a queen."

Just then the wise old woman of Hollowbush, who had the amiable peculiarity of appearing just when people most needed her, stopped before the window, and said, as she looked up at her young friend, "You were wishing for a diamond necklace, my child. What would you do if I should tell you of a country where diamonds are as plenty as flowers are here?"

"What would I do?"—and the child laughed at the idea of there being but one thing she could do.

"I would go to it at once, and fill my hands with the shining, beautiful things. But you don't mean that there really is such a place," she added, after a pause.

The old lady smiled, and said, "If you really love gems better than anything else in the world, I can tell you where to find all and more than all you want."

"That would be impossible," answered the child. "I could never have more than enough. But what a beautiful country it must be! Do tell me where to find it."

Still smiling, this wonderful old lady, who knew all manner of strange secrets, called the child to her, and having whispered in her ear, pointed in the direction of the woods just beyond the village.

The girl's face looked serious, as if she were perhaps a little frightened at what the old lady had told her; but if she could get all the jewels she wanted, it was worth more than one fright, she thought; so off she started without a word.

The shy little blossoms that hide their faces from the sunlight grew here and there in the woods.

White star-flowers and purple hepaticas nodded on their slender stems, while the crimson and white wood-sorrel fairly ran wild, creeping in and out through bush and brier, like a host of fairies in striped petticoats.

"A nice place enough," said the child, tossing her head, "for those who know of nothing better; but I can't stop to admire such simple things. Gems and jewels are the only flowers I care for."

The shadows were growing longer and deeper all around her, for the sun was almost down, and as she looked up through the trees she could see the pale face of the young moon peeping down at her through the branches.

"Oh, if the wise old woman had only come with me!" said the child, in a whisper. The shadows took on strange, ghostly shapes, and the tall pine-trees, so high that their topmost branches seemed to rest against the sky, sang softly and slowly and all together,

"Take care—take care—oh—oh—ough."

She had never realized before how full of sounds the stillness of the deep woods may be, and it seemed to her as if the rustling of the leaves and the singing of the wind were strange unearthly voices calling out to her and warning her to go back. But in spite of the rustling leaves and the mournful sighing of the pines the little girl hurried on. Perhaps, just because of them, she hurried all the faster, for she felt quite sure that she was nearing the place to which she had been directed. And in a few moments she saw just before her the gray moss-grown rocks piled one above another which the wise old woman of Hollowbush had described, and heard far below the rushing and tumbling of a brook.

Surely I must have been deceived! she thought.

Here was no strange country sown with jewels, but simply a rocky ravine, where ferns waved in the wind, clinging to the rocks, and catching the spray from the water as it bubbled and hissed and fell in a snowy pool below.

"This can't be the place," said the child, as she looked around; "but while I am here I may as well see what it is."

So she clambered over the loose stones and decaying logs till she reached the level of the stream, and there, strangely enough, scattered among broken bits of granite, were small bright stones of a deep wine-color. "These are not diamonds," she said to herself, "but they are too pretty to lie neglected here, whatever they may be."

She gathered them one by one, tying her handkerchief into four knots at the corners for a basket; and so absorbed was she that she had quite forgotten the weird shadows and the strange noises in the wood, until she was startled by a voice close beside her.

Her heart gave a sudden bound, as if it were going to jump away from her without so much as saying by your leave, and turning quickly, she saw, not the old woman—although the voice had sounded curiously like hers—but a quaint pale-faced little man, with small faded-looking blue eyes that blinked in the moonlight as if the brightest of June-day suns had been shining upon him.

"So you are fond of gems, my little maiden?" said the small man, in a small thin voice, winking and blinking good-naturedly as he spoke.

"SO YOU ARE FOND OF GEMS, MY LITTLE MAIDEN?"

The child stood staring at her companion, too much astonished to answer him a word, for she, nor you, nor I, I believe, had ever seen such a curious being before. He was so small that she could have tucked him under her arm and run away with him, but his pale blue eyes had a strange light in them, like nothing seen above the ground, and she might have gone on staring at him from that day to this if her handkerchief had not slipped from her fingers, letting her stones roll here and there over the ground, whereupon she uttered a low cry of disappointment.

"Oh, never mind those," said the little man, smiling; "they are nothing but garnets. Just come with me, and I will show you stones a thousand times more beautiful."

"Do you live in the country where gems grow instead of flowers?" said the child, recovering her voice and her self-possession at the same time.

"Yes," he answered; "I am the keeper of the gate, and if you will come with me, I will show you more beautiful things than any you ever dreamed of."

This invitation was just what the child wanted, and she followed the gate-keeper without another word.

What a strange place it was, this country of his into which he was leading her! It was so dark that she could see nothing but gleaming lights shining through the darkness, red and yellow and green and crimson, like tiny magic lanterns hung at intervals high above her head against the wall.

She began to perceive that they were going deep down under the earth, and she shivered, partly with cold and partly with fear, as she stepped carefully and slowly over the uneven path down which she and her guide were descending.

"Is it far we have to go?" she asked at length, rather timidly.

"Oh no," answered her companion. "This is simply a long corridor that runs through the base of the hills, but we have almost reached the end of it. In a few moments I shall lead you into the presence-chamber of the king."

"The king!" echoed the child, hardly knowing whether to be frightened or pleased. "And am I to go before a king?"

"Yes, yes," laughed the little man. "You don't suppose we are a people without a king?"

As he spoke he knocked three times against the wall, and a voice from within called out, "Who's there? who's there? who's there?"

"Alarik the gate-keeper," answered her companion, and immediately a door flew open.

[TO BE CONTINUED.]

WILD-BOAR HUNTING IN JAPAN.

BY WILLIAM ELLIOT GRIFFIS.

WINTER is the harvest-time of the Japanese hunter. The snow-covered ground is a great tell-tale, and the deer, bears, rabbits, and wild hogs can be easily tracked. Though the Japanese hunter often uses a matchlock or rifle, his favorite weapons are his long spear and short sword. He covers his head with a helmet made of plaited straw, having a long flap to protect his neck, and keep out the snow or rain. His feet are shod with a pair of sandals made of rice straw, his baggy cotton trousers are bound at the calves with a pair of straw leggings, and in wet weather he puts on a grass rain cloak. To see a group of hunters stalking through the forests in Japan, as I have often seen them, reminds one of bundles of straw out on a tramp.

I once enjoyed a dinner of fresh boar-steak at the house of a famous Japanese hunter named Nakano Kawachi, who lived in a village at the top of a mountain, between the provinces of Omi and Echizen. I had been travelling all the morning on snow-shoes through the forests of Echizen. The snow was full of tracks of deer, hogs, rabbits, woodchucks, weasels, martens, porcupines, monkeys, and ferrets. The hunters were out in force, and their shouts made the forest ring with echoes. Our path lay through a valley, with rocks on either side.

Just as we were within a mile of a village named Tsuné, a wild boar, closely pressed by a man with a spear, rushed down through the woods, and around a huge mass of

SPEARING A WILD BOAR.—From an Original Japanese Drawing.

rocks. The hunter, knowing every inch of the ground, sprang round a shorter curve, and reached the path at the end of the gully just as the boar at full trot leaped down. Levelling his long weapon, with all his might he drove the blade with a terrific lunge between the boar's ribs, just back of the heart. So great was the impetus of the swift animal that the hunter was nearly taken off his feet, while the boar turned a complete somersault. We expected to see the blade of the lance snap, or the handle wrench off; but no, steel and wood were too true. The boar struggled and rolled over the bloody snow, but was helpless to get on his feet again. The hunter quietly drew out the steel, wiped it with a bunch of dead leaves, and then, with equal coolness, drew his sword and severed the jugular vein of the dying boar.

By this time the hunter's two sons, who had helped to start the animal from his lair, came down the hill. Passing two strands of rope made of rice straw around the carcass, they inserted a thick bamboo pole under the withers. Then swinging the pole over their shoulders, they started off on a dog-trot to the village, shouting as they went. We followed them, and when near the village gate heard a bedlam of unearthly yells and whoops of triumph from all the boys and girls of the village, who were proud of their famous hunter. We had entered into conversation with him, and learned that his name was Nakano Kawachi.

Our party, at the invitation of the hunter, entered his house, first taking off our shoes. We all sat round the fire, which was in a great square hearth in the middle of the floor, while the chimney was a gaping black funnel in the ceiling. My party consisted of three of my students from the government school of Fukui, my interpreter, a brave soldier named Inouyé, and my body-servant Sahei. The six mountaineers with huge wide snow-shoes, whom I hired for the size of their feet to beat a path in the snow-drift for our party, remained outside with the villagers. They, with their children, stood in crowds outside to catch a sight of me, as they had never seen an American before.

Our host, first unstrapping his sword, carefully wiped and cleansed his spear, which he stands on its iron butt in the corner. We all sit around the fire, on which turnips and rice are boiling and omelet is frying. All around the ceiling from the smoky rafters hang strings of large dried persimmons, almost as sweet and luscious as figs. These we munch while Nakano cuts tenderloin steaks from half the carcass of a boar which he speared the day before. In a few moments seven hungry travellers are watching the sputtering, sizzling boar-steak as it wafts its appetizing odors everywhere, as it seems, but up the chimney.

"Is this the second wild hog you've speared this winter?" asks Iwabuchi, the interpreter.

"No, your honor," answers Nakano; "the snow began to fall ten days ago, and this is the eighth hog I have killed; but yesterday I speared my first boar this winter."

"How long have you been a hunter?"

"Hai! your honor, ever since I was a boy. I speared my first hog when I was fifteen."

"What do you do with the boar's tusks?"

"Hai! your honor, they are the most valuable part of the animal. I sell them to an agent of an ivory-carving shop in Tokio, who comes through these parts in the spring. The Tokio men carve nétsukés from them. They are not as good as ivory, but they do for bimbo [poor men]. My own nétsuké is of boar's tusk."

"Meshi shitaku" (rice is ready), cried the housewife, at this moment, and conversation was suspended. A little table of lacquered wood a foot square and four inches high was set before each man of our party. With chop-sticks for the rice and knives for the boar-steak, we partook of the hunter's fare. The march of eight miles in the frosty air, plodding our way through drifts, and stepping on snow-shoes, which furnished good exercise for our legs, had made us ravenously hungry. When full, and all had said "Mo yoroshio" (even enough) to the polite girls who waited on us, we walked out to the front, where a gaping crowd gazed at the American white-face, as if they were at Barnum's, and he was the Tattooed Man. I rushed at them, pretending to catch the children, when they scattered like sheep. In their fright they tumbled over each other, until a dozen or more were sprawling on the snow or had tumbled head-foremost in the drifts. A smile, and the distribution of some sugared cakes of peas and barley, made them good friends again. After an hour's rest we bade the hunter, the villagers, and our snow-shoe men good-by, and resumed our journey in single file over the mountains to Tokio.

SEEKING HIS FORTUNE

BY MRS. W. J. HAYS.

A BOY sat whistling on a fence. He was a lad of twelve years, and worked at all sorts of odd chores on the river farm, which sent most of its produce down to the city on the barges which one sees on the Hudson River, headed by little steam-tugs, and which are commonly called "tows." This boy, Tom Van Wyck, was a poor

was somewhat cleaner, a
his gaze. There was so
himself until hunger ag
was most inviting—raw
boiled eggs, salad, string
of pies. He went in at
"Fifty cents," was the r
countenance and well-oil

Tom glanced at his p
possessed, so he turned a
other window of the sam
and the viands staler; a
beer bottles, was a queer
empty oyster shells. He
so hungry, that a man al
was not meant to be unki
"Vat for you comes here
Ve vant some one to op
one supper here to-nigh
If you can do the vork,
meal." Tom hardly und
aided him, and putting
on the cellar steps. Tal

him and passed on. This was not very promising. It was now late in the day, and he was far from the steam-boat landing. He knew nobody, and was just wondering where he should pass the night, when a boy with a box strung by a leathern strap over his shoulder jostled him. He was a rough fellow, about his own age, but there was a twinkle in his eye which emboldened Tom to speak to him.

"Do you know where I can get any work to do?"

The boy put his fingers aside of his nose, winked violently, and made a grimace, but said nothing.

"I'm in earnest," said Tom. "I want work badly."

"Yes, in my eye!" was the response, regarding Tom's more decent apparel.

"Oh, but I do. What is your trade?"

"Now see here, feller-citizen, if you've any idea of comin' on my beat, I jist warn ye ye'd better git at once," and he shook his fist in Tom's face to make the reply more emphatic.

"But I have not," said Tom, anxiously. "I only want work of some sort, and a decent lodging. I'm just from the country, and don't know a soul in this town; besides, I've hurt my hand, and it pains a good deal."

"Let's see. I'm a crack doctor on all the fellers' cuts."

Tom unbound his hand, and the youthful Æsculapius gazed at it with great interest.

"That 'll knock you up yet," was the comforting diagnosis, with a wise shake of the head. "Bad place to git a cut. Jim Jones had one jist in that spot, and it festered, and hurt him so he had to go to the hospital."

"Pshaw!" said Tom.

"Ye'd better get yer granny to poultice it."

"I tell you I don't know a human being in this city, and I haven't an idea where I am going to sleep to-night."

The boy surveyed him doubtfully.

"You might go to the station-house."

"Not if I know it," said Tom, whose visions of grandeur, though dimmer, were not to be brought down so low.

"Then there's the Newsboys' Lodging-House."

"Could I get in there? But I don't know the way."

"Come along with me; I'll show yer. I sleep there most o' the time."

This was, indeed, unforeseen good fortune, and Tom embraced it heartily. As they walked along, Tim got out of him his whole story; and when it was finished, he said to him: "You were a big fool to leave a good home and try your luck here. For one that swims, a hundred sinks. Why, half the time I'm hungry, and the way we fellers gits knocked about is jist awful."

They reached the Lodging-House, and Tom, with his companion's aid, registered his name, got his ticket, and secured a bed. He was so tired he could hardly speak, and the pain in his hand was increasing. In the morning his friend had gone. The matron seeing his suffering dressed his hand, and led him on to tell her who he was and what was his errand to the city. Kindly and patiently, she pointed out to him the great wrong of his beginning, the wickedness of leaving his aunt in ignorance of his whereabouts, the mistake of supposing that it was an easy matter to work one's way up from obscurity to places of trust and honor; that if his endeavors were sanctioned by those in authority over him, and kind friends were willing to assist him and procure him occupation, he yet would find that it would only be by patient labor and constant effort that he could maintain himself, and that larks ready cooked no longer dropped into open mouths. All this and more came home to the sorrowful Tom with great force, for the dirt and jargon of the city were to him very distasteful. His castles were crumbling as he wended his way again to the docks. It was a weary time he had to find the boat which would carry him back, and it was with a grieved spirit that he found himself again at the door of the little red house by the hill. Grieved and weary and hungry, Aunt Maria, whose eyes were red with weeping, perceived him to be, and with wonderful wisdom she kept down her questions, and silently made him comfortable. Little Jane was full of curiosity, and more than one neighbor put their heads in to have a word to say.

A year afterward, as Tom, Ned Green, and Jonas were busy husking corn in the calm stillness of the fall, when the stacks were all about them, like Indian wigwams, and the stubble only of the golden pumpkins was left in the field, and the beautiful river wound itself away in the distance, bearing all kinds of craft, Tom told them about his day in the city, and said he had concluded that the country was good enough for him, and he meant to be a farmer all the days of his life.

A GREAT CATHEDRAL.

I REMEMBER well, when a child, hearing the Cathedral of St. Peter, in Rome, spoken of as being so immense that I thought of an ideal cathedral little less than a mountain in size, and the dome to be seen only as if looking at the stars. When the real cathedral was seen, of course that exaggerated idea had then long been tempered to something like the reality. Yet it was not without a certain pleasure to find that to get a good view, particularly of the dome, it was necessary for me to go from it several miles—to the Pincian hill, or a terrace of the beautiful Villa Doria-Pamfili. The latter view is one of the finest, as nothing else of all Rome is seen. The cathedral stands on the site of Nero's Circus, where many Christians were martyred, and where the Apostle Peter is said to have been buried after his crucifixion. In the year 90 an oratory was built there, and in 306 Emperor Constantine erected a church. It was the grandest of that time, and exceeded in size all existing cathedrals except two, yet was only half the size of the present building.

This cathedral was begun in 1506, and after forty years all the foundations were not built. Then Michael Angelo, though seventy-two years old, was persuaded to be the architect. His predecessor had wasted four years in making a model of the proposed edifice, at a great cost, but he, with marvellous energy, completed his model in a fortnight. Though the work went rapidly on, he knew he could not live to see his cathedral finished, and he patiently made a wooden model of the great dome of exact proportions. From this model his idea was carried out. Twenty popes came and went, pressing the work to completion; eighteen architects planned and replanned, and expended $100,000,000, brought from the four quarters of the globe; and a hundred and fifty years rolled around before St. Peter's was finished. Sixtus V. employed six hundred men, night and day, ceaselessly at work upon the dome.

The cathedral was consecrated on the 18th of November, 1626, the thirteen-hundredth anniversary of a similar rite in the first cathedral. It covers 212,321 square feet of ground, nearly twice the area of the next largest cathedral, that of Milan, which is a little larger than St. Paul's, of London. Its length is about equal to two ordinary city blocks, its width to that of a short block, and its total height that of a long block, or a little less than the height of the Great Pyramid of Egypt. The circumference of the base of the dome is such that two hundred ten-year-old boys and girls clasped hand to hand would just about stretch around it. The dome rests upon four buttresses, each seventy feet thick, and above them runs a frieze carved in letters as high as a man. Then, one above another, are four galleries, from the lower one of which a fine view of the inside of the church can be had.

The little black things seen crawling on the pavement away down below are grown men and women. The whole inside of the dome is of mosaic work, and set in this are mosaics of the evangelists—colossal figures, you may know, as the pen which St. Luke holds is seven feet long.

The roof of the cathedral is reached by means of an easy slope, up which one could ride on a donkey. Emerging on the roof, all Rome is seen, the country from the mountains, and the blue Mediterranean Sea in the distance. The roof holds a number of small domes, and dwellings for the workmen and custodians, who live there with their families. But stranger still is a fountain fed from the rain caught upon the roof. There we would be as high as the top of many church steeples, but away above us, like a whole mountain, would rise the dome, with a little copper ball on the summit. If our courage and knees did not fail us, we would ascend to that ball by staircases between the internal and external walls of the dome, and find it large enough to hold a score of persons.

So vast is the cathedral's interior that it has an atmosphere of its own—in winter slowly losing the heat of the preceding summer, and in summer slowly warming up for another winter. In cold weather the poor of Rome go there for comfort, as a Roman winter sometimes brings frosty days and ice. A traveller says he once saw a great sheet of ice around the fountain before the cathedral, and some little Romans awkwardly sliding on it. For the sake of doing what he never thought to do in Rome, he took a slide with them. The mosaic pictures, statues, and monuments are almost numberless, and the pavement of colored marble stretches away from the doors like a large polished field. Formerly, on Easter and June 29, the dome, façade, and the colonnades of the cathedral were illuminated in the early evening by the light of between four and five thousand lamps. It was called the silver illumination, and is described as having been very grand and delicate. Suddenly, on a given signal, four hundred men, stationed at their posts, exchanged the lamps for lighted pitch in iron pans fastened to the ribs of the dome. Then the dome shone afar as a splendid flaming crown of light.

THE LYNX.

AN ugly and savage member of the great cat family is the lynx, a creature very numerous in Canada and in the wild forests of our most northern States. It is found all over Northern Europe as well, and in Germany and Switzerland; a smaller variety, called the swamp lynx, is also an inhabitant of Persia, Syria, and some portions of Egypt.

The Canada lynx is a beast about three feet long, with a short stubbed tail, and might easily be mistaken for a large wild-cat. Its fur, which is short and very thick, and of a beautiful silver gray, is much used for muffs, tippets, and fur trimming. The lynx is a cowardly beast, and seldom attacks anything larger than hares, squirrels, and birds. It will sometimes rob a sheep-fold, as the gentle and pretty lambs have no means of defense against its terrible claws.

It is very much hunted for its valuable fur, and some years thousands of these beautiful skins are sent to market. The ears are very curious, having a tuft of bristling hair on the very point; indeed, this ear ornament is a distinguishing characteristic of all the varieties of the lynx tribe.

The large and powerful dogs which are found in Canada and the northern portions of Michigan, Minnesota, and other border States, where they are used as train dogs to drag the mail sledges over vast wastes of snow during the winter, are natural enemies of the lynx, and pursue it furiously through the snow-bound forests. Their loud barking often warns the hunter before he himself catches sight of the game that the desired prize is treed, and awaits its fate, with arched back and fur bristling, after the manner of an enraged cat.

The Canada lynx is a very stupid beast, and easily trapped—a method of catching it generally adopted by the Hudson Bay Company, as in this way its beautiful fur is uninjured by bullets.

The European lynx is a much larger, stronger, and more ferocious beast than its Canadian brother. Its great hairy paws are like those of the lion and tiger, which, strange as it may seem, are also members of the pussy-cat family. It lives in wild Siberian forests (where large numbers of trappers subsist on the proceeds of its valuable fur), in Norway and Sweden, in Switzerland, and also in other countries where wild forests exist. Vast numbers roam through the steppes of Asia and the uninhabited portions of the Eastern world.

So much is this creature dreaded in Switzerland for its depredations on the flocks that the shepherds whose sheep feed on the mountain pastures do all in their power to exterminate this cruel enemy of their fold, and a prize is offered by the government for every one killed.

Driven by hunger, the European lynx will often attack deer and other large animals. A story is told of a lynx in Norway which, much against its will, was forced to take a furious ride on the back of a goat. The winter had been very severe, and failing to find food in the forests and rocky barrens, a young lynx spied a flock of goats feeding among the dry stubble of a field. Giving a quick spring, it landed on the back of a large goat, with the purpose of tearing open the arteries of its neck—its method of killing large animals. But the goat, feeling its unwelcome rider, set out at a gallop for the farm-yard, followed by the whole herd, all bleating in concert. The claws of the lynx had become so entangled in the heavy beard of its intended victim that escape was impossible, and the farmer by a skillfully aimed shot put an end to its life.

Patience is largely developed in the lynx. It will lie stretched out for hours on a branch of a tree, watching for its prey. If anything approaches, it crouches and springs. Should the rabbit or bird escape, the lynx never pursues, but slyly creeps back to its branch, and resumes its patient watch.

When captured very young, lynxes may be tamed, and have been known to live on friendly terms with domestic animals, such as dogs and cats. But they are never healthy away from their native woods, and usually die in a short time. Even in the wild state the lynx is short-lived, and is said rarely to reach the age of fifteen years. In confinement the lynx never thrives. Specimens kept in menageries never become friendly, but grow sullen and suspicious. Spending the day in sleep, at night they walk

restlessly up and down their cage, giving vent to hideous howls and yells.

The glistening, piercing eyes of the lynx were formerly the subject of strange superstitions. In the days of Pliny it was known to the Romans by the same name it still bears. Specimens were first brought to Rome from Gaul (the country now called France), and so terrible was the glaring eye that it was said to be able to look through a stone wall as through glass, and to penetrate the darkest mysteries. Hence, no doubt, the expression "lynx-eyed," which is so often used to indicate keen and sharp watchfulness from which nothing can escape.

THE DEAD-LETTER OFFICE.

BY MRS. F. L. COLLINS.

OF course, dear readers, all of you have heard of the Dead-letter Office at Washington, and I suppose you have the same vague idea that I had until I went there and learned better—that it is a place where letters are sent when they fail to reach those for whom they are intended, and are thence returned to the writers. Really, now, I believe this is what most grown-up people think too; but in truth, it is such a wonderful place that I am sure you will be surprised when I tell you of some of the things you may find there, and I think when you come to Washington it will be one of the first places you will wish to visit.

Probably you have never written a great many letters, and I do not doubt that each one had its envelope neatly addressed by your father or mother, while you stood by to see that it was well done. I hope, too, that in due time your letters had the nice replies they deserved. You would have been much disappointed if any of them had been "lost in the mail," as people say, wouldn't you? You will not forget your stamp, I am sure, after I have related the following incident:

There was once a little girl, only ten years old, who was spending six months in the city of New York, just previous to sailing for Europe. Her heart was filled with love for her darling grandpapa, whom she had left in New Orleans, and she wrote to him twice every week. Her letters were in the French language; at least, the one that I saw was, and it began "Cher Grandpère cheri." She said, "I hope that you have received the slippers I embroidered for you, and the fifteen dollars I sent in my last letter to have them made." But, alas! the package containing the slippers had reached the "cher grandpère cheri," while the letter and money were missing. Then this old gentleman wrote to the Dead-letter Office, and said that it was the only one of his granddaughter's letters he had ever failed to receive; that it could not have been misdirected; and his carrier had been on the same route for many years, so he *knew* him to be honest; therefore the money must have been mysteriously swallowed up in the D. L. O.

What was to be done? Do you imagine the Dead-letter Office shook in its shoes?

Not a bit of it. It turned to a big book, and found a number which stood opposite the little girl's letter, and then straightway laid hands upon the letter itself, and forwarded it to the indignant "grandpère."

Now why all this trouble and delay, and saying of naughty things to the D. L. O., without which he might never have seen either his letter or his money? Simply this: the dear child had dropped her letter into the box *without a stamp.*

You will be surprised to learn that something over four millions of letters are sent to the Dead-letter Office every year.

There are three things that render them liable to this: first, being unclaimed by persons to whom they are addressed; second, when some important part of the address is omitted, as James Smith, Maryland; third, the want of postage. All sealed letters must have at least one three-cent stamp, unless they are to be delivered from the same office in which they are mailed, when they must have a one or a two cent stamp, according to whether the office has carriers or not.

For the second cause mentioned above about sixty-five thousand letters were sent to the Dead-letter Office during the past year; for the third, three hundred thousand, and three thousand had no address whatever.

When these letters reach the Dead-letter Office, they are divided into two general classes, viz., Domestic and Foreign, the latter being returned unopened to the countries from which they started.

The domestic letters, after being opened, are classed according to their contents. Those containing money are called "Money Letters;" those with drafts, money-orders, deeds, notes, etc., "Minor Letters;" and such as inclose receipts, photographs, etc., "Sub-Minors." Letters which contain anything, even a postage-stamp, are recorded, and those with money or drafts are sent to the postmasters where the letters were first mailed, for them to find the owners, and get a receipt. From $35,000 to $40,000 come into the office in this way during the year; but a large proportion is restored to the senders, and the remainder is deposited in the United States Treasury to the credit of the Post-office Department.

When letters contain nothing of value, if possible they are returned to the writers. There are clerks so expert in reading all kinds of writing that they can discern a plain address where ordinary eyes could not trace a word. For instance, you could not make much of this:

A dead-letter clerk at once translates it:

Mr. Hennison King,
Tobacco Stick,
Dorchester County,
Maryland.

In haste.

And such spelling! Would you ever imagine that Galveston could be tortured into "Calvesdon," Connecticut into "Kanedikait," and Territory into "Tearteir"?

Recently the Postmaster-General has found it necessary to issue very strict orders about plain addresses, and a great many people have tried to be witty at his expense. I copied this address from a postal card:

Alden Simmons,
Savannah Township,
Ashland County, State of Ohio;
Age 29; Occupation, Lawyer;
Politics, Republican;
Longitude West from Troy 2°;
Street Main
No. 109;
Box 1008.

Color, White;
Sex, Male;
Ancestry, Domestic.
For President 1880, U. S. Grant!

About once in two years there is a sale of the packages which are detained in the office for the same reason that

System, punctuality, industry, belong to the Dead-letter Office. It seems to embrace every other branch of business, and, as I have shown you, even to know how to treat such unwelcome guests as a nest of live serpents.

HOW MOTHER ROBIN CALLED A NEW MATE

BY E. JAY EDWARDS

CHARLEY BENNET'S GHOST STORY.

BY MRS. MARGARET EYTINGE.

"IT is a sin to steal a pin,
As well as any greater thing."

sang little Al Smith, in a loud, shrill voice.

"Very good sentiment, but very poor rhyme," drawled Hen Rowe (whose father was a poet), patting the singer's flaxen head in a patronizing manner.

"Talking of stealing," said Charley Bennet, dropping the pumpkin he was turning into a lantern, "did I ever tell you fellers about the time I went down to old Pop Robins's to steal apples, and came back past the barn where the horse-thief hung himself years and years ago, 'cause he knew the constables—they called 'em constables in those times—were after him, and that he'd be hung by somebody else if he didn't? No! Here's a ghost story for you, then, and I hope it will be a warning to you all never to take anything that doesn't belong to you, 'specially apples.

"You see, Billy Evans and I were staying with our folks at the hotel in Bramblewood that summer, and about two miles away was Pop Robins's farm. He used to bring eggs and chickens and vegetables and fruit to the hotel; and, oh my! wasn't he stingy!—you'd better believe it. He wouldn't even give you two or three blackberries, and if you asked him for an apple, he'd tremble all over. A reg'lar old miser *he* was, with lots of money, and a bully apple orchard. 'Let's go there some night and help ourselves,' says Billy Evans, one day. 'Dogs,' says I. 'Only one,' says he; 'I know him, and so do you—old Snaggletooth; I gave him almost all the meat we took for crab bait the day we didn't catch any.' 'All right,' says I.

"'THERE IT IS,' SAYS BARNEY."

"But when the night we'd agreed on came, Billy had cousins—girls—down from New York, and he had to stay home and entertain them. I don't care much for girls myself, and I was afraid they might want me to help entertain them too, so I made up my mind to go down to Pop Robins's alone. It was a splendid night; the moon shone so bright that it was almost as light as day. I scudded along, whistling away, until I got within half a mile of the orchard, and then I stopped my noise and walked as softly as possible, till I came to the first apple-tree. I shinned up that tree in a jiffy (old Snaggletooth didn't put in an appearance), filled my bag with jolly fat apples, and slid down again. But when I came to lift the bag up on my shoulder, I found it was awful heavy to carry so far, and I was just agoing to dump some of the apples out, when I remembered all of a sudden that if I cut across the meadow to the plank-road, I could get back to the hotel in a little more than half the time it would take to go the way I came.

"So I shouldered my load, and was nearly across the meadow before I thought of the haunted barn at the end of it. It wasn't a nice thing to remember; but I wasn't agoing to turn back, ghost or no ghost, and I tried to whistle again, when all at once that thing Al Smith was singing just now popped into my head, and says I to myself, 'That's so, Charles F. Bennet; you and your chums may think it's great fun to help yourselves to other people's apples and water-melons and such things, but it's just as much stealing as though you went into a man's house and stole his coat.' It doesn't seem as bad when you're going for 'em; but when you're coming back, up a lonely road, all alone, at ten o'clock at night, a lot of stolen apples on your back, and a haunted barn not far off, it seems worse.

"All the same, I held on to the apples. And when I faced the barn I determined I'd whistle if I died in the attempt; but, boys, I don't believe anybody could have told *that* 'Yankee Doodle' from 'Auld Lang Syne.' I tell you my heart jumped when I passed the tumble-down old place; but it *stood still* when, as I marched up the plank-road, I heard a step behind me. I wheeled around in an instant, but there was nothing to be seen. The moon shone as bright as ever, but there was nothing to be seen! 'I must have imagined it,' says I to myself, and I walked a little faster, listening with all my might, and sure enough pat, pat, pat, came the step after me. Again I wheeled round. Not a thing did I see. And again I started on, the apples growing heavier and heavier. Pat, pat, pat, came the step. It wasn't like a human step. That made it more dreadful. 'It *must* be the ghost,' I thought; and I don't mind telling you, fellers, I never was so frightened in my life. The time I fell overboard was nothing to it. I made up my mind, when I reached the bridge that crossed a little brook near our hotel, I'd streak it (I hadn't exactly run yet, for I was saving my strength till the last). But before I got to the bridge, says I to myself—and I must have said it out loud, though I didn't mean to—'Perhaps he wants the apples.'

"'Apples!' repeated a hoarse voice, with a horrid laugh.

"I tell you, boys, those apples flew, and I flew too. Over the bridge I went like lightning, and ran right into Barney Reardon, one of the stable-men, who was coming to look for me. 'Something has followed me,' I gasped, 'from the haunted barn—the ghost!' 'Did you see it?' says he. 'No,' says I, 'though I turned round a dozen times to look for it. But I heard it pat, pat, pat, behind me all the way.' 'And it's behind you now,' says Barney, bursting into a loud laugh. I jumped about six feet. 'There it is,' says Barney, roaring again, and pointing to—Pop Robins's tame raven! The sly old thing looked up at me, nodded its shining black head, croaked 'Apples!' and walked off. It had followed me from the barn, and every time I wheeled quickly round, it hopped just as quickly behind me, and so of course I saw nothing but the long road and the moonlight on it. But I never want to be so scared again, and if ever any of you boys go for anything belonging to other people, don't you count me in."

"What became of the apples?" asked Jerry O'Neil.

"If you'd 'a been there I could have told you," said Charley.

THE HOUSE THAT BELL BUILT;

Or, the Sad End of a Little Girl's Romance.

SITTING alone in the fire-light's glare,
This is the house that Bell built.

This is the girl with the golden hair,
That lived in the house that Bell built.

This is the garden fresh and fair,
Where played the girl with the golden hair,
That lived in the house that Bell built.

These are the peaches sweet and rare,
That grew in the garden fresh and fair,
Where played the girl with the golden hair,
That lived in the house that Bell built.

This is the great and terrible bear,
That ate the peaches sweet and rare,
That grew in the garden fresh and fair,

Where played the girl with the golden hair,
That lived in the house that Bell built.

This is the prince with noble air,
Who killed the great and terrible bear,
That ate the peaches sweet and rare,
That grew in the garden fresh and fair,
Where played the girl with the golden hair,
That lived in the house that Bell built.

This is the wedding beyond compare,
In which the prince of noble air,
Who killed the great and terrible bear,
That ate the peaches so sweet and rare,
That grew in the garden fresh and fair,
Married the girl with the golden hair,
That lived in the house that Bell built.

This is the house-maid, Biddy McNair,
With face so red and arms so bare,
Who took the poker without a care,
And slew the prince of noble air,
Who killed the great and terrible bear,
That ate the peaches so sweet and rare,
That grew in the garden fresh and fair,
And married the girl with the golden hair,
That lived in the house that Bell built.

Flower-Pots for Rooms.—Fill a pot with coarse moss of any kind, in the same manner as it would be filled with earth, and place a cutting or a seed in this moss: it will succeed admirably, especially with plants destined to ornament a drawing-room. In such a situation plants grown in moss will thrive better than in garden mould, and possess the very great advantage of not causing dirt by the earth washing out of them when watered. The explanation of the practice seems to be this: that moss rammed into a pot, and subjected to continual watering, is soon brought into a state of decomposition, when it becomes a very pure vegetable mould; and it is well known that very pure vegetable mould is the most proper of all materials for the growth of almost all kinds of plants. The moss would also not retain more moisture than precisely the quantity best adapted to the absorbent powers of the root—a condition which can scarcely be obtained with any certainty by the use of earth.

The Advantages of Foreign Tongues.—In the *Letters of Charles Dickens*, recently published, occurs this pleasant child's story: "I heard of a little fellow the other day whose mamma had been telling him that a French governess was coming over to him from Paris, and had been expatiating on the blessings and advantages of having foreign tongues. After leaning his plump little cheek against the window-glass in a dreary little way for some minutes, he looked round, and inquired in a general way, and not as if it had any special application, whether she didn't think 'that the tower of Babel was a great mistake altogether.'"

Vancouver, Washington Territory.

Mamma takes the *Bazar*, papa the *Weekly* and *Magazine*. I have the first and second numbers of *Young People*. I like it very much, but I like "The Brave Swiss Boy" the best. I am ten years old. I saw in your letter to us that you wanted us to write to your paper. I think it must have been very funny to come across the plains in a wagon. I came across from Fond du Lac, Wisconsin (where I was born), in the cars, and not in the big trains of wagons.

Our Reader read "Two Ways of Finding It," from the first number of *Young People*, in school last Friday.

The pets I have are gray and Maltese kittens. I did once have a chicken that would come and eat wheat out of my hand, and fly into my room.

Jessie H.

I live a little way from Scranton, Pennsylvania, and a friend takes *Harper's Young People* for me. I have had a great deal of fun trying to draw a pig with my eyes shut. It is very funny to do it, with your eyes shut, and try to fool another person with a pencil. Daisy.

Morristown, New York.

I wanted to write to you, and tell you how much I liked your new paper. I like the story of "The Brave Swiss Boy" best. I live with my grandpa and grandma, who are very good to me, and I love them very much. Please print this, and oblige

Harry W. T.

Pretty communications are received from Frederick B., Brooklyn, New York; Perkins S., New York city; Annie L., New London, Connecticut; Mary E. H., Albany, New York; Mabel L., New York city; and Lottie S. B., Boston, Massachusetts.

A. M. S.—As it may interest other young readers, we print the whole list of portraits on the United States postage-stamps in use at present, as well as the one you require: One cent, Franklin; two cent, Jackson; three cent, Washington; five cent, General Taylor; six cent, Lincoln; seven cent, Stanton; ten cent, Jefferson; twelve cent, Clay; fifteen cent, Webster; twenty-four cent, Scott; thirty cent, Hamilton; ninety cent, Commodore O. H. Perry.

Bessie G.—Your "Bran Pudding" is excellent, but it came too late for use. We shall reserve it for next Christmas, as it is good enough to keep.

Correct answers to Christmas Puzzle in No. 8 are received from Charlie G. G., Gussie L., Birdie G., J. S. D., Fred A. O., Herbert W. B., Emily J. M., Nina R. T., Willie C., Herbert B., Bobette C. Van B., and William W. F. The answer will be published in our next number.

The following easy puzzles from very young readers are offered for other very young readers to solve:

No. 1.

WORD SQUARE.

My first is a lamb.
My second is a girl's name.
My third is not cooked.

K. S. (nine years old).

No. 2.

ENIGMA.

My first is in store, but not in coal.
My second is in pin, but not in hole.
My third is in rod, but not in pole.
My fourth is in bear, and also in mule.
My fifth is in bread, but not in gruel.
My sixth is in meal, and also in stale.
If you can not guess this, you are not witty,
For my whole is found in every city.

C. G. (eleven years old).

No. 3.

NUMERICAL CHARADE.

I am a word of 10 letters.
My 1, 2, 3, 4 is a kind of labor.
My 8, 9, 10 is a weight.
My 5, 6, 7 is what a boy of a certain race is often called.
My whole was a great man.

R. D. C.

No. 4.

NUMERICAL CHARADE.

I am a word of 6 letters.
My 1, 5, 3 is a man.
My 3, 4, 5 is a biped.
My 6, 1, 2 is a verb.
My whole is a city in Europe.

F. C.

No. 5.

ENIGMA.

My first is in cold, but not in hot.
My second is in pan, but not in pot.
My third is in nap, but not in sleep.
My fourth is in sold, but not in keep.
My fifth is in flute, but not in drum.
My sixth is in example, but not in sum.
My whole is useful in the dark.

M. L.

No. 6.

DOUBLE ACROSTIC.

A girl's name. A measure. A fur cat. A girl's name. A verb. An explanation. The answer is two cities of the United States.

M. L.

No. 7.

RIDDLE.

Decline ice-cream.

M. L.

No. 8.

NUMERICAL CHARADE.

I am composed of 18 letters.
My 17, 18, 9 is the Latin name of an animal.
My 10, 11, 4, 13, 8 is a young animal.
My 14, 11 is a prefix.
My 6, 2, 12, 7 is a word applied to old clothes.
My 1, 5, 3 is a pronoun.
My 16 is a vowel.
A good many little folks like my whole very much.

M. F. B.

Answers to the above puzzles will be given in *Young People* No. 15.

Old Books for Young Readers.

Arabian Nights' Entertainments.

The Thousand and One Nights; or, The Arabian Nights' Entertainments. Translated and Arranged for Family Reading, with Explanatory Notes, by E. W. Lane. 600 Illustrations by Harvey. 2 vols., 12mo, Cloth, $3 50.

Robinson Crusoe.

The Life and Surprising Adventures of Robinson Crusoe, of York, Mariner. By Daniel Defoe. With a Biographical Account of Defoe. Illustrated by Adams. Complete Edition. 12mo, Cloth, $1 50.

The Swiss Family Robinson.

The Swiss Family Robinson; or, Adventures of a Father and Mother and Four Sons on a Desert Island. Illustrated. 2 vols., 18mo, Cloth, $1 50.

The Swiss Family Robinson.—Continued: being a Sequel to the Foregoing. 2 vols., 18mo, Cloth, $1 50.

Sandford and Merton.

The History of Sandford and Merton. By Thomas Day. 18mo, Half Bound, 75 cents.

Published by HARPER & BROTHERS, New York.

☞ HARPER & BROTHERS will send any of the above works by mail, postage prepaid, to any part of the United States, on receipt of the price.

The Fairy Books.

THE PRINCESS IDLEWAYS. By Mrs. W. J. Hays. Illustrated. 16mo, Cloth, 75 cents.

THE CATSKILL FAIRIES. By Virginia W. Johnson. 8vo, Illuminated Cloth, Gilt Edges, $3 00.

FAIRY BOOK ILLUSTRATED. 16mo, Cloth, $1 [illegible].

PUSS-CAT MEW, and other New Fairy Stories for my Children. By E. H. Knatchbull-Hugessen, M.P. Illustrated. 16mo, Cloth, $1 [illegible].

FAIRY BOOK. The Best Popular Fairy Stories selected and rendered anew. By the Author of "John Halifax." Illustrated. 16mo, Cloth, $1 [illegible].

FAIRY TALES. By Jean Macé. Translated by Mary L. Booth. Illustrated. 12mo, Bevelled Edges, $1 75; Gilt Edges, $2 [illegible].

FAIRY TALES OF ALL NATIONS. By E. Laboulaye. Translated by Mary L. Booth. Illustrated. 12mo, Cloth, Bevelled Edges, $2 00; Gilt Edges, $2 50.

THE LITTLE LAME PRINCE. By the Author of "John Halifax, Gentleman." Illustrated. Square 16mo, Cloth, $1 00.

FOLKS AND FAIRIES. Stories for Little Children. By Lucy Campbell Lawrence. Illustrated. Square 4to, Cloth, $1 00.

THE ADVENTURES OF A BROWNIE, as Told to my Child. By the Author of "John Halifax, Gentleman." Illustrated. Square 16mo, Cloth, 90 cents.

Published by HARPER & BROTHERS, New York.

☞ Sent by mail, postage prepaid, to any part of the United States, on receipt of the price.

"A book beyond the pale of criticism."
N. Y. DAILY GRAPHIC.

THE

Boy Travellers in the Far East.

ADVENTURES OF

TWO YOUTHS IN A JOURNEY

TO

JAPAN AND CHINA.

Illustrated, 8vo, Cloth, $3 00.

A more attractive book for boys and girls can scarcely be imagined.—N. Y. Times.

The best thing for a boy who cannot go to China and Japan is to get this book and read it.—Philadelphia Ledger.

[illegible]—N. Y. Journal of Commerce.

[illegible]—Providence Press.

Published by HARPER & BROTHERS, N. Y.

☞ Sent by mail, postage prepaid, to any part of the United States, on receipt of the price.

WHAT MR. DARWIN SAW

In His Voyage Round the World

In the Ship "Beagle."

ADAPTED FOR YOUTHFUL READERS.

Illustrated, 8vo, Cloth, $3 00.

A capital book on natural history for young readers.—Hartford Courant.

A superb volume filled with maps and pictures of beasts, birds, and fishes, as well as the faces of all sorts of men, and with all this a most delightful story of real travel round the world by a very famous naturalist.—Christian Intelligencer, N. Y.

[illegible]—Philadelphia North American.

[illegible]—U. S. Press, Phila.

Published by HARPER & BROTHERS, New York.

☞ Sent by mail, postage prepaid, to any part of the United States, on receipt of the price.

"A Rare Gift for Children."
PROVIDENCE TELEGRAPH.

THE PRINCESS IDLEWAYS,

A FAIRY STORY.

Illustrated, 16mo, Cloth, 75 cents.

Written in a simple but charming manner, and illustrated by beautiful pictures, so that a youngster just past the first reading-book would appreciate every word.—Christian Intelligencer, N. Y.

The illustrations are worthy of special commendation. Anything dainty, pretty, and full of grace, have rarely appeared in any American book for children.—Hartford Courant.

The language in which it is told is so pure and agreeable, that parents and good teachers [illegible] it a pleasure to read it aloud to the little ones.—Boston Courier.

Published by HARPER & BROTHERS, N. Y.

☞ Sent by mail, postage prepaid, to any part of the United States, on receipt of the price.

"A most enchanting story for boys."
PROVIDENCE TELEGRAPH.

AN INVOLUNTARY VOYAGE.

By LUCIEN BIART,

Author of "Adventures of a Young Naturalist."

TRANSLATED BY

Mrs. CASHEL HOEY and Mr. JOHN LILLIE.

ILLUSTRATED.

16mo, Cloth, $1 00.

A very charming book, brimming full of adventures, and has not an uninteresting page between its covers.—Baltimore Gazette.

[illegible]—Philadelphia Bulletin.

A most enchanting story for boys. * * * It is a story of adventure, and also contains much interesting and useful information.—Pittsburgh Telegraph.

A narrative crowded with adventure, told in the lively and graphic style for which the French writers of books for boys are so noted.—Cleveland Herald.

[illegible]—Observer, N. Y.

Published by HARPER & BROTHERS, N. Y.

☞ Sent by mail, postage prepaid, to any part of the United States, on receipt of the price.

A BOOK FOR EVERYBODY.

Ninth Edition now Ready.

HOW TO GET STRONG, AND HOW TO STAY SO. By WILLIAM BLAIKIE. With Illustrations. 16mo, Cloth, $1 00.

Your book is timely. Its large circulation cannot fail to be of great public benefit.—Rev. HENRY WARD BEECHER.

It is a book of extraordinary merit in matter and style, and does you great credit as a thinker and writer.—Hon. CALVIN E. PRATT, of the New York Supreme Bench.

A capital little treatise. It is the very book for ministers to study.—Rev. THEODORE L. CUYLER, D.D., in New York Evangelist.

It is unquestionably one of the most practical and useful books on this topic which have ever been published in this country.—N. Y. Evening Express.

We know of no man in America more capable of writing such a book, or who has a better right to do so.—Portland Daily Herald.

[illegible]—Springfield Union.

A veritable treasury of muscular common-sense.—Charleston News and Courier.

Published by HARPER & BROTHERS, New York.

☞ Sent by mail, postage prepaid, to any part of the United States, on receipt of the price.

CATASTROPHE No. 1. "You better stop!"

CATASTROPHE No. 2. "You better get out of the way!"

THE EGG TOMBOLA.

A VERY amusing toy can be made out of an egg, to resemble Fig. 1 in our picture. The one from which our drawing is copied was constructed in half an hour. The way to do it is this: Get a clean, well-shaped fresh egg. With a strong needle make a hole at each end about the size of a large shot, then suck out the contents of the egg. Now you have the hollow shell. Through one of the holes drop in about half a tea-spoonful of shot and the same quantity of pellets of bees-wax or tallow. Now take a small bit of bread and work it between the fingers till it becomes a paste; with this stop up the hole at the big end of the egg. Then procure a cup of boiling water, and hold the egg in it till the wax is melted, taking care to hold it quite upright, so that all the shot will settle in the big end. This will take about five minutes. Then hold the egg in very cold water till the wax has cooled. This will take about five minutes more. You will now find that the egg will stand upright on the table, no matter in what position you may lay it down. The next thing is to paint or draw on it the figure of an old gentleman like our picture, and you have the Tombola complete. If the figure be painted with oil-colors, the Tombola can be made to perform his pranks in a basin of water.

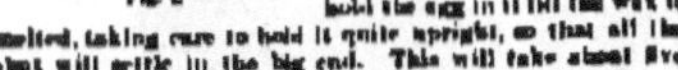

Fig. 1.

Fig. 2 shows the interior of the egg and the position of the shot and wax.

Fig. 2.

STORIES OF DOGS.

WE are sure all young people will read with pleasure the following description of a very remarkable dog which belonged to the Hon. Alexander H. Stephens. This dog, which is mentioned in the *Life of Mr. Stephens*, was a very large and fine white poodle, named Rio, a dog of unusual intelligence and affection, to which Mr. Stephens became very strongly attached. While Mr. Stephens was in Washington, Rio staid with Linton Stephens, at Sparta, Georgia, until his master returned. Mr. Stephens would usually come on during the session of Greene County court, where Linton would meet him, having Rio with him in his buggy, and the dog would then return with his master. When this had happened once or twice, the dog learned to expect him on these occasions. The cars usually arrived at about nine o'clock at night. During the evening, Rio would be extremely restless, and at the first sound of the approaching train he would rush from the hotel to the dépôt, and in a few seconds would know whether his master was on the train or not, for he would search for him through all the cars. He was well known to the conductors, and if the train happened to start before Rio had finished his search, they would stop to let him get out. But when his search was successful, his raptures of joy at seeing his master again were really affecting. His intelligence was so great that he seemed to understand whatever was said to him; at a word he would shut a door as gently as a careful servant might have done, or would bring a cane, hat, or umbrella. He always slept in his master's room, which he scarcely left during Mr. Stephens's attacks of illness. In a word, Mr. Stephens found in him a companion of almost human intelligence, and of unbounded affection and fidelity, and the tie between the man and the dog was strong and enduring.

"For nearly thirteen years he was," says Mr. Stephens, "my constant companion, when at home, day and night, and until he became blind, a few years ago, he always attended me wherever I went, except to Washington. You may well imagine, then, how I miss him!—miss him in the yard, in the house, in my walks; for though blind, he used to follow me about the lot wherever I went. When I was reading or writing, he was always at my feet. At night, too, his bed was the foot of my own. His beautiful white thick coat of cord was soft as silk. Who that knew him as I did could refrain from shedding a tear for poor Rio?"

Of course he was properly interred, in a coffin, in the garden, and placed in the position in which he usually slept, with his face on his fore-feet.

The smartest Newfoundland dog yet discovered lives at Haverhill, Massachusetts. He meets the newsboy at the gate every morning, and carries his master's paper into the house; that is, he did so till the other day, when his master stopped taking the paper. The next morning the dog noticing the boy passing on the other side without leaving the newspaper, went over and took the whole bundle from him, and carried them into the house. That's the kind of dog *he* is.

Bob and Tommy know that Aunt Patty is awfully afraid of Tramps, and so they rig up this figure, and knock at the door. Dreadful scare, wasn't it?

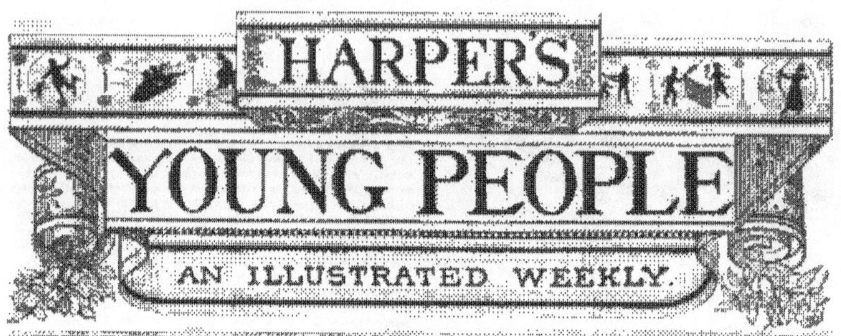

Vol. I.—No. 12. | Published by HARPER & BROTHERS, New York. | Price Four Cents.

Tuesday, January [illegible] | Copyright, [illegible] | [illegible] per Year, in Advance.

OUR OWN STAR.

"AS we have already," began the Professor, "had a talk about the stars in general, let us this morning give a little attention to our own particular star."

"Is there a star that we can call our own?" asked May, with unusual animation. "How nice! I wonder if it can be the one I saw from our front window last evening, that looked so bright and beautiful?"

"I am sure it was not," said the Professor, "if you saw it in the evening."

"Is it hard to see our star, then?" she said.

"By no means," replied the Professor; "rather it is hard not to see it. But you must be careful about looking directly at it, or your eyes will be badly dazzled, it is so very bright. Our star is no other than the sun. And we are right in calling it a star, because all the stars are suns, and very likely give light and heat to worlds as large as our earth, though they are all so far off that we can not see them. Our star seems so much brighter and hotter than the others, only because it is so much nearer to us than they are, though still it is some ninety-two millions of miles away."

"How big is the sun?" asked Joe.

"You can get the clearest idea of its size by a comparison. The earth is 7920 miles in diameter, that is, as measured right through the centre. Now suppose it to be only one inch, or about as large as a plum or a half-grown peach; then we would have to regard the sun as three yards in diameter, so that if it were in this room it would reach from the floor to the ceiling."

"How do they find out the distance of the sun?" asked Joe.

"Until lately," replied the Professor, "the same method was pursued as in surveying, that is, by measuring lines and angles. An angle, you know, is the corner made by two lines coming together, as in the letter V. But that method did not answer very well, as it did not make the distance certain within several millions of miles. Quite recently Professor Newcomb has found out a way of measuring the sun's distance by the velocity of its light. He has invented a means of learning exactly how fast light moves; and then, by comparing this with the time light takes to come from the sun to us, he is able to tell how far off the sun is. Thus, if a man knows how many miles he walks in an hour, and how many hours it takes him to walk to a certain place, he can very easily figure up the number of miles it is away."

"Why," said Gus, "that sounds just like what Bob Stebbins said the other day in school. He has a big silver watch that he is mighty fond of hauling out of his pocket before everybody. A caterpillar came crawling through the door, and went right toward the teacher's desk at the other end of the room. 'Now,' said Bob, 'if that fellow will only keep straight ahead, I can tell how long the room is.' So out came the watch, and Bob wrote down the time and how many inches the caterpillar travelled in a minute. But just then Sally Smith came across his track with her long dress, and swept him to Jericho. We boys all laughed out; Sally blushed and got angry; and the teacher kept us in after school."

"Astronomers have the same kind of troubles," said the Professor. "They incur great labor and expense to take some particular observation that is possible only once in a number of years, and then for only a few minutes. And after their instruments are all carefully set up, and their calculations made, the clouds spread over the sky, and hide everything they wish to see. People, too, are very apt to laugh at their disappointment.

"There would, however, be no science of astronomy if those who pursued it were discouraged by common difficulties. To explain the heavenly bodies they sometimes try to make little systems or images of the sun and the planets; but they are never able to show the sizes and distances correctly. If they were to begin by making the sun one inch in diameter, then the earth would have to be three yards off, and as small as a grain of dust; some of the planets would have to be across the street, and others away beyond the opposite houses. So when you look at these little solar systems, as they are called, you must remember that the sizes and distances are all wrong.

"Still, you can get from them some idea how the sun stands in the middle, and the earth and other planets go round, and how the earth, while going round the sun, keeps also turning itself around. You have seen how a top, while spinning, sometimes runs round in a circle. That is just the way our earth does. And if you imagine a candle in the centre of the circle that the top makes, you will see why it is sometimes day and sometimes night. When the side of the earth we are on is turned toward the sun, we have day; and when we have spun past the sun, night comes.

"The sun seems to go past us, and people used to think it really did. But we know now that it is as if we were in a rail-car, and the trees and houses seemed to be rushing along, when we ourselves are the ones that are moving. The sun and all the stars seem to move through the sky from east to west; but it is only our earth that is turning itself the other way, and carrying us with it."

"What makes summer and winter?" asked Joe.

"I think that the top will help you to understand that too. You have noticed that when it spins it does not always stand straight up, but often leans over to one side. So sometimes the upper part of it would be over toward the candle, and sometimes over away from it. The earth leans over too in this same manner; and that is the reason why we have summer and winter. When by this leaning our part of the earth is toward the sun, we get more heat, and have a warm season; when we are leaning away from the sun, and are more in the shadow, the cold weather comes, and continues until we get into a good position to be warmed up again.

"A kind Providence brings this all around very regularly, and there is no danger of our being kept so long in the cold that we would freeze to death. Everything works like a clock that is never allowed to run down or get out of order. In spinning, the earth carries us round twelve or fifteen times as fast as the fastest railway train has ever yet been made to run; and in making its circle round the sun, it moves as fast as a shot from a gun."

"Oh! oh!" exclaimed the children; and Joe asked, "Why are we not all dashed to pieces?"

"Because," said the Professor, "we do not run against anything large enough to do any harm; and we do not realize how fast we are moving, or that we are moving at all, because we do not pass near anything that is standing still. You know that in riding we look at the trees and fences by the road-side to see how rapidly we are going. The hills in the distance do not show our speed, but seem to be following us. Unless we look outside we can not know anything about it, excepting, perhaps, we may guess from the noise and jostling of the vehicle. But as the earth moves smoothly and without the least noise, we would think it stood entirely still did not astronomers assure us of its wonderfully rapid motion. It took them a great while to find it out. When they began to suspect it there was a great dispute over it. Some said it moved; others said it did not. The two parties were for a time very bitter against each other; but now all agree in the belief of its rapid motion."

"A queer thing to quarrel about, I must say," remarked Gus. "I wouldn't have cared a straw whether it moved or not, if I could only have been allowed to move about on it as I pleased."

"I hope you are not getting uneasy, Gus," said Joe.

"There is evident reason," observed Jack, "to suspect that his appreciation of the marvels of science is insufficient to preserve—"

"Oh, bother! Jack, don't give us your college stuff now, after the Professor has told us so much. We like to hear him, of course. I do, for one, a great deal better than I thought I should. But then a fellow can't help getting tired."

BABY'S EYES.

When the baby's eyes are blue,
  Think we of a summer day,
Violets, and dancing rills.
  When the baby's eyes are gray,
Doves and dawn are brought to mind.
  Brown—of gentle fawns we dream,
And ripe nuts in shady woods.
  Black—of midnight skies that gleam
With bright stars. But blue or gray,
  Black or brown, like flower or star,
Sweeter eyes can never be
  To mamma than baby's are.

(Begun in No. 11 of HARPER'S YOUNG PEOPLE, January 13.)

LADY PRIMROSE.

BY FLETCHER READE.

CHAPTER II.

"Infinite riches in a little room."

THE words of the wise old woman of Hollowbush were true, then. Here was a place where gems were more abundant than flowers; and as the child stood on the threshold gazing into the diminutive but wondrously beautiful apartment that had opened so suddenly before her, she saw that she was indeed in the presence-chamber of a king.

The walls were of pure white marble, studded with diamonds, and from the ceiling, which she could almost touch with her hand, hung slender chandeliers of the same material. In each of these, instead of lamps, were innumerable sapphires, throwing a soft blue light over all the place. In every stone a star seemed to be burning steady and clear and wonderfully brilliant. It was the asteria, or star sapphire, which was alone considered worthy to light even the outer courts of the king over a country so rich in gems as this.

The child clapped her hands, and would no doubt have shouted with delight if she had not found herself encircled by tiny men, all looking exactly alike, and all winking and blinking at her just as the gate-keeper had done.

Before she could speak, or even clap her hands a second time, they had entirely surrounded her, joining hands, and wheeling round and round, singing as they went:

"Workers are we—one, two, three—
And merry men all, as you see, as you see:
Deep under the ground,
Where jewels are found,
We work, and we sing
While we dance in a ring.
But a mortal has come to the caves below,
So, merry men all, bow low, bow low,
For our sister she'll be—one, two, three."

Three times did these strange and merry little people sing their song, and three times did they whirl around the new-comer, thus introducing themselves and welcoming her to their dominions.

Then one of them, but whether the gate-keeper or another she could not tell, stepped forward, and making a low bow, said, "I am the king of the mineral-workers and the workers in stone. These are my people; but because you are a mortal, we one and all bow before you."

At these words all the little people bowed and waved their hands. Then the king continued:

"Henceforth you are to be known as the Princess Bébé;" and he mounted a marble footstool that stood close by, standing on tiptoe, and placing on the head of the new-made princess a tiny coronet of pearls. Dumb with astonishment, the Princess Bébé listened quietly to all that was said to her, and allowed herself to be led away by one of the little men, who had been appointed her chamberlain.

It was now getting late, and she was glad enough to be shown to her own room, that she might think over the many wonderful things which she had seen.

But here were new wonder and new riches.

Instead of being covered with a carpet, the floor was laid in squares of jasper, the windows were of pure white crystal instead of glass, and the curtains were made of a fine net-work of gold, caught back with a double row of amethysts.

The furniture was of gold and silver, exquisitely carved, and the quilt, which lay in stiff folds over the bed, was a marvel of beautiful colors that seemed to be now one thing and now another.

The Princess Bébé held her breath. "It will be like going to sleep on a rainbow," she said to herself, for the opal bed was full of changing colors, now red, now green, and then purple and soft rose-pink, and then, perhaps, green again. "There was never anything so beautiful as this!" exclaimed the princess, throwing herself down; but the next moment she was ready to cry with vexation, for there was neither warmth nor softness in the opal bed, and she lay awake all night, alternately shivering and crying.

"I won't stay in this place another moment," she said, the next morning, when the chamberlain knocked at her door.

The chamberlain bowed, and held before her a silver cup filled with jewels. "These are a present from the king to the Princess Bébé," he said, holding it up for her inspection.

There was first of all a diamond necklace, just what she had been wishing for; then there were ear-rings and bracelets of lapis lazuli of a beautiful azure color; string after string of pearls; emeralds set in buckles for her shoes; amethysts; sapphires as blue as the sea; and last of all a large topaz, which shone with a brilliant yellow light, as if it had been sunshine which some one had caught and imprisoned for her.

The Princess Bébé forgot for a moment her hard bed and sleepless night, and ran to the king to thank him for his presents.

"I am glad to find that you are pleased with your new home," said the king, graciously. "Did the princess sleep well during the night?"

"Oh, not at all well," she answered, forgetting her errand. "And I was very cold, besides."

"Cold! cold!" said the king, sharply. "We must see to that."

Turning to one of his attendants, who held a crystal cup on which were engraved the arms of the royal family, he took from it a stone of a dark orange color, and said,

"This is a jacinth, my dear princess. Whenever you are cold, you have only to rub your hands against it, and you will feel a delicious sense of warmth stealing through your limbs."

The princess rubbed her hands against the smooth stone as the king suggested; but she almost immediately threw it away again, crying out with pain.

"Oh, I don't like it at all," she exclaimed. "It pricks and hurts."

"It is nothing but the electricity," answered the king. "You will soon get accustomed to it, and I have no doubt will be quite fond of your electrical stove."

"I don't want to get accustomed to it," answered the princess. "I want to go home."

Then the king's face grew dark, and his pale blue eyes

winked and blinked until they shone like two blazing lights.

"No one comes into our country to go away again," he said at length. "You are the Princess Bébé, adopted daughter of the king of the mineral-workers and the workers in stone, and with him you must stay for the rest of your life."

In spite of her diamond necklace, the princess was actually crying, although it is almost past belief that any one with a diamond necklace could cry; but the merry little mineral-workers, seeing the tears in her eyes, crowded around her, and tried their best to comfort her.

"Come into the garden," said one; and "Come to the gold chests," said another, "and see the diamonds."

"Diamonds!" exclaimed the princess, angrily and ungratefully: "I hate the very sight of them. But I would like to see the garden," she added, more gently.

Aleck, the gate-keeper, offered to act as escort, and the princess dried her eyes. He at least was her friend, she thought; and on the way to the garden, being very hungry, she ventured to ask him when they were to have breakfast.

"I AM THE KING OF THE MINERAL WORKERS."

"Breakfast!" he said. "Why, we don't have breakfasts here."

"Well, then, dinner," suggested the princess, meekly.

"Nor dinners either," replied the little man. "Why should we have dinners!"

"But at least you have suppers," said the princess, desperately, and feeling ready to cry again.

"What are you thinking of?" asked the gate-keeper, with an air of surprise.

Then the princess grew angry.

"What am I thinking of?" she cried, at the top of her voice. "I am thinking of something to eat—that's what I'm thinking of, and I'm almost starved."

The little gate-keeper looked up, with a curious smile on his face, and answered:

"Well, then, my dear princess, if that is what makes you unhappy, pray don't think of it any more. No one ever eats anything here. Indeed, I can not imagine anything more absurd."

Then, being at heart a very kind and obliging little person, he came close to the princess, and said:

"I am sorry for you—indeed I am, but don't give way to tears. They won't turn stones into bread. I beseech you, my dear Princess Bébé, to look at our fruit trees and flowers. They are considered very beautiful. I have no doubt but the sight of them will help you to bear this strange feeling which you call hunger." Then, kissing the princess's hand, he added: "I must leave you now and go to the gate. Amuse yourself in the garden, my dear princess, till I return."

It was a wondrously beautiful garden, as any one could see, but somehow the Princess Bébé did not get much comfort from it.

"Oh, if there were only real apples!" she sighed, for there were what seemed to be apple-trees in great abundance. But the apples were of malachite—a hard opaque stone of two shades of green—and when she tried to taste the grapes, she found they were only purple amethysts arranged in graceful clusters. The cherries were all of stone, instead of having a stone in the middle; and the plums were just as bad and just as beautiful—the cherries were deep red rubies, and the plums were made of chrysoprase. Nothing but hard glittering gems wherever she turned her eyes.

The poor princess seemed likely to die of starvation in spite of her riches, but she thought she would be almost willing to endure hunger if she could only have a rose that would smell like the sweet-brier roses which grew in Hollowbush in her own little garden. For what she had at first taken to be roses were, after all, nothing but pink coral cunningly carved, the daffodils were of amber, and the forget-me-nots were one and all made of the pale blue turquoise.

"It is very certain that I must die," said the princess, sadly, and also covered her face with her hands, crying bitterly, and praying that if death must come to her, it might come quickly.

[TO BE CONTINUED.]

JOE AND BLINKY.

BLINKY was a poor dirty little puppy whom somebody had lost, and somebody else had stolen, and whose miserable little life was a burden to himself until Joe found him. It happened one warm day in July that Joe, whose bright eyes were always pretty wide open, saw a group of youngsters eagerly clustering about an object which appeared to interest them very much. This object squirmed, gasped, and occasionally kicked, to the great amusement of the little crowd, who liked excitement of any sort. Joe put his head over the shoulders of the children, and saw a wretched little dog in the agonies of a convulsion. Now, instead of giving him pleasure, this sight pained him grievously, as did any suffering, and Joe pushed his way through the crowd, asking whose dog it was. No one claimed it; and Joe was watched with great interest, and warned most zealously, as he took the poor little creature by the nape of its neck to the nearest pump.

"You'd better look out. He's mad. See if he isn't."

"What yer goin' to do?—kill him? My father's got a pistol; I'll run and get it."

"No, you needn't," said Joe.

There was no pound in the town, and so the dog was worthless, and after a while the crowd of children found something else to interest them.

Joe bathed the little dog, and rubbed it, and soothed its violent struggles, and carried it away to a quiet corner on the steps of a house where a great elm-tree made a refreshing shade. Here he sat a long time, watching his little patient, and glad to find it getting quieter and quieter, until it fell fast asleep in his arms. Joe did not move, so pleased was he to relieve the poor little creature, whose thin flanks revealed a long course of suffering. There were few passers in the street, and Joe had no school duties, thanks to its being vacation, so he was free to do as he chose. After more than an hour the poor little dog opened its eyes, which were so dazzled by the light that Joe at once named him Blinky, and presently a hot red little tongue was licking Joe's big brown hand. That was enough for Joe; it was as plain a "thank you" as he wanted, and he carried his stray charge home to share his dinner.

From that day Joe was seldom seen without Blinky; and after many good dinners, and plenty of sleep without terrible dreams of tins tied to his tail, Blinky began to grow handsome, and Joe to be very proud of him. Blinky slept under Joe's bed, woke him every morning with a sharp little bark, as much as saying, "Wake up, lazy fellow, and have a frolic with me," and then bounced up beside him for a game. And how he frisked when Joe took him out! The only thing he did not enjoy was his weekly scrubbing, and the combing with an old coarse toilet comb which followed. But he bore it patiently for Joe's sake. Vacation came to an end, and school began. This was as sore a trial to Blinky as to Joe, for of course he could not be allowed in school, though he left Joe at the door with most regretful and downcast looks, which said plainly, "This is injustice; you and I should never be parted," and he was always waiting when school was out.

Joe hated school; he would much rather have been chestnutting in the woods, gay with their crimson and yellow leaves, or chasing the squirrels with Blinky; but he knew he had to study, if ever he was to be of any use in the world, and so he tried to forget the delights of roaming, or the charms of Blinky's company. But when the first snow came, how hard it was to stick at the old books! How delicious was the frosty air, and how pure and fresh the new-fallen snow, waiting to be made use of as Joe so well knew how!

"Duty first," said Joe to himself, as with shovel and

"FIRE AWAY!"

broom he cleared the path in the court-yard, and shovelled the kitchen steps clean. He did it so well that his father tossed him some pennies—for he was saving up to buy Blinky a collar—and he turned off with a light heart for school, with Blinky at his heels.

The school-mistress had a hard time that day; all the boys were wild with fun, one only of them not sharing the glee. This one was a little chap whose parents had sent him up North from Georgia to his relatives, the parents being too poor after the war to maintain their family. He was a skinny little fellow, always shivering and snuffling, and his name was Bob.

Now Bob wasn't a favorite. The boys liked to tease him, called him "Little Reb," and he in turn disliked them, and was ever ready to report their mischievous pranks to the teacher. If there was anything pleasant about the boy, no one knew it, because no one took the trouble to find out. Bob did not relish the snow; he was pinched and blue, and whenever he had the chance was huddling up against the stove; besides, he liked to read, and would rather have staid in all day with a book of fairy tales than shared the gayest romp they could have suggested. This afternoon Joe had made so many mistakes in his arithmetic examples that he was obliged to stay late, and do them over; but he was sorely annoyed and tempted at hearing the shouts and cries of joy with which the boys saluted each other as they escaped from the school-room, and he spoke very crossly when a little voice at his elbow said,

"Please may I go home with you?"

"No," said Joe.

"Ah, please!"

Joe turned, and saw that it was Bob. This provoked him still more. "I said no, 'tell-tale.' What do I want to be bothered with you?"

Bob turned away, disappointed. Joe kept on at his lesson; it was very perplexing, and he was out of humor. Besides, the fun outside was increasing; he could hear the roars of laughter, the whiz of the flying snow-balls, and the gleeful crows of the conquering heroes. He was the only one in the school-room. Presently there was a hush, a sort of premonitory symptom of more mischief brewing outside, which provoked his curiosity to the utmost.

"Five times ten, divided by three, and— Oh, I can't stand this," said Joe, as he gave a push to his slate, and ran to the window.

The boys had gone off to the farthest corner of the vacant lot on which the school-house stood, and by the appearance of things were preparing to have an animated game of foot-ball; but by the gestures and general drift of motions Joe saw, to his horror, that poor little Bob was evidently to be the victim. Already they were rolling him in the snow, and cuffing him about as if he were made of India rubber, and deserved no better treatment.

Joe's conscience woke up in a minute, for he knew that if he had allowed Bob to wait for him as he had wanted to do, the boys would not have dared to touch him, and he felt ashamed of his unkindness and ill humor as he saw the results.

The child was getting fearfully maltreated, as Joe saw, not merely on account of their dislike for him, but because in their gambols the boys were lost to all sense of the cruelty they were practicing, and they tossed him about regardless of the fact that his bones could be broken or his sinews snapped.

Cramming his books in his bag, and snatching up his cap, Joe dashed out of the door. Blinky was ready for him, and did not know what all this haste meant, but dashed after his master, as in duty bound.

"I say, fellers, stop that!" he shouted, repeating the "stop that!" as loud as his lungs could make the exertion. The din was so great that it was some moments before they heard him, but Blinky barked at their heels, and helped to arrest their attention.

"Stop! what shall we stop for?" asked one of the bigger and rougher ones.

"You are doing a mean, hateful thing—that's why."

"Oho! that's because you haven't a share in it," was the sneering reply.

"If you'll stop, I'll run the gauntlet for you," said Joe. There was a pause. Perhaps that would be better than foot-ball; besides, Joe never got mad, and little Bob was crying hard. "Let Bob go home, fair and square, and I'll run," repeated Joe.

"All right," they shouted. "Come on, then."

Joe helped to uncover Bob, shook the snow off his clothes, wiped his eyes with the cuff of his coat, and sent him on his way. Then the boys formed two lines, each with as many snow-balls as he could hurriedly make, and Joe prepared for the run. Blinky was furious, and as Joe shouted, "Fire away!" and started down the line, he barked himself hoarse. Hot and heavy came the balls, or rather cold and fast they fell on Joe's back and head and school bag. But he was a good runner, and tore like mad from his pursuers, screaming, as he ran, "Fire away! fire away!" until he reached a cellar door, where he knew he could take refuge. Here he halted; but Blinky was in a rage at having his master thus used. Joe did not mind it in the least, and was as full of fun as he could be. When he got home he found his mother making apple pies; she had baked one in a saucer for him. It looked delicious, but as he was about to bite it, he said, "Mother, may I just run over to Mrs. Allen's for a minute?"

"Oh yes," was the reply.

Wrapping up the pie in a napkin, he carried it with him. By the side of the stove, with his head aching and bound up in a handkerchief, he found poor little Bob. Without a word, he stuffed the nice little pie in Bob's hands, and then rushed out again.

It is hardly necessary to say that in the future Blinky had a rival, and that rival was Bob.

A SAIL ON THE NILE.

BY SARA KEABLES HUNT.

DID you ever go sailing on the Nile? Come, then, and imagine yourselves, on a clear warm January day, afloat on the river of which you have so often heard. What a sensation we should create if we could go sailing up the Hudson some sunny morning, our broad lateen-sail swelling in the breeze, and the Egyptian flag flying behind!

Let us take a walk over the boat which for two months will be to us a floating home, and to which we shall become really attached before we leave its deck, and the shores of the Nile. It is a queerly shaped vessel, entirely different from any other which has ever carried you over the waters. The length is about seventy-two feet, and the width between fourteen and fifteen feet at the broadest part. It has a sharp prow, and stands deep in the water forward; it is flat-bottomed, like all Nile boats, on account of the shallow water in the spring.

Here, a little way from the bow, is the kitchen—a small square place, where the cook holds undisputed sway, and gratifies your palate with novel and delicious dishes. This little spot is a very important part of the boat, I assure you, for sailing on the Nile gives you a keen relish for good dinners.

Somewhat back of here is the mast, rising thirty feet or more, and the long yard, suspended by ropes, large at the lower part, but tapering toward the extreme point, where floats the pennant which you have secured for the occasion.

This long yard bears the large triangular lateen-sail, its huge dimensions necessary to catch the wind when the river is low and the banks high. The sides of the boat are protected by a low railing not more than six inches in height, over which the sailors can easily step, as they will have occasion to do many times during the voyage. The main-deck is usually occupied by the crew, and from here are stairs leading to the quarter-deck, over the cabin and saloon, where we will take seats under the awning by-and-by, and watch the scenery on the banks of the river.

Let us go down these few steps leading to the saloon. We find ourselves in a room occupying the breadth of the boat; there are windows on each side, with long divans below them, a round table in the centre, chairs, cupboards, and book-case completing the furniture. Now let us open these glass doors, walk along this narrow passage, and take a look at the sleeping-cabins. They measure six feet by four, half of which is filled by the bed, which gives you girls little room in which to arrange your toilet; but you will not care to devote many hours to that while here.

Such is our floating home, and though limited in space, you can be most comfortable if you have a contented disposition, and a heart and mind to appreciate the wonders around and above you.

And now let us ascend to the quarter-deck. It looks

very cheerful, with its centre table loaded with books and papers, its bright-colored divan and easy-chairs; so we will be seated while I introduce you to the crew.

There is the reis, or captain—Hassaneen by name—a grave, quiet little old man, standing there at the bow of the boat, with a long pole in hand, sounding the water now and then, and reporting the depth. You will always find him there, reserved, thoughtful, his whole attention apparently fixed on his employment.

Do you see that old gray-bearded man with his hand on the rudder? That is Abdullah, always there, even when we are at anchor. Then a heap of blue and a gray burnouse in the same place tell us Abdullah is asleep. We need never fear while that old man is at the helm, for he will guide us safely by sand-banks and bowlders to the destined port.

Of the remainder of the crew I can not give so good a report. They are a curious assemblage of one-eyed, forefingerless, toothless men, bare-legged, in robes of dark blue, and gray turbans, it being a common custom to render themselves thus maimed in order to escape military conscription. There is Mohammed, a good-natured fellow, ready to do just as his companions do, whether it be good or bad. There is Said, a cunning, deceitful-looking man, but a good sailor. Just to the right is Hassan, black as coal, with glittering eyes, a tall form, and tremendous muscle; he is a faithful fellow, willing to obey to the letter, but without any judgment. There are Suleiman and Ali, the laziest ones on board, strong as any, but the first to cry out, "Halt," and the sleepiest couple on the Nile. There is Yusuf, always at his prayers, and more willing to pray than work. There is Achmet, watching his chance to run away. Then comes Mustapha, whose duty it is to clean the decks, scour the knives, and wait on the travellers generally. And last but not least is little Benemie, called "el walled" (the boy), who does more work and takes more steps than all the rest of the crew together. Ah, these boys!—they're worth a dozen men sometimes. He makes the fires, waits on the crew, and is at everybody's beck and call, from the howadji to the sailor. He is a dark-eyed, shy little fellow, not particularly neat in his appearance, and always sucking sugarcane, which probably is one of the attractions to the flies that gather continually on his face and eyes.

So there they are—a lazy set of fellows, take them all together; lazy in general when there is no present labor on hand. I think they work well, though, when a necessity arises. It is not an Arab's nature to look ahead; he sees only the present.

And now our sail is shaken out—we are off, the American flag floating aloft at the point of our tapering yard, and we seated in our easy-chairs or reclining on the divan of our decks, watching the scenery as we glide along. There before us are endless groups of masts and sails. The western shore is like a rich painting, with its palms and Pyramids, while opposite, half hidden in shining dark acacias, are palaces of the pashas, with their silent-looking harems and latticed windows. Cangias (small row-boats) are fastened to the banks, and the moan and creak of the sakias (water-wheels) tell us we are indeed upon the enchanted Nile.

Behind us rise the shining minarets of the city, and the Pyramids follow us as we go, photographing their outlines on our memory forever; the soft green plain slopes gently to the river; and as if stirred to life by the witchery of the surroundings, our bird-like boat flings her great wings to the breeze, and skims the waters, bounding along, as if with conscious joy, between the green plains of the Nile Valley.

The river is alive with boats, all bound southward, fine diahbeehs sweeping along, and looking proudly down on the lesser craft, and huge lumbering country boats laden with grain.

The landscape is not monotonous, though there is a sameness in its character, for the lines in that crystal air are always changing, and day after day the panorama unrolls, with its fields of waving tobacco and blossoming cotton, where workers are lazily busy.

We are passing the ruins of ancient cities as we sail onward, or are dragged along by the crew harnessed together by ropes, which task they call tracking. They never perform this labor reluctantly, or with any ill temper, but always accompanying their work with a monotonous sing-song in a slightly nasal twang, till the air is filled with these perpetual sounds of "Allah, haylee sah. Eiya Mohammed."

We see in this a relic of by-gone days, for the ancient Egyptians are painted on the tombs accompanying their work with song and clapping of hands.

As we are borne on through and into the creamy light of this glowing atmosphere, where the sunshine seems to pour into and blend with everything, we can hardly wonder that sun worship was an instinct of the earliest races, or that the little child believes that the East lies near the rising sun.

On, on we go, past the ruins of ancient cities, never pausing in the upward journey; it is only on the return that you visit the places of renown.

There lies Karnac, with its myriads of gigantic columns. Yonder sits Memnon, "beloved of the morning," which was said to give forth a note of music when the rising sun shone upon it. There is Luxor, Denderah, Thebes. Sometimes amid the warm light your thoughts will go away thousands of miles, where the frosts shiver upon the windows, the snows lie heavy upon the hills, and warm hearts are praying for the traveller; but the days will creep swiftly by on the Nile, and too soon will come the hour when, the journey ended, we must leave the river, the palms, the Pyramids, and bid a long adieu to our pleasant floating home.

THE WHITE BEAR OF THE ARCTIC REGIONS.

THE polar bear, the nannook of the Esquimaux, has its home in the desolate and icy wastes which border the northern seas. It has many characteristics in common with its brothers which live in warmer countries. It is very sagacious and cunning, sometimes playful, but is not a very savage beast, and will rarely attack a hunter unless in self-defense, or when driven by hunger to fall upon everything which comes in its way. Dr. Kane, the great arctic traveller, says he has himself shot as many as a dozen bears near at hand, and never but once received a charge in return. The hair of the polar bear is very coarse and thick, and white like the snow-banks among which it lives. Its favorite food is the seal, which abounds in the northern regions; it will also eat walrus, but as that animal is very strong, and possesses a pair of formidable tusks, bears are sometimes beaten in their attempts to capture it. Wonderful stories are told of bears mounting to the top of high cliffs and pushing heavy stones down upon the head of some unwary walrus sleeping or sunning himself at the foot, and then rushing down to dispatch the stunned and bruised animal, but arctic travellers disagree upon this point. A very hungry bear will sometimes attack a walrus in the water, for the polar bear is a powerful swimmer; but in his peculiar element—and he is never far from it—the walrus is the best fighter, and his tough hide serves as an almost impenetrable armor.

As seal hunter the polar bear displays much cunning. It will watch patiently for hours in the vicinity of a seal hole in the ice, and the instant its prey comes out to bask in the sun, the sly bear crouches, with its fore-paws doubled up under its body, while with its hind-legs it slowly and noiselessly pushes and hitches itself along toward the desired game. Does the seal raise its head to look around,

SLAIN IN DEFENSE OF HER YOUNG.

the bear remains motionless, its color making it hardly distinguishable, until the unsuspecting seal takes another nap. When the bear is near enough, with a sudden movement it seizes the innocent and defenseless victim, and makes a fat feast. Unless it is very hungry, it eats little besides the blubber, leaving the rest for the foxes. It is said that arctic foxes often follow in the path of bears, and gain their entire living from the refuse of the bear's feast.

The nest of the she-bear is a wonderful illustration of instinct, and a proof of the fact that a thick wall of snow is an excellent protection against cold. Toward the month of December the bear selects a spot at the foot of some cliff, where she burrows in the snow, and, remaining quiet, allows the heavy snow-storms to cover her with drifts. The warmth of her body enlarges the hole so that she can move herself, and her breath always keeps a small passage open in the roof of her den. Before retiring to these winter quarters she eats voraciously, and becomes enormously fat, so that she is able to exist a long time without food. In this snuggery the bear remains until some time in March, when she breaks down the walls of her palace, and comes out to renew her wandering life, with some little white baby bears for her companions, which have been born during her long seclusion.

Many funny and exciting stories are told by arctic travellers of encounters with bears. During Dr. Kane's expedition a scouting party who were away from the ship, and sleeping in a tent on the ice, were awakened by a scratching in the snow outside. On looking out they saw a huge bear reconnoitring the circuit of the tent. Their fire-arms were stacked on the sledge a short distance off, as had they been kept inside the tent, the frost from the men's breath would have clogged them and rendered them useless. There was nothing to be done but to keep quiet, and hope his bearship would go away. But the bear was bent on discovery, and his big head soon appeared through the fold of the tent. Volleys of lucifer matches and burning newspapers which were thrown at him did not disturb him in the least, and he quietly proceeded to make his supper upon the carcass of a seal. One of the men then cut a hole in the rear of the tent, and crawling cautiously out, was able to reach the guns, and soon sent a bullet through the body of the huge beast.

The mother bear's affection for her little ones is so strong that she will lose her life defending them. Two arctic huntsmen once saw a bear taking a promenade on an ice island with two little cubs. Chase was given at once, but the bear did not perceive the hunters until they were within five hundred yards of her. She then stood up on her hind-legs like a dancing bear, gave one good look at her pursuers, and started to run at full speed over the smooth ice, her cubs close at her heels. She had the advantage of the hunters, as the feet of the polar bear are thickly covered with long hair—nature's wise provision to keep the animal from slipping; but the ice soon broke up into a vast expanse of slush, and here the little cubs stuck fast. The faithful mother seized first one and then the other, but proceeded with so much difficulty that the hunters were soon near enough to fire at her. The little ones clung to their mother's dead body, and it was with great difficulty that the hunters succeeded in dragging them to the camp, where they stoutly resisted all friendly advances, and bit and struggled, and roared as loud as they could.

Bears often annoy arctic travellers by breaking open the caches, or store-houses, left along the line of march for return supplies. Dr. Kane relates that he found one of his caches, which had been built with heavy rocks laid together with extreme care, entirely destroyed, the bears apparently having had a grand frolic, rolling about the bread barrels, playing foot-ball with the heavy iron cases of pemmican, and even gnawing to shreds the American flag which surmounted the cache.

Roast bear meat is very palatable and welcome food to travellers in the dreary frozen arctic regions, and at the cry of "Nannook! nannook!" ("A bear! a bear!") from the Esquimaux guides, both men and dogs start in eager pursuit. The bear being white like the snow, it often escapes detection, and Dr. Kane mentions approaching what he thought was a heap of somewhat dingy snow, when he was startled by a "menagerie roar," which sent him running toward the ship, throwing back his mittens, one at a time, to divert the bear's attention.

Polar bears are sometimes found upon floating ice-cakes a hundred miles from land, having been caught during some sudden break up of the vast ice-fields of arctic seas, and every year a dozen or more come drifting down to the northern shores of Iceland, where, ravenous after their long voyage, they fall furiously upon the herds. Their life on shore, however, is very brief, as the inhabitants rise in arms and speedily dispatch them.

A NORSK STORY.

ON one of the *fjords*, or bays, which so deeply indent the coast of Norway lived two lads, sons of well-to-do farmers, who, besides their fields of rye and wheat, their *marks*, or pasture fields, and their *sæters*, or hay-making fields, farther away, had also an interest in the fisheries for which Norway is so famous. The salmon, the herring, and the cod are all caught in great numbers; so also is the shark, and used for its oil, which passes for cod-liver oil.

The fathers of Lars and Klaus were, however, peasants. They worked on their farms, and above their green pastures rose lofty mountains clad in fir-trees, dusky pines, mottled beeches, and silver birches. Klaus and Lars explored together the recesses of these mountains; together they hunted for bears; together they sailed over the blue waters of the *fjord*, in and out of the swift currents, and on and up into the streams fed by the great ice *fjelds*. They were always together. If any one wanted Klaus, he asked where Lars had gone; and if one had seen Lars, he knew Klaus would soon follow. It was their delight to see which could excel the other in the management of their fishing *jagts*, those square-sailed slow craft, and for days they would cruise about the haunts of the eider-duck—not to kill it, for that is forbidden, the bird being too valuable, but to filch from the sides of its nest the lovely down which the birds pluck from their own breasts.

They went to school, too, in the winter, and both were confirmed by the village pastor as soon as they had been well prepared for that solemn rite, which is of so much social as well as religious importance in their country.

In the short hot summer they helped the fishermen split the cod and spread them on the rocks to dry, or they made lemming traps and sought to see how many of the hated vermin they could capture.

In short, their life was active, hardy, and full of keen enjoyment; they were good-natured, and did not quarrel. Both were tall, finely grown as to muscle, but they would have been handsomer had they eaten less salt fish and more beef.

In a quaint little house at the foot of the mountains, near where tumbled in snowy foam a beautiful *foss*, lived an old woman and her grandchild Ilda. They were really tenants of Klaus's father; and in their wanderings the boys often stopped for a glass of milk or a slice of *fladbröd* (oat-cake), which the old woman was glad to give them. Ilda, too, in her red bodice and white chemisette, and her pretty, shy ways, was almost as attractive as the birds or beasts they were seeking. Neither the old woman nor Ilda often left their cottage, and so the boys were the more welcome for the news they carried.

They were able to give them the latest bit of gossip—how many men were off on the herring catch; if any strangers had come through the town in their *carrioles* on their way to the noted and beautiful Voring Foss and Skjæggedal Foss (two water-falls of great renown); or who had the American fever, and were going to emigrate. Or they talked about the ducks and geese of which Ilda was so proud, and of the pigeons which Klaus had given her when they were wild, but which had grown tame and lovable under her gentle care. Then the old woman related in turn many a legend and fable, tales of the saintly King Olaf, or the doings of Odin and Thor.

Thus the days glided by, and the boys became men, and still they were together in their work as they had been in their play. In the rye fields and the potato patches they toiled side by side, and in the last nights of summer—the

three August nights which they call iron nights, because of the frosts which sometimes come and blight all the wheat crop—they watched and waited, hoping for the good luck which did not always come to them: for the soil is a hard one to cultivate, and many are the trials which farmers have to meet in that bleak land. Soon after they became of age they were called upon to share the grief of their friend Ilda, whose grandmother died. After this they did not go so often to the cottage. One bright evening, however, as Lars was on his way up the mountain, he saw Klaus emerging from the little door beneath the shed of which they had so often sat. As they met, Klaus turned his face away, remarking, however, upon the beauty of the evening. Lars thought his friend's manner somewhat strange, and asked him if Ilda was well. Klaus said she was quite well—was he going to see her?

"Yes," said Lars. "I have some fresh currants from our garden, the only fruit which will grow in it, and I thought perhaps she might care for them, poor little thing. She is so lonely now!"

Klaus turned off down the road, whistling, while Lars went into the cottage. To his surprise he found Ilda crying, but supposing that the sight of Klaus had revived recollections which were painful, some sad thoughts of her grandmother, he tried to soothe her. She shook her head mournfully at his kind words, and told him that she had just done a cruel thing, that Klaus had asked her to be his wife, and she had said no to him. This came upon Lars very much like a thunder-bolt, for he had no idea that Klaus had any such wish; and much as he pitied his friend, he was not entirely sorry that Ilda had said no. So he asked her why she had refused to be Klaus's wife, when, with much embarrassment, she told him that she cared more for some one else.

Lars did not urge her to say any more, but leaving his currants, he followed Klaus down the mountain.

A few days after this, to the surprise of every one, Klaus bade his friends good-by, and took passage on the little steamer to Christiansand, from whence he would cross the Skagerrack, and sailing down the coast of Denmark, past Holland and Belgium, through the English Channel, he would be on the broad Atlantic, which was to bear him to a new home in the far western land.

Lars was not merely surprised, he was stunned, and thought his friend almost an enemy to go in that manner without consulting him, without even asking his advice or company. They had never before been separated. He could not understand it; and when Klaus bade him good-by he looked into his face as if to seek the reason for this strange conduct, but Klaus gave him no chance to ask it. He simply grasped his hand in silence, giving it a close clasp, and then he was off.

Days, weeks, months, went by, and no one heard from Klaus; at last his mother had a letter from him. He wrote cheerfully; said he liked America, but that he could not make up his mind to go far away to the prairies, where he could never see the blue ocean or the white gulls, or hear the splash of oars.

Meanwhile Lars was very unhappy. Everything seemed to go wrong with him—the crops failed, his share in the fisheries was small, and his father was hard and close with him. He missed his friend sadly; he cared no longer to do the daring things they had attempted together. He had never been to see Ilda since the day she had told him that she did not love his friend Klaus. As the spring advanced into summer, he met her one day in the pine woods near her cottage, and she looked so pleased to see him that he was tempted to tell her of all his troubles, especially of how disappointed and hurt he was by the departure of Klaus; and this reminded him of what she had told him about caring for some one else; but when he asked her who it was, to his great happiness she told him that he, Lars, was the one, and that was the reason why Klaus had gone away. Then, for the first time, he saw how generously his friend had acted; he had gone away that he might not interfere with his friend, for Klaus had found out that Ilda loved Lars. So in due time they were married in the simple fashion of the Norwegian people. But the crops were not more flourishing; and work as hard as he would, Lars could not do as well for himself as he would have liked. So he took all his money and bought a bigger jagt, and carried klip (or split) fish to the south, from whence they would be sent to Spain.

This separated him from Ilda and the little yellow-haired Hanne, his child; and his voyages were not very prosperous, so at last they determined to do as did the Norsemen and Vikings of old, set sail for the land of the setting sun.

It was hard to give up Norway, but Ilda was willing to do that which was for the best, and quietly filled the big boxes and chests with the linen she had spun herself, and made stout flannel clothes for little Hanne, and said "good-by" to every one she knew, and then they got off as fast as the slow jagt would carry them; off, out of the beautiful fjord with its green banks and snowy-topped mountains, away from the rocks and *fjelds* so dear to them, on to the broad, the mighty ocean.

They sailed and sailed for many a day, and Ilda knit while the little lassie, Hanne, played at her feet, and Lars smoked his pipe, and talked of the glorious land of liberty and fertile fields which they were approaching.

They had pleasant weather for a long while, and it did seem as if the kind words, the *lyksomme reise*, or lucky journey, which their friends had wished them, was really to be experienced. Little Hannchen was a merry, bright little companion, and made all the rough sailors love her. Her evening meal was milk and fladbröd, and she always threw some over the ship's side for the "poor hungry fishes," while she prattled in Norsk to the sailors, who were mostly Swedes and Finns. But whether they understood her or not, they liked to watch her blue eyes sparkle, and her yellow hair fly out like freshly spun flax, as she merrily danced about the slow old jagt; and they called her "Heldig Hanne," or "happy Hanne." But they were now approaching land, and fogs set in which were more to be dreaded than high winds, and the helmsman looked anxious, and Lars could not sleep. The atmosphere seemed to get thicker and thicker, and where they could for a while see the faint yellow twinkle of the stars all was now an opaque film.

One night as Ilda was singing a little song to Hanne a great crash came, a terrible thump, and then a queer grating sound. All had been still on deck, but now came hoarse shouts and cries, and Lars rushed down to the cabin, saying, "We are on the rocks! we are lost, Ilda!"

Ilda clasped little Hanne still closer as she said, tremulously, "Is it true, Lars? is there no way of escape? are we so near land?"

"Yes; come up on deck. The ship is already settling. We must try to get you and the child off in one of the boats."

"Not without you, Lars; we will not move an inch without you."

"See," he replied, as he helped her up the steps, "the gulls are flying over our heads; land must be near."

It was horribly true that the vessel was thumping and bumping on the rocks; the surf was roaring, and it seemed impossible for a boat to be launched. The sailors were making ready to cast themselves into the sea. Some were cursing, others praying, and others tying and lashing themselves to spars which they had taken from their fastenings. Two of them came up to Lars.

"Sir, for the sake of the child there, we will swim, if we can, to the shore, and get help."

"It would be useless," said Lars.

"Oh no," said Ilda; "let them try. They are brave. Perhaps they will succeed."

They nodded, and went off, Lars looking after them hopelessly as he muttered: "I might have known this; it is just my luck. Oh, Ilda! Ilda! why did I bring you with me?—and poor little Hanne!"

The child clung to her mother, her blue eyes dilated with fear, and her little hands about her mother's neck.

"Hush, Lars," said Ilda; "where thou art, there I would be, and so would Hannchen. God is yet able to save us."

The moments seemed like days; presently the vessel gave a great lurch to one side, and Lars had just time to tie Ilda to him as the waves broke over the jagt.

"*Farvel!*" was all he said to her, as they were plunged into the water; but as he saw the waves closing about them, he heard a cry from the sailors—a cry of joy, of welcome—and he felt a strong hand reached out to him, and a coil of rope flung about them. He had his arm under the fainting Ilda, but surely he had seen the face of the brave fellow who took Hanne in his arms from Ilda's clasp. He could not think; he only knew that they were saved at last—that a dozen strong men, some on land, some in the water, were dragging them to shore.

Ah! what rest and peace and thankfulness after a night like that! and with what strange and solemn emotions did Lars and Ilda look about them when they discovered that the house they were in belonged to the one who had carried their little Hanne in his arms from the ocean, and was none other than their old friend Klaus. Klaus the fisherman, Klaus the sailor, as he was known on that shore. The same Klaus, merry and brave, with a house of his own and a wife of his own, ready to share all he possessed with Lars, if Lars would only stay and settle near him. The jagt had gone down with all Lars's worldly goods; but Ilda was safe and Hanne was safe, and with so good a *friend* as Klaus, surely Lars could begin the world anew. And so he staid; and the tide turned, and fair weather prevailed.

CADDY'S CLOCK PARTY.

THE great hall clock was not asked to the party, but it was there, all the same. It was Milly Holland's birthday party. Milly was just fourteen years old; and most of the boys and girls near her own age whom she knew had been invited, and among them little Caddy Podkins, too little and young to care for at all, Milly thought; but kind Mrs. Holland had asked Caddy, because she was the only child of her nearest neighbor, and used to sit for hours in the bay-window across the way as if she did not have anything to amuse her.

The Hollands lived in a large, handsome house, and to-day it was pleasanter than usual, there were so many flowers about the rooms, and pretty moss baskets, and vines twisted around the chandeliers.

At half past five, the hour set for the party to begin, Milly's guests began to come; and Milly herself, in a soft white merino dress, came down the wide stairs to the polished oaken landing, and received them as they came up the lower steps from the big hall doors. There were nearly fifty boys and girls—more girls than boys—and as the party would be over at ten o'clock, they wisely lost no time, and came almost all at once. It made a pretty sight as they shook back their wrappings from their gay dresses, and crowded around Milly. It was as if a good-natured giant had spilled a huge basket of red and white rose-buds over the oaken landing and stairs, up which the children followed Milly to the dressing-room and the parlors, where the fires glowed in the cheerful grates, and the lamps in beautiful tinted globes made a brightness that seemed to the children more wonderful than day.

Now it is not so much about Milly's party as about one little girl who was in it that I am going to tell you; because parties are very commonplace things, and little girls, at least some little girls, are not.

When the party had been going on for a long time, and the children were being taken in to supper—and a very nice supper, too, with plenty of milk, white bread, and sparkling jellies—one of the largest girls stopped with Milly Holland for a moment where the staircase turned and looked down upon the oaken landing. There stood the tall, old-fashioned clock, looking very old and rather proud in its rich dark case, and against it leaned a very little girl, not more than eight years old, with a good deal of brown hair, and big gray eyes. Her folded hands and her little cheek were pressed against the edge of the clock case. The hall lamp from the bracket overhead shone on her hair and her crumpled dress, and left her face in the shadow.

"Who's that?" asked the other girl of Milly.

"What! don't you know Caddy Podkins?" said Milly. "The idea of mother asking such a baby as *that* to *my* party!"

Then the two girls went to supper. The supper-room was farther from the landing than the parlors, and when the door had closed, the hall became quite still. All at once Caddy thought the clock ticked louder than she had ever heard a clock tick in all her life before. And she was quite right, for the clock was trying to speak to Caddy, and except just to state, without a single needless word, the hour, this clock had never tried to speak before. But the clock liked Caddy very much. It had seen that Caddy was very bashful, and that the other children took hardly any notice of her, or any care for her pleasure, and it liked the feeling of Caddy's little cheek and warm hands upon its side.

Now Caddy had a little invisible key. It was finer than refined gold, and stronger than adamant (which is the very hardest kind of stone there is, you know), and there was not a lock—no, not even the lock of the tongue of a clock—which could help opening to Caddy's little key. Caddy herself knew nothing about this key, not even its long name—*Im-ag-i-na-tion*. But the key did not need to have Caddy know; it staid in a little pearl of a room full of the brightest thoughts of Caddy's mind, and whenever these thoughts began to stir about and say, "I wonder," away the little key would fly, and open some new delightful secret to Caddy. There are thousands and thousands of children who have keys of this sort; but, oh! there's such a difference in the keys and in the secrets that they find! Caddy's key was one of the very best, and even while she was noticing that the clock ticked so loud, her little key had turned itself in the very centre of the wheels, and the clock whispered, close in her ear, "Caddy, little Caddy, shall I—tick-a-tack—talk to you?"

Caddy was not at all surprised or bashful with the clock, but asked, quickly, "Were you ever at a party?"

"Hundreds of them," said the clock. "Tiresome things, parties are."

"Guess you don't get any supper, perhaps," said Caddy, with a queer little smile.

"Guess you are hungry, perhaps," laughed the clock, with a dozen little sharp ticks all together. "Now, you dear little Caddy, I'm a clock of a very good family. As far back as I can remember—and that's a very long time—there has never been a clock in my family which did not keep perfect time, and tell the truth exactly to a second every time it spoke, and I know how a little girl who is invited to a party ought to be treated, so I invite you now, Caddy Podkins, to my party."

"What! a really, truly clock party?" exclaimed Caddy, and in the same moment the big clock had swung its long pendulum wire around her waist, and lifted Caddy as if she were a feather, whirled her so fast that Caddy saw nothing at all, and then set her down very gently in a room whose floor was shaped like the flat side of a wheel, and the edges of the floor were notched just like the edges of the wheels in a clock. The walls of the room were like brass that has been rubbed very bright, and were covered with net-work of fine curling wire. In the middle of the room was a long table, set with wheel-shaped plates, which were heaped with large sweet raisins and nut meats, fresh flaky biscuits, and there were the most delicious fruits, so ripe you could see through to the seeds and stones in their cores. Over the table hung a chandelier, shaped like a pendulum, which gave a soft yellow light. The big clock stood at the head of the table, tapping her fore-head with her long minute-finger. She smiled at Caddy's wonder, and ticked out, merrily,

"Well, Caddy, Caddy, Caddy,
Tick-a-tock-tick-tock!
How's this for a clock?
Ha! ha! It's not so bad—eh?"

Caddy leaned against her tall friend, and asked, very comfortably, "Are your little clocks coming?"

At this question the old clock ticked slowly off on her minute-finger,

"Inty-minty-cuty-corn,
Apple seeds and apple thorn,
Wire brier, limber lock,
Three wheels in a clock!"

At that last word suddenly the curling wires all over the walls gave out a curious tinkling, and letting themselves swiftly down in long slender spirals, like the dandelion curls you make in the spring, each set a tiny little clock on the floor. Then all the wires snapped back to their places on the wall. There were as many as fifty of these little clocks, beautifully made, and no two of them alike, though they all had little brass hands reaching out of the sides of their cases, and they all had little brass feet, on which they hopped about nimbly, and they all ticked together in the funniest way.

"Tick-a-tock-tarty,
It's Caddy's party,"

said the old clock, and the little clocks instantly made a circle around Caddy, and each bent one knee and slid back one little brass foot in the most polite courtesy to Caddy. One of the oldest of the little clocks then hopped off to a tiny wire harp that stood in a corner, and began to play a sweet lively waltz with her queer brass fingers. The rest of the clocks came one after another and led Caddy out and waltzed with her. Caddy had never danced so much in all her life, and had never liked it half so well.

"Tick-a-tock, step feet,
Little Caddy must eat,"

said the old clock. And, oh! what a supper that was to hungry, happy little Caddy! and how happy the little clocks were to have such a good little girl as Caddy with them! They gave her the best of everything upon the table, and waited to see that she had all she wished before they even thought of eating for themselves. They told her all sorts of droll stories, and one little clock astonished Caddy very much by opening her little silver tunic and showing Caddy—who had not quite believed it before—that the little wheels actually did eat up the juicy fruits. "I wonder if *I* am full of little wheels," said Caddy. Then Caddy's little key sighed, for it was just the least bit tired, and Caddy's "I wonder" meant work for the key. But the old clock suddenly exclaimed,

"Tick-a-tock, 'most ten,
Little Caddy, come again."

CADDY LEANED AGAINST HER TALL FRIEND.

"Caddy! Caddy Potkins!" said Mrs. Holland, in great surprise. The children were putting on their things in the dressing-room up stairs, and Mrs. Holland had just noticed that Caddy was not with them, and coming hastily down stairs, saw Caddy, just as we did, leaning against the tall old clock. "My poor little dear, why, how cold you are! Have you been asleep? Milly ought to have taken care of you. I'm afraid you have not had a good time."

"I've had a clock party," said Caddy, rubbing her eyes, while Mrs. Holland tied on her hood, "and I'm to come again."

FAIR PLAY.

DEAR little May sat grieving alone,
  With a pout on her lip and a tear in her eye,
Till kind old grandmamma chanced to pass,
  And soon discovered the reason why.
"The children are planning a fair," sobbed she,
"And 'cause I'm so little, they won't—have—me!"

So grandmamma thought of a beautiful plan,
  And whispered a secret in little May's ear—
Something which brought out the dimples and smiles,
  And scattered with sunshine the pitiful tear.
Then off to grandmamma's room they went,
On something important very intent.

Well, the fair came off on a certain day,
  And what do you think was the first thing sold?
A beautiful pair of worsted reins,
  All knit in scarlet and green and gold.
The "big girls" wondered how came they there—
"The prettiest thing in the children's fair!"

Then out stepped May, with her cheeks so red:
  "You said there was nothing that I could do,
'Cause I was little; but I made these,
  And now, I guess, I'm as big as you!"
So little May at the fair that day
Was the reigning queen, it is fair to say.

THE WHITE PEBBLE PIT.—It has frequently happened that miners have discovered curious traces of former workings, hundreds of years ago, and tools have been found which belonged to the ancient miners, and many other relics.

A singular discovery was made, a few years since, by some workmen engaged in the Spanish silver mine known as the White Pebble Pit. Whilst digging their subterranean passages they suddenly found a series of apartments, in which were a quantity of mining tools, left there from a very remote period, but still in such good preservation that there were hatchets, and sieves for sifting the ore, a smelting furnace, and two anvils, which proved that the earliest miners had great experience in their operations.

In one of the caverns there was a round building, with niches, in which were three statues, one sitting down, and half the size of life; the other two were in a standing position, and about three feet in height. This building is supposed to have been the temple of the god who was believed, in pagan times, to preside over miners. Several objects of art, and some remarkable instruments, were also found, which have led scientific persons to think that the workings might have been made by the Phœnicians, the people who, as is well known, were, in the time of Solomon, famous for their manufacturing and commercial genius.

In 1864 a discovery was also made by some miners excavating on the other side of the mountain on which the White Pebble Pit is situated; this was a fine figure of the heathen god Hercules, which was found in an old working.

In digging for copper on the shores of Lake Superior, in this country, the miners have made many similar discoveries, showing that the mines were worked ages ago.

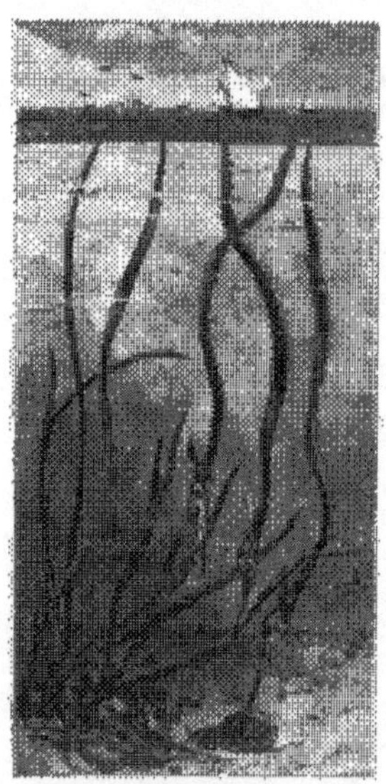

GRASS-FISH (NEMICHTHYS).

THE curious fishes with the tremendous name, the last part of which means snipe-billed, are very long and defenceless, and are invariably found among the leaves of a long sea-grass, which very nearly resembles them in form and color. Their head is quite long, and they always seem to stand on it, and when a hungry fish comes along, he would have to look long and well to tell which was the grass and which the fish. These grass-fish well earn their right to be called "mimics." These strange features in such low animals teach an interesting lesson: they show more strongly the wise governing of the great Maker, and correct the mistake, often thoughtlessly made, that the lower animals have no feelings, thoughts, or pleasures. If they do not show them as we do, it is none the less true that they possess them, but in different degrees.

Little Jack Horner.—The origin of the nursery rhyme has been said to be as follows: When monasteries and their property were seized, orders were given that the title-deeds of the abbey estates of Mells, which were very valuable, should be given up to the commissioners. The abbot's chosen [illegible] of sending them was in the form of a pasty to be sent as a present from the abbot to one of the commissioners in London. Jack Horner, a poor lad, was chosen as the messenger. Tired, he rested in as comfortable a corner as he could on his way. Hungry, he determined to taste the pasty he was carrying. Inserting his thumb into the pie, he found nothing but parchment deeds. One of these he pulled out and pocketed, as likely to be valuable. The Abbot Whiting of Mells was executed for having withheld the missing parchment. In the Horner family was discovered years afterward the plum that Jack had picked out, one of the chief title-deeds of Mells abbey and lands.

OUR heartiest thanks are due to our youthful readers who have sent us pretty and gracefully written New-Year's wishes from all parts of the United States. We would like to print every one of these welcome letters, but they are so numerous it would be impossible. Our young friends, however, may be sure that whether we print them or simply acknowledge them, they are alike pleasing and gratifying to us.

Robin Tozier (eleven years) writes that he punches a hole in his *Young People*, and ties the numbers together with a ribbon, adding the new numbers as fast as they come. This is an excellent suggestion, as it prevents the numbers from getting scattered and lost.

South Evanston, Illinois.

I have a little canary-bird. He is quite young, but is a beautiful singer, and almost always when he sings he says, "Pretty, pretty," so plain you could not mistake it. He is also very tame, and when I let him out of his cage he comes and stands on my shoulder, and hops around me. If I put my finger in his cage, he gets very cross, and waves his wings and pecks at me, and makes a queer noise as if he were scolding.

Edith T. (twelve years).

I am a little girl nine years old, and I live in Stockbridge, Massachusetts. I see that one little girl has written about her pet pigeon. I have a pet squirrel. He is so tame he will run all over me. Last summer we let him run out in the front yard, and papa put him in a tree, but he would not climb it. Papa has subscribed for *Young People* for me. I like it very much, and look forward with pleasure to the time for it to come. Thank you for making it larger; it is just nice.

John S. E.

Fort Wayne, Indiana.

I received *Young People* for Christmas, and like the stories very much. I like "Phantasm and Nycteris" so much that I can hardly wait till the next number comes. The engravings are very nice. I think that there was never a paper so interesting. I thank you for the "Wiggles" and other games. Happy New Year.

Walter C.

[illegible], Pennsylvania.

I am ten years old. I like *Young People* the best of any paper I ever saw. It is the first paper my papa has ever taken for me. He takes the *Weekly*. I think the *Young People* is just the right size for binding, and I am going to have it bound at the end of the year.

[illegible].

I am very much interested in your paper. I am going to save up my money to take it. I am nine years old. I have a pony named Coly. I enjoy him very much. He is a Texan pony. I live in Richmond, Kentucky, where the grass is so blue.

Bura Ware.

Letters are acknowledged from Mamie J. W., Dayton, Washington Territory; Daisie Ballard, Schuylerville, New York; Lorean C., Manitowoc, Wisconsin; Fred E. H., Cambridge, Massachusetts; Harry E., Winona, Minnesota; H. W. Singer, Cincinnati, Ohio; Minnie W. Jacobs, Indiana, Pennsylvania; Percy W. Shedd, Aylesbury, New York; Lizzie C., Utica, New York; Willie Hamilton, Allegheny City, Pennsylvania; Zella Thompson, Boston, Massachusetts; O. R. Heimer, Allentown, Pennsylvania; Frederick L. B., Brooklyn, Long Island; and Lyman C., M. C. B., and William F. B., New York city.

"Tel.," Zanesville, Ohio.—Flat cribbage-boards can be bought at a very low price, and folding ones which hold the cards are not expensive. You might make one from a piece of thick pasteboard, but as there must be sixty-one peg-holes for each player, it would not be easy to cut them neatly.—It is more customary to leave a card for each person called upon, especially where the visit is formal.

George H. H.—Harper's new School Geography gives Wheeling as the capital of West Virginia.

Fannie G.—Even if you are only seven years, you are old enough to read a boys' book about wild animals. Lions will catch and eat nearly all beasts that come in their way. They will even overpower a giraffe or a buffalo. The elephant and rhinoceros are almost the only quadrupeds a lion dare not meddle with.

OUR CHRISTMAS PUZZLE.

Lovelands, Ohio.

I think I have correctly worked the Christmas Puzzle in *Young People*. I had to study some time over "Yay," never having heard of such a fish. It was only by finding what letters I needed in the columns 13, 8, 9 that I saw they were Y-a-y. On looking in the dictionary I found there was a fish called by that name. "Yard" also puzzled me a great deal. The other words were easily found.

M. F. C.

Williamstown, Delaware.

My brother Bertie and I have had a nice time finding the answer to your Christmas Puzzle in No. 8 of *Young People*. We thank you very much for your kind wish, and wish you the same in return. Can your young readers tell what it is we wish you?

Lillie J.

All these boys and girls have also told our Christmas Puzzle wish correctly: Maynard A. M., M. A. S., and F. V. R., Alexina K. D., F. E. Cummin, Willie J. M., Virgil C. M., Amy L. H., Etta Douglass, Annie G. Long, Willie D. S., Lilian Forbes, Jamie D. H., Huntington W., A. A. R., Mamie M., Nellie P., Emie B., Fred D. H., Zaide H. D., Edna Heimen, Seabury O. P., E. A. De Lima, Claudie M. Tice, Louie A., J. H. Wolfe, Carroll O. B., George F. D., S. K. S., Ellie E. T., O. M. B., Ada and Clara, Florence D., Alice P., E. C. Repper, and George Henry.

The answer to Christmas Puzzle in *Young People* No. 8 is, "I wish you a merry Christmas and a happy New-Year."

"*Learning made pleasant.*"
N. Y. Evening Post.

SCIENCE FOR THE YOUNG.

By JACOB ABBOTT.

ILLUSTRATED.

4 volumes, 12mo, Cloth, $1 50 each.

I. HEAT. III. WATER AND LAND.
II. LIGHT. IV. FORCE.

If a mass-meeting of parents and children were to be held for the purpose of erecting a monument to the author who has done most to entertain and instruct the young folks, there would certainly be a unanimous vote in favor of Mr. Jacob Abbott. Two or three generations of American youth owe many of their most pleasant hours of recreation to his story-books; and his latest productions are as fresh and youthful as those which the parents and guardians of to-day once looked forward to as the most precious gifts from the Christmas bag of old Santa Claus. The series published under the general title of "Science for the Young" ought to be called "Learning made Pleasant." An interesting story runs through each, and beguiles the reader into the acquisition of a vast amount of useful knowledge under the genial pretence of furnishing amusement. No intelligent child can read these volumes without obtaining a better knowledge of physical science than many students have when they leave college.—*N. Y. Evening Post.*

Jacob Abbott is almost the only writer in the English language who knows how to combine real amusement with real instruction in such a manner that the eager young readers are quite as much interested in the useful knowledge he imparts as in the story which he makes the pleasant vehicle of instruction.—*Buffalo Commercial Advertiser.*

Mr. Abbott has avoided the error of slurring over the difficulties of the subject through the desire of making it intelligible and attractive to unlearned readers. The numerous illustrations which accompany every chapter are of indispensable value in the comprehension of the text, and come next to actual experiment as an aid to the reader.—*N. Y. Tribune.*

Published by HARPER & BROTHERS, New York.

☞ *Sent by mail, postage prepaid, to any part of the United States, on receipt of the price.*

"*A book beyond the pale of criticism.*"
N. Y. Daily Graphic.

THE

Boy Travellers in the Far East.

ADVENTURES OF TWO YOUTHS IN A JOURNEY TO JAPAN AND CHINA.

Illustrated, 8vo, Cloth, $3 00.

A more attractive book for boys and girls can scarcely be imagined.—*N. Y. Times.*

The best thing for a boy who cannot go to China and Japan is to get this book and read it.—*Philadelphia Ledger.*

Juvenile literature seems to have come to a climax in this book. In literary quality and in mechanical form it is a decided improvement on anything of the kind ever before produced in America.—*N. Y. Journal of Commerce.*

One of the richest and most entertaining books for young people, both in text, illustrations, and binding, which has ever come to our table.—*Providence Press.*

Published by HARPER & BROTHERS, N. Y.

☞ *Sent by mail, postage prepaid, to any part of the United States, on receipt of the price.*

Old Books for Young Readers.

Arabian Nights' Entertainments.

The Thousand and One Nights; or, The Arabian Nights' Entertainments. Translated and Arranged for Family Reading, with Explanatory Notes, by E. W. LANE. 600 Illustrations by Harvey. 2 vols., 12mo, Cloth, $3 50.

Robinson Crusoe.

The Life and Surprising Adventures of Robinson Crusoe, of York, Mariner. By DANIEL DEFOE. With a Biographical Account of Defoe. Illustrated by Adams. Complete Edition. 12mo, Cloth, $1 50.

The Swiss Family Robinson.

The Swiss Family Robinson; or, Adventures of a Father and Mother and Four Sons on a Desert Island. Illustrated. 2 vols., 18mo, Cloth, $1 50.

The Swiss Family Robinson—Continued: being a Sequel to the Foregoing. 2 vols., 18mo, Cloth, $1 50.

Sandford and Merton.

The History of Sandford and Merton. By THOMAS DAY. 18mo, Half Bound, 75 cents.

Published by HARPER & BROTHERS, New York.

☞ HARPER & BROTHERS *will send any of the above works by mail, postage prepaid, to any part of the United States, on receipt of the price.*

The Fairy Books.

THE PRINCESS IDLEWAYS. By Mrs. W. J. HAYS. Illustrated. 16mo, Cloth, 50 cents.

THE CATSKILL FAIRIES. By VIRGINIA W. JOHNSON. 8vo, Illuminated Cloth, Gilt Edges, $3 00.

FAIRY BOOK ILLUSTRATED. 16mo, Cloth, $1 50.

PUSS-CAT MEW, and other New Fairy Stories for my Children. By E. H. KNATCHBULL-HUGESSEN, M.P. Illustrated. 16mo, Cloth, $1 25.

FAIRY BOOK. The Best Popular Fairy Stories selected and rendered anew. By the Author of "John Halifax." Illustrated. 16mo, Cloth, $1 25.

FAIRY TALES. By JEAN MACÉ. Translated by MARY L. BOOTH. Illustrated. 12mo, Bevelled Edges, $1 75; Gilt Edges, $2 25.

FAIRY TALES OF ALL NATIONS. By E. LABOULAYE. Translated by MARY L. BOOTH. Illustrated. 12mo, Cloth, Bevelled Edges, $2 00; Gilt Edges, $2 50.

THE LITTLE LAME PRINCE. By the Author of "John Halifax, Gentleman." Illustrated. Square 16mo, Cloth, $1 00.

FOLKS AND FAIRIES. Stories for Little Children. By LUCY RANDALL COMFORT. Illustrated. Square 16mo, Cloth, $1 00.

THE ADVENTURES OF A BROWNIE as Told to my Child. By the Author of "John Halifax, Gentleman." Illustrated. Square 16mo, Cloth, 90 cents.

Published by HARPER & BROTHERS, New York.

☞ *Sent by mail, postage prepaid, to any part of the United States, on receipt of the price.*

"*A most enchanting story for boys.*"
Pittsburgh Telegraph.

AN INVOLUNTARY VOYAGE.

By LUCIEN BIART,

Author of "Adventures of a Young Naturalist."

TRANSLATED BY
Mrs. CASHEL HOEY and Mr. JOHN LILLIE.

ILLUSTRATED.

16mo, Cloth, $1 25.

A very absorbing book, bristling full of adventures, and has not an uninteresting page between its covers.—*Baltimore Gazette.*

A book that is at once novel and entertaining. * * * All the book is lively, and the voyagers have varied adventures, the telling of which is as entertaining as any book of Jules Verne's, besides having nothing in them that is unpalatable or extravagant.—*Philadelphia Bulletin.*

A most enchanting story for boys. * * * It is a story of adventure, and also contains much interesting and useful information.—*Pittsburgh Telegraph.*

A narrative crowded with adventure, told in the lively and graphic style for which the French writers of books for boys are so noted.—*Cleveland Herald.*

One of the most attractive books of the season. * * * Spirited sketches of travel and adventure on the ocean wave, among the islands and on distant coasts. All these delightful. But the main point which gives them their highest [illegible] is the [illegible] during our late civil conflict.—*Observer, N. Y.*

Published by HARPER & BROTHERS, N. Y.

☞ *Sent by mail, postage prepaid, to any part of the United States, on receipt of the price.*

A BOOK FOR EVERYBODY.

Ninth Edition now Ready.

HOW TO GET STRONG, AND HOW TO STAY SO. By WILLIAM BLAIKIE. With Illustrations. 16mo, Cloth, $1 00.

Your book is timely. Its large circulation cannot fail to be of great public benefit.—Rev. HENRY WARD BEECHER.

It is a book of extraordinary merit in matter and style, and does you great credit as a thinker and writer.—Hon. [illegible], *of the New York Supreme Bench.*

A capital little treatise. It is the very book for ministers to study.—Rev. THEODORE L. CUYLER, D.D., *in New York Evangelist.*

It is unquestionably one of the most practical and useful books on this topic which have ever been published in this country.—*N. Y. Evening Express.*

We know of no man in America more capable of writing such a book, or who has a better right to do so.—*Hartford Daily Herald and* [illegible].

It will pay any person—whether a farmer or a lawyer, laborer or idler, school-girl or housewife—to buy and read it, and follow its teachings.—*Springfield Union.*

A veritable treasury of muscular [illegible].—*Charleston News and Courier.*

Published by HARPER & BROTHERS, New York.

☞ *Sent by mail, postage prepaid, to any part of the United States, on receipt of the price.*

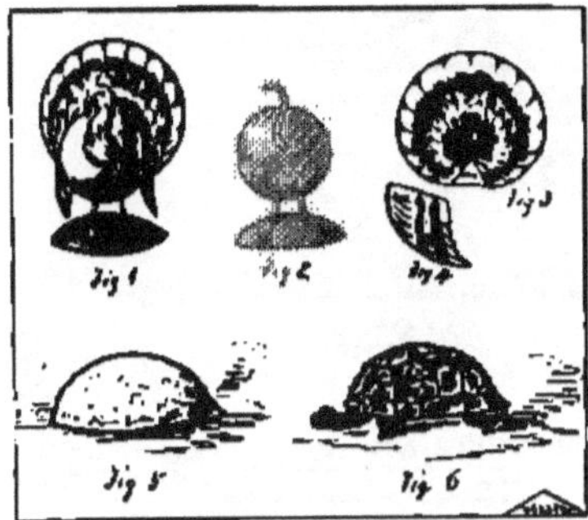

Johnny and Mary drive out in the Park,
And doubtless are having no end of a lark;
She holds Baby Rose with a motherly air,
And he handles his spirited horse with great care.

ART MANUFACTURES.

A GREAT many things can be made out of other things. A very fair turkey can be made out of a horse-chestnut, or even a common chestnut.

Look at Fig. 1 in the above picture: there you have the turkey complete. I will tell you how I made him. I first took a nice round chestnut, and stuck into it a bent pin to represent the neck; then I stuck in two other pins to represent the legs; then I took a piece of putty (dough, or bread worked up to the consistence of dough, will do), and made a stand into which I stuck the legs. He then looked as he is represented in Fig. 2. I then took a small piece of putty, and modelled on to the bent pin the head and neck of the turkey. After this I drew with pen and ink on thick paper, and cut with a pair of scissors, a thing like Fig. 3, and two things like Fig. 4; these were the tail and wings. I fastened them in their proper places with thick gum (short pins will do). Then with some red paint I painted the head and feet of the bird, and I had a very excellent turkey, but I felt thankful that I need not eat it for my dinner.

Figs. 5 and 6 show how a walnut shell may be changed into a turtle shell. Fig. 5 is the walnut shell, and Fig. 6 is the turtle; and I would not give a fig for the boy who, with a pen and ink and a little putty (dough will do), is not smart enough to make it.

Spiders that Kill Birds.—Everybody knows that spiders catch flies and other insects; but that some of them kill little birds may not be so generally known. A traveller in Brazil tells us that he caught one of them in the very act, while going through a forest in the Amazons. The spider was a hairy fellow, with a body two inches long, and eight legs measuring seven inches each, from end to end. The writer describing the incident says: "I was attracted by a movement of the monster on a tree trunk; it was close beneath a deep crevice in the tree, across which was stretched a dense white web. The lower part of the web was broken, and two small birds, finches, were entangled in the pieces. One of them was quite dead, and the other nearly so. I drove away the monster, and took the birds, but the second one soon died. The fact of species of Mygale, to which genus this spider belongs, sallying forth at night, mounting trees, and sucking the eggs and young of humming-birds, has been recorded long ago by Madame Merian and Palisot de Beauvois; but, in the absence of any confirmation, it has come to be discredited. From the way the fact has been related it would appear that it had been merely derived from the report of natives, and had not been witnessed by the narrators. The Mygales are quite common insects: some species make their cells under stones, others form artificial tunnels in the earth, and some build their dens in the thatch of houses. The natives call them Aranhas caranguejeiras, or crab-spiders. The hairs with which they are clothed come off when touched, and cause a peculiar and almost maddening irritation. The first specimen that I killed and prepared was handled incautiously, and I suffered terribly for three days afterward. I think this is not owing to any poisonous quality residing in the hairs, but to their being short and hard, and thus getting into the fine creases of the skin. Some Mygales are of immense size. One day I saw the children belonging to an Indian family with one of these monsters secured by a cord round its waist, by which they were leading it about the house as they would a dog."

GETTING A HITCH.

Get, get behind! The faster old Dobbin goes, the lighter grows his load.

ASSURANCE.

"Strike out, Nancy; Sis and I will hold you up."

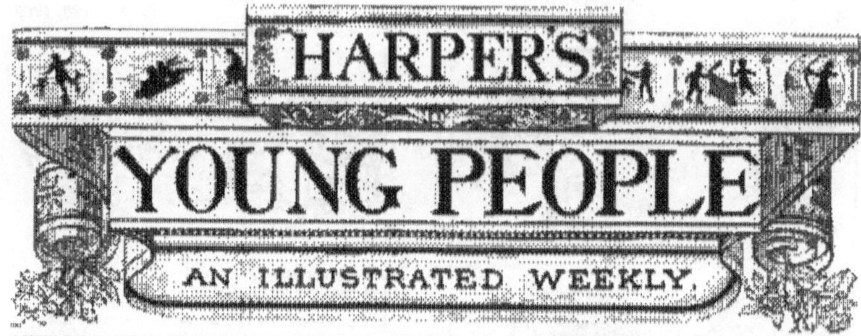

Vol. I.—No. 13. | Published by HARPER & BROTHERS, New York. | Price Four Cents.
Tuesday, January 27, 1880. | Copyright, 1880, by Harper & Brothers. | $1.50 per Year, in Advance.

THE DANCE IN THE KITCHEN.

On that winter afternoon,
Such a merry, merry tune
As the jolly, fat tea-kettle chose its singing to begin!
'Twas a lilting Scottish air,
And it sounded, I do declare,
As though bagpipes played by fairy were faintly joining in.

Then the bagpipes ceased to play,
And another tune straightway
Sang the kettle, shriller, louder, till its voice grew very high;
And the feet of laughing girls
(Lassies with shamrock in their curls)
You could almost hear a-tapping time to that old Irish jig.

Darling, smiling, cunning Bess
Grasped with tiny hands her dress,
And a pretty courtesy making, while the kettle made a bow,
"I'll your partner be," said she;
"Forward, backward, one, two, three;"
And pussy cried, "Bravo! my dears," in one immense me-ow.

And they danced right merrily
Till 'twas nearly time for tea,
The kettle tilting this way and then that way—oh, what fun!
And its hat bobbed up and down
On its sooty and steamy crown,
With a clatter falling off at last, and then the dance was done.

THE OLD MAN OF MONTROSE

THERE was an old man of Montrose
Who had a remarkable nose,
So long and so thin,
And so far from his chin,
'Twas always in danger of blows.

One day the old man of Montrose
Went out without muffling his nose;
And it grieves me to tell
That this organ of smell
As stiff as an icicle froze.

Soon after, in sneezing, "Ker-chew,"
His nose into smithereens flew,
And left but a stump,
A ridiculous lump,
That even in summer looked blue.

The frost-bitten man of Montrose
Used words that were equal to blows;
And so great his disgrace,
He soon quitted the place,
And where he has gone no one knows.

"THE BRAVEST OF THE BRAVE."

IN the small but strongly fortified town of Saar-Louis, on what was then the borders of France, in Rhenish Prussia, there was born, a little more than a hundred years ago, a child whose future intrepid career earned for him the title of "the bravest of the brave." His father's trade was nothing more warlike than that of a cooper; his home life and training were not different from those of many of his playmates; and yet before he was sixteen years old he had entered a regiment of hussars, or light cavalry, and before he was thirty had attained the high rank of general of division.

But those were warlike days; the French Revolution had just begun; all Europe was echoing with the clash and tread of such armies as the world had never before seen; and living as he did in the shadow of fortifications constructed by France's greatest military engineer, Vauban, it is not so strange that the youth became filled with an intense desire to taste the glory and share the danger of a soldier's life.

Michael Ney, Marshal of France, Duke of Elchingen, Prince of Moskwa—for by all these titles, commemorative of some one or other of his numerous victories, was he known—early rose in the confidence and estimation of the great Napoleon, and was by him intrusted with the most responsible commands in Switzerland, Prussia, Austria, and Spain; and it was not until he met Wellington at Torres Vedras, in the Peninsula, that he met his superior in the art of war; and even then, by a happy mixture of courage and skill, Ney was enabled to mitigate to a great extent the bitterness of defeat. But to relate his whole career would be to fill a volume, so we will only consider one or two incidents in his life.

In 1812, Ney took an active part in the invasion of Russia, and by his address and energy contributed largely to the French victory at the battle of the Moskwa, called by the Russians the battle of Borodino.

When the Russian Bear turned upon the invader, and the ever-memorable retreat commenced, with all its attendant horrors of cold, hunger, and physical pain, to Ney was assigned the honorable but arduous task of protecting the rear of the fleeing troops. At the start Ney's force numbered 7000 men, and on leaving Smolensk he found himself confronted by an army four times as large.

He was summoned to surrender before commencing the attack, and his characteristic reply, "A Marshal of France never surrenders," has passed into history, though it must be confessed that, in the light of recent events, history does not always bear out the assertion. Repeatedly driven back with awful loss, Ney determined to outwit the enemy; so, under cover of darkness, he and his troops made a wide circuit, and reached the bank of the river Dnieper far in advance of the pursuers.

But here a new foe confronted the gallant Marshal. How should he cross the stream! He had no boats, and although the weather was intensely cold, the rapid current was covered only by a thin coating of ice that bent beneath the weight of a single man. However, no time to deliberate was to be lost; so, dividing his forces into small companies, he caused the advance to be sounded, himself stepping first upon the glassy surface.

What a subject for a painter is here presented!—the frozen snowy landscape; the bare skeleton trees; the broad serpentine course of the frost-bound river, with here and there patches of open water showing darkly against the snow-covered ice; the scattered groups of soldiers treading carefully, and with the possibility before them that at the next step the treacherous floor might precipitate them into an icy grave.

But the hazardous passage was safely effected, and after a series of conflicts with forces in every case far superior to his own, Ney succeeded in rejoining the Emperor at Orsha, where he was received with open arms, and hailed as "the bravest of the brave"—a name which clung to him from that time.

After Napoleon left the army, Ney still continued to fight in the rear against the ever-increasing hordes of Russians that harassed the flanks of the fugitive army. Three times was the rear-guard that he commanded melted away by death, captivity, or flight, and as often was it re-organized by the indomitable Marshal who "never surrendered."

At last, with a poor remnant of only thirty men, Ney defended the gate of the town of Kovno—the last place in the Russian dominions through which the French retreated—against the pursuers, while the main body escaped through the gate at the other end of the town. He was himself the very last man to retire. Snatching a pistol from one of his men, he fired the last shot in the faces of the Russians, flung the weapon into the river Niemen, plunged in after it, and amid a storm of bullets swam the stream, and gained the neighboring forest, successfully eluded his pursuers, and joined his comrades, who had mourned him as dead, in the Prussian territory.

Ney's end was as unfortunate as it was unworthy so brave a soldier. When Napoleon was banished to Elba, Ney, who had previously incurred his displeasure, gave his allegiance to the restored Bourbons, and when the great Emperor re-appeared in France, Ney was placed in command of the army sent to oppose him, promising his new superiors to bring back Napoleon "like a wild beast in a cage."

There is no reason to doubt Ney's sincerity in this unhappy episode of his career. He was of a brave, impulsive disposition, one accustomed to act on the spur of the moment; so, when he drew near to the Emperor, and found that the men he commanded, nearly all of whom had fought at some time or other under the Emperor, were fixed in a resolve not to fight against Napoleon, it is not so much to be wondered at that Ney became Napoleonist with as much ardor as ever. And when Napoleon called on him by his old title, "the bravest of the brave," to once more rally under his standard, Ney responded with alacrity, as though the name possessed a magic spell he could not resist.

After Waterloo, when all that pertained to the cause of the dethroned Emperor was irretrievably lost, Ney was brought to trial by the re-restored Bourbons on the charge of treason, and was condemned to be shot on December 7, 1815. He met death with that same unflinching bravery which he so many times displayed, during his eventful career, on most of the great battle-fields of Europe.

On December 7, 1853, exactly thirty-eight years after his death, a statue was raised to the memory of the intrepid Marshal on the precise spot on which his execution occurred.

(Begun in No. 11 of Harper's Young People, January 13.)

LADY PRIMROSE.

BY FLETCHER READE.

CHAPTER III.

"A primrose by the river's brim
A yellow primrose was to him,
And it was nothing more."

"PRINCESS BÉBÉ! Princess Bébé! Princess Bébé!"

It was the little gate-keeper, running at the top of his speed, and shouting at the top of his voice.

Very much heated and very red in the face was the little man as he stood before the princess, holding out to her a loaf of bread almost as large as himself.

"This is for you," he said, in a choked voice, for he had run so far and so fast that he could hardly speak at all. "The wise old woman of Hollowbush sent it. Now eat, eat. Let me see what it is like—let me see how you do it."

While the princess ate her loaf of bread with more eagerness than any member of royalty ever displayed before or since, the gate-keeper watched her with wondering eyes.

"Well, I never saw anything like that before," he said at length. "And you go through that remarkable performance every day! Every day!" he repeated, in a tone of the most intense astonishment.

"But where did you find it?" asked the princess, who was more interested in the bread than in the gate-keeper.

"Find it!" he exclaimed. "I didn't find it. That wise old woman of Hollowbush, who has discovered the secret of the three knocks, knocked on the wall, and when I had opened the door, she thrust it in, saying she would bring you a fresh loaf every day."

"Then she has not quite forgotten me," sighed the princess, thinking of her last conversation with this same wise old lady. "But does she know that I must stay here the rest of my life?"

"Oh yes," answered the gate-keeper, shaking his head, and looking very wise. "That is—there is a secret—did it never occur to you, my dear princess," he added, suddenly, "that there might be a way of making your escape?"

"Oh, you dear delicious little gate-keeper!" exclaimed the princess, seizing him in her arms, and tossing him up and down. "I see how it is: you will let me out—you will do it. Oh, I am sure you will!"

"Not so fast, my dear," said the little man, struggling to free himself. "Put me down, and I will tell you all about it. But first of all you must promise to keep the whole matter a profound secret: if you should tell any one, the plan would fail."

"Oh, I can keep a secret," said the princess, smiling, and beginning to feel quite happy again.

"Well, then," said the gate-keeper, seating himself by the fountain—which was not a fountain at all, but only an imitation very skillfully done in aquamarine—"you are to stay here a year. Then, when the spring comes you are to be changed into a primrose, if you will consent to it, and grow up out of the ground like other flowers. Hidden deep within the woods, you must wait patiently, through sunshine and rain, till some one finds you, and breaks you from the stem. Whoever he may be, rich or poor, young or old, if he loves the flower well enough to take it home, and place it carefully in a vase of water, he will have the power of transforming it into a mortal, and you will be restored to your home in a world where the sun shines and where flowers grow."

"Dear! dear!" said the princess, "I suppose I must consent, if that is the only way of making my escape. But what if no one comes into the woods, and what if no one cares enough for the primrose to pick it?"

"Then it will wither on its stem, and you must come back to us, and be the Princess Bébé for another year."

The trial which was proposed to her seemed a very hard one, and the year which followed seemed very long. If it had not been for the kindness of the gate-keeper, who amused her by showing her all the curiosities which the kingdom of the mineral-workers contained, and explaining how the gems were cleaned and polished and cut, I am afraid the poor Princess Bébé would have died of homesickness long before spring. But at last the year came to an end, as all years must, and she started on her journey into the upper world.

Day after day she struggled through the earth, pushing her roots deep down into the soil, and stretching her slender leaf-like arms up into the sunlight. The dew came and kissed the little flower-bud with sweet moist lips, the sunshine warmed it, and the south wind sang to it, until at last a yellow primrose opened its eyes in the dark woods.

Day after day it lived there, trembling at the sound of every footstep, and wishing and praying deep down in its flower-heart for a friend.

June days had never seemed so long as these, for, despite her prayers, no one came, and the lonely primrose grew faint and weary with disappointment.

At last, however, a party of children playing in the woods caught sight of her bright face, and one of them—a merry, rosy-cheeked boy—broke the flower from its stem. He held it up to his companions, and they ran laughing after him.

"Oh, it's nothing but a yellow primrose," he said, as they tried to snatch the flower from his hand; and with these words he threw it away.

So it was all in vain that the little flower had lived and died, for the next day the Princess Bébé found herself back in the kingdom of the mineral-workers.

Her diamond necklace was just as beautiful as ever; her opal bed seemed all alive with trembling colors, soft white and flashing crimson; and the king welcomed her right royally, without a word of reproach for her long absence.

But for all that, her heart grew heavier every day. Even the attentions of the gate-keeper became tiresome; and when he tried to make her laugh with his merry ways, she could only smile sadly, and say, "Oh, it was such a disappointment to be picked, and then thrown away."

"Never mind—never mind," he would answer, cheerily: "better luck next time." And so the days dragged slowly by until another spring.

Then the princess began to hope once more; and when she found herself actually lifting her head into the sunlight, and felt the soft air blow over her, she wondered how she could ever have believed for a moment that anything was better or more beautiful than the deep blue sky above one, and the green earth beneath.

Contented and happy, she waited patiently through wind and rain, until it seemed as if her patience were to be rewarded.

A young man on a jet-black horse came riding through the woods. His face was bright and handsome, and he looked out upon the world with as merry a pair of eyes as you would care to see.

"Oh, if he would only take me home!" thought the flower. "I should like to be rescued by such a handsome youth as he." And in spite of her yellow primrose face, the little flower actually blushed.

"What a bright little flower!" said the young man, as

he rode along. "If it were not so much trouble getting off my horse, I would carry it home to Marjorie. But it's only a commonplace little primrose after all," he added, and so rode on.

That night the little flower cried itself to sleep among the shadows, and before morning it had withered on its stem.

"I will never make the attempt again," said the Princess Bébé, when she found herself once more in the kingdom of the mineral-workers.

"Oh yes, you will," said the gate-keeper, who had come forward to meet her. "If life is worth having, it is worth struggling for. Next year I shall send you up for your trial, whether you consent or not."

"If that is the case, I suppose I may as well consent at once," said the princess, and so yielded the point.

And when the long, long days of another year had come and gone, she left the kingdom of the mineral-workers for the third time. For the third time she struggled through the ground, lifting up her head among the blue-eyed violets and slender waving grasses.

She shook out her petals in the sunlight, and smiled as sweetly as a primrose can smile; but the spring days went by, and the summer was almost over, before any one took any notice of her.

THE PRINCESS BÉBÉ AND ALECK.

The poor little primrose was almost ready to die of despair, when one day, looking up quite suddenly, she saw the face of an old man bending over her.

He had gray hair and kind gray eyes; and as he looked at the flower he smiled tenderly, as if he were looking at something that he loved.

The flower smiled in turn, but could not speak.

"You must go home with me, little primrose," said the old man, stooping over the flower.

The fact that this gray-haired, gray-eyed old man was a poet will account, perhaps, for his talking to a flower as if it could understand what he said. At all events, he broke it from the stem, and when he reached his home placed it in a glass of water, saying,

"There you must stay, my little flower, until I can write a poem worthy of your bright face."

No sooner had he uttered these words than he saw standing before him a young girl with golden hair and softly shining eyes.

"Bless me! bless me!" exclaimed the old man, in great surprise, taking off the spectacles which he had so carefully adjusted across his nose, "where did you come from, my lady?"

"I came from the flower," she said; and she threw her arms round his neck and kissed him on the lips.

She was so delighted at her escape that she was not wholly responsible for her actions; and if she cried a little, I don't think any one will blame her.

Laughing and crying at the same time, and half wild with excitement, she told her new friend the story of her life for the past few years; and he, in his turn, smiled and wept a little, perhaps, and then he kissed her on the lips, and said,

"Henceforth, my dear girl, you shall be known as the Lady Primrose, and you shall stay with me as long as you will."

Whether or no he ever wrote a poem about her I can not tell. All I know is that she lived with him for the rest of her life, and was the sweetest and happiest Lady Primrose imaginable.

The house was as full of flowers as it could hold, and when the wise old woman of Hollowbush, who, you may be sure, had not forgotten her, asked her if she did not want another diamond necklace, Lady Primrose would answer:

"I don't care if I never see another diamond. The simplest flowers that grow in the woods are the loveliest jewels God ever made, and so long as I can have them, the lifeless flowers of the underground world may bloom for those who do not know of how little value the jewels they prize so highly really are."

THE END.

EIGHTY YEARS OF A BIRD'S LIFE

BY MRS. AMELIA E. BARR.

YOU must understand, my dear young readers, that the Raven of this tale is not at all an ordinary bird. It is true, he could not sing even as well as the smallest wren, but then he could talk, and it was generally believed that he knew a great deal more than the wisest of men and women supposed. He was, too, the very last representative of an extremely ancient family of Ravens, who had inhabited some rocky hills just behind the little cottage for hundreds of years—a family, indeed, so ancient that they had watched the battle-fields of Celts, Romans, Saxons, Danes, and Normans, and had had among them very wise birds, who croaked quite learnedly on the subject.

Now at the bottom of the lofty rocks which they inhabited was a rich and beautiful valley, and here, four hundred years ago, a Norman lord, who was a great fighter, built himself a fine castle. The Ravens and he got on very well together, and became great friends. His hunting and fighting supplied them with food, and it is said they told him a great many things that only a bird can know. He called his castle Ravensfield, and very soon people began to call him Ravensfield, and then the birds and he grew more friendly than ever. And it is said that when he was dying he told his son always to be good to the Ravens, for that just as long as the Ravens lived on Raven's Rock, the Ravensfields would own the rich lands below it.

For two hundred years everything went well; the knights grew rich and powerful, and the birds fat and numerous. Then the Ravensfields began to go to London, and spend money, and do all sorts of foolish things, and get into all kinds of troubles, and though the Ravens croaked and croaked until they were hoarse, they would not be prudent, and stay at home and mind their own business.

So the end of the matter was that every Ravensfield got poorer, and the fine old castle fell into ruins, and the colony of Ravens among the rocks also got smaller and smaller, until one morning the last knight of Ravensfield found in a deserted nest the last of this once powerful family of birds. It was half fledged and half starved, and he brought it home, and gave it to his sister to nurse. "Sister Mabel," he said, sadly, "this is the luck of Ravensfield; nurse it carefully, and to-morrow I will buckle my sword to my belt and go to India. I do believe this bird will live to see the old house rebuilt, and the glory of our family restored."

So the young Lord Stephen went over the seas, and Miss Mabel nursed the bird, and talked hopefully to it for fifteen years. But poor Lord Stephen was killed in a great Indian battle, and soon after there came to Miss Mabel a little lad who was Lord Stephen's only child. His father had left him a little money, and his aunt Mabel took great pains with him, and sent him to the best schools; and when he was twenty years old, she buckled his sword on his belt, and kissing him tenderly, sent him away also to India. "For, Stephen," she said, "you must win fame and gold to buy back the house and lands of Ravensfield."

All these twenty years the Raven had been growing large and splendid, and when the second Lord Stephen went away, he looked after him with a queer sidewise glance that filled Miss Mabel's heart with fear. But he was a bold, brave youth, and sent happy letters over the sea, and Miss Mabel told the Raven all the news, and I have no doubt they comforted each other very much. After nine years had passed, the Raven suddenly grew silent, and then there came a sad, sad letter: the second Lord Stephen had

NANNETTE FEEDING THE RAVEN.

been killed fighting under his flag, and his sickly little baby girl was sent home to his aunt in England.

Poor Miss Mabel was now sixty years old, and her heart and hopes were quite crushed. She had little love left for the desolate child, and she seemed to take a dislike to the poor Raven. At any rate, she never spoke to it, and the bird became the companion of the little girl. They played and ate and slept together, and when little Nannette went out to gather primroses or berries, the Raven always walked solemnly beside her.

One morning (the very morning when somebody drew this picture of them) her aunt was cross—she had a heart-ache, and a toothache too, poor old lady!—and Nannette took her porringer of bread and milk out of the cottage, and she and the bird were enjoying it together, when some one called out, "Nannette, I am going to shoot that ugly old bird!"

Then Nannette's little heart stood still in her terror, and she dropped her breakfast and ran to the boy, crying out that she should die if it were killed, for it was the only thing in all the world she had to love her.

The boy saw that she had great brown eyes, and beautiful brown hair, and a little mouth like a rose-bud, and he thought, "How lovely she is!" and dropped his gun, and said so many comforting words to Nannette, that always after it they were the very dearest of friends. And the Raven seemed to approve of Reginald also—for Reginald was the little boy's name, and he was very proud of it, being, as you know, a little out of the common; he would perch on his shoulder, and what he said to him as years went by I can not tell; but Reginald became thoughtful, and talked to Nannette continually about going away, and growing rich, and then coming home to marry her and make her a great lady. But Reginald did not have money enough to go away, and so he was often very sad and silent.

One day he came to Nannette with a paper in his hand. "See!" he cried, "the squire's son has been lost in the hills while hunting, and there is one hundred pounds to be given to whoever finds him. I know all about the hills, and shall certainly find the young squire." Then he said good-by to Nannette, and would have done so to the Raven, but the bird flew away before him, and for all his mistress's cries he would not come back. So together they went up the rocks, and Nannette watched them quite out of sight.

And Reginald, who knew a great deal about birds, watched the Raven, and saw that he flew continually over one spot in a narrow ravine; and there he found the poor young squire. His horse had been killed by the fall, and there he lay with a broken leg, and almost dead with hunger and thirst and pain. After this piece of good luck, Reginald's way was clear. Every one was then talking about a new country full of gold, called California; and though it was at the other end of the world, Reginald bravely sailed away into the West. Aunt Mabel shook her head, and the Raven nodded his head, and Nannette cried and laughed, and bid him "come quickly back, and build again the beautiful castle of Ravensfield"; and Reginald said, gravely, "I will surely do it," whereat the Raven nodded his wise-looking head harder than before.

"How long will he be away, Aunt Mabel?" said Nannette, sadly.

"Twenty years at least, my dear. I shall never see him again. I am seventy-five years old now."

"And I am fifteen. Ah! I shall be an old woman when Reginald comes back, and he won't know his little Nannette any more!" Then the Raven said something to Nannette, and she laughed, and his "Croak! croak!" sounded very like "Yes! yes!" It did, indeed.

Four years after Reginald went away, a very singular thing happened. Two pairs of strange Ravens came to Raven's Rock, and built nests and reared their young there. Nannette's Raven went very often to see them, and seemed to be altogether a changed bird. For though he was getting near sixty years old, he began to plume his feathers, and to sit continually at the cottage door, watching, watching, watching, as if he expected somebody.

It affected Nannette at last. "I think, aunt," she said, timidly, "that Reginald must be coming home. Just look at that bird!"

"Nonsense, child! How should he know?"

And indeed I don't understand how this wonderful bird knew, but he did; for that very night, just as Nannette was going to light the candle, she heard Reginald's step on the crisp snow, and the old lady heard it, and the Raven heard it, and there was the gladdest meeting you can possibly imagine; and if ever a bird said "I told you so," that Raven said it at least a hundred times that night.

Besides, Reginald had come home with hundreds and hundreds and hundreds of pounds; and he married lovely Nannette, and rebuilt Ravensfield; and dear, patient Aunt Mabel, after sixty years of waiting, went back to the stately old house, and ended her days in the little parlor where she had kissed her brother Stephen farewell.

As for the Raven, he showed himself to be a bird of a very aristocratic nature. He stepped proudly about the fine halls and gardens, and never went near the little cottage or the village streets again. He lived until his fine plumage began to turn gray, and Nannette's oldest son was almost big enough to put on a scarlet coat and a sword; and when he was nearly eighty years old he died on Nannette's knee, his foot in her hand, and the last thing he was conscious of was her tears dropping upon it.

Very likely, children, some extremely wise men and women will say, "I would not believe too much of this story, boys and girls." But when you have lived as long as I have lived, you will know that extremely wise men and women *don't know everything*. At any rate, there are plenty of Ravens on Raven's Rock now, and plenty of Ravensfields in the splendid castle; and if ever you go to England, you can see them if you want to.

A HARD SWIM.

BY DAVID KER.

THERE are few things more delightful than to be at sea on a fine summer day, with a bright blue sky above and a bright blue sea below, while the fresh breeze fills your sails, and the great smooth waves toss you lightly along, and spatter you at times with their glittering spray, like frolicsome giants. But it is a very different thing to be out in the teeth of a real equinoctial gale, with the whole sky black as ink, and the whole sea one sheet of boiling foam, and a huge wave coming thundering over the deck every other minute, sweeping everything before it, and making the whole vessel tremble from stem to stern.

So, doubtless, thought Olaf Petersen, captain and owner of the Norwegian schooner *Thyra*, of Bergen, when just such a storm caught him half way across the North Sea. It *did* seem rather hard, after escaping all the storms of blustering March, that fresh, genial April should serve him such a trick; but so it was, and instead of having a short and easy run northeastward to Bergen, as he expected, he found himself flying away to the west, driven by a gale which seemed strong enough to blow him right round the world, if it did not happen to sink him by the way.

All the sails had long since been taken in, and the little craft was scudding under bare poles, no one being on deck but the two men at the wheel (who had quite enough to do keeping her head straight) and the captain himself. A fine picture Olaf Petersen would have made as he stood there, with the spray rattling like hail upon his drenched tarpaulins, and his clear bright eye looking keenly out through the wet hair that was plastered over his face. It might be seen by the firm set of his mouth that he meant to fight it out while a plank would swim; but he looked grave and anxious, nevertheless.

And well he might. This time it was not only his vessel and the lives of himself and his crew that were in danger: his young wife was on board, after whom the *Thyra* had been named, and it was now too late to blame himself for having granted her entreaty to be allowed to sail along with him, instead of being left at home by herself for so many weary weeks, without knowing whether he was alive or dead.

Still it blew harder, and harder yet. Had not the *Thyra* been as good a sea-boat as ever swam, it would have been all over with her. Even as it was, she could barely hold her own against the mountains of water that came plunging over her deck with a force that seemed sufficient to rend a rock. More than once the captain's stiffened fingers were almost torn from their hold upon the weather rigging, while the men at the wheel were under water again and again. Vainly did Olaf strain his eyes to windward in the hope of seeing a break in the inky sky. All was grim and gloomy, and amid the blinding spray and the deepening darkness it was hard to tell where the sea ended and the sky began.

All that night and all the next morning they drove blindly onward, not knowing where they were; for the sun had not been seen for two whole days, and no observation could be taken. But Captain Petersen, who had those seas by heart, began to fear that they were being driven in among the Orkney Isles, and he knew only too well what chance the stoutest three-decker would have against those tremendous rocks with such a sea running.

Toward afternoon the wind fell suddenly, though the sea still ran high; but *now* came something worse than all—one of those terrible Northern fogs which turn day into night, and make the oldest sailor as helpless as a child. The lanterns were lit and hoisted, the ship's bell was kept constantly tolling, and the captain ordered up two "look-outs" besides himself; but the fog grew thicker and thicker, till those on the forecastle could barely make out the foremast.

Ha! what was that huge dim shadow that loomed out suddenly just ahead, like a threatening giant? Could it be a rock?

"Port your helm!—port!" roared the captain, at the full pitch of his voice.

But it was too late. The next moment there came a deafening crash, a shock that threw them all off their feet, and the vessel, with her bows stove in, was sawing and grinding upon the sharp rocks that had pierced her through and through, with the water rushing into her like a cataract.

The next few minutes were like the confusion of a troubled dream—a shadowy vision of a huge dark mass overhead, a short fierce struggle amid swirling foam and broken timbers—and then the captain and wife found themselves upon one of the higher ledges, hardly knowing how they had reached it, while the crew, with bleeding hands and sorely bruised limbs, dragged themselves painfully up after them.

They were not a moment too soon. Scarcely had the last man gained the ledge, when a mountain wave took the vessel aback. She slid off the rocks which had held her up, and went down so quickly that the captain, turning at the shouts of his men, just caught a glimpse of her topmasts vanishing under water.

The situation of the shipwrecked crew was now dreary enough. Alone upon a bare rock in the midst of a stormy sea, with no means of escape, and no food but the few brine-soaked biscuits in their pockets, there seemed to be nothing left for them but to give themselves up and die. But, of all men living, a sailor is the least apt to think his case hopeless, however dark it may appear. Having just been saved from apparently certain death, the stout-hearted seamen were in no mood to despair so easily; and settling themselves snugly in a sheltered cleft of the rock, they ate their scanty meal (a good share of which had been reserved for Mrs. Petersen) as cheerily as if they were lying at anchor in Bergen Harbor.

Just as the meal ended, the fog suddenly rolled away like a curtain, and the last gleam of the setting sun showed them an island several miles to the north, on the shore of which the keen-eyed captain made out a few white specks that looked like fishermen's huts.

"Lads," cried he, "if the wind rises again, it'll blow us all into the sea; and even if it don't, we shall freeze to death if we stick here all night, with no room to move about. There's just *one* chance left for us, and I'm going to take it. Somebody must swim to that island for help, and as I believe I'm the best swimmer among us, I'll be the one to do it."

"Olaf!" cried his wife, catching him by the arm, "you won't think of it! It's certain death!"

"Pooh, pooh!" said the captain, cheerily. "I haven't swum across Bergen Bay and back for nothing. It's certain death to sit here and freeze, if you like; but you'll soon see me coming back with half a dozen stout fellows, and we'll all have a good supper before the night's out. Keep your heart up, dear. God bless you!"

The next moment he was in the water, and vanishing from the eager eyes that watched him into the fast-falling shadows of night. Then came a long silence. The men looked at each other, no one daring to utter the thought which was in every one's mind, while Thyra Petersen hid her face in her hands, and prayed as she had never prayed before.

Meanwhile Captain Petersen, who had told no more than the truth in calling himself a good swimmer, was breasting the waves manfully. But he soon found the difference between attempting a long swim when quite fresh and vigorous, and doing the same thing after a hard night's work, on short allowance of food, and with limbs stiffened by wet and cold. Moreover, the sea, although much quieter than it had been, was still rough enough to tell sorely against him. Before he had gone a mile he felt his strength beginning to fail; but he thought of his wife, and of all the other lives that now depended upon him alone, and struggled desperately onward. But now came a new trouble. In the deepening darkness the island for which he was heading soon disappeared altogether, and he found himself swimming almost at random. Every stroke was now a matter of life and death, and yet each of these strokes might be taken in the wrong direction. It was a terrible thought. Heavier and heavier grew his cramped limbs, harder and harder pressed the merciless sea. He sank—rose—sank again, and as he came up once more, lifted his voice in a despairing cry, feeling that all was over.

"Hist, laddies! there's some ane skirling" (screaming), shouted a hoarse voice near him.

There was a sudden splash of oars, a clamor of many voices, and then a strong hand clutched him as he sank for the last time. So utterly was he spent that he could barely force out the few words needful to tell his story; but these were quite enough for the Orkney fishermen, who at once put about and steered straight for the rock.

It was a glad sight for the weary watchers, when the boat came gliding toward them out of the darkness. But when they recognized their captain, whom they had long since given up for lost, they gathered their last strength for a feeble cheer, while poor Thyra sprang into the boat, and threw her arms round his neck without a word.

So ended Captain Petersen's daring swim, which brought him good in a way that he little expected; for when the news of the feat reached Bergen, the towns-people at once started a subscription to buy him another vessel, in which he is voyaging now.

SOME CURIOUS ART WORKS AND ARTISTS.

THE Marquis de Veere once gave each of his household a sufficient quantity of the richest white silk damask for a suit. Charles V. was about to make him a visit, and the marquis wished his court to make a splendid appearance when assisting him to receive the emperor. His painter, Mabuse, who was always in debt, was granted the privilege of seeing to the making of his own suit of clothes. Mabuse, however, sold the damask for a good price, and having made a paper suit, painted it so perfectly to represent the damask that when he appeared in it all were deceived.

When the marquis called the emperor's attention to the

beautiful clothing of his court, and asked which suit he most admired, the emperor at once selected that of Mabuse. The joke was then explained to the emperor, but he would not believe that the suit was not of real damask until he had touched it with his hands.

It no doubt took Mabuse considerable time to paint his damask, but a much more celebrated artist once made a wonderful drawing almost in an instant. At the time of the Cæsars there was at Rome a panel on which was to be seen nothing but three colored lines. The lines were drawn one on top of the other, each thinner line dividing the next wider. This was considered one of the most wonderful art works at Rome.

The Grecian painter Apelles went one day into Protogenes's studio, and finding that artist out, drew on a panel the widest of the three lines in such a peculiar and beautiful manner that Protogenes knew at once his caller. When Apelles called the second time he found that Protogenes had drawn a colored line upon the first line, dividing it with the most delicate accuracy. Seeing this, Apelles divided the second line, to every one's astonishment. Protogenes lived at Rhodes, and the panel was taken to Rome to be admired by all who saw it. When the imperial palace was destroyed, the panel unfortunately shared a like fate.

In comparison, what a delicate flower is to a huge log, so the work of Apelles would be to such a vast oil-painting as the "Apotheosis of Hercules," painted by Lemoine, a Frenchman. This picture measured sixty-four feet one way by fifty-four feet the other, and the ultramarine to paint the clouds on it alone cost two thousand dollars.

Another huge painting, said to be the largest in the world, is Tintoretto's "Paradise," at Venice. It contains an almost innumerable multitude of figures, and fills the end of a large hall, over three hundred feet long and half as wide.

One of the most minute and beautiful of art works now at Florence is a glory of sixty saints carved on a cherry stone. It was carved by the Italian sculptress Rossi, who executed other similar carvings, besides working in marble.

Some of the old artists had peculiar methods of working. Aspertino taught himself to paint with both hands at the same time; and Goya, who died in this century, frequently used a stick or a sponge rather than a brush. There are pictures of Goya's done entirely with his palette knife and finger-ends.

One of the oddest of all artists was Bazzi, called Il Sodoma. Not only did he dress peculiarly, but his house was full of strange pet animals, such as monkeys and queer birds. Among the birds was a raven that could perfectly imitate his voice and manner of speech.

Sir Joshua Reynolds painted with brushes the handles of which were a foot and a half long, and used them so rapidly that he would paint a portrait in four hours. The finest of his pictures were those of children.

Other painters were noted also especially for their rapid work. One morning when some citizens called upon the Spanish painter Serra with an order for an altarpiece, he invited them to stay to dinner, and in the mean while to pass the time in his garden. When dinner-time came, the citizens were perfectly amazed to see Serra walk into their presence bearing the finished picture.

Rizi, another Spanish painter, went in early life to Salamanca to study theology, but he arrived there without money, and found that to be received at the college he must pay a hundred ducats. The abbot of the college gave Rizi but two days in which to get the money, or be refused as a student. Within that time, however, Rizi painted and sold a picture for the desired amount. He continued to paint to pay for his education, and in addition to becoming a famous painter he was made a bishop just before he died.

A celebrated painter of fairs and festivals such as took place among the Dutch was David Teniers. He usually painted on small or moderate-sized canvases, but the figures often were so numerous that one of his pictures contains nearly twelve hundred figures, while others with two hundred and three hundred figures are not rare. Teniers could imitate the style of other painters. At Vienna is a picture of his representing a gallery in which he and a gentleman are standing, and on the wall before them are hung fifty pictures of other artists. The pictures, of course, are quite small, but any one comparing them with the originals sees how striking is the imitation of different styles.

Another clever imitation of a very different kind was that of Peredo's, whose wife, a lady of rank, wished to have a servant with her whenever any one called. Peredo was not wealthy enough to keep merely ornamental servants, and he painted an old lady with glasses sitting in a chair, and who, apparently, when visitors saluted her, was so busily engaged in sewing as not to hear them.

HARES, WILD AND TAME.

THE hare family is one of the largest of the great animal kingdom, for Master Lepus is found in almost every corner of the earth, and whether hiding in tropical thickets, or scampering on Alpine heights, or through the frozen regions of the North, it is always the same agile, shy, and stupid little beast. It has very long ears, tipped with black, and heavy whiskers growing from each cheek. Its hind-legs are very long. It is a swift runner, and can jump a great distance.

Hares are very common throughout the Northern United States, their favorite haunts being overgrown old clearings, and thickets where are many snug places of concealment. They change their fur during winter, throwing off the pretty reddish-brown summer coat, and donning one of white and dark fawn-color. The color of the fur, however, is so varied that it is difficult to find two specimens exactly alike.

This little creature will eat any juicy, tender food, such as the young buds and sprouts in the spring, berries, and leaves. It is fond of cabbage leaves and young grain, and often does much mischief to the crops. It generally sleeps through the day, and morning and evening jumps about in search of food, scampering here and there wherever it can find a sweet morsel to nibble. It does not burrow its nest in the ground, like its cousin the rabbit, but scratches together a little heap of dry grass, which makes a very good temporary lodging. The hare's nest is called a "form," and is so in harmony with surrounding objects that it is scarcely noticeable. One may pass very near without suspecting that under such a heap of dry rubbish a cunning little animal lies concealed. On English heaths the hare makes its "form" in the little stubbly furze-bushes. Inside this mass of prickly leaves it hollows out a soft little bed, where it sleeps away the long sunny day, crouched close to the ground, its ears laid flat on its back.

Hares have no means of defending themselves, except their sharp toe-nails, which they rarely think of using, and they fall an easy prey to the many enemies which beset them. They are vigorously hunted by men and dogs on account of the delicate flavor of their flesh, and it has been thought necessary to place them under the protection of the game-laws. They are also the prey of foxes, wild-cats, weasels, and many other animals. Although defenseless, they still are in a measure protected by their keen ear, which catches the sound of the least rustle or movement, and warns the little beast against approaching danger.

The hare is the worst mother in the world. When her little ones are four or five days old, she leaves them unprotected in their nest, and scampers away to enjoy herself, returning once or twice, perhaps, to nurse her forlorn babies, and then leaving them to shift for themselves. Many little ones, thus neglected, die of cold and hunger, or are swooped up by hawks and owls. It is a strange fact that

HUNTING FOR SUPPER.

the mother hare makes no attempt to protect her babies, but will run away at the least signal of danger, and leave them to their fate. Hares have even been known themselves to bite their children to death. A young hare family remain together until they are half grown, when they separate, continuing to live near their native spot, for hares are not travellers, and, unless disturbed, seldom change their home. They are very short-lived, and seldom attain the age of ten years.

Hares are very plentiful in Switzerland, and are found high up among the ice and snow of the most lofty mountains. These Alpine hares are subject to a very strange change of costume. In December, when the Alpine world is one vast expanse of snow, the fur of the hare is the purest white, only the ears preserving the distinguishing black tip. As spring comes on, gray-brown hairs appear in the white fur, until, about the end of May, the animal is entirely covered with a gray-brown coat, which with the first snows of the autumn begins, in its turn, to change again into white. Ice hares, which are found as far north as the Parry Islands, are also subject to the same change, with the exception that the warm weather continues only long enough to spread a gray mantle along the back of the little creature, which quickly disappears as the temperature declines. The ice hare lives on the bark and twigs of the arctic willow and the dry moss and stubble of the desolate regions it inhabits. It makes its nest among the rocks, and in winter digs a hole in the snow.

Hares are good swimmers, but will not enter the water unless to avoid a foe. There is, however, one species of aquatic hare, found only in the Southern United States. It is amphibious, like the musk-rat, is a most expert swimmer, and makes its nest, or "form," on the edge of the morass, where it sleeps all day, sallying forth morning and evening for a swim in search of the delicate water-plants upon which it feeds. The young ones enter the water at a very early age, and may be seen paddling about with the mother on a hunt for breakfast.

Tame hares make very pretty pets. They are very stupid about learning tricks, and are said to have very short memories. Hares which have escaped from their masters, and have been recaptured after a few days of freedom, have been found to be entirely wild, as if they retained no remembrance, even for that short time, of all the petting which had been bestowed upon them. Dr. Benjamin Franklin is said to have had a pet hare which lived on the most friendly terms with a greyhound and cat, and would share the hearth-rug with them in the winter.

William Cowper, the English poet, had three pet hares, to which he was much attached, and about which he wrote many pretty things. They were given to him when they were leverets, as a hare is called during the first year of its life, and he named them Puss, Bess, and Tiney. He built them houses to sleep in, and always kept them near him. Bess, who died soon after he was full grown, "was," writes Cowper, "a hare of great humor and drollery. Puss was tamed by gentle usage; Tiney was not to be tamed at all." Once poor Puss was sick. His master nursed him with the greatest care. He says: "No creature could be more grateful than my patient after his recovery—a sentiment which he most significantly expressed by licking my hand, first the back of it, then the palm, then every finger separately, then between all the fingers, as if anxious to leave no part of it unsaluted; a ceremony which he never performed but once again, upon a similar occasion."

Upon Tiney the kindest treatment had no effect. If his master ventured to stroke him, he would grunt, strike with his fore-feet, spring forward, and bite. Tiney lived to be nine years old, and died from the effects of a fall. Puss survived him two years. A memorandum found among Cowper's papers reads: "This day died poor Puss, aged eleven years, eleven months. He died between twelve and one at noon, of mere old age, and apparently without pain."

The poet was so fond of his pets that he buried them in his garden, and wrote an epitaph on Tiney, from which we take the following stanzas:

"Here lies—whom hound did ne'er pursue,
  Nor swifter greyhound follow,
Whose foot ne'er tainted morning dew,
  Nor ear heard huntsman's hallo—

"Old Tiney, surliest of his kind,
  Who, nursed with tender care,
And to domestic bounds confined,
  Was still a wild Jack hare.

"Though duly from my hand he took
  His pittance every night,
He did it with a jealous look,
  And, when he could, would bite.

"His diet was of wheaten bread,
  And milk, and oats, and straw;
Thistles, or lettuces instead,
  With sand to scour his maw.

"On twigs of hawthorn he regaled,
  On pippin's russet peel,
And when his juicy salads failed,
  Sliced carrot pleased him well."

CHARADE

OUT on the sea, when the tempest is blowing,
  Over the waters dark and wild,
Guide I the sailor, his pathway showing
Over the shoals and the currents flowing;
  Never through me is the ship beguiled.

Many a wandering step have I guided;
  Children at school have I often taught;
Many disputes through me are decided;
Oft has my help, though sometimes derided,
  Even the Muse of History sought.

Off with my head! I'm a living creature;
  Trembling I follow, I guide no more:
Large-eyed and gentle, of kindly feature,
Hunted by man; in the wilds of nature,
  When he is coming, I fly before.

Cut off my head again, and for ages
  Long have I kindled the spirit of man.
Worshipped by artists, adored by the sages,
Present and past combine in my pages;
  There all the secrets of beauty you scan.

WHEN SKATES WERE BONES.

THOUGH it appears to be impossible to fix on the time when skating first took root in England, there can be no doubt that it was introduced there from more northern climates, where it originated more from the necessities of the inhabitants than as a pastime. When snow covered their land, and ice bound up their rivers, imperious necessity would soon suggest to the Scands or the Germans some ready means of winter locomotion. This first took the form of snow-shoes with two long runners of wood, like those still used by the inhabitants of the northerly parts of Norway and Sweden in their journeys over the immense snow-fields. These seem originally to have been used by the Finns, "for which reason," says a Swedish writer, "they were called 'Skrid Finnai' (Sliding Finns)—a common name for the most ancient inhabitants of Sweden, both in the North saga and by foreign authors."

When used on ice, one runner would soon have been found more convenient than the widely separated two, and harder materials used than wood; first bone was substituted; then it, in turn, gave place to iron; and thus the present form of skate was developed in the North at a period set down by Scandinavian archæologists as about A.D. 200.

Frequent allusions occur in the old Northern poetry, which prove that proficiency in skating was one of the most highly esteemed accomplishments of the Northern heroes. One of them, named Kolsno, boasts that he is master of nine accomplishments, skating being one; while the hero Harold bitterly complains that though he could fight, ride, swim, glide along the ice on skates, dart the lance, and row, "yet a Russian maid disdains me."

In the "Edda" this accomplishment is singled out for special praise: "Then the king asked what that young man could do who accompanied Thor. Thialfe answered that in running upon skates he would dispute the prize with any of the countries. The king owned that the talent he spoke of was a very fine one."

Olaus Magnus, the author of the famous chapter on the Snakes of Iceland, tells us that skates were made "of polished iron, or of the shank bone of a deer or sheep, about a foot long, filed down on one side, and greased with hog's lard to repel the wet." These rough-and-ready bone skates were the kind first adopted by the English; for Fitzstephen, in his description of the amusements of the Londoners in his day (time of Henry the Second), tells us that "when that great fen that washes Moorfields at the north wall of the city is frozen over, great companies of young men go to sport upon the ice. Some, striding as wide as they may, do slide swiftly; some, better practiced to the ice, bind to their shoes bones, as the legs of some beasts, and hold stakes in their hands, headed with sharp iron, which sometimes they strike against the ice; these men go as swiftly as doth a bird in the air, or a bolt from a cross-bow." Then he goes on to say that some, imitating the fashion of the tournament, would start in full career against one another, armed with poles; "they meet, elevate their poles, attack and strike each other, when one or both of them fall, and not without some bodily hurt."

Specimens of these old bone skates are occasionally dug up in fenny parts of Great Britain. There are some in the British Museum, in the Museum of the Scottish Antiquaries, and probably in other collections; though perhaps some of the "finds" are not nearly as old as Fitzstephen's day, for there seems to be good evidence that even in London the primitive bone skate was not entirely superseded by implements of steel at the latter part of last century.

One found about 1839 in Moorfields, in the boggy soil peculiar to that district, is described as being formed of the bone of some animal, made smooth on one side, with a hole at one extremity for a cord to fasten it to the shoe. At the other end a hole is also drilled horizontally to a depth of three inches, which might have received a plug, with another cord to secure it more effectually.

There is hardly a greater difference between these old bone skates and the "acme" and club skates of to-day, than there is between the skating of the Middle Ages and the artistic and graceful movements of good performers of to-day. Indeed, skating as a fine art is entirely a thing of modern growth. So little thought of was the exercise, that for long after Fitzstephen's day we find few or no allusions to it, and up to the Restoration days it appears to have been an amusement confined chiefly to the lower classes, among whom it never reached any very high pitch of art. "It was looked upon," says a recent writer, "much with the same view that the boys on the Serpentine even now seem to adopt, as an accomplishment, the acme of which was reached when the performer could succeed in running along quickly on his skates, and finishing off with a long and triumphant slide on two feet in a straight line forward. A gentleman would probably then have no more thought of trying to execute different figures on the ice than he would at the present day of dancing in a drawing-room on the tips of his toes." Even as an amusement of the common people it is not alluded to in any of the usual catalogues of sport so often referred to.

THE MONKEYS OF INDIA.

A MISSIONARY in India gives an interesting account of the monkeys that live in that far-away country. He says that in the morning, during the cold season, the monkeys are always very listless, but as soon as they are warmed with the rays of the sun, they are as playful as kittens. They will jump over each other's backs, slap each other's faces, pull each other's tails, and even make pretense to steal each other's babies.

The gray and the brown species are found nearly all over the continent of India; the former is more daring and destructive, and the latter more mischievous and cunning. They both form themselves into separate parties, or tribes, and rarely go beyond a certain boundary. They seldom migrate, except it be for food or water in times of drought and scarcity. This wild citizenship seems to be respected, for they very rarely trespass on each other's ground. Each tribe has a leader, or king, which can easily be recognised, and from the manner in which he conducts himself, he is evidently aware of the dignity of his position.

Like nearly all other wild animals, they have a keen sense of danger, and when a certain whoop is given, however scattered or tempted to stay, in a few moments they are hidden on the tops of the highest trees in the locality. They have the bump of destructiveness largely developed, and it is no small calamity when a tribe locates itself near a village. Scarcely anything in the shape of fruit or grain comes amiss to them, and when neither are to be had, in the hottest part of the year they eat the stems of the young leaves. When they commence upon a field of lentils, pulse, or peas, they always pluck up the plant by the root, pull off one pod, and then fling the plant away, so that it does not require many days to clear a whole field. Ripe mangoes have a special attraction, and it requires no small amount of vigilance to keep them away from the groves.

Dogs, however strong and fleet, are of very little use to drive them away, for the monkeys are sagacious enough to know that their safety is in keeping near the trees. When the dog has spent himself with barking and screaming at the foot of the tree, a monkey will come down to the lowest branch, and wag his long tail within a few inches of the dog's face, and when the poor dog has retired, completely foiled, a monkey will soon be after him to tempt him to a second encounter.

Mischief is certainly in their hearts, for, not content with stealing the produce of the gardens and fields, they will pull off the thatch from the native huts, fling the tiles from the better-built houses and shops to the ground, and we have even seen them try their best to rift the stones from the temples. A native town in one of the zemindary estates was so mutilated by them that it looked as if it had sustained a siege.

Some years ago, after making our arrangements for our encampment at night, we constantly had our peaceful rest broken by a tribe of brown monkeys. They evidently thought that long possession had given them a prior claim to the grove. For our own comfort it was felt by all that some means must be adopted to drive them away. Accordingly one was shot. Death was not instantaneous, and quite a number came around to see it die. They looked with startling interest into its face, but as soon as life was extinct they bounded away. Fear had fallen upon them all, and not a sound was heard from them during the night. Early next morning they assembled in an adjoining field. The sharp and quick manner in which they turned their faces first in this way and then in that was a sight not soon to be forgotten. They had instinct enough to see that their only safety would be in flight. In the course of an hour the king headed the tribe, and away they went, and not a solitary monkey was seen in that region for years afterward. The natives dared not openly commend us, but they were not a little pleased that we had rid them of creatures so destructive to their homesteads.

The monkeys are very numerous in the sacred cities, and especially in Benares and Pooree. Within a few miles of the temple of Juggernaut there are many hundreds, if not thousands. They are so tame that they will come down from the trees and eat rice from the hands of the pilgrims. When the pilgrim presents his hand with the rice in it, the monkey seizes it with his left paw, and he will never let go his grip until he has taken every grain. Very few persons are injured by monkeys, but they will sometimes seize a basket, if there be fruit in it, when carried by a woman or child. The natives often say that "monkeys can do everything except talk, and they would do that were it not for the fear of being made to work."

THE LITTLE DELINQUENT.

"LUCIE, my Lucie, wilt thou not forgive thy little Fritz!" pleaded the mother of two children whose father had been a soldier in the Prussian army, and whose bravery had been rewarded with a medal which was worn on his coat lapel.

Lucie answered, with a deep sigh, "He was so cruel, dear mother; he pushed me down so rudely on the hard floor!"

"Yes, I saw that push; but he was angry."

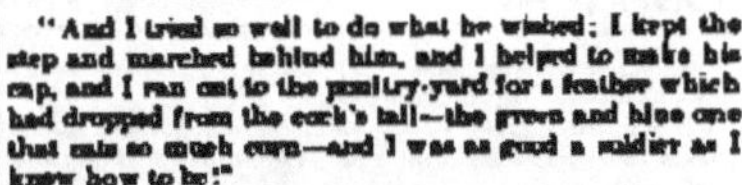

"And I tried so well to do what he wished; I kept the step and marched behind him, and I helped to make his cap, and I ran out to the poultry-yard for a feather which had dropped from the cock's tail—the green and blue one that eats so much corn—and I was as good a soldier as I knew how to be!"

"Well, what was the matter?"

"Why, I had my dear Rosa in my arms, and Ludwig looked over the fence, and laughed at Fritz for having a girl with a doll in his regiment, and Fritz became very cross, and said he would not play. Then I put my Rosa down, and went marching again; but that dreadful great cock came and pecked at her eyes, and I *could* not see her suffer; so I hid her in my apron while Fritz was not looking, and we came into the house to fill our knapsacks; then Fritz saw Rosa, and he said I was a disobedient soldier, and he pulled her out of my arms, and tossed her down and broke her, as you see—oh, my dear, my good Rosa!"

"But I think Fritz is sorry. See! he has been tied to the table a long while for punishment. Can you not forgive him?"

Lucie did not answer; her little soul seemed much disturbed.

"Come, I will tell thee a story, my Lucie, of two other children, and then, perhaps, thou wilt be more ready to let Fritz go free. Far away up in the mountains where are the chamois, and where the rocks are rough and the forests dark, lived Hans and Gretchen. They were wild as the chamois themselves, and their old grandfather could scarcely keep them by his side long enough to tell them the story of the Saviour's love, or teach them even to read. They knew the haunt of every wild creature of the woods, and many were their quarrels over a nest of young birds, or the possession of the animals they trapped. They had no kind mother; their words were often harsh, and sometimes hunger made them really cruel to each other. They were much to be pitied, for their grandfather was lame as well as old, and could do little for their support.

THE LITTLE DELINQUENT.

"One day, in an eager chase after a rabbit, Gretchen gave Hans a great push, which sent him down over a rocky ledge on to some stones. She was frightened to see that he did not move, and still more frightened when she found he was moaning with pain. She ran to get help, and the neighbors came and lifted Hans and carried him home; but he never walked again: his spine was hurt. Ah! what sorrow then was Gretchen's! How she wished she had never been so unkind!

"How she missed her companion in her wild rambles, and in her search for the Edelweiss flowers which she sold to travellers, and so gained a little money! Little by little she learned how to be a better girl—learned to be patient with Hans, who was often very cross; and as she grew older, and could better care for the house and her old grandfather, they came to love her very much.

"But do you not think that little children who have been taught to be kind, and to love the dear Father in heaven whose Son died on the cross, should be willing to forgive when quarrels arise?"

Both little faces had grown sad, one with earnest resolve never again to be harsh with his sister, the other with tender re-get. At last Lucie said, "My mother, I forgive Fritz; but what shall I do for poor Rosa?"

"Rosa shall have a new head when I have saved kreutzers to buy one," said Fritz; and so they kissed and made up.

THREE FAMOUS DIAMONDS.

A MAGNIFICENT diamond, belonging to the Emperor of Russia, bought by the Empress Catherine, weighs over one hundred and ninety-three carats. It is said to be the size of a pigeon's head, and to have been purchased for ninety thousand pounds, besides a yearly sum for life to the Greek merchant from whom it was bought. This diamond formed one of the eyes of the famous idol Juggernaut, whose temple is on the Coromandel coast, and a French soldier, who had deserted into the Malabar service, found the means of robbing the temple of it, and escaped with it to Madras. There he disposed of it to a ship captain for two thousand pounds, and by him it was resold to a Jew for twelve thousand pounds. From him it was transferred for a large sum to the Greek merchant. This diamond now surmounts the imperial sceptre.

The diamond of the Emperor of Austria, which formerly belonged to the Grand Dukes of Tuscany, weighs one hundred and thirty-nine and a half carats. Its estimated value is one hundred and fifty-five thousand pounds. This stone is of a lemon yellow color, which greatly lessens its value.

Among the Prussian crown jewels is the famous Regent or Pitt diamond, discovered in the Pasteal mine at Golconda. It weighs one hundred and thirty-six and three-quarters carats, and is remarkable for its form and clearness, which have caused it to be valued at one hundred and sixty thousand pounds, although it cost only one hundred thousand pounds. It was stolen from the mine and sold to Mr. Pitt, grandfather of the great Earl of Chatham. The Duke of Orleans purchased the diamond for presentation to King Louis the Fifteenth.

After the fall of Louis the Sixteenth, the people insisted that the crown jewels should be exposed to the gaze of the mob, and with them the Regent diamond was shown. So little, however, did the exhibitors confide in the honesty of these patriots that great precautions were taken to prevent the consequences of too strong an attraction. The passer-by who chanced to demand, in the name of the sovereign people, a sight of the finest of the jewels, entered a small room, within which, through a little window, the diamond was presented for sight. It was fastened by a strong steel clasp to an iron chain, the other end of which was secured within the window through which it was handed to the spectator. Two policemen kept a vigilant watch on the momentary possessor of the gem, until, having held in his hand the value of twelve millions of *francs*, according to the estimate in the inventory of the crown jewels, he again took up his hook and basket at the door and disappeared.

This diamond, which decorated the hilt of the sword of state of the first Napoleon, was taken by the Prussians at Waterloo, and now belongs to the King of Prussia.

ON THE TRACK.

In former times, superstition attributed to the diamond many virtues. It was supposed to protect the possessor from poison, pestilence, panic-fear, and enchantments of every kind. A wonderful property was also ascribed to it when the figure of Mars, whom the ancients represented as the god of war, was engraved upon it. In such cases the diamond was believed to insure victory in battle to its fortunate owner, whatever might be the number of his enemies.

For a long time diamonds were sent to Holland to be cut and polished, but this art is now well understood in England, and has been recently introduced into this country.

Diamonds are not only worn as ornaments of dress, or rare objects of art, but they are employed for several useful purposes, as for cutting glass by the glazier, and all kinds of hard stones by the lapidary.

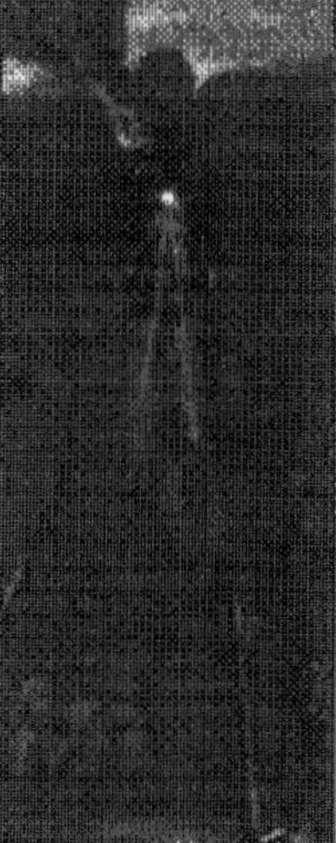

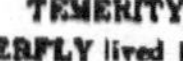

TEMERITY.

A BUTTERFLY lived like a princess in a green and golden wood, guarded day and night by the trees; but as there was never a butterfly yet that did not prefer sunshine to safety, she came fluttering out one morning, and after dazzling all the flowers in the neighborhood, spread her wings for a long flight.

There was no one to warn her of the dangers abroad, so when she came to the railroad track she just settled upon it, with no more fear than if it were a twig. An ugly brown worm that had been sunning himself on a sleeper crept up to her.

"You are in a dreadfully dangerous place," he groaned.

"Why?" asked the little rainbow, not a bit scared.

"There is a great monster coming soon. He crushes everything he meets; he has no heart; his bones are made of iron."

"How funny!" exclaimed the butterfly.

"See how dark the sky is getting; he will soon be here," went on the worm, solemnly.

"Oh, pshaw! it's only a shower coming up," said the butterfly, stretching her wings.

"No, it is the monster; don't you feel the ground shake? The storm is coming, but the monster is coming too. Get into this hole under the track; I beg you, I entreat you, get into this hole and be saved."

"Nonsense!" laughed the butterfly.

The rail was trembling, and in the distance a strange wild shriek was heard, a great puff of smoke went rolling up to the sky.

"Quick! quick!" implored the worm. "Do as I do, or you will be killed. There is no time to lose."

But the only answer he got was a laugh.

The monster was getting nearer and nearer, and the worm, with one more vain petition to the butterfly to follow him, squirmed into a crevice under the rail.

On came the monster, its great iron limbs pounding back and forth. A rattle, a shriek, a puff of smoke; he had come and gone. The worm—where was he? Limp and dead in his little hole under the rail. And the butterfly—the poor beautiful butterfly?

Oh, she had simply flown away.

NEW YORK CITY.

IN a short paper entitled "The Paradise of Insects," in *Young People* No. 10, some interesting facts are told of small sand-flies, called zancudos, which abound on the Upper Amazon and other swampy localities of South and Central America. Boys will like to know the origin of their name. Stilts are called zancos in Spanish, and these flies, a species of mosquito, are called zancudos—more properly spelled zancudos—on account of their very long, slender legs and disproportionately small bodies, which remind one of a very small boy on very high stilts. Flies on stilts is a funny idea, but not more funny than the appearance of these troublesome little insects. [illegible].

I am a little girl twelve years old, and live at Fort Supply, Indian Territory. My father is a captain in the Twenty-third Infantry. We live in huts made of logs, and the cracks filled with mud to keep out the cold, and the inside lined with canvas. We have frequent visits from the Indians. Not long ago a party of about fifty Indians were here, some of whom were on the war-path last fall. We have a school, and about sixteen scholars. If it were not for school I should be very lonesome, as I have only one playmate. There are plenty of children here, but they are all too small to play with. I take *Young People*, and it is a great addition to my small fund of amusements.

GRACE W. HUTTON.

[illegible], TENNESSEE.

DEAR "YOUNG PEOPLE,"—I thought when you made your first appearance that you were as pretty and interesting as possible, but when you arrived in your new dress, looking so fresh and bright, wishing us a "Merry Christmas," I was still more delighted with you. I hope the number of your subscribers will grow as fast as you have; you are such a dear little paper.

ANNA C. B.

The two following letters are from very young readers, who wrote in big capitals with their own little hands:

NEW YORK CITY.

I am so glad you have published *Young People*. I am five years old. I have a little kitten, and my papa says it will soon be a cat. I wish it wouldn't.

JENNIE B.

SYRACUSE, NEW YORK.

I thought I would drop you a line or two about the *Young People* and the "Wiggles," and I will. I send you what I make of the last number of the "Wiggles," and I like the new paper. So good-by. From

[illegible] REYNOLDS (six years).

Here are two more little folks, who employ an amanuensis:

DELAWARE.

I thought I would write you a letter to let you know how I like *Young People*. Grandpa takes it for me. I am only eight and a half years old. Grandpa is going to copy this, as I can not write very well.

EDGAR E. [illegible].

NEW YORK CITY.

I am only five years old, and can not read or write yet, but my mamma reads me the stories in *Young People* every week, and I like them very much, and the pictures and the letters; and papa says I ought to send you a letter, and tell you how much I like it. So does my little sister Lulu, and she is only three years old, and I have got a little brother only three weeks old, but he hasn't any name yet. I told papa I would write a letter, but I could not write it, and he said it would be fair if Nurse Belle would write, only I must tell her what to put in—I and nobody else—and so I did it.

LAURA F.

LANSING, MICHIGAN.

A few days ago I was walking with a friend when we saw a rabbit in the road. We ran to catch it, but could not, for it ran too. Suddenly it stopped. My friend whistled, and then it ran right up to her, and we caught it. I suppose that rabbits like music.

LOTTIE B.

EPSOM, NEW HAMPSHIRE.

I am going to tell you about a butterfly my brother Willie brought in from the woods this winter. It flew about the rooms for a few days, till one morning he seemed almost dead. Mamma took him to the door, and he flew away up over our barn and some great tall pine-trees. I am ten years old this winter.

L. MABEL [illegible].

What color were the butterfly's wings, and how large was it?

HOBOKEN, NEW JERSEY.

I once had a pet rabbit. He was gray and white, and I named him Mac, after papa. Once I gave him a peach, and another rabbit ran away with it; then he stood up on his hind-legs and begged for another.

HARRY F.

George D. R. and Cora B. E., both of Pittsburgh, Pennsylvania, also write of pet rabbits, and Spitz and Newfoundland dogs.

NEW YORK CITY.

I have a chicken that I hatched out by putting the egg in cotton. While I am writing this letter it is sitting on my hand. When I call it, it comes to me. I have also four white mice, which are as tame as the chicken. I did have a squirrel, but it died. I wish you would tell me how to feed my mice.

JOSIE P.

White mice will eat seeds of all kinds, canary-seed, and various other grains. They will also nibble bread and cake. They must have plenty of water, and like a little milk now and then. They should be given a soft, warm nest of dry moss or of flannel.

J. G. D.—In all rooms where meal is kept, the worms generally breed much faster than they are wanted. The meal-moth is very pretty. Its fore-wings are light brown, with a dark chocolate-brown spot on the base and tip of each. It is often to be seen clinging to the ceiling of kitchen or store-room, with its tail curved over its back. This moth deposits its eggs in the meal, and in a short time the worm is hatched, which soon forms itself into a cocoon, from which the moth again comes forth. You may find this worm crawling in old flour-barrels or some box in which meal has been kept; and if you keep a box of meal standing open in some warm place, the moth will be very likely to find it, especially in the summer-time, and use it as a deposit for her eggs. Meanwhile you can feed your mocking-birds on meal and milk, mixed now and then with very finely chopped raw beef and with bits of fruit. You can also buy prepared food for them. Be sure to give them plenty of clean gravel in the bottom of the cage.

"[illegible]," Moline, Illinois.—Hephaistos is the correct Greek spelling of Vulcan's name, but Hephæstus is the accepted English spelling of the word. Either is correct.—The translation of *Don Quixote* has become such a standard English work that the ordinary English pronunciation of the name is allowable. In Spanish it is pronounced Ke-ho-tay, with a slight accent on the second syllable.

Favors are acknowledged from Belle R., Tennessee; Willie P. T., Indiana; Robbie R. H., St. John, New Brunswick; Alpha T. K., Pennsylvania; from Illinois—Mamie Ripley, Tommy C. H., Edith Patterson, Joseph K.; from Massachusetts—[illegible], L. Tyler P., Stanley K. H., Harry R., F. E. T.; from Ohio—Lulie H., Oscar R., Willie Gordon, Ralph M. F., Hattie Mitchell; from Michigan—Nellie M. C., L. A. Waldron, Edward D. K.; from New York—Fred L. Caldwell, A. M. Tucker, R. G. Gilmore, Eddie R. Bernard, Toronto, Canada.

Correct answers to puzzles received from Walter S. Dodge, Washington, D. C.; Morton L. T., Massachusetts; James A. S., Connecticut; Sallie V. R., Nebraska; R. A. W., Canada; Harry Lewis, Kentucky; H. M. J., Ohio; from Pennsylvania—R. O. Lowry, George N. Hayward, Walter Lowry, Chester B. F., Florence M.; from New Jersey—K. R. Talbot, Cora M. Rae; from California—Viola A. Francis, F. T. Scott; from New York—R. O. S., Florence, Main, Perkins S., G. A. Page, Van Rensselaer, Kate R., Edna F. Smith, "Oscar," Nellie H., R. F. W., F. K. Dodd.

NOSES OUT OF JOINT.

You needn't cry and look so sad;
  I love you, pussy dear, the same—
I truly do—as I loved you
  Before this cunning kitty came;
But things are changed a little now,
  You know, and 'cause he's very small,
I've got to 'tend the most to him.
  Your nose is out of joint, that's all.
Don't you remember that cold day
  They left me hours and hours in bed,
And when nurse came for me at last,
  "Your nose is out of joint," she said,
"A baby's come to live with us!"
  Well, then, that's what's the matter now;
You might have known how it would be—
  Oh dear, my head! Please don't me-ow,
Or I must send you out the room;
  Nice little *girls* don't make a noise
When their mammas give almost all
  Their kisses to small red-faced boys.
I tell you, puss, you are too big
  To sit with kit upon my knee,
And it's no worse for you to have
  Your nose put out of joint than me.

"WHAR IS YER GWINE TO, MELINDY?"

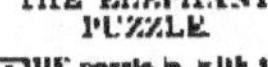

THE ELEPHANT PUZZLE.

THE puzzle is, with two cuts of the scissors to make this elephant stand on all fours.

INSTRUCTIONS.—Trace or copy the accompanying figure on a piece of Bristol-board or thick writing paper, and then go to work with your scissors and see what you can do.

The solution will be given in our next.

Ants that Bite.—Foraging ants by countless thousands are met with everywhere on the banks of the Amazons. Some of them are dwarfs not more than one-fifth of an inch long, while others are giants ten times as long, with monstrous heads and jaws. When the pedestrian falls in with a train of these ants, the first signal given him is a twittering and restless movement of small flocks of plain-colored birds (ant-thrushes) in the jungle. If this be disregarded until he advances a few steps further, he is sure to fall into trouble, and find himself suddenly attacked by numbers of the ferocious little creatures. They swarm up his legs with incredible rapidity, each one driving its pincer-like jaws into his skin, and with the purchase thus obtained doubling in its tail, and stinging with all its might. There is no course left but to run for it; if he is accompanied by natives, they will be sure to give the alarm, crying, "Tauoca!" and scampering at full speed to the other end of the column of ants. The tenacious insects that have secured themselves to his legs then have to be plucked off one by one—a task which is generally not accomplished without pulling them in twain, and leaving heads and jaws sticking in the wounds.

BLISSFULLY UNCONSCIOUS.

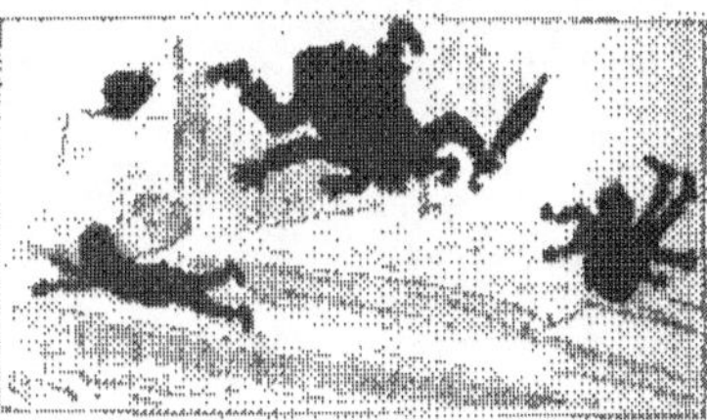

PAINFULLY CONSCIOUS.

VOL. I.—NO. 14. | PUBLISHED BY HARPER & BROTHERS, NEW YORK. | PRICE FOUR CENTS.
Tuesday, February 3, 1880. | $1.50 per Year, in Advance.

THE HOUSE-SPARROW.

THE English house-sparrow, a pert, daring little bird, which is seen in crowds in almost all cities of the Northern United States, was first brought to this country about twenty years ago. It is said the first specimens were liberated in Portland, Maine, where they immediately made themselves at home, and began nest-building and worm-catching as eagerly as when in their native air. Others were soon brought to New York city, and set free in the parks. At that time New York, Brooklyn, and other cities were suffering from a terrible visitor, the loathsome measuring-worm, which made its appearance just as the trees had become lovely with fresh spring green. It infested the streets in armies, hung in horrible webs and festoons from the branches of the shade trees, and ruined the beauty and comfort of the city during the pleasantest season of the whole year. About the first of July, when the worm finished its work, the trees appeared stripped and bare, as if scathed by fire, and a second budding resulted only in scanty foliage late in the season. A month after the worm disappeared, its moth—a small white creature, pretty enough except for

FEEDING THE SPARROWS.

its connections—fluttered by thousands through the city, depositing its eggs for the worm of another year. Desperate measures seemed necessary to stop this nuisance, and the question of cutting down all the trees was seriously considered. But relief was at hand. A gentleman, an Englishman, proposed an importation of sparrows, and soon hundreds of these brown-coated little fellows were set loose in different cities. They at once became public pets. Little houses were nailed up on trees and balconies for them to nest in, sidewalks and window-sills were covered with crumbs for their breakfast, and boys were forbidden to stone them or molest them in any way.

Now although the sparrow is very willing to feed on bread-crumbs and seeds, and save itself the trouble of hunting for its dinner, by a wise provision of nature the little ones, until they are fully fledged, can eat only worms and small flies and bugs. As the sparrows have three or four broods during the warm weather, they always have little ones to feed at the very season when worms and other insects destructive to vegetation are the most plentiful. An English naturalist states that in watching a pair of sparrows feeding their little ones, he saw them bring food to the nest from thirty to forty times every day, and each time from two to six caterpillars or worms were brought. It is easy to see from this estimate how quickly the tree worms would disappear, as proved to be the case in the cities where the sparrows were set free.

A very few years after they were introduced not a worm was to be seen. The trees now grow undisturbed in their leafy beauty all through the summer, and many children will scarcely remember the time when their mothers went about the streets where shade trees grew carrying open umbrellas in sunny days and starry evenings to protect themselves from the constantly dropping worms.

It is no wonder that every one is gratefully affectionate to the sparrow. They are very social little birds, and are entirely happy amid the noise and dirt and confusion of the crowded street. They are bold and saucy too, and will stand in the pathway pecking at some stray crust of bread until nearly run over, when they hop away, scolding furiously at being disturbed. They are fond of bathing, and after a rain may be seen in crowds fluttering and splashing in the pools of water in the street. The cold winter does not molest them. They continue as plump and jolly and independent as ever, and chirp and hop about as merrily on a snowy day as during summer.

In the New York city parks these little foreigners are carefully provided for. Prettily built rustic houses may be seen all over Central Park, put up for their especial accommodation. During the summer, when doors and windows are open, the sparrows hold high revels in the Central Park menagerie. They go fearlessly into the eagle's cage, bathe in his water dish, and make themselves very much at home. In the cages occupied by pigeons, pheasants, and other larger birds, the sparrows are often troublesome thieves. They can easily squeeze through the coarse net-work, and no sooner are the feed dishes filled with breakfast than they crowd in and take possession, scolding and fluttering and darting at the imprisoned pigeons and pheasants if they dare to approach.

The smaller parks of New York city contain each about two hundred houses for the sparrows. Some of them are of very simple construction, being made of a piece of tin leader pipe about ten inches long, with a piece of wood fitted in each end. A little round doorway is cut for the birds to enter, and they seem perfectly happy in these primitive quarters. Feed and water troughs are provided, and it is the duty of the park keeper to fill them every morning. The birds know the feeding hour, and come flying eagerly, pushing and scolding, and tumbling together in their hurry for the first mouthful. The greedy little things eat all day. School-children come tramping in, and share their luncheon with them, and even idle and ragged loungers on the park benches draw crusts of bread from their pockets, and throw the sparrows a portion of their own scanty dinner.

It is very easy to study the habits of the sparrow, for it is so bold and sociable that if a little house is nailed up in a balcony, or by a window where people are constantly sitting, a pair of birds will at once take possession, bring twigs and bits of scattered threads and wool for a nest, and proceed to rear their noisy little family. Chirp, chirp, very loud and impatient, three or four little red open mouths appear at the door of the house, the parent birds come flying with worms and flies, and then for a little while the young ones take a nap and keep quiet, when they wake up again and renew their clamor for food.

If houses are not provided, the sparrow will build in any odd corner—a chink in the wall or in the nooks and eaves of buildings. A pair of London sparrows once made their nest in the mouth of the bronze lion over Northumberland House, at Charing Cross. They are very much attached to their nest, and after the little speckled eggs are laid will cling to it even under difficulties. The sailors of a coasting vessel once lying in a Scotch port frequently observed two sparrows flying about the topmast. One morning the vessel put to sea, when, to the astonishment of the sailors, the sparrows followed, evidently bent upon making the voyage. Crumbs being thrown on the deck, they soon became familiar, and came boldly to eat, hopping about as freely as if on shore. A nest was soon discovered built among the rigging. Fearing it might be demolished by a high wind, at the first landing the sailors took it carefully down, and finding that it contained four little ones, they carried it on shore and left it in the crevice of a ruined house. The parent birds followed, evidently well pleased with the change, and when the vessel sailed away they remained with their young family.

Much has been written about the mischievous doings of the sparrow, and war has been waged against it to a certain extent both here and in England. But the sparrow holds its ground well, and proves in many ways that even if it may drive away robins, and injure grain fields now and then, it more than balances these misdeeds by the thousands of caterpillars, mosquitoes, and other insects which it destroys, thus saving the life of countless trees and plants. The whole year round it is the same active, bustling, jolly creature, and our cities would be lonely and desolate without this little denizen of the street.

A BRAVE PATRIOT.

IN 1780, after the fall of Charleston, the British commander had issued a proclamation to the people of South Carolina, calling upon them to return to their allegiance, and offering protection to all who did so. The men inhabiting the tract of country stretching from the Santee to the Pedee selected one of their number to repair to Georgetown, the nearest British post, to ascertain the exact meaning of the offer, and what was expected of them.

In accordance with his instructions, Major John James sought an interview with Captain Ardesoif, the commandant of Georgetown, and demanded what was the meaning of the British protection, and upon what terms the submission of the citizens was to be made.

He was informed roughly that the only way to escape the hanging which they so justly deserved was to take up arms in his Majesty's cause.

James, not relishing the tone and manner of the British officer, coolly replied that "the people whom he came to represent would scarcely submit on such conditions."

Ardesoif, unaccustomed to contradiction, and enraged at the worthy major's use of the term "represent," which smote harshly on his ears, sprang to his feet, and, with his hand on his sword, exclaimed, "Represent! If you dare speak in such language, I will have you hung at the yard-arm."

Major James was weaponless, but in his anger was equal to the occasion. Seizing the chair upon which he had been sitting, he floored his insulter at a blow, and giving his enemy no time to recover, mounted his horse and escaped to the woods before pursuit could be attempted.

His people soon assembled to hear his story, and their wrath was kindled at hearing how their envoy had been received.

Required to take the field, it needed not a moment to decide under which banner, and the result was the formation of Marion's Brigade, which won such fame in the swampy regions of the South.

A LATIN WORD SQUARE.

Behold my first! In her palmy days
(In the time of my second, you understand)
She had many poets who sang her praise,
Had soldiers and statesmen and wealth to amaze,
Her fame was unrivalled in many ways—
She had no equal in all the land.

Again to the time of my second refer,
And spell that backward, my third behold—
A hero of monstrous strength. They aver
He held up a temple its fall to defer,
And ate forty pounds (but I hope 'tis a slur)
Every day for his food, both hot and cold.

Now spell my first backward, my fourth appears,
The greatest power of any time.
All poets have sung of its hopes and fears,
All men have known it with smiles and tears;
It has ruled and will rule for years and years
In every nation and every clime.

Now take my word square and look all about,
Sideways, across, and down the middle,
Not a word can be found there by any devout
Which can not be spelled upside down, inside out,
All in Latin, you know; but now I've no doubt
You've guessed every word of this easy riddle.

A TERRIBLE FISH.

AMONG the inhabitants of the sea which, from their size or strength, have been termed "monarchs of the ocean," are the saw-fish and the sword-fish, which are formidable enemies to the whale; but it is not merely on their fellow-inhabitants of the deep that these powerful fishes exercise their terrible strength. Some singular instances are related of their attacking even the ships that intrude upon their watery domain. An old sea-captain tells the following story:

"Being in the Gulf of Paria, in the ship's cutter, I fell in with a Spanish canoe, manned by two men, who were in great distress, and who requested me to save their lines and canoe, with which request I immediately complied, and going alongside for that purpose, I discovered that they had got a large saw-fish entangled in their turtle net. It was towing them out to sea, and but for my assistance they must have lost either their canoe or their net, or perhaps both, and these were their only means of subsistence. Having only two boys with me at the time in the boat, I desired the fishermen to cut the fish away, which they refused to do. I then took the bight of the net from them, and with the joint endeavors of themselves and my boat's crew we succeeded in hauling up the net, and to our astonishment, after great exertions, we raised about eight feet of the saw of the fish above the surface of the sea. It was a fortunate circumstance that the fish came up with his belly toward the boat, or he would have cut it in two.

"I had abandoned all idea of taking the fish, until, by great good luck, it made toward the land, when I made another attempt, and having about three hundred feet of rope in the boat, we succeeded in making a running bowline knot round the saw, and this we fortunately made fast on shore. When the fish found itself secured, it plunged so violently that I could not prevail on any one to go near it: the appearance it presented was truly awful. I immediately went alongside the Lima packet, Captain Singleton, and got the assistance of all his ship's crew. By the time they arrived the fish was less violent. We hauled upon the net again, in which it was still entangled, and got another three hundred feet of line made fast to the saw, and attempted to haul it toward the shore; but although mustering *thirty hands*, we could not move it an inch. By this time the negroes belonging to a neighboring estate came flocking to our assistance, making together about one hundred in number, with the Spaniards. We then hauled on both ropes nearly all day before the fish became exhausted. On endeavoring to raise the monster it became most desperate, sweeping with its saw from side to side, so that we were compelled to get strong ropes to prevent it from cutting us to pieces. After that one of the Spaniards got on its back, and at great risk cut through the joint of the tail, when the great fish died without further struggle. It was then measured, and found to be twenty-two feet long and eight feet broad, and weighed nearly five tons."

An East Indiaman was once attacked by a sword-fish with such prodigious force that its "snout" was driven completely through the bottom of the ship, which must have been destroyed by the leak had not the animal killed itself by the violence of its own exertions, and left its sword imbedded in the wood. A fragment of this vessel, with the sword fixed firmly in it, is preserved as a curiosity in the British Museum.

Several instances of a similar character have occurred, and one formed the subject of an action brought against an insurance company for damages sustained by a vessel from the attack of one of these fishes. It seems the *Dreadnought*, a first-class mercantile ship, left a foreign port in perfect repair, and on the afternoon of the third day a "monstrous creature" was seen sporting among the waves, and lines and hooks were thrown overboard to capture it. All efforts to this effect, however, failed; the fish got away, and in the night-time the vessel was reported to be dangerously leaking. The captain was compelled to return to the harbor he had left, and the damage was attributed to a sword-fish, twelve feet long, which had assailed the ship below water-line, perforated her planks and timbers, and thus imperilled her existence on the ocean.

Professor Owen, the distinguished naturalist, was called to give evidence on this trial as to the probability of such an occurrence, and he related several instances of the prodigious strength of the "sword." It strikes with the accumulated force of fifteen double-handed hammers; its velocity is equal to that of a swivel-shot, and it is as dangerous in its effects as a heavy artillery projectile would be.

The upper jaw of this fish is prolonged into a projecting flattened snout, the greatest length of which is about six feet, forming a saw, armed at each edge with about twenty large bony spines or teeth. Mr. Yarrel mentions a combat that occurred on the west coast of Scotland between a whale and some saw-fishes, aided by a force of "thrashers" (fox-sharks). The sea was dyed in blood from the stabs inflicted by the saw-fishes under the water, while the thrashers, watching their opportunity, struck at the unwieldy monster as often as it rose to breathe.

The sword-fish is also furnished with a powerful weapon in the shape of a bony snout about four or five feet long, not serrated like the saw-fish, but of a much firmer consistency—in fact, the hardest material known.

THE STORY OF OBED, ORAH, AND THE SMOKING-CAP.

BY MRS. A. M. DIAZ.

A COZY room, a wood fire, bright andirons, and a waiting company. The Family Story-Teller promised the children he would come, and the whole circle, young, older, oldest, are expecting a good time; for the Family Story-Teller can tell stories by the hour on any subject that may be given him, from a flat-iron to a whale-ship. He once told about a flat-iron—and nothing can be flatter than a flat-iron—a story half an hour long. It began, "Once there was a flat-iron."

But where is he? Has he forgotten? Did the snow-storm hinder? Has he missed his horse-car? Hark! a stamping in the entry. Dick runs to open the door, and shows Family Story-Teller upon the mat, tall and erect, brushing the snow from his cloak, his whiskers, and his laughing eyes.

Miss Flossie declared that he must be "judged" for coming so late.

Said Dick, "I judge him to tell as many stories as we want."

This judgment being thought too easy for a person like him, to make it harder he was "judged" to tell the stories all about the same thing. It was left to grandpa to say what this thing should be, and grandpa said, with a laugh, "going to mill."

"Very well," said Family Story-Teller, "I will begin at once, and tell you the entertaining story of 'Obed, Orah, and the Smoking-Cap.'" He then began as follows:

Once upon a time, in the pleasant village of Gilead, dwelt Mr. and Mrs. Stimpcett, with their four young children—Moses, Obadiah (called Obed), Deborah (called Orah), and little Cordelia. Mrs. Stimpcett, for money's sake, took a summer boarder, Mr. St. Clair, a city young man, who wished to behold the flowery fields, repose upon the dewy grass, and who had also another reason for coming, which will be told presently.

On the morning after Mr. St. Clair's arrival, Mrs. Stimpcett said to grandma that, as the noise of four young children at once would be too much for a summer boarder until he should become used to it, Obed and Orah would go and spend the day with their grandfather's cousin, Mrs. Polly Slater. Mrs. Polly Slater lived all alone by herself in a cottage at another part of the village of Gilead. Obed was six and a half years old, and Orah nearly five.

The two children set forth early in the morning. Orah wore her pink apron and starched sun-bonnet, and Obed wore his clean brown linen frock and trousers, the frock skirt standing out stiff like a paper fan. As his second best hat could not be found, and his first best was not to be thought of, he was obliged to wear his third best, which had a torn brim, and which he put on with tears and sniffles and loud complaints.

It happened very curiously that as Obed and Orah were walking through the orchard, Obed still sniffling, they saw, under a bush, a beautiful smoking-cap. Obed quickly threw down his old hat, and put on the smoking-cap in a way that the loose part hung off behind.

This beautiful smoking-cap belonged to the summer boarder, and was presented to him by a young lady who liked him very much. It was wrought in a Persian pattern slightly mingled with the Greek, and was embroidered with purple, yellow, crimson, Magenta, sage green, invisible blue, écru, old gold, drab, and other shaded worsteds, dotted with stitches of shining silk and beads of silver, the tassel alone containing skeins of écru sewing silk. The young lady lived not very far from Mr. Stimpcett's, and she was that other reason why Mr. St. Clair became a summer boarder in the pleasant village of Gilead.

Spry, the puppy dog, probably carried the smoking-cap to the orchard; but all that is known with certainty is that Mr. St. Clair, the evening before, then wearing the cap, reclined upon several chairs with his head out of the window, gazing at the moon, and there fell asleep, and that, as on account of the abundance of his hair it was a little too small, the cap fell off his head, and that when he awoke the pain in the back of his neck and the lateness of the hour caused him to forget all about it.

Now when Obed and Orah arrived at Mrs. Polly Slater's, they found her doors shut and locked. Mr. Furlong, the man who lived in the next house, called out to them, "Mrs. Polly Slater has borrowed a horse and cart, and gone to mill; she will stay and eat dinner with your aunt Debby." Then he added, "I am harnessing my horse to go to mill; how would you like to go with me, and ride back with Mrs. Polly Slater in the afternoon?"

Obed and Orah liked this so much that they ran and clambered into the cart as fast as they could, Orah climbing in over the spokes of a wheel. Mr. Furlong fastened Obed's cap on by tying around it a stout piece of line.

When they had ridden several miles on their way to mill, they met a boy on horseback galloping at a furious rate. The moment this boy saw Mr. Furlong, he pulled up his horse—he nearly fell off behind in doing so—and said he, "Mr. Furlong, your sister at Locust Point has heard bad news, and wants to see you immediately."

Mr. Furlong drove as fast as he could, until he came to the road which turned off to Locust Point. Here he set the children down, and showed Obed, not quite half a mile ahead of them, a large white building with a flag flying from the top. "There," said he, "your aunt Debby, you know, lives next to that white building. It is a straight road. I am sorry to leave you. Keep out of the way of the horses, and go directly to her house." Mr. Furlong then drove to Locust Point.

Now after the two children had walked a short distance, they came to a road which led across the road in which they were walking, and along this cross-road were running boys and girls, some barefoot, some bare-headed, some drawing baby carriages at such a rate that the babies were nearly thrown out; and all that these boys and girls would say was, "Baker's cart! baker's cart!" At last Obed and Orah found out that a baker's cart had upset in coming through the woods, and had left first-rate things to eat scattered all about. Our two children found a whole half sheet of gingerbread, which was not sandy, to speak of; and as they sat eating it, they looked through some bushes down a hill, and saw there something which looked like a molasses cooky. They scrambled down, the blackberry vines doing damage to their clothes, and found two molasses cookies, and each took one. But before Orah had finished hers she leaned her head on a grassy hummock, and fell asleep. When she awoke, sad to relate, they turned the wrong way, and went farther and farther and farther into the woods. After walking a long time, they came to a brook, and stopped there to drink. They had to lie flat on the ground, and suck up the water. Orah took off her shoes and stockings, because there was sand in them, and dipped her feet in the brook. Obed pulled hard, but he could not pull her stockings on over her wet feet, and she had to carry them and her shoes in her hand. The woods became thicker as the children walked on, and the trees taller. Obed began to cry. "Oh dear!" he said; "we are lost! we are lost!"

"Oh, I want to see my ma! I do! I do!" said Orah, and burst out crying. Crying!—roaring!—so the man said who heard it.

This was a charcoal man who happened along just then, driving an empty charcoal cart. He kindly asked them where they lived, and whither they were going. After Obed had told him, he said to them, "You poor little children! You are dirty and ragged, and you are a long way from your aunt Debby's. I shall pass near your father's house, and would you like to take a ride with me?" Then, as they seemed willing, he helped them into his cart, dropping them at the bottom as the safest place. Obed, however, by putting his toes into knot-holes and cracks, climbed high enough to put his head over the top, and Orah found a loose board which she could shove aside, and so push her head through and look up at Obed.

Now as they were rattling down a steep hill not a great way from home, a slender young lady started from the sidewalk, and ran after them, shouting and waving her parasol in the most frantic manner. The charcoal man did not hear her. This frantic and slender young lady was the young lady who made for Mr. St. Clair the smoking-cap done in the Persian pattern slightly mingled with the Greek, and embroidered with the shaded worsteds before mentioned, mingled with stitches of silk and beads of silver.

It is not strange that upon seeing that smoking-cap, which had cost her so much time and labor and money, appearing over the top of a charcoal cart on the head of a sooty little boy—it is not strange, I say, that the slender young lady went to Mr. St. Clair and asked what it all meant. She found Mr. St. Clair sitting upon the door-step, watching the sunset sky. Mr. St. Clair declared that he had spent the whole day in looking for the smoking-cap, and that it must have been stolen. Mr. and Mrs. Stimprett came out, and said *they* had been looking for the cap all day, and had felt badly on account of its loss. At this moment, grandma, who was confined to her room with rheumatism, called down from a chamber window that there were two little beggar children coming round the barn—colored children, she thought.

"Why," cried the slender young lady, "that's the very boy!"

Mr. St. Clair rushed out to the barn. Just as he left the door-step who should drive up to the gate and come in but Mrs. Polly Slater. "I have been to the mill," said she, "and I came home by this road, thinking you would like to hear from Debby."

"But where are Obed and Orah?" cried Mrs. Stimprett, in alarm.

"I have not seen them," said Mrs. Polly Slater.

As she said this, Mr. Furlong stopped at the gate. He said that as he was passing by he thought he would ask how Obed and Orah got on in finding their aunt Debby's.

"*Aunt Debby's!*" cried Mr. Stimprett, Mrs. Stimprett, grandma, and Mrs. Polly Slater—"*Aunt Debby's!*"

On hearing at what place Mr. Furlong had left her children, Mrs. Stimprett fainted and fell upon the ground. Then all the people tried to revive her. The slender young lady fanned with her parasol, Mrs. Polly Slater fetched the camphor bottle, Mr. Furlong pumped, Mr. Stimprett threw dipperfuls of water—though owing to his agitation not much of it touched her face—and grandma called down from the chamber window what should be done.

In the confusion no one noticed the approach of a new-comer. This was the charcoal man, bringing shoes and stockings. "Here are your little girl's shoes and stockings," said he. "She left them in my cart."

"They are not my little girl's," said Mr. Stimprett, throwing a dipperful of water on the ground.

"She said she was your little girl," said the charcoal man. "But there she is"—pointing to the barn; "you can see for yourself."

Mr. Stimprett ran to the barn, and was amazed to find that the two beggar children were his Obed and Orah. Mr. St. Clair was scolding them, and the tears were running down their cheeks in narrow paths. Mr. Stimprett led them quickly to Mrs. Stimprett. Seeing their mother stretched as if dead upon the ground, they both screamed, "Ma! ma! m—a!"

The well-known sounds revived her. She opened her eyes, raised herself, and caught the children in her arms.

The slender young lady advised that the smoking-cap be hung out-doors in a high wind, and afterward cleansed with naphtha. The clothes of Obed and Orah were also hung out, and Mr. Stimprett, for fun, arranged them in the forms of two scarecrows, which scared so well that the birds flew far away. The consequence was an enormous crop of cherries, all of which, except a few for sauce, Mr. Stimprett sent to the charcoal man.

Mr. St. Clair and the slender young lady were married the next year at cherry-time, and it was said that during

their honey-moon they subsisted chiefly upon cherries. And now my story's done.

"How is this, Mr. Story-Teller?" cried the children's mamma. "The story is a story, no doubt, but it can not be counted in, for Obed and Orah did not really go to mill."

Family Story-Teller said, looking around with a calm smile, that he could tell plenty more, and that in his next one Grandma Stimprett should really go to mill, and should meet with surprising adventures.

PUSSY'S KITTEN (?).

Once a tiny little rabbit strayed from home away;
Far from woodland haunts she wandered, little rabbit gray.
Our old Tabby cat, whilst sitting at the kitchen door,
Thought she saw her long-lost kitten home returned once more.

Gave a pounce, and quickly caught it, with a happy mew,
Ere the frightened little wanderer quite knew what to do.
Gently Tabby brought her treasure to the old door-mat,
Purred, and rubbed, and licked and smoothed it—motherly old cat!

But what puzzled pussy truly, and aroused her fears,
Was the length to which had grown her kitten's once small ears.
Most amazing, most alarming, was that sight to her;
Green and round her eyes were swelling, stiff and straight her fur.

"Poor wee kitty! what a pity you're deformed!" thought she;
"Surely this has somehow happened since you went from me.
But you're welcome home, my kitten; mother's love is strong,
Though I will confess I wish your ears were not so long."

So the tiny little rabbit grew contented quite,
And our visitors like to call and see the pretty sight
Of nice old Tabby playing with her rabbit-kitty gray;
And she doesn't dream of her mistake, although, the truth to say,

Her own true kitten went the road that many kittys go;
For John the coachman took it to the horse-pond just below.
But I think it is most cruel to drown a little cat;
And I trust all girls and boys will have too much heart for that.

THE BOYS AND UNCLE JOSH.

BY W. O. STODDARD.

"HEY, Billy, my boy! Going skating?"

"Yes, Uncle Josh, Joe Pearce and me. The big pond's frozen solid."

"Is it safe?"

"Charley Shadders he says it's twenty feet thick in some places."

"Twenty feet thick! I declare! That's pretty thick ice. How did he know?"

"I don't know. I guess he guessed at it. He's an awful guesser."

"I should say he was. Twenty feet thick! Why, Billy, the water's only five feet deep in summer."

"Oh, but," exclaimed Joe Pearce, who had been listening with all the eagerness of twelve years old, "it swells water to freeze it, Uncle Josh."

"So it does, so it does. But I never heard of a swell like that." And Uncle Josh—for he was uncle to all the small boys in the village—shook his fat sides with laughter, but it was not all about the remarkable ice, for his next question was, "But, Billy, you've put all your skating on one foot. How's that?"

"'Cause it's all in one skate."

"Well, it's big enough. Why don't you divide it, and give the other foot a fair share?"

"I've got mine on the other foot," shouted Joe, trying to balance himself on one leg and hold up an uncommonly large skate for inspection.

How those skates were strapped on! They were even steadied with pieces of rope, and had bits of wood and leather stuffed in under the straps to make them fit.

"You see, Uncle Josh," explained Billy, "my brother Bob he went away to college, and left his skates, 'cause, he said, the college was out of ice this winter. And Joe Pearce he didn't have any. And Christmas forgot to give me any. And so we divided 'em, and took the sled, and we're going to the big pond."

"That was fair. Only you haven't divided the sled."

"The sled won't divide," said Joe, with a solemn shake of his curly head; "but I'd like to divide my skate with my other foot."

"I'll tell you what, boys," suddenly exclaimed Uncle Josh, "let's have a little Christmas of our own."

"Have you got any?" asked Billy.

"I guess I have. **Come right along to the store with me.**"

"Come on, Joe. Keep your skate on. **Don't limp any** more'n you can help."

But both he and Joe cut a queer figure as they followed Uncle Josh up the street; for when a boy makes one of his legs longer than the other, and slips and slides on that foot, it makes a good deal of difference in the way he walks.

Everybody knew Uncle Josh, and although he was a deacon and a very good man, everybody expected to see a smile on his face, and to hear him chuckle over something when they met him. So nobody was half so much surprised as Joe and Billy were, and their surprise did not come to them until they reached the store. But it came then.

"Skates for these boys," said Uncle Josh, as they went in. "One for each foot, all around. Straps too."

That was it, and now the boys were doing more chuckling than Uncle Josh himself.

"Billy," asked Joe, "do you know what to say?"

"Why, we must thank him."

"Yes, I s'pose so. But that doesn't seem to be half enough."

"Can't we thank him big, somehow?"

"Enough for two pair of skates?"

"That's so. We can't do it."

They had to give it up; but they did their best, and Uncle Josh cut them short in the middle of it.

"Come, come, boys, we can't stay here all day. There won't be another Saturday again for a week, and then it may rain. Don't put your skates on. Wait till we get to the pond. Bring along the big ones. They'll do for me."

"Why, are you going, Uncle Josh?"

"Of course I am. If the ice is twenty feet thick, I want to skate on it. That kind of ice 'll bear anybody."

And so the boys tied the big skates upon the sled, and were starting off, when Uncle Josh exclaimed:

"No, boys, give 'em to me. I haven't had a pair of skates in my hand for twenty years. I want to see how it would seem to carry them."

There were not a great many people to be met in a small village like that, but every one they did meet had a smile for Uncle Josh and his skates, till they reached the miller's house, just this side of the pond. And there was Mrs. Sanders, the miller's wife, sweeping the least bit of snow from her front stoop.

"Joe," said Billy, "do you see that?"

"And Charley Shadders was guessing, then. **He said** snow wouldn't light on her stoop."

"There isn't but mighty little of it, and it didn't cost her anything."

But just at that moment Mrs. Sanders was resting on her broom, and looking very severely at Uncle Josh, and saying,

"Now, Deacon Parmenter, where are you going with those boys? Skates, too, at your time of life."

"Good-morning, Sister Sanders. I declare, if you'll go with us, I'll trot right back and get a pair of skates for you. I'd like to see a good-looking young woman like you—"

"Deacon Parmenter! Me! To go skating? **With you** and a couple of boys? I never!"

But she did not look half so angry as she did at first. She was a plump and rosy woman; but she had a pointed nose, and her lips were thin. Billy whispered to Joe Pearce, "Aunt Sally says it'd keep any woman's lips thin to work 'em as hard as Mrs. Sanders does hers."

They were almost smiling just now, for Uncle Josh went on: "Now, Sister Sanders, I know it's a little queer for an old fellow like me, but it's just the thing for young folks. Just you say the word, and you shall have 'em. You're looking nicely this morning, Sister Sanders."

"Billy," whispered Joe, "how red in the face Uncle Josh is getting!"

"So is she," said Billy. "If he goes on that way, she'll come along and spoil the fun."

"No, she won't."

Joe was right, for Mrs. Sanders brought her broom down on the front step with a great bang with one hand, and she smoothed her front hair with the other, as she answered Uncle Josh: "No, Deacon Parmenter, I couldn't bring myself to set such an example. You must take good care of the boys, and see that they do not get into any mischief. If I was their mothers, I'd feel safer about them to know you was with 'em."

Uncle Josh had a spell of coughing just then, and it seemed to last him till he and the boys were away past the miller's house, and going down the slope toward the pond.

It was frozen beautifully, for the weather had been bitterly cold, without any snow to speak of. The pond was all one glare and glitter, and more than twenty men and boys were already at work on it, darting around like birds on their ringing, spinning, gliding skates. Only that some of the smaller boys put one more in mind of tumbler pigeons than of any other kind of birds.

It was quite wonderful how quickly Joe and Billy had their new skates on, and Uncle Josh looked immensely pleased to see how well they both knew how to use them.

"Why, boys, you haven't tumbled down once. How's that?"

"Oh, we know how," said Billy; "and the ice is great. Thick ice always skates better'n thin ice."

But Uncle Josh had seated himself on the sled, and was hard at work trying to put on Brother Bob's big skates.

They fitted him well enough, but he seemed to have a deal of trouble in getting hold of the straps.

"Seems as if my feet were farther away from me than they were twenty years ago."

"Joe," said Billy, "let's help. We can strap 'em for him."

"That's good, boys. Pull tight. Tighter. Let me stamp a little. There—one hole tighter. Now buckle."

And so they went on, till Uncle Josh's skates were strapped, as Joe Pearce said, "so they couldn't wiggle."

"That's all right," said Uncle Josh. "Now, you boys, just skate away, anywhere, and I'll enjoy myself."

They hardly liked to leave him, but off they went, for the boys to whom they wanted to show their new skates were away over on the other side of the pond.

"I don't know if this ice is twenty feet thick," muttered Uncle Josh, as he pulled his feet under him, "but it looks twenty miles slippery. Ice on this pond always freezes with the slippery side up. Steady, now. There! I'm glad I've got the sled to sit down on."

It was well it was a good strong sled, with thick ice under it, for Uncle Josh sat down pretty hard, and he was a fat, jolly, heavy sort of man.

He sat right still and laughed for a whole minute, and then he tried it again.

This time he succeeded in standing up, and he was just saying to himself, "I wish Jemima Sanders had come along to see me skate," when one of his feet began to slip away from him.

"I know how," he shouted. "There's no help for it. I must strike right out."

So he did, and his first slide carried him nearly a rod on that one skate before he could get the other one down. He did that, however, and it worked finely, for he had been a good skater when he was a young man. He had kept hold of the rope-handle of the sled, and it was following him. That is, when he struck out with a foot he swung his long arms too, and the sled swung around on the ice as if it was half crazy.

"What can be the matter with my ankles?" he said to himself. "They used to be good ankles."

No doubt; but then the last time he had skated before that, they had not had so much to carry.

"Billy," exclaimed Joe Pearce, "Uncle Josh is agoing!"

"How he does go! Ain't I glad it's thick ice!"

"Let's go. Come on, boys."

Other eyes than theirs had been watching Uncle Josh, for everybody knew him, and nobody had ever seen him skate, and Joe and Billy were followed by almost all the boys on the pond.

"Hurrah for Uncle Josh!"

"Can't he skate, though!"

"See him go."

Right across the pond, as if he were in a desperate hurry to reach the opposite bank before the ice could melt under him, went Uncle Josh, and with him, all around him, swung the sled.

It may have served as a sort of balance-wheel, and helped to steady him, but it could not steer him. Neither could he steer himself, and the next thing he knew he was headed down the pond, and skating for dear life toward the dam.

"If I stop, I shall come down," he said, with a sort of gasp. "I'm getting out of breath. Good! I'm pointed for the shore again, and there's a snow-bank."

All the boys were racing after him now, but they had stopped shouting in their wonder at what could have got into Uncle Josh. He himself was beginning to feel very warm, for it was a good while since he had done so much work in so short a time.

"Here comes the shore!" But just as he said it, there he was, and the skate he was sliding on caught in a chip on the ice.

The wind had been at work to keep the pond clean when it piled that snow-bank, and had left it all heaped up, white and soft and deep, and into it went Uncle Josh, head first, while the sled was pitched a rod beyond him.

"Get the sled, Billy," said Joe.

"He skated himself right ashore."

"Guess he isn't hurt."

"Hurt? No, indeed!" shouted Uncle Josh, as he came up again through the snow. "That's the way we used to skate when I was a boy. Billy, where's that sled?"

He did not seem in any hurry to stand up, but Joe Pearce found his hat, and handed it to him.

"Thank you, Joseph. Billy, you may bring the sled right here in front of me."

"He wants to sit down," said one of the boys.

"He's sitting down now," said Joe. But Billy brought the sled, and Uncle Josh carefully worked himself forward upon it, and began to brush away the snow.

"I'm as white as a miller," he chuckled to himself. "Boys, I guess you may do the rest of my skating for me to-day."

"Don't those skates fit?" asked Joe.

"Oh yes, they fit well enough. It's the ice that doesn't fit. It's too wide for me."

"Well," said Billy, "we'll pull you across. Take hold, boys."

"I declare!" began Uncle Josh; but the boys had seized the rope, and were off in a twinkling.

"It's fun," they heard him mutter; "but what would Sister Sanders say?"

"There she is!" exclaimed Billy, "right down by the shore. She's come to see us skate."

"Hold on, boys! hold on! Let me get my skates off."

But there were so many boys pulling and pushing around that sled that before they could all let go and stop it, the pond had been nearly crossed, and there was Mrs. Sanders.

Uncle Josh did not seem to see her at all, and only said, "Now, boys, just unbuckle my skates for me, will you?"

It would have been done more quickly if there had not

been so many to help, and by the time one skate was loose, Uncle Josh was laughing again.

"Deacon Parmenter!"

"Is that you, Sister Sanders? They're all safe—every boy of them. Just wait a moment now, and they'll be ready for you."

"Ready for me! What can you mean? I'm just aneared and upset, Deacon Parmenter. A man like you, to be cutting up in such a way as this!"

Brother Bob's skates for him. I hope you'll all have a good time."

He was edging and sliding along toward the shore while he was talking, and the last they heard him say was,

"I can skate well enough, but I'm afraid somebody else 'll have to do my walking for me for a week or two."

"He's just the best man in the village," said Joe Pearce.

"So he is," said Billy; "but I'm glad the ice was thick. What would we have done if he'd broken through?"

"That's why fat men like him don't skate, Billy. Did you see what a hole he made in that there snow-bank?"

He had, and so had the rest, but they all skated a race across the pond to take another look at it, and wonder how he ever managed to get out.

"HURT? NO, INDEED!"

"There they are, Sister Sanders. You can put 'em right on. Come and sit down on the sled. They're a little large for me, but they'll just fit you; I know they will."

Uncle Josh had very carefully risen to his feet, and was holding out to her Brother Bob's big skates, straps and all. Her face grew very rosy indeed as she looked at them.

"Fit me!" she exclaimed—"those things fit me! Why, Deacon Parmenter, what can you mean?"

"Too small, eh? Well, now, I'd ha' thought—"

But Mrs. Sanders turned right around and marched away toward her own house without saying another word.

"Boys," said Uncle Josh, "the skating is fine, but there isn't any more of it than you'll want. Billy, take care of

SHIPS OF COLUMBUS. NORWEGIAN SHIP OF THE TENTH CENTURY.

THE FIRST OCEAN STEAM-SHIP. THE "MAYFLOWER."

OCEAN STEAM-SHIP OF TO-DAY. AMERICAN CLIPPER SHIP.

SHIPS PAST AND PRESENT.

On page 161 are given illustrations of six different styles of vessels, all of which are correct drawings of ships that in different ages have acted important parts in the history of this continent.

The upper right-hand picture represents a Norwegian war ship of the tenth century, and in such a one Scandinavian traditions assert that, early in the eleventh century, Olaf Ericsson and his hardy crew sailed into the unknown west for many a day, until at length they reached the shores of America. On the authority of these same traditions, some people assert that the structure known as the "old stone mill of Newport" was erected by this same Olaf Ericsson, and left by him as a monument of his discovery.

If Ericsson and his men did make the voyage across the unknown ocean, it was a very brave thing for them to do, for as the picture shows their ship was a very small affair when compared with the magnificent vessels of to-day, and was ill fitted to battle with the storms of the Atlantic. She was of about ten tons burden, or as large as an oyster sloop of to-day, and carried a crew of twenty-five men. A single mast was stepped amidships, and this supported the one large square sail which was all that ships of those days carried. Well forward of the mast was a single bank of oars, or long sweeps, that were used when the wind was unfavorable, or during calms.

Although this style of craft appears very queer to us, in those days it was considered the perfection of marine architecture, and in these little ships the fierce Scandinavian Vikings, or sea-rovers, became the scourge and terror of the Northern seas.

The upper left-hand picture represents three ships very different in style from the first, but still looking very queer and clumsy. They are the ships in which, in—who can tell the date?—"Columbus crossed the ocean blue," and made that discovery of America which history records as the first. These caravels, as they were called, were named the *Santa Maria*, *Pinta*, and *Niña*. The first-named was much larger than the others, and was commanded by Columbus in person; but large as she was then considered, she would now be thought very small for a man-of-war, as she was, for she was only ninety feet in length. She had four masts, of which two were fitted with square and two with lateen sails, and her crew consisted of sixty-six men. In old descriptions of this vessel it is mentioned that she was provided with eight anchors, which seems a great many for so small a ship to carry. The other two vessels were much smaller, and were open except for a very short deck aft. They were each provided with three masts, rigged with lateen-sails.

From this time forth a rapid improvement took place in the building of ships. They were made larger and stronger, as well as more comfortable; a reduction was made in the absurd height of the stern, or poop, and much useless ornamentation about the bows and stern was done away with.

In the third picture is shown a model ship of the seventeenth century, which is none other than the *Mayflower*, in which, in 1620, the Pilgrims crossed the ocean in search of a place for a new home, which they finally made for themselves at Plymouth.

During the eighteenth century trade increased so rapidly between the American colonies and the mother country that the demand for ships was very great, and the sailing vessels built then and early in the present century have not since been excelled for speed or beauty. But a great change was about to take place; and early in this century people began to say that before long ships would be able to sail without either the aid of wind or oars, and in 1807 Robert Fulton built the first steamboat. Twelve years later the first ocean steamer was built, and made a successful voyage across the Atlantic. She was named the *Savannah*, and our fourth picture shows what she looked like.

The last two pictures are those of a full-rigged clipper ship of to-day under all sail, and one of the magnificent ocean steamers that ply so swiftly between New York and Liverpool, making in eight or nine days the voyage that it took the *Savannah* thirty days to make.

THE RABBITS' FÊTE.

BY MRS. E. F. PERRIN.

"Good-night, little girl. Go to nurse, and ask her to pop you right into bed."

The front door was shut, and Ellie hurried up stairs to the great hall window, and looked out to see her mamma and pretty Aunt Janet get into the sleigh and drive off. "Hark!" she says to herself, "how nice the bells sound! They keep saying,

'Jingle bells, jingle bells,
Jingle all the way;
Oh, what fun it is to ride
In a one-horse open sleigh!'

It's just as light as day out-doors. The moon makes the snow look like frosted cake. I can see the croquet ground as plain as can be, and it looks like a great square loaf. There's the arbor, and the seats in it have white cushions on them. How funny it would be to play croquet on the ice! Only the balls would go so fast we should have to put on skates to catch them. I can see ever and ever so far—'way over to the woods where Jack sets his traps. He says they are chock-full of rabbits; but I don't believe him, for he never catches any. What's that moving on the edge of the grove? What can it be? Oh, it's lots of them! They are coming this way, and I can hear them laughing and talking."

Ellie watched, and soon saw a troop of rabbits hopping along toward the lawn.

"Why, I do believe it is a rabbit party. How lucky it is I haven't gone to bed!"

On they came, chattering in the funniest way, and dressed in the top of the fashion. One who seemed to be the leader said: "Ladies and gentlemen, this is the spot. You see how level it is for dancing, and we can have a game at croquet if you choose. The band will now strike up; and take partners, if you please, for a waltz."

Ellie wondered where the band was, but the strains of "Sweet Evelina, dear Evelina," came floating on the air, and, looking up, she saw two crows perched on the bar from which the swing hung in summer. One had a little fiddle, and the other a flute.

"That's the queerest thing yet," thought Ellie. "The idea of a crow being able to play on anything, when they make such a horrid noise cawing! The night crows must be different from the day ones."

After the waltz was ended, and the couples were promenading, Ellie took a good look at the young ladies and their lovely dresses. There was one so beautiful she was charmed by her. She was as fair as a lily, and so gentle and sweet Ellie called her the belle of the ball. A little gray fellow never left her side, and could not do enough for her. He called her Alicia, and Ellie did not wonder he seemed so fond of her. She noticed, too, a tall young lady who had a white face with a black nose. She looked very cross, but was much dressed in a scarlet silk, with a long train, which gave her no end of trouble, for it was always in the way. Ellie heard her say, in the crossest way: "I suppose Alicia thinks she looks well to-night with that high comb in her head. I call her a perfect fright."

"You only say so because you haven't one," answered her companion. "I think it is very becoming, and it makes her veil float out beautifully behind."

The leader called out, "Take partners for the Lancers!" and they quickly formed into sets.

They danced to perfection: even the "grand square" was got through without a blunder. The leader was unlucky enough to step upon the scarlet train, and its wearer turned upon him, crying out: "I do wish, Mr. Hopkins, you wouldn't be so clumsy! You will tear my dress off me."

He humbly begged her pardon, but told his partner he should look out and not get in the same set with Matilda again; she was as disagreeable as ever. "Just because her grandmother was French, she gives herself great airs. She is no better than the rest of us."

After the Lancers was finished, Matilda went to the arbor to get her train pinned up. It was sadly torn. While one of the matrons was at work upon it, Ellie listened to the conversation.

"Why isn't Mrs. Gray here to-night?" asked one.

"Don't you know she has eight little ones a week old to-day?"

"Oh, indeed! Her hands must be full. I have been so busy with my own affairs I know nothing about my neighbors'. But who is that who has just arrived? Mr. Hopkins will surely break his neck trying to get to him."

"That must be *Lord Lepus*; he belongs to the Hare family, one of the most aristocratic in England. I heard he was to be invited. What an honor!—a nobleman at our New-Year's fête."

Matilda grew impatient, and pulled her dress away, saying. "That will do: I hope you've been long enough about it," and without a word of thanks hurried to join the young people.

"How very rude she is!" thought Ellie. "I always thought that French people were polite."

Her attention was drawn to the new arrival. "He must be what Jack calls a swell," thought she, "with that long coat almost touching his heels, and his button-hole bouquet of carnations, heliotrope, and smilax. How does he keep that one eyeglass in his eye? It never moves, and yet he skips about like a grasshopper."

"Shall I present your lordship to one of the ladies?" asked Mr. Hopkins. "Any of them will be only too happy to dance with you."

"Aw, really now?" answered Lord Lepus. "'Pon my word, they are all such charming creatures, it is hard to choose. Who is the little one with the blue veil standing with the gentleman in demi-toilet of gray?"

"That is Alicia. The gentleman is Mr. Golightly. They are to be married soon."

"How extremely interesting! Pray present me."

His lordship secured the blushing Alicia for a waltz, and was so well pleased with his partner he danced with her again and again.

After the last dance, Ellie saw Mr. Hopkins setting out the wickets for croquet. The balls were lady apples with different colored ribbons tied to the stems, and the mallets were cat-o'-nine-tails, with the pussy end going the other way.

"Well," thought she, "I don't see but that rabbits know as much as people. I wonder how they will play."

She did not have to wonder long, for they were at it almost before she had done thinking. Lord Lepus was a fine player. Alicia was his partner, and with his help her balls went flying through the wickets in a twinkling. Golightly and Matilda were in the same game, and did their prettiest; but his lordship was too much for them.

At last when Alicia sent Matilda's ball spinning, and struck the stake for her partner and then for herself, Matilda flew in a rage, and lifting her mallet, struck Alicia a blow on the head, which drove the teeth of her comb down into the pretty white skin. Poor Alicia gave one cry, and dropped senseless. Golightly was beside himself with grief, and pushing Lord Lepus aside as he sprang to her aid, cried, "Away! away! You took her from me in life: she is mine in death."

"I beg pardon—" politely began his lordship, but was interrupted by Mrs. Muff, Alicia's chaperon, who calmly ordered Golightly to stop his noise, and help Mr. Hopkins carry her charge to the arbor.

"Oh, what shall we do?" groaned Golightly, beating his brow with his hand.

"Do," repeated Mrs. Muff; "why, send for a porous plaster. Here, Skipjack, run to Dr. Pine as fast as you can, and fetch me one."

In a moment he was back with it, and Mrs. Muff quickly clapped it upon Alicia's head. Ellie looked on with breathless interest, and soon Alicia slowly opened her eyes, and looking up, said, in a soft voice, "Dear Golightly!"

Mrs. Muff skillfully jerked off the plaster, and Ellie saw the teeth of the comb sticking to it.

"Bless my soul! it's the most extraordinary thing," cried his lordship.

"Oh, that's nothing," replied Mrs. Muff; "I always use them when my children are teething, with great success. But where is Matilda?"

"The poor girl was terribly cut up, you know, and ran away toward the woods," answered Lord Lepus. "How does the charming Alicia find herself? Well enough to join us, I hope."

"She must rest awhile. A short nap will entirely restore her," said Mrs. Muff.

At that moment Mr. Hopkins put his head in the arbor, and announced supper was served.

"Now," said Mrs. Muff, "while you are at supper Alicia shall go to sleep, and I will watch her."

Ellie looked out, and saw a table spread on the croquet ground. "Well, well, how quick rabbits are! I wonder what they have to eat;" and she ran along with the rest of the party to find out. The table was loaded with nice things—apples and celery in abundance, and piles and piles of popped corn. Lord Lepus had never seen any before, and was so much pleased with it, Mr. Hopkins ordered a waiter to fill a bag and give it to his lordship when he left. "How strange," thought Ellie; "mamma says it is very impolite to carry away anything to eat when you go to parties. But perhaps it is different with rabbits."

When they had finished supper, Mr. Cawkins and son—the band—came flapping down and picked up everything that was on the table. "I suppose that playing makes them hungry," thought Ellie; "but how fast they do eat!"

When the last kernel of popped corn had disappeared, the crows flew back to their perch and began to play the liveliest, merriest tune Ellie had ever heard. Mr. Hopkins said to Lord Lepus, "Will your lordship join us in dancing the merry-go-round? It is our national dance, and we always have it on New-Year's Eve."

"I shall be most happy; and here comes the fair Alicia, looking as fresh as a daisy. I will secure her for my partner."

But Mr. Hopkins formed them into a circle, and they began to dance around, singing as they went. Ellie listened, and caught the words,

"Come dance, come dance the merry-go-round,
With sprightly leap and joyous bound.
We'll grasp each hand with right good cheer,
And welcome in the glad new year.
Oh, the merry-go-round, the merry-go-round,
We'll dance till day is dawning."

They flew around fast and faster, till Ellie could not tell one from another. They looked like a streak on the snow.

"Dear me, how dizzy they will get! Poor Alicia will certainly have the headache," thought Ellie; but still quicker went the music, and still faster flew the dancers. All of a sudden Ellie was startled by a loud "caw." She felt some one shaking her shoulder, and a voice in her ear said, "Wake up, Miss Ellie, wake up. The hall clock has just struck half past nine, and to think of your being out of bed at this hour! What will your mamma say! That giddy-pate Sarah told me she would undress you, for I was called away."

"I am so glad," said sleepy little Ellie, "for I have seen the merry-go-round."

Nurse gathered her up in her arms, and bore her to the nursery.

"Nursey," asked Ellie, "are English hares better than our rabbits?"

"Yes, miss, much better for soup."

"Soup!" cried Ellie; "how dreadful, when he was so beautifully dressed!"

"Yes," said nurse, "we like to have them dressed; they are so hard to skin."

"What do you mean?" exclaimed Ellie. "He wore such a beautiful long coat, and had on a locket and three rings."

"Dear me," thought nurse, "she has been in the moonlight so long I am afraid it has turned her brain. She certainly seems a little looney. The sooner she is undressed and in her bed, the better."

"Oh, nursey, the next time baby has any teeth coming, put on a porous plaster, and it will pull them right through his gums."

"Bless the child! What is she talking about now? Hares and plasters! The moon is a dangerous thing, and Sarah shall be well scolded for her neglect."

As Ellie laid her head on the pillow, she said, "They danced the merry-go-round, and at the end of every verse they sang, 'Oh, the merry-go-round, the merry-go-round, we'll—dance—till—day—'"

Nurse looked, and saw that little Ellie was fast asleep.

A WISE DOG.

MANY anecdotes have been published respecting dogs, proving that, besides giving evidence of being endowed with certain moral qualities, they possess and exercise memory, reasoning powers, and forethought; they can communicate with each other, form plans, and act in concert. The subject, however, is by no means exhausted, and dog stories almost always meet with a welcome reception, especially from juvenile readers.

The following story gives an instance, in the first place, of two dogs combining to perform a certain action; in the second place, it shows that one of these dogs evidently understood from the conversation of his master and another man the consequences likely to result from this action, and that he thereupon formed and carried out a plan to avoid them.

A farmer who resided in a town on the borders of Dartmoor was the owner of a valuable sheep-dog. So skillful was this dog in collecting and driving the sheep, that he almost performed the part of a shepherd. If the farmer, on his return from market, wanted the sheep to be driven to the field, he had only to say, "Keeper, take the sheep to field," and the dog would collect the flock and drive them to the field without suffering a single one to stray. But the proverb, "Evil communications corrupt good manners," is as applicable to dogs as to men. Keeper got acquainted with another dog, which proved to be of disreputable character, and like other disreputable characters, had a habit of rambling about at night. When the farmer was smoking his evening pipe by the kitchen fire, and Keeper was stretched along the hearth, apparently asleep, a low bark would be heard outside; Keeper would prick up his ears, and when the door was opened, would make his escape and join his companion, and then away would go both dogs on a ramble.

This game was carried on for some little time; Keeper's bad habits were not suspected at home, and he did his duty by his master's sheep as faithfully as ever. In the mean time it became known in the town that a few miles distant many sheep had been "worried" by dogs, but as yet the culprit or culprits had not been discovered. It may, perhaps, be as well to explain that by "worrying" sheep is meant that they have been attacked by dogs, which seize the sheep by the throat, bite them, and suck the blood, and then leave them to perish. In a single night one dog has been known to "worry" forty sheep. No wonder such animals are a terror to farmers. Besides, if a dog once takes to "worrying" sheep, he never leaves off the habit.

One evening as the farmer sat by his fire smoking and conversing with a neighbor, Keeper as usual basking by the fire, and waiting the expected call of his dog companion, the conversation turned on the great number of sheep that had been lately "worried" and destroyed, and the loss that would ensue to the farmers.

COME OUT AND HAVE SOME FUN.

"Well," said the neighbor, "we caught one on 'em, with his mouth and coat bloody, and we hanged him up on the spot. They do say thy dog Keeper was with un."

"It is too true, he was there," replied the farmer; then looking at the apparently sleeping dog, and shaking his head at him, he said, "Thee knows thee has been with un. Thy turn will come next. We'll hang thee up to-morrow."

Keeper lay still, pretending sleep, but with his ears open. He had heard his death-warrant, and was determined that it should not be carried into execution if he could prevent it. When the outer door was opened, he slunk off quietly, and was never seen again.

What became of him was never known.

Who will say after this that dogs do not understand the conversation of men, especially when it relates to "worrying" sheep, and the punishment it entails on the guilty dogs?

A Fox went out in a Hungry Plight.
2 He came at first to a Farmer's yard,
Where the Ducks and the Geese declared it hard
That their nerves should be shaken and their rest be [marred]
By the visit of Mr. Fox O, Fox O, Fox O.
3 He took the grey Goose by the sleeve;
Says he, "Madam Goose, and by your leave,
I'll take you away without reprieve,
And carry you home to my den O, den O, den O."
4 He seized the black Duck by the neck,
And swung her all across his back,
The black Duck cried out, "Quack, quack, quack,"
With her legs hanging dangling down O, down O, down O.
5 Old Mrs. Slipperslopper jumped out of bed,
And out of the window she popped her head,
"John, John, John, the grey Goose is gone,
And the Fox is off to his den O, den O, den O."
6 Then John he went up to the hill,
And he blew a blast both loud and shrill;
Says the Fox, "This is very pretty music—still
I'd rather be at my den O, den O, den O."
7 At last the Fox got home to his den,
To his dear little Foxes, eight, nine, ten;
Says he, "You're in luck, here's a good fat Duck,
With her legs hanging dangling down O, down O, down O."
8 He then sat down with his hungry wife;
They did very well without fork or knife;
They never ate a better Goose in all their life,
And the little ones picked the bones O, bones O, bones.

THAT our youthful correspondents may not think we slight any of their favors, we would say that we regret exceedingly that our limited space compels us to print so few of their prettily worded and neatly written letters. We thank you all for your praise and hearty good-will, but while we read all your comments on *Young People* with attention, as in that way we learn what pleases you best, we must choose for printing those letters which tell something of interest to other young readers.

To one thing we would call your attention. When you send drawings of "Wiggles" and other picture puzzles, be careful to do it on a separate piece of paper. Your letters are all recorded, and filed away; and if your idea for a "Wiggle" is drawn on the same piece of paper on which you write your letter, it makes confusion. We hope our young correspondents will pay attention to this suggestion.

[illegible]

In *Harper's Young People*, No. 13, Mr. Lossing wrote about "Putnam's Narrow Escape." He said his informant was [illegible]. Please tell Mr. Lossing that [illegible] was my great-grandfather. I am nine years old. [illegible]

Ben Ryland Hill.

[illegible]

I am two years old, and live away out in the Rocky Mountains. [illegible] Washington. [illegible]

Wallace B.

[illegible]

I am eleven years old. My father tells me lots of stories about Indians, and [illegible] were killed by them. [illegible] My father says [illegible] is a very old place, and the Pilgrims came here [illegible] I take *Young People*, and hope I shall always get it.

Clarence E. C.

[illegible]

I want to tell you about my dogs. I have two [illegible] I trained them all myself. [illegible] I drove the dogs when I was five years old.

Albert F.

[illegible]

My uncle gave me a little [illegible] on New-Year's day, [illegible]

[illegible]

[illegible]

I have a canary. His name is Willie. [illegible]

Mary.

Sometimes canaries will not bathe in cold weather. You must give your bird tepid water, otherwise it will get chilled, and sicken. Try putting the bath dish in its cage and leaving it there. Some canaries will never bathe if they are watched.

[illegible]

I have two Maltese [illegible] What can I do for her?

Hattie T. H.

Your kitty has a very funny appetite. Keep her in a warm corner by the fire, and give her plenty of warm milk to drink, and her cold will get well. A little weak catnip tea mixed with the milk would do her good.

Robbie I. G. has a kitty which climbs up on the balusters every morning and tries to open his chamber door; Carlotta P. writes that her kitties Betsy and Beatie play with balls, and run up the curtains as if they were climbing trees; Charlie B. S., Annie C. and Maggie W., Mattie V. S., and Ida R. L., also write of pet cats and dogs and birds.

Maynard A. M.—Your story and poems are very pretty, and show much fancy and imagination for a boy of your age, but we have not room to print them. We return them to Detroit, Michigan, the only address you give.

"Mystic."—Your drawing is very well done, but we can not use it.

Miss A. T.—There is no commentary on Pope's translation of Homer, but many interesting papers have been published on the subject.

Edward M. Van C.—Your letter was a long time reaching its destination, as it first took a trip to the Dead-letter Office at Washington, and was forwarded to us from there. Like the little girl mentioned in the paper on the Dead-letter Office in *Young People*, No. 11, you posted it without a stamp.

S. L. M.—You write a very pretty letter considering that you are "only a little girl nine years old," and you need not feel nervous in future.

Mrs. E. W.—Many thanks for the charming letter and poem you so kindly forward from the bright little nine-year-old girl, Jessie Lancaster, of Marshall, Texas.

Annie W. P.—The quotation you wish is probably this: "Nothing in his life became him like the leaving it." It occurs in Shakespeare's play of *Macbeth*, act first, scene fourth.

George O. R.—We are very sorry you are so unfortunate, and trust the weekly visit of *Young People* will continue to brighten the monotony of your illness.

W. T. Duff.—The incident you mention must be taken as an exception to a general rule, as the personal observation of many students of natural history establishes the statement to which you demur.

Ethel S. M.—Either spelling of the word is correct. The form you object to is more often used by American writers than the one you found in your English history.

Favors are acknowledged from Esther B., Minnesota; Osborn D., Arkansas; Bert C. S., Iowa; Tillie F. W., Maryland; [illegible], Washington, D. C.; Willie [illegible], Massachusetts; Louis C. V., New Jersey. From Connecticut—Annie H. L., "Daisy." From New York—R. Cohn, Addie and A. Goodnow. From Missouri—Charlie B., Theodore W. H. From Illinois—[illegible] M. H., Marion Peters. From California—Mary M. Case, Arthur White.

Correct answers to puzzles are received from Charlie A. T., Illinois; R. W. Sager, Ohio; Florence and Pauline W., California; J. T. Newcombe, Michigan; Ida V. R., Minnesota; John K. [illegible], Georgia; S. Addison W., Maryland; C. S. C., Connecticut; J. H. Hassett, New Hampshire. From Massachusetts—A. A. Gillmore, Stanley King, C. H. A., A. F. C. From New York—Thomas H. Van T., F. W. F., Mabel L., William MacG., Walter L., H. and B. [illegible], W. T., E. S., F. [illegible]. Oscar F., New Jersey.

Many of these answers are given in very neat operations in figures.

Answers to Mathematical Puzzles in No. 10:

No. 5.—While selling their apples separately the boys received an average price of two and one-twelfth cents per apple. The boy who sold the whole lot together received only two cents per apple, losing one-twelfth of a cent on each. This loss on sixty apples amounted to five cents.

No. 6.—Mother's age, sixty-five; oldest daughter's, thirty; second daughter's, twenty; youngest daughter's, fifteen.

PUZZLE PICTURE.

THE envelope in the middle of this picture is supposed to contain a number of letters. These letters taken from the envelope, and correctly placed before the several objects shown in the picture, will transform them into wild animals.

THROWING LIGHT.

I AM intangible; can't be seen, yet can be felt; am apparent to the taste—certainly to the touch, for I am pocketed daily, and there is no one who would not gladly grasp me at any time when offered; at the same time, I am almost always disagreeable, and very rarely desired. Too much of me is dangerous, and yet how could any one have too many of me? though even a sip is more than any one craves. No one was ever heard to say he was tired of me, and yet how many tears I have made children shed!

I am the means of making people happy, yet I am dangerous under certain circumstances, though, to be sure, if I make people sick, I also make them well. Once I made a dreadful disturbance in New York, but yet I doubt if there is any city in this country where more of me, if as many, pass from people's hands.

I cost nothing, any body can have me that wants me, yet no one if poor can keep me, though I am easily bottled. You can't confine me, though you can shut me out, for there is nothing to take hold of, but a little package will hold many hundreds of me. I am a fluid, yet I am only air. I can be made by a stroke of the pen, but the greatest care must be exercised in making me properly; but when I am made artificially I am not half as refreshing as when Nature makes me. You can carry me in your pocket, but you can not take hold of me. You may swallow me, but you can not touch me. What am I? Let some one else throw a light.

Answer to Charade.—Answer to Charade on page 146 of Harper's Young People No. 13 is "Chart."

Answer to the Elephant Puzzle.—To solve the Elephant Puzzle presented in No. 13 of Harper's Young People make two cuts with the scissors as shown by the white lines in Fig. 1, and transpose the sections thus cut out, placing it in the position shown by the white lines of Fig. 2.

Fig. 1.

IT BEING DICK'S BIRTHDAY, HE IS ALLOWED TO STAY HOME FROM SCHOOL.

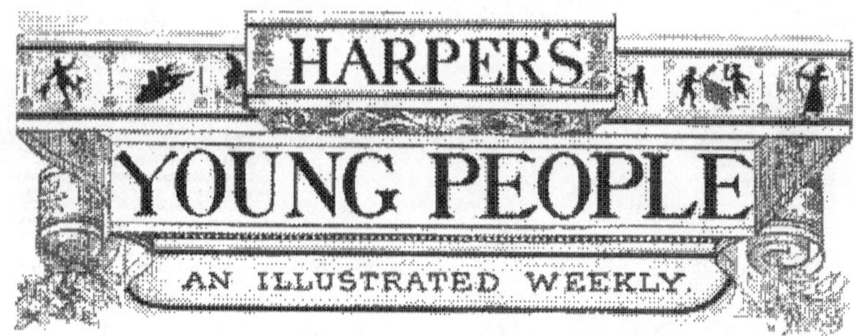

Vol. I.—No. 15. | Published by HARPER & BROTHERS, New York. | Price Four Cents.

Tuesday, February 10, 1880. | Copyright, 1880, by Harper & Brothers. | $1.50 per Year, in Advance.

OLD FATHER TIME.

"PROFESSOR," said May, turning on the sofa where she was lying, "Jack has brought me a calendar that runs for ever so many years. You know the doctor says I'll not be well for two whole years, or perhaps three. I have been wondering what month among them all I shall be able to run about in; and then I began to think who could have made the first calendar, and what led him to do it."

"That's very simple, May. Old Father Time just measured the days off with his hour-glass in the first place, and marked them down with the point of his scythe. The world has known all about it ever since."

"Please don't, Jack. Let the Professor tell."

"It would be hard, May, to tell who made the first calendar," answered the Professor. "All nations seem to have had their methods of counting the years and months long before they began writing histories, so that there is no record of the origin of the custom. The Book of Genesis mentions the lights in the heavens as being 'for signs and for seasons, and for days and years.' And Moses uses the word *year* so often that

A WINTER MORNING.

we see that it must have been common to count the years among those who lived before him."

"The number 1880 means that it is so many years since the birth of Christ, does it not?" asked Joe.

"Yes," said the Professor, "it has been the custom among Christian nations to reckon the years from that great event. They began to do this about the year of our Lord 532."

"Why did they wait so long?" asked Joe.

"You know," he said, "that at first the Christians were very few and weak; during the first three hundred years they had all they could do to escape with their lives from their enemies. But after that they became very numerous and powerful, and were able to establish their own customs. So in 532 a monk named Dionysius Exiguus proposed that they should abandon the old way of counting the years, and adopt the time of the birth of Christ as a starting-point. He thought this would be a very proper way of honoring the Saviour of the world. So he took great pains to find out the exact time when Christ was born, and satisfied himself that it was on the 25th day of December, in the 753d year from the foundation of the city of Rome. The Roman Empire at one time included most of the known world; and the Roman people, proud of their splendid city, counted the years from the supposed time of its being founded. At first the Christians did the same; but they were naturally pleased with the idea of Dionysius."

"Was he the first man who tried to find out what day Christmas came on?" asked Joe. "I should think everybody would have been anxious to know all about it."

"Doubtless there was much interest on the subject. But you know the early Christians had no newspapers, and very few books. Scarcely any of them could even read. Besides, it was very difficult in those times to travel or gain information; and it was dangerous to ask questions of the heathen, or for a man to let them suspect that he was a Christian. And then when we consider that the calendar was in confusion, because even the wisest men did not know the exact length of the year, and there were various ways of counting time, we need not be surprised that the Christians disagreed and made mistakes as to the time when the Saviour was born. In the fourth century, however, St. Cyril urged Pope Julius I. to give orders for an investigation. The result was that the theologians of the East and West agreed upon the 25th of December, though some of them were not convinced. The chief grounds of the decision were the tables in the public records of Rome.

"But let us return to Dionysius. His idea of making the year begin on the 25th of December was thought to be rather too inconvenient, and so the old commencement on the first day of January was retained, as the Romans had arranged it. But the plan of Dionysius was carried out with regard to the numbers by which the years were to be named and called. Thus the year which had been known as 754 became, under the new system, the year 1. And the succession of years from that year 1 is called the Christian era. To get the numbers of its years you have only to subtract 753 from the years in the Roman numbering."

"If we add 753," said Joe, "to 1880, will we get the number of years since old Rome was founded by Romulus and Remus?"

"Yes," said the Professor; "the rule works both ways. There is, however, some uncertainty as to whether the Romans themselves were correct in regard to the age of their city. Very early dates are hard to settle."

"Where did the months get their names?" asked May, "and how did months come to be thought of at all?"

"The months were suggested by the moon. In most languages the word *month* is very nearly like *moon*, as you see it is in ours. From new moon around to new moon again is about twenty-nine days, which is nearly the length of a month. The exact time between two new moons is a very puzzling problem. It always involves a troublesome fraction of a day, and is, in fact, never twice alike. So it was found convenient to divide the year into twelve parts, nearly equal, and to call each one a month."

"Why didn't they make them just equal?" asked Gus.

"To do so would have made it necessary to split up some of the days, which would have been awkward. If you divide the 365 days of the year by twelve, there will be five remaining."

"How was it found out that the year had 365 days in it?" asked Joe.

"It took the astronomers to do that," said the Professor; "and until nations became civilized enough to study astronomy accurately, they did not know the number of days in the year. This, however, did not prevent them from being able to count the years, because they could know that every time summer or winter came, a year had passed since the last summer or winter. But now the length of the year—that is, the time occupied by the earth in going completely round the sun—is known within a fraction of a second."

"Was it worth while to go into it so precisely?" asked May. "Would it not have been enough to know the number of the days?"

"By no means," said the Professor. "For then the calendar could not have been regulated so that the months and festivals would keep pace with the seasons. If 365 days had been constantly taken for a year, Christmas, instead of staying in the winter, would long since have moved back through autumn into summer, and so on. In about 1400 years it would travel through the entire circle of the seasons, as it would come some six hours earlier every year than it did the last. In like manner the Fourth of July would gradually fall back into spring, then into winter; and the fire-works would have to be set off in the midst of a snow-storm. The old Romans saw the difficulty; and, to prevent it, Julius Cæsar added an extra day to every fourth year, which you see is the same thing as adding one-fourth of a day to each year, only it is much more convenient. This was done because the earth requires nearly 365¼ days to move round the sun. The year that receives the extra day is called, as you know, leap-year. But even this did not keep the calendar exactly right. In the course of time other changes had to be made, the greatest of which was in 1582, when Pope Gregory XIII. decreed that ten entire days should be dropped out of the month of October. This was called the change from Old to New Style."

"It was rather stupid," said Gus, "to shorten the pleasantest month in the whole year. I would have clipped December or March."

"Please don't forget to tell us," said May, "how the months got their names."

"The first six of them were called after the heathen deities, Janus, Februus, Mars, Aphrodite, Maia, and Juno; July was named after Julius Cæsar, the inventor of leap-year; August after Augustus the Emperor. The names of the last four months simply mean seventh, eighth, ninth, and tenth."

"But," said Joe, "December is not the tenth month, nor is September the seventh."

"That is true," said the Professor; "but those names are supposed to have been given by Romulus, who arranged a year of only ten months, and made it begin with March. His year only had 304 days in it, and was soon found to be much too short. So the months of January and February were added, and instead of being placed at the end, they came in some way to stand at the beginning."

"Now please tell us about the names of the days of the week, and we will not ask any more questions."

"They were called after the sun, moon, and five planets known to the ancients, Mars, Mercury, Jupiter, Venus, and Saturn. You easily recognize sun, moon, and Saturn.

Tuesday, Thursday, and Friday are from names given by some of the Northern tribes of Europe to Mars, Jupiter, and Venus. Mercury's day seems scarcely at all connected with his name, but comes from Wodin, who was imagined to be chief among the gods of these barbarous tribes."

TOMMY'S VALENTINE.

BY MRS. M. D. BRINE.

He was only a little street sweeper, you know,
  Barefooted, and ragged as one could be;
But blue were his eyes as the far-off skies,
  And a brave-hearted laddie was Tommy Magee.
But it chanced on the morning of Valentine's Day
  Our little street sweeper felt lonely and sad;
"For there's no fun," thought he, "for a fellow like me,
  And a valentine's something that *I* never had."

But he flourished his broom, and the crossing made clean
  For the ladies and gentlemen passing his way;
And he gave them a smile, singing gayly the while,
  In honor, of course, of St. Valentine's Day.
Now it happened a party of bright little girls,
  All dainty and rosy, and brimming with glee,
Came over the crossing, a careless glance tossing
  To poor little barefooted Tommy Magee.

But all of a sudden then one of them turned,
  And running to Tommy, thrust into his hand,
With a smile and a blush, and the whispered word "Hush,"
  A beautiful valentine. You'll understand
How Tommy stood gazing, with wondering eyes,
  After the group of wee ladies so fine,
As with joy without measure he held his new treasure;
  And this is how Tommy got *his* valentine.

LOST IN THE SNOW.

AMONG the dangers of the winter in the Pass of St. Gothard is the fearful snow-storm called the "guxeten" by the Germans, and the tourmente or "tormenta" by the Swiss. The mountain snow differs in form, as well as in thickness and specific gravity, from the star-shaped snow-flakes on the lower heights and in the valleys. It is quite floury, dry, and sandy, and therefore very light. When viewed though a microscope it assumes at times the form of little prismatic needles, at other times that of innumerable small six-sided pyramids, from which, as from the morning star, little points jut out on all sides, and which, driven by the wind, cut through the air with great speed. With this fine ice-dust of the mountain snow, the wind drives its wild game through the clefts of the high Alps and over the passes, particularly that of St. Gothard. Suddenly it tears up a few hundred thousand cubic feet of this snow, and whirls it up high into the air, leaving it to the mercy of the upper current, to fall to the ground again in the form of the thickest snow-storm, or to be dispersed at will like glittering ice-crystals. At times the wind sweeps up large tracts of the dry ice-dust, and pours them down upon a deep-lying valley amid the mountains, or on to the summit of the passes, obliterating in a few seconds the laboriously excavated mountain road, at which a whole company of rutters have toiled for days. All these appearances resemble the avalanches of other Alps, but can not be regarded in the same light as the true snow-storm, the tormenta or guxeten. This is incomparably more severe, and hundreds on hundreds of lives have fallen sacrifices to its fury. These have mostly been travelling strangers, who either did not distinguish the signs of the coming storm, or, in proud reliance on their own power, refused to listen to well-meant warnings, and continued their route. Almost every year adds a large number of victims to the list of those who have fallen a prey to the snow-storm.

History and the oral tradition of the mountains record many incidents of accidents which have been occasioned by the fall of avalanches. During the Bellinzona war, in 1478, as the confederates, with a force of 10,000 men, were crossing the St. Gothard, the men of Zürich were preceding the army as van-guard. They had just refreshed themselves with some wine, and were marching up the wild gorge, shouting and singing, in spite of the warnings of their guides. Then, in the heights above, an avalanche was suddenly loosened, which rushed down upon the road, and in its impetuous torrent buried sixty warriors far below in the Reuss, in full sight of those following.

On the 12th of March, 1848, in the so-called Plangger, above the tent of shelter at the Mättelli, thirteen men who were conveying the post were thrown by a violent avalanche into the bed of the Reuss, with their horses and sledges. Three men, fathers of families, and nine horses were killed; the others were saved by hastily summoned help. But one of their deliverers, Joseph Müller, of Hospenthal, met a hero's death while engaged in the rescue. He had hastened to help his neighbors, but in the district called the "Harness" he and two others were overwhelmed by a second violent avalanche, and lost their lives. In the same year the post going up the mountain from Airolo was overtaken by an avalanche near the house of shelter at Ponte Tremola. A traveller from Bergamo was killed; the rest escaped.

History tells of a most striking rescue from an avalanche on the St. Gothard. In the year 1628, Landamman Kaspar, of Brandenburg, the newly chosen Governor of Bellenz, was riding over the St. Gothard from Zug, accompanied by his servant and a faithful dog. At the top of the pass the party was overtaken by an avalanche which descended from the Lucendro. The dog alone shook himself free. His first care was to extricate his master. But when he saw that he could not succeed in doing this, he hastened back to the hospice, and there, by pitiful howling and whining, announced that an accident had happened. The landlord and his servants set out immediately with shovels and pickaxes, and followed the dog, which ran quickly before them. They soon reached the place where the avalanche had fallen. Here the faithful dog stopped suddenly, plunged his face into the snow, and began to scratch it up, barking and whining. The men set to work at once, and after a long and difficult labor succeeded in rescuing the Landamman, and soon afterward his servant. They were both alive, after spending thirty-six fearful hours beneath the snow, oppressed by the most painful thoughts. They had heard the howling and barking of the dog quite plainly; and had noticed his sudden departure, and the arrival of their deliverers; they had heard them talking and working, without being able to move or utter a sound. The Landamman's will ordained that an image of the faithful dog should be sculptured at his feet on his tomb. This monument was seen till lately in St. Oswald's Church, at Zug.

THE STORY OF GRANDMA, LORENZO, AND THE MONKEY

BY MRS. A. M. DIAZ.

THE children told the Family Story-Teller they did not believe he could make a story about a grandma going to mill. "Especially," said the children's mother, "a grandma troubled with rheumatism."

Family Story-Teller smiled, as much as to say, "You shall see," took a few minutes to think, and began:

In Grandma Stimpett's trunk was a very small, leathery, beady bag, and in this bag was a written recipe for the Sudden Remedy—a sure cure for rheumatism, sprains, bruises, and all lamenesses. The bag and the recipe were given her by an Indian woman. To make the Sudden Remedy, grandma got roots, herbs, barks, twigs, leaves, mints, moss, and tree gum. These were

"THIS BOTTLE CONTAINS THE SUDDEN REMEDY."

scraped, grated, or pounded; sifted, weighed, measured, stewed, and stirred; and the juice simmered down with the oil of juniper, and bumble-bees' wax, and various smarty, peppery, slippery things whose names must be kept private for a particular reason. The Sudden Remedy cured her instantly; and as meal was wanted, and no other person could be spared from the place, she offered to go to mill.

She went in the vehicle—an old chaise which had lost its top—taking with her her bottle of the Sudden Remedy, in case, as Mr. Stimpcett said, the rheumatism should return before she did.

"Shall you be back by sunset?" asked Mr. Stimpcett, as he fastened the bag underneath the vehicle.

"Oh yes," said she; "I shall eat dinner at Debby's, and come away right after dinner. You will see me back long before sunset." Her daughter Debby lived at Mill Village.

Mr. Stimpcett shook his head. "I don't know about that," said he.

"If I am not back before sunset," said she, "I will give you—give you five hundred dollars."

The people laughed at this; for all the money grandma had was only about twenty dollars, put away in case of need.

Now when grandma had driven perhaps two miles on her way to mill, she stopped at a farm-house to water her horse; and here something curious happened. A woman came to the door of the house, and the next moment a large boy, named Lorenzo, hopped out on one foot and two canes, and began stumping about the yard at a furious rate, cackling, crowing, and barking.

"That's the way he does when he can't sit still any longer," said the woman. "He has to sit still a great deal, on account of a lame knee, which is a pity," said she, "for a spry fellow like him; a good, true-spoken fellow he is, too." The woman then told how he lamed his knee.

Lorenzo said he wanted very much the use of his legs that day, because there was to be a circus just beyond Mill Village. He said he wanted to go to the circus so much he did not know what to do. He said he began when he was four years old to go to circuses, and he had been to every circus that had come around since. "Now this circus is only a little more than two miles off," said he, "and here I am cooped up like a hoppled horse."

Grandma smiled, and took out the bottle. "This bottle," said she, "contains the Sudden Remedy—a quick cure for rheumatism, sprains, bruises, and all lameness. Rub on with a flannel, and rub in briskly."

Lorenzo rubbed on with a flannel, and rubbed in briskly, and then seated himself upon a stone to hear the stories grandma and the woman were telling of people who had been upset, or thrown from horses, or had fallen over stone walls, into wells, or down from trees, rocks, house-tops, or chamber windows. Lorenzo told some stories, and at last, in acting out one, he thrust forward his lame leg, without thinking of it, and found it was no longer lame. He tried it again; he sprang up; he stepped; he walked; he leaped; he skipped; he ran; he hurrahed; he flung his canes away.

Grandma then invited Lorenzo to ride with her to Mill

THE LAME MONKEY.

Village, near which the circus was to be; and he quickly took a seat in the vehicle, and having no time to put on his best clothes, he put on only his best hat, tipping it one side in order to give himself a little of a dressed-up look.

When grandma and Lorenzo reached Mill Village, Lorenzo got out at a pea-nut stand, and grandma drove on to her daughter Debby's. She had just stepped from the vehicle when Lorenzo came running to beg that she would bring her Sudden Remedy to the miller's house, for the miller had been taken that morning with the darting rheumatism, and the mill was not running, and people were waiting with their corn.

Lorenzo drove grandma to the miller's house, and in two hours' time the miller was in the mill, the wheel turning, and the corn grinding—grandma's corn among the rest.

Something which was very important to the circus will now be told. The Chief Jumper—the one who was to do the six wonderful things—lamed his foot the night before, and could not jump. Now when the man who owned the circus was looking at the Chief Jumper's foot, a circus errand-boy in uniform passed by. This errand-boy had been to the mill to get corn for the circus horses, and he told the man who owned the circus that a woman had just cured the miller of the darting rheumatism, and told the name of the medicine.

The circus owner took one of the circus riding wagons and the errand-boy in uniform and set off immediately to find the woman who had the Sudden Remedy, and found grandma at her daughter Debby's, just stepping into the vehicle to go home. Lorenzo was there, fastening the bag of meal securely under the vehicle. The circus owner offered grandma five dollars if she would go and cure his Chief Jumper, and as there was time to do that and reach home before sunset, she went, Lorenzo driving her in the vehicle. The circus owner and the errand-boy in uniform kept just in front of them, and some children who knew no better said that that kind-looking old lady and the great boy belonged to the circus, and had their circus clothes in the bag underneath.

Grandma was taken into a tent which led out of the big tent, where she saw the Chief Jumper in full jumping costume, and the Dwarf, and the Fat Man, and the Clown, and the Flying Cherub; and the Remedy worked so well that the Chief Jumper thought he might jump higher than ever before.

The Clown led grandma to the cage where monkeys were kept, and asked her if she would be willing to cure a poor suffering monkey whose leg had been hurt by a stone thrown by a cruel boy. Grandma said, certainly, for that she pitied even an animal that had to suffer pain. The Clown then took the monkey, and held its paw while grandma patted its head and stroked its back, and poured on the Remedy, the Flying Cherub standing near by to see what was to be done.

The circus owner invited grandma to stay to the circus; but as she had not time, he paid her eight dollars, and led her to the vehicle.

Now we are coming to the most wonderful part of my story. People going home from mill had told the tale of the miller's cure, and on her way back grandma was stopped by various people, who begged her to come into their houses and cure rheumatism, sprains, bruises, and other lamenesses. This took a great deal of time; but the kind-hearted old lady was so anxious to ease pain that she forgot all about her promise to Mr. Stimpcett, and when she reached home it was ten minutes past sunset.

Three buggies stood near Mr. Stimpcett's house. Grandma thought they were doctors' buggies. "Oh dear!" she said to herself, "something dreadful must be the matter!" She counted the children playing at the door-step. They were all there—Moses, Obadiah, Deborah, and little Cordelia.

At this moment Mr. Stimpcett came forward and said to grandma that three gentlemen had come, one after another, and had each asked to have a private talk with her. There was a large fleshy man in the front room, a chubby little man in the kitchen, and a sleek, long-faced man in the spare chamber.

Grandma talked with these, one at a time. They were all medicine sellers. Each one wished to buy the recipe for making the Sudden Remedy, and would pay a good price for it. For they knew that thousands and thousands of barrels of this Remedy could be sold all over the United States, Mexico, Canada, and Central America, and enormous sums of money made by the sale.

The summer boarder, Mr. St. Clair, said that the man who would pay the most money for it ought to have the recipe. Grandma brought from her trunk the small, leathery, beady bag which contained the recipe, and Mr. St. Clair stood in the vehicle, held up the bag, and said: "Bid! gentlemen, bid! How much do I have for it?"

The bidding was interrupted by a Jumper. It was a circus Jumper, but not the Chief Jumper. While the people were all looking at Mr. St. Clair, a monkey sprang from the meal bag underneath the vehicle and jumped upon grandma's shoulder, nearly knocking her over. It was the same one she had cured. On account of his lameness, he had been loosely tied, and from a feeling of thankfulness, no doubt, for being cured, he had run away and followed grandma.

THE TWO-CENT SIDE-SHOW.

The Stimpcett children—Moses, Obadiah, Deborah, and little Cordelia—shouted and capered so that the selling of the recipe could hardly go on; but at last it was sold, leathery, beady bag and all, to the sleek, long-faced man, for nine hundred dollars, of which grandma gave five hundred to Mr. Stimpcett, according to the promise she made before going to mill.

The circus people were written to, but as they did not

send for Jacko, he was kept for the children to play with. Mrs. Stimpcett dressed him in a pretty suit of clothes, with a cap and feather on his head. He showed much affection for grandma, followed her about daytimes both in-doors and out, and would sleep nowhere at night but at the foot of her bed, where a bandbox was at last placed for him. The children loved him dearly; but poor Jacko did so much mischief in trying to knit, and to cook, and to weed the garden, that it was finally declared that something must be done about that monkey; and grandma gave him to Lorenzo, with money enough to buy a grand harmonica.

Lorenzo came for the monkey toward the close of a calm summer's day, and fed him with frosted cake, which caused him to feel pleased with Lorenzo. There was a string fastened to his collar; Lorenzo took the string in one hand, and some frosted cake in the other, and led Jacko away. The children—Moses, and Obadiah, and Deborah, and little Cordelia—following on for quite a distance, all weeping.

Lorenzo went about for some time with a circus company. Evenings he staid inside the big tent to see the doings, and daytimes he had a two-cent side-show in a small tent of his own, where the monkey played wonderful tricks, and marched to the music of the grand harmonica.

At last he came to grandma, and told her that as for the Clown, he was a kind-hearted, sensible man, but that the others were commonly either drunk, or cross, or both, and that he had to travel nights, wet or dry, and that he was sick of that kind of life. He sold the monkey to a hand-organ man, and went back to live in his old home; and the last that was known of Jacko he was seen in the streets of a town carrying round the hand-organ man's hat for pennies.

It was grandma and Mr. Stimpcett who saw him, as they were riding past in the vehicle; and he saw them, and gave a bound, and broke his string, and leaped into the vehicle, and clasped his paws round grandma's neck; and the hand-organ man was obliged to place six maple-sugar cakes in a row upon the sidewalk before Jacko would return to him.

The sleek, long-faced man made his fortune by selling the Sudden Remedy, but few of those who bought it and took it knew what old lady it was who sold him the recipe for it.

The Family Story-Teller's next was a story of mistakes, and odd mistakes they were.

THE CHILDREN'S WEDDING.

IT very often happens that children of royal families are by their parents or by wise statesmen engaged to marry each other almost as soon as they are born, but the actual weddings do not generally take place until the children are grown up. One of these weddings did, however, actually take place, a great many years ago, between two children, and the story of it is as follows:

January 15, 1478, was the day appointed, when Richard, Duke of York, second son of Edward IV., aged four years, and created already Duke of Norfolk, Earl Warren and Surrey, and Earl Marshal of England, in right of his intended wife, was to lead to the altar the little girl whose tiny hand would bestow upon him the immense estates and riches of the Norfolk inheritance.

The little Lady Anne, who was, as an old book informs us, the richest and most noble match of that time, appears to have been two years older than her intended husband, and must have reached the advanced age of six years! She does not appear to have objected to the match, but to have been quite ready to act her part in the pageant, and no doubt the little Duke was eager to receive the notice and applause of the courtly throng, whilst both children looked with astonishment at the sumptuous preparations and the costly splendor of their own and the spectators' dresses.

The ceremony began by the high and mighty Princess, as the little bride was called in the formal language of the day, being brought in great state and in solemn procession to the King's great chamber at Westminster Palace. This took place the day before the wedding, on the 14th of January. The bride, splendidly dressed, most probably in the bridal robes of white cloth of gold, a mantle of the same bordered with ermine, and with her hair streaming down her back, and confined to her head by the coronet of a duchess, was led by the Earl of Rivers, the bridegroom's uncle. She was followed, of course, by her mother, and by the noblest of the court ladies of rank, and the gentlewomen of her household, whilst behind came dukes, earls, and barons, all in attendance on the little bride.

As soon as she had arrived in the lofty hall of Westminster Palace she was led to the dais, or place of estate, as it was called, where, under a canopy, and seated on a chair of estate, or kind of throne, she kept her estate, *i. e.*, sat in royal pomp with the King, Queen, and their children seated on either hand, whilst her procession of peers and peeresses stood around and waited upon her. Refreshments were then brought "according to the form and estate of the realm," which must have been a very wearisome and formal ceremony for a little girl of six years old, and which ended that day's ceremony.

On the 15th the Princess came out of the Queen's rooms, where she had slept, and led on one hand by the Earl of Lincoln, nephew to the King, and on the other by the Earl of Rivers, she passed through the King's great chamber in the palace into the White Hall, and from there to St. Stephen's Chapel. She was followed by a long suite of ladies and gentlewomen. Meanwhile the little bridegroom, the Queen, and a noble procession of lords and gentlemen, had already entered the chapel and taken up their places on the seats appointed for them, ready to receive and welcome the bride. There were also present the King and the Prince of Wales, the King's mother, and the three Princesses who acted as bridesmaids, Elizabeth, Mary, and Cecily.

As soon as the bride drew near to the door, between her two noble supporters, the Bishop of Norwich came forward and received her at the chapel entrance, intending to lead her and the bridegroom to their proper places and begin the service. Then the bishop asked who would give the Princess away? In answer the King stood up and took her hand, and gave it to the bishop, who placed it in the bridegroom's, and went on to the rest of the service, concluding with high mass. When this part was concluded, the Duke of Gloucester brought into the chapel basins of gold filled with gold and silver pieces, which he threw amongst the crowds of people who had pressed in to see the wedding, and who were highly delighted with this part of it.

Then followed the usual wine and spices, which were actually served out to the royal party in the church itself. The bridal party then left the chapel, the little bride and bridegroom, escorted by the Duke of Gloucester and the Duke of Buckingham (Richard's two uncles) on either side. They returned to St. Edward's Chamber in the palace, where a splendid banquet was prepared, and their numbers were increased by the bride's mother, who staid at home, strange to say, instead of accompanying her daughter and the Duchess of Buckingham. Another guest who now presided at a table on one side of the room with many ladies, whilst the Earl of Dorset, the Queen's son by her first husband, sat opposite at another side table, was the Earl of Richmond, afterward Henry VII., who, wonderful to say, was present, and whom Edward IV. must have invited to get him into his power. However, as soon as the marriage feasts were over, he managed to escape abroad without being stopped by the King.

The banquet completed the festivities of the wedding day, and, tired and wearied, the baby couple must have been glad to close their eyes in sleep.

No marriage, however, was complete without a tournament, and so on the 18th, when the children had recovered the fatigue of their wedding, a grand tournament took place, when the bride became the "Princess of the Feast," took up her place at the head of the first banqueting table, and there, supported by the Dukes of Gloucester and Buckingham, gave her largess to the heralds, who proclaimed her name and title in due form.

All the royal family were present, and the foreign ambassadors, and one of the most distinguished spectators was "my lord of Richmond." The coursers were running at each other with either spear or sword, and at the close of the jousts, the Princess of the Feast, with all her ladies and gentlewomen, withdrew to the King's great chamber at Westminster to decide upon the prizes. First, however, the high and mighty Princess called in her minstrels, and all the ladies and gentlewomen, lords and knights, fell to dancing right merrily. Then came the king-at-arms to announce to the Princess the names of those whose valor deserved the rewards she was to give away, as the principal lady on whom the duty devolved. But the little lady was both very young and bashful, and so to help her the lovely Princess Elizabeth, then a girl of fourteen, was appointed, and a council of ladies was held to consider the share each should take.

The prizes were golden letters, A, E, and M, the initials of Anne, Elizabeth, and Mowbray, set in gems, and were delivered to Elizabeth by the king-at-arms. The A was to be awarded to the best jouster, the E to the best runner in harness, and the M for the best swordsman. The first prize was then presented by the little bride, aided by Elizabeth, to Thomas Fynes, on which the chief herald cried out, "Oh yes! oh yes! oh yes! Sir William Truswell jousted well; William Say jousted well; Thomas Fynes jousted best; for the which the Princess of the Feast awarded the prize of the jousts royal, that is to say, the A of gold, to him," quoth Clarencieux.

Then the other prizes were given with the same ceremonies, the king-at-arms, Clarencieux, proclaiming in a loud voice before each, "Right high and excellent Princess, here is the prize which you shall award unto the best jouster," which Elizabeth received and then handed to her little sister-in-law, until all had been given, and the tournament was over. And now the infant marriage, with its pretty pageantry and joyous festivities, was concluded, and the children returned to the daily routine of play and lessons, whilst the wonderful wedding must have gradually faded from their memories.

A HUNTING ADVENTURE.

WHILE travelling in India, an English officer once spent a night in a small village, the inhabitants of which were much alarmed by a large panther which lurked in the jungle just beyond their houses. They begged the officer to kill it before he proceeded on his journey. He succeeded in finding and wounding it the next morning, but before killing it, had a terrible struggle, which he describes as follows:

"Having warned the village shikaree to keep close behind me with the heavy spear he had in his hand, I began to follow the wounded panther; but had scarcely gone twenty-five yards, when one of the beaters, who was on high ground, beckoned to me, and pointed a little below him, and in front of me. There was the large panther sitting out unconcealed between two bushes a dozen yards before me. I could not, however, see his head; and whilst I was thus delayed, he came out with a roar, straight at me. I fired at his chest with a ball, and as he sprang upon me, the shot barrel was aimed at his head. In the next moment he seized my left arm, and the gun. Thus, not being able to use the gun as a club, I forced it into his mouth. He bit the stock through in one place, and whilst his upper fangs lacerated my arm and hand, the lower fangs went into the gun. His hind claws pierced my left thigh. He tried very hard to throw me over. In the mean while the shikaree had retreated some paces to the left. He now, instead of spearing the panther, shouted out, and struck him, using the spear as a club. In a moment the animal was upon him, stripping him of my shikar-bag, his turban, my revolving rifle, and the spear. The man passed by me, holding his wounded arm. The panther quietly crouched five paces in front of me, with all my despoiled property, stripped from the shikaree, around and under him. I retreated step by step, my face toward the foe, till I got to my horse, and to the beaters, who were all collected together some forty yards from the fight.

"I immediately loaded the gun with a charge of shot and a bullet, and taking my revolver pistol out of the holster, and sticking it into my belt, determined to carry on the affair to its issue, knowing how rarely men recover from such wounds as mine. I was bleeding profusely from large tooth wounds in the arm; the tendons of my left hand were torn open, and I had five claw wounds in the thigh. The poor shikaree's arm was somewhat clawed up, and if the panther was not killed, the superstition of the natives would go far to kill this man.

"I persuaded my horse-keeper to come with me, and taking the hog-spear he had in his hand, we went to the spot where lay the weapons stripped from the shikaree. A few yards beyond them crouched the huge panther again. I could not see his head very distinctly, but fired deliberately behind his shoulder. In one moment he was again upon me. I gave him the charge of shot, as I supposed, in his face, but had no time to take aim. In the next instant the panther got hold of my left foot in his teeth, and threw me on my back. I struck at him with the empty gun, and he seized the barrels in his mouth. This was his last effort. I sprang up, and seizing the spear from the horse-keeper, drove it through his side, and thus killed him."

EAGLES AND THEIR WAYS.

THE great golden eagle is one of the most distinguished members of its mighty family. It is found in many parts of the world, a kingly inhabitant of mountainous regions, where it builds its nest on rocky crags accessible only to the most daring hunter.

This noble bird is of a rich blackish-brown tint on the greater part of its body, its head and neck inclining to a reddish color. Its tail is deep gray crossed with dark brown bars. Some large specimens which have been captured have measured nearly four feet in length, while the magnificent wings expanded from eight to nine feet.

The golden eagle is no longer found in England, but is still plentiful in the Scottish Highlands, where it makes its nest on some lofty ledge of rock among the mountain solitudes. Swiss naturalists state that it sometimes nests in the lofty crotch of some gigantic oak growing on the lower mountain slopes, but Audubon and other eminent ornithologists declare that an eagle's nest built in a tree has never come under their observation.

The nest of this inhabitant of the mountains is not neatly made, like those of smaller birds, but is a huge mass of twigs, dried grasses, brambles, and hair heaped together to form a bed for the little ones. Here the mother bird lays three or four large white eggs speckled with brown. The young birds are almost coal-black, and only assume the golden and brownish tinge as they become full grown, which is not until about the fourth year. Eaglets two or three years old are described in books of natural history as ring-tailed eagles, and are sometimes taken for a distinct species of the royal bird, while in reality they are the children of the golden eagle tribe.

Eagles rarely change their habitation, and, unless disturbed, a pair will inhabit the same nest for years. It is very faithful to its mate, and one pair have been observed living happily together through a long life. Should one die, the bird left alone will fly away in search of another mate, and soon return with it to its former home. Eagles live to a great age; even in captivity in royal gardens specimens have been known to live more than a hundred years.

Eagles are very abundant in Switzerland. Although not so powerful as the great vulture, which also inhabits the lofty mountains, they are bolder and more enduring. For hours the golden eagle will soar in the air high above the mountain-tops, and move in wide-sweeping circles with a scarcely perceptible motion of its mighty wings. When on the hunt for prey, it is very cunning and sharp-sighted. Its shrill scream rings through the air, filling all the smaller birds with terror. When it approaches its victim its scream changes to a quick kik-kak-kak, resembling the barking of a dog, and gradually sinking until sufficiently near, it darts in a straight line with the rapidity of lightning upon its prey. None of the smaller birds and beasts are safe from its clutches. Fawns, rabbits, and hares, young sheep and goats, wild birds of all kinds, fall helpless victims, for neither the swiftest running nor the most rapid flight can avail against this king of the air.

The strength of the eagle is such that it will bear heavy burdens in its talons for miles until it reaches its nest, where the hungry little ones are eagerly waiting the parent's return. Here, standing on the ledge of rock, the eagle tears the food into morsels, which the eaglets eagerly devour. It is a curious fact that near an eagle's nest there is usually a storehouse or larder—some convenient ledge of rock—where the parent birds lay up hoards of provisions. Hunters have found remains of lambs, young pigs, rabbits, partridges, and other game heaped up ready for the morning meal.

Over its hunting ground the eagle is king. It fears neither bird nor beast, its only enemy being man. In Switzerland, during the winter season, when the mountains are snow-bound, the eagle will descend to the plain in search of food. When driven by hunger, it will seize on carrion, and even fight desperately with its own kind for the possession of the desired food. Swiss hunters tell many stories of furious battles between eagles over the dead body of some poor chamois or other mountain game.

Eagles are very affectionate and faithful to their little ones as long as they need care; but once the young eaglets are able to take care of themselves, the parent birds drive them from the nest, and even from the hunting ground. The young birds are often taken from the nest by hunters, who with skill and daring scale the rocky heights during the absence of the parents, which return to find a desolate and empty nest. But it goes hard with the hunter if the keen eyes of the old birds discover him before he has made his safe descent with his booty. Darting at him with terrible fury, they try their utmost to throw him from the cliff; and unless he be well armed, and use his weapons with skill and rapidity, his position is one of the utmost peril.

EAGLES FIGHTING OVER A CHAMOIS.

The young birds are easily tamed; and the experiment has already been tried with some success of using them as the falcon, to assist in hunting game.

The golden eagle is an inhabitant of the Rocky Mountains, but is very seldom seen farther eastward. Audubon reports having noticed single pairs in the Alleghanies, in Maine, and even in the valley of the Hudson; but such examples are very rare, for this royal bird is truly a creature of the mountains. It fears neither cold nor tempestuous winds nor icy solitudes.

The eagle's plume is an old and famous decoration of warriors and chieftains, and is constantly alluded to, especially in Scottish legend and song. The Northwestern Indians ornament their head-dresses and their weapons with the tail feathers of the eagle, and institute hunts for the bird with the sole purpose of obtaining them. Indians prize these feathers so highly that they will barter a valuable horse for the tail of a single bird.

Royal and noble in its bearing, the eagle has naturally been chosen as the symbol of majesty and power. It served as one of the imperial emblems of ancient Rome, and is employed at the present time for the regal insignia of different countries. The bald eagle, the national bird of the United States, belongs to the same great family as its golden cousin, and is a sharer of its lordly characteristics.

THE HIDDEN BEAUTIES OF THE SNOW.

IN the falling of the snow we have *snow showers* and *snow storms*. In the *snow shower* the air is filled with light, fleecy flakes, which descend gently and noiselessly through it, and either melt away and disappear as fast as they alight, or else, when the temperature is below the point of freezing, slowly accumulate upon every surface where they can gain a lodgment, until the fields are everywhere covered with a downy fleece of spotless purity, and every salient point—the tops of the fences and posts, the branches of the trees, and the interminable lines of telegraph wire—are adorned with a white and dazzling trimming. In such a fall of snow as this the delicate process of crystallization is not disturbed by any agitations in the air. The feathery needles from each little nucleus extend themselves in every direction as far as they will, and combining by gentle contacts with others floating near them, form large and fleecy flakes, involving the nicest complications of structure, and filling the air with a kind of beauty in which the expression of softness and gracefulness is combined with that of mathematical symmetry and precision.

In a snow *storm* the force of the wind and the intensity of the cold usually change all this. The progress of the crystallization, which to be perfect must take place slowly, and under the condition of perfect repose, is at once hastened by the low temperature, and disturbed by the commotion in the air. Across the broad expanse of open plains, along mountain sides, through groves of trees, and over the smooth surface of frozen lakes and rivers, millions of misshapen and broken crystals are driven by the wind, piled up in heaps, or accumulated in confused masses under the lee of every obstruction, having been subjected on the way to such violence of agitation and collision that the characteristic beauty and symmetry of the material is entirely destroyed.

If we examine attentively the falling flakes, whether of snow *showers* or of snow *storms* at different times, under the varying circumstances in which snow forms and descends, we shall be surprised at the number and variety of the forms which they assume.

They may be received and examined upon any black surface—the crown of a hat, or a piece of black cloth, for example—previously cooled below the freezing-point. At any one time the crystallizations are usually alike, but different snow-falls seem to have each its own special conformation. Sometimes, however, a change takes place from one style of flake to another in the course of the same storm or shower, and during the period of transition both varieties fall together from the air. Persons interested in such observations may easily make drawings with a pen of the different forms that present themselves from time to time, and thus in the course of a winter make a very curious and interesting collection.

The number and variety of the forms which the snowy crystallizations assume seem greatest in the polar regions, and the celebrated scientific navigator Scoresby studied them there with great attention during his various arctic voyages. He made drawings of ninety-six different forms, and the number has been increased since, by more recent observers, to several hundred.

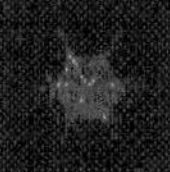

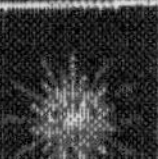

It will be observed that all the forms have a hexagonal character. They consist of a star of six rays, or a plate of six angles. There is a reason for this, or rather there is a well-known property of ice in respect to the law of its crystallization which throws some light upon the subject. The law is this: that whereas every crystallizable substance has its own primitive crystalline form, that of ice is a rhomboid with angles of 60° and 120°, and consequently all the secondary forms which this substance assumes are controlled by these angles, and derive from them their hexagonal character.

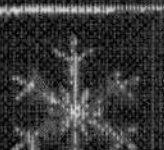

The most striking of the methods adopted for the inspection of ice crystals is one discovered by Professor Tyndall, and consists of melting the ice from *within*. This is done by means of a lens, by which the sun's rays are brought to a focus within the mass of ice, so as to liquefy a portion of it in the interior without disturbing that at the surface.

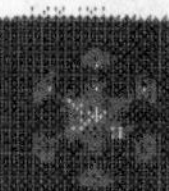

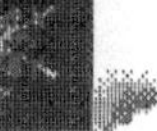

NETTIE'S VALENTINE.

BY AGNES CARR.

"THEY are all so lovely, I hardly know which to choose," said Nettie Almer to herself, as she paused at the entrance of a large stationer's shop to gaze in at the window, where was spread a tempting display of valentines of all kinds and sizes, from the rich, expensive ones in handsome embossed boxes to the cheap penny pictures strung on a line across the entire casement.

"I want them to be the prettiest ones there," continued Nettie to herself, and she gave her little pocket-book a squeeze inside her muff as she thought of the bright two dollar and a half gold piece which Uncle John had given her that morning to spend all for valentines; for Nettie was invited that evening to a large party, given by one of her school-mates, and after supper a post-office was to be opened, through which all her class were to send valentines to each other. Great fun was anticipated, while at the same time there was considerable rivalry as to who should send the handsomest missives, and at school nothing else had been talked of amongst the scholars for a week.

"Please, miss, buy just a little bunch." The words sounded close to Nettie's ear, and she turned to encounter a pair of pleading blue eyes gazing into hers, while the plaintive voice repeated, "Please buy a little bunch of flowers; I haven't sold one to-day, and Minna wants an orange so much."

It was a pitiful little figure that stood there, with an old shawl over her head, and her feet hardly protected from the icy pavement by a pair of miserable ragged shoes, while the tiny hands, purple with cold, held a small pine board on which were fastened small bouquets of rose-buds, violets, and other flowers, which she tried to sell to the passers-by, most of whom, however, pushed her rudely aside or passed indifferently by.

"Who is Minna?" asked Nettie, gently, after a moment's survey of the little girl.

"She is mine sister, and she is so bad, so very bad, with the fever. She cried all last night with thirst, and begged me to bring her an orange to cool her tongue. Please, miss, buy some of my flowers."

Nettie's tender heart was touched, and her eyes filled with tears in sympathy with the poor child, who was now crying bitterly. "Has she been sick very long?" she asked.

"Oh yes; and the Herr Doctor says she will die if she does not have wine to strengthen her. But where could we get wine? The mother can hardly pay the rent, and I sell flowers to buy bread; but I can only make two or three cents on a bunch, and some bad days they fade before I can get rid of them; so I'm afraid Minna must die. But please give me enough to get her an orange."

"An orange! of course I will," exclaimed Nettie; "and more than one. Come with me;" and she caught the child eagerly by the hand, and drew her toward the street. At this moment, however, her eye fell on the valentines in the window, and she stopped, hesitating. Should she give up the pretty gifts for her little friends, and lose half of the evening's anticipated enjoyment, or should she let this poor girl—of whose existence she was ignorant five minutes before—go home empty-handed to her sick sister? There was an instant of sharp conflict as she thought of how mean she should appear in her school-mates' eyes, and then, with a resolute air, Nettie turned her back on the fascinating window, and conducted the little flower girl to a fruit store near at hand.

A basket was supplied by the kind-hearted proprietor of the store, to whom Nettie explained what she wanted, and this she filled with golden Havana oranges and rich clusters of white grapes—a delicious basketful for a feverish invalid. This, Nettie found, took nearly half the money, and the remainder she gave to the grocer, begging him to get her a bottle of the best sherry wine, which was quickly done, and added to the basket.

"Now," she said, turning to her poor companion, who had stood meanwhile, hardly believing the evidence of her eyes, "take me home with you, and we will carry these to Minna right away."

"Oh, miss, thou art too heavenly kind! It will save Minna; she need not die now." And with smiles chasing away the tears, the happy child took hold of one side of the basket, while Nettie carried the other, and together they wended their way to a poor tenement-house in a dark narrow street, and climbed the rickety stairs to a back room on the fourth floor.

As they pushed open the door, a low moan was heard from within, and a weak voice asked, "Gretel, is it thou? Hast thou brought the orange?"

Gretel sprang to the bedside, and in an eager voice exclaimed: "Oh, Minna, yes, yes, I have the oranges, and so much more! See this good little lady, and what she has brought thee. Look! oranges—grapes—wine! Oh, Minna, sweetheart, thou wilt soon be well now!"

The pale child, reclining among the pillows, her golden hair brushed back from a brow on which the blue veins showed painfully distinct, stretched forth a thin little hand for the grapes, and said to Nettie, "Oh, I have dreamed of fruit like this; thou art an angel to bring it to me."

Gently Nettie brushed back the fair hair of the little patient, and pressed the cool grapes to her parched lips, while Gretel poured some of the wine into a cracked tumbler, and administered it to the sick girl, who, being too weak to talk much, soon sank into a quiet, refreshing slumber, with one of Nettie's hands clasped tightly in both her own; and as Nettie sat by the humble pallet she felt fully repaid for the loss of her valentines.

And Minna still slept when the German mother entered, who, after listening to Gretel's whispered story, exclaimed, as Nettie rose to depart, and stole softly from the room: "May Gott in Himmel bless thee, young lady, for what thou hast done this day! It is weeks since my Minna has slept like that." And throwing her apron over her head, the poor woman burst into happy tears.

It was with a light heart that Nettie tripped homeward, and she never even glanced at the great window where the brilliant hearts and Cupids gleamed as gayly as ever in the bright sunlight.

"Well, Pussie, how many valentines have you bought?" asked Uncle John, meeting Nettie in the hall as she entered the house.

"Only one; but it was a very nice one, and you mustn't ask any questions," answered Nettie, with a blush, as she ran up stairs to avoid further questioning.

It was rather trying, though, when evening came, and Nettie, dressed in her white dress and blue ribbons, stood among the other girls in the dressing-room, and they all crowded round inquiring how many valentines she had for the post-office, to be obliged to confess that she had none, and to bear the whispered comments of, "How mean!" "I didn't think that of Nettie Almer."

She kept her spirits up, however, by thinking of Minna, and the joy of her mother and sister, and soon forgot the valentines entirely, while dancing and joining in the merry games with which the first part of the evening was passed.

But after supper the mortification and almost regretful feelings returned, when the other children drew forth mysterious packages, and confided them to Mrs. Hope, the mother of the young hostess; and she was becoming quite unhappy when a servant entered, saying some one wished to see Miss Nettie Almer.

Gladly she hastened from the room; but what was her surprise when a messenger handed her a box addressed to

"Nettie, from St. Valentine, in return for the valentine she sent Minna and Gretel."

On removing the lid, the box was found to contain a dozen small bouquets of sweet, fragrant flowers, and a card saying they were intended as valentines for her little friends. Nettie shrewdly suspected them to be the same bouquets Gretel had tried so unavailingly to sell in the morning; but she did not know that Uncle John had been an unobserved spectator of the little episode in front of the stationer's, and that he had made a later call at the humble tenement, and gladdened the poor family a second time that day by buying all Gretel's flowers, and paying a good price for them, too.

It was with very much happier feelings that Nettie re-entered the parlor, and handed in her contribution for the letter-box; and when the office was opened in the back drawing-room, and Mr. Hope, disguised as St. Valentine, distributed the mail, all said none of the valentines could equal Nettie's, for in the centre of each bouquet was hidden a tiny golden heart, inclosing a motto appropriate to the occasion.

Nettie always said that that 14th of February was the happiest day she had ever spent; and it was also a turning-point in the fortunes of the German family, for Mrs. Almer having heard from Uncle John of her little daughter's *protégés*, interested some of her friends in them, who gave work to the mother, and when summer came, found a pleasant cottage on a farm for them in the country; and with the mother now happy and hopeful, Gretel well clad and rosy, and Minna quite restored to health, they were sent away from the dark, dreary tenement to a happy home among "green fields and pastures fair." And it all came about through Nettie's valentine.

AUNT SUKEY'S FIRST SLEIGH-RIDE.

"OH, Nan, look how the snow comes down! I thought it would never snow at all this winter. Just look at it! Now that's what I call tip-top," said Tom Chandler, gazing at the fast-whitening landscape, and drumming a cheerful tattoo on the window-panes with his fingers.

For some time the children stood in silence, watching the snow-flakes as they whirled and danced and floated like so many feathers, only to fall and pile up and cover the brown earth and the bare branches as with a lovely mantle of swan's-down.

Suddenly a thought seemed to have entered Tom's curly head, and he broke the silence with an air of profound mystery, saying: "I say, Nan, can you keep a secret? Well, look square in my face and say, 'Upon my word and sacred honor, I'll never, never, never tell anybody what Tom's going to tell me!' There! do you think you could keep it? It's the awfulest jolliest thing you ever heard of."

"Why, Tom," returned Nan, with dignity, "did I ever tell anybody anything that is a secret when you told me not to? Now do tell me this one."

"Let me see, now; haven't you told lots of my secrets, madam? Who went and told pa about my painting the white gobbler's feathers black, hey? Who told about my putting the mouse into Aunt Sukey's soap? Who told about my tying the clothes-line across the grass last summer? Who told about my—"

"That's real mean; you know I couldn't help it, ma was so vexed. You can keep your old secret; I won't listen to it—there!"

Seeing there was danger of one of Nan's showers, as Tom called her sudden tears, that young gentleman lowering his voice said, soothingly, "Never mind, old girl; just say, ''Pon honor' once more, and that you will never tell if you are shot for it, and I'll tell you what it is."

"That's what I call a solemn promise," exclaimed Tom, as Nanny concluded the prescribed speech. "Well, here goes."

Just what was said in Nan's ear we may never know, but that it was pleasing to both parties may be judged by what followed. The moment the grand secret became the property of two, there was such a clapping of hands, and whooping and laughing, and such a dancing up and down the room as made the boards tremble, and brought old Aunt Susan from her realms in the kitchen to the dining-room door.

"Bress de Lor', chillun, what dose yer mean cuttin' up like dat! yous 'll bring de roof down, an' no mistake! Stop dat noise! I guess yous disremember dere's comp'ny in de spare room yonder, gettin' ready fo' tea."

"Now you never mind the company, Aunt Sukey. Nan and I are only practicing a war jig we've got to dance for Miss Almira to-night."

"Drat your war jigs, an' have like 'spectable chillun! Ring de tea-bell, and make yo'selves useful; you's got younger bones dan dis ole Susan, tank de Lor'!"

"Remember!" said Tom, with a warning gesture to Nan, for he heard footsteps coming.

The next morning after breakfast Tom walked into the kitchen, where Aunt Sukey was putting the finishing touches to a dozen or more pies, for it was baking-day.

"Look here, Aunt Susan," exclaimed the youngster, "I've heard you say how much you would like to see 'Marse Linkum,' haven't I? Well, you've never had a sleigh-ride since you come North, have you? And I was just thinking last night that I'd take you for one when Nan and I go to school this morning. There! it won't take more'n a few minutes. Get your hood and shawl, and come along; it's only beyond Deacon Johnson's. Marse Lincoln would like to see you first rate."

"Oh, bress de Lor', honny, who tole you dat? Has ole aunty libbed to lay her eyes on de savior ob her people? Yous two dun wait for ole Aunt Susan, and she'll be wid you in a jiffy."

"Hurry up! Jocko's waiting," screamed Tom, as the old lady hustled off to get her "fixin's."

"But, Tom, what 'll ma say? and she's got company, too," asked Nan, uneasily.

"Why, it's all the better for our fun. She'll have some one to help her. Miss Almira can turn to and do up the pies and things, and make herself useful as well as ornamental."

The war of the great rebellion was nearly over, and the old woman, like many of her people, had made her way North, and this was her first winter; so Tom and Nan expected great sport over her new experience—a sleigh-ride. With considerable trouble, for aunty was stout and unwieldy, and the little cutter was narrow and high, she was at last bundled in, Nan and Tom following, to the infinite satisfaction of Jocko, the pony, which was pawing the snow and jingling his bells impatiently.

When the robes were all tucked in, Tom gave the word, and away they rushed down the lane into the road. Speeding on, they turned a curve so sharply that Aunt Sukey was wild with alarm; her eyes rolled, and her teeth glistened from ear to ear, as, with mouth distended, she screamed, "Oh, Marse Tommy, fo' de Lor's sake, hole in dat beast! I's done gone an' bin a fool to trust my carcass to a hoss like dat! Oh, Marse Tommy, Massa Tommy, yous 'll be de deff of ole Aunt Susan! Oh, fo' de Lor's sake, stop 'im!"

"Hooray, Jocko! go it, old boy!" was Tommy's laughing response.

"Oh, bress us an' save us! Missy Nanny, be a good chile, an' make Marse Tom stop dat yere beast, or we'll be upset, an' break ebery bone in our bodies!"

"Don't mind, aunty. Jocko knows every step of the way, and we won't let you get hurt," cried Nan, with a patronizing air.

"O Lor' hab mussy on a pore ole nigger, an' bring her safely to her journey's end, for mussy dese chillun hab none!" ejaculated Aunt Susan, as another sharp curve was so rapidly turned that the very trees and fences seemed rushing madly away in an opposite direction.

In less than twenty minutes, and the minutes seemed ages to affrighted Susan, Jocko, with a snort and an extra jingle of his bells, stood stock-still in front of the school-house.

A score of eyes peeped from the windows as Tom, alighting, with much ceremony handed out Nan and Aunt Susan, exclaiming, "Ladies, we shall soon be in the presence of 'Marse Linkum.'"

"Oh, tank de Lor', dar's no bones broken! and we's really gwine to see de blessed Marse Linkum, arter all!"

"There, now, Nan, take Aunt Susan up on the stoop, till I blanket Jocko and put him in the shed."

"Now, Missy Nan," whispered Aunt Susan, when they found themselves alone on the piazza, "does I look 'spectable nuff to see de President?"

"You look awful nice, aunty," replied Nanny, turning away her head to conceal her laughter. "Ah! here comes Tom."

"Now, Aunt Susan," exclaimed that youngster, "when I introduce you, say this: 'I hope I find your Excellency well, and all the people of color in the South send you greeting.'"

"Wa'al, now, what a genius dat chile is, to be shuah!" muttered Susan, walking behind Tom and Nanny.

"Mr. Lincoln," exclaimed Tom, advancing toward that gentleman, with a merry twinkle in his roguish eyes, "allow me to present to you a new pupil, Aunt Susan Whittingham; she has come all the way from Louisiana to see you."

"Oh, bress de Lor' dat hab given dis ole woman de privilege ob laying her eyes on de gloriousness ob de man who hab saved all her people, an' has strucken off de chains what held dem fast, an' made dem free forebber and forebber! Hallelujah! hallelujah! amen! Oh, bress me, I's done gone an' make a mistake arter all. Oh, your Presidency—no, your Elegancy, I hopes I find you well. All de people ob color in de Souf send you—send you—greetin'!"

"Aunt Susan, I am very sorry; but that little rascal, Tom, has been deceiving you all the time. I'm not the 'Marse Linkum' you take me for, I'm sorry to tell you, for I am only plain James Lincoln, school-master of the district. Tom, I say, how did you dare to treat Aunt Susan and myself in this way? I have a mind to punish you."

"Oh, de Lor' forgib Marse Tommy dat he fool a 'spectable ole body like me; an' de Lor' save me! all my pies an' tings goin' to construction, an' de missus all alone to hum wid comp'ny! It's too much—it's too much fo' shuah!"

"Come, aunty," cried Tom, soothingly, for he was beginning to be afraid himself, "we'll drive home ever so slow. Come, now, forgive us, and don't get us a whipping."

"I's mos' ready to forgib yous now; but jes you dis-remember how de chillun in de Bible war eaten up along o' de bars for sayin', 'Go up, ole bal'-head!' an' don't you nebber, nebber agin fool ole Aunt Susan."

Almira had "turned to," as Tom predicted, and was helping his mother with the dinner, when that lady exclaimed: "This is another of that boy's tricks; but boys are boys, and there's no help for it. I hope Aunt Susan's enjoying the ride."

Everything was in "apple-pie order" when the party returned, apparently in fine spirits. Tom thought it mighty queer that nothing was said about his escapade, and dying to tell it, he felt his way cautiously for an opportunity, and it came. In the evening, when the family were discussing nuts and cider around the glowing fire, he related the morning's adventure with such gay good humor that Pa and Ma Chandler and Augustus and Al-

"AWAY THEY RUSHED DOWN THE LANE."

mirs made the walls ring again with their laughter, bringing old Aunt Susan to the sitting-room door, where, poking her head in, she had courage to say, "'Pears to me youn folks is havin' great sport over Aunt Susan's fust sleigh-ride."

RUINS OF TRINITY CHURCH, 1776.

NEW YORK'S FIRST GREAT FIRE.

THE first great fire in New York happened in September, 1776, just after Washington had been driven from the city. New York was then a small but beautiful town: it reached only to the lower end of the Park, but Broadway was lined with shade trees, and its fine houses stretched away on both sides to the Battery. Trinity Church stood, as now, at the head of Wall Street. St. Paul's—a building of great cost and beauty for the times—almost bounded the upper end of Broadway. The British soldiers marched into the pleasant but terrified city, the leading patriots fled with Washington's army, and in the hot days of the autumn of 1776 New York seemed to offer a pleasant home for the officers and men of the invading forces. They took possession of the deserted country-seats of the patriots at Bloomingdale or Murray Hill, and occupied the finest houses on the best streets of the town. Here they hoped to pass a winter of ease, and in the spring complete without difficulty the rout of the disheartened Americans.

But one night in September the cry of fire was heard, and the flames began to spread from some low wooden buildings near Whitehall, where now are the Produce Exchange and Staten Island ferries. In those days there were no steam-engines nor hydrants, no Croton water nor well-organized fire-companies. But as the flames continued to advance, the British soldiers sprang from their beds and began to labor to check the fire with all the means in their power. They used, no doubt, buckets of water brought from the cisterns and the river. They found, it was said, several persons setting houses on fire, and in their rage threw them into the flames. But their labor was all in vain. All night the fire spread over the finest quarter of New York. From Whitehall it passed up Broadway on the eastern side, devouring everything, until it was stopped by a large new brick house near Wall Street. It crossed to the western side, and laid nearly the whole street in ruins. It fastened on the roof and tower of Trinity Church, and soon, of all its graceful proportions, only a few shattered fragments remained. Then the flames passed rapidly up to the west of Broadway from Trinity as far as St. Paul's; houses and shops crumbled before them; a long array of buildings seem to have fed the raging fires, until at last they reached the walls of the great church itself, and were about to envelop it in ruins. But here, it is said, the zeal of the people checked their progress. They mounted the roof of the church, covered it with streams of water, put out the sparks that fell on it, until at last the building was saved, the flames died out, and St. Paul's stands to-day almost as it stood in 1776, the monument of the close of the great fire.

It is not difficult to imagine the melancholy change wrought in the appearance of the city. Broadway, once so beautiful, remained until the end of the war in great part a street of ruins. From Wall Street to the Battery, from St. Paul's Church to the Bowling Green, the miserable waste was never repaired. Up its desolate track paraded each morning the British officers and their followers, shining in red and gold, to the sound of martial music; but they had no leisure nor wish to repair the ravages of war. On the wasted district arose a collection of tents and hovels, called "Canvas Town." Here lived the miserable poor, the wretched, the vile; robbers who at night made the ruins unsafe, and incendiaries who never ceased to terrify the unlucky city. The British garrison was never suffered to remain long at ease.

It was said that the great fire of 1776 was the work of the patriots, who had resolved to burn New York, and drive the invaders from their safe resting-place. The question of its origin has never been decided. It may have been altogether accidental, or possibly the work of design. But it was followed by a singular succession of other fires, during the period of the British ascendency, that seem to show some settled plan to annoy and discourage the invaders. The newspapers of the time are filled with accounts of the misfortunes of the garrison and the royalists.

TO MY VALENTINE.

BY M. M.

In love and hope
These blossoms fair
I lay at your dear feet!

Deep-folded,
In the rose's heart
You'll find my secret, sweet!

OUR POST-OFFICE BOX.

[illegible], MASSACHUSETTS.

I would like to know how old is the festival of St. Valentine's Day. I have painted some little cards myself, and am going to send them to my friend-[illegible]. I think that is better than buying them, even if I cannot make them quite so pretty. I am going to copy a little verse on the back of each [illegible]. [illegible] has chosen the verses for me. A. F. W.

There is no clear record of the origin of St. Valentine's Day. St. Valentine himself was a priest of Rome who was martyred some time during the third century, but he had nothing to do with the peculiar observance of his day. In ancient Rome a great part of the month of February was devoted to feasts in honor of Pan and Juno, during which the young men drew by lot the names of their companions for the festivities. It is supposed that this ancient custom changed gradually into the present observance of the day. Many allusions to St. Valentine's Day are found in English poetry of the earliest date, as the festival was much more generally observed four centuries ago than now.

[illegible], NEW YORK.

I am a little boy eight years old. I want to tell you that papa heard a bluebird sing in a chestnut-tree on January 11. I have six cats and three ducks. One of my cats died last week, and I buried her. Poor [illegible]! S. B. H.

The little bluebird must have left its winter-quarters in the Southern States, and travelled with the warm wave which swept northward in January. It is to be hoped it will escape being frozen to death, and live to sing its sweet spring song at a more seasonable time.

[illegible], TENNESSEE, JANUARY [illegible].

I send you some flowers which grew in the front yard. The buttercups and purple [illegible] are blooming also, but I could not press them to send them to you. I have seen some bluebirds and red-birds. Many of our flowers are blooming. It is just like summer outdoors. E. B. [illegible].

[illegible], [illegible].

I have a little rabbit I like very much. It lives with the hens in winter. Papa brought two in [illegible]. They travelled to Washington in a peach basket. When papa brought them home he gave one to me. The other was drowned last summer in a hard shower. My rabbit likes apples, potato skins, clover, grass, hay, and corn, and I must not give it [illegible] anything greasy. CARRIE E. [illegible].

[illegible], PENNSYLVANIA.

I have a little dog named Fanny, who shakes hands, and [illegible] when she gets a chance. She [illegible], and she shows her teeth when she laughs, and [illegible] when she is pleased.

LAURA B. W. (eight years).

[illegible], WEST VIRGINIA.

As you have asked us to write about household pets, I thought I would tell you about a pet fish we kept in a stone basin about three feet square and two feet deep. We caught the fish in [illegible] Creek, and brought it home in a basket, and placed it in the basin. It was a yellow bass about ten inches long and very pretty. It soon got very tame, and would take a fishing-worm out of my fingers. It committed suicide one night by jumping out on the floor and killing itself. I have a minnow in the basin now, but I don't expect it will ever get so tame. There are four or five pretty rabbits staying in our yard, and lots of [illegible]. SAMUEL J.

NEW YORK CITY.

In YOUNG PEOPLE No. 11 there is an article on the Dead-letter Office at Washington which mentions some curious things to go through the mail. There are three more very queer things I would like to mention. The first is two centipedes, which are on the shelf with the snake; the second is an iron [illegible] post; and the third is a live alligator about a foot and a half long. There is an old record in the office of 1775, which looked at that time eleven years, but which, a clerk said, would last now about fifteen minutes. K. P.

OSBORNE H. WEBSTER.—Coons are very fond of fish, and you might bait your trap with salt codfish roasted to give it a strong smell. The sense of smell of a coon is very acute, and it will rarely pass a trap baited with any provender it can scent.

LOUIS K.—The song you require is not yet published, but will probably be issued before long.

L. H. [illegible], JUN.—Any letters sent to the care of Harper & Brothers will be forwarded.

M. AND E. N.—Early numbers of YOUNG PEOPLE can be obtained on application to the publishers.

F. A. [illegible] AND [illegible] A. F.—You must inquire at your post-office for missing numbers. They have all been mailed to your address.

CHARLES W. L.—The best way to understand the construction of certain kinds of puzzles is to study the answers and puzzles together. You will find many answers given in this number which will help you.

"[illegible]," M. E. H., AND OTHERS.—We can not print puzzles unless accompanied with full name and address, as guarantee that they are original. Correspondents will please pay attention to this, as we have been compelled to reject some very pretty puzzles because they came without address. Never send old puzzles, as some have done, for they are worthless. Be very careful to give a clear and correct definition of words used in word squares, diamond puzzles, beheadings, acrostics, and charades. One poor definition will spoil an otherwise excellent puzzle. Do not take a name little known, like that of some Western town, to form an enigma, for children in some other part of the country will find it difficult to solve.

Favors are acknowledged from "[illegible]," Canada; [illegible] A. [illegible], [illegible]; H. [illegible] F., [illegible], Germany; [illegible], Wisconsin; [illegible] A. J., Minnesota; A. R. H., [illegible]; Florence [illegible], Michigan; [illegible] H., Washington Territory. From [illegible]—W. A. [illegible], [illegible] W. F., H. L. T. From [illegible]—[illegible], [illegible] and Hattie. From [illegible]—[illegible] H. F., [illegible] J. [illegible], James W. B. From Pennsylvania—Frank H., Amy F. From New York—George J. R., [illegible] Weller, Hattie [illegible], Anna L. A., [illegible], [illegible] F., Charlie L.; M. A. T. and F. V. [illegible], Kentucky; [illegible] R. H., Massachusetts; Bertie, Washington, D. C.; [illegible], New Jersey.

Correct answers to puzzles received from N. L. [illegible], Washington, D. C.; [illegible] A., West Virginia; Florence [illegible], Delaware; Nellie [illegible], Oregon; [illegible] B. Cooper, Tennessee; Arthur F. A., Wisconsin; [illegible], Indiana; Albert W. J., Illinois; H. D. C., Michigan. From Ohio—[illegible] H., Nellie B., Fannie [illegible], R. H. R. From Pennsylvania—"Little [illegible]," Laura B. W., Eddie H. H., "[illegible]," Charles M. C., [illegible] and Florence M., Charles W. [illegible], Charles H. H. From New York—Frank H. [illegible], F. W. F., O. B. [illegible], V. C., [illegible] D. D., George H. [illegible], W. E. [illegible], Pauline O., [illegible] A. S., Bertie [illegible], J. E. [illegible]. From Connecticut, [illegible]; [illegible], New Jersey; [illegible] R. H., Maine. From Rhode Island—[illegible] W., F. R. [illegible], H. W. [illegible], Annie Parker. From Connecticut—William H. H., "[illegible]." From Massachusetts—[illegible] G. [illegible], E. A. Abbot, Frank H. [illegible], E. Allen Cushing.

PUZZLES FROM YOUNG CONTRIBUTORS.

No. 1.

ENIGMA.

My first is in good, but not in bad.
My second is in [illegible], but not in sad.
My third is in [illegible], but not in [illegible].
My fourth is in [illegible], but not in found.
My fifth is in pen, but not in [illegible].
My sixth is in [illegible], but not in blue.
My whole is a musical instrument. [illegible].

No. 2.

[illegible].

A [illegible]. A vegetable. A South African animal. [illegible]. A [illegible]. [illegible] (twelve years).

No. 3.

ENIGMA.

My first is in food, but not in [illegible].
My second is in [illegible], but not in [illegible].
My third is in [illegible], but not in [illegible].
My fourth is in friend, but not in foe.
My fifth is in [illegible], but not in go.
My sixth is in [illegible], but not in [illegible].
My seventh is in [illegible], but not in [illegible].
My eighth is in grain, and also in bran.
My whole was the name of an eminent man.
E. S. C. (twelve years).

No. 4.

[illegible] ENIGMA.

I am composed of [illegible] letters.
My [illegible] is a school-boy's game.
My [illegible] is something most children like.
My [illegible] comes from the [illegible].
My [illegible] is part of a church organ.
My [illegible] is not cold.
My [illegible] is a boy's name.
My [illegible] is used in making bread.
My whole is the name of an interesting story for children.
[illegible] B. (twelve years).

No. 5.

[illegible].

To [illegible]. To regret. A [illegible]. [illegible]. To [illegible]. Answer—two great military commanders.
N. L. [illegible].

No. 6.

WORD SQUARE.

First, a [illegible]. Second, a [illegible]. Third, [illegible]. Fourth, departed.
N. L. [illegible].

Answers to Puzzles in No. 11.

No. 1.

W A R
A U A
R A W

No. 2. [illegible].
No. 3. Washington.
No. 4. [illegible].
No. 5. [illegible].
No. 6.

N [illegible] A
E [illegible] L
W [illegible] B
A [illegible] A
R [illegible] N
K [illegible] Y

Newark, Albany.

No. 7. [illegible], I thank you.
No. 8. HARPER'S YOUNG PEOPLE.

Old Books for Young Readers.

Arabian Nights' Entertainments.

The Thousand and One Nights; or, The Arabian Nights' Entertainments. Translated and Arranged for Family Reading, with Explanatory Notes, by E. W. Lane. 600 Illustrations by Harvey. 2 vols., 12mo, Cloth, $3 50.

Robinson Crusoe.

The Life and Surprising Adventures of Robinson Crusoe, of York, Mariner. By Daniel Defoe. With a Biographical Account of Defoe. Illustrated by Adams. Complete Edition. 12mo, Cloth, $1 50.

The Swiss Family Robinson.

The Swiss Family Robinson; or, Adventures of a Father and Mother and Four Sons on a Desert Island. Illustrated. 2 vols., 18mo, Cloth, $1 50.

[illegible]

Sandford and Merton.

The History of Sandford and Merton. By Thomas Day. [illegible]

Published by HARPER & BROTHERS, New York.

[illegible]

MRS. MORTIMER'S BOOKS FOR THE NURSERY.

Lines Left Out.

Lines Left Out; or, Some of the Histories Left Out in "Line upon Line." [illegible] By Mrs. Elizabeth Mortimer. 16mo, Cloth, 75 cents.

[illegible]

More about Jesus.

More about Jesus. Illustrations and a Map. By Mrs. Elizabeth Mortimer. 16mo, Cloth, 75 cents.

[illegible]

Streaks of Light.

Streaks of Light; or, Fifty-two Facts from the Bible for Fifty-two Sundays of the Year. Illustrated. By Mrs. Elizabeth Mortimer. 16mo, Cloth, 75 cents.

[illegible]

Reading without Tears.

Reading without Tears; or, A Pleasant Mode of Learning to Read. Illustrated. Small 4to, Cloth. By Mrs. Elizabeth Mortimer. Two Parts. [illegible] complete in One Volume, [illegible]

[illegible]

Published by HARPER & BROTHERS, New York.

[illegible]

DU CHAILLU'S STORIES OF ADVENTURE IN AFRICA.

Stories of the Gorilla Country.

By Paul B. Du Chaillu. Illustrated. 12mo, Cloth, $1 50.

[illegible]

Wild Life under the Equator.

By Paul B. Du Chaillu. Illustrated. 12mo, Cloth, $1 50.

[illegible] —*N. Y. Evening Post.*

Lost in the Jungle.

By Paul B. Du Chaillu. Illustrated. 12mo, Cloth, $1 50.

[illegible] —*Philadelphia Ledger.*

My Apingi Kingdom:

With Life in the Great Sahara, and Sketches of the Chase of the Ostrich, Hyena, &c. By Paul B. Du Chaillu. Illustrated. 12mo, Cloth, $1 50.

[illegible] —*N. Y. Herald.*

The Country of the Dwarfs.

By Paul B. Du Chaillu. Illustrated. 12mo, Cloth, $1 50.

[illegible]

Published by HARPER & BROTHERS, N. Y.

[illegible]

No. 8

No. 9

WIGGLES.

HERE are some of the answers to the Wiggle published in No. 10 of HARPER'S YOUNG PEOPLE. So many were sent in that it was impossible to publish them all, and so our artist selected those that he considered the best. Those that he used were sent in by J. R. S., J. B. G., M. E., A. T. Jones, Paul, D. C. Gilmore, H. and B., and Bert W. S., several of whom sent a number of different figures.

Others, and some of them very good, were sent in by W. R. R., Ethel M., S. A. W., Jun., John Priddle, C. F., Nettie S. H., Willie H. S., Mabel M., E. H. S., Betty, M. Ward, Philip M., Annie E. A., Willy H., H. W. P., J. L., Mary P., Archie H. L., C. B. F., R. S. M., W. A. Burr, Percy H. M., Paul B. T., E. S., C. F. C., Grace C., Eva M., and Anita R. S. Figure No. 8 is what our artist made of the Wiggle; and Figure No. 9 is a new Wiggle in two parts, which must be combined in one drawing, though they must retain their relative positions.

THE LONG-EARED BAT.

A long-eared bat
Went to buy a hat.
Said the hatter, "I've none that will do,
Unless with the shears
I shorten your ears,
Which might be unpleasant to you."

The long-eared bat
Was so mad at that
He flew over lands and seas,
Till in Paris (renowned
For its fashions) he found
A hat that he wore with great ease.

Another Sagacious Dog.—In No. 11 of HARPER'S YOUNG PEOPLE a story was told of a sagacious newspaper dog. Having read this, a Western editor sends the following story of his dog, in which he says: "My dog is a beautiful Gordon setter, and has been so well trained that while the carrier is delivering papers on one side of the street, Bob, the dog, delivers on the other. He receives his papers folded, half a dozen at a time, and going to the first place, lays the whole bundle down, and then picks it up, all but one, and so on till they are all gone."

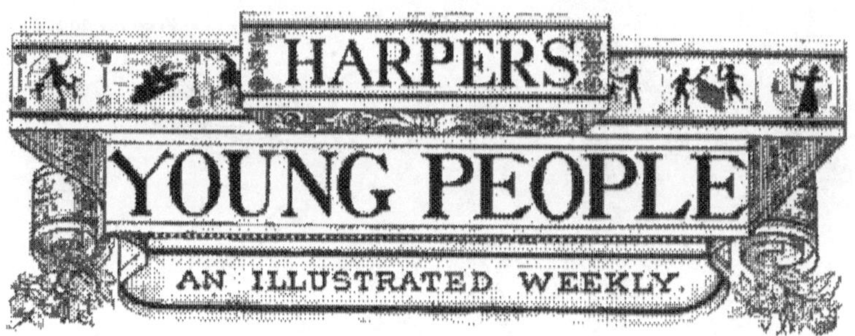

Vol. I.—No. 16. | Published by HARPER & BROTHERS, New York. | Price Four Cents.

Tuesday, February 17, [illegible] | Copyright, [illegible], by Harper & Brothers. | [illegible] per Year, in Advance.

"DON'T YOU WISH YOU COULD GET IT?"

GENERAL PRESCOTT AND THE YANKEE BOY.

BY BENSON J. LOSSING.

GENERAL PRESCOTT, commanding the British forces on Rhode Island in 1777, was a petty tyrant, imperious, irascible, and cruel. He would command citizens of Newport who met him on the streets to take off their hats in deference to him, and if not obeyed, he would knock them off with his cane. If he saw a group of citizens talking together, he would shake his cane at them, and shout, "Disperse, you rebels!" For slight offenses citizens were imprisoned and otherwise ill-treated. This unworthy conduct made the people despise and hate him. His tyranny became unbearable.

Prescott's summer quarters were at Mr. Overing's house, on the borders of Narragansett Bay, a few miles from Newport. On a warm but showery night in July, 1777, Lieutenant-Colonel Barton, with a few resolute men, went down the bay from Providence, in a whale-boat, landed near Prescott's quarters at about midnight, secured the sentinels, entered the house, and ascended to the door of his bedroom in the second story. It was locked. A stout colored man who accompanied Barton, making a battering-ram of his head, burst open the door. The General, in affright, sprang from his bed, but was instantly seized, and without being allowed to dress himself, was conveyed to the boat, and taken quickly across the bay to Warwick. Thence he was sent, under guard, to Washington's head-quarters in New Jersey.

In the spring of 1778 Prescott was exchanged for General Charles Lee, and returned to Rhode Island. Soon afterward the British Admiral invited the General to dine with him and his officers on board his ship, then lying in front of Newport. Martial law yet prevailed on the Island, and men and boys were frequently sent by the authorities on shore to be confined in the ship as a punishment for slight offenses. There were several on board at that time.

After dinner the free use of wine made the company hilarious, and toasts and songs were frequently called for. A lieutenant remarked to the Admiral, "There is a Yankee lad confined below who can shame any of us in singing."

"Bring him up," said the Admiral.

"Yes, bring him up," said Prescott.

The boy was brought into the cabin. He was pale and slender, and about thirteen years of age. Abashed by the presence of great officers, with their glittering uniforms, he timidly approached, when the Admiral, seeing his embarrassment, spoke kindly to him, and asked him to sing a song.

"I can't sing any but Yankee songs," said the trembling boy.

"Come, my little fellow, don't be afraid," said the Admiral. "Sing one of your Yankee songs—any one you can recollect."

The boy still hesitated, when the brutal Prescott, who was a stranger to the lad, roared out,

"Give us a song, you little rebel, or I'll give you a dozen lashes."

This cruel salutation was innocently met most severely by the child, when, encouraged by kind words from the Admiral, he sang, with a sweet voice and modest manner, the following ballad, composed by a sailor of Newport:

"'Twas on a dark and stormy night—
The wind and waves did roar—
Bold Barton then, with twenty men,
Went down upon the shore.

"And in a whale-boat they set off
To Rhode Island fair,
To catch a redcoat General
Who then resided there.

"Through British fleets and guard-boats strong
They held their dangerous way,
Till they arrived unto their port,
And then did not delay.

"A tawny son of Afric's race
Them through the ravine led,
And entering then the Overing house,
They found him in his bed.

"But to get in they had no means
Except poor Cuffee's head,
Who beat the door down, then rushed in,
And seized him in his bed.

"'Stop! let me put my clothing on!'
The General then did pray;
'Your clothing, massa, I will take;
For dress we can not stay.'

"Then through rye stubble him they led,
With shoes and clothing none,
And placed him in their boat quite snug,
And from the shore were gone.

"Soon the alarm was sounded loud:
'The Yankees they have come,
And stolen Prescott from his bed,
And him have carried hum.'

"The drums were beat, sky-rockets flew,
The soldiers shouldered arms,
And marched around the grounds they knew,
Filled with most dire alarms.

"But through the fleet with muffled oars
They held their devious way,
And landed him on 'Gansett shores,
Where Britons hold no sway.

"When unto land the captors came,
Where rescue there was none,
'A bold push this,' the General cried;
'Of prisoners I am one.'"

The boy was frequently interrupted by roars of laughter at Prescott's expense, which strengthened the child's nerves and voice; and when he had concluded his song, "I thought," wrote a gentleman who was present, "the deck would go through with the stamping." General Prescott joined heartily in the merriment produced by the song, and thrusting his hand into his pocket, he pulled out a coin, and handed it to the boy, saying,

"Here, you young dog, is a guinea for you."

The boy was set at liberty the next morning, and sent ashore.

CLIMBING A MOUNTAIN THREE MILES HIGH.

THE ice-bound peak of the Alps known as the Matterhorn, situated between Switzerland and Italy, forty miles northeast of Mont Blanc, and twelve miles west of Monte Rosa, towers skyward nearly 15,000 feet, presenting an appearance imposing beyond description. The peak rises abruptly, by a series of cliffs which may properly be termed precipices, a clear 5000 feet above the glaciers which surround its base. There seemed to the superstitious natives in the surrounding valleys to be a line drawn around it, up to which one might go, but no farther. Within that invisible line good and evil spirits were supposed to exist. They spoke of a ruined city on its summit wherein the spirits dwelt; and if you laughed, they gravely shook their heads, told you to look yourself to see the castles and the walls, and warned you against a rash approach, lest the infuriate demons from their impregnable heights should hurl down vengeance for your audacity.

Previous to 1865 several attempts had been made by daring tourists to reach its summit, but no one got beyond 13,000 feet, the remaining 2000 feet being generally regarded as inaccessible. But in the year just mentioned a little party of hardy English climbers accomplished the ascent. The achievement was made, however, at the cost of four human lives.

The story, as told by one of the leaders of the party, Mr. Edward Whymper, who had already made seven unsuccessful attempts, is an exciting one.

The ascent was made in July, in company with Lord Francis Douglas, Mr. Hudson, Mr. Hadow, and three guides. On the first day they did not ascend to a great height, and on the second day they resumed their journey with daylight, as they were anxious to outstrip a party of Italians who had set out before them by a different route. Difficulty after difficulty was surmounted. The higher they rose, the more intense became the excitement. What if they should be beaten at the last moment? The slope eased off; at length they could be detached from the rope which bound the party together; and Croz and Mr. Whymper, dashing away, ran a neck-and-neck race, which ended in a dead-heat. At 1.40 P.M. the world was at their feet, and the Matterhorn was conquered. Hurrah! They had beaten the party of Italians, whom they saw on the southwest ridge, 1250 feet below, and who did not prosecute the ascent farther. For an hour the successful climbers revelled in the scene which lay at their feet. There were black and gloomy forests, bright and cheerful meadows; bounding water-falls and tranquil lakes; fertile lands and savage wastes; sunny plains and frigid *plateaux*. There were the most rugged forms and the most graceful outlines; bold perpendicular cliffs and gentle undulating slopes; rocky mountains and snowy mountains, sombre and solemn, or glittering and white, with walls, turrets, pinnacles, pyramids, domes, cones, and spires. There was every combination that the world can give, and every contrast that the heart could desire.

Alas! their naturally triumphant feeling of pleasure was but short-lived. They had commenced their descent, again tied together with ropes. Croz, a most accomplished guide and a brave fellow, went first; Hadow, second; Hudson, as an experienced mountaineer, and reckoned as good as a guide, third; Lord F. Douglas, fourth; followed by Mr. Whymper between the two remaining guides, named Jaugwalder, father and son. They were commencing the difficult part of the descent, and Croz was cutting steps in the ice for the feet of Mr. Hadow, who was immediately behind him. A few minutes later a sharp-eyed lad ran into the Monte Rosa Hotel, saying that he had seen an avalanche fall from the summit of the Matterhorn on to the Matterhorngletscher. The boy was reproved for telling idle stories; he was right, nevertheless, and this was what he saw: Michel Croz had laid aside his axe, and in order to give Mr. Hadow greater security, was taking hold of his legs, and putting his feet one by one into their proper positions. "At this moment," says Mr. Whymper, "Mr. Hadow slipped, fell against him, and knocked him over. I heard one startled exclamation from Croz, then saw him and Mr. Hadow flying downward; in another moment Hudson was dragged from his steps, and Lord F. Douglas immediately after him. All this was the work of a moment. Immediately we heard Croz's exclamation, old Peter and I planted ourselves as firmly as the rocks would permit; the rope was taut between us, and the jerk came on us both as one man. We held; but the rope broke midway between Jaugwalder and Lord Francis Douglas. For a few seconds we saw our unfortunate companions sliding downward on their backs, and spreading out their hands, endeavoring to save themselves. They passed from our sight uninjured, disappeared one by one, and fell from precipice to precipice on to the Matterhorngletscher below—a distance of nearly 4000 feet in height. From the moment the rope broke, it was impossible to help them. So perished our comrades."

The bodies of three of the men who thus miserably perished were afterward recovered; but that of Lord Francis Douglas was never again seen. It was a melancholy ending, and may well excite a feeling of surprise that so many brave and useful men can thus be found year by year hazarding their lives for what is in many cases no higher purpose than that of pleasure or sport.

THE GOLD DIGGINGS OF IRELAND.

ALTHOUGH Ireland is not generally regarded as one of the gold-producing countries of the world, gold has been found there in paying quantities, especially in the county of Wicklow.

Tradition commonly attributes the original discovery of the Wicklow gold mines to a poor school-master, who, while fishing in one of the small streams which descend from the Croghan mountains, picked up a piece of shining metal, and having ascertained that it was gold, gradually enriched himself by the success of his researches in that and the neighboring streams, cautiously disposing of the produce of his labor to a goldsmith in Dublin. He is said to have preserved the secret for upward of twenty years, but marrying a young wife, he imprudently confided his discovery to her, and she, believing her husband to be mad, immediately revealed the circumstance to her relations, through whose means it was made public. This was toward the close of the year 1795, and the effect it produced was remarkable. Thousands of people of every age and sex hurried to the spot, and from the laborer who could wield a spade or pickaxe to the child who scraped the rock with a rusty nail, all eagerly engaged in the search after gold. The Irish are a people possessed of a rich and quick fancy, and the very name of a gold mine carried with it ideas of inexhaustible wealth.

During the interval which elapsed between the public announcement of the gold discovery and the taking possession of the mine by the government—a period of about two months—it is supposed that upward of two thousand five hundred ounces of gold were collected by the peasants, principally from the mud and sand of Ballinvally stream, and disposed of for about ten thousand pounds, a sum far exceeding the produce of the mine during the government operations, which amounted to little more than three thousand five hundred pounds.

The gold was found in pieces of all forms and sizes, from the smallest perceptible particle to the extraordinary mass of twenty-two ounces, which sold for eighty guineas. This large piece was of an irregular form; it measured four inches in its greatest length, and three in breadth, and in thickness it varied from half an inch to an inch; a gilt cast of it may be seen in the museum of Trinity College, Dublin. So pure was the gold generally found, that it was the custom of the Dublin goldsmiths to put gold coin in the opposite scale to it, and give weight for weight.

The government works were carried on until 1798, when all the machinery was destroyed in the insurrection. The mining was renewed in 1801, but not being found sufficiently productive to pay the expenses, the search was abandoned. There prevails yet, however, a lingering belief among the peasants that there is still gold in Kinsella, and only the "lucky man" is wanting.

THE STORY OF THE SUMMER BOARDER, MOSES, AND THE TWO VISITORS.

BY THE FAMILY STORY-TELLER.

I WARN you, said Family Story-Teller, looking round upon the family circle the next evening, that this is a story of mistakes. It will be a hard story to follow, and unless you pay close attention, you will forget which is Evelyn and which is the other girl, and why it was that Mrs. Stimpcett thought her boy Moses had broken his leg. I mean, of course, Mrs. Stimpcett of the village of Gilead.

Mrs. Stimpcett's summer boarder, Mr. St. Clair, was forgetful. He liked well to gaze at a brook, a pond, the clouds, the blue sky, the flowery fields, and often he forgot to stop doing so, and kept on gazing when it was meal-time, or bed-time, or some other time.

Mrs. Stimpcett took also another summer boarder, a rich lady of the name of Odell. Mrs. Odell was tall, and slim, and pale, and in her cap, just above her forehead, was set in a row three pink muslin roses. Mrs. Odell was silly enough to be proud of being rich, and stingy enough to like to save her own money at other people's expense.

Mrs. Odell had a six-year-old niece named Evelyn, a pale, delicate little girl, who lived in the city, and this Evelyn was coming to Gilead to visit her aunt Odell. She was coming in the cars to Mill Village in care of the conductor, and her aunt Odell was to send a carriage to the station to fetch her to Gilead. If the carriage was not there when the cars arrived, she was to stay with the station-man till it should arrive. I trust my story is plain thus far.

It happened that Mr. Stimpcett was going to Mill Village that same day, to get some corn ground, and Mrs. Odell, though it would take him very far out of his way, asked him to go round by the station and get Evelyn. This would save hiring a carriage.

Now Mr. St. Clair thought it would be a pleasant thing to go to mill, and asked if he might go in the place of Mr. Stimpcett. Mr. Stimpcett said, "Oh yes, if you will be sure to bring back the meal." So Mr. St. Clair went to mill: and Moses Stimpcett, a boy about nine years old, went with him, for the sake of the ride, and to see his aunt Debby, who lived not far from the mill.

They set off soon after the hour of noon. Moses wore his Zouave cap, and his second-best summer clothes, and Mr. St. Clair wore a black alpaca coat, a blue neck-tie tied in a bow, a broad-brimmed straw hat, a white vest, and white trousers. Moses drove the horse, and they reached

EVELYN.

the mill without accident. While the miller was taking in the corn, Moses bought a roll of lozenges at a store near by, and as he came out with them a man passed that way, leading a small but valuable dog. Said this man to Moses, "I wish you would hold my dog while I step into the mill;" and Moses took the string.

Mr. St. Clair hitched his horse a little way from the mill, and then said to Moses, "When the man takes his dog, you can go to your aunt Debby's. I will call for you there, after I have been to the station and got the little girl." Mr. St. Clair then walked up the bank of the stream to see the waters flow.

Moses led the dog along to the mill, and leaned against the building awhile; then sat down on a barrel. Soon the barrel began to move. The reason of this was that it stood on an elevator. Moses had not noticed that the barrel stood on an elevator. First he wondered what the matter was, and second, he thought he would jump; but by that time the barrel was quite a way off the ground, and, besides, he was troubled by holding the string of the dog, and the lozenges. The barrel rose higher and higher, and when the little dog found himself swinging in the air, he kicked and yelped, and jerked the string so that Moses was obliged to let it go, and also to drop the lozenges, for he had to grasp the barrel with both hands. The dog fell, and broke one of his legs. [Please remember that it was the *dog*, and not Moses.] Moses and the barrel were taken in at the third story. A traveller passing through the place heard of this elevator accident, and told of it that afternoon at a house in Gilead. But this person understood that it was the *boy* who broke his leg—"a Stimprett boy," he said, in telling the news. Mrs. Stimprett heard of it soon after milking-time; but this will be spoken of farther on in the story.

Mr. St. Clair walked far up the bank of the stream, and when he came back, the miller told him that his bag of meal had been put into his cart. He went out, and seeing a cart with a bag of meal lying at the bottom, he stepped in, and drove around to the station.

Now this cart which Mr. St. Clair took belonged to a man who came from Cherry Valley. Here, you see, was a mistake. But Mr. St. Clair not only took the wrong cart, he took the wrong little girl, as will now be told. He drove in haste to the station, knowing he had staid too long walking up the bank of the stream. On the platform of the station sat a roly-poly, chubby-cheeked little girl, with a carpet-bag and a heavy bundle. He asked her, "Are you waiting for some one to come for you?" "Yes, sir," she answered. "All right," said Mr. St. Clair; and he helped her into the cart. I hope you understand that this very fleshy child was not Evelyn Odell. She was Maggie Brien. Maggie Brien lived with her grandmother, not far from the station. Her mother did the cooking in a family two miles away, and she had promised to send that day for Maggie to come and make her a visit, and Maggie was sitting on the platform waiting for the man to take her.

Mr. St. Clair took her, and drove from the station, thinking to go to Aunt Debby's and get Moses, and set off for Gilead; but while he was gazing up at the sky, the horse—which you will remember was not Mr. Stimprett's horse—turned into a road which led to his own master's house at Cherry Valley. Mr. St. Clair had now the wrong horse and cart, the wrong meal, the wrong girl, and the wrong road. Presently the horse trotted up to the door of a farm-house, and stopped. Three heads of three young maidens popped out of three chamber windows, and a bare-armed woman, wiping her hands on her apron, rushed to the door. "Where is my husband?" she cried. "Is he hurt? Is he killed? Tell me the truth at once!"

MOSES LETS THE DOG FALL.

"I assure you, madam," answered Mr. St. Clair, mildly, "that I have not seen your husband."

"Why, then, have you come with his horse and cart?" she asked.

"This horse and cart, madam," said Mr. St. Clair, still mildly, "belongs to Mr. Stimpcett, of Gilead."

"Do you think I don't know our horse and cart?" cried the woman, in an angry tone. "Besides, here's my husband's name on the bag—I. Ellison."

"I must have taken the wrong horse and cart," said Mr. St. Clair. "I will go back at once and find Mr. Ellison."

"The quicker the better," said the woman, as he turned the horse.

Just after Mr. St. Clair had passed from the Cherry Valley road into the mill road, a man came out of a wood path and sprang at the horse, crying, "Stop thief!"

"Where is the thief?" asked Mr. St. Clair, looking all around.

"You are the thief!" cried the man. "You have stolen my horse and cart."

Maggie Brien began to cry.

"Are you Mr. I. Ellison?" asked Mr. St. Clair.

"Yes, I am," said the man, angrily.

Mr. St. Clair explained his mistake, and gave up the horse and cart to Mr. I. Ellison. He then took Maggie's carpet-bag and heavy bundle, and walked all the way to Aunt Debby's.

By the time they reached Aunt Debby's it was nearly dark, and as for Moses, he was already travelling home in his father's cart. It happened in this way. Aunt Debby heard that Mr. St. Clair had been seen driving off, and knew he must have taken the wrong horse and cart, for Mr. Stimpcett's was still standing near the mill. Therefore, as Moses had already waited until after supper, she let him take his father's horse and cart and drive home behind a man with an ox team who was going by a roundabout way to Gilead.

Now as soon as Moses had driven off, Aunt Debby locked her doors and went to an evening meeting, so that when Mr. St. Clair came there on foot, with Maggy Brien and her bag and bundle, to find Moses, he found no one. He questioned some boys standing by a fence, and they told him that Moses had gone home in his father's cart, behind an ox team. Maggy Brien began to cry again. "Don't cry, dear," said Mr. St. Clair. "I'll hire a buggy."

He hired from the stable a buggy, a fast horse, and a driver, and away they started for Gilead, and reached Mr. Stimpcett's house at about half past eight o'clock in the evening. Moses had not arrived.

Mr. St. Clair found Mrs. Stimpcett, with her bonnet and shawl on, walking the floor, sobbing and sighing and wringing her hands. Grandma, also crying, was wrapping a bottle of the Sudden Remedy in a piece of newspaper.

"Oh, how *is* Moses?" cried Mrs. Stimpcett. "*Will* it have to be taken off?"

"Is not Moses here?" asked Mr. St. Clair, in a mild voice.

"Here!" cried Mrs. Stimpcett. "How can he be here, when he has broken his leg? I am going to him as soon as Mr. Stimpcett can borrow a horse."

Mr. St. Clair thought that Moses must have fallen from the cart on his way home; but before he had time to speak, Mrs. Odell came in.

"Where is my niece?" she cried. "Where is Evelyn?"

"Here she is," said Mr. St. Clair, presenting Maggie Brien.

"What do you mean?" shrieked Mrs. Odell. "That my niece? No! no! no! Oh, Evelyn! Evelyn! Evelyn! Dear child, where are you?"

Maggie Brien began to cry bitterly.

"Alas! what a wretch I am, to have made this mistake!" cried Mr. St. Clair. "But I'll find your Evelyn. I'll go for a horse. I'll take this child back. Don't cry, little girl. I won't rest till I find your Evelyn;" and he rushed from the house, almost knocking down several children in the passageway—the Stimpcett children; for Obadiah, Debby, and little Cordelia had been awakened by the noise, and had come down in their night-gowns.

But the lost Evelyn was near, and coming nearer every moment. You will remember that Maggie's mother, Mrs. Brien, was to send for Maggie to come and visit her. The man whom she sent went back and told her that he could not find Maggie, and that her grandmother was afraid she had been stolen from the station. Mrs. Brien hired a horse and wagon, and drove to the station, and inquired of the station-master. A stable-boy who stood near told her he saw a little girl who looked like Maggie riding off

"'HERE SHE IS,' SAID MR. ST. CLAIR."

in a buggy with a man, and that the man hired the buggy to go to Gilead.

"The wretch!" cried Mrs. Brien; "to be stealing away my child! I will keep on to Gilead. I will follow him up."

"I wish you would let this little girl ride with you to Gilead," said the station-master. "She has been waiting a long time for some one to call and take her to Mr Stimpcett's, and Mr. Stimpcett will help you find your Maggie." He then brought out a slender, flaxen-haired little girl, and placed her in Mrs. Brien's wagon. This child was Evelyn Odell, and Mrs. Brien took her to Gilead.

It happened that they reached Mr. Stimpcett's just as Moses was driving into the yard with his father's horse and cart, and they three, Mrs. Brien, Moses, and Evelyn, went into the house together.

Scarcely had they entered before Mr. Stimpcett, and then Mr. St. Clair, arrived in haste, each with a horse and wagon. Mr. Stimpcett rushed in to get his wife, and Mr. St. Clair to get Maggie. There they found Mrs. Stimpcett with her arms around Moses, Mrs. Odell with hers around

"Fairy, paint me a picture, here on the smooth surface of the toad-stool, for I have never seen one."

Tintabel stopped his wailing to think how wretched was the elf who had never seen a picture.

"Ah! elf," he said, "I have neither pencil nor colors.

an answer quite as smart as his questions, and that was just what he liked.

One day a soldier came to him with a dispatch, and Suvoroff, seeing that he was quite a young, simple-looking fellow, thought it would be good fun to try his hand upon *him*.

"How many fish are there in the sea?" he asked.

"Just exactly as many as haven't been caught yet," answered the lad at once.

The General was rather taken aback, but he went on, nevertheless:

"If you were in a besieged town, without food, how would you supply yourself?"

"From the enemy."

"How far is it from here to the moon?"

"Two of your Excellency's forced marches."

Suvoroff smiled and looked pleased, for he was very proud of being able to move his men so quickly, and had won many a victory by it.

"Which of your officers do you like best?" was the next question.

"Captain Masloff."

Now this Captain Masloff happened to be a very handsome young fellow, while Suvoroff himself was frightfully ugly, so he thought he would catch the soldier in a trap by asking him, "What's the difference between your captain and myself?"

"Why," said the soldier, looking slyly at him, "my captain can't make me a corporal, but your Excellency has only to say the word."

The General burst into a loud laugh, and clapping him on the shoulder, said, "Well, then, I do say the word: you're a corporal from this day forth, and a right good one you'll make. If I can find another man as smart as you, I'll make him a sergeant."

Two or three months after this adventure, Suvoroff and his army were down on the Lower Danube, keeping watch over the Turks, in the middle of the hardest winter that had been known in that country for many a year. But of course, being Russians, they didn't mind *that* much, and Suvoroff went about in the snow and the frost as if he didn't know what cold was.

Well, one bitter night in the beginning of January, the old General was making the round of the camp, as usual, to see that his sentinels were all keeping good watch at the outposts, when suddenly he came upon a sentry who seemed to have got the coldest place of all, for he was right down upon the bank of the river, with the cold wind blowing through him as if it would cut him in two.

"Good-evening, brother," said the General, speaking as if he were only a common soldier too.

"Good-evening," answered the sentinel, pretending not to know him, although he had recognized the General's voice in a moment.

"Plenty of stars out to-night," went on Suvoroff, looking up at the frosty sky. "Can you tell me how many of them there are altogether?"

"Just wait a bit, and I'll count," said the soldier, quite coolly. And forthwith he began: "One, two, three, four, five, six," and so on, as if he were never going to leave off.

At first Suvoroff was rather amused at his smartness; but he soon found the game getting much too cold to be pleasant, for he was in his usual light dress, while the sentry at least had on a good thick frieze coat. Keener and keener blew the bitter night wind, till the poor old General felt as if he should never be warm again. For a while he bore up manfully, hoping the soldier would get tired and leave off; but when the man got up to a thousand, and was still counting away as if he meant to keep it up all night, Suvoroff could stand it no longer.

"What's your name, my fine fellow?" asked he, as well as his chattering teeth would let him.

"Vasili [Basil] Pushkin,"* answered the soldier, "private in the Seventh Foot."

"Very good," said the Marshal; "I won't forget you. Good-night."

The next morning Pushkin was sent for to the General's quarters; and Suvoroff, turning to his staff officers, said:

"Gentlemen, here's a man whom I tried to fool last night, but I met my match, and something more. I said I'd make any man a sergeant who was smart enough for that, and I must keep my word."

And he did so that very day.

THE SONG OF THE WREN.

BY MRS. MARGARET EYTINGE.

IN a certain wild but beautiful country place, far from this great city, stood a little white cottage all by itself, there being no other house for ten or twelve miles, over which, in summer-time, the wild rose vines clambered until they reached the very chimney, where, clinging to the red bricks, they flung out in merry triumph slender flower-laden branches like pennons on the breeze. Under the cottage eaves some swallows built their nests every spring, and to the garden came, as soon as the yellow and white honeysuckles and blue larkspurs and many-colored four-o'clocks bloomed, myriads of humming-birds, looking like rubies, and diamonds, and opals, and emeralds, and topazes, and sapphires, that had taken to themselves wings, and flown from all parts of the world to visit the living gems in this lovely spot. In the autumn, when the leaves, dressed in their gayest dress, were bidding farewell to the sunshine and the wind and each other, hundreds of robin-redbreasts—"God's birds"—hopped like little flames about the ground, and in a hollow tree near the cottage door a pretty red-brown wren and his mate had found shelter for a long time, and reared several broods. As for the saucy, chattering, busy, fearless sparrows, they had feather-lined nests wherever a sparrow's nest could be placed, and that is almost everywhere—on the pump, behind the wood-pile, in the barn, among the trees—and these nests they never forsook all the year round. What wonder that the cottage was called Bird House, and the dear wee girl whose home it was answered to the name of Birdie? No brothers or sisters had the innocent, blue-eyed child, and, save the birds, no little friends. But they loved her dearly, and were always near her; so she never grew lonely, but was happy and contented from morning until night. At early dawn, when a soft light in the eastern sky told that the sun was coming, they tapped on her window-panes to waken her; and when she appeared at the cottage door, they flew to meet her, lighting on her fair head, her shoulders, her outstretched hands, with loud, sweet, twittering welcomes. Even strange birds just passing that way would join the merry throng, and joyfully and gratefully partake of the crumbs the dear one scattered for her friends. And often at night, when Birdie awoke from a pleasant dream, and found her room filled with the silver of the moon, she would hear the sparrows and swallows say—still dreaming they—"Birdie, sweet Birdie!"

She had learned their language when she was but a babe, and knew when they were glad or sad; when they praised or scolded; when they gave warning that the spirits of the storm were abroad; when they said to their young, "Courage, little ones; it is time to try your wings"; when they softly chirped, "To sleep, to sleep"; and when they sang songs of love or farewell.

And so it happened that she understood every word of the song that the wren sang to her that winter afternoon. The snow had been falling, and the sunshine was just

* All purely Russian names end either in "off" or "in," the "ski's" being all Polish, and the "ko's" all Cossack.

BIRDIE AND HER LITTLE FRIENDS.

coming back, when she went out in the garden, in her Little Red Riding-hood cloak, to share her bread with the sparrows and snow-birds. Around her they flew, uttering cries of joy, when suddenly the wren, forgetting his rhymes, appeared among them; and this is the song he sang:

"In the time of violets,
When the Spring came dancing
O'er the meadow, through the wood,
Sunbeams round her glancing—
'Birdie's sweet, sweet, sweet,
Sweet,' sang the swallow,
'And where'er her footsteps roam,
I will follow, follow.'

"When the roses blossomed and blushed,
And the fragrant Summer
Kisses warm and sparkling smiles
Gave to each new-comer—
'Birdie's sweet, sweet, sweet,'
Sang the blackbird clearly;
'Sweet as daisy-buds, and I
Love her dearly, dearly.'

"When the autumn leaves began
Gold and crimson turning,
Robin-Redbreast sang—his breast
Bright as sunset burning—
'Birdie's sweet, sweet, sweet,
Sweet as dewy clover,
And her praises shall be sung
All the wide world over.'

"Wrens and sparrows—all the birds,
Dear, that fly above thee,
For thy gentle words and ways,
For thy beauty, love thee.
Birdie sweet, sweet, sweet—
Happy be forever!
While the birds can guard thee, sweet,
Harm shall reach thee never."

"Thank you, dear wren—thank you, dear birds," said Birdie, with tears in her beautiful blue eyes, when the song was ended; and she went away to her own little room and said a prayer of thankfulness.

And from that time the child's heart was lighter than ever, and she sang all day long like a tuneful mocking-bird, blending all the sweet strains of her friends in one delightful song, until winter passed away, and the snow melted, and the snow-drop peeped out of the ground, and said, timidly, "I am here: spare me, O Wind!" and while the spring covered the earth with daisies and dandelions and May buds and brave honest grass, and flung delicate blossoms all over the orchards. Then came the summer once more, and started millions of lovely "green things a-growing," and filled the trees with thousands of joyous young birds.

And one glowing July day, early in the morning, Birdie wandered off to the woods, as she had often done before, to look for wild flowers, and gather some green food for her feathered pets. "I'll be back again in a little while, mamma," she said, as she left the cottage. But the hours went by, and noon came, and she had not returned.

"Where is my little maid?" called her father, cheerily, as he came in to dinner from the field where he had been working; but no little maid replied.

"She has gone for bird weeds and flowers," said her mother. "She will be here in a few moments."

But the dinner was eaten, and the father went back to his work, and still no Birdie came.

The clock struck one—struck two—struck three, and then, her heart growing heavier and heavier at every step, the frightened mother started out to look for her darling. North, south, east, west, half a mile each way from the cottage, she ran, stopping every few minutes to call, "Birdie! Birdie!" but only the echoes answered her call. At last to the field where her husband was working she flew. "Leave the plough," she cried, wringing her hands, "and look for the child."

North, east, south, west, a mile each way from his home, went the father, shouting, "Birdie! Birdie, little maid!" and the echoes repeated, "Birdie! Birdie, little maid!" but no other sound he heard except the rustling of the leaves and the whir of insect wings. The sun was beginning to sink in the west when, tired and heart-sick, he came back again. "Perhaps she is there now," he thought, a ray of hope lighting up his face as he neared the garden gate; but a glance at his wife's tearful eyes as she came to meet him told him he had hoped in vain. "I'll saddle the horse and ride to the village," he said, "and every father there will join me in the search for my child. And we'll find her, never fear."

"God grant that you may—and alive!" sobbed the poor mother. "My darling! oh, my darling!"

At that moment a flock of birds came in sight—so large a flock that, wheeling around the head of the sorrowing mother, it almost shut out from her the light of day.

Round and round her the birds circled, uttering strange, eager sounds; then flew away a short distance, to return with louder calls than ever.

"They miss her," said the father, who was just about to mount his horse. "They have come to be fed."

"They have come to lead us to her," cried his wife, her whole face growing glad and bright. "Look at them! They are asking us to follow."

And the birds turned as she made a few steps forward, and flew slowly before her. To a narrow path up the nearest hill they led—so narrow that the horse had to be left behind, and the father, who in his impatience had ridden on in front, was obliged to dismount and follow on foot. Over the hill and across a bridge that spanned a wide stream they went, then up some steep rocks, and down, down into a tiny green valley, from which another flock of birds arose with welcoming cries; and there, in a little cave, imprisoned by a huge stone that had fallen from the rock above across its mouth, the trees and shrubs around her black with watching birds, sat Birdie, her little hands patiently folded in her lap, a smile on her pale lips, and faith shining from her heaven-blue eyes. And for once—her heart being full to overflowing with love for her wee daughter, and gratitude to the good God and them—the mother too understood the language of the birds as they sang,

"Birdie, sweet, sweet, sweet,
 Happy be forever!
While the birds can guard thee, sweet,
 Harm shall touch thee never."

WILD BOARS.

THE wild boar is one of the most dangerous of beasts. Although it belongs to the same great family as the lazy, good-natured pig that lies in utter contentment in the farmer's pen, it is an altogether different creature, and few animals are so difficult to hunt.

In appearance it has the same general characteristics as domestic swine, with the difference that it is larger, covered with coarser bristles, has fiery, glowing eyes, and is armed with two terrible tusks, sometimes ten inches long, with which it can inflict dangerous wounds.

Formerly wild boars roamed in great numbers through the forests of Great Britain, but for many years they have been extinct in that country. They are still found in some parts of France and Spain, and are very numerous in Germany and the wild jungles of India. They are also found in Poland, Southern Russia, and Africa. Du Chaillu, the African traveller, mentions encountering a hideous red-haired wild hog in the wondrous equatorial forests of the "dark continent." Notwithstanding its size it was tremendously savage, and very agile, jumping and running like a cat.

Wild hogs are gregarious, and are found in herds. They are fond of living near water, in which they like to roll and wallow; indeed, a bath appears almost indispensable to them, as they will sometimes travel miles to obtain it. Their food consists of roots, nuts, and all kinds of fruits and grains. In Egypt and India they do much injury to the vast tracts of sugar-cane, the thick growth affording them excellent hiding-places and shelter against attack.

It is said that wild hogs will not attack a man unless hunted or enraged; but as they are not only daring, but also very cautious and watchful, they suspect the least approach to be offensive, and proceed to defend themselves.

The sow guards her little ones with great care, and becomes wild with fury if they are touched. She will run with great speed if she hears them call, and few hunters have succeeded in capturing young specimens without first killing the parent. A man once riding through a forest in Germany came upon two little wild pigs which had strayed into the pathway. Delighted with his prize, he rolled the piggies in his horse-blanket, sprang to his saddle, and hastened on his road. But the smothered squealing of her babies reached the ears of the mother, and the man soon heard a loud grunting. On turning round he saw a furious sow, with gleaming eyes, coming after him at full speed. Being unarmed, he was compelled to fling the little pigs on the ground, and ride for his life.

The wolf, the lynx, and even the sly fox are terrible enemies of wild hogs, for with patience and cunning watchfulness they often succeed in making off with very young pigs, which form a most savory repast.

Wild-boar hunting has been held for ages as a royal sport, and in former times no banquet was considered perfect unless the table was graced by a boar's head. Kings and emperors rode to the hunt in those days with numerous followers and huntsmen, all armed with the cross-bow and boar-spear, in search of this royal game. At present wild-boar hunting is carried on to some extent in Germany; but in India it is a favorite sport, as the boar of that country is the largest and fiercest of any in the world, not fearing even the tiger, its savage companion of the jungles. Stories are told of dead boars and tigers being found together, each bearing the marks of a terrible and evenly balanced fight.

In India boars are hunted on horseback, the chief weapon used being a spear with a stout two-edged blade. A horse must be thoroughly trained to this sport, and must possess great fleetness of foot, as the boar is a very

A WILD BOAR AT BAY.

rapid runner. The time chosen for the hunt is at day-break, as the boar has probably been eating sugar-cane or other food all night, and is sleepy and heavy in the morning, and less capable of a long run. Savage and powerful dogs are used in the chase, which often prove serviceable in bringing the beast to bay. For dogs the boar has a most violent hatred, and will rush at them blindly often, with its superior strength and formidable tusks overpowering them, unless the hunter be near to use a spear or send a bullet through its heart.

In this country the hog was unknown originally in a natural condition, having been introduced by settlers from the Old World; and the wild boar in our Western and Southern States, and in Canada, is merely the domestic animal relapsed into a primitive state of wild ferocity.

TAKING—NOT STEALING.

BY HANNAH SHEPPARD.

"SO that's your game, is it, my lads? Guess I can help you a bit. I'll try, anyhow, if it's only for the love I bore your fathers before you. And you're fine fellows too; but you've got a wrong twist somewhere, or you'd never in the world do such a thing as that." And quickening his step at the close of his soliloquy, "Captain Dan," as he was called, came up behind two boys who were standing in front of the principal fruit and candy store of the busy town of Hamilton.

A large bag of pea-nuts, with many other things, was displayed outside under the window, and the old man's attention had been attracted by seeing the elder of the boys carelessly pick up a nut as he chatted with his companion, who soon followed his example. Evidently neither one had any thought of doing wrong as they stood eating the nuts and crushing the shells in their fingers.

They started as he laid a hand heavily upon the shoulder of each, but answered his greeting so cordially that it was easy to see they were warm friends. He stopped them, as, linking their arms in his, they began to turn him around, by saying: "Going toward home, are ye? Well, I don't mind if I do go a piece with you after a bit, if you'll go down to the shore first, for I want to take another look at that vessel I had a sight of a good hour ago, and see if I can find out where she hails from. There'll be a fine sunset, too, with the clouds piled like yon"—as he pointed seaward. "I 'most wonder you're not out in the *Firefly*. How is it, Dick?"—turning to the lad on his right hand.

"Why, you see, Captain Dan," replied the boy, slowly, as if bringing his thoughts back from a long distance, "Ethel wanted Maurice to row her over to the Island, though I don't think he knows much more about a boat than May."

"Did they take her with them?" asked the captain, eagerly.

"Yes," answered Dick; "and I'm sure mamma would not have let her go if she'd been at home. But she was out riding with papa, and May begged so hard that Ethel would take her in spite of all I could say."

"Oh, well, there's no great harm done that I know of," quoth Captain Dan, "though I'm free to confess that I don't think your cousin knows as much of boats as he does of his books. However, as you feel uneasy, we'll wait about the landing till they come, and they can climb the cliff with us if they like. Many's the time little 'May bird' has gone up it on my shoulder, little pet!" Then, as he noticed how intently Dick was watching, he added, "They'll surely be back before long, and it won't hurt us to talk here awhile, 'specially as I've a word to say to you, my hearties."

"That's all right," responded Dick, good-humoredly; "for you know Theo and I like nothing better than to have you spin us a yarn—eh, Theo?"

"Yes, indeed," chimed in Theodore Murray, giving a vigorous kick to a stone which lay in the captain's path.

By this time they had reached the shore, and after looking off toward the Island and seeing nothing of their boat, they all sat down on a rock, which seemed almost as though it might have been shaped for a seat, only that it was rather roughly finished.

"You really needn't look so anxious, my boy," said Captain Dan, turning to Dick, "for I don't think your party could possibly come to harm. Why, the water is as smooth as glass, and we can see them the moment they round the corner of the cove."

"If Ethel only wasn't so awfully polite," groaned Dick, "but would just take the oars herself, I'd not mind a bit, for she can row beautifully; but Maurice hasn't an idea how to manage a boat, though he's first rate on land. We're all ready for your yarn, though, captain, as soon as you've got your breath ready to begin to spin it."

Captain Dan smiled, half sadly. "It's no 'yarn' to-night, my lads. But, Dick, what would you call a man who took what didn't belong to him?"

"Why, a thief, of course," answered the boy, promptly.

"And what would you say if any one called your father's son a thief?" pursued the old man.

"Tell him he lied!" exclaimed Dick, quickly, springing to his feet, and confronting his questioner with flashing eyes. "What ever do you mean, sir, by such strange talk?"

"Sit down quietly again, and I'll tell you; for though I saw both you and Theo helping yourselves to what didn't belong to you this afternoon, yet I never could find it in my heart to call you thieves; for I suppose you would say it was only 'taking,' and not 'stealing.'"

"What do you mean?" asked Theodore, who had been listening in silence, but with a most puzzled face.

"Just this—that as I walked up the street I saw each of you take a nut or so from the bag which stands in front of Mr. Baker's store."

"Oh," said Dick, drawing a long breath of relief, "that was all, was it?"

"Why, that wasn't *stealing*, Captain Dan," broke in Theodore, eagerly.

"Oh, I beg your pardon," observed their friend, dryly. "I didn't know you'd paid for the nuts, or I'd not have mentioned the matter."

"Paid for them!" exclaimed both boys at once. "Of course we'd not paid for them; but then that's not stealing, you know, for we only each took one or two, and we were right there in open sight. It's a totally different thing."

"I beg leave to differ entirely from you," answered the captain, in his slow way. "But suppose there'd been a water-melon lying there on the step, would either of you have carried it off without paying for it, or eaten it there, either?"

"Of course not," said Dick, indignantly; but Theodore broke in, abruptly, as he sprang up, his cheeks glowing with shame:

"I never thought of it so before! Why, it's just dreadful, Dick; for Captain Dan is right—we were stealing, though we never meant it. Oh, what would my mother say?" he added, with a choke in his voice.

"I don't see it in that light at all," persisted Dick, sturdily; "it was only a pea-nut or so, and we didn't do it 'on the sly,' as we would if we'd been 'stealing,' as you say. Why, the very word makes me mad all over"—doubling up his fists as he paced up and down before them, now and then giving himself a shake like a great dog.

"Hold on a minute, my son," said the old man, gently, "and I think I can make it clearer. Suppose a basket of apples was standing in Smith's grocery store. On my way home I stop in to buy a pound of tea, and while it is being weighed out I pick up an apple to eat. You drop in next

d you take one while waiting.
is him for a pound of cheese, and

"Gently, laddie," said the captain; "remember we
must all have a learning: and no doubt you did as badly

THE FIRST VALENTINE.

"Ah, Jamie, don't you understand
The little heart that's in my hand?
The plain white heart with rosy band;
Can you not read the simple sign?
It is your first sweet Valentine.

"Come here and take it from me, dear;
It will not hurt, you need not fear;
You'll see, if you will come more near,
It only bears one little line,
'To Jamie! My first Valentine!'"

Then Cupid, laughing, said, "Ah me!
How calm this baby beau can be!
But wait awhile, and we shall see
What toys, with gold and jewels fine,
He'll send to some sweet Valentine.

Just leave your heart, Miss Leonore,
He'll take it soon, and long for more;
The little lad is only four.
Some day, a hero bold and fine,
He'll send full many a Valentine."

THE KING'S BABY

BY THE AUTHOR OF "THE CATSKILL FAIRIES."

THE baby was put to bed, as usual, in his wooden cradle, and his mother had rocked him to sleep, singing some national cradle song, like the mothers of all lands. He was a stout little fellow of five months old, with dimples in his brown cheeks, curly dark hair as soft as silk, and great black eyes, such as the children of Spain and Italy alone possess. When the baby was asleep, his parents busied themselves with their duties of the evening, and at an early hour also went to bed.

Their home was located in the province of Murcia, in Spain. The house was built of stone, half in ruins, and was surrounded by a poor little farm. Before going to bed the father had looked out of the door to see that all was safe for the night. Spain is a country where little rain falls, because armies long ago destroyed the forests covering mountain slopes, in time of war. Now the traveller sees these hills as bare rocks, with deserted towns on their sides, and the beds of rivers become heaps of dry stones for the majority of the year, parched with summer drought. In the city of Alicante two years sometimes pass without a drop of rain falling. The season of the year (1879) was very different. In the late summer and autumn fearful storms of thunder and lightning burst over several provinces usually so dusty and arid; persistent rains followed, until the channels of the rivers became filled with rushing torrents from the heights where springs have their source. The waters of the Guadalquivir rose five meters in a few days.

The baby's father looked out of the door on a valley flooded by one of these swollen rivers which had overflowed its banks, and felt safe, as his home was perched on a slope, and the village, with its church, convent, and steep streets of old houses, was between the farm and the stream. Then he had gone to rest, and sleep soon settled on the household. The night was dark, and no sound was to be heard except the drip of the rain or the rustling murmur of the distant river.

At two o'clock in the morning the church bell pealed wildly. "Quick! Danger is at hand, good people: save yourselves!" the bell seemed to say, and its vibrating note rang out on the awful darkness, chilling all hearts with sudden fear.

Stupid with sleep, the baby's father rose. Water was trickling along the floor of the chamber; outside was a deep sound of roaring waves, the crashing of trees, and the fall of buildings, mingled with the clang of the bell and the cries of human beings. Nothing could be more terrible. An embankment had given way, and the river, which already had spread over the lowlands, now deluged the village, sweeping away many houses, and surrounding the poor little farm, where the baby slumbered peacefully in his cradle. Already the cottage swayed and shook on its foundations. The mother awoke, and wept. She had no time to snatch the baby in her arms, for the father opened the door, and lifted the cradle near it. He returned for his wife; and just then a wave entered the door, and washed away the baby. It was not a moment too soon. There was a snapping, grinding sound, and the house fell apart and slid into the dark waters as if it had been a house of cards. The whole country was like a sea, and the church bell no longer rang, because the bell-ringer strove to save himself from being drowned.

The little waif, cast to the mercy of the wind and the flood, did not sink. God watched over it. The wooden cradle became a tiny boat; the baby waked up, stretched out his little hands, and cried; then, in the midst of frightful peril, fell asleep again, rocked by the motion of the stream.

At length the day broke, a cold gray mist seeming to blot out everything except the sheet of water, which was of a muddy and yellow color, and rolled along with giddy swiftness, gathering everything in its course. In some places the trees had their roots under water, and their branches, still dry, gave shelter to whole families. These cried out:

"Oh, look at the little baby! Who will save it?"

But the cradle sailed on, while the trees often bent beneath the wave. The boiling eddies of the current swallowed many objects, and caught the cradle, and spun it about in circles as if it had been a walnut shell, until the baby cried with fear; but then a friendly wave was sure to rescue it, and once more bear it onward.

Ah, at last! The poor baby must be drowned. A great tree had fallen into the river, with all its tangled roots high in the air, and the stream snapped off the smaller twigs and branches as it moved along. Every moment it struck some floating object with its gnarled roots and forest of branches; occasionally the shock was so great that the trunk rolled from side to side; but the object always sank, whether broken boat or dead animal, while the tree floated on. The baby's cradle was alone on the waste of waters; the tree approached slowly and surely. The cradle tossed up and down, and then—the forked branches caught and held it firmly just above the water-line. The tree became a raft.

The young King Alfonso of Spain stood on the shore, near a town, surrounded by officers in brilliant uniforms. Large boats full of his guards had ventured out from shore to try to save objects swept down from the country. They saw a tree with a cradle caught in the branches. Was the cradle empty? No, a little black head could be distinguished inside. Bravely the boat approached; the tree swerved about, and struck it so rudely that it nearly upset; but at that moment the soldier in the bow leaned over, and caught the baby by his little gown. Away whirled the tree on the swift tide, and the cradle, detached by the shock, drifted apart, overturned.

How the people ran about and talked! How the women cried, and caressed the little stranger thus safely brought to shore! The King saw it all, and approached.

"He shall be my child, and I will adopt him," he said.

"May he grow up to serve you, sire!" said one of the councillors, who wore a glittering star on his breast.

Then the "King's Baby," saved in a little wooden cradle from the perils of the night, crowed and smiled.

"ME AND MY LITTLE WIFE."

GEORGE WASHINGTON.

He was black as the ace of spades, you see,
And scarcely as high as a tall man's knee;
He wore a hat that was minus a brim,
But that, of course, mattered nothing to him;
His jacket—or what there was left of it—
Seemed his little black shoulders to fit;
And as for stockings and shoes, dear me!
Nothing about such things knew he.

He sat on the curb-stone one pleasant day,
Placidly passing the hours away;
His hands in the *holes* which for pockets were meant,
His thoughts on the clouds overhead were intent;
When down the street suddenly, marching along,
Came soldiers and horses, and such a great throng
Of boys and of men, as they crowded the street,
With a "Hip, hip, hurrah!" the lad sprang to his feet,

And joined the procession, his face in a grin,
For here was a good time that "dis chile is in!"
How he stretched out his legs to the beat of the drum,
Thinking surely at last 'twas the *jubilee* come!
Then suddenly wondering what 'twas about—
The soldiers, the music, and all—with a shout
He hailed a small comrade, "Hi, Cæsar, you know
What all dis percession's a marchin' for so?"

"Go 'long, you George Washington," Cæsar replied,
"In dis yere great kentry you ain't got no pride!
Dis is Washington's Birfday; you oughter know dat,
Wid yer head growed so big, burst de brim off yer hat."
For a moment George Washington stood in surprise,
While plainer to view grew the whites of his eyes;
Then swift to the front of the ranks scampered he,
This mite of a chap hardly high as your knee.

The soldiers looked stern, and an officer said,
As he rapped with his sword on the black woolly head,
"Come, boy, clear the road; what a figure you are!"
Came the ready reply, "*For George Washington, sah!*
But I didn't know nuffin about my birfday
'Till a feller jist tole me. Oh, golly! it's gay!"

Just then a policeman—of course it was mean—
Removed young George Washington far from the scene.

[illegible]

Yes, you have found them first. It is very remarkable to find them at all in January in the locality where you live, but as the buds set in the autumn, the singularly mild weather of January has made them swell and burst thus early in the season. Thank you for so promptly reporting these first signs that spring is near. Now let us see when the "pussies" will appear in other sections of the country.

[illegible]

Maggie M. M. has a big Newfoundland dog, just her own age, nine years, which is her faithful friend.

Belle Metzger, Jessie Edna, C. F. Cooper, Harry B., and Charles Bentley all send pretty accounts of domestic pets, which we would be glad to print if there was space to spare.

EVA MITCHELL.—*The Virginians in Texas* is published in "Harper's Library of American Fiction," and will be sent by mail, postage prepaid, to any part of the United States on receipt of seventy-five cents.

L. K.—Chapman's Drawing-Books are the best to use in beginning your studies.

[illegible]

You can feed guinea-pigs on cabbage leaves, bits of bread and cake, and all kinds of fruit. They like carrot tops better than any other food, especially in the spring, when the green is fresh and tender. You must give them plenty of water.

N. L. COLLAMER.—Your monthly magazine is very well edited. It is difficult to determine the correct spelling of Shakespeare's name, as equally reliable authorities disagree.

"LITTLE MARIE."—Your puzzle is very neatly done; but as "every large city" is not so favored as the one where you live, we fear it would not be easy to solve.

ELLA W.—You may send the one entirely original, and if it is pretty and very short, we might use it.

RICHARD S. C.—Your plan for a magnetic motor is very ingenious, and the machine would no doubt make a pretty and curious toy.

WILLIE H. S.—We will endeavor to send you the solution of your puzzle.

Eddie L. A., Minnesota, after expressing great pleasure in YOUNG PEOPLE, writes: "My papa thinks I am a pretty smart boy. I am eleven years old, and I milk the cow, and do most of the work, and go to school besides." You are a smart boy, Eddie, if you do all that, and do it well. If you persevere in that course, always attending to school duties and home work besides, there is every prospect that you will grow to be a smart man.

[illegible]

Ferdinand Wrangell, a Russian baron and traveller, who was born near the close of the last century, and died in 1870, commanded a sledge expedition which explored the polar sea north of East Siberia about 1821. In 1867 Captain Long, in traversing that part of the sea navigated by Wrangell, discovered a large tract of land which the Russian explorer had vainly endeavored to reach, and which he named Wrangell Land.

HARRY W. E.—Every harpoon thrown into a whale before he dies is entitled to a share of the oil.

W. S. ATKIN.—The sun is supposed to be moving slowly through space, carrying the earth and all the planets along with him. The great astronomer Herschel assigned the constellation Hercules as that toward which we are moving, and the calculations of more recent astronomers have also pointed to that same direction.

ANITA E. N.—The "good news" mentioned in the ballad is not recorded in history, and although many inquiries have been made concerning it, no satisfactory conclusion has yet been arrived at.

G. FUNNELL.—The oldest inhabited building in the territory of the United States is an ancient house built of adobes, or sun-dried brick, in the city of Santa Fé, New Mexico. Before the annexation of New Mexico, St. Augustine, Florida, which was settled in 1565, was the oldest town, and contained the most ancient buildings.

[illegible]

[illegible]

We acknowledge only those answers to puzzles which are mailed previous to date of publication of solutions.

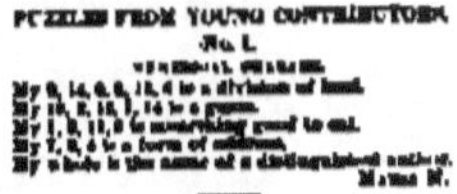

PUZZLES FROM YOUNG CONTRIBUTORS.

No. 1.

[illegible]

My whole is the name of a distinguished author.

No. 2.

WORD SQUARE.

[illegible]

No. 3.

ENIGMA.

[illegible]

No. 4.

[illegible]

No. 5.

[illegible]

Old Books for Young Readers.

Arabian Nights' Entertainments.

The Thousand and One Nights; or, The Arabian Nights' Entertainments. Translated and Arranged for Family Reading, with Explanatory Notes, by E. W. LANE. 600 Illustrations by Harvey. 2 vols., 12mo, Cloth, $3 50.

Robinson Crusoe.

The Life and Surprising Adventures of Robinson Crusoe, of York, Mariner. By DANIEL DEFOE. With a Biographical Account of Defoe. Illustrated by Adams. Complete Edition. 12mo, Cloth, $1 50.

The Swiss Family Robinson.

The Swiss Family Robinson; or, Adventures of a Father and Mother and Four Sons on a Desert Island. Illustrated. 2 vols., 18mo, Cloth, $1 50.

The Swiss Family Robinson.—Continued; being a Sequel to the Foregoing. 2 vols., 18mo, Cloth, $1 50.

Sandford and Merton.

The History of Sandford and Merton. By THOMAS DAY. 18mo, Half Bound, 75 cents.

Published by HARPER & BROTHERS, New York.

☞ Sent by mail, postage prepaid, to any part of the United States, on receipt of the price.

BOOKS FOR YOUNG MEN.

Character.

Character. By SAMUEL SMILES. 12mo, Cloth, $1 00.

It is, in design and execution, more like his "Self-Help" than any of his other works. Mr. Smiles always writes pleasantly, but he writes best when he is telling anecdotes and using them to enforce a moral that he is too wise to preach about, although he is not afraid to state it plainly. By means of it "Self-Help," at once became a standard book, and "Character" is, in the way, quite as good as "Self-Help." It is a wonderful storehouse of anecdotes and biographical illustrations.—Examiner, London.

Self-Help.

Self-Help; with Illustrations of Character, Conduct, and Perseverance. By SAMUEL SMILES. New Edition, Revised and Enlarged. 12mo, Cloth, $1 00.

The writings of Samuel Smiles are a valuable aid in the education of boys. His style seems to have been constructed entirely for their tastes; his topics are admirably selected, and his mode of communicating excellent lessons of enterprise, truth, and industry [illegible] and [illegible] if these words did not convey an idea which is only applicable to lessons of an opposite character and tendency taught in the more attractive style. The popularity of this book, "Self-Help," should [illegible] a powerful instrument of good, and many an English boy has risen from its perusal determined that his life will be moulded after that of some of those set before him in this volume. It was written for the youth of another country, but the wealth of instruction has been [illegible] by its translation into more than one European language, and it is not too much to predict for it a popularity among American boys.—N. Y. World.

Thrift.

Thrift. By SAMUEL SMILES. 12mo, Cloth, $1 00.

The mechanic, farmer, workingman, clerk, merchant, and a large circle of readers outside of these classes will find in the volume a wide range of counsel and advice, presented in perspicuous language, and marked throughout by vigorous good sense; and while, while deriving from it useful lessons for the guidance of their personal affairs, will also be imbibing valuable instruction in an important branch of political economy. We wish it could be placed in the hands of all our youth—especially those who expect to be merchants, artisans, or farmers.—Christian Intelligencer, N. Y.

In this useful and sensible work, which should be in the hands of all classes of readers, especially of those whose means are slender, the author does for private economy what Smith and Ricardo and [illegible] have done for national economy. * * * The one step which separates civilization from savagery—which renders civilization possible—is labor done in excess of immediate necessity. * * * To inculcate this most important and most homely of all virtues, we have met with no better teacher than this book.—N. Y. World.

Published by HARPER & BROTHERS, New York.

☞ Sent by mail, postage prepaid, to any part of the United States, on receipt of the price.

MRS. MORTIMER'S BOOKS FOR THE NURSERY.

Lines Left Out.

Lines Left Out; or, Some of the Histories Left Out in "Line upon Line." The First Part relates Events in the Times of the Patriarchs and the Judges. Illustrated. By Mrs. ELIZABETH MORTIMER. 16mo, Cloth, 75 cents.

This volume is an attractive juvenile book, handsomely brought out, rendering Scripture incidents into pleasant paraphrases.—Northwestern Christian Advocate, Chicago.

More about Jesus.

More about Jesus. Illustrations and a Map. By Mrs. ELIZABETH MORTIMER. 16mo, Cloth, 75 cents.

It consists of a series of stories, embracing the whole of the events in the life of our Blessed Lord, told in a plain, simple style, suited to the capacities of children of seven or eight years of age. But better still, all good children's books are good for adults; and this will be found equally useful to put into the hands of very ignorant grown-up people, who may learn this leave the story of man's redemption in an intelligent manner. Many of the lessons are illustrated with pictures of the places mentioned.

Streaks of Light.

Streaks of Light; or, Fifty-two Facts from the Bible for Fifty-two Sundays of the Year. Illustrated. By Mrs. ELIZABETH MORTIMER. 16mo, Cloth, 75 cents.

"This little work," says the author, "has received the distinguished honor of being appointed to be one of the class-books of the famous Cotteglians, and has been made to subserve the highest of all purposes—the preaching of the Gospel. To that purpose it is adapted when the lessons are thoroughly, intelligently, and appealingly taught. Each lesson can be understood by those who have no previous knowledge, and each is calculated to be the first address to one who has never before heard of God or his Christ."

Reading without Tears.

Reading without Tears; or, A Pleasant Mode of Learning to Read. Illustrated. Small 4to, Cloth. By Mrs. ELIZABETH MORTIMER. Two Parts. Part I., 75 cents; Part II., 75 cents; complete in One Volume, $1 25.

An easy, simple, and pleasant book for the tiny scholars of the nursery classes. It contains a picture for every word of spelling capable of pictorial explanation. The reading lessons have been carefully selected, being composed of the preceding spelling lessons, by which means, together with the picture meanings, the words are easily impressed on the memory of a very young child.—Athenæum, London.

Published by HARPER & BROTHERS, New York.

☞ HARPER & BROTHERS will send any of the above works by mail, postage prepaid, to any part of the United States, on receipt of the price.

TOO FAT AND TOO THIN.

A fat cat sat
On the parlor mat,
When through the room came whirring,
Right up to where the cat was purring,
A strange and ill-conditioned rat,
As though to tempt the pussy fat.
But, "No," said Puss, "this is too thin;
Such dodges may take Skye-terriers in.
I've had too many first-class meals
To try to eat a rat on wheels."

The Ribbon Dance.—Children's balls are now in great vogue in France. The latest novelty for them is the ribbon dance. Eight ribbons of different colors are attached to a ring in the ceiling. Four girls and four boys hold the ends of the ribbons. The orchestra strikes up, and the eight children dance a measure which enables them to plait the ribbons. The orchestra then starts another measure, the children another step, and the plait is unplaited. Each of the dancers may be dressed according to the color of the ribbon that he or she holds, and the mingling of the colors will be all the more brilliant. The idea might easily be taken for a cotillion figure.

A CAUSE FOR WORRIMENT.

Ada, on the morning of her birthday party, looking at the clock and feeling her pulse. "Oh dear! I wonder if I will be well enough for the party to-night!"

Search, if you like, the wide world over,
Barnum's the very best fellow that's known;
Now that we young ones are left here in clover,
Here's for a jolly good show of our own.

BROKEN RHYMES.

(Behead the word that completes the first line, and you have the word necessary to complete the second. This in turn beheaded gives the word that will complete the third line.)

"BEWARE the ice!" I heard him ——,
"Which is not safe unless 'tis ——;
Take my advice, for I am ——,
And do not venture here."
"But, oh! we want so much to ——.
He's like the dog," said saucy ——,
"Who could not eat what others ——,
Yet barked when they came near."

"But do not go so near the ——;
'Tis safer far within the ——;
The water here's so dark so ——;
To go would be a sin."
They heeded not, and in a ——,
Like little birds that feed on ——,
The merry girls flew o'er the ——;
And now, alas! they're in.

But when he heard the dreadful ——,
And saw the drowning maidens ——,
He hurried with his stick of ——
Along the slippery ground.
And others came, and with a ——
They crept around the dangerous ——,
And lifted dripping o'er the ——
The maids so nearly drowned.

SHADOWS OF GREAT MEN.

WHO can turn this old woman into the Duke of Wellington, and the rough-looking man with a broken nose into Napoleon III.? You will not need any fairy wand nor magic sentence to do it; just trace the heads upon a piece of thick paper, and cut them out carefully with a pair of sharp scissors; then place them so that their shadows may fall clearly upon a sheet of paper, and the change is complete. You can make many different surprises of the same kind by drawing other heads yourselves.

Vol. I.—No. 17. | Tuesday, February 24, 1880. | Published by HARPER & BROTHERS, New York. | Price Four Cents. | $1.50 per Year, in Advance.

COLD MORNING IN A COUNTRY SCHOOL.

TRACKING A BURIED RIVER.

THE ADVENTURE OF TWO SAILOR BOYS.

"THE sum of 2000 francs ($400) will be paid by the Scientific Association of Morlaix to any one who shall succeed in tracing the course of the Larve, and ascertaining whether it has any under-ground communication with the sea. FÉLIX DELAMOTTE, President."

Such was the announcement which, posted in the quaint three-cornered market-place of the old French town of Longchamp, attracted a good many readers, and among the rest two lads in sailor costume, one of whom remarked to the other:

"What a holiday we'd have if we could earn it! eh, Pierre, my boy?"

"I should think so! But nobody will earn *that* reward very soon. Don't you remember how, a *year* ago, they widened the cleft into which the stream falls, and let down a man with a lantern, and how, before he'd gone thirty feet, he got bumped against a rock, and broke his lantern, and hurt himself so badly that he had to be hauled up again?"

"True; it's not a very likely job. Well, come along, and let's get the boat out."

Pierre Lebon, the younger of the two, was a little, olive-cheeked, merry little fellow, whose slim figure and jaunty black curls contrasted markedly with the burly frame and thick sandy hair of his chum, Jacques Vaudry. The latter ought rightly to have been called Jack Fordrey, for he was an English boy, born in Guernsey; but having been adopted by a Breton fisherman after his father's death, both he and his name had got considerably "Frenchified."

The two boys had to manage by themselves the boat of which they were joint owners, for old Simon Lebon, Pierre's real and Jack's adopted father, was now too aged and rheumatic to help them in their work, except by advising them when to start and where to go. But his advice was always good, for in his time he had been one of the best fishermen on the coast, and the lads were usually very successful.

On this particular day, however, their good luck seemed to have forsaken them, for, try as they might, they could catch nothing worth mentioning. Possibly they were thinking too little of their work, and too much of the reward offered by the Scientific Association; for three thousand francs would have been quite a fortune to them both. Moreover, the idea of tracking an under-ground river had a spice of romance and adventure about it which was the very thing to tempt them.

The little stream of the Larve had long been the acknowledged puzzle of the whole neighborhood. After skirting the town for some distance, it vanished into the earth through a narrow cleft, and was seen no more. Where it went to after that, no one could tell; and, as we have seen, the first attempt to find out had succeeded so badly that nobody felt much inclined for a second.

Tired out at length, the unsuccessful fishers went home, inwardly resolving to try whether they might not have better fortune by night than by day. Pierre, indeed, when the night came, began to have some doubts about the wisdom of the idea, having heard his father say once and again that it was a very dangerous thing to attempt at that season. But the hardest thing in the world for a boy to do is to draw back from anything simply because it is dangerous. Rather than let Jack think him afraid, Pierre would have gone to sea on a hen-coop; so they stole out of the cottage as noiselessly as possible, and away they went over the dim grey waste of sea, half lighted by the rising moon.

The "take" of fish was a very good one this time, and the boys began to think their night voyage a lucky idea; but they were rejoicing too soon. A little after midnight the sky began to cloud over and the sea to rise in a way which showed that there was a storm brewing. They put about at once, and made for the shore, but long before they reached it the storm burst upon them in all its fury.

In an instant the boat was half full of water, and it was all they could do to keep her from foundering outright, as they flew through the great white roaring waves, thumped and banged about from side to side, and drenched to the skin at every plunge by the flying gusts of spray. Pierre grasped the tiller in his half-numbed hands, while Jack held on with all his might to the "sheet" that steadied their little three-cornered sail, at which the wind tugged as if meaning to tear it away altogether.

The little craft held her own gallantly, and the young sailors began to hope that, after all, they might make the entrance of the bay without accident. But just then an unlucky shift of the wind tore the sail clean away, and the boat, falling off at once, was swept helplessly toward the formidable cliffs beyond.

"Not much chance for us now," said Jack, shaking his head. "Pierre, my boy, I'm sorry I've brought you into this mess; it's all my fault."

"Not a bit, old fellow. I ought to have warned you of what I'd heard my father say. However, if the worst comes to the worst, we can swim for it."

However, there seemed to be little hope, for not a foot of standing-room was to be seen on the rocky sides of the vast black precipice upon which they were driving headlong. All at once Jack shouted:

"Port your helm, Pierre—port! We'll do it yet."

His keen eye had detected a cleft in the rock, just wide enough for the boat to enter.

Pierre had barely time to obey, when there came a tremendous crash, and the boys found themselves floundering amid a welter of foam, nets, sand, dead fish, and broken timbers, in a deep dark hollow that looked like the mouth of a cave.

"There goes father's boat," spluttered Pierre, as soon as he could clear his mouth of the salt-water.

"And there go our fish," added Jack. "Here's that loaf that we put in the locker, though; and even wet bread's better than none, in a place like this. Now, then, let's be getting higher up, for the tide will be upon us here in no time."

But to get higher up was no easy matter. They were in utter darkness, and (as they had already found by groping about) on the brink of a chasm of unknown depth. The ledge upon which they had been cast was evidently very narrow, and almost as slippery as ice; and Jack, being encumbered with the loaf, and Pierre badly bruised against the rocks, they were not in the best condition for climbing.

But the roar of the next wave as it came bursting in, splashing them *from* head to foot where they sat, was a wonderful quickener to their movements, and away they scrambled through the pitchy blackness, clinging like limpets to the rough side of the cavern as they felt their feet slide upon the treacherous rocks, and thought of the unseen gulf below.

Onward, onward still, deeper and deeper into the heart of the cold, silent rock, fearing at every moment to feel their way barred by a solid wall, and find themselves cut off from escape, and doomed to be drowned by inches. But, no; the strange tunnel went on and on as if it would never end, their only consolation being that they were unmistakably tending *upward*, and already (as they calculated) beyond the reach of the flood-tide.

Suddenly Jack uttered a shout of joy:

"Hurrah, Pierre! here's one of the lantern candles in my inner pocket, and I know I've got my matches somewhere. We'll be able to see where we are at last, my boy!"

The matches (luckily still dry) were produced, the candle was lighted, and our heroes took a survey of their surroundings.

They were in a long narrow passage, rising to a considerable height overhead, and with another ledge on its opposite side, steeper and more broken than the one on which they were. In the centre lay the chasm already mentioned; but instead of the frightful depth which they had imagined, it was only six or seven feet deep at the most, and more than half full of water.

"There's our terrible precipice," laughed Jack, stamping over it. "I don't think *that* would hurt us much. But—hollo! I say, Pierre, this isn't sea-brine; it's *fresh*-water, running water! It's a stream that's tunnelled its way through the rock; and if we follow it *far* enough, we'll get out. Hurrah!"

"Hurrah!" echoed Pierre, brightening up. "We shan't run short of water, anyhow; and as for food, we may as well have a bite of that loaf before starting again."

The under-ground breakfast was soon finished, and the adventurous lads started once more.

But the pain of Pierre's bruises, which he had manfully concealed hitherto, began to master him at last. His tired limbs began to drag more and more heavily; his feet slipped again and again, and only the strong hand of his comrade saved him from more than one serious fall.

"Better sit down and rest a bit, old fellow," said Jack, kindly; "there's no hurry, for this candle will burn a long while yet. I know you won't own it, but you *did* get a nasty bump against that rock yonder."

"I fancy you're right there," answered Pierre, sinking

wearily upon the ledge. "But we don't need the candle while we're sitting still, you know. Blow it out, and light it again when we start."

Jack did so, and they sat silent in the darkness. All at once Pierre heard his comrade call out,

"I say, don't you hear water falling somewhere?"

"To be sure I do," replied Pierre, after listening a moment. "We must be close to the place where this stream falls down into the tunnel, and now we'll have a chance of getting out at last. Bravo!"

Jack slapped his hands together, with a shout that made the cavern echo.

"I've got an idea, Pierre, my boy! What a fool I was not to think of it before! This stream that we've been following is the Larve, and we've got to the very place where it falls through the cleft. Now if we can only get out with whole bones, it's fifteen hundred francs apiece to us. Come along, quick!"

All Pierre's weariness was gone in a minute. Already, in his mind's eye, he saw his ailing father comfortably provided for, and Jack and himself standing out to sea in a brand-new boat. The instant the candle was lighted they were off again at a pace which would have seemed impossible a few minutes before.

Guided by the increasing din of the water-fall, they were not long in reaching a huge perpendicular funnel or chimney in the rock, down one side of which poured a stream of water, while through a cleft above, dazzlingly radiant after the darkness of the buried passage, came a bright gleam of *sunshine*. Just then a big stone, flung from above, came thundering down into the chasm, falling close to the feet of the two explorers.

"That's the boys at their fun," said Jack, laughing. "I've done it many a time myself. Above there—boy!"

The only answer was a howl of terror and the sound of flying feet. Pierre, alarmed at the thought of being deserted, shouted in his turn,

"Help, comrades! help!"

"Who's that calling?" asked a gruff voice from above, while the light was obscured by a broad visage peering down into the hole.

"Hollo, Gaspard! is that you?" cried Pierre, recognizing the voice of one of his father's fisher cronies.

"What, Pierre Lebon! you down there? Well, who ever saw the like! Just wait a minute, while I run for a rope."

But before he could return there were already more than a hundred people gathered around the hole, for the news of a human voice having been heard out of the "Larve Chimney," as the chasm was called, had spread far and wide.

The water-fall on one side and the sharp rocks on the other made it no easy matter to draw the boys up safely. But at length they were dragged forth into the daylight, to be embraced and shouted over by the whole town, and to receive, a few days later, the praises of the entire Scientific Association, together with the three thousand francs which they had so bravely earned.

BIDDY O'DOLAN.

BY MRS. ZADEL B. GUSTAFSON.

CHAPTER I.

DO you remember Biddy O'Dolan, the little rag-picker and ash girl who found Lily De Koven's broken doll in the ash-can that cold winter's morning? I have not forgotten my promise to tell you the rest about her.

Biddy had a boy-friend, a little Irish boy, who called himself "Chairlie-Shaugy." I suspect his name was Charley O'Shaughnessy. He was just as poor and alone in the world as Biddy, and almost always staid in the same cellar at night.

When Biddy ran off with her doll that cold morning, she not only thought of the hospital and the little girl who had there brought her the flowers, but she thought how she would tell Charley that night about her doll.

The first thing to be done was to get Dolly a dress, and this was the way Biddy managed it. She took an old knife and hacked out a piece of her skirt, then she pulled out of her dingy pocket a little wad. A wad of what? Pins. Pins that she had picked up on the street in the summer, when she swept the street crossings, and had stuck thick and "criss-cross" in a bit of woollen rag. With some of these pins Biddy fastened together the two sides of the cut in her skirt. Next she took the piece of cloth she had cut out, and punched her tough little forefinger through it in two places, and through one of these holes pushed the whole arm and through the other the broken arm of her doll, and pinned the cloth together in the back.

Thus Dolly was dressed, and nearly as well as Biddy, too. Biddy had been very quick about this, and had often looked over her shoulders to see who came in and out of the cellar.

You who do not live in a cellar, and do not get shoved about and slapped as Biddy did, can hardly imagine how glad she was that no one happened to take notice of her.

She hid Dolly under the straw where she was to sleep at night, and then hurried out to pick over as many more ash cans and barrels as she could, in hopes of finding something this time which would please Mrs. Brown, so that she could dare to show her doll, and perhaps be allowed to sit up and play with it a little.

Mrs. Brown was the cross old woman who kept the cellar, and the children on the street called her "Grumpy."

Biddy did not find anything in particular, and got fewer pennies than usual for errands and for showing people the way to places, so that old Mrs. Brown was very cross indeed, and Biddy went to bed without daring to pull Dolly out where she could see her. She lay awake, with her hand on it, waiting for Charley.

Charley was a newsboy, but he was not a lucky little boy. He had the large and beautiful deep blue eyes you may often see in the children of Irish immigrants. But he was weak in body, and very shy. He lived as Biddy did, among rough people, who were all the more rough because they were so poor and miserable. So he got knocked about a great deal, and stood no chance at all among other newsboys, who shoved him aside, and called their papers so loud that Charley's thin voice could not be heard. Some newsboys make money selling papers—make so much that they can start in other kinds of business for themselves, and get on very well in the world among other successful men. I have seen this kind of newsboy. They have bright, sharp, old-looking faces. They have wiry, strong bodies, good health, and seem to be afraid of nothing.

Charley wasn't this sort of boy at all. He got poked, and pushed, and cuffed, and tripped up, and laughed at. The girls called him "fraid-cat," because they thought he was a coward. The boys said he was just like a girl, and shouted, "Hallo, Polly!" when they saw him. Charley did not say much to all this. He went with his papers every day, and managed to sell a few; and, besides, he did errands quickly and well. In these ways he earned enough to pay for his straw in Mrs. Brown's cellar, and to buy enough to eat to keep life in him.

Charley's straw was next to Biddy's straw, and when he came in that night Biddy whispered to him all about her doll, telling him especially how one of its arms was broken off at the elbow. Charley put out his hand in the dark, and asked her to let him take the doll a moment. He felt it over carefully, and gave it back without saying anything. Biddy whispered a little more, and then they went to sleep.

One day Biddy happened to come in a little after noon. She was going right out again; but first she stooped, and felt under her straw—the doll was gone! Biddy sat down, quite faint for a moment; then she sprang to her feet, darted up the cellar steps, and around the corner where old Mrs. Brown sat behind her apple and candy stand. Biddy reached over and put both hands in the knot of gray hair in the old woman's neck, pulling as if she would carry her off, stand and all.

Biddy's face was pale, and her eyes were like white-hot coals, as she gasped out:

"Give it me! Give it me! I'll never leave go till ye give it me!"

"Howld on, an' lave go av me!" cried the old woman. She grasped Biddy's wrists, and drew them toward her to ease the strain on her hair; but Biddy's little fingers were strong. She tugged hard, and kept on gasping.

"I'll never, never leave go till ye give it me. Oh!"

Never had such an "Oh!" come from Biddy's lips before, and with the very sound of it she had torn herself away from Mrs. Brown, and had seized and almost knocked over little Charley, who had vainly been making signs at her as he came up behind Mrs. Brown.

MENDING THE DOLL.

Mrs. Brown rubbed her neck, smoothed down her apron, and jabbering fiercely, came panting up to the children. Biddy had let go of Charley, and was sitting right down on the cold pavement holding her doll, and looking with wild delight and wonder at its wooden arm, new from the elbow. Charley knew an old man who used to whittle out all sorts of things with his jackknife, and who seemed as ready to give away as to sell his work. Charley had taken Biddy's doll to this man, who had willingly and quite skillfully mended it. He was on his way back to get it hid under Biddy's straw for a surprise for her, when he found Biddy struggling with Mrs. Brown. Charley's plan was perfect. The trouble was that he couldn't plan for Biddy too, and she had spoiled everything without knowing it.

"How ever *could* ye git a new arm?" said Biddy. "It's a miracle."

"Sorra a bit wid yer mary-cles?" exclaimed old Mrs. Brown, snatching the doll, holding it high out of reach, and spreading out her other hand to keep Biddy off.

But Biddy did not spring at her this time. She stood up, and put her hands together, and twisted them till the knuckles were white, and she spoke as if there were cotton in her throat when she begged the old woman to give her the doll. She promised never to be a bad girl any more; to give every cent she could get to Mrs. Brown—every one; to do everything Mrs. Brown asked her to do; and she called her over and over again "*good* lady," and "*dear* lady."

Mrs. Brown kept on talking too fast to be understood. She was very angry, and slapped Biddy's cheeks, and pushed her toward the cellar. Biddy stumbled along as she was pushed, and kept on praying for her doll, and making every promise she could think of to the old woman. When they reached the cellar steps, Charley pulled Mrs. Brown's dress, showed her a bright new quarter dollar, and said she might have it if she would give up the doll to Biddy.

Mrs. Brown took the quarter, looked at it, rang it on the step, and then handed the doll to Biddy, telling her that she might have it that night, but that she must pay extra every day for what she called the "crayther's board an' lodgin'."

This idea seemed to please Mrs. Brown very much, for she called it a great joke, and put her hands on her hips and laughed. Then she looked savage again, and said she would keep the doll herself on nights when Biddy could not pay extra. She went off to her fruit stand, with her hands on her hips, laughing and muttering by turns. Biddy sat down with her doll. Now and then she looked at Charley and smiled, and seemed to be thinking very hard about something.

[TO BE CONTINUED.]

NEW YORK PRISONS IN 1776-77.

THOSE who tread the floor of what was recently the Post-office, once the great Middle Dutch Church, and now a Brokers' Exchange, at the corner of Nassau Street and Cedar, can scarcely believe that it was once a military prison, that its walls re-echoed the groans and cries of sick and dying patriots, that a large part of Washington's army was once confined on the very spot where now the broker is selling his stocks and the photographer fitting his lenses. The fine church in 1776 was converted at once into a royal prison. Its pews were torn out, its interior defaced, but the walls are the same that shut in the unfortunate Americans, and their only shelter was the lofty roof that still rises among the haunts of trade. The ancient building is one of the most touching of the historical remains of the early city. The number of persons shut up at once within its precincts is variously estimated; one account gives 800, another 3000, as the probable limit. It is certain that they were crowded in with no care for comfort, no regard for health or ease; that one aim of the royal captors was to "break their spirit" by ill usage, and win them back to their loyalty by no gentle means.

As the motley train of prisoners came down to the city after the capture of Fort Washington, they were met by the royal officers with every mark of contempt and hate. They were stripped of their arms and uniforms, robbed of their money, insulted with rude taunts and even blows. War had not yet been robbed of some of its brutality by the slow rise of knowledge, and the British officers had not yet learned the politeness of freemen. A savage Hessian made his way up to Graydon, the young American officer, and threatened to kill him. "Young man," said to him a Scotch officer of more humanity, "you should never rebel against your king." The prisoners were taken before the British provost-marshal to be examined. "What is your rank?" said the officer to a sturdy little fellow from Connecticut, ragged and dirty, who seemed scarcely twenty. "I am a *heppen*," said he, in a resolute tone; and the British officers, clad in scarlet and gold, broke into shouts of laughter. It was not long before they were flying before the "heppens" of New Jersey and New York, glad to escape from the rabble they despised.

When they had been examined, plundered, ridiculed, the unlucky prisoners were divided into companies, and marched away to the different prisons of New York, that were for so many weary months to be their homes or their graves. Those who were confined in the Middle Dutch Church were probably the most fortunate of all; they had air and light; but two of the prisons are covered with some of the saddest memories of the war for freedom. One of them was a common jail in the Park, now the Hall of Records, and the other was the old Sugar-House in Liberty Street, next to the Middle Dutch Church. The jail was so crowded with the captured Americans that they had scarcely room to lie on the bare floor. The air was stifling, the rooms pestilential, full of filth and fever.

But the most painful circumstance of their lot was the character of the keeper. His name was Cunningham; he seems to have been a monster. Many years afterward he was executed in England for some hideous crime, and boasted that he had put arsenic in the flour he served to the prisoners. It was under this man—one of those horrible natures war often brings into use—that the young men of New York, Connecticut, and New Jersey were to pass their miserable captivity. Soon even the English officials were forced to take notice of the horrors of the jail in the Park. The neighbors complained that they could get no sleep for the outcries and groans of the prisoners. Cunningham ruled over them with lash and sword. They were starved, reviled, beaten, "to win them," he said, "to their duty." The chill winter and the hot summer found them crowded in their pestilential prisons. The old Sugar-House in Liberty Street was also under Cunningham's care. It was a tall building, several stories high, with small windows, low ceilings, and bare walls. Every story was filled thickly with the captured Americans. They starved, pined away, died by hundreds. Cunningham withheld their food, and cheated even the miserable sick and dying. They froze to death in the chill winter of 1776–77. Sometimes the famished prisoners would come to the narrow windows of the old Sugar-

JAIL IN CITY HALL PARK.—[FROM MRS. MARY L. BOOTH'S "HISTORY OF THE CITY OF NEW YORK."]

House, crying for charity to those who passed, but the sentries drove them back. They pined away in the dark corners of the crowded rooms, dreaming of the old homestead in Connecticut, Thanksgiving cheer, and smiling friends. When they were brought out for exchange, Washington wrote indignantly to Sir Henry Clinton, "You give us only the sick and dying for our healthy, well-fed prisoners." Such were the sorrows our ancestors bore for us. They were the authors of our freedom. And he who treads the floors of the old Dutch Church, or seeks out the spot where stood the Sugar-House in Liberty Street, may well pause to think how much we owe to those who

once pined within their walls. Such, too, is war. Modern intelligence has shorn it of some of its horrors. It may be hoped that education will at last banish it altogether, and the people of Europe and America join to force upon their governments a policy of peace.

ZACHUR WITH THE SACK.

A STATELY-LOOKING man, wearing suspended on his left side by a strong strap a simple gray sack, while a well-filled leather purse hung on his right, was one day slowly wandering through the crowded bazar of Bagdad. He remained standing before one of the stalls, and there, after a little reflection, proceeded to purchase the largest and softest carpet there—one of those in which the foot seems gently to sink down, and the sound of each step is completely hushed.

The merchant was greatly surprised to see the richly dressed stranger without retinue, and said, politely, "Sir, as your slaves are not at hand, I will send one of my young men with you to carry the carpet."

"It is not necessary," said the purchaser, as he paid the price in shining gold pieces; "I can manage it myself."

He quickly took up the immense roll of carpet, and pushed it slowly but surely into his sack. Then, without heeding the amazement and shaking of the head of the dealer, he passed on.

His desire of purchasing seemed now to be thoroughly roused. Twelve flasks of otto of roses, from Schiras, found their way into his sack; ten pounds of the finest Turkish tobacco followed them; then came, quite appropriately, a magnificent nargileh, with a long tube and a yellow amber mouth-piece, on the top of which he carelessly threw a heavy ebony box, inlaid with copper.

Notwithstanding the crowd, he attracted continual notice, and a dignified-looking man had long been following him attentively, without, however, addressing him. But when he had reached the middle of the bazar, where the best and most costly wares are exposed for sale, and when, as though intoxicated by the sight, he seized the most incongruous things, and untiringly pushed them into his sack—pearls from Ormus and blades from Damascus, tons of Mocha coffee, and bales of silk, fishes and rings, bracelets and dates, watches, saddles, and diamonds—then the Caliph, for it was no less a personage who was following him, could contain himself no longer, and said:

"I have seen many wonders, O stranger, and by the beard of the Prophet, thou art not the least. Have, then, thy purse and thy sack no end? Why does thy sack not burst? How canst thou carry it? How canst thou find but one of the thousand things which thou art unceasingly cramming into it? And tell me, how will those poor tender pearls, which were too dear for me to buy for Zuleika, fare among tons and crates?"

Zachur—such was the name of the stranger—crossed his arms on his breast, and bowed low.

"Ruler of the Faithful," he said—"for it is in vain that thou hidest thy noble figure under a homely dress; thy portrait, painted by a Giaour, and offered to me in Frankistan, is also in my sack, and I recognize thee at once—Allah is great, and His gifts are wonderful. Thou carest for the lovely daughters of the shell? Look here!"

He quickly put his right hand into the sack, and brought forth unhurt, from the very midst of sabres and boxes, the double row of large milk-white pearls, which he respectfully presented to the Caliph.

The Caliph was astonished at Zachur's riches and dexterity, rejoiced at his present, and was curious to learn more concerning him.

"Then we will sit down there, on the broad stone steps at the foot of the murmuring fountain," said Zachur; and in a minute he had spread out his soft carpet, and lighted two nargilehs filled with the costly aromatic herb.

They sat down, with their legs crossed under them, peacefully sent little blue clouds into the air, and the stranger began his tale:

"I am the son of a poor man, O sire, and seemed doomed to poverty. But there stood a good fairy by my cradle, and laid on it this bag and this purse, saying:

"'Grow up, Zachur, and look around thee in the world. Buy what pleases thee. Pay for it out of this purse, which will not become empty, and preserve it in this sack, which will not become full; but especially pack in all that is valuable—the weight of it will not weary thee.'

"It has held more than she promised. All that I have ever possessed or loved is contained, imperishable, safe forever, and always at hand, in this sack."

"Wonderful, highly singular, and wonderful!" said the Caliph. "But tell me more, friend."

"Details would take too long to relate, but the whole is soon said," answered Zachur. "Thou wast surprised today at my rapidity in purchasing—thou shouldst have seen me in my young days! When the world still looked sunny and bright to my childish gaze, when thousands of objects attracted me, my hand was rarely out of my purse and my sack. I took long journeys over sea and desert, through lonely villages and large cities, and whatever pleased me I bought, and joyfully put into my capacious sack. Indeed, it filled itself, without aid from me; shining green birds and brilliant snow-white blossoms flew into it.

"The first impetuous joy was, however, soon stilled. Sometimes a feeling of indifference came over me, and I passed unmoved by the most beautiful things, because I already possessed so much that was lovely. 'Another opportunity will occur,' I thought, 'if I should ever wish for it.' But it never came, just as no moment of time ever returns; and now I mourn over many a neglected chance.

"Then, again, I comfort myself with the thought of how many things I possess, and take old and new out of my sack, according to my inclination—a quilted silk counterpane from Japan in which to envelop myself, or the Egyptian phœnix to lull me to sleep.

"Besides, the world is still large, and Zachur is not old yet. I have still time to buy; and sometimes the old longing is very strong within me. Thus to-day, O sire, when I entered thy city, I gave praise to Allah that He had enabled man to form, out of the dirty wool of the sheep, the brilliant carpet on which we are sitting, and caused the fragile amber now between our lips to rise up from the sand of the sea—that He brought the gold from the bowels of the earth, and the pearls from the depths of the sea! And eagerly I seized the things, O sire, until the eye of thy favor rested on me, and the blessed breath of thy mouth reached me, and gave me what can not be purchased with gold and silver—the honor and delight of thy presence!"

"Well spoken!" said the Caliph, delighted, as he blew a thick cloud before him; "it is easy to see that thou hast travelled, and been in courts too, friend Zachur. But one thing, before I again forget it in my amazement. The Prophet, praised be his name! has forbidden to make a likeness or picture of man, the image of Allah. But as thou possessest mine, done by some unbelieving dog—I can not conceive how he found time and opportunity to do it—"

"They paint rapidly," interrupted Zachur; "and are quick in all evil arts."

"True, very true. I should like to look at the thing. The people need know nothing about it. Couldst thou not take it out for me to have just one glimpse of it?"

"Thy wish is a command to me," answered Zachur, who was already fumbling in the sack, but for some time in vain.

"Well," called the Caliph, getting angry, "art thou sorry that thou hast promised? Or—"

"Here it is, O sire," said Zachur, breathing freely; and the anger of the ruler disappeared as he gazed with curiosity on a small silver medal.

"It is I, and yet it is not," he said, shaking his head. "It is my fez, with the ruby clasp, and the embroidery on my state dress; but I do not really look so stiff. Where are the brown cheeks, the brightness of the eyes, the coloring, friend? And—what do I see?—the thing is broken; look here! there is a crack across it that separates the feet of my horse from his body. Therefore thou canst not keep all thy things unhurt in that sack—thou canst not find them all in a minute: confess thou hast also lost some entirely."

"I am the son of a poor man," answered Zachur, blushing, "but I learned two things when only a boy: to use a sword, and to speak the truth. Yes, I have lost many a thing; and when I was boasting just now that I had everything in my sack, I was guilty of exaggeration, as men of limited capacity are, in the use of the two words *everything* and *nothing*. I should have said *most things*."

At this moment appeared two outriders on swift Arab steeds, and behind them came a gilt carriage, drawn by four Barbary horses. At sight of them Zachur sprang to his feet.

Without for a moment losing sight of the approaching procession seeing the Caliph rise too, he quickly pushed his carpet and nargileh into his sack, and exclaimed, with sparkling eyes, "To whom does this magnificence belong? Though how can I ask? for who but thou, O sire, could call such splendor his own?

"How beautifully the Nubian in his purple contrasts with the gray horse, and the pale Christian slave in the blue silk with the shining black steed! If only thou wert a merchant with this equipage for sale!"

"Princes do not barter," said the Caliph, as he put a little silver whistle to his mouth, and blew a shrill blast, when horses and carriage suddenly stood still by the side of the fountain.

"But thou hast made me a handsome present, friend Zachur, and what is more, given me a pleasant hour. Take what thou praisest so enthusiastically; be my guest to-day, and to-morrow, or when it pleases thee, drive away into the wide world in this carriage—it must be weary work dragging such a sack."

Zachur crossed his arms on his breast, bowed low, and answered: "Thy favor is like dew on a barren land, even for the richest, and if I had not promised a sick friend to be with him this evening, I would willingly enter within the shadow of thy halls. Therefore let me go in peace; but these beautifully kept horses and carriage shall not go through the dust of the suburbs."

Saying this, he quietly pushed the Nubian with his gray steed, the black horse and his rider, the carriage and horses, into the sack, bowed down to the ground again, and then stepped lightly and erect toward the city gate.

The Caliph shook his head as he looked after him, went home full of thought, and hung the double row of pearls round Zuleika's neck.

Then he sent for his private secretary and said:

"Take a swan quill and a sheet of the finest parchment, and write down carefully what I shall dictate: the story of Zachur with the Sack."

Many of our young readers have doubtless long since seen the meaning of this tale shine forth through its thin veil. We should all be surprised at a Zachur, and yet, like him, we have each a faithful capacious sack—*memory*—into which, from our youth upward, we have crammed what is noble and common, pearls and pebbles, and yet it does not become full, nor our purse—our power of comprehension—empty.

THE DIFFERENCE.

Who warms his slippers for papa
  When he comes home at night?
Who meets him with a joyous laugh,
  And blue eyes beaming bright?
Who climbs upon his ready knee,
With kisses sweet as kiss can be?—
  Our Kitty.

Who teases poor old grandmamma,
  And pulls her work away,
And with her gold-rimmed spectacles
  Too often tries to play?
Who's full of mischief, sport, and fun,
From early morn till day is done?—
  Our Kitty.

Whose little arms "hug mamma tight"?
  Whose lips give kisses sweet?
Who follows nurse about the house
  With little restless feet?
Who sings to Dolly, scolds her, too,
And tries to act as "big folks" do?—
  Our Kitty.

Who, bent on mischief, truth to say,
  Like any little elf,
Within the pantry hides to taste
  The "goodies" on the shelf?
Who bothers cook, where'er she goes,
And makes her scold, you may suppose?
  Our Kitty.

But lest our Kitty chance to get
  More than her share of blame
For mischief, I'll explain there is
  Some difference in the name:
Our Kitty is our child, you see;
The other, Kitty's c-a-t!

A PEEP INTO ROYAL TREASURIES.

THE Hasné, or imperial treasury, of Constantinople, contains a costly collection of ancient armor and coats of mail worn by the Sultans. The most remarkable is that of Sultan Murad II., the conqueror of Bagdad. The head-piece of this suit is of gold and silver, almost covered with precious stones; the diadem surrounding the turban is composed of three emeralds of the purest water and large size, while the collar is formed of twenty-two large and magnificent diamonds.

In the same collection is a curious ornament, in the shape of an elephant, of massive gold, standing on a pedestal formed of enormous pearls placed side by side. There is also a table, thickly inlaid with Oriental topazes, presented by the Empress Catherine of Russia to the Vizier Baltadji Mustapha, together with a very remarkable collection of ancient costumes, trimmed with rare furs, and literally covered with precious stones. The divans and cushions, formerly in the throne-room of the Sultans, are gorgeous; the stuff of which the cushions are made is pure tissue of gold, without any mixture of silk whatever, and is embroidered with pearls, weighing about thirty-six hundred drachmas. Children's cradles of solid gold, inlaid with precious stones; vases of immense value in rock-crystal, gold, and silver, incrusted with rubies, emeralds, and diamonds; daggers, swords, and shields, beautifully wrought and richly jewelled—all tell a story of ancient grandeur and wealth, when the Ottoman power was a reality, and Western Europe trembled before the descendant of the son of Amurath.

Notwithstanding these jewelled riches of Turkey, however, they are surpassed by the splendor of the Shah of Persia's treasury, the contents of which have accumulated in successive periods.

Nadir Shah of Persia, in the first half of the eighteenth century, amassed enormous riches by the spoils of war. He is said to have had a tent made so magnificent and costly as to appear almost fabulous. The outside was covered with fine scarlet broadcloth, the lining was of violet-colored satin, on which were representations of all the birds and beasts in the creation, with trees and flowers; the whole made of pearls, diamonds, rubies, emeralds, amethysts, and other precious stones; and the tent poles were decorated in like manner. On both sides of the peacock throne was a screen, on which were the figures of two angels in precious stones.

This splendid tent was displayed on all festivals in the public hall at Herat during the remainder of Nadir Shah's reign.

It would be impossible to describe in a short article the splendor of the Persian treasury. One extraordinary object may be mentioned: a two-foot globe covered with jewels from the north pole to the extremities of the tripod on which the gemmed sphere is placed. His Majesty had coats embroidered with diamonds and emeralds, rubies, pearls, and garnets; he had jewelled swords and daggers without number; so because he did not know what else to do with the rest of his jewels, he ordered the globe to be constructed, and covered with gems; the overspreading sea to be of emeralds, and the kingdoms of the world to be distinguished by jewels of different color.

WINGED FREEBOOTERS.

THE great goshawk, a bird in a coat of blackish-brown covered with blotches of black and reddish-white, is a terrible enemy to wild rabbits, hares, and squirrels, and to all the small feathered inhabitants of field and forest. It is about two feet long, and although it is not a bird of very rapid flight, its cunning and strength are such that its prey rarely escapes. Should the terrified hare hide itself in some thicket, the goshawk patiently perches on an elevated branch near at hand, where it will wait hours, motionless, until the poor hare, thinking its enemy departed, ventures from its retreat, when in an instant it is swooped down upon, and struck dying to the ground.

Goshawks are found in the Middle and Western States during the autumn and winter. In the summer they go far to the northward to rear their young. They build a large nest of twigs and coarse grasses on some lofty branch of a tree, and lay three or four eggs of dull bluish-white slightly spotted with reddish-brown.

These savage birds are very common in Maine, where they make great havoc among the flocks of wild-ducks and Canada grouse, and will even, when driven by hunger, venture an attack on the fowls of the farm-yard. Its sharp eye always gleaming and on the alert, the goshawk sweeps over fields and woods, changing its course in an instant by a slight movement of its rudder-like tail whenever any desired prey is sighted. It is the most restless of birds, and is almost constantly on the wing, seldom alighting except for breakfast and dinner.

Audubon relates a curious instance of sagacity in a goshawk, which he himself witnessed. A large flock of blackbirds flying over a pond were pursued by one of these birds, which, dashing into the flock, seized one after the other of the poor little victims, apparently squeezing each one with its powerful talons, and then allowing it to drop on the surface of the water. Five or six had been captured before the fleeing blackbirds gained the shelter of a thick forest. The goshawk then swept leisurely back, and with graceful curves descended to the pond and collected its victims, taking the dead birds one by one and carrying them away as if laying up a store for its evening meal.

Instances have been known where this bird has itself fallen a victim to its own designs. Dead goshawks have been found with their talons hopelessly entangled in thorn and furze bushes, upon which they had pounced with the object of seizing some little rabbit or squirrel which had sought shelter beneath the undergrowth. A hunter once witnessed such an occurrence, the rabbit scampering away in safety across the field, while the great bird remained entangled in the bush. The hunter forbore to shoot at the little rabbit which had made so fortunate an escape, and killed the wicked bird of prey instead.

Goshawks are found in nearly every portion of Europe, and have sometimes been trained to assist in hunting; but as they are more ferocious than the falcon, they are less easily controlled, and are always on the watch to regain their liberty.

A DASH FOR LIFE.

A smaller variety of the great hawk family, but one spreading equal terror among small birds, is the sparrow-hawk—a bold, provoking bird, with dark brown back and wings, and breast of rusty brown or grayish-white crossed by narrow bars of a darker tint. The sparrow-hawk feeds mostly upon small birds, but it will also catch moles, field-mice, and even grasshoppers. It flies low, skimming along but a few feet from the ground, its sharp little eyes always on the watch for prey.

When tamed, the sparrow-hawk becomes affectionate toward its owner, but will rarely accept civilities from any other person. One of these birds, which had been tamed by a lady, was accustomed to perch on the shoulder of its mistress, and eat from her hand. It was intensely jealous, and would fly savagely at any one to whom its mistress showed the least favor. This particular pet proved as troublesome as a thieving cat, for was any fine fat chicken or partridge left lying on the kitchen table, if the cook's back was turned for a moment, the prize was either mangled or borne away to a hiding-place by the mischievous bird.

The sparrow-hawk is not a nest-builder, but will usurp the nest of the crow or some other large bird. If a deserted nest can be found, the sparrow-hawk will immediately take possession; but if no such presents itself, this bad-hearted, quarrelsome bird does not hesitate to depose the rightful owner, and proceed to occupy a home to which it has neither right nor title.

The sparrow-hawk, the malicious hen-hawk, and cruel pigeon-hawk, are very common throughout the United States and Europe.

THE WRECK OF A COASTER.

UNCLE PHIL'S THIMBLE.

BY ELINOR ELLIOTT.

"A RAG-PICKER!"

"That's just what I am," sighed a poor girl who stood at one of the long tables in the rag-room of a large paper-mill. Down each side the table stood a row of girls, some older, some younger, than herself, all miserably clothed, and all with worn, pinched faces.

These girls came each day to their work with an eager look in their eyes, which burned brightly in the morning, flickered fitfully through the day, and faded out at night, leaving the patient, tired look which want and hunger and disappointment bring, and which is always ready to take courage and look forward once more; for in a pile of rags there sometimes lay a treasure—an odd penny, an old knife, a pair of scissors—something that might be taken to the little pawn shop round the corner and sold.

A little while ago a girl—a *lucky* girl—had a "find," a bright silver quarter. Her good luck had been whispered up and down the row, but no one betrayed her fortune. When the overseer came through the room, no exultant look nor envious glance suggested anything unusual, for this band of "rag-pickers" had its honor, which it held to as closely as the most compact trades-union in the land.

To some of the girls the thought sometimes came, "Is what we find really ours?" but long generations of workers in the mill had appropriated these "finds," and it had become a custom if not a right.

To-day Nance, at the head of the table, felt a keener longing than usual to secure something. She had never felt the utter dreariness of her loneliness and poverty so strongly as she had in the last bright Christmas season, which had been to her only a vision; not the sweet reality that it becomes to us, who bring it close to us in happy anticipation weeks before it really comes, who live in its light and peace and cheer, in its sweet givings and receivings, and keep its memory with us throughout the year.

For a whole year Nance had been at work in the mill,

and had had nothing but her regular five-cent salary. Now her long nervous fingers ran rapidly through the pieces, making four divisions, as she called, "Linen, cotton, woollen, silk—linen, cotton, woollen, silk," and the different bits dropped into their proper piles like falling leaves; while the girl on her right took the cottons, and assorted them, and the girl on her left went through the woollens in the same way, and a girl further on took the silks.

A stranger was always amused to watch the long rows of quiet bodies, nimble fingers, and moving lips, and to hear the half-whispered counting and calling of colors as they divided the pieces.

To-day Nance had a bag to pick from. Here lay her chance. The girls who took the rags from the bags were the most apt to find treasures, and their turn came only once a month.

She was fast nearing the bottom of the last bag. Every time she thrust her hand in, her heart beat fast, and she thought, "Shall I keep it, if I find anything?"

Once more, and her hand touches something cold; her fingers close round it, and she draws it out. Her head swims, she clutches the table with her other hand to keep from falling—perhaps, after all, it is only a button. She collects herself, and peeps slyly into her hand.

A gold thimble!

No one has seen it, no one knows, and Nance slips it into her pocket, and goes on with her work; but somehow it doesn't run smoothly. It is "Silk, cotton, woollen, linen," and then "Cotton, woollen, linen, silk," and the girls find fault because the piles are "mixed," and then the bell rings, and they are free for to-day.

Cautiously Nance makes inquiries about the "finds." How much did they sell things for, if they found any?

"My aunt," said one girl, "onst foun' a gol' ring, an' the jew'ler give her a dollar for't."

"He melted it down," explained another. "They allus does that. He told me one day that if ever I found a gold breas'pin or a bracelet, 'which 'tain't noways likely you will,' ses he, 'fetch it to me, an' I'll give you what's right for it.'"

So Nance's "find" was really worth money. More money, too, than she could earn in many days' steady toil. What would it not buy! Food, clothing, warmth, everything, seemed within her reach now that she held that source of wealth in her hand.

"'Tain't stealin', I hope," thought Nance. "Course not. I don' know who it belongs to."

When alone, Nance took out the thimble. What a dainty little thing it was! She tried it on each of her hard, bony fingers, and laughed to see the poor grimy things wearing a golden crown.

Why, there were letters on it!

"Reel writin'!" cried Nance, as she paused under a street lamp to spell the word by its light.

"Onst I could read writin'. That first mus' be a capertin—that's what they call them big fellers that stands first—a kin' of a Generel with his soljers. Oh! I don' know the capertins—never got acquainted when I went to school; common letters was good enough for me.

"That tall one, that's *l*, an' there's round *o*, then *r*, an' then *i* with a dot. L-o lo, r-i ri, lori; *m*, *e*, an' then another tall *l* on the end—that's m-e-l mel, lorimel. Now what's the capertin's name?—lorimel, lorimel; I've heerd that name somewheres. Why, it's her that came that day mother lay a-dyin' an' spoke so soft like; an' the gennelman with her he called her 'lorimel'—no that warn't it—Florimel, Florimel, that's the name!

"'Tain't yourn now, Nance. You know where it belongs. You ain't got no right to it now."

And then came other thoughts.

"What's a gold thimble to her? She can buy all she wants—gold thimbles, and gold scissors, and gold needles; and sit in a gold chair, and sew on a gold gown. She hadn't no business leavin' a gold thimble in a rag bag. Them that's careless has to pay for it."

The curtains were drawn in an elegant house on the Avenue. A bright fire burned in the grate, throwing a warm glow on the delicate walls, the beautiful pictures, and the snowy marble statues, and reflecting itself in the long mirrors, seemed, as it sparkled and glowed, the only thing of life in the room: for the young girl who lay back in the luxurious depths of the large chair by the hearth, with her fair hands lying listlessly in her lap, was as white and motionless as the statues around her.

Now and then her lip quivered, and an occasional tear stole from under her long lashes, but she did not look up till a gentleman entered the room. Then she sprang into his arms, and sobbed out, in reply to his question of how she had spent the day,

"I've been perfectly miserable, papa. I've lost my thimble—the thimble Uncle Phil gave me. I'd give everything in the world to see it again."

"Why, my dear little girl, that would hardly be worth while, when you can get another for a few dollars. We'll go to-morrow and buy the prettiest—"

"Ah! papa, you don't understand. All the money in the world can't buy a thimble to take the place of the one Uncle Phil gave me. It was the last thing he ever bought."

"Was it, darling?"

"Yes: and he said that morning, 'Florimel, can you sew pretty well?' and I laughed, and said, 'Of course not, Uncle Phil; what's the need of my sewing?' 'Great need, great need, little niece,' he said. 'Sewing is woman's most womanly work, and though you may never need to sew for yourself, if you know how, you might teach hundreds of poor girls to sew and clothe themselves and their families.'"

"My little daughter teaching a sewing-school! How funny it would be!"

"So that afternoon we went into Shreve's and selected one, and had my name engraved on it; and that night Uncle Phil was taken ill. So of course I feel badly, papa; don't you see why?"

"Yes, Florimel; but perhaps we shall find this thimble. Have you had Janet search for it?"

"Indeed I have, all day long. I had it yesterday at work on my Kensington, and think Janet must have taken it up among the bits of worsted when she put them into the scrap bag; and Ann sold all the scraps last night to the ragman. Oh dear! I shall never see it again."

"Hif you please, sir," said Jacobs, appearing in the doorway, "there's a vagrant at the basement door. Three times hi've sent 'er away, han' three times she 'as returned, hevery time hasking for Miss Florimel, han' sayin' she *must* see 'er."

"To see me! At the basement door? How strange!" and Florimel forgot her tears in her eagerness to see what the poor child at the door could want.

Her papa hurried down stairs after her, and saw her face radiant with joy as she held in her hand a gold thimble, while a scantily clothed girl stood beside her awkwardly twisting the corner of her shabby shawl.

"Oh, papa! this girl Nancy found my thimble among some rags, and brought it back to me. Oh, what can I do for her, papa?"

"How did you know whose the thimble was, my child?"

"I warn't sure, sir," faltered Nance, whose honor had outweighed her longing for money and the comfort it would bring, and had brought her through the long city to seek the rightful owner of the thimble—"I warn't *sure*; but I knew her name, for herself an' a gennelman came onst to see mother long ago."

"That was Uncle Phil," said Florimel. "He used often to take me when he went to visit the poor. But how did you know where I lived?"

"I knew the house, 'cause he told me to come here onst for some soup for mother, an' I came an' got it."

"How is your mother now?"

"She's dead, miss," sobbed Nance.

"And so is Uncle Phil;" and the two girls—the one so fair and beautiful and carefully guarded, the other so pale and pinched and friendless—forgot for a moment all but their sorrow, their longing for the dear dead faces they could never see again.

But Florimel's papa called Janet to see that Nancy was warmed and fed after her long cold walk, and took Florimel into the library to see what they really could do for this poor but honest girl.

Florimel at first insisted upon having her for her own little maid, but her papa convinced her that Nancy was too ignorant for such a position; and they finally decided that the best thing to do for her would be to give her a good home, where she could learn to do all kinds of nice work, and could also go to school.

"Why, papa, I know the very place for Nancy. Nurse Susan lives all alone, now her niece has gone out to service, and Nancy could live with her."

"That is a very bright thought, little daughter. It would be a comfort to Susan to have a young girl with her, and the money we should pay for Nancy's board would lighten her expenses. Let us send now for Nancy, and see if she likes the idea."

Did Nance like the idea?

Did she like to think she need never go back to the bustling, dusty mill; that she need not go again to that miserable tenement-house which she called home, where she shared one tiny room with seven other girls; that she need not know again what it was to battle with hunger and cold? Did she like to feel that she should have a home in the sweet fresh country; that her work should be in a garden, in a dairy, in a neat little cottage; that clothing, food, and the learning to be a good woman would lie within her reach?

LIFE ON BOARD A TRAINING-SHIP.

Training-ships, on board which boys are taught to become first-rate seamen, form an important portion of every navy; and in the accompanying sketches our artist has endeavored to convey correct ideas of the daily life of these boys to those of our readers who live far inland, are not familiar with ships and sailors, and who perhaps have never seen the sea.

FURLING SAIL.

The first sketch is one showing the boys undergoing a part of their sail drill, and engaged in furling the mizzen top-gallant-sail and royal. The sails of a man-of-war are furled and stowed with the utmost care and precision, so that the ends of the yard look exactly alike, and sometimes the boys have to do their work over and over again before the critical eye of the officer watching them is satisfied. In storms, when the great ship rolls so that the yard-arms sometimes touch the water, lying out on them and furling sails is very difficult and dangerous work,

BATH-ROOM.

SCHOOL-ROOM.

and it is only on account of the constant drill they have received during fair weather that the boys are able to accomplish the task under these circumstances.

Above all things, on these training-ships the boys are

DINNER-TIME: EIGHT BELLS.

obliged to keep themselves neat and clean. They are expected to bathe frequently, and are always compelled to do so on Sunday. The bath-room, provided with tubs, basins, and a plentiful supply of water, is located in the bows, in the extreme forward part of the ship.

Generally amidships, but sometimes in the stern of the ship, is the school-room; for sailor boys have other things to learn besides the practical sailing of a ship. In this school-room the young sailors spend four or five hours of each day, and are taught reading, writing, arithmetic, history, geography, and grammar.

At noon, or eight bells, as they say on shipboard, the bugles sound the dinner call, and from all parts of the ship the boys tumble down the hatchways to the berth-

ORLOP DECK, OR COCKPIT.

SERVING OUT BREAD AND TREACLE.

GUN PRACTICE.

deck, where in a long row of short tables swung from the ceiling, and where the young sailors eat the bountiful dinner provided for them as only healthy, hearty boys can eat.

The fourth or lowest deck of the ship is called the "orlop deck," and it is here that the boys stow away their muskets and cutlasses after drill. On this deck also the boys receive at four bells, or six o'clock in the evening, the allowance of bread and molasses, or treacle, that composes their regular supper.

Next to the sail drill, perhaps the most important is the gun drill, or practice with the heavy guns. This gun drill is not important merely because the guns are to be used in case of a fight, but because they are also used in the firing of salutes. These salutes must be fired whenever another man-of-war comes into port or a distinguished officer comes on board, on national holidays, and at many other times; therefore it is very important that the boys should be familiar with the great guns. Each gun has its crew, each one of whom has an especial duty to perform. The long cord that the boy in the last picture holds in his hand is called a lanyard; and as he pulls it with a smart jerk, a hammer falls on the breech of the gun, and with a roar that shakes the ship, the great gun is fired.

SAN FRANCISCO, CALIFORNIA.

I am twelve years old, and go to the Lincoln School. It is so called because it has a statue of Abraham Lincoln in front of it. It was built in [illegible], and is the best school in the city. I have been making money out of [illegible] eggs to send East to my cousins. The eggs come from the Farallon Islands, twenty-one miles outside of the Golden Gate. They are of a blue color, and have marks on them that look like hieroglyphics. The birds that lay them are a species of gull. I was born in San Francisco, and have lived here most of my life. Four years I spent up in the mountains on a farm, or ranch, as they call it here. CHARLES W. K.

Farallon, the name of these islands near the entrance to San Francisco Bay, is a Spanish word signifying a small pointed islet in the ocean. The islands, of which there are six, are so called because they consist of rugged towering peaks of granite. A more desolate place could not well be imagined. There is nearly always a fierce wind blowing, and the waves dash wildly into the numerous spouting caves along the rocky coast. There is a lighthouse here three hundred and sixty feet above the sea, and its keepers are the only human inhabitants of the desolate sea-bound rock; but thousands of sea-lions congregate upon the cliffs, and vast numbers of gulls and wild sea-birds make their home there. During the egging season men visit the islands, and gather thousands of eggs for the San Francisco market. A very interesting account of these islands is given in Mr. Nordhoff's book on *Northern California, Oregon, and the Sandwich Islands*.

FORT ASSINABOINE, MONTANA TERRITORY.

I am always glad to see YOUNG PEOPLE come with papa's mail. Out here in the wilderness we do not often see nice papers, but here we see what city people never see—plenty of Indians. Many of them are very poor, and so hungry that they pick bread and scraps of meat out of the swill barrels to eat—old stuff that the soldiers have thrown away. I think people should send the poor Indians something to eat. I send you a picture of some Indians as they look hunting for food this cold day. I am only nine years old, and can not draw very good pictures. BERTIE BROWN.

[illegible], WASHINGTON TERRITORY.

I [illegible] in Washington Territory, and thought I would tell you something about this [illegible] country. We live near the [illegible] Mountains. They are covered with evergreen trees. We can see the snow-capped mountains every day in the year—Mounts [illegible], Hood, St. Helen's, and Adams. It snows here sometimes in winter, but the wind comes up from the sea, and takes it away in a few days. I do not like to go to school, but I study and recite my lessons at home. We [illegible] at the new town of [illegible], there is an academy, and [illegible]. I am [illegible] years old, and was born in this country. Sometimes troops of Indians come riding past on their spotted ponies. They bring salmon from the Columbia River, [illegible] from the mountains, and [illegible] to sell. I am very fond of reading, and am delighted with YOUNG PEOPLE. I read every word in it. [illegible]

[illegible], ARKANSAS.

I am a little girl eight years old. I take YOUNG PEOPLE, and like it very much. I have a doll named Laura Martin. I live on a cotton plantation on the Arkansas River, and I can stand on the front gallery of our house and see all the boats that pass. We have never been to school, and we [illegible] governess now; so mamma has to teach us. We have a great many [illegible] trees here, and there is a pond near our house with a boat on it, and my sister and I row sometimes. CLAUDIA R. SMITH.

[illegible], NEW YORK.

I am six years old. My birthday was the 12th of January, and mamma gave me a little party. We had a nice time, and my mamma let us all [illegible] without any grown people. I have two birdies; they will put their little heads clear out of the cage, and take seeds from my mouth. Sometimes they nip my tongue, and one birdie will fly and light on the top. I keep [illegible] in. I taught them to eat in that way by not letting them have anything until they would take it. FRANK L. CARTER.

Papa brought me the numbers of YOUNG PEOPLE a few days ago. I had been waiting anxiously for them, and I was so delighted when he gave them to me. I have known all about Harpers' publications for a long time. [illegible] says that papa took Harper's Magazine long ago, before the war. I like the stories, [illegible], and puzzles in YOUNG PEOPLE very much, and I have succeeded in getting answers to some of the puzzles. My pets are cats and dogs, and I would like to get a pigeon. Alabama was my native place, but now I live in Maryland. LAURA B. DUNN.

[illegible], ARKANSAS.

I thought you might like to know about "Dr. Peter's lamp," as I promised to write you a letter. I am [illegible] and [illegible] their [illegible] are First, [illegible], and Charley. Papa takes HARPER'S [illegible] and [illegible] the BAZAR, and when YOUNG PEOPLE was advertised papa promised that each of us give something and take that too. We have here [illegible] just one hundred dollars picking cotton last fall, so we all contributed. We like the paper very much, and watch for its coming; and we read everything in it. WILL H PERCY.

[illegible], [illegible].

I am ten years old. My uncle takes YOUNG PEOPLE for me, and I can hardly wait until it comes. I have got the elephant on his four legs, and he looks well. I have a little [illegible] named Jenny. It lives in a hole in the yard, where I think it must have a good nest, for I feed it lots of hay and [illegible] in the hole. It comes to the house almost every day to get something to eat, and seems glad to see me. I have [illegible] a little dog named Trick, only I [illegible] one-half because he [illegible] for [illegible], and [illegible] a [illegible] three [illegible]. We [illegible] like the [illegible] to play with. Can you tell me what kind of a place a junk-shop is? HUBERT E. [illegible].

A junk-shop is where old ropes, old anchors, old iron, and cast-off cable and chain of all kinds are kept for sale. There are many such shops to be found in every large city, and if it is a sea-port, they are generally located near the water-front, as a vast quantity of such rubbish is picked up along the wharves. In New York city junk-dealers drive wagons round the streets, and buy old stoves or any worn-out household goods.

[illegible], ARKANSAS.

I found in grandma's front yard, near a brick wall, a little pansy, which I send you. It bloomed out the 26th of January. KATIE F. B.

It was fortunate for the little pansy that it was picked and pressed, for Katie Black writes, also from Arkansas: "There was a very pretty snow-storm here on the 2d of February. It began in the morning, and snowed all day."

WARD A. F.—Your puzzle is nicely done, but as we have already published one having the same solution, we can not use it.

[illegible], WEST VIRGINIA.

Can you tell me what five words in the English language end in "cion"? S. R. W.

Can any correspondent answer this question?

J. B. H.—Jupiter will be evening star until March 15; morning star until October 8. Mars will be evening star until October 25. Saturn will be evening star until April 7, morning star until October 18. Venus will be morning star until July 13, evening star the rest of the year.

KATIE.—You may write us any interesting things you know about prairie dogs in Kansas.

"INDIANAN."—You will find brief accounts of the ancient Roman road-builders in any history of Rome, also in Appleton's *Encyclopædia* under "Roads." Lemprière's *Classical Dictionary* also contains much information, especially of the Appian Way.

MAY W. T.—"The Youthful Philomathean" would be a pretty name for your literary society. Philomathean is a Greek word signifying loving to learn, or lover of knowledge.

WALTER S. DOWD.—The picture on the first page of YOUNG PEOPLE No. 14 is a fac-simile of a pencil drawing reproduced by a photographic process.

Very neat "Wiggles" are received from R. V. R., Hattie [illegible], and F. B. Myers, which we regret being unable to publish.

LOUISE B.—You write so prettily that we are sorry your enigma is not good enough to print. Do not be discouraged. Try again, and the next time see if you can not make rhymes.

JOHN P. S.—Persevere with your locomotive-engine drawing, and some day you may be able to put it to good use. Engines and machinery of all kinds are good things for a boy to become familiar with, and if you are really fond of them cultivate your mechanism all you can.

Netta Franklin, Freddie C., Emma S., Percy N., and Robbie V. B. are very youthful correspondents who favor us with letters printed

INDIANS HUNTING FOR FOOD.—DRAWN BY BERTIE BROWN.

WORCESTER, MASSACHUSETTS.

I have a canary, which is the only live pet I ever had. It was eight months old the 13th of February. I plant canary-seed, and let it grow until it is about two inches high, and then I give it to my canary. It likes to eat it very much. LOUIS E. WARE.

[illegible] remarkable [illegible]. May [illegible] also writes a very legible "Wiggle." When you learn to print, little girl, write again.

Acknowledgments [illegible] [illegible]

Correct answers to puzzles received from [illegible]

ANSWERS TO PUZZLES IN NO. 14.

The following solution to "A Latin Word-Square," on page 186, is from a correspondent in Pennsylvania:

R O M A
O R I N
M I L O
A M O R

The square is made of magic spells
That speak of Heaven and of Rome;
The third the glory that was Greece,
The first the grandeur that was Rome.

[illegible]

[illegible]

Answer to "Flaming Light," on page [illegible]—[illegible].

We have received numerous answers to the Puzzle Picture on page 188, which are correct with the exception that more beasts are there than any one has yet discovered. A great many little folks have found seven. Only one has found eight. There are nine concealed in the picture, and we give one more week in which to hunt for them before publishing the answers.

ADVERTISEMENTS.

HARPER'S YOUNG PEOPLE.

HARPER'S YOUNG PEOPLE will be issued every Tuesday, and may be had at the following rates—payable in advance, postage free:

SINGLE COPIES $0 04
ONE SUBSCRIPTION, one year ... 1 50
FIVE SUBSCRIPTIONS, one year ... 7 00

Subscriptions may begin with any Number. When no time is specified, it will be understood that the subscriber desires to commence with the Number issued after the receipt of order.

Remittances should be made by POST-OFFICE MONEY ORDER or DRAFT, to avoid risk of loss.

ADVERTISING.

The extent and character of the circulation of HARPER'S YOUNG PEOPLE will render it a first-class medium for advertising. A limited number of approved advertisements will be inserted on two inside pages at 75 cents per line.

Address

HARPER & BROTHERS,
Franklin Square, N. Y.

CANDY [illegible] C. F. GUNTHER, Confectioner, [illegible] MADISON STREET, CHICAGO.

CHILDREN'S PICTURE-BOOKS.

Square 4to, about 300 pages each, beautifully printed on Tinted Paper, embellished with many Illustrations, bound in Cloth, $1 50 per volume.

The Children's Picture-Book of Sagacity of Animals.

With Sixty Illustrations by HARRISON WEIR.

The Children's Bible Picture-Book.

With Eighty Illustrations, from Designs by STEINLE, OVERBECK, VEIT, SCHNORR, &c.

The Children's Picture Fable-Book.

Containing One Hundred and Sixty Fables. With Sixty Illustrations by HARRISON WEIR.

The Children's Picture-Book of Birds.

With Sixty-one Illustrations by W. HARVEY.

The Children's Picture-Book of Quadrupeds and other Mammalia.

With Sixty-one Illustrations by W. HARVEY.

Published by HARPER & BROTHERS, New York.

Sent by mail, postage prepaid, to any part of the United States, on receipt of the price.

Old Books for Young Readers.

Arabian Nights' Entertainments.

The Thousand and One Nights; or, The Arabian Nights' Entertainments. Translated and Arranged for Family Reading, with Explanatory Notes, by E. W. LANE. 600 Illustrations by Harvey. 2 vols., 12mo, Cloth, $3 50.

Robinson Crusoe.

The Life and Surprising Adventures of Robinson Crusoe, of York, Mariner. By DANIEL DEFOE. With a Biographical Account of Defoe. Illustrated by Adams. Complete Edition. 12mo, Cloth, $1 50.

The Swiss Family Robinson.

The Swiss Family Robinson; or, Adventures of a Father and Mother and Four Sons on a Desert Island. Illustrated. 2 vols., 18mo, Cloth, $1 50.

The Swiss Family Robinson.—Continued; being a Sequel to the Foregoing. 2 vols., 18mo, Cloth, $1 50.

Sandford and Merton.

The History of Sandford and Merton. By THOMAS DAY. 18mo, Half Bound, 75 cents.

Published by HARPER & BROTHERS, New York.

Sent by mail, postage prepaid, to any part of the United States, on receipt of the price.

BOOKS FOR YOUNG MEN.

Character.

Character. By SAMUEL SMILES. 12mo, Cloth, $1 00.

It is, in design and execution, more like his "Self-Help" than any of his other works. [illegible] —*Examiner*, London.

Self-Help.

Self-Help; with Illustrations of Character, Conduct, and Perseverance. By SAMUEL SMILES. New Edition. Revised and Enlarged. 12mo, Cloth, $1 00.

The writings of Samuel Smiles are a valuable aid in the education of boys. [illegible] The popularity of this book, "Self-Help," [illegible] —*N. Y. World*.

Thrift.

Thrift. By SAMUEL SMILES. 12mo, Cloth, $1 00.

The mechanic, farmer, apprentice, clerk, merchant, and a large circle of readers outside of these classes will find in this volume a wide range of counsel and advice, presented in [illegible] language, and marked throughout by vigorous good sense; and who, while deriving from it useful lessons for the guidance of their personal affairs, will also be imbibing valuable instruction in an important branch of political economy. [illegible] —*Christian Intelligencer*, N. Y.

[illegible] —*N. Y. World*.

Published by HARPER & BROTHERS, New York.

Sent by mail, postage prepaid, to any part of the United States, on receipt of the price.

THE FIRE-FLY GAME.

THE game of fire-fly is very graceful and amusing for dull days or winter evenings in the house. Out of a piece of Bristol-board (an old playing-card will do) cut a figure in the shape of the annexed diagram. If you have water-colors, and can paint it brightly in red and green or red and yellow stripes, all the better. Lay it flat on the cover of a book so that part of one of the wings projects over the edge; hold the book at a slight angle, pointing toward the ceiling, and then with a pencil or pen-holder give the projecting wing a smart blow, so as to send it flying upward; it will go twirling through the air toward the ceiling, and then return twirling back to the neighborhood of your feet. The game consists in trying to catch it on the cover of the book when it comes back. If you succeed, it counts you ten points; if you fail, you allow the fly to lie where it has fallen. Your adversary now takes his turn, and if he fails to catch his fly, then you see which fly has fallen nearest to a certain line on the floor on which you have previously agreed, and the owner of the nearest fly scores five. Whoever first scores one hundred wins the game.

A School in Morocco.—If one, happening to be in the south of Spain some day, should run across the Straits of Gibraltar in a southwesterly direction, he would come to the ancient city of Tangier, in Morocco. Here he would see many curious sights, but none more picturesque than the schools for children, of which there are several. A row of tiny slippers at the door and a hum of childish voices inside prompt the passer-by to look in. He sees a room, empty of furniture, and lit only by the open door. The school-master, a veritable Moses in appearance, is squatted on his haunches in the centre, and around him squat his pupils. Each has his slate before him, and repeats his lesson with monotonous chant, keeping his body moving backward and forward as if he were rowing hard the whole time against stream. The school-master's whip is of sufficient length to reach every boy around him, and now and then, without rising from his seat, he touches one or other up in the same manner as the driver of a mail-coach takes a fly off his leader's ear. The imperturbable gravity of the master, and the comical looks and quaint attire of the boys, form a picture which could not be transferred to canvas.

THE CHICKEN PUZZLE.

HERE is an orange. With four cuts of the scissors and the prick of a pin transform it into a chicken.

CHARADE.

My first belongs to an ancient race;
They say his pedigree he can trace
  To the time of the ark, and before;
But this I know, though his family tree
Be spread as wide as the sounding sea,
  He was not a companion of Noah.

My next in death plays a cruel part,
And yet 'tis dear to a woman's heart,
  And sets her pulse beating high.
Of all sizes and shapes, it can fly or bound;
When most 'tis inflated it trails on the ground;
  When least, then it soars in the sky.

My whole is extracted from earth and from sea;
Compounded with care, from obstacles free,
  'Tis dear to the Yankee, I own.
'Tis famous in song, and famous in story,
And yet 'tis indebted for most of its glory
  To the time when 'twas taken alone.

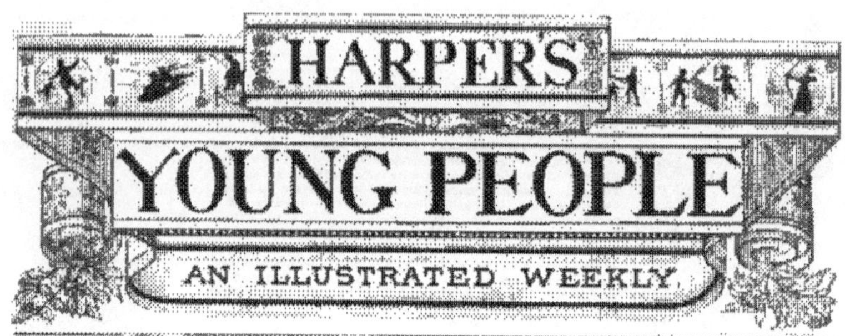

Vol. I.—No. 18. | Published by HARPER & BROTHERS, New York. | Price Four Cents.

Tuesday, March 2, 1880. | Copyright, 1880, by Harper & Brothers. | $1.50 per Year, in Advance.

PASSING THE BATTERIES.

A HUNTING ADVENTURE.

I HAD been travelling in the interior of Africa, in company with a Portuguese ivory trader, for several weeks, greatly enjoying the wild and exciting life we were compelled to lead. The exercise had steadied and braced my nerves, which before setting out were in a shattered condition from the effects of a severe and long attack of fever. Constant practice had also made me an expert shot and a successful hunter. Indeed, if one only knew how to handle a gun, and went to work with proper precaution, the amazing abundance of animal life everywhere to be met with could not fail in making him more or less of a sportsman.

In hunting the large game, such as the lion, the elephant, and the rhinoceros, there was always a spice of danger, and I had in two or three several instances found myself in positions of extreme peril, from which nothing but presence of mind or good fortune brought me safely out. But the danger incurred only lent additional charms to the pursuit; while a proud feeling of exultation would steal over the heart when thinking that an insignificant and feeble man should be more than a match for such huge creatures in spite of their gigantic strength.

One day, in our several canoes, we were paddling up a broad river; on either bank stretched an apparently impenetrable forest, many of the trees of which approached to the very water's edge, while the ends of creepers fell into, and huge plants actually raised their heads out of, the river itself. From the branches of the trees curious-looking monkeys gazed inquisitively at us, chattering to each other as if inquiring what business we had in invading their domains; numbers of brilliantly colored birds hovered on the wing, making the air resound with their varied and peculiar notes; the gentle gazelle would timidly approach to slake his thirst at the water; the noble lion would stalk out in all his majesty for the same purpose, while ever and anon, now close to the canoes, now yards away, a loud snort would startle us, and the huge ugly head of a hippopotamus would be thrust above the surface.

Journeying thus by water is a pleasant and restful change from the everlasting tramp, tramp, through the forest, which, although enjoyable, sometimes becomes a little wearisome. This particular day of which I speak made the third we had thus progressed without any startling adventure occurring to interrupt our voyage; it was not, however, to have so peaceful a close as the other two.

When within some few miles of the spot where we intended camping for the night, as our larder was low, I told the trader I would land and procure some fresh meat for supper, and that I would meet him before long at the trysting-place. My canoe was accordingly directed to the shore. Taking with me four of the natives, to carry my spare gun and what game I might shoot, I plunged into the forest.

I did not go very far from the banks of the river, for, as the day was drawing to a close, I was in hopes of meeting with plenty of game on their way to the water; so I followed the course of the stream toward our camping-place.

The sudden plunge from the dazzling brilliancy of the sun to the solemn gloom of the forest made it almost impossible to see anything clearly until my eyes got accustomed to the peculiar light; so I was perforce obliged for a short time to grope my way cautiously along.

My four attendants followed: one, a lad, bearing my spare gun; two armed with long lances; and the fourth—whom I always called Nacko, and who was one of the best native hunters I have ever known, active, brave, and cool in the presence of danger—carrying a gun of his own, which he could use with something like skill.

Nacko always kept close to my heels, for I think he looked upon himself as my shield and guardian, and thought his protection necessary to insure my safety; otherwise I should run into danger, and come to inevitable grief. His coolness and courage had on more than one critical occasion aided me very materially.

After a quarter of an hour's trampling through grass and bush and prickly thorn, a fine deer offered himself as a target to my rifle; he was on his way to the river, when, hearing our approach, he stopped to listen, and in so doing turned his shoulder toward me. Lifting my rifle, I took quick aim, and fired. The noble beast sprang into the air, and then, falling forward on his knees, gave a few convulsive struggles, and lay perfectly still.

Leaving two of the natives to convey the carcass to the boat, I pushed on with the others, hoping to get another shot. I had not proceeded far, when Nacko expressed his opinion that there were lions in the neighborhood.

"What leads you to think so, Nacko?" I inquired.

Before he could reply there was a rustling in the foliage, and a graceful gazelle bounded into view, evidently fleeing from some pursuer. Quick as thought my gun was at my shoulder, and in an instant he was rolling over.

Then, and only then, I became aware that his pursuer was close at hand, as the roar of a lion fell upon my ear. I began quickly to reload my rifle, but before I had rammed down the bullet a large lion sprang on the body, while a lioness with her half-grown cub followed at his heels.

With his two fore-paws placed on the body of the gazelle, the lion stood erect, and turned his face in our direction. No sooner did he see us than he gave utterance to a savage roar, but seemed uncertain what to do—whether to keep possession of the slaughtered prey or attack the new. Meanwhile the lioness crouched, growling, down by the side of the dead body, while the cub licked the blood trickling from the wound.

I never stirred, but kept my eyes fixed upon the lion, telling the lad with the spare gun to be ready to hand it to me when I should require it. Nacko stood prepared for what might follow.

For a minute we stood thus. I was unwilling to lose the gazelle, but hesitated to fire at the lion, for, even should I be fortunate enough to kill him, there would be the lioness to contend with. I determined to run the risk.

Taking a steady aim, I fired. The explosion was followed by a terrific roar. The bullet had not touched a vital part; I had only succeeded in dangerously wounding him. I had now an angry and formidable foe to encounter.

Throwing down my empty rifle, I put my hand behind me to receive the other from the boy. He was a few steps from me, and before he could place it within my reach, I saw the lion making ready for the fatal spring.

"Fire, Nacko," I cried, as the animal bounded into the air.

Swift as thought the flame leaped from his barrel. I heard the thud of the bullet on the body of the lion, but it could not check the impetus of his spring, and in another moment I was hurled violently to the ground, and for a moment lay stunned by the shock.

A dead heavy weight upon my body and legs soon brought me back to consciousness. Opening my eyes, I found my face within an inch or two of the lion's.

Nacko, seeing me knocked over, had thrown his own gun to the ground and picked up the spare one, and was now approaching to give the lion his *coup de grâce*. The animal watched the hunter's motions, but was unwilling, or too badly wounded, to leave me and attack him.

The bold black approached within six paces of the foe, and aiming behind his ear, fired. A shuddering quiver ran through the mighty frame; I felt a sudden relief from the oppressive weight which confined me to the ground as the lion rolled over, dead.

Nacko assisted me to my feet, running his hands over my body to ascertain if any bones were broken; but with the exception of several severe bruises, and a feeling of general soreness all over my body, I was unhurt. We looked round for the lioness and her cub; they were nowhere to be seen, and must have decamped during my encounter with the lion, for which I felt not a little thankful, as I had no wish for another such encounter.

BIDDY O'DOLAN.

BY MRS. ZADEL B. GUSTAFSON.

CHAPTER II.

MRS. BROWN was not quite so bad as her word, for she did not take away Biddy's doll every night when Biddy could not give her extra pay. Of course there were many nights when Biddy could not do this, even with Charley's help. She had, in the first place, to pay for her straw, her soup, and her bread. Whenever she had earned more than enough for this, Mrs. Brown had

ny had agreed,
a block or two,

said Biddy; "I
the soup when
ept at all till I
"

id Biddy; "I'll

He was a good

in the mornin'; an' if I git a home, I'll speak for ye. Do ye mind that, Charley! They'll be after wantin' of a boy as much as a girl; an' I can give ye a fust-rate riccommend, so I can."

Biddy made him take the card, and punched him once or twice to make sure of his attention.

"Did ye look at him, Charley?" she asked as they walked along. "Did ye mind the two kind eyes of him? The minute ever he looked at me I warn't a bit afeard; an' I felt as I could work my fingers to the bone for him."

Biddy went the next day to the place written on the card Mr. Phil Kennedy had given her. She teased and coaxed Charley a long time before she could get him to go with her, for he was very bashful, and hung back all the way. While she stood at the foot of the steps, looking up to be sure about the number, Mr. Phil Kennedy himself came to the door, and called her in. He looked just as kind and smiling as on the day before, and Biddy bobbed her curly head up and down, to show him how glad she was. She was so eager that she did not think to say "Good-morning"; but she cried out, in a glad, piping voice, "Here's Charley, sir; an' the best boy ye can ever see! If ye wants a boy to take care of the furnise an' fetch the coal; an' he can run of errands faster nor me; an' he mended me doll. Charley—"

While Biddy talked she kept making little springs and jumps at Charley, who kept edging away, so that Biddy was likely to get half way down the block, when all at once Charley turned, and showed his speed by running out of sight very quickly indeed. Biddy looked as if she was going to run after him; but Mr. Phil Kennedy, who stood laughing in his doorway, called after her, and Biddy came back. He led her through the hall, into a very pleasant room. There was an open fire, a bright rug in front of it, a mocking-bird in a cage in the window, and a beautiful lady sitting in an arm-chair, with her feet on a cushion. The lady was pale; her hands were thin and white; there were crutches beside her chair; but she looked as if she were very happy; and when she smiled at Biddy, Biddy could not have told why she felt as if her heart was filling her whole body.

"Let her sit here near me, Phil," said the lady. Then, when Biddy was seated between them, they asked her a great many questions, and Biddy answered them all as well as she knew how. Both spoke so kindly, sometimes the lady and sometimes the gentleman, and seemed to care so much to know all about her, that Biddy took a new interest in her own story, and told it very well. Like the stories of thousands of other friendless children, Biddy's story was very simple. She didn't know where she was born. She had never seen her parents. She didn't know if she had any brothers or sisters; she did know she had never seen any. She had never been at school. She had never slept on a real bed only when she was in the hospital. She had had a "reel good time" in the hospital. A little girl had given her some flowers. She had a friend; his name was Charley; and if they wanted a boy to do things, he was the best boy. He had mended her doll. She wanted a home for her doll. Grumpy wouldn't let her have her doll; that was why she wanted a home. And if they would let her bring her doll, she would do all she could, and try hard to please them.

When Biddy came to the end of her story, Mr. Phil Kennedy said:

"This lady is my sister. She is the only near friend I have in the world, Biddy. If you come to live with us, we will take good care of you, and you must take good care of her. She is lame, and can only walk a very little. You must watch, and learn to save her trouble. She will teach you the things she wants to have you do, but you must not make her tell you the same things over and over again."

Biddy sat very still, and when Mr. Kennedy paused, she waited for him to speak more. He seemed to think for a few minutes very deeply, then he said:

"After you have learned what you are to do, Biddy, I shall want you to help me find some other little girl who has no friends, and needs a home just as you do, and I can perhaps find a home for her too. I have heard all you have said about Charley. There are reasons why I can not help him just at this time. But I promise you that I will remember about him, and will see what I can do for him as soon as I can. Now, Biddy"—and Mr. Kennedy smiled, with a very merry look—"what wages do you think we ought to pay you?"

Biddy did not seem to even hear this question, she was so much interested in the other things Mr. Kennedy had said; and the moment he stopped speaking she asked if she might really have her doll, and when they had satisfied her on this point, she told them Charley would bring it. Then she seemed to suddenly feel how great a change had come in her life. She jumped down from her chair, looked round the room, her breath coming quick, then at her new friends.

"Oh, it's home it 'll be! An' if ye'll let me begin," she cried, "I'll try to be so good, so I will!"

[To be continued.]

"BLESS ME! IF IT ISN'T PHIL KENNEDY."

HELPING HIMSELF TO CAKE

BY M. E.

FAST asleep fell Madeline,
  Fairy-book held in one hand,
In the other slice of cake—
  Slept, and drifted to the land
Where the spirits of the dreams
  Many wondrous visions keep—
Visions that are only seen
  When the eyes are closed in sleep.

Dreamed the little Madeline
  That she was a princess fair,
Beautiful as that proud maid
  Famous for her golden hair.
And at splendid feast she sat,
  And a prince sat by her side,
Handsome as the prince who won
  "Sleeping Beauty" for his bride;

Dreamed a cake—a wedding cake—
  She dispensed to courtly throng,
Cutting it with knife of gold,
  While the "Blue Bird" sang a song.
Largest piece received the prince,
  And he whispered, "This is bliss,"
As he kissed her hand and gave
  Ring of diamond with the kiss.

But ere long the dream grew dim.
  Feast and courtiers vanished quite,
Diamond ring and lover too
  Softly faded from her sight;
And the only prince she saw
  (She was once more wide-awake)
Was a little prince of mice
  Nibbling at her slice of cake.

VIÂ BRINDISI.

BY HARLAN H. BALLARD.

WE left India in a bag of leather. Dark and narrow it was, but greater messengers than Postal Cards have to wait a while in darkness before the time comes for them to tell their message. Flowers have to—so do butterflies.

Do not think from this that I was lonely. Oh no. I rode next to a grand Letter in white, and not far from a partly Circular in buff. However, as he was not of my class, I shunned him. The Letter, on the contrary, charmed me; he seemed so self-contained, so wrapped up in his own thoughts. Besides, he bore a crest and a monogram and a superscription to be proud of. He was quite reserved; but before we passed Aden his singularity had so far worn off that I learned that he was commissioned to bear a message to a dainty young lady in the southwest of England. What the message was I could only guess. Letters are not nearly so frank about such matters as I have been taught to consider proper. Still, it must have been something very delightful, for one could tell from his crest and monogram that the Letter had been sent by a person of gentle blood, and in fact he told me that his master was a handsome young man in a military coat. Moreover, he said that this young man had given him a very warm pressure of the hand at parting (which had left a deep impression on him), and had even touched him lightly to his lips.

Possibly you have never reflected upon the fact that Postal Cards and Letters have any feelings. But wait. Perhaps one of our race is waiting at this very moment to undeceive you. After the right one comes along and tells you his message, you will know thenceforward that we are quite alive, and have great power over the affections.

Post-office clerks have no sentiment. All along the way they handled us as rudely as if we had been mere blank pieces of pasteboard. One or two of them coolly stared at me till I was very red in the face, and then turned me over and stared again, until I felt as if I were getting read in my back. I am told that such rudeness is not uncommon. As if this were not enough, the fellow then laid me upon my back, and picking up a heavy instrument, struck me a violent blow in the face. It was as if I had been stamped upon, and I carry the marks of it to this day. Why he did it, I do not know, unless it was because I was a *foreigner*.

The gentleman for whom I was travelling was a student, and I was carrying a glad message to an old chum of his in Massachusetts. I lived with this student some weeks before he sent me on my errand. As I lay in a pigeon-hole of his desk, I often saw him get out his books and study. He sometimes read them aloud. He liked Horace best of all. He would light a cigar, put his feet on the desk, and read Satires as if he were very happy indeed. I soon became fond of Horace too. I liked to listen to his queer stories of life in Rome, of his love of country life, and of his dear friends Virgil and Mæcenas.

My favorite story was the "Trip on a Canal-Boat." I used to picture to myself the jolly poet sitting by the prow of the quaint boat, watching the twinkling lights

alongshore, and listening to the loud songs and rude jests of the barge-men. So when I learned that I was to be sent on a long journey, you may believe it was no small comfort to me to learn that I was to go "*viâ Brindisi*." I was to visit the very town to which the poet had travelled so long ago. Perhaps between here and Rome I might even catch a glimpse of the old canal. Fortunately there was a little crack in the side of the bag where I lay, and I managed to get a peep of the town. I could not see anything which satisfied me much. Brindisi is not what Brundusium was. When Virgil died there, when Cæsar marched against it with golden eagles, when Antony threatened there the man who afterward became Augustus, it was a great city. It had an excellent harbor, strong fortifications, and sixty thousand inhabitants. Now it is nothing.

I can not tell you of all the interesting places I passed on my way. In fact, I hardly know myself where I did go, for I slept most of the time, and when awake, my bruised head ached so badly that I did not care to be curious.

In fact, until I reached Brindisi I had only once attempted to peep out. I did wish to view the Suez Canal. But for that I should have been obliged to go around the Cape of Storms. To be sure, in that case I might have caught a glimpse of Table Mountain and its vaporous "table-cloth," and have seen the rocky isle where Napoleon was caged. But that would have been small compensation for the tedious voyage. So I regarded the Suez Canal as in some sort a friend, and I tried to see it. But the vulgar yellow Circular I told you of edged himself directly in front of me, and hid the view completely. I had no more remarkable adventures until we reached the Post-office in London. I did not suffer at all on the Channel, though my courtly friend the Letter and his pages were all quite distressed. He was unkind enough to say that my escape was probably due to the fact that I had nothing inside. I excused the discourtesy, under the circumstances, and was heartily sorry to part from him at London. Here I was taken out and given a breath of fresh air. But here, also, I suffered. Another clerk seized me, and struck me a violent blow on the breast. He certainly left a red mark upon me. I think that I shall not recover from my ill-treatment.

I have lived long enough to reach the one to whom I was sent, and to give him glad congratulations on his—But, there! I almost told my secret. It is my greatest fault.

My life is nearly over. I meant to tell you of Bombay, its race-course, its fine harbor which gives it its name, its wealthy Parsees, and good Sir Jamsetjee Jejeebhoy, but I am too much worn out. I have had my face photographed for you. You can see my scars. You must not turn me over and read my glad message. That would not be fair. I too have a superscription. I have been of use. I have been told that after my death I may live again; that I may, perhaps, live in white, and become a grand letter. I may even get a monogram and a crest. It is not impossible. Other messengers of glad tidings die and live again. Flowers do—and butterflies.

POP'S IDEA OF FUN.

BY MRS. FRANK McCARTHY.

ONLY this morning Pop punched me in the ribs, and winked, and whispered behind his hand, "Any more sprees on hand, Bob?" I was disgusted, and didn't say anything. If he'd been a boy of my size just then, things would have been different; but Pop is a kind of man it isn't pleasant to offend. I smiled in a sickly way, but I was never more disgusted in my life. Any more sprees! I should think not. I'll leave it to any one if his kind of sprees pay. "Count me in for the next racket, Bob," he said at the breakfast table, and then he winked again. I declare I was that sick I let my buckwheat cake get cold.

Here's the way it was. We live in a nobby kind of place, you see. Almost everybody owns his own house and grounds, and spends all his spare time in fixing up. Most of the gentlemen go over to New York to business every day, but before they go, and after they come back, they're always fussing around, making little alterations, and what they call improvements. It makes 'em awful mad if the place is out of order the seventieth part of an inch. The ladies raise flowers, fix baskets and vases, and all that kind of gimcracks, and the men go pottering about, making more fuss over their plots of ground than a big farmer out West does over his thousands of acres. Well, we boys get together sometimes and arrange everything to suit ourselves. In a single night it 'll be like a transformation scene at a pantomime—maybe not so pretty, but every bit as funny. Fun! We've laughed ready to split our sides to see the poor old barber come limping up for his pole in front of the doctor's, and the doctor go blustering down there for his hitching post; a lot of paving-stones against the door of the real-estate office, and the cows and chickens running loose about town.

But this particular lark was what we called a specialty. Only gates were to be touched, and these were to undergo a regular tribulation. The weather was about right—muggy—and the mud in some places knee-deep. We arranged all the preliminaries at recess, and Tom Jones was to go around about nine o'clock and let us know if the coast was clear; but he wasn't to give our regular call—all the place knows that. It goes something in this way, "Ki-yuah-yuah, yoo-o," with a prolonged howl at the end. We always drop it when anything secret's on hand. It was agreed upon that Tom Jones should go to each house, if all was right, and have a coughing and sneezing spell that wouldn't arouse suspicion; then we were to creep out, when the folks were gone to bed, and go to work. And it happened to be work that time, you'd better believe!

We were all sitting around the table when the clock struck nine. Pop had his spectacles on, and was reading an editorial to ma, the girls were busy with their lessons, and I had finished my last example, when all at once we heard a terrible coughing and sneezing out in the street. That was the worst of Tom Jones—he always overdid his part. If he'd had pneumonia, whooping-cough, asthma, and bronchitis, and been hired to go round with a cough medicine to cure 'em, he couldn't have turned himself further inside out. Of course Pop began to notice it, and ma looked up in alarm. "Why," said ma, "that boy's got a terrible cold!"

"Fearful!" said Pop, with a queer twist of his under lip; and when Tom Jones, like a big donkey, went across the street to Jim Clancy's house, and began the whole thing over again, Pop wanted to know why that boy's cold was like the paper he held in his hand. We all gave it up, and Pop said because it was *periodical*. Ma and the girls looked mystified, but I was afraid then he'd tumbled to something, and couldn't help getting red, to save my life. That's the worst of my plagued skin—it's so thin the blood shows right through it.

There were no more of the boys' houses in our avenue, and pretty soon we all went to bed. I slept in the little room on the second floor off the hall; it was an easy thing to climb out the window, and down by the Virginia creeper to the front garden. I went around to our place of meeting, and there they all were. The wind had sprung up pretty brisk, and there was a thin coating of ice over the mud; but that was all the better for the gates we wanted to bury. We owed a grudge to old Jake Van Couter, and we made up our minds he'd have a nice time getting his gate back. The miserable old caboodle was rusty, and nearly tore our nails off, but we got it loose at last, and hauled it off to a marshy lot, where we sunk it in the mud. Then we changed the doctor's gate to the judge's, and to avert suspicion we took our own gates off with the rest. We were getting pretty well tired out and ready for home, and had laid my gate up against a neighboring fence, when who should be standing right there in the shadow of the wall but Pop! We were all so thunder-struck that we didn't move, and to my surprise Pop began to laugh and beckon to the boys to come closer. They were not to be caught by that bait, and stood off pretty considerably, when Pop whispered over to us, in quite a jolly tone of voice: "Don't be afraid, boys. I like to see you enjoy yourselves. I was a boy once myself. Bless your hearts! I like fun yet as well as anybody."

Then he laughed ready to split, bent himself double, and we all began to feel easy, and laugh too. Tom Jones said he wished *his* father was like mine, and Pop began to encourage us to do more. We were so spurred on by him that we hardly left a gate in the place where it belonged, Pop going along with us, acting as a kind of scout, he said, and seeing that nobody was near to disturb us. Once or twice he gave a signal of alarm, and we all crouched down as still as mice, Pop stiller than any of us. I never was so dumfounded in my life, for I'd never seen Pop very jolly that way before. The boys were delighted with him; they all agreed to make him president of our club, and Pop said he'd take the position when he got back from the Legislature.

Well, we'd come to the conclusion the place was completely done, and Jim Clancy proposed we should go home. Jim had torn his hands rather badly with Uncle Jake's gate, and didn't feel very good, when suddenly Pop said:

"Yes, boys, of course we'll go home pretty soon, when we're through, you know; but we must put *all the gates back in their places again first!*"

We all looked at each other aghast for a minute. "Back again!" cried the fellows. "Well, I guess not!" "Not much!" "Hardly!" and all sorts of derisive refusals went round.

Pop stood among us, whirling his cane, smiling all the time, and said: "Oh, yes you will, boys, when you think of it a minute. You've had your fun, you know; but it won't do to go too far. I'm a justice of the peace, you see, and this innocent little racket comes under the head of 'malicious mischief.' You could all be sent to jail; and no matter how badly I'd feel, I'd have to act under the law. There's where it is, you see; people are so hard on boys they won't let them enjoy themselves. It's too bad; but never mind, we've had our fun anyway. Now let's get to work in earnest. Here, we'll begin with this gate. Lift it up there, Jim; hold on the other side, Bobby, my boy. Now we have it—all together." And as true as you live, we actually found ourselves walking along with the gate between us. From that gate we went to another, and another. I don't know how it was, but we just plodded along, and did what Pop said. He was laughing, and joking, and flourishing his cane; but, oh, how tired we were! How our hands and our feet and our hearts ached, and how sickening it all was! The most sickening of anything was to hear Pop laugh and carry on all the time, as if this was the cream of the joke. I tell you, we were all mad enough; and when we got to old Jake Van Couter's, we just rebelled. We all hated Jake, anyhow; and Tom Jones he stood right out in the road, and said Jake was a mean old curmudgeon; and then Pop got hold of Tom before we knew it, and down came his cane with a whack.

"Now, boys," says Pop, "fun's fun, and I'm as fond of it as anybody, but I don't see any use of spoiling a good time in this kind of way. Jake couldn't put that gate back, to save his life, and it goes to my heart to hear hard words against the poor old man. He's bent double with rheumatism, he's old and he's poor, and he's no subject for your fun. Take a fellow like me if you want fun. I don't mind it. Do what you like to me, but spare poor old Jake."

Well, we just looked at one another in mute disgust, but we didn't care to dispute any further with Pop. We plunked along that nasty old freezing road, and we yanked Uncle Jake's gate out of the mud, and carried it half a mile, our nails hanging off, and tears of rage and mortification rolling down our cheeks, with Pop laughing like a good one all the while, declaring that he didn't see how anybody *could* be so hard on boys; they *would* have their fun, and for his part he thought it did them good, and it took him back to his youth again; he hadn't had such a spree for many a year.

We groaned and looked at each other, and each of us dropped off silently and gloomily at our separate doors. A whole month has gone by without a proposition for fun of any kind, and I'll leave it to anybody if it ain't enough to disgust a fellow to have Pop winking at me behind his hand, and telling me to count him in for the next racket.

ALMOST TIME!

ALMOST time for the pretty white daisies
  Out of their sleep to awaken at last,
And over the meadows, with grasses and clover,
  To bud and to blossom, and grow so fast.
Almost time for the buttercups yellow,
  The ferns and the flowers, the roses and all,
To waken from slumber, and merrily hasten
  To gladden our hearts at the spring's first call.

Almost time for the skies to grow bluer,
  And breezes to soften, and days to grow long;
For eyes to grow brighter, and hearts to grow gladder,
  And Earth to rejoice in her jubilant song.
Almost time for the sweetest of seasons:
  Nearer it comes with each new-born day,
And soon the smile of the beautiful spring-time
  Winter's cold shadows will chase away!

REMARKABLE ANIMALS.

AUSTRALIA and Tasmania possess many specimens of strange animal life; even in the latter, or Van Diemen's Land, are found several species which exist only on that small bit of the earth's surface. Tasmania, which is separated from the southern extremity of Australia by a strait about one hundred and forty miles in width, was first discovered in 1642, by Abel Tasman, a famous Dutch navigator, who supposed it to be a portion of Australia, then known as New Holland. The celebrated Captain Cook visited it one hundred and fifty years later; but it was not until about 1800, when Captain Flinders, exploring the southern coast of Australia, discovered the strait, that Tasmania was known to be an island. As Mr. Bass, surgeon of a British ship which had cruised in those waters, had already affirmed that such a strait existed, Captain Flinders named it Bass Strait in his honor.

At the beginning of this century a few tribes of natives were the sole human inhabitants of Tasmania, but about 1803 a party of English military, with a gang of convicts under their charge, came from New South Wales and formed a settlement, which is now a flourishing English town called Hobart Town. Sheep-raising is now the principal industry of this island, and large exports of wool are made yearly.

The scenery of Tasmania is very picturesque. Grand basaltic headlands tower along the coast, while inland are lofty mountains, broad lakes, untrodden jungles, and wide-spreading plains covered with rich and luxuriant vegetation.

Australia and Tasmania are the residence of the curious family of animals with pouches, called Marsupialia, from *marsupium*, signifying a purse or bag. One variety of this species, the opossum, is found in the United States, and a few live in South America and Mexico, but in the Australian regions are more than seventy different kinds of these singular creatures. The leader of them all is the great kangaroo, which stands about five feet high when resting upon its hind-feet and haunches. When running it springs from the ground in an erect position, holding its short fore-arms tight to its chest, like a professional runner, and it will go as far as sixteen feet at one jump. From twenty to thirty species of kangaroos are found in Australia and the surrounding islands.

A member of the Marsupialia family which does not exist out of the small island of Tasmania is the zebra-wolf, the most savage and destructive of all the marsupials. This ferocious beast is about the size of the largest kind of sheep-dog. Its short fur is of a yellowish-brown color, and its back and sides are handsomely marked with black stripes. It is a fleet runner, propelling itself with its hind-legs, which are jointed like those of a kangaroo, although it goes on all fours. Its gait is a succession of quick springs—a peculiarity of nearly all the animals of Tasmania.

The zebra-wolf is very troublesome to the sheep-raising farmers, and constant watch is required to prevent its depredations on the flocks and herds. It inhabits caverns and rocks in the deep and almost impenetrable glens in the neighborhood of the high mountain ranges, from whence it sallies forth at night to scour the great grassy plains in search of food. It preys on the brush kangaroo, the great emu, and any small birds or beasts it can capture.

Another strange beast is the porcupine ant-eater, or Tasmanian hedgehog. It is much larger than the English hedgehog, and can not roll itself into a ball. Its back is covered with very stout spines protruding from a coat of thick gray fur, and in place of a mouth it has a round bill about two inches long. One of these strange creatures was once presented to an English lady living at Hobart Town. For safety she placed it at the bottom of a deep wooden churn until better lodgings could be provided. Shortly after, on going to look at her captive, she found it clinging by its long claws to the top of the churn, with its funny little head peeping over. The bill gave an indescribably droll expression to its queer pursed-up face, while its bright eyes peered restlessly about from their furry nooks. There was something so pitiful, pleading, and helpless in the expression of the little creature, that the lady, fearing she could not make it happy in captivity, at once set it free in her garden. It immediately began to burrow, casting up a circular ridge of earth, beneath which in a moment it vanished, and never was seen again.

The duck-bill is a near kinsman of the porcupine ant-eater. It is a mole-like quadruped, with a large bill like a duck's. It spends most of its time in the water, but lives in a burrow on the shore. Its feet are very curious, as they can be changed at the pleasure of their owner. When in the water they are webbed like a duck's, but if the creature comes on shore, the web shrinks, and leaves long sharp claws ready for burrowing.

There is also a small, clumsy, inoffensive animal called the wombat, which is never found outside of these Australian regions. Its head resembles that of a badger. It has very small eyes, short legs, and its fat, squab body is covered with coarse gray hair. It lives in rocky places and mountain gullies, and feeds on the roots of plants. It is easily tamed, and makes a very affectionate pet. Some English children living in Tasmania once had a pet wombat. It became so mischievous, however, that they determined to carry it back to its native forest. But the wombat having tasted the comforts of civilized life, had no desire to dig for its living again. Three times it was carried away, the last time to a wood beyond a deep river; but every time, when night came, a well-known scratching was heard at the door, and the wombat presented itself, drenched and weary, but determined not to suffer banishment from its comfortable home. Its master, touched by so much attachment, at length allowed it to remain, and it passed the rest of its days in peace.

The kangaroo-rat and kangaroo-mouse, the opossum-mouse, the flying opossum, and some other odd little creatures, inhabit Tasmania. They are all marsupials, having a pouch for their little ones, and jumping on their hind-feet like a kangaroo.

An enormous bird is found in the Australian countries, called the emu. In its habits and general appearance it resembles the ostrich, although it does not possess the exquisite plumage of that bird. The long drooping feathers of the emu are brownish-black in color, and covered with hairy fibers. A full-grown bird is five or six feet in height. It never flies, but, like the ostrich, is a very swift runner, and as it is very shy, is difficult to capture. Its nest is a hole scraped in the ground, where it lays six or seven dark green eggs. Emus are much hunted by the Bushmen, as a fine clear oil is prepared from the skin, which is highly prized for its medicinal qualities.

Many varieties of remarkable and beautiful birds are found in Australia and Tasmania: the lyre-bird, with its wonderful tail feathers; the odd owl-like "morepoke," which screams its own name through the forest solitudes all night long; glistening bronze-winged pigeons; strange and gorgeous parrots; and others, to describe which would fill a large volume. In this locality are nearly a hundred species of birds and beasts not found in any other portion of the world, and they are all, with scarcely a single exception, the oddest and strangest of existing creatures.

EMU AND ZEBRA WOLVES.

A RIDE IN THE PARK.—Drawn by P. De Lisle.

NED'S SNOW-HOUSE.

A True Story.

LITTLE Ned Bancroft stood by the window, and as he looked at the fast-falling snow and the sidewalks deeply covered, he thought, "What a fine time I shall have this afternoon shovelling snow, for it is Friday, and I shall have no lesson to learn!"

His mamma then called to him, "Come, Ned, it is nearly nine o'clock; you must start for school."

So off he trudged, delighted with the idea of battling the storm, his feet well protected with high rubber boots, and his hands covered with warm mittens made by his loving grandmamma.

Ned was an only child, the pride of his papa and mamma, and the great pet of aunties and uncles. As for grandmamma, she never tired of kissing his sweet round little face.

Not long after he had gone to school it stopped snowing, and men with large shovels were seen in the streets, pulling the door-bells, and asking, "Want your snow shovelled?"

Mrs. Bancroft engaged one of these men, and ordered him, before cleaning the sidewalk, to clear up the back yard by shovelling the snow into a pile in one corner, as Jane wanted to hang out the clothes.

When Ned came home to lunch, he saw with delight the great mound of snow the man had made, and he resolved to make a house in it when school was over.

His aunt Lou, who lived in New York, came in on her way to grandmamma's while Ned and his mamma were eating their lunch, and Ned heard auntie ask his mother to go with her, and mamma consented, and he heard her say, "I will not get home before six o'clock." How well he remembered this remark, some hours afterward, we shall see, but at the moment he paid little heed to it, as his mind was full of the afternoon's sport. He kissed them good-by as he left the table, and was soon back at school, which was only a few blocks off.

Ned was only ten years old, but his mother had taught him to be careful with his books and toys, and put them in their proper places when he had done with them.

When school was out he ran home, put his spelling-book on the shelf in his little room, took out his shovel from the box where he kept his playthings, and went into the yard.

He began to work immediately, digging out a hole in the bottom of the pile of snow, which was to be his house. His shovel was small, and it took a long while to make a place large enough to creep into. But he enjoyed the sport, tossing each shovelful of snow as high as he could, and across the yard.

For a short time he had a companion, Eva Roslyn, a little girl who lived next door, who peeped through a crack in the fence, and could just see him at work.

"Didn't I throw that shovelful high, Eva?" he called out.

"Oh, I can hardly see you," said Eva. "I wish you would cut this hole larger, Ned."

"I will some day," replied Ned. "But run and ask your mother to let you come in here and help me dig out my house."

"Well," said Eva, and went in-doors, and up stairs to her mamma, whom she found in the parlor talking with a lady who had brought her little girl to play with Eva.

Eva and her friend were soon busy with their dolls and baby-house, and poor Ned was entirely forgotten. He had by this time made his house just large enough to allow him to get inside. He said to himself, "I will try it myself before Eva comes," and bending his head quite low, crept into the hole.

The stooping position was very uncomfortable, and he thought, "I must make my house higher inside," and moved slightly backward, intending to get out. Suddenly he found himself unable to stir, and entirely surrounded with darkness: his house had caved in, and the poor boy was deeply buried in the snow.

The brave little fellow, although terribly frightened, began at once to consider what was best for him to do. He thought there were three ways in which he might get released from his imprisonment. He had seen the clothes hanging on the lines; Jane would come out to take them down, and when she did, he would call to her for help. If she didn't hear him, then—oh, how well he remembered the hour!—mamma would be home at six o'clock. He knew she always closed her blinds before lighting the gas; he would call to her as loud as he could, and she might hear him. But he began to wonder a little how long should he have to wait. If neither Jane nor mamma heard him, he must then wait for papa, who would surely not sit down to dinner without searching for his little son. He thought of Eva, but didn't expect any assistance from her, because he knew when she came to the door and didn't see him in the yard she would return home.

Then he happened to remember what his teacher had told the class in school that very day—that any one would soon smother to death unless he could have fresh air to breathe, and he thought, "I shall soon use all the air in here. If I could only make a little hole to let in some fresh air from outside!" He felt very tightly packed in, his chin resting on his knees, and his back almost bent double. He tried so hard to change his position, but could at first only move backward and forward the fingers of his right hand; this he continued to do until he could slightly move his arm. He worked with it until at last he felt the cold air blowing upon his hand. How cold it felt! but he kept it outside, making as much motion with it as he could, hoping Jane would see it when she came out for the clothes, and wondering what it was, would come to his relief.

But he found it impossible to hold his little hand out long, for it began to ache and grow stiff; so he pulled it in, and comforted himself with the ray of light that came through the hole, and the thought of the fresh air he now had to breathe.

He hadn't once called out loudly for help, as most boys would naturally have done, for, as we have seen, he was thoughtful as well as brave, and knew that if he cried out now, when no one was near, he might not have any strength left to call to Jane when she came out, or to his mother when she opened the window.

How slowly the time passed! The small ray of light was getting dim, his courage began to fail, when the sound of an opening door came to his ears. It must be Jane, he thought, and his heart beat faster with hope.

Out she came, singing loudly,

> "'Now, Rory, be aisy,' sweet Kathleen would cry,
> Reproof on her lip, but a smile in her eye,"

and poor little Ned's smothered voice was not heard as he called, "Jane! Jane! come and help me; I'm under the snow!"

It seemed to him but a minute before all was still again: the clothes were taken from the line, and Jane was back in her warm kitchen, without a thought of suffering Ned.

One of his three hopes had failed, but Ned took courage. It must be nearly six now, for hardly any light was coming in through the hole, and mamma would soon open the window to close the blinds. How still he kept, listening for every sound! and at last his heart gave a thump.

"Surely that was the window opening." Not a second did he lose. "Mamma! mamma! I'm here under the snow; do come here!" he called, with all his strength, over and over again. It is no wonder that the tears began to fall thick and fast from Ned's eyes as the window closed, and the dreadful still darkness was around him, and the hope of making mamma hear him lost.

Now he had only to wait for papa, and our little hero stopped his sobs, fearing he might lose one sound of those expected welcome steps. He would try to be as patient as possible, not a doubt entering his mind of papa's finding him.

Mrs. Bancroft had come home, and after taking off her cloak and bonnet, as usual closed her blinds, entirely unconscious of the little voice appealing to her for help. She thought her boy was sitting in the library learning his lesson, or was perhaps listening to one of Jane's Irish stories in the kitchen, Jane being very fond of him; she had been his nurse when he was a baby. Yet mamma was rather surprised that Ned had not run up stairs to see her after the long afternoon's absence.

She went down stairs to meet Mr. Bancroft, whom she heard opening the front door; they walked together into the library, papa saying, "Where's Ned?"

"He must be in the kitchen," said Mrs. Bancroft. "I've not seen him since I came home at six o'clock."

Mr. Bancroft went into the hall, calling aloud, "Ned, where are you?"

How joyfully would Ned have answered could he have heard papa's dear cheerful voice!

There was no response, and Mrs. Bancroft rang the library bell. "Jane, send Master Ned up stairs," she said, as Jane made her appearance.

"Sure I've not seen him the whole afternoon, ma'am."

Mrs. Bancroft looked at her husband with an alarmed face, saying, "Where can the child be? He never staid out so late before."

After searching every room in the house, they went to the front door, looking in vain up and down the street. Mr. Bancroft then went to the houses of several neighbors whose little boys had often played with Ned, but none had seen him since school-time.

The parents were now truly frightened, for Ned had never been in the habit of going anywhere without permission; but now they thought he must have strayed away, and some accident befallen him.

"Oh, Edward," said Mrs. Bancroft, the tears falling from her eyes, "what shall we do to find our boy?"

Dreading to alarm her, Mr. Bancroft didn't mention his fears, but with a heavy heart put on his hat, and again went into the street, his wife returning to the library convulsed with sobs.

Where could he go but to the nearest station-house, thought Ned's anxious father, and started thither; but when he reached the corner of the street he turned round again, disliking the idea of going far from the house where it was most natural to see the boy.

"I will go back and examine his playthings. He has always been an orderly child. I can easily tell whether he has used any of them this afternoon."

Once more he entered the door, and went directly to Ned's room. The spelling-book was in its place, but his overcoat and hat were not to be found. The box of playthings was next examined. It was open, showing Ned had been there, and his little shovel was missing.

Why he immediately went into the yard, Mr. Bancroft could afterward never tell. It must have been a good fairy that led him to the back door, where he stood a few seconds looking out into the darkness, longing for a sight of the little face which always welcomed him home.

It must have been the same fairy that moved him to walk to the back of the yard, where a black spot in the snow attracted his attention. His heart gave a leap; it was Ned's shovel. And what was that faint moaning sound that came to his ears? Was Eva in any distress in the next yard? He listened.

"Papa! oh, papa! I'm here, under the snow!"

"Ned, my boy, where are you?"

"Here, papa, under the snow."

With the same little shovel the father now worked with all his might, cheering his child by the continued sound of his voice, saying, "Papa will take you out in a minute. Be a brave boy. Papa will soon get you."

Mrs. Bancroft, who was waiting in-doors, heard, as she thought, persons talking in the yard, and opened the library window, when her husband called to her: "Send some one here to help me! Be quick; Ned is here under the snow."

Jane overheard, and rushed out with her coal shovel, and began to dig with the strength and energy of a man, and crying, "Me darlint, me darlint, is it here ye are?"

When at last the brave little fellow felt the loving arms of his father tight about him, he simply whispered, "Oh, papa, I'm so glad you came!"

Can any of my young readers imagine with what happiness both father and mother kissed and hugged their cold and stiff little darling? They carried him with gentle hands into the house, and hurriedly sent Jane for the doctor, as poor Ned was now quite exhausted.

When old Dr. Gray looked down at the child he said little, but with a serious face administered stimulants, and with his own hands assisted in rubbing back life into the almost frozen body of our young hero.

If Ned had been many minutes longer buried in the snow, this story could never have had such a cheerful ending.

AN HONEST MINER.

IF you go into a mining district in Cornwall, England, you will see, not far from the mine works, rows of neat little cottages; most of them are extremely clean in the interior, and here the miners may be found seated at comfortable fires, frequently reading, or in the summer evenings working in their little gardens or in the potato fields. Frequently they become experienced floriculturists, and at the flower shows that occur annually in several of the Cornish towns they often carry off the prizes.

A pleasing anecdote is recorded of the honesty of a poor Cornish miner. There lived at St. Ives a lady named Prudence Worth, whose charity was remarkable. A miner living at Camborne had his goods seized for rent, which he could not pay. He had heard of the many good deeds done by "Madam" Worth, as she was usually called, and he determined to apply to her for assistance. He said:

"Madam, I am come to you in great trouble. My goods are seized for rent, and they will be sold if I can not get the money immediately."

"Where do you live?" inquired Mrs. Worth.

"In Camborne, and I work in Stray Park Mine."

"I know nothing of you," observed the lady, "and you may be a drunkard, or an impostor."

"Madam," replied the miner, with energy, "as I live, I am neither; and if you will lend me the money, I will return it in four months."

The money was lent, the period of *four months* elapsed, and, true to his promise, the poor miner, notwithstanding that bad luck had attended him, had managed to get the amount borrowed together, and set off on foot with it. Arriving at Hayle River, he found the tide coming up, but to save a journey of three miles round by St. Erith Bridge, he resolved to cross the water, which appeared to him shallow enough for this purpose. The poor fellow had, however, miscalculated the depth, and was drowned. When the body was brought to shore, his wife said that he had left home with three guineas in his pocket for Madam Worth. Search was made in his pockets, and no money was found, but some one observed that his right hand was firmly clinched. It was opened, and found to contain the three guineas.

BABY.

BY K. M. M.

What are you looking at, Baby dear,
With your wide-open serious eyes,
That were made from the depths of heaven's
own blue,
Stolen away from the skies?

What do you think of this great wide world
That you gaze on with such surprise?
I should like to know, if you only could tell,
You look so grave and so wise.

The professor himself, who has studied for years,
Has not half so sage an air
As this baby of ours when he sits all alone
In the lap of the great arm-chair.

And what are you talking of, all by yourself,
In those words which none of us know?—
We forget so soon the language of heaven,
In this work-a-day world below.

But teach us those accents strange and sweet
That you've learned from the angels above,
For we must become like this little child
Ere we enter God's kingdom of love.

KNITTED SCARF.

LITTLE girls who like to knit will be glad to know how to make this pretty scarf. It is knitted with two threads, one of white and the other of chinchilla zephyr worsted, and wooden needles, crosswise, in rounds going back and forth. Strands of worsted are knotted in the ends for fringe. Begin the scarf with a thread of white and a thread of chinchilla worsted, cast on 87 st. (stitch), and knit as follows: 1st round.—(Slip the first st. of each round, and carry the working thread to the wrong side, slipping it through between both needles; the last st. is always knit off plain with both threads, catching them together. This will not be referred to further.) Lay the chinchilla worsted on the needle from the front to the wrong side, knit the next st. plain with the white thread, * carry the chinchilla thread underneath the needle and over the white thread to the front, lay the white thread on the needle from the front to the wrong side, purl the next st. with the chinchilla worsted, lay the latter on the needle from the front to the wrong side, carry the white thread underneath the chinchilla thread to the next st., and knit this plain, and repeat from *. 2d round.—Lay the chinchilla thread on the needle from the front to the wrong side, purl the next st. which appears purled on this side, together with the thread thrown over, with the white thread, * lay the white thread on the needle from the front to the wrong side, carry the chinchilla thread underneath the white thread to the next st., and knit this plain together with the thread thrown over, carry the white thread from the wrong side to the front underneath the needle, and over the chinchilla thread, lay the latter on the needle from the front to the wrong side, purl the next st. together with the thread thrown over, with white worsted, and repeat from *. 3d and 4th rounds.—Like the 1st and 2d rounds, but in the 3d round always purl the st. which appear purled on the working side, and knit plain those which look as if knit plain. Repeat always the 1st to 4th rounds, transposing the design (see Fig. 2). Finally, cast off the st. loosely with both threads.

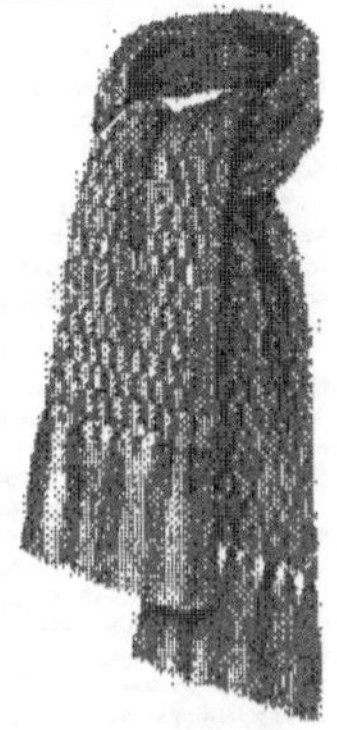

Fig. 1.—Knitted Scarf. [See Fig. 2.]

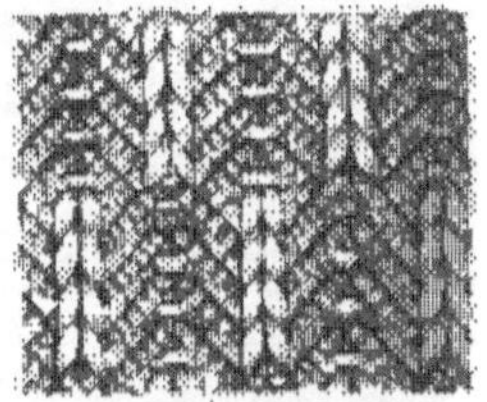

Fig. 2.—Detail of Scarf, Fig. 1.

BISHOP HATTO.

THE story goes that there once lived in Germany, in a handsome, spacious palace, a selfish, fat old Bishop. His table was always spread with the choicest dainties, and he drank in abundance wine of the very best; he slept long and soundly, and looked so comfortable and happy and fat that the people whispered to each other, "How grand it must be to be a Bishop!"

One summer, in the neighborhood where the Bishop lived, the rain came down in such torrents and continued so long, that the grain was utterly ruined, and when autumn arrived, there was none to be gathered. "What shall we do," said the poor fathers and mothers, "when the long winter comes, and we have no food to give our children?"

Winter arrived, bringing the cold winds and the snow and the frost. The little ones begged for bread, and the poor mothers were compelled to say the bread was all gone.

"Let us go to the Bishop," at last said the poor pining creatures. "Surely he will help us. He has far more food than he needs, and it is useless our starving here when he has plenty."

Very soon from his palace window the Bishop saw numbers of the poor people flocking to his gates, and he thought to himself: "So they want my corn; but they shall not have it; and the sooner they find out their mistake, the better." So he sent them all away. The next day others came. Still the Bishop refused, but still the people persevered in calling out for food at his gates.

At last, wearied with their cries, but still unmoved by their pitiable condition, the Bishop announced that on a certain day his large barn should be open for any one to enter who chose, and that when the place was full, as much food should be given them as would last all the winter.

At last the day came, and for a time forgetting their hunger, the women and children, as well as the men, both old and young, crowded up to the barn door.

The Bishop watched them, with a smile on his deceitful old face, until the place was quite full; then he fastened the door securely, and actually set fire to the barn, and burned it to the ground. As he listened to the cries of agony, he said to himself, "How much better it will be for the country when all these *rats*," as he called the poor sufferers, "are killed, because while they were living they only consumed the corn!"

Having done this, he went to his palace, and sat down to his dainty supper, chuckling to himself to think how cleverly he had disposed of the "rats."

The next morning, however, his face wore a different expression, when his eye fell upon the spot where the night before had hung a likeness of himself. There was the frame, but the picture had gone: it had been eaten by the rats.

At this the wicked Bishop was frightened. He thought of the poor dying people he had spoken of as rats the day before, and he turned cold and trembled. As he stood shivering, a man from the farm ran up in terror, exclaiming that the rats had eaten all the corn that had been stored in the granaries.

Scarcely had the man finished speaking when another messenger arrived, pale with fear, and bringing tidings more terrible still. He said ten thousand rats were coming fast to the palace, and told the Bishop to fly for his life, adding a prayer that his master might be forgiven for the crime he had committed the day before.

"The rats shall not find me," said Bishop Hatto, for that was his name. "I will go shut myself up in my strong tower on the Rhine. No rats can reach me there; the walls are high, and the stream around is so strong the rats would soon be washed away if they attempted to cross the water."

So off he started, crossed the Rhine, and shut himself up in his tower. He fastened every window securely, locked and barred the doors, and gave strict injunctions that no one should be allowed to leave the tower or to enter it. Hoping that all danger was over, he lay down, closed his eyes, and tried to sleep. But it was all in vain; he still shook with fear. Then, all at once, a shrill scream startled him. On opening his eyes he saw the cat on his pillow. She too was terrified, and her eyes glared, for she knew the rats were close upon them.

Up jumped the Bishop, and from his barred window he saw the black cloud of rats swiftly approaching. They had crossed the deep current, and were marching in such a direct line toward his hiding-place that they might have been taken for a well-marshalled army. Not by dozens or scores, but by thousands and thousands, the creatures were seen. Never before had there been such a sight.

"Down on his knees the Bishop fell,
And faster and faster his beads did he tell,
As louder and louder, drawing near,
The gnawing of their teeth he could hear.

"And in at the windows, and in at the door,
And through the walls helter-skelter they pour,
And down from the ceiling and up through the floor,
From the right and the left, from behind and before,
From within and without, from above and below,
And all at once to the Bishop they go.

"They have whetted their teeth against the stones,
And now they pick the Bishop's bones.
They gnawed the flesh from every limb,
For they were sent to do judgment on him."

Such was the horrible fate of Bishop Hatto; and whether it be perfectly true or not, it is a striking illustration of the folly, as well as the cruelty, of selfishness.

FUN IN THE WOODS.

Little Lake, California.

I am assistant teacher here in Little Lake district. I have a class of seven boys, among whom I am dividing the year's subscription of Young People. The "Parrot Story" I read aloud in school, and am now doing the same with the "Brave Swiss Boy." I read a chapter in the morning, and those who are tardy lose the story till they can borrow the paper. Every number is missed, and the boys are much pleased with our charming little paper and the beautiful stories. The story about the "Flower that lives in a Cellar" [illegible] wards. The puzzles and "Wiggles" are all discussed, but some of the boys [illegible] "wouldn't be right." A great California owl flew into the school-room the other night through the top of a lowered window, and [illegible] our heads, with his great [illegible] eyes [illegible] We have made "Tomboles," and they are very funny. We are so glad you are publishing this paper; it is just what we wanted.

Jennie E. Byrd.

Portland, Oregon, January [illegible].

My brother Harry and I have just picked a bunch of willow "pussies" for our mamma.

Clara Teel.

Palmyra, Missouri.

I am six years old. I see a good many little girls write letters to Young People. I like the paper to read, and so does brother Will. He is a big boy thirteen years old, and can skate. We are having a very warm winter here in Missouri, and not much ice.

Hattie Carrington.

[illegible], California, February 5.

The other day we had a snow-storm. It was the first time I ever saw snow. We have a large garden, and there are a great many birds in it. Last summer there was a bird's nest in the ivy, and now the little birds which were born there are coming back. We have beautiful flowers in California, but I would like to see some of the Eastern flowers. I am eight years old.

[illegible]

[illegible], Long Island.

I am ten years old, and am visiting my grandma. She lives by the sea-shore. We had a hard snow-storm the other day, and the tide came nearly up to the steps of our boat-house, and the next day it was away down in the eel-grass. My aunt teaches school in the village, and the tide was up to the railroad track, so she had to ride home. What makes the tide so high and then so low? Grandma says the day it was so high the wind was east, and the next day it was west, and it blew very hard.

Bertha A. P.

[illegible], Connecticut.

I could not tell you how happy Young People makes my brother and me. We cannot wait for the week to go by. We haven't any pets except our little brother Maxwell, who is three years old. He is so funny and full of mischief that we would rather have him than all the other pets in the world. He talks as funny as the baby that wanted Daisy to come back, but my brother Jimmie and I can always understand every word he says, even when mamma cannot. He is almost three years old.

Paul H.

[illegible], Massachusetts.

I am nine years old. I have a cat. She is three years old. There is a strange cat comes in our cellar. I gave her some milk, and she would not drink it. She runs away from me. I have a [illegible], and have been making some [illegible] to-day.

Agnes N. B.

[illegible], Pennsylvania.

There are a great many coal mines near where I live. Six little girls, [illegible], went down in one of them once with the superintendent, who explained to us how they mined coal. We girls each took a miner's pick and knocked off a piece of coal, so that we could say we had mined some ourselves. I take Young People, and I like it ever so much.

E. H. A.

[illegible], Massachusetts.

I have a [illegible], and [illegible] I can [illegible] We [illegible] all the [illegible] I am [illegible] in school.

Annie C. [illegible]

[illegible], Pennsylvania.

When I read Harry P. H.'s letter about his kitten that eats peanuts, I thought I would tell you about a dog I know. It's name is Sport, and he lives at my grandfather's farm, not far from here. As soon as he sees me he runs toward me, and wags his tail, and jumps up and down. He follows me everywhere. I give him corn and apples to eat, and he jumps to take them from my fingers. When he is very hungry he will always eat corn and apples. Do all dogs like such things?

W. A. Lewis.

Fort [illegible], [illegible].

I live in a fort by the seashore. Our post takes Harper's Weekly, and I read the Young People, which comes with it. We have splendid boating and fishing. We catch cod-fish, mackerel, [illegible], and lobsters. We catch the lobsters in nets. I have two pet pigeons, and two kittens exactly alike. Their names are Spunk and Punk. Spunk will run up my back when I hold out a piece of meat.

Campbell F. Hamilton.

West Troy, New York.

I would like to know what to do with my parrot. He talks, sings, and whistles very nice, but he picks his feathers all out, and looks almost naked. I had a canary, but it died two years ago. It was almost twenty years old. Can any little boy or girl tell me what to do for my parrot?

Nellie B.

H. L. Murray.—A big, strong Newfoundland dog will be the best to harness to your little carriage. Newfoundland dogs are very wise and gentle, and, if treated kindly, are easily trained.

Charley D. M.—The trouble with your fish probably comes from the want of air in the water. If you will make a reed or elder-bush squirt-gun, closing the lower end, and making a number of small holes near the bottom, you can use it for forcing air into the tank. This will make the water "alive," and your fish will flourish. It will be well also to put two or three fresh-water crabs and snails and a little vegetation into the tank.

T. H. Knox.—An owl, or an owl's head, would make a good badge for your literary society. You can buy very pretty owls' heads under glass, arranged to wear as a scarf-pin. They are not expensive. Or if you wish something original, a small gold eagle's quill would be appropriate.

Fred C. S.—The United States government has never offered to purchase cancelled stamps.

I. U.—Sheep have front teeth, or nippers, only on the lower jaw, the upper having instead a firm elastic pad. There are eight of these nippers in a full-grown sheep. There are six grinders, or back teeth, on each side of both the upper and lower jaws.

Edith J. P.—You will find information about gold-fish in Young People No. 6.

Zella T.—The origin of April-fools' Day is unknown. It is observed as a season of practical jokes in nearly every country. Even the Hindoos have a festival terminating on the 31st of March, during which they also send their friends on all manner of absurd errands, and enjoy a laugh at their disappointment. In Italy and France the victims of practical jokes of the 1st of April are called "April-fish."

D. R. T.—If you wish to keep the skin of your greyhound very soft and delicate, feed it on bread and milk, sugar, cake, crackers, and dainty food of any kind. It will eat meat fast enough, if you allow it to do so, and a little beef, cut very fine, will make it stronger and do it good. Always give it plenty of fresh water.

Sadie E. P.—The saw-fish (*Pristis antiquorum*) is most plentiful in tropical seas, although a few species are found in the arctic regions. Its weapon is a flat prolongation of the head, and has on either edge hard tooth-like projections. One species is found all along our coast, from New England to Florida. It has no other common name.

Gussie C.—Your theory that the pecking and the scolding noise made by a canary are simply to show its affection for its friends, and really a sign of pleasure, is very pretty, but we are not sure it is right. It is true that a canary will not often act in that way when approached by a stranger, for a new voice frightens it, and makes it shrink into a corner of its cage, but it will show a great deal of fight, and peck vigorously, when disturbed by a familiar finger. But either way, if it is loving or enraged, a canary is always the same dear downy little pet, and deserves the tenderest care and affectionate treatment.

A. H. Texas.—Peter Minuit—more correctly Minnewit—was born at Wesel, Holland, some time during the later part of the sixteenth century. He was appointed third Director-General of New Netherland in 1625—Cornelis May having been the first and William Verhulst the second—and arrived at Manhattan the following May. To him belongs the honor of having purchased Manhattan Island from the Indians, as up to this period (1626) the *Dutch* had possessed it only by right of occupation. Minuit opened negotiations with the native proprietors, and purchased the entire island for the Dutch West India Company "for the value of sixty guilders"—about twenty-four dollars of our present currency. He died at Fort Christiana, Delaware, in 1641.

A. L. W., Washington Territory, sends a neat "Wiggle," which we are sorry came too late to be printed.

Dorsey Coate.—Many thanks for your pretty valentine.

Mary N. C., Cuba.—The beautiful little moth which flew on your table while you were writing, and which you inclose, resembles the *Deiopeia bella*, which lives on the meadows of our Northern fields. The size and markings are precisely the same, but the cross-bars on the fore-wings of the Northern moth are buff, while those of its Cuban cousin are delicate pink.

Anna M. M., and Agnes and Willie, Scotland.—We are very glad to learn from your neatly written letters that little folks in Scotland derive so much pleasure from reading the "American stories in Young People."

Pretty favors are acknowledged from Frederick [illegible], Nicholas F. G., Tillie F. [illegible], George [illegible] F., John H. [illegible], F. L. W., Eddie R., Randall [illegible], E. G. B., Carrie L. Holman, Jay H. [illegible], Lillie R. W., Mamie [illegible], S. G. McKnight, [illegible] M. H., L. N. M., Willie B. M., T. H. Marsh, F. V. Griffin, Alfred [illegible], Henry M. C., J. B. [illegible], George N. M., M. H. V., Mary B. K., Florence M. L., Carrie [illegible], Flora, Rose, and Sallie, Freddie Haggerty.

Correct answers to puzzles received from Paul [illegible], G. J. B., Nettie A. Randolph, Mabel Lovett, Abby H. Vail, Laura H. White, [illegible], William F. B., Nora [illegible], Amy B. Turner, Willie H. [illegible], Maggie M. [illegible], [illegible] B. [illegible], N. V. B., Tillie M. Jones, John R. Glen, Mary H. Martin, M. White, J. [illegible], J. M. Waldo, N. L. Collamore, E. S. May, Harry C. M., "Phœnix," [illegible] F., Maud Miller, [illegible] H. M., H. Blodie [illegible], Philip T. Cragor, Dorsey E. C., R. F. H., "Harley."

No. 1.

ENIGMA.

My first is in cinders, but not in well.
My second is in write, but not in spell.
My third is in taste, but not in hill.
My fourth is in turkey, and so [illegible].
My fifth is in window, but not in door.
My sixth is in ceiling, and in floor.
My seventh is in wrong, but not in right.
My eighth is in dark, but not in light.
My ninth is in true, but not in false.
My tenth is in [illegible], but not in walls.
My whole is a large city in the United States.

W. F. C.

No. 2.

GEOGRAPHICAL DOUBLE ACROSTIC.

An island off the coast of Massachusetts. A city in Ireland. A city in Cochin China. A river in New York State. A city in Italy. One of the United States. A river in the Northwestern United States. A city in Kentucky. A lake in North America. Answer—a city in the United States, and the State of which it is the capital.

Daisy (twelve years).

No. 3.

ENIGMA.

My first is in carriage, but not in gig.
My second is in fairy, but not in [illegible].
My third is in laughter, but not in mirth.
My fourth is in girdle, but not in girth.
My fifth is in curl, but not in curry.
My sixth is in pear, and also in cherry.
My whole lies underground. C. L.

No. 4.

WORD SQUARE.

First, a firm, hard substance of dull white color. Second, elliptical. Third, an iron pin. Fourth, a girl's name. WILLIAM F. B.

No. 5.

DIAMOND PUZZLE.

A consonant. A beverage. Bright. A part of the head. A consonant. M. L.

No. 6.

NUMERICAL CHARADE.

I am composed of 14 letters.
My 8, 5, 7 is a kind of [illegible].
My 11, 12, 6, 8 is [illegible] from the earth.
My 13, 4, 6 belongs to a boat.
My 3, 14, 10, 4 is a girl's name.
My 2, 9, 13, 8 is part of a bird.
My whole was a great man. FANNIE (12 years).

ANSWER TO PUZZLE PICTURE IN No. 14.

[illegible]

ANSWERS TO PUZZLES IN No. 15.

No. 1. Collar.
No. 2. [illegible]

No. 3. Franklin.
No. 4. Washington and [illegible].
No. 5. [illegible]
Grant, Perry.

No. 6. [illegible]

ADVERTISEMENTS.

MORE WILLING THAN ABLE.

A Brave Princess.—In one of the Sandwich Islands in the South Seas, is a volcanic mountain with a huge lake of ever-burning fire. This was the reputed abode of the goddess Pélé and her fiery companions, the worship of whom was the central superstition of the islanders. The young Princess Kapiolani was converted to Christianity through the teaching of the missionaries. Grieving for the ignorance and misery of her people, she resolved to visit the burning mountain of Kilauea, and dare the dreaded Pélé to do her worst. There a priestess met her, threatened her with the displeasure of the goddess if she persisted, and prophesied that she and her followers would inevitably perish. In defiance of this threat, she and her Christian followers went down to the edge of the burning lake, and, standing erect, she thus spoke: "Jehovah is my God. He kindled these fires. I fear not Pélé. If I perish by the anger of Pélé, then you may fear the power of Pélé; but if I trust in Jehovah, and He should save me from the wrath of Pélé, then you must fear and serve the Lord Jehovah."

PERPETUAL MOTION.

TOMMY was only ten years of age, but still he was determined to obtain it. At last, one day, he ran into his father's office in ecstasies, and shouted, "Hurrah! Pop, I've got it!"

"Got what, my son?"

"Perpetual motion!" cried Tommy. "I've been watching it for the last half hour, and it works bully!" Then grasping "Pop" by the hand, "Come up in the garret and see it."

His father went up, and, sure enough, there was perpetual motion—that is, as long as there was any life left in the dog and that piece of roast beef hung to his tail.

CHARADE.

FIRST.

I am rocked in the arms of the sea,
  Or tossed on the flowing main;
Then fold my white wings in some peaceful bay,
  And am bound to the earth with a chain.

SECOND.

There's a fruit with its hue of gold
  From the land of the tropical sun;
I make it a cooling draught to hold
  To the lips of the thirsty one.

WHOLE.

With the tread of many feet,
  And the changeless roll of the drum,
With a deadly volley my foe to greet,
  Mid the flash of steel, I come.

THE SOAPBOXTICON, OR HOME-MADE MAGIC LANTERN.

WOULD you like to have a magic lantern? Very well: I will tell you how to make it. In the first place you must procure a burning-glass, such as you can get at any toy store for a few cents; or you may, perhaps, have the glass out of an old telescope. You also want a soap box (or any other kind of square box), a cigar box, and a piece of white muslin or linen as large as a pocket-handkerchief. Make a hole in the cigar box to fit your magnifying-glass, and put the glass into it. Now look at Fig. 1, and see how the cigar box is placed inside the soap box. Stretch the muslin over the opposite side of the soap box (from which, of course, you have removed the bottom), and tack it to the edges of the box. Put a lighted candle in the cigar box as represented in the illustration, and if you hold a drawing or a photograph opposite the glass in the cigar box, it will be reflected on the muslin stretched over the end of the soap box, and you have a magic lantern.

One thing more. By looking at Fig. 1 you will see that there are two bars and a cross-bar to hold the picture. These can easily be fixed, and will save you the trouble of holding the picture in your hand, and will be more steady. By carefully looking at the different drawings, you will soon see how to make one yourself.

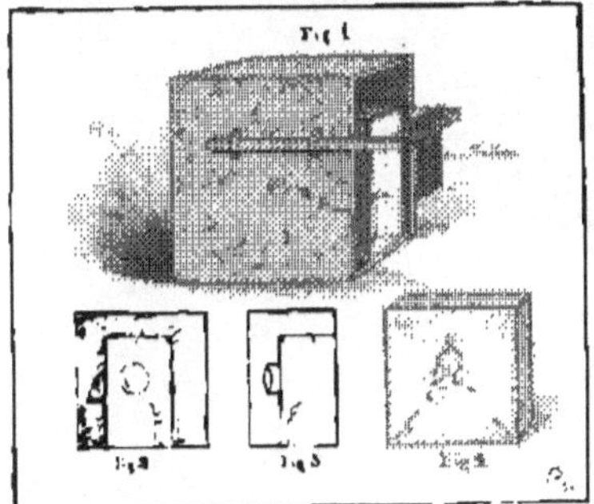

Fig. 1 is the perspective view; Fig. 2 is the back view; Fig. 3 is the side view (or section); Fig. 4 is the front view, showing the picture.

"WILL IT RING, MAMMA, IF I PULL?"

Vol. I.—No. 19. | Published by HARPER & BROTHERS, New York. | Price Four Cents.
Tuesday, March 9, 1880. | Copyright, 1880, by Harper & Brothers. | $1.50 per Year, in Advance.

ACROSS THE OCEAN: OR, A BOY'S FIRST VOYAGE.

A True Story.

BY

J. O. DAVIDSON

CHAPTER I.

THE FIRST NIGHT AT SEA.

P. M. STEAMSHIP *Amazon* sails this day at 1.30 P.M. for China and the East, [illegible]. Freight received until 4 P.M. Hands wanted.

"I guess that's what I want," muttered a boy, who was comparing the printed slip in his hand with the above notice, conspicuously displayed from the yard of a huge ocean steamer alongside one of the North River piers at New York.

Not a very heroic figure, certainly, this young volunteer in the battle of life: tired, seemingly, by the way in which he dragged his feet; cold, evidently, for he shivered every now and then, well wrapped up as he was; hungry, probably, for he had looked very wistfully around him as he passed through the busy, well-lighted market, where many a merry group were laughing and joking over their purchase of the morrow's Christmas dinner. But with all this, there was something in his firm mouth and clear bright eye which showed that, as the Western farmer said, on seeing Washington's portrait, "You wouldn't git that man to leave 'fore he's ready."

Picking up the bag and bundle which he had laid down for a moment, our hero entered the wharf house.

"Clear the way there!"

"Look out ahead!"

"Stand o' one side, will yer?"

"Now, sir, hurry up—boat's jist a-goin'!"

"Arrah, now, kape yer umbrelly out o' me ribs, can't ye? Sure I'm not fat enough for the spit *yet!*"

"Hallo, hub! it's death by the law to walk into the river without a license. Guess you want to keep farther off the edge o' the pier."

The boy's head seemed to reel with his sudden plunge into all this bustle and uproar, to which even that of the crowded streets outside was as nothing. Men were rushing hither and thither, as if their lives depended on it, with tools, coils of rope, bundles of clothing, and trucks of belated freight. Dockmen, sailors, stevedores, porters, hackmen, outward-bound passengers, and visitors coming ashore again after taking leave of their friends, jostled each other; and all this, seen under the fitful lamp-light, with the great black waste of the shadowy river behind it, seemed like the whirl of a troubled dream.

And the farther he went, the more did the confusion increase. Here stood a portly gray-beard shouting and storming over the loss of his purse, which he presently found safe in his inner pocket; there a timid old lady in spectacles was vainly screaming after a burly porter who was carrying off her trunk in the wrong direction; an unlucky dog, trodden on in the press, was yelling; and an enormously fat man, having in his hurry jammed his carpet-bag between two other men even fatter than himself, was roaring to them to move aside, while they in their turn were asking fiercely what he meant by "pushing in where he wasn't wanted."

Suddenly the clang of a bell pierced this Babel of mingled noises, while a hoarse voice shouted, "All aboard that's going! landsmen ashore!"

The boy sprang *forward*, flew across the gang-plank just as it began to move, and leaped on deck with such energy as to run his head full butt into the chest of a passing sailor, nearly knocking him down.

"Now, then, where are yer a-shovin' to?" growled the aggrieved tar, in gruff English accents. "If yer thinks yer 'ead was only made to ram into other folks' insides, it's my b'lief yer ought to ha' been born a cannon-ball."

But the lad had flown past, and darting through a hatchway, reached the upper deck, where a group of sailors were gathered round a cannon. On its breech an officer had spread a paper, which a big good-natured Connaught man was awkwardly endeavoring to sign. After several floundering attempts with his huge hairy right hand, he suddenly shifted the pen to his left.

"Are you left-handed, my man?" asked the officer.

"Faith, my mother used to say I was whiniver she gev me annything to do," answered Paddy, with a grin; "but this is my right hand, properly spaking, ounly it's got on the left side by mistake. 'Twas my ould uncle Dan (rest his sowl!) taught me that thrick. 'Dinnis, me bhoy,' he'd be always sayin', 'ye should alvers l'arn to clip yer finger-nails wid the left hand, *for fear ye'd some day lose the right.*'"

This "bull" drew a shout of laughter from all who heard it, and the officer, turning his head to conceal a smile, caught sight of our hero.

"Hallo! another landsman! Boatswain, hold that gang-plank a moment, or we'll be taking this youngster to sea with us."

"That's just what I want," cried the boy, vehemently. "*Will* you take me, sir?"

"Run away from home, of course," muttered the officer. "That's what comes of reading *Robinson Crusoe*—they all do it. Well, my lad, as I see it's too late to put you ashore now, what do you want to ship as? Ever at sea before?"

"No, sir; but I'll take any place you like to give me."

"Sign here, then."

And down went the name of "Frank Austin," under the printed heading of "Working Passenger." The officer went off with the paper, the sailors dispersed, and Frank was left alone.

Gradually the countless lights of New York, Brooklyn, and Jersey City sank behind, as the vessel neared the great gulf of darkness beyond the Narrows. Tompkins Light, Fort Lafayette, Sandy Hook, slipped by one by one. The bar was crossed, the light-ship passed, and now no sound broke the dreary silence but the rush of the steamer through the dark waters, with the "Highland Lights" watching her like two steadfast eyes.

Of what was the lonely boy thinking as he stood there on the threshold of his first voyage? Did he picture to himself, swimming, through a hail of Dutch and English cannon-shot with the dispatch that turned the battle, the round black head of a little cabin-boy who was one day to be Admiral Sir Cloudesley Shovel? Did he see a vast dreary ice-field outspread beneath the cold blue arctic sky, and midway across it the huge ungainly figure of a polar bear, held at bay with the butt of an empty musket by a young middy whose name was Horatio Nelson? Was it the low sandy shores of Egypt that he saw, reddened by the flames of a huge three-decker, aboard of which the boy Casabianca

"stood on the burning deck,
Whence all but him had fled"?

Or were his visions of an English "reefer" being thrashed on his own ship by a young American prisoner, who was thereafter to write his name in history as "Salamander" Farragut? Far from it. Frank's thoughts were busy with the home he had left; and amid the cold and darkness, its cosy fireside and bright circle of happy faces rose before him more distinctly than ever.

"Wonder if they've missed me yet? The boys 'll be going out to the coasting hill presently to shout for me; and sister Kate (dear little pet!), she'll be wondering why brother Frankie don't come back to finish her sled as he promised. And what distress they'll all be in till they get my first letter! and—"

"Hallo, youngster! skulking already! Come out o' that, and go for'ard, where you belong."

"I didn't mean to skulk, sir," said Frank, startled from his day-dream by this rough salutation.

"What! answering back, are ye? None o' yer slack. Go for'ard and get to work—smart, now!"

Frank obeyed, wondering whether this could really be the pleasant officer of a few hours before. Down in the dark depths below him figures were flitting about under the dim lamp-light, sorting cargo and "setting things straight," as well as the rolling of the ship would let them; and our hero, wishing to be of some use, volunteered to help a grimy fireman in rolling up a hose-pipe.

But he soon repented his zeal. The hard casing bruised his unaccustomed hands terribly, and it really seemed as if the work would never end. It ended, however, too soon for him; for the pipe suddenly parted at the joint, and splash came a jet of ice-cold water in poor Frank's face, drenching him from head to foot, and nearly knocking the breath out of his body.

"Why didn't you let go, then?" growled the ungrateful fireman, coolly disappearing through a dark doorway, hose and all, while Frank, wet and shivering, crawled away to the engine-room. Its warmth and brightness tempted him to enter and sit down in a corner; but he was hardly settled there when a man in a glazed cap roughly ordered him out again.

Off went the unlucky boy once more, with certain thoughts of his own as to the "pleasures" of a sea life, which made Gulliver and Sindbad the Sailor appear not quite so reliable as before. He dived into the "'tween-decks" and sank down on a coil of rope, fairly tired out. But in another moment he was stirred up again by a hearty shake, and the gleam of a lantern in his eyes, while a hoarse though not unkindly voice said, "Come, lad, you're only in the way here; go below and turn in."

Frank could not help thinking that it was time to turn in, after being so often turned out. Down he went, and found himself in a close, ill-lighted, stifling place (where hardly anything could be seen, and a great deal too much smelled) lined with what seemed like monster chests of drawers, with a man in each drawer, while others were swinging in their hammocks. He crept into one of the bare wooden bunks, drew the musty blanket over him, and, taking his bundle for a pillow, was asleep in a moment, despite the loud snoring of some of his companions, and the half-tipsy shouting and quarrelling of the rest.

[TO BE CONTINUED.]

A FAIRY FLIGHT.

BY ROSE TERRY COOKE.

A fairy lived in a lily bell—
  Ring, ring, columbine!
In frosts she stole a wood-snail's shell,
  Till soft the sun should shine;
And spring-time comes again, my dear,
  And spring-time comes again,
With rustling showers, and wakened flowers,
  And bristling blades of grain.

And, oh! the lily bell was sweet—
  Ring, swing, columbine!
But the snail shell pinched her little feet,
  And suns were slow to shine.
It's long till spring-time comes, my dear,
  Till spring-time comes again;
The year delays its smiling days,
  And snow-drifts heap the plain.

The fairy caught a butterfly—
  Swing, cling, columbine!
The last that dared to float and fly
  When pale the sun did shine;
For spring is slow to come, my dear,
  Is slow to come again,
And far away doth summer play,
  Beyond the roaring main.

She mounted on her painted steed—
  Ring, cling, columbine!
And well he served that fairy's need,
  And hot the sun did shine.
The spring she followed fast, my dear,
  She followed it amain;
Where blossoms throng the whole year long
  She found the spring again.

Oh, fairy sweet! come back once more—
  Ring, swing, columbine!
When grass is green on hill and shore,
  And summer sunbeams shine.
What if the spring is late, my dear,
  And comes with dropping rain!
When roses blow and rivers flow,
  Come back to us again.

ANIMALS THAT LOVE MUSIC.

MUSIC affects animals differently. Some rejoice, and are evidently happy when listening to it, while others show unmistakable dislike to the sound.

For some years my father lived in an old Hall in the neighborhood of one of our large towns, and there I saw the influence of music upon many animals. There was a beautiful horse, the pride and delight of us all, and like many others, he disliked being caught. One very hot summer day I was sitting at work in the garden, when old Willy the gardener appeared, streaming with perspiration.

"What is the matter, Willy?"

"Matter enough, miss. There's that Robert, the uncanny beast; he won't be caught, all I can do or say. I've give him corn, and one of the best pears off the tree; but he's too deep for me—he snatched the pear, kicked up his heels, and off he is, laughing at me, at the bottom of the meadow."

"Well, Willy, what can I do? He won't let me catch him, you know."

"Ay, but, miss, if you will only just go in and begin a toon on the pianner, cook says he will come up to the fence and hearken to you, for he is always a-doing that; and maybe I can slip behind and cotch him."

I went in at once, not expecting my stratagem to succeed. But in a few minutes the saucy creature was standing quietly listening while I played "Scots, wha hae wi' Wallace bled." The halter was soon round his neck, and he went away to be harnessed, quite happy and contented.

There was a great peculiarity about his taste for music. He never would stay to listen to a plaintive song. I soon observed this. If I played "Scots, wha hae," he would listen, well pleased. If I changed the measure and expression, playing the same air plaintively, he would toss his head and walk away, as if to say, "That is not my sort of music." Changing to something martial, he would return and listen to me.

In this respect he entirely differed from a beautiful cow we had. She had an awful temper. She never would go with the other cows at milking-time. She liked the cook, and, when not too busy, cook would manage Miss Nancy. When the cook milked her, it was always close to the fence, near the drawing-room. If I were playing, she would stand perfectly still, yielding her milk without any trouble, and would remain until I ceased. As long as I played plaintive music—the "Land o' the Leal," "Home, Sweet Home," "Robin Adair," any sweet, tender air—she seemed entranced. I have tried her, and changed to martial music, whereupon she invariably walked away.

HOW MANY WORLDS?

"PROFESSOR," asked May, "are there more worlds with people on them like this one of ours?"

"That is a hard question," said he. "For many ages it was believed that there could be *only one*. More recently, when astronomers learned by the aid of their telescopes the countless number of the heavenly bodies, it began to be doubted whether such an immense creation could be destitute of intelligent creatures like man; and it was argued that most likely the Almighty had supplied the heavenly bodies with inhabitants, but had for some good reason thought best not to reveal the fact to us, perhaps because our attention might be too much drawn away from the truths that He wished us particularly to remember. At last, however, men of science, continuing their researches, seem to be settling back in the first opinion."

"Why is that?" asked Joe.

"Because they find reasons for thinking that our earth has had human beings on it only a very little while in comparison with its own existence. And if this world was millions of years without man, then, of course, any or all the heavenly bodies may still be without any such creature on them."

"Is there no better reason than that?" asked Joe.

"Yes, there is considerable evidence that the bodies nearest to us can not be inhabited by any creatures at all like man. On the moon, for instance, there is no air to breathe and no water to drink. And without air and water there can be no grass, trees, or plants of any kind, and no food for any animal. And besides starving, all creatures that we know of would immediately freeze to death; for the moon is excessively cold. The nights are about thirty times as long as ours, and allow each portion of its surface to get so cold that nothing could live."

"How did the moon get so cold?" asked Joe. "What became of the heat?"

"It went off into the surrounding space, which is all very cold. Empty space does not get warmed by the sun, whose heat seems chiefly to lodge in solid bodies and dense fluids."

"But some of the planets are larger than the moon, are they not?" asked Joe.

"Yes, Jupiter, for instance, is very much larger than the moon and the earth; and Professor Proctor tells us it will take Jupiter millions of years to become as cool as the earth, while the moon was as cool as the earth millions of years ago. Here is a picture of the planet; but its surface is changing so constantly, that it seldom appears the same on two nights in succession. Jupiter at present is wrapped in enormous volumes of thin cloud that rises up from a melted and boiling mass in the centre. Professor Newcomb supposes that there is only a comparatively small core of liquid, the greater part of the planet being made up of seething vapor. So you see it would be about as difficult to live on Jupiter as in a steam-boiler, or a caldron of molten lead. Since last summer a great red spot has been noticed on the surface of the planet, which has attracted much attention. Some think it is an immense opening, large enough for our earth to be dropped through."

"Are the other planets such dreadful places?" asked May.

"Saturn seems to be in about the same condition as Jupiter. Mars is thought to be solid, and to have land, water, and air. It has also two brilliant white spots on opposite sides, which are supposed to be vast fields of ice and snow. But the water seems to be disappearing; and the time when the planet could be inhabited is thought to be long gone by."

"Where does the water go?" asked Joe.

"Probably it sinks into the cracks or fissures which form in the crust of the planet when it begins to shrivel up with the cold."

"Then it must be like a great frozen grave-yard," said May. "But is there no other planet that is pleasanter to think about?"

"The one that seems on the whole to be most like our own is Venus, and so Professor Proctor calls it our sister planet. It is so close to the sun that it is hidden most of the time, being only seen for a while before sunrise, and at other times a while after sunset. In the one case it is called the morning, and in the other the evening star. Also there is Mercury, still nearer the sun, and hidden almost all the time."

"Then," said May, "there seems to be no way of knowing anything about there being people like us in other worlds; and the more we look into it, the more uncertain we become."

"That is about the way the case stands," said the Professor. "But if science continues to make as rapid progress as it has lately done, we may hope that it will yet throw more light on the question."

"How many planets are there?" asked Joe.

"Until quite recent times there were supposed to be only the five we have mentioned. Since the beginning of the present century about two hundred little planets, called asteroids, have been discovered between the orbits, or paths, of Mars and Jupiter. Then there are Uranus and Neptune, very far off from the sun and from us, so much so that the latter was mistaken for a fixed star."

"Professor," said May, "you mentioned the moon as being near to us. Can you explain to us how its distance is measured, so that we can understand it?"

"And then, Professor," said Jack, "I would like to know what *parallax* means."

"There," said Gus, "is another big word of Jack's—pollywogs, knickknacks, gimcracks, slapjacks!"

"Hush, you goose."

"I think," said the Professor, "I can answer May's and Jack's questions both at once, as they are very closely connected. Suppose that at night, when you look down the street, you see two gas lamps, one much farther off than the other. Then if you go across the street, the nearer lamp will seem to move in the opposite way from what you did. Thus, in the diagram, when you are at A, the nearer lamp is on the right of the other, and when you go over to B and look at it, it is on the left. This change in direction is called *parallax*. Now we can imagine the nearer one of the lights to be the moon, and that an observatory, or tower with a telescope in it, is located at A, from which the direction of the moon is carefully noted at six o'clock in the morning. Then by six in the evening the earth, spinning round on its axis, will have carried the observatory about 8000 miles away from A, and placed it at, say, B. If the moon's direction be again noted, it is very easy to calculate her distance by a branch of mathematics called trigonometry, which Jack, I have no doubt, has already studied."

THAT NAUGHTY, NAUGHTY BOY.

"Gimme more pie-er!"

A FOUR-FOOTED MESSENGER.

JUST after the raising of the siege of Fort Stanwix, in the Mohawk Valley, the neighborhood continued to be infested with prowling bands of Indians.

Captain Gregg and a companion were out shooting one day, and were just preparing to return to the fort, when two shots were fired in quick succession, and Gregg saw his comrade fall, while he himself felt a wound in his side which so weakened him that he speedily fell.

Two Indians at the same time sprang out of the bushes, and rushed toward him. Gregg saw that his only hope was to feign death, and succeeded in lying perfectly still while the Indians tore off his scalp.

As soon as they had gone, he endeavored to reach his companion, but had no sooner got to his feet than he fell again. A second effort succeeded no better, but the third time he managed to reach the spot where his comrade lay, only to find him lifeless. He rested his head upon the bloody body, and the position afforded him some relief.

But the comfort of this position was destroyed by a small dog, which had accompanied him on his expedition, manifesting his sympathy by whining, yelping, and leaping around his master. He endeavored to force him away, but his efforts were in vain until he exclaimed, "If you wish so much to help me, go and call some one to my relief."

To his surprise, the animal immediately bounded off at his utmost speed.

He made his way to where three men were fishing, a mile from the scene of the tragedy, and as he came up to them began to whine and cry, and endeavored, by bounding into the woods and returning again and again, to induce them to follow him.

These actions of the dog convinced the men that there was some unusual cause, and they resolved to follow him.

They proceeded for some distance, but finding nothing, and darkness setting in, they became alarmed, and started to return. The dog now became almost frantic, and catching hold of their coats with his teeth, strove to force them to follow him.

The men were astonished at this pertinacity, and finally concluded to go with him a little further, and presently came to where Gregg was lying, still alive. They buried his companion, and carried the captain to the fort. Strange as it may seem, the wounds of Gregg, severe as they were, healed in time, and he recovered his perfect health.

WILL'S BELGIAN NIGHT.

BY MATTHEW WHITE, JUN.

"JUST like so many sheep!"

This was Will Brooks's exclamation, as he waited, with his elder brother Charlie, at the Northern Railroad station, in Paris. And truth to tell, the passengers were driven about and distributed somewhat after the manner of flocks, for, having purchased their tickets, they were obliged to pass along a corridor, opening into which were medium-sized waiting-rooms, separated from one another only by low partitions, and labelled, so to speak, as first, second, and third class. Here they were compelled to wait until five or ten minutes before the train was to leave, during which interval everybody endeavored to obtain the place nearest the door, so as to be sure of a choice of seats in the cars. Will and his brother had succeeded in getting pretty near the knob, where they were nearly suffocated with bad air, and much bruised by the satchels and umbrellas of their fellow-travellers.

"Now, Will, be ready," said Charlie, as a man was seen to approach with a key in his hand.

"All right; America to the front!" returned his patriotic brother; and at the same moment the doors were flung open, and in his nasal French tones the guard sang out, "Pour Liege, Aix-la-Chapelle, et Cologne!"

With a rush as of the sudden breaking away of a long pent-up mountain stream, the crowds surged forth from their "pens," and ran frantically up and down the long platform in search of the carriages for which they were respectively booked. The first-class compartment which Will and his brother had selected was speedily occupied by the six others required to fill it, their companions consisting of a gentleman and his wife, an old lady and a little boy, and two young men, evidently all French. Everybody had got nicely settled, the luggage was arranged in the racks overhead, and the train was just about to start, when a lady mounted to the doorway, with a little girl in one hand, and a bag, basket, and umbrella in the other. With a great volume of French she endeavored to thrust the child into the compartment, but was forced to desist from the attempt in deference to the remonstrances of the majority of those who already occupied it.

"C'est complet! c'est complet!" was the cry, and in the

SHINNY ON THE ICE.

midst of the confusion the guard approached to close the doors preparatory to starting. To him the distressed lady appealed in behalf of her offspring, for whom, she declared, there was no room in any of the carriages, and further stated that she herself was obliged to remain with her youngest, who was at present in charge of her next to the youngest in another car. The guard was finally obliged to settle matters by delaying the train, and adding thereto another carriage.

The conversation incidental to the foregoing episode had been interpreted to Will by his brother, whose French had been polished up considerably during his three weeks' stay in Paris. He and Will were over for an autumn tour in Europe, and having "done" the British Isles and the capital of France, they were now on their way to Germany.

Will had enjoyed his trip thus far immensely, even though he knew no modern language but his American English, and he now looked forward to seeing the wonders of the father-land with all the bright anticipations of fourteen.

"What's that for, I wonder?" he suddenly exclaimed, catching sight of a small triangular piece of looking-glass set in the upholstery at the back of the front seat of the compartment. "Read what it says underneath, Charlie;" which the latter accordingly did, reporting that it was a device for calling the guard in cases of emergency, the way of doing so being to break the glass and pull a cord which would be discovered in the recess thus exposed, which cord communicated with the engine. But if the glass be broken, the notice went on to state, without sufficient cause, a heavy fine would be imposed on the offender.

"But suppose I couldn't read French, as indeed I can't," surmised Will, "and were in here alone—that is, alone in company with a crazy man who was about to murder me—how could I ever imagine that by smashing that bit of glass I might stop the train, and so be rescued? Besides—"

"Nonsense!" interrupted his brother. "Don't you see the directions are repeated both in English and German underneath?" and Will looked and saw, and immediately turned his attention out of the window, leaving Charlie to peruse his French newspaper in peace.

There was, however, not much of interest to observe in the somewhat barren-looking country through which the railroad ran; and voting France (Paris excepted) a very slow place indeed, Will buried himself for the rest of the afternoon in a boy's book of travels. Nevertheless, the journey proved a very tedious one, and after stopping for dinner at six, the two brothers endeavored to bridge over the remaining hours with sleep.

"Verviers!" shouted out by the guard, was the sound that caused them both to awake with a start. The train had stopped, and all the passengers were preparing to "descend," as the French have it.

"Now, Will," said Charlie, sleepily, trying to read his guide-book by the light of the flickering lamp in the roof of the compartment, "this is the Belgian custom-house; but all trunks registered through to Cologne, as ours is, they allow to pass unopened; but it seems that everybody is required to get out and offer their satchels to the officers for examination; but, as we've only one between us, there's no use in our both rousing up, so you just take this, and follow the crowd."

"All right," responded Will, now thoroughly wide-awake; "then I can say I've been in Belgium;" and snatching the small hand-bag from the rack, he hurried off, leaving his brother to continue his nap.

"Wonder which room it is?" surmised Will, for the platform was deserted, and there were four waiting-apartments opening out on it. It did not take him long, however, to discover the proper one for him to enter, and he was soon among the jostling crowd that surrounded the low counter, behind which were the customs officials, who sometimes opened a bag and glanced over the contents, and then hastily marked on it with a piece of chalk, but oftener simply chalked it without examining anything whatever, which latter harmless operation was all to which Will's effects were subjected.

Rejoiced at getting through so easily, he turned to hasten out to the cars again, but the door by which he had entered was now closed, and guarded by a gendarme. From the gestures the latter made when he attempted to pass him, Will understood that he was to go out by another exit into an adjoining waiting-room, where he found most of the other passengers assembled in the true flock-of-sheep style; but while he was wondering where he might be driven to next, he saw through the window the train, containing his brother, his ticket, and his power of speech, whirl suddenly away into the darkness, and disappear.

"Hallo here! let me out!" cried Will, rushing up to the officer stationed at the door. "I'm going to Cologne on those cars, don't you understand?"

But the man evidently did not understand, for he shook his head in a most stupid fashion, at the same time feeling for his sword, as though afraid "le jeune Américain" were going to brush past him with the energy characteristic of the nation.

Seeing that it was now too late for him to catch the already vanished train, even if he should succeed in gaining the tracks, Will gave up the attempt, and resigned himself to his fate.

"But why are not the other passengers in as great a state of anxiety as I am?" he thought, as he looked around at his sleepy fellow-travellers, who had disposed themselves about the room in various attitudes of weariness and patience. "Perhaps, though, they're not going to Cologne; very likely they're all bound for some place in Belgium here, on another road. And now what's to become of me, a green American, with no French at my tongue's end but 'oui' and 'parlez-vous,' not a sign of a ticket, and with but six francs in my purse? Oh, Charlie, why did you send me out with this bag?" and Will paced nervously up and down the waiting-room, trying to think of a way out of his predicament. Suddenly a happy idea struck him.

"I'll go out by the door that opens into the town, and walk along till I come to the end of the station building, and then perhaps I can make my way around to the inside, and so see if the train really has gone off for good. Very likely it was only switched off, and will soon back down again."

Putting this plan into execution, Will was soon out in the streets of the queer Belgian city, wandering along in the darkness, striving to find the end of the dépôt, and then of a high board fence, which latter seemed to be interminable. At length, however, he reached an open space, and was about to leap across a telegraphic arrangement that ran beside the tracks, when one of the inevitable gens-d'armes sprang up from somewhere behind, and gave Will to understand that he was not allowed to put himself in the way of being killed by an engine.

Poor boy, he was now completely bewildered, and wished with all his might that he had studied French instead of Latin. As it was, he screamed out, "Cologne! Cologne!" with an energy born of desperation, and the officer, faintly comprehending his meaning, at last muttered a quick reply in his unknown tongue, and hurried Will off back to the dépôt with an alacrity that caused our young American to have some fears he might be taking him to quite another sort of station-house. But, notwithstanding their haste, when they entered the waiting-room it was empty, and the flashing of a red lamp on the rear car of a departing train told whither its former occupants had gone.

And now Will understood it all. The passengers had

been locked up while some switching was done, simply to prevent them from becoming confused.

"What a blockhead I was!" he thought, quite angry with himself. "If I'd just staid quietly where I was put, and not gone racing off, with the idea that I knew more about their railroads than the Belgians themselves, I'd never have gotten myself into such a scrape. And now what am I to do? I suppose Charlie's still fast asleep in the cars, being carried further and further away from me; and here am I, left at nine o'clock at night in an entirely foreign country, without a ticket, and, for the matter of that, without a tongue in my head. Why didn't some of the other passengers explain matters to me, and— But, pshaw! what good would it have done if they had? I couldn't have understood a word."

All this time the gendarme had been talking with the ticket agent, and pointing to Will as though the latter had been a stray dog not capable of saying anything in his own behalf. What should he do? where should he go? and how could he manage to pass away the time that might elapse till his brother should miss him and return in search of him? And now the officer came up, and began to question him, speaking very slowly, and in an extremely loud tone. Notwithstanding, poor Will could only understand a word here and there, and at length, in despair, he determined to try a new plan.

Taking out his purse, he showed the money therein to the gendarme, at the same time exclaiming, "Hotel! hotel!" and pointing to himself. The officer evidently comprehended this pantomime, for, with a nod to the ticket agent, who had all the while been grinning through his little wicket, he motioned for Will to follow him out into the street.

The Hôtel du Chemin de Fer (Railroad Hotel) was close at hand, and having in a few rapid sentences explained the situation to the landlord, the gendarme left Will to his own resources.

The latter thought for a moment that he had stepped into pandemonium itself, for opening on the right into the main hall of the hotel was a large apartment decorated with a sort of stage scenery to represent trees and lakes, the room itself being filled with little tables, around which were seated men smoking and drinking beer, while a thin-toned brass band discoursed popular music from a gallery overhead.

Will stared at this strange sight with all his eyes, and then suddenly became conscious at one and the same moment that he was hungry and being talked at by the proprietor. Encouraged by his former success with one-word speeches, Will simply said "Coffee," and then sat down at one of the little tables, where he was speedily served with a generous cup of the invigorating beverage, together with a plentiful supply of bread and butter.

"What a queer adventure!" thought the youth, his spirits much improved by the warm draughts of coffee, to say nothing of the lights and music. "But now how shall I ever be able to make the man understand that I want to stay here all night? Charlie's sure to come back for me in the morning. Oh, I have it! I'll register my name on a piece of paper, hand it to the landlord, and exhibit my purse again;" which plan succeeded admirably, and "William C. Brooks, New York, America," was immediately shown to a good-sized room on the second floor, where he lost no time in retiring to rest after his eventful evening.

His sleep, however, was not undisturbed, for all night long he imagined himself to be an American locomotive towing an English steamer across the Atlantic, and crashing into several icebergs on the way.

The next morning Will opened his eyes in a flood of sunshine, and at first could not recollect where he was, but the whistling of an engine near by soon recalled to him his situation, causing him at the same time to hurry with his dressing, that he might hasten over to the station for news of his brother. He did not have to go as far as that, however, for as he was going down stairs he ran against Charlie coming up, and Will had never been so glad to see anybody or anything since the time when he used to open his eyes on Christmas mornings to behold the well-filled stocking hanging from the mantel-piece.

Over the breakfast, which the brothers ate together in the theatrical dining-room, the elder explained how he had not missed Will till the train had left Verviers a good distance behind. "And then when I awoke from my nap," continued Charlie, "you can imagine the fright I was in when I found the cars going, and *you* gone. We had just passed Aix-la-Chapelle when I made the dreadful discovery, or I might have driven back here from there with a carriage, for it is only twenty miles off; but as it was, I could do nothing but fret till we arrived at Cologne, from which city I at once telegraphed to the station-master here, and ascertained that you were safe and sound, and fast asleep in bed."

"But why didn't they wake me up, and let me know that you knew that—" broke in Will, but choked the remainder of his speech with a swallow of coffee and a slice of bread, from a sudden remembrance of the crashing of icebergs, which might have been knocks on the door he had heard in his sleep.

"The whole thing was my fault, though," summed up Charlie, as, having settled with the smiling landlord, they walked over to the station. "I should not have let you go off alone in a new country; but then," he could not help adding, "you should not have left the rest of the flock, when you were shut up in the pen."

"I never will again," said Will, as they took their places in the train for Cologne; "I'll be in future the meekest lamb they ever drove. But anyway," he continued, as the cars rolled slowly away from the dépôt, "I can say I have been in Belgium, even though it was only by mistake, and so have experienced not an Arabian but a Belgian Night."

HETTY.

BY MRS. W. J. HAYS.

THEY were all in the sitting-room. Matilda Ann was trimming a bonnet to wear to the concert which was to take place that very evening in the Town-hall, and the roses did look so pretty that Hetty wished she was grown up enough to have some one come for her in a brand-new buggy, and take her to a concert; but where was the use of wishing? Every one told her she must not be too childish, and then every one said she mustn't think herself a young woman, and want long gowns and trains, and big braids and puffs—that there was "time enough yet." She wondered what "time enough" meant. It seemed to her as if it must be the time of freedom, and certainly that was a long way off.

Jane was sewing strips of woollen cloth together for the big balls that were to make carpet, and their mother was darning stockings, and they were all talking about the school-teacher who had lately come to the little brown house next to the district school. Jane said she was "hity-tity," mother said she didn't like to see so many furbelows, and Matilda Ann criticised her manner of wearing her hair; so Hetty ventured to say, "I don't think it matters much what she wears, or how she looks, if she can teach the children."

"Yes," said the mother, "**it does matter; for children** need a good example."

"Of course she ought to be neat," said Hetty.

"Yes, and simple, and not be sticking on jewelry every day."

"For that matter, Aunt Maria says people in the city wear diamonds when they go to market."

HETTY AND JIM.—Drawn by T. [illegible]

"That does not make it any more sensible; fools are to be found everywhere."

"But, mother, Miss Martin isn't a fool; she is very nice. I think you would like her."

"Perhaps so," said the mother, somewhat doubtfully; adding: "She had on a flounced skirt the last time I saw her. It takes a great deal of time to do them up nicely. Only rich folk ought to wear them."

"Suppose some one gave her her fine clothes?" said Hetty.

"Not very likely; but that would make it a little better."

Hetty went out to take a swing under the elm-tree, wondering why big people couldn't find something better to talk about than what other people wore. Then Jane spoke up:

"Hetty always hates to hear others spoken of when they can't take their own part."

"She's a good little thing, anyhow," said Matilda Ann, who was standing before the looking-glass, in high good humor, with the new bonnet on, and turning her head from side to side, so that she could the better survey the trimmings.

"Well," said Mrs. Hall, "you've stood there long enough, Matilda Ann. I never did see such an amazin' amount of vanity as there is nowadays."

"Oh, mother, I dare say you were just as silly when you were young," said Jane.

"No," said the mother, severely. "I never was given to fineries; my heart was set on higher things."

"I don't see, then, how father ever got the chance to do any courting."

"Jane," said Mrs. Hall, "Jedediah Hall would never have married me if I had been like the girls of the present day, who scorn to churn, and to wash, and to do housework of any sort. He respected a woman who could make her family comfortable."

"But the courting—did he ever talk nonsense, mother?"

"The courting was over in short order, I can tell you. Nonsense?—no, there was no nonsense about him. Well, well, it's a long time ago." And she arose, and went out into the kitchen. The table was set for tea, and the biscuits were ready for the oven. She went to the cellar to skim the cream, and found a large bowl of custard had been left over from the dinner. There was more than would be eaten on their own table. What would she do with it? Pretty soon Hetty heard her mother calling her: "Hetty! Hetty!"

She ran in quickly from the garden.

"How would you like to take some of this custard to Miss Martin?"

"Splendid!" said Hetty. "But, mother," she said, hesitating, "I thought you didn't like her?"

"Pshaw, child, I didn't say so. I said I didn't approve of too much dress. Get your hat and a tin pail. Here;" and she poured out the custard. "Now go, and mind you come home in time for tea."

It was a level road, and the afternoon a pleasant one late in the fall. Hetty could not chase the squirrels, for fear of upsetting her pail; neither could she pick berries, for they were all gone. And so she trudged on silently, wishing she were as old as Matilda Ann, so that she might go to the concert. As she passed a lot which was covered with stubble, a boy appeared, leaning over the fence. He was a big fellow, and the son of an old neighbor, and Hetty liked him, but there were people who said he was mischievous, and told tales of him, which perhaps made him somewhat shy. He nodded pleasantly enough to her, however, and asked her where she was going.

"Down to Miss Martin's," was Hetty's reply.

"I say, Hetty," said Jim, "do you think Miss Martin thought it was me who tried to frighten her the other night?"

"No," said Hetty.

"Well, I was afraid she did. Give a dog a bad name, you know, and he never gets rid of it."

"But, Jim, you don't mean to speak of yourself that way?" said Hetty.

"Yes, I do; people believe anything of me, and I half the time get the credit of doing things that never came into my head."

"I only heard a little about Miss Martin's fright; some one chased her, I believe."

"Yes, Sam Tompkins made believe he was a tramp, and scared her 'most out of her wits. He ought to have been shot. I licked him when I heard he had tried to make out it was me who did it, and I'll lick him again, too."

"Oh, don't, Jim; you had better forget all about it."

"Indeed I won't; I mean to make him repent it. See here, Hetty, I've got some tickets for the concert. Don't you want to go?"

"Don't I?" said Hetty; "I guess I do; but I can't, you know."

"Why not?"

"Oh, I am not big enough yet," said Hetty, blushing.

"Now I'll tell you what I'll do. If you will ask Miss Martin to go, I'll take you both, for, you see, I want to be sure that she doesn't hold any ill-will against me; and if she goes, all the people hereabouts will know that I was not the mean sneaking coward who tried to frighten her."

"All right," said Hetty. "I understand; and I will go on now as fast as I can, and coax Miss Martin to go."

"Let me know what she says when you come back, and I'll get the horse hitched, for father said he'd let me have the wagon."

"I will," said Hetty, already hastening on her way.

The teacher was sitting in rather a lonely and dejected mood at her window as Hetty's bright face appeared before her. She was a young girl, with soft brown eyes and a patient expression. It was her first experience at district-school teaching, and she found it laborious. Hetty soon told her errand, and in her eagerness so mixed up the concert and the custard and Matilda Ann's new bonnet that Miss Martin was bewildered, but after a while made out what it all meant.

"So James Stokes wants me to go to the concert?"

"Yes, ma'am, and me too."

"Have you permission?"

"I'll get it, Miss Martin. I'm sure mother'll say 'yes,'

"STRAYS."—From a Painting by B. H. Carter.

and I sha'n't tell any one but her. I want to surprise Matilda Ann, and I will get ready and come here, so that Jim Stokes needn't go to our house."

"Please thank your mother kindly, Hetty, for the custard; it is so nice. And tell James I shall be happy to go. I know he was not the one who frightened me."

Away Hetty flew, as fast as possible, to arrange the matter at home. Mrs. Hall could not say no, and Hetty soon exchanged her every-day clothes for her best gown and ribbons.

The Town-hall was crowded, and Hetty heard some one in a pink bonnet say, "Why, there's our Hetty: how did the child get here?" Then she turned her smiling face upon Matilda Ann in triumph.

When the concert was half over, and the singers were taking a rest, a very grand-looking person came to Miss Martin and said: "How do you do, my dear Amy? I am so glad to see you! And who is this little friend with you?"

Then the teacher spoke very kindly of Hetty as one of her best pupils, and Jim was also introduced, and the grand-looking lady said some very pleasant things to them.

"Who is that?" whispered Hetty.

"It is my aunt," replied Miss Martin—"the one who gives me so many pretty things. She would like me to live with her, but I prefer to maintain myself. I could never dress half so tastefully if she did not give me such nice clothes."

"Oh," said Hetty, much pleased to hear this confirmation of her own charitable supposition. "May I tell mother about it?" she asked.

"Certainly," said Miss Martin; "I wish you would, for I don't want to be thought extravagant."

From that time Miss Martin had no stancher friends than Jim and Hetty; and when one day Jim's big brother led her up the aisle of the village church as a bride, there were two young people behind her in white gloves and ribbons who looked almost as bright and happy as the chief actors of the day.

A LITTLE GIRL'S IMPRESSIONS OF MADEIRA.

BY KATIE C. TORRE.

IT was a beautiful clear day in October when I had my first view of Madeira. The high blue mountains, the green shores, and the white city of Funchal gleaming in the distance, looked very lovely to us as we approached the island.

About noon we anchored at a little distance from the city, and swarms of row-boats came around the ship. Some of them were full of half-naked brown boys, and if we threw a piece of money into the beautiful blue water, they would dive down and catch it before it reached the bottom. Some of the other boats were full of men, who came on board, bringing fans, canary-birds, parrots, feather flowers, basket-work, filigree jewelry, and many other things to sell.

We and some of the passengers got into a row-boat, after a good deal of trouble, because there is always a heavy swell there, so one minute the boat was very high up, and the next very low down. When we had managed to get in, we rowed to the city. There were great waves dashing up on the shore, and four or five bare-legged men rushed into the water, and drew the boat on land just as a wave came in.

What was our surprise to see waiting for us, instead of a horse and carriage, a great sleigh drawn by bullocks. This is called a bullock-car in English, and a *carro* in Portuguese. We got into one of them, with a great deal of laughter, and drove to the hotel. The driver walked by the side of the *carro*, and threw the end of a greasy rag first under one runner and then under the other, to make it run more easily.

When we arrived at the hotel, we found it was a great white building, with a lovely garden, which contained mango, guava, banana, custard-apple, and many other trees. Among them was what was called the moon-tree; it was covered with great white bell-like flowers, and was very beautiful. There were a great many gorgeous flowers and curious plants that we do not have in this country. The garden was surrounded by a wall eight feet high, and there were some fish-geraniums which reached above the top of it. There was a little arch covered with the night-blooming cereus, and that evening, when the buds had opened, we went out to see them in the moonlight. They were beautiful white blossoms, as large as your head, and had a faint perfume.

Next day we took a hammock ride about the town and surrounding country. Each hammock was fitted out with a mattress, pillows, and canopy, and slung on a long pole carried by two men. We reclined lazily against the pillows, and enjoyed the ride very much. The men, when they went up hill, carried us feet downward, but once they forgot, and carried us feet upward, and as the hill was very steep, we felt as if we were standing on our heads.

The houses of Funchal are low, and covered with white stucco, which looks very neat, but those of the poor have only one window without any glass, and are very dark and dismal inside. The streets are narrow, and some of them very steep. We often passed gardens surrounded by high walls, over which hung lovely flowering vines. Out in the country there were lantanas, geraniums, and fuchsias which seemed to be growing wild, and great cactus plants everywhere.

PENCIL DRAWING.—No. 1.

THIS beautiful and graceful art may be acquired by every girl and boy in the land who will take the necessary steps. And they are pleasant steps.

A pretty drawing-book, a nicely cut No. 2 Faber's drawing pencil, a piece of *black* India rubber, some pieces of tissue-paper to cover the drawings, unless the drawing-book is furnished with tissue-paper. These are the implements required. In this pencil drawing which I now recommend there are no lines, straight and slanting, repeated to utter weariness. This is *object* drawing, and drawing *from nature* also, and the *objects* are inexhaustible, being the *leaves* which nature gives to every plant and tree.

Drawings of leaves are beautiful when well done. The writer knew a young girl of twelve or thirteen years who began with drawing simple, easy leaves, and went on to more difficult ones season after season. Her drawing-books were charming; and not this alone, for she acquired a fund of pleasant knowledge, which loses none of its delight as time goes on. She began with leaves, picked from the house plants which her mother cultivated.

As the spring came on, she sought the *wild* leaves in the woods. No one who has not tried it can judge of the interest felt in the beauty and wonderful variety in the growth and shapes of leaves. They seem endless; and when to these are added the leaves of forest trees, the enchanting maples, beeches, birches, and hosts of others, it may be imagined that young fingers may find ample employment in portraying these, to say nothing of the wild flowers which come on in the New England woods—the early anemones, hepatica, bloodroot, and all the flowery train—as the season advances.

This young girl learned to draw with great accuracy, and to this day (for it is years since she began) her ready pencil can sketch any object with ease and skill, the beginning of which was the effort to draw a leaf of smilax.

I have a few simple outlines of leaves ready, but will reserve them for another time.

[Begun in No. 17 of HARPER'S YOUNG PEOPLE, February 24.]

BIDDY O'DOLAN.

BY MRS. ZADEL B. GUSTAFSON.

CHAPTER III.

ANY one who had seen Biddy O'Dolan in the old hard days, when she was dirty and ragged and wretched and rude, and lived in the street, and slept in a cellar, would hardly have known her if he had seen her three weeks after she came to live with the Kennedys.

Biddy was not pretty, but she had a clear skin—now the dirt was washed off—and bright, earnest eyes. Now, too, she wore neat and pretty clothing. Her dark curly hair was nicely brushed, and tied with fresh ribbons. She had a small, pleasant room all for herself and her doll, and Miss Kennedy had taught her how to keep it in order.

Biddy had given a great deal of trouble to this gentle lady at first, because Biddy had many unpleasant habits. She used bad words; she did not seem to think it any harm to tell lies; she was not at all neat; she was sometimes willful and disobedient; she was often careless, broke dishes, tore her clothes, and put things out of order. These things were a much greater trouble to Miss Kennedy than Biddy knew. Miss Kennedy was so good and kind and true that Biddy's faults grieved her much, and carelessness and disorder were like pain to her, she was herself so neat and pure, like a fine white pearl.

But Miss Kennedy never forgot what poor Biddy's life had been, and Biddy was so affectionate and grateful, and tried so hard, that Miss Kennedy grew to love her dearly, and little by little Biddy conquered her old bad habits.

She did not see much of Mr. Kennedy, who was very busy, and was away a great deal. When she did see him, he had always a kind word and a pleasant smile for her, which made Biddy feel as if he took care of her.

Charley had brought her the doll, as Biddy said he would. But she could not make him come within a block of the house; and when he saw Biddy so fresh and clean in her pretty new garments, he had blushed and run away almost without speaking. She did not see much of him. She met him sometimes when she was out on an errand. The last time she had seen him he had looked very much pleased, but she had not been able to get him to speak to her. She thought him more bashful than ever.

Biddy did not forget Charley, or cease to wish he might have a nice home in the same house with her; but she was kept so busy with her easy but constant duties in waiting upon Miss Kennedy, who was also teaching her to read, that time flew very fast with Biddy, and it was midsummer when one day she went out on an errand, and—did not come back!

Miss Kennedy waited and wondered; and when it began to grow dark, and Biddy had not come back, she grew really alarmed. One of the servants had been sent out twice to look for Biddy, but in vain. At last, just as Miss Kennedy was about to send for him, Mr. Kennedy came in. As soon as he learned the cause of his sister's alarm, he comforted her in the very best way by starting out to search for Biddy himself.

He had not gone more than twenty steps before a boy, who had watched him come out, stopped him, and to his great surprise gave him a message from Biddy.

Mr. Kennedy ran back and spoke with his sister, and then went quickly away with the boy who had brought Biddy's message.

Now this is what had happened.

After Biddy had done her errand, she thought about Charley, and felt a great wish to see him. She was prettily dressed, and it came into her head that it would be a grand thing if she could walk by Mrs. Brown's stand, and see if the old woman would know her. For a long time after she ran away from Mrs. Brown, Biddy had been afraid to go near her old home for fear Mrs. Brown might claim her, and perhaps in some way be able to hide her from her new friends. But she had lost most of this fear, and now thought it would be great fun to step up to the stand and buy something, and see what the old woman would say.

The old days when she and Charley used to be so much together came into Biddy's mind as she walked along, swinging her parasol. She remembered a great many little things about him and his quiet kindnesses to her, which she had hardly noticed at the time, and she thought with new pleasure of Mr. Kennedy's words to her in the morning. He had passed her in the hall as he was going out, and had laid his hand on her head and said: "I think I shall be able to do something for Charley very soon. Will you like that, Biddy?" And Biddy, as usual, when her heart was very full, had not said a word. "I'll tell Charley," she thought to herself.

At last when there was only one more block to walk before reaching Mrs. Brown's stall, and Biddy was just beginning to think about what she should say to the old woman, she noticed an unusual stir down the street. People old and young were darting about, running around and forward, yelling at the tops of their voices; and there was another low hoarse sound Biddy could not make out. Nearest were some children running in her direction and screaming. Biddy stopped near a pile of empty boxes. She was full of wonder and fear. One of the children was Charley. He saw Biddy at the same moment she saw him, and it seemed as if he flew, he came toward her so fast. As he came up with her he grasped her arms, turned her around, and pushed her toward the boxes with one quick movement.

"Up wid 'ee, Biddy! Quick—oh, quick!" he called to her.

His white face and his piercing cry made Biddy obey him without a thought of asking why. She clutched at the boxes, and scrambled up, and Charley helped her by his hands and his shoulders. The boxes did not stand even, and they tottered as she climbed, but Charley leaned his little body against them, and stretched out his arms, and held them steady. Biddy was not a moment too quick. As she threw herself forward across the topmost box, the shuffle and clatter of many feet and the shouting and screaming seemed to be all around them. Biddy could not look down. She was so frightened, and had climbed so fast, she could hardly breathe, but she heard a snapping and crunching of jaws and a hoarse rattling breath beneath her. She was not able to think; she only clung with all her might, so dizzy that it seemed as if she and the boxes were swimming. Several shots were fired, and it seemed as if there were more noise and confusion than before. Then some one said,

"Poor children!"

Biddy felt herself lifted down. She was shaking all over. There were a great many people around her, but they didn't make so much noise now. She heard some one saying,

"It's Griffith's blood-hound—a good dog enough, too, if those idle scamps had let him alone. But it wouldn't stand no nonsense—that sort of dog never does. By heavens! it snapped that great chain like a pipe stem, and was after them like a tiger in no time!"

Then another voice said: "Did you see the little boy? He's almost the smallest little fellow you ever saw. But he was a hero. He saved the little girl's life; he gave up his own for it. I saw and heard the whole thing from the window overhead here, and I'll never see a braver deed done. I tell you, he's a hero; his father can be proud of him."

"*His father!*" said another and rougher voice. "*That* boy hain't got any one belongin' to *him*. Take a look at his clothes—what's left of 'em from that brute's teeth! *He's* never had too much to eat nor too much to wear, you kin just bet yer life on that. But you're right, mister; he *was* a hero, an' no mistake. He held as still as a mouse, an' with a grip like death, while that durned critter chawed up his legs."

Biddy was beginning to understand; so were the other children, the little boys and girls who had known and laughed at and nicknamed Charley all his silent, bashful life.

They stood around, gazing horror-struck at the dead hound that lay just beyond the curb-stone, and at Charley, lying all mangled and perfectly still in the arms of a policeman. A cart with cushions in it backed up to the curb, and just as the policeman was trying to move Charley so as to lay him on the cushions, he moaned and opened his eyes. He looked at the children. They saw this look, and crowded up to the cart, sobbing.

One of them exclaimed, "Oh, Charley, we'll never call ye 'Polly' no more!"

Another boy leaned close over Charley, and said, "The men sez as ye're a real hero, Charley; just ye brace up!"

A faint smile passed over Charley's face. He turned his eyes, with the same kind, calm look in them, among the people, till he saw Biddy. Then the tired eyes flashed with joy. He saw that she was quite safe. He moved his hand a little toward her. Her lips quivered; she reached out her arms; and they placed her in the cart on the cushions by Charley's side. Just before it started, Biddy asked the little boy who had last spoken to Charley to go and tell Mr. Kennedy what had happened, and to say that she should stay with Charley till he got well. When Mr. Kennedy reached the hospital, Biddy was crying as if her heart would break, and poor, brave, tender, bashful little Charley had got quite well, and had gone home to be with his Father.

The shock and the sorrow of little Charley's death changed Biddy very much. It was long before Mr. and Miss Kennedy could persuade her that she was not to blame for it. It seemed to the poor child as if she had been cruel to climb into safety, leaving Charley to such a fate. But she had really not been at all to blame. She had obeyed Charley's startling and earnest cry, without thinking, or even having time to think, until it was too late to act in any other way.

After a time the sharpness of this sorrow passed away, and the thought of Charley became full of comfort and help to Biddy. As she grew older she could understand that if Charley had lived, he could not have been very happy, he was so feeble, and shrank from people so much. And she could feel, if she did not understand, that his death was a noble one, an act of love so simple and so whole that it was a gift, the gift of a great example, helping every one who knew of it to be more brave and true.

Biddy lived on with the Kennedys, and she has helped Mr. Kennedy from time to time to find out little children as wretched as she once was. In this way she has already been the means of getting six poor children into good homes, where they have a chance to learn how to live. She remembers so well her sad childhood that she understands, even better than you or I would, how to speak to and help these poor children when they first begin to do better, and get so discouraged because their old bad habits pull them down, and make it hard for them to do well. Biddy goes to see them, and talks with them so kindly, and with so much patience and love, that they are comforted and ready to try harder than ever. When she tells them that she was once just as dirty and rough and naughty as they have ever been, and they see how sweet and good she has become, it fills them with courage and hope. You can very well suppose that Biddy did not always find it an easy thing to help these children. Perhaps you think that any little girl would jump at the chance of being taken from the street and put in a good and pleasant home. Biddy thought so, until she tried to help Katy Kegan. She was the second little girl Biddy found for Mr. Kennedy. Biddy had known Katy Kegan all her life, and liked her better than any other little girl when they used to be living on the street. Yet when Biddy became better off, and tried to make things just as nice for Katy, that little girl didn't see it as Biddy did at all, and gave her more care and worry than all the other five. I'll tell you something about this.

I AM THE LAD IN THE BLUE AND WHITE.

BY MARY A. BARR.

I am the lad in the blue and white—
    Sing hey! the merry sailor boy.
My head is steady, my eyes are bright,
My hand is ready, my step is light,
My brave little heart, all right, all right—
    Sing ho! the merry sailor boy.

I am the lad in the blue and white—
    Sing hey! the merry sailor boy.
I sit in the shrouds when the soft winds blow,
The light waves rock me to and fro;
I run up aloft or down below—
    Sing ho! the ready sailor boy.

I am the lad in the blue and white—
    Sing ho! the merry sailor boy.
When the skies are blue and the sea is calm,
The air is full of spice and balm,
And the shore is set with shadowy palm,
    Oh, glad is the merry sailor boy!

"What will you do when the great winds blow?
    What will you do, my sailor boy?"
When great winds blow, and are icy cold,
Never you fear, for my heart is bold:
I'll watch my captain, do what I'm told—
    Sing ho! the ready sailor boy.

"If a foe should come—in such a plight,
    What would you do, brave sailor boy?"—
Run up the "Stars and Stripes" in his sight,
Stand by my captain, wrong or right,
And give the foe an up-and-down fight—
    Sing ho! the gallant sailor boy.

I am the lad in the blue and white—
    Sing hey! the merry sailor boy.
I carry my country's flag and name;
I never will do her wrong or shame;
I'll fight her battles and share her fame—
    Sing ho! the gallant sailor boy.

With spirit. CHAS. F. BOWEN.

I am the lad in the blue and white—Sing hey! the merry sailor boy. My head is steady, my eyes are bright, My hand is ready, my step is light, My brave little heart, all right, all right—Sing ho! the merry sail-or boy.

OUR POST-OFFICE BOX.

A [illegible]. A [illegible]. [illegible].—Two [illegible]. CHARLES L. B.

No. 3.

[illegible]

My first is in [illegible].
My second is in [illegible].
My third is in [illegible].
My fourth is in [illegible].
My fifth is in [illegible].
My whole is something good to eat. MART.

No. 4.

WORD SQUARE.

First, [illegible]. Second, a [illegible]. Third, [illegible]. Fourth, [illegible]. M. L.

No. 5.

NUMERICAL ENIGMA.

I am composed of 27 letters.
My 16, 26, 5, 23 is a wild animal.
My 8, 7, 21 is a tree.
My 10, 3, 6, 17 is not hard.
My 14, 2, 6 is what we all must do.
My 20, 13, 11 is what most all of us can do.
My 4, 25, 19, 9 is a [illegible].
My 1, 24, 18 is a large body of water.
My 12, 22, 15, 16, 8, 21 is a school-book.
My [illegible] is a ruler of a country.
My 1, 9, 19 is an adverb.
My [illegible] is used for measuring.
My whole is a proverb. MARY B. N. (9 years).

No. 6.

[illegible]

A [illegible]. A [illegible]. A long-legged bird. A period of time. A [illegible]. E. K. C. M.

ANSWERS TO PUZZLES IN NO. 18.

No. 1. Charles Dickens.

No. 2.
H A I L
A N N A
I N N S
L A N T

No. 3. Bayonne.
No. 4. Bonaparte.
No. 5.
B er L
E [illegible] N
[illegible] N
L [illegible] D
[illegible] O
N [illegible] N
Berlin, London.

[illegible]

Shold, gold, old. | Tribe, rice, ice.
[illegible] | [illegible]
[illegible], ink. | [illegible]

ADVERTISEMENTS.

HARPER'S YOUNG PEOPLE.

HARPER'S YOUNG PEOPLE will be issued every Tuesday, and may be had at the following rates—payable in advance, postage free:

SINGLE COPIES $0 04
ONE SUBSCRIPTION, one year.... 1 50
FIVE SUBSCRIPTIONS, one year.. 7 00

Subscriptions may begin with any Number. When no time is specified, it will be understood that the subscriber desires to commence with the Number issued after the receipt of order.

Remittances should be made by POST-OFFICE MONEY ORDER or DRAFT, to avoid risk of loss.

ADVERTISING.

The extent and character of the circulation of HARPER'S YOUNG PEOPLE will render it a first-class medium for advertising. A limited number of approved advertisements will be inserted on two inside pages at 75 cents per line.

Address

HARPER & BROTHERS,
Franklin Square, N. Y.

CANDY

Send one, two, three, or five dollars for a sample box, by express, of the best Candies in America, put up elegantly and strictly pure. Refers to all Chicago. Address

C. F. GUNTHER,
Confectioner,
78 MADISON STREET, CHICAGO.

"SWEET LITTLE CHERRIES," "Kiss [illegible]" — [illegible]. Dodworth's "New Knickerbocker," [illegible]. FREDERICK BLUME, 861 Broadway.

The Child's Book of Nature.

The Child's Book of Nature, for the Use of Families and Schools; intended to aid Mothers and Teachers in Training Children in the Observation of Nature. In Three Parts. Part I. Plants. Part II. Animals. Part III. Air, Water, Heat, Light, &c. By WORTHINGTON HOOKER, M.D. Illustrated. The Three Parts complete in One Volume, Small 4to, Half Leather, $1 31; or, separately, in Cloth, Part I., 53 cents; Part II., 56 cents; Part III., 56 cents.

A beautiful and useful work. It presents a general survey of the kingdom of nature in a manner adapted to attract the attention of the child, and at the same time to furnish him with accurate and important scientific information. While the work is well suited as a class-book for schools, its fresh and simple style cannot fail to render it a great favorite for family reading.

The Three Parts of this book can be had in separate volumes by those who desire it. This will be advisable when the book is to be used in teaching quite young children, especially in schools.

Published by HARPER & BROTHERS, New York.

☞ Sent by mail, postage prepaid, to any part of the United States, on receipt of the price.

CHILDREN'S PICTURE-BOOKS.

Square 4to, about 300 pages each, beautifully printed on Tinted Paper, embellished with many Illustrations, bound in Cloth, $1 50 per volume.

The Children's Picture-Book of Sagacity of Animals.

With Sixty Illustrations by HARRISON WEIR.

The Children's Bible Picture-Book.

With Eighty Illustrations, from Designs by STEINLE, OVERBECK, VEIT, SCHNORR, &c.

The Children's Picture Fable-Book.

Containing One Hundred and Sixty Fables. With Sixty Illustrations by HARRISON WEIR.

The Children's Picture-Book of Birds.

With Sixty-one Illustrations by W. HARVEY.

The Children's Picture-Book of Quadrupeds and other Mammalia.

With Sixty-one Illustrations by W. HARVEY.

Published by HARPER & BROTHERS, New York.

☞ Sent by mail, postage prepaid, to any part of the United States, on receipt of the price.

BOOKS FOR YOUNG MEN.

Character.

Character. By SAMUEL SMILES. 12mo, Cloth, $1 00.

It is, in design and execution, more like his "Self-Help" than any of his other works. Mr. Smiles [illegible] enough without philosophy, but he writes best when he is telling anecdotes, and using them to enforce a moral [illegible], although he is not afraid to state it plainly. By means of it "Self-Help" at once became a standard book, and "Character" is, in its way, quite as good as "Self-Help." It is a wonderful storehouse of anecdotes and biographical illustrations.—Examiner, London.

Self-Help.

Self-Help: with Illustrations of Character, Conduct, and Perseverance. By SAMUEL SMILES. New Edition, Revised and Enlarged. 12mo, Cloth, $1 00.

The writings of Samuel Smiles are a valuable aid in the education of boys. His style seems to have been constructed entirely for their tastes; his topics are admirably selected, and his mode of communicating excellent lessons of enterprise, truth, and [illegible] [illegible] which is only applicable to lessons of an opposite character and tendency taught in the same [illegible] style. The popularity of this book, "Self-Help," abroad, has made it a powerful instrument of good, and many an English boy has risen from his present [illegible] that his life will be moulded after those of some of those set before him in this volume. It was written for the youth of another country, but its wealth of instruction has been recognized by its translation into more than one European language, and it is not too much to predict for it a popularity among American boys.—N. Y. World.

Thrift.

Thrift. By SAMUEL SMILES. 12mo, Cloth, $1 00.

The mechanic, farmer, apprentice, clerk, merchant, and a large circle of readers outside of these classes will find in the volume a wide range of counsel and advice, presented in perspicuous language, and marked throughout by vigorous good sense; and who, while deriving from it useful lessons for the guidance of their personal affairs, will also be imbibing valuable instruction in an important branch of political economy. We wish it could be placed in the hands of all our youth—especially those who expect to be merchants, artisans, or farmers.—Christian Intelligencer, N. Y.

In this useful and sensible work, which should be in the hands of all classes of readers, especially of those whose means are slender, the author does for private economy what Smith and Ricardo and [illegible] have done for national economy. * * * The one step which separates civilization from savagery—which renders civilization possible—is labor done in excess of immediate necessity. * * * To inculcate this most necessary and most homely of all virtues, we have met with no better teacher than this book.—N. Y. World.

Published by HARPER & BROTHERS, New York.

☞ Sent by mail, postage prepaid, to any part of the United States, on receipt of the price.

THE DARWINOGRAM.

THE object of this game is to discover from what prehistoric animal you are descended. You select any one of the numbers, and follow the line to which it belongs with the point of a pencil to the other end, and there you will find your original ancestor, according to the theory of Mr. Darwin. It may prove to be a butterfly, or it may prove to be a goose.

THE LITTLE SPANISH DANCER.

THIS lively little fellow is very easily made. Take an old kid glove and cut off the fingers—this is for the foundation. Upon it you may sew any bits of bright silk or cloth you like to look like a jacket, and hide the doubled-up fingers. Make two little mittens, and two little socks with stuffed toes, remembering to stuff one sock higher than the other, as your fore-

finger is shorter than your middle finger, and you want your dancer to have both legs the same size. After dressing up your hand to your satisfaction, paint on the back of the wrist a face with water-colors, mixing a little gum with them if they will not "lay," and the little Spaniard is ready to dance as long as it pleases you.

CHARADE.

My whole most mischievous appears;
  Yet, if I you offend,
Cut off my first, and swiftly will
  You bring me to my end.

Freed from my last, I'm gayly off,
  Yet would you me detain:
Cut off my last, and, lo! for time
  Without end I'll remain.

My first the teamster causes his nag
  That helps to draw the load,
As toward my last their journey tends
  Along the country road.

When, eagerly, we are my first,
  My last to thus pursue,
We're anxious most to shun my whole,
  While yet my whole we do.

SPRING SPORTS—TWO EPISODES OF "TOP-TIME."

HARPER'S YOUNG PEOPLE

AN ILLUSTRATED WEEKLY.

VOL. I.—NO. 20. | PUBLISHED BY HARPER & BROTHERS, NEW YORK. | PRICE FOUR CENTS.

Tuesday, March 16, 1880. | $1.50 per Year, in Advance.

Copyright, 1880, by Harper & Brothers.

FRANK MEETS WITH AN ACCIDENT.

[Begun in No. 19 of Harper's Young People, March 9.]

ACROSS THE OCEAN; OR, A BOY'S FIRST VOYAGE.

A True Story.

By J. O. DAVIDSON.

Chapter II.

THE FURNACE-ROOM.

HAD Frank lain awake he would have seen a curious sight; for there are few more picturesque scenes than the "forecastle interior" of an ocean steamer at night, lit by the fitful gleam of its swinging lamp. This grim-looking man, fumbling in his breast as if for the ever-ready knife or pistol, must be dreaming of some desperate struggle by his set teeth and hard breathing. That huge scar on the face of the gaunt, sallow figure beside him, whose scaled red shirt and matted beard would just suit the foreground of a Nevada gully, might tell a strange tale. That handsome, statuesque countenance yonder, again, faultless but for the sinister gleam of its restless eyes—what can it be doing among these coarse, uncultivated men, not one of whom can tell why they should all shrink from it as they do? What a study for a pirate any artist might make out of this shaggy, black-haired giant, whose lion-like head is hanging over the side of his bunk! His weather-beaten face looks hard as a pine knot; but a child would run to him at once, recognizing, with its own unerring instinct, the tender heart hidden beneath that rough outside. Next to him lies a trim, slender lad, who looks as if he knew more of Latin and Greek than of reefing and splicing, and whose curly brown head some fond mother has doubtless caressed many a time; yet here he is, an unknown sailor before the mast, with all his gifts wasted, and doomed perhaps to sink lower still.

But these are the exceptions; the majority are sailors of the ordinary type, careless, light-hearted, improvident, never looking beyond the present moment—content to accept the first job that "turns up," and quite satisfied with a day's food and a shirt to their backs. Some are coiled up on lockers and spare sails, others sleeping off their last night's "spree" on the bare planks, and rolling over and over with every plunge of the vessel.

Whew! what a stream of cold air comes rushing down the hatchway, as it opens to let in the deck watch, glad enough to get below again out of the cold and wet! Their shouts, as they dash the brine from their beards and jackets, and chaff the comrades who are unwillingly turning out to relieve them, arouse Frank, who for a moment can hardly make out where he is. Then it all flashes upon him, and he "tumbles up," and goes on deck.

Certainly, if any one ever could feel dismal at sea, it would be during the hour before dawn, the most cheerless and uncomfortable of the whole twenty-four. After spending the night in a lively game of cup and ball, with yourself for the ball, and an amazingly hard wooden bunk for the cup, you crawl on deck, bruised and aching from top to toe. While gazing upon the inspiring landscape of gray fog and slaty blue sea, you suddenly feel a stream of cold water splashing into your boots, while an unfeeling sailor gruffly asks "why in thunder you can't git out o' the way!" Springing hastily aside, you break your shins over a spar which seems to have been put there on purpose, and get up only to be instantly thrown down again by a lee lurch of the ship, amid the derisive laughter of the deck watch. Meanwhile a shower of half-melted snow insinuates itself into your eyes, and up your sleeves, and down the back of your neck; and all this, joined to the agonizing thought that it will be at least two hours before you can get any breakfast, speedily fills you with a rooted hatred of everything and everybody on board the ship.

Well might poor Frank, contrasting his dismal surroundings with the comfortable rooms and piping-hot breakfasts of his forsaken home, begin to think that he had made a fool of himself. But he choked down the feeling as unworthy of a man, and tried to turn his thoughts by watching the two quartermasters at the wheel, who were straining every muscle to keep the ship's head to the mountain waves that burst over the bow every moment with the shock of a battering-ram.

Breakfast came at last, but was not very satisfactory when it did. The old saying of "salt-horse and hard-tack" exactly described the food; and Frank, eating with one hand while clinging desperately to the long narrow table with the other, had quite enough to do in keeping his knife from running into his eye, and himself from going head over heels on the floor. At every plunge below the water-line the mess-room, already dim enough, became almost dark, while the faces of the men looked as green and ghastly as a band of demons in a pantomime. And, to crown all, one of Frank's neighbors suddenly sent a tremendous splash of grease right over him, coolly remarking,

"Now, Greeny, you won't get hurt if you fall overboard—ile calms the water, you know."

At which all the rest laughed, and Frank felt worse than a murderer.

Breakfast over, our hero was "told off" to go below with the firemen. Down he went, through one narrow hole after another, past deck after deck of iron grating—down, down, down—till at last, as he emerged from a dark passageway, a very startling scene burst upon him.

Along either side of a long narrow passage (the iron walls of which sloped inward overhead) gaped a row of huge furnace mouths, sending out a quivering glare of intense heat, increased by the mounds of red-hot coals that heaped the iron floor. Amid this chaos, several huge black figures, stripped to the waist, and with wet cloths around their sooty faces, were flinging coal into the furnaces, or stirring the fires with long iron rakes—now standing out gaunt and grim in the red blaze, now vanishing into the eddies of hissing steam tossed about by the stream of cold air from the funnel-like "wind-sail" serving as a ventilator.

A shovel was thrust into Frank Austin's hand, and he was set to keep the doorway clear of the coal that came tumbling into it from the bunkers where the coal-heavers were at work. In this way he labored till noon, and then, with blistered hands and aching back, crawled up the iron ladder, worn out, grimy, and half dazed, to his dinner.

But what a dinner for Christmas-day! No appetizing turkey and plum-pudding, eaten in the midst of loving faces and merry talk and laughter; nothing but coarse salt-junk and hard ship-biscuit, hastily snatched among rough, unsympathetic men, who neither knew nor cared anything about him. And as soon as the meal was over, back again to his weary toil in the coal bunker, which was fated, however, to be cut short in a way that he little expected.

For a time he worked away manfully; but the heat of the room and the monotony of his occupation combined to make him careless. Little by little his thoughts wandered away to his pleasant home beside the Hudson, and the little garden patch where he used to work, and the cozy fire, in the ashes of which he and his brothers roasted their chestnuts, and—

"Look out there!"

The warning cry came too late. There was a sudden shock—a deafening crash—and poor Frank was seen lying on his back senseless and half buried beneath the huge heap of coal that blocked the doorway.

[TO BE CONTINUED.]

WHAT THE BOYS AND GIRLS PLAYED TWO THOUSAND YEARS AGO.

BY HATTIE B. CRAFTS.

DO you ever think about the little boys and girls who lived so long ago? Well, in the celebrated country of Greece they were as fond of sports as children of the present day, only they had not so many wonderful toys made for them as are manufactured now. But could we look back upon them at some of their sports, we should find them very happy children, and it might surprise you to know how many games have been played century after century, and are still played and enjoyed to-day.

The babies had their rattles and bright-colored balls, the children their hoops and balls, and what we call "Blindman's-buff" was a favorite game among them. Perhaps you know about the old giant Polyphemus, who was master of a race of one-eyed giants, and who devoured the Greeks that were round his cave, until they succeeded in putting out his eye, and how he still groped around and endeavored to find them, but in vain. Well, the boys and girls of Greece used to represent this story by this very game of "Blindman's-buff." The one blindfolded was called Polyphemus, and the others would hide and pretend they were the Greeks whom he was to find. Another way of playing this game was for the children to run round about the blindfolded person, and one of them touch him. If he could tell correctly who it was, the two exchanged places.

In Athens, and in other cities and towns as well, you might almost any day see a whole group of children hopping along on one foot, as though the other was hurt; but, no, it was only for the fun, as every child of every nation knows, of seeing who could hop the farthest. Sometimes one boy would be allowed the use of both his feet, and the others would try to overtake him by hopping on only one foot, and for those who could do this it was accounted a great victory.

In one of their games they set up a stone, called the Dioros, and each of the players was to stand at a certain distance from it, and in turn throw stones at it. But the one who missed had rather a difficult task to perform, for the rule of the game was that he must be blindfolded and carry the successful player round on his back until he could go directly from the standing-point to the Dioros. A sport not requiring quite so much skill, and one which many of you have perhaps practiced, consisted in setting a stick upright in the soil wherever it was loose and moist, and trying to dislodge it by throwing other sticks at it, keeping, of course, at a certain distance.

Who will attempt to enumerate the many games played by a ring of children running about one in the centre? There must be a wonderful charm about them, so much are they played by both boys and girls in every country. Whether little Sallie Waters had her origin in Greece I will not pretend to say, but we do know that games were played in a similar manner. Here are some, enjoyed especially by the boys. One boy sat on the ground, and the others, forming themselves into a ring, ran round him, one of them hitting him as they went; if the boy in the centre could seize upon the one who struck him, the captive took his place. This did very well for the smaller boys, but the older ones had an arrangement a little in advance of it. The one in the centre was to move about with a pot on his head, holding it with his left hand, and the others, running around, would strike him and cry, "Who has the pot?" To which he replied, "I, Midas," trying all the time to reach one of them with his foot, and the first one touched was obliged to carry the pot in his turn.

One of their most interesting games, and one which you would all enjoy, was the twirling of the ostrakon. A line was drawn on the ground, and the group of boys separated into two parties. A small earthenware disk, having one side black and the other white, was brought forward, and each party chose a side, black or white. It was then twirled along the line, the one throwing it crying, "Night, or day," the black side representing night, and the white day. The party whose side came up was called victorious, and ran after the others, who fled in all directions. The one first caught was styled "ass," and was obliged to sit down, the game proceeding without him. And so it was continued until the whole number were caught. This was excellent exercise, and often played by the hour together.

A favorite game among the girls was played with five little balls or pebbles. They would toss them into the air, and endeavor to catch many on the back of the hand or between the fingers. Of course some of them would often fall to the ground; but these they were allowed to pick up, provided they did so with the fingers of the same hand on which the others rested, which required considerable skill. The French girls have a very pretty game of this, which is played with five little glass balls.

We must not omit the ancestors of Punch and Judy, who lived in those early times, though probably under different names. But however they were called, they were just as queer-looking a family; and their arms would move, their shoulders shrug, their eyes roll, and their feet cut as strange capers as those of their descendants; and I have no doubt afforded the little ones, and perhaps some older persons, as much pleasure then as now.

GARDEN-LORE.

Every child who has gardening tools
Should learn by heart these gardening rules:
He who owns a gardening spade
Should be able to dig the depth of its blade;
He who owns a gardening rake
Should know what to leave and what to take;
He who owns a gardening hoe
Must be sure how he means his strokes to go;
But he who owns a gardening fork
May make it do all the other tools' work;
Though to shift, or to pot, or annex what you can,
A trowel's the tool for child, woman, or man.

THE ROBBER BLUEBIRD.

BY A LITTLE GIRL.

ONCE upon a time there lived in a beautiful house two little brothers, called John and Harry, and they were almost always very good boys.

But one day they got angry at each other, and they looked just like two turkey-gobblers, their faces were so red, and they blustered about so. John declared that he would thrash Harry; and Harry made faces at John, and dared him to fight.

What do you think all the quarrel was about? Why, nothing but a little piece of cake that the cook had given to Harry. Now just as they were going to strike one another, they saw a beautiful bluebird, with a lovely crest upon its head, fly down into the yard and pick up a large worm.

He was just going to fly off with it, when another bird, just like himself, dived down and tried to take the worm from the one that had first found it.

Before the two brothers could say a word, the birds were flying at each other, and tearing off their beautiful crests and coats.

Harry and John stood watching them, and quite forgot that they had a fight on hand of their own.

Just as the naughty bird that was trying to rob his brother bluebird had seized the worm, and was about to fly away with it, there was a sudden rush and flash, and Pussy Cat ran under the house with the wicked little robber tight between her teeth.

Then the other bird, trembling with fear, flew up into a tree to rest.

"Oh, John!" cried Harry, "just think if that had been you and me, and a lion had come and carried one of us off, and ate us up!"

"Only—only it would not have been you, Harry. He would have carried me off, because it was I began the quarrel. Cook gave you the cake, and I wanted to take it from you, just like the robber bluebird did. Let us kiss and be friends, Harry."

"Yes, and you can have half of my cake, John."

"And I hope my little boys will never do so again," said mamma, who had been watching, and heard all.

And years afterward, when John and Harry were away from their mamma and home, they often reminded each other of the lesson they had learned from the fate of the robber bluebird.

DREAMING.

"He is dreaming. Guess of what, now."
"Well, I guess that in his hand
Is a marble—such a beauty!
And he dreams of wonder-land.

"Dreams a dream of giants rolling
Giant marbles—oh, such fun!
See, he smiles, for he has seen one
Bigger, brighter, than the sun."

CHAMPION.

BY MRS. L. G. MORSE.

HETTY had five brothers and sisters, and Champion, the dog, felt that he had too much to do. There were plenty of people in the cottage at Lenox, where they lived in summer, to take care of the children, but there is a certain sort of responsibility which dogs of good, sound character are not willing to intrust to anybody. The baby was always with his mother or nurse, and Champion found it easy to take care of the other little ones, for they were not allowed to venture outside of the garden gate, and if that were carelessly left open, he had only to station himself in front of it, and to gently tumble them over on the grass if they attempted to pass through it. He had never hurt them, and their mother thought that they could not be under any better protection than that of good old faithful "Cham."

But Hetty, who was seven years old, and Rudolph, who was nine, worried the dog terribly, and caused him to wear almost a perpetual scowl of anxiety upon his face. He evidently looked upon them as not old enough to be trusted by themselves, and it was a serious annoyance to him that they were too big to be rolled over on the grass, and so kept within the limits of the garden.

One lovely summer morning Hetty was missing. She had run away with a beautiful ripe plum, which her cousin Francis had picked in order to show her that the bloom upon it was exactly the color of old "Greylock" in the distance. So she climbed the nearest hill, to compare the colors of the mountain and the plum. Looking away over the valley, the child saw too much beauty all at once. Clasping her hands behind her, she took in a long sweet breath of morning air, and did not know what it was that filled her whole soul with joy. She laughed aloud up at the clear sky, and spreading her arms as if they were the wings of a bird, she ran down the hill-side. Oh, there were so many robins! And butterflies flew around her in little clouds. The fields were like fairy-land, they were so full of flowers. She picked baby daisies, and put them inside of the wild-carrot heads, not in blossom yet, which grew in the shape of nests. When she climbed over a stone wall to the road, a squirrel ran across her path, into the woods on the opposite side. "There!" she whispered, softly, "maybe I can find his hole." And she ran after him.

It was a great pity that Champion had so much to do that morning. When dinner was ready, and no Hetty appeared, Rudy called the dog, and asked, "Cham, where's Hetty?"

Champion whined piteously, and looked first down the road, then up at Rudy, and then down the road again.

"Come and eat some dinner, Rudy," said his mother, shading her eyes, and looking anxiously toward the woods. "Hetty will feel hungry, and come home soon now." But she looked proudly after Rudy when he clapped his hat on with a thump, and said, "Never you mind about me, mother; I'll eat more if I find Het first," and went racing after Champion, who bounded over the ground as if he meant to run all the way to the mountain.

At the edge of the woods Rudy waited, and whistled to Cham. "Hold on!" he said; "maybe she's hiding." And for a while he looked about the laurel bushes in the

places where they were accustomed to play, and sang lustily.

"A-roving, a-roving,
I'll go no more a-roving
With thee, fair maid."

But after a while he ceased his singing, and answered one of Champion's whines by ramming his hands in his pockets, and saying, "Look a-here, Cham! If anything has happened to Het, I'll—" The thought brought such a film over his honest brown eyes that he had to rub his cuff over them a good many times before he could see well enough to go on with his search. Fortunately, dogs don't cry tears, and Champion's eyes seemed to grow brighter as Rudy's grew dim. He seemed to say to himself: "If Rudy is going to give up, and cry about it, I've got to take matters into my own hands. Hetty's got to be found, and I can't waste my time waiting for a boy to get the better of his feelings. He oughtn't to *have* any feelings until after our business is settled!" And Champion gave Rudy's boot a good-by lick, and raced away alone.

Rudy dried his eyes, and had no more idea than the dog had of giving up the search. Dogs are just as apt to misunderstand boys as boys are to misunderstand dogs.

Rudy ran over woods and fields, up and down the neighboring hills, calling Hetty and Champion, whistling and shouting, until he was hoarse. He could not find Hetty, and Champion did not return.

After a while he got angry at the dog, and said, between his teeth, "I'll give it to Cham for running away from *me*, just when I want him to help me find Het!" But his anger melted into grief when the terrible thought came that perhaps some dreadful thing had happened to his sister. Once he lay down flat upon his face, and cried aloud at the sudden memory of how he had teased her that very morning by running away with one of her doll's shoes, which he had only just that moment switched out of his pocket. In a few moments, however, he jumped up again, looked at the little shoe tenderly, and tied it carefully in a corner of his handkerchief, saying, "There! I'll give it back the minute I find her, and I'll fix her something for the baby-house, to make up."

He started off once more, this time without stopping to think where Hetty would be likely to go, only rushing about in a sort of desperate way, calling her by name, and shouting for Cham.

He stopped on top of a high hill called the Ledge, and looked down the steep side of it a moment. Hark! He certainly heard the whine of a dog. He clambered down a little way, and called his loudest. The dog's whine answered him again. With a new hope in his heart, he called, and listened until the whine grew louder and louder, and he recognized Cham's bark. Catching at branches, stumbling, sliding, and blundering, he made his way down the hill-side, until suddenly the dog's bark was almost at his ears. And at last, there, farther round the side, on a ledge, just where a light motion would send her rolling down a steep declivity, lay Hetty; and Champion—stanch old Champion—sat upright before her, like a brave, resolute soldier on guard, pricking up his ears, barking loud in answer to Rudy's calls, his body quivering all over, and his feet restless on the ground. But Rudy knew that Hetty could roll no farther, and that Champion would sit there until help came. He did not wait to waken Hetty, but climbing to her, he patted Cham on the head, and bade him watch her till he returned. Then he planted a rough, glad, boyish kiss on her unconscious cheek, and hurried home as he had never hurried in his life before.

The mother's pride in her boy that night made her face shine, as she sat by Hetty, who lay on the sofa, waited upon by everybody, because of her ankle, which was slightly sprained. And she said nothing about the chips Rudy was making, against all regulations, on the floor, as he was whittling into shape a bench for Hetty's doll's kitchen.

"I'll tell you what, though, Het," said Rudy, "when you want to go off again to see whether mountains are plum-colored or not, you'd better take somebody along who knows that a carrot-weed's a flower, and that stumps and stones are stumps and stones. You'd better take a person—like me, you know," he said, winking comically at Hetty—"who won't mistake a frightened squirrel for the king of the brown elves off on a hunting spree, or for anything else that never was born, except inside of your topsy-turvy head."

Hetty laughed, and blushed rosy red. "I guess I won't," she said; "but if you had found yourself, Rudy, sliding and tumbling and running like lightning down that hill, I guess *your* head would have been topsy-turvy for once. And I don't know which is the funniest, to faint away, or to wake up and find Cham licking me. Dear, good, darling Cham! I never *will* go away again without Cham."

Champion licked Rudy's face as he and the boy rolled over on the rug together, and blinked at both the children as if he understood and quite approved of Hetty's good resolution.

THE LITTLE SHIPS OF THE WATER STREETS.

BY JAMES B. MARSHALL.

IF the jolly uncle of certain Venetian girls and boys comes home from China, and says, "Hurra, children! let's go take a ride, and have a good time," they don't imagine it will be in an open carriage behind swift-footed horses.

They would think of a beautiful little ship, about thirty feet long, four or five wide, and as light as cork, called a gondola, which means "little ship." It would be painted black, like every other gondola, and the prow would be ornamented with a high halberd-shaped steel piece, burnished to a dazzling glitter. This steel prow would act as a counter-balance to their rower,

A GONDOLA ON THE GRAND CANAL.

who would stand on the after-end, and row with his face in the direction they wished to be taken. The rowlock would be simply a notched stick, and he would row with one long oar, pushing swiftly along.

He would row so gracefully and easily that you might think you could quickly become a good gondolier if you tried. You would change your mind, however, after the laughable experience of rowing yourself overboard several times, and admit that rowing a gondola requires no small skill.

It was the people called the Veneti who, more than a thousand years ago, settled Venice, and invented these little ships. The fifteen thousand houses of Venice are built on a cluster of islands, over one hundred in number, and divided by nearly one hundred and fifty canals, or water streets. However, one may visit any part of the city without the aid of a gondola, as the islands are joined together by three hundred and seventy-eight bridges, and between the houses lead narrow crooked passages, many not wider than the width of one's outspread arms.

The canals are salt, and offer at high tide fine salt-water bathing. As most of the houses rise immediately from the water, it is not an uncommon sight, at certain hours, to see a gentleman or his children walk down his front-door steps arrayed for bathing, and take a "header" from the lower step. That sounds very funny, but to the Venetians such proceedings are quite a matter of course.

In the lagoon around the city are numerous exasperating sand islands, exposed to view at low tide. The amateur gondolier seeks this lagoon, to be safe from scoffers at his clumsy rowing, and often, right in the midst of his "getting the knack of it," the tide leaves him stuck fast on a sand island, to wait for its return.

Excepting the Grand Canal, the canals are narrow, and make innumerable sharp turns; so that it requires more skill to steer a gondola than it does to row, if such a thing is possible. The gondoliers display great skill in both rowing and steering, and they cut around corners and wind through openings seemingly impassable, always warning each other of their intentions by certain peculiar cries.

During Venice's prosperity, gondola regattas were held, and were events of great pomp and display. They took place on the Grand Canal, when the whole city gathered on its banks, or in many gondolas on its surface, and what with the music, the display of flags and banners, and the bright-colored clothing of the color-loving people, the spectacle certainly must have presented a scene of great brilliancy. The prizes were money and champion flags, and with the lowest was also given a live pig—a little pleasantry corresponding to the leather medal in American contests.

Once a year the Doge, or chief ruler of Venice, and his officers went in a vessel of royal magnificence, called the *Bucintoro*, out upon the Adriatic Sea, followed by a grand procession of gondolas, and there he dropped overboard a gold ring, after certain impressive ceremonies, thus signifying Venice's espousal with the sea, and her dominion over it.

This *Bucintoro* was a two-decked vessel propelled by one hundred and sixty of the strongest rowers of the Venetian fleet. Its sides were carved and gilded, some parts gold-plated, and the whole surmounted by a gold-embroidered crimson velvet canopy. The mast is still preserved in the arsenal at Venice, but the vessel was purposely destroyed to secure its gold ornaments.

It is only in the severest winters—of rare occurrence—that gondolas can not be used; but then the young Venetians may perform the—to them—wonderful feat of walking on the water, and tell of it years after. Some two hundred years ago the ice lasted the unheard-of time of eighteen days, and such an impression did the event make upon the Venetians that the year in which it happened is known to the present day as the *anno del ghiaccio*—"year of the ice."

THE GREAT LILY'S MISSION.

BY MRS. J. B. McCONAUGHY.

FORTY-THREE years ago last New-Year's Day a native boat was gliding along through one of the small rivers of British Guiana, when it came to a spot where the stream widened into a little lake. A celebrated botanist was a voyager in the little canoe, and all at once his attention was fixed on a wonderful plant he found growing along the margin of the lake. All his weariness and the many discomforts of his situation were forgotten in the enthusiasm of that moment. Never before had he seen such a flower. One might fancy a giant had been raising lilies to present to some fair giantess.

Imagine the rippling water covered with thick leaves of pale green, lined with vivid crimson, each one almost large enough to cover your bed, while all about were floating massive lilies, whose single petals of white and rosy pink were more than a foot across, and numbered over a hundred to a blossom.

The flower was sent home to England, and awakened great enthusiasm among the lovers of science, but no one surmised that the fair stranger was destined to effect a great revolution in the architecture of the world. Yet all great enterprises have generally taken a very roundabout way before they came to perfection. You could hardly forecast them when you looked at their beginnings.

Such a royal lily well deserved a royal name. So it was christened the *Victoria Regia*. Had it been a beautiful princess they were anxious to make contented in her adopted land, they could not have taken more pains to humor her tastes and whims. Mr. Paxton, the great gardener who had it in charge, determined that the baby lily should never know that it was not in its native waters, growing in its native soil, under its own torrid skies. So he made up a bed for its roots out of burned loam and peat; the great lazy leaves were allowed to float at their ease in a tank of water, to which a gentle ripple was imparted by means of a water-wheel, and then a house of glass, of a beautiful device, was built over it all, and the right temperature kept up to still further deceive the young South American.

With all this pampering it grew so fast that in a month it had outgrown its house. A new one must be had forthwith, or the baby lily would be hopelessly dwarfed. Mr. Paxton was not disconcerted by this precociousness of his wayward pet, but at once put his talents to work to provide it with suitable accommodations. The greenhouse he next built was a more novel and elegant conservatory, and might rightly be styled the first Crystal Palace.

It was just at this time that the word had gone out over all the earth that its nations were invited to a great World's Fair at London. And now a very serious question came up about the building in which to house them. The committee, of course, decided on a structure of orthodox brick and mortar, and then began a fierce war in the papers with regard to the project. How would their beautiful Hyde Park be spoiled by letting loose in it such an army of shovellers, bricklayers, hewers, and all manner of craftsmen! What a spoiling of its ornamental trees, and what a cutting up of its smooth drives by the heavy carts loaded with brick and mortar enough to build a pyramid!

Mr. Paxton read in the *Times* these many objections, and the thought flashed through his mind that they could all be removed by building on the plan of his lily-house. A succession of such structures enlarged and securely joined together would produce just such a building as was wanted. All could be prepared in the great workshops of the kingdom, and brought together with almost as little noise and confusion as was Solomon's great Temple.

The building committee were hard to convince. They were joined to their idols of brick and mortar. But good Prince Albert, and Sir Robert Peel, and Mr. Stephenson, the engineer, were all on the side of iron and glass, and at last they won.

Such a beautiful fairy-like structure as went up, almost like Aladdin's palace, by New-Year's Day, 1851, the world had never seen. The great lily had, all unconsciously, accomplished a wonderful work. Over and over again has its crystal house been copied, and not the least beautiful of such structures is our own grand Centennial Main Building.

THE MISHAPS OF AN ARAB GENTLEMAN.

THE Orientals differ in many respects from the Europeans and Americans in their customs and manners, their dress, and the furniture of their houses. The dress of the men consists of a red cap, wide baggy cloth trousers, silken girdle, and a jacket. The houses in Syria are invariably built of stone, and in the south of Palestine entirely so. The floors of the rooms are paved with marble or granite. At the entrance of every room is a space of several feet square, paved with figured marble, and never carpeted, generally used as a receptacle for shoes and slippers, which the Orientals remove from their feet on entering a room. The rest of the floor is raised about half a foot higher. The Orientals sleep on the ground, *i. e.*, on mattresses laid on carpets, or mats spread on the floor.

In an Arab family one of the members became ambitious of transforming himself into a European. This young gentleman had received an excellent education, being familiar not only with the Arab literature, but master of the ancient and modern Greek.

His first step toward the desired end was to study English and French. When he had gained a fair knowledge of these languages, he applied for the position of interpreter to the American consulate, to which he succeeded in being appointed.

His so-far satisfied ambition would no longer allow him to wear the Oriental dress, and he soon showed himself to an admiring world of natives in European costume. One day he was asked how he liked his new costume.

"Not at all," he replied. "I feel as if tied hand and foot in a tight-fitting prison."

A few weeks later he one day startled some of his European friends by asking them, with a thoughtful seriousness, whether they often tumbled out of bed.

"Tumble out of bed!" they exclaimed. "Why, of course not. How could one?"

"I would much rather find out how a person could not," was his reply.

He was asked what put such an idea into his head.

The rest is best told in his own words.

"I furnished my rooms with European furniture. Bad luck to the day I was foolish enough to do so! A few nights ago, after having locked my door and put out my light—things I never did before—I got up into the bedstead. My sensations were those of being put away on a high shelf in a dark prison. I wondered whether Europeans experienced such feelings every night. Finally I fell asleep, comforting myself that I might get used to it. How long I slept in that bed I shall never know, for when I awoke, it was to find myself in the grave. I was cramped in every limb; I felt the cold pavement under me, and icy walls round me. For clothing or covering I found nothing within reach but what at the time seemed a shroud. Where was I? What had happened? Suddenly the idea came to me that I must have fainted, been mistaken for dead, buried, and now recovered consciousness in my grave. So convinced was I, that I shouted at the top of my voice that I was not dead, and begged to be taken out of the tomb. The noise I made soon awoke the whole house, and as I had locked my door, no one could get in. I heard my mother and brothers uttering pious ejaculations to exorcise the evil spirit which they believed had got hold of me, while I trebled my frantic yells for deliverance. By vigorously shaking the door, they finally burst it open, and then I was surprised to see that I was not in my grave, but that I had tumbled out of bed, and rolled along the floor till I landed in the space by the door."

"But did you not wake with the fall?"

"No; I felt nothing till I awoke, as I believed, in my tomb, but really in the shoe receptacle; and since you all assure me that Europeans never tumble out of their beds, I resign all hopes of ever being transformed into one. I shall in the future, as I have done in the past, sleep on the ground, from which there is no danger of tumbling."

THE HIPPOPOTAMUS.

THE hippopotamus, or river-horse, is found exclusively in the great rivers, lakes, and swamps of Africa. Fossil remains of extinct species have been discovered in both Europe and Asia, but ages have passed since they existed. This animal is amphibious, and can remain under water five minutes or more without breathing. When it comes to the surface it snorts in a terrible manner, and can be heard at a great distance. It is never found far away from its native element, to which it beats a retreat at the least alarm. Travellers along the White Nile and in Central Africa often encounter enormous herds of these ungainly creatures sometimes lying in the water, their huge heads projecting like the summit of a rock, sometimes basking on the shore in the muddy ooze, or grazing on the river-bank; for this animal is a strict vegetarian, and the broad fields of grain and rice along the Upper Nile suffer constantly from its depredations.

The hippopotamus is a hideous-looking beast. It has an enormous mouth, armed with four great tusks that appear viciously prominent beneath its great leathern lips. These tusks are so powerful that a hippopotamus has been known to cut holes through the iron plates of a Nile steamer with one blow. Its eyes are very small, but protruding, and placed on the top of its head. Its body resembles a huge hogshead perched on four short, stumpy legs. A full-grown animal will sometimes measure twelve feet in length and as much in circumference. The hide of this beast is very thick and strong, and is used to make whips. Ordinary bullets, unless they strike near the ear, rattle off the sides of this King of the Nile like small shot. Sir Samuel Baker, the African traveller, relates an encounter with a large bull hippopotamus which was taking an evening stroll on the bank of the river, quietly munching grass. Baker and his attendant were armed only with rifles. They aimed and fired, hitting as near the ear as possible, but the great beast only shook its head and trotted off. At the sound of firing the remainder of the party hurried up, and poured a volley of musketry at the retreating beast, but the hippopotamus walked coolly to the edge of a steep cliff, about eighteen feet high, and with a clumsy jump and a tremendous splash vanished in the water. As the flesh of the hippopotamus, which is said to resemble pork in flavor, was much desired as food by the soldiers under Baker's charge, he had a small explosive shell constructed, which, fired into the creature's brain, seldom failed to leave its huge body floating dead on the surface of the river.

The natives are very fond of hippopotamus flesh, and resort to many expedients to secure the desired delicacy. Hunting this beast is dangerous sport, for in the water it is master of the situation, and will throw a canoe in the air, or crunch it to pieces with its terrible jaws. In Southern Africa, Dr. Livingstone encountered a tribe of natives called Makombwé who were hereditary hippopotamus-hunters, and followed no other occupation, as, when their game grew scarce at one spot, they removed to another. They built temporary huts on the lonely grassy islands in the

FIGHT WITH A HIPPOPOTAMUS.

rivers and great lakes, where the hippopotami were sure to come to enjoy the luxurious pasturage, and while the women cultivated garden patches, the men, with extraordinary courage and daring, followed the dangerous sport which passes down among them from father to son. When they hunt, each canoe is manned by two men. The canoes are very light, scarcely half an inch in thickness, and shaped somewhat like a racing boat. Each man uses a broad, short paddle, and as the canoe is noiselessly propelled toward a sleeping hippopotamus not a ripple is raised on the water. Not a word passes between the two hunters, but as they silently approach the prey the harpooner rises cautiously, and with sure aim plunges the weapon toward the monster's heart. Both hunters now seize their paddles and push away for their lives, for the infuriated beast springs toward them, its enormous jaws extended, and often succeeds in crushing the frail canoe to splinters. The hunters, if thrown in the water, immediately dive—as the beast looks for them on the surface—and make for the shore. Their prey is soon secured, for the well-aimed harpoon has done its work, and the hippopotamus is soon forced to succumb. Should it be under water, its whereabouts is indicated by a float on the end of the long harpoon rope, and it is easily dragged ashore.

Travellers on the Nile are often placed in great peril by the attacks of these beasts, which although said to be inoffensive when not molested, are so easily enraged that the noise of a passing boat excites them to terrible fury. Baker relates being roused one clear moonlight night by a hoarse wild snorting, which he at once recognized as the voice of a furious hippopotamus. He rushed on deck, and discovered a large specimen of this beast charging on the boat with indescribable rage. The small boats towed astern were crunched to pieces in a moment, and so rapid were the movements of this animal, as it roared and plunged in a cloud of foam and wave, that it was next to impossible to take aim at the small vulnerable spot on its head. At length, however, it appeared to be wounded, and retired to the high reeds along the shore. But it soon returned, snorting and blowing more furiously than ever, and continued its attack until its head was fairly riddled with bullets, and it rolled over and over, dead at last.

Young hippopotami have been captured and placed in zoological gardens, but as they become old they grow savage, and are very hard to manage. Some fine specimens were formerly in the Jardin des Plantes at Paris. They ate all kinds of vegetables and grass, and slept nearly all day, generally lying half in and half out of the big water tank provided for them.

The hippopotamus is supposed by many to be identical with the behemoth of Scripture, which is described as a beast "that lieth under the shady trees, in the covert of the reed and fens." It is also spoken of as one that "eateth grass as an ox," and that "drinketh up a river," and the "willows of the brook compass him about."

THE CAT'S-MEAT MAN.

In one corner of Fulton Market in New York city is the snug little stall of the cat's-meat man. He is a jolly, merry-looking fellow, as you may see by his picture; and he sings and whistles as he works. In the morning he goes about the streets feeding his cats; but his afternoons are devoted to preparing their food for the next day.

Most of this food is raw meat, which, with a sharp knife, he cuts up into very small pieces, until several hundred pounds are thus prepared. Sometimes a small portion of the meat is boiled; but this cooked meat is only intended for cats who are not very well, and who need something more delicate than raw meat. Once a week—on Thursdays—the cat's-meat man cuts up fish instead of meat; for on Fridays all his cats have a meal of fish, of which they are very fond, and which is very good for them.

PREPARING CAT'S MEAT IN FULTON MARKET.

After the meat or fish has been nicely cut into bits, it is all done up in small brown-paper parcels, each of which weighs a pound; and these parcels are packed into great strong baskets. Each basket

STARTING OUT

holds forty or fifty of these pound packages, and is pretty heavy for the cat's-meat man to carry.

Bright and early in the morning, soon after sunrise, the cat's-meat man begins to feed his cats, starting out from the market with a big basket of meat on his shoulder, and threading his way through the crooked streets and lanes of the lower part of the city to the homes of his little customers.

Everywhere the cats and kittens are anxiously waiting and watching for him, and sometimes they run out and meet him at the corners half a block or more away from their homes. Often when he is feeding the cats on one side of the street, those living on the other side run across, and rubbing against his legs, mewing and purring, seem to beg him to hurry and get over to their side.

Of course these cats do not belong to the cat's-meat man, though he takes just as much interest in them, and is just as fond of them, as though they were his own. They are the cats that live in the stores and warehouses of the lower portion of the city, where they are kept as a protection against the armies of fierce rats that come up from the wharves, and do terrible damage wherever the cats are not too strong for them. For this reason the cats are highly prized and well cared for in this part of the city, and the cat's-meat man finds plenty of work to do in feeding them. He is paid for this by the owners of the cats, and as he has about four hundred customers his business is quite a thriving one.

SOME DOWN-TOWN CATS.

The cats all know and love him, and are generally expecting him; but if he opens the door of a store where one of his cats lives, and she is not to be seen, he calls "Pus-pus-pus," and the kitty comes racing down stairs, or from some distant corner, so fast that she nearly tumbles head over heels in her hurry to get at her breakfast.

Some of the cats are only fed every other day, and they know just as well as anybody when it is "off day," as the cat's-meat man calls it. On these off days they lie perfectly still as he passes, paying no attention to him; but on the days they are to be fed, these "every-other-day cats" are the most eager of all, and travel the greatest distances to meet their friend.

Besides the cats, several dogs are fed daily by the cat's-meat man, and of these the most interesting is Carlo. Carlo used to be a sailor dog, but now he lives quietly in a store on Old

CARLO.

A CHARITY CAT.

THE MORNING CALL.

Slip. His first master was a sea-captain, with whom Carlo made voyages to many different parts of the world. At last his kind master, who was as fond of Carlo as though he had been an only child, became very sick with a terrible fever, and when his ship reached New York, he was taken to a hospital to die. Carlo went to the hospital with him, and just before the dying sailor breathed his last, he begged a kind gentleman who stood beside his bed to take care of Carlo. The gentleman promised to do so, and has ever since kept his promise by giving Carlo a good home in his store, and paying the cat's-meat man to feed him every day. Carlo repays this kindness by keeping the store free from rats, and his reputation as a famous ratter has spread far and wide through the neighborhood.

Many stray cats watch for the coming of the cat's-meat man, for they know that he will befriend them, and many a tidbit does he give to some lean hungry creature as he merrily trudges along through the winter snow-drifts.

At certain corners the cat's-meat man is met by one of his assistants, with whom he exchanges his empty basket for a full one. These halting-places are well known to all the forlorn and homeless cats and dogs, and at them a number of them always await his approach. He most always throws them a few bits from his well-filled basket, for which they seem very grateful, though they look as if they would be very glad of more.

Besides feeding cats and dogs, the cat's-meat man cares for them when they are sick, preparing special food for his patients, and sometimes giving them small doses of medicine. So, you see, the cat's-meat man is a real benefactor, and it is no wonder that all the cats and dogs in the lower part of the city watch for his coming, and are glad when they see him.

MY TARTAR.

BY DAVID KER.

MOST of us have read descriptions and seen pictures of those sallow, flat-faced, narrow-eyed, round-headed hobgoblins who, under the name of Tartars (a wrong one, too, for it should be Tatâré), used to amuse themselves by conquering Eastern Europe every now and then some hundreds of years ago. But it is not every one who has had the pleasure of travelling alone with one of these fellows over nearly a thousand miles of Asiatic desert in time of war—a pleasure which I enjoyed to the full in 1873.

And a very queer journey it was. First came a range of steep rocky hills (marked on the map as the Ural Mountains), where we had to get out and walk whenever we went up hill, and to hold tight to the sides of our wagon, for fear of being thrown out and smashed, whenever we went down hill. Then we got out on the great plains, where we came upon a post-house of dried mud (the only house there was) once in three or four hours; and here we used to change horses by sending out a Cossack with his lasso to see if he could catch any running loose on the prairie; for there are no stables in that country.

Next came a sand desert, where we harnessed three camels to our wagon instead of horses. Here the people lived in tents instead of mud houses, while a hot wind blew all day, and a cold wind all night. One fine evening we had a sand-storm, which almost buried us, wagon and all; and the sand stuck so to my Tartar's yellow face that he looked just like a peppered omelet.

After this came a "rolling prairie," where the people lived in holes under the ground, popping up like rabbits every now and then as we passed. Beyond it was a large fresh-water lake (called by the Russians "Aralskoë Moré," or Sea of Aral), where the musquitoes fell upon us in good earnest. Here we were both boxed up in a mud fort for seven weeks by a Cossack captain, on suspicion of being spies, like Joseph's brethren. When we got out again, we had to go up a great river (called the Syr-Daria, or *Clear Stream*, though it was the dirtiest I ever saw), fringed with thickets, and huge reeds taller than a man, where the musquitoes were doubled, and we had the chance of meeting a tiger or two as well. Then came some more deserts, and then some more mountains; and so at last we got to the capital of the country—a big mud-walled town called Tashkent, or Stone Village—I suppose because there is not a single stone within twenty miles of it.

All this while, Murad (for so my Tartar was named) had been like a man of stone. He never complained; he never smiled; he never got angry. When our food and water ran out; when the sand-flies and musquitoes bit us all over; when we lost our way on the prairie at midnight in a pouring rain; when the jolting of our wagon bumped us about till we were all bruises from head to foot; when we had to sit for hours upon a sand-heap waiting for horses, with the sun toasting us black all the time; when our wheels came off, or our camels ran away—honest Murad's heavy, mustard-colored face never changed a whit. At every fresh mishap he only shrugged his shoulders, saying, "It is my *kismet*" (fate); and when he had said that, he seemed quite satisfied. I never even saw him laugh but once. That once, however, I had good reason to remember; and this was how it happened.

On getting to Tashkent we took up our quarters at a native hotel (*caravanserai* they call it there), where we were kindly allowed a stone floor to sleep on, provided we brought our own beds and our own food along with us. However, we were pretty well used to that sort of thing by this time; so I got out my camp-kettle, and proceeded to make tea, while Murad, like Mother Hubbard in the song,

"Went to the baker's to buy him some bread."

By this time our daily mess of food had become a *mess* in every sense. Bumped and jolted about as we had been, it was no uncommon thing for me to find my bottle of cold tea standing on its head with the cork out, my soda powders fraternizing with the salt and pepper, and my brown loaf taking a bath in the contents of a broken ink-bottle, the splinters of which would be acting as seasoning to the mashed remains of a Bologna sausage. I was not surprised, therefore, to discover a piece of chocolate half buried in my last packet of tea, and by way of experiment I decided to boil the two together, and try how they agreed.

But apparently they didn't agree at all, for I had hardly taken a sip of my first tumbler* when I became aware of the most horrible and astounding taste imaginable, as if a whole apothecary's shop had been boiled down into that one glass. The second tumbler was, if possible, even worse than the first; but this time I noticed a white froth on the top, such as I had never seen upon any tea before. A frightful suspicion suddenly occurred to me. I emptied out my camp-kettle, and discovered—with what emotion I need not say—that the supposed chocolate was nothing less than a piece of brown soap!

Just at that eventful moment in came my Tartar. One glance at the soap, my distorted visage, and the froth in the glass, told him the whole story; and the effect was magical. To throw himself on the floor, to kick up his heels in a kind of convulsive ecstasy, to burst into a succession of shrill, crowing screams, like a pleased baby, was the work of a moment; and he kept on kicking and crowing, till, provoked as I was, I could not help laughing along with him. Then he suddenly sprang up and stood before me with his usual solemn face, as if it were somebody else who had been doing all this, and *he* were utterly shocked at him. But he never afterward alluded to the occurrence, nor did I ever again see him laugh, or even smile.

* The Russians drink tea in tumblers, with lemon-juice instead of milk.

[Begun in No. 17 of HARPER'S YOUNG PEOPLE, February 24.]

BIDDY O'DOLAN.

BY MRS. ZADEL B. GUSTAFSON.

CHAPTER IV.

LITTLE Katy Kegan had the blackest hair and eyes you ever saw, and she was very pretty, with color like the cream and red of the lady-apples packed in tempting pyramids in the fruit stalls. She was the kind of girl who keeps you always expecting, without your knowing what it is you expect. Katy was very bright, quick as a dart in her motions, but as rough and sharp as a prickly-briar if things didn't go to suit her. She had all the bad habits which friendless little children learn from living on the streets, with no one to care what they do or how they feel. She was saucy and bold, and used very bad words, and thought it smart to steal fruit and pea-nuts when she could; and she would tell a lie about her thefts, or indeed about anything else, as glibly as a toad swallows a fly. If you ever saw that done, you know that it is pretty swiftly done; and just as a toad, when it has swallowed a fly, looks as if it had never so much as heard of such an insect, so Katy, when she told a lie, would look straight at you, and smile with an air of such innocence that you would find it hard to not believe her. These sad faults were Katy's misfortunes. She did not know how wrong they were.

But you can see, if you think a moment, that such habits would be a great trouble in the way of her finding a home, because good people would not like to take a little child with such naughty ways into their homes, to be with their own dear children. Still, Katy's pretty face and bright mind, and the love she was so quick to give to any one who was kind to her, made people feel like trying to see what they could do for her.

Three times Mr. Kennedy placed Katy in good homes, in the care of noble people, who wished to help him in such work. In each instance Katy had been loved, because she was so bright and sweet and lovable when she felt like being so; but her sudden fits of anger, and the strange and naughty things she would say and do, made her new friends feel anxious and troubled. Yet Katy had never been sent away from these homes. Perhaps she might have been, but she never waited for that; she ran away of her own accord each time, without saying a word about it, and nothing that Biddy or Mr. Kennedy could say could make Katy agree to go back when once she had run away.

One day Miss Kennedy, who had thought a great deal about this willful child, said to her brother, "Don't be discouraged about Katy; you and Biddy will save the dear little thing yet."

"But I do feel a little discouraged," said Mr. Kennedy. "You see, she is so uncertain; she's tricky as a kitten, and you can never tell what she'll be at next. If the trouble only all came to us, you know, we would be glad to bear it, for there is something very dear about little Katy that pays for care and bother. But how can I go on asking our friends to put up with such a little harum-scarum! And she *will* take things that don't belong to her, and she will deny it. I really don't know what to do."

Biddy sat sewing, but she listened, and looked very earnest. Miss Kennedy smiled.

"I've thought of something, Phil," said she. "I think we have been making a mistake all along in fixing things too easy and pleasant for Katy. I think she needs to have a weight put on her."

"A weight! How do you mean?"

"Well, I mean this. Katy is very loving, and she is more full of active, bounding life than any one I ever saw. I don't think she wants to have things done for her; I think she wants to do things herself. I think she needs to feel that some one, in some real plain way, depends on her, needs her, so that she can not do without her. I have seen feelings in Katy that make me think a weight of this kind would hold her."

Mr. Kennedy looked pleased, and sat some moments thinking. Then he asked: "Well, sister, how will you find such a weight for Katy? I wouldn't like to have her bright wings too closely clipped."

"I've thought of that, Phil, and I've thought it would be well to let Biddy—Katy loves Biddy with all her warm little heart—to let Biddy coax her to go to Mrs. Raynor."

"Mrs. Raynor!" cried Phil.

"I know you are thinking of such a madcap as Katy in Jenny Raynor's sick-room. But that is just my reason. I've talked with Mrs. Raynor, and she is quite willing to try Katy, if we can only get her there to be tried. If there's any one in this world who can tame Katy's wild humors and turn them to good uses, it is Mrs. Raynor. And Jenny needs some one to care for her all the time. Katy can not help loving them, and between them I think they will find a way to hold Katy till she grows to see what a little girl's life means."

The very next day Biddy went out to look for wayward Katy, for it was Katy's having run away again from her third home which had led to this talk between Mr. Kennedy and his sister. Biddy found Katy sitting on some steps on Fulton Street, eating pea-nuts, and tossing up the shells. She looked so happy that Biddy felt a new wonder about her. She remembered how she had longed for a home, and here was Katy liking nothing so well as to run about the streets, and seeming to think home was a great bother. Suddenly a thought came to Biddy, and made her say, quickly, as she reached Katy, "Oh, Katy, did you ever have a doll?"

"Hallo! that you?" said Katy. "Want some pea-nuts? No, I never had no dawl—don't want no dawl—seen lots of 'em—think they're silly. Dawls is only pretendin'—Hallo! catch 'em;" and she tossed a handful of pea-nuts to Biddy.

Biddy sat down on the steps by Katy, and told her as kindly as she could that she wanted her to try once more to like a good home. She held a bit of Katy's skirt in her hand, for fear Katy would run; but she did not think Katy knew she had hold of her dress, till Katy said, "No need to hold on to me—ain't goin' to run."

"Oh, Katy, what have you done with your pretty shoes?" exclaimed Biddy.

"Guv 'em to gal 'at wanted 'em—likes to go barefoot," said Katy, promptly; then she turned her black eyes on Biddy with a queer, sharp look, and said, "Needn't ask no more questshuns—sha'n't answer."

After a little more talk, in which Katy insisted that she didn't think she could stay in a home, though she was willin' to try, 'cause she liked to see insides of houses, they started off together.

The Raynors lived in a larger and more beautiful house than the Kennedys, and a well-behaved maid showed the children into a room which was so dark that Biddy and Katy could hardly see anything at first. Biddy felt Katy twitch at her hand as if she would dart off and rush out into the merry sunlight again. All the way up stairs Katy had been making droll faces at the maid, who went on before them, and mimicking her walk in the funniest manner. Biddy had not seemed to notice, though she had found it hard not to laugh right out at Katy's mischief. Now Biddy held fast to the little hand that wriggled in hers, and as their eyes grew used to the dimness, they saw a large bed with folds of lace hanging around, but drawn away at the sides, and in this bed lay the whitest little girl they had ever seen, with soft eyes looking at them kindly, and close to them was a tall, handsome lady. But what ailed Biddy?

She looked at the white-faced child in the bed, and she

looked at the lady. A flush came in Biddy's cheek, and her eyes opened so wide they were almost as round as marbles. It was the most puzzled little face Mrs. Raynor had ever seen.

"I expected you, and I'm very glad to see you," said she.

In an instant Biddy turned and threw her arms around Katy, who stared, and looked as if she would "cut," as she called it when she ran away.

"Oh, Katy! Katy!" said Biddy, with a queer little quick shake in her voice, "it's the hospital lady, and the hospital little girl that gave me the flowers!" Jenny Raynor's eyes were getting to be as round as Biddy's had been. "Oh, don't you remember the little bit of a girl that was run over, and lay in the hospital on Christmas-day, ever and ever so long ago?" cried Biddy.

Biddy stopped, as had always been her way when feeling became very strong. Mrs. Raynor made her sit down by the bed, and then put out her hand to Katy, who stood so still in the centre of the room. All the bright color had gone out of Katy's cheeks, so that her black eyes looked darker than ever. She staid just where she was, she put her hands down in her apron pockets, raising her small shoulders in doing so. She was the picture of a little elf that might vanish if any one stirred. She looked at Biddy, and said, "Is that gal in the bed the hospital gal what guv ye the flowers?"

Biddy said, "Yes."

"What's matter of 'er?"

"She has been sick a long time," said Mrs. Raynor.

"Stay in bed all time?" asked Katy, still looking at Biddy.

"Oh yes; I shall never get up any more," said Jenny Raynor. "Will you come up here, close to me, little girl?"

Katy came forward a little. "Miss Kennedy says you like to run about a great deal," said Jenny; "I used to like that very much."

Katy came close to the bed. She took her hands out of her pockets; they were full of pea-nuts. She laid them on the bed, and nodded to Biddy. "I'll stay here," said she.

And Katy Kegan kept her word. She didn't get over her faults right off. She had a hard fight with them; but for the first time in her life she tried hard to get rid of them, and soon showed she had great strength to do what she had made up her mind to do.

But Miss Kennedy was right. All Katy had needed was to *be needed*. This was her "weight."

She was the very best thing that could have been brought into Jenny Raynor's sad and shut-up life. Jenny was a good little girl, but no little child can be easily content and cheerful who can not go out into the sunlight, and enjoy the sweet full life of the birds and flowers, and the merry games with other little girls and boys. It is very hard for a child to lie always in bed, and be shut out from all other children's lives. Now Katy Kegan was so wild, so merry, so constantly full and running over with bright ideas of how to get fun out of everything and anything, that she was a whole play-ground in her one little self; and she brought all this life into the room where Jenny lay, and made a new world for Jenny there. Katy was as good as a theatre, for she imitated people, and did it quite wonderfully, so that Jenny could tell just whom she meant; that is, if she had ever seen the person Katy was taking off. And Katy would show her all that she had seen or noticed on the street, in just this way by imitating, so that Jenny seemed almost to make new acquaintances with people whom she had never really seen, by means of Katy's droll mimicry. When Katy saw how all her pranks and fun made Jenny laugh and look so pleased, she took good care to find out some fresh thing to amuse her with whenever she went out.

"BIDDY SAT DOWN ON THE STEPS BY KATY."

When Jenny Raynor gave the flowers to poor Biddy in the hospital so long ago, she could not know that the little kindness would come back to her a thousandfold through another little girl whom she had then never seen at all.

Least of all would you imagine that an old broken-armed doll fished out of an ash-can could be the means of doing so much good, and leading to so much happiness in so many lives. For the good that began in these little things goes on, and may reach into countless lives in time to come. Nothing stops, and nothing stands quite apart by itself from other things. You will find this out, and think of it more and more, as you grow older. As for Biddy O'Dolan, she is quite a young woman now. Of course she does not play with her doll any more. But she keeps it. No money could buy it, with that little wooden arm on it which Charley made. She calls it her first friend, and I think it was a very good friend, don't you?

THE END.

ALICE'S QUESTION.

SOFTLY, gently upward
  A strain from the organ floats,
And the children at play in the nursery
  Listen awhile to the notes.

Stop, and are silent a moment—
  They are almost tired of play,
And the shadows of evening are falling,
  Making twilight out of the day.

Then down the broad old staircase
  Comes the patter of little feet,
And in through the open doorway,
  Drawn by the sounds so sweet.

Then close to the organ stealing,
  With awe-struck eyes they gaze
At the player, and listen intently
  To the deep clear notes of praise.

Then drawing nearer and nearer,
  Made bold by the twilight gray,
Little Alice looks up, and whispers,
  "Did God teach you how to play?"

THE CARE OF PARROTS.

PARROTS are among the most intelligent of household pets, and much attention should be bestowed upon them. No large a bird suffers if kept constantly confined in a cage, but a parrot is so destructive that it is impossible to allow it the liberty of a house, as chairs, carpets, in short, every article of furniture, will soon show the marks of its strong beak. If there is a garden, the parrot should be given a daily promenade during warm weather. It is a necessity to this bird to exercise its beak, and if kept in a cage, it should often be given a chip of wood to tear to pieces. A parrot will amuse itself for hours biting a chip into small fragments. The cage and feed dishes should be thoroughly cleaned every day, and fresh gravel kept in the bottom of the cage.

Parrots are fond of canary and hemp seed, and should always have fresh water, in which a little cracker may be soaked. A little sweetened weak coffee and milk, with bread crumbed in it, may be given about once a week. Apples, pears, and oranges are healthy food, and should always have the seeds left in, as a parrot will eat them first, carefully peeling them, and devour the meat afterward. A slice of lemon and a small red pepper should be given occasionally, also English walnuts.

Cleanliness is essential to the health of a parrot, and as it will not bathe itself like most other birds, it should occasionally be stood in a pan containing an inch or two of tepid water, and its back sprinkled gently. The bird will scream and rebel, but will feel better after it. It should be left in its bath for a few moments only (as it easily gets chilled), and then placed on its perch, where it can not feel any wind, to dry and plume itself. During a warm summer shower it is well to stand the cage out-of-doors for a short time. The parrot will usually spread its wings to receive the drops, and scream with delight, as that is its natural way of bathing. Parrots have very tender feet, and they often suffer if their claws are not kept perfectly clean. The perch should on this account be wiped dry every day. Meat, or anything greasy, is harmful to a parrot, and parsley will kill it, although lettuce, and especially green peas in the pod, are healthy diet.

Parrots are almost always savage to strangers, but so affectionate to the person who tends them that they fully repay for the care bestowed upon them.

PENCIL DRAWING, No. 2.

SIMPLE as it may seem to draw *leaves*, there must be care, and patience, and faithful effort. After a while, the young student who *succeeds* will go on to *flower* drawing, which is more difficult, but very delightful, and will be illustrated by-and-by.

At present we must try *easy leaves*. I make a few illustrations, enough to begin with. Nos. 1, 2, and 3 are fuchsia leaves; No. 4, oxalis. These may be drawn again and again. A whole page of fuchsia leaves of different sizes is very pretty, and so of any leaf. By a skillful hand they may be arranged with artistic grace.

Attention to a few points will give a precision and interest to the drawing. Let the drawing be *lightly* rather than heavily done. Learn to draw the *double lines* of *stems* and *veins* with great correctness. Make a darker line on the under edge of leaves, and on one side of the stems. By turning the leaf on the wrong side the veins can be distinctly seen, and easily drawn. Do not be discouraged, but *persevere*. Begin to-morrow, or to-day; these beginnings may help you to become a skillful sketcher, and will give to you a delightful occupation that will grow dearer to your heart every day of your life.

This number of Harper's Young People completes the thirteen issues [illegible] to subscribers to Harper's Weekly for 1880, and is therefore the last number to be sent out with that paper. Any one of our little friends who may thus be deprived of a weekly visit from Harper's Young People, and who wishes to continue acquaintance with us, may receive the remaining thirty-two numbers of our first volume, which will conclude with the number dated October 26, 1880, by sending One Dollar to the publishers, who will, on receipt of that amount, forward those numbers weekly, postage free, to any address in the United States or Canada. Those who wish the back numbers, as well as the remainder of the volume, should send One Dollar and Fifty Cents, the price of a year's subscription. The publishers assure their subscribers that they will make every effort to please their young patrons by providing weekly an attractive and instructive variety of illustrated reading.

[illegible]

Are any correspondents informed about the health and present condition of the whale?

[illegible]

C. H. Williamson.—All of Jacob Abbott's books for the young are in print. Valuable works on Long Island history have been published by the Long Island Historical Society of Brooklyn. Hitchcock's Geology and Gray's Lessons in Botany will be of service to you.

C. F. Allen.—Danger Island is in the Chagos Archipelago, on the west end of the great Chagos Bank, Indian Ocean.

Here is a very pretty experiment, sent by F. V. S., Madison, Wisconsin: "Take an ordinary water-pail. Lay across the top two pieces of stout wire, about two inches apart. Then lay a lump of ice on the wires. In about half an hour go and look at it, and you will find that the wires pass through the middle of the lump of ice, but you can not see how they came there."

The following tribute to the egg tumbler is from Ella W.:

[illegible]

Margaret Cooper.—The directions given to Charley D. M., in Young People No. 16, will probably apply to your fish.

Ella Fuller and Helen Thompson.—We fear there is no remedy for your unfortunate animals.

Henry B. H.—Excellent directions for the construction of a cheap telescope are given in Young People No. 1.

Charles Cooper.—We can not undertake any such commissions.

J. H. Thayer.—Pages of advertisements are almost always given in weekly papers. You will find them in every bound volume of Harper's Weekly, and similar publications.

"North Star."—You understand the art of making puzzles, but you must be more careful with your spelling. There is only one "c" in [illegible].

Albert Hyland.—Box-wood only is used by engravers on wood, as it has a fine grain and the requisite hardness. It can be got out in small pieces only, and these are either glued or screwed together to form large blocks. When a picture is to be engraved in haste, the block is taken apart and the pieces are given to several engravers, in order to save time. Sometimes thirty or more engravers are employed at once on a single block.

Lochian R. R.—If you send four cents in postage stamps to the publishers the number you require will be forwarded to you.

A. H. Ellard.—Your handwriting is very neat and distinct for a boy of your age. In a Numerical Charade each figure represents a letter of the solution. Supposing the answer to be "America," you could make "one" from the sixth, seventh, and fourth letters, and proceed in this way until you had used every letter of the solution.

[illegible]

[illegible] and rose bushes are beginning to send out tender green shoots. "Pansies" have been reported by [illegible]; and [illegible] sends a spray of [illegible] which he accompanied with a very pretty printed border. It is now time to begin to watch for violets and anemones, and other early flowers.

Answers to question by [illegible] in Post-office Box, No. 17, are received from [illegible] and others. [illegible] words have been sent. [illegible] There is also [illegible] These are, besides, several obsolete words with the same ending not to be found in modern English dictionaries.

[illegible]

[illegible]

[illegible]

[illegible]

PUZZLES FROM YOUNG CONTRIBUTORS.

No. 1.

[illegible]

No. 2.

[illegible]

No. 3.

[illegible]

No. 4.

[illegible]

No. 5.

[illegible]

No. 6.

[illegible]

THE TRAMP PUZZLE.

WITH one straight cut of the scissors get out of this tramp a handsome Peruan and a sea-cow.

A PERSONATION: WHO AM I?

MY enemies declare I was alike faithless to friend or foe; my partisans, that I was a martyr. In either case, I expiated my follies and weakness with my life, as had my grandmother before me. I was born at Dunfermline, November 19, 1600, and died January 30, 1649—not an old man, as you see. I was heir to great possessions, and held a high position, but I lost land, fortune, and honor. When young, my great friend, also a favorite with my father, obtained a hold on me, and induced me, as soon as I succeeded my father in my inheritance, to begin my career by paying no heed to my people's wishes. I was very obstinate, and as determined as my people to carry my point, and we soon fell out. What I could not gain fairly, I tried to obtain by treachery, and the result can be readily guessed. I introduced many measures; none of them were liked, and the struggle as to who would conquer—the one or the many—began. My habits were extravagant, but then I had fine tastes; collected many beautiful pictures, which, alas! at my death, were scattered, never again to be a collection. The painter Vandyck was a favorite of mine, and when he lay dying I sent my own doctor to attend him, but in vain. He painted several likenesses of me and my family. I had very warm friends, who stood by me in all my troubles, but nothing could save me; and at last, January 15, 1649, I was put on trial for my life. My judges were prejudiced against me, and I was not allowed to plead my own cause, so was adjudged worthy of death. All agree, friends and foes, that I met my fate bravely, and when you find out who I am, "remember" the last word I spoke. My family were scattered and poor. Afterward my eldest son avenged my "murder," as he considered it, but three of my judges escaped, and found shelter in America. There was, however, a taint of falsehood in all of us, and my children's children were at last dispossessed of what had been my inheritance.

What most grieved me was not my losses, but remembering how many friends suffered with me; and, spite of all my faults, few have been more loved.

WILL IT BITE?

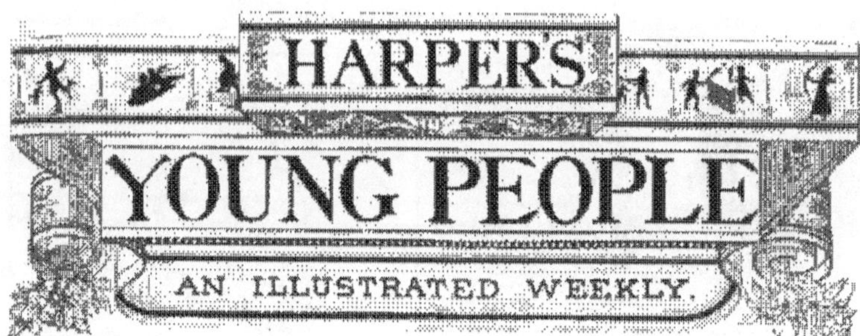

Vol. I.—No. 21. | Published by HARPER & BROTHERS, New York. | Price Four Cents.

Tuesday, March 23, 1880. | Copyright, 1880, by Harper & Brothers. | $1.50 per Year, in Advance.

A DUET.

BY MARGARET EYTINGE.

Sunshine on the meadow,
  Sunshine on the sea;
Green buds on the rose-bush,
  Blossoms on the tree.
Two wee children singing
  In a rapt delight—
One as fair as morning,
  One as dark as night.
Hymn-book held between them
  With the greatest care,
Though they can not read a word
  That is printed there.

"Jesus, Saviour, meek and mild,
Friend of ev'ry little child,
Once a child Thyself, we pray
Thou wilt guard us day by day;
For such helpless things are we,
We can only sing to Thee!"

Standing in the doorway,
  Arunah smiles to hear
Bird-like voices blending
  Sweet and loud and clear.
"'Pears to me de angels
  Mus' be lis'nin' too—
Lis'nin' an' a-lookin'
  From de hebbens blue;
Lookin' an' a-smilin'
  At de pretty sight;
An' in dar eyes—bress de Lord!—
  Hope dem chillun's white."

"HOPE DEM CHILLUN'S WHITE."

EASTER FLOWERS.

BY F. E. FRYATT.

"COME, Nell, and you too, Harry. I have planned a delightful trip for you, and we must be off bright and early."

"Where—where, Miss Eleanor?" cried both children together.

"To the large greenhouses just beyond the city line. You remember the minister said on Sunday, 'Let every person bring flowers, if but a single lily or a rose, to make God's house beautiful on Easter-day'! There are millions of flowers in blossom now at the greenhouses, and I wish you to see them, and learn how the florists make them bloom out of season."

"I hope you will tell us something about it," said Harry, as we rattled swiftly over the rails in the steam-dummy; "that is, when we get out of this noisy old trap."

In a few minutes we alighted at the city line, and Harry, taking my arm, declared himself ready for more "flower talk."

"Suppose," said I, "that a florist wishes to have several thousand plants in bloom for Easter, does he allow them plenty of water and sunshine, and opportunity to bloom several months in advance of the day? No; he stows them all away to rest, or sleep, as he calls it, for weeks and weeks, in cool, dry, shady places, some on shelves, some in sand, and some in pots 'in cool houses.'

"After a time the bulbs are taken out of the sand, and placed in earth, and with the other plants are allowed to enjoy a little warmth and sunshine.

"The rose-bushes are pruned, bound, and tied in trim forms, and placed in rows, and though destitute of foliage, look so healthy and neat one can not but admire them. In a week or two, as if by magic, thousands of buds are swelling and bursting into leaf on every stem.

"Five weeks ago I visited the greenhouses we are now going to, and as I stood in the Easter 'rosery,' I thought it must be quite delightful to be a young rose in training for Easter, the sunshine was so warm and golden, the air so soft and dewy sweet. Every bush showed signs of coming buds—very, very tiny, but they were there. The bulb houses were stocked with rows and rows of cherry-red pots filled with rich brown mould; in some the point of a tulip or hyacinth leaf peered up green and bright, in others there were already brave crowns of strong leaves.

"'Ah,' thought I, 'these will surely please the florist's eye;' but I assure you they had a very different effect, for he looked at them with a frown that said, plainer than words, 'My brave young folks, wouldn't you like to blossom before Easter, and spoil my fine show for me? Indeed you shall not.' He thought that, of course; for the next minute he cried out, 'John, take these forward bulbs and put them back in the "cold house."'"

"What a pity!" murmured Nell.

"Not at all," replied I, "for soon they would have had spikes of fine blossoms; then Madam Hyacinth and Mr. Tulip might bid farewell to all thought of going to church on Easter-day, for long before that time their gay clothes would be faded and spoiled."

"What is the 'cold house'?" inquired Harry.

"A greenhouse where the mercury stands below 50°. Jonquils, tulips, hyacinths and lilies, and most other Easter plants, need warmer air than that to grow rapidly in. The 'cold houses' are not neglected, for they have a certain amount of moisture and sunshine allowed them too, or the plants would die.

"As the happy day draws nearer and nearer, great activity reigns in the greenhouses: batches of plants are seen going back to the 'warm houses,' and such a showering, sponging, snipping and training, and general potting going on, that if plants had any brains, they would go mad with it all. But as they are not troubled with brains, they enjoy the warm sunshine, and the gentle vapors that rise steaming from the earth, and just set themselves to blossoming and looking as lovely as they can."

"So it takes earth, sunshine, wind, and water to raise flowers!" said Harry.

"Yes, and labor and knowledge."

Here the flower lecture ended, for we were at the greenhouse gates. In another moment a door was opened, and we were ushered into a world of beauty.

"How lovely!" cried Nell, looking down the green aisles of the "azalea house."

"They look like swarms of great white butterflies among the dark leaves," remarked Harry.

"Or giant snow-flakes ready to melt or blow away," suggested Nell.

"If you call those white azaleas so handsome, I wonder what you will say to these?" exclaimed the florist, opening wide the door of a "lily house."

"Come here, children," cried I. "Was there ever a more heavenly sight than these hosts of lilies holding up their white chalices to the flooding sunshine?"

"Or anything more delicious?" murmured Nell, bending lovingly over a group of Ascension lilies.

Further on there were ranks and ranks of tall callas, stately as sceptred queens, starry narcissus, white as snow, and jasmine bouvardias, with ivory tube-like blossoms in fragrant clusters.

Something "new, and strange, and sweet" greeted us at every step. Here it was a Deutzia, with starry cup-like blossoms; there a Spiræa, with spikes of milk-white plumes; here sprays of creamy Lantanas, and yonder clusters of tasselled Ageratum.

"Don't go yet," pleaded Nell and Harry, as I turned to leave.

"You'll admire the 'rosery' more than this," said the gardener, opening another door, and standing aside.

A marvellous fragrance saluted us as we looked down the long ranks of tall symmetrical shrubs laden with hundreds of silken buds and opening blossoms, in every shade from lemon to purest white.

How dainty!—how exquisite! Here and there a full-blown rose showed its closely folded center, and long slender petals so delicately hung that a breath might scatter them.

Along the walls were trained vine-like Marechal Neils, with great golden buds and blossoms, while below rows of Safranos lifted fragrant cups rivalling in tint the bloom of an apricot's cheek.

In a second "rosery" we were fairly smothered in sweets. Scores of pale pink Hermosas, blushing Bon Silenes, and Plantiers—living balls of snow—and white Lamarques mingled their spicy breaths in one soft cloud of incense. Pink and white, ruby, buff, and golden, they hung and nodded on every stem, till, like Aladdin in the magician's garden, we knew not which way to turn.

As for the "carnation houses," they made us think of spice islands floating on seas of green; the "pansy houses" were beds of gold and amethyst; the "violet houses" and "smilax greeneries," perfect visions of spring.

There were, besides, ferns, lilies of the valley, camellias on tall tree-like shrubs that made quite a respectable forest in a house by themselves, and rows upon rows of dainty pink, crimson, and white primroses.

Like a true artist, the florist had reserved his most wonderful picture for the last. As he opened the door of an Easter bulb house, he said, "What do you think of that?"

With a cry of delight, as the glory of colors burst upon her, Nell stood entranced in the doorway. Down the middle of the house hundreds and hundreds of potted tulips flamed and glowed with vivid dyes.

On either side the long walks, on the shelves, stood rows and rows of hyacinths in splendid bloom.

Here vases and urns of yellow, purple, saffron, scarlet, pink and white, pied and streaked with living flames.

There bells of ivory, azure, lilac, rose, and buff, fluted, feathered, fringed, and spicy sweet.

It seemed as if some fairy alchemist had melted in magic crucible topaz, ruby, sapphire, gold, and amethyst, to deck each fragrant cup and bell.

THE SHORTEST BAMBOO; OR, HOW TO CATCH A THIEF.

AN EAST INDIAN STORY.*

THERE was a terrible stir in the barracks of the —th Native Infantry at Sekundurabad (Alexander's Town) one bright morning at the beginning of the "dry season." Some money had been stolen from the officers' quarters during the night, and all that could be made out about it was that the theft must have been committed by one of those inside the building, for nobody had got in from without.

The officers' native servants and the sepoy soldiers, to a man, stoutly declared that they knew nothing about it; and the officer of the day, with very great disgust, went to make his report to the Colonel.

Now the Colonel was a hard-headed old Scotchman, who had spent the best part of his life in India, and knew the Hindoos and their ways by heart. He heard the story to an end without any sign of what he thought of it, except a queer twinkle in the corner of his small gray eye; and then he gave orders to turn out the men for morning parade.

When the Colonel appeared on the parade-ground, everybody expected that the first thing would be an inquiry about the stolen money; but that was not the old officer's way. Everything went on just as usual, and the thief probably chuckled to himself at the idea of getting off so easily. But if so, he chuckled a little too soon. Just as the parade was over, and the men were about to "dismiss," the Colonel stepped forward, and shouted, "Halt!"

The men wonderingly obeyed. The Colonel planted himself right in front of the line (carrying a small bag under his arm, as was now noticed for the first time), and running his eye keenly over the long ranks of white frocks and dark faces, spoke to them in Hindustanee:

"Soldiers! I find there are dogs among you who are not 'true to their salt,' and after taking the money of the Ranee of Inglistan [Queen of England], steal from her officers. But such misdeeds never go unpunished. Last night" (here the Colonel's tone suddenly became very deep and solemn) "I had a dream. I dreamed that a black cloud hovered over me, and out of it came a figure—the figure of Kali."

At the name of this terrible goddess (who holds the same place in the Brahmin religion as the Evil One in our own) the swarthy faces turned perfectly livid, and more than one stalwart fellow was seen to shiver from head to foot.

"'There is a thief among your soldiers,' she said, 'and I will teach you how to detect him. Give each of your men a splinter of bamboo, and the thief, let him do what he may, will be sure to get the *longest*; and when he is found, let him dread my vengeance.'"

By this time every soldier on the ground was looking so frightened that had the Colonel expected to detect the thief by his looks, he might have thought the whole regiment equally guilty. But his plan was far deeper than that. At his signal each man in turn drew a bamboo chip from the bag which the Colonel held; and when all were supplied, he ordered them to come forward one by one, and give back the chips which they had drawn.

He was obeyed; but scarcely had a dozen men passed, when the Colonel suddenly sprang forward, seized a tall Rajpoot by the throat, and shouted, in a voice of thunder, "You're the man!"

"Mercy, mercy, Sahib" (master), howled the culprit, falling on his knees. "I'll bring back the money—I'll bear any punishment you please—only don't give me up to the vengeance of Kali."

"Well," said the Colonel, sternly, "I'll forgive you this once; but if you're ever caught again, you know what to expect. Dismiss!"

"I say, C——, how on earth did you manage that?" asked the senior Major, as he and the Colonel walked away together; "I suppose you don't want me to believe that you really *did* get that idea in a dream?"

"Hardly," laughed the Colonel. "The fact is, those bamboo chips were all exactly the same length; and the thief, to make sure of not getting the longest, *bit off the end of his*, and so I knew him at once. Take my word for it, there'll be no more thieving in the regiment while *I'm* its Colonel."

And indeed there never was.

* This story is perfectly true, and was told by its hero, Colonel C——, of the Ninety-first Highlanders.

[Begun in No. 19 of HARPER'S YOUNG PEOPLE, March 9.]

ACROSS THE OCEAN; OR, A BOY'S FIRST VOYAGE.

A True Story.

BY J. G. DAVIDSON.

CHAPTER III.

OUR HERO'S FIRST FIGHT.

IT was well for Austin that he had been struck by the small coal instead of the heavier pieces, or he might have been killed outright; as it was, after a dash of cold water, and a short rest in his bunk, he was almost as sound as before. But the accident had worse results than a few bruises. He was at once set down as an "awkward landlubber," dismissed from his coal-shovelling, and ordered to do duty in the lamp-room.

This was a dismal hole in the lowest part of the ship, where even what little light there was had to struggle through an iron grating. Behind the counter that ran half way round it stood several large iron tanks, strongly padlocked, labelled "Soap," "Oil," "Waste," "Lamp Wicks," etc. The floor was covered with various necessaries for engine use, and from the beams overhead swung lamps of all shapes and sizes, while the walls were covered with bolts, bars, hammers, and tools of every kind.

This pleasant place usually fell to the charge of some one who was fit for nothing else; and its present occupant was a lanky youth known as "Monkey"—a name fully warranted by his narrow watery eyes, enormous under-jaw, and huge projecting bat-like ears. He had been cruising backward and forward in the *Arizona* for years, till he seemed quite to belong to her, and although he disappeared as soon as she reached port, he always found out the day of her departure in time to join her again—how, no one knew, for he could neither read nor write.

Frank's appointment, of course, displaced Monkey, and neither was pleased with the change. Monkey much preferred even the dismal lamp-room (where he had only to serve out a certain quantity of stores daily, and to see that nothing was lost or stolen) to the harder work of scrubbing the engine-room, which now fell to his share; while Austin, used as he was to out-door exercise, felt quite miserable in this dungeon-like hole, where he could not even see to read. He was on duty from dawn till dusk, and even liable to be roused up at night should anything be wanted. His meals were given him after all the rest were served, and only very rarely did he get the chance of ask-

STORE-ROOM

ing a question, or learning anything that he wished.

Nor did his troubles end here. The men, who in Monkey's time had been allowed to help themselves pretty freely to the ship's stores, were enraged at finding that their new store-keeper could neither be bribed nor bullied into letting them have anything without orders. One of Frank's greatest troubles was the giving out of soap—a priceless luxury in the forecastle of a steamer, where the "grit," coal-dust, and irritating brine are unbearable if not promptly washed off. For a piece of soap (the ship's allowance being unusually small), shirts, stockings, and even tobacco, were gladly bartered; and those who had been shrewd enough to lay in a stock before sailing drove a brisk trade.

This gave our friend Monkey a chance which he was not slow to use. He began by hinting to the crew that Frank's care of the stores was meant to "curry favor" with the officers; and then he went on to losing or stealing whatever he could, and laying the blame on Austin. Nor were these the most serious tokens of his ill-will. One day he managed to give Frank a push which sent him down through a trap-door, though he luckily escaped unhurt. Another time, a similar trick hurled him into the well in which the ship's pump worked, and he only avoided serious injury by clinging to the shaft.

At last, as Frank was serving out stores one afternoon, Monkey suddenly darted off with a bar of soap, and being pursued into the engine-room by Austin, declared that the latter had been about to sell it to one of the men, and that *he* had just come in time to prevent him—a statement confirmed by the sailors. In vain poor Frank denied the charge; he was roughly ordered to hold his tongue, and give up the store-room keys to their former possessor, Monkey.

This was hard indeed; but, as the proverb says, "It is a long lane that has no turning," and our hero's affairs suddenly took a turn which neither he nor any one else could have foreseen.

The pride of a steamer is her machinery, and at all hours of the day men may be seen polishing it with balls of cotton "waste," till it shines like silver; but if you venture to touch the glittering surface, you find it burning hot, and scorch your fingers pretty smartly. One day Frank was polishing the broad round top of the cylinder, protected by a thick rope mat from the burning metal, when Monkey, sneaking up behind, suddenly jerked away the mat, throwing him right on to the hot surface. Smarting with pain, Austin sprang to his feet, and regardless of his enemy's superior bulk and strength, flew at him like a tiger. The two grappled, and rolled on the floor, Frank undermost.

Monkey's small, cunning eyes gleamed wickedly as he saw that they were close to the edge of the "crank-pit" (the space in which the crank of the shaft revolves), and he exerted all his strength to fling Austin into it. But the latter, who had not played foot-ball for nothing, suddenly wrenched himself free, and dodging round behind his enemy, sprang upon his back, and grasped his throat like a vise. Down went the valiant Monkey upon the hard grating with a whack that made his big mouth swell up bigger than ever; and, pinned beneath Frank's knee, he howled shrilly for help.

His cries were answered by a loud laugh from the skylight above, through which several of the crew had been watching the combat. At the same moment the second engineer appeared on the scene.

"What! fighting? You young imps, is *that* how you do your work? Here, Williams, take 'em both to the first officer, and report 'em for fighting on duty."

[TO BE CONTINUED.]

FRANK'S FIGHT WITH "MONKEY."

"LONG LIVE THE KING!"

THE BABY KING.

"I, Henry, born at Monmouth,
Shall small time reign and much get.
But Henry of Windsor shall long reign and lose all,
But as God will, so be it."

THIS strange bit of doggerel is said to have been composed and repeated by King Henry V. of England on the birth of his only child Henry. The baby first saw the light of day in Windsor's royal palace, where he was born on the 6th of December, 1421, and was welcomed with delight by the English nation as the son and heir of their idolized King.

Before little Henry was more than nine months old, the King his father was dead. The poor little baby was already King of England, and within another month his grandfather, Charles VI. of France, was also dead, and another heavy crown was burdening the infant's brow.

No sooner had Queen Katherine, the mother of the little King, fulfilled her duty of seeing the funeral rites belonging to her husband properly accomplished, than she hastened to Windsor to embrace her child, and pass in solitude the early months of her widowhood. She was only in her twenty-first year, and had many arduous duties before her. The first of these was to see her baby King properly received and acknowledged as their sovereign by the nation. The sanction of Parliament was required, and accordingly the Queen removed from Windsor to London, passing through the city on a moving throne drawn by white horses, and surrounded by all the princes and nobles of England. In her lap was seated the infant King, and "those infant hands," says one of the chroniclers, "which could not yet feed himself, were made capable of wielding a sceptre, and he who was beholden to nurses for milk, did distribute support to the law and justice of the realm!" "The Queen, still holding her baby on her knee, was enthroned among the lords, whom, by the chancellor, the little King saluted, and spake to them his mind at large by means of another's tongue." It was declared that during this scene in Parliament the baby King conducted himself with marvellous quietness and gravity. Henry VI. had been already proclaimed King of France, at Paris, before even he thus held his first Parliament on his mother's lap. For as soon as the last service had been performed over the dead body of Charles VI., and the body lowered into the vault belonging to the royal Kings of France, the impressive ceremony followed of the ushers belonging to the late King breaking their staves of office, throwing them into the grave, and reversing their maces, whilst the king-at-arms, or principal herald, attended by many heralds, cried in a loud, solemn voice over the tomb, "May God show mercy and pity to the soul of the late most puissant and most excellent Charles VI., King of France, our natural and sovereign lord!"

Hardly had these solemn words rolled echoing through the vaulted roof, striking the hearts of the 25,000 spectators with mournful awe, than the herald raised his voice again, and twice demanded their prayers, for the living this time, and not the dead. And thus he cried, "May God grant long life to Henry, by the grace of God King of France and of England, our sovereign lord!"

Then, when an infant ten months old had been proclaimed King over two of the greatest kingdoms in Europe, the sergeants-at-arms and ushers turned their maces, and shouted together, "Long live the King! long live the King!"

The Duke of Bedford was now sole Regent of France, whilst a council of prelates and peers, with the Duke of Gloucester at its head, governed England in the baby King's name, making use of the amusing fiction of issuing all their decrees and mandates as though they were dictated by the mouth of an infant still in arms.

Sometimes Henry misbehaved, or rather showed the natural temper of a baby. In 1423, when his Majesty was nearly two years old, he was taken by his mother to London to hold another Parliament. It was Saturday when they left Windsor, and at night the Queen and her baby King slept at Staines instead of going on. On the Sunday the Queen wished to proceed, and had her son carried to her car, when, instead of comporting himself with his usual dignity, "he shreeked" (says the quaint chronicler), "he cried, he sprang, and would be carried no further; wherefore they bare him into the inn, and there he abode the Sunday all day. But on the Monday he was borne to his mother's car, he being then merry and full of cheer, and so they came to Kingston, and rested that night. On Tuesday, Queen Katherine brought him to Kennington, on Wednesday to London, and with glad semblance and merry cheer, on his mother's barm [lap] in the car, rode through London to Westminster, and on the morrow was so brought into Parliament." The old historian would make us believe that Henry refused to travel on Sunday, even at two years old.

The guardianship of the baby King had been intrusted to the Earl of Warwick, and in the pictorial history of this Earl he is represented as holding the King, a lovely baby of fourteen months old, in his arms, while he is showing him to the lords around him in Parliament. The Earl, however, only held his sovereign lord on public and state occasions, leaving the young King in his private walks and hours of retirement to the care of a certain Dame Alice Boteler, his governess, and his nurse Joan Astley. "We request," says his infant Majesty, in a quaintly worded document proceeding from his council, but as usual written in his name, and in regal form, "Dame Alice from time to time reasonably to chastise us as the case may require, without being held accountable or molested for the same at another time. The well-beloved Dame Alice, being a very wise and expert person, is to teach us courtesy and nurture, and many things convenient for our royal person to know."

It was whilst Dame Alice was still in power as the King's chastiser that we again find the royal child noticed as holding the opening of Parliament in 1425. Katherine entered the city in a chair of state, with her child sitting on her knee as before. But Henry was now four years old, and no longer needed to be held on Warwick's arm or placed upon his mother's lap. As soon then as he reached the west door of St. Paul's Cathedral, the Protector lifted the child King from his mother's chair, and set him on his feet, whilst the Duke of Exeter, on the other side, conducted him between them to the high altar up the stairs which led to the choir. At the altar the royal boy knelt for a time upon a low bench prepared for him, and was seen to look gravely and sadly on all around him. He was then led into the church-yard, placed upon a fair courser, to the people's great delight, and so conveyed through Cheapside to his residence at Kennington. There he staid with his mother until the 30th of April, when he returned through the city to Westminster in a grand state procession. The little King was again held on his great white horse, and when he arrived at his palace, the Queen seated herself upon the throne of the White Hall where the House of Lords was held, with her child placed upon her knee. This procession drew the people in crowds to see and bless their infant sovereign, whose features they declared were the image of his father.

His tutor, the Earl, was now always with him, whilst his young friends had distinct and separate instructors, for whose reception and entertainment were carefully provided by the Privy Council. Henry's governor, Warwick, was ordered by the King's guardians (speaking, as usual, in the King's person) "to teach us nurture, literature, and languages, and to chastise us from time to time according to his discretion." Unfortunate little Henry! we find more said about his being chastised than about his being rewarded, as if he were of a rebellious and obstinate temper. On the contrary, he was remarkable for his mildness and the meek submission of his character, and we fear the blows which he had to endure only saddened and subdued him, and rendered him unfit to cope with the ambitious and high-spirited nobles who surrounded him.

Little Henry was no sooner eight years old than it was determined by his uncles and his council that he should be crowned King of England in London, and afterward King of France at Paris. So, after much delay, the royal child was taken to Westminster on the 6th of November, 1429, and there crowned with much pomp and state, amongst the acclamations of the people. As soon as the ceremony was over, the little King, in his robes and crown, created, under the direction of his governor, thirty-six Knights of the Bath. Then followed a sumptuous feast in the great Hall of Westminster, where a noble company were assembled, and nobody of note allowed to be absent. Immediately after this, Henry and a great escort of nobles went to Paris, where he was crowned King of France.

His journey to France, his coronation there, the homage and presents he received from French subjects as their King, must often in his after-life have appeared like a dream.

When Henry VI. returned to England he was eleven years old, having been allowed the pleasure of having far more of his own way than he could have obtained in England. Perhaps the ceremony of his coronations, the homage, smiles, and deference shown him, the young companions whose acquaintance could not then be refused, had some exciting influence on his naturally meek and quiet temper. Certain, however, it is that he began at this time to rebel, and demanded from his Privy Council freedom from personal chastisement, which appears to have tried him sorely. The poor boy, however, gained little by his petition, for the Earl addressed the council, and complained that certain officious persons "had stirred up the King against his learning, and spoken to him of divers matters not behoveful," and he begs that he may "have power over any or all of those belonging to his household, and to exchange them for others if he should find it necessary. Also that none be admitted to have speech with the King, except he or some persons appointed be present." He besides besought them to stand by him when the King begins "to grudge and loathe his chastising him for his faults, and to impress their young King with their assent that he be chastised for his defaults or trespasses, and that for awe thereof he forbear to do amiss, and entered the more busily to virtue and to learning."

So Henry, like any other school-boy, submitted, and said no more until he entered on his sixteenth year, when he demanded to be admitted into the council, and to be made acquainted with the affairs of his kingdom. This was granted, and he was after this allowed to conduct his own affairs.

CHILDREN'S SAYINGS.

GEORGIE was a sharp-eyed little fellow still in frocks, who saw everything, and blurted right out what he thought of it. One morning, while he was playing with his toys at his mother's feet, a lady called, bringing with her one of the homeliest little pug-nosed pet dogs that ever lived. Georgie was all attention at once, and his eyes followed Pinkie wherever he went. Presently the little dog came and sat right down before him, and looking straight in his face, wagged his tail, and seemed delighted to see him. Georgie stared at him for a while, and then looked up earnestly into the lady's face, then at the dog, and then at the lady again, as if trying to make out a puzzle. Finally, when he had settled it, out it came. "Mamma," he asked, "hasn't Mrs. Duncan dot a nose just like Pinkie's?" and the worst of it was that it was true. Mamma tried to smooth the matter over, but Mrs. Johnson never forgave Georgie.

Everybody has heard of the little girl who, on being asked, after her first visit to an Episcopal church, how she liked the service, replied that it was "all very nice, only the man preached in his shirt sleeves." That story may or may not be true, but it is true that a little girl in New Jersey said on a similar occasion, "Oh, mamma, the minister had on a long white apron to keep his clothes clean."

Another young church-goer, the daughter of a well-known Baptist clergyman in Brooklyn, who was a critic in her way, and who had a faint suspicion that anecdotes generally were "made up" for the occasion, went one day with her father to hear his Thanksgiving sermon. He told a melting story about his poor blind brother who, notwithstanding his infirmity, was always cheerful and happy. The audience was deeply impressed, and many, including the speaker himself, were moved to tears. On her return home, Mary, we will call her, said, with deep earnestness, "Papa, when you were telling that about Uncle Nat this morning, did you say the real truth, or were you only preaching?"

A four-year-old Sunday-school girl did the best she could with a question that was asked of the infant class. Said the teacher, reading from Isaiah, xxxvii. 1: "'And it came to pass, when King Hezekiah heard it, that he rent his clothes.' Now what does that mean, children—he rent his clothes?" Up went a little hand. "Well, if you know, tell us."

"Please, ma'am," said the child, timidly, "I s'pose he hired 'em out." (This is an actual fact, and the name of the town where it occurred begins with "M.")

A pretty anecdote is told of a little girl to whom the unseen world is very real. "Where does God live, mamma?" she asked, one evening, after saying her prayers.

"He lives in heaven, my dear, in the Celestial City whose streets are paved with gold."

"Oh yes, I know that, mamma," she said, with great solemnity; "but what's His *number*?"

Doubtless she expected to go there one day, and wanted to make sure of finding the way.

"How does the Lord make cats?" asked an inquisitive little fellow, who was always trying to find out the whys and wherefores of things. "Does He make the cats first, and sew the tails on, or does He make the tails first, and sew the cats on?" Every clergyman who comes to the house is asked the same question, but no satisfactory reply has yet been given. He threatens now that unless he finds out very soon, he will take his favorite Topsy all to pieces, and see for himself.

A little girl in Oil City is just recovering from a severe attack of scarlet fever. During her illness she has been greatly petted by her indulgent parents, who bought her any number of toys and nice things. A few days ago, as she was sitting up, she said, "Mamma, I believe I'll ask papa to buy me a baby carriage for my doll." The brother—a precocious youngster of only six years of age, spoke up at once, and said, "I would advise you to strike him for it right away, then; you won't get it when you get well."

A little girl went timidly into a store at Bellaire, Ohio, the other morning, and asked the clerk how many shoe-strings she could get for five cents.

"How long do you want them?" he asked.

"I want them to keep," was the answer, in a tone of slight surprise.

It was just after Christmas, and Kenneth's mind was full of the story of the Babe who was born at Bethlehem. When, therefore, he was taken into mamma's room to see his new little brother, he looked with wonder on the dainty cradle, trimmed with lace and ribbons, wherein the little baby lay, and asked, in an awed whisper, "Mamma, is that a manger?"

A neighbor asked a little girl the other day if her father wasn't one of the pillars of the Mianus M. E. Church. "No, indeed," she warmly replied; "they don't have any *pillows* there."

I SHOULD LIKE TO KNOW.

When in budding trees
  Bluebirds sweetly sing,
And the pretty early flowers
  Come to welcome spring,
"No more cold," we think,
  "No more sleety rain";
But sometimes old Winter turns,
  Mocking, back again.

Then the bluebirds hide,
  And the buds stand still,
And the flowers droop and shrink
  With a sudden chill,
And the young vines stop
  Growing in the wood,
Waiting patiently until
  He is gone for good.

But when, some fine night,
  In a friendly throng,
From the swampy places where
  They have slept so long
Hop the frogs, and all
  Loudly croak together,
Then there will be, we are sure,
  No more wintry weather;

And the birds rejoice,
  And the buds unfold,
And the sun upon the grass
  Lies in bars of gold.
Now I'd like to know,
  For it's surely so,
How when spring is really here
  Frog-folks chance to know.

THE CHAMOIS AND THEIR FOES.

THE only European species of the antelope family are the chamois (*Antilope rupicapra*), which inhabit the highest regions of the Alps, the Pyrenees, and the Caucasus. On inaccessible cliffs and rocky crags these graceful mountaineers make their home, and except when disturbed by the approach of man, lead a peaceful and harmless life. The chamois resembles the wild goat of the Alps, but is more elastic and airy. It is especially distinguished from it by the absence of beard, and by its black glistening horns, which are curved like a hook and pointed.

In the spring the chamois is very light-colored, but as summer advances, its coat assumes a reddish-brown hue, which by December often becomes coal black. Its eyes are large, black, and full of intelligence, and its delicate hoofs are surrounded by a projecting rim which renders it firm-footed and able to march with ease over the great glaciers or along narrow ledges of rock.

These pretty animals live in herds, five, ten, and sometimes twenty together. They are merry, wise creatures, graceful and agile in their movements, and spring from cliff to cliff and across chasms with extraordinary lightness and sureness of foot.

In the winter the chamois seek the upper forests on the mountain slopes, where, under the shelter of the widely branching umbrella fir, the drooping boughs of which hang almost to the ground, they find snug quarters, and long dry grass for winter provender.

The opening of spring in the Swiss Alps is attended by many wonderful phenomena. It would seem that no power was strong enough to break the icy chain in which the high Alps are bound fast; but there comes a day, generally early in April, when beautifully tinted veils of cloud form over the southern horizon, and a death-like stillness prevails in the mountains. The eye of the experienced hunter detects this sign in a moment, and knows it to be the token of approaching danger. If among the glaciers, he hastens to the valley below, where he finds the villages in commotion. Sheep and cattle are being hurriedly housed, and everything being secured against the dreaded *Föhn*, which is surely coming from beyond those rose-tinted clouds in the south. The *Föhn* is a warm wind which, in the spring, comes blowing northward from the hot African desert. On a sudden the stillness is broken by a terrible rushing sound, and a burning breath like fire strikes on the snowy pinnacles and glaciers. All nature is soon in an uproar. Mighty banks of snow, loosened from their winter resting-place, roar and rumble down the mountain-side in avalanches, bearing huge rocks and giant trees in their arms. The whole winter architecture of the mountains crumbles to ruins before the burning desert wind.

When the storm is over the great ice beds and banks of snow cease their pranks, and peace reigns once more in the mountains. But the strength of winter is broken. The *Föhn* returns again and again, and soon patches of bluish-green begin to appear here and there among the high precipitous crags. When the highest mountain pastures are open, the chamois leave their forest retreat, and troop upward into the most lofty regions. Here they lead a happy life. They are most frolicsome in the autumn, and may be seen for hours together gamboling and chasing each other upon the very smallest ledges of rock, where it would seem almost impossible to maintain a foothold. There are sometimes bitter fights, too, between the male chamois, terrible contests for leadership. Grappling each other with their horns, they battle until the superiority of strength is decided.

The chamois is very shy, and is always on the alert. Its sense of hearing, of smell, and of sight is very acute, and the most skillful hunter will sometimes search the mountain pastures for days without securing his game. When the troop is grazing, a sentinel is always appointed, who stands on the watch sniffing the air. At the least approach of danger the careful sentinel gives a shrill whistling signal of warning, and instantly the troop is filing off between the rocks and along the chasms, where no human foot could follow, all whistling together as they march. The only chance of the hunter to escape detection by these watchful creatures is to approach them from above, for, as if conscious that there are few so daring as to penetrate the upper regions of eternal snow, the sharp eye of the sentinel is on the look-out for danger from below.

As the greatest skill and courage are required to secure this valuable game, a good chamois-hunter is a person of importance in the wild Swiss valley where he lives, and the family of which he is a member glory in his deeds, and relate them to awe-struck listeners around the evening fireside. Chamois-hunting is the central point around which cluster all the charms of romance and dangerous adventure; it is the subject of many popular ballads, and its hold upon the imagination of the people is wonderful. Chamois skulls adorned with the black hooked horns may be seen among the most precious treasures of many a Swiss household, each one suggestive of some tale of wonderful bravery and endurance.

BATTLE OF THE CHAMOIS.

The chamois-hunters of Switzerland lead a strange life. None knows when he departs from his home in the morning with his gun, ammunition, and alpenstock, if he will ever return from the mysterious misty heights towering before him far aloft in the clouds. The pursuit of the chamois will often lead him to the narrowest boundaries between life and death, to overhanging cliffs, and across gorges where even the falling of a bit of turf or the loosening of a stone would be fatal. Up, up, the hunter must go in search of the running game, until lost among the cliffs, and blinded by the thick mists which appear as clouds to those in the valley below, he may often wander in the trackless solitudes for days, with the terrible roar of avalanches sounding in his ears, before being able to return to his home. And yet in face of all these dangers, the Swiss, apart from the price they obtain for the flesh, skin, and horns of the chamois, have an inborn love of this sport, and stories are told of many celebrated hunters, men to whom every rock, tree, and path on the high mountains was as familiar as the streets of their native village, and who feared neither fogs, snow-storms, nor avalanches. But few of these hunters, however, have died at home in their beds, for in the end accident overtook them, and their lofty hunting ground became their grave.

THE RED WILLOW AND ITS USES.

INDIANS AND RED WILLOW.

TO the Indians of the great Western plains the red willow, which is only found in that country, proves so very useful that its loss would be greatly felt by them. It is a bushy growth, never reaching more than fifteen or twenty feet in height, and is found along the river-banks, where it grows rapidly and in great abundance.

The Indian most values the red willow because from its bark he makes what to him is a very good substitute for tobacco. To do this he strips one of the long, slender shoots of its leaves, and with his knife cuts the bark until it hangs from the wood in little shreds. Then he thrusts the stick into the fire, but not so that it will burn, only so that the bark will become thoroughly dried. When this is done, he carefully rubs it between his hands until it is crumbled almost to a powder.

This willow-bark powder he mixes with a small quantity of real tobacco, if he has any; if not, he mixes it with the dried and crumbled leaf of a small and very bitter shrub that grows on the mountain-sides, and has a leaf looking somewhat like our box-wood. The Indians call it killikinick, and often mix it with tobacco when they have no red willow. So fond are the Indians of their red-willow tobacco that they prefer it to the real unmixed article, which seems to be too strong for them.

The squaws use the red willow to make temporary shelters or wick-i-ups, which are used instead of the heavy skin lodges, or tepees, when the Indians are on the move, and only camp in one place for a night or so.

When a pleasant spot by some running stream, where there is plenty of red willow, has been fixed upon for a camping-place, and a fire has been lighted, the squaws cut a quantity of the willow, and, making a rude framework of the larger branches, of which the butt-ends are fixed firmly into the ground, and the small ends bound together to look like a small dome, they weave the smaller branches and twigs in and out until the whole affair looks like a great leafy basket turned upside down. The entrance is very low, and when once inside, a grown person can only lie or sit down, for if he should stand up, he would probably lift the house with him.

While the squaws are building the wick-i-ups the Indian has been stretched on the ground, smoking his long-stemmed pipe, with its stone or iron bowl, or else he has been kneeling beside the fire preparing his much-loved red-willow tobacco. Over the same fire is hung a jack rabbit, skinned; and spitted upon a slender red-willow stick, and from a tree near by the baby swings in his red-willow cradle.

From the same red willow the squaws make baskets and mats. On its tender twigs the ponies browse in winter, when the grass is covered deep with snow. And to these same red-willow thickets the Indians go in winter in search of deer or antelope, which are pretty sure to be found browsing among them.

So you see the Indian has good reason to be fond of the red willow, and he dreads the approach of white farmers, who clear it off from the rich bottom-lands wherever they locate, for it is on these lands that they can raise their heaviest crops of corn.

"THIS LITTLE PIG STAID AT HOME."

BY MARY DENSEL.

SIX tow heads bobbing about a pen in the big barn. In the pen were thirteen small pigs, all squealing as only small pigs know how to squeal.

The owners of two of the tow heads soon departed. They were Solomon and Isaac. Being fourteen years old, they were too ancient to care much for pigs. Eliza and John also went away. They had business elsewhere in the shape of woodchuck traps. Philemon would fain have lingered near, had he not made an engagement to play "two old cat" with Tom Tadgem.

As for Romeo Augustus, no charm of bat or ball would have drawn him from that pen, since he had seen one of the small pigs stagger about in a strange fashion, and then sink down in a corner. Something was wrong with that pig.

Romeo Augustus peered and peeped. At last into the pen he climbed, and caught the little pig in his arms.

Then there was a hubbub indeed. Up rushed the mother in terrible excitement. Round and round spun the twelve brothers and sisters, each crying, "No, no, no, no," in a voice as fine as a knitting-needle, and as sharp as a razor edge.

But Romeo Augustus kept a steady head. Back over the pen he scrambled, pig and all, and sat down on the barn floor to find out the trouble.

Ah! here was enough to make any pig stagger. Two little legs dangled helplessly—one fore-leg, one hind-leg. The bones were broken.

At first Romeo Augustus was tempted to weep. What good would that do? It was far better to coax the bones into place, put sticks up and down for splints, and bind one leg tight with his neck-tie, the other with his very best pocket-handkerchief.

It was not an easy job. The pig did writhe and twist, while the frantic mother danced up and down in the pen behind, and drove the surgeon nearly crazy with her noise. But he toiled bravely on, and when at last the operation was done, the heart of Romeo Augustus was knit unto that small pig in bands of deep affection.

"I love him as if he was my—*daughter*," said Romeo Augustus, solemnly. He did not confide this to his twin brother Philemon: Philemon would have jeered. He told it to Elias, who was poetical, and had a soul for sentiment. Elias nodded, and said,

"Just so!" That showed sympathy. He also added, "Why don't you keep him for your own, and call him Leggit or Bones?"

"No," answered Romeo Augustus, with dignity; "his name shall be Mephibosheth, for the man who followed King David, and was lame in both his feet."

For five weeks Romeo Augustus nursed and fed and tended that pig. In time the legs grew strong. Mephibosheth was as brisk as any pig need be. Romeo Augustus rejoiced over him, and loved him more and more. So the days went on, until a certain morning dawned.

The sun rose as usual; the cocks crowed as cheerfully as they always did. Solomon and Isaac had gone to drive the cows to pasture, as was their wont. Elias and John were peacefully skinning their woodchucks in the shed. Philemon had been sent back to his chamber (as he was every morning of his life) to brush his back hair. There was nothing to suggest the storm which was to break over Romeo Augustus, who stood by the kitchen stove watching the cook fry fritters.

"Fizz, fiz-z-z, fiz-z-z," hissed the fritters.

"*Aren't* they going to be good?" said Romeo Augustus, smacking his lips.

Suddenly came a voice. It was Romeo Augustus's father speaking to the man-servant:

"Those little pigs are large enough to be killed. How many are there? Never mind. Carry them all to market to-morrow, and sell them for what they will bring. I don't want the trouble of raising them."

Romeo Augustus listened in horror. "Large enough to be killed?" "Carry them all to market?" "*All!* ALL?" Why, that included Mephibosheth. Terrible thought!

Not a fritter did Romeo Augustus eat that morning. After breakfast he roamed aimlessly about the farm. He would not go near the barn. How could he look upon poor doomed Mephibosheth?

Once he thought of going to his father, and pleading with him for his pig's life. But Romeo Augustus was shy, and somewhat afraid of his father, who was a stern man. So he kept his grief to himself, and meditated.

Elias unconsciously deserted him at this time of need, and curdled Romeo Augustus's blood by asking twice for pork at dinner. Ask for pork? Why, speaking coarsely, Mephibosheth was also—pork. How could any one eat pork with such a relish? Romeo Augustus shivered, and kept his own counsel. All that afternoon he pondered. Then the darkness of night came on.

The next morning off started the man-servant with his load of little pigs.

"Have you all?" asked Romeo Augustus's father.

"I would ha' swore, sir, there was thirteen, but it seems there was only twelve. Yes, sir, I has 'em all;" and away he drove.

As for Romeo Augustus, a change came over him. Far from shunning the barn, he hung about it constantly. Moreover, he was always present when the cows were milked, morning and night. He had a playful trick of dipping his own tin cup into the foaming pail, and scampering away with it full to the brim. Nobody objected to that. If he chose to strain a point, and drink unstrained milk, he was welcome to do it.

"And if you see fit to save half your dinner, and give it away, I am willing," said his mother, who was busy, and hardly noticed what Romeo Augustus asked her. "But you must *not* soil your jacket fronts as you do. This is the fifth time within a week I have sponged your clothes."

Soon after this, Philemon and Romeo Augustus were out in the barn, rolling over and over, burying themselves in the sweet-smelling hay.

Suddenly Philemon pricked up his ears.

"What's that?" quoth he. "I heard a little pig squealing. Where can he be?"

"Philemon," said Romeo Augustus, earnestly, "let's climb to that top mow, and jump down. Hurrah! It's a good twenty feet. Come on, if you dare!"

If he dare! Of course he dared. It was great fun to launch one's self into space, and come whirling down on the hay. There was just enough danger of breaking one's neck to give spice to the treat. How Romeo Augustus did scurry about, hustling Philemon whenever he stopped to breathe, and urging him on, shouting at the top of his lungs,

"One more jump, old boy. Hurrah! Hurray!"

Philemon had no spare time in which to wonder if he heard a small pig squeal.

That very night, when all the family was wrapped in slumber, Elias felt a hand on his shoulder. Another hand was on his mouth, to prevent any exclamation.

"Come with me," whispered Romeo Augustus; and he held out Elias's jacket and trousers. Elias took the hint, also the clothes. Down the stairs crept the two. Out the front door, which would creak, into the moon-lit yard stole they. Elias's eyes were snapping with excitement; for, as I said, Elias was poetical, and, like all poets, he was always expecting something to turn up. At this present he was on the look-out for what he called "the Gibbage."

Elias himself had grown to believe the marvellous stories he told his brothers. He had full faith in the Lovely Lily Lady, who lived in the attic; in the Mealy family, with their sky-blue faces and pea-green hands, in the cobwebby meal chest under the barn eaves; in the Peely family, who inhabited the tool-box in the shed, and whose heads were like baked apples with the peel taken off; in the big black bird, which came from the closet under the stairs at night, and flew through the chambers to dust the boys' clothes with its wings.

And now Elias had suspected in his own mind that there existed a creature, somewhat like a mouse, somewhat like a red flower-pot, which glided around during the night-watches to sharpen slate-pencils, smooth out dog-ears from school-books, erase lead-pencil marks, polish up marbles, straighten kite strings, put the "suck" into brick-suckers, and otherwise make itself useful. If there were not such a creature, there ought to be, and Elias became daily surer that there was. He called it "the Gibbage."

Perchance Romeo Augustus had caught a glimpse of it. No wonder Elias's eyes snapped as he was hurried across the yard, and led back of the barn, where there was a space between the underpinning and the ground. By lying flat one could wriggle his way under the barn, and when once beneath, there was room to stand nearly upright.

"Elias," said Romeo Augustus, breathlessly, "I keep Mephibosheth under here."

"Sakes and daisies!" gasped Elias.

That was a very strong expression. When somewhat moved, Elias often exclaimed, "Sakes!" but when he added, "and daisies!" it was a sign he was stirred to his inmost depths.

"Sakes and daisies!" said Elias.

"Yes," Romeo Augustus went on, "I heard father say he didn't want the trouble of raising him, so I concluded I would. But nobody must see him till he's raised, and Philemon he heard him this very day. I must take him somewhere else. Where, Elias, oh, where can I carry him?"

Elias frowned and pondered. He was grieved not to have discovered "the Gibbage," but he would do the handsome thing by Romeo Augustus.

Half an hour later the jolly old moon nearly fell out of the sky for laughing. There were Elias and Romeo Augustus straining and tugging, coaxing and scolding, trying with might and main to stifle the expostulations of Mephibosheth, as they bore him down to an unmowed meadow.

The ox-eye daisies opened their sleepy petals to see what all the stir was about. The buttercups and dandelions craned themselves forward to peep.

Down in the meadow the boys drove a stake, and to it they fastened Mephibosheth. It was no joke taking food to him now. The unmowed meadow was in sight of the house, and it seemed as if one or another of the boys was always at the window. But Elias aided Romeo Augustus, and between them Mephibosheth got his daily rations. Surely he was safe at last. Far from it.

"Who has been trampling the grass in the north pasture?" asked Romeo Augustus's father, a fortnight later. "I followed the path made by feet that had no right there. At the end I found a stake. Tied to the stake I found a—"

Solomon and Isaac looked surprised. John and Philemon shook their heads. They knew nothing of the matter. Elias and Romeo Augustus quaked.

"At the end I found a—" repeated their father, gazing sternly round the table—"I found a—"

"*Pig*," said Romeo Augustus, in the smallest possible voice; and he fled from the table in an agony of tears. His labor had been in vain. After all, Mephibosheth must die. How could he endure it? He dared not glance out of the window of the chamber where he had taken refuge, lest he should behold Mephibosheth led to slaughter. It seemed as if his heart would break in two.

But listen! What is that noise? A clatter as of falling boards. There is a sound as of hammering. At first it seems to Romeo Augustus like Mephibosheth's death-knell. Thud, thud, thud, go the blows. Drawn almost against his will, Romeo Augustus stealthily approaches the window. He glances fearfully out. What does he see? His father pounding busily, making—what is he making? Can it be? It is—it is *a pen*.

"Father!" gasps Romeo Augustus.

His father looks up and smiles. "Your pig must have a house to live in," says he. "I can't have my meadow grass trampled."

Before noon Mephibosheth was in his new quarters. There was a parlor with two pieces of carpet on the floor; there was a chamber with plenty of straw, whereon Mephibosheth could repose; there was a dining-room, with what, in common language, might be termed a trough.

Such a life as that pig led! He was cared for tenderly. He was washed all over every morning, and put to bed every night. He was not a very brilliant pig as far as his intellect went, it must be confessed. He could do no tricks with cards; he could not be taught to jump through a hoop.

One year passed; Mephibosheth was large. Two years went by; Mephibosheth was wonderful. I would I could say he was *plump*; that word does not begin to express his condition. It would be pleasant to call him *stout*; that would not give the glimmer of an idea of his size. *Corpulent* would be a refined way of stating it. Alas! corpulent means nothing as far as Mephibosheth is concerned. That animal measured *seven feet and twenty-two inches* round his body. He weighed—truth is great, and must be spoken—he weighed *five hundred and fifty and two-third pounds*.

He could not walk; his legs were pipe-stems under him. He could scarcely breathe. That is the excuse for what happened.

One day Romeo Augustus came home from school. Mephibosheth's pen was empty. Mephibosheth's pen would be empty for evermore. That is a gentle way of telling the story. In vain it was explained to Romeo Augustus that Mephibosheth's life had become a burden; that common humanity demanded his departure. In vain Philemon offered three fish-hooks and a jack-knife by way of solace. In vain Solomon was sure his father would present a calf to the mourner for a pet.

Elias was the only one who gave the least comfort.

"We will make a tombstone, and I will write an epitaph," said he.

Soon he brought a board, on which were drawn an urn and a couple of consumptive weeping-willows (for Elias was an artist as well as a poet), and underneath were these lines, which being written partly in old English spelling, were so much the more consoling:

Sacred to the Memorie
of
MEPHIBOSHETH.

Kinde Reader, pause and drop a teare,
Ye Pig his bodie lieth here;
Ye Auguste third of fiftie-nine
Was when his sun dyd cease to shine.
He broke two legs, which gave him woe;
He doctored was by Romeo,
Who cherished him from yeare to yeare,
As by this notice doth appeare.
He fed him till he waxed soe big
He was obliged to hop the twig.
Ye friends do sadly raise their waile,
And fondly eke preserve his tayle.

"And here's his tail," said Elias, presenting the pathetic memento.

"The only trouble is in the line, 'Ye Pig his bodie lieth here,'" sobbed Romeo Augustus. "It doesn't lie here. He's been sold to a butcher."

"It's Elias who '*lieth* here,'" remarked Isaac.

That was a heartless joke. No one was so low as to laugh at it.

"They often have monuments without the—the—the body," said Elias, with great delicacy.

Romeo Augustus was content.

He is a grown man now, but to this very day he keeps Mephibosheth's monument. It is nailed on the wall of his chamber. He sometimes smiles when he looks at it, but he does not take it down.

THE TAILOR AND THE WOLVES.

TRANSLATED FROM THE GERMAN.

EVER so long ago there lived a tailor's apprentice, a merry, light-hearted fellow, but with a large hump, so that he always looked like a country-woman going to market on a Saturday, carrying her goods on her back.

One night, as he was returning from some festivity in the town, he had to go through a thick wood, in which it was so dark that he could not see his hand before his face. As he was dawdling along quite merrily, and whistling the tune of the last waltz that he had danced, he lost his way, and fell into a deep pit, so that sight and hearing forsook him, and he gave himself up for lost. But when he found out that he was unhurt after the fall, he began to cry pitiably and to call for help, till he suddenly heard talking not far off.

In the pit, which sloped sideways far down into the earth, lived a large wolf with his wife and two little ones, and when they had heard the tailor's fall and screams, the old wolf said, joyfully, to his wife,

"Be quick, my dear, hang the pot over the fire: I think we shall have something good to-night."

These words reached the ears of the tailor, who, in the deepest anxiety for his life, became as still as a mouse.

But the wolf opened the door of his den, put a lamp in his paw, and peered all round till he had discovered the tailor, whom he then seized by the legs, and, without more ado, dragged into his sitting-room.

When he was about to be killed, the poor fellow cried and bemoaned himself in such a heart-rending manner that the wife, who was a good soul, put in a word for him to her husband.

"Well, then," said the wolf, "he may live, but he must never return to men, or he would betray us; he must stay here and become a wolf."

"Most joyfully," said the tailor, "for I would rather live as a wolf than be cooked and eaten as a man."

Whereupon the wolf fetched one of his old furs out of the cupboard, and his wife had to sew the tailor into it.

So the tailor staid with them, soon learned to howl perfectly, and to walk on all fours; besides which, he became quite expert in catching rabbits.

One day, when they had all gone out hunting together, it happened that the King of the same land was also hunting in the wood. As soon as the hunters came near the wolves, they and the tailor took to their heels.

They ran into a neighboring thicket, and hid themselves behind some bushes, when the old wolf whispered to the others to keep quiet, without fear, for he had seen no dogs, and without their help no huntsmen would find them.

He spoke truly, for it so happened that a wild boar had killed every single dog.

Then it occurred to the King to take a pinch of snuff; after which he sneezed violently.

The tailor, who had not yet lost his knowledge of polite ways, said, respectfully, "Your health, sire!"

When the King heard these words he rode toward the bush, and all his huntsmen followed him.

Here they perceived the wolves, and the King and his companions set up a loud shout of joy. They threw their spears so well that only the old wolf could escape; and the tailor was the last to be seen, because he had hidden himself so well, but before the huntsmen could aim at him, he had rolled himself, howling piteously, toward the King, saying,

"I beg your pardon, sire; I am really a tailor's apprentice, and only by accident among the wolves."

Then they all began to laugh, and a huntsman cut him out of his skin. A horse also was brought, that he might ride by the King's side and relate his tale.

"Tailor," then said the King, very graciously, "you have caused me much amusement, and if you like you may remain with me."

This speech pleased the little man right well, and he rode straight away to the castle, where he lived in joy and luxury for some time, as the King's court and private tailor.

But the old wolf, who had escaped with his life, felt raging anger against all human beings, especially toward the tailor, who had been the cause of the death of his wife and children, and he determined to revenge himself.

So he lay continually on the watch, and any man who appeared in his sight was a child of death. The whole land was full of grief and sorrow, for hardly a day pass-

HAVING A LITTLE FUN.

AN EASTER EGG.

ed in which at least one human being did not meet with a sorrowful end in the grip of the fierce old wolf.

But he said, "It is not yet enough; they must all come to it; and the tailor shall suffer the most for bringing about the death of my wife and children, because he could not hold his tongue."

Saying which he went to the castle, where the tailor was just looking out of the window smoking a pipe.

"Fellow!" said the wolf, "you must die, or I can not rest."

Terror seized the little man, and he told the King what the wolf had threatened.

"Wait, tailor," answered the King; "it is now high time that we should catch this wretch, even if it costs me my only daughter. He has not even respect for the court tailor; so what will such conduct lead to? And besides, he is eating up all my subjects, which I can not allow; for if I have no subjects, I can no longer be a king."

He spoke, and caused it to be proclaimed through the whole land that he who brought the wolf alive should be his son-in-law.

The tailor had not dared to leave the castle for days, for fear of the monster; but at length he could sit still no longer, and went into the garden one bright summer's day. Suddenly the wolf sprang from behind a tree, caught the poor fellow by the tail of his coat, and dragged him far into the wood, in spite of all his wriggling and screaming.

"Rascal of a tailor!" said he; "you have brought me into misery, therefore you must die."

Then, in his dire need, a cunning, artful idea occurred to the tailor, and he exclaimed, "Look! there come the huntsmen!" and as the wolf turned round in alarm, the tailor leaped on to his back, and held his hands tightly over the creature's eyes.

Then the wolf ran as he had never run in his life before, so that each moment he thought his hated rider must fall to the ground.

And as the creature could not see, the tailor guided him toward the castle, to an open stable door; there got down, pushed him into one of the stalls, and then bolted the door on the outside.

The King was highly delighted that the tailor was such a cunning fellow, and consented that the betrothal to his daughter should take place at once.

The wolf was hanged, and his skin, which the tailor received among his wedding gifts, has been preserved to the present day, and just now lies under the table, belonging to the author of this little tale.

THE TALE OF A TAIL.

There was a rat lived in a mill—
Heigh oh! says Tidley Pill;
If she's not dead, she lives there still—
Heigh oh! says Tidley Pill.

This rat she had a great long tail—
Heigh oh! says Tidley Pill;
One day she caught it on a nail—
Heigh oh! says Tidley Pill.

She pulled so hard she pulled it out—
Heigh oh! says Tidley Pill;
And then she turned herself about—
Heigh oh! says Tidley Pill.

At home I've got a little babee—
Heigh oh! says Tidley Pill;
I wonder if she will know me—
Heigh oh! says Tidley Pill.

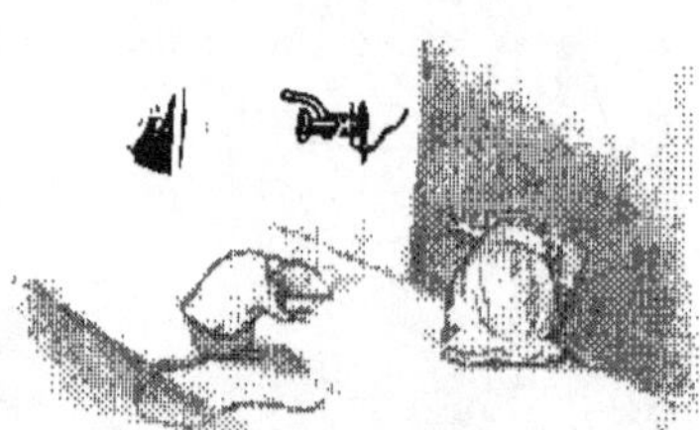

Oh, mother! mother! where's your tail?—
Heigh oh! says Tidley Pill.
Yonder it hangs upon a nail—
Heigh oh! says Tidley Pill.

It gives us the greatest pleasure to receive all the pretty letters which come to us in every mail from all parts of the country. Those communications which we think will be of interest to other children we print whenever we can make space for them, and all, without any exception, are carefully read, and their receipt acknowledged. These letters give pleasant, satisfactory glimpses into many homes, and we see the group of eager young faces watching, as they tell us, "for papa to bring the paper." Do not be disappointed, any of you, when you fail to find your pretty letter, which you have written so carefully and neatly, printed in the Post-office Box. We can not print all. If we did, you would have no stories to read, no pictures to look at—nothing but letters; for your busy little brains and fingers would fill the whole paper every week if we did not crowd some of you out. But keep on writing, for we like to hear what makes pleasure for you most, and in what subjects you are most interested. In that way there is always a mutual understanding between us, and our acquaintance is more likely to be intimate and lasting. We are also very much interested in what children write about the seasons in different regions of the country, showing how spring advances from Texas up into the far northern State of Oregon. Such letters are always interesting and instructive. One request we would make, that is, always write your signature very distinctly. Often we can not make out even your initials, and your name may be misprinted in our acknowledgments.

[illegible]

The wind-flower is found in the early spring growing among dry leaves and in sunny nooks by old stone walls, sometimes in open pasture lands where the soil is damp. The blossom, which are pale pinkish-white, grow on a stem from two to four inches in height. There is only one drooping flower on a stem. This plant is more properly called anemone, from *anemos*, a Greek word signifying wind. It is interesting to know that it was called *anemone* by the ancient Romans. Pliny alludes to it, and says it was called wind-flower because it opened its petals only when the wind blew.

[illegible]

Answers to S. R. W.—[illegible]

George F. Pinney, Willie G. Lee, Frank [illegible], M. Paul Martin, and Fred A. [illegible] [illegible] trouble with the [illegible], but if they persevere, and carefully follow directions, they will soon have a pretty one.

[illegible]

Who among our young correspondents can answer this question?

[illegible]

John H. M., Nicholas P. G., and Robbie C. write pretty stories of their pet cats, dogs, and foxes, which we regret having no room to print. In answer to Robbie's question, we would say that the bite of a fox is painful, but not dangerous like that of a dog.

Willie B. C.—When you recover from your illness, and can write your "print well," we will print your letter if it is interesting.

Louise [illegible] and Harry D.—Pigeons like to eat bird seed, broken corn, or any kind of grain, and enjoy that kind of food much better than bread-crumbs. They need fresh water to drink, and will bathe now and then, like a canary, if they have a bath dish large enough to flutter in.

W. M. L.—There is many a man much older than you who would be glad to know an easy and quick way to make ten dollars. Unfortunately we can not tell you how to accomplish your object.

May.—Your poetic line of beauty is very pretty, and shows much imagination for such a little girl.

Bessie D. L.—Call your bird Birdie, and your kitty Clover. There was once a big Maltese cat named Clover who did many funny tricks, and lived to be very old. If you name your kitty after her, perhaps she will live as long.

Mary B.—Your plain form picture scrap-book is very good. Try to select some pictures of historical localities and celebrated buildings, and then, when you show your book to your little friends, you will have something interesting to tell them.

Clara B. H.—Your "old bachelor uncle" is very kind to send you Young People, and you will be glad to hear that a large number of other uncles have made their little nieces happy in the same way.

Favors are received from [illegible]

Correct answers to puzzles received from [illegible]

PUZZLES FROM YOUNG CONTRIBUTORS.

No. 1.

ENIGMA.

My first is in rhythm, but not in [illegible].
My second is in [illegible], but not in [illegible].

[illegible]

No. 2.

[illegible]

No. 3.

[illegible]

No. 4.

[illegible]

No. 5.

[illegible]

No. 6.

[illegible]

ANSWERS TO PUZZLES IN NO. 16.

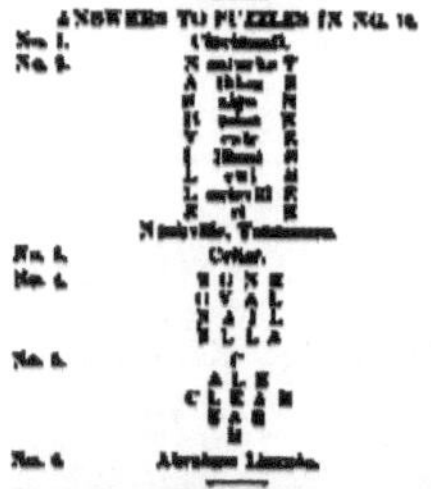

[illegible]

EASTER REVENGES.—"Break, break, break,
For the tables are turned, we see;
And the damaged heads of the boys that are 'bumped'
Are warnings to you and me."
TENNYSON (*altered appropriately for the occasion*).

WIGGLES.

DRAWINGS of Wiggle No. 9, given on page 184 of HARPER'S YOUNG PEOPLE No. 15, have been sent in by Alph A. H., J. M. W., E. B. C., F. H. Denman, Arthur H. Spear, G. L., Isabelle Oakey, "Trombone-blower," J. H. G., John Peckle, Laura C. Parmelli, F. S. J., John T. Hall, Fred Houston, Ettie Houston, J. G. T., Harry Austin, D. W. C. F., Willie H. Speller, M. D. J., Lena E. Schtabl, Harry Moore, G. H. Fisher, Miriam Hill, John G. Wilson, William Atkinson, Mabel Lowell, Walter Stillman, Mabel H., J. R. G., R. S. G., J. S. E., Josie Vail, W. C. N., Willie R. B., E. J. B., K. T., Entomologist, Bertha Childs, J. R., John H. Greene, J. H. G., R. C. Jopp, Karol, R. R. I., I. H. J., George Town, Ross, C. T. Hamilton, Leon M. Forbes, W. F. Pinkham, E. T. J., M. H. V., Jeny Kessler, Annie O. Alger, Frank M. Richards, Morton D. H., F. G. Wardman, K. T., Herbie Ferguson, C. H. Thebernth, Willie H. Spiller, J. K. M., Dollie Murdoch, Theo. F. John, Percy and George, Annie R. H., G. S. D., Matthew Lado, Julia West, Olive Russell, Charles Conner, Willie R. C. Carson, Effie E. Parks, Margaret E., Carter Colquitt, M. O. K., Mattie L. F., B. H. Smith, Irwin McDowell, C. H. A., F. E. G., and E. We have only room to publish some of the best of the many drawings offered. Fig. No. 10 is a new Wiggle; now let us see what you can do with it.

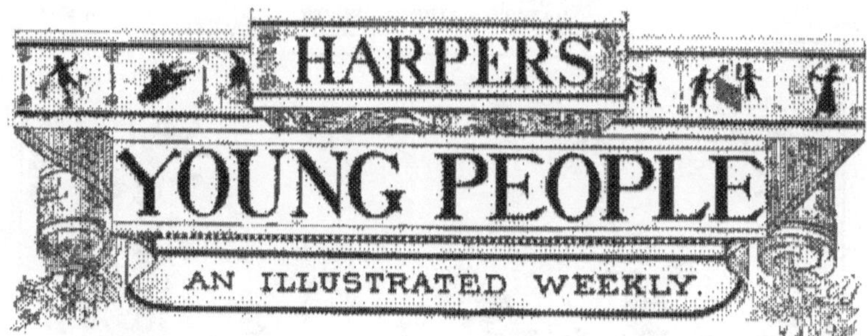

VOL. I.—No. 22. Tuesday, March 30, 1880. | PUBLISHED BY HARPER & BROTHERS, NEW YORK. | PRICE FOUR CENTS. $1.50 per Year, in Advance.

A DELUSION AND A SNARE.

"APRIL-FOOL!"

BY MARGARET EYTINGE.

THERE was one boy in the Merrit Academy who never joined in any of the games; never went skating; never went swimming; never made a snow man or threw snowballs; never came to the meetings of the debating society, where such questions as, "If a fellow ask a fellow for a bite of a fellow's apple, which is the politer way to give it to a fellow—to bite off a piece yourself, or let a fellow bite for himself?" were debated with much mock gravity and real fun.

He looked with horror on all kinds of fighting; had no admiration for great generals; thought war should be abolished; shuddered at tales of cruelty and suffering; was constitutionally timid and extremely credulous; hated thunder and lightning; liked birds, flowers, pretty verses, and fairy tales; believed in ghosts and supernatural beings; was very fair haired, very blue eyed, tall, slender, and named Harold Lord. But after the first week or two of his attendance at school—he was a day scholar—his real name was never heard, for his school-mates, quickly finding out his peculiar characteristics, skillfully turned it into "Lady Harriet," and Lady Harriet he remained for for many a long year. Of course, being so girlish in his appearance, ways, and tastes, and of so reserved and gra-tle a disposition, the other boys rather looked down upon him, and, after the manner of boys, made him the subject of much chaff and many practical jokes; and so it came about when Charley Bennet and Ned Morningstar and Ben Rowe began on the afternoon of the 31st of March to talk about the 1st of April, they hit upon Lady Harriet as a boy who would make a capital "April-fool."

"We can have no end of fun with him," said Charley. "You know he lives all alone with his grandmother—"

"A Little Red Riding-hood," interrupted Ben Rowe.

"—down by the cedar woods," continued Bennet. "But the question now in order is, what kind of fun shall it be?"

"Dress up like Indians, and pretend you're goin' to scalp him," proposed little Al Smith, who had joined the party—a thing no other small boy in that establishment would have dared to do; but then Alfred, as his aunt called him—and a very cross old aunt she was, too—had no father nor mother, and was such a good-natured, willing, reliable young chap that his older school-mates made quite a pet of him, and allowed him many liberties they would have allowed to no one else in his class.

"Nonsense, Smithey," said Ben Rowe. "Ghosts is the thing;" and striking an attitude, he quoted:

"'I am thy father's spirit:
Doom'd for a certain term to walk the night;
And, for the day, confined to fast in fires....
I could a tale unfold, whose lightest word
Would harrow up thy soul; fre-e-eze thy young blood;
Make thy —'"

"That's quite enough of that, Rowe," said Bennet. "A band of young desperadoes is my idea. The papers are full of 'em just now—fellows living in caves and other queer places, and robbing right and left (result of reading too many dime novels; heard the Professor say so this morning). Been 'round here too; stole Uncle Jeff's calf day before yesterday; and his grandmother goes to sewing society to-morrow night."

"The calf's grandmother?" asked Ben Rowe.

"Didn't know you had any grandmother," said Bennet.

"Charley's hit on the very thing," declared Ned Morningstar. "We'll let three or four other fellows into the joke, and I'll be captain, and we'll wear masks, and all the old clothes we can beg, borrow, or take, and get ourselves up prime as a No. 1 band of reg'lar young villains. Aha! your money or your life!" making a lunge at small Al.

"But you won't really hurt Lady Harriet?" said the little fellow, an anxious look coming into his soft brown eyes. "He's good to me, and gives me candy, and took me fishin' once."

"Took you fishin'!" repeated Charley Bennet, counterfeiting the greatest astonishment. "If he did, I'll bet he never let you catch a fish. He'd 'a fainted when he saw it a-wriggling on the hook."

"He did too," answered Al, stoutly. "I caught four, and six crabs, and he got eight," adding, frankly, "but he said he didn't like to catch them, only his grandmother said he must."

"Very reprehensible old lady," said Ben Rowe, gravely, "to allow her greediness for fish to trample on the softest feelings of her grandson's head—I mean heart. But don't be afraid, Smallbones"—stroking Al's dark curls—"we won't hurt him, not a bit; make your mind easy about that. He shall live to take you a-fishin' again."

"It does him good to wake him up once in a while," added Ned Morningstar, "he's such a turtle. I think I see his face when we all shout 'April-fool'!"

At dusk the next evening, after Grandmother Lord had gone to the sewing society, six or seven dreadful-looking objects came splashing through the mud up the road which led to her cottage. They were dressed in uncouth garments of all sizes and colors. Hats, brimless, or with brims very much turned up or very much turned down, two flaming red turbans, and a round handleless basket, through the open wicker-work of which the hair of the wearer straggled in the most outlandish and porcupinish manner, constituted their head-gear. The leader carried a gun. The others were armed with hatchets, knives, and clubs. All their faces were hidden by paper masks painted in various colors. "This is the house," said one of them, in a voice that seemed to come out of the ground beneath his feet, as they ranged themselves on the front porch, and he rapped sharply on the door with the stick he carried. It opened, and there stood Lady Harriet, gazing out with horror-stricken eyes upon the motley gang. "Your money or your life!" demanded he of the gun, at the same time pointing the weapon at the trembling boy.

Lady Harriet turned pale, and shrank back. "I have no money," he said, in a faltering voice.

"Then we must have your life," was the gruff reply, "unless you consent to become one of us. Seize him and search him!"

"*Do* go away, and leave me alone," implored the boy, falling upon his knees and clasping his hands. "There is no use—making me—join your gang," he continued, with chattering teeth. "I—couldn't be a—a—what you are—to save—my life."

But the young desperadoes paid no attention to his entreaties, and while two of their number rifled his pockets, the others, lighting a couple of lanterns they had brought with them, followed their leader on a tramp through the house, with much noise and deep growling. On the return of the latter, the pocket-searchers presented the captain with half a stick of peppermint candy, a penknife, a dime, a small book (*The Language of Flowers*), and some violets wrapped in a handkerchief.

"Prisoner," said the captain, sternly—that is, as sternly as the pebble he had under his tongue would allow—"if you make an attempt to escape, the consequences be on your own head. Right about face! March!"

And away they went, dragging poor Lady Harriet, begging and imploring to be set free, with them.

"Did you ever see any fellow so scared in all your life?" whispered Charley Bennet to Ben Rowe, as their victim began to cry and scream.

"Never," said Rowe. "I begin to feel sorry for him. But what a baby he is! Why don't he break and run? He can make good time with those long legs when he's a mind to."

"Halt!" cried the captain, when they reached the cedar woods. "This has gone quite far enough. We want no cowards among us. Boy, you are—" And the mouths of his followers simultaneously opened for a tremendous shout, when—

"I perfectly agree with you," interrupted the prisoner, quickly, wresting himself at the same time with a dexterous movement from the grasp of the two boys who had held him; and then he went on in his usual soft voice and slow way: "I mean this joke's gone quite far enough. You came half an hour or so before I expected you, but I think we've all acted our parts first-rate. Good-evening, Captain Morningstar. Good-evening, desperadoes. Farewell, April-fools." And he turned and walked leisurely toward his home again.

"Jiminy!" exclaimed Ned Morningstar, snatching off his mask and pulling a long face. "Somebody has—"

"Blundered," said Ben Rowe.

"Fools to the right of me,
Fools to the left of me,
Fools ev'ry side of me—
Oh, how they wondered!

But what's the use of being glum about it. I've an idea

it serves us right. Three cheers for Lady Harriet. He's not such a fool as he looks."

"As we look, I think," said Roy Wheeler.

And then, like the jolly boys they really were, they gave the cheers with a will, and followed them up with a roar of laughter that wakened all the echoes for miles around.

GENERAL SCHUYLER AND THE TORIES.

BY BENSON J. LOSSING.

THE Tories of the Revolution were the most bitter and annoying foes of the patriots who were struggling for their independence. The relation of the Whigs and Tories was that of belligerents in a civil war—cruel and uncompromising.

General Philip Schuyler, whose sleepless vigilance acquired for him the title of "the Eye of the Northern Department," was the terror of the Tories in Northern New York, from Sir John Johnson down to Joe Bettys. Schuyler was, for a long time, commander of the Northern Department. In 1781 he was not in military command. He lived at his country-seat at Saratoga a part of the year, and the rest of the time at his fine mansion situated in the southern suburbs of Albany. The British, under Burgoyne, having destroyed his mansion at Saratoga, and that place being exposed to incursions of the British and Indians, he made his residence permanently at Albany.

Early in August, 1781, an attempt was made by some Tories and Indians to capture him, that he might be used in exchange for some prominent British prisoner, and also to get rid of the watchfulness of that dreaded "Eye." In Saratoga lived a man named Walter Myers, who knew Schuyler well. He had eaten at his table in Albany, and knew the character of his house and its surroundings. Myers had joined the Tory Rangers of Colonel Robert Rodgers—a famous partisan on the northern frontier. The British authorities in Canada employed Myers, who had become a captain under Rodgers, to seize General Schuyler, Governor Clinton, and other prominent patriots in the region of the Hudson River, as far down as Poughkeepsie. Myers was at the head of the party of Tories and Indians above alluded to, who attempted to carry off Schuyler. I will let the General tell the story of that attempt in the following letter to General Washington, dated "Albany, August 8, 1781." I copied it from the original:

"On Saturday, the 28th, while with the commissioners for detecting conspiracies, I received information that a certain Captain Myers, of Rodgers's Rangers, from Canada, lurked in the vicinity of this place, with an intent to take or assassinate me. This corroborated intelligence given to General Clinton by a person escaped from Canada. On the Monday following I was informed by a Tory (whose gratitude for favors received surmounted the influence of his principles) that a reward of 200 guineas had been offered by the government in Canada to bring me there.

"On Sunday last, Major McKinstry wrote me by express from Saratoga that a party under Captain Jones had ambuscaded some time about Saratoga, that he had certain intelligence that I was their object, and that another party was down here with the same intentions. I took every precaution, except that of requesting a guard from General Clinton.

"Last night, about nine o'clock, Myers, with about twenty others, made the attempt. He forced the gate of a close court-yard, and afterward my kitchen door, from which servants, who had taken alarm, flew to their arms, and by a gallant opposition at the door of my house, afforded me time to retire out of my hall, where I was at supper, to my bedroom, where I kept my arms. After having made prisoners of two of the white men, wounded a third, and obliged the other to make his escape out of the house, some surrounded it, and others entered it. Those in the quarter exposed to my fire immediately retired. Those who had got up into the saloon to attempt, I suppose, the room I was in, retreated with precipitation as soon as they heard me call, '*Come on, my lads! surround the house; the villains are in it.*' This I did to make them believe that succor was at hand, and it had the desired effect. They carried off two of my men, and part of my plate. The militia from the town and some of the troops ran to my assistance, and pursued the enemy, but too late to overtake them."

Thirty years ago, Mrs. C. V. R. Cochrane, of Oswego, the youngest child of General Schuyler, told me the story substantially as it is told here. Her father also related that when the family fled up stairs from the hall, in affright, the baby was left behind in the cradle. Mrs. Schuyler was about to rush down stairs for the child, when the General interposed, saying, "Your life is more valuable." Her daughter Margaret, then about twelve years of age, hearing this, ran down for the baby, snatched it from the cradle, and started up the stairs with it. An Indian threw a tomahawk at her. It grazed the infant's head, cut a hole in Margaret's dress, and lodged in the mahogany stair rail. That infant became Mrs. Cochrane, and Margaret became the wife of Stephen Van Rensselaer, the Patroon, at Albany. The mansion yet stands; and well up the stairway may be seen the scar made by the keen blade of the tomahawk in the rail.

YOUNG DIAMOND MERCHANTS.

A NOTED traveller, who wrote about the diamond mines of India a very long time ago, describes the work done by the children. In speaking of a visit to the principal mine of Golconda, he says:

"A very pretty sight is that presented every morning by the children of the master-miners and of other inhabitants of the district. The boys—the eldest of whom is not yet over sixteen, or the youngest under ten years of age—assemble, and sit under a large tree in the public square of the village. Each has his diamond weight in a bag, hung on one side of his girdle, and on the other a purse, containing sometimes as much as five or six hundred pagodas.

"Here they wait for such persons as have diamonds to sell, either from the vicinity or from any other mine. When a diamond is brought to them, it is immediately handed to the eldest boy, who is tacitly acknowledged as the head of this little band. By him it is carefully examined, and then passed to his next neighbor, who, having also inspected it, gives it to the next boy. The diamond is thus passed from hand to hand, amidst unbroken silence, until it returns to that of the eldest, who then asks the price, and makes the bargain. If the eldest boy is thought by his comrades to have given too high a price, he must keep the stone on his own account.

"In the evening the children take an account of their stock, examine their purchases, and class the diamonds according to their water, size, and purity, putting on each stone the price they expect to get for it. These children are so perfectly acquainted with the value of all sorts of gems, that if one of them, after buying a stone, is willing to lose one-half per cent. upon it, a companion is always ready to take it."

The diamond mines of Brazil were discovered by a curious circumstance in 1730. Some miners in searching for gold found some curious pebbles, which they carried home to their masters as curiosities. Not being considered of any value, they were given to the children to play with. An officer who had spent some years in the East Indies saw these pebbles, and sent a handful to a friend in Lisbon to be examined. They proved to be diamonds. A few were collected and sent to Holland, and were pronounced to be equal to those of Golconda. The news soon reached Brazil, and those who possessed any of the "pebbles" soon realized large sums of money. The Portuguese government laid a claim upon all diamonds that might be found thereafter, a search was made, and mines were discovered.

[Begun in No. 19 of HARPER'S YOUNG PEOPLE, March 9.]

ACROSS THE OCEAN; OR, A BOY'S FIRST VOYAGE.

A True Story.

BY J. O. DAVIDSON.

CHAPTER IV.

A DARING FEAT.

LUCKILY for our hero, Mr. Hawkins, the first officer, was a shrewd, clear-headed man, and had his own opinion of Master Monkey. The latter told his tale confidently enough, but a few pointed questions confused him at once: he stammered, contradicted himself, and was finally turned out in disgrace. Austin then gave *his* version, and the officer, after questioning him closely, appeared satisfied.

"Here, my lad," said he, writing a few lines on a slip of paper, "take that to the chief engineer—you'll find him in his bunk, I reckon."

In his bunk, sure enough, lay the "chief," groaning dismally. He was a tall, fine-looking fellow, with bright blue eyes, and an arm like a blacksmith's; but when a man is on his back from sea-sickness, how can he look heroic?

"So, my boy, you've run away to sea, eh? Humph: that's just what *I* did when I was your age—and much good I've got by it! It was all through reading those precious sea-stories, which made me think I'd only to start to be made a captain at once. Wish I'd never learned to read—ugh!"

Here came a terrible spasm of sickness, to the great amazement of Frank, who had never dreamed of such a thing as a seasick sailor. Such cases, however, are not uncommon; and Nelson himself, one of the greatest sailors on record, never got over this weakness at all.

"This is how *I* am for the first week of every voyage," resumed the engineer; "and I always vow that every cruise shall be my last; but when I get ashore, I can't be happy till I'm afloat again—ugh! oh!"

And another spasm followed, worse than the first.

Frank said nothing, but his pitying face spoke for him; and the sick man, evidently touched by it, went on in a cheerer tone:

"Well, youngster, you're lucky not to be sick like me. Your name's Frank Austin, eh? Well, go and tell Mr. Harris to give you some work in the engine-room."

This promotion was the beginning of a new life for our hero. Now, at last, there was a chance of learning something; and the men, in whose estimation he had risen greatly since his defeat of Monkey, were always ready to answer his eager questions. He was never weary of admiring the huge machine which did with one smooth and regular movement the work of hundreds of strong men, obeying the slightest turn of a tiny wheel, yet capable of tearing the whole ship to pieces should its irresistible strength ever break loose.

And now, as they began to enter the tropics, everything grew warm and bright. Flannels were doffed, and an awning spread over the after-deck. The wind, though it still blew strongly, was now in their favor; and foretopsail and mainsail, jib and spanker, were set to catch it, till the ship staggered under her press of canvas, and careened as if about to dip her very yards.

So passed several days, during which nothing special occurred; for by this time everything had got "shaken into its place," and the routine of the ship's duties proceeded as regularly as clock-work. Frank, now restored to his place at the mess table, and high in favor with the crew (who henceforth reserved for Monkey the cuffs and jeers formerly bestowed upon our hero), was beginning to feel quite at home in his new life, when it was suddenly broken by a very startling adventure.

One evening, about dusk the machinery slackened suddenly, and an unusual bustle was heard on deck. A man running past thrust an oil-can into Frank's hand, and bade him carry it to one of the engineers upon the starboard (right-hand) paddle-box. On deck all was confusion. Men were rushing hurriedly to and fro, while the paddle-box itself was occupied by an excited group of officers and engineers; and it was some time before Frank could make out what was the matter.

An obstruction of some kind had impeded the turning of the shaft in the "outboard bearing," which had grown dangerously hot. It was this that had caused the "slowing down" of the engine, which could not be set working again till the impediment was removed and the "bearing" oiled.

Looking over the side, Austin saw a man hanging by a rope on the outer face of the paddle-box, like a spider on its thread, and laboring stoutly, with hammer and oil-can, to set matters to rights. Suddenly the ship plunged, and the man disappeared into a surging wave. He rose again, vanished a second time, re-

MAN OVERBOARD!

appeared once more, and again the blows of his hammer were heard, and again the boiling whirl of foam swallowed him up. At every plunge Death seemed to gape for him; but drenched, gasping, and half stifled as he was, he still worked bravely on.

On the deck all was now deadly still; and in that grim silence the hard breathing of the excited crew could be heard as they watched the solitary man at his fearful task. Would it *never* be over? Crash after crash the cruel waves came bursting upon him, and all could see that his strength was beginning to fail.

But the work is nearly done! A few more hammer strokes and he is safe. Already the anxious crew are beginning to breathe more freely, and even to greet their hero with encouraging shouts, when suddenly a mountain wave is seen coming right down upon him.

"Look out, Allen!" roar the sailors, with one voice.

Allen casts one glance up at the overhanging mass, and then twines his arms and limbs around the "open-work" of the paddle-box with the strength of desperation. The next moment there comes a stunning shock and a deafening crash, and all is one whirl of blinding spray and seething foam, amid which nothing can be heard and nothing seen. But when the rush passes, the brave man is still there.

A shout of joy arises, but is instantly followed by a terrible cry. *The safety-line around Allen's body has parted!*

"Grapple him with boat-hooks, some o' ye!" roars the boatswain. "Fling him a rope!—quick! or he's lost."

But before any of the hands stretched toward the doomed man could reach him, his stiffened fingers lost their hold. For one moment he was seen balanced in mid-air, with his imploring glance cast upward at the stanch comrades who were powerless to save him, and then down he went into the roaring sea.

There was an instant rush to the life-boat; but it was barely half way to the water when a huge sea dashed it against the ship's side, crushing it like an egg-shell. This was the last chance. An arm tossing wildly through the foam of a distant wave, a faint cry borne past on the wind, and poor Allen was gone forever.

Then, amid the dismal silence, was heard, clear and strong, the firm voice of the captain:

"Lads, I won't *order* any of you to run such a risk; but this job must be done somehow, or we shall all go to the bottom together. Fifty dollars to any man who'll volunteer!"

OILING THE OUTBOARD BEARINGS.

A dozen men sprang forward at once; but quick as they were, there was one before them—and that one was Frank Austin. Unnoticed by all, he had knotted a rope around his waist, fastened the other end to an iron stanchion, and before any one could stop him, down he slid to the perilous spot, escaping, as if by miracle, several heavy seas which came rolling in, one upon another.

For a moment the whole ship's company stood as if thunder-struck; and then one of the sailors, muttering, "Guess he'll want *them*, anyhow," lowered a hammer and oil-can, which Frank dexterously caught. The work was so nearly done that a few blows of the hammer sufficed to complete it; and a deafening cheer greeted the young hero as he prepared to climb up again.

"Smart, now, lad!" shouted half a dozen voices; "here's another sea comin'."

But Frank saw at once that the wave would be upon him before he could reach the deck, and that there was only one way of escape. Thrusting his slim figure between the beams of the open-work, where no full-grown man could have passed, he held on with all his strength. Crash came the great billow against the side, making the whole ship quiver from stem to stern; but Austin remained unhurt. The next moment he was safe on deck.

And now came a scene that might have served any painter for a study of Horatius among the Romans after his defense of the bridge. Frank was snatched up and carried shoulder-high to the forecastle by the cheering crew, who kept shouting the news of his exploit to all that had not seen it. His hands were shaken till they tingled, and his shoulder-blades ached with friendly slaps on the back from the sledge-hammer fists of his admirers. Every one was eager to give something to the hero of the hour. Offers of pipes, clasp-knives, tobacco, etc., rained upon him from the very men who had cuffed and kicked him like a dog but a few days before; and even his refusal of these gifts, which would formerly have been set down to conceit and "uppishness," was now taken in perfectly good part. In fact, that one deed of promptitude and courage had raised him from the last to one of the first among the whole crew. So true is it that they who succeed best are not always the bravest, or the wisest, or the strongest, but simply those who keep their wits about them, and never miss a chance of doing something.

[TO BE CONTINUED.]

A STRANGE FELLOW-VOYAGER.

I'VE had many a queer voyage in my time, said Captain M——, but the queerest I ever had was one that I made (somewhat unexpectedly, as you will see), upon the Great Fish River, in South Africa, on my way back from a hunting excursion.

As I neared the bank I saw that the river was in full flood, more than twice its usual breadth, and running like a mill-race. I knew at once that I should have a very tough job to get across, for a flooded African river is no joke, I can tell you. But I knew also that my wife would be terribly anxious if I didn't come back on the day I had fixed—South Africa being a place where a good many things may happen to a man—and so I determined to chance it.

Just at the water's edge I found an old Bushman that I knew well, who had a boat of his own; so I hailed him at once:

"Well, Kakoomi, what will you take to put me across the river?"

"No go fifty dollar this time, baas" (master), said the old fellow, in his half-Dutch, half-English jargon. "Boat no get 'cross to-day; water grood" (great).

And never a bit could I persuade him, although I offered him money enough to make any ordinary Bushman jump head-first down a precipice. Money was good, he said, but it would be no use to him when he was drowned; and in short he wouldn't budge.

"Well, if you won't put me across," said I at last, "lend me your boat, and I'll just do the job for myself; I can't very well take my horse with me, so I'll just leave him here in pledge that I'll pay for the boat when I come back."

"Keep horse for you, master, quite willing; but s'pose you try cross to-day, you never come back to ask for him."

He spoke so positively that, although I'm not easily frightened, I certainly did feel rather uncomfortable. However, when you've got to do a thing of that sort, the less you think of it the better, so I jumped into the boat and shoved off.

I had barely got clear of the shore when I found that the old fellow was right, for the boat shot down the stream like an arrow. I saw in a moment that there was no hope of paddling her across, and that all I could do was just to keep her head straight. But I hadn't the chance of doing even that very long, for just then a big tree came driving along, and hitting my boat full on the quarter, smashed her like an egg-shell. I had just time to clutch the projecting roots, and whisk myself up on to them, and then tree and I went away down stream together, at I don't know how many miles an hour.

At first I was so rejoiced at escaping just when all seemed over with me, that I didn't think much of what was to come next; but before long I got something to think about with a vengeance. The tree, as I've said, was a large one, and the branch end (the opposite one to where I sat) was all one mass of green leaves. All at once, just as I was shifting myself to a safer place among the roots, the leaves suddenly shook and parted, and out popped the great yellow head and fierce eyes of an enormous lion.

I don't think I ever got such a fright in my life. My gun had gone to the bottom along with the boat, and the only weapon I had left was a short hunting knife, which against such a beast as that would be of no more use than a bodkin. I fairly gave myself up for lost, making sure that in another moment he'd spring forward and tear me to bits.

But whether it was that he had already gorged himself with prey, or whether (as I suspect) he was really frightened at finding himself in such a scrape, he showed no disposition to attack me, so long at least as I remained still. The instant I made any movement, however, he would begin roaring and lashing his tail, as if he were going to fall on me at once. So, to avoid provoking him, I was forced to remain stock-still, although sitting so long in one position cramped me dreadfully.

There we sat, Mr. Lion and I, staring at each other with all our might—a very picturesque group, no doubt, if there had been anybody there to see it. Down, down the stream we went, the banks seeming to race past us as if we were going by train, while all around broken timber, wagon wheels, trees, bushes, and the carcasses of drowned horses and cattle, went whirling past us upon the thick brown water.

All at once I noticed that the lion seemed to be getting strangely restless, turning his great head from side to side in a nervous kind of way, as if he saw or heard something that he didn't like. At first I couldn't imagine what on earth was the matter with him, but presently I caught a sound which scared me much worse than it had done the lion. Far in the distance I could hear a dull, booming roar, which I had heard too often not to recognize at once: we were nearing a water-fall!

I had seen the Great Falls of the Fish River more than once, and the bare thought of being carried over those tremendous precipices made my very blood run cold. Yet being devoured by a lion would hardly be much of an improvement; and as I hadn't the ghost of a chance of being able to swim ashore, there really seemed to be no other alternative.

Faster and faster we went; louder and louder grew the roar of the cataract. The lion seemed to have quite given himself up for lost, and crouched down among the leaves, only uttering a low moaning whine every now and then. I was fairly at my wits' end what to do, when all of a sudden I caught sight of something that gave me a gleam of hope.

A little way ahead of us the river narrowed suddenly, and a rocky headland thrust itself out a good way into the stream. On one of the lowest points of it grew a thick clump of trees, whose boughs overhung the water; and it struck me that if we only passed near enough, I might manage to catch hold of one of the branches, and swing myself up on to the rock.

No sooner said than done. I started up, hardly caring whether the lion attacked me or not, and planted myself firmly upon one of the biggest roots, where I could take a good spring when the time came. I knew that this would be my last chance, for by this time we were so near the precipice that I could see quite plainly, a little way ahead, the great cloud of spray and vapor that hovered over the great water-fall. Even at the best it was a desperate venture, and I can tell you that I felt my heart beginning to thump like a sledge-hammer as we came closer and closer to the point, and I thought of what would happen if I missed my leap.

Just as we neared it, it happened, by the special mercy of God, that our tree struck against something, and turned fairly crosswise to the current, the end with the lion on it swinging out into mid-stream, while my end was driven close to the rock on which the clump of trees grew.

Now or never! I made one spring (I don't think I ever made such another before or since), and just clutched the lowest bough; and as I dragged myself on to it I heard the last roar of the doomed lion mingling with the thunder of the water-fall, as he vanished into the cloud of mist that overhung the precipice.

As for me, it was late enough that night before I got home, and I found my poor wife in a fine fright about me; so I thought it just as well, on the whole, to keep my adventure to myself, and it wasn't till nearly a year later that she heard a word about my strange fellow-voyager.

EASY BOTANY.

MARCH.

THE delightful science of botany treats of the forms and habits of plants.

This study leads the steps away from the busy town to the quiet woods and hills, giving a charm to every stroll, and making for each young student hosts of friends whose sweet faces will greet him through life with unaltering truth and beauty.

Gathering wild flowers is a pleasure too well known to need dwelling upon, but studying plants botanically involves more than this, as the student will soon find out. And there are difficulties, such as hard Latin words of many syllables which must be pronounced, and, worse still, *spelled*—a trying process even to the experienced. Care must also be taken to write down everything distinctly, and there must be patience, faithfulness, and resolute perseverance. But the reward comes, and one feels paid for his trouble when he is able to pick a flower, to sit down and *find it out*, and give to it its hard botanical name.

It is now spring, and the tears and smiles of April will quickly awaken the sleeping wild flowers. Let me urge the young people to take up the study of these "darlings of the forest." Gray's *First Lessons in Botany* will help along beginners, and before the flowers come we will tell them where to find them.

Let each one have a ruled blank book of *good size* to write down the botanical and common name of every flower. How many flowers do you think you can find in April? and who will find the most?

NOBLESSE OBLIGE.

BY V. G. SMITH.

THOSE of you who have studied French can translate this motto, and those who have not may perhaps guess that it means "nobility obliges"; but it is a favorite expression with so many different people, and it seems to mean such different things to different persons, that perhaps it may be worth while to tell a few anecdotes about what nobility has been supposed to oblige us to do.

When James I. of England was a little boy in Scotland, he had an extremely clever tutor, George Buchanan. Now Buchanan was a great Latin scholar. He wrote verses, and was called the Scotch Virgil. Of course he was very ambitious that his royal pupil should be a good Latin scholar too, and the books say he "*whipped* so much knowledge into him" that James was called the "British Solomon." This was the approved way in Great Britain at that time to educate boys. But there is a fact about which most of the books are silent: Buchanan and his friends reasoned that though it was quite true that James could never learn Latin unless some one was whipped, it would be a dreadful thing to strike a boy of the blood royal, and so they arranged that another boy should live at court, who should be whipped every time James failed in his declensions and conjugations.

This seems to have been a very satisfactory arrangement, and you see, in this case, "nobility obliged" somebody else to be punished when the "nobility" had done wrong.

This is the sense in which a great many splendid and magnificent people, with crowns on their heads and sceptres in their hands, have understood the motto.

Tradition does not say what James himself thought about it. Perhaps he worked all the harder with his lessons, and felt that "nobility obliged" him not to let any one else suffer for his faults. If that was so, it was not a bad plan, after all.

There is a better sense in which some have understood the motto. Perhaps some of you have read the touching letter of the Prince Imperial before he went to the fatal Zululand, where he was so cruelly murdered. The poor boy felt as if he had no object in England. He thought of the great deeds of the other Napoleons, and was stung at his own inaction. There seemed to be no duty left for him to do, in the way of fighting; but fight he must, to show he was as brave as the rest of his family. They say he was a gentle, affectionate, noble-spirited boy, and it seems as if he thought others would suppose he was weak unless he did some deed of daring. *His* nobility obliged him to be foremost in the most desperate places; and so he died, and the world mourned for him.

I think, as you read history more and more, you will believe, as I do, that men, and even children, of high birth, are surer to be brave and courageous than those in more obscure station. They may have other faults—dreadful ones—but it seems as if they dare not be cowards, because their whole race is looking at them, and expecting them to be noble. In this country, where we know so little about our ancestors, we need a still higher courage to make us do as grand things from yet higher motives.

For, much as I pity and admire the little Prince, I think there is even a better way than his to understand the old motto.

Perhaps you have been reading lately some account of the wedding festivities of the young King Alfonso of Spain; but it is not very long since he was married to his first wife, sweet little Princess Mercedes, who died within a few months after her marriage. Indeed, their nobility often obliges kings who lose their wives to be married again very soon.

It is of Queen Mercedes I wish to tell you. When she was about thirteen or fourteen years old she was sent to school to a convent in France. The convent was full of lovely and noble ladies, who had gone there because they had met with misfortunes of one kind or another. These ladies taught the young girls under their care very gently; still, there were certain light punishments for those who were careless or idle. I think one of these was that the offender should stand in a corner for a certain length of time.

Although most of the girls were of high birth, the little Princess, soon to be Queen, was of higher rank than any of the others. Her seat was a little apart from theirs, and by various small tokens of this kind her position was recognized.

Now one day it happened that Mercedes committed some fault. Perhaps she was late in rising, or failed in some other way to carry out the convent rules. The fault was not serious, and the Sisters did not think it necessary to enforce the punishment; but Mercedes, blushing very much, went of her own accord to the corner where she knew she ought to stand, and staid the appointed time. You see she felt that if she was of too high rank to receive punishment from others, the duty of inflicting it upon herself was her own. *Noblesse oblige.*

Although the illustrations I have given you have all been from royal families, where, I suppose, the motto originated, I am sure you will be able to apply it to hundreds of other cases, and will believe that nobility of character obliges us with still more force to do the best things always, though we are bound by no outward law.

THE SUN AT MIDNIGHT.

THERE are portions of our globe, away toward either pole, where the sun remains above the horizon for about two months of the year, making one long day. During this period the pleasant alternations of morning, day, evening, and night, are unknown in those regions; and there is also a long season of night, when the sun is not seen at all. This must be still more unpleasant, because it is winter-time. The pale cold moon sheds a chilling light at times over the snow and ice, and the aurora borealis flashes its splendors through the heavens. The cold is so great that old chroniclers, writing about the arctic regions, pretended that when the inhabitants tried to speak, their very words froze in coming out of their mouths, and did not thaw out till spring. It is not safe to believe all that old chroniclers tell us, and perhaps in this case they only tried, in an extravagant way,

to make their readers understand how very cold it was in that Northern land.

Our next picture shows the pleasanter side of arctic life, when the sun is above the horizon most of the time.

stood on the very edge of the cape one July midnight—that is, it was midnight by the clock—and saw the sun descend nearly to the horizon, and then begin to rise again. Far to the northward stretched the deep blue wa-were little patches of dwarf birch, scarcely a foot high, crouching close to the ground to escape being torn away by the furious winds that sweep over the land. There was none of the abundant life that we see around us in our fields and woods. A spider, a humble-bee, and a poor little wanderer of a bird, were the only living things Du Chaillu saw.

But he beheld the sun at midnight. As the hour of twelve approached, the pale orb sank almost to the horizon, the line of which it seemed to follow for a few moments, as it shone serenely over the lonely sea and desolate land. It was a sight never to be forgotten by one who had travelled hundreds of miles to witness it.

Sailors and explorers in the far Northern regions find it hard at first to accustom themselves to the long arctic day; and animals carried on board ship from lower latitudes are entirely at a loss when to go to sleep. There is a curious story of an English rooster that seemed to be utterly bewildered because it never came night. He appeared to think it unnatural to sleep while the sun was shining, and staggered about until he fell down from exhaustion. After a while he got into regular habits, but was apparently so disgusted to wake up in broad daylight, instead of the gray dawn to which he was accustomed, that he discontinued crowing. Perhaps he thought he had overslept himself, and was ashamed to crow so late.

It seems almost incredible that the dreary regions of which our pictures afford a glimpse enjoyed, ages ago, a climate even warmer than our own. The chilling waves that dash against the base of the dreary North Cape once washed shores clothed in luxuriant vegetation. Stately forests stood where now only stunted shrubs struggle a few inches above ground. The mammoth, and other animals that require a warm climate, roamed in multitudes through those regions. Their bones, found in great abundance when the banks of the lakes and rivers thaw out and crumble away in the spring, form an important article of traffic.

The people who live in the dreary regions of the far North are, generally speaking, industrious, sober, simple-minded, and contented. They have few pleasures, and their lives are toilsome. But in whatever region we find them—in the fishing villages of the northernmost coast of Norway or Lapland, and even in Greenland—they fondly believe their country to be the best and most favored part of the world. We must beg leave to differ with them. We love our changing seasons, that gradually come and go, the sweet succession of day and night, the joyous life that fills our fields and woods, and the comforts, luxuries, and all the advantages of civilization. But it is a great blessing to mankind that, wherever our lot may be cast in this great and wonderful world,

"Our first, best country ever is at home."

A BOARDING-SCHOOL CLUB.

BY ELINOR ELLIOTT.

"WELL, Mildred, what does she say?" asked Dr. Clifford of his pretty eldest daughter, as she came to the end of her long letter; and the shower of questions following showed how eager were all at the breakfast table to hear from the sister away at boarding-school.

"She says so much," laughs Mildred, "that I will read it to you."

[illegible], —— 12, 1880.

DEAR MILLY,—I am rejoiced to know your first party was a success, and that you were spared the ignominious fate of "full many a flower born to blush unseen, and waste its sweetness on the"—ball-room wall.

Your dress must have been a beauty, but I do not envy you. "Fine clo'" I have forsworn, and I would not exchange my jolly school-days for all your festive parties.

Tell papa I must have some new boots—very thick, with broad soles and low heels—and entreat him not to send them C. O. D., for I truly can't pay the expressage.

We girls have formed a club for the "Abolition and Extirpation of Grotesque Idiotic Style."

Our initials, A, E, G, I, S, as you see, spell "Aegis," which is to be our shield (its literal meaning) from aristocratic sneers. I dare say I shall not be received in polite circles when I go home, but when I look at my ring, on which is engraved A E G I S, I shall gain such invulnerability that all sneers will glance aside ineffective.

There is a curious fact about our club and motto. Like the old English Cabal, we have five members whose initials form the name, viz.,

Anna Clifford,
Enid Evans,
Gertrude West,
Ida Langford,
Sallie Peterson.

I have given up curling my hair, and braid it. Of course it isn't becoming, but we Aegises stoop not to vanity. I have gained five pounds since Christmas; so when my spring suit is made, tell the dress-maker to put the extra material into the waist, and not waste it (a pun, but very poor) in puffs and paniers, for we have abolished them. We try to get along with the bare necessities of life.

I'd give a good deal to see you all, but I'm not the least bit homesick.

Good-by. Give my double-and-twisted love to everybody, and kiss the dear pink of a baby a hundred times for me.

Lovingly, ANNA I. CLIFFORD.

P.S. When you send the boots, perhaps if you put them in a fair-sized box, there'll be room for a cooky or two. A. I. C.

"Isn't that a happy letter?"

"Think of our dainty, exquisite Anna so independent! her pretty brown curls straightened out in a braid, and her dresses shorn of puffs and ruffles!"

"That's the kind of 'society' for school-girls to form," says papa. "I'll order the thickest boots I can find to be sent up; also a chicken for Bridget to roast; and as she has given us so delicate a hint, perhaps you can find something else to put in the box."

Afternoon finds the Clifford family again assembled in the dining-room, intent upon packing the boots and "cookies"; and from the size of the box on the table one would infer that the boots must be No. 17's, and the cookies as large as cheeses, or, more correctly, that something more is to be added.

"Wouldn't it be fine to send five things for the club individually?" asks one.

"Capital!" "Good!" "Just the thing!" cry all.

"And have their initials spell Aegis."

"What shall the first be?"

"A—Apples!" sounds a full chorus.

"It is a vote. And the next?"

"E—Eels," suggests fourteen-year-old Dick, whose suggestions are apt to be more ludicrous than elegant.

"Eggs; hard-boiled eggs are always dear to my heart in the scenes of my childhood."

"Bridget, put on a dozen eggs, to boil ten minutes."

"G—Ginger-snaps."

"Grapes."

"Gum-arabic," from Dick.

It takes so long to decide this important point that Dr Clifford calls out the fourth letter:

"I."

A hush falls upon them, but, as Dick would say, made no noise, and did no damage in falling. No one can think of anything but ice-cream. And I challenge you: put your hand over your eyes, and name two other edibles beginning with "I."

At last Dick, in an ecstasy of inspiration, starts up, and cries, "Inch-worms!"

A peal of laughter, and each one suggests some impossible or awful article; and then the dauntless Richard again: "A few *Ideas*."

"If we had them to spare," says papa, dryly.

"Irish potatoes would be like coals at Newcastle."

"I feel it in my bones that Bridget would suggest *Johnny*."

"Apropos of that," says Milly, "I think we shall have to adopt the sound, and send *English* walnuts, as Anna loves them dearly."

"Now for the last letter."

"S—Sardines."

The things are collected, and stowed away in the box; it is sent off by express, and in a few days the following letter announces its arrival.

E—— HALL, —— 16, 1880.

DEAR, DEAR, DEAR FAMILY,—I know I can't show you my delight better than by telling you all about it.

Yesterday we Angles were out walking all the afternoon, and when we came home, hungry as wolves, were cheered by a chorus from the piazza:

"A Clifford box, a Wood box—
A Clifford box, a Wood box."

Perhaps you have an appetizing association with a wood-box, but the news quickened our steps, and inspired us with the elasticity of a quintette of rubber balls as we bounded up the steps, and fell upon our boxes with all the love of a father upon a returned prodigal.

I sat down on my box, and Gertie on hers, and there we sat, as happy as two enthroned queens, with sixth and seventh standing near. Has every girl in school bribed us last night?

"George has driven Madame over to town, and won't be back till late," said Enid, coming from her expedition to the basement in search of George. (George is the man-servant who "does the chores" and "plays boss" for the school.)

"How can we ever get them up stairs?" asks Gertie.

"Carry them ourselves," cried a brawny girl; "we'll all help."

So, with a girl at each corner of each box, we struggled up stairs. Mine was not very heavy, but Gertie's was; and one girl let her corner slip, which threw us all into confusion, and in the midst of the hurly-burly we became aware of a majestic presence at the head of the stairs, and there stood—Miss Cunningham, the first assistant. Our hearts stood still, for we had not asked permission; but Sallie, whom nothing ever daunts, cried out,

"Oh, Miss Cunningham," she called, "do come and help us!" and she actually stepped down and caught it as the girls were losing control of it, and engineered it into our sitting-room.

You know we five Angles have one sitting-room, with three bedrooms opening out of it. As she turned to go, I thought I saw in her face a longing to stay, and be a girl with the rest of us, and I said,

"Don't go, Miss Cunningham; stay and see what is in the boxes."

"Thank you; I know you will enjoy yourselves more alone. Madame told me to give you five young ladies permission to have supper in your own room to-night."

"Why?" we all cried. "What made her?"

"Because it is Miss Wood's birthday."

"My birthday!" cried Gertie, in amaze. "I didn't once think of it;" while the girls flew at her ears.

"I don't see how any one could forget such a thing—do you, Miss Cunningham?" I asked, as she stood in the door.

"No; I could not forget mine," she said. "This is mine too."

When I told the girls it was Miss Cunningham's birthday too, they unanimously proposed to give her a present, and ran to their rooms for their purses.

"There are just ten of us," said Enid, counting.

"Pass round a hat," said Ida.

"This will do," cried Sallie, seizing an India-rubber shoe, and taking up the collection. "If you have little, give little; but if you've got a lot, give a good deal. Six dollars and ninety cents," said Sallie, counting it. "Now what shall we get?"

"Flowers? They fade so quickly."

"Let's get something she can keep."

"Well, what?"

"A gold thimble. You know hers rolled down the register, and was lost."

We agreed upon the thimble. Then Enid went to Miss Cunningham, and gained permission for us to go down to the jeweller's. So the five other girls left the selection of the thimble to us, and went down stairs.

"Wasn't 'Cunny' good?" said Sallie. "Little did she suspect our object."

"Would it be a bad idea to ask her to feast with us to-night?"

"Not at all bad. Do you believe she'll come?"

"Very doubtful. Who will ask Madame if we may have the feast?"

"I," said Sallie; "my life for my country."

We bought a beautiful gold thimble for six dollars, and spent the rest for flowers; then hurried home to open the boxes, and get everything ready before study hour.

"What shall we do for a table-cloth?"

"Take a fresh sheet," said Sallie.

"Isn't there anything better?" asks Ida.

"Positively nothing," answered Sallie, throwing a sheet at her. "Take this, and be thankful it isn't sheet lightning that strikes you. Now I start for my interview with Madame."

"Good luck attend you! Enid, put the flowers in the centre, with a lemon pie at one side and a [illegible] at the other."

"Here is a roast chicken," I cried. "Ida, put it at one end."

"Enid," called Gertie, "here's a duck in my box; put him opposite the chicken."

"'*Dulce et decorum*,'" said Enid.

"Well," answered Gertie, "I'm glad she didn't eat them all."

Here Sallie came in, triumphant.

"I showed her the thimble, girls, and told her all about everything, and she says we five and the other five and Miss Cunningham—Elsie, she called her—can come up here right after prayers, and stay till ten o'clock."

"Could anything be jollier?"

"She says Elsie was our age when she first came here, and was as full of fun as we are."

Then I found your note, saying there were *Apples* for Anna, *Eggs* for Enid, *Grapes* for Gertie, *English* walnuts for Ida, and *Sardines* for Sallie. We saw how hard up you were for I's, but we'd rather have the nuts than anything.

We had just got everything in order when the study bell rang. You can scarcely mention a "goody" that was not in one of those boxes. Gertie had a birthday cake with fifteen tapers on it, which we lighted.

I can't begin to tell you what a jolly time we had when we came back up stairs. All our invitations were accepted. Miss Cunningham was charmed with the thimble. We "toasted" all you good people at home who were the cause of our joy, and sent the flowers to Madame when our revelry was o'er.

By the way, the boxes are exactly right. Now, with the love and thanks of all the Angles, I must close, for I haven't touched a lesson for to-morrow.

Lovingly, gratefully, and thankfully yours,

ANNA E. CLIFFORD.

THE BABY ELEPHANT.

ON the 10th of this month an event occurred in Philadelphia that has aroused universal curiosity and interest. It was the birth of a baby elephant, which immediately became famous as being the first of his kind, so far as is known, ever born in captivity. All other elephants brought to this country for exhibition, or used in Eastern countries as beasts of burden, have been captured and tamed; and it has heretofore been regarded as an unquestioned fact that they would not breed in captivity.

The mother of the cunning little fellow who is attracting so much attention is a large black Asiatic elephant named Hebe, and belongs to the Great London Circus. She is acknowledged by all the other elephants of the circus as their queen, and they are all loyally devoted to her. She and six other large elephants have been spending the winter in a stable at the corner of Twenty-third Street and Ridge Avenue, Philadelphia. Here the elephants stand in a large room, each with their hind legs chained to posts.

Immediately upon the birth of the little elephant the others seemed to become crazy with joy. They had been very quiet, but they now set up the most tremendous bellowing and trumpeting imaginable. Some of them broke their chains, and danced about in the most grotesque manner, besides performing all the tricks they had been taught in the circus ring. The general excitement communicated itself to Hebe, and in a moment she became the most frantic of them all. Snapping the chains that bound her to the posts as though they were threads, and apparently

THE EXCITED ELEPHANTS.

becoming, for the first time, aware of the presence of her baby, she seized him with her trunk and threw him with great force, twenty yards or more, to the opposite side of the room. He fell close beside a large stove, around which was a railing of heavy timbers. Rushing after him, his crazy mother beat down this railing, threw over the stove, and in her madness would probably have killed her baby, had not her keeper, who had fled for his life upon the first outbreak, returned with help, and attracted her attention. With considerable difficulty she was secured and again chained to the posts, and the other animals were also quieted. During all the confusion the baby had stood motionless in the place to which his mother had flung him, and had regarded the whole scene with a look of wise solemnity such as only a baby can assume.

When quiet was restored, he became very frisky, and was willing to make friends with everybody. He ran about with his mouth wide open, and his little trunk pointing upward in the funniest way possible. He blundered about here and there, running against all sorts of things, and finally seemed overjoyed to be taken back to his mother, who has ever since shown the greatest fondness for him. He is thirty-five inches high, and weighs 211 pounds, so that he is about the size of a large Newfoundland dog. He is fed by means of a nursing-bottle made of a yard of rubber hose and a large funnel. One end of the hose is put in his mouth, and the other is attached to the funnel, into which the keepers pour warm milk until the baby shows that he has had enough by throwing down his end of the tube.

PRACTICAL JOKES.

BY FRANK BELLEW.

AS a general rule, practical jokes are a kind of fun that should not be encouraged; but there are a few harmless ones which may be made the means of a good deal of innocent merriment.

Tom Hood, who was one of the most kindly and genial of men, as well as one of the greatest of poets, was very fond of playing little practical jokes on members of his own family and immediate circle of intimate friends. On one occasion, when his wife had made a magnificent English plum-pudding, as a Christmas present for some German friends, Hood surreptitiously got hold of it, and filled it with wooden skewers, which he ran through in every direction, and in this condition it was sent by the unsuspicious Mrs. Hood to her friends in Germany, who no doubt thought English cookery a most eccentric art.

On another occasion he wrote as follows, from London, to an intimate friend, one Lieutenant Franck, of the Prussian army:

"I also send for yourself an imitation gold-fish. It appears that there is something in the color or taste of the gold-fish which renders it irresistible to other fish as a bait. They are quite mad after it. It appears to be intended to be sunk with a weight, and pulled about under water, or else to float on the top; but they say it is taken in anyway."

This wonderful bait was made of wood, and painted yellow, or covered with gilt paper, and presented an appearance like the annexed engraving.

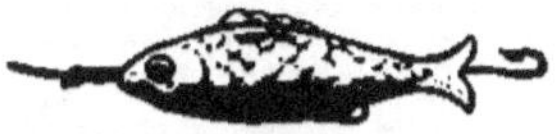

Fig. 1.

But under this innocent exterior lurked Tom Hood's joke. The fish was made of two pieces of wood, like Fig. 2, glued or gummed together, only one of which was attached to the line, and on this piece was burned, with a red-hot knitting-needle, the words, "*O, you April fool!*"

Fig. 2.

Of course, after the sportsman had dragged this about in the water for some time, the glue melted, the loose half of the bait floated away, and when he hauled in his line to see how things were getting along, he discovered the inscription, and at the same time that he had been made a *fool of*, whether it happened to be April or not.

THE CLOCK BEWITCHED.

I was once at one of those little social gatherings which the Scotch call a "cooky-shine," and the English a "tea fight," where two young ladies appeared escorted by a rustic beau (for be it known this was in the country), who, like many beaux from both city and country, had a very well developed opinion of his own shrewdness and sagacity, of which opinion he gave several rather obtrusive illustrations during the course of the evening. This peculiarity, added to the fact that, quite early in the festivities, he displayed an anxiety to hurry the young ladies home in the midst of their enjoyment, made him anything but popular. The fact was that the young man, having exhausted his limited stock of conversation, grew bored and sleepy, and wanted to go home himself. Not being able to accomplish this, he seated himself in an obscure corner

WHAT TIME IS IT?

of the room, where he soon dropped off into a doze. Now among the company was a little imp of a boy, a son of the hostess, who seemed to feel himself called upon to amuse the rest of the guests. He whispered a few words in his sister's ear, and then left the room. In about fifteen minutes the drowsy beau woke up with a start, and asked what o'clock it was.

"I really don't know," responded one of the ladies. "What time was it when you went to sleep?"

"Sleep—sleep! I haven't been to sleep—wake all the time."

"Indeed you have," chorused the party; "nearly two hours, and saying all sorts of things."

The youth looked blank, and rather frightened, but tried to brave it out. "Oh, pshaw! two hours. Sleep!—why, I haven't been to sleep ten—that's to say, I've been awake the whole time. Now we'll see." And he arose and walked into the next room, which was rather dimly lighted, to look at the clock. He remained there a long time, shuffling about, and emitting sundry whiffs and snorts, and then rejoined the company, rubbing his eyes, and rumpling his hair all over his head, with an expression of bewilderment on his countenance which set every one present tittering.

"All right," he said. "Guess't's 'bout time to start home."

"Oh no, not yet," answered the hostess. "We are going to have some cider and doughnuts."

The cider and doughnuts were brought in and handed round, the sleepy beau receiving his last. He took a good fresh bite. A pause. Something was the matter. He pulled, he gnawed, he wrestled, he grunted, he struggled: it was no use; that doughnut was too much for him. Suddenly, with a quick motion worthy of the late lamented Mr. Grimaldi, he whipped the doughnut out of his mouth and into his pocket. He thought he was unobserved, but a roar of rustic laughter from all sides of the room soon undeceived him. We will draw a veil over the scene, etc., etc., as the novels say. In a few seconds his two fair charges, in charity, proposed to go home; and they went.

Now what was this all about? I will tell you. When the young imp left the room, as before mentioned, he slipped into the back parlor, turned down the lights, and carried the clock off into the kitchen, where with some Indian ink and a brush he marked on its face half a dozen extra hands. He then replaced the clock on the mantelpiece in the parlor, and returning to the kitchen, procured two small balls of cotton batting, which he soaked in some batter the cook was using for doughnuts, and these he fried till they exactly resembled the genuine article the cook had just made. He had previously let the ladies into the secret, so that when the sleepy beau went into the back parlor to look at the clock, as they took care he should, they perfectly knew the bewildered frame of mind he was in while trying to find out the time. The sister, too, while handing round the doughnuts, managed to reserve the cotton ones for the same gentleman.

The next day our hostess received a polite note from the discomfited escort, thanking her for the gift of the doughnut, which he said had been of infinite value to him, as he had given it to a neighbor's dog which kept him awake all night, and the dog had since died. So he took it good-naturedly, after all.

THE JOLLY DOG'S PRACTICAL JOKE.

'Twas near dinner-time, and the pudding was hot.
So Nelly, her cheeks all aglow
(The master liked icy-cold pudding), ran out,
And popped the dish into the snow.

For though on that morn smiling April was here,
A snow-heap that March left behind,
When he hastened away, in a dark corner lay
Of the garden, blown there by the wind.

Singing merrily, back to the kitchen went Nell,
When a jolly dog came up the lane.

"Aha! something good!" and he stopped and he sniffed,
Looked around, cocked his ears, sniffed again.

Then, the gate being open, he boldly walked in,
Going straight to the snowy spot where
The dish sat a-cooling—three great gulps he gave,
And a pudding no longer was there.

Down the steps flew the maid. "I must now take it in,
For I'm sure by this time it is cool."
Said the dog, running off, "Pray don't trouble yourself;
I have taken it in—April-fool!"

OUR POST-OFFICE BOX

Correct answers to puzzles are received from [illegible].

PUZZLES FROM YOUNG CONTRIBUTORS.

No. 1.

ENIGMA.

My first is in left, but not in [illegible].
My second is in fire, but not in [illegible].
My third is in [illegible], but not in [illegible].
My fourth is in [illegible], but not in [illegible].
My fifth is in [illegible], but not in [illegible].
My sixth is in [illegible], but not in [illegible].
My seventh is in [illegible], but not in [illegible].
My whole is a game of which you have heard.

[illegible]

No. 2.

[illegible]

To whittle. A [illegible]. A [illegible]. Something [illegible]. [illegible]. Answer—[illegible]. [illegible]

No. 3.

[illegible]

[illegible]

No. 4.

NUMERICAL CHARADE.

I am composed of 15 letters.
My 14, [illegible], 7 is a [illegible] of walking.
My [illegible] is a fruit.
My 10, 12, 11, 13, 9 is a [illegible].
My whole is a common Latin phrase.
Also the name of a flowering plant. W. F. R.

No. 5.

[illegible]

A vowel. An insect. A [illegible]. A [illegible] plant. A consonant. H. N. T.

No. 6.

ENIGMA.

[illegible]

F. W.

ANSWERS TO PUZZLES IN NO. 18.

No. 1. [illegible]

No. 2. [illegible]

No. 3. [illegible]

No. 4.

W A R M
A [illegible]
[illegible]
M [illegible]

No. 5. Trifles often lead to serious results.

No. 6. [illegible]

[illegible]

THE MAGIC LANTERN.

We have received numerous letters from correspondents about the [illegible]. Some report great success in making it, while others have been unable to make it work right. To the unsuccessful ones we would say that you probably do not [illegible] your lens box far enough from the muslin screen, your outer box not being quite long enough. In this case, you can move the lens box out of the other box as far back as you please. The lens we use is about two and a half inches in diameter, but the size is of little consequence. The main conditions are to keep the light well to one side, that no direct rays pass through the lens to illuminate the screen, and to concentrate as bright a light as possible on the picture, and on that alone. There should be no other light in the room when the experiment is tried, and the picture should be very clear and distinct. Two double [illegible] placed one at each end of a tube of cardboard will act better than one lens alone.

Fig. 1. Fig. 2.

Fig. 3.

MISFITS.

BOB has discovered another amusement. The other evening he suddenly commanded me to "draw a head" on a piece of paper that he placed before me.

"Don't let me see it, nor my body. Now fold it back, and leave a little bit of the neck showing. Now I'll draw the body."

Which he did, and again folded the paper.

"Now, papa, you draw the legs."

Papa obediently took the pencil, and had his turn at the paper.

"Now, Mamie, you name it. Call it after somebody you know, if you like."

So Mamie named it Miss Fust, in honor of her school-teacher, the most stately of maiden ladies. Then Bob unfolded the paper, and displayed to us a most comical mixture of flesh and fowl.

"More like a sight, than Miss Fust," said papa.

"There! that's what I'll call 'em," exclaimed Bob—"misfits. That's just what they are, you know—misfits."

"She's a duck, anyway," said Mamie.

"Looks more like a goose," said Bob.

We afterward tried another, in which Mamie had a hand with the pencil. I named it after myself, and was rewarded for my vanity by finding "Nelly" a more ungainly object than even "Miss Fust."

In making "Misfits" you must remember to leave a small piece of one picture projecting into the other, in order to have them join properly. You will also find it better to draw them on a larger scale than the pictures we give.

CHARADE.

A sudden spring, a noiseless tread,
A playful poise of the restless head,
A sleepy song of sweet content,
While slyly on schemes of mischief bent:
'Tis thus the days of my first are spent.

To do my second is surely human;
They say the fault was first with a woman.
'Tis a little word, but its power was great,
To change the course of a happy fate.

My third is seen in many a land,
Where ancient temples ruined stand,
Like a grim sentry, placed before,
To guard an open palace door.

My whole, with slow and measured grace,
Among the lowly takes its place;
Nor dream its future yet shall be
A wondrous thing of mystery.

SOLUTION OF CHICKEN PUZZLE.

THE Chicken Puzzle given on page 216 of HARPER'S YOUNG PEOPLE, No. 17, has proved too difficult for any of our readers to solve, and not a single correct answer to it has been sent us. The puzzle was to make a chicken out of an orange with four cuts of the scissors and the prick of a pin. In Fig. 1 of the above diagram the dotted lines on the stalk and the white lines on the orange show where the cuts with the scissors are to be made, and Fig. 2 shows the pieces put together, and the chicken complete.

LITTLE TOMMY'S NIGHTMARE, AFTER SPENDING AN UNUSUALLY BUSY DAY KITE-FLYING.

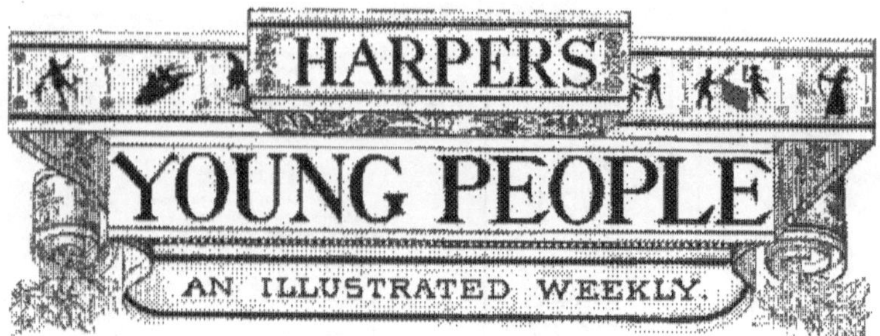

VOL. I.—NO. 23. PUBLISHED BY HARPER & BROTHERS, NEW YORK. PRICE FOUR CENTS.
Tuesday, April 6, 1880. $1.50 per Year, in Advance.

A RABBIT DAY.

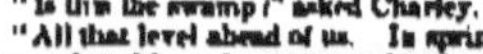

BY W. O. STODDARD.

"JIM," said Charley, "has that dog of yours gone crazy?"

"Old Nap? No. Why? What's the matter with him?"

"Just look at the way he's diving in and out among the trees. He'll run full split right against one first thing he knows."

"No, he won't. He's after rabbits. We're 'most to the swamp now, and Nap knows what we've come for as well as we do."

There was no mistake but what he was a wonderfully busy dog just then. It looked as if he was trying to be all around, everywhere, at the same time; and every few moments he would give expression to his excitement in a short sharp yelp.

"He means to tell us he'll stir one out in a minute," said Jim. "It's a prime rabbit day."

"Are there more rabbits some days than there are others?"

"Easier to get 'em. You see, there came a thaw, and the old snow got settled down, and a good hard crust froze on top of it; then there was a little snow last night, and the rabbits 'll leave their tracks in that when they come out for a run on the crust. Old Nap knows. See him; he'll have one out in a minute."

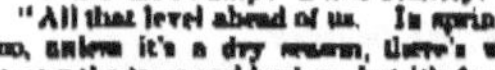

"Is this the swamp?" asked Charley.

"All that level ahead of us. In spring, and in summer too, unless it's a dry season, there's water everywhere among the trees and bushes; but it's frozen hard now."

"What is there beyond?"

"Nothing but mountains, 'way back into the Adirondacks. We'd better load up, Charley."

"Why, are not the guns loaded?"

"No. Father never lets a loaded gun come into the house. Aunt Sally won't either. Shall I load your gun for you?"

"Load my gun! Well, I guess not. As if I couldn't load my own gun!"

Charley set himself to work at once, for the movements of old Nap were getting more and more eager and rapid, and there was no telling what might happen.

But Charley had never loaded a gun before in all his life. Still, it was a very simple piece of business, and he knew all about it. He had read of it and heard it talked of ever so many times, and there was Jim loading his own gun within ten feet, just as if he meant to show how it should be done. He could imitate Jim, at all events; and so he thought he did, to the smallest item; and he hurried to get through as quickly, for it would not do to be beaten by a country boy. And then, too, there was

JIM AND CHARLEY IN THE WOODS.

old Napoleon Bonaparte—that is to say Nap—beginning to yelp like mad.

They were just on the edge of the swamp, and it was, as Jim said, "a great place for rabbits."

"He's after one! There he comes!"

"Where? Where? I see him! Oh, what a big one!"

Bang!

Charley had been gazing, open-mouthed, at the rapid leaps of that frightened white rabbit, and wondering if he would ever sit down long enough to be shot at, with that dog less than half a dozen rods behind him.

He was in a tremendous hurry, that rabbit, and he would hardly have "taken a seat" if one had been offered him; but he was down now, for Jim had not only fired at him—he had hit him.

"One for me. I meant to let you have the first shot. Never mind; you take the next one. Keep your eyes out. He may be along before I'm loaded."

Old Nap's interest in a rabbit seemed to cease the moment it was killed, for he was now ranging the bushes at quite a distance.

"Here comes one. Quick, Charley! He's stopped to listen for the dog."

So he had, like a very unwise rabbit, and was perking up his long ears within quite easy range of Charley's gun as he levelled it.

"Cock it! cock it!" shouted Jim. "Cock your gun!"

"Oh, I forgot that."

But he knew how; and when he once more lifted his gun, and pulled the triggers, one after the other, they came down handsomely.

"Only snapped your caps!" said Jim. "I never knew that gun to miss fire before. He's gone."

The rabbit had taken a hint from the bursting of the caps, and was now running a race with Napoleon Bonaparte across the swamp.

Charley looked at his weapon very gravely, and put on another pair of caps, remarking, "I never had a gun miss fire like that with me before."

Jim's own gun was ready again in short order, but there was a queer questioning look stealing into his face, and he said,

"Take mine, Charley; I'll look into that business."

Charley traded guns, and stood anxiously watching for another rabbit, while Jim "looked into" both barrels of the offending piece, and tried them with the ramrod.

"Got enough in 'em; no mistake about that. Guess I'd better draw the charges."

There was a corkscrew on the end of the ramrod for that sort of thing, and in a moment more Jim had a wad out of each barrel.

"Hullo! Powder? I declare! Why, Charley, you've put your ammunition in wrong end first. You might have cracked caps on that thing all day. Your shot's all at the bottom."

"Is that so? Well, you see, I never used that kind of a gun before, and—"

"Here comes Nap! Big rabbit. There's a chance for you. Take him on the run."

He tried. That is, he raised Jim's gun, and blazed away with one barrel, but all the harm he did that rabbit was to knock down a whole bunch of bright red mountain-ash berries from a branch twenty feet above him.

"Quick, Charley! Your other barrel. He's turning on Nap, around those sumac bushes."

Charley had held his gun a little loosely, and it had given him a smart kick in consequence; but he saw what Jim meant, and his reputation as a sportsman was at stake. He knew, too, that Jim was trying his best not to laugh, and he was determined to get that rabbit.

"Bow-ow-ow-wow!"

Rabbit and dog seemed somehow to come within range of that gun at the same instant, just as it went off. It was a grand good thing for old Nap that his master's city cousin aimed so high, and that the gun kicked again. As it was, the astonished dog was now making the snow fly in a whirl, as he dashed around in it after the tip of his tail, where one of the little leaden pellets had struck him.

That was only for a moment, however, and then he came gravely marching across the crust, and looked up in the faces of the boys, one after the other, as much as if he was asking, "Which of you was green enough to take me for a rabbit?"

He had not been very badly hurt, except, perhaps, in his sense of justice; but now Charley suddenly gave a shout, and sprang forward.

"I hit him! I hit him!"

"Fact," said Jim; "so you did. Come here, Nap. Poor fellow! How's your old tail now?"

Charley was back in a twinkling with his own rabbit and the one Jim had killed, but there was a wide difference between them. There was shot enough in the latter to have killed half a dozen, while all the mark they could find on Charley's game was one little spot at the roots of his ears.

"So much for making the shot scatter. If I hadn't put in a double load of shot, you'd have lost 'em both."

"There wasn't but one," said Charley.

"I mean that rabbit and old Napoleon Bonaparte. Come on now. Your gun's all right. Let's try the other side of the swamp."

He pointed out a rabbit, sitting among some bushes, on the way, and Charley's gun went off finely, now that the powder had been put in first.

"Don't you ever shoot them when they're sitting still, Jim?"

"No; and you won't when you're used to it. There's one coming for me. I'll take him as he goes by."

Nap was entirely safe this time. Indeed, he seemed inclined all the rest of that morning to do his rabbit-hunting at a somewhat unsociable distance from his friends.

There were plenty of rabbits in the swamp, and the boys were more than a little proud of their success, especially Charley; but when the time came for going home, it was curious how ready they both were to go. So was Napoleon Bonaparte. Truth to tell, it had been hard work, and the boys declared the rabbit a remarkably heavy beast for his size, by the time they reached home with their game.

THE AWAKENING.

BY M. E.

Down all the rugged mountain-slopes,
  Through all the mossy dells,
There comes a gentle purling sound,
  Like peals of fairy bells.

A tinkling, rippling, gurgling song
  Is borne on every breeze;
Mysterious whispers seem to stir
  The grim old forest trees.

The tiny grasses wave their hands
  And gayly nod their heads
To lazy buds, still half asleep
  In cosy winter beds.

And now the riotous sunbeams come;
  They draw the curtains wide;
Nor leave untouched the smallest nook
  Where sleepy buds may hide.

"Awake! awake!" the whole Earth cries:
  "King Winter's reign is past;
His crown he yields to his fairest child,
  And Spring is Queen at last."

SALT AND ITS VALUE.

ALL our young readers know the value of that familiar and useful substance, salt, which enters so largely into our daily wants, and is so essential to our existence. Formerly prisoners in Holland were kept from the use of salt; but this deprivation produced such terrible diseases that this practice was abolished. The Mexicans, in old times, in cases of rebellion, deprived entire provinces of this indispensable commodity, and thus left innocent and guilty alike to rot to death.

This mineral is frequently mentioned in the Bible. The sacrifices of the Jews were all seasoned with salt, and we read of a *covenant of salt*. Salt was procured by the Hebrews from the hills of salt which lie about the southern extremity of the Dead Sea, and from the waters of that sea, which overflow the banks yearly, and leave a deposit of salt both abundant and good.

Among ancient nations salt was a symbol of friendship and fidelity, as it is at present among the Arabs and other Oriental people. In some Eastern countries, if a guest has tasted salt with his host, he is safe from all enemies, even although the person receiving the salt may have committed an injury against his entertainer himself.

Among the common people all over Scotland, a new house, or one which a new tenant was about to enter, was always sprinkled with salt by way of inducing "good luck." Another custom of a curious nature once prevailed in England and other countries in reference to salt. Men of rank formerly dined at the same table with their dependents and servants. The master of the house and his relations sat at the upper end, where the floor was a little raised. The persons of greatest consequence sat next, and all along down the sides, toward the bottom of the table, the servants were placed according to their situations. At a certain part of the table was placed a large salt vat, which divided the superior from the inferior classes. Sitting *above* the salt was the mark of a gentleman or man of good connections, while to sit *beneath* it showed a humble station in society.

Salt is found in greater or less quantities in almost every substance on earth, but the waters of the sea appear to have been its first great magazine. It is found there dissolved in certain proportions, and two purposes are thus served, namely, the preservation of that vast body of waters, which otherwise, from the innumerable objects of animal and vegetable life within it, would become an insupportable mass of corruption, and the supplying of a large proportion of the salt we require in our food, and for other purposes. The quantity of salt contained in the sea (according to the best authorities) amounts to *four hundred thousand billion* cubic feet, which, if piled up, would form a mass one hundred and forty miles long, as many broad, and as many high, or, otherwise disposed, would cover the whole of Europe, islands, seas, and all, to the height of the summit of Mont Blanc, which is about sixteen thousand feet in height.

If salt, however, were only to be obtained from the sea, the people who live on immense continents would have great difficulty in supplying themselves with it; and here you see how kindly Providence watches over the comfort of human creatures, for nature has provided that the sea, on leaving those continents, all of which were once overspread with it, should deposit vast quantities of salt, sufficient to provide for the necessities of the inhabitants of those parts. In some places the salt is exposed on the surface of the ground in a glittering crust several inches thick; in others, thicker layers have been covered over with other substances, so that salt now requires to be dug for like coal or any other mineral. Salt is found in this last shape in almost every part of the world; though in the vast empire of China it is so scarce that it is smuggled into that country in large quantities.

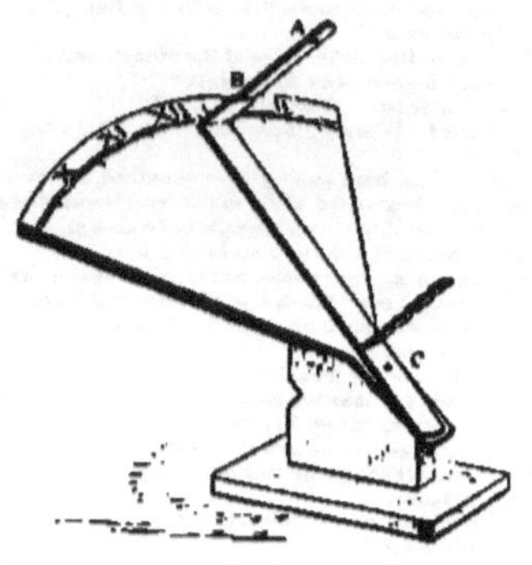

A SUN-DIAL.

OUR young friends would, we doubt not, like to know how to make a sun-dial that will give the time very accurately. Common sun-dials depend on the shadow of a post, which is thick and heavy, and affords only a very rough idea of the time. But the one we are going to tell them about will show the time as precisely as a clock. And it is quite easy to make. It has, in the first place, a *face* set up slanting on a pedestal. The proper slant answers to the latitude of the place. At and near New York it should be about forty-one degrees from the perpendicular, or a little more than half upright. The *face* is divided into hour spaces, just like the face of a clock, but the whole circle is not used. A semicircle is all that the sun can traverse, except in the long days of summer. The fourth part of a circle is about all that can be used in ordinary windows. It will answer for the hours between nine o'clock and three. It is divided into six equal parts for the hour spaces, and each of these is subdivided for the minutes. If the radius of the circle be one foot, the minute spaces will be about one-sixteenth of an inch, or about the same as on the *face* of a watch. The dividing is easily done with a pair of compasses, a ruler, and a sharp lead-pencil.

Now we will explain the indicator. It is made of three pieces—a base and two uprights. The base is fifteen inches long, three wide, and three-quarters of an inch thick. The uprights are of the same thickness, and about seven inches high. They are morticed into the base, and have the shape shown in the picture. A hole half an inch in diameter is bored through the upright at A, and another at B. Over each of these holes pieces of tin are tacked, with a little hole in the centre about as large as a pin's head. When the sun-dial is placed in position, the sun shines through these holes, and makes a little bright circle on the other upright. The upper hole, A, is for summer, when the sun is high, and the lower one, B, for winter. The indicator is pivoted by a large screw to the centre, C, of the *face*, so that it can be turned round like the hand of a clock. At the upper end of the indicator a little pointer is fastened directly over the scale of hours and minutes. A needle, or a pin with the head cut off, makes a good pointer.

After the sun-dial is made, the next thing is to set it in its proper position, which is so that when the pointer is at XII. it will also be directed exactly south, while the lower end of the indicator is to the north. Then, at noon by sun time, the sun will make its little bright circle exactly in the middle of the lower upright. A line should be drawn up and down to show the middle; then this line will cut the sun circle equally in two. To find out the time before and after noon, the indicator is moved so that the sun circle will fall on the same middle line, and the pointer will show the time. This sun time differs somewhat from clock time. The difference for every day in the year is given by the almanacs, and very exactly by the Nautical Almanac. This difference being added or subtracted, makes known the true clock time. Thus, for the 1st of March, clock time is twelve minutes faster than sun time. Hence noon by the sun-dial is just that much later than noon by the clock. Any of our readers who have a little mechanical skill can make a sun-dial, on the plan described, that, when put in proper position, will be more reliable than the best of clocks, and that will be found a convenient means of setting them right. But don't despise the clocks; for very likely you will have to resort to one in order to get the sun-dial in position; and then, too, remember that the sun does not shine all the while, but is very fond of hiding behind clouds.

—

(Begun in No. 18 of Harper's Young People, March 2.)

ACROSS THE OCEAN; OR, A BOY'S FIRST VOYAGE.

A True Story.

BY J. O. DAVIDSON.

Chapter V.

FRANK AND THE CAPTAIN.

AUSTIN was still the centre of an admiring group, when a deep voice made itself heard from behind.

"Say, mates, ye'd better let the lad git on some dry duds, 'stead o' fussin' over him that way; why, he's as wet as the lee scuppers."

Frank recognized old Herrick, the quartermaster, who had roused him from his nap on the coil of rope the first night of the voyage.

"Come, youngster," pursued the old man, "hurry up and git a dry shirt on. What d'ye look so queer for?—hain't ye got nary one?"

Frank explained that his bag and bundle had "disappeared somehow," before they had been two days at sea.

"Stolen, I reckon," growled a sailor; "but 'twarn't nobody on the fo'c'stle as done it, anyhow. It's been some o' them blessed firemen—thievin' wharf-rats every one!"

"Ay, they're the boys for hookin' things," added another. "Last v'y'ge I made, there was a fireman we called Sandy, as I'd seen hangin' around my sea-chest just afore I missed suthin'. So I fixed a fish-hook to the lock, and nex' day Mr. Sandy had a precious sore finger somehow; and from that day for'ard we never called him nothing but 'Sandy Hook'. (A loud laugh from the rest applauded the joke.) But I'll lend the younker a shirt, willin'."

"And I."

"And I."

"Well, look'ee here, boys," said old Herrick, "let's give him poor Allen's chest and kit. He'll never need it more, poor fellow, and I've heerd him say he'd nary relative ashore. Seems to me Frank's the one as ought to have it: what say ye all?"

All agreed, and the drowned man's chest was pulled out and rummaged. Out came caps, jackets, trousers, shirts, sea-boots. Out came three or four letters and a photograph, which were laid aside to be handed over to the purser; and lastly, out came a small, well-thumbed Bible of old-fashioned look, which Herrick (after eying it thoughtfully for a moment) put into his own pocket.

"Whew! who'd ha' thought Allen kep' a Bible?"

"I have seen him spellin' in it, though, once and again; but he always shet it up when anybody come nigh him."

"Well, well, 'twarn't it as brought him his ill luck, anyhow. Now, young un, let's see how the duds fit you."

But, as might have been expected, everything was "fallen too big," and bagged about him in such a way as to make one of the men remark, with a grin, that "if he carried so much loose canvas, he'd founder in the first squall."

"We must take in a reef or two, then, that's all," said Herrick. "Bear a hand, my boy, and we'll soon turn you out ship-shape."

To work went the two amateur tailors, while Frank seized the chance of taking a good look at his new friend. The old tar was certainly well worth looking at. Tall, broad-shouldered, active, with his brown hard face framed in iron-gray hair and beard—a pleasant twinkle in the keen blue eyes that looked out from beneath his bushy brows, and a kindly smile flickering over his rugged features ever and anon, like sunshine upon a bare moor—he looked the very model of one of those sturdy old sea-dogs who held their own against England's stoutest "hearts of oak" in the old days of '76

FRANK AND OLD HERRICK.

As he worked on, making stitches which, though they would have horrified a fashionable tailor, were at least strong and durable, he began to pour forth a series of yarns, a tithe of which would "set up" any novelist for life. Fights with West-Indian pirates; hair-breadth escapes from polar icebergs; picturesque cruises among the Spice Islands; weary days and nights in a calm off the African coast, on short allowance of water, with the burning sun melting the very pitch out of the seams—were "reeled off" in unbroken succession, while Frank listened open-mouthed, and more than once forgot his tailoring altogether.

But the stroke of a bell overhead broke in upon the talk.

"My watch on deck," said the old man, springing up as nimbly as a boy. "Now, lad, slip on them togs agin. Ay, now you look all a-taunto."

Frank was indeed improved. His shore clothes, which, with grease, coal-dust, tar, salt-water, and the rents made by the fight with Monkey, were (as the boatswain said) "not fit for a 'spectable scarecrow to wear of a Sunday," were exchanged for a blue flannel shirt and a pair of trim white canvas trousers. A neat black silk handkerchief was knotted around his neck, and his battered "stiff-rim" replaced by a jaunty sailor cap.

"Hello, youngster! the cap'n wants yer," shouted a sailor, as Frank appeared on deck.

"You're in luck, my boy," said Herrick. "Keep a stiff upper lip, but don't speak unless you're spoken to, and then say as little as you can."

On entering the captain's room Frank found the latter busied in "pricking out" the ship's course on the chart, and was thus able to survey him at leisure. Captain Gray's plain black suit and standing collar, his grayish-brown hair, close-cut whiskers, and mild expression, made him look more like a preacher than like one who had led a forlorn hope over the ruins of Fort Sumter, and had captured, single-handed, the ringleader of a dangerous mutiny in the West Indies. This mutiny, however, had occurred aboard another vessel, for nothing of the sort had ever been heard of on his own. The crew "froze to him" in all he did or said; and any "sea-lawyer" who tried to breed a disturbance soon found the *Arizona* too hot for him.

"Talk 'bout the officers as ye like," was the constant saying on the forecastle, "but nary word agin the old 'deacon.'"

For, strange to say, Captain Gray was a deacon when ashore, and not a few of his best hands were members of the old white church at home in Nantucket.

His room was like himself—simple, but perfectly orderly. A neat bed, with snow-white coverlet and pillow; a little cupboard beside it, containing a pitcher and wash-basin; a Bible in a neat wooden rack on a small table; a rifle, cutlass, and two revolvers, all bright and clean, hanging on the wall above it; a cabinet of books, mostly works of travel and navigation; several chairs, on one of which lay the captain's coat and cap; and a curtain along the wall, above which appeared various articles of clothing hung on pegs.

Presently the captain looked up, and after "figuring" a moment on a slip of paper, touched a bell. Instantly a panel flew open, and a hoarse voice shouted, "Ay, ay, sir!"

"How's her head now, quartermaster?"

"S.E. by S., sir."

"All right; keep her so."

"Ay, ay, sir;" and the panel closed again.

Then, for the first time, the captain appeared to become aware of Frank's presence, and bending forward, fixed upon him a look that seemed to read his very soul. It was a proverb with the crew of the *Arizona* that "no rogue could ever face the old man's eye;" and although

THE CAPTAIN'S ROOM.

he was never known to utter an oath or unseemly word, his very glance had more effect than any amount of bluster and bullying.

"So you're the boy who oiled the outboard bearing to-day? I hear you've been fighting with Monkey. We won't say any more about that now, but don't let it happen again. Can you read and write?"

"Yes, sir."

"Is this your handwriting on the ship's articles, and in the store-room account-book?"

"Yes, sir."

"Have you studied arithmetic? Well, then, work me out this example."

Austin obeyed.

"Right," said the captain, glancing at the result. "After this, Mr. Hurst (the chief engineer) will put you in the place of the oiler who was lost this morning. The fifty dollars reward is in the purser's hands, where I advise you to leave it till you really need it. You may go now. Good-night."

"What! couldn't they make ye nothin' better'n a bottle-iler?" growled old Herrick, on hearing the result of the interview; for, like a true sailor of the old school, he abominated everything connected with "that 'ere new-fangled steam." "A *sailor's* what you're cut out for, and a sailor's what every man ought to be as can. Howsomdever, there's no fear but you'll git on well enough with the old man; for he's a good feller, if ever there was one. We shipped together for our first v'y'ge, him and me, when we were no bigger'n you are; and if we ever part comp'ny agin, 'twon't be *my* fault, anyhow."

[TO BE CONTINUED.]

HOUSEHOLD PETS.

AN amusing story is told of a modern puss which sailed across the seas. A Polynesian missionary took a cat with him to the island of Raratonga, but Puss, not liking her new abode, fled to the mountains. One of the new converts, a priest who had destroyed his idol, was one night sleeping on his mat, when his wife, who sat watching beside him, was terribly alarmed by the sight of two small fires gleaming in the doorway, and by the sound of a plaintive and mysterious voice. Her blood curdling with fear, she awoke her husband, with wifely reproaches on his folly in having burned his god, who was now come to be avenged on them.

The husband, opening his eyes, saw the same glaring lamps, heard the same dismal sound, and, in an agony of fright, began to recite the alphabet, by way of an incantation against the powers of darkness. The cat on hearing the loud voices felt as much alarm as she had caused, and fled in the darkness, leaving the worthy pair much relieved.

A short while afterward Puss took up her quarters in a retired temple, where her "mews" struck terror into the breasts of the priest and worshippers who came with offerings to the gods. They fled in all directions, shouting, "A monster from the deep! a monster from the deep!" to return with a large body of their companions in full war array, with spears, clubs, and shields, and faces blackened with charcoal. The cat, however, was too nimble for them, and escaped through the midst of their ranks, sending these brave warriors flying in every direction.

That night, however, Puss, tired of her lonely life, foolishly entered a native hut, and creeping beneath the coverlet under which the whole family were lying, fell asleep. Her purring awoke the owner of the hut, who procured the help of some other models of valor, and with their assistance murdered poor Pussy in her tranquil and confiding slumbers.

But cats, though thus at first misunderstood, were afterward welcomed in Raratonga, which was devastated with a plague of rats. The missionaries imported a cargo consisting of pigs, cocoa-nuts, and cats.

A youthful clerk who was once appointed to make out an invoice of shipments on a Mississippi steamer, was perplexed by the item of "Four boxes of tam-cats." On inquiry, the mystery was solved. "Why," said the indignant sutler, "that means four boxes of *tomato catsup*. Don't you understand abbreviations?"

An amusing reason is given for cats washing their faces after a meal. A cat caught a sparrow, and was about to devour it, but the sparrow said,

"No gentleman eats till he has first washed his face."

The cat, struck with this remark, set the sparrow down, and began to wash his face, on which the sparrow flew away. This vexed Pussy extremely, and he said,

"As long as I live I will eat first, and wash my face afterward."

Which all cats do even to this day.

Here is another cat and sparrow fable:

"I wonder," said a sparrow, "what the eagles are about, that they don't fly away with the cats! And now I think of it, a civil question can not give offense." So the sparrow finished her breakfast, went to the eagle, and said: "May it please your Majesty, I see you and your race fly away with the birds and the lambs, that do no harm. But there is not a creature so malignant as a cat; she prowls about our nests, eats up our young, and bites off our own heads. She feeds so daintily that she must be herself good eating. Why do you not feed upon a cat?"

"Ah!" said the eagle, "there is sense in your question. I had a worm here this morning, asking me why I did not breakfast upon sparrows. Do I see a morsel of worm's skin on your beak, my child?"

The sparrow cleaned his bill upon his bosom, and said, "I should like to see the worm that made that complaint."

"Come forward, worm," the eagle said. But when the worm appeared, the sparrow snapped him up and ate him, after which he went on with his argument against the cats.

HOW HE BROUGHT HIS ENGINE DOWN.

BY CHARLES BARNARD.

IT was one of the most difficult parts of the whole line. A range of high hills lay directly north and south, and the railroad ran nearly east and west; that is, the stations on each side of the range of hills lay east and west, but to cross the range the road wound about in the most complicated and curious fashion. At the summit of the range, where the line crossed, there was a water tank, and a cross-over switch, and a house for the line-man. This place was eight miles from the station, on the east side, as the crow flies; by rail it was seventeen miles, a steady up grade all the way. All the west-bound trains had to have help in getting over this seventeen-mile grade, and for this service there were several pushing-engines kept there to go behind the trains, and help them up the grade. When the top of the grade was reached, the trains went on, for there were no passengers to be taken or left there. The line-man's house was the only house within five miles, and all the rugged hills round about were covered with deep woods. The pushing-engines that came up the grade usually stopped for a moment or two for water, took the cross-over switch, and ran back on the down track without using steam, as it was down grade all the way. Of course all east-bound trains, both freight and passenger, came down without help, and, in fact, without using steam, except to get a good start at the top.

One day a long freight train moving west came to the foot of the grade, and took on an extra engine to help it up the hill. This extra engine stood on a siding, and when the freight had passed, it drew out on the main line, and took its place behind the train. It was not coupled to the train, as its duty was merely to push behind. There were about thirty-five cars in the train, chiefly empty grain cars going west, and with a "caboose" behind. There were half a dozen brakemen and the conductor scattered along the train on top of the cars. All these points you must remember, to understand what happened soon after.

The line for the seventeen miles up the grade is very crooked, with several high embankments and very sharp turns. Not a nice bit of road for a fast run with a heavy train. Nearly all the distance is through thick woods, so that the brave engineer's deeds were not seen by any one save the few men who were on the train, and in the greatest peril.

The two engines and long line of cars crept slowly up the grade, and without accident, till almost at the top. The forward engine reached the top, and kept straight on; there was no need to stop; and when the train fairly passed the summit, and began to descend the grade on the western side of the hills, the pushing-engine merely stopped, and was left behind. Just then something very singular happened. The engineer reversed his engine, and started to run back to the cross-over switch that was just below. He intended to take the down track, and return to the station, seventeen miles below. The station-master was at the switch, and had already opened it. Suddenly the fireman gave a cry, and the engineer looked out his forward window to see what had happened. The train was still in sight up the line, but it was moving down instead of up. It had broken apart. A coupling had given way, and some of the cars were rolling down the grade right on to his engine. He could see the men on top waving their hands for him to get out of the way.

THE HOBBY-HORSE REGIMENT.

WHEN the Thirty Years' War was finally brought to a termination by the treaty of peace of Westphalia, which was concluded at Nuremberg in 1560, the authorities of that place ordered in commemoration public rejoicings of various kinds—banquets, balls, fire-works, etc. But among all these public diversions, none was more distinguished for singularity and originality, and perhaps childish simplicity, than the procession of lads and boys on sticks or hobby-horses. Thus mounted, they rode, regularly divided into companies, through the streets, and halted before the hotel of the Red Horse, where was staying the Imperial Commissioner, Duc D'Amalfi.

The Duke was so pleased with the novel cavalcade that he requested a repetition of the same procession at an early day of the following week, which they performed in much larger numbers. On arriving before his hotel, the Duke distributed amongst them small square silver medals which he had in the interval caused to be struck. The coin represented on the obverse a boy on a hobby-horse with whip in hand, and the year 1560 was inscribed in the centre, while the reverse represented the double eagle and armorial bearings of Austria, with the inscription, "Vivat Ferdinandus III., Rom. Imp. vivat!"

THE HOBBY-HORS[E]

THE LITTLE SWISS MAN.

THERE was once a little Swiss man who had a mind and will of his own. He was one inch high, and carved out of wood by the busy people of Brienz, in the long cold winter season. Perhaps the bit of wood out of which he was cut was unusually hard, and even knotted; but certainly he had more character than his companions, the pretty birds perched on boxes, the deer and chamois supporting vases, and all the trinkets made in that town, where the wooden hous[es] with projecting roofs, and balconies filled with flowers, on th[e] border of Lake Brienz, are precisely like the tiny toy mansi[ons] in shop windows.

When he was finished, the little Swiss man was very proud of himself. He wore gaiters, a jacket, a broad straw hat

[illegible] ON THE MARCH

[illegible] carried a creel on his back [illegible] mountain, laden with butter, cheese [illegible] The contents of the workshop were scattered like a handful of leaves in the wind. The chamois were sent to Paris and London, the little birds on the boxes journeyed as far as Russia

"I am sure to be much admired wherever I go," said the little Swiss man, with a smile, which was none the less conceited because it was a wooden one.

Soon he found himself in the window of a shop at Geneva, and he was not immediately bought, to his own surprise. However, he was in very good company, although he took upon himself to look down on his companions, and he only an inch high!

The shop was located on the Rue du Rhone, but the small window where the toys were exposed opened on the rear. The river Rhone, of a beautiful color, as pure as ice, quitting the Lake Leman above, swept down under the bridges past this window, dividing the city of Geneva. Had the little Swiss man possessed any eyes except for his own importance, he would have found the view from his shelf interesting. On the right the Isle Rousseau was visible, where the ducks and swans live; opposite, a foot-bridge crossed the rushing Rhone; and below were the tall old houses of the island, with plants in the windows, terminating in a clock tower. Along the river margin the Geneva washer-women toiled all day, not like those of America, scrubbing at a steaming wash-tub, but under long sheds which appeared to float on the surface of the stream, and dipping their linen in the flowing water.

The little Swiss man could not understand why he was not bought immediately. To be sure, the next shop displayed sparkling heaps of crystal, veined agate, [illegible] he found himself better than all. Children [illegible] the pane and laughed with delight, pointing out [illegible] objects. Our hero took all this admiration to himself as his due. On the same shelf was a game, wearing top-boots, the Ulster of a tourist, a bag fastened over his shoulder with a boy in India rubber, from Nuremberg; a beautiful paste-board theatre, with a lady of blue paper advancing from a side scene; tiny Swiss houses in boxes; two rope-dancers hanging over their cord; balls and tops. The shelf below held the most tempting dishes, representing cakes and dessert, in china, ever placed on the table of a doll-house; wax babies rocking in cradles; tiny lamps; sewing-machines; miniature goats and cows.

The little Swiss man observed especially a large bear of Berne, wearing a cotton night-cap with a red tassel, and a white shirt collar, who carried a hand-organ, and a good St. Bernard dog, with the flask suspended about his throat, ready to help the poor wanderers lost in the snow. Beyond was an interesting company of monkeys on a music-box, some playing harps, others scraping violins in obedience to the head monkey, who stood in the attitude of a leader of the orchestra, wearing a black coat with long tails. The vain little Swiss man fancied the passers-by paused only to admire him.

Night came, and the master of the shop closed the door, placed shutters before the show-cases, and seated himself at his desk. The little window in the rear was still uncovered, and revealed the light on the desk where the master wrote. He heard the scratching of his pen on the paper, and the patter of rain-drops outside, for the night was stormy. There was another sound in the shop, softer than fall of the rain, and finer than chirp of a cricket, or humming sound of a mosquito: the toys in the window were talking together.

"I have been here for a month, and everybody says I am too dear at five francs," said the goose in top-boots.

"How could you expect to sell, when I am in the same window?" growled the bear.

"What do you say?" cackled the goose, indignantly.

"He is only a bear," said one of the rope-dancers, cutting a caper.

"Do you know who I am?" retorted the bear, with dignity. "I am the Bear of Berne. You will find me on the shield of the city, and kept in a pit by the citizens to this day."

"What is the use of boasting?" interposed the St. Bernard dog, pettishly. "The bears of Berne live in idleness; they walk about in a pit all day, or stand on their hind-legs begging for nuts. A St. Bernard dog is better employed, I should hope. We save the travellers in the snow who lose their way on the great St. Bernard mountain. If you wish to see the dog Barry, who saved fifteen lives, look for him in the Berne Museum, stuffed, and kept in a glass case."

The bear was very cross at this reply. He pulled his cotton night-cap over his right eye, which gave him a very savage appearance, and turned the handle of his organ as if his life depended on it.

"I am not Swiss; I am a German," said the Nuremberg fat boy, puffing out his India rubber cheeks.

"Hear him!" cried the lady made of blue paper, on the stage of the little theatre—"hear the rubber boy boast of being a German, when there are French toys about!"

At this all the little babies made of pink wax, in the cradles, laughed; and even the goats shook their heads.

At this moment something happened. A boy pressed his face against the pane, and stared at the toys. Crack! —a stone hit the glass, and the boy ran away. The wind and the rain swooped in together, upsetting the theatre, and knocking the dolls about. The master hastened to close the shutter.

The little Swiss man had fallen outside.

In the morning a porter passing by kicked the tiny bit of wood toward the parapet, and the next comer sent it spinning into the river.

"Pride goes before a fall," said the St. Bernard dog.

"Why did he feel so superior to the rest of us?" inquired the goose.

"It was all in the grain of the wood," said the leading monkey.

Below Geneva the Rhone joins the Arve, and the two rivers remain distinct for a long while—the Rhone like a green ribbon, and the Arve whitened by glacier torrents. Here a poor boy was fishing. What he caught was the little Swiss man, bobbing along on the stream, and he took this prize to the stone cottage, his home.

"I am glad to be out of the water," thought our wooden hero. "All the same, I wish I was back in the shop window. Ah! I did not know gratitude, as the Edelweiss said."

THE CANARY'S MUSIC LESSON.

"Now teach me your song, Canary," said Maud with the roguish eyes.
"And when father comes home with mother, I'll give them such a surprise;
They'll think I am you, Canary, and wonder what set you free,
And nearly die a-laughing, when they find it is only me.
Teach me your song, Canary; I'll whistle it if I can;
Now open your throat, dear Tiptoe, and sing like a little man."

Tiptoe, the pretty fellow, cocked up his bright black eye,
As if to say, "Little mistress, it will do you no harm to try."
Then taking some slight refreshments, and polishing off his bill,
Broke into a rapture of singing that ended off with a trill;
And Maud, with her head bent forward, sat listening to his lay,
And fast as he sang, she whistled, till gathered the twilight gray.

Then she crept down to the parlor as quietly as a mouse;
The maids were in the kitchen, and no one else in the house.
And when the key in the doorway the dear little mischief heard,
She whistled away so sweetly, they thought it was surely the bird.
Hither and thither she flitted, behind the sofa and chairs;
Her mother cried, "Mercy, Edward! the bird! Is the cat down stairs?"

Wildly they stared around them, till, "It's me, it is me, papa!"
Said Maud, from her corner springing. Ah, then what a loud "Ha! ha!"
Rang through the room. Her father, convulsed, on the sofa sat.
Gravely appeared among them their sober old pussy cat.
Maud merrily laughed and shouted, "A cunning old cat like you—
To think you should mistake me for a little canary too!"

MODEL YACHT-BUILDING.

A SLOOP-YACHT.

teenths at the stern; the stern-post (*e t*) is laid off, and the outer line of the stern (*t f*); and finally the curved lines *a f* and *a r* are drawn, completing what is called the sheer plan.

In copying from the drawings it must be kept in mind that they are exactly one-fourth the full size, so that any distance taken from them with the dividers must be laid off four times on the block.

To copy the curved lines, their distance from some line, as A B or W L, is measured on each of the two-inch lines, by which a number of points on the curve are found, and a line drawn as nearly as possible through all of them by means of a flexible ruler, held in place by pins.

The block must now be cut away to the outline *a f t s r*, after which lines two inches apart are drawn on the top, the line A B drawn entirely around the block in the centre of the top, bottom, and ends, and Fig. 1 drawn on top, both halves being of course the same.

The block is next cut to the line *a b c d*, Fig. 1, the widest part being, not on deck, but along the line *c d*, as there is some "tumble home" from *b* to the stern.

The outline of the deck is *a b e f*, the stern being a segment of a circle of five inches radius.

A piece of thin board must be cut of the shape of Fig. 5 (which is half size), which is the widest part of the boat, and is fourteen inches from the bow, and by using it for a guide, both sides may be cut out exactly alike.

The stem piece, half an inch thick, and the stern-post, five-sixteenths of an inch, are sawed out, and tacked in place temporarily, and a wooden keel of the shape shown in Fig. 4 (marked "Lead Keel"), half an inch thick, tapering to five-sixteenths where it joins the stern-post, is fitted in between them.

The shaping of the hull may now be completed, using a gouge, spokeshave, and rasp, keeping the midship section for a guide, and running the curved surfaces smoothly and evenly into the sides of the keel, stern, and stem, the latter tapering to five-sixteenths of an inch forward.

The hole for the rudder-stock is next bored, one-fourth of an inch in diameter, and burned out with a moderately hot iron to five-sixteenths of an inch; then, should the stock swell when wet, it will not stick in the charred wood, but will still turn freely.

The keel, stem, and stern are removed, to avoid injury to them, and the line *l m n o p*, Fig. 1, is drawn, after which the wood inside is cut away with a large gouge or carving tool, until it is one-fourth of an inch thick, care being taken to have it all an even thickness, and not to cut through at any point, and also to leave the wood solid around the rudder-hole.

After the hollowing out is completed, a rabbet one-eighth of an inch wide and deep is cut to receive the deck, its outer line being *g h i k*, Fig. 1. Then a light deck beam is set in amidships, the mast step put in, and the inside of the hull and the bottom of the deck painted. The deck is of pine, one-eighth of an inch thick, and after being cut out should have lines scratched in with the compasses three-eighths of an inch from each edge to represent the water-ways, and parallel lines one-fourth of an inch apart scratched in to represent the joints of the deck plank.

Now the deck is laid and tacked down, and the joints painted, and calked if needed, the stem and stern-post replaced permanently, and the bowsprit screwed to the deck and stem.

The length of the bowsprit is eight and a half inches from the point *a*, Fig. 4, to the outer end, three-sixteenths of an inch in diameter, and three inches from *a* to the inner end, where it is framed into the bitts, the inner end being half an inch square.

A piece (*x*, Fig. 4) is next fitted on deck at the stern, forming the after portion of the bulwarks, which on the sides are one-eighth of an inch thick, flaring out at the bow, where they are nailed to the bowsprit, and tumbling in aft, where they are nailed to the piece *x*, a strip one-eighth of an inch thick (shown in Fig. 5) being first tacked to the deck, and the bulwarks nailed against it. Small brads should be used in nailing.

The rail is of walnut or mahogany, one-fourth by three-thirty-seconds of an inch, nailed on top of the bulwarks, and running out on the bowsprit to a point (Fig. 3).

For a sailing model a leaden keel of about two pounds is needed, a mould being made in plaster of Paris from the wooden pattern, and the melted lead poured in, after which it is smoothed with a plane. It is put on temporarily, and the boat, when rigged, put in the water; then enough may be planed off to make her trim properly, and the keel put on permanently.

The mast is twenty-one inches from deck, where it is half an inch in diameter, to cap, where it is a quarter of an inch square, and the topmast is eleven inches long, projecting eight inches above the lower mast.

The boom is twenty-two inches long, fitted to the mast by wire staples; and the gaff, fourteen inches long, has two jaws embracing the mast.

All spars are of yellow pine; the rigging is of fishing-line; and the blocks, five-sixteenths of an inch long, and the dead-eyes, one-fourth of an inch in diameter, are cut out of any hard wood. The lower one of each pair of dead-eyes has a wire looped around it, the other end being turned up, and driven into the boat's side, as in Fig. 5.

The upper end of each shroud has a loop spliced in, which goes over the mast-head, and a dead-eye is spliced into the lower end.

The forestay has a loop at the top, and runs through the bowsprit, forming a bobstay.

Davits are placed on each bow for the anchor, and two on each side for the boats, and a capstan stands just forward of the mast.

The sky-lights and companion-way are of mahogany, and with the decks, spars, and rail, are varnished, the rest of the hull being painted black, white, or green, and that

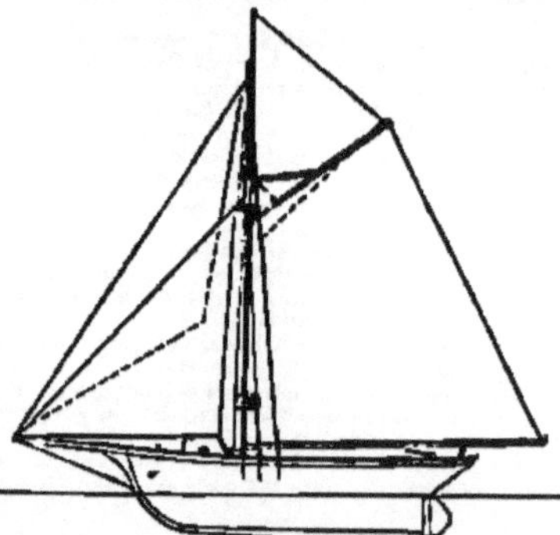

portion below the water-line being varnished, and dusted over with bronze powder, and when perfectly dry, varnished again, giving the appearance of metal sheathing.

The sails are of muslin or lawn, and are laced to the boom and gaff and to curtain-rings on the mast, or for the jibs the common "eye" used for dresses makes a capital jib hank, and will slip readily up and down the forestay.

The drawings show all the remaining details, and by following them carefully a handsome and able boat may be built.

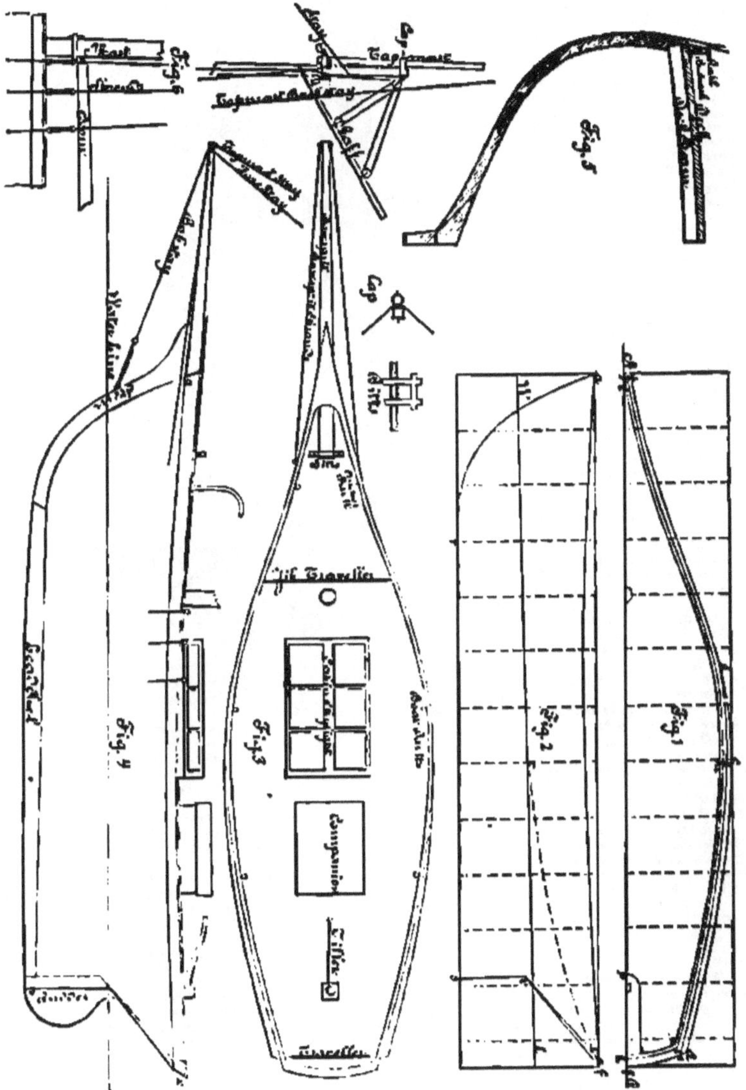
Fig. 1
Fig. 2
Fig. 3
Fig. 4
Fig. 5
Fig. 6
Companion
Tiller
Traveller
Jib Traveller
Water Line
Bobstay
Topmast
Gaff
Cap
Rudder

THE WHITE RABBITS AND THE TAR BABY

BY AGNES CARR.

TEN little white rabbits once lived on the edge of a wood, in a snug little hole at the foot of a tall tree; and they were as happy as ten rabbits could be, for every day a good little girl, who lived just back of the wood, brought them their breakfast of white rolls and brown gingerbread; and near by there was a beautiful stream of clear, sweet water, where they went to drink, and which sang a merry tune to them as it went rippling along.

But one morning when the little rabbits went for their water, they found the brook full of sticks and stones, and the water so muddy they could not drink it at all.

"Who has done this?" asked Frisky, the oldest and wisest of the rabbits.

"It was old Reynard the fox," said the brook; "and I am so choked up I can not sing."

So the little rabbits set to work to clear away the dirt and rubbish, and did it so well that before long the brook began its gay song again, and the water was clear enough for them to drink.

Next day, however, the stream was filled up again, and they had all the work to do over, until their little paws ached. So when, on the third morning, they found the water as muddy as ever, they all sat down on the bank and cried.

At last Frisky jumped up and said, "It is no use to cry over muddy water; but we must do something to punish this old rascal of a fox, and make him leave our brook alone."

"But what can we do?" asked his brothers and sisters.

"Come with me, and I will show you."

So the little rabbits followed Frisky to a pile of tar and pitch that some men had left; and out of it they made a black tar baby, which they set up on a rock close by the edge of the brook, with a piece of gingerbread in its mouth; and when night came, and the moon shone bright, they all hid behind a tree to see what would happen.

Pretty soon the old fox smelled the gingerbread, and spied the baby on the rock.

Then he came up close and said, "Little girl, little girl, give me a piece of your gingerbread, or I'll box your ears."

The baby did not answer, so the old fox climbed up on the rock, and boxed her on the ear; and his paw stuck so fast he could not pull it away again.

Then he said, "Little girl, little girl, give me a piece of your gingerbread, or I'll box you on the other ear."

The baby did not say a word, so he boxed her on the other ear, and his other paw stuck fast.

Then he said, "Little girl, little girl, give me a piece of your gingerbread, or I'll bite off your nose." Still the baby would not answer, so the fox bit at her nose, and his teeth stuck tight in the pitch, and he was almost choked with the tar.

The little rabbits then all came out and danced around the wicked old fox, saying, "Now you can't choke the pretty brook, for your own mouth is choked with tar!"

At last Frisky asked, "Now what shall we do with him?"

"Leave him to starve," said one. "Set fire to his tail," said another. And they all proposed something, except Snowflake, the youngest and prettiest of the family, who said nothing until Frisky turned to her and asked, "And what would you do?"

"I should let him go," replied Snowflake, "if he would promise not to trouble the water again."

"Snowflake is right," said Frisky; "he has been punished enough. We will let him go."

So they first loosened his mouth, and rubbed his teeth with butter to take off the tar, and when he had said three times, "Hope my tail may drop off if I ever hurt you or the brook again," they set his paws free, and he scampered off, and hid himself in his den in the wood.

And the little rabbits lived happy forever after.

OUR POST-OFFICE BOX

[illegible] by the wind.

Charlie Culbbery, Lizzie Brown, Blanche T. F., [illegible] write pretty stories of gold-fish, canaries, squirrels, goats, and other pets, which we sincerely regret we have no room to print.

PUZZLES FROM YOUNG CONTRIBUTORS.

No. 1.

[illegible]

No. 2.

[illegible]

No. 3.

[illegible]

No. 4.

[illegible]

No. 5.

[illegible]

No. 6.

[illegible]

ANSWERS TO PUZZLES IN No. 22.

[illegible]

[illegible]

Correct answers to puzzles are received from [illegible]

ADVERTISEMENTS.

HARPER'S YOUNG PEOPLE.

HARPER'S YOUNG PEOPLE will be issued every Tuesday, and may be had at the following rates—payable in advance, postage free:

SINGLE COPIES	$0 04
ONE SUBSCRIPTION, one year	1 50
FIVE SUBSCRIPTIONS, one year	7 00

Subscriptions may begin with any Number. When no time is specified, it will be understood that the subscriber wishes to commence with the Number issued after the receipt of order.

Remittances should be made by POST-OFFICE MONEY ORDER or DRAFT, to avoid risk of loss.

ADVERTISING.

The extent and character of the circulation of HARPER'S YOUNG PEOPLE will render it a first-class medium for advertising. A limited number of approved advertisements will be inserted on two inside pages at [illegible] cents per line.

Address

HARPER & BROTHERS,
Franklin Square, N. Y.

CANDY [illegible]

[illegible] MADISON STREET, CHICAGO.

KEEP YOUR BIRD IN HEALTH AND SONG by using SINGER'S PATENT GRAVEL PAPER. [illegible]

OUR CHILDREN'S SONGS.

Our Children's Songs. Illustrated. 8vo, Ornamental Cover, $1 00.

[illegible]

Published by HARPER & BROTHERS, New York.

[illegible]

CHILDREN'S PICTURE-BOOKS.

Square 4to, about 300 pages each, beautifully printed on Tinted Paper, embellished with many Illustrations, bound in Cloth, $1 50 per volume.

The Children's Picture-Book of Sagacity of Animals.

With Sixty Illustrations by HARRISON WEIR.

The Children's Bible Picture-Book.

With Eighty Illustrations, from Designs by [illegible]

The Children's Picture Fable-Book.

Containing One Hundred and Sixty Fables. With Sixty Illustrations by HARRISON WEIR.

The Children's Picture-Book of Birds.

With Sixty-one Illustrations by W. HARVEY.

The Children's Picture-Book of Quadrupeds and other Mammalia.

With Sixty-one Illustrations by W. HARVEY.

Published by HARPER & BROTHERS, New York.

Sent by mail, postage prepaid, to any part of the United States, on receipt of the price.

Old Books for Young Readers.

Arabian Nights' Entertainments.

The Thousand and One Nights; or, The Arabian Nights' Entertainments. Translated and Arranged for Family Reading, with Explanatory Notes, by E. W. LANE. [illegible] Illustrations by Harvey. 2 vols., 12mo, Cloth, $3 00.

Robinson Crusoe.

The Life and Surprising Adventures of Robinson Crusoe, of York, Mariner. By DANIEL DEFOE. With a Biographical Account of Defoe. Illustrated by Adams. Complete Edition. 12mo, Cloth, $1 50.

The Swiss Family Robinson.

The Swiss Family Robinson; or, Adventures of a Father and Mother and Four Sons on a Desert Island. Illustrated. 2 vols., 18mo, Cloth, $1 50.

The Swiss Family Robinson.—Continued: being a Sequel to the Foregoing. 2 vols., 18mo, Cloth, $1 50.

Sandford and Merton.

The History of Sandford and Merton. By THOMAS DAY. 18mo, Half Bound, 75 cents.

Published by HARPER & BROTHERS, New York.

Sent by mail, postage prepaid, to any part of the United States, on receipt of the price.

THE BOSSY PUZZLE.

RE-ARRANGE this picture so as to get a rustic group out of it. It is left to your own ingenuity to find out of what the group consists.

HOW TO MAKE INDIANS AND MICE.

BY BESSIE GUYTON.

FIGS and raisins seem very queer things to make an Indian of; but with a bit of wire, two figs, a handful of raisins, a few feathers, a dash of red and blue paint, a piece of red flannel, and two beads, a very savage old fellow can be produced.

Take a piece of fine wire fourteen or fifteen inches long, and draw it through a round, plump fig, pushing the fig to the middle; bend the wire together, and slip one large raisin on the double wire, close to the fig: now we have the head and neck. Spread the wires, and put through a fig larger than the head, for the body; fill both wires with raisins, for the legs, turning up the length of one for the feet; pass a piece of wire three or four inches long through the upper part of the body fig, and string both ends with raisins, which makes the arms, with a turn on the ends for the hands. Stick a few feathers around the head (a duster can be robbed for the purpose), set black or white beads for eyes (peas or beans have a very startling effect when large eyes are required). Make use of your paint-box for mouth, nose, brows, war-paint, etc., according to taste, pin a square of bright flannel about the shoulders, and you have an alarmingly startling likeness of a Pi-ute chief. A boy handy with his penknife can add a wooden tomahawk.

Apple seeds can be converted into the 'cutest little mice imaginable by following these directions:

With a fine needle draw black sewing silk through the pointed end of a good fat apple seed, and clip it short enough to appear a proper length for ears; then with a sharp penknife shave a narrow strip from the under or flat side of the seed, and turn it out at the other end for the tail. Now pass the needle through a white card, and through the seed near the tail, and again through the card, and draw down snugly to the card; repeat the same at the ear end, and the little chap stands on all fours, a very realistic mouse. Two or three tiny muslin bags, filled with cotton, marked, "The malt that lay in the house that Jack built," and sewed on one corner of the card, with half a dozen or so of these miniature pests headed toward it, furnish a very unique trifle, the making of which will give an hour's pleasure.

ANSWER TO THE PUZZLE OF THE TRAMP TRANSFORMED.

THE Tramp Puzzle given in YOUNG PEOPLE No. 21 is solved as follows: The dotted line *A B* indicates the cut you are to make with the scissors. The brim of the man's hat, his pipe, and his nose will fit into the spaces *C*, *D*, and *E*. The other piece off the hat represents the sea-cow. The few lines marked *F* represent the reflection of the sea-cow in the water.

Tricking Bruin.—The Lapps and Finns have an idea that when they kill an animal it has the power of haunting them if it condescends to take that advantage. When therefore they have slain a bear, they surround the body and utter loud lamentations, expressive of the deepest regret. Presently one of them asks, in pitying tones, "Who killed thee, poor creature? Who destroyed thy beautiful life?" Another of the party replies on behalf of the bear, "It was the wicked Swede who lives across the mountain!" And there is a chorus of "What a cruel deed! What a dreadful crime!"

HARPER'S YOUNG PEOPLE

AN ILLUSTRATED WEEKLY.

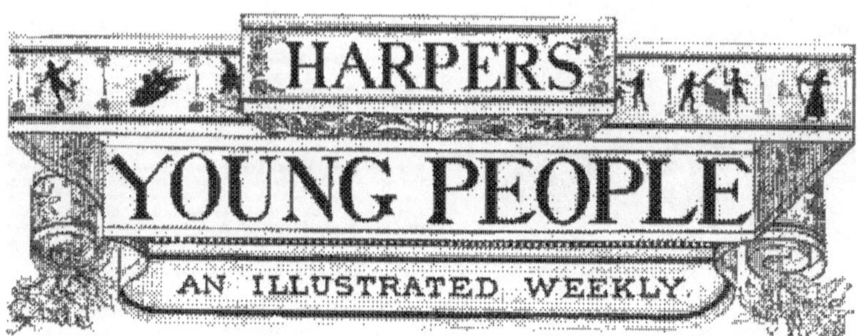

Vol. I.—No. 24. | Published by HARPER & BROTHERS, New York. | Price Four Cents.

Tuesday, April 13, 1880.

$1.50 per Year, in Advance.

MISS NANCY TAKES LEAVE OF THE OFFICERS.

NANCY HANSON'S PROJECT.

BY HOWARD PYLE.

IT was in the old Quaker town of Wilmington, Delaware, and it was the evening of the day on which the battle of Brandywine had been fought. The country people were coming into town in sledges, and in heavy low carts with solid wheels made of slices from great tree trunks, loaded with butter, eggs, milk, and vegetables; for the following day was market-day. Market-day came every Fourth-day (Wednesday) and every Seventh-day (Saturday). Then the carts drew up in a long line in Market Street, with their tail-boards to the sidewalk, and the farmers sold their produce to the town people, who jostled each other as they walked up and down in front of the market carts—a custom of street markets still carried on in Wilmington.

Friend William Stapler stopped, on his way to market

in his cart, at Elizabeth Hanson's house, in Shipley Street, to leave a dozen eggs and two pounds of butter, as he did each Tuesday and Friday evening. Elizabeth came to the door with a basket for half a peck of potatoes. William Stapler took off his broad-brimmed hat, and slowly rubbed his horny hand over his short-cut, stubbly gray hair.

"Ah! I tell thee, Lizabeth, they're a-doin' great things up above Chadd's Ford. I hearn th' canning a boomin' away all day to-day. Ah, Lizabeth, the world's people is a wicked people. They spare not the brother's blood when th' Adam is aroused within them. They stan' in slippery places, Lizabeth."

"Does thee think they're fighting, William?"

"Truly I think they are. Ah! I tell thee, Lizabeth, they're differen' 'n when I was young. Then we only feared the Injuns, 'n' now it's white men agin white men. They tuck eight young turkeys of mine, 'n' only paid me ten shillin' fer 'em."

"But, oh, William, I do hope they're not fighting! I expect my son-in-law, Captain William Bellach, and his friend Colonel Tilton, will stop here on their way to join General Washington; and they may arrive to-night."

"Ah, Lizabeth, I've lifted up my voice in testimony agin the young men goin' to the wars an' sheddin' blood. 'F a man diggeth a pit an' falleth into it himself, who shall help him out thereof? Half a peck o' potatoes, did thee say, Lizabeth?"

During the evening rumors became more exciting, and it was said that the Americans had been defeated, and were retreating toward Philadelphia. Late that night Captain Bellach and Colonel Tilton arrived at Elizabeth Hanson's house.

"I've heard the rumors, mother," said Captain Bellach. "I don't believe 'em; but even if there was a file of British at the door here, I would be too tired to run away from them."

Pretty Nancy Hanson spoke up. "But, Billy, they would not only send thee and thy friend to the hulks if they caught thee, but they might be rude to us women were they to find thee here."

"Yes, sister-in-law, if I thought there was any danger, I would leave instantly; but the British, even if they have beaten us, will be too tired to come here to-night."

"I agree with my friend Will, Mistress Nancy," said Colonel Tilton. "Moreover, our horses are too tired to take us farther to-night."

About two o'clock in the morning the silence of the deserted streets of the town was broken by a rattling and jingling of steel, the heavy, measured tread of feet, and sharp commands given in a low voice.

Nancy Hanson awakened at the noise, and jumping out of bed, ran to the window and looked out into the moon-lit street beneath. A file of red-coated soldiers were moving by toward the old Bull's Head Tavern. The cold moonlight glistened on their gun-barrels and bayonets as they marched. Nancy ran to her mother's room and pounded vigorously on the door.

"Mother! mother! waken up!" she cried; "the British are come to town, sure enough!"

The family were soon gathered around the dull light of a candle, the gentlemen too hastily awakened to have their hair en queue, the ladies in short gowns and petticoats; Elizabeth Hanson wore a great starched night-cap perched high upon her head.

"You were right, sister-in-law," said Captain Bellach, "and I was wrong. The best thing we can do now is to march out and take our chances."

"So say I," assented the Colonel.

"It's all well enough for thee, Billy, to talk of marching out and taking thy chances," said Nancy; "thee has thy black citizen's dress; but Colonel Tilton is in uniform."

"True; I forgot."

"It does not matter," said the Colonel.

"Yes, but it does," cried Nancy. "Stay now until morning, and I think I can get thee citizen's clothes. I have a project, too, to get thee off. For mother's sake, though, we must hide thy uniform, for if it is found here, she will be held responsible. Billy, thee will have to go with thy friend back to the bedroom and bring us his things as soon as he can take them off. Thee must lie abed, Colonel Tilton."

Nancy's plans were carried into execution. The bricks in one of the up-stairs fire-places were taken up, the sand beneath them removed, and the Colonel's uniform deposited in the vacant place, over which the bricks were carefully replaced.

In the gray of the morning Peggy Allison and Hannah Shallcross, on their way to market, each with a basket on her arm, met in front of Elizabeth Hanson's house. A company of soldiers had halted in Shipley Street, and their arms were stacked before Elizabeth's door. The red-coated soldiers were lounging and talking and smoking. Some officers sat around a fire near by warming their hands, for the morning was chill.

"'Tis a shame!" said Hannah Shallcross, vigorously—"'tis a shame to see these redcoats parading our streets as bold as a brass farthing. I only wish I was John Stedham the constable; I'd have 'em in the Smoke-House* or the stocks in a jiffy, I tell thee!"

She spoke loudly and sharply. A young British officer, who was passing, stepped briskly up, and tapped her on the arm.

"Madam," said he, "do you know that you are all prisoners? Be advised by me, and return quietly home until the town is in order."

However patriotic Hannah might be, she did not think it advisable to disregard this order, and both dames retreated in a flutter. As the young officer stood looking after them, the house door opposite him opened, and Nancy Hanson appeared upon the door-step. She had dressed herself carefully in her fine quilted petticoat and best flowered over-dress, and looked as pretty and fresh as an April morning.

"Friend," said she, in a half-doubtful, half-timid voice. The young officer whipped off his cocked hat, and bent stiffly, as you might bend a jackknife.

"Madam, yer servant," he answered. He spoke with a slight brogue, for he was an Irish gentleman.

"We have a friend with us," said Nancy, "who hath been compelled for a time to keep his bed. He was brought here last night on account of the battle, and was too weary to go further. Our neighbor Friend John Stapler, across the street, hath thick stockings, and I desire to get, if I can, a pair from him, as, thee may know, in cases of dropsy the legs are always cold. I am afraid to cross the street with these soldiers in it. Would thee escort me?"

"Madam, you do me infinite honor in desiring me escort," said the young officer, bowing more deeply than before; for Nancy was very pretty.

Friend John Stapler was a very strict Friend, and as such was inclined to favor the royalist side; still, he was willing to do a kindly turn for a neighbor. He was a wrinkled, weazened little man, whose face, with its pointed nose and yellowish color, much resembled a hickory nut.

"Hum-m-m!" ejaculated he, when Nancy, who had left the officer at the door, stated the case to him—"hum-m-m! thus it is that intercourse with the world's

* The Smoke-House was a small stone structure something like a sentry-box, only with an iron door and grated windows. In this prison, petty criminals, vagrants, and drunkards were confined. It stood at the junction of the two most important streets of the town.

people defileth the chosen. Still, I may as well help thee out o' the pother. Hum-m-m! I suppose my small-clothes would hardly be large enough, would they?" and he looked down at his withered little legs.

"I hardly think so," said Nancy, repressing a smile, as she pictured to herself the tall dignified Colonel in little John Stapler's small-clothes.

"Well, well," said he, "I'll just step out the back way, and borrow a suit from John Benson. He's the fattest man I know."

He soon returned with the borrowed clothes, which they wrapped up in as small a bundle as possible, after which Nancy rejoined the officer at the door.

"'Tis a largish bundle of stockings," observed he, as he escorted her across the street again.

"They are thick stockings," she answered, demurely.

When they reached home, she invited her escort and his brother officers, who were gathered around the fire near by, to come in and take a cup of coffee—an offer they were only too glad to accept, after their night march.

"Gentlemen," said Nancy, as they sat or stood around drinking their hot coffee, "I suppose you have no desire to retain our afflicted friend a prisoner? The doctor, who is with him at present, thinks it might benefit him to be removed to the country. I spoke to my friend whom I saw this morning, and he promised to send a coach. May he depart peaceably when the coach comes?"

"Faith," said the young Irish officer, "he may depart. He shall not be molested. I command here at present."

"What is the matter with the invalid?" inquired another officer.

"He appeareth to have the dropsy," answered Nancy, gravely.

In about half an hour an old-fashioned coach, as large as a small dwelling-house, and raised high from the ground on great wheels, lumbered up to the door. The steps were let down, or unfolded, until they made a kind of step-ladder, by which the passenger ascended to the coach which loomed above. The door stuck, in consequence of being swelled by the late rains, and was with difficulty opened. The officers stood around, waiting the appearance of the invalid, and the young Irishman who had been Nancy's escort waited at the door to help her in, for she was to accompany her afflicted relative to the ferry.

The house door opened, and she appeared, bearing a pillow and blanket to make the sick man comfortable. She arranged them, and stepped back into the house to see him moved. Then, with a shuffling of feet, the pretended victim of dropsy appeared, dressed in plain clothes, and so enormously puffed out that there was scarcely room for him in the passageway. The so-called doctor, dressed in black, and wearing a pair of black glass spectacles, assisted the invalid on one side, and Nancy supported him on the other. The dropsical one groaned at every step, and groaned louder than ever as they pushed, squeezed, and crowded him up the steps and into the coach. Nancy and the doctor followed, and the Irish officer put up the steps and clapped to the door, while Nancy smiled a farewell through the window to him as the great coach rumbled away toward the Christiana River.

"Oddsnooks!" exclaimed one of the officers, "that is the fattest Quaker I ever saw."

He would have been surprised if he had seen the fat Quaker draw a stout pillow from under his waistcoat after the coach had moved away, while the doctor stripped some black court-plaster from the back of his spectacles, and instead of the invalid and the physician appeared two decidedly military-looking gentlemen.

The coach and its occupants had lumbered out of sight for some time, and the young officer still remained lounging near the door of Mistress Hanson's house, when an orderly, splashed with mud from galloping over yesterday's battle-field, clattered up to the group.

"Which is Major Fortescue?" he asked, in his sharp military voice.

"I am," answered the young Irish officer.

"Order for you, sir!" and he reached the Major a folded paper, sealed with a blotch of wax as red as blood. He opened it, and read:

"You will immediately arrest two men, officers in the rebel army, known respectively as Colonel Tilton and Captain Bellach. Information has been lodged at head-quarters that they are now lying concealed at Mistress Elizabeth Hanson's in Wilmington town. You will report answer at once. By order of

Colonel Robert Wycherly, R. A.,
Com. 5th Div. H. M. A.
in the Province of Pennsylvania.

"To Major Allan Fortescue,
Commander at Wilmington,
In the Lower County of Newcastle."*

"Stop them!" roared Major Fortescue, as soon as he could catch his breath. He gave a sharp order to the soldiers lounging near; they seized their arms, and the whole party started at double quick for the ford of the Christiana River, half a mile away, whither the coach had directed its course.

Meanwhile the fugitives had arrived at the bank of the river, where they found that the ferryman was at the other side, and his boat with him. He was lying on the stern seat, in the sun, and an empty whiskey bottle beside him sufficiently denoted the reason of his inertia. When the Colonel called to him, he answered in endearing terms, but moved not; and when the officer swore, the ferryman reproved him solemnly. Affairs were looking gloomy, when Captain Bellach, who had been running up and down the embankment that kept the river from overflowing the marsh-lands that lay between it and the hill on which the town stood, gave a shout which called the Colonel and Nancy to him. They found that he had discovered an old scow half hidden among the reeds; it was stuck fast in the mud, and it was only by great exertions that the two gentlemen pushed it off the ooze into the water. The Colonel then took Nancy in his arms, and carried her across the muddy shore to the boat, where he deposited her; then pushing off the scow, he leaped aboard himself.

"Lackaday for my new silk petticoat, all spotted and ruined!" cried Nancy. "I'd rather have been taken prisoner at once!" And she looked down ruefully upon the specks of blue marsh mud that had been splashed upon that garment.

Neither of the men answered. The boat leaked very badly when it was fairly out in the water, and the Colonel was forced to bail it out with his hat. The Captain sat in the middle of the boat, paddling it with a piece of board. His hat had blown off, and his black silk small-clothes were covered with mud. The tide was running strongly, and as the boat drifted down the stream, it was swung round and round in spite of the Captain's efforts to keep it straight, while the leak gained on them, until Nancy, with a sigh, was compelled to take her best beaver hat, ribbons and all, and help the Colonel bail.

They were scarcely more than half across when Major Fortescue and his squad of soldiers dashed up to the bank. They ran along the embankment, keeping pace with the boat as it drifted with the tide.

"Halt!" cried the officer; but no one in the boat answered. "Halt, or I shoot!" But Captain Bellach only paddled the harder.

"Make ready! Take aim!—"

* Newcastle County, Delaware, formerly a portion of Penn's Proprietary Government in the Americas.

"Down, for your life!" cried Colonel Tilton, sharply, dragging Nancy down into the bottom of the boat, where Captain Bellach flung himself beside them. It was the work of a moment. The next instant—"Fire!" they heard the royalist order, sharply, from the bank.

"Cra-a-a-ack!" rattled the muskets, and the bullets hummed venomously around the boat like a swarm of angry hornets.

None of the fugitives were hurt, though two of the bullets struck the side of the boat; but Nancy's petticoat was entirely ruined by the mud and water in the bottom. Before the redcoats could reload, they had reached the further shore, and run into a corn field near by, in which they were entirely hidden. Captain Bellach wanted to go up the stream and thrash the drunken ferryman; but the Colonel and Nancy dissuaded him, and they made the best of their way to Dover, which they reached after a very weary journey. There Nancy, who considered it safer to absent herself from home while the British retained possession of Wilmington, found herself the heroine of the hour; and she was fêted and dined and made much of, until it would have completely turned a less sensible little head than hers.

In after-years, when her husband presented her to President Washington, "Ah, Mistress Tilton," said his Excellency, "your husband should indeed value an affection that not only endangered a life, but even sacrificed a fine silk petticoat, for his sake."

[Begun in No. 18 of Harper's Young People, March 2.]

ACROSS THE OCEAN; OR, A BOY'S FIRST VOYAGE.

A True Story.

BY J. O. DAVIDSON.

Chapter VI.

AN OCEAN PRAIRIE.

FRANK found his new work tolerably easy, though it required constant attention, for every joint of the machinery had to be watched, and oiled afresh the moment it began to get dry and hot. There being two other oilers, he now stood his regular watch of three hours at a time, having the rest of the day to himself. Most of this leisure time was spent in talking with Herrick, or studying the ins and outs of the machinery; and Frank soon learned to "take a card" as well as any man on board. This is done as follows: a slip of paper is rolled round a brass tube attached to the valve of the engine cylinder, and a pencil fixed so as to trace certain curved lines on the paper as it turns, the shape of which shows the exact working condition of the engine.

IN THE SARGASSO SEA.

On the fourth afternoon of his new duties Austin heard himself hailed from the upper deck by a familiar voice:

"Hello, Frank, my boy! come up and have a look at Daddy Neptune's pasture-ground."

Up went Frank with all speed; but his first glance around made him start. Instead of the deep blue water that had surrounded her a few hours before, the ship was now in the midst of a smooth green plain, extending as far as the eye could reach, and covered, to all appearance, with coarse grass and broad-leaved plants. Nothing was wanting, in fact, to complete the picture except a few sheep and cattle.

For a moment our hero really thought he must be dreaming; and then he suddenly recollected his school-book pictures and stories of the famous Sargasso Sea, where, for thousands of acres together, the water is quite hidden by a thick growth of "Gulf weed," and knew at once that this must be it.

And certainly this ocean prairie was a wonderful sight. As the steamer ploughed its way through the matted weeds, Frank could see in the narrow openings their trailing roots hanging far down into the clear cool depths below. Above these open spaces thousands of sea-birds were hovering with shrill cries, while ever and anon one of them would swoop down into the water, re-appearing instantly with a fish wriggling in its beak.

In the purple shadow of the weed beds bright-colored fish were moving lazily to and fro, but these darted swiftly away at the approach of the steamer. On every side queer little crabs and turtles were plumping into the water, scared by the plashing wheels, while, stranger still, birds' nests and eggs were seen here and there amid the huge broad leaves of the stronger plants, to the great delight of Frank, who thought the idea of birds nesting in the middle of the Atlantic the finest joke he had ever heard.

A mass of the tangle was hauled on board, and the men amused themselves by stamping on the hollow air-cells which give the weed its buoyancy, producing a series of cracks like the explosion of fire-crackers.

"I've heerd tell, though I can't say I've seen it myself," observed a sailor, "as there's places whar them weeds are so thick and strong that a man can walk on 'em all the same as dry land."

"Well, they can stop a ship, anyhow, whether they can carry a man or not. A chum of mine as v'y'ged here in a Portigee steamer told me that she once got reg'lar jammed among the weed, and only 'scaped by reversin' her *engines*."

"Well, it's a fact that somewhar in these seas there's a place they call the Lumber Yard, 'cause of all the driftwood and floatin' spars and bits o' wreck and sich gittin' jumbled up together; for all the currents sort o' meet there, like them puzzles whar every road leads in and none out. If a ship once gits in *there*, good-by to her: for there ain't no wind, nor tide, nor nothin', and you jist stick there till you rot."

Here old Herrick muttered, dreamily, as if speaking to himself, "*I've* seen that, and I sha'n't forget it in a hurry."

The men nudged each other, and there was a general silence; for it was but seldom that Herrick could be got to spin a yarn, and he was now evidently about to "get off" one of his best.

"I was cruising in these waters," he went on, "'bout twenty years ago, when one afternoon we sighted a sort o' mound in among the thickest of the weed, with somethin' like a ship's mast standin' up from it. The 'old man' came out to look at it, and then gave orders to lower the boat, and we pulled for the wreck with a will. But as we neared her, the very look of her seemed to strike cold upon us all. Her hull had such an old-fashioned build that it might ha' been afloat for a hundred years and more; and all up the sides and over the deck great slimy coils of weed had trailed, like them eight-armed squids that clutch men and drag 'em down. As we came nigher, the very sun clouded over, and all was chill, and gray, and dismal, and the wreck itself looked so unearthly, with no sign or sound of life about it, that I guess I wasn't the only one who felt queer when we ran alongside at last.

"Up we scrambled, our very tread soundin' hollow and uncanny in that awful silence. Not a livin' thing was there aboard, not even a mouse. The mainmast was gone, all but a stump, and the moulderin' tackle lay on the deck all of a heap. The plankin' was rotten and fallin' to bits, and the place on the stern where her name had been was clean mouldered away. All at once our coxswain, Bill Grimes, gives a jump and a holler as if he'd trod on a rattlesnake; and when we ran for'ard, what should we see, half hid among the weeds, but the skeleton of a man, fastened to the bulwarks by a rusty chain!"

The speaker ceased, and looked round the attentive circle with the air of a man who feels that he has made a hit.

"A slaver, I reckon," said one, at length.

"Or a pirate."

"Or some craft that had got starved out."

"Ay; but how cum that skeleton there? Did you never find out nothin' 'bout her, old hoss?"

"*Never*," said the old man, solemnly. "That's how many a gallant ship has ended—just a mark of 'missing' opposite her name in the owner's list, and a few poor souls watchin' and waitin' for them that 'll never come back. Ay, boys; for as bright and pretty as these waters look, there's many a black story hid aneath 'em as 'll never be known till the day when the sea shall give up its dead."

They were now east of the Azores, and within four days' run of Gibraltar, which was their first halting-place. So the men were set to work to scrub the deck, polish the rails, new paint the boats, mend such of the signal flags as were torn, and "smarten" up the vessel generally; for a sea-captain is as proud of his ship as a landsman of his wife, and likes to bring her into port as trim as possible.

Frank, always ready to be of use, took his share of the work, though he had plenty to occupy him without it. He was never tired of watching the sun make rainbows in the spray of the bow, and the pretty little sea-fairies, called by sailors "Portuguese men-of-war," float past with their tinted shells and outspread *feelers*; while at night the moon was so gloriously brilliant, and the sea so clear and smooth, that he often staid on deck till midnight to enjoy the spectacle. But another sight was in store for him, even more to his taste than these.

One evening, just before sunset, two sail (the first for several days) were descried by the look-out, quite close to each other. Herrick, after eying them keenly for a moment, pronounced them to be a British steamer and a full-rigged American clipper ship.

"How on earth can you tell that?" asked the wondering Frank, who could see nothing of the strangers but their topmasts.

"Easy enough. That un's a steamer, by her smoke; and she's a Britisher, by the *look* o' the smoke, for they

AN OCEAN RACE.

mostly burn soft coal. T'other's a clipper, by her rig, and the lot o' handkerchiefs [studding sails] she has aloft; and she's a 'Merican, for nothin' else could hold its own with a steamer. But what can they be doin' so close together? Ah! *I've* got it—they're a-racin'."

When the two vessels came near enough to be signaled, and to reply, Herrick was found to be right in every particular, and the excitement aboard the *Arizona* rose to a height. The captain himself came out to watch the race, and every man who was not on duty below hastened on deck.

"See how Johnny Bull's a-pilin' the coal on!" cried old Herrick, pointing to the eddying smoke, which grew blacker every minute. "But he don't whip *that* craft—not much! Canvas agin tea-kettles any day! Hooray!"

"Right you air, old hoss! Guess some o' them clippers can show as good a record as any steamer afloat. Why, didn't the old *Nabob* run 7389 miles in thirty days out thar in the Indian Ocean?—and that's 246 miles a day for a whole month, anyhow."

The two racers were now crossing the *Arizona*'s bows, and every one crowded forward to look at them. The steamer's passengers were seen clustered along the side like bees, while the crew were bustling to and fro, setting every sail that would draw. But still on the starboard quarter hung the beautiful clipper, gliding along smoothly and easily, one great pyramid of snow-white canvas from gunwale to truck, while the look-out and the two men at the wheel (the only persons visible on board) grinned from ear to ear at the "Britisher's" vain efforts. Just as the clipper passed, the Stars and Stripes fluttered out jauntily at her peak.

"Come, boys!" cried Herrick; "let's give the old 'gridiron' a cheer."

Mingling with the hearty shout that followed (in which Frank joined with a will) came three sharp blasts from the *Arizona*'s steam-whistle, by way of salute. Instantly the clipper's crew sprang up from behind the bulwarks, and, waving their caps, sent back a rousing cheer, answered by the Englishman with a short whistle of defiance as he swept by.

Little by little the racers, still close together, melted into the fast-falling shadows of night; but there were not a few who declared that, when last seen, the clipper was getting the best of it, and their belief in the superiority of wind over steam was greatly strengthened thereby.

[TO BE CONTINUED.]

APRIL'S TEARS.

April's tears are happy tears,
  Joy when the arbutus sweet
  Creeps about her dancing feet.
When the violet appears,
When the birds begin to sing,
  When the grass begins to grow,
  Makes her lovely eyes o'erflow.
She's a tender-hearted thing,
Bonny daughter of the spring!

BILLY'S GREAT SPEECH.

BY WILLIAM O. STODDARD.

BILLY was the youngest member of the debating society; that is, the other members were all grown-up men, though none of them were very old, and he was not yet quite fourteen years of age. Some of the boys he knew told him he had been let in by mistake, and some said it was a joke; but there he was, week after week, every Friday evening, sitting on a front bench, and as much a member as the president, or the secretary, or either of the three vice-presidents.

One of the names of that village debating society was "The Lyceum," but it wasn't much used, except when they had distinguished strangers to lecture for them, and charged twenty-five cents apiece for tickets.

The regular weekly debates were "free," and so there was always a good attendance. The ladies, of all ages, were sure to come, and a good many of the boys. Billy never missed a debate; but he had not yet made so much as one single solitary speech on any subject. Nobody knew how often he had entered that hall with a big speech in him, all ready, or how he had always carried it out again unspoken.

A little after the Christmas and New-Years' holidays spoken. He knew very well what a troublesome thing a speech was to keep in, and without any cork.

Billy thought he had never known men to talk so long as they did—two young lawyers, three young doctors, the tutor of the village academy, the sub-editor of the *Weekly Bugle*, Squire Toms's son that was almost ready to go to college, and the tall young man with red hair who had just opened the new drug store.

That was the man who did Billy the most harm, for his argument was nothing in the wide world but a string of quotations from Daniel Webster. He called him the Great Expounder, and a great statesman, and a number of other names, and wound up by asserting that the opinion of such a great man as that settled the matter. There was a good deal of applause given to the red-headed young man as he was sitting down, and Billy took advantage of it; that is, before he knew exactly what he was doing, he was on his feet, and shouted, "Mr. President!—ladies and gentlemen—"

"Mr. Morton has the floor," remarked the president, very dignifiedly; and Billy, as he afterward said of himself, "was pinned."

There was no escape for him now, and when Grandfather Morton pounded with his cane, and shouted, "Platform!" dozens of other people took it up, and it was "Platform!" "Platform!" "Platform!" all over the hall. He knew what it meant. All the favorite speakers were sent forward in that way, and it was a great compliment; but Billy thought he must have walked forty miles, from the tired feeling in his legs, when he got there. Oh, how hot that room was just then, and what a dreadful thing it was to have a crowd like that suddenly begin to keep still! They must have been holding their breaths.

Billy knew his speech was in him, for it had been swelling and swelling while the others were speaking, but he could not quite get any of it very close to his mouth at that trying moment.

But Billy kept thinking, all the way home, "What would he have said if I hadn't forgot the rest of it?"

That was years ago, and Billy is a great lawyer now; but he says he has never forgotten what it was that made his first speech so very good.

THE CZAR'S FISH.

BY DAVID KER.

ONE fine July morning, a few years ago, there was a great stir among the villagers of Pavlovo, on the Lower Volga, for the news had got abroad that the Czar was coming down the river, on his way to his Summer Palace in the Crimea. So, of course, every one was on the look-out for him; for the Russian peasants of the Volga are a very loyal set, and many old men and women among them, who have never been out of their native village before, will tramp for miles over those great, bare, dusty plains on the chance of catching a passing glimpse of "Alexander Nikolaievitch" (Alexander the son of Nicholas), as they call the Czar.

Among those who talked over the great news most eagerly were the family of an old fisherman, who was known as "Lucky Michael," on account of his success in catching the finest fish, although hard work and experience had probably much more to do with it than any "luck."

But of late "Lucky Michael" had been very unlucky indeed. His wife had been ill, to begin with; and one of his two sons (who helped him with his fishing) had been disabled for several weeks by a bad hurt in his arm. Moreover, his boat was getting so crazy and worn out that it seemed wonderful how it kept afloat at all; but the news of the Czar's coming seemed to comfort him for everything.

"If Father Alexander Nikolaievitch would only give us money enough to buy a new boat!" said old Praskovia, Michael's wife, as she put away what was left of the huge black loaf that had served for breakfast; "but I suppose it wouldn't do to ask him."

"Of course not!" said Michael, who was an independent old fellow; "he's done quite enough for us already, in making us freemen, when we were all slaves before.* Now, then, let's get to work. Come, Stepan [Stephen], come, Ivan (John), and let us see what God will send us."

But at first the luck seemed to be still against them, for they drew their net twice without catching anything. The third time, however, the net felt unusually heavy, and there was such a tugging and kicking inside of it that it was plain they had caught a pretty big fish of some kind. John, who was the first to look in, gave a loud hurrah, and shouted, "Father! father!—a sturgeon! a sturgeon!"

There, sure enough, lay the great fish amid a crowd of smaller ones, in all the pride of its spiky back, and smooth, brown, scaleless skin. All three rejoiced at the sight, for a sturgeon will always fetch a good price in Russia, and the two lads began to think at once how far this would go toward paying for a new boat.

siderable excitement. But there was not much time to talk it over, for, two days later, young Stephen, who had been sent to look out for the Czar's steamer, came running to say that it was in sight. So Michael put his sturgeon into the boat, and away they pulled. It was a hard pull against that strong current, but at last they got near enough to hail the steamer and be taken in tow.

Up went Michael, fish and all, and the captain led him aft to where the Czar and his officers were standing. Many of them were handsome, stalwart men, all ablaze with lace and embroidery; but the old fisherman, with his tall, upright figure, clear bright eye, and hale old face framed in snow-white hair, looked, despite his rough dress, as fine a man as any of them.

"See here, father," said he, "this is the finest fish I ever caught, and so I've kept it for *you*. I want nothing for it; take it as a free gift."

"Thank you, brother," said the Czar; "it's a royal fish, indeed, and I'll have it for dinner this very day, and drink your health over it. What's your name?"

"Michael Ribakoff, father, from the village of Pavlovo."

"Good—I won't forget you. Good-by!"

When the villagers heard what had happened, they all thought Michael rather a fool for giving his fish away, when the Czar would have paid a good price for it. But a week later came a fine new fishing-boat for "Michael Ribakoff," in the stern locker of which were a complete suit of fisherman's clothes and a new net, with a piece of paper inscribed, in the Czar's own handwriting, "*A midsummer gift from Alexander Nikolaievitch.*" And old Michael always said that he valued the paper far more than the boat.

THE HERMIT AND THE ROBBERS.

A GENTLE hermit, one day, proceeding on his way through a vast forest, chanced to discover a large cave nearly hidden under-ground. Being much fatigued, he entered to repose himself awhile; and observing something shining in the distance, he approached, and found it was a heap of gold. At the sight he turned away, and hastening through the forest again as fast as possible, had the misfortune to fall into the hands of three fierce robbers. They asked from whom he fled, and he answered, "I am flying from Death, who is urging me sorely behind."

The robbers, not perceiving any one, cried out, "Show us where he is." The hermit replied, "Follow me," and proceeded toward the grotto. He there pointed out to them the fatal place, beseeching them at the same time to abstain from looking at it. But the thieves, seizing upon the treasure, began to rejoice exceedingly. They afterward permitted the good man to proceed on his way, amusing themselves by ridiculing his strange conduct. At length they began to consider what they should do with the gold. One of them observed, "We ought not to leave the place without taking this treasure with us."

"No," replied another, "we had better not do so; but

on their part, while he had been away, had come to the conclusion of killing him on his return, in order that they might divide the money among themselves, saying, "Let us fall upon him the moment he comes, and afterward eat what he has brought, and divide the money between us in much larger shares than before."

The robber who had been into the city now returned with the articles he had bought, and was immediately killed. The others then began to feast upon the provisions prepared for them, and were seized with violent pains, and soon died. In this manner all three fell victims to each other's avarice and cruelty, without obtaining their ill-gotten wealth.

ANIMAL-PLANTS.

THE aquarium presents a field for delightful and ever-varying study, as its inhabitants belong to the most curious and interesting of ocean and fresh-water creatures. Fishes alone are well worthy of close observation; and when to these are added odd little reptiles, queer shell-fish, and different classes of the wonderful zoophytes, an aquarium presents a constantly changing picture of the marvels of ocean life.

The zoophytes are the most remarkable of all marine creatures. The name zoophyte comes from two Greek words—*zoön*, an animal, and *phyton*, a plant—and therefore has the literal signification of animal-plant.

An important member of the zoophyte family, and one often introduced into aquaria, is the actinia, or sea-anemone, sometimes called sea-rose. Sea-anemones were for a long time considered as vegetables, beautiful and gayly colored flowers of the ocean, and only comparatively recent investigation has discovered them to be animals, and blood-thirsty, voracious little robbers and murderers of the worst character.

One of the most common among the many varieties of sea-anemones is the *Actinia mesembryanthemum*. The polypus-hunter who finds this living flower clinging to sea-coast rocks, and bears it home as an addition to his aquarium, unless he is already acquainted with the nature of his prize, will behold with astonishment and delight the wondrous variations in the appearance of this little creature. Clinging to the rocks, the anemone probably appeared like a round leathery bag drawn in at the centre; but when placed on the miniature cliffs of the aquarium, a wondrous transformation takes place. The bag gradually expands, a mouth appears in the centre, and from it unfold a multitude of petals of a variety of colors—pale scarlet, blood-red, orange, and white—which wave gently back and forth like a graceful nodding flower. Now drop a small earth-worm or tiny fish in the water. The instant it touches the least of these petal-like tentacles the whole flower is in commotion, all the arms reaching toward the struggling victim, and holding it in a grasp so firm that escape is impossible, and it is soon drawn into the capacious and hungry stomach. Every animated thing that comes within reach of the tentacles of the anemone is mercilessly seized and devoured. Even small mollusks and crustacea are unable to resist the power of the grasping threads, and crabs are often conquered and swallowed by this voracious living flower. For this reason sea-anemones are dangerous inhabitants of an aquarium stocked with creatures having the power of locomotion, and are best placed in a tank with other zoophytes like themselves. How often they eat when free in their natural element is unknown, but weekly feeding is said to be sufficient to sustain them in an aquarium. Small bits of meat are acceptable food, which can be dropped into the water. The instant a descending morsel touches the petals, or tentacles, of a hungry anemone, it is eagerly seized and drawn into the open, greedy mouth. The *Actinia mesembryanthemum* is a very long-lived creature, and certain specimens are reported to have lived over twenty years in aquaria in England.

There are many varieties of sea-anemones, and although all possess the same distinguishing characteristics, they vary in the form and color of the open flower. The *Actinia gemmacea*, which is like a gorgeous sunflower, is said to be the most voracious of its kind. An English naturalist describes a specimen which swallowed a shell as large as a saucer, its own diameter not being over two inches. Its elastic stomach extended sufficiently to receive this enormous prey; but as the shell completely

CARNIVOROUS OCEAN PLANTS.

A VISIT TO THE OLD HOME.

separated the upper half of the animal from the lower, a new mouth began immediately to form, through which to convey nourishment to the lower portion, thus presenting the curious spectacle of a double-headed monster in miniature. So remarkable are the anemones in their reproductive power, that if the tentacles are injured or broken off, new ones immediately form, and if the animal be cut in two, new mouths form, and soon two perfect animals are waving their graceful tentacles to and fro in the water.

The locomotive power of the anemone, or actinia, is very sluggish. It will remain days and weeks in the same spot, and it moves only by sliding one edge of its base very slowly along the object to which it is fastened, and drawing the other after it. It can therefore never pursue its food, and appears to have no sense except that of touch, as a worm or shiner may float in the water all about the anemone without causing it the slightest agitation; but if the tiniest tip of one of its tentacles be touched, or brushed even, the whole creature is alive in an instant, and grasping for its prey. In the centre of the illustration are two specimens of this animal-plant, the wondrous flesh-eating flower of the ocean. To the left may be seen a specimen of the *Eledone moschata*—a small and very common member of the octopus family. The eledone is a hideous-looking beast. Its small eyes, which it can open and shut at will, are glistening, and of changing iris. Its long arms are strong enough to grasp a mussel shell, and hold it firmly until its contents are devoured. At the least touch a dark color instantly appears spread over the whole body of this curious creature, and dark prickly spines arise, which impart a stinging sensation when handled, like the anemone and sea-nettle.

The two odd-looking things in the background of the engraving are specimens of the limulus, or arrow-tailed crab. The upper side of the limulus is covered with two smooth overlapping shields, in which are two tiny eyes. Armed with six pairs of nippers, the limulus often fights its companions in the aquarium, and boldly engages in battle with the eledone, which, with its long arms, is more than a match for the pugilistic crab, whose retreat and utter discomfiture generally end the battle, for, thrown on its back, it can with difficulty right itself. If a limulus and alcione be confined in the same tank, almost daily must the former be rescued from the arms of the latter.

The palm-like creature to the right of the picture is a *Spirographis*, or tube-worm. This savage little beast lives in a tube formed of particles of lime or grains of sand, and stretches its gill-like threads upward, in search of food, in the form of a spiral wreath. It is very sensitive, and at the least touch on the surface of the water, or on the walls of the tank, the threads are instantly withdrawn into the tube.

In the background may be seen the waving, bell-like *Medusa aurita*, armed with prickly threads. It belongs to the jelly-fish family, and loves to lie near the surface of the water, but it is with great difficulty kept alive in an aquarium. When it dies, it dissolves itself into the watery element of which it is so largely composed, and its fairy-like skin can scarcely be discovered in the tank.

EASY BOTANY.

APRIL.

NOW it is April, and the time has come to explore the woods and wilds.

Let us hasten to welcome the first blossom, so delicate and yet daring to face the uncertain sky of early spring.

Happy are they who live in the country, who have the freedom of rural roads, rocky banks, wooded hills, and smiling meadows! The young botanical student can not expect to become acquainted with all the wild plants in his vicinity in one summer, nor is this desirable; the pursuit will last for a lifetime, becoming more and more enchanting. But every one can make a pretty collection; and if, in addition to studying out the flowers, and keeping an accurate list of them, and pressing some of the most interesting, the young student will learn to draw with pen or pencil a few of the most simple and graceful, the pleasure will be greatly increased. A great deal of information might be given on botanical subjects, but in this brief article little more can be done than to mention the names of those plants which may be looked for during the month, and the localities they choose. Most of the flowers mentioned are found from Maine to Florida, and West and South as well, though some that are abundant in the Middle States and on Western prairies avoid the chills of New England. The wild flowers delight in the semi-seclusion of pastures and meadows, and spring up along the lines of old fences in fields and on the hills and in the dim woods.

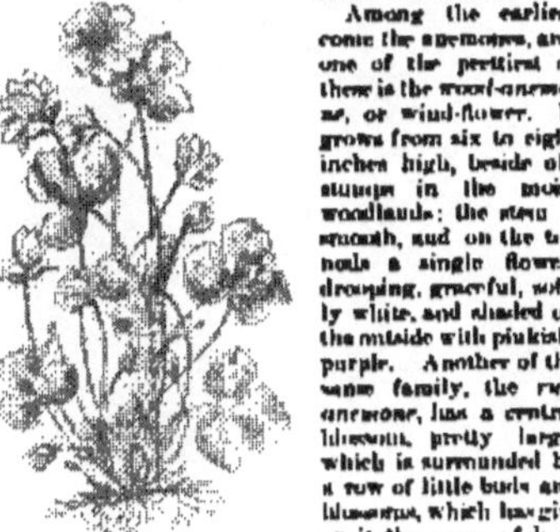

Among the earliest come the anemones, and one of the prettiest of these is the *wood-anemone*, or wind-flower. It grows from six to eight inches high, beside old stumps in the moist woodlands; the stem is smooth, and on the top nods a single flower, drooping, graceful, softly white, and shaded on the outside with pinkish-purple. Another of the same family, the *rue-anemone*, has a central blossom, pretty large, which is surrounded by a row of little buds and blossoms, which has given it the name of leu-

Another delightful April flower is the *hepatica*, growing sometimes in New England woods, but abundantly in the Middle States. This charming little plant is fond of the loveliest shades of deepest blue, fading into the palest purple and white, and on the Orange mountains, in New Jersey, are clumps of the most beautiful rose-color. The hepatica grows finely if transplanted.

DRABA VERNA.

Do not fail to find the snow-white bud of the *bloodroot*, which comes up wrapped in a charming little green cloak, and also the smallest of all the floral tribe, the *Draba verna*, with stems of white flowers, and stems only an inch or two high. Some plants that may be easily found are:

Wood-anemone, margins of fields; New England.
Rue-anemone, same localities; New England.
Hepatica, woody hill-sides; Middle States.
Bloodroot, rich open woods; New England.
Blue violet, fields, meadows, hills; everywhere.
Draba verna, sandy fields and road-sides.
Spring beauty, moist open woods; New Jersey, South.
Wild geranium, open woods and fields; New England.
Epigæa, damp soil; New York, Pennsylvania.
Quaker ladies, road-sides, fields; everywhere.
Dandelion, road-sides, fields; everywhere.
Azalea, New England woods and elsewhere.
Benzoin—spice-bush—damp woods; New Jersey, Pennsylvania.
American mistletoe, New Jersey and South.

TWO ANCIENT FAMILIES.

A PAPER READ BEFORE THE "LITTLE LITERATI" BY MOTHER.

I FEAR I appear before you but illy prepared for the evening duties, as, mother-like, my week has been full of cares—unusually so. Being left to choose my own subject, I thought to speak briefly of a worthy but almost extinct family, or, indeed, I should say two families.

Many grown persons persist in declaring that the families have passed entirely out of existence, but I find there are a few of them to be found still on the rugged mountain-sides, on the plains, and down in the deep green valleys. Little children know them best, as they seem to be modest, retiring families, seldom or never intruding themselves on the notice of others. I conjecture, from the freedom with which little children use their names, that they must be a kindly, simple people. My little Mary, or Minnie, tells me almost every day of little Johnnie He or little Sallie She, and in my mind's eye I see little Johnnie He coming through his father's gate on his way to school—a plump, rosy-cheeked little fellow in white pants and blouse.

> Most amiable and fair he looks,
>   That little Johnnie He,
> While following close behind his heels
>   Is little Sallie She.
> With flaxen curls and laughing eyes,
>   This little girl we greet,
> Exclaim, "How fair is Johnnie He!
>   And Sallie She, how sweet!"

Very little is known of the ancestors of these simple

were a worthy, renowned family in their day and generation; but, alas! history has given us all too little of them. It is known that they were born hundreds of years ago, living bright and useful lives in the earliest ages of civilization. History speaks freely of one who may have been the great-great-grandfather of the present Hes (much less is known of the Shes), and while speaking of him forgets not to take his travelling artist along to sketch him. This noble ancestor is Mr. Zaccheus He, and he is in the act of performing the feat that saves his name from utter oblivion. The deed is made doubly impressive by the travelling artist sketching the same. The poet too lends his sublime aid to render the act one never to be forgotten. In the present age of the world, many parents, from some deep-seated prejudice, strive to blot out this unpretending family entirely; but little children with tearful eyes bring the Historian, the Artist, and the Poet at once to the rescue, exclaiming, "Then why does the book say,

"'Zaccheus He
Did climb the tree?'"

CHIN-FAN, THE CANTON BOAT-BOY.

BY THOMAS W. KNOX.

HOW many readers of Harper's Young People are aware that in China, on the other side of the world, there are thousands and thousands of boys and girls that live in boats? There is a great city in China called Canton, and at this city there is a river which is so crowded with boats that it is not easy to get around among them. They are not large boats like the great steamers on American rivers, and they do not have comfortable rooms where you can sleep as well as in a bed on shore. Some of them are so small that they can only hold three or four persons, and there is no space for walking around; but these three or four must live there from day to day and from week to week, and if they ever go on shore at all, it is only for a few minutes at a time. A whole family will often be found living on a boat which we would hardly think large enough to cross in from one side of the Hudson River to the other. They cook and eat and sleep on the boat, and they manage to earn a little money by carrying passengers over the river, or doing other work. The kitchen where they do their cooking is only a little heap of coals that a man might put in his hat, and it rests on a box of

quaintance. The strange baby smiled in reply; and then Chin-Fan held out his chubby little hand to lift him out of the water. Of course the other one held up a hand to meet him, but he could not reach far enough. Then Chin-Fan reached down, while the stranger reached up, and pretty soon Chin-Fan lost his balance, and tumbled into the water.

Wasn't he in a dangerous place! His mother did not know what had happened, and she kept on rowing the boat right away from where the poor little fellow was struggling and trying to keep from being drowned. An American baby would have screamed and sunk, but Chin-Fan was not American, and so he did nothing of the sort. He dropped all thoughts of the strange baby, and considered nobody but himself; he managed to get hold of the billet of wood to which his cord was fastened, and by holding on firmly he kept his head out of water. The current of the river carried him along, and very luckily it carried him to where a ship was anchored, with her great cable sloping down the stream. He struck against this cable, and as he did so, he let go of the billet, so that it went one side of the cable, while Chin-Fan went the other. Then he took hold of the cable with both his chubby hands, and next he screamed as loud as his little lungs would let him.

A sailor on the bow of the ship heard the scream, and was not long in finding that it came from the cable. Chin-Fan kept it up until he was rescued, and just about the time he was taken on board the ship he was missed by his mother. She came paddling down the river in search of him, and shouted to everybody she met that her baby was missing. The sailor held little Chin-Fan up so that she could see him, and in a very short time he was back in his place on the deck of the boat.

For a good while after that incident Chin-Fan kept at a respectful distance from the side of the boat, and he did not show any desire to make the acquaintance of strange babies in the water. His mother taught him how to swim, and he became a boatman at Canton, and afterward he was a sailor on one of the great steamers that run between San Francisco and China. He did a great many brave things in and on the water, and his mother was very proud of him; she said she always knew he would be a famous sailor, when he showed so much good sense and coolness at the time of his first plunge.

BIRTH-PLACE OF WASHINGTON.

From early boyhood Washington had a strong liking for a soldier's life. He used to train his school-mates as soldiers, was an eager student of drill and tactics, expert in the use of the sword, and a skillful horseman. At that time the Indians swarmed through the forest in the back country, and were often urged on by the French (who claimed the Ohio and Mississippi valleys as their own) to attack the whites. So the colony of Virginia had to keep a good many men under arms to protect the homes and the lives of the people. When Washington was about twenty-two years old he became a Major in this little army, and devoted a great deal of time and hard work to training his men.

In 1755 the French and Indians became so troublesome that quite a large army was sent over from England to clear the borders of them. General Braddock was at their head, and he asked Washington to go with him, with the rank of Colonel, as one of his aides; that is, to be always with him, and help him with advice, or in carrying orders, and in any way he could. The gallant young officer was glad to go. The English General did not know much about fighting in the woods, and his slow and stately march toward the Ohio did not suit Washington's ideas, for he knew that nothing could be done against the French unless it was done swiftly.

When the army neared the French fort, at what is now Pittsburgh, Washington, who was on his back in an ambulance, sick with fever, insisted on going to the front, for he knew there would soon be fighting, and hard fighting, too. The fighting began before it was looked for. The British troops crossed the Monongahela River, and marched up a wooded hollow toward the French fort. As they swept up the hollow in close ranks, with gay red uniforms and gleaming arms, there suddenly blazed upon them, from unseen guns on every side, a murderous fire, before which they shrunk quickly back. Startled, but not cowed, their officers rallied them again and again; but they could not see the enemies whose fire was mowing them down, and they slowly and in great disorder tried to get back across the river.

General Braddock was mortally wounded. More than half the army were killed or wounded. Colonel Washington behaved "with the greatest courage and resolution." He rode from point to point carrying orders, and seemed reckless of death. "I had four bullets through my coat," he wrote to his brother, "and two horses shot under me, yet I escaped unhurt, although death was levelling my companions on every side of me."

Fifteen years later an old Indian, who was in the fight on the French side, told him that he had fired at him many times, and ordered his young warriors to do so. None of the shots hit, and the Indians, thinking the young officer was under the special care of the Great Spirit, ceased to fire at him.

After this battle, Colonel Washington was kept in bed for four long months with a fever, which was made worse by his exposure on the battle-field. He had little more hard fighting to do, but he learned many a good lesson from the war—especially to rely on himself, and to study his own way out of any troubles that he met. His fame went, too, to the other colonies, and the young Colonel of Militia was becoming known as a man on whose courage and faithfulness and sound good sense it would do for his country to lean in time of trial.

[TO BE CONTINUED.]

PUCK AND BLOSSOM.

From the German of Marie von Olfers.

PART I.

ONCE upon a time Puck and his little sister Blossom lived together in a great big egg.

"It's too close in here," said Puck; "let's go and see how it looks outside." Bang! went his head, right through the wall.

Outside it was raining, so he drew back his head in a hurry; but the rain came pattering in after him. "Oh, my doodness!" moaned Blossom, "is *that* how it is outside! Now we shall det wet to the skin."

"Come," said Puck, "let's go find us another house; it 'll be better by-and-by."

So they went, and they went, till they came to old Mother Bee, who lived with her children in the leafy house of the linden-tree.

"Oh, come in," said she; "but you must sit quite still, or else my children will sting you. As for me, I must go and gather honey."

For a little while they sat quite still. "Sister Blossom," said Puck, "it's too close in here. I must go see where they keep the honey." He was starting off that very

minute, but all the Bee-children flew up in such a rage, and fastened themselves upon Puck and Blossom, that they got away, they hardly knew how.

"I didn't even get a taste of their old honey, and I'm all stung up," sobbed Blossom.

"Never mind," said Puck, comfortingly. "It 'll be better by-and-by."

On the meadow whom should they meet but Master Stork. "Oh, take us with you up to your nest!" cried Puck. Master Longlegs, being quite willing, quickly snatched up the children in his long bill, and set them down in his nest.

"Sit still," said he, "then you'll have plenty of room."

For a little while they sat quite still. "Sister Blossom," said Puck, "it's too close in here. I've seen

young storks fly. I know how they do it; I can do it too. Come, now, you do just what I do." He spread his little arms, she spread her little arms, and—

Thump!—they lay on the ground.

[TO BE CONTINUED.]

[illegible]

Have any of our correspondents had experience in taming wild rabbits?

[illegible]

You would better give your alligator a piece of board to crawl up on, for it will die if compelled to remain constantly in the water.

[illegible]

Your caterpillar must have passed some time in the chrysalis state before it became a butterfly. It is very interesting to watch the process of transformation from a caterpillar to a chrysalis, and nothing is prettier than the butterfly or moth creeping out of its cell, and expanding its wings for the first time.

[illegible]

If you intend to devote your time to making clothes for poor little girls like Biddy O'Dolan, your sewing society is an excellent idea; and we hope you will carry it out. If you stop to look about you, there are many poor children within your reach whose lives you can make brighter and more comfortable. You can not realize the good you can do until you begin, and see the effects of your work.

MILLIE B. S.—The fact that you take YOUNG PEOPLE through a news agent makes no difference whatever. "Wiggles," puzzles, and other favors from our young readers all receive the same attention, and are equally welcome.

C. H. W.—Ceres, called Demeter by the Greeks, was the goddess of agriculture. She was pictured by the ancients holding a torch and sheaf of corn, a basket filled with flowers at her side, and a garland of wheat ears interwoven in her hair. Her festival fell on the 19th of April, the beginning of seed-time. There is a pretty legend that Persephone, the daughter of Ceres, was stolen by Pluto, who allowed her to leave his subterranean kingdom only during the period between spring-time and autumn, and that Ceres, enraged at the theft of her daughter, refused to bless the earth with fruits and flowers during those months when she was deprived of Persephone. The name Ceres is derived from the Sanskrit, and signifies to create. Vulcan, whose Greek name was Hephæstus, was the son of Jupiter and Juno, and the god of fire. He was lame and ugly, but was worshipped as the patron of all craftsmen who worked at the forge. He is represented by ancient artists as a powerful, bearded man clad in a workman's cap and short tunic, surrounded by smith's tools. His festival fell on the 23d of August, when the young men of Athens ran torch races in his honor. You can obtain an answer to your other question by inquiring at the rooms of the Society, corner of Court and Joralemon streets, Brooklyn.

HARRY VAN N.—Wheeling is the capital of West Virginia. The *New Hampshire Gazette*, published at Portsmouth, New Hampshire, is the oldest paper in the Union which has been continued without interruption or change of name. It was established by Daniel Fowle in 1756. The Worcester *Spy*, still in existence, was established in 1770, and there are several other papers of equal age. The New York *Commercial Advertiser* is one of the oldest dailies. It was established in 1793 as the *Minerva*, but soon assumed its present name. The New York *Evening Post* first appeared in November, 1801. You will find a complete history of American newspapers in Frederic Hudson's *Journalism in the United States*, published by Harper & Brothers.

Willie S. W.—There are no rules by which one can train cats. They are not so easily taught as dogs and birds, still, with patience and kindness, you may accomplish your purpose.

"Nobody Knows."—Your puzzle is very neatly and correctly made; but we can not use it, as we have recently published one with the same solution. Do not be discouraged, but try again. The book you inquire for is published by Henry Holt & Co., and is a very useful little volume.

C. W. Lee.—The dauw (*Equus burchellii*) is a South African quadruped, intermediate between the zebra and the quagga. It is found in numerous herds in the wide plains north of the Orange River. It is somewhat larger than the zebra, but more easily domesticated.

Willie B. A.—Read the paper on "Gold-Fish" in Young People No. 8.

PUZZLES FROM YOUNG CONTRIBUTORS.

No. 1.

[illegible]

The [illegible] in the following sentence form the name of a great poet, which is composed of 11 letters. A little girl was in the garden [illegible]. The gardener was at work [illegible] a [illegible] to eat. Then a poor fellow came up the road [illegible] if [illegible] might give him a piece of bread.

Phil.

No. 2.

[illegible]

Each dash represents a letter. The whole is a familiar proverb.

[illegible]

A. T.

No. 3.

ENIGMA.

My first is in battle, but not in fight;
My second is in darkness, but not in night;
My third is in brightness, but not in cheer;
My fourth is in [illegible], but not in [illegible];
My fifth is in kind, but not in tie;
My sixth is in [illegible], but not in sight;
My whole is a tropical fruit.

Katie [illegible] (11 years).

No. 4.

DOUBLE ACROSTIC.

A vegetable. A [illegible]. A [illegible]. A [illegible]. A [illegible]. [illegible]. A unit of value. An affirmation. Answer—Two branches of an important study.

C. P. T.

No. 5.

[illegible]

First, a province. Second, to [illegible]. Third, [illegible]. Fourth, a girl's name. Fifth, [illegible].

E. M.

No. 6.

ENIGMA.

My first is in [illegible], but not in done;
My second is in [illegible], but not in fun;
My third is in [illegible], and also in spoon;
My fourth is in lake, but not in moon;
My fifth is in chain, but not in run;
My sixth is in cake, but not in [illegible];
My seventh is in [illegible], but not in begun;
My eighth is in [illegible], but not in [illegible];
My whole was a noted French general. C. W. J.

ANSWERS TO PUZZLES IN NO. 21.

No. 1. [illegible]
No. 2. Story of Robinson Crusoe.
No. 3. Athens, Orleans, Sparta, Dover, Granada, Naples, Madrid, Paris, Berlin, Berlin, Lodz.
No. 4. Candy.
No. 5. Hudson, Wabash.
No. 6. Wellington.

Favors are acknowledged from [illegible], Roy Thompson, William R., [illegible], [illegible] W., William H. M., Frank [illegible], [illegible] A. [illegible], Charles L. M., [illegible], Robert Hoyt, Amy [illegible], [illegible], Mary Thurston, [illegible], Walter M. and Clara M., [illegible], [illegible], [illegible], [illegible], C. B. Adams, [illegible], Lillian [illegible], [illegible], [illegible].

Correct answers to puzzles are received from [illegible], C. H. [illegible], George W. [illegible], [illegible], Willie Atkinson, Grace J. Richards, [illegible], [illegible], Hugh [illegible], [illegible], Fannie and Florence M., [illegible] C., May Fields, Agnes [illegible], [illegible], Walter [illegible], [illegible], [illegible], [illegible], [illegible], and [illegible].

ADVERTISEMENTS.

I'M ALL READY.

DECAPITATED CHARADE.

My whole a churchman is of weight,
Summoned his grievances to state,
Where, in the lofty audience-hall,
The bishops are assembled all.
His head cut off reveals his plan,
Which he will do as best he can.
What's left, again beheaded, shows
The state of mind in which he goes,
As, mounted on his good gray steed,
He rides along through vale and mead.
Behead that word, and, lo! 'tis plain
Why all his efforts were in vain.
Dejected now, at close of day,
He, sighing, takes his homeward way.
Behead once more; see what he did
Ere sleep fell on each weary lid.

A GEOGRAPHICAL GAME.

AN amusing and instructive geographical game has just been invented by M. Levasseur, a well-known French geographer. It is called "Tour du Monde," and is played on a large terrestrial globe, richly illustrated, and divided into 252 spherical rectangles, each of which is marked with a number corresponding to a number on a list which indicates gains or losses in the game. A brass rib or meridian running from pole to pole of the globe, but raised above the latter, is perforated with a row of eighteen holes; and there are eighteen tiny flags provided for the purpose of being planted in the holes. Each flag corresponds to one of the principal states of the world, from China the most populous to Holland the least populous.

To play the game the globe is set revolving, and a player, commencing at the south pole, plants a flag into each hole one after another at each revolution of the globe, and advances northward. The score of the player, which may be either a gain or a loss, is determined by the nature of the facts indicated on the rectangular space above which a flag may stand when the globe stops revolving; and this is, of course, the interesting and humorous part of the game. London, for example, counts thirty, Paris twenty, and so on, according to population. A coal mine, a Manchester cotton factory, a grain mart, all are reckoned gains; but an encounter with a Zulu or a lion in Africa, a storm in the Atlantic, a polar iceberg, a crocodile on the Nile, naturally go for serious losses.

A PERSONATION; WHAT IS MY NAME?

BY ELEANOR JOY.

I WAS a queen of royal birth. I was married on the 8th of September, 1761, to a certain King of England, with whom I lived for fifty-seven years. I had fifteen children, all of whom lived to grow up except two. The king whom I married had never seen me, and was only attracted toward me by my writing him an eloquent letter on the miseries and calamities of war. I was brought to England in a yacht covered with streamers and flowers. I was not very handsome, and the king, my husband, winced when he saw I was not so beautiful as some of his ladies at court. But he soon began to love me, and I lived happily with him till my death. Who am I?

THE METRIC SYSTEM IN COINS.

IT may not be generally known that we have in the nickel five-cent piece of our coinage a key to the tables of the linear measures and weights of the metric system. The diameter of this coin is two centimeters, and its weight is five grams. Five of them placed in a row will, of course, give the length of the decimeter; and two of them will weigh a decagram. As the litre is a cubic decimeter, the key to the measure of length is also the key to measures of capacity. Any person, therefore, who is fortunate enough to own a five-cent nickel may be said to carry in his pocket the entire metric system of weights and measures.

GIVING THE BABIES AN AIRING.

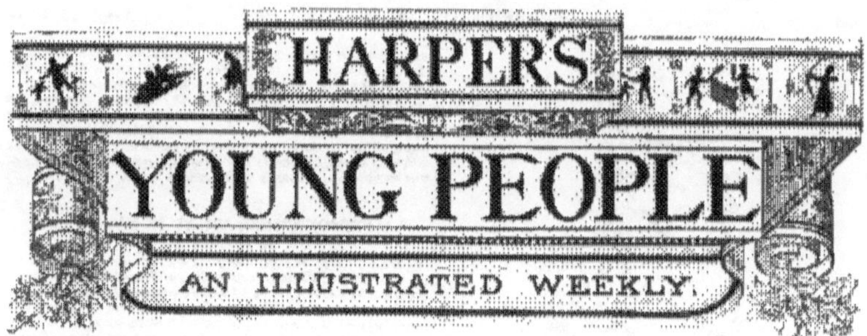

Vol. I.—No. 25. | Published by HARPER & BROTHERS, New York. | Price Four Cents.

Tuesday, April [illegible], 1880. | Copyright, 1880, by Harper & Brothers. | $1.50 per Year, in Advance.

SIM VEDDER'S KITE.

BY W. O. STODDARD.

THE kite fever visited Hagarstown every year, and caught all the boys over five before it subsided. It generally crept in slowly, a boy and a kite at a time; but this year it came as if a big wind brought it.

Yesterday there had been three kites up at one time in the main street, and Squire Jones's pony had been scared into a canter. The Squire, and Mrs. Jones, and the three

Misses Jones, and Aunt Hephzibah had all been in the carry-all at the time, and they had all screamed when the pony began to canter. So the Squire had told the boys he "could not have any more of that dangerous nonsense in the streets," and they had all come out to Dr. Gay's pasture, on the side-hill, to-day, and they had eight kites among them.

"Sim Vedder's coming, boys," said Parley Hooker. "He's been making a kite."

"He?" exclaimed Joe Myers. "He's a grown-up man. What does he know about kites?"

"There he comes now, anyway."

They all turned toward the bars and looked, for not one of them had sent up his kite yet.

"Oh, what a kite!"

"It's as tall as he is."

"No, it isn't. He's carrying it on his shoulder."

"It's just an awful kite."

Sim Vedder was the man who worked for Dr. Gay, and he was as thin as a fence rail. So was his face, and his hooked nose had a queer twist in it half way to the point.

He was coming with what looked like an enormous kite trying all the while to get away from him.

All the boys wanted to ask questions, but they didn't know exactly what to ask, so they kept still.

"Kiting, are you? Well, just you let me look at your kites, and then you may look at mine. One at a time, now. Keep back. Make that kite yourself, Parley?"

"Yes, I made it."

"Had plenty of wood around your house, I guess. Your sticks are bigger than mine, and your kite is only two feet high, and mine's five. Look at it."

He turned the back of his kite toward them as he spoke, and they saw that the frame-work of it was made of a number of very slender slips of what looked like ash or hickory wood.

"Mine's made of pine," said Parley. "And yours 'll break, too."

"No, it won't. Well, maybe yours 'll fly. Set it agoing. There's plenty of wind."

Parley obeyed, and, mainly because there was indeed a good deal of wind, his heavy-made kite began to go up.

"Joe," said Sim Vedder, "hand me that kite of yours."

"Mine's a di'mond. I don't know how to make any other."

"Do you suppose it 'll stand steady, with those fore-bands so close together? No, it won't. Up with it, and see how it 'll wiggle. Bob Jones, is that yours?"

The third kite was meekly handed to him, for the more the boys stared at Sim's big kite, the more they believed he knew what he was talking about.

"It isn't a bad kite, but those fore-bands are crossed too low. It 'll dive all over."

"There's plenty of tail, Sim. It can't dive."

"Tail!—and a bunch of May-weed at the end of it! How's a kite of that size to lift it all? I'll show you," replied Sim.

He was unfastening the fore-bands as he spoke, and now he crossed them again over his little finger, and moved them along till the kite swung under them, almost level.

"That 'll do. Now I'll tie 'em hard, and you can cut off your May-weed. There'll be tail enough without it. When I was in China—"

"Was you ever in China?"

"Yes, I was. That was when I was a sailor. I saw kites enough there. They spend money on 'em, just as we do on horses; make 'em of all shapes and sizes. Don't need any tails."

"Kites without tails?"

"Well, some of 'em have, and some of 'em haven't. It's a knack in the making of 'em. I've seen one like a dragon, and another like a big snake, and they floated perfectly. Only a thin silk string, either."

"String's got to be strong enough to hold a kite," said Parley Hooker. "Look at yours."

"Yes, mine's strong: it's made of fine hemp. But it isn't any heavier than yours. What do you want of a rope, with a kite of that size?"

"It isn't a rope."

"It's too heavy, though. Besides, you've tied pieces together with big knots in them. You can't send up any travellers."

"What's that?"

"I'll show you. Some call 'em messengers."

Just then Parley exclaimed, "Sim! Sim! mine's broke! it's coming down!"

"Broke right in the middle, where you notched your big sticks together."

"Just where it needs to be strongest," said Joe, knowingly.

"No, it doesn't. Look at mine."

It was the biggest kite they had ever seen, and it came down square at the bottom; but it was not a great deal wider than Parley's. The curious part of it was the cross-sticks and fore-bands. What did he need of so many?

"So many?" said Sim. "Why, the bands take the strain of the wind. If you put it all on the sticks, they'd bend or break. Don't you see? There's a band tied every two inches, and they all come together out here in the centre knot. It just balances on that."

"Your tail's a light one."

"It's long enough, and it spreads enough to catch the wind. It isn't the mere weight you want in a tail, if your kite's balanced. The wind blows against the tail as hard as anywhere else."

"Won't yours ever dive?"

"Of course it will, with a cross puff of wind; but it 'll come right up again. That won't happen very often. I'll send her up. You wait and see."

The other kites were all up now, except Parley's broken one, and most of them were cutting queer antics, because, as Sim explained, their fore-bands were tied wrong, and their tails "did not fit them."

"The Chinese could teach us. But, the way we make kites, there's as much in the tail as in anything else."

"Oh, but our kites are covered with paper, and you've put some old silk on yours."

"Of course I have. It isn't much heavier. The Chinese use thin paper that's as good as silk. It won't wet through."

"Wet? Oh, Sim, it looks as if a storm is coming now."

So it did, and Sim's big kite was going up, up, up very fast, and he was letting the strong brown string run rapidly off from a sort of reel he held in his hand.

"Pull in your kites, boys," shouted Parley. "Let's cut for home."

"I want to see Sim fly his."

"You all pull in yours, and we'll go into the cattle shed. It's only a shower. I can fly mine from the door."

The shed was close at hand, and the door was a wide one. In three minutes more, just as the first drops came down, there was quite a crowd of boys behind Sim, as he stood a little inside, and watched his kite. His reel was almost empty now, and the big kite looked a good deal smaller than when it started.

"How steady it is!"

"It pulls hard, though."

"There comes the rain."

"Thunder and lightning too."

Sim had fastened his wooden reel against the door-post, on a hook that was there, but he kept his hand on the string.

"I declare, boys! Feel of that! The string's wet, and it's making a lightning-rod of itself."

Parley and Joe and Bob and two or three others, felt of it at once.

"Lightning? Why, Sim," said Bob, "I know better than that. I've had an electric shock before."

"That's all it is," said Parley.

"Well," replied Sim, "didn't you ever hear of Dr. Franklin? We're doing just what he did. He discovered electricity with a kite. A wet kite string was the first lightning-rod there ever was in the world."

"Lightning?" exclaimed Bob. "Don't you bring any in here. I won't touch it again."

"Did lightning ever strike anybody when he was flying a kite?" asked Joe.

"Not that I ever heard of," said Sim. "But it's beginning to pour hard. I'll reel in my kite till the storm's over."

He unhooked his reel as he spoke, but it was well he took a good strong hold of it. The wind must have been blowing a gale up where the kite was, and the string was a very strong one for its size.

"I declare! Why—"

But the next the boys knew, Sim Vedder was out in the rain, with that kite tugging at him. He would not let go, and he could not stop himself, and the sloping pasture before him was all down hill. On he went, faster and faster, till his foot slipped, and down he went full length. He held on, though, like a good fellow, and there he lay in the wet grass, with the rain pouring upon him, tugging his best at his big kite.

The wind lulled a little, and Sim began to work his reel. Slowly at first, then faster; and about the time the rain stopped, the wind almost died out, and the wonderful kite came in.

"There isn't a stick of it broken," said Sim, triumphantly, "nor a fore-band. That's because they were made right, and put on so they all help each other."

"Oh, but ain't you wet!" exclaimed three or four boys at once.

Well, yes; he was, indeed, very wet.

TWO NARROW ESCAPES.

BY UNCLE NED.

ONE evening last winter the children called upon their uncle Ned, who is a sailor, and just home from India, for a story. He willingly granted their request, and at once proceeded to tell them of a narrow escape he once made, as follows:

"At the time of the occurrence I was staying at a small village called Yealah, in India, with a young friend in the civil service, who had a bungalow there. We used to amuse ourselves picking up shells on the beach in the cool of the evening, and later, sitting out enjoying the breeze and smoking our cheroots. One evening, however, our conversation was interrupted by a herd of buffaloes rushing past us at full speed, which we imputed to their being chased by a tiger. On the following morning our surmise proved correct, and we learned that a tiger had carried off a buffalo within two or three hundred yards of where we had been sitting on the previous evening. My friend, who was a keen sportsman, resolved to track the tiger; and I accompanied him, with a number of natives, who took care to keep at a safe distance in the rear. Following the broad track through the jungle, we soon arrived at the spot to which the tiger had dragged his prey, and here we found the mangled remains of the buffalo, but the tiger had betaken himself elsewhere to enjoy his siesta after gorging himself. We proceeded on cautiously; but as the jungle got very thick and tangled, my friend decided it would be imprudent to proceed any further, and we halted. We brought the butts of our rifles to the ground, and being of a botanical turn, I stooped to pick up a flower. At that moment a tremendous roar echoed through the forest, and seemed to stun me. I staggered a little, as if from a blow; but recovering myself, grasped my rifle, for I immediately guessed it was the tiger. My friend, with an exclamation, 'What an escape!' dashed away to the right, and I was about to follow, I knew not exactly whither, when he made his appearance, to my intense satisfaction.

"His first exclamation was, 'The brute has got away. Just like my luck.' And then he added, 'What a lucky escape you had!'

"'What do you mean?' said I.

"'Why, don't you know that, as you stooped down to pick the flower, that tiger sprang at you, and missed you by a few inches?'

"I confess a cold sweat broke out over me, and I inwardly thanked the Almighty for my providential escape.

"As my story is rather a short one, I will tell you another of a lucky escape I witnessed; though first I should mention that soon after this affair my friend paid with his life for the temerity with which he tracked tigers in the jungle.

"The brig to which I belonged was proceeding from Rangoon, and one evening, after having come to an anchor abreast of a small inlet just above Elephant Creek, at the mouth of the Irrawaddy, I accompanied the skipper and a friend in the boat up the inlet to a small village to procure a supply of fruit. On our return my companions expressed their determination to bathe; but as I did not feel inclined to do so, I seated myself in the stern, and taking out of my pocket one of Scott's novels, amused myself with reading until they should have completed their bath.

"About five minutes had elapsed, and the skipper was alone in the water, when my attention was aroused by shouts and screams from the villagers, who were hurrying down to the water's edge. Turning round, I saw my captain, for whom I had no great affection, exerting every muscle to gain the bank, from which he was still at a considerable distance. Not seeing anything to account for the hubbub, my first impression was that a child had fallen into the water, and that he was swimming to the spot of the accident to save it. In an instant I directed the Lascars to 'give way' with the oars, and seizing the helm, steered as nearly as I could guess in the direction to which the gestures of the Burmese appeared to point. Before I reached the point the skipper disappeared beneath the water; but, full of the preconceived impression, I imagined that he was diving in search of the child. A few strokes and we were at the spot, but it was not until the Lascar crew lashed their oars violently into the water that the truth flashed upon me. It must be an alligator that was pursuing him; and soon all doubt was removed, when the master, a few moments later, rose at a short distance from us in a spot where he could feel the bottom, and ran quickly ashore, his shoulder bleeding profusely. The whole transaction occupied a very short time, and the wounded master was conveyed on board the brig with all dispatch.

"On inquiry I learned that the alligator had been first seen by the Burmese, who gave instant notice of his approach, as before described, and the warning was as quickly comprehended by the captain. All his exertions to escape were, however, unavailing, and he felt himself seized a little below the shoulder. By a convulsive effort he succeeded in shaking off his cruel antagonist, and again struck out. The animal, however, again advanced, and seizing him nearly by the same place, dragged him under the surface for an instant or two, when the splashing of the oars compelled him to relax his hold. On examination it proved that the arm, although severely lacerated, was not so much injured as to incur the necessity of amputation; and being placed under medical care at Rangoon, the skipper was soon enabled to resume his duties."

(Begun in No. 18 of Harper's Young People, March 2.)

ACROSS THE OCEAN; OR, A BOY'S FIRST VOYAGE.

A True Story.

BY J. O. DAVIDSON.

Chapter VII.

TOWED BY A WHALE.

"HAVE you ever seen a whaler, lad?" asked old Herrick, as Frank came on deck the next morning. "Well, here's one for you now, anyway!"

There, sure enough, on the very edge of the great weed prairie which was now almost left behind, lay a large vessel, with her sails hanging loosely against the masts. Alongside of her floated a huge black and white mass, which a second glance showed to be the carcass of a whale, while the thick black smoke that rose from between her masts told that the work of "trying out" the oil was going briskly forward. This was just the sight for Austin, who, in the long winter evenings at home, had devoured every account and engraving of the whale-fishery that he could lay his hands on. He was still gazing, when Herrick touched his arm.

"See them two boats yonder, my boy? They've struck another whale, or my name ain't Herrick."

The whaler's boats were about three miles off, pulling as if for life and death. The other end of the line attached to each was under water, but the disturbance of the surface showed that some large object was in violent motion below. Suddenly both crews "backed water," while a man leaped into the bow of each boat, axe in hand, ready to cut the rope should the whale attempt to drag them under.

The next moment the huge black body broke through the seething foam with a lash of its tail, which, as Herrick said, "sounded like a church tower a-fallin' flat on an acre o' planks." In flew the boats, one on each side, up sprang the harpooners, with went the well-aimed weapons, and the wounded whale, giving a leap that set the whole sea boiling, turned and came right down upon the *Arizona*, as if taking *it* for the assailant.

Frank turned pale in spite of himself, for the charge of this moving mountain seemed able to crush the strongest ship like an egg-shell. But just as it was about to strike the bow, the monster turned again, and made for the distant whaler, towing the two boats after it with the speed of a locomotive.

"Bully for you, mates!" shouted a harpooner, as they flew past. "Ye've turned the critter for us, and now she'll tow us aboard without our pulling a stroke!"

On the sixteenth night of the voyage, Frank was sitting on the fore-hatch, admiring the brightness of the moon. Eight bells (8 P.M.) had just been struck, when the ship's officers were seen crowding together on the after-deck with an appearance of considerable excitement. Before any one could guess what was the matter, one of the men uttered a cry of astonishment, and pointed upward.

THE ECLIPSE.

The moonlight had become suddenly obscured, not by mist or clouds, but by a huge circular shadow, which moved steadily across the bright disk, blotting it out inch by inch.

"It's a 'clipse, that's what it is," said one; "and I heerd Mr. Hawkins say this minute as some feller ashore, months and months ago, said it 'ud come this very day and hour. Queer, ain't it, for any land-lubber to be so 'cute?"

The darkness steadily increased, till the men could barely see each other's faces; and with the unnatural gloom, a solemn silence fell upon one and all. Not a word was spoken, not a sound heard, save the rush of the steamer through the great waste of black waters. But the return of the light at length unchained all tongues, and many a quaint comment was made upon what they had just seen.

"Guess the moon's got one side bright and t'other dark, and when she slews round, she brings the dark part broadside on."

"Not much, I reckon; it's them wet clouds goin' back'ard and for'ard over her that spile her polish, same way as the spray rusts our b'ilers."

"Shouldn't wonder; for a book-l'arned feller told me once that the sun hisself's all black inside, and them spots ye see on him's jist the black a-showin' through the gildin', like a darky's skin through the holes in his shirt."

The signs of their approach to land now became unmistakable. The sea took a greenish tinge; numerous vessels were seen heading the same way as themselves; and various birds, of a kind never met far from shore, came fluttering around them. Frank, too much excited to go below, perched himself in the rigging, and strained his eyes to catch the earliest glimpse of Europe. But Africa came first, in the shape of the Tangier Light; nor was it till 4 A.M. that the haze lifted, and a huge dark mass was seen looming on the port bow, the sight of which made the boy's heart leap, for it was the Rock of Gibraltar.

TOWED WITH THE SPEED OF A LOCOMOTIVE.

As the dawn brightened, all the grand features of the scene came forth in their full splendor. The long purple range of the African mountains, ending in the bold headland of Ceuta, far away to the southeast; the wide blue sweep of the bay, with the dainty little white town of Algeciras planted on it, like an ivory carving; the flat sandy neck of "neutral ground" between the Rock and the mainland, with all its countless memories of war, from the old-world battles of Spaniard and Saracen to the day when the combined fleets of France and Spain swept it with the fire of 1800 cannon; the bristling masts of the harbor; the long gray curve of Europa Point; the mighty fortress itself, with the narrow eyes of levelled cannon peering watchfully through the terraced rocks that loomed against the bright morning sky like a thunder-cloud; the blue Spanish hills, wave beyond wave, melting at last into the warm, dreamy horizon; and right in front the white houses of Gibraltar, huddled together along the base of the cliff, as if (to quote old Herrick) "they'd been playin' snow-sled, and all slid down in a heap"—all were there.*

To get into Gibraltar Harbor is no easy matter; but the *Arizona*, following in the wake of an English mail-steamer, reached her berth at last, and had barely cast anchor when she was surrounded by a perfect fleet of "shore-boats" freighted with oranges, figs, bananas, cocoa-nuts, monkeys,† parrots, and everything else that any sailor could be expected to buy.

The screams of the parrots, the chattering of the monkeys, the bumping of the boats against each other, the clatter of the oars, the angry outcries of the boatmen, in Spanish and broken English, whenever a monkey or a parrot fell overboard, or a fruit basket got upset, made a deafening uproar. An English man-of-war, anchored close by, was similarly beset; and a mischievous sailor had just lassoed a monkey out of the nearest boat, against which outrage both Jocko and his master were protesting with all the power of their lungs. Frank lost no time in buying a stock of oranges, and tossed a quarter to the tall, black-eyed boatman, whose embroidered jacket, brown handsome face, and round flat hat with a jaunty cockade on one side of it, made a very striking picture. The Spaniard rang it on a knife-blade, tested it with a hard bite from his strong white teeth, and then tied it up in the handkerchief around his head, with a bow and a "Gracias, señor" (thanks, sir), worthy of any grandee in Spain.

* Most engravings of Gibraltar give a very imperfect idea of its position, which may be best conveyed by representing the Spanish coast as a door, and the Rock as the knob of its handle. The latter's seaward face is a pretty close copy of the Hudson Palisades.

† The Rock of Gibraltar is the only spot in Europe where monkeys are found running wild.

A GIBRALTAR FRUIT BOAT.

"What a fine fellow!" cried Frank, enthusiastically.

"Ay, ain't he!" growled an old tar who overheard him. "If I'd a loose tooth in my head, I'd yank it out 'fore comin' here, for fear some o' them 'fine fellers' ud steal it!"

"You don't say!"

"Fact; and that's why we never let none on 'em aboard. I guess the old sayin's true enough, 'The Spanish wines

THE ROCK OF GIBRALTAR.

steals all heads, the Spanish women steals all hearts, and the Spanish men steals everything.'"

The captain, purser, and doctor had gone ashore with the ship's papers; but to the no small dismay of the crew (who had expected a long stay in port) a signal was suddenly reported to "up anchor" at once. So the chain-cable was passed around the capstan, the bars manned (for the convenient fashion of getting up the anchor by steam was not yet adopted by the *Arizona*), and to work they went.

The slack of the chain came in easily enough; but to "break" the anchor out of the mud was a harder matter. Up came more men—up came even the "trimmers and heavers" from the engine-room; the bars bent with the pressure of six sturdy fellows apiece, but the anchor never budged. The perspiration rolled down the bronzed faces of the sailors, and their brawny chests heaved like bellows with the strain; but all to no purpose.

Suddenly a "flaw" of wind made the vessel heel, bringing more pressure on the chain. The crew made a desperate effort, and seemed about to conquer, when snap went a bar. The capstan spun back, the men were dashed along the deck like nine-pins, and one poor fellow, jammed between the chain and the hawse-pipe, had his hand cut in two as if by an axe.

"Hello, Yankee Doodle!" shouted a voice from the British ship, "can't git up yer mud-hook, eh? Shall we send a boy down to lift it for yer?"

Frank's eyes flashed fire at the taunt, and the roar of laughter that followed. Forgetting everything in the passion of the moment, he sprang upon the capstan, and shouted:

"Mates, are we going to let that Britisher laugh at us? Not much! Come—all together; now!"

The excited men answered with a deafening cheer, and bent to their work like giants. One tremendous heave, and up came the anchor at last. Round and round they spun, leaping over the cable, which was now coming rapidly in; and while Frank cheered and waved his cap like a madman, they ran the anchor up "chock-a-block," just as Captain Gray and his officers came up the side.

[TO BE CONTINUED.]

THE ROYAL BLACKSMITH.

BY FLETCHER READE.

THERE was born one day in the grandest palace that ever the sun shone upon a child whose life was for many years a sad and weary one. He was a cripple from his birth; and the Queen his mother, whose heart was so full of pride that there was no room left in it for love, hated the innocent babe, and refused to take him in her arms.

He, poor fellow, would no doubt have been as handsome as any of us if he had been consulted about the matter; but as no one asked him whether he would prefer being ugly or beautiful, he could hardly have been to blame for coming into the world with one leg longer than the other.

The Queen, however, did not stop to think of this. The longer she looked at him, the more angry she became, until at last, when no one was looking, she snatched him from his cradle, and threw him out of the window.

Down through the blue air fell the baby boy; still down and down, till he reached the sea. Stretching out their arms as if to welcome such a royal playfellow, the waves clapped their white hands, until the little Prince crowed and cooed for joy.

Far away beneath the waves lived two nymphs named Eurynome and Thetis, who, when they heard what had happened, decided to adopt the child. Hastening to his assistance, Thetis took him in her arms, and the two hurried along under the sea until they reached the home which they had made for themselves in one of the loveliest of the ocean caverns.

Here the boy lived for many years, but he could not forget his old home among the mountains of Olympus.

"I shall never be happy," he said to himself, "until I regain my rightful place among the sons of Zeus."

He had already displayed great skill in carving, and the little grotto of Thetis was like a piece of wonder-land, fitted and furnished with all manner of curious ornaments made by the lame boy, Hephæstus.

As he grew older he resolved to turn his talents to account, so he made friends with the Old Man of the Sea, an elderly gentleman of uncertain temper, who spent his time in sailing over the ocean in an enormous shell drawn by sea-horses.

To him Hephæstus brought a trident, hoping that the gift would induce him to offer the young exile his assistance in making peace with the Queen.

Now this trident was a magical three-pronged spear, with which the owner could still the waves in their wildest fury. It was therefore almost invaluable to the old sailor; but although he accepted the gift, and praised the workmanship, he forgot to thank the workman, and sailed grandly away.

It was not long after this that the lame Prince, walking one day through the woods, fell in with a band of wandering musicians.

Some were dancing; others were singing; and as he examined them more closely, he saw that they had legs and hoofs and even long ears like goats.

While he stood looking with wondering eyes at these fantastic beings, the leader of the band suddenly approached him, and said,

"What aileth thee, my brother? Tell me thy trouble, that I may make thee glad again, for I can not abide a sorrowful countenance."

"I am called Hephæstus," replied the Prince; "but I know not who you may be, to call me brother."

"You will be wiser when you are older," laughed his *new friend*. "It is enough for you to know now that I am a son of Zeus. But I like not the solemn grandeur of the court, so I live in the woods, keeping holiday all the year. These fauns and satyrs are my friends; and if you will join our company, I can promise you a merry life and a long one."

But Hephæstus shook his head.

"I can never be happy," he said, "until I have won the love of the Queen-mother. To do that I must show her that I have gifts quite as valuable as beauty; but I have no one to plead my cause, and I, alas! do not know the way to Olympus."

"If that is all your trouble," answered the merry man of the woods, "set your heart at rest, for I myself will present you at court."

With these words, the good-natured Bacchus threw the skin of a wild beast over his shoulders, and the two travellers became the best of friends as they journeyed together along the road which lies between the wooded heights where the satyrs dance, to the hill where the Olympian palace hides half its rosy towers among the clouds.

The Queen at first would not recognize her son; the unhappy Prince hung his head, and the assembled courtiers laughed long and loud at the awkward silence of the youth.

Bacchus, however, was not to be frightened by laughter, however inextinguishable, and he pleaded his brother's cause so well that the Queen finally consented to overlook his ugliness, and ordered that a palace be built for him.

"All I ask," said the Prince, "is a workshop, a pair of bellows, and a forge."

"Then you are not my son, after all," exclaimed the Queen. "You are nothing but a poor blacksmith."

"'Tis true I am a blacksmith," he answered, "but I will show you that I am no common workman."

Concealing her astonishment, the Queen ordered his request to be granted, and Hephæstus, glad but silent, limped away.

Day after day found him at his work; and at length one morning, when the King and Queen were sitting in their banqueting hall, the doors were thrown open, and there appeared at each entrance a golden table laden with nectar and ambrosia.

One by one the tables walked across the hall as if they had been alive, and close behind followed Hephæstus, supported on either side by lovely maidens, fashioned, like the tables, out of gold.

To the King he presented a golden sceptre and thunderbolts, which no one but Zeus himself could hold.

"Thou art indeed our son," cried the King. "Choose what thou wilt, and it shall be given thee."

Looking around the court, the eyes of Hephæstus rested at last on Venus—a Princess so beautiful that she was supposed to have been made of sea-foam.

"Grant me, O Zeus, that I may have this lady for my wife," said Hephæstus.

The request was granted almost before it was asked, and the wedding which followed was one of the most brilliant that had ever taken place in the country of Olympus.

Venus, however, was as false as she was beautiful, and Hephæstus was often unhappy; but he consoled himself as best he could by keeping perpetually at work, sometimes making a brazen shield for one friend, or forging a suit of armor for another.

So it came to pass that the lame boy Hephæstus, exiled from his father's court on account of his ugliness, became the world-renowned royal blacksmith, honored by all for his patient endurance of wrong, for his matchless skill, and for his loving service.

THE BLUE GROTTO.

BY JAMES B. MARSHALL.

"DID you ever see any blue-colored people?" asked Miss Bertha, aged ten, shortly after my introduction to that young lady at Naples. I was forced to confess that, though my acquaintances had shaded from white to black, and brown to red, I had never been fortunate enough to boast of a blue one.

"Oh, I saw 'most a hundred the other day!" said she, triumphantly. "Then did you ever see a silver-colored man?"

"A silver-colored man! Miss Bertha dear, I have an idea that you have been to fairy-land."

"He was a real silver-colored man," said she, very earnestly.

"I suppose he was the King of the fairy-land you went to."

"Oh no, he wasn't; he was a big boatman. But it was just like fairy-land; it was splendid!—really, just splendid!"

It proved that the dear little enthusiast had been, a few days previous, on a visit to the Island of Capri to see the famous Blue Grotto; since which she had been startling people with her descriptions of blue folks and a silver man.

Seeing that I couldn't have a better guide than Miss Bertha, the next morning we and a jovial party went on board of the tiny steamer that plies between Naples and the eighteen miles distant Island of Capri, hollowed under the cliffs of which the Blue Grotto is situated. The Bay of Naples, you know, is called the most beautiful in the world, and a sail across it is a lovely thing in itself. There are such glorious blue skies overhead, and such clear blue waters underneath, that the steamer appears to bear one through the air between two skies. Then, close to Naples, is seen that wonderful volcano, Vesuvius, with always a cloud of smoke curling lazily out of its crater. And, besides, the white houses of Naples are so built on a hill-side, the streets climbing to the top, that a few miles away that too is a handsome sight. Miss Bertha told me that they were the marble steps to the giant's palace, whose bird was carrying us to the enchanted island to show us the giant's jewel-room. Capri then looked like a distant light-house, merely a brown rock rising out of the sea.

As we went bobbing over the waves it grew higher and higher, which Miss Bertha explained was the correct thing for it to do, until, when the steamer anchored a little distance from its cliffs, it rose straight up from the water to a dizzy height. A flock of little skiffs crowded around the steamer for the passengers, and Miss Bertha, taking charge of me, led me into one.

"But the Grotto, where is it?" I asked, staring at the huge cliffs, straight at which our red-sashed boatman was rowing us as if to destruction.

Skiff after skiff ahead of us was seen to be swallowed up in the cliffs in the most amazing way, and not an opening in the rocky wall to be seen. "You mustn't be afraid," said my sweet little guide, assuringly; "it won't hurt;" and she gave me her hand, that—perhaps I shouldn't tell—trembled a little, and directly its mate stole into my grasp.

"Lie low down," said our boatman, when the skiff was within a few feet of apparently smashing against the cliff.

"And shut your eyes tight," said Miss Bertha, screwing up her eyes so tight that she showed all of her pretty white teeth in the funniest way. The skiff scratched and bumped on the rocks a few times, and then floated clear.

The bright sky was gone, the gulls flying about the cliffs were gone, the steamer was gone, and the cliffs themselves were gone: we had slipped under them, through a tiny opening, and were in the Blue Grotto. The blue roof rose high above us, and there was ample room within the Grotto for many times the numerous blue skiffs filled with blue-haired blue people, all dressed in blue clothes, and breathing blue air. That is just the way we appeared. The water was lighter-colored than the air, and when a boatman jumped overboard, his every action being distinctly seen, he seemed to be flying in air, and not diving in water. It gave one a weird ghostly feeling to see him, and when he came to the surface it seemed to be the most natural thing for him to tumble back to us after capering around in the sky. Then he crawled out on a rock to allow the water to drain off his clothes, and then it was that Miss Bertha's promise of a silver man was made good. He stood there a moment, appearing like a burnished silver statue, and the trickling drops as they fell from him sparkled with silvery glitter.

An oar splashed in the water sent the drops flying into the blue air, to glimmer there in silver brightness a moment, like a patch of the starry Milky Way on a frosty night.

"Isn't it lovely!" said Bertha, clapping her hands joyfully; "and you can get a whole handful of silver by just reaching for it, but you can't keep it." She grasped the blue water as she spoke, and it escaped through her fingers in glittering drops, as if a handful of coins was melting in her palm. Whatever is held in the water assumes, for the time, this silver color, and the blades of the oars shone as though the Capri boatmen were so rich that they had made them of pure silver.

For hundreds of years the Grotto was known to exist somewhere under the cliffs of the island, but so small is the entrance that it was not rediscovered until this century. It can not be entered except the sea around the island is very calm; and as all the beautiful effects are due to the refraction of light, the bright mid-day sun should be shining without.

THE ALBATROSS.

FAR away in the desolate South Seas there lives a large and beautiful bird called the albatross, the giant member of the petrel family. The wandering albatross (*Diomedea exulans*) is the largest of its tribe. Specimens have been captured measuring four feet in length, and with an expanse of wing from ten to fourteen feet. The body of this bird is very large, its neck is short and stout, and its head is armed with a powerful hooked beak from six to eight inches long. It is snowy, glistening white, its long wing-feathers tipped with black.

Its mighty strength of wing renders it the admiration of all navigators, who fitly name it the lord of the stormy seas. In the desolate regions where it lives the sailors hail its appearance with delight, as it comes sailing around the ship with majestic, careless flight, rising, sinking, now swooping down to seize some cast-off mouthful of food, now poising high above the mast-head, moving with the ship at the most rapid speed, and yet with scarcely a perceptible movement of its gigantic wings.

In storm or calm the albatross is master of the wind and waves. Sailors, straining every nerve to guide the laboring, struggling ship through tempestuous seas, look up, and see far above their heads the albatross calmly breasting the gale, its majesty unruffled, and its great outstretched wings as motionless as on a still, sunny day. Its strength of flight is marvellous, and is said to be superior to that of any other bird. Sailors have captured these royal inhabitants of southern polar regions, and marked their glistening breasts with spots of tar, that they might distinguish them and determine their power of endurance; and in several instances the same bird has followed a ship under full sail, before the wind, for seven days and longer, circling round and round, and apparently taking no rest, its sharp eye always watchful for any refuse of food cast overboard by the sailors.

The albatross is very voracious, and easily caught, as it is neither cunning nor shy. As it lives in desolation, and has little to do with men, it knows nothing of trickery, nor dreams of the plots laid against its royal freedom. An interesting account is given of the capture of an albatross by an officer of a French ship. It was a sunny, windy day, and the vessel was speeding along near the dreary Tierra del Fuego, when a great shadow like a cloud passed over the deck. On looking up, the officer saw an immense albatross, its white breast glistening like snow, floating aloft with wide-spread wings. Wishing to examine the bird more closely, he gave orders for its capture. Fastening a piece of fat pork to a strong hook attached to a line, a sailor threw it overboard, and allowed full forty yards of cord to run out. The albatross soon descried the tempting morsel, and sweeping down in graceful circles to seize it, was soon securely hooked. The only show of resistance it made to being drawn on board was to extend its wings, and utter loud discordant cries. Once on deck, its grace and majesty vanished. It showed no fear, and the hook, still fastened in its beak, did not seem to annoy it; but no landsman could have been more awkward than was the albatross on the smooth rocking deck. It staggered and waddled clumsily, and tried in vain to lift itself with its wings. It showed considerable temper, and snapped furiously at all who approached, and the captain's dog, which came trotting up, full of curiosity over the strange visitor, received a terrible blow from the hooked beak, which sent him howling with pain to the most distant corner of the deck. As the officer was desirous to preserve the beak, breast, wings, and feet of this magnificent creature as souvenirs, he ordered the sailors to kill it, although he states that it impressed him as though he were commanding the execution of some royal personage.

A SKIMMER OF THE SOUTHERN SEAS.

The albatross is an expert swimmer, and floats on the waves like a piece of cork, riding in undisturbed serenity over the lofty foaming crests of stormy billows. It is not, however, a good diver, and is obliged to subsist on whatever food comes to the surface. It might be called the vulture of the seas, for dead fish, floating carcasses of whales, and other sea refuse form its main diet.

The habits of the albatross during the breeding season are still partially veiled in mystery, as the desolate mossy headlands of Tristan d'Acunha, Inaccessible Island, and other lands lying far to the southward, where the albatross makes its nest, are visited only at rare intervals. The island of Tristan is circular, and almost entirely volcanic, and on the summit of its cliffs, which rise a thousand feet above the sea, on broad dreary plains of dark gray lava, the albatrosses gather some time during November, and prepare themselves nests. Selecting some space free from tussock-grass, the bird scrapes together a circle of dried grass and clay, in which it lays one egg about the size of a swan's, white, with a band of small brick-red spots round one end. But few naturalists have been able to visit these great breeding warrens, and none have determined how the albatross lives and feeds its young during its absence from the ocean. It is certain that the great bird rarely leaves its nest, for there is a wicked little robber gull ever on the watch to break and eat the egg, should the mother-bird desert it for a moment.

The young, when hatched, are snow-white, and covered with a soft woolly down. A traveller once climbed up the dangerous precipice of Tristan d'Acunha, and saw these young helpless things lying in the nests, while several hundred pair of parent birds were stalking awkwardly about. They all snapped their beaks with a great noise, and ejected from them an offensive oil—their only means of defense. The same traveller visited the place five months later, when he found all the young albatrosses sitting in their nests as before, but the old birds had all disappeared. It is supposed that an albatross must be a year old before it can fly; and as the parents depart some time in April for their ocean hunting grounds, and are never seen to return until the breeding season again comes round, it is astonishing what feeds and supports the young until they are able to hunt for themselves. Naturalists wonder over this point, and advance many different theories, but as yet no facts have been discovered in regard to the diet of the young and helpless bird.

"KITTY, YOU CAN'T HAVE MY APPLE."—Engraved from a Picture by F. Dielman, by Permission of R. E. Moore, American Art Gallery, New York.

The albatross was formerly regarded with superstitious reverence by sailors, who considered this majestic companion which came around the ship in desolate icy seas as a bird of good omen; and to kill one was considered a crime that would surely be punished by disaster and shipwreck. Coleridge, the English poet, has written a wonderful poem on this superstition, called the "Rime of the Ancient Mariner," to which Gustave Doré, a French artist, has drawn a series of illustrations picturing the lonely frozen ocean, and the majestic, lordly albatross which the unhappy sailor shot with his cross-bow, thereby bringing misfortune and death on the goodly ship and its crew.

A BEAR STORY

BY EMILY H. LELAND.

A GOOD many years ago, when the century was young, there came to live in the big forests of Northern Vermont a man and his wife and their little boy. Partly because they liked to be high up out of the fogs and damp, and partly because there was little else but hilly land in that part of the country, they built their cabin at the top of a nice baby mountain, which was covered at the back with an immense orchard of maples and butternuts, but which was quite bare and steep at the east side, and had rocks cropping out which the farmer thought would be fine for building a good stone house with some day.

It was long, hard work starting a farm in a place where there was nothing but woods; but after a year or so had passed by, and enough trees had been cleared away to make room for a corn field and a potato patch, and a little chicken-house and cow-shed had been added to their log-cabin, the young farmer used to sit down before their rough stone fire-place, with its bright crackling fire, and trot his boy to sleep upon his knee, while he watched the pretty young mamma putting away the supper things, thinking all the time what a rich and happy man he was. And when at last a pig-pen was joined to the cow-shed, and two cunning little pink-nosed pigs had been bought of a neighbor five miles away, and placed in it, he felt richer and grander than many a man does nowadays who owns a railroad.

And how they grew, those pink-nosed pigs! They had a southern exposure, good drainage, plenty of dry leaves and moss for bedding, and an abundance of milk, with an occasional handful of cracked corn or a pint of mashed potatoes. How could they help growing! The farmer took great delight in feeding them, and his wife would sometimes ask him, with a laugh, "Now, Stephen, which do you love the most—the pigs or our little 'Lisha?"

Elisha was the baby's name. They hadn't thought of such names as Carl and Claude and Clarence in those days.

One fine moon-lit night, late in the fall, after the corn had been husked and carried into the loft, and some of the big yellow pumpkins had been cut into strips and hung on long poles near the kitchen ceiling to dry, and others had been stored away for the cow's luncheons and the Thanksgiving pies, and the potatoes were safe in the cellar, and the onions hung in long strings above the mantel-shelf, this young farmer covered up the glowing coals in the fire-place with ashes, so they would keep bright and hot for the morning fire, and went to bed feeling quite well prepared for winter, for he had that day "banked" the house clear up to its queer little windows, and made the cow-shed and pig-pen and hen-house very cosy with loads of hemlock and spruce boughs.

He was just dozing off to sleep, when all at once there sounded through the still, frosty air a long and terrible squeal from the pig-pen.

The farmer did not wait for it to end, but bounced out of bed, tore away the clumsy fastening of the door, and rushed out with a war-whoop that could have been heard a mile away if there had been anybody to hear it. As he rushed he caught up a corn stalk that happened to lie in his way. A corn stalk was a foolish thing for him to pick up, but people seldom stop to think twice in such moments. He was around by the pig-pen in no time, and there he saw a great burly *something* just lifting one of his dear little pigs over the top of the pen. He rushed upon him, and struck him over the head with the corn stalk. There was a joint in the corn stalk nearly as hard as a crust of bread, and the *something* seemed to almost feel it through his thick fur, for he turned about and looked at the farmer, as if saying,

"What do you want of me?"

And there he was—a great, black, full-grown bear!

"Drop him! drop him!" yelled the farmer; and he brought the corn stalk down upon the bear's nose. The bear dropped the pig very quickly, but he grabbed the man in place of it, and then commenced a grand wrestling match. The farmer was a strong man, and he was "fighting for the right." The bear was strong too, and being a little tired of wild honey and beech-nuts, he had made up his mind to have a little spring pig for his family's supper. As they pushed and pulled this way and that, the bear tripped against a stump, and down they came, bear and man, to the ground; and being near the steep hill-side, in about ten seconds they began rolling down, over and over, and faster and faster, bumping over rocks and hummocks, but never letting go, and never stopping until the bottom of the hill was reached.

And then—

Up got Mr. Bear, and made off down the valley at a slow trot, never stopping to say "good-night" or anything. And up got the farmer, and scrambled up the hill as fast as his bruised legs could carry him, and feeling of his ribs as he went, expecting to find half a dozen of them at least punching out through his night-gown. But they were not.

At the door he was met by his wife keeping guard with the birch broom over her sleeping boy.

"Oh, Stephen! what was it?" she said, in a shivering whisper.

"Oh! nothing but a bear, nothing but a bear," said the farmer.

But the little pigs slept in the hen-house for the rest of the night, and the next day they had a stout log roof built over their heads.

PROFESSIONAL DIVERS.

ONE of the diver's earliest experiences is a disagreeable "roaring" sensation in the ears for some time after his first descent; but this is little felt after he becomes accustomed to his work. It is caused by the air pressure, which increases with depth. From the same cause the diver often experiences a sensation amounting to earache, which any one may test for himself by descending in a diving-bell. With regard to the mode of working, it is noteworthy that, instead of moving gradually outward after reaching the bottom, the diver usually gropes at once to the full length of his tether in the required direction, and then works slowly back to the starting-point. He considers this the safer method, partly because it leaves him at the finish directly at the place whence he has to rise.

The length of time during which a diver can remain under water depends very much upon his own strength and experience, the steady care with which the air-pump is managed, and other circumstances. M. Freudenberg states that in the repair of the well in the Scharley zinc mines, in Silesia, two divers descended to a depth of eighty-five feet, remaining down for periods varying from fifteen minutes to two hours. Siebe, another authority on the subject, relates that in removing the cargo of the ship *Cape Horn*, wrecked off the coast of South America, a diver named Hooper made seven descents to a depth of no less than two hundred and one feet, and at one time remained down forty-two minutes—supposed to be the greatest diving feat ever achieved.

JOE.

BY MRS. MARGARET E. SANGSTER.

Honest brown eyes and tangled hair,
  Rosy cheek beneath the tan,
Fearless head on shoulders square—
  That is Joe, the little man,
  Helping mother all he can.

Father is away at sea
  (Oh, the vessel tarries long!):
Lonely would the cottage be,
  Many a weary day go wrong,
  But for Joe, with shout and song.

Rough the weather, fierce the gales,
  Wild the nights upon the shore;
Oft the dear wife's courage fails,
  When she hears the breakers roar,
  Lest her sailor come no more.

Joe, with true heart and leal,
  Tells her it is safe outside;
That the deep sea does not feel
  All the troubles of the tide;
  That the good ship safe will ride.

Mother leans her comforter:
  He is only eight years old,
But his earnest words to her
  Are as rubies set in gold—
  Precious with a worth untold.

MR. THOMPSON AND THE BUMBLE-BEE.

BY ALLAN FORMAN.

"BUZZ, buzz-z, buzz-z-z," scolded old Mr. Bumble-Bee, flying around Mr. Thompson's head. Mr. Thompson didn't understand him, however, and only brushed at him impatiently, and said, "Get out!" in a tone anything but sociable; but the old bee kept flying around just the same, and complained in his drowsy voice: "Buzz, buzz-z, buzz-z-z. I wish you would go away. I want to get into my house, and I don't want you to see me. My family are in there, and we are making bread to-day, and unless I get home with the flour, my wife will scold awfully. Buzz, buzz-z, buzz-z-z."

But in the mean time Mr. Thompson had fallen asleep, and the old bee sat down on the fence-rail and watched him. "Hum, hum, hum," he murmured. "I guess that he has gone to sleep. I don't see what men want to stay awake for, anyway; they are not half so much trouble when they are asleep. And only listen how nicely he can buzz through his nose!—he really seems to be quite like a sensible bee."

Now Mr. Thompson says he did not go to sleep at all; he says that he only closed his eyes, and in a few minutes he could understand every word that the old bee said.

"He's a pleasant-looking man," hummed the bee. "I wonder if he likes honey?"

Mr. Thompson answered through his nose that he was very fond of it.

"Sensible, too," said the bee, who thought (all bumble-bees do) that anybody who agreed with him must be sensible. Then, turning to Mr. Thompson, the bee murmured, in a more pleasant buzz, "If you like honey, try some of this." As he said it he alit on Mr. Thompson's lips, and pressed some of the honey he had with him into his mouth.

Mr. Thompson began to grow smaller, and as he shrunk in size, his light alpaca duster became gauzy, and formed itself into wings. Just as he had begun to wonder how long it would take him to shrink into nothing, the bee said, "There, I guess that will do."

Mr. Thompson stretched himself, and found to his surprise that he was in reality nothing more than a large black bumble-bee. He shook his wings, arose, and, flying around for a few moments, settled on the fence rail. He has since told me that if it is true, as Mr. Darwin says, that men were evolved from the lower orders of animals, they made the greatest mistake of their lives when they left off their wings.

"Well," remarked the old bee, "you look quite presentable. Won't you drop in and take dinner with me? My wife would be delighted to see you."

Mr. Thompson thought how much he resembled a certain highly respectable old gentleman who was wont to invite his friends to his humdrum dinners, and buzz them unmercifully in the same drowsy way. But as he did not like to offend his new friend, he answered, politely, that he would be most happy, and followed him under the rail into a round hole that was the door of the bumble-bee's house.

They entered a long cylindrical corridor, or, as the old bee expressed it, "arched at the top, sides, and floor." It was lined with the fibres of the wood, and was as soft as velvet. After walking some distance along the hall, they reached a part where it widened into a sort of parlor. Here Mrs. Bumble-Bee was seated, resting from the labor of bread-making.

"Well, you are home at last," she buzzed, angrily. "I'll be bound you forgot the flour."

"Why, my dear, don't you see it? I have it here," answered Mr. Bee, soothingly, pointing to two little yellow bundles on his legs.

After greeting her guest, Mrs. Bee excused herself on the score of domestic duties, and busied herself in carrying the flour, or pollen, into the corridor above. Soon she returned, and after they had made a meal of bee-bread and honey, Mr. Bumble-Bee proposed to show his guest through his mansion. They passed through several long corridors, so constructed that the rain could not beat into the living-rooms, as Mr. Bee explained. One end of one of the upper galleries was securely walled up, and in another compartment lay three or four worm-like insects almost covered with bee-bread.

"What is this room used for?" inquired Mr. Thompson.

"This is the nursery," answered Mr. Bee, proudly.

"Ah, indeed! And what are those white, ugly-looking grubs?"

Mr. Bee looked aghast for a moment, but his surprise quickly turned into indignation, as he buzzed, angrily: "Grubs! grubs! ugly-looking grubs! Those, sir, are my children, sir, and I flatter myself that a more charming family does not exist. Grubs, forsooth! Out of my house, base insulter!" And before Mr. Thompson could apologize, Mr. Bee had pushed him out, and stung him on the end of his nose.

He fell, and as he dropped from the rail he began to grow larger, and when he reached the ground he had assumed his natural proportions. He found himself lying in the same place beside the fence that he had occupied when the bee first spoke to him.

When he related the story to his friends, some one suggested that he had dreamed the whole adventure. He gently touched his inflamed and swelled nose, and answered, in a grieved tone, "I suppose I dreamed this too."

This argument was unanswerable, and Mr. Thompson is now engaged in writing a lecture on the habits and customs of the bumble-bee. Among other things he says, "Bumble-bees only consider those people sensible who agree with them"; and again, "Bumble-bees invariably think their own children the most beautiful and interesting creatures in existence."

Which facts, if they are true, show the great superiority of men over bumble-bees.

THE STORY OF GEORGE WASHINGTON.

BY EDWARD CARY.

Chapter II.

After the close of the French and Indian war, Washington, then in his twenty-seventh year, married Mrs. Martha Custis, and settled down to a Virginia planter's life at Mount Vernon. His neighbors elected him again and again to the House of Burgesses of the colony—a body much like one of our State Legislatures. Here he did not talk much, but he kept close watch of matters, and knew, as nearly as he could, all the facts that were needed to make up his mind, so that he had a good deal of weight with other members, and yet was very modest. When he first took his seat in the House, the Speaker was directed to thank him, in the name of the people, for his great services as an officer. This the Speaker did in glowing terms, quite unexpectedly to Washington. Washington rose to reply. His face flushed; he struggled to speak; but could only stammer, and stood speechless and trembling. "Sit down, Mr. Washington," said the Speaker, with a smile. "Your modesty equals your valor, and that surpasses the power of any language that I possess."

After Washington had been some ten years at Mount Vernon, looking forward to the peaceful and easy life of a wealthy farmer, certain things happened which seemed then of small account, but which were to lead to a great change in his career. The government of Great Britain undertook to raise money in America for use on the other side of the ocean. This government was made up of the King and the Parliament, and the Parliament was for the most part chosen by the people of England. The people of America were not allowed to choose any of its members, and when the British government declared that the Americans must raise money for it, the Americans had no one to vote for them or speak for them on that question. They thought that this was not fair. They were willing to pay the expenses of their own governments, because they had some voice in them, but they would not help pay the expenses of the British government, in which they had no voice.

The British government passed an act which said that every written promise to pay money must be upon stamped paper, which could only be got by buying it from British officers. If the promise was not on this kind of paper, the man who signed it need not pay. The British thought this would bring in a good deal of money. But the Americans would not use the stamped paper. They seized that which was sent over, and burned it. Other kinds of taxes were tried, but the Americans would pay none of them. Washington took the side of his countrymen with great zeal. He wrote to a friend: "I think the Parliament of Great Britain have no more right to put their hands into my pocket, without my consent, than I have to put my hands into yours." But the British government insisted, and sent over troops to Boston to try and force the people to submit.

Washington was one of a number who proposed that a Congress, or great meeting, should be called to arrange

WASHINGTON TAKES COMMAND OF THE ARMY.

for resisting the taxes, and he was chosen to go to the Congress, which was held at Philadelphia in September, 1774. Meanwhile more soldiers were sent over. An attempt was made on the 19th of April, 1775, to seize some powder which the Americans had at Concord, near Boston, and the result was the battle of Lexington, where a good many Americans were killed, but where the British soldiers were finally driven back. Large numbers of men took their guns and gathered at Boston to watch the British troops, and keep them in the city. They came from Massachusetts and the other colonies called New England—from Connecticut and Rhode Island, and from New Hampshire and Maine.

The Congress came together again in May, 1775, and Washington was also there. The battle of Lexington had been heard of, and the people were everywhere angry and excited.

The Congress resolved to resist all attempts by the British to force the country to submit. It called for troops and guns and powder from the various colonies. It adopted the soldiers around Boston as a part of the "Continental Army," or the army of the whole country; it chose Washington as commander-in-chief, to have the direction of all the soldiers. When this was made known to him, he thanked Congress for the honor, but he added, "I beg it may be remembered by every gentleman in this room that I this day declare with the utmost sincerity I do not think myself equal to the command I am honored with." He also refused to take any pay for his services. "I will keep an exact account of my expenses," he said. "These, I doubt not, Congress will discharge, and that is all I desire." Washington hastened to Boston, learning of the battle of Bunker Hill on the way. He found some seventeen thousand men around Boston, and took command of them on the 3d of July, under a great elm-tree, on the common in the village of Cambridge. He was then forty-three years old, and a very tall and fine-looking man. His features were large, his eyes were of a pure blue, usually grave, but full of kindness, and at times very merry. His manners were gentle, but full of dignity, and they often seemed very cold to those not well acquainted with him, though at heart he was not cold.

[TO BE CONTINUED.]

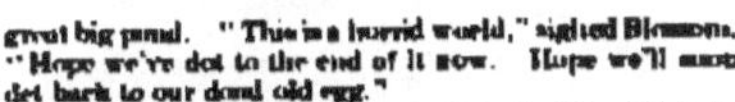

PUCK AND BLOSSOM.

From the German of Marie von Olfers.

PART II.

"OW!" sobbed Blossom, "that hurt."

"Never mind," said Puck, comfortingly, "things never go right the first time; it 'll be better by-and-by."

Then they went and they went, till they came to a great big pond. "This is a horrid world," sighed Blossom. "Hope we're dot to the end of it now. Hope we'll soon det back to our dood old egg."

"But let's go see how it is over there first," said Puck. "Ducky, ducky, come and carry us across."

"Ow! but then my little white frock will det all dirty," said Blossom.

"What does that matter?" answered Puck; "we shall see how it is over there." Over there was very much the same as it was over here. The duck ducked them finely.

"So you'll know how it is down here too," he said.

Dripping, they stood upon the shore.

"Ow! ow!" sobbed Blossom, looking very miserable indeed; "if it doesn't get better soon, I don't want to see any-

thing more at all, I don't."

"Of course it 'll get better," said Puck; "the sun 'll dry us." The sun looked out condescendingly from the

clouds for a moment, and then disappeared. "Come,

Blossom," said Puck, "who cares for the old sun! Just as though there wasn't fire anywhere but up there! There's some down here too. I know where it lives—down there in that little house."

Yes, down there in that little house.

"In the ashes, inside the stove," said the cat, who was looking after things while the cook was away.

"It's asleep," said Puck. "Wait; I'll soon wake it up." So he blew and he blew, but it would not wake up at all. The sparks looked out at him with grim and wrathful eyes, while Puck blew more and more madly on.

At last it did wake up. It sprang out of the stove, wild and raging; it grew bigger and bigger; the children fled, the fire behind them—Blossom ahead, terrified, shrieking, screaming.

The fire had caught Puck, had wrapped him round in a great sheet of flame!

But Blossom cried, and cried, and cried, so bitterly that the fire was all put out, and there was nothing left but a great black smoke.

Then Puck gathered together all there was left of him, and they went sorrowfully on their way to find their egg.

Ah me! it was broken in two, and gone. But the nest was still hanging on the tree. In great haste they climbed in, never venturing to leave it again, and if they are not dead, they are sitting there still.

THE END.

OUR POST-OFFICE BOX.

signs that winter is passing away, are always [illegible] welcomed. The buds form in the [illegible] on the brown twigs, and with the first warm spring sun, long before anything green has started, they swell, and burst open the brown scaly covering, disclosing a soft, downy white [illegible], or blossom, resembling the toe of a white kitty. This resemblance is perhaps the reason why children call these early blossoms "pussies."

A. [illegible].—Directions for feeding mocking-birds are given in Post-office Box of Young People No. 13.

Lillie T.—Your rabbit-hutch should be in a dry place, and should have two apartments. The sleeping-room should be boarded in, and you must have a door which you can open to clean it and supply it with fresh straw. The other apartment should have grated sides, and there is where the food should be placed. You must feed your rabbits regularly two or three times a day. They should have oats or bran for dry food, and carrot tops, cabbage leaves, and fresh clover frequently. If you have a yard, let them run in the grass an hour or more every day during warm weather.

K. [illegible]'s request in Young People No. 23 for long English words, has been answered by Bertha F. H., H. F., Hattie N., Thomas J. F., Albert H. E., Kent K., Emily J. M., Fanny S., Bessie C., H. H. M., Edith C., Willie H. H., Herbert S. T., [illegible] A. Page, and others. To print all the words sent would occupy too much space. We give only a few of the longest. [illegible], [illegible], [illegible], [illegible], [illegible]. [illegible] and [illegible] have also been suggested, as one has a mile, the other a league, between the beginning and the end.

[illegible] are acknowledged from [illegible]

Correct answers to puzzles are received from [illegible]

PUZZLES FROM YOUNG CONTRIBUTORS.

No. 1.

[illegible]

I am composed of 8 letters.
My 4, 2, 6 is a boy's name.
My 1, 2, 7, 8 is a [illegible].
My 3, 8, 5, 1 is to [illegible].
My whole was an ancient king.

A. M. S. (13 years).

No. 2.

[illegible]

My first is in [illegible], but not in [illegible];
My second is in [illegible], but not in [illegible],
My third is in [illegible], but not in [illegible],
My fourth is in [illegible], but not in [illegible],
My fifth is in [illegible], but not in [illegible],
My sixth is in [illegible], but not in [illegible],
My seventh is in village, but not in town,
My whole is a fairy of [illegible].

E. S. G. M.

No. 3.

[illegible]

In blood. A girl's name. A reptile. [illegible]. In blood.

A. L. B.

No. 4.

WORD SQUARE.

First, a multitude. Second, a musical instrument. Third, to [illegible]. Fourth, a portion of time.

[illegible]

No. 5.

[illegible]

My whole is a South American [illegible] of 9 letters.
My [illegible] is a period of time.
My [illegible] is a portion of the earth.
My [illegible] is [illegible].

E. L.

No. 6.

[illegible]

A [illegible]. A [illegible]. [illegible]. A [illegible] of the [illegible]. [illegible]. A [illegible] for a [illegible] purpose. Surrounded by water. To [illegible]. [illegible].

Rip Van Winkle.

ANSWERS TO PUZZLES IN No. [illegible]

No. 1. [illegible]

No. 2. [illegible]

Daisy, Pansy.

No. 3. [illegible]

No. 4. [illegible]

No. 5. [illegible]

No. 6. [illegible]

Charade on page [illegible]—Caterpillar.

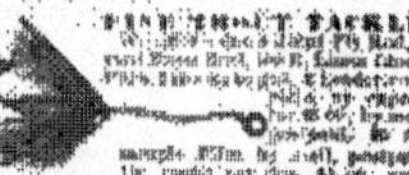

"SPRING, SPRING, BEAUTIFUL SPRING."

A Wonderful Clock.—The most astonishing thing ever heard of in the way of a time-piece is a clock described by a Hindoo Rajah as belonging to a native Prince of Upper India, and jealously guarded as the rarest treasure of his luxurious palace. In front of the clock's dial was a gong, swung upon poles, and near it was a pile of artificial human limbs. The pile was made up of the full number of parts of twelve perfect bodies, but all lay heaped together in seeming confusion. Whenever the hands of the clock indicated the hour of one, out from the pile crawled just the number of parts needed to form the frame of one man, part joining itself to part with quick metallic click; and when completed, the figure sprang up, seized a mallet, and walking up to the gong, struck one blow that sent the sound pealing through every room and corridor of that stately palace. This done, he returned to the pile, and fell to pieces again. When two o'clock came, two men arose and did likewise; and so through all the hours, the number of figures being the same as the number of the hour, till at noon and midnight the entire heap sprang up, and marching to the gong, struck one after another each his blow, and then fell to pieces.

THE PENGUIN PUZZLE.

With two straight cuts of the scissors change this fish into an alarmed penguin catching a herring.

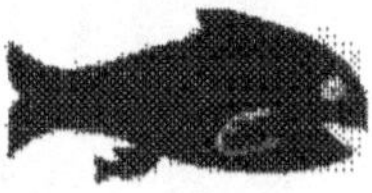

CHARADE.

An Emperor kneels in sore dismay,
  For his enemy cometh apace.
In this hour of need to whom shall he pray?
  From which of his gods seek grace?
To his father's God, the One, the Alone,
  He cried, and the answer burst
On his wondering eyes: a marvel shone,
Pledge of hope and help from the God unknown,
  And that answering sign was my *first*.

Some voyagers weary of wooden walls
  Are treading the land once more.
The father around him his children calls,
  Their God, who had saved, to adore.
Seven angels all hasten God's answer to bring,
  Of His promise the seal and the sign;
Arrayed is each one as the child of a King;
Together they rival the flowers of spring,
  And together my *second* they shine.

King Henry hath crossed over into France
  With his lords and his nobles gay.
He would teach the Frenchman quite a new dance,
  And bid him the piper to pay.
Such his design; but the end who can tell?
  Who the fortunes of battle control?
One thing I aver, and none will demur:
If King Henry succeeds, 'twill be by the deeds
  Of his soldiers, who carry my *whole*.

An Ancient Castle.—The Czarowitz recently visited, with King Oscar II., the famous old castle of Gripsholm, in Sweden. The old keeper showed the Czarowitz a heap of straw, and told him that his father, the present Czar, had used it as his bed in the year 1838. Alexander in that year accompanied his father, Czar Nicholas, to Sweden, and it was during their visit to the castle that that severe parent insisted upon making his son sleep on straw. It is popularly believed in Russia that the stern Nicholas never allowed his son and heir to sleep upon any more comfortable bed.

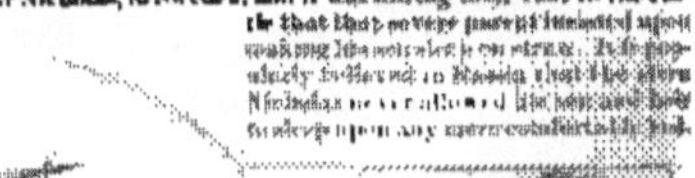

Vol. I.—No. 26. | Published by HARPER & BROTHERS, New York. | Price Four Cents.
Tuesday, April 27, [illegible] | $1.50 per Year, in Advance.

SPANISH SAILORS IN A STORM.

[Begun in No. 19 of Harper's Young People, March 9.]

ACROSS THE OCEAN; OR, A BOY'S FIRST VOYAGE.

A True Story.

BY J. D. DAVIDSON.

Chapter VIII.

A "WHITE SQUALL."

HURRAH for the Mediterranean! Hurrah for the tide-less sea, with its sunny skies and sparkling waters, blue and bright as ever, while English moors and German forests are being buried in snow by a bitter January storm!

Well might one think that these handsome, olive-cheeked, barefooted fellows in red caps and blue shirts, who cruise about this "summer sea" in their trim little lateen-rigged fruit boats, must be the happiest men alive. Yet there was once an English sailor who, plunging into a raw Channel fog on his return from a twelvemonth's cruise in the Mediterranean, rubbed his hands, and cried, gleefully, "Ah, this is what *I* calls weather! None o' yer lubberly blue skies *here!*"

Frank, having seen for himself that the Straits of Gibraltar are thirteen miles wide, instead of being (as he had always thought) no broader than the East River, was prepared for surprises; but he could not help staring a little when Herrick told him that this bright, beautiful, glassy sea is at times one of the stormiest in the world, and that many a good ship has gone down there like a bullet, "as you'll see afore long, mayhap," added the old sailor, warningly.

The sunset that evening, however, seemed to contradict him point-blank. It was so magnificent that even the careless sailors, used as most of them were to the glories of the Southern sky, stood still to admire it, and pronounced it "the finest show they'd ever seen, by a long way." Not a cloud above, not a ripple below; the steamer's track lay across the glassy water like a broad belt of light. All was so calm, so clear, so bright, that it was hard to tell where the sea ended and the sky began. The ship seemed to be floating in the centre of a vast bubble.

Suddenly the sun plunged below the horizon like a red-hot ball, and a deep voice muttered in Frank's ear.

"We're a-goin' to catch it!"

At that moment, as if to bear out this gloomy prophecy, the boatswain's hoarse call was heard:

"Stand by topsail sheets and halyards! Man the downhauls! Clear away, and make all snug!"

Instantly all was bustle and activity. While some stripped the yards and clewed up the sails, others battened down the hatches, looked to the lashings of the boats, and made everything fast. Still, though he strained his eyes to the utmost, not the least sign of a storm could Frank see, and at last he whispered to Herrick,

"How can they tell that it's going to be rough?"

"The glass is falling, lad, and that's always enough for a sailor; but there'll be more'n *that* afore long. Ay, sure enough—see yonder!"

A streak of pale phosphorescent mist had just appeared on the port bow, which spread and spread till it blotted out sea and sky, and all was one dim, impenetrable pall. From the far distance came a strange, ghostly whisper, while the sea-birds, which had hitherto kept close to the vessel, flew away with dismal shrieks.

"Below there!" roared the boatswain. "Tumble up there, smart!"

Up flew the men, each darting at once to his own post—and not an instant too soon. A huge white cloud seemed to leap upward through the inky sky like smoke from a cannon, a long line of foam glanced like a lightning flash across the dark sea, and then came a rush and a roar, and over went the ship on her beam ends, and every man on board was blinded, deafened, and strangled, all in one moment, while crash followed crash, as doors, sky-lights, and port-shutters were torn away or dashed to atoms.

Frank, who was just stepping out of one of the deck-houses when the storm burst, was spun across the forecastle like a top, and would have gone overboard had not a sailor clutched his arm, and pressed him down on the deck by main force till the ship righted.

"Lie snug, young 'un," said his rescuer, "for them 'white squalls' ain't to be sneezed at, that's a fact. Look at my shirt."

This was easier said than done, for honest Bill had no shirt left to look at, except the collar and wristbands, all the rest having been torn clean away.

But as Austin glanced round him he saw other proofs of the wind's force even more convincing than this. Two of the boats had been literally smashed to pieces, the strong iron davits that held them being twisted like pin-wire. Down in the engine-room the flying open of the furnace doors had flooded the whole room with blazing coal, and four of the tubes had burst at once, scalding several firemen so severely that they had to be carried to the surgeon forthwith.

Suddenly a cry for help was heard from the wheel-house. Three or four brave fellows rushed across the reeling deck at the risk of their lives, and tearing open the door, found one quartermaster lying senseless and bleeding in a corner, while the other, with a broken arm, was actually keeping the wheel steady with *the remaining hand and his knee*, which he had thrust between the spokes!

But the stout-hearted crew, not a whit daunted, coolly set about repairing damages. The injured men were carried below, the decks cleared of the fragments of wreck, and the coals drawn from the furnaces, into which the firemen, swathed in wet blankets, crept by turns along a plank (relieving one another as the stifling heat overpowered them) to close the flues again by hammering strong wooden plugs into the leaks.

By twelve o'clock the gale was at its height. Even with four men at the wheel, the *Arizona* could barely hold her own against the tremendous seas that came thundering upon her like falling rocks, and old Herrick himself began to look grave.

"Get out a drag!" shouted the officer of the watch.

The boatswain repeated the order, to the no small amazement of our hero, who, having always associated a drag with the wheel of a coach, was puzzled to imagine how it could be applied to a ship.

But he was not long in finding out. Pieces of timber from the broken boats, worn-out sails, old iron, and various odds and ends were hastily gathered into a heap, lashed together with chains, and launched overboard, with two strong hawsers attached. The chains and pieces of iron made the buoyant mass sink just deep enough to steady the vessel, and keep her head up to the wind, which toward night-fall began to show signs of abating.

Just before darkness set in, a Spanish bark crossed their bows. The storm had left its mark on her upper spars, which were terribly shattered; but the crew, instead of clearing away the wreck, were groaning and praying around a little doll-like image of the Virgin, while their officers vainly urged them to return to their duty.

"Skulkin' lubbers!" growled old Herrick; "they should git what that feller in the song got. D'ye mind it, Frank, my boy?

"'The boatswain he rope's-ended him, and "Now," says he, "just work!
I read my Bible often, but it don't tell men to *shirk*;
The pumps they are not choked as yet, so let us not despair:
When all is up, or when we're saved, we'll join with you in prayer."'"

The next morning they sighted the craggy islet of Zembra, which Jack Dewey, the wit of the forecastle, said should be called "Zebra," for its cliffs were curiously veined with stripes of blue, red, and black, as regular as if painted with a brush. A few hours later appeared the larger island of Pantellaria, standing boldly up from the sea in one great mass of cloud-capped mountain, with the trim white houses of the little toy town scattered along its base like a game of dominoes.

By sunset that evening the gale seemed to have fairly blown itself out. But now came another enemy almost as dangerous. A little after midnight the ship was hemmed in by a perfect wall of fog, through which neither moon nor star was to be seen; and all that could be done was to set the bells and fog-horns to work, making an uproar worthy of a Chinese concert.

About three in the morning came a faint answering chime of church bells; and the *Arizona*, "porting" her helm, kept circling about the same spot for two hours more ("playin' circus," as Jack Dewey said), till the morning breeze suddenly parted the fog, displaying to Frank's eager eyes the rocky shores of Malta, and the entrance of Valetta Harbor.

"There's one thing here as you're bound to see, lad," said Herrick, "and that's a sort o' under-ground tunnel, like ever so many streets buried alive, and pitch-dark every one of 'em. They calls it the Cat-and-Combs [Catacombs]. I never could tell why, for it ain't got nothin' to do with combs, nor yet with cats neither. But you've got to take guides and lights with yer, and stick mighty close to 'em, or ye're a gone 'coon. Guess *I* ought to know that!"

"Why, did you ever get lost there?"

"That's jist what I did, sonny, though I can't think how; but, anyway, there I was, all *in* ones, right away from the rest, and all alone in the dark. I tried to holler, but my throat was so dry with the dust and what not that I made no more noise nor a frog with a sore throat. 'Twarn't pleasant neither, I can tell ye, to feel my feet kickin' agin skulls and bones in the dark, and to think how my bones 'ud be added to the collection 'fore long, when the rats had picked 'em clean. At last I concluded that I'd jist make matters worse by steerin' at hap-hazard, and that my best way was to anchor, and wait for the rest o' the convoy.

"Jist then I spied *two eyes* a-shinin' in the darkness, and 'fore I could say 'Knife,' slap came somethin' right in my face, givin' me sich a start that I jumped five ways at once. But by the soft, furry feel, I guessed what 'twas; so I sang out, 'Puss! puss!' and the thing came rubbin' agin my feet, and what should it be but a stray cat! Thinks I, 'Here's somethin' to keep off the rats, anyhow!' and I sat down in a corner, and took the cat in my lap, and, if you'll b'lieve me, off I went sound asleep! Fust thing I knew after that, all my mates was around me agin, laughin' like anythin' to find me nussin' a cat that way. But I wouldn't go that job over agin, not to be made a Cap'n!"

[TO BE CONTINUED.]

SOMETHING ABOUT FANS.

KAN SI was the first lady who carried a fan. She lived in ages which are past, and for the most part forgotten, and she was the daughter of a Chinese Mandarin. Who ever saw a Mandarin, even on a tea-chest, without his fan? In China and Japan to this day every one has a fan; and there are fans of all sorts for everybody. The Japanese waves his fan at you when he meets you, by way of greeting, and the beggar who solicits for alms has the exceedingly small coin "made on purpose" for charity presented to him on the tip of the fan.

In ancient times, amongst the Greeks and Romans, fans seem to have been enormous; they were generally made of feathers, and carried by slaves over the heads of their masters and mistresses, to protect them from the sun, or waved about before them to stir the air.

Catherine de Medicis carried the first folding fan ever seen in France; and in the time of Louis the Fourteenth the fan was a gorgeous thing, often covered with jewels, and worth a small fortune. In England they were the fashion in the time of Henry the Eighth. All his many wives carried them, and doubtless wept behind them. A fan set in diamonds was once given to Queen Elizabeth upon New-Year's Day.

The Mexican feather fans which Cortez had from Montezuma were marvels of beauty; and in Spain a large black fan is the favorite. It is said that the use of the fan is as carefully taught in that country as any other branch of education, and that by a well-known code of signals a Spanish lady can carry on a long conversation with any one, especially an admirer.

The Japanese criminal of rank is politely executed by means of a fan. On being sentenced to death he is presented with a fan, which he must receive with a low bow, and as he bows, *presto!* the executioner draws his sword, and cuts his head off. In fact, there is a fan for every occasion in Japan.

THE BOYS' SCHOOLS OF ENGLAND.

BY AMELIA E. BARR.

I SUPPOSE there are few boys who have not heard of Westminster Abbey, and who do not know that within its ancient and splendid walls the Kings of England are crowned, and the great, the wise, and the brave of every age are buried. But few, perhaps, are aware that the Abbey also contains the oldest and one of the most famous boys' schools in the world. It is true that the statutes of the school, as they now exist, are of a less remote date than those of Eton and Winchester schools—being framed by Henry the Eighth and Elizabeth—but they no more represent the origin of Westminster School than the Reformation represents the origin of the English Church.

Westminster Abbey was built by Edward the Confessor, and the Master of the Novices sitting with his disciples in the western cloister was the beginning of Westminster School. It was, without doubt, this school that Ingulphus—the writer of a famous chronicle (A.D. 1043-1051)—attended; for he tells us that Queen Edith often met him coming from school, and questioned him about his grammar and logic, and always gave him three or four pieces of money, and then sent him to the royal larder to refresh himself—two forms of kindness that a school-boy never forgets. Ingulphus afterward became the secretary of William the Conqueror. In his day there was no glazing to this cloister, and the rain, wind, and snow must have swept pitilessly over the novices turning and spelling out their manuscripts. They had, indeed, a carpet of hay or rushes, and mats were laid on the stone benches, but it must have been a bitterly cold school-room in winter.

At the Reformation, Henry the Eighth drew up new plans for Westminster School, and Elizabeth perfected the statutes by which the school is still governed. It was to consist of forty boys, who were to be chosen for their "good disposition, knowledge, and poverty, and without favor or partiality"; and even at the present day there is no admission as a "Queen's Scholar" at Westminster except by long and arduous competition between the candidates for the honor.

No one who has witnessed the mode of election will ever forget it. The candidates are arranged according to their places in the school, and the *lowest two boys* first enter the arena. The lower of these two is the challenger. He calls upon his adversary to translate an epigram, to parse it, or to answer any grammatical question connected with the subject. Demand after demand is made, until there is an error. The Master is appealed to, and answers, "It was a mistake." Then the challenger and the challenged change places, and the latter, with fierce eagerness, renews the contest. Whichever of the two is the conqueror, flushed with victory, then turns to the boy above him, and if he be a really clever lad, he will sometimes advance ten, fifteen, or twenty steps before he is stopped by a greater spirit. This struggle—which is peculiar to Westminster, and highly prized by its scholars—frequently extends over six or eight weeks, and the ten who are highest at its close

A VIEW OF WESTMINSTER.

are elected "Queen's Scholars," in place of those advanced that year from Westminster to Oxford or Cambridge.

This mental tournament is a very ancient custom, for Stow says that the Westminster scholars annually stood under a great tree in St. Bartholomew's Church yard, and entering the lists of grammar, chivalrously asserted the intellectual superiority of Westminster against all comers; and Stow, as you very likely know, died about A.D. 1605. There is, therefore, as you may see, a very great honor in being a "Queen's Scholar"; besides which, the prizes to be divided among them are very valuable. These consist of three junior studentships of Christ Church, Oxford, tenable for seven years, and worth about £120 a year; Dr. Carey's Benefaction, which divides £600 a year among the most needy and industrious of the scholars in sums of not less than £50, and not more than £100; and three exhibitions at Trinity College, Cambridge, of yearly value about £27, tenable until the holder has taken his Bachelor of Arts degree. The Queen's Scholars are partially maintained by the school; but all other boys, of which the average number is about one hundred and fifty, pay very handsomely for their education.

The government of this school is an absolute monarchy in the hands of the Head-Master, though the Dean and Chapter of Westminster can exercise a certain control of the Queen's Scholars, and the reigning sovereign of England is by the statutes Visitor of the School. In 1846 the father of one of the Queen's Scholars complained to her Majesty that his boy had been cruelly treated by three of the other scholars, and she ordered an immediate trial, and punishment of the guilty parties.

Westminster, from its earliest records, has been famous for its Masters. Before the great Camden—the Pausanias of England—were Alexander Nowell, Nicholas Udall, and Thomas Browne. Nowell was Master in Queen Mary's reign, and Bonner intending to burn him, he fled for his life. On Elizabeth's accession he again became Master, and was also one of Elizabeth's preachers, and reproved her so plainly that on one occasion she bade him "return to his text." You know, boys, it is so easy and so natural for school-masters to tell people when they are wrong, and the Masters of Westminster have been noted for the habit.

Dr. Busby's name is forever associated with Westminster, and he ruled the school with his terrible birch rod for upward of fifty-seven years. "My rod is my sieve," he said, "and who can not pass through it is no boy for me." So many able boys, however, passed through it, that he could point to the Bench of Bishops, and boast that sixteen of the spiritual lords sitting there at one time had been educated by him. The height to which he carried discipline is exemplified by his accompanying King Charles through the school-room *with his hat on*, because "he would not have his boys think there was any man in England greater than himself." Dryden was one of Busby's scholars, and received from the great Master many a severe flogging, yet Dryden always spoke of Dr. Busby with the greatest reverence. Flogging is now only administered on very grave occasions, by the Head-Master, and in the presence of a third party, who must be one of the boys.

In Dr. Busby's time the upper and lower schools were divided by a curtain, about which there is a remarkable story. A boy, having torn this curtain, was saved from one of Busby's terrible floggings by his school-mate assuming the fault, and bearing the rod in his place. This brave lad in the civil war took the King's side, became implicated in a futile rising, and was condemned to death at Exeter. But his judge happened to be the very boy whose place he had taken under Busby's rod, and he was not unmindful of the favor, for he hastened to London, and begged from Cromwell his friend's life. If you will get No. 313 of the *Spectator*, you can read the whole story, and it is a very beautiful as well as truthful one.

The school-room at Westminster is one of the most interesting rooms in the world. It was the dormitory of the old monks; and when I saw it, thirty years ago, its walls were quite covered with the names of boys who had studied there, and who had cut with their penknives these rude autographs. Many of the names have since become famous all over the world, and will never be forgotten. At that time "John Dryden" was deep and plain in the solid bench where he cut it, for not one of all the thousands of Westminster boys who have sat in his place since have been mean or thoughtless enough to deface it.

The dormitory of the Queen's Scholars stands where the granary of the monks stood, and is a chamber one hundred and sixty-one feet long by twenty-five broad. It is interesting because it is the theatre where for centuries the "Westminster Play" has been acted. This "play" was expressly ordered by Queen Elizabeth for "her boys," and those of Terence were chosen by her. In 1847 there was a movement to abolish the "Westminster Play," but a memorial, signed by more than six hundred old Westminsters, pleaded for its continuance, and it is still one of the great features of a London Christmas.

Westminster is pre-eminently a classical school, but no school has a longer or more splendid list of great scholars. Of Church dignitaries it counts nine Archbishops and more than sixty Bishops: among the latter Trelawney, Francis Atterbury (the friend of Pope, Swift, and Gay), Isaac Barrow, and the witty, loyal Dr. South, who, when but an Upper Boy at Westminster, dared to read the prayer for

THE SCHOOL-ROOM.

Charles the First an hour before he was beheaded. Still more famous was Prideaux, the great Oriental and Hebrew scholar, and the wise Dr. Goodenough, whose sermons before the House of Lords elicited the lively epigram from some Westminster boy.

* "'Twas well enough that Goodenough before the Lords should preach, For sure enough that bad enough were those he had to teach."

Among famous lawyers, Westminster educated Lane, the eloquent defender of Strafford; Glynne, the great Commonwealth lawyer; the Earl of Mansfield, the pride of Westminster School, and the glory of Westminster Hall, Lord Chief Justice of England for more than thirty years; and the late Sir David Dundas. Among statesmen, Westminster counts the younger Vane, whom Milton so nobly eulogizes, as

"young in years, but in sage counsel old,
Than whom no better senator e'er held
The Roman helm";

Halifax, the accomplished "Trimmer" of the Revolution, about whom you must consult Macaulay; Warren Hastings; Sir Francis Burdett; Sir James Graham; and John, Earl Russell.

Among warriors, five of the seven officers not of royal blood who rose to the rank of Field-Marshal between 1810 and 1856 were Westminster boys, and one of these five was Lord Raglan.

Her list of literary sons is so long that I can only name a few of the best-known names—Rare Ben Jonson, Cowley, George Herbert, John Dryden, Christopher Wren, John Locke, the two Colmans, Richard Cumberland, Cowper, Gibbon, and the all-accomplished Robert Southey.

The chief amusement of Westminster boys is boating; for which the proximity of the Thames affords great advantages; also cricket, racket, quoits, sparring, foot-races, leaping, and single-stick. The school has always been noted, also, for the strong bond of fraternity uniting the boys: to the end of life Westminster boys acknowledge this tie, and in many a national crisis it has been, "All Westminsters together!"

THE LAST CHECK.

BY MRS. W. J. HAYS.

"I HAVE hunted high and low for that check, Sam, and I can not find it."

"I thought it was careless, when I saw you parading it about here."

"Well, you see, I felt rich. Father never sent me such a lot of money before."

"It was your birthday, wasn't it?"

"Yes, and the governor came down handsomely. He knows I am saving up for a trip to the Adirondacks. Well, if it is gone, it is gone."

"It could not go without hands; but I hope it will turn up yet. In future you had better put such documents in a safe place."

Will Benson heard this conversation between two fellow-clerks in the warehouse where he also was employed, and it troubled him much. He was a young fellow about fifteen or thereabouts, but so steady and reliable a youth that already many matters of importance were intrusted to him. He had seen Charlie Graham flourishing a check about, and had heard him talking very largely of his plans, etc. He had also seen the valuable bit of paper lying about, and had asked Charlie to pocket it; but he had also seen some one else do that in a very quiet way, and it had so peculiarly affected him that when Charlie asked him about it, he had colored up violently, and was so confused, that had Charlie been of a suspicious nature, he would have had good reason to suppose that Will knew more about the affair than he cared to tell—which was the truth. But Charlie was neither suspicious nor careful, and, in addition to leaving the paper about, he had also indorsed it.

Will listened to the inquiries and the comments in silence, not knowing what to say. Had he been very impulsive, he would have come out instantly with his suspicions; but he had a habit of reflection, and was inclined to consider before acting or speaking. At this moment, however, his thoughts were confused, and finding that his writing was suffering in consequence, he thrust his pen behind his ear, and sat down on a box at the office door to see if he could not think himself out of his difficulty.

WILL CONSIDERS THE SITUATION.

He was quite sure that a theft had been committed, and that he had witnessed it. What should he do?—tell Charlie Graham, have the man arrested and sent to prison, as he deserved, or keep the matter quiet, wait, and see how the thing would turn out?

As he sat there in the soft spring morning a little bird perched itself on a budding bough, and began to chirp. As it turned its head from side to side, and peeped coyly at him, it reminded him, by one of those unconscious flights of association, of another bird, which hung in a gilded cage very near the couch of his invalid mother. He could see the little warbler doing his best to entertain the weary moments of one who seldom heard the wild birds, or set her foot in the woods. He could also see the soft draperies about the window, the climbing ivy and growing ferns, and the much-used books and work-table, and from all these homely but precious belongings came uppermost the sweet smile of affection, the placid face which, in spite of age and sorrow and suffering, had always so tender a beauty for him. Quickly he turned back to his desk, and wrote a long letter to his mother. She would set him aright, she would solve his difficulty. Happy the boy who has such a mother!

Of course he had to wait some time for the answer, and the waiting was tedious. Charlie gave up the check as lost, and said no more about it, and Will took so great an aversion to the porter, who he was sure was the thief, that he hated to come in contact with him. But the mother's letter was worth waiting for, and Will acted on its advice.

Late one afternoon he wended his way to the narrow street where lived Grimes, the porter. It was a noisome locality. Will could not help thinking what a contrast it was to the quiet, clean town where he was born, and where his mother still lived! These dirty, narrow, crowded city slums, what wonder that all sorts of crime are born in them!

He found the house, and through the dark wretched stairway at last came to a door, at which he knocked.

"Come in," was the response.

He entered, stumbling over heaps of unwashed clothing. Two or three forlorn-looking children were eating at a wretchedly uninviting table in the midst of these surroundings. A feeble-looking woman was on a bed.

"Is Grimes at home?" asked Will.

"No, sir, he's not; and I beg pardon for letting you come in. My washing was half done when I was took down with a turn, and Grimes is looking now for some one to do what I am unable to do."

"Will he soon be in, do you think?"

"Yes, sir; have a chair; he'll be in presently."

"I will wait outside," said Will, glad of the excuse to get out. He waited in the dim light of a dirty window outside, and wished he had about a gallon of Cologne water at hand. Soon Grimes came, looking tired and cross. When he saw Will he grew pale, but asked him, in a smothered voice, what he wanted.

"I have come to speak about that check of Charlie Graham's," said Will.

Grimes grew red and angry, swore roundly that he knew nothing of it, and threatened to pitch Will down stairs.

Will very firmly replied that he had seen Grimes take it, and that unless he was willing to make reparation, his employers would have to be told of it.

At this the man wavered a little, but still stoutly denied the theft. At this moment the door, which was ajar, was pushed wider open, and the woman's head came peering out; then the children followed, but they were speedily sent down into the street.

Grimes retreated into the room; Will followed, not without some tremors, but that letter of his mother's was in his pocket.

"Sure and are ye found out?" said the woman, impetuously. "Didn't I tell you so? didn't I say no good could come of stalin', Grimes, my man?"

Grimes tried to hush her, but she would not listen to him. She had drawn a shawl about her, and was the picture of woe, with her pale face, her unkempt hair, and her glittering eyes. She took Will by the hand. "As you are a gintleman, and the son of a lady, have mercy on Grimes. If it's the bit of paper ye want, I have it; here it is;" and she drew it from the folds of her dress. "I knew no good could come of it, and I would not let him use it, miserable as we are. But spare him, and God will bless you."

"I have no wish to injure him," said Will, "and my mother thinks if this is a first offense, and he is at all sorry, I had better not make his dishonesty known."

Grimes was hanging his head in sullen silence, but at this he raised it eagerly. "Never in my life before have I taken anything—but you see our misery. I thought she would be the better for something this money could buy."

"Hush!" said the woman. "I might better die than live by stalin'. You will forgive him, misther; I know you will; I see it in your kind eyes."

Will promised silence, except to Charlie Graham, to whom he should be obliged to reveal the theft, as well as to make restitution; and gladly turned away from this scene of misery.

Charlie and he had a long talk that night. They concluded to abide by Mrs. Benson's advice.

"It was very wrong as well as silly for me to leave that check where it could tempt a poor fellow; and if it wasn't for the Adirondacks I'd send the whole amount to Mrs. Grimes," said Charlie, generously.

"No, that would not be wise," said Will; "but I tell you what, let's club together and send her some decent food and clothing."

Their kindness was not thrown away. Grimes never repeated the wrong-doing. With better times came better health and strength for his wife, and when Will went home for a holiday he took to his mother a bit of Irish lace, which Mrs. Grimes had begged him to carry to her.

A CHEAP CANOE.

BY W. P. S.

THE labor and ingenuity expended in one season by a boy who has any taste for the water in building rafts, and converting tubs and packing-boxes into sea-going vessels, would, if well directed, build a good-sized ship; but, from lack of knowledge and system, the results of such attempts are generally failures.

After some experience with rafts that *would* sink, scows that *would* leak, and other craft that showed a strong preference for floating with keels in the air, we found in the canvas canoe a boat at once handsome, speedy, and safe, and capable of a great variety of uses, while the small cost and easy construction place it within reach of all young ship-builders.

To produce a good canvas boat care and patience are more necessary than great skill with tools, though it is supposed that the young mechanic can use his rule correctly, saw to a line, and plane an edge reasonably straight.

The first proceeding in any building operation, after the plans are decided on, is to make out a "bill of materials" and an "estimate," and ours will read as follows:

Keel, oak, 1 in. square, by 15 ft. long. / 10 rib-bands, oak, 1 × ½ in., by 15 ft. long. / 2 gunwales, oak, 1 × ⅝ in., by 15 ft. long.	Sawed from an oak board 15 ft. × 6 in. = 7½ ft. @ 5c.	$0 38
Keelson, 3 × 1 in., 10 ft. long. / Bow, stern, coaming, and ridge pieces.	10 in. pine board	85
Moulds. / Floor boards.	2 pine boards 13 × ¾ in., 13 ft. long = 26 ft., @ 3c.	78
Paddle, 1⅛ in. spruce plank, 4½ in. × 12 ft.		25
Canvas, 5 yds., 40 in., @ 65c.		3 25
Canvas deck, 5 yds., 28 in., @ 25c.		1 25
1 package 1 in. No. 7 brass screws		50
Tacks, nails, and screws		50
Rubber cloth for apron		50
Sawing moulds and paddle		50
Paint		1 00
		$[illegible]

Having all our material ready, it will be best to mark out the different pieces, and have them all sawed at once by a steam-saw.

Beginning with the bow and stern, we will lay off on one corner of the ten-inch board a line two feet long, representing the dotted line *c d* in Fig. 1.

A line is drawn half an inch from the edge from the point 11 to 12, making a notch for the end of the keelson; and the two feet are divided into four parts, and perpendiculars drawn at each point.

Now measure off on the line *c d* nine and a half inches, giving the point *a*; on the others three and a quarter inches, an inch, and a quarter of an inch; then draw a line from *a* to *c* through all these points.

The shape of the inner line is not important, so it may be drawn by eye, making it thick enough for strength.

As the bow and stern are alike, two of these pieces are needed.

The keelson must be cut from the same board, being three inches wide at the centre, tapering to one inch at the ends.

To obtain the shapes of the moulds or sections we must enlarge Fig. 4 four times to its full size.

The horizontal lines in the drawing are one-fourth of an inch apart, so in our large drawing they will be one inch; then taking the line marked 2 (Nos. 1 and 13 require no moulds), we find the distance of the point *g* to be one and seven-sixteenths inches from the centre line, so we make it four times as much, or five and three-fourths inches, and continue with the other points until we have enough to determine the line pretty closely, after which we join them with the line *g h*, giving the shape of one-half of our first mould.

The lines on the right represent the half sections in the fore end of the boat, and those on the left the after end.

When all are drawn, they should be transferred to the half-inch board, each mould, however, being a whole and not a half section.

The outline of the paddle being drawn also, all may be taken to a saw-mill and sawn out, or else they may be sawn by hand with a compass-saw.

Having all cut out, we will first screw the bow and stern to the keelson, and secure the three pieces on a plank set upright, the upper edge being curved to fit the keelson, which is a little rockered.

Moulds Nos. 2, 3, 4, 5, 9, 10, 11, and 12 are next notched to fit the varying widths of the keelson, the first and last also fitting over the bow and stern; then they are put in place, and the gunwales notched into them, and also into the bow and stern.

The moulds for Nos. 6, 7, and 8 are sawn from three-quarter-inch oak or ash, each being in two pieces. The inner edge of No. 6 is shown by the dotted line K C, Fig. 4, and of Nos. 7 and 8 by *m b*. They are put in place the same as the others.

Now the rib-bands are planed off and tacked in place, being spaced amidships as shown in Fig. 4; then the points where they cross the bow and stern and all the moulds are marked, and notches one inch by one-fourth of an inch cut to receive them, the edges of the bow and stern being tapered off at the same time to half an inch; then all the parts are placed in position again, and fastened with one-inch screws, except where the keelson joins the bow, stern, and moulds, where one inch and a half screws are used. Each screw is dipped in white lead before inserting, and the head afterward puttied over.

The highest point of the deck is at No. 6, where a deck beam is placed, the shape of it and of the deck at No. 9 being shown in Fig. 4.

The other moulds may be easily shaped by using these as guides; then pieces two inches wide and three-fourths of an inch thick are notched into each mould, down the centre of the deck, from No. 6 to the bow, and from No. 9 to the stern, making a ridge over which the canvas is stretched.

A piece of one-inch pine is next set in between Nos. 9 and 6, and screwed to each, as well as to Nos. 7 and 8 and the gunwales, and forming the sides of the well.

The frame is now carefully sandpapered off, and painted with two coats; then a floor of half-inch pine is screwed to moulds Nos. 6, 7, and 8.

The canvas, forty inches wide, is first oiled, and then laid on the frame-work, and tacked along the centre of the keelson from No. 2 to No. 12; then it is tacked lightly to the gunwales; then cut to fit the curved bow and stern, and tacked, the edges overlapping half an inch, after which it is stretched tightly over the gunwales, and tacked on the *inside*.

The deck is of drilling, twenty-eight inches wide, tacked around the gunwale (a half-round bead being screwed over the joint), and turned up and tacked around the coaming, which is of three-eighth inch pine, rising an inch and a half above the deck, and screwed to the side pieces, mould No. 9, and the deck beam at No. 6.

The keel is of straight-grained oak, one inch deep from No. 3 to No. 11, tapering to one-half by three-eighths of an inch at the ends, and may be soaked in hot water before bending. When cold, it is screwed to the keelson and the bow and stern, the canvas under it being painted.

The stretcher for the feet rests against a strip nailed to the floors, and a small block on each gunwale.

A half-inch hole is bored in bow and stern for the painter.

The paddle is seven feet long, six and a half inches wide, and three-sixteenths of an inch thick at the edges; the handle being an inch and a quarter in diameter at the middle, tapering to seven-eighths where it joins the blades. A rubber ring is slipped over each end to prevent the water running down. In using, it is grasped about seven inches on each side of the centre, keeping the hands about the width of the body apart. The stroke should be as long and steady as possible.

It will be found at first that the boat will rock from side to side in paddling, and the paddle will throw some spray; but both these faults disappear with practice, and the boat should be perfectly steady at any speed. A slight twist as the paddle leaves the water, hard to describe, but easily found on trial, shakes off all drip.

For an apron, a strip of pine one-quarter by one and a half inches is fastened to each side of the well by brass straps hooking over the coaming, shown in Fig. 6.

A piece of rubber cloth is gored to fit around the body, and is tacked to each side piece, a rubber cord fastened to each strip, and running around the front of the well, serving to keep it down, and the after ends being tucked in between the backboard and the body, all falling off in an upset.

The backboard, Fig. 5, is seventeen inches long, the strips being two and one-fourth inches wide, and the same distance apart; it swings on the coaming at the back of the well.

Two coats of paint should be put on, and the paddle varnished.

A deck of half-inch pine, laid from No. 9 to No. 10, under the canvas, allows the canoeist to sit on deck sometimes in paddling.

In entering the boat, step in the centre (facing the bow), and, with a hand on each gunwale, drop into the seat.

When not in use the canoe should be sponged out and stored on shore.

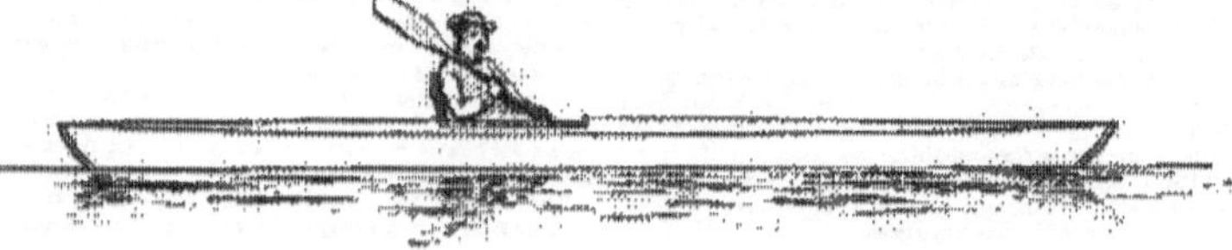

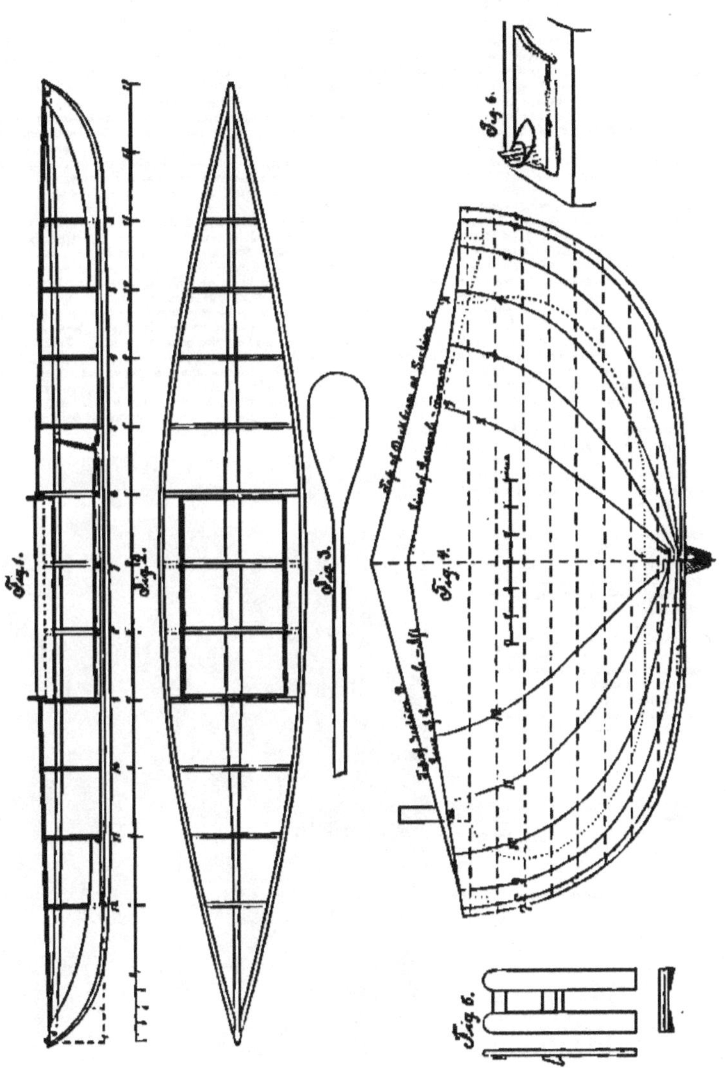

MAHMOUD THE SYCE.

BY SARA KEABLES HUNT.

ONE of the most novel and interesting sights which attracts the traveller's attention when he first arrives in Egypt is the syce running before the horses as they go through the narrow, closely packed streets. How the crowd scatters, and the donkey-boys bustle their meek property out of the way as one of these runners comes bounding along, shouting, in the strange Arabic tongue, "Clear the way!" The sun shines upon his velvet vest, glittering with its spangled trimmings, the breeze fills the large floating sleeves till they wave backward like white wings. Then on dash the spirited horses, dogs bark, children squeal, beggars dodge, men swear, and women, holding their face-veil closer, ejaculate fiercely.

On springs the syce; what cares he for man or beast? while proudly following rolls the rich equipage, or prances the Arab steed with its turbaned rider and Oriental robes.

Mahmoud, the subject of this little sketch, was the syce of a rich Pasha in Cairo; he was a favorite with his master, and everybody loved him—even the horses would neigh joyfully at his approach, and eat from his hand as gently as a dog. His life was an easy one, for, being a favorite, no arduous duties were placed upon him, and his strength was encouraged and sustained by the master for the swift running which commands so much admiration. So agile did he become, that no name among the syce of Egypt was more renowned than that of Mahmoud. Often at the latticed windows bright eyes of hidden beauties followed him through the narrow streets, and watched for his coming as he led the way for his master each morning in his rides. Sometimes they threaded their way through the crowded bazars amid scenes of the *Arabian Nights*, breathing wonderful Eastern perfumes, gazing on rare gems and exquisite embroideries; and again, down the road to the Pyramids, with the soft air blowing in his face, trees waving overhead, and birds singing merrily; or, in the blood-red sunset, passing down the Choubra Road, the fashionable drive of Cairo, with its shade of gnarled old sycamores, and crowded with conveyances of every description. Sometimes he led the way for the harem carriage, very proud of the honor.

One morning the Pasha sat in his garden under the blossoming orange-tree, smoking his chibouque, and talking with his friend the Bey from Alexandria, whose horse stood in the path champing impatiently at his bit, and held by his syce, Abdullah, in his gay costume. They talked of politics, the condition of the country, its financial troubles; they spoke of their religion and their mosque, of the Suez Canal, the improvements of the city, the Khedive's new palace, their own dwelling-places. By-and-by the conversation ran upon their horses and their favorite syce.

"Abdullah can outrun them all," said the Bey.

"Not so," replied the Pasha; "my Mahmoud is the fleetest runner in Cairo—ay, in all Egypt."

"Sayest thou so?" cried the Bey. "Come and let us test their skill."

"Most surely," answered the Pasha, "and I will give a prize to the boy who wins."

The news soon spread over Cairo that Mahmoud and Abdullah were to run a race, the winner to receive a costly girdle of rich embroidery, finished with a clasp set with gems. Great was the interest, and on the day appointed crowds assembled to see the race, gathering long before the competitors appeared.

What a motley group there was! Camels with their riders, stylish carriages with pretty French children, rosy-cheeked English girls, Italian singers, American officers and tourists, English lords, wild desert Arabs, swarthy-faced fellaheen, pistachio and pea-nut dealers, donkey-boys, beggars, and peddlers. A Turkish band played a quick reveille. Here they come! The crowd cheers—the signal is given—they are off! The general sympathy is with Mahmoud, but Abdullah is a strong fellow, of tremendous muscle, more experience, and mighty will, so that little Mahmoud has a rival of no mean powers.

Every eye is fixed upon those two figures, side by side, leaping onward in graceful bounds. Forward they fly, past the cotton field, around the curved path; but look!—Abdullah is ahead; Mahmoud seems far behind. The band plays quicker. Abdullah is flying; he will win; he—But no; Mahmoud is gaining; he nears his rival. Abdullah sees and strains every nerve, but in vain. Mahmoud swings his light wand over his head, and shoots by like an arrow. It is over; the goal is reached. Mahmoud has won, and amid the loud cheers of the crowd the Pasha descends from his carriage, and places the glittering sash around the victor's waist. Abdullah approaches, gives his successful rival a hearty salam, which awakens fresh applause. Somebody scatters a shower of gold coins over them, and the crowd disperses.

THE SYCE ON DUTY.

[By special arrangement with the author, the cards contributed to this Leaflet series, by W. J. Rolfe, A.M., formerly Head-Master of the Cambridge High School, will, for the present, first appear in Harper's Young People.]

CAMBRIDGE SERIES
OF
INFORMATION CARDS FOR SCHOOLS.

The English Language.
BY
W. J. ROLFE, A.M.

THE inscription on the Soldiers' Monument in Boston, written by the President of Harvard College, has been much admired. It reads thus:

TO THE MEN OF BOSTON
WHO DIED FOR THEIR COUNTRY
ON LAND AND SEA IN THE WAR
WHICH KEPT THE UNION WHOLE
DESTROYED SLAVERY
AND MAINTAINED THE CONSTITUTION
THE GRATEFUL CITY
HAS BUILT THIS MONUMENT
THAT THEIR EXAMPLE MAY SPEAK
TO COMING GENERATIONS

What is to be said is here said in the simplest way. There is no waste of words, no attempt at display. It is a model of good English, brief, clear, and strong. If a school-boy had written it, he would have thought it a fine chance for using big words. He would have said, "The citizens of Boston who sacrificed their lives," not "the men who died"; and "preserved the integrity of the Union," not "kept the Union whole"; and "erected," not "built." And some men who have written much in newspapers and books would have made the same mistake of choosing long words where short ones give the sense as well or better.

A great preacher once said that he made it a rule never to use a word of three or two syllables when a word of two syllables or one syllable would convey the thought as well; and the rule is a good one. In reading we want to get at the sense through the words; and the less power the mind has to spend on the words, the more it has left for the thought that lies behind them. Here the simple words that we have known and used from childhood are the ones that hinder us least. We see through them at once, and the thought is ours with the least possible labor.

Those who urge the use of simple English often lay stress on choosing "Saxon" rather than "Classical" words, and it is well to know what this means.

The English is a mixed language, made up from various sources. Its history is the history of the English race, and the main facts are these:

Britain was first peopled, so far as we know, by men of the Celtic (or Keltic) race, of which the native Irish are types. The names of the rivers, mountains, and other natural features of the land are mainly Celtic, just as in this country they are mostly Indian. About fifty years before the Christian era the Romans conquered Britain, and held it for about 500 years. They brought in the Latin language; but few traces of it now remain except in the names of certain towns and cities. The mass of the people kept their old Celtic tongue. Between the years 450 and 550 A.D. Britain was invaded and conquered by German tribes, chiefly Angles and Saxons. It now became *Angleland*, or *England*; and the language became what is called *Anglo-Saxon*, except in the mountains of Wales and of Scotland, where Celtic is found to this day. In the ninth and tenth centuries the Danes invaded England, and ruled it for a time, but they caused no great change in the language. In the year 1066 the Norman Conquest took place, and William the Conqueror became King of England. Large numbers of the Norman French came with him, and French became the language of the court and of the nobility. By degrees our English language grew out of the blending of the Anglo-Saxon of the common people and the Norman French of their new rulers, the former furnishing most of the *grammar*, the latter supplying many of the words. Now the French was of Latin origin, and the English thus got an important Latin or "Classical" element, which has since been increased by the adding of many Greek and Latin words, especially scientific and technical terms.

The two great events in the history of the English language, as of the English people, are the Saxon and the Norman conquests. To the former it owes its grammatical frame-work, or skeleton; to the latter much of its vocabulary, or the flesh that fills out the living body.

It must not be inferred that our grammar is just like the Anglo-Saxon because this is the basis of it. The Anglo-Saxon had many more *inflections* (case-endings of nouns and pronouns, etc.) than the French; and in the forming of English most of these were dropped, prepositions and auxiliaries coming to be used instead. It was not until about A.D. 1550 that the language had become in the main what it now is. Some words have since been lost, and many have been added, but its grammar has changed very little. Our version of the Bible, published in 1611, shows what English then was (and had been for fifty years or more), and has done much to keep it from further change.

As a rule the most common words—those that chiefly make up the language of childhood and of every-day life—are Saxon; and very many of them are words of one syllable. In the inscription above, every monosyllable is Saxon, with *Boston*, *grateful*, and *coming*; the rest are French or Latin. In the case of pairs of words having the same meaning, one is likely to be Saxon, the other Classical. Thus *happiness* is Saxon, *felicity* is French; *begin* is Saxon, *commence* is French; *freedom* is Saxon, *liberty* is French, etc. The Saxon is often to be preferred, though not always; but, as has been implied above, if a short and simple word conveys our meaning, we should never put it aside for a longer and less familiar one. In such cases the chances are that the former is Saxon, and the latter Classical. Thus above, *citizens*, *sacrificed*, *preserved*, *integrity*, and *erected* are all Classical.

THE STORY OF GEORGE WASHINGTON.

BY EDWARD C. CARY.

Chapter III.

WASHINGTON spent about nine months with the army around Boston. Several times he was ready to attack the British, and to try and drive them from the city; but his officers were afraid the army was not strong enough. So Washington had to wait and watch—he had a good deal of waiting and watching to do all through the war, for that matter. At last, in March, 1776, the Americans around Boston having gradually pushed closer and closer, the British found that they must either leave or fight. Their General did not feel strong enough to fight, so he put his men on ships and sailed away to Halifax. Of course the Americans were greatly rejoiced. Washington got much praise, and deserved it, for he had shown great good judgment and skill in his management of the army.

Washington knew that the British would soon come back, and thought they would come to New York. So he took nearly all his army, and marched them westward to that city.

Early in July the British came, as Washington had expected, and made their camp on the beautiful hill-sides of Staten Island. They brought with them what they called propositions for peace. These were simply offers to pardon the Americans for resisting the British tax laws, if they would now obey them. But this would only have left things exactly as they were in the beginning; it came too late. The Americans had already made up their minds that they would not obey the British laws which taxed them, nor any laws of Great Britain, but that in the future they would make their own laws in such manner as seemed to them most just. This purpose was written out in a long paper called the Declaration of Independence, and was signed on the Fourth of July, 1776, by the members of Congress. General Washington caused the Declaration of Independence to be read to his soldiers. "Now," he said to them, "the peace and safety of our country depend, under God, solely on the success of our arms," and he appealed to "every officer and soldier to act with fidelity and courage."

The year 1776 was a very gloomy one. All efforts to hold New York failed. A hard battle was fought around Brooklyn (August 27), and the Americans were badly beaten. Washington had to give up New York, and content himself with trying to keep the British from going to Philadelphia. Late in the fall he got across the Delaware River, with the British close on his heels. Soon the river filled with ice, as the cold weather came on, and the two armies lay one on one side and the other on the other. The American troops had dwindled away until there were only about three thousand of them.

Washington resolved that something must be done to raise the spirits of the country, or the people would lose all hope of resisting the British with success. At Trenton, on the opposite side from his own army, lay a force of Hessians, who were German soldiers, hired by Great Britain to come to America to fight, and Washington formed the plan of capturing them.

On Christmas-eve, 1776, he crossed the Delaware with 2400 men. The night was bitterly cold; a pelting hail-storm was falling; ice in great blocks was running down the stream, and hindered the boats, so that the army did not get across until four o'clock in the morning. Then the soldiers formed in ranks in the darkness, and being divided into two parties, started for Trenton, nine miles below. Washington led one of the parties, and General Sullivan the other. As they plodded along through the hail and snow, some of the men, exhausted, fell by the road-side, and of these two froze to death before they could be rescued.

As the men under Washington reached Trenton, and began to capture the Hessian soldiers set as sentinels to watch the road, they heard firing on the other side of the town, and knew that Sullivan's men had come up. Then both parties rushed swiftly toward the centre of the town, and with very little bloodshed a thousand prisoners were taken. This was a great success of itself, and had the effect which Washington had hoped for: it gave the whole country new courage.

Washington then started back toward New York, and so rapid was his march that the British commander became frightened lest the Americans should retake the city, and he too went quickly back, and gave up all thought of reaching Philadelphia that year.

[TO BE CONTINUED.]

A DISOBEDIENT SOLDIER.

BY DAVID KER.

"NOW, lads, there's the battery; remember the Emperor himself is watching you, and carry it in true French style. The moment you get into it, make yourselves fast against attack; and mind that any man who comes out again to pick up the wounded, even though I myself should be among them, shall be tried for disobedience as soon as the battle's over."

So spoke Colonel Lasalle to his French grenadiers just before the final charge that decided the battle of Wagram. Then he waved his sword, and shouted, "*En avant!*"

Forward swept the grenadiers like a torrent, with the shout which the Austrians opposed to them already knew to their cost. Through blinding smoke and pelting shot they rushed headlong on, with mouths parched, faces burning, and teeth set like a vise. Ever and anon a red flash rent the murky cloud around them, and the cannon-shot came tearing through their ranks, mowing them down like grass. But not a man flinched, for the same thought was in every mind, that they were fighting under the eye of their "Little Corporal," as they affectionately called the terrible Napoleon.

Suddenly the smoke parted, and right in front of them appeared the dark muzzles of cannon, and the white uniforms of Austrian soldiers. One last shout, which rose high above all the roar of the battle, the bayonets went glittering over the breastwork like the spray of a breaking wave, and the battery was won.

"Where's the Colonel?" cried a voice, suddenly.

There was no answer. The handful of men that remained of the doomed band looked meaningly at each other, but no one spoke. Strict disciplinarian as he was, seldom passing a day without punishing some one, the old Colonel had nevertheless won his men's hearts completely by his reckless courage in battle; and every man in the regiment would gladly have risked his life to save that of "the old growler," as they called him.

But if he were not with them, where was he? Outside the battery the whole ground was scourged into flying jets of dust by a storm of bullets from the fight that was still raging on the left. In such a cross-fire it seemed as if nothing living could escape, and if he had fallen *there*, there was but little hope for him.

"*I see him!*" cried a tall grenadier. "He's lying out yonder, and alive, too, for I saw him wave his hand just now. I'll have him here in five minutes, boys, or be left there beside him."

"But you mustn't disobey orders, Dubois," said a young Captain (now the oldest surviving officer, so terrible had been the havoc), hoping by this means to stop the reckless man from rushing upon certain death. "Remember what the Colonel told you—that even if he were left among the wounded, no one must go out to pick them up."

"I can't help that," answered the soldier, laying down his musket and tightening the straps of his cross-belts. "Captain, report Private Dubois for insubordination and breach of discipline. I'm going out to bring in the Colonel."

And he stepped forth unflinchingly into the deadly space beyond.

They saw him approach the spot where the Colonel lay; they saw him bend over the fallen man, shielding him from the shot with his own body. Then he was seen to stagger suddenly, as if from a blow; but the next moment he had the Colonel in his arms, and was struggling back over the shot-torn ground, through the dying and the dead. Twice he stopped short, as if unable to go farther; but on he came again, and had just laid his officer gently down inside the battery, when, with his comrades' shout of welcome still ringing in his ears, he fell fainting to the earth, covered with blood.

By the next morning Colonel Lasalle had recovered sufficiently to amaze the whole regiment by putting under arrest the man who had saved his life; but the moment it was done, the Colonel mounted his horse, and rode off to head-quarters at full gallop. In about an hour he was seen coming back again, side by side with a short, square-built man in a gray coat and cocked hat, at sight of whom the soldiers burst into deafening cheers, for he was no other than the Emperor Napoleon.

"Let me see this fellow," said Napoleon, sternly; and two grenadiers led forward Pierre Dubois, so weak from his wounds that he could hardly stand.

"So, fellow, thou hast dared to disobey orders, ha?" cried the Emperor, in his harshest tones.

"I have, sire. And if it were to be done again, I'd do it."

"And what if we were to shoot thee for insubordination?"

"My life is your Majesty's, now as always," answered the grenadier, boldly. "And if I must choose between dying myself and leaving my Colonel to die, the old regiment can better spare a common fellow like me than a brave officer like him."

A sudden spasm shook the old Colonel's iron face as he listened, and even Napoleon's stern gray eyes softened as few men had ever seen them soften yet.

"Thou'rt wrong *there*," said he, "for I would not give a 'common fellow' of thy sort for twenty Colonels, were every one of them as good as my old Lasalle here. Take this, *Sergeant* Dubois"—and he fastened his own cross of the Legion of Honor to Pierre's breast. "I warrant me thou'lt be a Colonel thyself one of these days."

And sure enough, five years later, Pierre Dubois was not only a Colonel, but a General.

THE NAUGHTY CUCKOO AND THE BOBOLINKS.

BY AGNES CARR.

SPRING had come, with its buds and blossoms, warm bright days and gentle showers, and the old apple-tree at the end of the garden was putting on its new spring dress of green leaves and tiny pink buds, which before long would open into sweet blossoms, and still later turn into ripe golden fruit, when a pair of Bobolinks came flying through the garden one fine morning house-hunting, or rather looking for a nice place to build a nest and go to housekeeping.

"Here is a good spot," said the little husband, whose name was Robert, perching on a limb of the old apple-tree and poking his bill into a crotch formed by a crooked branch.

"So it is," said Linny, his wife, "for the leaves will soon be out and hide the nest from sight;" and they began to chatter so fast about the nice home they would have there, that it sounded like nothing but "Bob-o-link, bob-o-link, spink, spank, spink," so that two little girls who were playing with their dolls under the tree said, "What a noise those Bobolinks make! what are they chattering so about?"

Soon, however, they saw the little birds flying back and forth, back and forth, with bits of hair and straw in their bills, and then they said to one another, "The Bobolinks are building a nest," and they hung pieces of cotton and bunches of thread on the lower limbs of the tree, and watched to see Robert carry them off to weave into the outside of the nest, while Linny made a soft lining of hair inside. And at last the little home was finished, and three pretty eggs laid snugly inside; when one day, while Robert and Linny had gone to stretch their wings by a short flight around the garden, an ugly old Cuckoo, who had seen the Bobolinks flying in and out of the tree, came and laid a big egg in the nest; for Cuckoos are lazy birds, and never build houses for themselves, but steal places to lay their eggs, and let somebody else take care of their children.

Now Robert and Linny had never been to school, and could not count; so when they came back they did not notice that there were four eggs in the nest instead of three, and Linny settled down on them, quite happy, while Robert sang a merry song to her, all about birds and flowers, and brought her nice fat worms and flies to eat, and was just the best little Bobolink husband in the whole garden.

And after a while a faint "*peep-peep*" was heard, the eggs all cracked, and out came four little blind birdies, without any feathers, and ugly enough, you would have said, but their papa and mamma thought them lovely. One, however, was as large as the other three put together, and took up so much room that Linny said "Oh dear, we have made the nest too small! When the children grow larger, some will be crowded out."

"That is strange," said Robert, "for it is the same size as the other Bobolinks have built, and they have plenty of room."

"Yes, but just see how big one of the babies is," said Linny.

Just then Robert saw the Cuckoo on a tree near by, winking one eye, and laughing until her sides shook, and exclaimed: "I see how it is; that old thief of a Cuckoo has laid an egg in our nest. I will throw her ugly child out, and she can look after it herself;" and he made a dive for the little Cuckoo, but Linny caught him by his tail-feathers, saying:

"No, no; poor little fellow, he will die if you throw him on the ground. Let him stay until he gets too big for the nest."

So the Cuckoo staid. But he was a very bad bird, for after a while, when he and the little Bobolinks got their eyes open, and had nice coats of feathers, he would peck at his companions, and take away all the best bits of bread and fattest worms that their papa and mamma brought them home for dinner, and was so cross and greedy that Robert would have pitched him out on the grass if Linny had not begged he might stay a little longer, and tried to make him behave better.

The apple-tree was now covered with pink and white blossoms, which grew around the little nest and made it like a bower. And now the birdies were learning to fly, and could go to the outer branches of the tree, where they sat in a row, while their father taught them how to sing.

"Bob-o-link, bob-o-link, spink, spank, spink," sang Robert. And

READY TO MOVE—MAY-DAY IN THE CITY.

the little ones, who could not speak plain, all repeated, "Bobo-link, bob-o-link, pink, pank, pink"—all except the biggest bird, who would only say, "Cuckoo, cuckoo," in a harsh voice.

At last, one day, Robert said, "Now, children, you are old enough to leave the tree, and to-day you must begin to go a little way into the garden."

"Yes," said their mother, "but take care, and never sit on the ground, for there is a great yellow cat who will surely eat you up."

"We will be very careful," said all the little Bobolinks.

After Billy, Bobby, and Jenny, as well as Cuckoo, had had their feathers brushed nice and smooth, they were sent out to try their wings; but the Cuckoo was stronger, and could fly farther than the Bobolinks.

Bobby flew over to the fence, to see what was on the other side, and the first thing he spied was the yellow cat creeping slowly along, and she fixed her eyes right on him. He tried to fly back, but just then the Cuckoo came behind, and gave him a push which sent him fluttering to the ground, right in front of Mrs. Pussie. Poor Bobby gave himself up for lost; but as the cat was about to spring on him, a great dog came bounding across the yard, which sent the cat scampering off in a hurry, and saved Bobby, who hastened home as fast as his little wings could carry him.

"Pshaw!" said the Cuckoo; "I thought there would be one out of the nest. But there is the cat under a bush, and Jenny is tilting on a twig just above, without seeing her." So the naughty bird flew to the rose-bush, and said, "Jenny, you look as if you were having a nice time."

"I am," said Jenny; "but don't come on this twig, it won't hold you."

"Oh yes, it will," said Cuckoo, leaning on the slender spray, which broke, and fell with Jenny, who was too frightened to fly; and quick as lightning the cat seized and carried her off in her mouth.

"Ha, ha, ha," laughed Cuckoo; "there will be room in the nest now." But at that moment the two little girls came out of the house, saw the cat with the bird, and made her drop Jenny on the grass. She was not much hurt, and they carried her gently back to the apple-tree, and gave her to her papa and mamma. The Cuckoo then went to look for Billy; but as he was passing the flower garden he saw a juicy white angle-worm lying in a bed of violets, and feeling hungry, stopped to take a little lunch.

The worm was very nice, and Cuckoo enjoyed it very much, when, just as he was swallowing the last morsel, the cat came stealing softly from under a wood-pile, and thinking if birds could lunch on worms, she could lunch on birds, pounced upon Cuckoo, and carried him off: and nothing more was ever seen of him, except a few feathers scattered near the door of the wood-shed. These Billy saw, and went home to tell the sad story.

OUR POST-OFFICE BOX

[illegible] are acknowledged from Charlie [illegible], Bessie H. M., [illegible], R. V. L., [illegible], Charles W. L., James H. R., [illegible] King, [illegible], T. [illegible], [illegible], Ralph W.

Correct answers to puzzles are received from Frank [illegible], Louisa [illegible], [illegible] Phillips, Emma L. E., W. G. [illegible], [illegible], Mary [illegible], Reginald F., [illegible], Mary [illegible], [illegible] Chapman, [illegible], Mary [illegible], [illegible].

PUZZLES FROM YOUNG CONTRIBUTORS.

No. 1.

ENIGMA.

My first is in run, but not in walk.
My second is in shout, but not in talk.
My third is in bull, but not in house.
My fourth is in pheasant, but not in grouse.
My fifth is in April, but not in May.
My sixth is in night, but not in day.
My seventh is in [illegible], but not in [illegible].
My eighth is in [illegible], and also in [illegible].
My ninth is in [illegible], but not in [illegible].
My tenth is in [illegible], but not in [illegible].
My eleventh is in [illegible], but not in [illegible].
My whole was the name of a Scottish king.
W. R.

No. 2.

RIDDLE.

What familiar word is composed of four S's, three M's, two I's, and one P?
C. L. S.

No. 3.

[illegible]

I am composed of 14 letters.
[illegible]
My whole is a [illegible].

No. 4.

[illegible]

[illegible]

No. 5.

[illegible]

[illegible]
C. P. T.

No. 6.

ENIGMA.

My first is in [illegible], but not in [illegible].
[illegible]
My whole is [illegible].
N. L. C.

ANSWERS TO PUZZLES IN No. 25.

No. 1. Sapphire.

No. 2.
[illegible]

No. 3.
[illegible]

No. 4.
[illegible]
Atlanta, Trenton.

No. 5. Christopher Columbus.

No. 6.
[illegible]

Fig. 1.

SOLUTION OF THE BOSSY PUZZLE.

The Bossy Puzzle given in No. 23 of Young People is solved by relieving the Bossy of her disfiguring black patches, and arranging them as in Fig. 1. Fig. 2 shows the rustic group that the artist

Fig. 2.

had in his mind when he invented the puzzle. The only correct solution to this puzzle that we have received was sent in by Eddie S. Hequembourg.

OPTICAL TESTS.

The eye is an organ which is very easily deceived, and needs constant training to enable it to judge correctly of the relative proportions of objects of different forms. Most of our readers are probably familiar with the optical test of guessing the height of an ordinary stove-pipe hat by measuring off the supposed height on the wall of a room. Those who have not heard of it will find it interesting to try the experiment. Take a stick, or walking-cane, and measure off on the wall of a room a height to which you suppose a stove-pipe hat would reach if placed on the floor immediately underneath, as represented in Fig. 1. Nine times out of ten the point selected will be a great deal too high.

Fig. 1.

Another point in which the proportions of a hat are very deceptive is this: The diameter, or distance across the crown, of a silk hat is greater than the height of the crown of the hat from the brim. Most people will be very positive that just the reverse is the case. We have all heard that a horse's head is as long as a flour barrel, and felt very much inclined not to believe it, though such is the fact.

There is also an optical test which is little known, and far more surprising: Take three tumblers of the same size, and place them in a row on the table, as represented in Fig. 2;

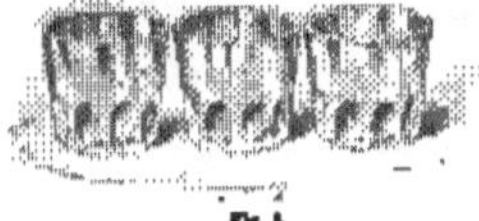

Fig. 2.

then withdraw the middle tumbler, and request any one present to place it at such a distance on the table from the other two tumblers—as represented in Fig. 3—that the measurements from C to D and from E to F shall be the same as from A to B. This test will prove very amusing at any small gathering. Each person in turn tries his hand; the distance he guesses is marked off on the table. Then the real distance is measured off, and the tumbler put in its right place, when it will probably be found that every one has fallen far short of the right measurement. In Fig. 3 we have only represented the relative positions of the tumblers; the correct distance is not given. Try it before you measure.

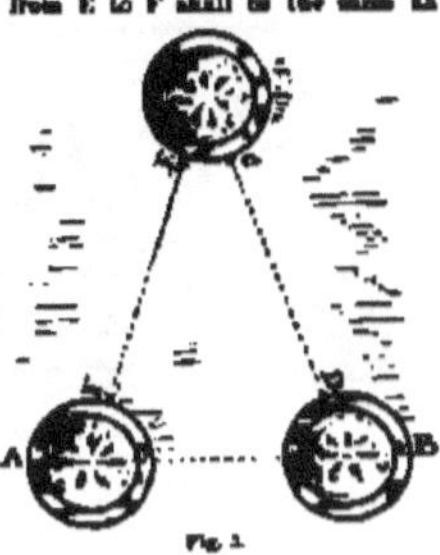

Fig. 3.

AUNT FLORA.

A BROKEN RHYME.

Aunt Flora was a precious——
Her sympathies were ever——
Her cranberry pies were always——
Aunt Flora.

Her homespun dress was neat and——
Her favorite conversation——
Kept her employed like Solomon's——
Aunt Flora.

I do not think she had a——
But everything she did was——
How much I've felt her blessed——
Aunt Flora.

Her heart was sweet and warm as——
And you would know from any——
Among the wise she was not——
Aunt Flora.

A BOY'S POCKETS.

Schoolmaster. "Are you quite sure you have got nothing more in your Pockets?"
Boy. "I've got a Hole in my Vest Pocket, Sir."
Schoolmaster (sternly). "Take your seat, Sir."

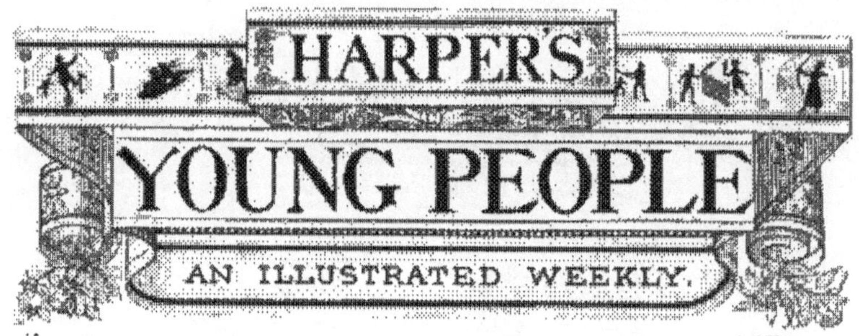

Vol. I.—No. 27. | Published by HARPER & BROTHERS, New York. | Price Four Cents.

Tuesday, May 4, 1880. | Copyright, 1880, by Harper & Brothers. | $1.[illegible] per Year, in Advance.

ROB'S NAVY.

BY W. O. STODDARD.

THE tide was just out on the Staten Island shore, and the water in the little cove below Mr. Drake's residence was as smooth as a pan of milk with the cream on.

Nothing in the shape of a ship ought to have tipped over in such water as that.

So Rob Drake had thought, but every time he shoved his new ship away from the flat rock at the head of the cove, over she went. First on one side, then on the other, it did not seem to make much difference which. She stood up well enough so long as Rob kept hold of her, but as soon as ever he let go, down she tumbled.

Rob was about twelve years old, and he believed he knew all about ships.

Did he not live on Staten Island, right across the bay from New York? Did he not go over to the city on the great ferry-boat every now and then, and see all the shipping at the wharves, and sail past all sorts of craft on the way there and back?

Some of them, he knew, came from almost all the countries in the world, and he had seen hundreds of them sail out of the harbor to go home again.

Of course Rob knew all about ships; but this one, on which he and Larry McGee had been whittling and working for a week, seemed determined to float bottom up.

What could be the matter?

"Larry, she's top-heavy."

"No, she ain't. It's ownly a sort of a thrick she's got. All she wants is practice."

Larry was Mr. Drake's hired man, and knew a little of everything, only he knew more about a horse than he did about any kind of sailing vessel.

"The boy's right, my hearty. She's more lumper than hull, and she's no ballast at all."

Rob and Larry looked behind them when they heard that. They had not heard him come along the sandy beach, they had been so busy, but there he was; a short, thin old man, with broad shoulders, dressed like a United States "man-o'-war" sailor, and with a wooden leg that was now punching its round toe deep into the sand.

"'Deed, sor," said Larry, "it's a good ship she is, or she wouldn't lie down that way."

"She's a ship, then? I'm glad to know that. It's a good sign for the boy that he's taken to ships. There's not many boys care for 'em nowadays."

"Why, of course it's a ship," said Rob, as he pulled his craft ashore and held her up to let the water drip from her wet sails. "Didn't you know what she was?"

"Old fellows like me don't know much nowadays. You've put in four masts, and a bowsprit at each end, and I couldn't tell just what she was."

"Oh," said Rob, "that's nothing. I saw a steamer with four masts the other day."

"There's no accounting for steamers, my boy. And I've heard men call 'em ships, too, that ought to have known better."

"Don't I know a ship?" proudly exclaimed Rob. "Can't I tell a schooner from a sloop, and a bark from a brig? I know. It's the masts and rigging make the difference."

"Well, now," said the old man, "you're a bright boy. What's your name?"

"Robert Fulton Drake."

The old man shook his white head solemnly, and took off his round Scotch cap. "Drake's a good name. There was a great sailor of that name once. He was an admiral, too. But Fulton—Robert Fulton—it's awful the mischief we owe to that man."

"Fulton? He a bad man?" said Rob, with all sorts of wonder in his face. "No, sir. He was a great man. He invented steamboats."

"So he did—so he did. More's the pity. Ships were ships till Fulton came. Now they're all great iron pots, and go by steam. No use for sailors now."

"Steam-ships have to have sailors."

"What for, my boy? Well, yes, they do have a few lubbers on board that they call sailors. And there are some ships left too—pretty good ones. But they don't have sailors nowadays like they used to. Robert Fulton spoiled it all. But I'm glad you like ships. Only you don't know how to make 'em. Come and see me some day. I'll show you."

"Where do you live?"

"Half a mile the other side of the ferry landing." He went on and gave Rob pretty full directions how to find his house; and Larry McGee added, quite respectfully,

"Ye're an owld sailor yersilf, sor?"

"Am I? Well, yes, I was once, before I lost my leg. The ships weren't all turned into iron pots then."

"Was it there ye lost yer lig?"

"There? Oh, you mean aboard ship? That's where it was, my hearty. Did you ever hear of Mobile Bay?"

"I niver did, sor."

"I did," exclaimed Rob.

"Did you, then? I'm glad of that, my boy. Did you ever hear of a sailor named Farragut?"

"The great Admiral? Admiral Farragut? Oh yes, indeed. Father's got a picture of him, up in the rigging of a ship, with a telescope in his hand. He was a great fighter."

"You're the boy for me. Do you know about that picture? That was the old ship *Hartford*; and when the Admiral was up in the rigging there, with the bullets flying round him, I was down on deck, getting my leg shot off."

Larry McGee took off his hat right away.

"Wuz that so indade, yer honor? Was it for that ye got the gould shtar ye're wearin'?"

"Star? No, indeed. I got a pension, but I didn't get any star."

"But it's a foine one."

So it was, and it was fastened by a strong, wide blue ribbon to the old man's left breast. It looked like solid gold, and it was curiously lettered and ornamented.

"I'm proud of that, my man. And I got it that day too."

"How was it?" asked Rob, who had dropped his four-masted ship to listen.

"How was it? I'll tell you, my boy. It was Farragut himself. He was the best sailor ever trod a plank, and he hated steam and iron pots to the day of his death. He came to see me and the rest, in hospital, like the true sailor he was, and he'd a good word all around. I'd been one of the crew of his own gig, and before he went he put his hand in his pocket, and seemed to be feeling for something. Belike his hand had been in that pocket pretty often, those days, for it looked as if he couldn't find a thing. When it came out, though, it had a piece of gold in it. An old Spanish doubloon he'd carried for a pocket-piece—"

"That's a gold coin?" asked Rob.

"The biggest there is, except a double-eagle, only there's not many of 'em nowadays. And says he to me, says he: 'Good-bye, Jack Peabody. Most likely I'll never see you again. Keep that to remember me by. I don't think you'll forget the old ship, nor Mobile Bay.'"

"Truth an' the owld fellow was right there," said Larry McGee.

"So I took the doubloon, but I was too weak to say much, and when I got out of hospital I worked that bit of gold into this here star, with the Admiral's name on it, and the date, and Mobile, and all the other things I could think of. There's a picture of the old *Hartford* on the other side. She was a ship, she was."

Rob and Larry took a long and careful look at the star, and then the old man stumped away.

"How thim owld sailors does hate the shtamers!" said Larry.

"I don't care, the sailing ships are prettier."

"So they be, but the shtamers goes betther. How'd ye loike to wait for a wind whin ye wanted to go to the city, insthid of shtamin' over in a ferry-boat?"

Rob talked with his father that evening, and showed him his four-masted ship with a bowsprit at each end.

"Rob, my boy, your old sailor friend is right. I think I'll take you over with me in the morning, and we'll walk up South Street, along the wharves, and I'll show you what he means."

"That's what I'd like."

"Wounded at Mobile Bay, was he? One of Farragut's men? I must hunt him up. Every American boy ought to touch his hat when he speaks of Farragut."

Mr. Drake was a little of an enthusiast about ships and sailors, and it was no wonder Rob took after him.

The next morning, when the great ferry-boat took over its biggest crowd of passengers, and ever so many teams and loaded wagons, Rob and his father were standing out in front by the railing, looking hard at every vessel they came near, and talking about them all.

When they landed in the city, they walked on from the ferry along South Street, which is lined on one side by warehouses, and on the other by docks and piers. The docks were all full of vessels, and the great bowsprits of the larger ships sometimes stuck half way across the street to the buildings.

They were both so busy with the shipping that they hardly noticed anything on the other side of them, but suddenly Rob heard a cracked voice exclaim:

"Robert Fulton Drake. That was his name. Drake's a good one; but then—Fulton! I say, boy, look here!"

Rob looked, and so did his father.

There sat the old one-legged sailor, Jack Peabody, on the stone steps of one of the warehouses, with his bright gold star on his breast, and a cane in his hand.

Just beyond him, however, on the upper step, stood a beautiful model of a brig, with a hull about two feet long. She was completely rigged, sails and all.

"Look at that, sir. She'll float. She isn't top-heavy. No danger of her tipping over. Made her myself."

"Father," said Rob, "it's the very man. Don't you see the star? Oh, what a pretty brig!"

There was a card stuck at the brig's mast-head, with "[illegible]" written on it.

"Will you? Why, then you'll have a navy. I hope they'll all float. Not all the ships they build nowadays make out to do that."

Rob hurried home with his brig, and he built his "navy," but it was just as the old sailor feared, not more than half of them would float.

GRANDPA'S BARN.

BY MARY D. BRINE.

Oh, a jolly old place is grandpa's barn,
  Where the doors stand open throughout the day,
And the cooing doves fly in and out,
  And the air is sweet with the fragrant hay;

Where the grain lies over the slippery floor,
  And the hens are busily looking around,
And the sunbeams flicker, now here, now there,
  And the breeze blows through with a merry sound

The swallows twitter and chirp all day,
  With fluttering wings, in the old brown eaves,
And the robins sing in the trees which lean
  To brush the roof with their rustling leaves.

O for the glad vacation time,
  When grandpa's barn will echo the shout
Of merry children, who romp and play
  In the new-born freedom of "school let out."

Such routing of doves from their cozy nests,
  Such hunting for eggs in the lofts so high,
Till the frightened hens, with a cackle shrill,
  From their hidden treasures are fain to fly.

Oh, the dear old barn, so cool, so wide!
  Its doors will open again ere long
To the summer sunshine, the new-mown hay,
  And the merry ring of vacation song.

For grandpa's barn is the jolliest place
  For frolic and fun on a summer's day;
And e'en old Time, as the years slip by,
  Its memory never can steal away.

[Begun in No. 19 of HARPER'S YOUNG PEOPLE, March 9.]

ACROSS THE OCEAN; OR, A BOY'S FIRST VOYAGE.

A True Story.

BY J. O. DAVIDSON.

CHAPTER IX.

ASHORE AT MALTA.

Instantly the English boatswain's shrill pipe was heard, and a crowd of sturdy fellows in clean "whites" and bare feet came racing aft, and cleared away the wreck in a twinkling, not without a few rough-hewn jokes at "Yankee seamanship," which the *Arizona's* men repaid with interest.

"Just as well you've got no navy, if *that's* how you handle a ship," shouted one of the English.

"Better have none at all than one made out o' cracked tea-kettles," retorted Herrick, who never lost a chance of having a fling against steam.

The pilot, who had been shaking in his shoes at the mishap, now began to hope that it would all end in a laugh; but he was not to escape scot-free, after all. As the *Arizona* forged ahead, a rotten egg, flung through one of the iron-clad's open ports, hit him full on the forehead, and exploded over his whole face, like a bombshell, making such an object of him as his own father would scarcely have recognized.

An American steamer does not touch at Valetta every day, and the *Arizona* soon had plenty of visitors. Most of the crew being busy, Frank was "told off" to act as showman, and for the first two days he had more than enough to do. From sunrise to sunset the decks were crowded with sight-seers of all ages and conditions—stiff, wooden-faced soldiers from the garrison; languid ladies, who looked much more at each other's bonnets than at the ship, and seemed to be always sitting down and never getting up; jaunty military officers, with uniforms as trim as their mustaches; huge red-whiskered sailors from the English men-of-war, who kept patting Frank on the head like a child, to his great indignation; and native Maltese, who seemed immensely astonished at all they saw, and chattered over everything like so many parrots. Some of these last mistook the white-painted iron of the engine for wood, and were seen trying to chip off pieces of it with their knives as mementos of the visit.

But when once he was off duty, Austin began to enjoy himself in earnest. There really seemed to be no end to the curious sights of the place—the steep, break-neck streets, almost like paved precipices; the tall, thick-walled, narrow-windowed houses, small fortresses in themselves; the shaven monks, who looked terribly hot in their heavy black robes; the slim, dark-eyed Greeks, with their jaunty red caps, and the gaunt, swarthy Moors scowling from under their huge white turbans; the queer little Maltese boats, with high prows and sterns, quaintly carved and painted; the files of donkeys plodding past under big baskets of fruit, with their bare-footed drivers yelling behind them; the huge forts built by the Knights of St. John (the former owners of Malta), nine thousand of whom had held them for eight months against thirty-five thousand Turks, during the great siege of 1565; and the stately English iron-clads, which seemed to be always exercising their men, or standing out to sea to bang at a floating mark with their big guns for hours together.

MALTA.

1. The Grand Harbor.
2. [illegible] (Maltese) Boat.
3. Landing-Place.
4. The [illegible].
5. Street in Malta.

But there were other and even more striking sights than these. There was the old city of Città Vecchia, with its ruined aqueduct. There was the Church of St. Paul (the first built on the island), the ceiling of which is covered with magnificent frescoes, while the floor is one mass of precious stones, worked into portraits of the great men who lay beneath it. There was a cave, said to have sheltered St. Paul after his shipwreck, and containing a fine statue of him. There was the garden of St. Antonio, which, in the glory of the dazzling Southern sunshine, seemed the most beautiful of all. There was the armory of the Knights of St. John, where Frank saw numbers of huge bows, battle-axes, and two-handed swords; quaint old cannon, made of copper tubes covered with coils of rope, which usually burst at the fifth shot; and last, but certainly not least, an enormous helmet, as heavy and almost as big as a wash-tub, said to have been worn by a gigantic knight of the order, who, after defending the gate of Fort St. Elmo single-handed against a whole battalion of Turkish Janizaries, had at length to be blown bodily away with cannon-balls.

Austin did not forget to visit the Catacombs, which fully bore out Herrick's description of them. Far and wide the earth was honey-combed with these gloomy galleries, in which, hundreds of years before, the Christians of Malta had found refuge, while everything above-ground was being wasted with fire and sword by the destroying rage of the Saracens. Crumbling stone crosses, rudely carved names, antique burial-places, seamed the gloomy walls in every direction, while the skulls and bones of men, women, and children lay under foot like shells upon the sea-shore. In the fitful glare of his torch, the long dark robe and white corpse-like face of the monk who acted as guide might well have passed for one of the dead about whom he told so many ghastly stories; and Frank was not sorry to find himself in the bright sunshine once more. But on looking round him, he saw with amazement that he was now right on the opposite side of the mountain, several miles from the spot where he had entered it. And then his monkish guide, by way of a satisfactory wind-up, proceeded to relate, in his most dismal voice, how a gay party of English naval officers descended into this gloomy maze to make a complete exploration of it, and were never seen again.

On the last night of their stay in Malta, the *Arizona's* officers and crew went in a body to the opera-house (a fine building of gray stone), to hear a young American singer in *La Sonnambula*. At first the Maltese seemed disposed to find fault with her; but all adverse demonstrations were speedily overwhelmed by the uproarious applause of the English and American sailors. Even when the heroine made a false step in her crossing of the bridge, and tumbled bodily on to the floor of the stage, the gallant blue-jackets applauded as lustily as if this were the best part of the performance, though Jack Dewey afterward observed that "'twas a bad sign of any craft to capsize that way in a calm."

Next morning they were off, but not without a "hitch" or two before starting. At the last moment, the man who had been hurt at Gibraltar had to be sent ashore invalided, and another hand shipped in his place. Then two of the firemen were found to be missing, and turned up just in time to scramble aboard in what the chief engineer called "a strictly unsober condition." One of them, who seemed to be in a quarrelsome humor, was beginning to shout and abuse every one, when Captain Gray suddenly appeared beside him.

"Stop that noise," said he, very quietly, "and go forward at once."

"Pretty tall talk, that," growled the brawler. "*I* ain't a-goin' for'ard for nobody. One man's as good as another."

The words were barely out of his mouth, when the "quiet" Captain's clinched fist flew right *into* it, with a shock that made his teeth rattle like dominoes, and sent him sprawling on his back.

"Put that man in irons, Mr. Hawkins, and pass him down 'tween-decks," said the Captain, walking aft as if nothing had happened.

"Ay, *he's* the one to settle 'em," muttered old Herrick, nodding approvingly. "I tell ye, Frank, my boy, it's as hard to git off any foolin' on our 'old man', as to git a 'pology out of a middy."

"How's that?" asked Austin, seeing by the twinkle of the old quartermaster's eye that there was a good story coming.

"Ah, don't ye know that yarn? Well, it's worth hearin', too; I got it from a Britisher last time I was here. Ye see, there was a young middy aboard one o' Nelson's ships in the old war, who was always in some scrape or other; and one day the third officer, Mr. Thorpe, got riled with him, and called him a confounded young bear.

"'Well,' says the mid, quick as winkin', 'if *I'm* a bear, you're not fit to carry bones to a bear, anyhow.'

"'What! what!' cries Thorpe—'mutiny, as I live! You whelp, I'll teach you to talk that way to *me!*' and off he goes to the Cap'n, and reports him for disrespect to his superior officer.

"Well, the Cap'n calls up Mr. Middy, and tells him this sort o' thing won't do nohow, and he must either 'pologize or leave the ship. So the mid takes off his cap with a reg'lar dancin'-school bow, and says, 'Mr. Thorpe, I said just now that you were not fit to carry bones to a bear; I was wrong, and willingly apologize, for I now see that you *are* fit to carry them.'

"'Sir,' begins the Cap'n, in a voice like a nor'east gale.

"'Oh, Cap'n Mayne,' says Thorpe (who wasn't bright 'nuff to see the joke), 'if the young gentleman sees his error, and takes back his words, I'm satisfied.'

"'Well,' says the Cap'n, bitin' his lips to keep from laughin', 'if *you're* satisfied, *I* am; but catch me ever trying to get an apology out of a midshipman again!'"

[TO BE CONTINUED.]

THE STORY OF GEORGE WASHINGTON.

BY EDWARD CARY.

CHAPTER IV.

IN the last chapter I told you how Washington kept the British out of Philadelphia during the winter of 1776 and 1777. The next year the British came around from New York by water with a large and fine army. Washington's army was badly trained, and many of them were new men. A bloody battle was fought below Philadelphia, on the Brandywine Creek, and the Americans were divided and beaten. The British marched into Philadelphia, and in spite of all that Washington could do, staid there that winter, and the Americans went into camp at Valley Forge, some twenty miles away. It was a terrible winter, and often the soldiers were "barefoot and otherwise naked," as Washington wrote to Congress, and food was often very hard to get. Some members of Congress found fault with Washington for not attacking the enemy. He answered, "I can assure those gentlemen that it is a much easier and less distressing thing to draw remonstrances in a comfortable room by a good fireside than to occupy a cold bleak hill, and sleep under frost and snow without clothes or blankets." During the winter Mrs. Washington came on from Virginia, and shared her husband's log-hut.

But after the long, hard winter at Valley Forge, the spring of 1778 opened with new hopes. The French government had signed a treaty with the United States, agreeing to aid them with men and money, and a fleet of French ships was sent to America. The British finding Philadelphia hardly worth the hard fighting it had cost, since they could not get far away from it, or hurt the American army very much while in the city, got ready to leave it and go back to New York. Washington followed hard after them, and a heavy battle was fought at Monmouth, in New Jersey, from which neither side gained a great deal. The British got back into New York, and Washington took his men up the Hudson, and kept them there, watching a chance to join in some attack with the French troops who came to Newport, in the State of Rhode Island.

For the next three years there was not any very hard fighting under Washington's own command, but his cares were scarcely less. He had to keep watch of all that was going on, and to have his army ready to strike at a moment's warning. Waiting and watching were tedious work. They tried his patience and his firmness. A weaker man would have given up, but Washington was not any more easily tired than he was frightened. He held steadily to his task, and tried hard to keep his countrymen, many of whom were weary of the war, up to their duty.

At one time the cause of liberty was nearly ruined by a traitor. General Benedict Arnold tried to sell to the British a fort at West Point, on the Hudson River. If the British could have got that, the States north and east of New York would have been cut off from the rest, and probably they would have all been conquered. Happily the plot failed. This was in 1780.

The next year Washington really closed the war by a splendid move. A large army of the British had been sent to Virginia, under Lord Cornwallis, in hopes to cut the troops who were farther south off from connection with the North.

Washington sent a gallant young French General, Lafayette, whom he loved and trusted greatly, to prevent this. Lafayette had a small force, but he was quick and brave and shrewd, and he managed to get the British shut up in Yorktown, near the Chesapeake Bay. There he learned that a French fleet, under Comte de Grasse, would soon arrive. He sent urgent word to Washington to come South right away.

Washington straightway marched, with nearly all his army, and most of the French troops, for Virginia. They arrived on the 14th of September, 1781, just in time. The French fleet sailed up the bay, the American and French troops came down on the land side, and between them they shut the British General in the little village of Yorktown, and there they laid siege to his army.

When they had got pretty close to the town, they had to drive the British from some redoubts, or walls of earth and stone, behind which they had planted their cannon. This was done by a party of Americans under the gallant Lafayette, and a party of French soldiers. They marched steadily up to the redoubts, and springing over the walls, under heavy fire, drove the enemy out with their bayonets. It was a brave assault, and successful, and it was the last hard fighting of the war. On the 19th of October, Lord Cornwallis, seeing that he could hold out no longer, surrendered his army prisoners of war. It was a great victory, and was won with less loss of life than there might have been if it had been less skillfully fought, for Washington had managed so quietly and so quickly that he had surrounded Lord Cornwallis with nearly twice as many troops as the British General had.

After the surrender at Yorktown, Washington returned North, and on his way stopped at his home at Mount Vernon. He had slept there on his journey southward, a few weeks before, for the first time in nearly seven years, and he had found it sadly injured in his absence. During his second visit, his wife's son, Mr. Custis, died, leaving a son and a daughter, whom Washington adopted as his own, and tenderly cared for as long as he lived.

[TO BE CONTINUED.]

MAKING MAPLE SUGAR.

WHEN in the early spring-time the snow and ice have been so softened by the ever-increasing warmth of the sun's rays as to put an end to coasting, skating, and other winter sports of the North, a new source of amusement, equally fascinating to the children, is provided. It is maple-sugar making, with all the delights of life in the camp, or "sugar bush," as it is more generally called.

When the heat of the sun is sufficient to melt the snow, it is also powerful enough to send the sweet sap of the rock and sugar maples rushing through all the delicate bark veins up toward the branches and twigs. At night, when the sun has set, and the air is full of a nipping frost, the sap does not run; so, as it must be collected during the daytime, the boiling is very often done at night.

As the first sap of the season is the sweetest and most abundant, the sugar-makers are on the ground and making ready their camps upon the first indications of "sap weather," as they call it. The sap runs, according to locality, from the last of February until late in April, and the sugar season lasts about four weeks in each place.

When the farmer thinks that sap weather is about setting in, he calls his boys together; they load the big kettles and camp material on the ox sleds, and start for the "bush," or grove of maple-trees, which is often many miles from the house. When they reach the maple grove, all hands find plenty to do. If it is a warm day, the trees must be immediately tapped, and a couple of boys are started off with a sled-load of iron spiles, each about six inches long, and a quantity of sap buckets or short wooden troughs that have been cut out during the long winter evenings. A slight cut is made through the bark of each tree, or an auger hole is bored, a spile driven in directly beneath it, and at the foot of the tree is left a trough so arranged as to catch the sap as it drips from the end of the spile.

While the trees are being tapped, the men left in camp have been busy enough building the rude shanties of logs and spruce boughs that are to shelter them while they remain in the bush, cutting quantities of fire-wood, and swinging the great kettles into place on the iron bar that rests on two forked posts solidly fixed in the ground. Sometimes great shallow pans of iron, set upon rude foundations of stone, are used instead of the kettles, and the shanty in which the men live is often a very permanent structure of logs, that can be used for many years.

Late in the afternoon the sleds, each carrying a large cask or hogshead, are sent around to the maple-trees, all the sap buckets are emptied, and finally the casks, full of what tastes like sweetened water, are drawn slowly back to camp. The sap is poured into the big kettles, the fires lighted, and the "syruping down" begins. The pans or kettles are kept constantly full from the barrels of sap standing near by, and sometimes the bubbling liquid boils over. When it does this, a bit of bacon is thrown in, and the troubled waters subside.

The boiling is continued until the watery sap has been changed into a rich syrup, when it is drawn off into casks for future use, or into other iron kettles to be boiled again until it becomes sugar. This second boiling must be done very carefully, or the syrup will become burned and spoiled. It is constantly stirred with a long-handled wooden paddle, and both eggs and milk are often thrown in to purify it. The scum that rises to the top is carefully removed, and thrown out on the snow, to the delight of the children, who watch for it to cool and partially harden. They call it "maple candy" or "taffy," and regard it as a treat.

When by testing on the snow, or in cold water, the syrup is found to have boiled long enough, it is run into moulds, where it cools into cakes of maple sugar, or the kettle is lifted from the fire, and its contents stirred and beaten as they cool, until they become coarse brown sugar that can be used in cooking.

A VOYAGE ON AN ICE-BLOCK.

BY DAVID KER.

THE breaking up of the ice in Russia is always a fine sight to look at, even upon a small stream like the Neva at St. Petersburg, which is a mere brook compared with the great rivers of the South. As soon as the spring thaw sets in, all the wooden bridges are removed, and nothing checks the descending ice but the stone piers of the Nikolaievski Bridge, named after its founder, the Czar Nicholas. Every morning, while the show lasts, the balustrades of this bridge are lined with a crowd of eager spectators, looking as intently at the wonderful sight as if they had never seen it before.

And a wonderful sight it is indeed. Far as the eye can reach, the smooth, dark surface of the river is one great procession of floating masses of ice, of all shapes and sizes, moving slowly and steadily downward.

But the place to see this famous sight at its best is the Volga, which, with its two thousand miles of length, brings down ice enough to overwhelm a whole city. At times the force of the current piles it up, sheet over sheet, into huge mounds, the crashing and grinding of which, as they dash against each other, make the very air shake. When the river is "moving," as the Russians call it, he would be a bold man who should attempt to take a boat across it; for, once caught between two of these moving islands, the strongest boat on the Volga would be crushed like an egg-shell.

So, doubtless, think the group of peasants who are standing upon the river-bank, one bright March morning, a mile or two below the great manufacturing town of Saratov, watching the endless procession of ice-blocks sweep past. Strange-looking fellows they are, with their flat sallow faces and thick yellow beards, their high boots smeared with tar instead of blacking, their rough caps pulled down over their eyes, and their heavy sheep-skin frocks with the wool inside. But, queer as they look, they are a merry set, laughing and joking unceasingly, and enjoying the spectacle like a party of youths at a circus.

"Come, now, Meesha [Michael], here's an open course; let us have a race across!"

"All right, Stepka [Stephen]; and as you're a friend of mine, I'll give you a half-minute start."

And then follows a loud laugh, for a little fun goes a long way in Russia.

But a sudden shout from one of the men draws everybody's attention, and he is seen pointing to a huge sheet of ice some distance up the stream. On its smooth white surface lies a dark, shapeless lump, perfectly still; and guesses begin to fly from mouth to mouth as to what this can be.

"A block of wood, I think."

"A dog, more likely."

"Too big—must be a bundle of hay."

A handsome young fellow, lately arrived in that district from the North, presses to the front, and fixing his keen eyes for a moment upon the mysterious object, says, emphatically, "Tchelovek!" (a man).

"A man!" echo two or three of his companions. "He must be frozen, then, for he don't seem to move a bit."

"Feodor [Theodore] has the best eyes among us, though," puts in another. "If he says a man, why, a man it must be."

"And so it is," shouts one who has run a little way up the bank; "and he's alive, too, for I saw him move his head just now."

By this time the ice-block had come near enough to let the strange object upon it be plainly seen. It was the figure of a man in a sheep-skin frock, doubled up in a crouching posture.

"We must help him, lads," cries Feodor; "it won't do to let a man perish before our eyes."

"Ah, my boy," answers an old man beside him, shaking his gray head, "it's easy to say 'help him,' but how are we to do it? Crossing the Volga when it's moving is not like dipping a spoon in a bowl of milk."

"I'll try it, anyhow," says Feodor, resolutely. "God cares for those who care for each other. I'll just run and get out my boat."

But as he was starting off to do so, a shout from the rest made him turn his head, and he saw something that stopped him short.

Just abreast of the spot where they stood three or four small islets, or rather sand-banks, lay close together in the centre of the stream. The huge fragment of ice upon which the man was crouching, turned sideways by the current, had just run upon the end of one of these banks, where it stuck fast.

"Now's the time," shouted Feodor, springing forward; "not a moment to be lost. A rope and a pole—quick!"

He was obeyed at once; for these rough fellows seemed to feel instinctively that *he* was the man for the occasion, and had a right to take the command. He twisted one end of the rope around his left arm, and running a little way up the bank, threw the other end to those who followed him, grasped the pole in his right hand, and bounded like a deer on to the nearest ice-block, the in-drawn breath of the excited lookers-on sounding like a hiss amid the dead silence.

Had any artist been there to paint the scene, it would have made a very striking picture. The sky had darkened suddenly, and a cheerless gloom brooded over the sullen river with its drifting ice, and the bare sandy ridges on either side, and the helpless figure stranded upon the islet, and the daring man winning his perilous way over the treacherous surface, and the group of anxious watchers on the shore, while the wind moaned drearily through the leafless trees, like a warning of coming evil.

But Feodor was not the man to be frightened by any such fancies, and on he went in gallant style, springing

MIGHTY QUAM.

"[illegible]"

lightly from block to block, while the ice creaked and groaned beneath his weight, and the water splashed up all around him. Twice a cry of dismay burst from his comrades, as the ice upon which he leaped gave way under his feet. Once his way was barred by a gap too broad to be cleared; but with his pole he drew a passing fragment within reach, stepped upon it, and went forward again.

But now came a new peril. The stranded mass of ice for which he was aiming, then stuck fast in the midst of the stream, formed a kind of breakwater, behind which the smaller lumps began to accumulate; and several of these, driven by the current beneath the great sheet, forced one end of it up, while the other was held fast by the sand-bank. Such a strain was too great to be long endured. Just as Feodor was almost within reach of the helpless man, the ice floe upon which the latter lay split in two with a deafening crash, and the pent-up masses behind, all breaking loose at once, came down upon Feodor like an avalanche.

"God help him, he's lost!" muttered an old peasant, clasping his hands.

But Feodor was not to be caught so easily. Quick as lightning he planted the end of his pole on the nearest block, and with one bound was safe upon the islet, just as the ice torrent went rushing and roaring past. The next moment his hand was on the shoulder of the prostrate man.

"Up with you, man!" roared he, shaking him violently; "up with you, quick!"

But the man never moved. Either cold or fright, or both together, had plainly rendered him quite helpless.

For an instant Feodor stood perplexed; and then he seemed to have made up his mind what to do. Planting his feet firmly upon the rough ice, he gave a powerful thrust with his pole, which pushed the block clear off the sand-bank; and another shove sent it fairly out into the stream.

"Now, lads," shouted he, to his friends on the bank, who still kept their hold of the connecting rope, "pull with a will."

The men, seeing at once what he meant to do, pulled at the rope with all their might, while Feodor guided the floating mass with his pole. More than once a huge block bore down upon him so swiftly that a fatal collision appeared certain; but the young hero's skillful hand and eye carried him through, and five minutes later the rescued man and his deliverer were both safe on shore.

"Bravo!"* cried his companions, crowding eagerly around him.

"Bravo!" echoed a strange voice from behind; and it was then seen that a handsome sleigh had halted beside the group, in which sat a tall, soldier-like man in uniform, at sight of whom the peasants doffed their caps and bowed low.

"What's all this?" asked the new-comer.

The story was soon told, and the stranger's face lighted up with a glow of hearty admiration as he heard it.

"Well done, my brave fellow!" said he, handing Feodor a bank-bill for twenty-five roubles ($19). "It's poor enough pay for such a day's work, after all; but if ever you're in want of money, come to me, and you shall have it, and welcome."

And away went the sleigh before Feodor could recover from his amazement, which was not lessened when half a dozen of his comrades, all speaking at once, informed him that this liberal stranger was no other than the Governor of Saratov himself.

---

* The Russian word is "molodetz" (literally "fine fellow"), answering to our familiar "bully boy."

A SUGAR BUSH AND CAMP
EMPTYING THE BUCKETS.

MAY'S BIRTHDAY.

DANCING round the May-pole—
  Oh, the merry sight!
Little lads and lassies
  'Neath the sunshine bright.
On her throne of daisies,
  Blossoms in her hair,
Laughing 'mid her blushes,
  Sits the May-Queen fair.

O'er the sunny meadow
  Clover blossoms grow;
Through the dainty grasses
  Spring's sweet zephyrs blow.
Buttercups and daisies
  Lift their pretty heads,
And watch the violets peeping
  From their fragrant beds.

Oh, the merry May-time
  With its charming hours,
With its skies so tender,
  And its dainty flowers!
Dance away, my children,
  Round your little Queen;
May's bright birthday honor
  With a "dance upon the green."

THE HAPPY CLUB.

A RECIPE FOR HAPPINESS.

TAKE six little girls about ten years old; add three or four nice little boys, and mix them with the girls, taking care not to stir them up too much. Then take—

But perhaps you will understand it better if I tell you just how we did it.

This is how it began: I have a little friend named Annie, who comes to see me every Saturday. She tells me "all about everything," and we have very good times together. One day she told me a story she had read in HARPER'S YOUNG PEOPLE about a poor little girl who finds a doll in an ash barrel.

"I think it is a very nice story," said Annie, "and that lady says that we could all make pretty things for sick children if we wanted to. Oh dear! I wish I had lots and lots of money!"

"It does not always take much money to make pretty things," I said. "You can make six elephants for thirty cents."

"True elephants!" asked Annie, opening her blue eyes so wide that I was afraid of an accident.

"No," I said, "but very tame elephants, made of gray flannel, and with red saddle-cloths."

"Oh, I don't think they are pretty," she said.

Then I told her how I had once bought two elephants, a big one and a small one, and sent them to a sick little girl. And how, when I had gone to see her, she had said to me: "Them ollifans is too nice for anything, and they don't never bite me at all. The big ollifan is the mother, and she keeps me company; and the little one comes and puts his big nose under my chin to get warm. Oh, I just love them!"

After that I bought one more elephant, and killed him, and used his skin for a pattern, and made several other elephants, to be loved by little children.

"I know what I will do," said Annie; "I will make some kittens. Won't that be nice?"

I thought it might be very nice, if we could get a good pattern. And as she wanted to begin immediately, we looked in a box where I keep all sorts of remnants, and found a piece of red plush, which Annie declared "would be just the loveliest thing for a kitten."

As I had never seen a red kitten, I was a little doubtful; but since that time I have seen kittens red and pink and blue, and the children to whom they are given always fall in love with them at first sight.

But our kittens were not made in one day. We found it so difficult to cut a pattern that would "look like anything" that we had to send to a special artist in the city; and during the winter we spent a whole dollar for patterns of animals.

How we became a club happened in this way:

Annie was so delighted with the idea of making pretty things for other children that she spoke of it to several little girls, who said that they would like to make pretty things too. Then they came to see me, and after talking it over we decided to go to work at once, and to call ourselves "a club." We were to meet every Saturday, in my sitting-room, and I was to be president, secretary, treasurer, cutter, and general manager.

At first it was to be strictly a "ladies' club"; but Louis, Annie's little brother, said he "wanted to be a club too," and as he is a very nice boy, we took him in, and also two other boys who applied for admission. There are ten of us—six girls, three boys, and myself.

Now I will tell you what we do, and how we do it.

The club meets a little before eleven o'clock every Saturday morning. The members bring their lunches, and all the pennies, toys, pieces, picture-books, and new "good ideas" they have been able to collect during the week. We sit around a table in a bright sunny room, with a large bay-window filled with green plants. On each side of the window are book-cases, and behind the glass doors of one of these you can see beautiful dolls, kittens, dogs, elephants, and a variety of other works of art. These are our "pretty things," which were, most truly, "born to be admired." A deep locked drawer under the shelves contains the raw material from which our wonders are made, and in the southeast corner of it is safely hidden the bank in which our precious pennies are kept.

During the first half hour we work, make plans, and exchange ideas. Then comes the request, "Please tell us a story; tell us about when you were a little girl." And as I am a very obedient "manager," I do as I am told.

At half past twelve we go into the dining-room, where we have "a picnic in the woods." The big table represents a shady grove, the sideboard is a hill, a large ivy at one end of the room is a summer-house, and we sit on rocks and fallen trees. This gives us a little change of air, and, as everybody knows, change of air gives people a good appetite.

When our picnic is over, we go to work again, and as we are all in pretty high spirits, we are very funny and witty, if not very wise. We relate anecdotes, recite short "pieces," sing, guess riddles and conundrums, we play "our minister's cat," and other games, and, as Louis says, "we have jolly old times."

Speaking of picnics reminds me of something that happened at our last meeting. The Saturday before, I had told my little friends about the French apple-tarts my grandmother used to make for me—"little pies," she called them. And as every member of the club wanted to know how they were made, I wrote nine short recipes, so that they would be sure to remember.

This gave me a good idea for "a secret."

When we went to the dining-room last Saturday, the children were surprised to find the table covered with a red cloth which was evidently hiding something.

Then I made a little speech: "We will not have a picnic to-day, but we will eat our lunch quietly on the top of our shady grove. Guess what I have for you."

"And guess what we have for you," answered nine little voices.

Instead of guessing, I lifted the cloth, while they opened their lunch-baskets. Then we all stared, and said, "Oh!"—a great big Oh!—for in a moment the table was all covered with apple-tarts, and in the middle of the tarts there was a large round apple-pie. You see, I had made the big pie for the children to eat, and several tarts to be taken home to their mothers; and *they* had all tried my recipe, and made tarts for the children, and some for me. So we had fifty-six tarts and the pie!

It would take too long to tell you everything about our little club; but so far it has been a success; and we have learned by experience how much pleasure can be given to others with a little trouble, and a great deal of good-will.

As we shall not be able to do much sewing when the warm weather comes, we intend to do garden-work, and send plants and flowers to our little friends who have no gardens of their own. We are already making delightful plans for flower beds, hanging baskets, and window boxes, filled with nasturtiums, sweet-peas, and mignonette. And our plans look so beautiful on paper that I can almost smell the flowers.

And now do you not think that we were right to call our club the "Happy Club"?

A LETTER FROM A LAND TURTLE.

BY ALLAN FORMAN.

MY young master said that he was going to write a letter to YOUNG PEOPLE about me, but Charley Bates just came in and asked him to go out and play, and I guess that he has forgotten all about it. My master don't know as much about me as I do myself, anyhow, and I have never told him anything, so I don't see how he could write. He has left me on his table, and I just looked over the edge, and it is 'most a mile high, I guess, so I won't try to get down. I'll take his pen and tell you some things about my life and adventures. You need not think that because I am only a turtle I have had no adventures.

I was born of an adventurous family. My great-grandfather was dropped by an eagle on the head of *Æschylus*, the Grecian poet, the eagle having mistaken the poet's bald head for a stone, and it is from my great-grandfather, who, as you see, was so closely brought into contact with one of the most learned heads of ancient Greece, I inherit my talent for literature. Another relation of mine, an uncle on my mother's side, was the principal in the great walking match which is so graphically described by *Æsop*. But enough of my family. I promised to tell you something about my life. I am so sleepy that I don't know as I can make it very interesting.

You see, we turtles stay awake all summer, and sleep all winter; we are *hibernating* animals, my master says. At first I thought that he meant that we were of Irish extraction, and as I am very proud of my Greek descent, the next time I saw the dictionary on the floor I found the word. If you don't know what it means, you had better look it out too: you will remember it better than if I told you.

My master read about a cousin of mine who lived for a time with a Reverend Mr. Wood, and ate bread and milk, and climbed on the footstool, and did all sorts of tricks; so he came and dug me out of the nice hole where I was asleep for the winter, brought me into his room, and before I was fairly awake thrust my head into a saucer of milk. Of course I would not eat. Then he tried to make me climb; but I was so bewildered that I drew in my head and shut up my shell. My master went out, saying, "Mr. Wood is a humbug, anyway." I waited till all was quiet, then I took a survey of the room. I began to feel hungry, as you may imagine, for I had eaten nothing since the first of November; so I crawled over to the saucer of milk, and drank it all. How I did laugh when my master came in and I heard him say, "That cat has been here and drunk all the turtle's milk"!

Since then he has watched me very closely. He gave me a piece of banana the other day, and it was very good. Sometimes he gives me a few earth-worms, of which I am especially fond; and there are four flies in the room—there were five, but I caught one and ate him: he was delicious. I mean to have the others before long. The way in which I catch them is this: I lie perfectly still in the sun, and when one comes along, I snap him. Flies are generally too quick for me, but I am very patient.

The first thing that I can remember is that I lived on a sand-bank with thirteen brothers and sisters. We used to eat flies and little insects then, and as we were very lively, we could catch them easily, and I think that the flies were more plenty. We grew very fast at first, and we soon wandered off, and were separated. For the next two years of my life I travelled, living near strawberry beds in the spring, then among raspberry and blackberry bushes, and finally in pear and apple orchards. I lived mostly upon insects, only taking a bite of strawberry or pear for a relish. I have heard my master say that I always picked out the best-looking pears to bite; but that is only fair, for if I did not eat up the insects, he would not have any best-looking pears at all, so I don't think that he ought to grumble.

It was in a pear orchard that one of the happiest events of my life took place. It was while eating pears that I met my Matilda Jane. Oh, she was the most lovely young turtle that you can imagine! Her beautifully rounded shell, with its delicate markings in black and "old gold," which was just then coming into fashion, her snake-like head and neck, and her beautiful bright yellow eyes, gave her the well-deserved name of "The Belle of the Village." We loved each other at the first, and for some time we were inseparable, until one morning, when my master's father was coming to the city, I was picked up, wrapped in a newspaper, and packed off to Brooklyn, that I might "kill the slugs in the garden," I heard my master say. For two weary years I lived alone in the garden, thinking only of my Matilda Jane. You can imagine my joy when, this fall, four more turtles were brought and placed in the yard, and one of them was my long-lost friend! I knew her immediately, from her having the letters "A. F., 1869," cut on her shell. Ever since that joyful meeting we have lived very happily together.

Of course we have troubles, like every one else, but they mostly arise outside our own household. There was one old turtle who used to put on airs because he had "Adam, year 1," cut on his shell; but my Matilda stopped his boasting by telling how she saw my master cut the name at the same time that he marked her. Old Adam, as we used to call him, sneaked off, and I have not seen him since.

I want to tell you one thing more, and then I will be done. Perhaps you don't know how the little turtles are born. The mamma turtle finds a quiet, secluded place where the soil is sandy; there she digs a hole, and lays from twelve to thirty eggs. The eggs are perfectly round, and about an inch in diameter. They do not have shells like birds' eggs, but they are covered with a coating like parchment. After she has laid her eggs she covers them up, and leaves them to be hatched by the heat of the sun. In about three weeks the young turtles make their appearance; they are not much larger than a silver fifty-cent piece. They are very lively, and are very cunning about hiding when any one comes near their home. They grow very rapidly, however, and in a short time wander away, as I did. I hope that you will all remember that turtles more than pay for the fruit that they eat by keeping your gardens free from worms and insects; and I trust that you will let your pet turtles sleep through the winter, and not keep them awake to study about them as my master has done.

Yours truly, LAND TURTLE.

FUN IN A CHINESE SCHOOL-ROOM.

BY WILLIAM ELLIOT GRIFFIS.

THESE five Chinese boys (except the one whose ear is being pulled) are having fine fun. The Fu-tsz, or old teacher, has gone out of the room for a few minutes to fill his tobacco pouch. Let us look round and see what kind of school-room they have in China, and how the pupils study.

The boys in this case are all of one family, and the old gentleman is their private tutor. He is white-bearded and shaven-pated, and has rather long finger-nails, as the fashion is in China among those who do not have to work with their hands. Long finger-nails with them are like white hands and tapering fingers among us.

The floor of the room is of stone set in squares like a checker-board. It is very pleasant and cool in summer-time, and in all weathers the lads keep on their velvet and maple-wood shoes. These are thick-soled and warm, slightly turned up at the end, but do not "draw" the feet, as our leather or rubber shoes do. The three younger boys wear embroidered coats. All except the "baby" have plaits of hair on the side of the head; but the little fellow, who is not yet six years old, still wears the very young child's circle of hair.

Every day or so their heads are neatly shaved; and when they are twelve years old, there will be a family party, and each one will lose his boyish locks, and begin to raise a "pigtail," or queue, which hangs down his back. Then they will feel as proud as our boys when they sport their first attempt at a mustache.

The walls of the school-room are plain, but are not complete without the usual picture of the bamboo swaying in the wind or sleeping in the moonlight. The Chinese have thousands of stanzas and ditties of which the graceful bamboo is the subject.

Notice the tables; they are of hard polished wood, with colored marble tops. The seats are of round hollow wood, with leather tops. They look like ginger jars with paper covers. On these the boys sit while tracing the characters which we see on *real* Chinese tea boxes (for those made in New York are almost always upside down, as if they had turned a somersault). Every boy must learn from two hundred to ten thousand of these characters, and many years of hard study are required. Their books, ink-stones, brush-pens, water-pot, and presents are all on the table. They use "India" ink, and write with a brush.

In learning their lessons the scholars study out loud, and a Chinese school-room is a very noisy place, and worse than the buzzing of many bee-hives.

When a boy has learned his lesson he comes to the teacher, and then "backs his book"; that is, he hands his book to the instructor, and then turns his back, so as not to see the page or face of the teacher, and then recites. At the same time he holds out two of his fingers, first of one hand and then of the other, beating them up and down alternately, like a music leader beating time.

The boys in the picture have become tired of so much sitting; so, as soon as the cat leaves the room, the mice begin to play. One of them mounts the table, taking the master's wooden seat with him. On this he poses himself, foot over knee, and dons Fu-tsz's hat, on which is the crystal button and horse-hair plume, of which all dignified men are very proud. He quickly anchors the huge goggle spectacles astride his nose, with the aid of the guy-ropes around his ears, seizes the empty pipe in one hand, and with fan in the other, calls out to the oldest boy to "back his book."

The big boy begins to see-saw his fingers up and down, and to bawl out his lesson; but quickly turns round to see the fun. The next oldest boy is pulling the ears of "the baby," who squeals out, while the boy on the floor, who pretends to be in disgrace, and can not rise, calls on the teacher to speak to the mischievous urchin.

But the old Fu-tsz has heard the squealing and the racket, and is hurrying along the corridor to see what is the matter.

What will be done? There will be no rattan or ruler used, or ears boxed, but each one will receive a lecture on propriety, and an extra lesson. The bigger boys will be ordered to learn fifty new characters, and the smaller ones will each have a longer copy to write after school.

MOTHER GOOSE'S MAY PARTY.

BY AGNES CARR.

IT was May-day, and the sun popped out of bed early that morning to wake up the little birds and flowers, that they might clear their throats and wash their bright faces in dew, by the time the old woman had swept the cobwebs from the sky, and left a beautiful blue roof over Goosetown village; for they knew it was the 1st of May, and that dear old Mother Goose, who taught the Kindergarten, or infant school, was going with all her little scholars to have a May party under the trees in the merry green wood.

And the children knew it too, and they were all on hand bright and early—Tommy Green and Johnny Stout, Humpty Dumpty and Little Bo-peep, Jack and Jill, Little Boy Blue in a brand-new suit of clothes, and Goldilocks with her yellow hair flying in the wind, Tom, the Piper's son, and poor Simple Simon, the dunce of the school, with many others that we have known and loved—and all brought baskets filled with good things for their dinner.

"Oh, won't we have fun!" said Margery Daw to Jacky Horner. "I hope you have got something nice in that big basket of yours."

"Yes, indeed," said Jack. "Cook made me a lovely pie, and stuffed it just full of plums. I will try and pull one out for you;" and he lifted up the napkin over the basket, and was trying to break a hole in the pie-crust, when Mother Goose came in, and seeing him, said, "Here, here, Master Jack! keep your fingers out of the pie. I never saw such a boy. He sticks his thumb into everything, from Christmas pies to inkstands."

"Oh, Mother Goose, do let us start!" shouted the children.

"Yes, yes, my dears, very soon. We are only waiting for Contrary Mary. I have sent Nimble Dick for her; and here they come now."

Sure enough, there was heard a jingling of bells, and in danced Mary, quite contrary, with her fingers covered with rings, and her apron filled with flowers from her garden, with which to make a wreath for the May-Queen.

And now they all started, walking two and two, with Mother Goose at the head, holding the youngest scholar, Baby Bunting, tight by the hand, for fear he should fall down and tear his new rabbit-skin overcoat, while Tom, the Piper's son, played "Over the hills and far away" on his pipe, and all the little folks danced and skipped along to the gay tune.

When they reached the pleasant wood, they were all glad to sit down on the green moss and rest awhile; and Mother Goose said, "The first thing is to choose a May-Queen: now who shall it be?"

"Goldilocks!" "Goldilocks!" shouted the children, for they all loved the dear little girl with pretty hair and sweet blue eyes.

"Oh, no, no!" said Goldilocks, and she hid behind Tommy Tucker.

But they made her come out and sit on a throne formed of Miss Muffet's tuffet, scattered over with wild violets and May-flowers, which grew all around; and Contrary Mary put a beautiful crown of "roses and lilies and daffadowndillies" on her golden curls, and she looked just the dearest little May-Queen in all the world.

Then all the children joined hands, and danced round the throne, singing,

"Hail to the Queen of May
On this our festal day!
Gay flowers we'll bring,
Sweet blossoms of spring,
To crown our Queen of May."

The little Queen then gave each one a flower, and let them kneel and kiss her tiny white hand; and then they scattered through the woods, and played "Oats, peas, beans," tag, and other games, until Little Boy Blue blew a blast on his horn, which meant "Come to dinner"; and when they all came running back at the call, they found Mother Goose had a table-cloth spread on the grass, and all the biscuits, cake, and fruit from their baskets set out on green leaves, while in the centre stood Jack Horner's pie, a bowl of curds and whey that Miss Muffet brought, and a plate of strawberry tarts sent by the Queen of Hearts; and Jack and Jill were bringing a pail of nice cold water from the spring.

How hungry they all were, too, and how good everything tasted! while they had such a laugh at little Miss Muffet, who screamed and ran away when a great daddy-long-legs walked across the table.

They ended the feast with the plum pie, which the little Queen cut, and gave every one a piece; and they all said it was so nice. Jack Horner felt quite proud, and thought he was a bigger boy than ever.

After everything was eaten up, Margery Daw and Little Bo-peep washed the dishes, while Little Boy Blue went fast asleep under the fence, and Mother Goose told all the little ones a story, until the cobwebs began to come over the sky, and the sun whispered to the little birds and flowers it was time to shut their peepers for the night, when they started for home, Goldilocks the Queen riding in the middle of the procession on big John Stout's shoulder; and when they bade their teacher a tired but happy good-night, all said they had had the nicest kind of a day, and hoped next year Mother Goose would give them another May party.

GOING HOME FROM THE PICNIC.—DRAWN BY JESSIE CURTIS.

AT PLAY ON SNOW-SHOES.

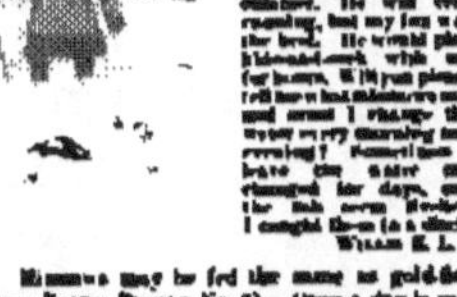

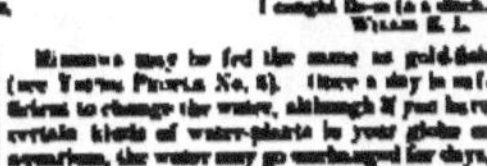

From internal evidence the middle of the fifteenth century has been fixed upon as the probable period of the composition of these wonderful tales.

R. E. S. VARIANT.—There are about 38,000 distinct words in the English language. About 23,000 of these are of Anglo-Saxon origin. The vocabulary of the new edition of Webster's *Unabridged Dictionary* contains about 118,000 words, including derivatives, compounds, etc.; 3000 or 4000, however, are all that are in common use for oral or written communication. The Old Testament contains 5642 different words, Milton uses about 8000, and Shakespeare about 15,000. Only about 300 words are in ordinary use for telegraphic business messages.

PUZZLES FROM YOUNG CONTRIBUTORS.

No. 1.

ENIGMA.

My first is in [illegible], but not in [illegible].
My second is in earth, but not in ground.
My third is in [illegible], but not in [illegible].
My fourth is in doubt, but not in guess.
My fifth is in [illegible], but not in [illegible].
My sixth is in [illegible], but not in [illegible].
My seventh is in [illegible], but not in [illegible].
My eighth is in [illegible], but not in [illegible].
My whole is a [illegible] painter's name,
Emblazoned high on the roll of fame.

NORTH STAR.

No. 2.

WORD SQUARE.

First, an article of [illegible]. Second, to [illegible]. Third, without end. Fourth, a Roman Emperor.

[illegible]

No. 3.

[illegible]

I am composed of 19 letters.
My 10, 2, 15, 11 is [illegible].
My 4, 3, 16, 5, 18 is a [illegible].
My 1, 6, 7 is a boy's name.
My 12, 8, 9, 6 is a flower.
My 14, 13, 8 is [illegible].
My 8, 3, 11 is a pronoun.
My whole is a noted event of the Revolutionary war.

W. R. S.

No. 4.

ENIGMA.

My first is in joy, but not in sorrow.
My second is in lend, but not in borrow.
My third is in [illegible], but not in [illegible].
My fourth is in [illegible], but not in [illegible].
My fifth is in [illegible], but not in [illegible].
My sixth is in better, but not in [illegible].
My seventh is in song, but not in hymn.
My eighth is in [illegible], but not in [illegible].
My ninth is in fancy, but not in whim.
My whole, a whole, when it is formed,
Is the name of a [illegible] much renowned.

[illegible]

No. 5.

[illegible]

In [illegible]. A song. A boy's name. A part of the body. In [illegible].

M. E. S.

No. 6.

DOUBLE ACROSTIC.

A [illegible]. A [illegible]. A [illegible]. Fish[illegible]. To enlighten. To [illegible]. Answer.—Primals form the first name and finals the second name of a celebrated man of the [illegible] century.

W. F. R.

ANSWERS TO PUZZLES IN NO. 21.

No. 1. Shakespeare.

No. 2. Birds of a feather flock together.

No. 3. [illegible]

No. 4. [illegible]

Geometry, Calculus.

No. 5. [illegible]

No. 6. Montcalm.

Decapitated Charade, on page 356.—Pirate.

A Perambulation, on page [illegible].—Queen Charlotte Sophia, wife of George the Third of England.

Favors are acknowledged from [illegible], [illegible] Werner, [illegible] Hamilton, [illegible], J. [illegible] Wolfe, Maggie [illegible], [illegible], Fred Lewis, J. [illegible], Nell B. [illegible], L. W.

Correct answers to puzzles are received from [illegible]

WIGGLES.

In answer to Wiggle No. 10, given in HARPER'S YOUNG PEOPLE No. 21, more than three hundred drawings have been sent in. Nearly one-third of these were correct answers to the Wiggle. Of the remainder a variety have been selected, and are published on page 376. With them is also given new Wiggle No. 11. The following list is of those who furnished drawings to the Wiggle, but who did not happen to catch our artist's idea:

[illegible]

ADVERTISEMENTS.

SOME ANSWERS TO WIGGLE No. 10, OUR ARTIST'S IDEA, AND NEW WIGGLE No. 11.

ALL those in the following list have caught our artist's idea, and have sent in Wiggles of chickens resembling his:

Wiggins, [illegible], Howard Rathbone, [illegible]

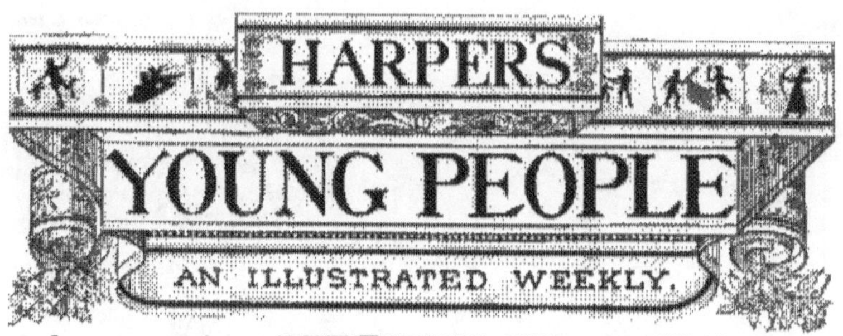

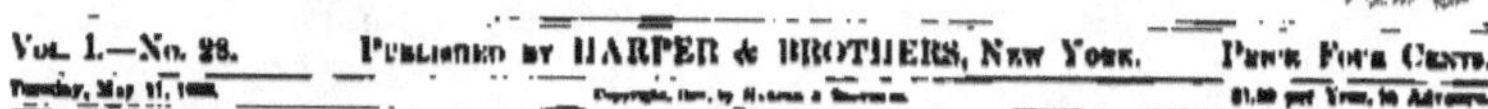
VOL. I.—NO. 28. PUBLISHED BY HARPER & BROTHERS, NEW YORK. PRICE FOUR CENTS.
Tuesday, May 11, [illegible] Copyright, [illegible] $1.50 per Year, in Advance.

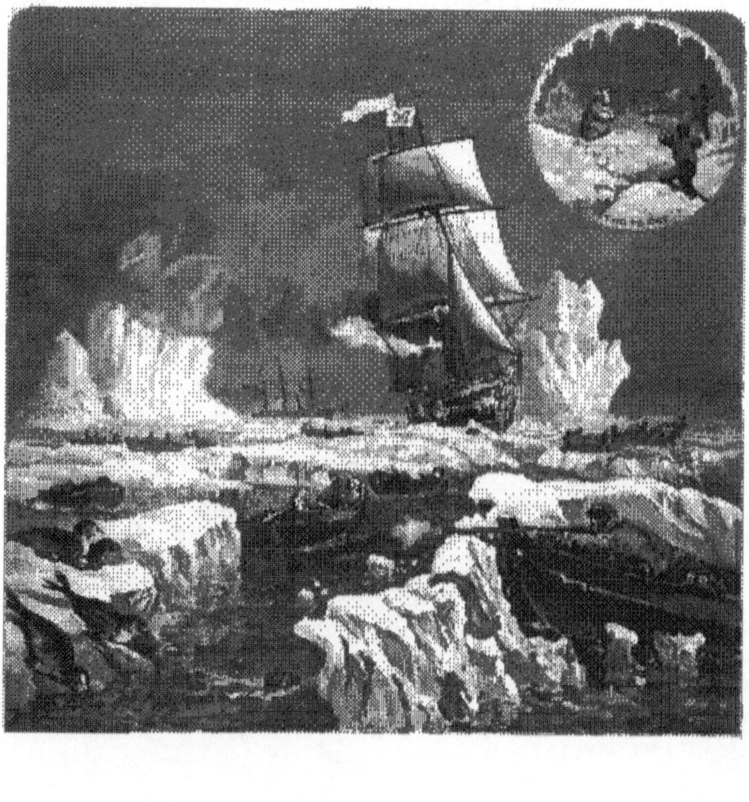

WHY?

"Why must I learn to sing?
 Why learn to fly?"
Said a young bird to its mother—
 "Why, oh, why?"

"All birdies learn to sing;
 All learn to fly,"
To the young bird said its mother;
 "And that's 'why.'"

HUNTING IN ARCTIC REGIONS.

ALTHOUGH in the remote and dreary ice regions of the extreme North a variety of game, including bear, whale, walrus, seal, reindeer, foxes, wolves, ptarmigan, ducks, and geese, is found and pursued by the hardy Esquimau, or Innuit, it is upon the capture of the seal that he expends the most time and labor. The seal is everything to him, and without it life could hardly be sustained. In the words of Captain Hall: "To the Innuit the seal is all that flocks and herds, grain fields, forests, coal mines, and petroleum wells are to dwellers in more favored lands. It furnishes him with food, fuel, and clothing."

"Nutchook" (the seal) is one of the most wary and suspicious of animals, and to capture him when he is on his guard requires an almost incredible amount of skill and perseverance. The Innuits say that "Ninoo" (the bear) taught them to capture the seal, and that if they could talk to Nutchook as cleverly as Ninoo does, they would capture him much oftener than they do. When Ninoo sees, at a distance upon the ice, a black spot that he knows to be Nutchook taking a nap beside his air-hole, he makes up his mind that he will dine that day off seal.

Nutchook's nap is a series of "cat-naps," each lasting about ten seconds, and after each he lifts his head and looks around. Ninoo crouches low upon the ice, and creeps along when the seal is napping. The moment his head is raised, the bear stops short and begins to talk to Nutchook. The sound that he utters while thus talking is quite different from his ordinary voice, and seems to charm the seal, who lays his head down for another nap, during which Ninoo again advances. At last the bear is within springing distance, and in a moment all is over with poor Nutchook.

Although seals are caught at all seasons of the year, the great hunts take place in the spring and early summer months. At this time the fur is in the best possible condition, and as they play in the open water lanes near the coast, or bask in great numbers on the ice, their capture is comparatively easy. During the summer the glare of the sun so affects the eyes of the seal that he becomes almost blind, and is easily approached.

Hundreds of vessels, many of them steamers, are engaged in the seal fishery, and on the first page of this number is a picture of the boats belonging to one of these "sealers" drifting cautiously down upon a number of seals that have been basking and frolicking on the ice, heedless of the approach of danger. Hundreds of thousands of seals are thus killed every year for the sake of their skins, which are shipped to every part of the world, and from which are made the beautiful sacques, muffs, tippets, and gloves with which most of our readers are so familiar. Only last month a disaster occurred that vividly illustrates the danger of sealing. A huge ice-field a hundred miles long, and bringing with it thousands of seals, drifted down from the North, and stranded on the coast of Newfoundland near St. Johns. For several days the people living along the coast ventured far out on the ice, and captured great numbers of the seals.

Suddenly, on the 8th of April, the northeast wind that had been blowing steadily for two weeks, and keeping the ice packed, changed to a warm southerly breeze. The ice-pack broke, became intersected in every direction by lanes of water, and began to drift out to sea, carrying with it more than two hundred of the hardy hunters. Many of these were rescued by steamers, but others were borne away into the fog, beyond the hope of rescue, far out to sea, where they have perished from starvation, freezing, or drowning. For weeks past dead bodies have been cast upon the rugged coast by the sea, but the fate of many of the lost will never be known.

Mr. Ninoo, who hunts the seal so successfully, is hunted in turn for the sake of his thick soft fur, and often falls a victim both to white men and Esquimaux. The latter sometimes kill him by rolling a thick piece of whalebone, about two feet long and four inches wide, into a small coil, and wrapping it in a piece of seal blubber so that it forms a ball. Placed outside the hut, it soon freezes hard. Provided with this frozen bait, the natives search for Ninoo. When they find him, they run away, and he chases them; but they drop the ball of blubber, and he, meeting with it, greedily swallows it whole. In a few minutes the heat of his body thaws the blubber and releases the whalebone. It uncoils with terrible force, and so tears his stomach that the great bear falls down in helpless agony, to which an end is quickly put by the hunter, who now hurries to the spot.

(Begun in Harper's Young People No. 24, April 13.)

THE STORY OF GEORGE WASHINGTON.

BY EDWARD CARY.

Chapter V.

SO now the war was as good as finished. There was no more fighting. The British government was nearly ready to give up to the United States, and own that they "were, and of right ought to be, free and independent," as the great Declaration had said more than five years before. But such things take a long time to settle, and General Washington thought that the Americans could make a great deal better terms of peace if they kept ready for war. How tired he was of the war! How he longed to get back to Mount Vernon, and to his peaceful farmer's life! His letters written about this time are full of these desires. He was a great General; and the whole country honored and loved him as a man whose courage and skill had made his countrymen free, but he often said that he would give all the glory he had won if he could go back to his crops and his trees, his horses and his hounds, and his beloved family, and rest. Yet he stood by his post to the very last. He begged his countrymen to keep up the army, and not to lay down their arms till everything was sure. He begged his officers and soldiers to be patient and stay with him, though they had much reason to complain. They had been poorly paid, or not paid at all. Many of them were actually ruined for their country, and, when they left the army, did not know where or how they should get a living. At this moment some of them thought they would be happier and better off under a King, if that King were Washington. They said to themselves: "It is all very well to be free, but here is a free nation which turns its old soldiers out to starve, which does not pay its debts, which hardly deserves freedom. We should have greater justice, and more peace and safety, with this wise, strong man as King." One of Washington's officers hinted as much to him. The General was filled with sorrow and anger and shame at the very thought. What had he done, that men should think he would consent to such treason? He wrote to the man who had suggested the plan, "If you have any regard for your country, or respect for me, banish these thoughts from your mind."

At last, in the spring of 1783, word came that a treaty of peace had been signed, and that the independence of the United States was no longer disputed. This joyful news was read to the American army on the 19th of April, just eight years after the first gallant fight at Concord in 1775. Washington wrote a farewell address to the army which he had led so long. It was like the wise and loving speech of a good father. He thanked them warmly for the noble spirit with which they had upheld him during the tedious and cruel years of war; he reminded them of the end for which they had fought, that the United States might be a free nation, with the right to govern itself as it thought best; and he prayed them to do all that they could to make their country just and wise in peace, as it had been brave and fortunate in war. It was winter before Washington had the affairs of his command settled so that he could leave the army and return to his home. On the 4th of December he met the principal officers of the army at New York to bid them farewell. They were gathered for that purpose at Fraunce's Tavern when he entered. Filling a glass, he turned to them, and said: "With a heart full of love and gratitude, I now take leave of you. I most devoutly wish that your latter days may be as prosperous and happy as your former ones have been glorious and honorable." Then one by one, as the officers came to him, he clasped hands with each, and embraced him in silence. Those brave men, who had faced death together, and had cheerfully borne untold privation, were not ashamed to weep at parting with their beloved friend and chief. When he had saluted them all, he passed through a corps of soldiers outside the door, and walked to the river-side, followed by the officers in solemn silence. He entered the barge, and raising his hat, he waved them farewell; and they, with the same loving gesture, watched the barge push off, and turned away. Washington took his journey to Annapolis, in Maryland, gave up his commission to Congress, and returned to Mount Vernon.

He reached his home on Christmas-eve, 1783. It was more than eight years and a half since he had left it to join the Continental Congress at Philadelphia, and he had seen it but twice in that long interval. When he went away he was forty-three years old—in the very prime of manhood; when he returned he was fifty-one, and felt that he was growing old. Constant labor, constant care, exposure in the camp and on the march, and the sad and fearful experience of battle, had told upon his naturally strong frame, and he welcomed the prospect of rest as simply and as gladly as a tired child. He wrote to his dear friend Lafayette, who had returned to France: "At length I am become a private citizen on the banks of the Potomac; and under the shadow of my own vine and fig-tree, free from the bustle of a camp and the busy scenes of public life, I am solacing myself with tranquil enjoyments...... I have not only retired from all public employments, but I am retiring within myself, and shall be able to view the solitary walk and tread the paths of private life with heart-felt satisfaction."

[TO BE CONTINUED.]

THE MAGIC SPINET.

BY MRS. J. E. McCONAUGHY.

THE gay people of Paris were one day invited to attend a musical entertainment, in which "a magic spinet" was to be the chief attraction. Its wonders were set forth in glowing terms, and a large audience gathered at the appointed time to witness its performance. The poor musician, whose all was at stake, looked on the assembly with rejoicing eyes, but perhaps with a little trembling lest his "magic" should not work as perfectly as at rehearsals.

After some playing by himself and his two little children, all stepped back, and at the word of command the instrument repeated the whole symphony. This marvel was well received, when the musician pretended to wind up his machine by a very hard-working winch, which made a terrible racket.

Now the wise ones thought it all explained. "Only a foolish contrivance of weights and springs, like a barrel-organ," they said. That was just what the musician wished them to think, as it would make his triumph more decided. He now proceeded to show them that the instrument had a mind capable of hearing and obeying. Calling his children away, he waved his wand, and in an authoritative voice commanded, "Spinet, play"—such a tune.

The instrument obediently played the tune. Then the order was given, "Spinet, be silent," and all was quiet.

"Spinet, give us a light flourish," and it instantly warbled forth the gayest melody, which was received with rapturous applause. Then the whole sentiment of the audience was changed, and all admitted that Jean Baptiste Raisin, the musician, was also a great magician.

Evening after evening he repeated his performance, and the gold poured in beyond his fondest dreams. His reputation spread far and wide, and at last reached the King. He would have this novelty brought to court, and let the Queen and the royal ladies enjoy such a wonderful entertainment.

Jean was not used to courts, but his passion for money was growing fast, and he determined fairly to settle himself in such a golden harvest field. His instrument was "instructed" to a most unusual degree, and at the appointed time was in good working order at the palace of Versailles. Everything proceeded famously until the organist carried on his old trick of "winding up." Royal ears were not used to such horrid discords as followed the working of that winch. The delicate nerves of all the ladies were dreadfully shocked, the Queen's in particular.

But I suppose a Queen's curiosity is much like other people's. She must have a view of the evil spirit inside the instrument, which seemed to play so unwillingly, judging from the shrieks it gave out on being wound up. The poor organist protested he had "lost the key." But that was of no avail.

"Can not some one break it open?" asked the King. Royalty has a very persuasive way, so Jean was forced at last to open the box; and what do you think they found within? A poor trembling little lad, not six years old, who operated a set of keys inside, which his father had constructed for him. The whole instrument was planned with this performance in view, the lad's small size and wonderful musical talent making the deception possible.

It was plain that the little one was half fainting with the stifled air he had breathed so long; and ready hands reached out to help him, and kind voices soothed and comforted him. When he was refreshed, all wished to hear him play in fair sight, and the praising and petting and confections and gold coins showered upon him would have turned a wiser head. Defeat was turned into a grand victory.

His father now invented a comedy, in which little Louis acted an important part.

A company appeared seated about a table, with a big black pudding before them. When the pudding was cut, a great outcry was heard within. Soon it began to roll about the plates, and at last out hopped a little pig. They chased it about awhile with skewers, and finally, just as it was caught, it changed into an imp, with horns and hoofs, and a sabre by its side. Of course the company were greatly frightened, and tumbled down on the stage, pell-mell, all in a heap. But one sad day a performer thrust too hard with his sharp skewer, and poor little Louis performed and played no more. They laid him away in the pleasant cemetery, and very soon a heart-broken little sister, who could not be comforted, was laid beside him.

[Begun in No. 19 of Harper's Young People, March 9.]

ACROSS THE OCEAN; OR, A BOY'S FIRST VOYAGE.

A True Story.

BY J. O. DAVIDSON.

CHAPTER X.

FIGHTING A WATER-SPOUT.

"ANYTHING wrong below, Smith?"

"Well, sir, she's got a precious list to port, and the water's runnin' into the fire-room like anythin'. Seems to come from under the coals."

"Have them shifted at once, then, and see what's wrong."

"Ay, ay, sir."

Frank had overheard the fireman's report to the first officer, and a thought struck him. Walking aft till he was right over the engine-room, he climbed out under the "guard," and looked keenly along the port quarter. Aha! There, just as he had expected, was a port-hole standing wide open, and letting in water at every plunge of the vessel.

"Well done, my boy! that's twice you've got us all out of a scrape," said Mr. Hawkins, to whom Frank hastily reported what he had seen. "How did you come to think of that port-hole?"

SHOOTING THE WATER-SPOUT.

"I'd noticed it when I was shovelling down there, sir, and I thought that must be it."

"Good! I like to see a youngster keep his wits about him. Send up the carpenter to fix it, will you? I won't forget to tell Captain Gray what you've done, depend upon it."

This, of itself, would have been a sufficient "event" for the first day out from Malta; but another was still to come. The next morning Frank noticed two new faces among the firemen, and asked Herrick who they were.

"Stowaways, lad," said the old tar. "We found 'em hid away among the cargo last night, and now we're making 'em work their passage. There was three on 'em altogether, but them two Britishers are all that's any good. The third was a Maltee lubber, who'd never done nothin' but wait at table, and sich; so we jist sent him aft to serve the officers."

That evening there was a sudden cry of "Fire!" and Frank, to whom the mere thought of a fire at sea had always been a perfect nightmare, was amazed to see how coolly the men got out their hose-pipes and took their appointed stations, without the slightest flurry or confusion. In *three* minutes all was ready; but happily it proved to be a false alarm.

IN THE SUEZ CANAL.

Ha! what is this long gray band along the southern sky, with one tall white line standing up from it like a mast, and two black bars stretching from its edge far into the bright blue waters? Can it be the coast of Egypt already? It is nothing else. The white streak is Port Said Light-house; the black bars are the walls of its breakwater, running their huge piled-up blocks of "concrete" nearly two miles out to sea.

Frank was greatly amused with the quaint little toy town of 2000 inhabitants, perched between the desert and the sea, where everybody shut up their stores and went to sleep in the middle of the day; where, thanks to the deep soft sand, carriages and horsemen went by as noiselessly as shadows; and where every gust of wind raised a dust-storm that hid people, houses, and everything else. Here, for the first time, he saw a *punka*, or monster fan, worked by a rope, and hung from the ceiling of a room. He was shown over the light-house by a trim little Arab boy and girl, who, to his great surprise, turned out to be man and wife; and altogether he had plenty of new impressions to think over when he at last found himself fairly afloat upon the Suez Canal.*

A narrow ribbon of light green water between two interminable sand-banks, growing gradually higher as they advanced southward; a huge "dredger" every here and there, lying like a castle upon the water, with a clamorous garrison of blue-shirted men and red-capped boys; an occasional tug-boat, disdainfully greeted by Herrick as "Puffing Billy"; a distant caravan, with its endless file of camels and horses and men, melting away in curve after curve, like some mighty serpent, far back into the quivering haze that hovered over the hot brassy desert—such were the main features of the famous passage, begun by Pharaoh-Necho, and finished by Lesseps. The sun was sinking as they cast anchor for the night before Ismailia, and saw the mouth of the Sweetwater Canal, and the docks and houses of the brand-new town which the late sovereign of Egypt built and named after himself, fading into the fast-falling darkness.

Starting again next morning, they passed Suez about noon (fortunately without having to halt at one of the ugliest and dirtiest towns in the world), and headed down the Red Sea. Frank took a good look, in passing, at the bold headland of Ras Attakah, which is said by the best authorities to mark the scene of the Israelite passage, and where, according to a grim Arab legend, the shrieks of Pharaoh's drowning host may still be heard at times mingling with the roar of the storm. Farther on, a break in the sea-board hills gave him one glimpse of the huge square dark gray mass of Sinai,† far away to the east; and then they were in the open sea once more.

Keeping well out to sea, they escaped the net-work of coral reefs which beset the Arabian coast for forty-five miles together; but they could not escape the heat, which overpowered not a few even of the old hands. Again and again strong men were carried fainting from the engine-room, to be tended by a surgeon almost as sick as themselves. The stiff breeze that was blowing, instead of refreshing them, seemed to bring with it the heat of all the African deserts at once, and a passing steamer signaled that she had lost *sixteen* men by it in two days.

"See that lubber of a mountain spoutin' fire, as if 'twarn't hot enough already!" growled Herrick, pointing to the volcanic islet of Jebel Teer. "That other island yonder's where the Arabs think their spirits go when they die; but I guess if *I* was a spirit, I'd like to have a cooler berth."

But once through the Straits of Bab-el-Mandeb (Gate of Tears) into the Indian Ocean, Frank's ideas of a tropical voyage were fully realized. Bright skies, smooth seas, a steady breeze abeam keeping all cool, porpoises frolicking around the ship by hundreds, gay-plumaged birds alighting in the rigging, and a dance on deck every night to the music of fiddle and concertina, with a roaring accompaniment of sea-chorus that might have pleased Captain Marryat himself. Frank's throat was sore for a whole day after his patriotic efforts to "give full mouth" to one of these, which began thus:

"May our good ship *Arizona* have fair winds to fill her sails!
She can race the King of Sharks, not to say the Prince of
Whales;
And she'll laugh at Arab roaches and at crawling British
snails,
As she goes sailing on."

The guns were got ready as they ran through the pirate-haunted Straits of Malacca; and though no pirate ventured to attack them, they had to face an enemy quite as dangerous that very afternoon. Frank, who had been looking at the blue Sumatra hills, with here and there a curl of smoke above the trees to show where the sandal-wood gatherers were at work, was suddenly startled by the cry of, "A water-spout!"

There it was, sure enough, the long dark pillar, topped by a mass of black cloud, moving swiftly over the sea. Two native fishing-boats were flying before it, one of which was speedily drawn into the swirling foam at the base of the column. The other, more fortunate, got under the lee of the steamer.

"Give him a shot, Herrick," shouted the Captain, and the old quartermaster obeyed. The first shell missed, though so narrowly that the spout was seen to quiver; but the second burst right upon the thinnest part of the column, which broke and fell, with a noise that might have been heard for miles. For a moment the whole air was dark as night with spray and smoke; then a torrent of rain burst upon them, and when it cleared away, not a trace of their terrible enemy was to be seen.

The morning after her water-spout adventure the *Arizona* sighted the light-ship marking the approach to Singapore; and after an exciting race with an English screw-steamer, ran safely over the bar into the harbor. This was certainly rather hard upon the native pilot-boat,

SINGAPORE PILOT-BOAT.

which had put out to her in the hope of a job; and the six black, half-clothed scarecrows who pulled it vented their feelings in a prolonged howl and a clatter of their diamond-shaped oar blades, to which Jack Dewey replied by asking, with an air of deep interest, how much they would take to "come on board and new pitch the boats with the tar off their elegant black hides."

[TO BE CONTINUED.]

STORIES FROM THE MINES.

MANY stories are told of the manner in which the first discoveries of gold in California were turned to account by ingenious speculators, and among them are the following: In one district the gold-dust was mixed with large quantities of fine black sand, which the miners—most of whom were raw hands—blew off from the gold in their anxiety to arrive at the ore itself. A keen old man turned their impatience to account by shamming lameness, and pretending that in his weakly state he was not equal to the toil of mining, and was thus compelled to resort to the poor and profitless branch of gathering the black sand, which he sold as a substitute for emery. He used to go about of an evening with a large bag and a tin tray, requesting the miners to blow their black sand upon it, and returning with it to his hut. By the aid of quick-

* Of the eighty-six miles of the canal, nearly thirty lie through the shallow lakes of Menzaleh, Timsah, and "Bitter Water," the channel being marked by posts or mounds. Its depth is twenty-six and a quarter feet, its mean breadth about seventy, and in the "sidings" nearly one hundred.

† Called by the Arabs "Jebel Musa" (Mountain of Moses).

silver he was able to extract the gold, double in quantity to that which was obtained by the hardest-working miner at the washings.

Tricks of every kind were played upon new-comers in search of the golden treasures. One story is told of some American associates who had been working at an unprofitable spot, putting up a notice that their "valuable site" was for sale, as they were going elsewhere. A few Germans who had just arrived offered themselves as purchasers. The price asked was exorbitant, as the proprietors stated that the "diggings" returned a large amount of gold, and the following day was appointed for the Germans to come and see what could be produced in the course of a few hours' working. The sellers went during the night and secreted the gold-dust in the banks, so that it would come to light, as a natural deposit, when the earth was turned up. The following morning the poor Germans were so delighted with the apparent richness of the place that they gave a large sum of money and two valuable gold watches for the property. The Germans were laughed at; but they went to work, and actually succeeded in raising a large amount of gold beneath the spot where the others had left off. The Americans were thus outwitted in turn, and endeavored to get repossession of the place by force; but another company of Germans arriving, they were obliged to decamp.

An old miner relates this story: "While working on Rock Creek, the weather being very hot, we always had near us a can of water, and close to it we put a tea-cup to hold the particles of gold as we collected them. One morning as we were at work a thirsty digger came by, who asked permission to take a draught of water, which being granted, he filled up the cup, and quaffed off the costly drink, without either drinking our healths or leaving the least sediment at the bottom. I suspected at first that some trick had been played upon us, and he had secreted the gold; but from the evident distress of the man, and the earnest manner in which he promised to repay us when he got work, I firmly believe that he had swallowed the gold, not having noticed it in the cup."

Scarcely twenty-three years have elapsed since the gold yield in California became an undoubted fact, and within that period many millions of dollars' worth of gold-dust has been added to the wealth of the world. But even these results have been eclipsed by the wonderful discoveries of gold in Australia. So extensively are the gold deposits distributed throughout that great country, that Melbourne, the capital, has been said to be paved with the rich metal, the broken quartz rocks which have been used to make the streets being found to contain gold.

A BOAT-RACE AT YARROW.

BY E. L. TALBOT.

YARROW is the place where I am at school while my father and mother are in Europe. My father was ordered to the Mediterranean: that's an awful word to spell. My chum, Sandy, says, "Remember from the Latin *Medi-terra*," but that's harder than the spelling. I am glad every day that I was sent here, because I don't believe there is another school in the world where you can have such fun. Mr. May is our teacher; and though he is pretty strict always, and sometimes, if a fellow tries to cheat or play sick, he's awful hard on him, yet when everybody is trying to do his best, Mr. May is the quickest to find it out, and it makes him mighty good-natured. Perhaps I should not think Yarrow such a good place to send a boy if it wasn't for the river that is within a stone's-throw from Mr. May's barn. We skate there in winter, and in summer row, swim, and drive logs. Last year we had nothing to row in but the old *Pumpkin Seed*, broad as she is long, and rows like a ship's yawl. Now she might fill and go to the bottom, for all we cared, for Nate Niles and I have had birthdays, and my uncle Tom sent us each the prettiest double shell, cedar decks, outriggers, spoon oars, and all. I tell you, they were beauties! My uncle knows what's what in a boat, as he used to row, and beat, too, when he was in college. He is always sending me things, because I'm his favorite relation, and my middle name is Thomas. Lately he gives things to Nate, because he is going to marry his sister. Before Nate got his boat, he said he'd a million times rather have her an old maid than have such a chap for a brother. Now, though, he's all right, he likes his boat so much.

Mr. May made a bargain that we were to study hard for a month, and he would give us boards and timber enough to build a boat-house. We couldn't leave such valuable boats as the *Arrow* and the *Edith* out-of-doors, and Nate said the cows would *hook 'em* if we left them in the barn. Mick Murphy (he's Mr. May's man) did most of the carpentering, but we boys helped. Sam Fish got so he could shingle as well as Mick, and keep the nails in his mouth. I pounded my thumb the first day I tried, and the biggest blood-blister I ever saw grew; so I had to give up hammering. Sam says if he can't be a Congressman, he means to be a first-rate shingler, and get the job of shingling all the spires in the country. I shan't be that, anyway. If I can't get on better with my arithmetic, and get to be an Admiral, I shall keep a stable, and let my father ride my horses—regular circus horses, and calico-spotted ones—very cheap. Sandy King (he's my chum) helped me that month over my lessons, so I got on swimmingly. Sandy can read Latin as quick as lightning, and knows *horse* in eight languages, not counting pigeon English. He's a splendid fellow, besides, and I shall never forget how good he was to me when I came to Yarrow, and was the only Democrat, except Mick and his family.

I painted the boat-house, because I had hurt my eyes when Sam's gun burst when I went after a partridge. It turned out to be one of Muffy Wilson's hens, who lives just across the river, and I had to pay a dollar and a half, and she only weighed four pounds. I thought I was dead, sure, when I dropped the gun, and Mick's boy said he thought so too. I only burned off my eye-winkers, and got some powder in my cheek. Mr. May was awfully severe, and said I broke one of the rules of the school. I guess he always says that when a fellow almost kills himself. He did when Nate lassoed the pig, and she bit him. I only know the dog and smoking rules. You can't keep one, because, Mr. May says, it eats what would keep a poor human being. I think, though, if I could find a dog that would eat only fat, I could keep him, because I always leave that, and no human being could live on that. Bridget hopes there isn't any such dog to be found, because she is so stingy over her old soap stuff.

When the house was done, the red roof just showing above the alders, and looking so pretty just at the bend in the river, we didn't feel a mite sorry for all the hard work we had put into it; though I do wish I hadn't let Sam try and get the paint off my trousers, for he took cloth and all. I have been mighty unlucky lately with my clothes. I scalded my best shoes, and Polly Burr didn't notice, and wore my best jacket common for two days, and got gravy on it. He's such a funny fellow! He used to use any boy's tooth-brush. We put salt on ours, and cured him of that, though we couldn't use ours for ever so long. My uncle wrote me a solemn letter a little while ago, and said, "Robert Ames, you must never forget you are a poor man's son." That was because I sawed my new gray trousers. I felt solemn for a long while, and now I'm afraid he will write another.

Nate named his boat the *Arrow*, because he said it went so well with Yarrow. He chose Sam Fish for his stroke, as he is the strongest fellow in the school. I named mine *Edith*, after my mother, and took Sandy for bow oar.

Sandy said he wasn't half so strong as Polly, and wanted to give up; but I wanted just no fellow but Sandy. And then Polly has been scared of boats, and rather a land-lubber, ever since his aunt got blown up on a steamer. Besides, he cares more about his menagerie, and was busy training his ant-eater.

We decided to have a race the 18th of June, as it was Mr. May's birthday. Sam wanted a silver cup for a prize, but we couldn't get money enough. Polly was mighty generous, and gave fifty cents for the prize. We appreciated Polly's generosity, for we knew he didn't care a pin for boating, and the express on his ant-eater cost him ninety cents. The three Freshmen, Fritz Davis, Phil Hayes, and Billy Butler, each gave twenty-five cents toward the prize, Sam a dollar, Nate all he had, forty-three cents, Sandy fifty, and I eighty-three. I hope it wasn't too much for a poor man's son. The boys made me captain and Polly treasurer of the Yarrow Boat Club.

Sandy and I rowed every minute we could get. Every time we got into the boat we liked her better and better: she rowed so easily, and sat like a duck in the water. Sandy got so he didn't dip too deep nor jerk, as he did first. We found out that Sam and Nate were training. They ate rare beef and ran two miles a day. Sandy wanted to train too, but I told him I couldn't, as I only liked the outside of beef, and my only shoes hurt my feet.

"Let them try one way, and we another; the 18th will prove which is best." Sandy and I were getting ready to anchor the *Pumpkin Seed* up the river for the turning stake on the day of the race, when Polly and his ant-eater came down the hill.

"Any more money, Polly?"

"Yes; great luck. Mick and Bridget each gave ten, and Mick's boy gave twenty-five for a chance to sell corn balls."

"Didn't you see the Sunday-school?"

"I forgot all about it until after they had put their money into the contribution box; but they all said they were coming, sure pop."

We anchored the *Pumpkin Seed* up the river just a quarter of a mile from the boat-house; that made the distance to be pulled half a mile. Sam sent to Boston for shirts and crimson handkerchiefs for his crew. They both looked splendidly, but Sam's broad back and long stroke rather scared us. Mrs. May fixed us shirts, but they wrinkled round the neck. Then we had two yellow handkerchiefs that Mr. May used to use. The day before the race the small boys made a *grand stand* at the Oxbow for the spectators. It looked strong, but Mr. May said it wasn't, so Mick had to do it over.

Polly told me the night before that he had kept the time of the two boats for a week, and ours had been the best every time. That would have been grand, if I only could have trusted Polly's watch. But it was a bad one, and he used to set it three times a day.

I walked to the village, and brought back the blue and yellow flag, with the letters Y. B. C. on it, which was to be the prize. The grand stand was to be saved for adults and girls, and Mick was to be in the *Pumpkin Seed* at the turn. He knows a good deal about races, as his brother owns a trotter. Mr. May was to keep the time, as he had some kind of a thermometer watch. Such a dinner as Mrs. May gave us! I had Sam's and Nate's pieces of lemon pie, as they couldn't eat anything but meat. Mr. May looked over his spectacles, and asked if I was the boy who was to row a race that afternoon.

At one o'clock boys began coming, and took seats on the stand. Mick had to tell them about the girls and adults. Those mean Wilson boys had built a stand in the night, and let the crowd in for five cents: so both banks were full. They are the meanest family in America. They promised to keep every one out of their field. We were mad enough, but we couldn't do anything then.

Sam and Nate were in the *Arrow* when we got to the river, and they cheered us as we got into our boat, and Polly shoved off our bow. I gave the stroke, and we pulled into the middle of the river, where the prize flag was waving, and looking pretty enough to pull a dozen races for.

"Lay on your oars, and wait the signal." It seemed an hour before Mr. May said, "One, two, three—go!" and Sandy and I began our work, not rowing as we meant to later. The *Arrow* was to hug the Wilsons' shore, and we our bank. I heard a cheer for the *Arrow*, and knew she was ahead. It was a strong temptation to look round and see how far ahead she was, and by a spurt bring our boat up with her if possible. I didn't, though, and just rowed away as well as I could, and tried to keep cool.

The boys on the bank kept shouting, "Go it, *Arrow!*" "You're ahead!" "Brace up, *Edith!*" We had passed the alders, and were nearing Mick and the turn. We held our port oars, and rounded neatly, and heard Mick say, "Well done, Bob!" Then I told Sandy to "give it to her," and by the spring in the boat I knew that Sandy had been saving his strength for the homestretch. We were doing our best. If we could not get ahead at that rate, the race was lost. But we weren't going to be badly beaten. "The *Edith*'s ahead!" "Good for you, Bob!" That was Polly's voice near us on the bank. When I knew we were ahead, I felt all right. We could row that way long enough, and if Sam and Nate hadn't been saving their strength, we could win. I could see we held our lead; if anything, we added to it.

"You're bating, Robert, you're bating." Bridget had promised to stand near the barn; so we knew we were nearing the boat-house. For saying that, Bridget should come in free, and I meant to return her ten cents.

"Handsomely, Sandy!" and we both put on a little extra muscle that we didn't know was left over, and shot by the flag, about three lengths ahead of the *Arrow*.

"Three cheers for Captain Bob!" "Well done, *Edith!*" "Now, Sandy!" Such yells as the boys gave! I've never heard anything like 'em since.

The girls waved their handkerchiefs, and Fritz Davis played his hand-organ. Sam handed the flag to me, and I put Sandy's brown hand on it, and we waved it, and started cheers for the *Arrow*, as loud as we could. When we rowed ashore, the boys put Sandy and me on their shoulders, and rode us up to the house. Polly waved the Yarrow flag, and Fritz ought to have played the "Conquering Hero," but he made a mistake, and played the "Cruel War." Mr. May says he has no ear. That isn't the matter though, for he has two, and big ones, too.

When we were changing our clothes, we four talked it all over. "By thunder! Bob, I thought we had lost when you ate those corn balls, after all that pie." I never saw Sandy so excited. He's a minister's son, and pretty calm.

"Stuff! Bob has it in him, and nothing he eats makes any odds." Sam thinks, because my father is a sailor, I can row. But father never rows a stroke.

"Well, Sam, the next one, don't let us go into training. I've been hungry ever since we began." Poor Nate had had a hard time of it, because he and I have the biggest appetites at school, and he didn't like rare beef, so he ate mighty little. He says he is always hungry, excepting Thanksgiving afternoons.

"When shall we try again, boys?"

"Fourth of July; and I'll get my father to give a prize," and Sam hit on the thing we all wanted—to try it again.

Mr. May invited all the boys and girls on our side of the river to stay and have lemonade and cake. Sam bought all the corn balls Pat had left, to celebrate the opening race and Mr. May's birthday. That's the way Mr. May served the sneaking Wilsons and their five-cent crowd. But Sam heard they said the cake was molasses gingerbread and the lemonade bitter, and we are going to make the mean sneaks take back every word the next time they bring the milk.

Mick said it was as well conducted a race as he ever saw; and Mr. May said his birthday never had been so honored before; and Sandy and I want to row just such another the coming Fourth of July.

THE LAST BATTLE OF THE REVOLUTION.

BY BENSON J. LOSSING.

DR. ALEXANDER ANDERSON, the father of wood-engraving in this country, died in Jersey City, in 1870, a few weeks before his ninety-fifth birthday. He was born in New York two days after the skirmish at Lexington, and had vivid recollections of some of the closing incidents of the Revolution in that city. From his lips the writer heard many narratives of those stirring scenes. One of them was an account of the last battle of the Revolution, of which young Anderson, then a boy between eight and nine years of age, was an eye-witness.

Anderson's parents lived near the foot of Murray Street, not far from the Hudson River. There were very few houses between them and Broadway. Opposite Anderson's dwelling was a boarding-house kept by a man named Day. His wife was a comely, strongly built woman, about forty years of age, and possessed a brave heart. She was an ardent Whig, and having courage equal to her convictions, she never concealed her sentiments.

On the morning of the day (November 25, 1783) when the British troops were to evacuate the city of New York, and leave America independent, Mrs. Day unfurled her country's flag over her dwelling. The British claimed the right to hold possession of the city until noon on that day. Cunningham, the notorious British Provost-Marshal, was informed of this impudent display of the "rebel banner" in the presence of British troops, and sent a sergeant to order it to be taken down. Mrs. Day refused compliance.

At about nine o'clock in the morning, while young Anderson was sitting on the porch of his father's house, and Mrs. Day was quietly sweeping in front of her own, he saw a burly, red-faced British officer, in full uniform, with a powdered wig, walking rapidly down the street. He halted before Mrs. Day, and roughly inquired,

"Who hoisted that rebel flag?"

"I raised that flag," coolly answered Mrs. Day, looking the angry officer full in the face.

"Pull it down!" roared the Briton.

"I shall not do it," firmly answered Mrs. Day.

"You don't know who I am," angrily growled the officer.

"Yes, I do," said the courageous woman.

Cunningham (for it was he) seized the halyards, and attempted to pull down the flag, when Mrs. Day flew at him with her broom, and beat him so severely over the head that she knocked off his hat, and made the powder fly from his wig. "I saw it shine like a dim nimbus around his head in the morning sun," said Anderson.

"CUNNINGHAM SEIZED THE HALYARDS."

Cunningham was an Irishman, detested by everybody for his cruelty to American prisoners in his charge. Mrs. Day had often seen him. He stormed, and swore, and tugged in vain at the halyards, for they had become entangled; and Mrs. Day applied her broomstick so vigorously that the blustering Provost-Marshal was finally compelled to beat a retreat, leaving the American flag floating in triumph in the crisp November air over the well-defended Day castle.

This was the last battle between the British and Americans in the old war for independence.

MARABOUS AND HYENAS.

THE ugliest storks in the world are found in Southern Asia and Central Africa. Their flesh-colored heads are only partially covered with stiff, wiry feathers, and hanging on the breast they bear a disgusting pouch, which answers the purpose of a crop. One of the largest of these storks is the marabou. It stalks about the great sandy plains of Central Africa with a composure and lordly grandeur, as if it were the most beautiful bird in the world. Its body feathers are of a dull metallic green color, and its wings and tail are dingy black. Looking at the awkward creature, no one would suspect that under its ungainly wings it carried the most exquisite and fairy-like little plumes, so airy that it takes basketfuls of them to weigh an ounce. They are pure white, and so much desired for trimming that the bird is vigorously hunted by the natives, who sell these dainty feathers to traders for a very large price.

Hunting the marabou is attended with great difficulty, as the bird possesses wonderful cunning, and often contrives to outwit the most skillful hunter. With laughable dignity it measures the ground between itself and its pursuer, and takes very good care not to exhaust itself by too rapid flight. If the hunter moves slowly, the bird at once adopts an equally easy pace, but if the hunter quickens his steps, the bird is off like an arrow. It is very difficult to get within gun-range of this calculating creature, but the natives adopt a novel means of capturing it, which the bird, with all its astuteness, is unable to comprehend, and falls an easy victim. A tempting morsel of meat is tied to the end of a long stout cord, which the skillful hunter flings to a great distance, as he would a lasso, the bait falling as near the fleeing bird as he can aim it. He then conceals himself hastily behind a bush, or crouches low on the sand. The marabou, which always keeps its eye on the hunter, seeing him vanish, quietly stops and devours the bait, when it is easily secured by the hunter, who runs toward it, coiling the rope as he goes.

The marabou feeds on carrion, like the vulture. Its throat is very large, and it will greedily eat everything that comes in its way. In the swamps and plains around Khartoum, on the Nile, are immense flocks of marabous, and they are so daring as to come to the slaughter-houses on the outskirts of the city in search of food, and whole ox ears, and shin-bones with hoof attached, have been found in the crop of specimens which have been killed.

This bird is a very skillful fisher. It haunts the low marshy islands in the rivers and lakes of Central Africa, with elephants, monkeys, flamingoes, and many varieties of birds for its companions, and gains its principal food from the water. It often goes in companies of ten or twelve to fish. Wading in the water, the birds form a circle which they gradually draw together, gathering the frightened fish in the centre as with a net, when with their long bills and quick movement they speedily provide themselves with a hearty meal.

Although marabou mammas have been seen proudly parading round with a brood of diminutive downy young ones, so shy and retiring is this bird in its domestic habits that naturalists have been unable to determine when and how it builds its nest. The natives assert that it nests in high trees, but their statement is not confirmed.

In captivity the marabou is lord of the inclosure, and in zoological gardens where specimens have been confined no other birds, nor even small beasts, dare approach the feeding trough until the hunger of this impudent bird is

MARABOU FIGHTING WITH HYENAS.

The hyena is a strange-looking beast. It has a big head and a heavy shaggy mane. The hind part of its body is much lower than its shoulders, and its hind-legs are short. This odd formation gives it an awkward shambling manner of walking, which is both ludicrous and hideous.

This creature rarely shows itself by day, but when the shadows of night fall on the plains and forests, it comes out from its home among the rocks and caverns in search of food. African travellers are much annoyed by it. When the camp is silent, and all are sleeping, the hyena comes prowling round, uttering hoarse human cries; and should it fail to find sufficient camp refuse to satisfy its hunger, some poor donkey is sure to be torn in pieces by

CHATTER-BOX AND CHATTER-BAG.

BY A. P. C.

DOUBTLESS you all know what a *chatter-box* is, but are any of you acquainted with a *chatter-bag?* I do not think the word is in the dictionary, and yet the article exists. Perhaps you would like to hear how it came to be invented.

Once upon a time a young lady, whom we will call Miss Matilda, entered upon her duties as teacher in a large school. There were about fifty girls in her department, and she had to be somewhat of a disciplinarian to keep them all in order. But things, on the whole, went quietly, until one morning a pleasant-faced old lady appeared, and introduced as a new pupil her granddaughter Anna Maria Spilkins.

Anna Maria S. was eleven years of age. She was a graceful little person, with large round blue eyes, rosy cheeks, and a quantity of short, curly, golden hair. Her face was very bright; she had the appearance of being uncommonly clever. But she was eminently a *chatter-box.*

This *fact* soon made itself felt. Miss Matilda had scarcely placed her at a desk, and bowed Madam Grandma out of the school-room, when the chattering commenced. Anna Maria leaned over and whispered something to the girl on her right hand, then something to the one on the left, then a word to the one in front of her, then a word to the one behind her. Miss Matilda looked at her gently, then gently reprovingly, then reprovingly, then sternly, and all the glances were totally lost on Anna Maria. Miss Matilda benevolently thought, Perhaps this child has never been to school before.

"Anna Maria," she said, in a serious tone.

"What, ma'am?" said Anna Maria, looking up with perfect innocence in her clear blue eyes.

"Did you ever attend school before?"

"Oh dear yes! Why, I went when I was only three years old. First I went to Mrs. McToole's, and then I went to Miss Smith's, and then I went to Mr. Brown's, and then—"

"There, that will do," exclaimed Miss Matilda. "You can tell me the rest some other time. What I wish to know now is, were you allowed to talk as much as you pleased in those schools?"

"Well, I don't know as I was," replied Anna Maria, looking down, and blushing a little.

"The rule here," continued Miss Matilda, "is *silence.* I hope, my dear, that you will never speak except when it is absolutely necessary."

"Yes, ma'am," said Anna Maria, in a subdued tone, after which she closed her lips very tightly.

Miss Matilda called up the first class in geography, and proceeded to hear the lesson. In about five minutes her keen ear became conscious of a faint whispering sound. She glanced quickly in the direction of Anna Maria: evidently it was her little tongue that was wagging. But it was wagging very gently, and its waggery was addressed to one of the best girls in school. Miss Matilda thought, Perhaps she is asking some necessary questions: I will not be severe with her the first day. So she said nothing. But in five minutes more the whisper had risen to quite a buzz, and Miss Matilda detected distinctly the words, "White, with three flounces, and a new pink sash."

"Anna Maria!" she exclaimed.

"What, ma'am?"

"Did I not tell you that you were not to speak unless it was absolutely necessary?"

"Oh dear yes! I beg your pardon, teacher. I forgot all about it."

"Well, my dear, I trust you will be perfectly quiet now."

"Yes, ma'am," said Anna Maria, very meekly. She closed her lips tightly again, and was quiet—for about five minutes.

Miss Matilda thought, To-morrow, when she has her lessons to recite, it will be different.

But Miss Matilda was mistaken; to-morrow, when she had lessons to recite, it was exactly the same.

Chatter, chatter, chatter, Anna Maria kept it up day after day, from one end of the week to the other. The industrious girls were seriously annoyed by it. To the idle pupils it was a new excuse for idleness; to the silly ones, a new excuse for giggling. And punishment seemed to make no impression on Anna Maria. Again and again she was ordered to stand up in the corner. She went meekly and stood there, and in two minutes was chattering with the girl who sat nearest to her. She was told to stay in after school a quarter of an hour; half an hour; an hour; an hour and a half. She never put her head down on the desk and cried, as some of the girls did when they were kept in; she staid her time out quite cheerfully, and chattered with all her fellow-culprits. Miss Matilda thought, This child is simply distracting.

Then she made a rule that Anna Maria was not to speak to any person in the school excepting her teacher. And what was the result? At all hours of the day, in the midst of the most important business, Miss Matilda would be interrupted with talk similar to the following:

"Oh, teacher, may I speak to you one minute?"

"Certainly. What is it?"

"I just want to tell you about my cousin Susie's new doll. You ought to see it; it is perfectly splendid!—wax face and hands and feet, and real hair, and—"

"Anna Maria, have I not told you repeatedly that you were not to speak about anything except what was absolutely necessary? Now do you think that such conversation is necessary?"

Anna Maria hung her head a little, and then she said, in a sort of apologetic way, "Well, teacher, it may not seem so, but really it is necessary *for me.* You see, I get thinking about something, and I can't stop thinking about it until I have told it to somebody else."

"Well, and when you have relieved your mind in this manner, at the expense of peace and quiet to the whole school, what then?"

"Oh, then I think about something else."

"Yes, and then you wish to chatter about that."

"But really, teacher, I can't help it. I always was so. Grandma says I talk more than all the rest of the family put together. In *fact,* the family have to be quiet because I talk so much. I always did, you know. It is one of those things that can't be altered."

"Ah," said Miss Matilda, a little dryly, "I was not aware of that. Thank you for the information. I am sorry you did not tell me before."

One bright December afternoon, when school was about to be dismissed, Miss Matilda arose and said:

"Girls, I have decided that this class is to receive a Christmas present—something which will be useful and agreeable to you all. As this article (which I will not at present name) requires some very neat sewing, I have further decided that Miss Anna Maria Spilkins, whom I heard mentioned as an excellent needle-woman, shall have the honor of making it."

The girls applauded, and Anna Maria looked very proud.

"Anna Maria," continued Miss Matilda, "do you think your grandmother has a nice piece of calico at home, about a yard and a half long, which she could let us have?"

"Oh dear yes," replied Anna Maria. "Why, she has lots. Last winter she made a patchwork quilt, and she went down to New York and bought everything new for it. Aunt Jemima thought she could have used some things that were in the house, but she thought she couldn't—and you never saw the like! One yard of this, and two yards of that, and three yards of the other—enough to make half a dozen quilts—and every bit of it perfectly lovely. Oh, there is one piece that is just splendid! It is pink, with flowers of every color you can think of all over it. It is so bright you can hardly look at it."

"That would be the very thing. Do you think she will let us have it?"

"Oh, I guess so. I'll talk her into it; you depend on me for that."

"Very well. And to-morrow you will bring with you the calico, a yard and a half of alpaca braid to match, and your sewing materials."

"Yes, ma'am."

"Also, a large brass-headed nail and a hammer."

"Why, what is that for?"

"You will see when the time comes. And you will be excused from your lessons in the last hour on Thursday and Friday, so that you can do this piece of sewing in school."

"Thank you, ma'am."

Anna Maria was delighted. She felt herself a very important personage; besides, she had something new about which to chatter. Some of the other girls, however, were quite sulky over the affair. "I don't see why one of us couldn't do it," said one. "Miss Matilda is dreadfully partial," said another. "Yes, she lets Anna Maria Spilkins do anything she likes," said a third. But all were equally curious about it. "I do wonder what it can be," was heard on all sides.

The next morning Anna Maria arrived, bundle in hand. With great pride she spread out its contents. The girls were fairly dazzled with the beauty of the pink calico. In the afternoon, at the beginning of the last school hour, Miss Matilda said, "Anna Maria, have you brought the things we spoke of yesterday?"

"Yes, ma'am," said Anna Maria, stepping **up to** the desk.

Miss Matilda examined them with satisfaction. "Now, Anna Maria, take that brass-headed nail in your left hand, and the hammer in your right."

"Yes, ma'am."

"Do you notice that bar of wood along the wall, about five feet from the floor?"

"Yes, ma'am."

"Now measure carefully, and find the spot exactly over the middle of your desk; then drive the nail in."

Anna Maria obeyed. The hammering resounded strangely through the quiet school-room. When this piece of work was over, Miss Matilda folded down the pink calico, and marked out two long seams to be run and felled. Anna Maria took the sewing to her seat, and stitched away complacently, while the other girls fretted and growled over "that horrid grammar lesson." When school was over, she brought the work to Miss Matilda, who put it away carefully in her desk.

"Ah, teacher, do tell us what it is!" some of the girls exclaimed.

"I think you will see to-morrow," Miss Matilda answered, quietly.

The next afternoon Anna Maria resumed her work.

"I do believe it is going to be a bag," whispered one of the girls, who was watching her.

"Why, yes, so it is," said another. "But what can it be for?"

"Do you think Miss Matilda could mean to have a Christmas grab-bag for us?" asked a third.

"I don't know why she should," said a fourth; "I don't see that we have been so *awfully* good as all that."

But a bag undoubtedly it was. Half an hour before school was over, Anna Maria had finished the string-case, and run the piece of pink alpaca braid through it. The work was done. She walked to the desk triumphantly, and presented it to her teacher. Miss Matilda examined it, commended the sewing, and then handed it back to her.

"And now, Anna Maria," she asked, "do you know what this bag is for?"

"No, ma'am."

"Have you no idea?"

"No, ma'am."

"*It is to put your head in!* In future I shall never reprove you for talking. You may talk as much and as often as you please, but all you say must go into this bag. When it is quite full of talk, draw the string tight, so that not one word escapes, and bring it to me. Then I will empty the chatter out of the window, where it will disturb no one, and return you the bag, to be refilled whenever you choose."

A wild shout of laughter rang through the school-room. Anna Maria turned crimson, and dropped the bag. She would have been glad if the floor had opened and swallowed her. She could make no answer—for once in her life she was dumb.

"Pick up the bag, Anna Maria," said Miss Matilda, "and hang it on the nail above your desk."

Very slowly and unwillingly the little girl obeyed. She took her seat, and then, for the first time since she came to school, put her head down on her desk and cried. Miss Matilda took no notice; she merely called the second class in grammar, and resumed the lessons.

When school was over, and all the other girls had gone, Anna Maria lifted her head, and exclaimed, "Oh, teacher, teacher, I can't stand it! Do let me take that hateful bag away!"

"No, my dear," said Miss Matilda, gently. "For three months you have disturbed the entire school with your perpetual chatter, and now for three months that bag is to hang over your desk. If by the end of that time you have learned to control your tongue, the bag shall be removed—not otherwise."

But it was strange to see how the three months changed her. Miss Matilda never again needed to say one word to her about talking; one glance at the bag was more efficacious than a dozen scoldings had been formerly.

Moreover, when her grandmother met her teacher, **she** said, "Oh, Miss Matilda, how Anna Maria has improved of late! She used to be such a terrible chatter-box; we sent her to school when she was only three years old, because we could not endure the noise of her tongue, but now she is growing so pleasant and sensible that we all enjoy her company."

THE WAYWARD DONKEY.

BY W. H. BEARD.

THERE was once a little donkey who gave his poor mother no end of trouble, he was so stubborn, unreasonable, exacting, and dreadfully saucy. Why, when angry, he didn't hesitate at all to call his mother an old donkey, right out. One day, when crossed in some particularly absurd desire, he declared he would run away. Immediately putting his threat into execution, off he trotted, heedless of his poor fond mother's entreaties. Away he went, sustained at first by his temper and pride.

But as the day wore on, he became weary, faint, **and** hungry. The matter of food and shelter became a question of serious alarm, and how to obtain them was a problem too great for his little donkey brain to solve. He now remembered that he had never had to trouble himself with all this before, all the needs and comforts of life having been provided for him without thought or care on his part.

The land over which he was travelling was quite poor, and only afforded a few little stunted thistles, which seemed to consist more of prickers than anything else, which pierced his tender little nose, and made it bleed. He saw plenty of oats and other grains, as well as nice vegetables, growing in fields, but so well guarded by high fences that he could not hope to get at them. Many times, when hun-

THE LITTLE PEACE-MAKER.

"Come, now, [illegible] to behave ourselves; [illegible] and be friends."

ger and fatigue had subdued his pride, would he have returned home; but he had wandered so far that he had not the least idea which way he had come. To add to his distress, he saw the sun was fast declining. Already he felt the chills of evening. But there was no use bemoaning his fate, and he must make the best of it.

At length, too weary to travel farther, he was forced to lie down to rest, and selected for the purpose an unfenced overgrown piece of ground of considerable extent. Here, as he lay among the weeds, nothing was visible of him above their tops but his two ears, which might easily have been taken for two stakes, or the roots of an upturned stump. As he lay shivering in the damp grass, he felt anything but comfortable. The sun went down, the moon arose and shed a cold light over the face of nature, which made him feel lonely indeed.

Suddenly there appeared above the grass several other pairs of ears, bobbing about, quite like his own. The sight thrilled him with something akin to pleasure, for he asked himself, "To whom can such ears belong but to little donkeys? and if young donkeys are around, they must have mothers, or a mother, near by, who, no doubt, would be very glad to adopt such a fine specimen of the race as I." The reader has already seen that he was a conceited little donkey.

So saying, he arose quickly to his feet; the others stood up also, though not as he did on their four feet, but on their hind-legs—that is to say, they stood up on their haunches—and looked at him in blank amazement; but as he approached them they bounded away so fast that it was useless to try to overtake them. When he stood still, they also stopped, and again stood upon their haunches, and peered at him over the tops of the weeds. Master Donkey did not try again to go to them, but expostulated with them upon their ill-breeding and unkind behavior, called them cousins, told them he was tired and hungry, and asked for food and shelter. This touched their tender little hearts, and they cautiously drew near, and made the acquaintance of their supposed cousin.

On a close scrutiny, however, they doubted his claim to relationship, and flatly told him so. But they good-naturedly said if he was hungry, it was no more than common humanity to first relieve his wants, and discuss the question afterward. Even murderous man would do as much as that, so they brought him carrots and other vegetables in abundance from a farm garden near by, from which they were accustomed to supply their own wants.

When his appetite was satisfied, his humility, such as it was, oozed out, and he became as arrogant as ever, and stoutly claimed that he was their big cousin, though, he said, he was not particularly anxious to be acknowledged by such a pack of little dwarfish thieving creatures as they were, who would steal through the farmer's fence to purloin vegetables for a cousin whom they impudently refused to recognize.

Their spokesman retorted, and said they claimed a right to a share, sufficient for their needs, of whatever grew upon the earth. To be sure, they were obliged to obtain it stealthily at night, as man claimed it all for himself, and it would be almost certain death to be found by him within his inclosure. Indeed, many of their unfortunate fellows had already suffered death for the exercise of this natural right. If, however, he regarded their act as a crime, he was himself a criminal, inasmuch as he had accepted the fruits, and profited by the act, knowing how the food had been obtained. To this the donkey could make no answer; at least he did not think it prudent to try, as night was still before him, and the question of shelter still unsolved.

Good-nature was soon restored, and the discussion renewed. The rabbits could see many points of difference, but two only of resemblance. It certainly could not be denied that the ears were remarkably like, and the complexion was very nearly the same; but the hard feet were so widely different from their own soft paws! And the tail, too, long and dangling like a cow's—what a tail for a rabbit! Then, again, they had observed that he *stood* while eating, whereas a true rabbit always crouched comfortably near the ground while taking his food. In the matter of voice, too, they flattered themselves there was a *wide* difference. However, all this might be changed or improved by judicious training, except the feet. The hoofs they despaired of. The tail they proposed to nibble off at a proper length from the body. This operation the donkey positively refused to submit to, but finally consented to hold his tail up over his back as much like a rabbit as possible, and, moreover, would at once set about his lessons to learn their ways, so that he might the sooner adapt himself to their habits, and become one of them.

Accordingly, one of the cleverest of their number was charged with his instruction, and immediately began with the important art of sitting on the haunches with his tail curled up upon his back. In this, though he strained every nerve to perform it, he made an ignominious failure. He could only maintain the position for a moment, and then pitch forward or fall backward, seeming to rock over on his curved tail, and cutting such a ridiculous figure that it made all the rabbits laugh. This made him very angry, and he began to use his heels in a most vigorous and unrabbitlike manner. All ran for their lives, but not all escaped unhurt. The "spraggly" forms of two or three of those nearest to him showed dark against the moon-lit sky before they limped off, and, joining their fellows, gathered in a little knot at a distance from their fractious pupil, and discussed his merits with great freedom. They voted him an ill-natured brute, a stupid dolt—in short, a perfect donkey. Scarcely had they arrived at this unanimous conclusion, when—pop! pop! bang! bang!—four loud reports, and four little rabbits lay in the agonies of death.

The farmer and his son, seeing by the moonlight strange movements in the field, had stolen upon them, in the unguarded moment of their excitement, with their double-barrelled guns, and, as the boy expressed it, bagged four rabbits and a donkey; for poor little donkey stood paralyzed with fear. He had never looked upon death before, and was an easy captive. Without troubling himself to inquire who the rightful owner was, the farmer took him for his own, housed him that night in a stall by himself, where he passed almost the entire night, notwithstanding the fatigues of the day, in such reflections as he was capable of; and though he grew up to be a great donkey, to be sure, the lessons of that day were never forgotten by him.

[illegible]

Unfortunately your drawings of Wiggle No. 10 came too late to be engraved. [illegible] were all excellent. In YOUNG PEOPLE No. 27 we gave you a new Wiggle, which you can practice upon, and send us what you make of it. The plan of your club is good, as it will afford you much amusement, and at the same time give you good exercise in drawing.

[illegible]

The gopher, or Canada pouched rat, is a very remarkable burrower, as it will dig underground passages, extending in lateral galleries in all directions. It is difficult to capture, as it keeps open a means of escape on every side. The mischief done by this creature is very extensive. It delights to burrow among the roots of fruit trees, which it gnaws, until often a large tree dies from the underground attacks of this troublesome animal.

E. A. C.—It is impossible for us to comply with your request.

W. H. H.—Flowers are beautiful pets, and repay well the attention bestowed upon them. The large plant, with its wide-spreading, bluish-green leaves, which bears the castor-bean, is raised from the seed, like any other bean. It is an annual, but it grows so rapidly that by midsummer it is already several feet high. In warm countries this plant is called palma-Christi, and is much valued as a garden ornament, as its pale green leaves form a beautiful contrast when growing among masses of dark shrubbery.

Annie P.—Your beautiful wild flower was so faded and crushed when it reached us that it was impossible to identify it.

G. H. Fisher and "Needham."—In an article soon to be published in YOUNG PEOPLE you will find all your questions fully answered.

"[illegible]," [illegible].—For directions for preserving insects, see answer to Kate R. F., Post-office Box, No. 27.

Mamie S.—Ocean Grove, Squan, or Seagirt, New Jersey; Vineyard Grove, Dukes County, Massachusetts; and many places along the New England coast.

[illegible] A. H.—Turtles should have a big tub of earth in which to bury themselves in the [illegible] winter. Or if they are left loose in a yard, they will take care of themselves, and appear again in the spring. Read the answer to Lyman C. in Post-office Box, No. [illegible], where you will find full directions for the care of turtles.

CHARLIE W. M.—Your charade is gracefully made, but too personal to be printed in YOUNG PEOPLE. Thanks for your pretty compliments.

Favors are acknowledged from Frank [illegible], [illegible] [illegible], "[illegible]," Katherine [illegible], [illegible] [illegible], Fanny [illegible], Lucy [illegible], Paul R. H., [illegible] [illegible], [illegible] [illegible], "[illegible]," [illegible] [illegible], [illegible] [illegible], [illegible] [illegible], [illegible] [illegible], Frank [illegible], [illegible] [illegible], [illegible] [illegible], J. H. [illegible], C. K. [illegible], [illegible] [illegible], [illegible] [illegible], [illegible] [illegible], Harry [illegible], Agnes S. [illegible], [illegible] Russell, Aubrey [illegible], [illegible] [illegible].

Correct answers to puzzles received from [illegible] [illegible], Edward Taylor, [illegible] [illegible], Lillie [illegible], J. F. [illegible], Robert R. [illegible], John Whelan, [illegible] and [illegible], [illegible], Mary [illegible], George H. [illegible], [illegible] [illegible], Clarence Howard, [illegible] [illegible], [illegible] [illegible], Willie C. [illegible], [illegible] and [illegible] [illegible], [illegible] and [illegible] Watson, Charley H. [illegible], Paul J. H., [illegible], [illegible] [illegible], [illegible] "[illegible]," William G. [illegible].

PUZZLES FROM YOUNG CONTRIBUTORS.

No. 1.

[illegible]

In [illegible]. In [illegible]. To [illegible]. A [illegible] shrub. To [illegible].

M. W.

No. 2.

GEOGRAPHICAL DOUBLE ACROSTIC.

A French city. A town near the mouth of the [illegible] River. An Italian city. A town in [illegible]. A city in Spain. A Mexican province. Answer—Two countries in Europe.

C. F. T.

No. 3.

[illegible]

I am composed of 11 letters.
My 3, 10, [illegible] is a boy's name.
My [illegible] is an animal.
My [illegible] is to [illegible].
My whole is beautiful and sweet.

JENNIE.

No. 4.

[illegible]

A familiar proverb:
[illegible]

[illegible]

No. 5.

[illegible]

My first is in [illegible], but not in [illegible].
My second is in [illegible], but not in [illegible].
My third is in [illegible], but not in [illegible].
My fourth is in [illegible], but not in [illegible].
My fifth is in [illegible], but not in [illegible].
My sixth is in [illegible], but not in [illegible].
My seventh is in [illegible], but not in [illegible].
My eighth is in [illegible], but not in [illegible].
My ninth is in [illegible], but not in [illegible].
My whole [illegible].

J. A. W.

No. 6.

[illegible]

I am a little word of [illegible] letters, yet you will find in me a [illegible], a [illegible], and [illegible]. I am as old as the [illegible], and [illegible] [illegible]. [illegible] [illegible]. What can [illegible]?

C. W. H.

ANSWERS TO PUZZLES IN No. [illegible].

Charade on page 344—[illegible].

ADVERTISEMENTS.

HARPER'S YOUNG PEOPLE.

HARPER'S YOUNG PEOPLE will be issued every Tuesday, and may be had at the following rates—payable in advance, postage free:

SINGLE COPIES	$0 04
ONE SUBSCRIPTION, one year	1 50
FIVE SUBSCRIPTIONS, one year	7 00

Subscriptions may begin with any Number. When no time is specified, it will be understood that the subscriber wishes to commence with the Number issued after the receipt of order.

Remittances should be made by POST-OFFICE MONEY ORDER or DRAFT, to avoid risk of loss.

ADVERTISING.

The extent and character of the circulation of HARPER'S YOUNG PEOPLE will render it a first-class medium for advertising. A limited number of approved advertisements will be inserted on two inside pages at 75 cents per line.

Address

HARPER & BROTHERS,
Franklin Square, N. Y.

[illegible]

[illegible]

[illegible], 126 and 128 Nassau St., N. Y.

OUR CHILDREN'S SONGS.

Our Children's Songs. Illustrated. 8vo, Ornamental Cover, $1 00.

The best compilation of songs for the children that we have ever seen.—New Bedford Mercury.

This is a large collection of songs for the nursery, for childhood, for boys and for girls, and sacred songs for all. The range of subjects is a wide one, and the book is handsomely illustrated.—Philadelphia Ledger.

Published by HARPER & BROTHERS, New York.

☞ HARPER & BROTHERS will send the above work by mail, postage prepaid, to any part of the United States, on receipt of the price.

FISHING OUTFITS.

[illegible]

B. SIMPSON, [illegible] Nassau Street, N. Y.

The Child's Book of Nature.

The Child's Book of Nature, for the Use of Families and Schools: intended to aid Mothers and Teachers in Training Children in the Observation of Nature. In Three Parts. Part I. Plants. Part II. Animals. Part III. Air, Water, Heat, Light, &c. By WORTHINGTON HOOKER, M.D. Illustrated. The Three Parts complete in One Volume, Small 4to, Half Leather, $1 31; or, separately, in Cloth, Part I., [illegible] cents; Part II., [illegible] cents; Part III., [illegible] cents.

A beautiful and useful work. It presents a general survey of the kingdoms of nature in a manner adapted to attract the attention of the child, and at the same time to furnish him with accurate and important scientific information. While the work is well fitted as a class-book for schools, its [illegible] and simple style [illegible] it a great favorite [illegible].

The Three Parts of this book can be had in separate volumes by those who desire it. This will be [illegible] where the book is to be used in teaching quite young children, especially in schools.

Published by HARPER & BROTHERS, New York.

☞ Sent by mail, postage prepaid, to any part of the United States, on receipt of the price.

Old Books for Young Readers.

Arabian Nights' Entertainments.

The Thousand and One Nights; or, The Arabian Nights' Entertainments. Translated and Arranged for Family Reading, with Explanatory Notes, by E. W. LANE. 600 Illustrations by Harvey. 2 vols., 12mo, Cloth, $3 50.

Robinson Crusoe.

The Life and Surprising Adventures of Robinson Crusoe, of York, Mariner. By DANIEL DEFOE. With a Biographical Account of Defoe. Illustrated by Adams. Complete Edition. 12mo, Cloth, $1 50.

The Swiss Family Robinson.

The Swiss Family Robinson; or, Adventures of a Father and Mother and Four Sons on a Desert Island. Illustrated. 2 vols., 18mo, Cloth, $1 50.

The Swiss Family Robinson—Continued: being a Sequel to the Foregoing. 2 vols., 18mo, Cloth, $1 50.

Sandford and Merton.

The History of Sandford and Merton. By THOMAS DAY. 18mo, Half Bound, 75 cents.

Published by HARPER & BROTHERS, New York.

☞ Sent by mail, postage prepaid, to any part of the United States, on receipt of the price.

CHILDREN'S PICTURE-BOOKS.

Square 4to, about 300 pages each, beautifully printed on Tinted Paper, embellished with many Illustrations, bound in Cloth, $1 50 per volume.

The Children's Picture-Book of Sagacity of Animals.

With Sixty Illustrations by HARRISON WEIR.

The Children's Bible Picture-Book.

With Eighty Illustrations, from Designs by STEINLE, OVERBECK, VEIT, SCHNORR, &c.

The Children's Picture Fable-Book.

Containing One Hundred and Sixty Fables. With Sixty Illustrations by HARRISON WEIR.

The Children's Picture-Book of Birds.

With Sixty-one Illustrations by W. HARVEY.

The Children's Picture-Book of Quadrupeds and other Mammalia.

With Sixty-one Illustrations by W. HARVEY.

Published by HARPER & BROTHERS, New York.

☞ Sent by mail, postage prepaid, to any part of the United States, on receipt of the price.

PLAIN-SPEAKING.

BY MARGARET EYTINGE.

A Mullingong met an Echidna one day,
  And he cried, "What a very odd nose!
So exceedingly *sharp*. Why, it's funnier far
  Than your porcupine coat and your toes."
Then most rudely he made all the echoes resound
  With "he-hees!" and "haw-haws!" and "ho-hoes!"

The Echidna made answer, "My merry young friend,
  If your own comic nose you could see,
Like a juvenile shovel exceedingly *flat*,
  I am sure you'd stop laughing at me;
For *perfectly lovely*, beside it, is mine.
  Ho! ho! and haw! haw! and he! he!"

A PERSONATION: WHO AM I?

THERE have been few people more written about, and yet there is very little known of me. I wish I had known, during my life, that I was to become so famous, for I might have taken pains to leave accurate accounts of myself. I wrote a great deal, yet there is much discussion even over my signature. I was born and brought up in the country, as you can easily judge from the many allusions to country pleasures and sights in my works. My parents were poor, and I had to depend on myself; and when still young decided to go to London—many say because I could not live happily with my wife, whom I had married when but eighteen. I sought and found employment in London in the theatres. I was anxious to return home (which I had left a poor lad) a rich man; so I worked early and late, and about twelve years after leaving home was able to buy one of the best houses in my native place. It has always been supposed I did not like my wife very much, because in my will I left her only my "second-best bed"; but then people forget that she also had her dower. I wrote over thirty-seven books, though some of the writings attributed to me are not mine, and scholars will dispute about me probably to the end of time.

Except that I was born, married, went to London, wrote, returned home, made a will, and died, there is nothing certainly known about me: everything else is conjecture, for, alas! I had no Boswell. My books have been translated into all civilized tongues, my sayings are as familiar in men's mouths "as household words," and though about me the world may know little, no one can be considered well educated who is not conversant with my books.

I forgot to tell you I was born on the 23d of April, 1564, and died on the 23d of April, 1616—not an old man, you see, to have gained such fame; yet every year many pilgrims visit my birthplace and my grave, the epitaph on which has alone enabled me to lie quietly in the country church-yard, for many would like to see me in Westminster Abbey, where there is a fine monument to me.

THE ABSURD PENGUIN PUZZLE.

THIS Puzzle appeared in No. 25, page 344. It was, with two straight cuts of the scissors, to change the fish, Fig. I, into an absurd penguin catching a herring, as is shown in Fig. II.

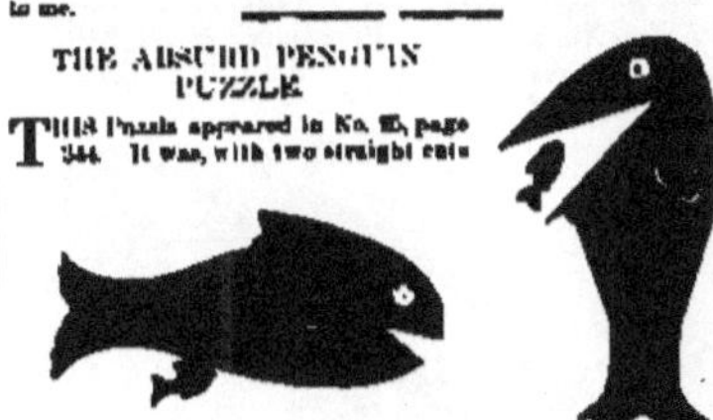

Fig. I. Fig. II.

A Spider's Instinct.—Spiders crawling more abundantly and conspicuously than usual upon the in-door walls of houses foretell the near approach of rain; but the following anecdote shows that some of their habits are the equally certain indication of frost being at hand. Quartermaster Disjonval, seeking to beguile the tedium of his eight years of prison life at Utrecht, had studied attentively the habits of the spider. In December of 1794 the French army, on whose success his restoration to liberty depended, was in Holland, and victory seemed certain if the frost, then of unprecedented severity, continued. The Dutch Envoy had failed to negotiate a peace, and Holland was despairing, when the frost suddenly broke. The Dutch were now exulting, and the French Generals prepared to retreat; but the spider warned Disjonval that the thaw would be of short duration. He contrived to communicate with the army of his countrymen, and its Generals relied upon his assurance that within a few days the water would again be passable by troops. They delayed their retreat. Within twelve days the frost had returned, and the French army triumphed.

"WHEN I WAS YOUNG AND CHARMING, I PRACTICED BABY-FARMING."

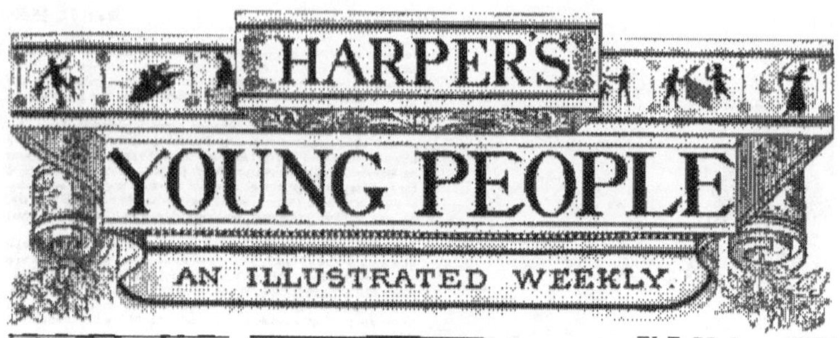

Vol. I.—No. 29. | Published by HARPER & BROTHERS, New York. | Price Four Cents.

Tuesday, May 18, 1880. | Copyright, 1880, by Harper & Brothers. | $1.50 per Year, in Advance.

[Begun in No. 19 of Harper's Young People, March 9.]

ACROSS THE OCEAN; OR, A BOY'S FIRST VOYAGE.

A True Story.

BY J. O. DAVIDSON.

CHAPTER XI.

AMONG THE "COOLIES."

THEY found the city one blaze of lanterns, banners, and many-colored fire-works. All the ships in the harbor were gay with brilliant bunting, and the air echoed with the boom of cannon and the snapping of fire-crackers, in honor of the Chinese New-Year. In fact, it was quite a Fourth-of-July celebration; and at night there began such a burst of sky-rockets and fire-balloons that the whole town seemed to be in flames.

Early next morning the *Arizona* opened her ports to receive cargo; and Frank, being told off to assist, saw for the first time one of the most picturesque sights in the world—a gang of coolies at work. On the other side of the "entering port," beside which he was posted, stood a Parsee merchant, whose long white robe, dark face, and high black cap made him look very much like a cigar wrapped in paper. Along the quivering line of sunlight that streamed through the port came filing, like figures in a magic lantern, an endless procession of tall, sinewy, fierce-looking Malays, and yellow, narrow-eyed, doll-faced Chinamen, carrying blocks of tin, rice sacks, opium chests, or pepper bags, and all moving in time to a dismal tune, suggestive of a dog shut out on a cold night.

Each man shouted his name in passing, and the merchant then handed Frank a short piece of cane. These canes were the "tally sticks," their different colors indicating the nature of the articles counted. At every tenth entry the Parsee cried, "Tally," and Austin, reckoning the sticks in his hand, and finding them correct, answered, "Tally."

Our hero soon found that these were not the *only* sticks employed. A rice sack burst suddenly, and all the coolies stopped their work to pick it up to the last grain, it being thought far too sacred to be wasted. They were not quite brisk enough about it, however, to please the worthy merchant, who, seizing a stout bamboo, with a shrill yell of "Bree! bree!" (hurry up) laid about him as if he were beating a carpet, till the hold echoed again.

"You take 'tick too; give 'em whack-whack," cried he, offering Austin another bamboo. "Dey no work proper widout 'tick; dat 'courage 'em."

"Hum!" thought Frank; "I don't think it would encourage me much."

The remedy seemed to answer, however, for the coolies at once quickened their movements, grinning as if the whole thing was a capital joke. But it was not long before Frank had to exercise *his* stick upon a fellow whom he caught in the act of dropping a package overboard, to be fished up and rifled later on—a common trick with the natives, who are most expert thieves. What with all this, and what with the constant counting, he found it very tiring work, and was not sorry when the gang "knocked off," and he went to hand in his accounts to the Captain.

"Very good, my boy; you've done capitally for a first trial. After this I'll rate you as supercargo, and give you a state-room on the officers' deck."

This was promotion indeed, and our hero, tired as he was, "turned in" with a light heart.

Next morning the work began again. Bags, boxes, chests, crowded so fast upon each other that Frank and the Parsee were soon forced to shift to one of the six huge barges that lay alongside, piled high with spices, pepper, and bundles of rattan. Two native servants stood by to fan them, while two others shielded them from the burning sun with huge umbrellas; and this group, together with the long file of black or yellow skinned figures below, pouring into the ship with their burdens like a stream of ants, and still chanting their strange, monotonous song, made a very curious picture.

About two o'clock (the sailors' dinner hour) the gang had a short rest, which the Malays employed in squatting about in groups, and chewing betel-nut. A piece of the nut was folded between two green leaves, and munched vigorously, the result being to cover their mouths with a red froth, which, as Frank thought, made them all look as if they had just had two or three teeth out.

After night-fall the work went on by lamp-light, and a very picturesque sight it was. Tired as they were, the men worked with a will, and by midnight the last package was stowed, the last receipt signed, and the *Arizona* all ready to sail the next day.

After his hard day's work, Frank slept like a top; but he was aroused soon after sunrise by a knock at his door, and in came a venerable old native in a long white robe, crimson girdle, and hat exactly like a stove-pipe, minus the rim. Shutting the door as carefully as if he were about to confess a murder, he opened a small silk bag, and flashed upon Frank's astonished eyes a perfect heap of precious stones of all sorts and sizes; then holding up the fingers of both hands several times in succession, he uttered the one word "Rupees."*

But the price, though low, was far beyond Austin's means. He shook his head, and the old gentleman bowed himself out as politely as if Frank had purchased his entire stock. Five minutes later came a second tap, and another native entered, with a basket of delicious fruits, answering our hero's "How much?" by pointing to a pair of worn-out shoes, and saying, "Can do." Before Austin could recover from his amazement at the idea of a country where men preferred old shoes to hard dollars, the fruit merchant had made his "salam" (bow), and departed with his prize.

He was hardly gone, when a third trader turned up, with a splendid collection of shells and coral, and the same scene was repeated. This time the "Can do" referred to some ragged old flannel shirts and pants that hung on the wall, in exchange for which the dealer handed over the entire contents of his basket. Frank, more puzzled than ever, went to old Herrick for an explanation.

"Well, lad," said the veteran, "these *natyve* fellers, d'ye see, are divided into so many 'castes,' one above t'other, like men and officers aboard ship, and the lower castes have got to pay toll to the higher 'uns. Now the high-caste crowd are too great swells to touch a furriner's clothes or shoes, though they'll touch his money fast enough; so them two chaps 'll be able to keep all you gave 'em, whereas if you'd paid 'em in dollars, they'd ha' had to go halves with the 'upper crust.'"

[TO BE CONTINUED.]

* The rupee is the standard coin of British India, and worth about fifty cents.

EASY BOTANY.

MAY.

MAY brings so many wild flowers that the mere names would easily fill all the space I can have.

But the young flower-hunter must get an idea of some of the flowers sure to appear in May, and those who will notice the habits of plants will soon discover where these fair friends dwell, and will learn which selects the valley, which the hill-side, finding that as a general thing they may be looked for with the certainty of being found in their favorite haunts.

Botanical authorities have arranged all known plants

arly, of most c
n damp, rich
up the shady

CONSTANCY.

BY E. B.

LITTLE Ruth looked at her dolly one day,
Said: "Dolly, they wish me to give you away;
They say you are old, and I know it's quite true;
But, dolly, dear dolly, I can't part from you.

"Your color has faded, your nose is quite gone,
Yet I love you as well as the day you were born;
You've great cracks on your face, and scarcely a hair,
Yet, dolly, my dear, to me you are fair.

"Though you're hurt, darling dolly, too often, I fear,
But you are so brave that you won't shed a tear;
And although you've one arm, one leg, and no nose,
You're dearer to me because of your woes.

"But what was the hardest and cruelest sting
Was that father once called you a horrid old thing:
He said, 'What a battered and wretched old fright!
Do take her away, pray, out of my sight.'

"And, dolly, he said that a new doll he'd buy;
To find me a nice one he really would try;
She should have two legs, and more than one arm:
I am sure that papa did not mean any harm.

"Pray what would they all say if I asked mamma
To go out and buy me a nice new papa,
Because father dear is old, bald, and gray?
I should like very much to hear what *he'd* say."

[Begun in Harper's Young People No. 24, April 13.]

THE STORY OF GEORGE WASHINGTON.

BY EDWARD CARY.

CHAPTER VI.

THE private life of Washington was very simple. He was very fond of farming, and studied it carefully, as he seems to have studied everything that he took in hand. Some of his letters to Arthur Young, a great English traveller, who was also a writer on farming, are very interesting. In reading them it is easy to forget the General and the public man, and to think only of the painstaking planter, eager to know what was the best way to plant his various crops, or to plough his different fields. He liked shade trees greatly, and had a great many kinds of them at Mount Vernon, set out under his own direction, and some of them with his own hand. Some of my readers may yet see them on the pleasant sloping banks of the Potomac, below the city of Washington. Even among the cares of the camp and the battle-field Washington found time nearly every week to write minute directions to his superintendent, who had charge of his farm, telling him just what work to do each day, and how to do it. When he got back to his home, he took up the task of seeing to things himself with the greatest enjoyment. Every morning after breakfast he mounted his horse and rode about his ample fields, and he seldom let anything prevent his doing so—neither bad weather, nor the claims of visitors, of whom he had a host, nor anything else. He laid out his time on an exact system. Each morning he arose before sunrise to write letters and to read, and on his return from his ride over his estate he again went to his study, and staid there attending to business until three o'clock in the afternoon. At three he dined, and gave the rest of the day and evening to his family and his guests. At ten he went to bed.

But he was not to enjoy this happy, peaceful life very long. His countrymen needed him as much in peace as in war, and soon called him again to public life. After the American States had cut loose from Great Britain, they found that their common affairs did not get on very well. They had borrowed a good deal of money to carry on the war, and the only way to pay it was by each State giving its part. But the people of the various States were jealous of each other, and quarrelled over the amount they ought to pay. There was danger that the States would divide from each other, and then be much less able to defend themselves against foreign governments. Washington dreaded such a thing. He believed that the only means by which the States could keep the freedom they had won was by uniting closely. He wished to see a national government formed, with power to raise money by equal taxes, to pay the common debts, and to make war if

WASHINGTON AT THE AGE OF FIFTY.
FROM A PORTRAIT BY COLONEL TRUMBULL.

need be. He wrote on this subject to many of his friends, who agreed with him.

After a while, by general consent, each State chose some of its ablest men to come together at Philadelphia and make a plan for a national government which should take charge of all public affairs not belonging to any one State by itself. This was done, and a plan was formed in the year 1787, and adopted by the people of all the States. This was called the Constitution of the United States. It set up a government of three parts. First, there was Congress, made up of men chosen, in one way or another, by the people. Congress was to make the laws. Second, there was the President, chosen by the people, who was to see that the laws were carried out and obeyed. The President was to be aided by a large number of officers of various kinds, whom he was to choose, with the consent of a part of Congress called the Senate. Finally, there were the Judges, who were to decide any disputes that might come up about the meaning of the laws. The Judges were also chosen by the President, with the help and consent of the Senate.

Of course the one man in the government who had more to do with it than any other was the President. As soon as it was seen that the new Constitution would be taken by the people, every one turned to General Washington as sure to make the best President. He had shown himself so wise and true in war, how could he be otherwise in peace? People knew that he would try to do his whole duty, and serve the country at any cost to himself. It was the same feeling the boys in school had had forty years before, when they chose him to be their captain, and left all their quarrels to him to settle. So Washington was elected President, and though he disliked to leave his tranquil home, his fields, and his trees and his horses, he felt that it was his duty to do so, and promptly accepted the office.

[TO BE CONTINUED.]

HOW JOHN GOODNOW GOT HIS OWN WAY.

BY MRS. Z. B. GUSTAFSON.

HE was all by himself in as pretty a patch of sunny green meadow-land as you could wish to see, yet he had plenty of company. To say nothing of the birds chattering on the fence, the tall thick grass was as full of hopping, fluttering, and creeping things as a wheat beard is of grain. These tiny little creatures seemed to find life so pleasant and comfortable, and the glisten and "swish" of John Goodnow's scythe so very odd and amusing, that they kept only a little out of his way as he mowed, and when he stopped to whet his scythe they flocked around and settled on his boot-legs, on the brim of his hat, and even in the creases of his shirt sleeves, to see how he did it.

John Goodnow was just sixteen. He was a manly boy, strong, straight, and good-looking. He had plenty of spirit and energy, and liked what he was doing well enough; but he had some ideas in his head which made him think he could do something else much—very much—better.

John's father did not happen to think about John as John thought about himself. This very often happens between parents and their children. Your parents are older and wiser than you, but then you boys and girls often think a great deal more, and with more good sense, than you get credit *for*. When your parents do not think as you do about what you are to be and do in life, it is hard to tell which is wisest, and there is no sure rule to help you out; but I will tell you one little thing that I think it will be good for you to remember; it is very much in your own power to decide for yourself, *to get your own way by giving it up*, as John did.

"I wish *father* could see this as I do," John thought.

He had put the whetstone in his pocket, and was once more leaning to the scythe.

"Of course I can be a farmer, and of course *farmers* are as necessary as Presidents; and a *farmer* can be a President, and eat potatoes and corn in the White House, instead of hoeing and hilling them in the field. But I want to be a lawyer, and that settles it *for me*. I just wish it would do as much for father. He *did* look queer when I told him I didn't believe a lawyer that was always hankerin' after a farm would amount to much in lawyerin'. Mother said, 'Do let the boy have his way; it's his life he's got to live, you know, not yours.'

"She's so sensible, and just the best mother in the world. I made up my mind, when she said that, that if I did get my way, I'd just like to be the one to fix Uncle Si. Stingy old fellow! I'd make him pay mother what he owes her. Guess he knows it, an' that's why he looks at me so sour, and tells father to 'keep him at the plough; he'll never come to nuthin' mooonin' over them lyin' lawyer books.'"

NOON-TIME IN THE MEADOW.

John smiled, with a bright, mischievous look, as if he had already won the case against his uncle.

Then he whistled till he came to the end of the swath. He liked the sweet, fresh smell that rose from the cut grass.

"I know farming is good, useful work," he thought, "and pleasant, when any one likes it; but I want to do what I can do best, and I'm sure it's law. When things happen, I want to know how they happen, and who was wrong, and how to fix things so that they'll happen right. It just makes me tingle all over when I can get hold of a case, and read up all about it, and I can talk it over with mother. She's smarter'n a steel-trap, and might have been a lawyer herself. But I can't show off to father at all. He shuts right down on me so—almost makes me think I don't know anything, after all. He's a real good father, though, and I hate to disappoint him."

John set his lips, and his young face looked troubled. He cut the swath very neatly to the edge of the brook as he went along.

"I told him I'd say no more about it now," John went on thinking, as he looked at the pretty rippling stream, which kept up such a merry little song over its round pebbles, "and I promised him I'd stick to the farm for this year, and do my best to like it, and so I will. Mother said, 'It isn't because he doesn't like you to be a lawyer; it's because he thinks you aren't old enough to judge, and he thinks good farming is the best and noblest work in the world, and that you can't help liking it if you try. But he won't stand in your way a moment, my boy, when he sees that you know your own mind. You just yield to him first, and he'll yield to you last.'"

It was nearing noon, and the sun was hot. John lifted his hat just enough to wipe his forehead; then resting the scythe upon the bank, he leaned against its curving handle. He looked well as he stood there, like a boy who would one day be a man of purpose, and will to carry out his purpose. He was tired, just tired enough to make rest sweet. He looked across the little hollow at the foot of the meadow toward his home. He was very hungry, and glad to see a little girl coming down the path through the hollow with a pail in her hand. "Thank goodness! there's Kitty coming with the lunch. I'm hungry enough to eat a crow, feathers and all. I know just what's in that pail—ham sandwich, a big slice of brown-bread, bottle of milk or sweetened water, and some of mother's apple-pie, with a slice of cheese. Hurry up!" he shouted aloud, in a strong, pleasant voice—"hurry up, Kitty dear; I'm as hungry as a cat."

When the end of the year came, Mr. Goodnow did not wait for John to speak. On New-Year's Eve, just before bed-time, he laid down his paper, crossed the room, put his hand on John's shoulder, and, as if only an hour instead of seven months had passed since he had last spoken of what he wished John to be, he said, "Well, my boy, speak out: will ye be farmer or lawyer?"

John rose quickly, and looked at his father. "I will be a lawyer, if I can," said he. "But, father, I do wish you could like it;" and his voice trembled a little.

"I do like it—I like it very much," said Mr. Goodnow, quickly; "for if ye can do so well as ye have done at a work ye don't take to, I'm sure ye'll prove a master-hand at what yer heart's so set on. Ye've helped me in my way, and I'll help ye in yourn. Ye shall have the best schoolin' in law that money can buy, and ye've shown ye'll do the rest yourself. Happy New-Year, my boy!" Mr. Goodnow held out his hand, and John took it with a grip that made his father wince and smile at the same time.

Then John went to his mother, who, of course, knew all about it, and was as happy, yes, happier, than her boy over the happiness which he had earned so well. When he went to his own room, he was so busy thinking, that it was some time before he looked up; but when he did he started, and shouted "Jerusalem!" as if the word had been a bullet and he the gun. On the wall over the table were three pictures which had not been there before. One was of Charles Sumner, one of Rufus Choate, and one of Abraham Lincoln. On the table beneath was this note in his mother's hand:

"I want you, my own good boy, to learn what you attempt to know as thoroughly, and do what you believe to be right as fearlessly, as Charles Sumner did. Rufus Choate had the great power to so move men's minds that they were like something melted which he could shape as he chose. If you can be as brave, tender, and good as Abraham Lincoln was, I shall wish with all my heart that you may have power like Rufus Choate's and opportunity like Charles Sumner's. You mustn't fret about father. He's as pleased and satisfied as we are. You won him just as I told you you would, by yielding. It is more than a month since he brought home the books you will find on your table. They are for your first term in the law-school. Now good-night, and a happy New-Year from your loving

"MOTHER."

Under the books on the table lay a flat package which his mother did not know about, as Mr. Goodnow had slyly placed it there the last thing before John went up to bed. John untied it, and found a fine picture of Horace Greeley, and this note from his father:

"You needn't be afraid of putting Horace Greeley along of them chaps your mother has given you. He can stand it if they can; and they'll make a good beginning of your picture-gallery. I've heard tell of lawyers getting to be editors, too, afore now. If you should ever run a paper, what you know about farming won't hurt it none."

Many years have passed away since John talked with himself as he mowed the home meadow on that pleasant summer morning. If I should tell you the real name of John Goodnow, you would know at once how well his good mother's wish had been granted in the noble career of her well-known son. And there isn't a father in the land prouder of his son than Farmer Goodnow of his son, Judge ——.

CAMPING OUT.

BY WILLIAM O. STODDARD.

"WHAT am I a-stoppin' for? Why, this 'ere's the eend of the road. It's as fur as I can git, even with one hoss and a buckboard."

It looked like it, for the word road had been getting dreadfully scrubby for a mile or so.

"Wade, was it like this when you and your father and the rest were here before?"

"A good deal like it. How far are we from Pot Lake now, Mr. Jones?"

The queer-looking old teamster was busily unfastening several small packages from the broad "buckboard" of his rude wagon, but he looked gruffly up to say, "'Bout a mile 'n' a half."

"It's all of that, Sid, but it's of no use to grumble. We've got to foot it the rest of the way. It's a plain enough path."

"Foot it! And lug all that?"

"Guess you'll be glad there ain't any more of it afore ye git thar."

Mr. Jones was right, for they were both of them glad already, considering how warm a day it was.

Neither of the boys was much over sixteen, but Wade Norton looked the older of the two, although his companion was fully as tall and strong. Standing together, they made a good "specimen pair" of vigorous, bright-eyed, self-reliant youngsters.

In three minutes more Mr. Jones and his pony and his buckboard were out of sight among the trees, and Sid and Wade were left to their own resources.

It was seven miles due south, and a good deal longer by the road, to the nearest clearing, and all to the north of them was wilderness—woods, lakes, and mountains.

"Now, Wade, how'll we divide the load? There's a heap of it."

"Guess we won't divide it. I'll show you—here's the hatchet."

"Go ahead. I'm a greenhorn yet. What are you going to do?"

Wade was too busy to answer, but he quickly had a pair of very slender ash saplings hacked down, trimmed clean, and laid side by side about two feet apart. To these he tied a couple of cross-sticks, six feet from each other. Then he spread his blanket on the ground, laid the frame in the middle, folded the blanket across, and pinned it firmly.

"Looks like a litter," said Sid.

"That's what it is. Put the tin box of hard-tack in the middle. It's the heaviest thing we've got; weighs ten pounds. Now the bacon; that only weighs five. Now the other things. The guns ain't loaded; lay 'em along the sides. And the fishing-rods. Now we're ready."

One boy in front between the poles, and one behind, and it was a pleasant surprise to Sid to find how easy it worked. Still, it was a dreadfully long and warm mile and a half over that rough forest path before they came out on the slope that led down to the blue waters of Pot Lake.

"It's just beautiful," said Sid, as they set down their load for a rest and a look.

"Hist! Let me get my gun."

A cartridge was slipped in like a flash; and then there came another flash, and a report.

"Thought you said it was unsportsmanlike to kill a partridge sitting?"

"So it is, my boy; but it's a question of dinner. Our breakfast was an early one. Look at 'em, will you?"

Sid was looking, and there was a very strong suggestion of dinner in that pair of barely full-grown young birds. Fat, plump, the very thing for a boy whose breakfast had been eaten early. There was a sort of natural "open" on that side of the little lake, and Wade led the way straight to it.

"Just as I expected. The old shanty's knocked all to pieces. The boards and the nails are there, though. They may be good for something."

"What next? Shall I unpack?"

"Hold up, Sid. Yes, there's the spring. Down yonder; that's where we'll pitch our tent."

"Needn't do that yet awhile."

"First thing always. We're not in camp till the tent's up."

"Go ahead. Don't you wish you had the tent poles here now?"

"Not if I had 'em to carry besides the other things. We can cut all we want."

As they talked they walked, and they were now standing by the spring, on the slope, not more than a hundred yards from the shore.

"There's the place for the tent."

"Isn't one spot as good as another?" asked Sid.

"You don't want to sleep slanting, do you? That isn't all, either. That little hump of ground in front of it's a tiptop fire-place."

"Don't look much like one."

"You'll see. Come on and let's cut some tent poles."

Two five-foot sticks, each with a "crotch" at the upper end, were soon set in the ground about six feet apart, and a ridge pole laid across them.

"You haven't set 'em deep enough," said Sid. "They'd go over too easy."

"No they won't. The strength of a tent is in the canvas and pegs, not in the poles," said Wade.

He was unrolling the great square piece of strong but light "cotton duck," and in a moment more it was flapping over the poles.

"Stretch it well, and peg it strong. That tent won't blow down."

"Can't stand up in it."

"That isn't what it's for. In with the supplies. The sun's as bad as rain would be, for part of 'em, spite of the tin boxes."

"Nothing extra—not even butter."

"Butter! There's one roll of it, but the bacon's the butter for us. Now for the butcher-knives. We must ditch our tent."

"What for?"

"To drain away the water, if it rains. We must cut a V."

The apex of the V was cut pretty deeply on the slope above the tent, and the arms were cut around it till they led out below.

"Water doesn't run up hill," said Sid. "We're drained. What next?"

"Fire."

"A day like this? Are you going to cook right away? I'd rather try the lake for some fish."

"Of course we will. But it takes an hour for an open fire to be fit to cook by. Got to have plenty of coals and ashes."

Fuel was plentiful enough, and a rousing fire was speedily blazing on the little hump of ground, a rod in front of the tent.

"Not near enough to set anything on fire. If that hump hadn't been there, we'd have made one."

As it was, he had levelled it on top a little, and the surface so made was barely two feet across.

Sid was a little curious about such a fire-place, but decided to wait and see what his friend meant.

Wade's father was an old army officer, and had taken his boy with him on more than one "camping-out" excursion, while Sid was taking his very first lesson.

"That'll do. Now for some fish. You go ahead, while I pluck the partridges."

"Guess not. I can do that as well as you can. Give me one of 'em."

It was easy work to strip the tender game and hang it in the tent, but the boys were thoroughly tired of mere "going into camp" by the time they started for the lake.

"Hullo, Sid! If there isn't the old dug-out floating yet!"

"That thing out there by the snag? We can't get at her."

"Can't we? Can't you swim as far as that? I can."

"Swim? Oh yes, of course we can. Shall you go now?"

"Why, no: not till we get in fish enough for dinner."

"That's it. We're Indians. Got to fish, hunt, or starve—or live on hard-tack and bacon."

Pot Lake was a great place for trout, and both of the boys knew how to handle a rod.

"No three-inchers; none of your speckled minnows," shouted Sid, as he landed a half-pound beauty.

"Here comes a bigger one. Oh, but isn't this fun?"

"Better fun than going into camp."

"Or tramping through the woods with a load. But don't you begin to feel hungry?"

"Begin? Well, you may say begin if you want to. Seems to me I began a little while after breakfast," replied Sid.

They had caught more fish than any two boys could eat; but Sid's first remark on reaching the tent with them was, "I do hate cleaning fish."

"Clean fish? Out here in the woods? While we're Indians? You wait till I find a bass-wood tree."

There were plenty of lindens, or bass-woods, in that vicinity, and the broad flat leaves were as good as brown paper to wrap up a trout in, fold over fold.

The fire had now burned long enough to supply Wade with a heap of hot ashes, which he raked out on one edge of it. All the little coals were carefully poked aside, the leaf-covered trout were put down and smothered an inch deep in their ashy bed, and then a pile of glowing cinders was raked over them.

"They'll cook, Sid. You go to the lake for a kettle of water, while I get out the frying-pan and the coffee-pot."

"Frying-pan! We won't need any bacon with all those fish and the partridges."

"We'll only broil one bird, but we must have some hard-tack. I'll show you."

Sid went for the water, but when he got back Wade was

putting the frying-pan on a bed of coals, with a couple of thin slices of bacon in it.

"They look lonely," said Sid.

"They'll have company enough. This coffee smells first rate."

"No milk, Wade, and nothing to settle it with."

"I thought I'd surprise you, Sid. I've brought some little cans of condensed milk."

"Why not a big can?"

"Spoils after it's opened, just like other milk."

"Next thing to having a cow. But, oh, won't the coffee be muddy!"

"I guess not. There, the bacon's beginning to fry."

Half a dozen ship biscuit, hard as dinner plates, were dipped for a moment in the water, and quickly transferred to the frying-pan.

It was wonderful how puffed up and soft they became, and what a fine flavor of bacon improved their taste when it came time to eat them.

Wade was at his coffee-pot before that, however.

Two heaping table-spoonfuls of the ground coffee were first poured into one of the tin cups, which were all the "table crockery" in that camp, and just covered with cold water.

That had been done before the bacon was put on, and now the coffee-pot full of water was sitting on a bed of coals and beginning to steam.

"She's boiling," shouted Sid.

In went the contents of the tin cup, and on went the cover.

"Let her boil awhile."

"The hard-tack's a-swelling."

"The fish must be done, too. Now for settling."

The cover of the coffee-pot was lifted, and half a cupful of cold water was suddenly dashed in, and then the pot was lifted from the coals to the grass.

"Let her stand a bit. Now for the fish. Have your tin plate ready."

"Ain't they splendid?"

CAMP LIFE.—Drawn by Charles Graham.

So they were, when they were dug out from the ashes, their leafy coats removed; and Sid discovered that by a careful use of his fork and fingers all the parts of the fish that he did not want seemed to come away together. A little salt and pepper improved both them and the hard-tack, and the coffee poured out beautifully clear and strong.

Just as he and Sid were getting ready to begin their meal, however, Wade took one of the partridges and spread him flat on the forks of a long crooked branch he had cut.

"That'll hold him just high enough above the coals."

"Yes, but you stuck him right into the heat, first thing."

"Always. That shuts up his outside coat, so he won't lose all his juice in broiling. Cook him slow, now. I've put a little salt and pepper on him, and a piece of butter as big as a chestnut. He'll do."

"We can't eat all we're cooking."

"Take our time to it."

So they did, and Wade went so far as to clean a small trout, and show Sid how to fry him.

"Always break up a little hard-tack fine as you can, and sprinkle it on the bottom of the frying-pan as soon as your bacon fat begins to smoke. Then your fish won't stick, unless your pan's too hot. You must look out for that."

Dinner was over at last, and then the boys went to the edge of the woods for a couple of strong forked stakes and a cross-stick to hang their kettle on.

"What are you setting the crotches so far from the fire for?" asked Sid.

"So they won't burn down. Besides, when you don't want your kettle on the fire, you can just slide it along; needn't take it off every time."

"Look, Wade—the sky isn't as clear as it was."

"That's so. May have rain. We must cut our bedding and lay in our wood-pile."

Plenty of small hemlock boughs were heaped on the bottom of the tent to spread their blankets on; and Sid almost rebelled at the amount of dry wood Wade insisted on piling up.

"May rain all day to-morrow, Sid. We must catch a lot of fish to-night."

"What are all these great slabs of bark for? Kindling?"

"I'll show you. It's mean work starting an open fire with wet wood."

The first day in camp was clearly a day of hard work; but the fish seemed to bite better than ever as the sun went down, and the boys had each a capital "string" before supper-time.

The old dug-out canoe was swam after, and brought to the shore.

"We can use it, Sid. It was a tottlish thing to get into, till father nailed a keel-board on the bottom of it. We'll bail it out to-morrow. I'm too tired for that sort of fun now."

"So am I. Let's go for supper. Let me make the coffee this time."

"All right. But don't put any more wood on the fire. I'll broil some fish instead of frying them. Clean 'em, and split 'em down along the backbone inside, and they'll lie flat. Spread 'em on a forked stick, so they won't touch the coals and ashes. Season 'em just a little."

Sid decided afterward that there was very little to be said against broiled trout.

They were both of them tired enough to go to bed early, but it was hardly eight o'clock when the rain-drops began to patter on the tent cover.

"We must keep our fire, Sid," said Wade.

He was raking it from the top of the "bump" as he spoke, and putting down there several solid pieces of dry wood. These he covered with the live coals and burning fragments, and these again with ashes; and than he made over all a sort of conical "wigwam" of his slabs of bark, putting flat stones against them at the bottom, so they would not easily blow away.

"Couldn't do that with too big a fire. Always make a camp fire as small as possible. So my father told me. That 'll keep, if it rains ever so hard."

"It's going to do that. Will our fish be safe?"

"Hanging in the water by the canoe? Of course they will. Who'll steal 'em? They'll be fresh, too, in the morning. We can't live on fish, though. I can show you twenty ways of cooking birds."

They had crept into the tent now, and the rain was pelting harder and harder.

"Glad the tent's well ditched," said Wade. "We'll be as dry as two bones."

"Oh, but isn't it fun! But I tell you what, Wade Norton, I feel as if I wanted to sleep about twenty-four hours."

—

FÊTE DAYS IN FRANCE.

THE French are a very merry nation, and for their *fête* or festival days have many jolly games to amuse both the children and older people. In one of these a weighted string is hung up at one end of a tent, and the children, starting from the other end, try to cut it with a pair of scissors. This would be easy enough, were it not that each player is blindfolded by a great hollow head with a grinning, ugly face, something like the comic masks we see in the shop windows. There are no holes for the eyes, and the head rests down on the shoulders of the player, like a great extinguisher, making her look like the caricatures in which little bodies are represented with big heads. The player turns around several times before starting, and having no idea of the proper direction, sometimes walks toward the sides, and snips the scissors in the faces of the spectators. A drummer marches toward the string, making a loud noise with his drum, but the sound oftener confuses than guides. If the player really succeeds in cutting the string, a present is awarded as a prize.

The same play-ground also serves at night as a dancing hall, for the French are very fond of dancing. Here

SCENE AT A FRENCH FAIR—TRYING TO CUT THE STRING.

is a little poem about French fêtes, which perhaps some of your grandparents will remember, as it was written about sixty years ago.

"Come with the fiddle, and play us a tune or two;
Lasses and lads, bring your dancing-shoes.
Here on the green in the light of the moon for you—
None but the lazy or lame can refuse.
Jig it with tweedledum,
Let fools wheedle 'em,
Making Anxiety laugh as she views.

"Come, little Annette, with tresses all curling bright,
Sporting and frisking like lambkin or kid,
Foot it so sprightly, and dance it all down aright—
Never for languor shall Annette be chid.
Right hand and left again,
Round about set amain,
Jokingly, laughingly, just as you're bid.

"See, there is Lubin and Javotte already there—
Hark! 'tis the fife and the jerked tambourine—
Mother and granddad sitting all steady there,
Smiling and nodding, enjoying the scene.
They will delighted be,
While all benighted we
Dance in the moonlight that checkers the green.

"Farewell to misery, poverty, sorrowing!
While we've a fiddle we gayly will dance;
Supper we've none, nor can we go borrowing;
Dance and forget in the fashion of France.
Long live gay jollity!
'Tis a good quality—
Caper all, sing all, and laugh all, and prance."

THE CARE OF DOGS.

As most of the young people love dogs, and many of them own one or more of these faithful pets, they will, perhaps, be glad of a few hints as to their proper care and treatment.

Dogs are subject to accidents, and swellings or tumors of various kinds on different parts of the body; and in such cases, if you do not know just what to do, it is better to consult some good authority, such as the editor of a first-class sporting paper, than to try experiments which may or may not be for the good of your favorite. In order that you may be able to describe minutely and accurately the part of the animal's body where the trouble seems to be, the diagram showing the "points" of a dog is given:

POINTS OF A DOG.

1. Nose.
2. Flews.
3. Nasal bone.
4. The stop.
5. The skull.
6. Occipital bone.
7. Dewlap.
8. Front of chest.
9. Top of the shoulder.
10. Top of the hip.
11. Shoulder-blade.
12. The rump.
13. The arm.
14. The elbow.
15. The fore-arm.
16. The [illegible].
17. The [illegible] joint.
18. The [illegible].
19. The tail, called by [illegible]
20. The [illegible].
21. The pasterns.

Nearly all dogs enjoy an occasional washing, and if they do not get it, their skin is apt to become foul, and vermin may collect, which will prove very troublesome and difficult to remove. When the dog is to be washed, get two large buckets full of soft water, a rough towel, and a cake of Spratt's soap, for which you may be obliged to send to a dog-fancier. The water in one bucket should be lukewarm, and that in the other cold. Tie the dog in the yard or on the grass under a tree, and begin by pouring a little of the warm water on his shoulder, at the same time rubbing on the soap. Keep on in this way until every inch of the dog's body is covered with a lather, washing the head last, and taking care not to let the soapy water get into either his eyes or ears.

After the dog is thus thoroughly covered with lather, wash it off with clean warm water, at the same time gently squeezing the hide and rubbing downward. When the soap is all rinsed off, dash a few dipperfuls of cold water over the dog, and rub his jacket briskly with the rough towel. Then untie him and let him have a good run, after which, and when his coat is nearly dry, is the time to give him a thorough combing and grooming, carefully unravelling every bit of tangle or "mat" you may find in his feather. (The long hair of a dog is called his "feather," not feathers.)

In order that a dog may be kept in good health, his kennel requires frequent attention. Not only should the bedding be always sweet and dry, but the place should be occasionally scrubbed with soap and boiling water, and left to become thoroughly dry in the sun before it is again occupied.

If your dog has a collar—and every well-behaved dog deserves a pretty collar to wear when he goes out for a walk—be sure and take it off as soon as he comes in. Remember, also, that while the outside of the collar must be kept clean and bright in order to look well, it is very important for the good of the dog that the *inside* should be kept clean as well, and not allowed to become foul.

A DINNER IN TOKIO.

Very strange dishes came upon the board at our New-Year's dinner at the hotel in Tokio. A preliminary pipe of mild tobacco was handed around. The tobacco was too mild an affair altogether to take the edge off one's appetite, if intended for that purpose. The first course consisted of sweetmeats, served upon lacquered plates. The whole meal was of a Frenchified character. Balls of golden, scarlet, and green jellies were among the things in this dish; rice, flour, and sugar made up the constituents of the other parts of it. Saki (rice spirit) and the ever-present tea were then served round. The second course consisted of soup, into which were shredded hard-boiled eggs. This was served in bowls, but without spoons. I had, however, my purchased spoon, fork, and knife always with me, and so escaped trouble. Then came a very strange dish: it was a collop cut from a living fish wriggling on the sideboard. The Japs are a great fish-eating folk, and this raw fish-eating is quite common. The steak cut for Bruce from the living ox, told of in his Abyssinian travels, occurred to one's memory. The live tidbit is supposed to be eaten with the Japanese "Soy"—a sauce that makes everything palatable—but I let my portion of it pass. It is not possible to comply with all Japanese fashions at once. Time is necessary to the acquirement of taste. Cooked fish was next served, and that in great variety, including shell-fish. A sort of lime or small lemon was used as the flavoring to this dish. Then came boiled beans, with ginger roots, and some fried fish and horse-radish. To follow that came boiled fish and clams, the latter cut up, and served with pears. Rice in tea-cups followed, and then a salad, and the dishes were ended. The hot saki and tea cups were sent round after each course. The health of our landlord was proposed in Japanese, and drunk in saki. He then rose to reply. I thought that he would never have done bowing before he began to speak. He appeared to speak very well, and easily,

MR. HARVEY'S HOUSEKEEPERS, AND NAN'S EXAMINATION-DAY.

BY E. COOMBS.

OF the four little housekeepers, Patty, the eldest, who was fifteen, was chief. Johnny came next. He was housekeeper number two. And then there was Katie, who was eleven, and Nan, nine. Their mother had died two years before, and when the housekeeper left, about a year afterward, Patty, in all the dignity of her fourteen years, decided to dispense with help in future, and that they could do the work among themselves. Mr. Harvey was absorbed in his business, and never greatly disturbed by any irregularities in his household, provided the children were generally peaceable and happy.

So Patty's decision was allowed to stand. Housekeeping had seemed a very easy thing to her, as she had seen her mother go about quietly doing one thing after another, without hurry or confusion. But she found doing the same things herself to be another thing. Oh, the trouble they had with the cooking! The same fire that would not bake the biscuits burned the steak to a crisp. After repeated efforts and experiments, however, bread, steak, and potatoes that could be eaten appeared on the table.

Then they decided to try some cake. Patty, and Johnny, who was always ready to help, knit their brows and puzzled their brains over the recipes. Johnny volunteered to read the directions from the cook-book, while Patty measured and mixed the ingredients.

He read, "'Four eggs, two cups sugar—'"

"Stop, Johnny—don't read so fast. I wonder if the eggs ought to be beaten?"

"Course they ought to; sh'd think any goose 'd know that," said Johnny, contemptuously.

"I don't believe they ought to be; the recipe doesn't say anything about beating." So the eggs were broken in with the sugar, and they were stirred together. Then the butter—a liberal quantity—and milk and flour. "'Two tea-spoons cream-tartar; flavor to taste,'" read Johnny.

At length the cake was in the oven, and they watched and waited for it to rise. But it never rose. The fire was made quick; then it was allowed to burn slower; still the cake was an inch below the top of the pan. More than an hour passed, then Patty took it from the oven. What could be the trouble? It was as heavy as lead. Johnny read the recipe over again carefully. "'One tea-spoonful soda'—that's the trouble, Pat; we forgot the soda."

Katie was the most unfortunate of the housekeepers. If she trimmed the lamps, she was sure to spill the oil; if she cooked the dinner, in spite of her wisest precautions it was sure to be burned. And Johnny used laughingly to warn her against looking at stakes, or nails, or twigs, as a rent in her dress was sure to be the result.

Then there was Nan. She did so hate dish-washing! Sometimes, if in the very midst of hot water and rattling crockery, she saw her girl friends outside at play, away she would go, not thinking again of her unfinished task until returning, perhaps half an hour afterward, she would find the towels wet and the water cold in the pan.

And it must be confessed that sometimes even Patty herself would drop her broom, and at the same time her dignity, and join the children, as eager as any of them, forgetful of the dinner hour and the uncooked dinner.

But the sewing—making the clothes—was the worst. Patty was so proud that she would not ask help from anybody—no, not if she ruined her eyes, and worked her fingers to the bone. Garments were picked to pieces, stitch by stitch, to learn how they were made. Dresses were puzzled over, and pulled this way and that; a little cut off here and a piece sewed on there to make them fit.

But now was coming the tug of war. In a week would be the examination at the grammar school to which Nan went, and she had not a thing fit to wear.

Patty wondered what she should do. She consulted her father.

"Why, buy her a dress," he said.

"But I can not buy one all made."

"Make her one, then," and he laid a crisp bill on the table.

So Patty was left to manage as best she might. Taking Nan with her, she went first to the shoe store, where she selected a pair of the daintiest, nicest-fitting boots; then to the dry-goods store, where she bought a number of yards of some sort of twilled goods of a lovely shade of blue. With these, a lace bib, and a large blue bow for her hair, Patty thought Nan would look very pretty.

Purchasing the material had been quite easy, but now came the cutting and making of the dress. The dresses of other girls were studied, fashion plates consulted by all the little housekeepers, and at last a style was decided upon. Then there was a laying on of patterns, and cutting, and basting, and ripping out, and sewing together, till at last the dress was completed. It is true that it was a little too long on the shoulder, and a little too short under the arm, and a little too scant in the skirt. But it was pretty, and the effect was good.

At length the day before examination came, and everything was ready. The lace had been basted into the sleeves, and the dress, French kid boots, bow, and collar were laid away in the best chamber.

But just before dark a lady living in another part of the city sent for Patty to come and spend the night with her, as she was alone. How could she go? There was Nan to be dressed in the morning. But then she could not disappoint her kind friend; so, after giving Katie and Nan many directions for the morning, she left them, promising to meet them at the school-house.

The next morning Johnny got the breakfast, and Nan and Katie cleared away the dishes. Then they went up stairs to dress. Nan had just finished her hair, having pinned on the blue bow, and was surveying its effect in the glass, when the sound of music on the street, just in front of the house, attracted her attention. She rushed to the window. There was a chariot painted in gay colors, and men in scarlet and gold uniforms, and such music! The new dress was forgotten, and she flew down stairs and out of the door. With a troop of children she followed the gaudy chariot and gayly caparisoned horses from street to street.

At length, before she realized how far she had gone, she found herself before the school-house door, and the clock was striking nine. There was no time to go back. She thought of the new dress. No matter; she had on the blue bow.

Patty had gone directly to the school-house, instead of first going home, and was awaiting Nan's appearance.

The bell rang for the second class to come down; and though trying to be calm and dignified, Patty could not help leaning eagerly forward, as the girls came trooping into the recitation-room. She wanted to see how Nan looked in the new blue dress and neat boots.

One by one the girls pushed forward and took their seats, until at last— Could that be Nan? Poor Patty's cheeks burned with mortification as she saw her pressing eagerly forward among the rest, her freckled face beaming with satisfaction. Instead of the beautiful blue dress, she had on a faded calico, considerably outgrown, and her coarse every-day boots with copper tips, half laced up, and much the worse for wear. But, in striking contrast, the blue bow was perched proudly on the top of her head. Then she had forgotten her pocket-handkerchief, and poor Patty was anything but soothed by the snuffs that she gave from time to time.

But when the recitations were heard Nan's dress was forgotten. Her answers were prompt, correct, and distinct; and Patty's feelings were somewhat soothed by the looks and words of praise that passed from one to another of the examining committee, as Nan, still fresh and unwearied, answered the last question correctly.

Then came the awarding of prizes. The silence of expectancy reigned in the school-room, unbroken, save by the whispered consultation of teachers and examiners. At last the principal called the second class forward to the recitation seats.

As the girls passed down the aisles, another great wave of mortification swept over poor Patty, as Nan, in striking contrast to the other girls, in their pretty dresses, still careless and eager, pressed forward among the rest. When the girls reached their places, and all had become quiet, one of the committee rose and said: "You have all done well. I am pleased with the interest which you seem to manifest in your school and studies, and with the industry and application shown by your ready responses. But for prompt, correct, and distinct answers, which her teachers tell me have been uniform throughout the term, I award to Miss Nannie Harvey the first prize." And as Nan, bright and unconscious as ever, stepped forward to receive it, an almost audible smile passed round the room, mingled with a murmur of applause.

But after this, as they trudged home together, Patty was almost as forgetful as Nan of the shabby dress and thick half-worn shoes.

BLUE VIOLETS.

BY E. M. M.

Listen! No; you can not hear them;
  Never do they make a sound,
All these thousand sweet blue flowers
  Starting up from out the ground.

Scattered are they up the hill-side,
  Hidden in the woodland nooks,
Sprinkled over sunny meadows,
  Nestled close by sparkling brooks.

Where, I wonder, have they sprung from?
  Do they live in worlds below?
Have they slept the livelong winter
  Underneath the soft white snow?

Ah! if only they had voices,
  What strange stories they might tell
Of the land where winsome fairies
  With the flowers love to dwell!

Oh, you dainty wee blue flowers!
  Brightest roses June may bring,
But they can not match your sweetness,
  Gentle messengers of spring.

WORK FOR GIRLS.

AN EMBROIDERED WORK-BAG.

This pretty work-bag has a foundation of splints, wicker-work, Manila braid, or whatever material of the kind may be found most convenient, fourteen inches

Fig. 1.—Embroidered Work-bag.

and seven-eighths long and ten inches and a half wide, which is sloped off on the corners, and trimmed with two strips of embroidery, separated by a bias strip of blue satin, which is turned down on the edges an inch wide on the wrong side, and gathered so as to form a puff. The embroidered strips are worked on a foundation of white cloth as shown by Fig. 2. For the corn-flowers use blue silk, and work them in chain stitch. The calyxes are worked in satin stitch with moss green silk, and the lilies-of-the-valley with white silk. The stems and sprays are worked in tent and herring-bone stitch with green silk in several shades. For the ends cut of blue satin two pieces each six inches and a half wide and seven inches and a quarter high, fold down the upper edge an inch and a quarter wide on the wrong side, and gather it twice. Having sloped off the lower corners of these parts, pleat them, and join them with the foundation. For the bag cut of blue satin one piece twenty-four inches wide and ten inches and a half high, sew it up on the sides, and fold down the upper edge two inches and a half wide on the wrong side, for a shirr, through which blue silk cord is run, and sew it to the upper edge of the foundation on the wrong side. The work-bag is trimmed on the outside with a ruche of blue satin ribbon seven-eighths of an inch wide. Light gray instead of white cloth forms a pretty and more serviceable foundation for the embroidered strips. Little girls who do not know how to embroider may make a very handsome work-bag from this pattern by using ribbon brocaded in bright colors, or a double row of ruching around the edge in the place of the embroidery. Bamboo handle.

Fig. 2.—Border for Work-bag.

"I AM THE LAD IN THE CADET GRAY."

BY MARY A. BARR.

I am the lad in the cadet gray—
Rat-a-tat, rat-a-tat, rat-tat, hey!
My buttons are bright, my jacket is tight,
My step is a soldier's, quick and light;
I'm ready to dance, I'm ready to fight—
Hurrah! hurrah! for the boy in gray.

I am the lad in the cadet gray—
Rat-a-tat, rat-a-tat, rat-tat, hey!
The bugle wakes me at dawn of day;
I'm out at drill in the morning gray,
Prompt and trig, not a hair astray—
Hurrah! hurrah! for the boy in gray.

I am the lad in the cadet gray—
Rat-a-tat, rat-a-tat, rat-tat, hey!
My hardest tasks are cheerfully done;
I'm under orders from sun to sun;
You should see me handle sword and gun—
Hurrah! hurrah! for the boy in gray.

I am the lad in the cadet gray—
Rat-a-tat, rat-a-tat, rat-tat, hey!
At "four-o'clocks," and at dress parade,
My chevrons, buttons, and fancy braid
Win smiles from many a lovely maid
For the handsome lad in cadet gray.

For the lad in gray the drum is rolled—
Rat-a-tat, rat-a-tat, quick and bold;
And when the days of drilling are through,
This is the thing that I shall do:
Doff cadet gray for the army blue—
The army blue with its stars of gold.

Braver and freer a thousandfold—
Rat-a-tat, rat-a-tat, true and bold.
Plume and sword in my silken sash,
After my country's foes I'll dash,
Where muskets rattle and sabres clash—
Hurrah! for the army blue and gold.

Hurrah! for the lad so brave and true,
In cadet gray or in army blue.
On his heart he wears his country's name,
And his hand will keep her spotless fame;
In gray or blue he is just the same—
Hurrah! for the lad in gray or blue.

Music by Chas. F. [illegible]

OUR POST-OFFICE BOX

while it is in a damp or pulpy condition. The practice dates back to the early part of the sixteenth century, and came into ... after the invention of printing. The mark is produced by pressure on the paper ... over a wire-gauze net, or under a roller, in its progress from the vat, the raised lines of the design making the paper thinner at the points of contact.

LOTTIE B.—We shall soon begin the publication of "The Story of the American Navy," by Benson J. Lossing.

H. H. SMITH.—Your idea of your "Wiggle" is entirely original, and very good. We are very sorry it arrived too late to be engraved among other answers.

PUZZLES FROM YOUNG CONTRIBUTORS.

No. 1.

[illegible]

[illegible]

No. 2.

[illegible]

No. 3.

[illegible]

No. 4.

[illegible]

No. 5.

[illegible]

No. 6.

[illegible]

ANSWERS TO PUZZLES IN No. 28.

[illegible]

[illegible]

THE TARANTULA.

A VERY comical and natural-looking toy spider can be made from very simple material. A cork, a jackknife, three hair-pins, the remains of an old brush or broom, are all the implements necessary. If you have a box of paints, so much the better. In the first place, cut the body of the spider out of a cork, as represented in Fig. 1; then paint it all over with flake-white; when that is perfectly dry, paint it as bright a yellow as you can; and after that, paint black stripes on it with lamp-black or India ink. Then get the hairs from an old brush, a few sticks of broom-corn will answer as well, and stick them into the body of the spider, as represented in Figures 1 and 2. Take three hair-pins, bend them into the proper form, run them through the cork, and you have the legs. Now your spider is complete except in two points: you must run a pin in the back to which to tie a thread or string to hold it up by, and two large pins into the place where you have painted the eyes. The bright heads of the pins make the eyes look very natural.

THROWING LIGHT.

I AM one, yet it takes many to complete me, though I am intangible. Motion is necessary to make me. I have no motion of my own, being incapable of voluntary action; still, were there not voluntary action on my part, commerce would be at a stand-still. I am necessary to vessels. I am a vessel. I am what vessels take. I am visited every day by some one; and though meant to hold a liquid, still, when there is my full complement, more solid food than liquid is needed to satisfy when I am on myself. If broken, I am useless; yet, when separated, I can be brought together again. I am most agreeable when made at will, am generally an ugly piece of domestic furniture, but need a strong hand to keep up proper discipline.

Treat us kindly, we would probably always be agreeable. I don't care how you treat me, provided you don't break me. There is nothing breakable about me, though you can bring me to an end at any moment. Of course I cost money, ordinarily a few pennies. There is a fixed tariff for our employment; contracts must be drawn up; yet I can be made as expensive as one chooses. Sometimes I am undertaken in the cause of science. I am generally in the kitchen, and we certainly need a kitchen and me to provide for our many and daily wants.

The Monkey and the Hawk.—There lives in the south of France a man of wealth whose château, or country place of residence, has around it very tall trees. The cook of the château has a monkey—a pert fellow, who knows ever so many tricks. The monkey often helps the cook to pluck the feathers from fowls. One day the cook gave the monkey two partridges to pluck: and the monkey, seating himself in an open window, went to work. He had picked the feathers from one of the partridges, and placed it on the outer ledge of the window with a satisfied grunt, when, lo! all at once a hawk flew down from one of the tall trees near by, and bore off the plucked bird. Master Monkey was very angry. He shook his fist at the hawk, which took a seat on one of the limbs not far off, and began to eat the partridge with great relish. The owner of the château saw the sport, for he was sitting in a grape arbor, and crept up to watch the end of it. The monkey picked the other partridge, laid it on the ledge in the same place, and hid behind the window-screen on the inside.

The hawk was caught in this trap, for when it flew down after the partridge, out reached the monkey, and caught the thief. In a moment the hawk's neck was wrung, and the monkey soon had the hawk plucked.

Taking the two birds to the cook, the monkey handed them to him, as if to say, "Here are your two partridges, master." The cook thought that one of the birds looked queer, but he served them on the table. The owner of the house shook his head when he saw the dish, and telling the cook of the trick, laughed heartily.

How the Pigeons Help the Doctor.—A celebrated English physician has found a new use for the carrier-pigeon, as a helper in his practice. Describing the operation, he says: "I take out half a dozen birds in a small basket with me on my rounds, and when I have seen my patient, no matter at what distance from home, I write my prescription on a small piece of tissue-paper, and having wound it round the shank of the bird's leg, I gently throw the carrier up into the air. In a few minutes it reaches home, and having been shut up fasting since the previous evening, without much delay it enters the trap cage connected with its loft, where it is at once caught by my assistant, and relieved of its dispatches. The medicine is immediately prepared, and sent off by a messenger, who is thus saved several hours of waiting, and I am enabled to complete my morning round of visits. Should any patient be very ill, and I am desirous of having an early report of him or her next morning, I leave a bird to bring me the tidings."

AUNT FLORA'S ANSWER.

Aunt Flora's scolding never made you ——,
Her sympathies, though cold, were never ——,
And her old pies were marvels of high ——.
Poor Flora.

Her homespun dress, though scant, was made with ——,
Her harmless cat would neither cure nor ——,
And, like the busy ant, she knew no ——.
Good Flora.

A nameless charm with face and form did ——;
No harm she did, but graciously would ——
Her arm to guide you safely to your ——.
Kind Flora.

A heart may seem of stone if grief it ——;
Her tone to you was ever like a ——;
One wise was she among the foolish ——.
Wise Flora.

BREAKERS AHEAD! AH, WHAT A MEETING THAT WILL BE!

Vol. I.—No. 30. | Published by HARPER & BROTHERS, New York. | Price Four Cents.
Tuesday, May 25, 1880. | Copyright, 1880, by Harper & Brothers. | $1.50 per Year, in Advance.

A MOTHER'S ANXIETIES—"WATER, WATER, EVERYWHERE!"

MEMORIAL FLOWERS.

BY M. M.

Bare violets ope their saintly eyes,
  Red columbines bend and sway,
White star-flowers twinkle in beds of moss,
  And, blooming, they seem to say,
"We bring you the red and the white and the blue
  To welcome Memorial-day."

So gather them, children, at earliest dawn,
  While yet they are fresh with dew,
And we'll scatter them over the sacred mounds
  Where slumber our soldiers true;
For we'll give them only the colors they loved—
  The red and the white and the blue.

HOW JONATHAN BEWITCHED THE CHICKENS.

BY MARY HICKS.

"HURRAH! hurrah! Now for a long play-day: the school-master's a witch, and we are free;" and some twenty boys came flocking and tumbling out of the school-house door, and went swarming up the street. Not much like the boys of to-day, except for the noise, were these twenty youngsters of nearly two centuries ago, who skipped and ran up the streets of Boston, dressed in their long square-skirted coats, small-clothes, long stockings, and low shoes with their cherished buckles of silver or brass. And very different from to-day were the streets through which they passed as they flocked homeward talking of the master.

"He'll have naught to do but learn of the Black Man now; they do say he rides his ferule and bunch of twigs high up in the air, like Mistress Hibbins used her broom-stick," cried William Bartholomew, the sneak of the school.

"He best have been switching thee with it, then," cried Jonathan Winthrop. "Thou never hast thy share of the whippings—does he, mates?" and frank-faced Jonathan turned to his companions.

"Truly thou and I, Jonathan, need not complain that we have not our share of the fun and the twigs," laughed Christopher Corwin, as he laid his arm on Jonathan's, and shrugged his shoulders at the thought of numerous beatings. For Jonathan Winthrop and Christopher Corwin, with their plots and pranks, were enough to make poor Master Halleck sell his soul to the Evil One, as report said he had done.

"His ferule was sharp as a knife," said overgrown Jo Tucker, the butt of the school.

"Truly," cried William Bartholomew, "sharper than thy wits, we doubt not; or thy knife either, for that was never known to cut aught."

"Keep thy tongue in thy head, Billy Mew; none ever said that was not sharp enough," put in Christopher Corwin.

"I do not believe he is a witch," said Samuel Sheldon, a quiet boy, dressed in very plain drab clothes, and a wider brimmed hat than the others.

"Oh, doesn't thee?" cried several.

"Thou art but a Quaker thyself, and a Quaker's as bad as a witch any day," shouted Robert Pike.

"There, muddle thy stockings in yon mud puddle for that speech, thou water-loving Baptist," cried Christopher Corwin, as he jostled Baptist Bob in some water by the way.

"Hurrah for the witch, and a long play-day!" cried the boys.

"Peace! peace! ye noisy urchins!" said Magistrate Sewall, as he stepped suddenly from a door-way. "The master has imps of the earth as well as the air, I see. Get ye home less noisily, or we must needs put ye in yonder prison with the master."

The awe of the magistrate's presence had the desired effect, and the crowd broke up in groups of two or three, and each took his way homeward quietly.

"Jonathan, dost thou believe the master dotted his i's and crossed his t's when he signed his name in the Black Man's book in the forest yonder?" said Christopher, as the two boys walked home together.

"Nay, I know not," said Jonathan, absently.

"Verily, I hope the Black Man cracked him across his knuckles, if he did not," said Christopher; and he thought of his own often-aching fists.

"Chris, thou art too wise to believe the poor master's a witch," said Jonathan.

"Nay, how could I be, when the magistrates themselves, and all the wise men of the town, believe it?"

"Thou dost not believe the master stuck pins in Job Swinnerton's stomach?"

"Nay," laughed Chris; "the green apples from Deacon Gedney's orchard were the cause of his pain."

"But, Chris, I'm afraid it will go hard with the master, for all the boys but thou and I seem bent on making him a witch."

"Well, trouble not thyself about it. As Billy Mew says, if the master's a witch, we will have the longer play-day. To-morrow I go to my grandfather's, in Salem, and thou come over with thy father some day; it will be rare fun to see the witch children act."

"Peradventure I may. It will be dull without thee, Chris; and with the rest of the boys making the master out a witch, they'll have no time for play."

"Well, take care of thyself, good fellow, and beware thou dost not provoke Dame Betty too far; she has a rare relish for calling people witches."

"Ay, that she has. There's a pail of water now at her door, and she's talking with our Debby. I doubt not; let's turn the bottom up to dry;" and in a wink the two boys were off for this bit of mischief.

In a few days all were off to Salem—Jonathan's father as one of the judges, the master to be tried for a witch, with those of the children whom he had afflicted as accusers, and jolly Chris to see the fun.

It was very lonesome for Jonathan at home, for he had no brothers or sisters, his mother was always sick, and Debby spent all her spare time talking with a crony across the way of the witch-woman, Bridget Bishop, then on trial for witchcraft.

So Jonathan made playmates of and amused himself with the chickens of the Rev. Deodat Parker, who lived next door. Now these chickens were the source of much pleasure to Jonathan, for the Winthrops had none, neither Jonathan nor Debby being deemed fit to be trusted with them; and Jonathan envied the Rev. Deodat Parker his yard full of staid old fowls and lively young chicks. Early in the spring Jonathan had loved to caress and cuddle up the little rolls of yellow and black down; but now that they were great stalking, ragged fowls, putting on all sorts of airs, they excited his ridicule, and he longed to tease them, and the last year's brood of clucking hens and crowing roosters, that didn't quite know what to make of these new-comers.

Once he would have gone over in the yard to play with and tease the chickens to his heart's content; but Dame Betty having traced the overturned pail and numerous other tricks to his door, he considered her an enemy in ambush, liable to fly out at any moment with a stout broom-stick or hot suds, and so wisely kept at a safe distance.

But roosted on the fence, with a handful of corn, Jonathan's fears were at rest, and he fed the chickens, drove the old roosters nearly wild with long and loud crowing, and sometimes made a hasty jump into the yard to set two ruffled, ambitious roosters fighting.

Now Jonathan teased and bothered the poor fowls so continually that they began to grow afraid of him, and would not come when he called them, much to his indignation. But one day he thought of a plan, and went straightway to work at it.

First he went to his mother's work-basket and got a spool of thread, then to the meal chest for a handful of corn. Sitting down on the door-step, he tied long strings of thread to each grain of corn, then climbed the fence, and commenced what was fun for him, but misery for the poor chickens.

"Chick, chick," called Jonathan; and he threw his handful of corn to the ground. "Now I've got ye, ye disobliging things," said he to himself, as the stout old hens and pompous roosters pushed the young ones aside, and gobbled up the corn.

Then Jonathan gave a sudden jerk to his strings, that caused the poor chickens to feel more uncomfortable in their stomachs than they ever had before, and made the roosters dance, and the poor old hens tumble and bob around in all directions. Mischievous Jonathan sat and laughed until he tumbled off the fence, which broke the strings, and set the poor fowls free.

This mischief Jonathan carried on for a few days, until the wily chicks would not come to get the corn when they saw him, and he had to hide behind the fence until the poor things had swallowed their uncomfortable morsel, and then he would pop up to see the fun.

But Betty had her eyes on Master Jonathan, and one morning, while waiting on table, spoke her mind as follows:

"Master, I know not what's to be done with that brat Jonathan Winthrop; now that his father's away, he behaves more unseemly than wont. The master on trial yonder has made him a witch, and he has bewitched our chickens."

"Why for, my good Betty?"

"Why for! Why, they scream and fly away from him on first sight; and then he bewitches them nearer, and they are filled with pain seemingly, and flutter and fly about as if in great distress."

"Some of his pranks, I doubt not. I'll speak to him. Serve a fowl for dinner, Betty;" and the Rev. Deodat Parker rose from the table, evidently not crediting Betty's story.

Well, the fowl was served for dinner, and the minister and his good wife ate heartily, likewise Dame Betty. But that night the minister had an uncomfortable time of it, for the fowl was a tough old hen, and didn't sit as quietly on the minister's stomach as she would on a nest full of eggs.

"To my thinking, that boy's a witch of the Black Man's own brewing," said Betty, the next morning. "He hath bewitched our chickens, for certain."

"Nonsense, Betty," said the minister and his good wife together.

"Verily, no nonsense," snapped back Dame Betty. "That hen was bewitched I killed and cooked yesterday, as the eating of it has proved to the master. Never hen had such legs, or was so hard to kill; and, hark ye! I could not keep water in the pot," said Betty, mysteriously.

"Verily, this is a matter to be looked into. Thou thinkest the boy a witch?" And the Rev. Deodat Parker, uncomfortable from his disturbed night, was more willing to believe.

And so, I can hardly tell how, in a short time it was whispered around that little Jonathan Winthrop was a witch, and had bewitched the Rev. Deodat Parker's chickens.

One day Dame Betty walked into the minister's study, and said, "Master, come and see for thyself."

So the minister called his good wife, and the three took their station behind a closed blind. And there, sure enough, was Master Jonathan astride the fence, waving his hands in the air, in what seemed to them some dreadful incantation, while on the ground four old hens and one miserable rooster were bobbing and squawking like things bewitched.

Now, unfortunately, the minister and his good wife and old Betty could not see the strings in Jonathan's hands, and so immediately believed him a true witch.

"Deodat, it must be seen to," said Goodwife Parker.

"Yes, I will go at once for a magistrate." And the old gentleman hurried off with unseemly haste, and returned in a short time with two magistrates and a brother clergyman, all considerably out of breath as they took their station behind the blind to see the wonderful manifestations.

And Jonathan was at it yet. Owing to the chickens being so hard to catch, he prolonged the fun when he did catch them. As the solemn magistrates peeped out, Jonathan gave a jerk to his threads that made the poor fowls fly toward him, fluttering and squawking like mad; and as he let the thread out again they ran away with all their might, only to be twitched back by their tormentor, who laughed until he cried at their antics.

The two magistrates and brother clergyman were old, as nearly all men in office were in those days, and their eyes saw no strings either. So they had a long talk, and decided Jonathan had best be arrested and tried, lest he should bewitch people next.

But on that day little Deliverance Parker, the minister's granddaughter, who lived out beyond the town, came to make a visit at her grandfather's, and she was told by Dame Betty that she must not play with Jonathan Winthrop as she used to do, for he was a witch, and had bewitched their chickens. And then Dame Betty showed her, as she had many others, from behind the blinds, Jonathan as he was plaguing the poor fowls.

Now little Deliverance had sharp eyes, saw the strings plainly, and took in the trouble at once; but Betty was so set and stupid she could not convince her, and they would not let her tell Jonathan of his danger.

Fortunately matters came to a crisis that afternoon. The magistrates had been waiting for Jonathan's father to come home; but as he was kept so long at Salem, they took matters in their own hands, and brought Jonathan before quite an assembly in the minister's study.

The poor boy was so frightened at all the stern faces before him that he didn't know what to say to the charge, and grew so confused and flustered, they believed him guilty at once.

But little Deliverance waited until the magistrates had finished talking, and then walked straight before them, and began to speak.

"Verily, he is no witch. He only ties strings to the corn that the poor fowls eat, and by the aid of the strings pulls them about."

"Thou art mistaken, little one; we saw no strings," said the magistrates.

"Yes, but there were;" and little Deliverance was so positive, and by that time Jonathan had found his tongue, and both children explained the affair so clearly, that the old magistrates looked rather foolish, and dismissed the case with a reprimand to Jonathan for wasting his time so foolishly. But some good came of the boy's prank after all. For his father, seeing how near Jonathan came being proved a witch, bestirred himself in favor of poor School-master Halleck, who was set free from prison in consequence.

[Begun in No. 19 of Harper's Young People, March 9.]

ACROSS THE OCEAN; OR, A BOY'S FIRST VOYAGE.

A True Story.

BY J. O. DAVIDSON.

Chapter XII.

THE "HEATHEN CHINEE" AT HOME.

THE first sight of China—that region of marvel and mystery, where everything seems exactly opposite to what one sees at home, and the fashions of three thousand years ago are supreme as ever—is a great event in any one's life. So thought Frank Austin, who was on the watch for the Chinese coast long before it came in sight, although the run from Singapore was an unusually quick one; for the *Arizona* exerted all her speed to "get in for a cargo" before a rival steamer, which had kept close to her all the way, coming so near at times that the respective officers could exchange a little good-humored "chaff" through their speaking-trumpets.

But our hero got a glimpse of the "Celestials" sooner than he expected. For the last two or three days of the voyage the sea was literally covered with Chinese junks, large and small, many of them strongly manned, and armed with cannon, to guard against the countless pirates of the "China seas." At every moment it seemed as if the *Arizona* must run some of them down; but just as the crash was about to come, the junk would veer, and slide nimbly away. When several of them came by together, the barking of dogs, crowing of roosters, and shouts of children made Frank *feel* quite as if he were in a town instead of on the open sea. So steadily do the "trade-winds" (here called "monsoons") blow from one quarter, that these junks, starting at the same time every year, often make a whole voyage without shifting sail at all.

Frank was delighted with the picturesque sight, and overwhelmed Herrick with questions, that the old tar answered readily enough.

"That's right, lad," he would say; "keep your eyes open, and when you don't know a thing, never be ashamed to ask. That's the way to git on—you see if it ain't! Why, there's that feller Monkey, now: 'stead o' lookin' about him when we were at Singapore, I found him fast asleep in the shadder o' the quarter-boat, never knowin' whether he was in Malacca or Massachusetts! If you'd been one o' *that* sort, 'stead o' bein' supercargo, you'd ha' been shovellin' coal down thar yet."

A CHINESE TRADING FLEET SAILING WITH THE MONSOON.

For some time past Frank had noticed a curious change in one of the men, who, after showing himself a brave and able seaman in the earlier part of the voyage, had suddenly, without any apparent reason, become so gloomy and miserable that his mates nicknamed him "Dick Calamity." The surgeon, though finding no sign of actual illness about the man, had pronounced him quite unfit for duty, and thenceforth the poor fellow would sit for hours looking moodily over the side, with a weary, hopeless expression, which, as Herrick truly said, "made a man's heart ache to look at."

One evening there was some music on the after-deck (there being several good musicians among the lady passengers who had come aboard at Singapore), and Frank, with some of the officers, stood by to listen. As the last notes of "Home, Sweet Home" died away, Austin's quick ear caught a smothered sob behind him. Following the sound, he discovered poor Dick crouching under the lee of one of the boats, and crying like a child.

Frank spoke to him kindly, but for some time could get nothing from him but sobs and tears. At last, however, the whole story came out. The man was homesick.

"I want to be home agin!" he groaned, "and I don't care to live if I can't. If I could just git one glimpse o' my little farm yonder among the Vermont hills, it 'ud be worth every cent I've got."

"But you'll soon be home now, you know," said Frank, cheerily. "We're close to Hong-Kong, and you can get a passage home from there whenever you like."

Dick only shook his head mournfully; but after a time he seemed to grow quieter, and went below. His mates—who had long since left off making fun of him, and now did all they could to cheer him up—helped him into his bunk, and recommended him to go to sleep.

The next morning an unusual bustle on the forecastle attracted Frank's attention, and he went forward to ask what was the matter.

"Poor Dick's gone and killed hisself,"* answered one of the men, sadly. "I was al'ays afeard that 'ud be the end of it."

It was too true. An hour later the poor fellow's body, sewn up in a hammock, and weighted with a heavy shot, was plunged into the sea; and Herrick, drawing his rough hand across his eyes, muttered, "*That's* what comes o' goin' to sea when you ain't fit for it."

On the seventh day of the voyage the Chinese coast was seen stretching like a thin gray cloud along the horizon. Presently the mountains began to outline themselves against the sky, and as the vessel drew nearer, the huge dark precipices and smooth green slopes grew plainer and plainer, while in the background towered the great blue mass of Victoria Peak, at the foot of which lies Hong-Kong.

* A fact.

CHINESE FISHING FLEET OFF CANTON.

Frank was not a little puzzled by a number of strange-looking brown objects that lay close inshore, tumbling and bobbing about like porpoises. But as the steamer approached, they turned out to be Chinese "sampans" and fishing-boats, hard at work. Some had white sails criss-crossed with strips of bamboo, others huge brown sails of woven matting, like bats' wings; and altogether—what with the brightly painted boats, the queer faces and gestures of the pigtailed fishermen, the barking of the big dogs which seemed to act as sentries, the glittering scales of the fish that came pouring out of the nets, and lay flapping on the deck, the general bustle and activity—it was a sight well worth seeing.

Over the after-part of each boat was an awning of straw or matting, under which the fisherman's family could be seen at work upon their morning meal of rice and fish, flipping it into their mouths with long knitting-needles, which Herrick said were the famous Chinese "chopsticks." They hardly took the trouble to look round at the steamer as she passed, seeming to care very little whether she happened to run them down or not.

And now larger junks began to appear, together with not a few foreign vessels, which seemed to start out of the solid mountain, for as yet no opening was to be seen. But all at once the *Arizona* made a sharp turn to port, around the elbow of a huge headland, and there, through a gap in the cliffs, appeared the beautiful harbor of Hong-Kong, right ahead.

"Dutch Gap, by hoe-cake!" cried a tall Virginian, with a joyful grin.

"Ah! don't I jist wish it was!" muttered another, who was beginning to feel a touch of poor Dick Calamity's complaint.

Gliding past the pretty little islet that sentinels the entrance, the *Arizona* ran in and dropped anchor, while the rival steamer, came slowly up behind her.

[TO BE CONTINUED.]

THE STORY OF A WINGED TRAMP.

BY FLETCHER READE.

TRAMPS, you think, are a modern invention, and a very disagreeable one, too; but if you had chanced to live so long ago as when the earth was young, you would know that the institution is a very old and honorable one.

You would have heard, too, in that far-off golden age, of the winged tramp—a beautiful youth who spent his life in travelling from place to place, sometimes on the earth, sometimes in the air, walking or flying as the humor seized him: a merry fellow withal, and the very Prince of the wandering brotherhood.

He was, indeed, a true Prince, for his father, Zeus, was King of Olympia, and his mother, Maia, was descended from the Titans, an ancient and royal family.

Instead of living in the grand Olympian palace, however, Maia preferred to remain in her own home—a beautiful grotto on the hill Kyllene, and it was here that the young Prince Hermes was born.

Even then babies were wonderful beings, as they are now, and always must be; but of all astonishing and precocious infants Hermes was certainly the most remarkable.

Cuddled and wrapped in his cradle, and six hours old by the sun, he leaped to his feet, and ran swiftly across the hard, uneven floor of Maia's cave.

Just outside the door he spied a tortoise.

"Aha, my fine fellow!" said this wonderful baby, "you are just the person I wished to see."

The tortoise was so taken by surprise that he could not find a word to say, and by the time he had made up his mind that the best thing for him to do was to get out of the way, there was nothing left of him to get away with, for the baby Prince had thrust out his eyes, and had converted his shell into a lyre.

Hermes smiled as he held it between his hands, and then,

her baby wore on his feet a curious pair of sandals, on each of which grew tiny wings.

She turned quickly to clasp him in her hands, for she knew by the sign of the winged shoes that he would soon fly away from the little grotto of Kyllene.

But Hermes sprang out of her reach, and laughed gayly as she chased him about the cave, hardly stopping to turn his head as he bounded past her, and out into the open air, carrying his lyre in his hand, and wearing on his head a funny little hat, on which were two wings like those upon his shoes.

Faster and faster he flew, now floating on the wind like a swallow, now bounding over the earth, and now rising just above the tops of the highest trees.

This was the little tramp's first journey, and his errand, I am sorry to say, was a very wicked and mischievous one; for no sooner did he see the cows of Prince Apollo feeding in the pastures of Pieria than he decided to steal a couple of them for his breakfast, and to let the rest stray away. Having accomplished this piece of mischief, he went back to his cradle, gliding through the open door as swiftly and softly as the summer wind.

Phœbus Apollo soon discovered what had happened, and started off in pursuit of the robber; but Hermes was by this time fast asleep.

"What! I steal your cows!" he exclaimed, rubbing his eyes, as Apollo stood at the door of Maia's cave. "I beg your pardon, but I do not even know what a cow is."

Then he laughed to himself, and hid his face under the clothes; but Apollo was not to be deceived, and Hermes was compelled to leave the pleasant grotto, and appear before Zeus to answer for his crime.

Still the little tramp denied the theft. "No, no," he said, "I never stole a cow in my life. I do not know a cow from a goat. I, indeed!" And the boy turned on his heel, laughing as he spoke.

"Hermes," said Zeus at length, from his royal throne, "it is useless for you to try longer to deceive us. Return the cows, make up the quarrel, and Apollo will forgive the theft."

Hermes saw that his secret was discovered, and confessed his fault as gayly as he had before denied it.

Prince Apollo was still somewhat out of humor, but as the boy led him back along the sandy shores of Pieria, he told such pleasant stories and sang such bewitching songs that the angry Prince began to smile, and at last declared that the music was worth the loss of a hundred cows.

Hermes, who was as generous as he was mischievous, immediately made Apollo a present of his lyre, and Apollo, not to be outdone, gave him in return a magic wand. This wand, which was so cunningly carved that it looked like two serpents twining around a slender rod, was called a caduceus, and Hermes carried it with him in all his wanderings.

After Apollo and Hermes had exchanged presents, they swore eternal friendship to each other; and then, having pointed out the place where the cows were hid, Hermes hurried back to Olympus.

Having once tasted the delights of travel, he could not endure the thought of a quiet humdrum life in the little cave at Kyllene, and he besought the King to send him on some foreign mission.

Zeus, pleased with the boy's adventurous spirit, appointed him his special Ambassador.

Light of foot and light of heart was the bright-haired messenger of the gods, the very merriest tramp that ever walked, or flew, or ran.

Sometimes he showed to travellers the road they had lost, and sometimes he led them far out of the way, stealing their purses, and then laughing at their tears.

On one occasion, having found Zeus in great distress because the Queen had determined to kill Io, a lovely young girl of whom the King was very fond, he declared that he alone would save her.

Zeus at first changed Io into a heifer, but the Queen discovered the secret, and sent Argus, a monster with a hundred eyes, to watch her.

It seemed impossible that the lovely Io could escape, and the poor old King was in despair.

"Trust me," said the cheerful Hermes, "I will manage the matter."

Swifter than a cloud that flies before the wind, he glided through the air until he reached the spot where the monster lay in wait for Io.

With one touch of his wand Hermes put the beast to sleep, and before he had time to wink even one of his hundred eyes Argus was dead.

It would take too long to tell of all the wonderful deeds which Hermes, the "Argus slayer," the messenger of the gods, performed.

Wherever he went he was greeted with prayers and songs and gifts, for although he sometimes wrought more harm than good, the winged tramp was always a welcome visitor both to gods and men.

[Begun in HARPER'S YOUNG PEOPLE No. 94, April 13.]

THE STORY OF GEORGE WASHINGTON.

BY EDWARD CARY.

CHAPTER VII.

"GENERAL" WASHINGTON was now "President" Washington. The man was the same, but the work he had to do was very different. And then it was all new. My readers have not yet got so used to doing things that they do not know that it is a great deal harder to do anything the first time than it is the second or the third.

Washington was not only the first President, but the whole government, in which he had so great a part, was a strange thing. No one understood exactly how it was going to work, and a great many people in each State were afraid of it. They thought that the President would have too much power, and that he would get to be as bad as a King after a while, and the people hated Kings bitterly in those days.

Some very earnest but not very just writers went so far as to say that the country had only got rid of George the Third (who was King of England), to set up in his place "George the First" (meaning Washington), and they said the change was like the one the frogs made from "King Log" to "King Stork."

What this meant you may find in *Æsop's Fables*. And I must say that our first President was a good deal more like a King in his manners and his notions than our Presidents are nowadays. Perhaps he was more so than he would be if he were President now.

He was a proud man—not a vain one, but proud of his office; and he wanted people to show their respect for his office by the manner in which they treated him. He dressed very richly, and had his wife dress richly too. He rode to and from the Capital in a coach with four horses, and sometimes even six, handsomely clad. He put his servants in a sort of uniform, like the "livery" which nobles' servants wear. He gave grand parties, where he and Mrs. Washington received their guests from a slightly raised platform, called a "dais."

On every occasion where he appeared as President of the United States he insisted that things should go on in a certain order, and with as much display as possible. But in his private life and conduct he was as simple and modest as any one could be.

In his public work Washington chose some of the best and ablest men in the country to help him. He called Alexander Hamilton from New York to take care of money matters, with the title of Secretary of the Treasury. Hamilton was an officer on Washington's staff during the Revolution, and had led the Americans over the British redoubts in the last fight at Yorktown. Washington knew him to be as honest and skillful as he was brave, and relied on him greatly. Then he called Thomas Jefferson from Virginia—a very clear-headed man, with many bold ideas—to take charge of any business that might come up with other nations. His title was Secretary of State, and he had a great deal to do, for the governments of Europe had not yet learned to respect the rights of the United States, or to care much for this country in any way.

General Washington took up his residence in New York, where Congress was then meeting. The first thing he did was to lay out an order in which business should be done, in such a manner that nothing should be neglected, and things should not get confused. His plans were made after asking advice from the chief men about him, for, great man as he was, he was always ready to take the counsel of others.

Nothing is more striking in reading Washington's letters than this habit of asking advice. It certainly did not come from any lack of courage, for when he had once made up his mind, he was very firm in carrying out his plans. And when he had to do so, he could act very quickly and wisely without advice, and during the war he frequently did what he thought best against the advice of his generals.

[TO BE CONTINUED.]

HOW TO MAKE AN AVIARY.

BY A. H. M.

ONE of the charms of having a good garden is the opportunity it affords for keeping different pets, caged or at liberty; and those who are fond of birds can find no easier way of watching their habits than by keeping them in an out-door aviary, such as any bright boy with a love for carpentering, and a few good tools, can build for himself.

There are certain rules and facts connected with carpentry to be borne in mind and acted upon: Buy only the best tools, and keep them *sharp*; keep your tools, when not in use, well out of the reach of little children, who would be glad to use your chisels, if not to dig out refractory tin tacks, at least as screw-drivers.

In doing any out-door work, such as a fern frame, dove's house, or what not, never put together any part of it inside the shop until you have ascertained that such portion will somehow get through the doorway. This remark brings us back to the aviary, and its general size.

If it is to be about seven feet square, the frame of each side can be set up in-doors; if larger than that, each piece of wood, when prepared, will have to be taken out, and the various parts joined together near where the aviary is to stand.

The materials we require consist merely of ordinary deal rafters, two inches square, and a good number of deal boards, five-eighths of an inch thick, planed on one side, with rebate and groove already cut—all of which may be obtained of any timber-merchant.

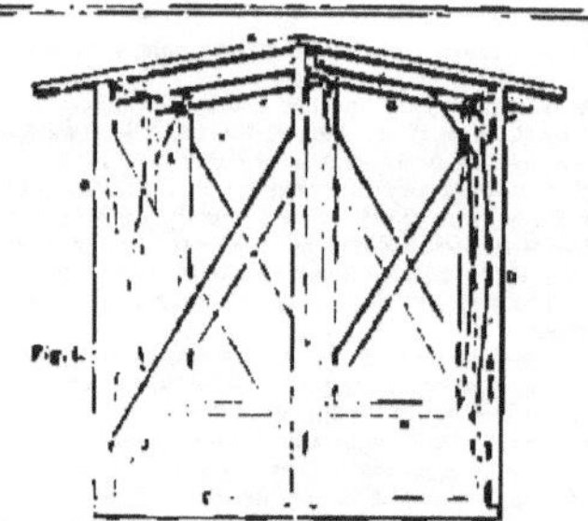
Fig. 1.

First, the frame of one side, as before stated, is put together, A B C D (Fig. 1), then that of the opposite side, E F G H, the various corners being mortised into one another (Fig. 2). Then the remaining parts of the frame having been got ready piece by piece, the whole may be set up. The two iron stays between each couple of upright rafters must on no account be omitted; nor yet the galvanized iron squares, similar to those used by shopkeepers to support their window-shelves, which will be found most useful to strengthen the angles.

Now get the mason to come with his cement and some bricks, and build up on the selected site a level foundation for the house to rest on, spreading a layer of cement along the top of the upper course of bricks, to which the base of the frame-work (which must be lifted on to it while it is moist) will adhere. Then, to give additional stability, and lessen the risk of the house being lifted or shifted by a gale (for, being open in front and sides, it will offer, like the inside of an open umbrella, far greater resistance to the wind than would be the case if glazed as a greenhouse is), an inner line of bricks is next cemented against the side of the bottom rafters all round, and flush with their surface, as seen at Fig. 3. Lastly, when the floor has been paved with bricks, the mason's job is finished.

Now comes the roof. This is made to play out widely for two purposes: to give our aviary a somewhat ornamental appearance, and also to carry the drip well clear of the walls and wire netting. First of all, the boards, B (Fig. 4), must be nailed on, planed surface downward, to form a smooth ceiling; then the whole is covered with strips of stout canvas, A, overlapping one another. The ends of the canvas are fastened tightly under the eaves, and the exposed selvedge of one strip, with the selvedge of the next beneath, is properly tacked to the wood. Finally the top piece, C, and the narrow strips of wood, B (Fig. 5), being securely nailed on over the canvas, the roof is complete; and when painted with *light* lead-color, it will be perfectly water-proof, and have the appearance, without the weight, of a real leaden covering.

There remain the sides to be walled up. The boards

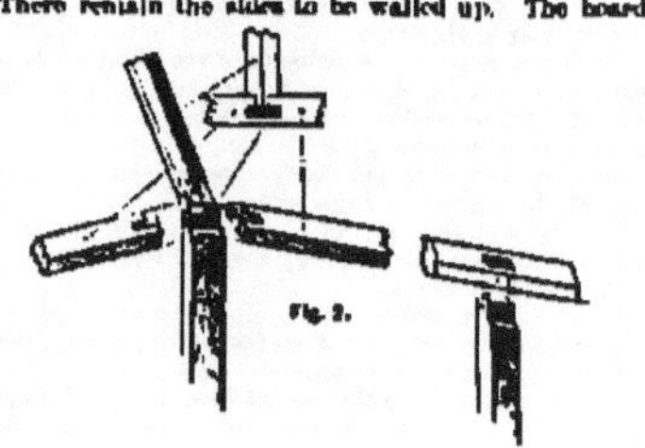
Fig. 2.

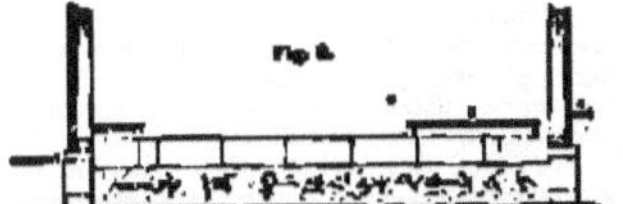

for these can now be nailed on from the bottom upward, with the exception of the pieces H H (Fig. 6), which must be left over until the wire netting has been attached to the upright pillars. A window two feet square, of a single pane of strong glass, well bedded in putty, to give more light to the interior, without extra draught, and with wire netting over the glass on the inside, is placed at the back, where also is seen the door, capacious enough for a person to get in and clean out the aviary when required; for which purpose three feet by two feet will give sufficient room. But we do not want the bother of unfastening this big door, and stooping down to the floor, every time we put in the saucers of food, besides running the risk of allowing some of

Fig. 4.

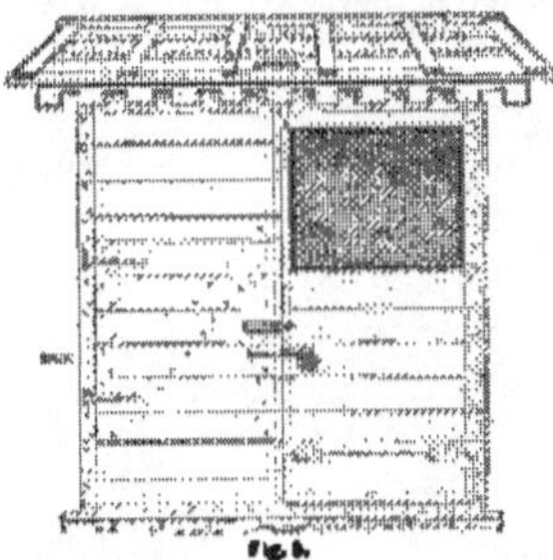

Fig. 5.

the birds to fly out during the operation; so we construct another one, much smaller, at the side (Fig. 7), at about the height of one's elbow when standing by it. Two brackets fixed to the door serve to keep it in a horizontal position when open, thus forming a table on which to place and fill the saucers with seed and bread

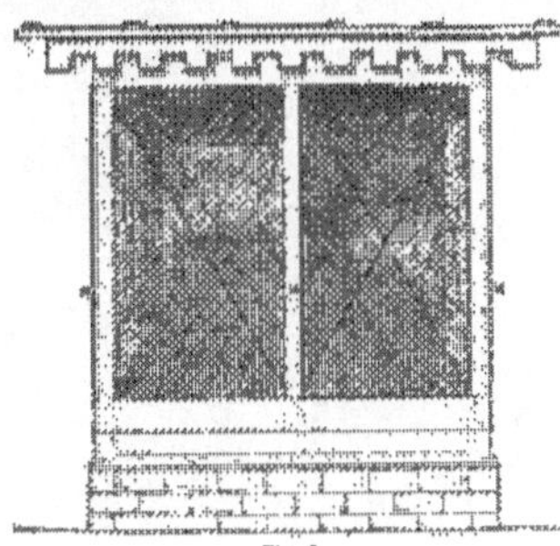

Fig. 6.

and milk, before transferring them to the wooden tray at the same level inside. Another little door, fourteen inches by four inches, with the bottom of it flush with the brick floor, A (Fig. 8), and a spring like that of a mouse-trap attached to the hinges to make it shut, will be large enough to admit a zinc trough one foot square, two inches deep, which will contain abundance of water to give all the birds a good bath daily.

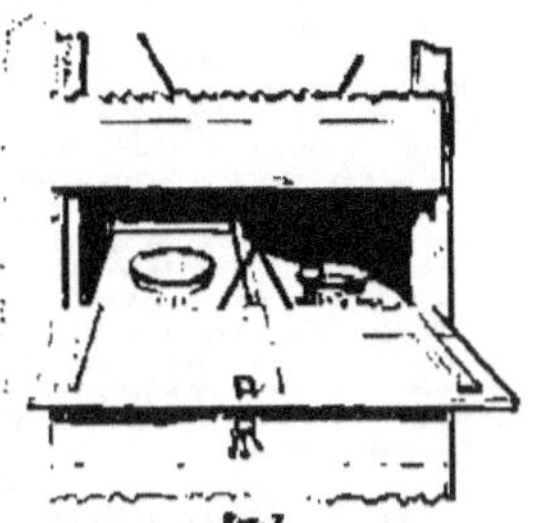

Fig. 7.

Two coats of lead-color painted over the whole outside wood-work, two coats of dark green over that and over the wire netting, three coats of light lead-color over the outside of the roof, with three coats of white paint over the walls and roof inside, will complete the work of the house itself.

The arrangement of perches and nesting-places may be left to the reader's judgment. The goldfinches will want some slender twigs close to the roof, and a swinging perch, such as in Fig. 9, as they love to get up as high as possible, and look down contemptuously on everybody else. The canaries will like another swing (Fig. 10) suspended from a stout perch above by a small swivel and chain, and placed in the front near the wires, where they can be swung to and fro by the breeze. It is pretty to watch the canaries singing as they swing.

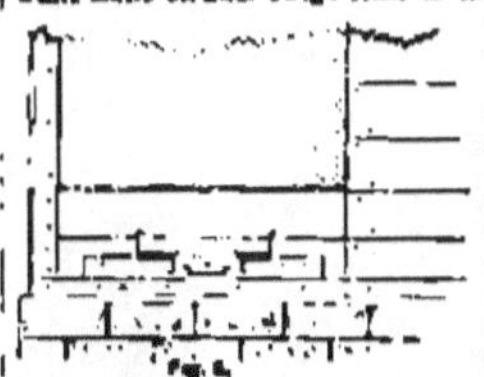

Fig. 8.

The site should be as sunny and sheltered as possible. If the front of the house can face south, and there be a hedge or spreading shrub on the eastern side, the birds will have nothing to complain of from spring to autumn.

By the first of November place a covering of thick warm felt over the whole roof, tacking it to the narrow slips above the canvas, so that a space is left between the boards and the felt, the warmth of a *double* roof is imparted to the interior, and the birds are made all snug and comfortable. This covering, together with a wooden shutter fitting closely over the top half of the netting on the weather side, may be removed again in March.

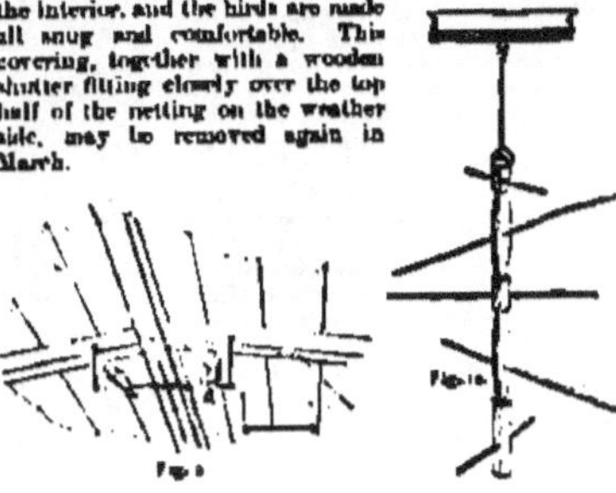

Fig. 9

Fig. 10.

One word more. It may happen that at feeding or cleaning-out time a cock bullfinch, or some valued bird, will slip out and escape. Nothing whatever will be gained by exclaiming, "What a pity!" nor would it be wise to chase the fugitive from bush to bush, because to pursue would merely frighten it farther afield. But if left alone, it will probably be too much astonished at the novelty of its freedom to think of flying at first farther than the nearest thick shrub. So, having noticed where it has flown to, we must fetch the trap-cage without losing a moment, put in a hen from the aviary as call-bird, a few grains of hemp as bait, stand the cage on a box, or anything else, close to the bush, and watch from some point out of sight. In less than ten minutes we shall most likely have caught the truant safely once more.

THE ERMINE.

THE silky white fur which forms the ornament of many a royal robe is the skin of the ermine—a graceful and saucy member of the weasel tribe. The ermine is found in all Northern countries. In the summer it is a reddish-brown creature, but no sooner does the reign of winter begin than it attires itself in purest white, with the exception of the tip of its tail, which is glossy jet black. It is thought by naturalists that the coat of the ermine changes color at the beginning of winter, but that the change in the spring is effected by shedding the white hairs, which are replaced by new ones of a brown tint.

The ermine (sometimes called stoat) is somewhat larger than the common weasel, but not unlike it in its habits. It lives in hollow trees and among rocks, wherever it can find a snug hiding-place. Although it often comes out to frolic in the sun, its hunting-time begins with the setting of the sun. Toward evening, when the shadows are rapidly lengthening across the clearings, the ermine may be seen issuing forth for its night campaign. Now it twists its lithe body like an eel in and out among the rocks and underbrush; now it stands for a moment motionless, peering about in search of a victim, its slender little body arched up in the middle like an enraged cat. It is always on the alert, whisking here and there, sniffing at every hole and corner where perchance some rat or rabbit may lie concealed.

Odd stories are told of the extreme boldness of the ermine, and some of them are no doubt true. A celebrated German hunter relates that, creeping through the forest in search of game, he came to the edge of a clearing, where he saw two ermine frolicking about on the ground. Seizing a stone, he threw it with such sure aim that one of the little creatures was knocked senseless, when, to his astonishment, the other, giving a loud cry, sprang at him, and running up his clothes with the rapidity of lightning, fastened its sharp teeth in the back of his neck. With the utmost difficulty he succeeded in freeing himself from the angry ermine, which bit his face and hands severely in the struggle.

The ermine is a cruel enemy of all small beasts, a despoiler of birds' nests, as it likes nothing better than a supper of fresh eggs, and a most heartless persecutor of the snow

grow conscious of their entire helplessness in the presence of this dangerous foe, and although they are swifter of foot, the bright, glittering eye of the ermine paralyzes them with terror; and should they attempt to fly, the ermine well understands the art of riding on the back of its victim, its sharp teeth fastened in its throat, until, exhausted and faint, the stricken hare is forced to succumb.

Even the powerful water-rat is no match for the ermine. It may spring into the pool by which it lives, and swim rapidly among the reeds; but the ermine, although its home is on land, is as good a swimmer as the rat, and fastening its teeth in its victim's throat, it drags it, helpless and dying, on shore.

In May or June the ermine seeks some soft, secluded corner, from whence it comes forth in a few days with five or six playful, tiny children. No pussy cat is a prouder, fonder mother than the ermine. It bestows the tenderest care and caresses on its little ones until they are three or four months old, and capable of shifting for themselves. Should danger threaten its children, the ermine will seize them all in its mouth, and fly to a place of safety; even if compelled to swim a deep river to escape capture, it will carry its babies safely over.

The fur of the ermine is very much valued. The species which inhabit Siberia and the most northern countries of Europe are the most sought after by traders, as the intense cold of those regions blanches the fur to silvery whiteness. These creatures are usually caught in traps, and specimens are sometimes kept by the trappers as pets. A Swedish gentleman relates his experience with one that was captured about Christmas-time, when its beautiful silky coat was of the purest white, with the exception of the pretty black tip on its tail.

It was first placed by its owner in a large room, where it soon made itself completely at home. It would run up the curtains like a mouse, twist itself into the smallest corners, and at length, one day, when it had been invisible for several hours, it was discovered snugly curled up in an unused stove funnel, its beautiful coat smeared with rust and soot.

When its cage was ready, the ermine, after being placed in it, developed an extraordinary temper. It would dash about, climbing on the wire, and uttering a loud hissing cry, as if protesting against confinement. When it went to sleep, it would curl up in a ring, twisting its little tail around its nose. It was fed with milk, which it drank eagerly, with hens' eggs, the contents of which it sucked, and with small birds, which it ate, leaving nothing but the feathers.

A large brown rat was one day put into the cage alive. At first the ermine curled in a corner, and allowed the rat to drink its milk, and range about the floor. But the daring rat approached too near the lord of the domain. With one quick spring the ermine was on the back of its antagonist, its long teeth buried in its throat. A terrible battle ensued, the rat several times freeing itself from the ermine, which returned again and again, until at length the rat was stretched lifeless and bleeding on the floor of the cage. The ermine then devoured it, leaving nothing but the head, skin, and tail, thus thoroughly disproving the assertion that the whole weasel family only suck the blood of their victims.

In our illustration the ermine is represented in deadly contest with a large brown rat (*Mus decumanus*), called the Norway rat in England, although the species is said to be unknown in the country after which it is named. This rat is supposed to have been brought into Europe from Asia early in the eighteenth century, and about one hundred years ago it made its way to America. The Germans call it the migratory rat, because, starting from its native place in the far East, it has made itself at home in nearly every country. It is one of the boldest and most destructive of its tribe, and a dreadful nuisance wherever it goes.

"FOR MAMMA'S SAKE"

A STORY OF NED AND HIS DOG.

BY MARY D. BRINE.

THERE was no mistake about it. Ned and his mother were very poor, and decidedly uncomfortable. Ned was so tired of living in one little room, where all day long mamma sat by the window and sewed till the daylight faded away; and sometimes, too, both he and mamma went to bed rather hungry, and when the little boy used to pat his mother's thin cheeks lovingly, after a sweet baby fashion he had, he could often feel the tears in her eyes, when it was too dark for *his* bright blue eyes to look upon her face. There was a cunning little dog, Fido, Ned's only playmate, which also lived with them in that small room, and his chief occupation was the constant wagging of a very bushy tail, and a readiness to accept the slightest invitation for a frolic from his small master.

As for *Fido's* meals, he had grown so used to circumstances that I don't believe he even remembered the taste of a good juicy bone such as he used to have in Ned's old home before the days of poverty came. Never mind what brought about a change of circumstances in the family, but the change had come sadly enough, and Ned and mamma had only the memory of the times gone by to comfort them. Fido had been a puppy in those days—they were only two years back, after all—and if dogs can remember, no doubt this doggie longed for the green fields and sunny lanes in the pretty country town where he and Ned ran races together, and never were hungry. The little boy was only six years old then, and now, on the day before my story begins, mamma had celebrated his eighth birthday by buying him a tiny sugar angel with gauze wings, which filled Ned with awe and delight. Eat it? No, not he! it was far too lovely for that; so he suspended the angelic toy by a string, and it soared above Ned's bed day and night, keeping sweet watch over all things.

But to Fido, the shaggy-haired, pug-nosed companion of his days, and sharer of his discomforts, Ned's heart clung with a love unbounded. He laughed, and Fido laughed, or, that is to say, Fido *barked*, which meant a laugh, of course. Ned cried, and Fido also wept, if a drooping of ears and tail, and a decided downcast expression of countenance, meant anything in the way of silent sympathy.

They were always together, and of the greatest comfort to one another, so that the "alley boys" (as they were called who lived by the tenement-house in which Ned lived) used to cry, jeeringly, whenever the little boy appeared for a breath of air, "How are you, Ned, and how is your dog?" or, to vary it occasionally, "How are you, doggie, and how is your Ned?"

I am telling this, so that my little readers can understand how hard it was for the little boy to do what he did, after a time, for mamma's sake.

It came about in this way. One afternoon late, when Mrs. Clarke had gone to carry home some work, and Ned and Fido were having a regular frolic on the floor, there came knocking at the door a Mrs. Malone, who collected the rent due from the several lodgers in the miserable building. With a frown on her face, when informed that Mrs. Clarke was out, the woman had bidden the boy tell his mother that "she'd wait no longer for the rent due her, and Mrs. Clarke might look out for herself."

Ned had cowered before her threatening face, but Fido, far from feeling any fear, had boldly barked at the intruder until he had nearly shaken his bushy tail from his small body. That made Mrs. Malone angry; and meeting Mrs. Clarke on the stairs, she repeated her threat to the weary, tired woman, who presently entered the room in tears.

Ned soon learned that the man from whom his mother had obtained sewing had dismissed some of his workwomen, and Mrs. Clarke amongst them; and now indeed there seemed distress before them. The boy was too young to fully comprehend all his dear mother's woes, but his loving heart grew sad and thoughtful, and he stood mournfully by the window looking up into the sky, where he knew papa was so safely living. Poor little Fido sat silently beside his master, wondering what had happened to break up the frolic so suddenly; and altogether, while mamma prepared the simple supper, things were very quiet and sad.

"Have you got much money, mamma?" asked Ned at last.

His mother could not help smiling at the question so plaintively asked. "Enough for the rent, dear," she replied, trying to speak cheerily. "And to-morrow maybe I'll find some new work. Don't look so sad, my little Ned; we'll manage to get along in some way if we trust in the dear Father above. You know we must have courage, Ned, and not despair."

"But I can't be glad when you cry, mamma," said the boy; and straightway his soft cheek was laid against mamma's, and he comforted her with his kisses till she smiled again, and the tears were all dried.

The next day mamma went out early, leaving Ned and Fido to take care of the room. She little knew what plans had developed themselves in Ned's small head during the night, when the little fellow had been unable to sleep, and had tormented himself with wishing he was "a big boy, and could earn money for his poor mamma." No, indeed, she knew nothing of any plans on his part. So she had kissed his sweet lips, sighed to herself over his pale cheeks, and telling him that she would not be home until afternoon, and he would find luncheon for himself and Fido all fixed on the closet shelf, had gone out into the streets to look for work from store to store.

But Ned knew what he had to do before mamma's return, and no sooner had she gone than he brushed his curly head, made himself neat and clean, and lifted his Scotch cap from its peg behind the door. That was the signal for Fido to sit up on his hind-legs and beg, as Ned had long before taught him, when preparing for a race in the street; and now he not only begged, but thumped his bushy tail impatiently against the floor, saying, dog fashion, "Come, do hurry up." He didn't appear to notice that his little master's face was sober this morning, and that once two big tears gathered in the blue eyes which were usually such merry eyes, as a boy's should be.

And finally, after Ned had written, in a very scrawly hand, "Dear mamma, Fido and I are going to take a walk just a little while," and placed the queer little note where his mother would see it if she came home before him, the two friends went down the narrow stairs, and through the alley into the street which led toward the City Hall. Fido looked inquiringly into his master's face to see what could be the reason that he walked so quietly along this morning, instead of, as heretofore, racing and chasing his four-footed little comrade from block to block. But Ned was swallowing several lumps in his throat, and had no heart for a frolic.

It was not long before the City Hall Square was reached; and a little timidly, now that he was in so large and strange a place alone, Ned seated himself upon the broad stone lower step of the great building, and lifted Fido in his arms. Then he mustered courage, and cried, feebly, although he fancied his voice was very loud and brave: "Anybody want to buy a dog? Dog to sell. Want a dog?"

But nobody seemed to hear him, and the noise of the streets frightened our poor little fellow into silence for a while. So he buried his face in Fido's shaggy back, and tried not to cry.

"Oh, my doggie Fido!" he murmured, "you've truly got to be sold. Oh dear! it is awfully hard, and I'll 'most die without you. But you must be sold, 'cause mamma is so poor."

Fido wriggled about, and objected to being held in Ned's arms, when he wanted to frisk about on the broad pavement; and so he whined and snarled a little, and even ventured a growl—something very rare with gentle Fido. But Ned did not dare let him go, and so held the tighter, until doggie tried the persuasive powers of his little tongue, and kissed his master's hand over and over again.

Then pretty soon a policeman came by, and eyed Ned severely. That was a terrible scare for the youngster, and he said, eagerly, "Please, sir, I ain't doing anything. I'm only waiting to sell my dog, 'cause my mother's so poor."

The burly guardian of the peace laughed and went his way, and Ned breathed freely again. But somebody had chanced to hear his words—a boy of ten or twelve years—and he came near to look at the dog in Ned's arms.

"Will you buy him, boy?" asked Ned, earnestly. "I'll sell him *real cheap*; and, you see, I must take mamma some money to-day."

The boy was ready enough to make the purchase, but though he turned his pockets inside out, he could not rake and scrape from them more than the sum of one dollar.

"Here's all I've got," he said. "My grandpa gives me lots of money; but it's all spent but this, and you won't sell him for a dollar, I suppose?"

Ned's eyes sparkled. "Oh yes, I will, too," he replied. "Oh yes, indeed. A dollar is a hundred cents, and I never had so many cents in my life, boy. You may take him now. Only let me kiss him good-by, please."

His voice faltered a little toward the last, as he hugged the dog tightly to his heart, and the tears streamed presently from his brave eyes, in spite of all the winking and blinking to keep them back.

"Oh, my Fido! my own little doggie!" was all he could say, while the dog wagged his tail, and wondered what the fuss was about.

"There, now you'll have to go," Ned said at last, smothering one more sob, and loosening his arms. "Take him, boy, please, quick as you can."

The boy promised to be very kind and good to Fido, and attempted to lift him from Ned's knee. But to this Fido would not agree, expressing his dislike of the new and extraordinary arrangement, which he couldn't comprehend, by a growl and short bark.

Ned apologized. "You see, I've had him an awful long time, ever since I was a *little* fellow, and I s'pose he don't want to leave me."

So the new master tied a string to Fido's collar, and Ned said, gravely, "Now, Fido, you smile and look pleasant, like a good dog;" and then the two old friends parted, Fido whining and tugging to break his string, and Ned wiping his eyes on his jacket sleeve as he hurried toward his lonely home.

He reached it just after mamma had come in, and his little note was in her hand. With a choking sob, he sprang into her arms, and thrust the dollar—small silver piece—into her hand. "Take it, mamma—oh, take it quick!" he cried, and then came the explanation concerning his morning's work. It was told with many tears and sobs, in which mamma was not ashamed to join, as she folded her brave little son in her arms.

For her sake he had parted with his one loved treasure, and his reward was great when she kissed and called him her comfort and little helper. But she did not let him know how almost useless his sacrifice had been, since the dollar would go but a small way toward the relief of their necessities. Oh no, she let him feel happy in the thought that he "*had* helped dear mamma," and the thought went far toward softening the grief of parting with his pet.

So days went by, until one morning Mrs. Clarke decided to answer in person an advertisement that called for "A Housekeeper," and took her son with her, lest he should miss more than ever his old companion and playfellow.

The house to which they were directed was a large, handsome house, having beside the door a small gilt sign bearing the name of Dr. ——. A spruce black servant admitted them, and presently the doctor entered the room. Satisfactory arrangements were made, the gentleman not objecting to Ned, whose plaintive little face strangely attracted him. And with a heart full of joy and gratitude Mrs. Clarke rose to take her leave, until she could return and enter upon her duties. But a boy came whistling through the hall, and presently—oh, the joy of it!—what should rush, with a scamper and joyous bark, pell-mell upon little Ned, but his own Fido! Such a shout of gladness! and Ned sat fairly upon the floor, and hugged his dog again and again, while the boy—none other than the doctor's grandson—explained to the bewildered old gentleman that "this was the boy who had sold him the dog."

So now, you see, it all turned out happily, and henceforth Fido had *two* masters, both of whom he served, although I think the largest part of his canine heart was given to the old and first master.

And as for Ned, once in a while he asked mamma this question—not because it hadn't been answered over and over, but because it kept suggesting itself to his heart—"Oh, mamma, isn't it the funniest thing?"

And the reply was always, "Yes, Ned, it really is."

A TINY SEED.

One May morning two green leaves
  Peeping from the ground
Polly and her brother Will
  In their garden found.
They a seed had planted there
  Just ten days ago,
Only half believing that
  It would ever grow.

"Oh, it's growed! it's growed!" they cried,
  "And it soon will be,"
Will proclaimed, now full of faith,
  "Like a little tree:
There will lady-slippers come,
  And they'll all be ours.
Oh, how good God is to turn
  Brown seeds into flowers!"

JAPANESE WINE-FLOWERS.

BY WILLIAM ELLIOT GRIFFIS.

ON both sides of the great wide street leading to Asakusa, in old Yedo, were shops full of toys of all kinds. At certain seasons of the year booths were hastily put up, and stocked with the curiosities of the season. For a few days before New-Year's one could buy ferns, lobsters, oranges, evergreens, and rice-straw festoons. In the second month appeared seeds, roots, bulbs, and gardeners' tools. Dolls and girls' toys came on in the third month, ready for the Feast of Dolls. Images of heroes, banners, toy horses, and boys' playthings, for the Feast of Flags, were out in the fifth month. Bamboo and streamers, in the seventh month, celebrated the meeting of the star-lovers. Chrysanthemums in autumn, and camellias in winter, could be bought, all having their special use and meaning. Thus throughout the different months Asakusa was gay with new things of all colors, and bustling with ten thousand people of all ages. Besides the shops and booths, a constant street fair was held by people whose counter was the pavement, and whose stock in trade, spread out on the street, must run the risk of dust, rain, and the accidents from passers-by.

Among these jolly peddlers was one Umé, a little rosy-cheeked maid of twelve years, who sold wine-flowers.

"Wine-flowers; what are they?"

If we open the boxes or paper bags sold by Umé, we see a pack of what seem to be tiny colored jackstraws or fine shavings. They are made by cutting out very thin slices of pith in the shape of men, women, birds, flowers, fishes, hats, tortoises, tools, and many other things. These are gummed, folded up, and pinched tightly, until each one looks like nothing but a shred of linen or a tiny chip of frayed wood. If you drop one of them into a bowl of hot water, it will open and unfold like a flower. They blossom slowly in cold water, but hot water makes them jump up and open at once.

Umé's blind grandfather and her mother made these wine-flowers for a living, and she went out daily and sat on the Asakusa street to sell them.

Sometimes they made "shell-surprises."

Out of a hard paste made from moss they cut the shapes of roses, camellias, lilies, daisies, etc., of real size, which they painted to a natural color. Then folding them in a ball, and squeezing them into a cockle-shell, they were ready for sale. They looked just like common white shells; but when dropped into hot water they opened at once, and the ball of gum inside, rising to the surface, blossomed into a flower of true size and tint.

"But why are they called wine-flowers?"

The reason is this. The Japanese drink their "wine" (saké or rice beer) hot, and in tiny cups about the size of a small half orange. When one friend is about to offer the cup to another, he drops one of these pith chips on the surface of the wine. It blossoms instantly before their eyes, and is the "flower of friendship."

The artist Ozawa has sketched the inside of a home in Japan, where the children are merrily enjoying the game of surprises. A Japanese mother has bought a few boxes of the pith toys from Umé. They have a lacquered tub half full of warm water. Every few minutes the fat-cheeked servant-girl brings in a fresh steaming kettleful to keep it hot. They all kneel on the matting, and it being summer, they are in bare feet, which they like. The elder one of the two little girls, named O-Kin (Little Gold), has a box already half empty.

"Guess what this one is," says she to her little brother Koso, who sits in the centre.

"It's a lily, or a pot of flowers—I know it is," cries Koso; "I know it, because it's a long one."

O-Kin drops it. It flutters like a feather in the air, then it touches the water, squirms a moment, jumps about as if alive, unfolds, and instead of a long-stemmed flower, it is a young lady carrying a lantern, all dressed for an evening call. "Ha! ha! ha!" laugh they all.

"You didn't guess it.—You try," said O-Kin, to O-Haya (Little Wave), her sister; "it's a short one."

"I think it's either a drum or a tai" (red fish), said O-Haya, looking eagerly.

It opened slowly, and a bright red fish floated to the top and swam for a second. Its eye, mouth, and tail were perfect. "I guessed it," said O-Haya, clapping her hands.

"Look, mamma," cried Koso, to his mother, "here are two heavenly rats (bats), but they can't fly; two of Fuji Mountain; two musumé (young ladies), a maple leaf, a plum blossom, a 'love-bird,' a cherry blossom, a paper swallow, and a kiku (chrysanthemum flower). They have all opened beautifully."

A GAME OF SURPRISES.

Then mamma dropped in a few from her box. They were longer and finer than O-Kin's, and as they unfolded, the children screamed with delight. A man in a boat, with a pole and line, was catching a fish; a rice mortar floated alongside a wine-cup; the Mikado's crest bumped the Tycoon's; a tortoise swam; a stork unfolded its wings; a candle, a fan, a gourd, an axe, a frog, a rat, a sprig of bamboo, and pots full of many-colored flowers sprung open before their eyes. By this time the water was tinged with several colors, chiefly red.

After the fun was over, the children carefully picked out the spent tricks with a flat bit of bamboo, and spread them to dry on a sheet of white paper; but they never could be used again.

Sometimes only flower tricks are used, and then the blossoms open in all colors, until the water contains a real floating garden or "water bouquet."

DANDELION.

BY AMY ELLA BLANCHARD.

"GOLDEN-HEAD, Golden-head,
The sun must have kissed you."
"So he did," said Golden-head,
"Just before he went to bed."

"Golden-head, you're a white head;
The frost must have nipped you."
"No; he would not be so bold;
I am only growing old."

"Puffy-ball, Puffy-ball,
Where's the wind taking you?
I'm afraid another day
You will all be blown away."

The only rules for taming birds, squirrels, or any other little creatures, are those consisting of patience, perseverance, and kindness.

There is really nothing known of the history of the mound-builders and cliff-dwellers, who were early inhabitants of our country. Their mounds and their dwellings remain, but they are silent monuments of an extinct people.

sible reason for such action is the great prevalence of counterfeits intended to defraud the government.

FRANK A.—An answer to your question respecting barbers' poles is given in Post-office Box No. 29. The blue is often added to the red and white by barbers in the United States for a very obvious reason.—For answer to your other question, see Post-office Box No. 12.

"BOB."—If the chest you inquire about was to be opened four hundred years after the death of the famous sculptor, the time has not yet arrived, as he died about 1563, only a little more than three hundred years ago.

DAVID H. M.—The specimen you send appears like common gravel mixed with fibres of last year's leaves. The white glistening bits are quartz. If there were any shells, they were broken past recognition before reaching us.

PUZZLES FROM YOUNG CONTRIBUTORS.

No. 1.

[illegible] PUZZLE.

Parts by which things are held. Checks for work. A rag. A sign. A [illegible]. A pile of [illegible]. Parts of a [illegible]. Centrals read downward spell a [illegible]. E. D.

No. 2.

[illegible]

My first is in [illegible], but not in [illegible].
My second is in [illegible], but not in sleep.
My third is in [illegible], but not in Cork.
My fourth is in [illegible], but not in [illegible].
My fifth is in [illegible], but not in [illegible].
My sixth is in [illegible], but not in [illegible].
My seventh is in [illegible], but not in [illegible].
My whole is a city in Germany. W. R.

No. 3.

GEOGRAPHICAL [illegible].

A cape in Africa. A mountain in Asia. A river in [illegible]. A cape in Spain. Mountains in the United States. Answer—Primals spell the name of a city, and finals the country in which it is situated. [illegible]

No. 4.

WORD SQUARE.

First, [illegible]. Second, a [illegible] plant. Third, a [illegible]. Fourth, a period of time. W. G. M.

No. 5.

[illegible]

(Each sentence spells one word.)

1. My [illegible]. 2. [illegible]. 3. No [illegible] in [illegible]. 4. [illegible]. 5. A war [illegible]. 6. I mean that rules. C. P. T.

No. 6.

[illegible]

My first is in bread, but not in [illegible].
My second is in [illegible], but not in [illegible].
My third is in [illegible], but not in [illegible].
My fourth is in [illegible], but not in [illegible].
My fifth is in [illegible], but not in [illegible].
My whole was a [illegible] long years ago. JAMES.

ANSWERS TO PUZZLES IN NO. 27.

No. 1. [illegible]

No. 2. [illegible]

No. 3. [illegible]

No. 4. [illegible]

No. 5. [illegible]

No. 6. [illegible]

Martin Luther.

Favors are acknowledged from [illegible].

Correct answers to puzzles are received from [illegible], George W. Raymond, Frank Hayward, "Zouzou," M. S. Brigham, May F. Willard, Mary L. Maclean, [illegible], "North Star," and "Little Lizzie," Lillie F., Alice E. Doyle, [illegible], John Larkin, [illegible], David H. Morford, Amy Dale, Harry P. Phillips, [illegible], J. W. Thompson, Alice Hammond, A. L. [illegible].

SPECIAL NOTICE.

OUR NEW ILLUSTRATED SERIAL.

In the next Number of HARPER'S YOUNG PEOPLE will be found the opening chapter of a new Serial Story, entitled

"THE MORAL PIRATES,"

written expressly for this paper by WILLIAM L. ALDEN, well known as the humorist of the *New York Times*. The story, which is full of amusing incidents and mishaps, describes the adventures of four boys during their summer vacation. Each Number will be illustrated from spirited original designs by A. B. FROST.

HARPER'S YOUNG PEOPLE

AS

A SCHOOL READER.

After an experience of fourteen and ten years, respectively, in teaching English reading, our success has reached high-water mark in using *Harper's Young People* as a school reader.

W. R. WEBB, } Principals of
J. M. WEBB, } Culleoka Institute,
Culleoka, Tenn.

My pupils are very much pleased with the *Young People*, and I find it ably assists in supplying them with reading matter, so necessary outside of their usual school-books. Such reading I have hitherto found difficult to procure, but I think *Harper's Young People* will prove very suitable for our purpose.

ELLEN MCCLEMENTS,
Sheboygan, Wis.

Please find enclosed a copy of the Resolution that the Board adopted this afternoon at my urgent request.

J. H. LEWIS, Supt. of Schools,
Hastings, Minn.

Resolved: "That *Harper's Young People* be and is hereby adopted by this Board as the text-book to be used for reading exercises in the intermediate grades of the public schools."

Please send 2 copies of your *Young People* for nine weeks, to my address. I am a teacher in a country school, near this city, and fully appreciate the advantages to be obtained from putting fresh reading matter constantly before my pupils.

CHAS. W. MOORE,
Minneapolis, Minn.

Please send me 100 copies of *Harper's Young People*, divided into 20 copies each of five different numbers. I want them for supplementary reading matter in the public schools.

EDWARD BURGESS, Supt. of Schools,
Poughkeepsie, N. Y.

Harper's Young People is quite popular here. Many of the schools read from it each week.

JOSEPH G. EDGERLY, Supt. of Schools,
Fitchburg, Mass.

I am delighted with my experiment in using *Harper's Young People* in my school in place of reading books. I get closer attention, and better reading in the class-room, as well as an increased interest in good reading matter outside of the school.

FRANK H. [illegible],
Carmel, N. Y.

I am a teacher in one of the public schools of this city. I take *Harper's Young People* to school with me, and my pupils enjoy it very much.

I have the oldest children in the building, and they can understand all of the pieces. I read them the articles as a reward for good behavior and well-learned lessons, and let them copy and work out the puzzles.

It would please you to see how anxiously they wait for each new issue, and how happy they are when it comes. * * * Permit me to congratulate you on the success your paper has achieved both here and abroad.

A TEACHER,
Buffalo, N. Y.

HAVING A GOOD TIME.

"HAVING a good time," are you?
  But, ah! what would mother say
If she knew of the two rogues rummaging
  In her bureau drawer to-day?
"Mamma's gone out," is that it?
  And nurse is "off duty" too?
And little mice, when the cat is away,
  Find mischief enough to do.

Well, little golden-haired burglars,
  What do you find for your pains?
Some garments folded so neatly away,
  And mamma's jewel-case are your gains.
You look at the jewels before you
  With innocent, joyous surprise:
But the jewels *I* like are your own precious selves,
  And like gems are your merry blue eyes.

But hark! I knew nurse would wonder
  What mischief you two were about:
"When those children are quiet," I once heard her say,
  "Some mischief I'm sure to find out."
Oh, dear little rogues, scamper quickly
  Away from temptation and fun;
Leave the jewels and drawer, ere your fingers
  Be guilty of harm yet undone.

THE PASHA PUZZLE.

HERE are two British gun-boats sailing up the Bosporus to rescue British subjects from brigands.

Here are three sea-gulls sailing over the British gun-boats.

Here are two Turkish cimeters to help the British gun-boats against the brigands.

Here are two Turkish bayonets to support the cimeters.

Here is a British shell ready to burst.

Here is a grim fortress on the banks of the Bosporus.

Now how are you going to make Hobart Pasha out of all this?

THE STREETS OF CANTON.

THEY are very narrow and dirty, to the first place, with an average width of from three to five feet. They are paved with long, narrow slabs of stone. Their names are often both devotional and poetical. We saw Peace Street, and the street of Benevolence and Love. Another, by some violent wrench of the imagination, was called the street of Refreshing Breezes. Some contented mind had given a name to the street of Early Bestowed Blessings. The paternal sentiment, so sacred to the Chinamen, found expression in the street of One Hundred Grandsons and street of One Thousand Grandsons. There was the street of a Thousand Beatitudes, which, let us pray, were enjoyed by its founder. There were streets consecrated to Everlasting Love, to a Thousandfold Peace, to Ninefold Brightness, to Accumulated Blessings; while a practical soul, who knew the value of advertising, named his avenue the Market of Golden Profits.

Other streets are named after trades and avocations. There is Betelnut Street, where you can buy the betel-nut, of which we saw so much in Siam, and the Cocoanut, and Drink Tea. There is where the Chinese hats are sold, and where you can buy the finery of a mandarin for a few shillings. There is Eyeglass Street, where the compass is sold; and if you choose to buy a compass, there is no harm in remembering that we owe the invention of that subtle instrument to China. Another street is given to the manufacture of bows and arrows; another to Prussian blue; a third to the preparation of furs.

The shops have signs in Chinese characters, gold letters on a red and black ground, which are hung in front, a foot or two from the wall, and droop before you as you pass under them.

One of the annoyances of the streets is the passage through them of mandarins in their palanquins, surrounded by guards, who strike the foot-passengers with their whips if they do not get out of the way quickly enough.

THE INTERRUPTED RIDE.

Vol. I.—No. 31. PUBLISHED BY HARPER & BROTHERS, NEW YORK. PRICE FOUR CENTS.

Tuesday, June 1, 1880. $1.50 per Year, in Advance.

THE MORAL PIRATES EXAMINE THEIR CRAFT.

THE MORAL PIRATES.

BY WM. L. ALDEN.

CHAPTER I.

"THE truth is, John," said Mr. Wilson to his brother, "I am troubled about my boy. Here it is the first of July, and he can't go back to school until the middle of September. He will be idle all that time, and I'm afraid he'll get into mischief. Now the other day I found him reading a wretched story about pirates. Why should a son of mine care to read about pirates?"

"Because he's a boy. All boys like piratical stories. I know, when I was a boy, I thought that if I could be either a pirate or a stage-driver I should be perfectly happy. Of course you don't want Harry to read rubbish; but it doesn't follow, because a boy reads stories about piracy, that he wants to commit murder and robbery. I didn't want to kill anybody: I wanted to be a moral and benevolent pirate. But here comes Harry across the lawn. What will you give me if I will find something for him to do this summer that will make him forget all about piracy?"

"I only wish you would. Tell me what your plan is."

"Come here a minute, Harry," said Uncle John. "Now own up: do you like books about pirates?"

"Well, yes, uncle, I do."

"So did I when I was your age. I thought it would be the best fun in the world to be a Red Revenger of the Seas."

"Wouldn't it, though!" exclaimed Harry. "I don't mean

it would be fun to kill people, and to steal watches, but to have a schooner of your own, and go cruising everywhere, and have storms and—and—hurricanes, you know."

"Why shouldn't you do it this summer?" asked Uncle John. "If you want to cruise in a craft of your own, you shall do it; that is, if your father doesn't object. A schooner would be a little too big for a boy of thirteen, but you and two or three other fellows might make a splendid cruise in a row-boat. You could have a mast and sail, and you could take provisions and things, and cruise from Harlem all the way up into the lakes in the Northern woods. It would be all the same as piracy, except that you would not be committing crimes, and making innocent people wretched."

"Uncle John, it would be just gorgeous! We'd have a gun, and a lot of fishing-lines, and we could live on fish and bears. There's bears in the woods, you know."

"You won't find many bears, I'm afraid; but you would have to take a gun, and you might possibly find a wild-cat or two. Who is there that would go with you?"

"Oh, there's Tom Schuyler, and Joe and Jim Sharpe; and there's Sam McGrath—though he'd be quarrelling all the time. Maybe Charley Smith's father would let him go. He is a first-rate fellow. You'd ought to see him play base-ball once!"

"Three boys besides yourself would be enough. If you have too many, there will be too much risk of quarrelling. There is one thing you must be sure of—no boy must go who can't swim."

"Oh, all the fellows can swim, except Bill Town. He was pretty near drowned last summer. He'd been bragging about what a stunning swimmer he was, and the boys believed him; so one day one of the fellows shoved him off the float, where we go in swimming at our school, and he thought he was dead for sure. The water was only up to his neck, but he couldn't swim a stroke."

"Well, if you can get three good fellows to go with you—boys that you know are not young scamps, but are the kind of boys that your father would be willing to have you associate with—I'll give you a boat and a tent, and you shall have a better cruise than any pirate ever had; for no real pirate ever found any fun in being a thief and a murderer. You go and see Tom and the Sharpe boys, and tell them about it. I'll see about the boat as soon as you have chosen your crew."

"You are quite sure that your plan is a good one?" asked Mr. Wilson, as the boy vanished, with sparkling eyes, to search for his comrades. "Isn't it very risky to let the boys go off by themselves in a boat? Won't they get drowned?"

"There is always more or less danger in boating," replied Uncle John; "but the boys can swim; and they can not learn prudence and self-reliance without running some risks. Yes, it is a good plan, I am sure. It will give them plenty of exercise in the open air, and will teach them to like manly, honest sports. You see that the reason Harry likes piratical stories is his natural love of adventure. I venture to predict that if their cruise turns out well, those four boys will think stories of pirates are stupid as well as silly."

So the matter was decided. Harry found that Tom Schuyler and the Sharpe boys were delighted with the plan, and Uncle John soon obtained the consent of Mr. Schuyler and Mr. Sharpe. The boys immediately began to make preparations for the cruise; and Uncle John bought a row-boat, and employed a boat-builder to make such alterations as were necessary to fit it for service.

The boat was what is called a Whitehall row-boat. She was seventeen feet long, and rowed very easily, and she carried a small mast with a spritsail. By Uncle John's orders an air-tight box, made of tin, was fitted into each end of the boat, so that, even if she were to be filled with water, the air in the tin boxes would float her. She was painted white outside, with a narrow blue streak, and dark brown inside. Harry named her the *Whitewing*; and his mother made a beautiful silk signal for her, which was to be carried at the sprit when under sail, and on a small staff at the bow of the boat at other times. For oars there were two pairs of light seven-foot sculls, and a pair of ten-foot oars, each of which was to be pulled by a single boy. The rudder was fitted with a yoke and a pair of lines, and the sail was of new and very light canvas. On one side of the boat was a little locker, made to hold a gun; and on the other side were places for fishing-rods and fishing-tackle. When she was brought around to Harlem, and Harry saw her for the first time, he was so overjoyed that he turned two or three hand-springs, bringing up during the last one against a post—an exploit which nearly broke his shin, and induced his uncle to remark that he would never rise to distinction as a Moral Pirate unless he could give up turning hand-springs while on duty.

Harry could row very fairly, for he belonged to a boat club at school. It was not very much of a club; but then the club boat was not very much of a boat, being a small, flat-bottomed skiff, which leaked so badly that she could not be kept afloat unless one boy kept constantly at work bailing. However, Harry learned to row in her, and he now found this knowledge very useful. He was anxious to start on the cruise immediately, but his uncle insisted that the crew must first be trained. "I must teach you to sail, and you must teach your crew to row," said Uncle John. "The Department will never consent to let a boat go on a cruise unless her commander and her crew know their duty."

"What's the Department?" asked Harry.

"The Navy Department in the United States service has the whole charge of the navy, and sends vessels where it pleases. Now I consider that I represent a Department of Moral Piracy, and I therefore superintend the fitting out of the *Whitewing*. You can't expect moral piracy to flourish unless you respect the Department, and obey its orders."

"All right, uncle," replied Harry. "Of course the Department furnishes stores and everything else for a cruise, doesn't it?"

"I suppose it must," said his uncle, laughing. "I didn't think of that when I proposed to become a Department."

The boys met every day at Harlem, and practiced rowing. Uncle John taught them how to sail the boat, by letting them take her out under sail when there was very little breeze, while he kept close alongside in another boat very much like the *Whitewing*. Harry sat in the stern-sheets, holding the yoke lines. Tom Schuyler, who was fourteen years old, and a boy of more than usual prudence, sat on the nearest thwart, and held the sheet, which passed under a cleat without being made fast to it, in his hand. Next came Jim Sharpe, whose business it was to unship the mast when the captain should order sail to be taken in; and on the forward thwart sat Joe Sharpe, who was not quite twelve, and who kept the boat-hook within reach, so as to use it on coming to shore. The boys kept the same positions when rowing, Tom Schuyler being the stroke. Uncle John told them that if every one always had the same seat, and had a particular duty assigned to him, it would prevent confusion and dispute, and greatly increase the safety of the vessel and crew.

It was not long before Harry could sail the boat nicely, and the others, by attending closely to Uncle John's lessons, learned almost as much as their young captain. So far as boat-sailing can be taught in fair weather, Harry was carefully and thoroughly taught in six or seven lessons, and could handle the *Whitewing* beautifully; but the ability to judge of the weather, to tell when it is going to blow, and how the wind will probably shift, can, of course, be learned only by actual experience.

[TO BE CONTINUED.]

KENSINGTON CLOVER.

BY MARCIA B. BRADBURY.

Such a hubbub in the meadow!
Such a rustling in the grass!
"I feel injured," sighed the daisy,
"Things have come to such a pass.
To be worked in colored worsted,
Ev'ry shade and line complete,
Isn't very compliment'ry
To a stylish marguerite."

"One might call it," said the poppy,
In a tone of sleepy fun,
"Flowers raised by cross culture—
Only, please, excuse the pun."
"Oh, don't joke on such a subject,"
Said an innocent, rather low,
While from sev'ral other quarters
Came a disapproving "No."

"Really," laughed a sweet red clover,
"I flushed up quite nervously
When I saw a head on canvas
So exceedingly like me.
If the honey-bee had been there,
He'd have buzzed about that leaf.
Ah! I only wish he had been;
'Twould have served him right—the thief!"

Suddenly through all this chatter
Came a voice, like music's flow,
From a little yellow violet
Growing in the marsh below.
All the flowers nodded silence
As she said—a little pause—
"What a foolish fuss, my field-mates,
You have made with no real cause!

"Are they fragrant? Can you smell them?
Though they are so bright and fair.
Do the breezes, when they touch them,
Carry incense on the air?
When they fade, will hidden blossoms
Take the places of those dead?
Shooting stems and growing leaflets
Crown the drooping plant instead?"
And the others, well contented,
When the violet's song was o'er,
Tossed their pretty heads and said they
Wouldn't worry any more.

A TREE ALBUM.

MANY of our boys and girls, we venture to say, would like to know how to make a collection of specimens illustrating the trees of their own neighborhood and of other parts of the country. We hardly need remind them that the only way to get a complete knowledge and to enjoy the beauty of natural objects is to examine them closely, and find out all their little peculiarities. We may take long walks through the groves and woods, and spend a great deal of time there, and yet when we get home we may know very little about them. We might remember that we had seen a great many trees, but not be able to tell of what kinds they were, how their branches and leaves were shaped, how tall they were, or anything about them.

Now such knowledge is very pleasant to have, and will afford a great deal of pure enjoyment. The more we know about the beautiful trees, the more we will value them, and find entertainment in admiring them.

It is a good plan to bring home from our rambles small portions of them, so that we can examine them minutely at our leisure. The bark, the leaves, and the blossoms are the most important; they are what we look at to recognize a tree, and we should have specimens of each. The first necessary step is to find some way of arranging and preserving them. A good method is to get some pasteboard or stout paper, and cut it into sheets of convenient size—say eight inches long and five wide. Then a box will be needed to keep them in, so that they will not get lost or soiled. Give one sheet to each tree, and upon it paste a piece of the bark, a leaf, and a blossom. The bark should not be taken from the tree where it is too coarse and clumsy, but where it is nearly smooth and perfect, and gives the best idea of the tree; nor should too thin a piece be taken, as when it gets dry it may wrinkle up and crumble to pieces. It may be well to take off with the bark a thin layer of the wood to stiffen it and keep it smooth. A piece of bark about three inches long and two wide would be of a good size.

The blossoms will have to be pressed and dried before they are attached to the sheet. Take care to lay them so as to show the face and the inside parts as plainly as possible. It may be well in some cases to press two or more blossoms, laying them in different positions, so that every part can be seen.

The leaves will be easy, as they are mostly flat. If they are small, several may be taken, or a little twig. If the under side of the leaf is very different from the upper, or is remarkable for its hairs, or for any reason, one leaf should be placed with the under side upward. Care should be taken to do the pasting neatly, so that the sheet will look pretty, and the parts can be readily examined by the eye alone, or with a magnifying-glass or microscope, which reveals many interesting facts that can not be discovered by the eye unassisted.

In this way the trees can be studied at any time, even in winter, when the world outside is bare and dreary, and the evenings are long, and afford fine opportunity for such amusement. And what is more important still, the sheets prepared as we have shown can be sent through the mail to distant parts of the land, where the trees displayed on them do not grow, and are wholly unknown.

Thus our young readers, scattered over the United States and Canada and elsewhere, can supply each other with specimens, so that each may make up a collection from the trees growing over a very wide area.

Most trees are very long lived, and some are still living that are known to be hundreds of years old. Certain kinds of wood, too, seem almost incapable of decay if protected from the weather.

Probably the oldest timber in the world which has been used by man is that found in the ancient temples of Egypt, in connection with the stone-work, which is known to be at least four thousand years old. This, the only wood used in the construction of the temple, is in the form of ties, holding the end of one stone to another. When two blocks were laid in place, an excavation about an inch deep was made in each block, into which a tie shaped like an hour-glass was driven.

The ties appear to have been of the tamarisk or shittim wood, of which the ark was constructed—a sacred tree in ancient Egypt, and now very rarely found in the valley of the Nile. The dovetailed ties are just as sound now as on the day of their insertion. Although fuel is extremely scarce in the country, these bits of wood are not large enough to make it an object with the Arabs to heave off layer after layer to obtain them. Had they been of bronze, half the old temples would have been destroyed years ago.

If those among our young friends who are alive to the charms of nature will arrange some specimens of trees on the plan we have explained, and label the sheets with the common names of the trees, and the scientific names also, if they can find them out from their parents, we will be glad to hear from them, and will publish their letters in the Post-office Box, so that they can make exchanges with each other.

Very little folks, who may find it too hard to get the bark and the blossoms, can begin by making collections simply of the leaves. Be careful to cut the sheets exactly of the size we have mentioned, so that when laid together they will make a nice even pile like a book. And, remember, don't send them to us; only write, and let the Post-office Box know when you have them ready for exchange. We will publish the fact in the Young People, so that you can send the specimens to each other, and make up the collections among yourselves.

[Begun in No. [illegible] of Harper's Young People, March [illegible].]

ACROSS THE OCEAN; OR, A BOY'S FIRST VOYAGE.

A True Story.

BY J. O. DAVIDSON.

Chapter XIII.

FRANK GETS PROMOTED.

FRANK AUSTIN'S duties as supercargo were soon over, and he decided to go ashore and look about him. The moment he was seen looking over the side, a clamor arose from the Chinese boats around the steamer, which reminded him of the chorus of monkeys and parrots at Gibraltar.

"Good boatee, my—no upset!"

"Fast sampan—no can catchee!"

"He good, my better!"

"Come see—here allee best sampan!"

Frank was confounded by the uproar, and not less so by observing that all the boatmen, and boat-women too (for there were plenty of the latter), seemed to be exactly alike, so that if he picked one, and happened to lose him, it would be no joke to find him again. As he stood hesitating, a good-looking Chinese girl hailed him from a neat little boat with a staring red eye painted on either side of its bow.

"Hi! say! My name Whampoa Sam; washee, keepee state-room, row boat—can do all for two bits fifty cents. Come tly!"

Such a list of accomplishments was not to be resisted, and Austin at once took his seat under the stern awning. The young woman spread her sail, and turned the boat shoreward, steering it with an immense oar.

Away they went, past huge high-pooped junks that looked like monster rocking-chairs; past stately English steamers, beside which the little painted sampans seemed mere toys; past big clumsy rice barges, and trim gigs pulled by sturdy Western sailors. While threading her way through this maze of shipping as dexterously as any seaman, the girl found time to answer Frank's eager questions upon all that he saw, down to the staring eyes on the bow of her boat, which, as she explained, were meant to "help boatee see go straight, allee same man's eye." The mystery of her masculine name, which had puzzled Austin not a little, was also cleared up.

"My Whampoa Sam *wife*; Sam up Canton side now—can catchee more pieece dollar there. My row boatee till come back. Work boatee, my, allee same man. Chop! you no b'lieve? Bime-by pickaninny Sam row boatee too, muchee ploper. Look see!"

She pushed aside a plank, and hauled out of a box underneath it a little round-faced "four-year-old," so like a big doll that Frank almost took him for one, till he saw the child grasp the steering oar in his little pudgy hands, and actually steer the boat to shore.

"Well," thought our hero, "the Chinese may well be good boatmen, if they begin as early as that."

But he afterward learned that on the great Chinese rivers thousands of families live altogether in boats, each of which has an allotted place of its own. In Canton alone these floating streets have a population of 300,000, and it is common to see two-year-old children toddling about with small wooden buoys on their backs, fixed there by their careful mothers in case they should fall overboard, which they do, on an average, three or four times a day.

For several hundred feet around the great stone quay extended a perfect army of Chinese boats, clustering together like bees; but Mrs. Sam soon made her way through them, and Austin leaped ashore. He had hardly done so when a crowd of sturdy natives surrounded him, with ear-piercing screams, asking if he wished to "ride in chair." This being a new idea, he accepted at once, and presently found himself being carried off in a sedan-chair by four sinewy fellows, who went at a

A CLIPPER-SHIP LOADING WITH TEA AT HONG-KONG.

LITTLE WHAMPOA STEERS THE BOAT TO SHORE.

long swinging trot, like the "palanquin bamals" of British India.

Six more runners were speedily added, for the way now led up a street made entirely of stairs, like the "Hundred-and-one Steps" at Constantinople. Then out into the open country, and away toward the summit of Victoria Peak. Up, up, they went, poor Frank getting so bumped about that he was sorely tempted to get out and walk; but he reached the top at last, and saw the whole town, the harbor, and miles upon miles of the inland country outspread below him like a map. The trip, when paid for, proved wonderfully cheap, though the reason given for this made Frank feel rather "cheap" himself:

"Large piecee man, two bob; small piecee man, *like you*, one bob. All right—chin-chin!"

During his rambles through the town Austin saw many curious sights. He was shown through a native bank, where three Chinese "tellers" were standing ankle-deep in gold, and counting so rapidly that the ring of the coins sounded like one continuous chime. In another place a house was being built *from the roof downward*, and he was told that "rain come, walls muchee hurt, so put up roof first!"

Having now reached the farthest point of his voyage, Frank began to think about getting home again, and finding that all who had shipped on the *Arizona* were entitled, by the terms of their agreement, to a free passage in the next homeward-bound steamer, he went down to the company's office to get his ticket.

As he passed the open window a familiar voice from within caught his ear. It was that of his Captain, who was having a talk with the company's agent.

"I really don't know whom to send with this cargo," said the agent. "It *must* go in a day or two, and none of my clerks can be spared. Do you know of anybody, Gray?"

"Well, there's a young fellow who came out with me, that might do. He's rather young, certainly, but I put him in charge at Singapore, and he did very well. Hello! there he is. Austin!"

Frank entered, cap in hand.

"My lad," said the Captain, "we're sending a cargo of tin and opium to Canton, and you might take it up, unless you'd rather go home."

"I was thinking of going, sir," said Austin; "but if you have anything for me to do till I can get letters from home, I shall be very glad to do it."

"All right, my boy. Just look in here to-morrow morning, and we'll arrange it."

The next morning, sure enough, Frank received his appointment, and set sail up the river for Canton a few days later, with a handful of the *Arizona's* picked men for his crew, and old Herrick as his second in command—the latter remarking, with a grin, that "'twarn't a bad start for a youngster to begin his first v'y'ge as coal-heaver, and end it as Cap'n."

Our hero's farther adventures in China—how he succeeded so well with his first cargo as to be at once intrusted with a second—how he received letters from home, reporting all well—how he studied the ins and outs of the "up-country" trade, and the ways of the Chinese, finding both very different from what he had imagined—and how he soon got a good appointment in the office, which he held for several years—would make too long a story to be told here. But he always bore in mind the last words of old Herrick, which were:

"Frank, my son, next time you meet a young feller wantin' to run away to sea, jist you tell him you've tried it yourself, and 'tain't so nice as it looks. If a lad goes to sea 'cause he's fit for it, and ain't 'fraid o' *hard work*, well and good; but if he goes 'cause he's quarrelled with his bread and butter, all along o' stuffin' his head with dime novels and sich like rubbish, I guess he'll end where you began—in the coal-hole. Now don't you forget them words o' mine." And Frank never did.

THE END.

STREET OF STAIRS, HONG KONG.

SETTING THE BROOK TO WORK.

BY WILLIAM O. STODDARD.

THE brook had never done a stroke of work in its life.

So long, at least, as Mart Benson could remember, it had gurgled across the foot of his father's garden, tumbling heels over head down the little fall in the middle, as if it knew it had got into some place that didn't belong to it, and was in a desperate hurry to get out.

Then it made a dive under the fence, into Squire Spencer's orchard, and then under another fence, and through a low stone archway across the river road.

That was the end of the brook, for the river let it right in without so much as saying, "How do you do?"

"It isn't more'n two feet across anywhere," said Mart to himself. "It isn't so much as that just above the fall, and it's a foot and a half below the top of the bank. I could make a dam there, and a flume."

Mart was a great whittler.

Mr. Jellicombe, the carpenter, used to say of him that when he wasn't whittling, it was because he had had to stop to sharpen his knife.

"Well," said Mart, in reply to that, "what's the fun of whittling with a dull knife? If you want a knife to cut straight and smooth, you've got to have an edge on it."

So there was always a pretty good edge on his, and it was curious what things he managed to carve out with it.

He had made a wooden chain out of a long square stick that Mr. Jellicombe brought to the house to mend a door frame with. He had made kites, walking-sticks, bats, wooden spoons and forks, a little wagon, and any number of other things, of which about all that could be said was that they gave him plenty of good whittling.

But Mart had been to the mill the day before, and had waited there two hours while his father was having a grist of corn ground. All those two hours had been spent by Mart with a shingle in one hand and his knife in the other, but at the end of them there was hardly a notch in the shingle, and Mart shut up his knife, and put it back in his pocket.

He had been watching the great water-wheel and the flume that brought the water to it from the pond. He had studied the dam, too, and had been thinking of the brook in his father's garden.

The more he looked at it now, the clearer he saw that it was high time for that brook to be doing something.

It was easy enough to gather flat stones and pile them in at the narrow place at the top of the fall. That was little more than a foot high, to be sure, but the dam would more than double it.

Then he begged a couple of old raisin boxes at the store where his father traded, and when the ends were knocked out of them, and they were firmly set in the top of the little dam, one behind the other, they made a good enough flume. The end of the foremost one stuck out beyond the stones, and the water came pouring from it beautifully.

It took all the rest of that day for Mart to get the brook penned in and compelled to run through the raisin boxes, for he had to keep on putting stones and sods and dirt behind the dam to strengthen it, as the water rose higher and higher. It would not do to make a pond of the garden, but so long as the brook did not overflow its banks it would do no harm. Sometimes it had run over in the spring, or after very heavy rain-storms.

The next day Mart hardly went near his new dam, and he was a very serious and busy boy indeed, considering that he was only thirteen.

A piece of wood had to be found first two and a half inches square, and about a foot and a half long. It took a great deal of work to shave down the four corners of that piece of wood till it had eight smooth sides all just alike. Then Mart was compelled to go over to Jellicombe's carpenter shop and put his piece of wood in a vise, so it would be held steady, while he took a saw and sawed a long groove, more than half an inch deep, in the middle of each one of those eight faces. Jellicombe told him he had done that job very well.

"Looks like a hub for something. Going to make a wheel this time?"

"I'll show you. May I take your inch auger and bore a hole in each end?"

"Go ahead. If you ain't keerful, you'll split yer timber."

Mart was careful then, but he had trouble before him. He had picked out a number of very straight shingles, and he was whittling away on these now as if he was being paid for it. He cut them down to six inches long, and shaved them at the sides, so that two pieces laid together were just a foot wide. With a little more whittling after that he fitted them all, one by one, into the eight grooves in his "hub," and his "water-wheel" was done. A proud boy was Mart, but he ought to have kept on being "careful."

"Look out!" said Mr. Jellicombe, as Mart rapped hard on one of the shingle pieces, to drive it in more firmly; but it was too late.

"Crack!" the hub was split from end to end.

"Got to go to work and make a new one," said Mart, ruefully.

"Guess I wouldn't. Just take a couple of two-inch screws, and screw that together again. It'll be stronger'n it was before."

That was a capital idea, and it only took a few minutes to carry it into effect.

"Make your end pins of hard wood," said Mr. Jellicombe; "and shave 'em smooth. Then they'll run easy."

That was easy enough, but one of those "end pins" was made of an old broom handle, and was more than a foot long.

"I see what you're up to," said the carpenter, with a grin. "You've made a right down good job of it, too. Grease your journals before you let 'em get wet."

Mart's "journals" for his end pins to run in were two holes he bored in a couple of boards. When these were stuck up on each side of the lower end of his flume, and the water-wheel was set in its place, Mart took off his hat and shouted,

"Hurrah! the brook's at work!"

So it was, for it was rushing fiercely through the two old raisin boxes, and down upon the wide "paddles" of Mart's wheel, and this was spinning around at a tremendous rate.

"You've done it!"

"Is that you, Mr. Jellicombe? I didn't know you'd come."

"You've done it. Now what?"

"Why, I'm going to put another wheel on this long end pin, and set another one above it, and put a strap over both of them."

"Oh, that's it. Going to make a pulley and band. All right. It'll run. There's plenty of water-power. But what then? Going to build a mill?"

"Guess not. All I care for is, I've set the brook to work."

"Why don't you make it do something, then, now you've found out how?"

"Don't know of anything small enough for a brook like that."

"I'll tell you, then. There's your mother's big churn that goes with a crank. You whittle out a wheel twice as large as that, and set it a little stronger, and raise your dam a few inches, and you can run that churn."

"Hurrah! I'll do it!"

There was a good deal of busy whittling before Mart finished that second job, but before two weeks were over there was butter on Mrs. Benson's dinner table which had actually been churned by the brook at the bottom of the garden.

HOW THE SECRET WAS STOLEN.

BENJAMIN HUNTSMAN, a native of Lincolnshire, England, was the inventor of cast steel. The discovery was kept a great secret, and as the success it obtained was very great, many efforts were made to find out how it was prepared.

One cold winter's night, while the snow was falling in heavy flakes, and Huntsman's manufactory threw its red glare of light over the neighborhood, a person of the most abject appearance presented himself at the entrance, praying for permission to share the warmth and shelter which it afforded. The humane workmen found the appeal irresistible, and the apparent beggar was permitted to take up his quarters in a warm corner of the building.

A careful scrutiny would have discovered little real sleep in the drowsiness that seemed to overtake the stranger; for he eagerly watched every movement of the workmen while they went through the operations of the newly discovered process.

He observed, first of all, that bars of blistered steel were broken into small pieces, two or three inches in length, and placed in crucibles of fire-clay. When nearly full, a little green glass, broken into small fragments, was spread over the top, and the whole covered with a closely fitting cover. The crucibles were then placed in a furnace, and after a lapse of from three to four hours, during which the crucibles were examined from time to time, to see that the metal was thoroughly melted, the workmen lifted the crucible from its place on the furnace by means of tongs, and its molten contents, blazing, sparkling, and spurting, were poured into a mould of cast iron. When cool, the mould was unscrewed, and a bar of cast steel was presented.

The uninvited spectator of these operations effected his escape without detection, and before many months had passed the Huntsman manufactory was not the only one where cast steel was produced.

A JOLLY DAY IN THE PARK.

BY F. S. PRYATT.

"HIP, hip, hurrah! to-morrow's my birthday, Miss Eleanor," shouted Harry Lewis, bursting into my garden like a young hurricane. "Cousin Jack's coming over from New York, Nell's got a holiday, and father says if you'll decide and go with us, we may have a jollification somewhere."

"How delightful! Of course I'll go, with the greatest pleasure. Suppose we choose Prospect Park?"

"Capital! Miss Eleanor, good-by; excuse haste. I'm off to tell Nell, and hurry mother with the birthday cake and the fixin's."

Old Prob predicted fair weather, and he was as good as his word, for the sun shone in the bluest of skies, and the morning was fresh and breezy, when Nell and I stepped into an open car, followed by Harry, Jack, and the family lunch basket.

Every one looked happy, and even the car horses trotted briskly along the broad avenue to the Plaza as if they knew we were anxious to be there.

Arrived at the Park, the two boys put their wise heads together, and gallantly agreed that I should be captain of the party, a decision they shortly after announced in an important manner.

"Follow your leader, then," said I, helping Nell into one of the large phaetons standing near the entrance.

"All right," responded Harry, as the whip cracked, and away dashed the horses in fine style.

Now we swept past velvety fields and wood-crowned hills; now we rolled softly under arches of tremulous green; then through miniature valleys between blossoming heights; now through shadowy forests, and away again beside open meadows.

"How lovely!" cried Nell, rapturously, as one moment we caught the glitter of a distant lake, the next the twinkle of a reedy pool overhung with hazel and alder bushes.

Even the boys were stirred to delight, when, crossing a rustic bridge, they could look down and see a dashing cascade tumble and foam over mossy precipices, till it reached a stony basin below, where it lay golden and clear as a topaz.

On and on we sped, past new wonders of blossoming groves and ferny hollows, to the end of our ride.

Which way to turn, after we left our basket at the Lodge, we knew not. Labyrinthine walks met us in every direction, leading to bowers and dells and wildernesses innumerable.

"Let us take the nearest," said I; and away we went, tripping it gayly, till the path ended unexpectedly at the loveliest bower imaginable, all hidden with clambering vines and shrubbery, from which peeped out a thatched roof, with two odd little peaks, surrounded by bird-houses.

Past its pretty arches, as we sat on the rustic seats, we could look upon acres of velvety meadow, dotted with wild flowers, and gay with groups of pleasure-seekers.

Near by, Madam Nurse trundled Miss Baby; yonder, a company of girls played at "bean bags"; further on, the croquet-players were busy with mallets and balls; while passing to and fro were troops of school-children making the most of their weekly holiday.

"Listen!" cried Nell, suddenly, as sounds of music were borne to us on the breeze.

"It's 'Nancy Lee': go for it!" shouted Harry, leaping over the railing, and darting across the meadow.

"Come on; follow the sound, girls," cried Jack, bounding after him.

Nell and I take the path sedately, "hastening slowly," for we can not help stopping to listen to the soft twitter of the birds, to admire the golden laburnums; we even wait to let a sparrow hop leisurely down the walk before us.

We have had time to spare, for when we arrive in sight of the "merry-go-round" in its pretty pavilion, the musical history of Nancy Lee is still being repeated.

But a pretty vision greets us. Whirl, whirl, whirl, flies a magic ring of boys and girls, with their fluttering ribbons, bright eyes, and tossing curls.

Click, click, clash a score of shining blades, as the eager riders, with parted lips, lean forward and try to pick off the rings from a projecting bar.

Now the music begins to die away; the circle moves slower, and slower, and slower.

"Count your rings!" shouts the man in charge. "The biggest number wins the free ride."

"Sixteen, eighteen, twenty," calls out Harry, triumphantly, adding, as he spies Nellie, "There's my sister; give her a ride."

Nothing loath, Nell is strapped on a gray pony, and waits impatiently for the music. The seats fill, the organ sounds forth, "I'm called Little Buttercup," and away they float as light as feathers.

"It is well they're so merry," groans the poor horse beneath them in the cellar, as he treads his weary beat; "they'd find it a sad-go-round if we changed places."

The noon hour strikes; the merry-go-round man is mortal, and wants his dinner, which reminds us that it is time to send for the lunch basket.

Choosing a lovely spot under a spreading elm in the meadow, we lay the cloth, set out our luncheon, brew a pitcher of fine lemonade, and sit down, the merriest of merry parties.

In the midst of our entertainment four uninvited but welcome visitors make their appearance. Guess who they are.

A toad came first, and sat blinking at us with the funniest airs imaginable. Then a robin-redbreast and two sparrows edged their way up to our table with great

PROSPECT PARK, BROOKLYN.—DRAWN BY L. W. ATWATER.

"I could do that too," said Nell, imitating the movements of the skaters.

"You shall try," replied I; and a minute later we were inside the square, bargaining for a lesson on the odd three-wheeled triangular arrangement, with its horse's head and handled reins.

"Plant your feet firmly on this brace," said the instructor, showing Nell the iron bar; "hold the reins well in hand, bend your right knee, and strike out with your foot as if skating; now your left, and away you go."

Sure enough, off shot Nell, managing to keep up a tolerable speed, then slacking, then increasing, then coming to a dead halt, as Jack, shouting, "Clear the track!" bore down on her car, almost upsetting it.

"A miss is as good as a mile," screams Harry, flying by on the other side, with flushed cheeks and sparkling eyes.

"Strike out, little girl!" cries a lad, giving Nell's car a push, and sending her speeding along. In and out, around and about, they fly, like mimic charioteers, until, fairly exhausted, they are willing to stop, and go over to the Rotary Yacht, whose snow-white wings are visible from the hill-top.

A pleasant walk across the sloping meadow and along by the side of a small lake brings us to this novel boat, which is merely a great hollow ring of seats, with oars and rowlocks for calm, and sails for breezy, weather.

We step in and sit down; the wind, coming in soft puffs from the south, sends us floating around and around with a dreamy, restful motion that our tired little charioteers thoroughly appreciate as they lean back and trail their hands idly through the cool water.

caution, winked at us with bright eyes, concluded we were trustworthy, and ventured to peck at the crumbs we scattered for them.

Gathering up the remnants of our feast, we wended our way to a pretty summer-house overlooking a small lake, in which sported a multitude of gold-fish, a pair of swans, some geese, and a bevy of ducks with lovely rings of red, purple, and gold-green feathers about their necks.

Here Nell and the boys found fine sport throwing crackers into the water, and watching the ducks and fishes rush for them, but came away in high disgust because one old drake gave the ducks and fishes hardly any chance at all, but darted and dived and bobbed about so fast that he grabbed a dozen pieces to their one.

"Good-by, old greedy; hope you'll never come up again!" cried Jack, moving away, as the nimble fellow dove head-first till nothing but his funny tail flirted above the water.

A peep at the deer, pony-rides for the boys, and a drive in the goat-carriage for Nell, varied our ramble to the Aerial Skating Rink, which we found on the other side of the Park.

As we came in sight of the elevated square of asphalt pavement, with its gay cavalcade of skaters flitting to and fro inside the railings, the boys hurrahed with delight.

"It's perfectly glorious; let's try it," shouted Harry, bounding down the hill-side, followed closely by Jack.

"Come, come," said I at last, "wake up for our row on the lake, sleepers, and then heigho for home and supper!"

"I was only fooling, Miss Eleanor; I'm fresh as a lark," cried Harry, leaping nimbly out on the platform.

"So am I," said Jack, lending a hand to Nellie.

"The Rotary Yacht will do for a rest, but this is what I call life," exclaimed Harry, as later he and Jack, with even sweep of the oars, sent our pretty boat skimming over the waters of the lake.

Now we sped around curving shores, and past grassy capes; now we skirted fairy islands and reedy shallows; then under hollow bridges, that gave back jolly echoes to Nell's laughter and the dip of the oars.

"Quick, quick—quick, quick," screamed a bevy of ducks, hurrying to shore, as we rounded a woody bend in the lake, and came upon them with a rush that sent the water in diamond showers over their backs.

"Tirra-la, tirra-la," whistled a wood-thrush in the grove; "tirra-la, tirra-la," answered another.

"Ah! that's a warning, children; he sings at sunset. See the light shooting gold green through the trees; that means that our happy day is over. And there's another sign; look over your right shoulder—the new moon."

"Tu-whit, tu-whoo, good-night to you," hooted an owl, as we turned our boat homeward.

"Don't be alarmed; we are going," sighed Harry, half sad that the jolly day at Prospect Park was ended.

A BATTLE ON THE BUFFALO RANGE.

BETWEEN the half-breeds who form a large portion of the population of the settlements of the Northwest, along the Red River of the North, and their neighbors, the Sioux, exists a bitter enmity. Peace is seldom declared between them, and when parties of Sioux and half-breeds meet, bloody battles are the result.

Although the half-breeds are more civilized than the Indians, and live in villages, generally near the forts or trading posts, they depend largely upon buffalo-meat for their winter food, and upon buffalo-robes, for which the traders give them guns, powder, shot, blankets, tea, coffee, sugar, and other necessaries and luxuries of their life. To obtain this meat and these robes they organize grand buffalo hunts every summer and fall, each of which lasts for several months, and in which hundreds of men engage. The hunters travel from their homes to the distant hunting grounds on horseback; but they take with them long trains of very curious-looking ox-carts, in which the women and children, who go with their husbands and fathers on these long trips, ride, and in which the buffalo-meat and hides are carried home.

The ox-carts, or "Pembina buggies," as they are often called, are very strong and clumsy, and are made entirely of wood, generally by their owners. The wooden wheels, turning on the ungreased wooden axles, make the most horrible creaking and groaning; and when, as is often the case, several hundred or a thousand of these carts are in one train, the noise they make can be heard for miles.

Each cart is drawn by a single ox, attached to the rude shafts by a simple and home-made harness of rawhide, with the aid of which the patient beast draws a load of a thousand pounds for hundreds of miles, at the rate of twenty or thirty miles a day.

As they approach the buffalo range, where they expect to find their game, the hunters know that at any moment they may run across hunting parties of the Sioux, and for them they keep a sharp look-out night and day.

Some years ago a brave hunter by the name of Jean Bedell, whose home was in Pembina, joined one of these great hunting parties, taking with him his wife and their little child, a baby of but a few months old. The party to which Jean belonged was so large that they had but little fear of Indians, and did not guard against being surprised by them as carefully as usual.

One morning as the brigade broke camp, and the long line of carts moved slowly away toward Devil's Lake, which could be seen gleaming in the distance, and near which the hunters felt sure they would find buffalo, Jean Bedell found that a portion of his harness had given out, and he must stay behind and mend it. He had just finished his task, and started on after the carts, the groaning and screeching of which could still be heard in the distance, when other and more terrible sounds, borne clearly to his ear, caused him to come to a sudden halt.

The sounds that so startled him were quick shots, almost as steady as volleys of musketry, and the terrible yell with which the Sioux charges upon his enemy. Far down the valley the hunter could see sharp flashes of fire pierce the cloud of dust that hung over the train of ox-carts, and the dark mass of Sioux warriors charging down the hill-side, lashing their ponies, firing and yelling as they went.

Alone, and cut off from his companions, with his wife and baby to protect, Jean Bedell had nothing to do but lie down, with his trusty rifle in hand, powder and bullets by his side, and wait, determined to sell his life as dearly as possible if worst came to worst.

For hours the hunter watched the fight, while his wife

crouched in the bottom of the cart, with her baby in her arms. He could see that the carts had been formed in a semicircle, and from behind them his comrades withstood charge after charge of the Indians, who would dash up to the barrier of heavy carts, pour in a volley, and sweep away beyond rifle range, until their own guns were reloaded.

At last, late in the afternoon, the battle came to an end. The Indians, finding it impossible to drive the hunters from behind their barrier, suddenly withdrew, and taking their dead with them, disappeared over the hill down which they had dashed in the morning. They might make another attack, but for the present all was safe, and Jean Bedell might rejoin his friends. When he reached them, he found that though they were rejoiced to have driven off the hated Sioux, their joy was mingled with much sorrow, for there were many dead to be buried, and many wounded to be cared for. Among the dead were several of the little children, to whom stray bullets had found their way; and when Jean Bedell and his wife saw the poor little bodies, they were very thankful that, on account of a broken harness, their own darling baby had been kept at a safe distance from the terrible battle.

[Begun in Harper's Young People No. 24, April 13.]

THE STORY OF GEORGE WASHINGTON.

BY EDWARD CARY.

Chapter VIII.

I HAVE said that the work which President Washington had to do was quite new to the country. The people had been used to having all their affairs attended to in their own States. None of the States was very large. Some of them were very small, compared with what the States are now, so that the public men in each were known by a greater part of the people than they now are. Then distance seemed greater than it does now. It took nearly as long to go from Boston to New York as it now does to go from Boston to California; there was no telegraph any more than there were railways and steamboats, and news travelled as slowly as men did themselves. You can see that it was harder for people in Georgia or New Hampshire to know what was going on in New York than it is now for people in Oregon or Florida to know what is being done in Washington. Where there is ignorance there is always more distrust and doubt. Men found it not easy to give up public business to a Congress, far away, that they did not know much about. Washington set himself earnestly at work to try and have things done so carefully, so honestly, and so wisely, that the people would learn to trust the national government, and live happily under it.

The national government had been meant especially to do three things: First, to raise money and pay the debts of all the States; second, to see that the country was rightly dealt with by other countries, and that other countries were justly treated by our own; and third, in a general way to do for the common good what no one State could do by itself.

The government has now for nearly a hundred years done this work very well, and that fact is largely due to the way George Washington began it. He was President for eight years.

It would not be easy to tell all the things he did in that time which have had a good effect ever since, but it will be well to remember a few of the principal ones. He always insisted on the full and honest payment of the public debt, that is, of money borrowed by the government to carry on the war, and so forth. He believed that a nation must keep its word as much as a man must, if it expects other people to deal fairly with it.

In order that the government might pay its debts, it was necessary for it to get money from the people by taxes, and President Washington showed very early that no man or set of men were to be allowed to refuse to pay a fair share of these taxes, as fixed by law.

The people chose the Congress, and the Congress decided how the taxes should be paid. When that was done, there must be no further dispute about paying. If the people did not like the laws Congress made, they could elect men to Congress who would change the laws, but until the laws were changed in this way, they must be obeyed.

A large number of persons in the State of Pennsylvania refused to pay a tax ordered by Congress, called an excise tax, which was a certain sum on every barrel of whiskey made in the country. When Washington learned of this, he sent word to these people that if they did not obey the laws, he should have to compel them to; and as they took no notice of this warning, he got together an army of 16,000 men, and sent it into the State. This soon settled the trouble, and there has never been any attempt, on a large scale, to resist a tax law in the United States since then.

It is easy to see that Washington knew better than to do such a thing by halves. He sent so large an army that to fight against it was hopeless, and so there was no fighting.

It would have been well for the country if this wise example had always been followed.

[to be continued.]

THE CHILD SINGER.

BY LAURA FITCH.

IN a narrow dirty street in the most miserable part of the great city of London, a group of children were playing beside the gutter. They were all dirty and ragged, and the faces of many were old and worldly-wise. One little girl, however, though her dress was as torn and soiled as that of any of the other dwellers in the filthy street, had a pretty childish face. She was a bright-looking little one, with matted brown hair hanging in tangled curls that had never known a brush, and a pair of sweet dark eyes looking out trustfully into the uninviting world around her. She stood a little apart from the others, leaning against the doorway of a rickety tenement-house, humming softly to herself.

A rough-looking boy in the group by the gutter, hearing her low tones, called out, "Louder, Nell; sing something."

The child obeyed; with her hands clasped, and her eyes fastened on the speck of blue sky to be seen between the roofs of the tall, smoky houses, she burst into a song. No wonder that the other children stopped their noisy play, and listened. It was not their ignorance of music that made the singing seem beautiful to those little street vagabonds. There was in the clear voice of the child singer a strange, wistful tone, of which she herself was unconscious, but which held the listener spell-bound.

Nell had been born and bred in those low surroundings. She had never seen the inside of a church, or heard other music than the whining tones of a street organ, yet there was in her the very soul of music. She lived in a wretched garret, with a dirty, slouchy woman whom she called aunt, and loved as only a child or a woman can love one from whom she receives no sign of affection. Miserable as such a life was, it might have been worse.

One day Nell's aunt was brought home on a shutter; she had been run over by a carriage, and instantly killed.

Now Nell was indeed destitute; no money, and no friends but her rough neighbors. But these, though rough, were not hard-hearted; they would have given her money, but they had none themselves, except what they earned or stole each day. So they told her, if she wanted her aunt buried properly, she must go out at night and sing, in which way she would very likely earn enough, as people would pity so young a child.

So that night poor little Nell set out on her work of love. She walked till she reached the broad streets and handsome houses that form the London which the world knows. Here she sang. In the clear silent night the childish voice rang out, and the hour and the stillness made its wistful tones sound wild and weird. Up one street and down another the little figure went singing, while its heart seemed breaking. A strange excitement bore her up, and she felt no fatigue.

Her pathetic appeal was not in vain; it seemed to touch the hearts, and, what is more difficult, the pockets, of all who heard her. When midnight came, she thought of stopping only because most of the houses had closed for the night, and there was little more to be obtained. So she took her last stand in front of a fine old house in Kensington Square, in whose windows lights were still burning. It was the home of Barach, the great musician. As the tones of Nell's voice broke on the stillness of the night, he paused in the work he was doing, and after a moment rose and threw open the window. With amazement he saw the little childish figure standing in the light of the street lamp, and while his artist's ear drank in the wonderful tones with delight, his fatherly heart filled with pity for the desolate child. When Nell ceased, he called to her, and descending, opened the door and took her in.

From that moment Nell was no longer destitute, no longer *friendless*. In Barach she had *found* a *friend* who never deserted her. Captivated by her voice, he took the little waif into his heart and home, and thenceforth she was protected, cared *for*, and educated. And he was amply rewarded when, in after-years, the *fame* of Helen Barach spread over England. No one then ever dreamed that the great singer began her career years ago, one dark night, under the stars, a little outcast singing for money to bury her dead.

"HE'S MY FRIEND."—A TRUE STORY.

BY AUNT FANNY.

CHARLEY was the son of a young, rich, and beautiful widow, who lived in one of the splendid up-town hotels of New York city. His mother was a very busy woman, for she was a manager of the "Children's Retreat," the "Children's *Relief*," the "Old Ladies' Mitigation Society," and ever so many other charities, and these took up so much of her time that her own poor little half-orphaned Charley was left pretty much to himself; for Lizzie, his nurse, spent most of her time laughing and talking with the other servants.

So Charley amused himself running up and down the stairs, and taking trips with the elevator man, who was very fond of the bright little fellow.

One day Charley wandered down the wide stairs, and along a corridor or hall. He was throwing up a little ball and catching it as he went. At the end of the hall he saw through an open door another flight of stairs, very narrow, and rather dark. It was the stairs for the servants' use.

"Hallo!" cried Charley, "here are some more stairs," and like the learned monkey that let nothing escape him on his travels, down the stairs went the boy on a voyage of discovery.

When he came to the bottom, which was *far* below the level of the street outside, he walked along to an open door, and saw something which dimpled his face all over with smiles; for, standing like a heron on one leg, leaning against the wall opposite the door, was *another boy*. He was twirling a little paper windmill fastened to a stick; his great black eyes were dancing with glee, and as he laughed he showed two rows of snow-white even teeth. At a stationary wash-tub was a big woman washing clothes, and singing softly to herself, "'Way down in ole Virginny."

Neither of them saw Charley, so, by way of introducing himself, he said, "Hallo, boy."

The woman turned quickly round, and exclaimed, "Why, honey, whar did yer come from?"

"I came down stairs; may I come in?" asked Charley, adding, quickly, "I want to play with that boy."

"Course you can; come right in," said the black woman, for she was nearly as black as ink, but there was a sweet, honest expression in her broad face, and a welcoming tone in her voice, which brought Charley quickly in, with a little laugh, to the side of the other boy.

And he—oh, how black he was! but as clean and neatly dressed as soap and water and nice clothes could make him, for Juliet, his mother, loved her little son, and she took good care that his manners were as nice as his clothes. He held out his hand to Charley, and, making a queer little bow, said, "How do you do, sir? I hope you are very well." Then he twisted one leg tighter than ever round the other, and gave a vigorous twirl to his paper windmill.

"Hey! I like that," said Charley. "Let *me* try to do it."

"Oh yes," said the other, "but this is the best way—to hold it straight out, and run fast."

So Charley took the windmill, and both boys went scampering and galloping round the room, the windmill flying round famously, until the boys were quite out of breath.

"What's your name?" asked Charley, as they were resting together in a large old rocking-chair.

"George Washington Johnson. What's *your* name?" asked the black boy, in return, rocking the chair as hard as he could.

"My name is Charley Lee. I like you. Will you be my friend?"

"Oh yes; will you be mine?"

"Yes, and we'll play together every single day."

Just then Juliet went away with a great basket of clothes, to hang them up in a room where they were quickly dried by steam; and Charley, taking George's hand, said, "Come up stairs with me, and take a ride in the elevator."

What a blissful invitation for George! They tumbled up stairs in their delightful hurry, ran through the door into the broad hall, to the elevator, and the moment it appeared, Charley cried out,

"Oh, Mike, open the door; George wants to ride up and down with me; *he's my friend*."

"Oh, he's your friend, is he?" said Mike, puckering up his eyes at George Washington; "and a very pretty color he is, too. Well, step in, Snowball."

"His name isn't Snowball; it's George Washington," said Charley.

The elevator man laughed, and the two boys got close together in a corner, pretending that it was a balloon, and they were sailing up and down in the air; and there they sat, in a state of perfect happiness.

The two boys never quarrelled. George had a sweet disposition, and was ready to do anything Charley proposed. They loved each other dearly, and many were the slices of bread and butter, spread thickly over with molasses, to which the two friends were treated by the good-natured washer-woman. They never sat down to eat them; oh no! they capered, and danced, and burst out laughing when they tumbled over a broomstick or a bench, and seemed to grow rosier and fatter every day. That is, Charley grew rosier, and George's smooth black skin grew shinier, which was the same thing—for him.

The little black boy was often permitted by his mother to go out toward Fourth Avenue, and run over one of the high arched bridges which covers the Fourth Avenue Railroad, and he did not think he was doing wrong when one day he asked Charley to go too.

"Oh yes, I will," he cried, in a great state of delight.

As soon as they arrived at the bridge, they began chasing each other over it; and then Charley said:

"Oh, George, let's play that we are travellers, hunting for a whale. I heard my mamma talking about one that was on ex-ex-exedition down by the river. She said that it was 'most a mile long."

"Gosh!" cried George. "What a mons'ous whale!"

So the boys ran down the street toward the East River a long, long way, and presently they got to some rocks, upon the top of which were a number of miserable wooden houses called shanties.

Geese, pigs, chickens, and a forlorn, starved-looking dog were poking about for something to eat. Near by was a great heap of coal ashes. Some bad-looking boys were raking the ashes up into a sort of mound on top of the heap; but a moment after, they ran away to see an organ-grinder and a monkey which had come upon the rocks. Charley and George would have run too, had not their ears caught the sound of a stifled piteous mewing, which seemed to issue out of the very middle of the ash heap.

"What's that?" asked both boys at once.

"Mew! me—ew!" came again from the ashes.

"It's a cat!" exclaimed Charley; "and it is inside of those ashes. I do believe those boys thought it was dead, and buried it. Let's hurry and dig it out."

Charley and George worked hard, but they had nothing but their hands to work with, and they threw the ashes all over their clothes; but the piteous mewing came quicker and louder, and in a few moments the gray head of a live kitten popped out of the ashes; then two gray paws, and soon the whole kitten was liberated.

"Oh, you poor little thing!" said Charley, trying with soft pats to get the ashes out of its fur, while George took out of his pocket a queer little pocket-handkerchief, six inches square, with A B C all round the edge, and a portrait of his great namesake in the middle, and said, in a tender tone, "Here, poor kitty, let me wipe your nose; don't cry any more;" and he wiped it so softly that it really seemed to comfort the afflicted little creature.

"Let's run home with it," said Charley.

"And give it some milk," said George.

"And wash it clean," said Charley.

"And dry it in the steam-room," said George.

No sooner said than done. Charley carried the kitten one block, and then George the next, and so on in turn, until at last they got back to the hotel, and rushed down into the laundry, where Juliet was beginning to feel worried at their long absence.

"La sakes!" she cried, when she saw the plight they were in, "whar have you ben gone? Why, you look jes like ole Bobby de ash-man. Whar you get dat ar cat? Why, George Washington! you's a disgrace to your raisin'! How you spec' I'se gwine' to make you look genteel if you cum home dat ar way?"

"Oh," said George, rolling his eyes at his mother—"oh, we've had such s'prising 'ventures; we went to see a whale."

"Whale! is dat what you call a whale?" said Juliet, pointing to the poor little kitten, which he was hugging tight to his breast.

Then Charley spoke up, and when Juliet had heard of the "surprising adventures," she was sorry she had been the least bit cross with the kind-hearted little fellows. To make up for it, she gave the kitten a saucer of warm milk, and taking off the soiled clothes of the boys, and washing their faces and hands, she put two funny little night-gowns upon them, and popped them into her bed, which was in a little room next to the laundry. Then she caught up their clothes—for there was no time to be lost—and popped *them* into a tub of hot water, with plenty of soap, and in ten minutes they were just as clean as soap, water, and hard rubbing could make them.

Then she wrung them out with a will, shook them out with a flourish, and running into the steam-room, hung them upon a horse—a clothes-horse, of course. In ten minutes more they were dry enough to iron, and she polished them with the hot and heavy irons at such a rate that

SUSPENSE.—Drawn by J. E. Kelly.

they fairly shone, and she shone too.

When the boys were called, and Juliet put on their clothes again, they looked cleaner, brighter, and happier than ever.

The kitten was adopted as a friend too, and had soon shook and licked itself clean, and it lived a very comfortable life down in the laundry.

One day, for a wonder, Charley's mother staid at home. She was expecting a call from her lawyer, Judge Spencer, upon some business. When he came he had a long talk with Charley.

Presently Charley said: "I want to tell you something. I've a friend; his name is George."

"Only one friend?" asked the Judge, laughing.

"But he's my 'tic'lar friend," explained Charley. "May I bring him to see you? He's real nice."

"Does he live in the hotel?" asked Charley's mother, who had never heard of him.

"Oh yes," replied Charley, "and he and I have a *lovely* kitten—we take care of it."

"Well, bring him in—the kitten too," said the good Judge; "that is, if your mother consents."

"Oh, certainly," said Mrs. Lee.

So Charley rushed down the narrow stairs, and found George playing with the kitten, and looking as neat and clean as a new pin.

"Come, George, come up with me to mamma's parlor. Judge Spencer is there; he wants to see you, and the kitten too."

They went up stairs, and softly opening the door of the parlor, and holding George's hand tightly, Charley walked quickly up to the Judge and said, "Here's my friend; he can't help being black!"

For one moment astonishment kept Charley's mamma and the Judge silent. Then the good man held out his hand to the black boy, and taking Charley on his knee kissed him tenderly. That warm, loving kiss told Charley that the Judge understood it all. His face grew radiant, his eyes rested affectionately on his friend, and then he leaned toward George, and put the beloved kitten in his arms. "You hold it now," he said.

With a cautionary wave of his hand, the Judge prevented Mrs. Lee from reproving Charley for his choice of a friend; then he sent them into the next room, and had a long talk with the widow, the result of which was that, after inquiring about George, and finding how good his "raisin'" was, as Juliet called it, Charley was still permitted to play with him. And to this very day (for all this has happened within a few months) if you ask Charley Lee who George Washington Johnson is, he will answer at once, "*He's my friend.*"

THE SOLEMN OLD LADY.

BY W. L. PETERS.

There was once a wee boy
With an excellent face,
Who was seen every Sunday
At church in his place;
And there this wee boy was accustomed to stare
At a solemn old lady with lavender hair,
Who used to sit opposite to him.

But when the long service
Was over at last,
He would wait at the
Vestibule door till she passed;
And then she would stop on her way from the pew,
And propounded a conundrum, which he never knew,
For she asked him the "drift of the sermon."

By and by, when the little boy's
Manhood came round,
The whole world an unanswered
Conundrum he found.
And he can no more answer it now, I declare,
Than he could the old lady with lavender hair,
Who used to sit opposite to him.

THE WEE BOY IN CHURCH.—Drawn by C. A. Northam.

OUR POST-OFFICE BOX

inclinations of these little housekeepers of the future are very pleasing, and we hope other little girls will send recipes for the cooking club, which should certainly be encouraged.

[illegible]

[illegible]

[illegible]

[illegible]

Mr. Du Chaillu is alive, and in excellent health. You will be pleased to know, also, that he is hard at work on new books, which promise to be of even greater interest than those already published.

A. H. [illegible].—See answer to B., Post-office Box No. 23.

E. A. S.—Rabbits eat cabbage, clover, crackers and milk, and almost all kinds of vegetables, herbage, or grain. Do not give them parsley, as it is said to be poisonous to them.

PUZZLES FROM YOUNG CONTRIBUTORS.

No. 1.

ENIGMA.

[illegible]

No. 2.

[illegible]

No. 3.

[illegible]

No. 4.

WORD SQUARE.

First, distant. Second, imagination. Third, previous. Fourth, a title.

No. 5.

ENIGMA.

[illegible]

No. 6.

[illegible]

Harry M.

ANSWERS TO PUZZLES IN No. 28.

No. 1. [illegible]

No. 2. [illegible]

No. 3. Cabbage-rose.

No. 4. Make hay while the sun shines.

No. 5. Mayflower.

No. 6. Noon.

A Persecution, on page 388—Shakspeare.

[illegible]

[illegible]

ADVERTISEMENTS.

HARPER'S YOUNG PEOPLE.

Harper's Young People will be issued every Tuesday, and may be had at the following rates—payable in advance, postage free:

Single Copies	$0 04
One Subscription, one year	1 50
Five Subscriptions, one year	7 00

Subscriptions may begin with any Number. When no time is specified, it will be understood that the subscriber desires to commence with the Number issued after the receipt of order.

Remittances should be made by POST-OFFICE MONEY ORDER or DRAFT, to avoid risk of loss.

ADVERTISING.

The extent and character of the circulation of Harper's Young People will render it a first-class medium for advertising. A limited number of approved advertisements will be inserted on two inside pages at 75 cents per line.

Address

HARPER & BROTHERS,
Franklin Square, N. Y.

OUR CHILDREN'S SONGS.

Our Children's Songs. Illustrated. 8vo, Ornamental Cover, $1 00.

[illegible]

Published by HARPER & BROTHERS, New York.

Harper & Brothers will send the above work by mail, postage prepaid, to any part of the United States, on receipt of the price.

CHILDREN'S PICTURE-BOOKS.

Square 4to, about 300 pages each, beautifully printed on Tinted Paper, embellished with many Illustrations, bound in Cloth, $1 50 per volume.

The Children's Picture-Book of Sagacity of Animals.

With Sixty Illustrations by Harrison Weir.

The Children's Bible Picture-Book.

With Eighty Illustrations, from Designs by Steinle, Overbeck, Veit, Schnorr, &c.

The Children's Picture Fable-Book.

Containing One Hundred and Sixty Fables. With Sixty Illustrations by Harrison Weir.

The Children's Picture-Book of Birds.

With Sixty-one Illustrations by W. Harvey.

The Children's Picture-Book of Quadrupeds and other Mammalia.

With Sixty-one Illustrations by W. Harvey.

Published by HARPER & BROTHERS, New York.

Sent by mail, postage prepaid, to any part of the United States, on receipt of the price.

Old Books for Young Readers.

Arabian Nights' Entertainments.

The Thousand and One Nights; or, The Arabian Nights' Entertainments. Translated and Arranged for Family Reading, with Explanatory Notes, by E. W. Lane. [illegible] Illustrations by Harvey. 2 vols., 12mo, Cloth, $3 50.

Robinson Crusoe.

The Life and Surprising Adventures of Robinson Crusoe, of York, Mariner. By Daniel Defoe. With a Biographical Account of Defoe. Illustrated by Adams. Complete Edition. 12mo, Cloth, $1 50.

The Swiss Family Robinson.

The Swiss Family Robinson; or, Adventures of a Father and Mother and Four Sons on a Desert Island. Illustrated. 2 vols., 18mo, Cloth, $1 50.

The Swiss Family Robinson.—Continued: being a Sequel to the Foregoing. 2 vols., 18mo, Cloth, $1 50.

Sandford and Merton.

The History of Sandford and Merton. By Thomas Day. 18mo, Half Bound, 75 cents.

Published by HARPER & BROTHERS, New York.

Sent by mail, postage prepaid, to any part of the United States, on receipt of the price.

PLAYING "BOGEY."

"Jimmy, I wonder if Bobby's out yet?"

A Good Samaritan who would not tell his Name.—Oberlin, the well-known philanthropist of Steinthal, while yet a candidate for the ministry, was travelling on one occasion from Strasburg. It was in the winter-time. The ground was deeply covered with snow, and the roads were almost impassable. He had reached the middle of his journey, and was among the mountains, but by that time was so exhausted that he could stand up no longer. He was rapidly freezing to death. Sleep began to overcome him; all power to resist it left him. He commended himself to God, and yielded to what he felt to be the sleep of death. He knew not how long he slept, but suddenly became conscious of some one rousing him and waking him up. Before him stood a wagon-driver in his blue blouse, the wagon being not far away. He gave him a little wine and food, and warmth returned. He then helped him into the wagon, and brought him to the next village. The rescued man was profuse in his thanks, and offered money, which his benefactor refused. "It is only a duty to help one another," said the wagoner, "and it is the next thing to an insult to offer a reward for such a service." "Then," replied Oberlin, "at least tell me your name, that I may have you in thankful remembrance before God." "I see," said the wagoner, "that you are a minister of the Gospel: please tell me the name of the Good Samaritan." "That," said Oberlin, "I can not do, for it was not put on record." "Then," replied the wagoner, "until you can tell me his name, permit me to withhold mine." Soon he had driven out of sight, and Oberlin never saw him again.

Earthquakes in Chili.—In some parts of South America men keep their "earthquake coats," which are dresses that can be put on instantaneously, with a view to a speedy exit from the house. The advisability of such a practice may be inferred from the picture of one of the features of life in Chili which is set forth in the following extract from a letter of a young Englishman, who settled at Valparaiso a few years ago. Under date of November 16 he writes: "I am in a most nervous state on account of having had three days and nights of successive earthquakes—fearful ones. The first night I walked the streets, and indeed every one else did the same; the second night I went to bed quite exhausted at about 3 A.M.; last night also at about 3 A.M., but I could not sleep, for we had about six shocks, though not so strong. The whole cornice of a house close to ours came down into the street, but luckily no one was passing at the time. The women rush into the street in their night dresses, screaming like lunatics, and one trembles from head to foot. I was crossing our street when the strongest shock came, and I was transfixed with fright, for the road was going up and down like waves. My hand even now shakes, for at any moment we may have another, and how strong it may be no one can tell. I can assure you I am afraid to take off my clothes. The large squares have been filled for the last three nights with beds and people wrapped up in blankets."

SOLUTION OF THE PASHA PUZZLE.

THIS is the solution of the Pasha Puzzle given on page 421 of YOUNG PEOPLE No. 30. The puzzle was to make Hobart Pasha by combining a fort, two sabres, two British gun-boats, two bayonets, a bomb-shell, and three birds; and here you have an accurate (?) likeness of the fire-eating Turk.

CHARADE.

My first is solemn and sedate,
  Or ought to be, that's certain;
But sometimes, owing to the state
Of human passions, or to fate,
It is a scene of fierce debate
And wrath; but ere it is too late
  I'll stop, and draw the curtain.

My second visits many lands,
  In bright and stormy weather;
'Tis fair to see across the sands,
Though never quite at rest it stands;
One mind alone its course commands;
Within are many hearts and hands
  Most strangely met together.

My whole is thought a happy time,
  Its praise is often sounded;
'Tis told in books, 'tis sung in rhyme,
In every age and every clime;
Of youth and manhood 'tis the prime,
Except when on the sordid grime
  Of avarice 'tis founded.

THE DOG PUZZLE.

Here is a picture of two dogs ready for a fight. With one straight cut of the scissors transform it into the illustration of an old fable.

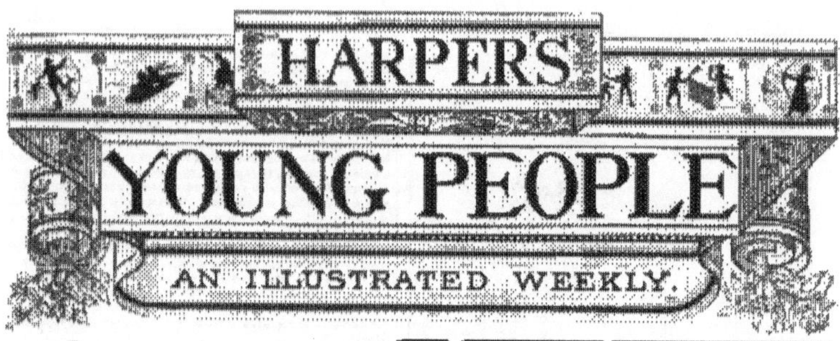

VOL. I.—NO. 32. PUBLISHED BY HARPER & BROTHERS, NEW YORK. PRICE FOUR CENTS.
Tuesday, June 8, 1880. $1.50 per Year, in Advance.

"THE TIDE WAS AGAINST THEM."

[Begun in YOUNG PEOPLE No. 31, June 1.]

THE MORAL PIRATES.

BY WM. L. ALDEN.

CHAPTER II.

WHEN Uncle John announced that the Department was satisfied with the ability of the captain and crew to manage the *Whitewing*, the day for sailing was fixed, and the boys laid in their stores. Each one had a fishing-line and hooks, and Harry and Tom each took a fishing-pole—two poles being as many as were needed, since most of the fishing would probably be done with drop-lines. Uncle John lent Harry his double-barrelled gun, and a supply of ammunition. Each boy took a tin plate, a tin cup, knife, fork, and spoon. For cooking purposes, the boat carried a coffee-pot, two tin cake-pans, which could be used as frying-pans as well as for other purposes, and two small tin pails. Harry's mother lent him several large round tin boxes, in which were stored four pounds of coffee, two pounds of sugar, a pound of Indian meal, a large quantity of crackers, some salt, and a little pepper. The rest of the provisions consisted of two cans of soup, two cans of corned beef, a can of roast beef, two small cans of devilled chicken, four cans of fresh peaches, a little package of condensed beef for making beef tea, and a cold boiled ham. The boat was furnished with an A tent, four rubber blankets and four woollen blankets, a hatchet, a quantity of spare cordage, a little bull's-eye lantern, which burnt olive-oil, and a few copper nails, a pair of pliers, a small piece of zinc, a little white lead, for mending a leak. Of course there was a bottle of oil for the lantern; and Mrs. Schuyler added a box of pills and a bottle of "Hamlin's Mixture" as medical stores. The boys wore blue flannel trousers and shirts, and each one carried an extra pair of trousers and an extra shirt instead of a coat. These, with a few pairs of stockings and two or three handkerchiefs, were all the clothing that they needed, so Uncle John said; though the boys had imagined that they must take at least two complete suits. He showed them that two flannel shirts worn at the same time, one over the other, would be as warm as one shirt and a coat, and that if their clothing became wet, it could be easily dried. "Flannel and the compass are the two things that are indispensable to navigation," said Uncle John. "If flannel shirts had not been invented, Columbus would never have crossed the Atlantic." Perhaps there was a little exaggeration in this; but when we remember that flannel is the only material that is warm in cold weather and cool in hot weather, and that dries almost as soon as it is wrung out and hung in the wind, it is difficult to see how sailors could do without it.

The boys agreed very readily to take with them only what Uncle John advised. Tom Schuyler, however, was very anxious to take a heavy iron vise, which, he said, could be screwed on the gunwale of the boat, and might prove to be very useful, although he could not say precisely what he expected to use it for. Joe Sharpe also wanted to take a base-ball and bat, but neither the vise nor the ball and bat were taken.

The *Whitewing* started from the foot of East One-hundred-and-twenty-seventh Street on a Monday morning in the middle of July, at about nine o'clock. Quite a small crowd of friends were present to see the boys off, and the neat appearance of the boat and her crew attracted the attention of all the idlers along the shore. When all the cargo was stowed, and everything was ready, Uncle John called the boys aside, and said, "Now, boys, you must sign the articles."

"What are articles?" asked all the boys at once.

"They are certain regulations which every respectable pirate, or any other sailor, for that matter, must agree to keep when he joins a ship. I'll read the articles, and if any of you don't like any one of them, say so frankly, for you must not begin a cruise in a dissatisfied state of mind. Here are the articles:

"'I. *We, the captain and crew of the* Whitewing, *promise to decide all disputed questions by the vote of the majority, except questions concerning the management of the boat. The orders of the captain, in all matters connected with the management of the boat, shall be promptly obeyed by the crew.*'

"Now if anybody thinks that the captain should not have the full control of the boat, let him say so at once. Very likely the captain will make mistakes; but the boat will be safer, even if the crew obeys a wrong order, than it would be if every order should be debated by the crew. You can't hold town-meetings when you are afloat. Harry, I think, understands pretty well how to sail the boat. Will you agree to obey his orders?"

All the boys said they would; and Joe Sharpe added that he thought the captain ought to have the right to put mutineers in irons.

"That, let us hope, will not be necessary," said Uncle John. "Now listen to the second article:

"'II. *We promise not to take corn, apples, or other property without permission of the owner.*'

"You will very likely camp near some field where corn, or potatoes, or something eatable, is growing. Many people think there is no harm in taking a few ears of corn or half a dozen apples. I want you to remember that to take anything that is not your own, unless you have permission to do so, is stealing. It's an ugly word, but it can't be smoothed over in any way. Do you object to this article?"

Nobody objected to it. "We're moral pirates, Uncle John," said Tom Schuyler, "and we won't disgrace the Department by stealing."

"I knew you would not except through thoughtlessness. Now these are all the articles. I did think of asking you not to quarrel, or to use bad language; but I don't believe it is necessary to ask you to make such a promise, and if it were, you probably would not keep it. So sign the articles, give them to the captain, and take your stations."

The articles were signed. The captain seated himself in the stern-sheets, and took the yoke lines. The rest took their proper places, and Joe Sharpe held the boat to the dock by the boat-hook. "Are you all ready?" cried Uncle John.

"All ready, sir!" answered Harry.

"Then give way with your oars! Good-by, boys, and don't forget to send reports to the Department."

The boat glided away from the shore with Tom and Jim each pulling a single oar. The group on the wharf gave the boys a farewell cheer, and in a few moments they were hid from sight by the Third Avenue Bridge. The tide was against them, but the day was a cool one for the season, and the boys rowed steadily on in the very best of spirits. There was a light south wind, but as there were several bridges to pass, Harry thought it best not to set the sail before reaching the Hudson River. It required careful steering to avoid the steamboats, bridge piles, and small boats; but the *Whitewing* was guided safely, and her signal—a red flag with a white cross—floated gayly at the bow.

Uncle John had made one serious mistake: he had forgotten all about the tide, and never thought of the difficulty the boys would find in passing Farmers-bridge with the tide against them. They had passed High Bridge, and had entered a part of the river with which the boys were not familiar, when Joe Sharpe suddenly called out, "There's a low bridge right ahead that we can't pass." A few more strokes of the oars enabled Harry to see a long low bridge, which completely blocked up the river except at one place, that seemed not much wider than the boat. Through this narrow channel the tide was rushing fiercely, the water heaping itself up in waves that looked unpleasantly high and rough. The boat was rowed as close as possible to the opening under the bridge; but the current was so strong that the boys could not row against it, and even if they had been able to stem it, the channel was too narrow to permit them to use the oars.

Harry ordered the boat to be rowed up to the bridge at a place where there was a quiet eddy, and all the crew went ashore to contrive some way of overcoming the difficulty. Presently Harry thought of a plan. "If we could get the painter under the bridge, we could pull the boat through easy enough if there was nobody in her."

"That's all very well," said Joe, "but how are you going to get the painter through?"

"I know," cried Jim. "Let's take a long piece of rope and drop it in the water the other side of the bridge. The current will float it through, and we can catch it and tie it to the painter."

The plan seemed a good one; and so the boys took a piece of spare rope from the boat, tied a bit of board to one end of it for a float, dropped the float into the water, and held on to the other end of the rope. When the float came in sight below the bridge they caught it with the boat-hook, and throwing away the piece of board, tied the rope to the painter. "Now let Joe Sharpe get in the bow of the boat, to keep her from running against anything, and we'll haul her right through," exclaimed Harry.

Joe took his place in the bow, and pushing the boat off, let her float into the current. Then the three other boys e always

would be
please sit
iazza and

ate-peg a
tub, what

it !"
came out,
ay.
own, and
t what in
. When
d. "How

played a
ughed fit
t was the

this. Som-

He looked over this story, and corrected the spelling for me, and told me to send it to the YOUNG PEOPLE. Only it is to be a secret that he helped me. I'd do almost anything for him, and I'm going to ask Sue to marry him just to please me.

A CHAT ABOUT PHILATELY.

BY J. J. CASEY.

PHILATELY? What is that?

Many years ago, beyond the longest recollection of the oldest of the young people, a school-teacher in Paris (so one story goes) advised her pupils to get specimens of different postage stamps, in order the better to study their geography. There was a general searching among old letters to secure these little bits of bright-colored papers. Parents and friends were asked to save the stamps from their letters; strangers at the post-office were pounced upon, the moment they received their letters, for the stamps; and from this little beginning sprang stamp-collecting.

At first it was limited to boys and girls; but the older

bums, to look over the numerous evidences of the growth of the postal system, or to help some young friend in the filling up of a modest little blank-book.

In spite of the ridicule which has been heaped upon the collector of stamps, the interest in stamp-collecting is as great to-day as it was a dozen years ago, and from Prince Edward Island to Australia will be found stamp "merchants," as they delight to call themselves, stamp papers, and stamp agencies, to supply the continually increasing demands of young and old collectors. Societies exist in several countries, at the meetings of which most learned papers are read to show the why and the wherefore of this or that stamp, and even the government at Montevideo has authorized a stamp society, lately established there, to use a private postal card.

This pursuit of stamp collecting is called Philately, from two Greek words, which have been translated "the love of stamps," and those who engage in the pleasure or the pursuit are pleased to call themselves Philatelists.

This little "chat" shall be closed by a reference to the illustrations of some curious or interesting stamps, and a notice of stamps that have been issued during the past few months.

Fig. 1

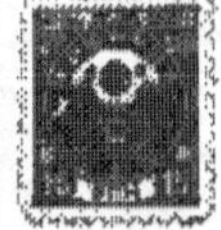

Fig. 2

Fig. 1 is one of the series of United States stamps for postage on large packages of newspapers and periodicals, and represents a value of forty-eight dollars. There is a higher value of sixty dollars. These stamps are perfect gems, and are among the most beautiful in the world.

Fig. 3

Fig. 2 represents one of the stamps in use to-day in Japan. It is only necessary to compare a specimen of this issue with the first stamps used in Japan to see how rapidly the Japanese acquire every modern improvement.

Fig. 4

Fig. 3 is one of the current Guatemala stamps, printed in Paris, which found their way to collectors before they were delivered to the government. The thick black line on either side is a bird's tail—the quezal, or national bird, one of the most beautiful on this continent.

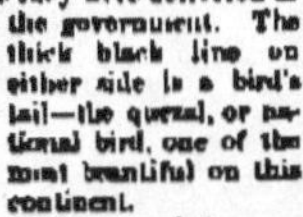

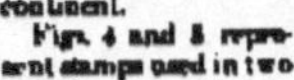

Fig. 5

Fig. 6

Figs. 4 and 5 represent stamps used in two of the native states of India. The native stamps of India, ugly as many of them are, are among the most interesting found in the collector's album, and quite difficult to obtain.

Fig. 6 is one from the South African Republic, or the Transvaal, lately seized by England.

Some of the newest issues are:

Antigua.—A new value, 4d., blue; and a postal card, 1½d., red-brown on buff.

Cape of Good Hope.—The 4d., blue, surcharged in red above, "Three Pence."

Dominica.—New values of ½d., yellow; 2½d., brown; 4d., blue; and a postal card of 1½d., red-brown.

Danish West Indies.—A new value, 50c., same type as current series, in mauve.

Gold Coast.—Stamps of ½d., golden yellow, and 2d., green; and card of 1½d., red-brown.

Great Britain.—The 2½d. stamp is printed in blue, and the 2s. changes from blue to red-brown.

Montserrat.—New stamps of 2½d., red-brown, and 4d., blue; and postal card of 1½d., red-brown.

Nevis.—New stamps of 2½d., red-brown, and 4d., blue; and postal card of 1½d., red-brown.

Peru.—A new series of stamps is in preparation, but for the present the authorities surcharge the current stamp with the words, "Union Postale Universelle" and "Plata," in an oval. The 1c. changes its color to green, the 2c. to carmine, and the 20c. is suppressed.

Roumelia.—This province of Turkey begins its stamp history with a postal card of the value of 10 paras, as expressed on the face, but in reality of 15 paras, at which it is sold.

BUTTERFLIES AND BEES.

Butterflies are merry things,
Gayly painted are their wings,
And they never carry stings.
Bees are grave and busy things,
Gold their jackets, brown their wings,
And they *always* carry stings.
Yet—isn't it extremely funny?—
Bees, not butterflies, make honey.

AN APRONFUL OF WATER-CRESSES.

BY MARGARET EYTINGE.

CISSY MOUNT came down to the gurgling, sparkling little brook at the foot of the hill, where Frank Hillborn and his brother Dave were gathering water-cresses.

"I'm going to Fairview, Frank," she said, "and came to ask you if you would look in on mother by-and-by, and see if she needs anything."

"Of course I will," said Frank. "But you're not going to walk to Fairview, Cissy? That's a long tramp for a girl."

"Yes, I am," she replied. "There's no other way I can go. Nobody that I know ever drives down there. Mother wants me to try and get her some sewing to do. You know there are five or six big stores there, and mother can sew and knit beautifully. I wish I had time to pick some wild flowers to take with me. Town-people like wild flowers."

"A good many of them like something fresh and green to eat better than they do wild flowers," said Frank; "so you just take along some of these water-cresses. Aren't they beauties? They're the first we've gathered this spring, and I hope they'll bring you luck."

"But I have no basket," said Cissy.

"Carry them in your apron. They won't hurt;" and as she held it up, he heaped it full of moist green bunches.

"That's just like you, Frank Hillborn," said Dave, when the girl had gone. "What's the good of our owning the only water-cress brook for miles if you're going to give 'em away to everybody that comes along?"

"Everybody that comes along?" repeated Frank, with a cheery laugh. "I've only given a basketful to Ezra Lee—he lent us his fishing-line when we lost ours—and an apronful to Cissy Mount. Poor Cissy! Guess there's hard times at her house since her father was killed on the railroad and her mother got lame. And you know she's going to ask for work, and it most always puts folks in good-humor if you carry 'em something nice."

"All right," said Dave; "but don't you give away any more, for we want to make five dollars out of 'em this season, anyhow."

Cissy Mount walked bravely on mile after mile, until

half of her journey had been accomplished. Then she stopped and looked around for a place where she might rest awhile. A pleasant little lane, on either side of which stood a row of tall cedar-trees, branched off from the main road. Into this lane she turned, and sat down on the grass near the side gate of a fine garden. And as she sat there peeping through a hole in the hedge at some lovely beds of hyacinths and tulips, radiant in the sunshine, a queer-looking little old gentleman, with no hat on, but having a wonderful quantity of brown hair, came scolding down the garden path, followed by a man carrying a camp-chair. The old gentleman as he talked grew more and more excited, and at last, to Cissy's great astonishment, grasped the abundant brown locks, lifted them completely off his head, waved them in the air an instant, and then gravely replaced them. As he came near, the child could hear what he was saying: "I sent word from Europe when this place was bought that if there were no water-cress stream upon it, one was to be made at once. That's a year ago."

"Beg pardon, sir," said the man, humbly, "but I did my best, sir. It isn't my fault, sir. Sometimes you can't make water-cresses grow, all you can do, sir."

"And what's to be done with the puddle—for it's nothing but a puddle, though a big one—that you've disfigured my grounds with?" asked the old gentleman.

"Miss Grace says it will be a capital place for raising water-lilies, sir," said the man.

"Oh, indeed! Very fine. But I can't eat water-lilies. There's no pepper about them, and it's the pepper I want."

"Perhaps I can find some cresses for sale somewhere near, sir. Shall I go and look, sir?"

"No," snarled the master. "By the time you came back with them, if you got them, ten chances to one I shouldn't want them. When I want things, I want them at once. Yes, I'd give five dollars for some fresh water-cresses this very minute;" and he again seized his wig and flourished it in the air.

With trembling fingers Cissy opened the gate, and walked in. The servant-man placed the camp-chair on the ground. The old gentleman sat down in it, first hanging his hair on the back, leaving his head as smooth and shining as an ivory ball, looked at the intruder with keen black eyes, and asked, sharply, "Well, what do *you* want?"

"To give you these water-cresses," she said, with a smile, holding up her apron. "They were gathered only a short time ago, and my apron's quite clean, sir."

"Bless me!" exclaimed the old gentleman, "what a wonderful coincidence! and"—taking a bunch and beginning to eat them—"what fine water-cresses! And I suppose you expect that five dollars, for of course you heard what I said."

"No, sir," said Cissy, shyly, "I never thought of the money. I know you only said that as people often say things. I'm glad to give them to you, sir, because you wanted them so *much*."

The old gentleman burst into a loud laugh, put on his wig, and asked her name. And then by degrees he got the whole story from her—the death of the father, the accident that lamed the mother, the gift of the cresses from Frank Hillborn, and the five miles yet to go in search of work. "And what was your mother's name before she was married?" was his last question.

"Prudence Kelly, sir."

"Prudence Kelly! I knew it!" he shouted, springing from his chair. And then, in a still louder voice, he called, "Grace! Grace!" and a pretty young lady came running toward him. "I've found your old nurse, my dear, your faithful old nurse that we have lost sight of for

years. This is her daughter. And she is in want. Take the carriage and go to her at once. What a blessing that I got up in a scolding humor this morning, and wanted water-cresses! Go with Grace, Cecilia my child, and when you get home, give this five-dollar bill to your friend Frank, and tell him it isn't the first time a little act of kindness has brought luck."

[Begun in Harper's Young People No. 24, April 13.]

THE STORY OF GEORGE WASHINGTON.

BY EDWARD CARY.

Chapter IX.

VERY soon after General Washington was elected President a war broke out between France and England. It was natural that people in this country should wish to help the French, who had helped us. But General Washington saw that if we once got in the way of taking a part in wars between other countries, where our own rights were not in danger, we should always be at war. He saw, too, that we were a small nation then, compared to the nations of Europe, and that we might easily lose the freedom we had fought so long for. He dreaded to put our freedom in danger unless compelled to. So he issued an order to the people, as he had a right to do, not to take part with one nation or the other, but to mind their own business.

This was wise, because the British government was only too ready to pick a quarrel with us. General Washington also went further. He made a treaty of peace and commerce with Great Britain, which kept war from our shores for twenty years, and gave the country a chance to grow. The people did not like this treaty much. There was a great deal of ill-feeling toward Great Britain, growing out of the long fight we had had with her. But General Washington, who was ready to fight for real rights, felt that it was wrong to get into a quarrel from mere angry feeling. He was very anxious to keep the two countries at peace until their people could get calm, and go to trading with each other, and learn to live together in friendship. Surely this was both sensible and good. It was fortunate for the country that a man was at the head of its government wise enough to see what was right, and firm enough to do it.

Just at the time Washington was elected President, the French people rose against their government, which had many faults, and drove away many of their rulers, and cut off their King's head. Among the leaders was Lafayette, who, however, was no party to the cruelties which were practiced. The other kings of Europe undertook to restore the King of France to power, and in the war which followed Lafayette was taken prisoner and closely confined. His wife wrote to Washington, asking him to try and get Lafayette released. Washington gladly did all that he could, but it was of no use. However, he sent money to Madame Lafayette, for her property had been taken away, and he brought over to this country one of Lafayette's sons, and took him into his family, and cared for him as if he were his own. The boy was named after Washington, and always remembered the President's kindness with thankfulness.

When the first term of four years for which Washington was elected came to an end, he was chosen again, without a single vote against him, though he was very anxious to go back to private life.

Finally, at the end of his second term, when he had been eight years President, he refused to serve any longer. Just as he had written a farewell address to his soldiers, after being eight years in command, he now wrote a farewell address to the American people. I hope all my young readers will read it as soon as they are old enough to understand it. It is written in a quaint and somewhat stiff style, for Washington always found it easier to act than to talk or write; but it is full of wisdom. Even now, eighty-four years after it was written, there is much in it which we ought to remember and try to carry out.

It was the spring of 1797 when Washington gave up the President's office, and returned to Mount Vernon. He had visited his beloved home frequently during his Presidency, and had kept a very careful watch over it in his absence. Again he took up with great delight the old round of peaceful duties. Every day he was up before the sun. Every day he was in the saddle, riding over his large farms, watching his laborers and his crops, planning changes and directing work. In the evening he saw much company—many, indeed, who had little claim on him, who came from idle curiosity, and wearied him with their presence. But he was always courteous. He enjoyed the society of his family and friends very keenly. He had no children of his own, but he had reared first the children, and afterward two of the grandchildren, of his wife in his home. He took great pleasure with them, and was as merry as he was loving. He hoped to live the remainder of his days in quiet in this circle.

[to be continued.]

LITTLE FATIMA.

BY SARA KEABLES HUNT.

IT was a beautiful Oriental picture, and I paused in my walk along the banks of the Nile to sketch her, that dark-eyed Arab girl, as she half reclined in the sand, the western sunlight flickering through the green boughs of a clump of palms, and falling upon the upturned face and purplish braids with their glitter of gold coins. In the background were a few broken columns, relic of some past grandeur, and at a little distance a camel crouched in the sand, gazing as mournfully as the Sphynx across the desert. The flowing Eastern dress of the child was pushed back from one beautifully rounded arm, but the other was concealed, as if she had tried to hide it from even the sunlight. It was crippled and pitifully deformed.

Poor little Fatima! I knew her sensitive spirit, and I put my pencil out of sight as I came nearer, for I saw on her face the shadow of a restless discontent. She smiled as she bade me welcome, but it was a sad smile, and changed to tears as she spoke.

"I am of no use," she said in Arabic. "If I were a boy, they would care for me; but a girl! They scorn me and my disfigured arm. I can never do any good in the world; never, never. And, oh, lady, there is a soul within me that longs to do something for somebody! I want to accomplish something; not to sit here day after day making figures in the sand, only to see them drift back again into a dull level. But I shall live in vain. What can I do with this poor crippled arm!"

It was a difficult task to soothe her; but I think, after awhile, she felt that the great Allah had done all things well, and peace crept over her tired little heart.

"But, dear child," I said, as I left her, "it may be that you can do more good with your one arm than I ever can with my two. We do not know what may happen."

And so I went home to my little cottage, taking the field path instead of the railroad track, as I usually did. When I reached the house, and called for my little girl-baby, who often came toddling out to meet me, all was silent, and in answer to my inquiries the nurse said she had just gone down the track a little way to meet me.

"Down the track! Oh, the train! the train! It's time for the train! Why do you stand here idle? Call Hassan and Mahomet. Run, and save her!"

I rushed wildly along the embankment. How plain it all is to me now, even to the bits of pottery gleaming in the sand, and the distant echo of an Arab's song as it floated over the hills! I saw the white dress of my darling far ahead, and stumbled on—how, I hardly knew. The train was coming! I could hear it plunging on; I could see the fearful light. Oh, if I might reach her!

But who is that? Can it be Fatima? It is Fatima, waving her arms wildly as she speeds onward. She is on the bank! She is there! She grasps the child! And the train plunges past me with a wild glare; and there, before me, is my baby, my golden-haired baby, safe and unharmed, but Fatima lay dying on the iron rail. I clasped her to my heart, and called her name amid my sobs. She lifted the long, dark eyelashes, and smiled. "Allah be praised!" she murmured. Then in her weak, broken English she said:

"Me do something wid dis poor arm; me die for you baby!" She fell back in my arms; and so we carried her to my home, white and insensible.

But she did not die. The deformed arm had to be severed from the shoulder, but her life was saved; and to-day, surrounded by all that grateful hearts can give, she is one of the happiest little creatures on the banks of the Nile.

A ST. ULRIC DOLL.

BY THE AUTHOR OF "THE CATSKILL FAIRIES."

THE steam-ship *Columbine* was crossing the ocean from Liverpool to New York. On the deck the passengers walked about, looking at the sea and sky. Occasionally they saw a flock of gulls circling about overhead, or a shoal of dolphins leaping up in the blue waves. Among these passengers was the shy gentleman. Now the shy gentleman was tall and large, with a full brown beard, which should have made him quite bold, but he was not. If a stranger spoke to him, he blushed, and if he tried to say something really wise, he merely stammered, so that his meaning was lost. As for tea-cups and wine-glasses, he always broke them with his elbow, or by allowing them to slip through his big fingers, while chairs and little tables seemed placed in his way for the sole purpose of his tumbling over them.

In his cabin was his portmanteau, filled with all sorts of treasures. A Paris doll and her wardrobe were given the place of honor. The beautiful blonde hair of this fashionable lady must not be disarranged, and the boxes containing her dresses and gloves, her boots, mantles, and parasols, required much space. She was a very important person. In a corner was wedged the case of one of those mechanical bears covered with black fur, and wound up by means of a key in his side. In the opposite corner were the Venetian lion of St. Mark, made of brass, trinkets of straw and glass, and a little Neapolitan boy in mosaic on the lid of a box. The St. Ulric doll, folded in a bit of tissue-paper, had been allowed to fall down anywhere. She was made of a single stick of wood, with a head carved on top, but without arms or legs, like the Italian babies, who are wound about with cloths until they resemble little mummies.

She remained quietly where she had been placed, between a flannel waistcoat and a pair of stockings, with her head resting on a meerschaum pipe. She thought of her home, and sighed. Yes, she was homesick, because she loved her own land as only the Tyrolese and the Swiss love their native mountains.

The shy gentleman had bought the St. Ulric doll at a booth under the stone archway of one of the streets of Botzen. He could not carry away with him the beautiful Austrian Tyrol, except as pictures in his own mind, and therefore he picked up the droll and ugly little St. Ulric doll.

"When I give the doll to Nelly, I will tell her about the mountain peaks where the hunters climb to shoot the chamois and the black-cock, and the valleys down toward Italy where the grapes ripen, and all about the castles perched like watch-towers along the Brenner route," thought the shy gentleman, wrapping the purchase in the bit of tissue-paper. "I must not forget to add that this Brenner Pass, where the traveller of to-day journeys on the railway from Munich to Verona, is one of the oldest highways in the world; the Etruscan merchants used to pass here, trading in iron with the Northern nations, long before the Romans."

One day a tremendous rattling was heard inside the case of the mechanical bear.

"What is the matter? Are you sea-sick?" inquired the lion of St. Mark.

"No," grumbled the mechanical bear. "I have been standing on my head too long, and if this voyage does not soon end, my machinery will be out of order. I shall growl at the wrong time."

"We must be gifts for children. I hope they will like us," said the St. Ulric doll.

"I hope we shall like *them*," said the French doll. "I came from a shop window on the Boulevard des Italiens. How can I live out of Paris!"

Just then the lid of the portmanteau was lifted, and a Custom-house officer looked in. The steamer had reached New York.

"Here he is, mamma!" cried a little girl, as a carriage paused before the door of a house on Gramercy Square.

She had been looking out of the window. Now she ran down stairs, and opened the front door. Two gentlemen got out of the carriage; one was her uncle Fred, and the other a traveller with a brown beard, whose arms were full of mysterious parcels and boxes. This was the shy gentleman, and Nelly had always found him a good friend. Soon the parcels were distributed. The mosaic box was for mother, the brass lion for Uncle Fred, and all the rest for Nelly. She was wild with delight. The Paris doll fascinated her. All her friends were invited to admire the lady from the Boulevards. Nelly could not eat, or sleep, or study her lessons. She tried on all the dresses, gloves, bonnets, and shoes.

The St. Ulric doll had been glanced at, laid on the table, and forgotten. At length Nelly wearied of so much splendor, and her mother found the Paris doll too fine for every-day play. Nelly noticed the St. Ulric doll then.

"You have no clothes, poor thing," she said.

She opened her own work-box, sought in a bag for a piece of blue flannel, and began to sew. Soon the St. Ulric doll was clothed. To be sure, her gown was like a bag tied about her neck.

Nelly's mother, a pretty widow, said, "I did not know he loved me."

Nelly whispered to the St. Ulric doll that her mother was to marry the shy gentleman.

"I thought there was a good reason for bringing us across the sea," said the St. Ulric doll to the mechanical bear and the Paris lady.

The latter was out of temper.

"Already the little girl loves you best, because she has made your gown herself," she said.

THE GRIZZLY BEAR.

THE grizzly bear is the most terrible of all beasts. Its great strength, its enormous size, its ferocity, and its courage render it a more formidable enemy than the lion. It ranges the westward-lying slopes of the Rocky Mountains from Mexico to British America, and is a constant terror to the regions it inhabits.

The average length of the grizzly bear is about seven feet, and its weight nine hundred to a thousand pounds, although much larger specimens have been killed in Arizona and other Southern regions.

Grizzlies do not often attack men unless surprised or infuriated, or driven by desperate hunger to seize upon everything which crosses their path; but all animals, from a

GRIZZLY BEAR AND BUFFALOES.

mouse to an enormous buffalo, fall an easy prey to this monarch of the far West.

The immense daring of the grizzly bear, and its entire confidence in its strength, are evident from the fact that it will not hesitate to attack buffaloes even when a whole herd are together. It has been known to kill a buffalo with one blow of its terrible fore-paw, and afterward to drag it away and bury it. It can easily dig a hole with its cimeter-like claws, and it usually buries what it can not devour, as a store to fall back upon when provisions are scarce.

Hunters tell many stories of sharp contests between grizzlies and buffaloes. The bear will prowl by the side of a herd, keeping under cover of the bushes until some big fat fellow comes within easy reach, when it rushes on its victim, and with one blow fells it to the ground. The other buffaloes may rush to the rescue of their comrade, but the powerful grizzly is generally a match for them all, and instances are rare where the savage beast has been driven to crawl away defeated.

The claws of this beast are longer than a man's finger, and are very much prized as ornaments by the Indians. To wear a necklace of bear's claws, taken from an animal killed by himself, is one of the highest ambitions of an Indian brave; for if he is thus decorated, his courage and superior strength are acknowledged by his whole tribe. An Indian will sell his horses, his blankets, everything he possesses, but nothing can induce him to part with his bear-claw necklace, which marks him as an invincible warrior. To obtain this coveted prize Indians will run the most extreme risks. Are the enormous foot-prints of a grizzly discovered in the vicinity of the camp, the men all set out in hot pursuit, and many a poor Indian has lost his life in fierce encounter with this monarch of the mountains. If the bear can be traced to its den among the rocks, the Indians will lay trails of powder leading from the lair in different directions, which, as they burn, set fire to the dry grass and stubble. As the animal, startled by the smoke and flame, rushes from its hiding-place, the Indians, who lie concealed behind rocks and bushes, pelt it with blazing pine knots, and fire volley after volley from their rifles into its body, until some lucky shot enters the heart or brain, and the monster staggers and falls dead to the ground.

This beast has a strong hold on life, and has often been known to run with great speed, and even to swim deep rivers, with twenty or more large rifle-balls in its body. It is so difficult to kill, and so furious when aroused, that a hunter will never attack the grizzly single-handed if the encounter can be avoided. The hunter may escape by climbing a tree; for although young grizzlies can climb like a cat, the old bears can do nothing more than stand on their hind-legs in vain endeavors to reach the branches where the man lies concealed, and growl spitefully. Their extreme heaviness, however, is thought by the Indians to be all that prevents them from climbing.

A hunter once took refuge in a tree from one of these savage beasts, and having vainly discharged all his ammunition at the monster, he endeavored to hit it in the eye with cones, thinking to drive it away. But the grizzly only became more infuriated, and began a brisk war-dance around the tree, howling all the while in a terrible manner. At length the branch upon which the hunter was sitting began to give way, and the unfortunate man felt himself doomed to certain death. Closing his eyes, he resigned himself to the worst, when, instead of falling, as he expected, into the open jaws of the huge beast, he, together with the heavy branch upon which he had been sitting, landed with a tremendous thump upon the grizzly's head. The animal was so astonished and frightened at this sudden and unexpected assault, that it took to its heels, and soon disappeared in the forest. Such miraculous escapes, however, are not frequent, and the number of Indians and hunters killed by grizzlies is very large.

Young grizzlies have often been captured, and when very small are as playful and affectionate as dogs. But they are not to be trusted, for as they grow older, their savage nature develops, and they are liable to become dangerous property. Unless they can be surprised away from the mother, their capture is attended by the utmost peril. Nothing can exceed the fury of the mother bear if her little ones are molested. Rising on her hind-legs for a moment to survey the object of her hatred, she will utter a hoarse "huff, huff, huff," and charge madly, and wary and courageous must be the hunter who can overcome this savage monster.

Hunting the grizzly is usually accomplished by parties of men well mounted, and with bands of trained dogs, but the huge beast will make a desperate fight for its life, and often severely wounds numbers of its assailants before being forced itself to succumb.

A MINIATURE YACHT REGATTA.—Drawn by F. S. Cozzens.—[See next Page.]

MINIATURE YACHTS.

ON the preceding page is an illustration of a miniature yacht regatta on the Lake in Prospect Park, Brooklyn. In that beautiful Park there are few sights to be seen as beautiful as this. The dainty yachts, perfect in every detail, look like graceful white-winged birds skimming over the water, and the announcement of a regatta on the Lake often attracts more spectators than similar announcements of "grown-up" regattas down the bay. Many of these spectators are very critical, and attend these regattas in order to study fine points of sailing, and to learn what models will show the greatest speed.

The little yachts are so carefully planned and built that they often serve as models for those of many tons. Some of the finest yachts of the New York, Brooklyn, Atlantic, and Seawanhaka Yacht Clubs are built from models furnished by winners of races and regattas on the lakes of Central and Prospect Parks.

Two regularly organized and officered clubs, the New York and Brooklyn Miniature Yacht Clubs, are the rivals of these lakes, and many exciting match races are sailed between the flyers of the two clubs. These races and all the regattas are governed by the regular rules of yachting, time allowances being made for differences of measurement, and the amount of canvas allowed each boat, as well as the course to be sailed, being accurately defined.

Of the miniature yachts, schooners of the first class are generally about sixty inches long, are heavily sparred—that is, they have very tall masts, long booms, and bowsprit—and are ballasted with very deep and heavy lead keels. They are either "built" or "cut"—that is, ribbed and planked, or worked out from a single block of wood.

They carry rudders merely to make them look shipshape, and are steered entirely by their sails. These are so arranged as to balance fore and aft, and the jib and main sheets are made of elastic rubber, so nicely adjusted that if the boat is inclined to sail too close to the wind, the main-sheet stretches, the mainsail is eased off, and she resumes her proper course, with the wind free. If she is inclined to "fall off" too much, and run before the wind, the jib-sheet stretches, the wind spills out of the jib, and the pressure upon her aftersails quickly brings her up on the wind again.

The fleet at Prospect Park this season numbers some fifty sail, from sixty-inch schooners down to ten-inch cat-boats, and contains schooners, sloops, cat-boats, catamarans, and one square-rigged steamer. An English cutter will probably be added to the fleet very soon, and interesting races between her and the boats of American model are expected.

EASY BOTANY.

JUNE.

JUNE has many beautiful flowering trees, and many rare and remarkable plants. Some of the anemones bloom in April and May, but several wait for June. Among these the rare red anemone is found on rocky banks in Western Vermont, in Northern New York, and Pennsylvania.

Among the pines and maples of Cape Ann, at Manchester, Massachusetts, we find the laurel-magnolia, or sweet-bay, with silky leaves and buds, and deliciously fragrant cream-white flowers. This charming shrub seems to belong to the South, but has strangely strayed away, and made for itself a cozy home on the "stern and rock-bound coast" of New England. This magnolia also grows in Pennsylvania and Southern New York.

Belonging to the same fair family is the tulip-tree, with large tulip-shaped flowers tinged with yellow, orange, and green. These trees are found in rich soil in the Middle, Southern, and Western States.

Another wonderful plant of June is the large water-lily the *Nelumbo luteum*, or water-chinquepin. This plant apparently belongs to the East Indies, and seems to be nearly related to the pink lotus, or sacred bean of India. The American species is rare, being found at but few places; but Connecticut professes to possess it in the Connecticut River, near Lyme; and it is found in the Delaware River, near Philadelphia, at Woodstown and Swedesborough, New Jersey, and in several Western lakes. The leaves are circular, from one to two feet in diameter, and raised high above the water; the fragrant flowers are pale yellow; the seeds, sunk deeply in a receptacle, are as large as acorns.

Our own beautiful white pond-lily is well known and well beloved; and few New-Englanders are unfamiliar with the serene ponds and still waters where the lily pads make a carpet on which rest the lovely heads of these delicious favorites.

At Sandwich and Barnstable, Massachusetts, and Kennebunk, Maine, are found lilies of a fine rose-color. The common cow-lily, as it is called, though not a beauty like its relatives, is a pleasing variety, being of a rich yellow color.

Next we come to the wonderful pitcher-plants, whose chosen homes are in the black mud of peat-bogs and swamps.

The one with which we are most familiar is favored not only with a botanical name of seven syllables, but has the common names of side-saddle-flower, pitcher-plant, and hunter's-cup—all referring more or less to the curious leaves, which are hollow, and shaped like little pitchers, and are always found partly filled with water. The flower, nodding on a tall stalk, is as singular as the leaves; it is of a deep reddish-purple color, the petals arching over a little green umbrella in the centre, which covers the stamens. This striking and interesting plant may be easily found by any enterprising young botanist who is not afraid of mud and water, as it grows from Maine to Illinois and southward.

Another queer little dweller in bogs and swamps and wet meadows is the sundew, one species of which may be found in June, and others later. The leaves of this peculiar plant are covered with fine reddish-brown hairs, or glands, which furnish small drops of fluid, glittering like dew-drops.

Three species of wild oxalis, or wood-sorrel, should not be overlooked. The *yellow*, which is found everywhere, is so common as to be unappreciated; but the *white*, with petals streaked with red lines, is very pretty: it is found in deep, cold woods in Massachusetts and the Middle States. The *violet* wood-sorrel is, however, the beauty of the family, and rare enough to require being searched for. It springs from a bulb in shady, rocky woods in New Jersey, Pennsylvania, and New York; three or four soft purple blossoms nod on a slender stalk, and it is a lovely little plant. All the wood-sorrels are attractive and interesting from the graceful and pathetic habit which they have of folding up and drooping their delicate leaves at night-fall, opening them at the early light of morning.

The showy wild lupine comes out with long racemes of purple, pink, blue, and white blossoms, covering sandy fields with a flush of color.

The dear wild roses make the wood paths beautiful, and the indescribably delicious fragrance of the sweet-brier betrays its location on the dry banks and rocky road-sides.

The flowering raspberry, found in moist woods and shady dells, is as beautiful as the rose, and the buds, if possible, more beautiful than rose-buds. The flowers are large, of a vivid deep rose-red, and the leaves maple-shaped, and very graceful.

In June, also, come six or eight species of *Cornus*, or dogwood, each beautiful in its way. These shrubs, which are generally found in rich soil in rocky, open woods, are rare in New England, but abundant in the Middle States.

The brilliant little bunchberry, however, which belongs to the *Cornus* family, delights in the deep cold woods of Maine, where it grows luxuriantly, its rich red berries charming the eye in the depths of the forest.

In the gloom of shady woods, at the roots of pine and oak trees, the young botanist may perhaps be startled to see an array of little *ghosts*, as it were, springing from dead leaves, and without one touch of the green of summer, but waxen-white in every part, leaves, stems, and all, sometimes having a faint shade of pink or tawny yellow. This is the Indian-pipe, with none of the healthful honesty of other plants, but stealing its existence from surrounding neighbors; and with this ghostly parasite we will close the list for June, not that it is exhausted, for hundreds stand waiting, but it would take a *book* to tell of them all.

FLOWERS OF JUNE.

COMMON NAME.	COLOR.	LOCALITY, ETC.
Alpine azalea	Wh., rose-color	White Mts., rocky hills; N. E.
Alum-root	Greenish-purple	Rocky woodlands; Conn. to Wis.
Alum-root, downy	Purplish-white	Rich woods; Lancaster, Pa.
American ipecac	Rose-color	Damp woods; N. Y., Pa., and West.
Arrow-wood	White, light blue berries	Wet places. Common North.
Bell-shaped sullivantia	White	Limestone cliffs; Ohio, Wis.
Bird's-eye primrose	Pale lilac	Shores of Western lakes; Mt. Kineo, Me.
Black snakeroot	Greenish-yellow	Copses, open glades. Common.
Black huckleberry	Reddish, berries black	Woodlands. Common.
Blue tangle	White, berries dark blue	Low copses; New England.
Bunchberry	White flowers, red berries	Damp, cold, deep woods; Me.
Burning-bush	Dark purple	Shaded woods; N. Y., Pa., South.
Bush honeysuckle	Honey yellow	Rocks and thickets; Northward.
Buttercups	Yellow	Banks and fields. Common.
Cassiope	Wh., rose-color	White Mts., Adirondacks, Me. Rare.
Chervil	White	Fields and copses; Lancaster, Pa., N. J.
Chinquapin, American lotus	Pale yellow	Conn., N. J., West. lakes. Rare.
Clustered bell-flower	Deeper blue	Road-sides; Danvers, Mass.
Coffee-tree	White racemes	River-banks, rich soil; N. Y., Pa., West.
Collinsia	Blue and white	Moist soil; N. Y., Pa., West.
Common elder	Flowers white, berries black	Banks, rich soil. Common.
Cornel, panicled	Flowers and berries white	Thickets and river banks.
Cornel, red osier	Whitish; berries white	Damp New England pastures.
Cornel, silky	White, berries pale blue	Wet places. Common.
Cow-lily	Bright yellow	Still waters. Very common.
Cranberry-tree	Wh., red berries	Low, damp grounds; N. J.
Crowberry	White	Mountains; New England.
Cuckoo-flower	Rose-color, wh.	Bogs, swamps; Vt., N. J.
Dahoon holly	Yellow-white	Swamps of Virginia.
Dwarf raspberry	White	Hillsides; N. E. to Pa. Common.
Dwarf wild rose	Deep pink	Dry rocky banks and fields; N. E.
Evening primrose	Pale yellow	Sandy fields; N. J. and South.
False indigo	Violet	River-banks; Pa., South, West.
Feverwort	Brownish-purple	Rich woodlands. Common.
Flowering dogwood	Purplish-white, red berries	Rocky woods; Conn., N. J., South.
Flowering raspberry	Deep red purple	Cañons, wooded banks; New Eng.
Fumitory, climbing	Purplish-white	Wet woods; West.
Great-spurred violet	Pale violet	Damp shady woods; Miss. Rare.
Great willow-herb	Pink purple	Low grounds, burned pastures, and woods.
Green violet	Greenish-white	Open woods; N. Y., Pa. Rare.
Green-weed	Yellow	Dry hills; Mass., Middle States, W.
Hedysarum	Violet-purple	Mountains; New England, Me.
Herb-robert	Red-purple	Shady ravines, wet woods; N. E.
High blackberry	White	Woods, pastures, banks. Common.
Ilex holly	Greenish	Moist woodlands; sea-coast, N. J.
Indian-pipe	Waxy white	Dark shady woods; New England.
Inkberry	White flowers, berries black	Sandy grounds; Cape Ann.
Labrador tea	White	Cold bogs and mountain woods; New England.
Leather-flower	Purple	Rich woods; N. J., N. Y., West.
Low blackberry	White	Low woods, road-sides. Common.
Magnolia, sweet bay	White	Cape Ann, Gloucester and Manchester woods.
Marsh five-finger	Purple	Cool bogs; New England to Pa.
Marsh violet	Pale lilac	White Mts., high lands N. Rare.
Meadow-sweet	White	Damp soil, banks; N. J., West.
Mountain laurel	Pink and white	Rocky hills, damp soil. Common.
Mountain sandwort	White	Mountains; New England.
Nine-bark	Wh., rose-color	Rocky river-banks; West.
One-flowered pyrola	White-pink	Deep cold New England woods.
Pale laurel	Light purple	Cold peat bogs and mountains.
Partridge-berry	Purple and white, red berries	Dry woods, creeping. Common.
Persimmon	Pale yellow	Woods and old fields; R. I., N. Y.
Pimpernel	Scarlet, blue, wh.	Waste sandy fields; Rare, N. J.
Pitcher-plant	Deep purple	Peat-bogs and swamps; New Eng.
Poison-ivy, climbing	Greenish	Rocky thickets, low grounds.
Poison sumac	Dull color, very poisonous	Swamps and wet pastures.
Pond-lily	White, pink	Ponds, pools, and still waters. Common.
Prince's-pine	Pale pink	Dry woods. Common.
Pyrola	Greenish white	Rich woods; Conn., N. J., N. Y.
Queen of the prairie	Peach-color	Open meadows; Pa., prairies W.
Red anemone	Red	Rocky hills; Vt., N. Y. Rare.
Red elder	Flowers white, berries red	Rocky woods; New England.
Round-leaved cornus	White, berries blue	Rich soil, copses; Middle States.
Roxbury wax-work, climbing	Red berries	Thickets; N. E., Middle States.
Seneca snakeroot	White	Rocky soil; N. E., West, South.
Sheep-laurel	Crimson	Hill-sides, pastures. Common.
Shrubby cinque-foil	Yellow	Wet grounds; N. E. Common.
Silver-weed	Yellow	Brackish marshes and meadows; New England, West.
Small cranberry	Rose-color	Peat bogs; N. E., Middle States.
Spotted wintergreen	Pink and white	Open woods; Middle States.
Staghorn sumac	Greenish	Hill-sides, dry banks. Common.
Strawberry-bush	Greenish-purple	Wooded banks; N. Y., Ill., South.
Sundew	White	Bogs, wet pastures; New Eng.
Sundrops	Yellow	Open fields; N. J., N. Y., Pa.
Supple-jack, climb'g	Greenish white	Damp meadows; Va. and South.
Swamp-honeysuckle	White-pink	Swamps; New England sea-coast.
Swamp-rose	Pink	Swamps and pastures. Common.
Swamp-saxifrage	Greenish	Bogs, wet pastures. Common.
Sweet-brier	Pale pink	Rocky banks, road-sides; N. E.
Sweet cicely	White	Rich moist Northern woods.
Tall bell-flower	Bright blue	Rich soil; N. Y., N. J., West.
Three-toothed cinque-foil	White	Brunswick, Me., White Mts., Cape Cod. Rare.
Twin-flower	Pale pink	Moist, mossy woods; Me., N. J., N. Y.
Valerian	Pale pink	Wooded banks; Lancaster, Pa., O.
Wild elder	Greenish-white	Rocky banks, thickets. Common.
Wild flax	Yellow	Wet, boggy grounds; New England, West. Rare.
Wild honeysuckle	Light yellow	Rocky banks; Catskill, Ohio, W.
Wild [illegible]	White	Sandy shores; Western N. Y.
Wild lupine	Purple, blue, pink, white	Sandy open fields; Mass., Conn.
Wild monk's-hood	Bright blue	Rich shady hills; N. Y., N. J., S.
Wild pea	Purple, white	Dry sandy soil; North and South.
Wild red raspberry	White	Thickets, road-sides; N. E., South, and West.
Wild sarsaparilla	White	Moist woods; North and West.
Wild touch-me-not	Orange, brown	Thickets, shades, beside streams. Common.
Wood-sorrel	Violet	Rocky, damp woods; Orange, N. J., South. Rare.
Wood-sorrel	White, red veins	Deep cold woods; Maine to Pa.
Wood-sorrel	Yellow	Copses and open fields; everywhere.
Yellow-wood	Showy white flowers	Rich woods and hills; Middle States.

THE ADVENTURES OF A RAT RACE.

BY JAMES B. MARSHALL.

THE carpenters came on a certain Monday morning to make some needed alterations about Mr. Wilson's stable at the rear of his house yard. And you know what a noise carpenters will make when working; far more than enough to disturb the most contented of rats.

Peggy O'Conner, who was moving to and from the

SWINGING "BRER RABBIT."—DRAWN BY PALMER COX.

kitchen hanging up linen to dry in the yard, said she saw no rat pass by her; but as a rat was found in the library, it must have come there by way of the side yard from the stable.

It was a rather warm summer morning, but with enough of a breeze blowing to start Uncle Leonard sneezing if he should drop off to sleep while sitting in a draught. Now, merry Uncle Leonard was asleep in an easy-chair down in the library, where the two window-sashes were raised and both doors were open. He had gone there, as usual, to read the morning paper, but gradually it drooped nearer and nearer the end of his nose, as usual, until it finally spread itself adroitly over his closed eyes, to fend off the flies. Then he began to make that soft steam-enginery sound that most stout gentlemen make when asleep, about as loud as the purring of "Cattegat," Lou and Amy's cat.

Cattegat always followed Uncle Leonard to the library if possible, to escape Lou and Amy, who, during their vacation, were trying to teach him to hold a lump of sugar on the end of his nose while seated on his hind paws. Cattegat, who liked the sugar but not the trick, had been so named by a Danish gentleman who had presented him to Lou and Amy.

The rat as it entered the library thought, doubtless, that it was a pretty comfortable-looking place, or else it wouldn't have gone about the room smelling and sniffing until it found a piece of sponge-cake, knocked by the canary from the wires of its cage.

That little breeze went on blowing across Uncle Leonard's head, and directly he gave a rousing "ashoo!" of a sneeze. Such an "a-a-sh-sh-shoo," that he actually sneezed himself into a sitting position. The rat was more startled at such a noise than at all the carpenters had made, and dropping the cake, peeped from behind an ottoman where it took refuge.

Cattegat jumped up and looked at Uncle Leonard as if to ask him if he had made that noise, and then glanced about the room.

"What can ail the cat?" exclaimed Uncle Leonard, as Cattegat went across the floor in about three springs. Then quickly closing the yard door, he called, "A rat! a rat!" as the rat ran from behind the ottoman.

Cattegat and the rat raced headlong around the room once, and Uncle Leonard nearly kicked himself off his feet as the rat slipped unhurt by him. Then away went the rat out of the library through the other door, along the hall, and up the front stairs; away tore Cattegat not far behind it; and quickly in pursuit trotted Uncle Leonard, calling, "Catch him, Cattegat; catch him, Cattegat!"

At the moment, Lou, a very handy boy about the house, was in a second-story room near the head of the stairs, and had just finished gluing in the leg of Amy's rocking-chair. He had taken the chair there to mend, because the floor was not carpeted, but smoothly varnished, and any glue dropped could be easily removed. Amy stood watching him as she slowly untied a package of prepared chalk for the teeth, with which she had shortly before returned from the drug store.

"Gracious! what's coming up stairs?" said Lou, placing the glue brush on the chair beside the glue-pot, and stepping to the door.

"Look out for the rat!" shouted Uncle Leonard.

Amy instantly sprang on the first object at hand, her just-mended rocking-chair, which gave way, of course, and over she went. However, she broke her fall by catching at the chair holding the glue-pot and brush, though the glue rolled to the right and the brush to the left. The package of prepared chalk, that had received an upward pitch as Amy had toppled over, then came down in time to plentifully powder both her and Lou.

The latter had turned to clear the way for the rat and Cattegat, not more than an instant later than Amy had taken alarm, but the glue had been spilled more quickly. And though Lou jumped over the pool of glue safely, he landed right under the shower of chalk, and directly upon the slippery glue brush. Presto! down went Lou, and shooting over the smooth floor, vanished under the bed at the far end of the room, as though he had been a clown playing in a pantomime.

Amy, so filled with laughter, could scarce manage to

climb on the second chair before the rat and Cattegat came whizzing through the doorway; both leaped clear of the spilled glue, and scampered in a flash across the floor into the next room, and so on through several other rooms that communicated.

"Oho! bravo, Cattegat!" said Uncle Leonard, as he came on, running at a wonderful rate for him. Right through the doorway he ran, but on seeing Amy, he was about to lessen his speed, and have her join in the chase, when he stepped in the pool of glue. Slip, slip, slide across the room, went Uncle Leonard, with his feet getting farther apart, as though the floor was the slipperiest of ice. He slid to and against a wash-stand, and then sank down slowly and gracefully at its foot in a way that would have done credit to a champion gymnast. But he shook the stand so violently that the water-pitcher was shaken over within its basin, and emptied half its contents upon his head.

Amy rushed to his aid, righted the pitcher, and inquired if he was hurt.

"Not a bit," said Uncle Leonard, getting again on his feet, smiling mirthfully at his own dripping coat, and giving one of those jolly laughs of his at Amy's chalk-powdered head. "Come along, my dear," continued he; "keep the chase up, or the rat will yet have the best of it. But where's Lou?"

"Here I am!" answered Lou, poking his laughing, powdered face from under the bed, and crawling out. And away they all followed the chase, Uncle Leonard kicking off his gluey slippers, and catching up a pair of Papa Wilson's.

Cattegat and the rat in the mean time had been racing up and down the front bedrooms, frightening Mamma Wilson and Aunt Laura into climbing up on one of the beds, and Cattegat had distinguished himself by knocking over a sewing basket and a screen. As the pursuers appeared upon the scene, rat and cat ran out into the hallway again, through a door that Aunt Laura had opened, hoping to get clear of them.

Then pat, pat, pat, again in chase went Lou and Amy's shoes; flap, flap, flap, followed Uncle Leonard's slippers; and Mamma Wilson and Aunt Laura brought up the rear with an irregular run and walk. Right through the length of the whole second story, through the hallway, and from room to room they rushed, with such a clatter and whoop as had never before been heard in that house, merry as were its people.

Cattegat will now surely catch that ferocious rat in the last room, thought every one. But no; straight down the back stairs plunged the rat, and jump, jump, followed Cattegat, still several feet behind it. And at the bottom of the stairway, closed by a door, the race would have been doubtlessly won by Cattegat, but Peggy O'Conner, hearing such an unusual commotion overhead, came to the door to inquire its cause. As Peggy opened the door she heard several voices call: "Don't open that door; Cattegat's after a rat."

Bang! went the door—closed quickly, I assure you; but something flew past Peggy, and she only shut the door in Cattegat's face.

As that something, very much like a rat, flew past Peggy, and vanished out of the kitchen, a piece of soap that Katie, the other girl, threw with a very bad aim, went flying after it. But frightened Peggy, in dismay, raised her hands, backed awkwardly against a tub of blue water on the floor, and before she could recover her balance, splashed down into the water, which flew about like the spray of a great fountain.

As the whole party filed down the back stairs, Katie was trying amidst her merriment to help wringing-wet Peggy out of her queer bath, and all but Cattegat had something to laugh at.

Cattegat seemed very much disappointed because the rat had escaped, and went out in the yard, and hid himself under a rose-bush.

As for the rat, Lou is pretty certain that he sees it occasionally capering about the stable, very much unlike a common rat that has never had an adventure.

THE MORNING MESSAGE.

BY E. N. M.

A BEAM was sent out by the morning sun
To carry the message that day had begun.

First the gay courier told his story
To the opening buds of the morning-glory.

The birds in their nest on the branch o'erhead
Heard every word that the sunbeam said,

And all at once in the trees was heard
The twittered "good-morning" of each little bird.

Then in at the window the messenger flew,
And all around him his gold he threw.

He scattered it here, and everywhere,
He gilded the braids of the mother's hair.

He glanced at the baby, who laughed with glee,
And danced for joy on his mother's knee.

And little Clara, the three-year-old,
Tried to catch at the shining gold;

And she said, "Mamma, if I'm good to-day,
Perhaps this beautiful sunbeam will stay."

OUR POST-OFFICE BOX.

ber in HARPER'S BAZAR. She is a very estimable and charitable lady, and universally respected.

RICHARD S. C.—The best thing for you to do is to visit some establishment where the article you require is for sale. There are so many kinds and so many sizes of bicycles that it is impossible for us to give you any idea of prices.

PUZZLES FROM YOUNG CONTRIBUTORS.

No. 1.

ENIGMA.

My first is in fortune, not in luck.
My second in calves, not in stock.
My third in squadron, not in fleet.
My fourth in company, not in band.
My fifth in bottle, not in wreath.
My sixth in rigging, not in sleeve.
My seventh in sailor, not in flag.
My eighth in [illegible], not in brag.
All these letters will show to you
An officer gallant, tender, and true.

MARY D.

No. 2.

[illegible] PUZZLE.

A familiar proverb:
[illegible]

C. K. S.

No. 3.

WORD CHANGES.

[illegible]

1. Love to hate. 2. Fret to [illegible]. 3. Cent to [illegible]. 4. Head to foot. 5. Bear to [illegible]. 6. Hare to [illegible]. 7. Oaken to [illegible].

C. P. T.

No. 4.

ENIGMA.

My first is in schooner, not in ship.
My second is in boat, but not in whip.
My third is in team, but not in steed.
My fourth is in chase, but not in heed.
My fifth is in pie, but not in cake.
My sixth is in shovel, but not in rake.
My seventh is in shin, but not in well.
My eighth is in tongue, but not in bell.
My ninth is in castle, but not in tower.
My whole is a fragrant, beautiful flower.

BELLE H.

No. 5.

NUMERICAL CHARADE.

My whole is a great composer of 11 letters.
My 11, 2, 3, 4, 5 is a celebrated tower.
My 3, 10, 9 is useful at night.
My 6, 8, 7 is a member of the family.

AVA.

No. 6.

[illegible] PUZZLE.

In [illegible]. A Spanish term. A [illegible]. A [illegible]. In [illegible].

M. V.

ANSWERS TO PUZZLES IN NO. 28.

No. 1. 1. Troy, Galveston. 2. [illegible], Trenton. 3. Mobile, Lima. 4. Utica, [illegible]. 5. Salem, Alton.

No. 2. [illegible].

No. 3.

```
O R G A N
R O L L A
G L O O M
A L O N E
N A M E S
```

No. 4. The [illegible] mystery.

No. 5.

```
    W
  A A R
W A L R S
  R E D
    S
```

No. 6.

```
N  [illegible]  N
A  [illegible]  A
P  [illegible]  S
L  ockpor  T
E  [illegible]  S
S  [illegible]  U
```

Naples, Nassau.

"Aunt Flora's Answer," a broken rhyme, on page [illegible]:

Start, tack, eat. Shut, [illegible], it.	Bread, tread, each. Saintly, [illegible], [illegible].

Answer to "Throwing Light," on page [illegible]—Crane, crown.

Correct answers to puzzles are received from Grace N. Whiting, [illegible], W. L. [illegible], "[illegible]," A. E. Ellard, "[illegible]," Allie and [illegible], E. [illegible], [illegible], [illegible], Mary E. [illegible].

Favors are acknowledged from W. [illegible], [illegible], J. E. R., [illegible], J. W. [illegible], Charles H. [illegible].

ANSWERS TO WIGGLE No. 11, OUR ARTIST'S IDEA, AND NEW WIGGLE No. 12.

INSTRUCTIONS TO WIGGLE CONTRIBUTORS.

[illegible]

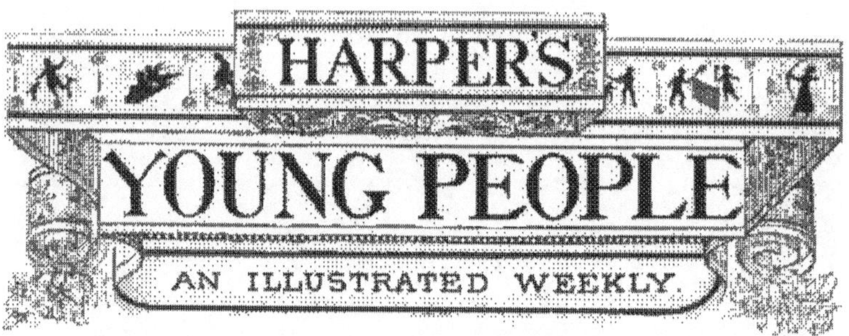

Vol. I.—No. 33. | Published by HARPER & BROTHERS, New York. | Price Four Cents.
Tuesday, June 15, 1880. | Copyright, 1880, by Harper & Brothers. | $1.50 per Year, in Advance.

CHARLEY'S BALLOON VOYAGE.

BY FRANK H. TAYLOR.

"BAL-LOON! balloon! Oh, Charley! where are you, Charley? There's a balloon a-comin'."

Charley's big brother Harry came running excitedly down the road, and vaulted the farm-yard fence in a state of great excitement. "Oh, Charley, come out quick and see the balloon."

Charley was nowhere to be found. He had wandered off home before to his favorite rock by the brook to have a "good cry." And this was the reason of it: One day, a short time before, he had been into the town of Wayneburg, not many miles distant, with Harry. Charley didn't often have a chance to go to town, and you may be sure he made the best use of his eyes. The one thing which he remembered above everything else was the big poster-board near the market, covered over every inch of it with bright-colored pictures of leaping horses, trick mules, flying riders jumping through hoops, comical clowns, and, above all, a big balloon just rising out of the crowd, everybody swinging their hats.

For two weeks Charley had talked of nothing, thought of nothing, dreamed of nothing but the coming show, and so, when his mother promised to take him to see it all, he was the happiest little boy in the county. But, alas! Charley's mother was taken sick just before the circus came, and there was no one else to go with him. Harry was too young and wild to be trusted, she said, and so poor Charley staid at home, and, sitting upon the big gate-post, watched the wagon-loads of people rattling merrily into town, bound for a day's fun. With swelling heart he wished he was a full-grown man. Then he strayed down by the creek, as I have said, to tell his grief to the fishes.

Harry, who had felt almost as badly as Charley, though he scorned to cry about it, kept on shouting until Charley peeped above the orchard wall to see what was wanted. Then he too spied the balloon. It didn't look bigger than his top, away up among the fleecy clouds, but it rapidly grew to the size of a pippin, and then over the hill came two or three galloping horsemen, swinging their hats, and shouting as they rode.

Now the balloon began to descend, and shortly disappeared behind the woods back of the house. Charley didn't know whether to run or stand still, and while he was doubting, the great yellow dome arose into sight again, and this time Charley could see the men in the basket. They were looking down, and calling to the men in the road to take hold of the long drag-rope, and pull them down.

This was not hard to do, as a balloon is so prettily balanced when in the air that in a light wind a little boy like Charley could pull it to the earth. It is not so easy when the balloon is going rapidly. I once saw a plucky dog catch hold of the rope with his teeth, and it jerked him along over fences and through a stubble field on his back, and I guess when he let go he had but very little hair left. Well, they pulled the balloon down, and before the men got out several large stones were put into the basket to hold it down, and the rope was tied to a strong post. One of the men was tall and stoop-shouldered, with a long sandy beard; they called him "Professor" (a queer title for a balloon man, is it not?). The second man was tall and good-looking; he belonged to the circus company. And the third was the artist, whose sketches you see in this paper.

After a little, Charley's mother came to the door, and invited the three strangers into the house, but they preferred to sit on the step; and the Professor took Charley upon his knee, and asked him how he would like to travel in the way they did. How odd! Why, that was the very thing he was wishing for at the moment. He had often watched the birds, and longed for their wings for a little while. The Professor said, "I'll tell you what we'll do, Charley; you and I will get into the basket, and tell them to let us up to the end of the rope." Charley's mother was afraid to allow him to go; but the tall man told her the Professor often took children up that way, where he came down when voyaging. Sometimes he had seen a dozen in the basket at once; so she consented, and shortly they were seated with plenty of stout hands hold of the rope, "paying out," as the sailors say. Above the barn they rose, then higher than the big elm. Up, up, until the folks below looked very short and funny, with all their faces turned up to the sky. Charley's mother didn't look larger than a doll.

I wish I could tell you all that Charley and the Professor saw as they sat there so high and secure. Away over the hill was the town, and, beyond, a winding river and another village that he had never seen before; indeed, there were several towns in sight. He was sure they must be Boston, New York, and Chicago. He thought he could see the ocean and the Rocky Mountains; but the one was only distant plains, and the other the Catskills, about fifty miles away.

The Professor told Charley a great many things about his voyages. Once he was blown out to sea, and when he had almost given up hope, the rope was overtaken by a sail-boat in pursuit, and he was towed ashore; again, he had floated over burning forests, and once came to the earth from the weight of snow on the balloon; and once, too, his balloon was torn in the top of a high tree.

Suddenly a great shout was heard from below, and the Professor looked down. He quickly said to Charley: "Now, my boy, don't be frightened. They have made a mistake down there, and let loose the rope. We are going up into the clouds, but I will bring you down all right."

Charley was a brave little fellow, and besides this, he had confidence in the Professor, who seemed to manage his "air-ship," as it is often called, so skillfully. What a great thing it is to have confidence in a leader!

The shouting below was very faint and distant now. They were among the clouds, and in a moment were enveloped in one of them. It was just like a fog. The soft white masses rolled and whirled close beside the basket; it was very cool and damp.

In a minute the Professor exclaimed, "Look, Charley; we are above the clouds."

"What a funny smell the clouds have!" said Charley; upon which the Professor laughed heartily, and showed him that the neck of the balloon was open, and some of the gas was flowing out. He explained that the gas took up more room as they arose, until it finally escaped in the way. Then he pulled on a small rope which was fastened to the top of the balloon, and a rushing sound was heard. This was caused by the escaping gas going through the valve. This interested Charley, who wanted to know the "why" of everything.

When he looked about again, they had once more passed through the clouds, and far below were square light and dark spots, which he knew were woods and fields. These kept growing in size, and finally right below appeared a mill where he had often gone with Harry for grist. What a commotion there was among the cattle and pigs and chickens! The miller and his men ran out and caught hold of the rope as it rattled noisily over the roof, pulling them down in the adjoining field. They were greatly astonished to find such a little fellow in the basket. As it was only five miles from where they had started, some of the horsemen who had been there were speedily at the mill. The Professor proposed that they should take the balloon back along the road to the town, which could easily be done. So the drag rope was tied to the axle of a heavy wagon with a number of men riding on it, and the balloon was allowed to float about a hundred feet from the ground. Charley still rode with the Professor in his basket, and so they reached his home. He was the hero of the day, and, to crown all, the town newspaper printed Charley's story of his trip, just as he told it to them, with his name in capitals at the top of the page.

I would like to be there, behind the door, when Charley gets this paper and sees the pictures. I advise him to cut them out and put them in a frame, and when he looks at them to resolve that he will always be as brave and manly as upon the day of his balloon trip.

A MANLY BOY.

MR. THOMAS HUGHES, author of *Tom Brown's School-Days* and *Tom Brown at Oxford*, relates many anecdotes of the boyhood of his manly brother George, a year older than himself. Many of the most noble traits of the boys of whom the author wrote were first exhibited in his brother George.

The two boys were sent to school at an early age, and before they had been there a week George showed the fine stuff he was made of. His young brother's class had a lesson in Greek history to get up, in which a part of the information communicated was that Cadmus was the first man who "carried letters from Asia to Greece." When they came to be examined, the master asked Thomas Hughes, "What was Cadmus?" This mode of putting it puzzled the boy for a moment, when suddenly remembering the word "letters," and in connection with it the man with the leather bag who used to bring his father's letters and papers, he shouted, "A postman, sir." At first the master looked very angry, but seeing that the answer had been given in perfect good faith, and that the answerer had sprung to his feet expecting promotion to the head of the class, he burst out laughing.

Of course all the boys joined in chorus, and when school was over Thomas was christened Cadmus. To this he would have made no great objection, but the blood kindled in his veins when the word was shortened into "Cad." The angrier he grew, the more eagerly some of the boys persecuted him with the hated nickname; especially one stupid fellow of twelve years old or so, who ought to have been two classes higher, and revenged himself for his degradation among the youngsters by making their small lives as miserable as he could.

A day or two after, with two or three boys for audience, he shut up little Hughes in a corner of the play-ground, and greeted him with the nickname he knew to be so offensive, "Cad, Cad," until the boy's wrath was beyond bounds. Suddenly a step was heard tearing down the gravel walk, and George, in his shirt sleeves, swept into the circle, and sent the tyrant staggering back with a blow in the chest, and then, with clinched fists, bravely confronted him. Bullies are invariably cowards, and Tom Hughes's persecutor, though three years older, much heavier, and stronger than his assailant, did not dare to face him. He walked off, muttering and growling, much to the disgust of the boys, who, boy-like, had hoped for "a jolly row;" while George returned to his comrades, after looking round and saying: "Just let me hear any of you call my brother 'Cad' again."

It is pleasant to relate that this manly, gallant-spirited fellow was a capital student. He rose from class to class until he reached the highest, amongst boys two years older than himself, and in the competition for prizes was invariably successful.

CAMBRIDGE SERIES
OF
INFORMATION CARDS FOR SCHOOLS.

No. 2.
The Sun as a Worker.

BY

W. J. ROLFE, A.M.

EVERYBODY knows that we are indebted to the sun for light and heat, but this is by no means all that we owe to him; or, rather, this includes a good deal more than we may see at first sight. The sun really does all, or nearly all, the work of the world. We talk of water-power, wind-power, steam-power, animal power, and the like; but all these are only kinds of sun-power. Let us look at them one by one, and see if the sunbeams are not the forces within or behind them all.

Water-power is the force exerted by falling or running water; and running water is falling water. In the most familiar forms of water-wheels, troughs—or buckets, as they are called—are arranged on the rim in such a way that the water runs into those on one side of the wheel near the top, making that side heavier, so that it descends. As the buckets go down, the water runs out of them, but those above are being filled in their turn, so that this side of the wheel is continually weighted with water, while on the other side empty buckets are going up. The wheel may turn mill-stones to grind wheat or corn, or may give motion to machinery for spinning and weaving cotton or wool; but is it the water-wheel that really does the work? "No," you will say; "if we trace back the force that moves the machinery, we find it in the falling water that fills the buckets of the wheel; it is the water-fall that is the real worker." So; it is the sun, which is a force behind the water-fall, or the water-fall is the force behind the wheel. What supplies the water-fall with its never-failing stream? The rain that fills the springs high up among the hills, where a little brook has its source—the rain that feeds the brook as it flows, and other brooks that join it on its way, until it becomes the river that descends in the water-fall. And what is the source of the rain? The sun, whose rays turn the waters of the earth to vapor, and lift them up to the clouds, whence they fall upon the hills. Were it not for the sun the rain would soon cease to fall, the springs in the hills would dry up, the brooks would run out, the river would dwindle away, the roar of the water-fall would die into silence, and the wheel would stop for want of power.

The wind, which is the motive force of windmills and of sailing vessels, is another form of sun-power. The atmosphere has been compared to a great wheel carried round by the heat of the sun. We know that when air is heated it rises, and that the tropical parts of the earth are hotter than the polar regions. In the tropics, therefore, the heated air rises, and the cooler air from the poles flows in to fill its place, while the place of the latter is filled by an upper current flowing back from the equator; and this goes on continually, and keeps the great atmospheric wheel turning. Whenever a wind blows, the process is similar: it is the sun that causes the wind, be it zephyr, or gale, or hurricane.

"But," you will say, "the sun does not run our steam-engines; it is artificial heat, not sunheat, that changes the water into steam." Very true; but how do we get this heat? By burning wood or coal. For the former we are clearly in debt to the sun, which made the trees grow that furnish the fuel; and the coal is the remains of plants that grew long before the creation of man, plants that were as dependent on the sunshine as those that flourish to-day. When we burn coal, the heat we get from it is nothing but the sunbeams that were caught and imprisoned by those ancient plants; our steam-engines use the force that was stored up by the sun millions of years before the steam-engine was invented.

All muscular power, whether of man or of other animals, may be traced to the same source. Animals get their food either from plants or from other animals that have fed upon plants; and the plants owe their existence to the sun. The animal is a machine, like the steam-engine; the food which it eats is the fuel that keeps the machine in action. With every movement we make, a portion of this fuel is burned up in our muscles. Every beat of our hearts is at the expense of such material; and the material is the gift of the sun. Our very thoughts are indirectly dependent on the sunbeams; for the brain, which is the organ of thought, requires food to maintain its activity, like the muscles and all the other machinery of the body.

There are other kinds of force less familiar than these—as electricity, magnetism, and chemical force—which can also be proved to come indirectly from the sun, but the proof can not be given here. We can detect the work of the sunbeams in the flash of the lightning and the roar of the thunder, in the turning of the compass-needle to the north, and in all the wonders of chemical science, as certainly as in the growing plant or the running stream.

The only form of force known to us which does not come directly from the sun is that of the tides. The tidal wave is raised and carried round the earth mainly by the attraction of the moon. The sun, though immensely larger than the moon, is so much farther off that it attracts the waters of the earth much less than the moon does. A tide-mill, which gets its motive power from the rise and fall of the tide, is therefore worked by the moon rather than by the sun.

[By special arrangement with the author, the cards contributed to this useful series by W. J. Rolfe, A.M., formerly Head-Master of the Cambridge High School, will, for the present, first appear in Harper's Young People.]

THE MORAL PIRATES.

BY WM. L. ALDEN.

CHAPTER III.

As Harry vanished, Joe's head appeared, as he climbed up the side of the bridge and joined his brother and Tom. Their anxiety was now for Harry, who had been swept through the channel under the bridge, and was manfully swimming toward the eddy where the boys had landed. He came ashore none the worse for his bath, and was delighted to find that Joe was not only safe, but dry. Joe explained that the boat had drifted against one of the piles of the bridge, and the current and the tow-rope together had forced one of her sides so low down that the water began to pour in. Joe thought that if the river intended to get into the boat, he had better get out; so he sprang up and caught one of the timbers of the bridge, and so climbed safely up to the roadway. The boat, relieved of his weight and freed from the tow-line, drifted quietly away, and was now floating peacefully on the river about twenty rods from the shore.

Luckily an old man in a row-boat saw the run-away *Whitewing*, and kindly caught her and brought her up to the bridge. As the boys bailed her out, they told him how the accident happened, and the gruff old man said it "served 'em right." "When you tow a boat next time," he continued, "you'll know enough to put all your weight in the stern. Did you ever see a steam-boat towing a row-boat with a man in the bow? If ever you do, you'll see him go overboard mighty quick. A boat 'll sheer all over creation if you tow her with a fellow in the bow. You just put the biggest of you fellows in the stern of that there boat, and she'll go through under the bridge just as steady as a church."

The boys gladly took the old man's advice. When the boat was bailed out, they floated the rope down again, and when it was made fast, Tom Schuyler, who was the heaviest of the boys, offered to sit in the stern. His weight brought the bow of the boat out of the water, and she was towed quickly and safely through. The boys resumed their places as soon as Harry had put on dry clothes, and after a short and easy row glided under the Spuyten Duyvel railway bridge, and found themselves on the broad and placid Hudson. They rowed on for nearly a mile, and then, having found a little sandy cove, ran the boat aground, and went ashore to rest. After a good swim, which all greatly enjoyed, including Harry, who said that his recent bath at Farmersbridge ought not to be counted, since it was more of a duty than a pleasure, they sat down to eat a nice cold lunch of ham sandwiches that Mrs. Wilson had kindly prepared; and when they were no longer hungry they stretched themselves lazily in the shade.

HARRY SWIMS FOR THE EDDY.

"Well, boys," said Harry, "we made a big mistake at the bridge; but we learned something, and we won't get the boat swamped that way again."

"I'm awfully obliged to Harry for jumping in after me," said Joe; "but it's the first time I ever heard of a captain jumping over after a sailor. When a sailor falls overboard, the captain just stands on the deck and looks around, kind of careless like, while the second mate and four sailors jump into a boat and pick the man up. That's the way it's done; for I know a fellow that saw a man fall overboard on a steam-ship, and he said that was how the captain did."

"All right," said Harry; "I won't jump in for you again, Joe. The fact is, boys, I oughtn't to have done it without waiting to find out whether there was really anything the matter with Joe. I'll tell you what we'll do. Joe is a first-rate swimmer, and we'll make a rule that whenever anybody is to jump into the river for anything, Joe shall do it. What do you say?"

"Oh, I'm willing enough," said Joe. "I don't care who jumps, as long as the captain don't. It won't look well for the captain to be all the time jumping overboard to pick somebody up."

"A better rule," remarked Tom, "would be that no fellow shall fall overboard."

"I move to amend that," cried Jim, "by forbidding any accidents to happen to any of us."

"But you can't do that," said Tom, who never understood a joke. "Accidents never would happen if people could help themselves."

"Well," said Harry, "if the rest of you will agree not to fall overboard, I'll promise that the captain sha'n't spend all his time in jumping after you. But if you are all ready, we'd better start on. There's a nice little breeze, and we can rest in the boat."

By this time Harry's shirt and trousers, which had been wrung out and hung up on a bush, were perfectly dry. He packed them away with his rubber blanket rolled tightly around them, and Jim attended to the duty of stepping the mast. Then the boys took their places, and Joe pushed the boat off with the boat-hook. The gentle breeze filled the sail, and the *Whitewing* went peacefully on her way up the river.

"Boys," said Harry, presently, "it's getting awfully hot."

"That's because we're sailing right before the wind," said Tom. "We are going just about as fast as the wind goes, and that's the reason why we don't feel it."

"Is this a lecture on wind, by Professor Thomas Schuyler?" asked Joe. "Because if it is, I'd rather hear it when it's cooler. Let's go over to the other side of the river, where we can get in the shade of the Palisades."

It was now about three o'clock, and the sun was very hot. The boat seemed to the boys to creep across the river, and the Palisades seemed to move away just as fast as they approached them. When they finally did come into the shadow of those huge rocks, they thought they had never known anything so delightful as the change from the scorching sunshine to the cool shade. Joe and his brother stretched themselves out, and put their blankets under their heads; presently they grew tired of talking, and in a little while they were fast asleep. Tom was not sleepy; but he was so delighted with the beauty of the shore, as seen from the boat, that he did not care to talk.

For a long time the boat glided stealthily along. The Palisades were passed, and a long pier projecting into the river from the west shore gradually came in sight. When the boat came up with the pier, half a dozen barges lay alongside of it, into which men were sliding enormous cakes of ice. The Sharpe boys woke up, and proposed to stop and get a little ice. The men let them pick up as many small pieces of ice as they could carry, and they went on their way so much refreshed that they chattered away as gayly as possible.

Uncle John had warned them to select a camping ground long before dark. They remembered this advice, and at about five o'clock they landed on a little low point of land a few miles below the entrance to the Highlands. They first hauled the boat a little way up the beach, so that it would be sure not to float off, and then began to take the tent, the cooking things, and the provisions for supper out of her.

"We want to pitch the tent and make a fire," said Harry, "and somebody ought to get some milk. Let's pitch the tent first."

"I'll do that," said Tom, "while you fellows get the supper."

"It takes two or three fellows to pitch the tent," said Harry; "you can't do it alone."

"I'll undertake to pitch it alone," replied Tom. "One of you can get fire-wood, one can go for milk, and the other can get out the things for supper. Here goes for the tent."

The tent was furnished with two upright poles and a ridge-pole, each one of which was made in two pieces, and joined together with ferules, like a fishing-rod. Tom se-

SAILING BY THE PALISADES.

lected a soft sandy spot close by the water's edge, where he spread out the tent, and pinned down each of the four corners with rough wooden pins, which he cut with the hatchet from a piece of drift-wood. Then he crept under the canvas with the poles. He put one of the upright poles in its place with the end of the ridge-pole over it, and then, holding the other end of the ridge-pole in one hand, he put the second pole in position with his other hand, and pushed the end of the ridge-pole into its proper place. The tent was now pitched; and all that remained to be done was to tighten the four corner pegs, and to drive in the other ones.

Meanwhile Jim had taken one of the pails, and gone toward a distant farm-house for milk. Joe had collected a pile of fire-wood, and Harry had lighted the fire, and put the other tin pail half full of water to boil over it. By the time the water had boiled, Jim had returned, bringing the milk with him. It did not take long to make coffee; and then the boys sat down on the sand, each with a tin cup of hot coffee at his side, and proceeded to eat a supper of ham sandwiches and cake. It was not the kind of supper that they expected to have on subsequent nights; but Mrs. Wilson's sandwiches and cake had to be eaten in order to keep them from spoiling. After the coffee was gone they each had a cup of cold milk, and then put the rest of it in a shady place to be used for breakfast. The provisions were carefully covered up, so as to protect them in case of rain, and then the beds were made. This last operation was a very easy one, since the sand was soft enough for a mattress, and all that needed to be done was to spread the rubber blankets on the ground as a protection from the damp. Then the boys rolled up their spare clothing for pillows, and, wrapping themselves in their blankets, were soon sound asleep.

[TO BE CONTINUED.]

THE BIG DOG'S LESSON.

BY W. O. STODDARD.

"THERE they are, Uncle Joe, the Dorking chickens, just where I found them."

"Pulled all to pieces."

"It was Mr. Bates's yellow dog—I know it was; and they've let him out again to-day. He'll be over, and kill some more."

"No, he won't, Parry," said Uncle Joe, as he leaned over the barn-yard fence. "Don't you see what I've done for him?"

"You've let the chickens all out. Yes, and there's Bayard. Isn't he pretty?"

"Yes, he's pretty enough, but that isn't all. What did we name him Bayard for?"

"'Cause he isn't afraid. But won't he hurt some of the other roosters?"

"I've shut 'em up. See him?"

The game-cock was indeed a beautiful fowl, and he seemed to know it too, for he was strutting around in the warm sun, and stopping every minute or so to flap his wings and crow. His comb and wattles were of a bright crimson, his wings and feathers of a brilliant black and red, and his long, arching tail feathers were remarkably graceful and glossy. He was not a large fowl, but he was a very well-shaped and handsome one.

"There comes that dog, Uncle Joe, right over the fence."

"Yes, there he comes."

"Won't you throw a stone at him, and drive him away?"

"Then he'd come again, some time when we were not here to throw stones at him."

Mr. Bates's yellow dog was a very big one. Perhaps he was not altogether a bad dog, either, but he had a sad weakness for teasing any animal smaller than himself. Cats, sheep, chickens, anything defenseless, would have been wise to keep out of his way if they could.

The two poor Dorking chickens had not been able to get away from him the day before, and so they had lost their feathers and their lives.

He had jumped the barn-yard fence now in search of more helpless chickens, and more of what he called fun.

A snap of his great jaws would have been enough to kill any fowl in that yard, and it would have crushed the life out of one of the little yellow "peepers" the old hens were now clucking to, if he had but put a paw on it.

But Bayard, the game-cock, was neither a Dorking, nor an old hen, nor a chicken, and he did not run an inch when the big dog came charging so fiercely toward him. He did but lower his head and step a little forward.

"Oh, Uncle Joe! He will be torn all to pieces."

"No, he won't. See!"

It was done almost too quickly for Parry to see, but the sharp spurs of the beautiful "bird" had been driven smartly into the nose of the big yellow dog, and the latter was pawing at it with a doleful whine.

The game-cock had not done with the barn-yard invader. He meant to follow that matter up till he had finished it.

"Clip!" he had hit him again—in the left shoulder this time—and the dog's whine changed to a howl.

Another, a deep one, in the fleshy part of one of his hind-legs; for Bayard seemed disposed to dance all around him.

That was enough, and Mr. Bates's yellow pet turned and ran yelping toward the nearest fence, while his conqueror flapped his wings and crowed most vigorously, and every hen in the yard clucked her admiration of his prowess.

Parry, too, clapped his hands, and felt as if he wanted to crow.

"He's such a little fellow, Uncle Joe, to fight such a big dog as that!"

"With teeth and claws, too, and a hundred times stronger than he."

"Did you know he could beat him?"

"Of course I did."

"He knew just how to use his spurs, didn't he?"

"That's it, Parry. He didn't have much, but he knew just what to do with it."

"Guess the dog knows it too now. He won't chase any more of our chickens."

"He'll keep out of this yard for a while. He's got his lesson."

So had Parry, and Uncle Joe would not let him forget it. It would be a shame, he said, for any boy to be less wise than a game-cock, and not to be able to use all the natural gifts he had.

THE CARPENTER'S SERMON.

BY DAVID KER.

"TELL ye what, mates, this sort o' thing won't do. Here we've been at it these six weeks, and not a penny of wages yet. It's all very fine to say, 'Stick to your work,' but a man won't git fat on workin' for nothing, that's sartain!"

"Right you are, Bill. S'pose we knocks off work, and tells Sir James we won't do no more without he pays us?"

"Gently, lads: remember what happened to the dog as dropped his meat in grabbin' at the shadder. If we stick to this job, mayhap we'll git our money some time; but if we knock off, we won't find another job growin' on every bush, mark ye."

"Well, that's true; but it's mighty hard luck for us, all the same."

So grumbled, under their breath, a gang of English workmen, who were repairing the interior of one of the great London churches, one fine summer afternoon in the time of George I. And certainly they had good reason to grumble. Sir James Thornhill, the court painter, whom the King had employed to restore and redecorate the building, had his head so full of his own fine plans and sketches, and of the grand show that the church would make when all was done, that he had quite forgotten such a small matter as the paying of his men's wages. So, although the poor fellows had been hard at work for six weeks and more, not a shilling of pay had any of them received yet.

"Look here, boys," cried a tall, gaunt carpenter, with a dry, keen-looking face, "I've always heard say as Sir James is a kind old gen'l'man at heart, and mayhap it ain't that he don't *want* to pay us, but only that he's forgot it, like. Let's just draw lots who shall go and tackle him about it, and then there'll be no mistake."

The suggestion was at once followed out, and the lot fell upon the tall carpenter himself.

This was more than the worthy man had bargained for, and he looked somewhat nonplussed. However, there was no drawing back for him now. Up he got, and away along the aisle he went toward the spot where Sir James Thornhill was standing.

But the nearer he got to him, the slower he walked, and the more chop-fallen did he appear. Indeed, Sir James looked such a grand old gentleman, as he stood there like a statue, in his laced waistcoat and silk stockings, with his powdered hair falling over his fine velvet coat, and his hand resting upon his silver-hilted sword, that poor Chips felt as bashful as if he were going before the King himself.

But, as the proverb says, "Fortune favors the brave," and the valiant carpenter was unexpectedly helped out of his dilemma by the very man who had caused it. Sir James suddenly turned round, and seeing him coming up, called out:

"Ah, my good fellow, you've come just in time to do me a service. You see, I want to be quite sure that that pulpit yonder, which we're just putting up, is in the right place; for, of course, when the clergyman goes up into it to preach, his voice ought to be heard equally well in every part of the church. Now suppose you step up there and make a speech of some sort, while I stand here and try if I can hear you plainly."

"But what be I to say, your honor?" asked Chips, scratching his head. "I haven't got the gift of the gab like you gen'l'men have."

"Oh, say whatever you like—just the first thing that comes into your head."

The carpenter's small eyes twinkled, as if a bright idea had suddenly occurred to him. Up he went, and leaning over the carved front of the pulpit, began as follows:

"Sir James Thorn'ill, sir! Me and my mates has been a-workin' for you, in this here church, good six weeks and more, and we haven't seen the color of your money yet; and now we ain't going to do another stroke, without you pays us all that's owing!"

"That 'll do, my man," said Sir James, hastily; "you may come down. Your elocution's perfect, but I can't say I quite admire your choice of a text."

However, the sermon was not thrown away. The very next morning the men received their wages in full, and Sir James gave the clever carpenter half a guinea extra for himself.

(Begun in HARPER'S YOUNG PEOPLE No. 24, April 13.)

THE STORY OF GEORGE WASHINGTON.

BY EDWARD CARY.

CHAPTER X.

IT is not pleasant to think that when Washington went back to his quiet home on the Potomac he was not as generally beloved as when he took his high office. He had had to disappoint a great many men who looked to him to help their private ambition at the expense of the country. He had had to enforce laws which some people looked upon as unjust. He had differed from various public men as to the war between France and England, and the payment of the debt, and other things, and it is so easy for all of us to think that a man who differs from us is in some way a bad man. A good many writers in the newspapers of that day had said hard things about him. But, after all, the moment the country got into trouble, all hearts turned toward him.

The men who had come into power in France after the Revolution of 1789 were proud, quarrelsome, and selfish. Because the Americans would not side with the French in their quarrel with England, these men directed American ships to be plundered. When the American agents in France complained, they were insulted; there was danger that such conduct would lead to war, and the American government began to get ready for it. The first thing was to choose a commander for the army, and again all eyes turned to Washington. In 1798 he was made Commander-in-chief, and for the next year and a half he was closely engaged getting the army ready for war. Happily it did not come.

In the midst of this work General Washington's noble life was brought to a sudden end. In December, 1799, he was taken with a violent disease of the throat, from which he died on the 14th of that month. In his last sickness he was brave, as he had been on the battle-field; patient, as he had been in public council; and unselfish, as he had always been. "I am not afraid to go," he said to those about him, and he begged them not to take too much trouble for him. The pain he bore was very great, but he never complained.

When he died, grief spread like a shadow over the whole land. In every home men felt that they had lost a faithful friend, a wise and loving guide. Wherever men gathered, words of sorrow for his loss, and praise for his great life, were spoken. Nor this alone. The French Generals, against whom he was preparing at the moment of his death to defend his country in arms, wrapped their flags in mourning in honor of his memory. The English ships in the Channel hung their flags at half-mast in sign of the grief of the English people. Surely no better proof of his high character could be given. It had won the love of those who had fought against him, and those who were on the point of going to battle with him.

It was found by the will which Washington left that he had given freedom to the slaves which he had held during his life, and whom he could not free before; that he had provided for all the aged and weak among them, and for the children; and that he had left large sums of money to give free schooling to the children of those in his neighborhood who could not get schooling otherwise. His last thoughts were of others, and how to do them good.

Indeed, the thing which made Washington so great was the earnest way in which he tried to find what was right, and to do it. Other men have had greater gifts of mind than he, and could do what he could not. But no man was ever more true to duty, small or great. At each moment he asked himself what he ought to do, and he spared no pains to make a true answer to that question. He carefully studied the rights of others as much as his own. He looked ahead to see what would follow his acts, that he might do no wrong by mistake. And when he had made up his mind what was right, he bent himself to do it. No fear for himself, no love of ease, no hope of gain, prevented him from going the way that he thought he ought to go. It was given to him to serve his country better than any other man has ever served it, and to leave a name which will be honored for a long time. But if we were to try to tell the secret of his greatness, it could be done in this short sentence: He always tried his best to do his duty.

THE END.

AN INDIAN GAME.

WHEN not on the war-path, or engaged in hunting, Western Indians spend much of their time in various games or contests of skill. Of these contests one of the most popular is flying the arrow, a sport to which the Indians of all tribes devote considerable time and attention.

When this game is proposed, each of those who wish to join in it lays on the ground something of small value, such as a pipe, quiver of arrows, a bow, spear, tobacco pouch, or knife, and when all have been collected, the value of the whole makes a prize well worth trying for.

Then bows are carefully examined, a dozen of the best arrows in the quiver selected, and the first of the competitors steps out in front of the rest, and prepares to shoot, not at a mark, but straight up into the air. His object is to have as many arrows in the air as possible at the same time; and he who can send up the greatest number, before the first touches the ground, wins the game and all the prizes.

But few of the most expert of the Indian bowmen have been known to put more than ten arrows into the air at once, and to do even this requires extraordinary skill and strength. The arrows, ten or twelve in number, are held in the hand that grasps the bow, and the rapidity with which each is fitted to the string and sent upward is truly wonderful.

FLIGHT OF THE ARROWS.

SHIP-BUILDING.

BY LIEUT. J. A. LOCKWOOD.

FEW people who are not sailors at all realize what a wonderful thing a ship is, and of how many different parts one is made up.

In the first place, a model of the proposed vessel has to be made. The model is an American invention. Formerly what was known as the draught of a ship took the place of the model. In the draught the proposed ship was represented on paper from three points of view. The first gave a complete view of the side, the second, or body plan, showed the breadth, having described on it every timber composing the frame of the ship; lastly came the horizontal plan, showing the whole as if seen from above. The model is much simpler than the old-fashioned draught. It is simply a miniature ship.

Once having a perfect model, the good ship-constructor feels that half his battle is already won. It may be as well here to mention the fact that, as a rule, the length of a ship is five times her greatest breadth of beam; her depth two-thirds of her breadth. Steamers are longer in proportion than sailing vessels. This is on account of the extra speed to be attained, even at the expense of strength.

After the model has been approved, the building of the ship begins. Most of

"A LITTLE SNAKE."

our ships are now built of wood from the South, where, since the war, entire forests can be bought for a song.

The keel of a ship has been likened to the backbone of a man, running, as it does, from stem to rudder. It consists of several timbers scarfed or pieced together, and under it is the shoe, a kind of second keel, but differing from the keel proper in that it is only loosely joined to it, whereas the keel is bolted to the ship's bottom through and through. The reason for this is that in case of grazing a rock a vessel having a shoe will, in most cases, part with the shoe, thus saving the keel, and escaping without serious injury. Corresponding with the keel outside is a set of timbers within the frames, known as the keelson. On each side of the keelson are assistant-keelsons to give greater strength.

On the after-end, and morticed into the keel, is the stern-post, another important timber, all the after-part of a ship curving gracefully toward this post. The rudder-stock works on the stern-post, which performs the double duty of supporting the after-timbers and the rudder.

Spaces are purposely left between a vessel's frames for "salting down." Sometimes this salt can be seen oozing out of her sides after a long voyage. Two hundred hogsheads of salt is not an unusual quantity for an ordinary-sized ship. It is the only thing that will prevent what is known as the "dry-rot" from attacking her timbers.

As a rule, every wooden vessel's ribs are of oak, and, for greater strength, preference is given to the best qualities of live-oak. As a ship's side curves, her outside planking has to be forced into place, and for the short curves near the bows and stern, the planks have to be steamed, and bent on while moist, as otherwise they would crack and split in the process. After these outside planks are all on, the calkers begin their work, which consists in filling in the spaces between the planks with oakum, mallets and calking-irons being used for this purpose. These seams are afterward covered with pitch.

In order to prevent barnacles from injuring a ship's bottom, sheathing is put on. This usually consists of a composition of zinc and copper, and covers all parts of a vessel exposed to the action of the water.

In Longfellow's beautiful poem, "The Building of the Ship," the reader is led to infer that the masts are "stepped" (*i. e.*, put in) before the launching occurs. But practically a ship is first launched, and then shears are rigged, and she is fitted out with her spars.

LIVING HONEY-COMBS.

BY CHARLES MORRIS.

"ISN'T it queer what dumb things animals are?" asked Harry Mason, as he looked up inquiringly into the face of his uncle. "Here's my dog Roger; why, he knows nothing except to hunt for bones, and to bark at tramps. And there are the cows, and the horses, and the pigs—what do they know that's of any account? I'd like somebody to tell me that."

"They know enough to know when dinner is ready, and I could not say that for some boys that I am acquainted with," replied his uncle, quizzically.

"Oh yes, that's me, I know," rejoined Harry, laughing. "But that's because I have something else to think of. Now they don't think of anything but their dinners. And they are always eating. That's about all they live for."

"Perhaps they think more than you imagine, Harry."

said his uncle, looking down from his arm-chair which he had leaned back comfortably against a tree. "They don't talk, it is true; but they have other ways of showing their thoughts. I could tell you some stories about the good sense of animals that would open your eyes."

"Oh yes, about elephants squirting water all over a tailor, and that sort of thing," said Harry, disdainfully. "I have read all that. But I mean something else. Why can't they build themselves houses, like men do, with chimneys and fires? And why don't they have farms, and roads to travel in, and barns?"

"And cows to milk?" broke in little Willie Mason; "and somebody to work for them and to fight for them—and—and pies, and candy, and such?"

Uncle Ben looked down with a comical expression upon the eager little fellow, with his bright young face and his sparkling blue eyes.

"Perhaps they do," he said.

"Oh, now, Uncle Ben!" cried Harry and Willie in chorus. "You're only funning now. Who ever heard of cows building houses?"

"I didn't say cows," replied Uncle Ben.

"But there can't be any animal that builds houses and barns, and raises crops," persisted Harry.

"Indeed there is, then," rejoined his uncle. "And milks cows, too, and has armies and workmen, as Willie says; and builds roads and bridges, and digs tunnels, and carries umbrellas. I don't know any that bakes pies, but I could name more than one that lives on candy."

"Now I know that Uncle Ben is funning," cried Willie, gleefully; "for he has got those wrinkles about his eyes, and he never has them except when he's funning."

"What kind of animals are they, I would like to know?" asked Harry, who was determined to put his learned uncle to the test. "I never came across any of their houses, I know."

"Indeed you have, then. I have seen you, more than once, shut their front doors for them, without asking leave or license."

Uncle Ben, as he spoke, had leaned over to the ground. He now rose, with a little black travelling speck on his finger.

"Here is one of them," he said, "out for an airing."

"That!" cried Harry, contemptuously. "Why, that's only an ant. I said animals. I didn't say ants."

"Oho! Is that it? An ant is not an animal, then?"

"I guess not," broke in Willie, decidedly. "Animals eat and drink, and walk and run, and—and climb trees, and whistle, and bark. Who ever heard an ant bark?"

"Or a cow?" rejoined his uncle. "As for running, I think this little fellow can run fast enough. And he eats, too. And he can climb trees. I don't say that he can whistle, but neither can a frog. I have no doubt that our ant can talk to his comrades as easily as your dog can converse with his friends."

"But ants," said Harry, doubtfully. "Don't you forget, Uncle Ben, you said they built houses and barns, and milked cows, and made roads and bridges, and had farms, and kept soldiers and workers?—I forget the rest. Yes, you said some of them lived on candy; and that is the queerest of all. I'd just like you to tell me what kind of candy it is, and how they make it; and I'd like to see one of their houses."

"Their houses are all built under-ground," replied Uncle Ben. "There are too many boys about, with clumsy feet, for them to build their delicate palaces above-ground. But if you were only to open an ant-hill, and trace out all its entries and passages, and its rooms and granaries, and its stairways and its nurseries, you might have more respect for these little creatures. If you want to see a larger ant-house, you will have to go to Africa. There the white ants build huge houses twelve feet high, and firm enough for a dozen men to stand on."

"And full of rooms," began Harry, but he was interrupted by his eager little brother, whose curiosity ran in another direction.

"Just tell us 'bout the candy, Uncle Ben," he demanded. "I don't care nothing 'bout the houses now. I want to know 'bout the candy."

"I think that Harry has the floor," said his uncle, reprovingly.

"Well, never mind the houses, and all the other queer things," said Harry. "Not just now, I mean; I want to know about the candy too."

Uncle Ben settled himself back in his chair, crossed his legs, and prepared for a story; while Willie hung to his knee on one side, and Harry stretched himself in the grass on the other, and Roger, the dog, went off on a butterfly hunt. He evidently was not interested in natural history.

"Ants are not the only animals that live on candy," said Uncle Ben, as he pinched Willie's ear. "There are bees, and wasps, and butterflies. And even such great creatures as bears. For bears sometimes break into bees' confectionary shop, and gulp down all its contents."

The two boys looked at each other dubiously. What in the world could Uncle Ben mean?

"It isn't honey you mean?" asked Harry, wonderingly. "That isn't candy."

"It is not cooked candy, I will admit," replied his uncle. "But it is flower candy. It is the candy that Nature makes, and lays up in her pretty blossom cups to feed insects that have a sweet tooth."

"But ants don't make honey-comb," cried Willie. "It is the bees do that. Nobody ever heard of an ant honey-comb."

"Don't be too sure of that, my boy; some folks have heard of many things that have never travelled to your ears. Why, there is an ant out West that makes a living honey-comb. Some of the ants themselves are turned into honey-combs to feed the others during the long winters."

Harry rose to his feet. He could not continue to lie down lazily when such marvellous stories as these were afloat.

"Living honey-combs!" he ejaculated.

"They are from the West, you know; the land of wonders," explained his uncle. "They are found in New Mexico. And they were discovered last summer in Colorado by a Philadelphia gentleman named Dr. McCook. This gentleman examined their mode of life, and brought some of them home with him, and tells wonderful stories about them."

"But won't you tell us all about them right away, Uncle Ben?"

"Yes, right away," echoes Willie.

"Well, then," began their uncle, "they live in nests dug in a stony soil, and having a great many rooms and passages. And in some of these rooms are found the queerest creatures that were ever heard of. Little living ants, with half their bodies turned into great bags of honey. They look exactly like great amber-colored peas, with a black pin's head stuck on one side of them. This black dot is the head and forward part of the ant. All the rest of its body is converted into a great honey-bag, and is swelled out with its sweet contents until it is as big as a large pea."

"And are all the ants like that?" asked Harry.

"No, only a certain number of them. The others go out foraging for honey. When they obtain it, they come back, hold their mouths to that of the honey-bag ant, and force the honey into its body. There are some three or four hundred of these honey-bearers in each ant-hill. And that is the way the ants lay up their winter provisions. These living honey-combs do not do anything; they are too heavy for that. They only hang by their feet to the ceiling of one of the under-ground rooms. If one of them happens to drop off, one of the other ants picks him up and drags him back again. It is no light task, either, for one of these little fellows to carry a great bag of honey, fifty times his own weight, up a perpendicular wall and across a ceiling."

"I should think not indeed," cried Harry.

"But how do they use the honey?" asked Willie, curiously. "I should think when these honey-ants eat it, that would be the end of it."

"They feed it back to the others as they require it," replied Uncle Ben. "When one of the ants is hungry, he goes up to a honey-bearer, taps him to let him know what he is after, and puts his mouth to his. The honey-bearer then seems to slightly compress his bag of sweets, until some of it flows out of his mouth into that of the other. When the latter is satisfied, he walks away, and the living honey-comb takes a rest until some other hungry individual calls upon him."

"Well, that is very curious, I know," cried Harry. "And does the honey last all winter? Is that all they have to feed on?"

"Yes, so far as is known."

"I guess the honey-bags must be pretty empty by spring, then," said Willie.

"I have not quite finished the story yet," continued Uncle Ben. "We have talked about how bears feed on the honey-comb of the bees. Now men feed on these living honey-combs."

"Oh, now, Uncle Ben!"

"Yes they do. In New Mexico it is the custom to have a plate full of honey-ants on the dinner table for dessert. The poor things can not get away, of course. After dinner the folks there pick them up one by one, squeeze the bags between their teeth, and suck out the honey, throwing the empty bags away."

"I don't like such a fashion as that," cried Harry, decidedly. "Why, they are regular cannibals."

"And what do the rest of the poor ants do for their honey?" asked Willie.

"I fear they must pass a hard winter, if they do not die of hunger," replied Uncle Ben.

BEAUTIES OF THE UNDERGROUND WORLD.

IT has often happened that in the course of excavations in search of minerals, the workmen have come upon some singular hollows or openings in the rock, caused by convulsions of the earth or earthquakes, or caverns through which torrents have flowed in former ages, and have left them for nature to ornament in the most beautiful and fantastic manner.

You will understand how the natural caverns are formed that you may have seen on the sea-coast; the moving waters, carrying with them gravel and sand, enter the cracks and crevices in the rocks, and increase their size by wearing away portions of the rock until caverns are formed. Some of these are of immense size, and the extent of many is unknown.

Many caverns are lined with beautiful crystals, called *calcareous spar*, or substances containing much lime, and generally colored by the impurities of the water that has dropped on them. Sometimes these crystals are of a pure white, and have, when the cave is lighted up, a richness and transparency that can scarcely be imagined. Others have the appearance of stone, moss, and shells, in every variety of color.

Caverns of enormous extent occur in Iceland; that of Gurtahellir being forty feet in height, fifty in breadth, and nearly a mile in length. It is situated in the lava that has flowed from a volcano. Beautiful black stalactites hang from the spacious vault, and the sides are covered with glazed stripes, a thick covering of ice, clear as crystal, coating the floor. One spot in particular is mentioned by a traveller, when seen by torch-light, as surpassing anything that can be described. The roof and sides of the cave were decorated with the most superb icicles, crystallized in every possible form, many of which rivalled in delicacy the clearest froth or foam, while from the icy floor arose pillars of the same substance, in all the curious and fantastic shapes that can be imagined. A more brilliant scene, perhaps, never presented itself to the human eye.

A WELL-MEANING LITTLE BUSYBODY.

BY MRS. L. G. MORSE.

THEY say I am full of mischief, but they don't speak the truth. Maria is the only one that knows, and she says I'm a busybody. Mamma hugs me tight, and says I will be a great help when I am big, but papa tosses me high up to the ceiling, and says I won't wait to grow up, and that I make the very best use of my time now. He knows as much as Maria, for that's just what I do—I use my time. I did so much work yesterday that I nearly got tired. First, mamma said she was going to Cousin Alice's wedding. I knew she was, for I saw her best bonnet out of its box on her bed. So, while she was talking to Katy in the kitchen, I climbed all the way up stairs, and dragged it down to her myself.

I don't know what they'd have done without me yesterday, for after mamma had gone, Maria was careless. She left the basin of water on Nelly's little table. She forgot all about it, so I went, like a good girl, to put it away for her, 'cause I was afraid that mamma might come back and knock it over on to the carpet. It wasn't my fault that it slid out of my hands and broke itself. *I* was careful, and Maria said nobody else but just me would ever have thought of putting it away for her.

My sister Bessie don't try half so hard to help people. She sat in her little arm-chair all the time, tying up Susan Hopkins's joints. She thinks Susan is the best of all our dolls, but I don't. Her joints are all loose, and her legs rattle. Bessie isn't so much use as I am. She kept out of the way, tending to Susan, while Maria had to change every one of my clothes, 'cause the naughty water sloshed; and Bessie didn't even pick up the broken pieces of basin for poor Maria! Maria told her not to touch 'em, for fear of getting her feet wet and cutting her fingers.

Afraid! They're afraid of everything. The very minute Maria had me dressed again, I began to pick up the pieces for her, and I didn't cry even when I *did* cut my hand, and the blood got all over my nice clean apron. I don't think it was very polite of Maria to set me down so hard on the masewing chine, and tell me not to move 'till she'd cleared up the floor.

Bessie is bigger than I am, but she isn't a busybody at all. She only plays while there's work going on; and only see how much work I've done this morning! I've fixed up mamma's work-basket for her, and I've stuffed all the rags and little pieces of our new dresses that were piled up on the machine into papa's collar drawer. Then I cleared up a whole lot of muss after Maria. She went to answer the door-bell, and while she was gone, I took papa's clothes-whisk and swept up a big pile of dust she left on the hearth, and dumped it where nobody can see it, in a dark corner of the closet, under mamma's dresses.

It was real lucky I went to the closet, too, for I found the waist of mamma's best walking suit. I heard her say one day that she was going to change the trimming on the sleeves, so I took it out, and got a needle and thread, and I'm going to do it my own self for her. Bessie's darning a stocking that Maria gave her, and I'll sit right in front of her, so I can see how she pulls the needle through. The ends of the lace get right in the way of the needle, though, and I don't know but what I'll have to cut some of it off, so as to sew it better. I am going to hurry fast, and see if I can get it done before mamma comes home from market.

TWO LITTLE SUN-BONNETS

Under the shade of the sun-bonnet's crown,
One head is golden, and one head is brown;
Blue eyes and hazel eyes sparkle with fun,
Hide and go seek, as the gay dimples run.

Four little hands overbrimming with flowers,
Four little feet tripping through the blithe hours;
Two little maidens, so happy and bright,
Busy all day, and so tired at night.

VOYAGE OF THE PAPER DOLLS.

BY MATTHEW WHITE, JUN.

IT was a hot summer afternoon, and the great play-room in the garret was deserted.

There was not even breeze enough blowing in at the open window to stir Angelina Mary, Matilda Agnes, and General Adolphus Popgun, as they lay upon their paper backs on the table.

"Oh dear," complained Angelina, with a sigh, "I do wish those girls wouldn't leave us in such attitudes when they go down to dress! It's so undignified."

"But you must remember, my love," rejoined her friend Matilda, "that it has a tendency to sprain our ankles if we remain long standing; and, by-the-way, did you not hear the children speak about our having some new paper-muslins?" and thereupon the two ladies fell to discussing dress with great animation, General Popgun growing meanwhile quite puffed out with pride, as he reflected on the fact that his blazing red coat, ornamented with yellow braid, and his jaunty cap with its conspicuous tricolored pompon, must be particularly becoming to him.

He was not as yet very well acquainted with his two companions, having only arrived at the post (as he professionally termed the garret) the previous day, and since then he had been obliged to attend so many drillings of the tin soldiers that he had enjoyed but few opportunities for social recreation. Now, however, he thought he would enter into conversation with the two fair members of his race beside him, and was just endeavoring to think of something new to say about the weather, when a great clattering was heard on the stairs, and the next instant two boys made their appearance in the garret, both breathing very hard, and looking as if they had been running races with the sun.

"I beat, anyhow," said one, as he sat down on an old trunk and wiped his face.

"All right," returned the other; adding, "and now what'll we get to put in the *Foam*?" and then the two rummaged around the room for a while, till suddenly one of them pounced upon the table where lay the paper dolls, and catching all three of them up in his hand, cried out: "Here! these'll do. Come on, Frank;" and the boys hurried down stairs again with even more racket than they had made coming up.

As may be imagined, Angelina Mary and Matilda Agnes grew paler than foolscap with fright when they felt Tom's fingers closing over them so roughly, and General Adolphus Popgun, although somewhat nervous himself, felt called upon to postpone his weather remarks, and endeavor, instead, to calm the fears of his companions.

"Pray don't be alarmed, I beg," he said; "I have no doubt we are being transported to a grand review of the Tin Regiment. It will be a very fine sight, and I shall try to provide seats for you in the grand stand."

The boys, however, did not stop at the garden play-house, where the tin soldiers were encamped, but kept straight on to the gate, passed through the latter, and then walked briskly off down the road. The General ventured to peep out between the fingers that inclosed him, and to his horror saw that Frank held in his hand a little boat six inches long, roughly whittled out of a common stick of wood.

And soon his dread anticipations were realized, for striking into a path that ran through a corn field, the boys made straight for the brook, where Frank proceeded to cut a long switch from a willow-tree, while Tom took out three pins from his coat, and deliberately impaled the two paper ladies to the stern, and General Popgun to the bow of the boat.

Fortunately the pin in each case pierced only some portion of the dress of the terror-stricken creature, otherwise the consequences might have been most tragical.

And now the *Foam* was launched, and the ladies and the General floated upon the rippling deep.

"Hi, don't they look fine!" cried Tom, as with the long willow switch he guided the little bark on its course down the stream, while his cousin walked by his side, much interested in the operation.

Having recovered from their first shock, the passengers began to look about them and enjoy their voyage.

"How very delightful!" exclaimed Matilda Agnes. "'Tis quite a pity, General, that you're not an Admiral."

"Oh yes. I always adored the navy," added Angelina Mary.

At these remarks the General blushed as red as the white paper out of which he was manufactured would allow, and hastened to change the subject by calling attention to the beauties of the country through which they were passing. He had just begun a poetical discourse on the wild flowers which an army tramples down on the field of battle, when Tom's switch happened to strike him in the face with such force as caused him to flutter for an instant like a sheet of paper in a high wind.

And now the ladies' fears returned, for the brook was growing wider and wider, and the *Foam* drifting constantly further and further from the bank.

Suddenly Tom, who had been busy talking about water

turtles with Frank, noticed this, and struck out with his willow branch to bring the truant back, but it was too late; the boat had got beyond his reach, and was now floating swiftly down the middle of the stream with the current.

The ladies screamed, and the General groaned; but as neither the screams nor the groans were louder than paper is thick, they were not heard by human ears.

"The boys will surely save us," said Matilda Agnes, hopefully. "We are too valuable to lose, to say nothing of the boat."

Before long, however, Tom exclaimed: "Oh, I'm tired trudging after the thing. Come on, Frank, let's go back home, and I'll beat you a game of croquet."

"But the dolls," the other ventured to interpose. "What 'll the girls say when we tell 'em what's become of them? They'll be mad, won't they?"

"Oh, I guess not, if we make up a nice story about their sailing off down to the ocean, and going to Europe and Africa, and seeing gorillas and bears, and kings and princes;" and with these words Tom gave up the pursuit, and, followed by Frank, soon disappeared in the woods.

Being thus cruelly abandoned, with not so much as a match at hand by means of which to row themselves ashore, the three paper voyagers gave up all as lost, and were beginning to bemoan their awful fate, when the General suddenly spoke out, in cheerful tones: "Perhaps somebody 'll pick us up."

"Or a steamboat may run us down," added Angelina Mary, somewhat spitefully.

"Maybe we'll land on a water-lily," murmured Matilda Agnes, with a poetical sigh.

But time passed, and none of these things happened. The little boat drifted on and on, through woods full of singing-birds, and by fields covered with waving grain, beside houses, around hills, under bridges, and over mill-dams. To be sure, when they emerged from the latter, the paper travellers were wet to the skin, but the *Forum* always came out right side up, and the sun soon dried them.

By-and-by the sun went down, and when the moon rose the little river had changed into a big one, and the tiny boat still floated down the middle of it, on and on, all through the night, and during the whole of the next day; and discovering that nothing terrible befell them, the three paper dolls began to grow quite contented with their life of constant change; and when they sailed down past the great city, with its many piers, big steamers, middle-sized ferry-boats, and little tugs, they forgot all about being frightened, so interested were they in gazing at the strange sights about them.

And thus they floated down the harbor, out at the Narrows, and so into the great broad ocean, and there they may be drifting to this very day.

At any rate, the girls say they are going to keep a good look-out for them when they go to Europe.

OUR POST-OFFICE BOX

The above letter is very gratifying, and we thank the writer heartily for her kind words on behalf of Young People.

This little housewife forgot to state the amount of flour required to complete her recipe, but any little girl's mamma will say how much is necessary to make the batter stiff enough for crullers.

[illegible] Any of [illegible] I would like to exchange for other kinds.

I saw a letter in YOUNG PEOPLE No. [illegible] from Samuel F. [illegible], of New Jersey, offering to exchange eggs. If he has any kinds not mentioned in my list, I would be very glad to exchange with him.

[illegible]
[illegible] Farm, Cherokee County, Georgia.

E. J. [illegible].—E. & F. N. Spon, New York city, can supply you with catalogues and books of all kinds relating to telegraphy.

WILLIE H. M.—The dates you require are given in "A [illegible]," on page [illegible] of YOUNG PEOPLE No. 28.

CHARLES L. S.—Fort Dodge, the military post, is in Kansas. There is a town in Iowa of the same name.

[illegible] A. H.—The shells of your doves' eggs are soft because the doves probably eat nothing from which the shell can be formed. A piece of cuttle-fish bone in the cage might answer the purpose; or, still better, the shells of hens' eggs broken in pieces and scattered in the cage. The doves also need plenty of clean gravel [illegible].—Your first favor was acknowledged in YOUNG PEOPLE No. 19.

[illegible] H.—In an article on "The House-Sparrow" in YOUNG PEOPLE No. [illegible] you will find out what kind of [illegible] "sparrow named [illegible]" will like best.

PUZZLES FROM YOUNG CONTRIBUTORS.

No. 1.

[illegible]

[illegible]
A. H. K.

No. 2.

WORD SQUARE.

First, to [illegible]. Second, a European city. Third, a boy's name. Fourth, [illegible]. "[illegible]."

No. 3.

[illegible]

What is it that goes to [illegible], [illegible], comes back, and yet never [illegible]?

No. 4.

[illegible]

1. A Carthaginian General: [illegible]
2. A [illegible]: [illegible]
3. A [illegible]: [illegible]

No. 5.

[illegible]

[illegible]
[illegible]
[illegible]
[illegible]
[illegible]
[illegible]
A [illegible] city and [illegible] land,
[illegible]
C. P. T.

No. 6.

[illegible]

A town on the Vistula River. A [illegible]. To [illegible]. [illegible]. A [illegible] in the possession of the English. A Northern [illegible]. A part of the [illegible]. [illegible] the second name of a celebrated Scottish [illegible].
"[illegible]."

ANSWERS TO PUZZLES IN NO. [illegible]

No. 1.
[illegible]

No. 2. [illegible]

No. 3. [illegible]

No. 4. [illegible]

No. 5. 1. [illegible]. 2. [illegible]. 3. [illegible]. 4. [illegible].

No. 6. [illegible]

[illegible] are acknowledged from C. G., [illegible], [illegible], [illegible], [illegible], Joseph [illegible].

Correct answers to puzzles are received from George W. [illegible], [illegible] H. Osborn, Frank E. [illegible], John A. [illegible], [illegible], [illegible], [illegible], Joseph Van [illegible], George H. [illegible].

OPENING OF THE BASE-BALL SEASON—THE FIRST HOME RUN.

THE IBEX.

THE ibex, or steinbok, is an Alpine animal remarkable for the development of its horns, which are sometimes more than three feet in length, and of such extraordinary dimensions that they appear to a casual observer to be peculiarly unsuitable for a quadruped which traverses the craggy regions of Alpine precipices. Some writers say that these enormous horns are employed by their owners as "buffers," by which the force of a fall may be broken; and that the animal, when leaping from a great height, will alight on its horns, and by their elastic strength be guarded from the severity of a shock that would instantly kill any animal not so defended. This statement, however, is but little credited.

To hunt the ibex successfully is as hard a matter as hunting the chamois, for the ibex is to the full as wary and active an animal, and is sometimes apt to turn the tables on its pursuer, and assume the offensive. Should the hunter approach too near the ibex, the animal will, as if suddenly urged by the reckless courage of despair, dash boldly forward at its foe, and strike him from the precipitous rock over which he is forced to pass. The difficulty of the chase is further increased by the fact that the ibex is an animal of remarkable powers of endurance, and is capable of abstaining from food or water for a considerable time.

It lives in little bands of five or ten in number, each troop being under command of an old male, and preserving admirable order among themselves. Their sentinel is ever on the watch, and at the slightest suspicious sound, scent, or object, the warning whistle is blown, and the whole troop make instantly for the highest attainable point.

OLD SCOTTISH COINS.

THE Edinburgh *Scotsman* reports a somewhat remarkable discovery made in the pretty little burgh of Fortrose, in Scotland. In raising the clay floor in the kitchen of an old house on the margin of the Cathedral Green, occupied by Mr. Donald Jones, for the purpose of replacing it with a floor of cement, the soil below was penetrated for some little depth, and the spout of what appeared to be a tea-kettle was exposed. On removing the earth from around it, a vessel, apparently of tarnished copper, was uncovered. It was some ten or eleven inches in height, of the familiar shape of the water ewer or flagon in use in Scottish families in the fourteenth and fifteenth centuries, the water being poured from it over the hands of guests and others previous to meals. The top was closed with a lid, formed of a piece of lead three-quarters of an inch in thickness, and apparently soldered to the flagon.

The vessel was remarkably heavy, and on removing the lead it was found to be filled with old silver coins. There was a quantity of dark-looking liquid in the vessel, and on this being poured out, the coins were left, with one or two exceptions, quite white and clean. They were over a thousand in number, and were all of the time of King Robert III. of Scotland, who reigned from 1390 to 1406. They are very thin, as is the general character of the silver coinage of that time, and larger than a shilling in the surface.

THE STUMP PUZZLE.

WITH two straight cuts of the scissors restore this old stump to life.

DOUBLE ACROSTIC CHARADE.

BY H.

INITIALS AND FINALS.

First friends, then foes, my first and last are reckoned,
My first called great, and really great my second;
Eager for fame, each led a soldier's life,
Each fell a victim to the assassin's knife.
My first died first; but when my second fell,
He fell before my first, by some strange spell.

CROSS WORDS.

1.

My first an Indian chief, who vainly sought
To exterminate the foe 'gainst whom he fought.

2.

Another Indian chief, entrapped, betrayed,
Whose haughty spirit broke in dungeon shade.

3.

A State whose boundaries were hard to fix,
Where lakes and streams their flowing waters mix.

4.

An ancient Greek, most famous in his age,
Renowned for eloquence and counsel sage.

5.

My fifth a novel, read with great applause
When Dr. Johnson wagged his ponderous jaws.

6.

My sixth a cycle of revolving time,
Which visits every nation, age, and clime.

THE LITTLE WASHER-WOMAN.

Vol. I.—No. 34. | Published by HARPER & BROTHERS, New York. | Price Four Cents.

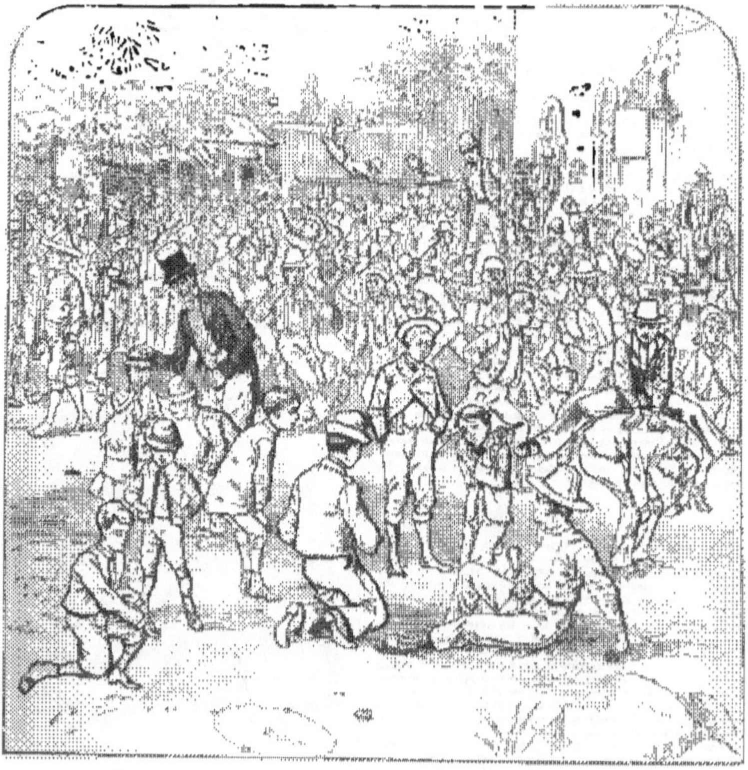

BABY, BEE, AND BUTTERFLY.

BY MARY D. BRINE.

BABY, Bee, and Butterfly,
Underneath the summer sky.

Baby, bees, and birds together,
Happy in the pleasant weather;

Sunshine over all around,
In the sky, and on the ground;

Hiding, too, in Baby's eyes,
As he looks in mute surprise

At the sunbeams tumbling over
Merrily amid the clover,

Where the bees, at work all day,
Never find the time for play.

Happy little baby boy!
Tiny heart all full of joy;

Loving everything on earth,
As love welcomed him at birth;

Ever learning new delights,
Ever seeing pleasant sights;

Taking each day one step more
Than he ever took before.

Shine out, sunbeams, warm and bright,
Lengthen daytime, shorten night,

Till so wise he grows that he
Spells *baby* with a *great big B.*

AN AMERICAN SOLDIER OF FORTUNE.

BY E. LOCKWOOD.

ONE hundred and twenty years ago there lived a plain, honest farmer in the beautiful town of Woodstock, in the province of Connecticut, by the name of Eaton. He belonged to the fine, intelligent New England stock, and did his duty like a man in the state of life to which God had been pleased to call him, working on his farm in summer, and teaching school in winter; for he needed all he could earn to put bread in the mouths of his thirteen children, who were taught early to help themselves, after the fashion of their stalwart Anglo-Saxon forefathers. One of Farmer Eaton's boys, named William, was born February 23, 1764, and was a high-spirited, clever, reckless little chap, keeping his mother continually in a state of anxiety on his account; indeed, if she had not been so used to boys with their pranks and unlimited thirst for adventures, I think Bill would have been the death of her, for she never knew what he would be about next. For all his love of sport and out-door amusement, the boy was so fond of reading that he nearly always managed to conceal a book in his pocket when he went out to work in the fields or woods, and often, when left alone, or when his companions stopped for rest or meals, Bill would steal time to read. When his elders caught him at it he would often get soundly scolded for not being better employed, but the very next chance he would be at it again.

One Sunday, when he was ten years old, he was returning from church, and passing a tree laden with tempting red cherries, climbed up in his usual reckless fashion to help himself; but either the branch broke or he lost his footing, for he fell to the ground with such violence that he dislocated his shoulder, besides being so stunned that he lay senseless for several days after he was picked up and carried home. The neighbors came in to offer their services when they heard of the accident, for though they no doubt shook their heads and remarked, "I told you so," "I knew how it would be," they were, all the same, very kind to the poor little chap who lay there, white and death-like, for so many long hours.

A neighbor, who was a tanner by trade, was sitting by his bed when at last he opened his eyes. I suppose the tanner was glad enough to see the boy come to life again; but all he said was, "Do you love cherries, Bill?"

"Do you love *hides?*" spoke up Bill, as quick as a flash.

You see, he came to the full possession of his senses at once after his long sleep, and wasn't going to let himself be taken at a disadvantage by any tanner in the land.

When Eaton was twelve our country declared itself free and independent, and all true patriots rose up to defend, by sword or whatever other means was in their power, the sacred cause of liberty.

Our young friend Bill fairly burned with desire to go off and do something great. His soul was on fire with patriotic ardor. How could he stay quietly in Woodstock, and lead a humdrum life, when the soldiers of the tyrant were threatening all the Americans held most dear? But his friends at home did not encourage his practical patriotism. He was told that he must stay at home, and work on the farm, and get ready for college; the country would get on very well without him; and so he did stay for four years, and the war seemed no nearer an end than ever. At last one night he could stand it no longer; so he ran away, and joined the nearest camp, where he enlisted. But the pride of the sixteen-year-old boy received a blow; they made him servant to one of the officers, and in this menial position he was obliged to stay. He found that he was far from being his own master now. He behaved so well, though, that he was placed in the ranks after a while, and in 1783 was made a sergeant, and discharged.

He went home, and taught, to support himself, while he prepared for college; for he had no father now to help him along. He entered Dartmouth College, and graduated honorably, though he had lost five years for study out of his young life. Not long after his graduation, while he was teaching again, he was given a captain's commission in the army for his service during the Revolution. A soldier's life suited his bold character far better than the quiet occupation of country teacher. Then he married, and went first west, then south, on military service, and saw plenty of wild life, and made enemies as well as friends, for the best of us can not expect to please everybody, and Captain Eaton had too strong a character not to make some people, who did not think as he did, very angry.

When he was about thirty-five years old, trouble rose between the United States government and some of the countries of Africa, and the President sent Eaton out to Tunis as consul. Tunis is one of the Moorish kingdoms of Africa that border on the Mediterranean Sea, and were called "Barbary States." The other Barbary States were Morocco, Algiers, and Tripoli. For a long time these countries had been nests of pirates, who made their living by preying on the commerce of Christian nations, and making slaves of their seamen, so that the black flags of their ships were the terror of the Mediterranean. These robbers had the daring to demand tribute of European nations, which many of them paid annually for the sake of not being molested, and lately they had tried to extort money from the United States on the same plea. Eaton managed so cleverly and successfully with the Bey, or ruler, of Tunis, that he made a very satisfactory arrangement with him, and then returned home; but the other agents did not manage so well, and at last war was declared, for the United States had no idea of being cowed and threatened by these pirates and murderers—far otherwise! The memory of her recent successful struggle with the greatest nation of the earth was too fresh to make it possible that an American ship should voluntarily lower its flag before a Moorish marauder. But what we would not do voluntarily we had to do by compulsion. The frigate *Philadelphia*, sailing in African waters, under Captain Bainbridge, was captured by the Bey of Tripoli, and towed into the harbor of that town. Her crew was carried off into slavery by the pirates, some languishing in hopeless imprisonment, others toiling their lives away under the burning sun of Africa.

Captain Decatur soon after sailed into the harbor in a vessel that he had captured from the Tripolitans, and retook and burned the *Philadelphia*; but, alas! brave as he was, he could not rescue his unfortunate countrymen. A few months later, in 1803, Eaton was sent back to the Barbary States as Naval Agent, and first stopped in Egypt. Here he made up his mind that he would bend all his energies toward rescuing the captives at Tripoli. He found that the rightful ruler of Tripoli, named Hamet Caramalli, had been driven away from his dominions by his brother Yusef, and was in Alexandria. Eaton offered to assist him to recover his throne, and collected a little army of five hundred men, most of them Mussulmans, a few Greek Christians, and nine Americans. With these followers he and Hamet marched across the desert toward Derne, in the kingdom of Tripoli. Eaton had not lost his boyish love of adventure yet, you see. This was just one of the bold, daring undertakings that he may have dreamed of in those early days when he stole away from his work to read with eager delight stories of wild venture and perilous escape in the peaceful shades of the forest around Woodstock. Doubtless these desert marches now entered upon far exceeded all his young imagination had pictured them.

It was a perilous journey, for the Arab sheiks and their followers, who made up most of his army, sometimes behaved in a very mutinous manner, and it took all Eaton's force of will and strict discipline to keep them in any sort of order, for Hamet showed very little decision of character, and proved that he was not very well fitted to be a ruler of men.

They were liable to be attacked by brigands from the mountains, too, so that ceaseless vigilance was needed. Some friendly Arab bands joined them on the road; so, when they reached Derne, Eaton found himself at the head of quite an army. Here he was met by two American ships, and with their help he bombarded the town, and took it by assault, driving the wild Arabs who were defending it back to the mountains. Now Eaton was in a situation to dictate his own terms to the usurper Yusef Bey, since he had brought Hamet Caramalli triumphantly into his own city of Derne, and had driven all enemies before him. He had laid his plans to march on Tripoli, drive off the usurper, and deliver his poor captive countrymen at the edge of the sword, when suddenly his successful career was brought to an end in rather a mortifying way. Yusef, frightened out of his defiance, consented to come to terms with Colonel Lear, American Consul-General at Algiers. If Colonel Lear had not been too hasty in concluding a treaty which forced the United States to pay sixty thousand dollars ransom money, when not a cent should have been given, and left the cruel Yusef safe on his throne, General Eaton might have marched on Tripoli with his victorious army, restored Hamet, and let the captives go in triumph.

Most people agreed that but for Eaton's promptness and bravery the troubles might have lasted much longer; and when he returned to America, soon after, he was received with great distinction by his countrymen, who made him quite an ovation. The Massachusetts Legislature voted him ten thousand acres of land in the district of Maine. The remainder of his life was passed in his pleasant home at Brimfield, Massachusetts, where he died June 1, 1811, at the age of forty-seven.

Aaron Burr tried to draw Eaton into his famous conspiracy, but Eaton was a firm patriot, and refused with horror to play the traitor. Wishing to make his true sentiments known, once for all, he gave this toast at a public banquet, in Burr's presence: "The United States—palsy to the brain that shall plot to dismember, and leprosy to the hand that will not draw to defend our Union!"

THE HARE AND THE BADGER.

A Story from the Japanese.

BY WILLIAM ELLIOT GRIFFIS.

A GOOD while ago there lived near the Clack-clack Mountains an old man and his wife, who, having no child, made a great deal of a pet hare. Every day the old man cut up food and set it out on a plate for his pet.

One day a badger came out of the forest, and in a trice drove away the hare, and eating up his dinner, licked the plate clean. Then, standing on his hind-legs, the badger blew out his belly until it was as round as a bladder and tight as a drum, and beating on it with his paws to show his victory, scampered off to the woods. But the old man, who was very angry, caught the badger, and tying him by the legs, hung him up head downward under the edges of the thatch in the shed where his old woman pounded millet. He then strapped a wooden frame to hold fagots on his back, and went out to the mountains to cut wood.

The badger, finding his legs pain him, began to cry, and begged the old woman to untie him, promising to help her pound the millet. The tired old dame, believing the sly beast, like a good-hearted soul laid down her pestle and loosened the cords round the beast's legs. The badger was so cramped at first that he could not stand; but when well able to move, he seized a knife to kill the old woman. The hare, seeing this, ran away to find the old man, if possible, and tell him. The badger, after stabbing the old woman, crushed her to death by upsetting the [illegible] upon her, and then threw her body into the mortar, and pounded her into a jelly. Setting the pot on to boil, he made the woman's flesh into a mess of soup, and ate all he could of it. Then the badger, by turning three double somersaults, turned himself into an old woman, looking exactly like the one he had just eaten. All being ready, he waited till the husband came home tired and hungry.

Soon the old man came back, thinking of nothing more than the hot supper he was soon to enjoy. Throwing down his fagots, he came into the house, and while he warmed his hands at the hearth, his wife (as he supposed) set the mess of soup and millet, with a slice of radish, before him on a tray. He fell to, and ate heartily, his wife (as he supposed) waiting dutifully near by till her lord was served. When the meal was finished he pulled out a sheet of soft mulberry paper from his bosom and wiped his old chops, smacking them well, as he thought what a good supper he had so much enjoyed. Just then the badger took on his real shape, and yelled out: "Old fool, you've eaten your own wife. Look in the drain, and you'll find her bones." And he puffed out his body, beat it like a drum, whisked his tail scornfully, and ran off.

Almost dead with grief and horror, the old man gathered up the bones of his wife, and decently buried them. Then he made a vow to take revenge on the badger. Just then the hare came back from the mountains, and after condoling with the old man, said he would also take revenge on the badger.

So the hare buckled on his belt, in which he kept his flint and steel, and made ready a plaster of red pepper.

Going into the forest, he saw Mr. Badger walking home with a load of fagots and brush on his back. Creeping up softly behind him, the hare set the bundle on fire. The badger kept on, until he heard the crackling of the burning twigs. Then he jumped wildly, and cried out, "Oh, I wonder what that noise is!"

"Oh, this is the Clack-clack Mountain; it always is crackling here," said the hare, looking down from the top of the hill.

The fire grew more lively, and the badger became scared. He fell down, and threw out his fore-paws wildly.

"Katchi-katchi" (clack-clack), went the dry fagots, as the red hot coals flew about.

"What can it be?" said Mr. Badger.

"This mountain is called Katchi-katchi (Clack-clack); don't you know that?" said the hare, coolly standing on the bridge, and leaning on his axe.

"Oh! oh! oh! help me!" howled the badger, as the blazing twigs began to burn the hair off his back. And running through the woods to a stream near by, he plunged in, and the fire was put out. But his running had only increased the fire and burning, and his back was all raw. When the hare found the badger at home in his house, he was howling in misery, and expecting to die from his burn.

"Let me take a look at your burn, Mr. Badger," said the hare; "I have some famous salve to cure it"—as he pretended to be very pitiful, and held up a bowl of what seemed to be fine salve in one paw, while in the other was a soft brush of fine hair. Then the hare clapped on the red-pepper plaster, and ran away, while the badger rolled in pain.

By-and-by, when the badger got well, he went to see the hare, to have it out with him. He found the hare building a boat. "Where are you going in that boat?" said the badger.

"I'm going to the moon," said the hare. "Come along with me. There's another boat."

So the badger, thinking to catch some fish by going on the water, got into the boat, and both launched away.

Now the boat in which Mr. Badger rowed was made of clay, which soon began to melt away in the water. Seeing this, the hare lifted his paddle, and with one blow sunk the boat, and the badger was drowned.

The hare went back and told the old man, who was glad that his wife had been revenged, and more than ever petted the hare to the end of his life.

(Begun in Young People No. 31, June 1.)

THE MORAL PIRATES.

BY W. L. ALDEN.

Chapter IV.

SOME time in the middle of the night Joe Sharpe woke up from a dream that he had fallen into the river, and could not get out. He thought that he had caught hold of the supports of a bridge, and had drawn himself partly out of the water, but that he had not strength enough to drag his legs out, and that, on the contrary, he was slowly sinking back. When he awoke he found that he was very cold, and that his blanket felt particularly heavy. He put his hand down to move the blanket, when, to his great surprise, he found that he was lying with his legs in a pool of water.

Joe instantly shouted to the other boys, and told them to wake up, for it was raining, and the tent was leaking. As each boy woke up he found himself as wet as Joe, and at first all supposed that it was raining heavily. They soon found, however, that no rain-drops were pattering on the outside of the tent, and that the stars were shining through the open flap.

"There's water in this tent," said Tom, with the air of having made a grand discovery.

"If any of you fellows have been throwing water on me, it was a mean trick," said Jim.

All at once an idea struck Harry. "Boys," he exclaimed, "it's the tide! We've got to get out of this place mighty quick, or the tide will wash the tent away."

The boys sprung up, and rushed out of the tent. They had gone to bed at low tide, and as the tide rose it had gradually invaded the tent. The boat was still safe, but the water had surrounded it, and in a very short time would be deep enough to float it. The tide was still rising, and it was evident that no time should be lost if the tent was to be saved.

Two of the boys hurriedly seized the blankets and other articles which were in the tent, and carried them on to the higher ground, while the other two pulled up the pins, and dragged the tent out of reach of the water. Then they pulled the boat farther up the beach, and having thus made everything safe, had leisure to discover that they were miserably cold, and that their clothes, from the waist down, were wet through.

Luckily, their spare clothing, which they had used for pillows, was untouched by the water, so that they were able to put on dry shirts and trousers. Their blankets, however, had been thoroughly soaked, and it was too cold to think of sleeping without them. There was nothing to be done but to build a fire, and sit around it until daylight. It was by no means easy to collect fire-wood in the dark; and as soon as a boy succeeded in getting an armful of drift-wood, he usually stumbled and fell down with it. There was not very much fun in this; but when the fire finally blazed up, and its pleasant warmth conquered the cold night air, the boys began to regain their spirits.

"I wonder what time it is?" said one.

Tom had a watch, but he had forgotten to wind it up for two or three nights, and it had stopped at eight o'clock. The boys were quite sure, however, that they could not have been asleep more than half an hour.

"It's about one o'clock," said Harry, presently.

"I don't believe it's more than nine," said Joe.

"We must have gone into the tent about an hour after sunset," continued Harry, "and the sun sets between six and seven. It was low tide then, and it's pretty near high tide now; and since the tide runs up for about six hours, it must be somewhere between twelve and one."

"You're right," exclaimed Jim. "Look at the stars. That bright star over there in the west was just rising when we went to bed."

TOM MAKES A CALCULATION.

"You ought to say 'turned in,'" said Joe. "Sailors never go to bed; they always 'turn in.'"

"Well, we can't turn in any more to-night," replied Tom. "What do you say, boys? suppose we have breakfast?—it 'll pass away the time, and we can have another breakfast by-and-by."

Now that the boys thought of it, they began to feel hungry, for they had had a very light supper. Everybody felt that hot coffee would be very nice; so they all went to work, made coffee, fried a piece of ham, and, with a few slices of bread, made a capital breakfast. They wrung out the wet blankets and clothes, and hung them up by the fire to dry. Then they had to collect more fire-wood; and gradually the faint light of the dawn became visible before they really had time to find the task of waiting for daylight tiresome.

They decided that it would not do to start with wet blankets, since they could not dry them in the boat. They therefore continued to keep up a brisk fire, and to watch the blankets closely, in order to see that they did not get scorched. After a time the sun came out bright and hot, and took the drying business in charge. The boys went into the river, and had a nice long swim, and then spent some time in carefully packing everything into the boat. By the time the blankets were dry, and they were ready to start, the tide had fallen so low that the boat was high and dry; and in spite of all their efforts they could not launch her while she was loaded.

"We'll have to take all the things out of her," said Harry.

"It reminds me," remarked Joe, "of Robinson Crusoe that time he built his big canoe, and then couldn't launch it."

"Robinson wasn't very sharp," said Jim. "Why didn't he make a set of rollers, and put them on the boat?"

"Much good rollers would have been," replied Joe. "Wasn't there a hill between the boat and the water? He couldn't roll a heavy boat up hill, could he?"

"He could have made a couple of pulleys, and rigged a rope through them, and then made a windlass, and put the rope round it," argued Jim.

"Yes, and he could have built a steam-engine and a railroad, and dragged the boat down to the shore that way, just about as easy."

"He couldn't dig a canal, for he thought about that, and found it would take too much work," said Jim.

"But we can," cried Harry. "If we just scoop out a little sand, we can launch the boat with everything in her."

The boys liked the idea of a canal; and they each found a large shingle on the beach, and began to dig. They dug for nearly an hour, but the boat was no nearer being launched than when they began. Tom stopped digging, and made a calculation. "It will take about two days of hard work to dig a canal deep enough to float that boat. If you want to dig, dig; I don't intend to do any more digging."

When the other boys considered the matter, they saw that Tom was right, and they gave up the idea of making a canal. It was now about ten o'clock, and they were rather tired and very hungry. A second breakfast was agreed to be necessary, and once more the fire was built up and a meal prepared. Then the boat was unloaded and launched, and the boys, taking off their shoes and rolling up their trousers, waded in the water and reloaded her. It was noon by the sun before they finally had everything in order, and resumed their cruise.

There was no wind, and it was necessary to take to the oars. The disadvantage of starting at so late an hour soon became painfully evident. The sun was so nearly overhead that the heat was almost unbearable, and there was not a particle of shade. The boys had not had a full night's sleep, and had tired themselves before starting by trying to dig a canal. Of course the labor of rowing in such circumstances was very severe; and it was not long before first one and then another proposed to go ashore and rest in the shade.

"Hadn't we better keep on till we get into the Highlands? We can do it in a quarter of an hour," said Tom.

As Tom was pulling the stroke oar, and doing rather more work than any one else, the others agreed to row on as long as he would row. They soon reached the entrance to the Highlands, and landed at the foot of the great hill called St. Anthony's Nose. They were very glad to make the boat fast to a tree that grew close to the water, and to clamber a little way up the hill into the shade.

"What will we do to pass away the time till it gets cooler?" said Harry, after they had rested awhile.

"I can tell you what I'm going to do," said Tom; "I'm going to get some of the sleep that I didn't get last night, and you'd better follow my example."

All the boys at once found that they were sleepy; and having brought the tent up from the boat, they spread it on the ground for a bed, and presently were sleeping soundly. The mosquitoes came and feasted on them, and the innumerable insects of the summer woods crawled over them, and explored their necks, shirt sleeves, and trousers legs, as is the pleasant custom of insects of an inquiring turn of mind.

"What's that?" cried Harry, suddenly sitting up as the sound of a heavy explosion died away in long, rolling echoes.

"I heard it," said Joe; "it's a cannon. The cadets up at West Point are firing at a mark with a tremendous big cannon."

"Let's go up and see them," exclaimed Jim. "It's a great deal cooler than it was."

With the natural eagerness of boys to be in the neighborhood of a cannon, they made haste to gather up the tent and carry it to the boat. As they came out from under the thick trees, they saw that the sky in the north was as black as midnight, and that a thunder-storm was close at hand.

"Your cannon, Joe, was a clap of thunder," said Harry. "We're going to get wet again."

"We needn't get wet," said Tom. "If we hurry up, we can get the tent pitched and put the things in it so as to keep them dry."

They worked rapidly, for the rain was approaching fast, but it was not easy to pitch the tent on a side-hill. It was done, however, after a fashion, and the blankets and other things that were liable to be injured by the wet were safely under shelter before the storm reached them.

[TO BE CONTINUED.]

NEW YORK PRISON-SHIPS.

ON the Long Island shore, where the Navy-yard now extends its shops and vessels around Wallabout Bay, there was in the time of the Revolution a large and fertile farm. A number of flour mills, moved by water, then stood there. The flat fields glowed with rich crops of grain, roots, and clover. Their Dutch owners still kept up the customs and language of Holland; at Christmas the kettles hissed and bubbled over the huge fires, laden with olykoeks, doughnuts, crullers; at Paas, or Easter, the colored eggs were cracked by whites and blacks, and all was merriment. The war no doubt brought its difficulties to the Dutch farmers; they were sometimes plundered by both parties, and they had little love for King George. They lived on in decorous silence, waiting for the coming of peace, remembering how their ancestors in Holland had once fought successfully for freedom against the Spaniards and the French. But in front of the quiet farm at Wallabout, and anchored in the bay, were seen several vessels, decayed, unseaworthy, and repulsive. They were the prison-ships of New York. Here from the year 1776 a large number of American prisoners were confined until the close of the war, and the tragic tales of their sufferings and fate lend a melancholy interest to the Wallabout shore.

The largest of the prison-ships—the old *Jersey*—was crowded with miserable captives. She was an old man-of-war, worthless, decayed; her low decks and dismal hold were converted into a jail; her crowded inmates were only thinned by the hand of death. The old *Jersey* may well be taken as one of the best symbols of the terrors of war. Her miserable captives pined away for months and years, deprived of all that makes life tolerable. In the chill and bitter frosts of winter no fires warmed her half-clad inmates; in the hot summer they faded away beneath the pitiless heat. Disease preyed upon them, yet no physician, it is said, was suffered to visit them. They were clothed in rags and tatters; their food was so scanty and often so repulsive that they lived in continual starvation. The fair youth of Connecticut and Rhode Island, the young sailors of New York and New Jersey, confined in these floating dungeons, were the sacrifices to the ambition of King George. They died by hundreds and even thousands during the war; the whole shore was lined with the unmarked graves of the patriot dead; the prison-ships were the scandal of the time, and their starved inmates seldom bore long the pains of the merciless imprisonment. It is said that the bones of eleven thousand dead were found upon the shore, and reverently buried in a common tomb.

Yet the prisoners of the old *Jersey* and the other ships were not left always without sympathy and aid. Often a boat was seen sailing from the rich farms on the Wallabout, laden with provisions for the famished patriots. The Dutch farmers from their own diminished resources gave bountifully to the sufferers. The ladies of the household worked warm stockings with the busy knitting-needle; the spinning-wheel was never idle; the fair Dutch damsels, demure and prudent, blushing with the rich complexions of Amsterdam, were never weary of their charitable toil; and many a poor prisoner was saved and strengthened by the gifts of his unknown friends. As the war advanced, too, the successes of the Americans seem to have convinced the royal chiefs that they were at least deserving of tolerable treatment. Some of the worst abuses of the system were removed. Hospital-ships were provided; the sick were separated from the healthy; the *Whitby*, the most infamous of the floating jails, was abandoned. Yet still, an observer relates, the dead were carried away every morning from the old *Jersey*, and still the horrors of captivity in the prison-ships exceeded all that had been known in every recent European war.

Several curious escapes are related. Once, in 1777, as a boat hung fastened to the old *Jersey* unnoticed, three or four prisoners let themselves down into it quietly, cast off the rope, and drifted away slowly with the tide. It was evening, and the darkness saved them. Their escape was discovered, and guns were fired at random after them; but they floated unharmed along the East River, passed what are now the Fulton and South ferries, and reached by a miracle the New Jersey shore. Here they found friends, and were safe. At another time, in the cold winter of 1780, fifteen half-clad, half-famished prisoners escaped in the night on the ice; others who followed them turned back, overpowered by the cold. One was frozen to death. It is almost possible to see in fancy the miserable band of shivering fugitives fleeing over the ice of the restless river in the deep cold of the winter's night, chased by the fierce winds, half lost in the blinding snow. They made their way to the Connecticut shore. A very remarkable escape from the Old Sugar-House is related of a Boston prisoner. He dug a passage under Liberty Street from the prison to the cellar of the house on the opposite side of the way. The difficulty of making the excavation will be plain to every one who looks at the labors of a party of workmen opening a trench for gas-pipes or water. Yet the Boston boy burrowed under-ground until he found himself free.

The prison-ships were retained in use until 1783. Several were burned at different times, either by accident or by the prisoners in their despair. At the close of the war the remaining ships were all sunk or burned. A few years ago the wreck of the old *Jersey* could still be seen on the Wallabout shore.

THE TIGER.

THE royal tiger of Asia is an animal celebrated for its beauty and its agility, cunning, and prodigious strength. Its skin is a bright tawny yellow, with glossy black stripes running downward from its back. Its tail, which is long and supple, is ringed with black, and its large head is marked in a very handsome manner. It is like a great cat. Its puffy cheeks are ornamented with white whiskers, and its big paws are like those of a pussy magnified fifty times. Its motions are very graceful, and whether lying down, its nose on its paw, sleeping, or walking through the paths of its native jungle with soft cat-like tread, it appears formed of muscle and sinew, without a bone in its body, so gracefully does it curve and twist itself as it moves.

The tiger is not considered a courageous beast by hunters, who say that if it is faced boldly, it will turn and slink away among the bushes, if it can. But if it can attack a hunter from behind, it will spring upon him, filling the air with its savage growls, and probably kill him with the first blow of its mighty paw.

The strength of this creature is almost incredible. It will break the skull of an ox, or even that of a buffalo, with the greatest ease. A story is told of a buffalo belonging to a peasant in India, which, while passing through a swamp, became helplessly entangled in the mire and underbrush. The peasant left the buffalo, and went to beg his neighbors to assist him in extricating the poor beast. When the rescuing party returned, they found a tiger had arrived before them, and having killed the buffalo, had just shouldered it, and started to march home to its lair with the prey. The tiger was soon dispatched by the peasant and his friends, and his beautiful skin was made to atone in a measure for the murder of the buffalo, which, when weighed, tipped the scales at more than a thousand pounds—a tremendous load for so small an animal as a tiger to shoulder and carry off with ease.

The tiger is very troublesome to the inhabitants of certain localities in India, as it attacks the herds, and makes off with many a fat bullock; and when unable to find other provender it will even attack the huts of the natives, sometimes tearing away the thatch, and springing in with a loud roar on a startled family. Instances are rare, however, of tigers attacking human beings, except when surprised and driven to self-defense. In some portions of the country they are very abundant, and may be heard every night roaring through the jungles in search of deer and other beasts upon which they prey. Even the savage wild boar of India does not terrify this queen of cats, and often bloody battles occur between these two powerful beasts.

As a mother the tiger is very devoted, and will fight for its pretty kittens to the last extremity. A story is told of an English officer who, while hunting in India, came upon the lair of a tiger, in which a tiny kitten, about a fortnight old, was lying all alone. Thinking that the mother was probably among the beasts killed by his party, the officer took the kitten to the camp, where it was chained to a pole, and amused the whole company with its graceful gambols. A few hours later, however, the whole camp was shaken by terrible roars and shrieks of rage.

A ROYAL BENGAL TIGER.

which came ever nearer and nearer. The kitten heard them, and became a miniature tiger at once, showing its teeth, and answering with a loud wail. Suddenly there leaped into the camp unawares a furious tigress with glaring eyes. Without deigning to notice the robbers of her baby, she seized the little thing in her teeth, snapped the small chain which held it with one jerk, and briskly trotted off with it into the jungle. Not a man in the camp dared move, and no one was malicious enough to fire at the retreating mother that had risked her life to regain possession of her baby.

Any one who has watched the feeding of caged tigers in a menagerie can easily imagine how terrible a hungry tiger would be, were he running free in his native jungle. As supper-time approaches, the tigers begin to roar and growl, and march restlessly up and down the cage. When the keeper approaches with the great pieces of raw beef, their roaring makes everything tremble. With ferocity glaring in their eyes, the tigers spring for the food, and begin to devour it eagerly. They often lie down to eat, holding the meat in their fore-paws like a cat, rolling it over and over while they tear it in pieces, growling savagely all the while.

The royal tiger is found only in Asia; for the beast called a tiger in South America and on the Isthmus of Panama is properly the jaguar, and its skin is not ornamented by stripes, but by black spots. It is not so powerful as its royal relative, but very much like it in its habits. Like the tiger, it is an expert swimmer, and as it is very fond of fish, it haunts the heavily wooded banks of the great South American rivers, and is a constant terror to the wood-cutters, who anchor their little vessels along the shore.

The crocodiles and the jaguars are at constant war with each other. If a jaguar catches a crocodile asleep on a sand-bank, it has the advantage, and usually kills its antagonist; but if the crocodile can catch its enemy in the water, the jaguar rarely escapes death by drowning.

Jaguars are not as plentiful on the Isthmus of Panama as formerly, before the scream and rumble of the locomotive disturbed the solitudes of the dense tropical forest. Still, large specimens are occasionally killed there, and their beautiful skins bring a high price when brought to market.

BICYCLING.

BY THE CAPTAIN.

ONE of the prettiest and most interesting sights ever seen in the gay city of Newport was the parade of bicyclers last Decoration-day, where, among the one hundred and fifty riders, were to be seen the uniforms of twenty-five crack clubs.

The illustration of the procession on next page shows it on Bellevue Avenue while passing the quaint and beautiful Casino Building. First of all rides the commander, Captain Hodges, of the Boston Bicycle Club, and directly behind him, riding three abreast, are the six marshals of the procession, who act as his aides. Then come the men of the New York Club, in gray and scarlet, riding in column of fours, and followed by the long line of glittering steel and gay uniforms that stretches for nearly a mile along the pleasant street.

Crowds of people have gathered to watch the procession, and their cheers, as some particularly well-drilled club passes, cause the men to ride with great care, and to preserve their lines so well that they move with the steadiness and precision of a body of cavalry.

Of all the riders in this long procession, the youngest was probably the best. Theodore R——, or "the young captain," as he is called, is but fourteen years old, and looks much younger. He lives in Philadelphia, and has practiced riding the bicycle in a rink in that city until his performances upon it are as wonderful as those of a circus rider on his horse.

In the picture of "the young captain" he is represented as mounted on his own machine, of which the driving-wheel is but forty-two inches in diameter. His most wonderful riding is, however, done upon a bicycle twelve or fourteen inches higher than this, and of which he can but barely touch the pedals as they come up. Thus he keeps the machine in motion by a succession of little kicks or pushes. He rides bicycles so tall that to gain the saddle he has actually to climb up the backbone of the machine after he has set it in motion with a vigorous push.

"The young captain" is a very bright boy, and excels in all games and feats of skill, while at the same time he is a good scholar, and stands well in all his classes.

Since the great Newport meet of bicyclers, or "wheelmen," as they are now generally called in this country, a number of letters containing questions about bicycles have been written by boys anxious to become riders, and sent to Young People. In the following hints to young riders I will try and answer all these questions:

Any active boy of ten years of age and upward may become a wheelman.

It is best to learn to ride on an old-fashioned wooden machine, or "bone-shaker," or on a bicycle so low that the rider may touch the ground with his toes. By this means he will learn to maintain his balance without getting any serious falls.

Anybody who can ride a "bone-shaker" can ride a bicycle, though in the latter case he must learn to mount his machine before he can ride it.

To learn the "mount" take your machine by the handles, give it a running push, place your left foot on the step, and, rising from the ground, maintain your balance as long as possible in that position without attempting to gain the saddle. After trying this a dozen times or more, try to take your seat in the saddle, not with a spring, but slide in easily, and do not let your body lean forward or you may pitch over the handles.

A beginner should have his saddle set well back on the spring. Although this position gives less power, it is much safer.

In going up hill lean well forward, and transfer the entire weight from the saddle to the pedals. Do not be ashamed to dismount in going up hill, but do so in every case rather than exhaust yourself.

In going down hill lean back as far as possible, and keep your machine under control. A little practice in back-pedalling, or pushing against the pedal as it comes up rather than as it goes down, will enable you to take your machine down very steep hills at ordinary walking pace. If your machine does escape from your control, throw your legs over the handles, and "coast," as you are less liable to get a bad fall while in this position than in any other.

Keep to the right of the road as much as possible. Always keep to the right when you meet a team, foot-passenger, or other bicycle, and in overtaking any of these always pass to the left. Dismount and walk past any horse that becomes frightened at your bicycle.

Always carry a light when riding at night.

Be careful not to use your whistle or bell more than is absolutely necessary, otherwise you will become a nuisance, and as such will not be a welcome addition to the ranks of wheelmen.

Remember that while you have rights for which you are bound to stand up, others have equal rights, which you are equally bound to respect.

In selecting a bicycle, be sure that it fits you perfectly. Do not gratify a mistaken ambition by trying to ride a wheel that is too large for you. The larger the wheel, the more difficulty you will find in driving it up hill.

As soon as you own a bicycle, make yourself familiar with every part of it, and especially with all its adjustments.

Never lend your bicycle.

Always clean and adjust it yourself. If it gets broken, send it to none but a first-class machinist for repairs.

FIRST GRAND MEET OF AMERICAN WHEELMEN.—Drawn by W. P. Snyder.

THE PIG'S PENNY.

BY W. O. STODDARD.

IT was the pig did it.

The bigger that pig grew, the more he squealed, and the less he seemed to like his pen.

Ben knew it, but for all that he wondered how it came to pass that he should find that pig in the village street, half way down to the tavern.

"Out of the pen into the barn-yard, and out of that into the street when the gate was open. Won't I have a time getting him home?"

There was little doubt of that, for the pig felt that it was his duty to root as he went, and he refused to walk quietly past any good opportunity to thrust his snub-nose into something.

Ben worked, and so did the pig.

"Hullo! What's that?"

The pig had turned up a clod of earth with something sticking on it, and Ben sprang forward to pick it up.

"It's a cent!"

It was round; it was made of copper; it was a coin of some kind; but it was black and grimy, and Ben rubbed hard to clean it.

"I never saw a cent like that before. I can't even read what it says on it."

"What have you found, Ben, my boy?"

"Guess it's a kind of a cent. The pig found it."

All the boys in the village knew old Squire Burchard, only they were half afraid of him. It was said he could read almost any kind of book, and that was a wonderful sort of man for any man to be.

"The pig found it? I declare! I guess I'll have to buy it of you."

"Don't you s'pose it'll pass?"

"Well, yes, it might; but it'll only buy a cent's worth. I'll give you more than that for it."

"Going to melt it over and make a new cent of it?"

"No, Ben, not so bad as that. I'll keep it to look at. It's a very old German coin, and I'm what they call a numismatist."

Ben listened hard over that word for a moment, and tried to repeat it.

"Rumismatics—I know; it's a good deal like what father says he has sometimes. Gets into his back and legs."

"Not quite, Ben; but it makes me gather up old coins, and put them in a glass case, and look at them."

"Father's is worse 'n that; it takes him bad in rainy weather."

"Well, Ben, I'll give the pig or you, just as you say, a quarter of a dollar for that cent."

Ben's eyes fairly danced, but all he could manage to say was, "Yes, sir. Thank you, sir. Guess I will."

"There it is, Ben. It's a new one. I don't care much for new ones. What'll you do with it?"

Ben hesitated only a moment, for he was turning the quarter over and over, and thinking of just the answer to the squire's question.

"It's a puppy, sir. Mrs. Malone said I might have it for a quarter, and father said I couldn't buy it unless I found the money."

"It'll be the pig's puppy, then? All right; but you can't make pork of him."

The pig was driven home in a good deal of a hurry, without another chance given him to root for old coins; and when Ben's father came in from the corn field that night, there was Ben ready to meet him with the puppy.

"Got him, have you?"

Ben had to explain twice over about the old cent and the Squire.

"Oh, the pig did it. Well, Ben, I don't see what we want of another dog; though that is a real pretty one. Too many dogs in this village, anyhow."

The next day Ben's father went to town with a load of wheat, and Ben went with him.

He had not owned that puppy long enough to feel like leaving him at home, so the little lump of funny black curls and clumsiness had to go to town with him.

Ben's father was in the store, selling his wheat, and Ben was sitting on top of the load in the wagon, when a carriage with a lady in it was pulled up in the street beside it.

"Is that your puppy, my boy?"

"Yes, ma'am."

"Will you sell it? I want one for my little boy."

"It's a real nice puppy—"

"What will you sell him for?"

Ben did not feel at all like parting with his new pet, but he knew very well what his father thought about it. Still, it might save him the puppy if he asked a tremendous price for it.

"I'll take five dollars, ma'am."

"Bring him to me, then. It's just such a dog as I thought of buying."

It seemed to Ben a good deal as if he were dreaming; but he did as he was told, and climbed back to his perch on the heaped-up bags of wheat to wait for his father.

It was not long before he had sold the wheat and came out.

"Why, Ben, where's your puppy?"

"There he is, father."

"Why, if that ain't a five-dollar bill! You don't say so!"

Ben explained, and added, "The pig did it, father."

"Well, yes, the pig did it. It just beats me, though."

"He won't know what to do with a five-dollar bill."

"Nor you either. But soon's I can throw off this load we must drive on up town. There's to be a horse auction."

Ben knew what that meant, for his father knew all about horses, and was all the while buying and selling them. So it was not long before the wagon was empty, and Ben and his father made their way to where the horses were to be sold.

"There's a good many of 'em," said Ben's father, "but the whole lot isn't worth much. I guess there isn't anything here I want."

Not many people were bidding for the horses, and they were indeed a poor-looking lot; but pretty soon a gray horse was led out that limped badly, and was as thin as if he had been fed on wind. One man bid a dollar for him, and another bid two, and there was a good deal of fun made about it; but Ben's father had very quietly slipped down from the wagon, and taken a careful look at the lame horse.

For all that, Ben was a little surprised when the auctioneer's hammer fell, and he shouted, "Sold! for five dollars, to— What's your name, mister?"

"Ben Whittlesey."

Ben's father said that. But it wasn't his name. His name was Robert.

"Ben," said his father, when he came back to the wagon, "hand me that five-dollar bill. If I can get that horse home, I'll cure him in a fortnight. There's no great thing the matter with him."

There was trouble enough in making the poor lame animal limp so many miles, and they got home after dark; but that was just as well, for nobody saw the new horse, or had a chance to laugh at him or his owner.

"It's the pig's horse," said Ben.

Ben's father was as good as his word about curing the lameness, and plenty of oats and hay, and no work, and good care, did the rest. The man who sold the gray for five dollars would not have known him at the end of two weeks.

It was just about two weeks after that that Ben's fa-they drove the pig's horse to town and back in a buggy, and with a nice new harness on. He stopped at the blacksmith's shop on his way home, and Mr. Corrigan, the blacksmith, seemed to take a great fancy to the gray.

"Just the nag I want, Mr. Whittlesey; only I've no ready cash to pay for him."

"I don't sell on credit, you know," said Mr. Whittlesey. "Anything to trade?"

"Nothing that I know of. Unless you care to take that vacant lot of mine, next the tavern. 'Tisn't doing me any good. I had to take it for a debt, and I've paid taxes for it these three years."

"Will you swap even?"

"Yes, I might as well."

There was more talk, of course, before the trade was finished, but it came out all right in the end. Before the next day at noon Mr. Corrigan owned the pig's horse; but the deed of the town lot was made out in the name of Ben Whittlesey, and not of the pig.

"Father," said Ben, at the tea table, "mayn't I let that pig out into the road every day?"

"No, Ben; all the pigs in the village can't root up another cent like that."

"He did it."

"Well, Ben, he did and he didn't. Do you know how he got the town lot for you?"

"Why, yes. Don't I?"

"Not quite. You saw him turn up the cent, and knew what to do with it; he didn't."

"Yes, father."

"And Squire Burchard saw the cent, and knew what to do with it; you didn't."

"Yes, father."

"And the lady saw your puppy, and knew what to do with it, and you didn't, nor I either. And I saw the gray horse, and knew what to do with him; the pig didn't."

"But I don't know what to do with the pig's town lot."

"No, nor Mr. Corrigan didn't, nor I either; but the man from town that's just bought the old tavern is going to build it over new, and wants to buy that lot to build on. I tell you what, Ben, my boy, there isn't much in this world that's worth having unless somebody comes along that knows what to do with it."

"Ben!" suddenly exclaimed his mother, as she looked out of the window, "there's that pig out in the garden!"

"Jump, Ben," said his father. "If he gets into your patch of musk-melons, he'll know just exactly what to do with them."

Before Ben got the pig out of the garden, the pig learned that Ben knew exactly what to do with a big stick.

MISS VAN WINKLE'S NAP.

BY MRS. W. J. HAYS.

Chapter I.

"MAMMA, will you please listen a moment?"

"How can I, Quillie dear? just see how busy I am," answered mamma, turning over a letter she was writing, while a man was bringing in trunks from the store-room, and another man was waiting for orders, and through a vista of open doorways was seen a dress-maker at work upon gingham slips and linen blouses.

"If you please, ma'am, a bit of edging will look none the worse on these cambrics, and the flannels need a touch of scarlet; even the wild flowers have vanity enough for a little color of their own."

"True enough, Ellen. Well, get your samples ready. Now, Quillie, I am going to address this letter, and then I promise to listen to you."

Quillie sighed—she found it so difficult to wait when she had so much to say. But she only fidgeted a little as mamma scrawled off an address in letters which Quillie thought would cover half her copy-book, then the little taper was lighted, the wax was melted, the pretty crest was imprinted on the seal, and mamma turned with a relieved smile to the little girl.

"Well, Quillie, what is it?"

"It's only this, mamma," began Quillie, impetuously; "I want to take a friend to the country with us."

"Who is the friend? why can not she go with her own people?" said mamma.

"Now, mammy dear, please don't hurry me; you know madame, our French teacher at school, has a little girl about my age—eight and a half. Well, if it wasn't for her, madame says she could go with some pupils to their country-seat, and teach them all summer, but they will not have her child, which is very hateful and disobliging, I think; and it popped into my head that perhaps you would let us have Julie with us, for the madame says she can not leave her alone in the city, and she has no relatives—hardly any friends—and I think it would make madame so happy not to lose this chance of giving lessons, and yet to have Julie, and—and—"

Mamma stooped down and kissed her little girl. "There," she said, in her quick, decisive way, "that will do. It was a kind thought, and I will consider it. Now run off and dig in the garden; your seeds are coming up nicely."

"But, mamma," said Quillie, not quite satisfied, "are you sure you won't forget?"

"I promise not to," was the answer, and she arose to change the coquettish cap and morning-gown for her street costume. Then she took out her pencil, and jotted down two or three errands in her memorandum-book, and gathering up the samples to match for Ellen's work, out she went.

It was a warm day, a balmy air, but one which induces languor, and as Mrs. Coit stopped at a street corner and bought a bunch of roses, she thought she would get the children out of town as soon as possible. Her eye was next attracted by some exquisite laces. She wanted a few yards, and stopped to price them. They were thread, filmy as cobwebs; they were costly; and as she held them in her hand, debating the purchase, she thought of Quillie's request; the cost of the lace would more than meet the expense of sending little Julie away. She concluded not to buy the laces. And so she went on with her errands.

At last she had finished, and turned off into a side street, got into a car, and was whisked away to a quiet place in the old part of the city. She stopped before a house which had in its day been fine; now it looked like a person who is keeping up appearances—a little shabby and worn, and wanting freshness. She rang the bell, and asked if Madame Garnier lived there. She was directed by a slovenly maid to a room on an upper floor, and left there. The air was redolent of garlic. She knocked at the door, and a little pattering of feet was heard, the door was opened on a crack, and a small head was to be seen, covered with a tiny handkerchief tied under the chin; a large checked apron concealed the rest of the small person. When the small person saw that the visitor was a lady, she no longer kept the door more than half closed, but throwing it wide open, she made a profound courtesy, and said, "Pardon, madame; please to enter."

Mrs. Coit paused, smilingly taking in the background of this interior. A sunny window full of plants, a bed with ruffled pillow-cases, a gilt clock, a canary, a table set out for two, a writing-desk and books in a corner, and a cooking stove, with a bubbling saucepan sending the cover dancing up and down. It was very close and warm, and the little hostess was pale, despite the heat.

Mrs. Coit had no time to spare. She asked the child if she were Julie Garnier, and if she wanted to spend two or three months in the country.

FRED'S STEAMBOAT.—DRAWN BY W. H. CARY.

The child opened her eyes in silent wonder. "Could madame be in earnest? Was it possible?"

Mrs. Coit explained, and in addition took out her pencil, and with rapidity wrote a note to madame.

The little Julie fairly wept with delight. To be in the country, with birds and bees and brooks—ah! it was too much felicity. Her mother would be wild with pleasure.

Then Mrs. Coit was going; but Julie could not let her depart without a taste of her *pot au feu*, which she was cooking for her dear *pauvre petite maman*—just one sip, if madame could take no more; and pushing a chair to the table, and hurriedly wiping off an old cracked faïence bowl, pretty enough in its day, the little eager hands dipped out a ladleful of soup. Mrs. Coit found it delicious. Warm as was the room and the repast, it was yet refreshing; so thanking the child for her hospitality, she at last took her departure.

A week from this time behold an eager group of little ones on the deck of a Hudson River night boat kissing their hands to Mr. and Mrs. Coit on the wharf. Nurse is on guard, and counts the heads to see if all are with her. Quillie's yellow locks are beside Julie's dark tresses; Fred and Willie come next; and little Artie, who scorns being the baby, waves in great dignity, as color-bearer, a small American flag. Long before the stars are out they beg to go to their state-rooms. They creep into the little beds, and imagine themselves on the tossing ocean. Nurse hears them discussing who shall be in the upper and who in the lower berths, and whether they shall be able to remain in them at all, for the vessel may pitch them all out; then Julie silences all with a vivid account of her travels. She gesticulates as she talks, occasionally rolls those dark eyes of hers, speaks of the great steam-ships, the mighty waves, the roar of the wind, the scream of the fog-whistle, and the terrible *mal de mer*. Instinctively they yield to her vast experience, and offer no more remarks, but silently prepare for their slumbers.

Quite with the early dawn they awake again, refreshed, eager, and taking in long draughts of the pure air into which they have come. Where are the docks and wharves and shipping? where the scenes of the night before? In the rosy flush of the morning lie the green hills and meadows. The birds are straining their throats with melody, the cocks are crowing, the geese cackling, and they hear the lowing of cows and the bleating of sheep.

"Is it paradise?" asks Julie.

"No, it is only Catskill," responds Quillie, tossing back her yellow locks.

"Hallo! there is Mr. Brown's wagon," screams Fred; and Will shouts till the farmer responds with a smiling nod.

Soon they are all safely stowed in the wagon, and jolting over the well-remembered roads, an hour or more bringing them to the comfortable farm. Then what savages more wild than they in their gambols! They roam from one haunt to the other, visit the cattle and the poultry, and expect a welcome from all. Breakfast waits, but no one comes. Nurse has to go after them. There they are on an old hay wagon, which Fred has made into a steamboat by dragging out of the lumber-room of the barn a piece of stove-pipe, and Artie's flag at the stern. Julie has her doll, and Will has the puppy he claims already, but Quillie emerges from some other corner with two darling kittens. What can nurse do to get them in to Mrs. Brown's table, with its wild strawberries, its crisp radishes, its cream, and golden butter, and piles of brown-bread? She hits upon a happy plan.

"Children, if you will all come in this moment, I will tell you something splendid."

Their ears were pricked at once. "What is it, nurse? what is it?"

"Not a word more till you obey me."

They scrambled down at that, and hastened into the house.

[TO BE CONTINUED.]

[illegible]

We are pleased to see that you take such an interest in botany, for it is a beautiful study, but as your list contains the names of thirty-seven different flowers, it is a little too long to print, especially as many of them are given in the paper on "Bee Flowers," in No. 26.

[illegible]

The following letter will be welcome to the many inquirers for this little flower girl of the Pacific coast:

[illegible]

Calif., Sacramento County, California.

[illegible]

Ferns and flowers should be laid carefully between two sheets of clean paper, the leaves artistically arranged in graceful shape, and placed under heavy pressure until they are dry. If the ferns are to be used for decoration, a warm iron, not too hot, must be passed over them, always placing clean paper between them and the iron, otherwise the heat of the room will curl them as soon as they are placed upon the wall. It is better not to iron them until they are dry, as the suddenly applied heat is liable to change the color of fresh ferns, causing them to look dull and faded. The sugar-maple leaf you send is well pressed, and beautifully varnished. What kind of varnish did you use? No doubt some little girls who are preserving leaves would like to know.

[illegible]

CATHY D. B.—Write again, and tell us how you amuse yourself while you are sick, and we will try to print it. Your last letter was so much a business communication that we could not put it in the Post-office Box.

[illegible]

Turtles like a diet of flies and small insects, and fruit. You will find directions for the care of different kinds of turtles in the Post-office Box of YOUNG PEOPLE No. 5 and No. 14. The "Letter from a Land-Turtle," in YOUNG PEOPLE No. 27, will also give you information.

[illegible]

The whip-poor-will is a native of North America, and is found from the Pacific to the Atlantic. In winter it travels southward, and spends the cold season in the forests of Central America. It is a brownish-gray bird, and has a huge mouth, armed with bristles at the base of the bill, with which it catches the moths and other soft-bodied insects upon which it feeds. It is a very shy bird, and hides itself all day, coming out at evening and early morning to skim along with noiseless flight near the ground, seeking its food. It is sometimes called the night-hawk. It makes no nest, but deposits two greenish eggs, spotted with blue and brown, in some snug corner, among fallen leaves, on the ground.

[illegible]

Your bug is probably one of the small [illegible] beetles, of which there are many varieties. As they move about in the light, the color appears to change, like the color of the head and throat of a South American humming-bird. [illegible] it will probably die of starvation some day.

GEORGE H. M.—A neat black walnut box about five inches deep, will make a good case for butterflies. Glue pieces of cork in the bottom, on which to mount your specimens, and have a tightly fitting glass cover. [illegible]

[illegible]

"[illegible]"—The *Passion Play*, which is celebrated once in ten years in the peasant village of Ober-Ammergau, in the Bavarian Tyrol, is a relic of the ancient Miracle Plays and Mysteries which were so popular among the common people throughout Europe during the thirteenth and fourteenth centuries. [illegible]

PUZZLES FROM YOUNG CONTRIBUTORS.

[illegible]

ANSWERS TO PUZZLES IN No. 33.

[illegible]

ADVERTISEMENTS.

HARPER'S YOUNG PEOPLE.

[illegible]

ADVERTISING.

[illegible]

HARPER & BROTHERS,
Franklin Square, N. Y.

FISHING OUTFITS.

CATALOGUE FREE.

[illegible], Nassau Street, N. Y.

The Child's Book of Nature.

The Child's Book of Nature, for the Use of Families and Schools: intended to aid Mothers and Teachers in Training Children in the Observation of Nature. In Three Parts. Part I. Plants. Part II. Animals. Part III. Air, Water, Heat, Light, &c. By [illegible], M.D. Illustrated. The Three Parts complete in One Volume, [illegible] [illegible]

[illegible]

Published by HARPER & BROTHERS, New York.

[illegible]

ELEMENTARY EDUCATION.

Books for the School and Family.

ARITHMETIC.

[illegible]

NATURAL SCIENCE.

[illegible]

FRENCH AND GERMAN.

[illegible]

OBJECT LESSONS.

[illegible]

Published by HARPER & BROTHERS, New York.

[illegible]

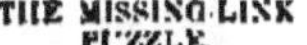

A LATIN WORD SQUARE.

BY H.

My first was highly prized of old;
They thought the future it foretold,
  And nothing did without it;
But now we listen with a smile
When once 'tis mentioned in a while,
  And hardly think about it.

My second has no proper hue,
Though white, red, yellow, black, and blue,
  'Tis called by one or t'other.
We pass it over night and day,
And yet when man becomes its prey
  They swallow each the other.

My second backward spells my third,
And shows what magic's in a word.
  It makes a part of being.
'Tis singular, and yet 'tis true,
Imperfect as it is, to you
  It shows how time is fleeing.

Now take my first, reverse its spell,
'Twill make my fourth; and *he*, note well,
  Could solve the problems mighty—
To square the circle, change to gold,
Perpetual motion to unfold,
  And make elixir vitæ.

THE MISSING-LINK PUZZLE.

PUT on your thinking cap, and see if you can not find out the true inwardness of these sausages.

THE GAME OF GEOGRAPHY.

AS ARRANGED BY C. E. BARTLETT.

THIS play, although instructive, can not fail to be amusing, as the best scholars can hardly help making blunders in the excitement and hurry of the game. Two leaders are chosen, who each select in turn, until all the players are taken, and are formed in two lines facing each other, a chair for each being placed behind him. The leader on one side calls out some letter, and says "Sea," or mentions some other body of water. The leader on the other side immediately names one beginning with the letter, and each one on his side gives another in rapid succession. If there is a pause, the leader of side No. 1 counts ten rapidly, and calls "Next"; the player who stands next answers, and the one who missed takes his seat. If a mistake is made by giving a wrong name to the piece of water called for, as by calling a river by the name of a sea or isthmus, or by giving the wrong letter as its first one, and it is not corrected by some member of the same side before the leader of the opposite side calls out "Miss," then all of side No. 2 must take their seats, which counts two for side No. 1.

The leader of side No. 2 requests all his side to again stand in line, with the exception of those who missed, and calls out some piece of land, as mountain, State, county, etc., and a letter, which the opposite side answer in the same way; and if every one succeeds in answering to the call, and each one gives a correct reply without mistake, they score three for their own side. The game is won by the side that first scores ten; and as all who have missed must keep their seats until the end of the play, they have abundant opportunity for laughing at the mistakes which are made by their friends. If it should happen that the leader of one side has no one to call upon to stand in line, he is obliged to answer alone; and if he also fails, the victory belongs to the other, even if they have not scored ten.

Another game of geography is played by each person taking pencil and paper, and in a given time—say, five minutes—writing as many geographical names, beginning with a certain letter, as he can remember. When "Time" is called, a player reads his list, and any name that he has, and the others have not, counts as many for him as there are players besides himself. Each then reads his list in turn, and the one who scores the greatest number, when all have read, wins the game. If during the reading any name is challenged, and the writer is unable to describe it, if it be a river, sea, bay, etc., or locate it if it is a city, town, or cape, every other player counts one.

[illegible]

VOL. I.—NO. 35. PUBLISHED BY HARPER & BROTHERS, NEW YORK. PRICE FOUR CENTS.
[illegible] Copyright, [illegible], by Harper & Brothers. $1.50 per Year, in Advance.

(Begun in YOUNG PEOPLE No. 31, June 1.)

THE MORAL PIRATES.

BY W. L. ALDEN.

CHAPTER V.

IT was a terrific storm. The wind swept down the river, raising a ridge of white water in its path. The rain came down harder, so the boys thought, than they had ever seen it come down before, and the glare of the lightning and the crash of the thunder were frightful.

"What luck it is that we got the tent pitched in time!" exclaimed Joe. "We're as dry and comfortable here as if we were in a house."

"Pick your blankets up quick, boys," cried Harry. "Here's the water coming in under the tent."

Joe had boasted a little too soon. The water running down the side of the hill was making its way in large quantities into the tent. To save their clothes and blankets the boys had to stand up and hold them in their arms, which was by no means a pleasant occupation, especially as the cold rain-water was bathing their feet.

"It can't last long," remarked Tom. "We're all right if the lightning doesn't strike us."

"Where's the powder?" asked Harry.

"Oh, it's in the flask," replied Joe, "and I've got the flask in my pocket."

"So, if the lightning strikes the tent, we'll all be blown up!" exclaimed Harry. "This is getting more and more pleasant."

A SOUP EXPLOSION.

wriggle out from under the tent. "We've got to get wet now, anyway; but perhaps, if we stay as we are, we can manage to keep the blankets dry."

The wet tent felt miserably cold as it clung to their heads and shoulders, but the boys kept under it, and held their blankets and spare shirts wrapped tightly in their arms. Luckily the storm was nearly at an end when the tent blew down, and a few moments later the rain ceased, and the crew of the *Whitewing*, in a very damp condition, crept out and congratulated themselves that they had escaped with no worse injury than a wet skin.

"Where are the rubber blankets?" asked Harry.

"Rolled up with the other blankets," answered everybody.

"It won't do to tell when we get home," remarked Harry, "that instead of using the water-proof blankets to keep ourselves dry, we used ourselves to keep the water-proofs dry. It's the most stupid thing we've done yet; and I'm as bad as anybody else."

"It was a good deal worse to pitch a tent without digging a trench around it," said Tom. "If I'd dug a trench two inches deep just back of that tent, not a drop of water would have run into it."

"And I don't think much of the plan of using only four pins to hold a tent down when a hurricane is coming on," said Joe.

"And I think the least said by a fellow who carries two pounds of powder in his pocket in a thunder-storm, the better," added Jim.

It took some time to bail the water out of the boat, for the rain and the spray from the river had half filled it. But the shower had cooled the air, and the boys were glad to be at work again after their confinement in the tent. They were soon ready to start; and rowing easily and steadily, they passed through the Highlands, and reached a nice camping spot, on the east bank of the river below Poughkeepsie, before half past five.

This time they selected a place to pitch the tent with great care. It was easy to find the high-water mark on the shore, and the tent was pitched a little above it, so as to be safe from a disaster like that of the previous night. Harry wanted it pitched on the top of a high bank; but the others insisted that, as long as they were safe from the tide, there was no need of putting the tent a long distance from the water, and that they had selected the only spot where they could have a bed of sand to sleep on.

This important business being settled, supper was the next subject of attention.

"We haven't been as regular about our meals as we ought to be," said Harry, "but it hasn't been our fault. We'll have a good supper to-night, at any rate. How would you like some hot turtle soup?"

"Just the thing," said Joe. "The bread is beginning to get a little dry; but we can soak it in the soup."

"About going for milk," continued Harry; "we ought to arrange that and the other regular duties. Suppose after this we take turns. One fellow can pitch the tent, another can go for milk, another can get the fire-wood, and the other can cook. We can arrange it according to alphabetical order. For instance, Tom Schuyler pitches the tent to-night, Jim Sharpe goes for milk, Joe gets the fire-wood, and I cook. The next time we camp, Jim will pitch the tent, Joe will get the milk, I will get the wood, and Tom will cook. Is that fair?"

The boys said it was, and they agreed to adopt Harry's proposal. Jim went off with the milk pail, and when the fire was ready, Harry took a can of soup and put it on the coals to be heated.

Jim found a house quite near at hand, where he bought two quarts of milk and a loaf of bread, and was back again at the camp before the soup was ready. He found the boys lying near the fire, waiting for the soup to heat and the coffee to boil.

"That soup takes a long time to heat through," said Tom. "There isn't a bit of steam coming out of it yet."

"How can any steam come out of it when it's soldered up tight?" replied Harry.

"You don't mean to tell me that you've put the can on the fire without punching a hole in the top?"

"Of course I have. What on earth should I punch a hole in it for?"

"Because—" cried Tom, hastily springing up.

But he was interrupted by a report like that of a small cannon: a cloud of ashes rose over the fire, and a shower of soup fell just where Tom had been lying.

"That's the reason why," resumed Tom. "The steam has burst the can, and the soup has gone up."

"We've got another can," said Harry, "and we'll punch a hole in that one. What an idiot I was not to think of its bursting! It's a good thing that it didn't hurt us. I should hate to have the newspapers say that we had been blown up and awfully mangled by soup."

The other can of soup was safely heated, and the boys made a comfortable supper. They drove a stake in the sand, and fastened the boat's painter securely to it, and then "turned in."

"No tide to rouse us up to-night, boys," said Harry, as he rolled himself in his blanket. "I sha'n't wake up till daylight."

"We'd better take an early start," remarked Tom. "We haven't got on very far, because we started so late this morning. If we get off by six every morning, we can lie off in the middle of the day, and start again about three o'clock. It's no fun rowing with the sun right overhead."

"Well, it isn't more than eight o'clock now; and if we take eight hours' sleep, we can turn out at four o'clock," said Harry. "But who is going to wake us up? Joe and Jim are sound asleep already, and I'm awful sleepy myself. I don't believe one of us will wake up before seven o'clock anyway."

Tom made no answer, for he had dropped asleep while Harry was talking. The latter thought he must be pretending to sleep, and was just resolving to tell Tom that it wasn't very polite to refuse to answer a civil question, when he found himself muttering something about a game of base-ball, and awoke, with a start, to discover that he could not possibly keep awake another moment.

The boys slept on. The moon came out, and shone in at the open tent flap, and the tide rose to high-water mark, but not quite high enough to reach the tent. By-and-by the wheezing of a tow-boat broke the stillness, and occasionally a hoarse steam-whistle echoed among the hills; but the boys slept so soundly that they would not have heard a locomotive had it whistled its worst within a rod of the tent.

The river had been like a mill-pond since the thunder-storm, but about midnight a heavy swell rolled in toward the shore. It came on, growing larger and larger, and rushing up the little beach with a fierce roar, dashed into the tent and overwhelmed the sleeping boys without the slightest warning.

[TO BE CONTINUED.]

THE OLD, OLD TOAD.

BY MRS. E. W. LATIMER.

"MAMMA," said one of my boys to me (they are "grown-up boys," but they take great pleasure in the weekly arrival of the YOUNG PEOPLE), "why don't you write a communication to the editor, and tell him how papa once saw a live toad in a slab of rock that had just been blasted?"

"Perhaps the editor would not believe me," I replied. "It seems a doubtful point among geologists and naturalists, and he says the fact has never been certified to by any scientific man."

"Well, wasn't papa a man of science?"

"No; he was a young civil engineer, with only science enough to be employed on the first surveys and construction of the Baltimore and Ohio Railroad. But he is one of the most accurate observers I have ever seen, and so careful in his statements that, as you know, he relates even a common fact as cautiously as if he were giving evidence in a court of justice."

"Well, I should like to hear it over again. Tell me the story."

"Your father was, as I said, a young engineer superintending the construction of the line of road west from Sir John's Run, near Berkeley Springs, in West Virginia. His men were engaged in blasting a mass of very hard rock—gneiss, he called it—which ran across the line. Coming up to where they were at work, immediately after a fresh blast, he found the block that had just been detached lying on the ground. It was a mass of stone about as large as the chair you are sitting on; the surface where it had just been severed from the parent rock was perfectly smooth, except that about the middle of it appeared a reddish blister, about the size of half an egg. This attracted your father's notice. He was curious to see what it could mean, and taking up a hammer that was lying near, he tapped upon it gently. It cracked like an egg-shell, and out came a toad, which moved rather feebly, was very weak, extraordinarily thin, and covered with a sort of red rust. He did not, however, live more than a few minutes. Whether the blow with the hammer had hurt him, or whether the fresh air was too much for him, nobody ever knew. He died, and there being no professional naturalist on the spot, his body was not preserved. The men of the gang gathered around his death-bed, and the contractor had some marvellous stories to tell of things of the kind he had met with in his experience.

"The spot where the toad lay in the slab of rock was probably, your father thought, about five feet from the surface, but he could not say with certainty. He was sure there was no fissure or opening in it communicating with the outer air."

"I should think, mamma, you would be glad the readers of YOUNG PEOPLE seem to be taking an interest in your friends the toads."

"So I am. I liked and protected them, for the sake of their beautiful eyes, long before I found out how useful they are in a garden. You recollect I used to tell you of a lady who had a splendid bed of mignonette one year, and the next had no mignonette at all, because her cruel gardener had killed off all the toads!

"A toad's eyes are the only things in nature which could not be represented without using gold. I fancy that the toad's eyes are the origin of the superstition about the 'precious jewel in his head.' As to their being poisonous, as the French peasants say, or making warts, as the old mammies tell us, that is pure nonsense. I have handled hundreds of them. Their tongues are as curious as their eyes are beautiful. The root of the tongue is just behind the under lip, and it folds backward.

"When Mr. Toad sees a fly, he darts his long and active tongue out so quickly that it is hard to see him do it, and jerks the fly alive down his wide gullet.

"Do you remember watering Darby and Joan, who have lived twenty years under our porch, when you were little boys? You thought they seemed to enjoy a rain so much that you would give them a shower. Poor Darby and his wife realized the proverb, 'It never rains but it pours.' A gentle, steady rain was agreeable enough; but you floated them out of house and home, and I do not think they ever resettled in the same spot.

"There is a charming story about a toad, called Monsieur le Vicomte."

ELM COTTAGE

BY M. M.

Now is the time when hither and yon
  Our city-people run
Seeking a home. And here, close by,
  Is the prettiest under the sun.

So dainty it is, so cosy and fresh,
  Its walls in a marvellous way
Are covered all over with tapestry
  In yellow and green and gray.

The ceiling is frescoed in light and shade,
  And the cottage stands so high
That the view extends to the mountains dim,
  Whose peaks are lost in the sky.

No window it has, but an open door
  Invites one to sweetest rest;
For my wee house, perched on a swaying elm,
  Is only an oriole's nest.

HOW DO THEY GROW?

WHILE the children were waiting for the Professor one bright summer morning, they overheard through the open window little Jennie asking John Grant, the gardener, "Where do the flowers come from?"

"Why, don't you see?" said he; "they grow up out of the ground."

"How do they grow?" continued the little questioner, whose curiosity was clearly on the increase.

Before John could collect his wits sufficiently to frame an answer, the Professor made his appearance with a pretty rose-bud in his hand.

"Will you not tell us," said Gus, "how flowers grow? There's John out there digging among them all day, but he seems to know nothing about them, after all."

"Oh yes, he does," said the Professor; "I presume he knows more about them, in a practical way, than either you or I. He can take care of them through the winter, and train them, and get them early into bloom, far better than I could, I am sure. But very likely I know more of what the books have to say on the subject, and can more readily find words to express what is called the theory in the case. The growth of plants has given rise, perhaps you know, to the science of botany."

"Please don't be very scientific," pleaded Gus, "but tell us in a plain way how they grow."

"Well, let us begin with the seed. In the first place, the sun warms the ground in which the seed lies buried. Then the seed swells and bursts, and sends downward a little root; the root drinks in the water from the soil, and so gets larger, and spreads around; and by-and-by it sends up a stem above the ground. As soon as the sunlight falls on the little plant, it gets stronger, and is able to take food as well as drink from the soil, so as to get its full shape and size and green color."

"Has it a mouth to eat and drink with?" asked Gus, in some doubt.

"Yes, a great many mouths scattered all over the root, or on very little branches reaching out from it. While it is under-ground in the dark, it is thirsty, and cares only to drink water; but as soon as it comes up, and has enjoyed the light and heat of the sun, it begins to get hungry, and takes in solid food with the water. The fresh air and sunshine sharpen its appetite, just as they do in our case."

"The little spring flowers seem to come up so suddenly," said Joe, "as if they did all their growing in one night. We don't see them at all until they are standing in full bloom."

"It takes them some days to develop and blossom," said the Professor. "The stem rises slowly from a little point, getting longer and longer, until it reaches its full size. Shrubs and trees begin in the same way, mounting upward until they reach their proper height. If you examine the ground closely, you will find plenty of little plants just peeping out. Most of them are grass, and keep on about the same as they begin; but some change very greatly, and take all kinds of shapes and directions. They soon put out their leaves, one by one, or two by two, along the stem, short spaces apart. Just above the leaves, in the larger plants, branches start out, and grow much like the stem, with their own leaves."

"How do the flowers come?" asked Gus.

"Sometimes they grow on a little stem of their own, called a scape, that springs up separately from the root. But usually the main stem or one of the branches is changed into a flower-stem. Now suppose we cut this rose-bud in two, and then I can show you."

"Please, Professor," said May, "don't cut the poor rose-bud. There is a book down stairs with one in it cut in two."

Gus brings the book, and the Professor exclaims, "That is what I want exactly. Here are lines pointing to the parts; and now I'll explain them. You see, S is the sepals."

"What are they?" asked Joe.

"The sepals are the outer covers of the flower. They lie all over and hide it when it is in the bud, but are folded back when the bud opens. There are five, which is a very common number for flowers to have. Some have only two or three, others none at all. The petals are marked L. They are the gayly colored parts that lie next to the sepals, and inside of them. Sometimes the petals are separate from each other, and sometimes all fastened together. They are also called the corolla, which means a little crown, and are the showiest portion of the flower. Wild flowers are apt to have only one row of petals, but those cultivated in gardens often have a large number. The good care that they get has the effect to make them deck themselves out with more petals, which are the parts chiefly admired for their brilliancy."

"What are these little threads near the middle?" asked Joe.

"They are called stamens. In the picture they are marked P. Inside of them, in the very centre, is what are called the pistils, T. Down below them are the seeds, in the middle of what becomes the fruit, as you have noticed in an apple or pear, which is somewhat like a rose when ripe, though very much larger. After the petals have fallen off the rose, the part that is left gets ripe with the seeds inside, just as if it were an apple or a pear."

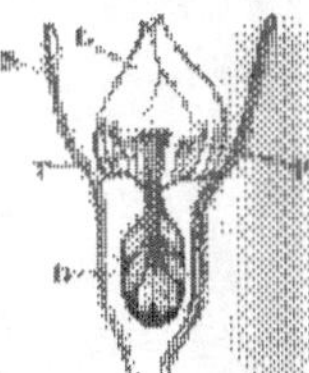

ROSE-BUD CUT VERTICALLY.

LITTLE JENNIE AND THE GARDENER.

MISS PAMELA PLUMSTONE'S PIANO.

BY SYDNEY DAYRE.

"WHAT do you say to Ned's taking a ride up to Miss Pamela's to-morrow?" said Mr. Weatherby to his wife.

"How? All by himself? A ride of twenty miles?"

"On horseback. Yes. Yes. Does that answer your three questions satisfactorily? Now *I'll* ask one. Why not?"

"Oh, I suppose there is no objection, only he has never taken such a long ride alone."

"Why, mother! I, a great fellow of fourteen! Of course I can go—that is, please let me. What for, father?"

"I have had a little dividend of fifty dollars paid in on Miss Pamela's morsel of horse-railway stock, and I know she always wants money as soon as it comes."

"Probably much sooner, poor soul—" said Mrs. Weatherby.

"Unlike most other people, eh, ma'am?" interrupted Mr. Weatherby.

"—and more than ever now, since she has taken those two girls of her good-for-nothing brother's. If they had been boys, they might have been some use on her mite of a farm. When I said so to her, she said: 'Yes, my dear, that's just the reason their mother's family don't want them; but, you know, girls have to live as well as boys. We're pretty sure of getting enough to eat, and as for the rest, I believe the Lord will provide.'"

"Her faith will be rewarded just now," said Mr. Weatherby, "for this is an unlooked-for dividend. The road has been doing better than usual of late."

"I'm very glad," said his wife. "I dare say it will be a real godsend to them all."

"I'll be off early in the morning," said Ned.

"All alone, and carrying money!" said his brother Tom, with an ominous shake of the head.

Ned *did* feel a little like a hero as he started on his long ride through a thinly settled country, and over a road passing through miles of thick woods. His suggestion that it might be well to carry a revolver had been smiled at by his father, and frowned down by his mother, and he had to confess to himself that he felt a little safer without it. His half-desire for just a trifling adventure was not to be gratified, for as noon approached he drew near Miss Pamela Plumstone's quaint old farm-

FISHERMAN'S LUCK.

house, and was soon warmly welcomed by that sprightly lady.

"Why, Master Ned, I am delighted! How good of you! Didn't you find the roads very bad? And how is your mother and the twins? And has your father quite got over his rheumatism? And when is she going to get out to see us again?"

"Very well, thank you. Yes, ma'am. No'm. Just as soon as the roads get settled, she says," said Ned, attempting to answer her rather mixed questions, as he perceived by her pause that she expected a reply.

"And what a fine big fellow you've grown to be, Master Ned! I am astonished to see how you improve."

Ned fully agreed with her, but modestly refrained from saying so, and made known his errand. How poor Miss Pamela's face shone!

"Oh, my dears, come here," she cried, running to a door. "Do come here and see what has come to us."

Ned looked curiously at the two girls who came in answer to her call. They had become inmates of Miss Pamela's house since his last visit to her, and he had never seen them before.

"The youngest one looks as if she might be pretty," he said to himself; "but how funny they do look!"

They did look funny. Miss Pamela's only ideas on the subject of dressing little girls were drawn from her memories of what she herself had worn forty years ago. Their pantalets reached almost to their heels, and their gingham aprons were almost as long, and cut without a gore. Their hair was drawn tightly back, and braided in two tails, those of the older one being long and dangly, and of the other short and stubby.

"See here, my dears," again exclaimed Miss Pamela, "here is some money I didn't expect. Didn't I tell you, Kitty Plumstone, that Providence would send you some new music somehow? She plays on the piano, Master Ned; I really do think she is going to make quite a musician. I teach her myself, you know. I can't play any.

more because of the stiffness in my fingers, but Kitty can play 'Days of Absence,' and 'Come, Haste to the Wedding,' already."

Ned was expressing pleasure at this pleasing proficiency, when Miss Pamela bustled away with a few words about dinner, which sounded agreeably to him after his ride.

A long ramble afterward on the farm, in company with the funny-looking girls, proved them to be as genial and companionable as they could have been had their dress included all the modern improvements, although Ned, who was rather critical in such matters, still thought it a pity they could not have blue streaks on their stockings, ruffles somewhere about them, and wear their hair loose.

They knew where the late wild flowers and the wild strawberries grew, and where the birds built their nests. They gathered early cherries, and promised Ned plenty of nuts if he would come in October. They had tame squirrels and rabbits penned up in the wonderful old ramshackle building which did duty as barn, stable, carriage-house, granary, and general receptacle for all kinds of queer old-fashioned lumber, the accumulations of many years. They were poultry-fanciers, too, in a small way; had a tiny duck-pond at one corner of the barn, where the great sweep of roof sloped down almost to the ground, forming a shed, and they all climbed upon it, and watched a quacking mother as she introduced her first brood of downy little yellow lumps to their lawful privileges as ducklings. And all agreed (the girls and boy, that is) that it was much nicer to be young ducks than young chickens; and there is no reason to doubt that the young ducks thought so too, as they realized the delights of the cold-water system.

But all agreed that nothing came up to the bantams—the proud little strutting "gamy" (Ned said that) roosters, all bright color and ambitious crow, and the darling wee brown mothers, scarcely larger than quails, whose cunning babies were no bigger than a good-sized marble. Kitty promised Ned a pair when they should be grown.

After tea he was called upon to admire Kitty's playing, but his praises of her performance were interrupted by Miss Pamela's profuse apologies for the condition of the piano.

"It is so terribly out of tune, you see, Master Ned." He was evidently looked upon as something of a critic in music. He rather liked to be so considered, and thought it unnecessary to assure them he knew nothing about it. The old piano sounded to him very much like the bottom of two tin pans mildly banged together; but if it had been a much better instrument, it would have been all the same to his unmusical ear.

"Oh, it sounds very well, I assure you, Miss Pamela," he said.

"You see," went on the lady, "it hasn't been tuned for four years or more. Mr. Scrutils went about the country for many a year tuning pianos; but he got old, and the last time he came he left his tuning key, or whatever you call it, saying he'd be round again if he could; but he never came. It's such an expensive thing, you know, to bring a man twenty miles to do it, that I've been putting it off, and putting it off. But we'll have it done now, eh, Kitty?"

"Why, Miss Pamela," said Ned, "I'll do it for you, if you have the thing they do it with."

"You, Master Ned! Can you tune a piano?"

"Well, I never did tune one, but I know exactly how they do it. I've seen Professor Seaflatt tune my mother's ever so many times."

"Oh, I'm sure you could do it, if you really feel as if you could take so much trouble; it would be a great kindness to us."

"Of course I'll do it, with the greatest pleasure in the world, ma'am. Let me see—I am to go home to-morrow afternoon; I'll do it the first thing in the morning." And rash Ned went to rest on Miss Pamela's feather-bed, in a room smelling of withered rose leaves. The bed was hung with old chintz curtains; the wall-paper displayed a pattern of large faded flowers. The swallows made a soft twittering in the wide chimney, as he closed his eyes with a glow of satisfaction at the thought of the kind action (and very clever one, too!) he had undertaken to perform.

He found it harder than he had expected. The screws were rusty and hard to move, and the tuning key was old, and *would* slip. But before noon he announced his task completed, and Miss Pamela and her two nieces gathered near, their faces beaming with interest.

The piano was small and narrow, with legs so thin as to suggest to Ned that it needed pantaloons. It had been the pride and glory of Miss Pamela's girlhood, and was still, in her eyes, an excellent and valuable instrument, although she, being of a modest turn of mind, was willing to acknowledge that it had probably seen its best days.

"It will be so nice to have it in good tune again!" she said, in a tone of great satisfaction. "I declare, Master Ned, what a thing it is to have such advantages as you boys are having!—to be able to turn your hand to 'most anything! Now, then, Kitty, play 'Days of Absence.'"

Kitty played it. But what could be the meaning of that fearful jumble of strange sounds? Surely that time-honored melody (modern hymn-book, "Greenville") never sounded so before. What was the matter? Miss Pamela's face fell a little, but she still smiled, and said,

"You had better get your notes, Kitty; you are playing carelessly."

Kitty got her notes, and played carefully, but the result was still, to say the least, most astonishing and unsatisfactory.

"Try 'Come, Haste to the Wedding,' then." But the jig ran riot to such an extent that Kitty lost her place, stumbled, and finally came to a dead stop.

Poor Miss Pamela listened with a face of deepening dismay, while Ned stood still, with cold chills running down his back, as he was suddenly struck with the appalling idea that he might have undertaken something entirely beyond his abilities, and that the ruin of the cherished old piano might be the possible dreadful result.

"Try a scale, Kitty," again suggested Miss Pamela, with a polite effort to look tranquil.

Oh, that scale—what capers it cut! what unheard-of combinations of fearful sounds it was guilty of! Up and down it jumped and flourished, careering about in a manner as far as possible removed from that of a sober, well-conducted scale. Bass notes and treble notes ran against each other; high notes and low notes played leap-frog—they groaned, shrieked, and wheezed in a horrid discord, which could not have been worse if a thousand imps had been let loose in the old oaken case.

Did you ever see an intelligent dog with a rustling paper ruffle tied round his tail, paper shoes on, and a fool's cap on his head? and as everybody laughed at him, and he *knew* they were doing so, do you remember his reproachful look of helpless, indignant protest against being made to appear ridiculous in spite of himself?

Just such an expression we may imagine that poor old piano would have worn, to any one who could have taken in the full absurdity of the position. A venerable instrument like itself, after thirty-five years of honorable service, thus to be forced to exhibit a levity so unbefitting its age and dignity!

"Well," and Miss Pamela sank into a chair, "it's very strange—*very strange indeed*."

Poor Ned was red-hot with mortification and chagrin. He certainly was to be pitied. It was very trying indeed to have been led into such a scrape by his boyish over-confidence in his own powers, and a real desire to do a favor. Even through her own surprise, and her distress at what she feared might prove a lasting injury to her precious old piano, Miss Pamela felt sorry for his embarrassment.

"Never mind, Master Ned," she said, in a kindly tone. "I dare say the tuning key was too old, or perhaps you understand modern pianos better. I don't believe any real harm is done, and you know I was going to have it tuned with some of the money you were so good as to bring me, so you see I am no worse off than I was before."

As she left the room, Kitty buried her face in her big gingham apron.

"Oh, Kitty, *don't cry!*" exclaimed Ned, his trouble greatly increased, if that were possible, by her evident emotion. "Kitty, I'll have it fixed the first thing—you see if I don't! I know it can be fixed."

Kitty raised her head, and Ned was wonderfully relieved at seeing that the tears in her eyes were caused by suppressed laughter.

"Oh, Ned, it's so funny!" she half whispered. "*If* Aunt Pamela knew I laughed, though, she would never forgive me."

"Kitty, what *is* the matter, anyhow?" asked Ned, pointing to the piano.

"Why, *I* don't know. Don't *you* know? I thought you knew all about music and pianos."

"No, I don't, Kitty," said Ned, in a burst of remorseful frankness. "I'm the only one of the family that don't. The only things I could ever sing were 'Greenland's Icy Mountains' and 'Oh, Susannah' (that's a song mother used to sing to us children), and I always got them mixed up, because they begin just alike; so I never dare to sing 'Greenland's Icy' in church."

Kitty's words of comfort were as kind as those of her aunt, but Ned felt very anxious to get away from the scene of his discomfiture, and was glad to find himself at last on the road home, where he arrived in due season, finding the family at tea. It was not until he was alone with his father and mother that he unburdened himself.

"Father," he began, with some effort, "will you allow me to send a person at your expense to tune Miss Pamela's piano?"

"At *my expense?* Well, I should want first to know why you ask it."

"The fact of it is, sir, I undertook to tune it myself, and—well, I'm afraid I made a bad business of it."

"*You did* WHAT?" asked his mother, turning on him a look of such comical amazement that he could not help laughing, although he turned redder than before.

"I tuned her piano."

"Where did *you* ever learn to tune a piano? I always thought you had no ear for music."

"I didn't do it with my ears, I did it with my hands, and it was hard enough work, too. They are all blistered, and my wrists ache, and I am as lame all over as if I had been sawing wood all day."

"How did you do it? and, in the name of all that is ridiculous, *why?*" gasped his mother.

"Well, I did it just as I've seen Heaflatt do yours. I screwed every wire up as tight as I could, and kept on fiddling with the other hand on the key to see if it kept on sounding, *just exactly* as he always does."

Ned never forgot the peal of laughter which came from his parents. Both keenly relished the joke, and when Ned learned that what he had done could easily be undone, he felt so much relieved as to be able to laugh with them.

"Yes," said his father, emphatically, when he could recover his voice, "I think you had better send Heaflatt up to Miss Pamela's as soon as possible, and set her mind at rest."

"And, oh, Ned," said his mother, "if ever you tune another piano, may I be there to see—and hear!"

"If ever I do, ma'am," he answered, with a vigorous shake of the head, "*I hope you may.*"

OLD TIMES IN THE COLONIES.

BY CHARLES CARLETON COFFIN.

No. I.

HOW THE INDIANS WERE WRONGED, AND THEIR REVENGE.

AT three o'clock Tuesday morning, December 11, 1688, James II., King of England, rose noiselessly from his bed, passed with stealthy steps from his palace, entered a carriage in waiting, and was driven rapidly to the bank of the Thames, where he stepped into a boat, and was rowed swiftly down the stream. As the boat shot past the old palace of Lambeth, he flung into the river the Great Seal of England, used in stamping all the royal documents to give them validity. He was fleeing from his palace, his throne, his kingdom, and from people whom he had outraged in his attempt to set up an absolute and personal government—to do just as he pleased without regard to law. He believed that the King had the right to be above all laws. The people had risen against him, and had invited his son-in-law, William of Orange, to come over from Holland to aid them in overthrowing James. William had landed at Torbay, and had been so warmly welcomed that James was seeking refuge in France with Louis XIV., where adopted daughter, Mary of Modena, as she was called, was James's wife.

"You are still King of England, and I will aid you in securing your throne," said Louis XIV.

It was not simply a generous act on the part of Louis to a fellow-sovereign who was in trouble, but there were ideas behind it. Louis XIV. believed with James in the absolute right of kings to do just as they pleased: that the people must do their bidding.

"*The state—it is me!*" said Louis, striking his hand upon his breast, to indicate that there was nobody else who had a right to say or do anything in regard to law and government.

The people of England, on the other hand, believed that they had the right to make their own laws through a Parliament of their own choosing, and that it was the duty of the King to obey and execute those laws.

James had done what he could to crush out the Protestant religion in England; Louis had driven the Huguenots, who were Protestants, from France, waging a cruel war upon them. Thousands had been killed. More than eight hundred thousand had been compelled to flee to other countries. The war was waged not merely that James might regain his crown, but it was a great struggle for civil and religious freedom. It extended to other countries; battles were fought on the banks of the Rhine, the Danube, the Po; in the meadows of Holland; on the plains of Germany; amid the vineyards of Italy; in the wilderness of North America; on the Penobscot, Piscataqua, Merrimac, and Mohawk.

All through the years Jesuit priests had been laboring to convert the Indians of Canada to Christianity, and had made them the allies of France. When the war broke out, all the Indians in Maine and New Hampshire sided with the French.

The English, especially the men who bought furs of the Indians, had not always treated them justly.

The traders cheated them when buying their beaver skins. They would put the furs on one side of the balance, and bear down the other with their hands, saying a man's hand weighed a pound. The Dutch fur-traders on the Hudson used their feet instead of their hands. The simple-hearted red men, knowing nothing of balances and weights, could only look on in astonishment, wondering at the lightness of the skins. The Indians of Maine and New Hampshire had a grudge against Major Waldron, who lived at Dover, New Hampshire.

"His hand weighs too much," they said.

But they had another and greater grievance. To understand it we must go back a little.

MAJOR WALDRON'S TERRIBLE FIGHT.

In 1675, Philip, who lived on a hill overlooking the peaceful waters of Narragansett Bay, began war upon the English, which lasted nearly two years, during which the New Hampshire Indians murdered some of the settlers. The Governor of Massachusetts sent Captain Sill and Captain Hathorn, with their two companies of soldiers, to seize all the Indians, although only a few had taken any part in the murders. Major Waldron invited the Indians to come to Dover; and they, regarding him as their friend, came from their wigwams along the lakes and rivers, to see what he wanted.

"Let us have a sham fight," he said.

The Indians agreed to it. They ranged themselves on one side, their guns loaded with powder only, and the white men on the other.

"You fire first," said Major Waldron.

The Indians fired their guns in the air, and the next moment found themselves surrounded by the white men, who made them prisoners, taking away their guns, putting them on board a vessel, sending them to Boston, and selling two hundred of them into slavery.

One Indian made his escape from the soldiers, ran into Elizabeth Heard's house, and the good woman secreted him in the cellar, and saved him from being sold into slavery.

The war between England and France began. The Jesuit fathers were making their influence felt among the tribes, winning them to the side of France.

Previous to this the Indians had made themselves at home in Dover, coming and going as they pleased. There were five strongly fortified houses in the town, in which the settlers slept at night.

It was the evening of the 27th of June, 1689, when two squaws called at Major Waldron's garrison, and asked if they might sleep there.

"Indians are coming to trade to-morrow," they said.

Major Waldron was pleased to hear it, for trade with the Indians always meant a good bargain to the white man.

"Supposing we should want to go out in the night, how shall we open the door?" asked the squaws.

They are shown how to undo the fastenings.

Major Waldron is eighty years of age, white-haired, wrinkled, but there is force yet left in his arm, and he is as courageous as ever. He has no fear of any Indian that walks the earth, and the vague rumors and whisperings of an uprising are as idle as the wind to him. He lies down to sleep. The lights in all the houses are extinguished. No sentinel walks the street. In the darkness dusky forms glide noiselessly through the town. The doors of the houses open. The terrible war-whoop breaks the stillness of the summer night. A half-dozen Indians burst into the room where the brave old man is sleeping. He springs from the bed, seizes his sword, and single-handed drives them from his chamber into the large room. In the darkness one steals behind him, strikes a blow, and he falls. It is their hour of triumph. He has been a ruler and a judge. The Indians can be sarcastic. They seat him in his arm-chair, lift him upon the table. It is his throne.

"Get us supper," is their command to the family.

They eat, and then turn to their bloody work. One by one they slash their knives across his breast.

"So I cross out my account," they say. They are settling an account that has been standing thirteen long years.

An Indian cuts off one hand. "Where are the scales? Let us see if it weighs a pound."

One cuts off his nose, another his ears. The old man's strength is gone, and as he falls, one holds his sword, so that it pierces his body.

In one of the garrisons is a faithful dog, whose barking awakes the inmates. The Indians rush upon the door. Elder Wentworth throws himself upon the floor, holds his feet against it, and braces himself with all his might. The bullets whistle over him, but do him no harm, and he holds it fast, keeping the Indians at bay, and saving the lives of those within.

Elizabeth Heard and her children on this evening have come from Portsmouth in a boat. They are belated, and the Indians are at their bloody work when they arrive. Her children flee, while she sinks in terror upon the ground. An Indian with a pistol runs up and stands over her, but he does not fire.

"No harm shall come to you," he says. He permits no one to touch her. It is the Indian whom she befriended thirteen years ago.

When the morning dawns it is upon the smouldering ruins of burning dwellings, upon the mangled bodies of twenty-three men and women, and upon twenty-nine women and children going into captivity—a long weary march through the woods to Canada to be sold as slaves to the French, or kept as prisoners by the savages. Yet amid the ghastly scene, through the blood and flame and smoke and desolation, there is this brightness—the remembrance of the kindness of Elizabeth Heard, and its reward.

HOW THE LITTLE SMITHS GOT THEIR FOURTH-OF-JULY MONEY.

BY MARGARET SIDNEY.

"WHAT did George Washington do, I wonder, on the Fourth of July?" said Harper Smith, rattling his tin money bank with an awful din.

"Mercy! I don't know," said Aunt Nancy, shielding her ears, and thinking twice as much about the noise as she did about the question. "Do pray be still! I'm sure I wish there wasn't any Fourth of July."

"Oh, Harp, you ninny!" cried his brother Joe. "There wasn't any Fourth at all till George Washington made it."

"You better study up," said Aunt Nancy, coming to her senses, as Harper, very much confused, stopped the rattling. "You don't begin to realize what the guns and the fire-crackers and the torpedoes, and all the other dreadful things that blow up people and knock off boys' fingers and toes, are for. It would be a great deal better if boys had more history in their heads and less money in their pockets. That's the way to celebrate, *I* think; and I mean to ask your father about it."

"Oh, don't, don't, Aunt Nancy—please *don't!*" cried both boys, in the greatest dismay, while Lucy ran in from the next room, with wide-open eyes, at the uproar. "Don't make father take away our money; we always have it, you know."

"You can have your money," said Aunt Nancy, putting up her spectacles to look at their distressed faces, and beginning to laugh at the sight; "but you ought to know what you're spending it for. *I* would, I know, be able to tell something about my country, and who fought for it."

When Mr. Smith came home the boys were both out in the barn, looking at a very new colony of kittens in an old barrel. So Aunt Nancy had about five minutes of peace and quiet, which she speedily made the most of, I can assure you—talking away so fast that Mr. Smith had to follow her pretty closely, with eyes as well as ears on the alert.

When she had finished, "Capital," was all he said. And then the boys came tearing in, and they had tea.

After supper, "Now for a story," cried Joe, getting possession of the chair next to Mr. Smith, while Harper flew for another.

"When does Fourth of July come?" asked Mr. Smith, abruptly.

"It's three weeks from day after to-morrow," cried Joe, springing up, and running for the almanac.

REVIEW OF THE CAVALRY BY THE INFANTRY.—Drawn by Sol. Eytinge, Jun.

"Well, what are you going to do on the Fourth?" said their father.

"Oh, *everything*," cried Joe, while Harper came in on the chorus; and Lucy beat a soft little tune on her father's shoulder with her hand.

"You said you'd give us more money *this* Fourth," cried Harper, seeing his chance. "Don't you remember? 'Cause we're bigger, you know."

"And so you'll try to blow off your heads harder than ever, I suppose," said Mr. Smith, with a twinkle in the eye next to Harper. "And then who's to pay the doctor's bills, I wonder?"

"If our heads were off, we wouldn't have to have the doctor," suggested Joe, dreadfully afraid the money wasn't coming.

"True enough," laughed his father. "Well, heads stand for everything else—all the hurts, I mean."

"I ain't goin' to blow off my head," declared Harper, getting up in an anxious way, and standing in front of his father. "Say, father, I promise you I won't. Do give us the money—do."

"Do you want more than you had before?" asked his father, pulling his ear.

"Yes, *sir*," emphatically declared Harper, all out of breath from his exercise; "I want forty cannons."

"Mercy!" ejaculated Aunt Nancy, in smothered accents, over in the corner by the window, with her mending basket.

"Well, then, I'll tell you how you can get it," said Mr. Smith, speaking very earnestly, and fastening his eyes intently on their faces.

"*Really*, papa?" cried Lucy, sitting up straight on his knee.

"*Really*," said Mr. Smith, bringing his hand down on the arm of his chair with convincing emphasis. "And I don't mind paying money for such an object—it's well spent, I can tell you. Now, boys, see here—and Lucy too;" and he leaned forward and began to talk in a way that made the children see that this was no funning, but sober earnest, every word of it. "If you all go to work for three weeks, beginning to-morrow morning—all the time you get out of school, I mean—and study up everything you can get hold of that concerns the history of our country; what Fourth-of-July's for, and all that; who made the country what it is, so that we can celebrate and bang away, and play with powder and guns— Stop! I haven't got through," as he saw both boys' mouths fly open to launch numberless questions at him. "Begin at the very foundation; get all the information you possibly can; find out all the names of the Presidents, for one thing, and all about the establishing of Congress; most of the principal battles, and all that—why, then, three weeks from to-morrow night, the one who knows the most, and can tell it in a sensible way that shows he knows what he's learned, and not like a parrot, *he* shall have the most money. And it *shall* be a large sum, I promise you, compared to what you had last year. That's all. Now you may speak." And Mr. Smith leaned back in his chair, and burst into a hearty laugh at the tumult he had raised around his ears.

At last Harper, in a lull of questions and answers that were flying back and forth, turned and fixed a reproachful glance over in the direction of the big mending basket. "'Twas all Aunt Nancy," he cried. "Oh dear! And she wasn't never a boy. And she don't know how we want things, she don't."

"We never can do it," cried Joe, in despair.

"Never's a long word," cried Mr. Smith, briskly. "Begin to-night. Come, boys, get out the maps, and we'll start right off, now, this very minute;" and he jumped up, and began to roll the big table up closer to the window.

"And I'm goin' to get that awful old history," cried Harper, rushing out, full of enthusiasm; "that'll tell lots."

"Do," cried his father, approvingly. "Go along too, Joe and Lucy, and get all the books you can; *then* we'll see."

So in two or three minutes three happy and excited children sat around the table, while their father showed them how to begin, explained the hard parts, and pointed out places on the map, while Aunt Nancy, over in the corner, smiled and nodded to herself more than ever.

All of a sudden a voice broke in on the absorbed group: "And *I'm* going to have a finger in this Fourth-of-July pie; so you needn't think you can keep me out."

Everybody looked up and stared.

"Yes, I am; so there, now!" repeated Aunt Nancy, decisively. "And the one that I find knows the most when you all get through in three weeks, why, there's some stray dollars in my purse that I don't know what to do with, and they might as well go along with your father's as anywhere else."

At this there was such excitement over by the table that nobody could hear anything, till Harper's voice finally got the high key. "And if anybody sees a bigger Fourth of July than *we'll* have, I'd like to know it, that's all."

"Three cheers for Christopher Columbus, and the whole lot!" cried Joe. "I wish 'twas Fourth twice a year, I do."

"We haven't got ready for *one* yet," said Lucy, deep in an atlas. "I'm goin' to make this a good one first."

"Three cheers for Christopher Columbus—and Lucy!" said Harper, taking the hint, and settling down to work.

"It *can't* be nine o'clock!" cried Joe, when Mr. Smith gave the word "To bed."

"Look at the clock, then," said their father; and all the flushed faces were turned up to the old time-piece in the corner.

"It's dreadfully nice," said Lucy, cuddling up to Aunt Nancy for a good-night kiss. "Oh, I'd love to sit up all night and study."

"Hold out to the end," said Mr. Smith; "that's what will tell." And off the three children flew to their seats, to dream of George Washington dancing a war-dance on Bunker Hill, while Pocahontas read the Declaration of Independence.

It all went very well for two days. The children got up early in the morning, and otherwise made the most of their time. Then Harper's great friend Chuckie Branson, who had received a wonderful dog from an uncle in the country, waxed so enthusiastic over the various tricks that the little spaniel performed that Harper couldn't help catching the fever. And it came to be quite the natural thing that when the little history class gathered around the big table, one of their number was missing, and Harper's book-mark remained stationary for many a long hour. And then, unfortunately *for* poor Lucy, who eagerly grasped every second from play-time to spend among the text-books and atlases, which by this time had become exceedingly fascinating, for her came one evening the final hour of study, and the last hope disappeared of her ever winning the coveted "First Prize." Hateful little red spots blossomed all over Lucy's face, as if by magic, so suddenly that no one noticed, until Joe, glancing up to find a word in the dictionary, discovered them, and nudged Aunt Nancy.

"Mercy!" said that individual, looking keenly over her spectacles at the little student—"if you haven't broken out with measles! Shut your book, child; it's dreadfully bad for the eyes. Now you mustn't read another word."

If Lucy was red as a rose before, now she was pale enough. All of the hateful little red spots seemed to run right in at the command, and hide their heads.

No more study! How could she give it up? Oh! and there were still ten days before the glorious Fourth!

With all Joe's sorrow for his little afflicted sister, with all his kindness of disposition, he couldn't help but rejoice just one wee bit at being sole conqueror—just for one minute, though. The next he said,

"See here, Lucy. I'll read 'em to you—every one of the questions, you know. There, don't cry, puss. And then you can learn the answers, and say 'em over and over; and—goodness me!—why, you'll learn a heap that way."

"I can't," moaned poor Lucy, screwing her fingers into her smarting eyes. "It 'll put you back; you might be studying all that while, Joe. Oh dear! dear!"

"That's very true," observed Aunt Nancy, whisking off something very bright from her cheek; "and that wouldn't be quite right, Lucy. It's all the same a good thing in you, Joe, to want to. There are some things better than prizes, or knowledge even. But I'll read to you, Lucy, and if you can have the patience to learn that way—it 'll be much harder, you know—but if you can do it, why perhaps you'll come off better than you think—who knows?"

So Lucy, with her father's old silk handkerchief tied over her eyes, sat on her little stool patiently day after day, while Aunt Nancy went over as much ground as could be covered in that slow way; and on the unequal battle waged.

"Of course I don't expect any prize," said Lucy, with a very big sigh, when the eventful evening of the 3d of July arrived; "but I know a little something, and that's nice. But, oh! to think of Joe!"

"Where's Harper?" said Mr. Smith, when the little circle was formed around him.

"Here," said a doleful voice from underneath the table. "I don't know anything, an' I ain't a-comin' out."

"I shouldn't think you did," said Mr. Smith, gravely. "Ah, Harper, my boy, play is pleasant enough at the time, but I tell you it hurts afterward; that is, if it's *all* play."

"And now," exclaimed Aunt Nancy, bringing them back to order, when a delightful hour of questions, anecdotes, and rapid answers had fairly whirled by—"the result."

"The first prize, of course," said Mr. Smith, smiling down into the two upturned, eager faces before him, "belongs, without doubt, to Joe; but if ever a prize ought to go, as fairly earned under difficulties, there should be one for my little girl!"

He put into Joe's hand a brand-new ten-dollar bill that crinkled delightfully; and then he took hold of Lucy's little hand, and opening it, he laid within one just like it.

"You've got one too!" screamed Joe, perfectly delighted. "Oh, Lucy, do look and see!"

"Have I?" cried Lucy, poking up one corner of the old handkerchief to see. "Oh, Joe, I have, I *have*!"

"And here is my part of the Fourth-of-July pie," cried Aunt Nancy, rattling down on them a goodly shower of silver quarters. "There! and there! and there!"

"The Fourth of July forever!" sang Joe, jumping up on the table, and swinging his arms. "Three cheers for the *Encyclopædia of Events* I'll get!"

"That's no better than the Histories I'll have!" crowed Lucy, triumphantly.

"And I," said a dismal voice under the table, "shall begin now for next year. Yes, I will."

MR. MARTIN'S SCALP.

BY JIMMY BROWN.

AFTER that game of mumble-te-peg that me and Mr. Martin played, he did not come to our house for two weeks. Mr. Travers said perhaps the earth he had to gnaw while he was drawing the peg had struck to his insides and made him sick, but I knew it couldn't be that. I've drawn pegs that were drove into every kind of earth, and it never hurt me. Earth is healthy, unless it is lime; and don't you ever let anybody drive a peg into lime. If you were to swallow the least bit of lime, and then drink some water, it would burn a hole through you just as quick as anything. There was once a boy who found some lime in the closet, and thought it was sugar, and of course he didn't like the taste of it. So he drank some water to take the taste out of his mouth, and pretty soon his mother said: "I smell something burning goodness gracious! the house is on fire." But the boy he gave a dreadful scream, and said, "Ma, it's me!" and the smoke curled up out of his pockets and around his neck, and he burned up and died. I know this is true, because Tom McGinnis went to school with him, and told me about it.

Mr. Martin came to see Susan last night for the first time since we had our game; and I wish he had never come back, for he got me into an awful scrape. This was the way it happened. I was playing Indian in the yard. I had a wooden tomahawk and a wooden scalping-knife and a bow-and-arrow. I was dressed up in father's old coat turned inside out, and had six chicken feathers in my hair. I was playing I was Green Thunder, the Delaware chief, and was hunting for pale-faces in the yard. It was just after supper, and I was having a real nice time, when Mr. Travers came, and he said, "Jimmy, what are you up to now?" So I told him I was Green Thunder, and was on the war-path. Said he, "Jimmy, I think I saw Mr. Martin on his way here. Do you think you would mind scalping him?" I said I wouldn't scalp him for nothing, for that would be cruelty; but if Mr. Travers was sure that Mr. Martin was the enemy of the red man, then Green Thunder's heart would ache for revenge, and I would scalp him with pleasure. Mr. Travers said that Mr. Martin was a notorious enemy and oppressor of the Indians, and he gave me ten cents, and said that as soon as Mr. Martin should come and be sitting comfortably on the piazza, I was to give the war-whoop and scalp him.

Well, in a few minutes Mr. Martin came, and he and Mr. Travers and Susan sat on the piazza, and talked as if they were all so pleased to see each other, which was the highest piece of hypocrisy in the world. After a while Mr. Martin saw me, and said, "How silly boys are! that boy makes believe he's an Indian, and he knows he is only a little nuisance." Now this made me mad, and I thought I would give him a good scare, just to teach him not to call names if a fellow does beat him in a fair game. So I began to steal softly up the piazza steps, and to get around behind him. When I had got about six feet from him I gave a war-whoop, and jumped at him. I caught hold of his scalp-lock with one hand, and drew my wooden scalping-knife around his head with the other.

I never got such a fright in my whole life. The knife was that dull that it wouldn't have cut butter; but, true as I sit here, Mr. Martin's whole scalp came right off in my hand. I thought I had killed him, and I dropped his scalp, and said, "For mercy's sake! I didn't go to do it, and I'm awfully sorry." But he just caught up his scalp, stuffed it in his pocket, and jammed his hat on his head, and walked off, saying to Susan, "I didn't come here to be insulted by a little wretch that deserves the gallows."

Mr. Travers and Susan never said a word until he had gone, and then they laughed till the noise brought father out to ask what was the matter. When he heard what had happened, instead of laughing, he looked very angry, said that "Mr. Martin was a worthy man. My son, you may come up stairs with me."

If you've ever been a boy, you know what happened up stairs, and I needn't say any more on a very painful subject. I didn't mind it so much, for I thought Mr. Martin would die, and then I would be hung, and put in jail; but before she went to bed Susan came and whispered through the door that it was all right; that Mr. Martin was made that way, so he could be taken apart easy, and that

I hadn't hurt him. I shall have to stay in my room all day to-day, and eat bread and water; and what I say is that if men are made with scalps that may come off any minute if a boy just touches them, it isn't fair to blame the boy.

[Begun in Harper's Young People No. 34, June 22.]

MISS VAN WINKLE'S NAP.

BY MRS. W. J. HAYS.

Chapter II.

"Now, nurse, what is it?" cried Quillie and Fred and Will and Artie, as they rushed from the deck of their odd craft, and after a hasty brushing, and a dip into the clear spring water, they made their way to the breakfast table.

"Yes, nurse *chérie*," echoed gypsy Julie, "please be so good as to inform—describe— Oh, what is the word?"

"Tell, tell—that is the word, little Frenchie," said Fred.

"Thanks, monsieur," said Julie, gravely.

Quillie whispered softly to Fred that his manner was rude, whereupon Fred, with a nonsensical bow, turned to Julie.

"My sister 'informs, describes' me as rude; am I?"

"A little, I think," said Julie; but she turned eagerly to hear what nurse had to say.

"Mr. Brown says that he will bring in his first load of hay to-day, and as many as choose can go to the 'Look-out' field and help him, and afterward he will give you all a ride."

"Splendid!" "Glorious!" said the boys.

"Won't it be nice?" said Quillie to Julie.

"Charming!" replied Julie; "but why is it called the Look-out field?"

"Because there is so fine a view from it of the mountains."

"The Catskills?"

"Yes, where old Rip Van Winkle slept for twenty years."

"Did he, truly?"

"So the story goes. Every time it thunders, we think the queer old mountain men are playing nine-pins."

"Do you?" said Julie, with eyes still wider open. "I should like to see them."

"The Indians used to say that an old squaw lived on the highest peak of the Catskills, and had charge of the doors of Day and Night. She hung up the new moons in the skies, and cut up the old ones into stars."

"Oh, Quillie, would it not be lovely to seek her, and find out more about the moons and stars?"

"Pshaw!" said Quillie, with scorn. "Do you believe such nonsense, Julie?"

"I don't know," said Julie, "but I think I should like to believe it."

Then they all concluded that they wanted no more breakfast, and there was another rush; for the trunks had come, and each desired some particular treasure—a garden tool, an old hat, a sun-bonnet, a tin pail, or a fishing-rod.

Nurse was too good-natured to refuse, and so the trunks were opened, and ransacked very thoroughly, until Mr. Brown summoned them; then, like swallows at twilight, they were again all on the wing, darting hither and thither. But in one little brain was a thought like a butterfly emerging from its chrysalis.

To Julie this jaunt from the city to the country had been the realization of a dream, or as if she had walked into a page of her story-books, and found the things and people all living and true. The scent of the sweet clover, the twittering of the birds, the deep blue of the sky and the deeper blue of the mountains, the snow-white daisies and the yellow buttercups, were things she had read about in the many lonely moments she had spent while her mother was out giving lessons; but in all her little life she had no actual experience of these things; and now here they were, and in addition it was the land of romance—a place where people could sleep for twenty years, a place where queer hobgoblin people played nine-pins. That squaw Quillie had told her about was fascinating; perhaps it was true that she still was living, and oh! how she should like to see her! Perhaps if she walked all day, she might reach the top of that great blue peak, and find in some strange little wigwam that old creature who cut up the old moons into stars, and then what a wonderful tale Julie would have to tell! It would be like visiting the old woman who swept the cobwebs from the sky. There would be no harm in trying. She had often been on errands alone in the great city, where everything was so confusing. Perhaps the squaw would be pleased, and give her some wonderful talisman; or she might relate to her stories of Indian life, which she (Julie) would write down and make into a book; and then no one, not even nurse, would be angry with her for daring to do so courageous a thing.

RIDING HOME FROM THE HAY FIELD.—Drawn by W. M. Cary.

Who would have imagined that, as the children tossed about the heaps of fragrant hay, this wild scheme was brewing beneath the brim of a tiny straw hat wreathed with daisies? And who thought to count the merry ones on the top of the wagon-load as it turned homeward? Not nurse, who was sewing beneath a tree, and who gathered up her work and went after her charge in blissful igassurance that one lamb had strayed from the fold.

With eager, hurrying steps Julie had left the meadow and sought a clump of trees; from these she emerged upon a road which seemed much travelled. It was very steep and dusty where it was not rocky, but she was not to be daunted at the outset; so on she went as rapidly as possible, for fear that, being missed, she might be overtaken, and prevented from accomplishing this great feat. At first she could hear the voices in the field beneath her, but as she hastened on all became silent but the stirring of the summer breeze in the tree-tops, and the far-away cackle of an industrious hen. The road, at first very sunny, had now wound itself beside huge crags, which made a welcome shade, and Julie saw with delight a little water-fall come tumbling down a narrow fissure, plunging into a pool below, and crossing the path. Warm and thirsty, she stopped to refresh herself and listen to the gurgling of the brook. But she must not dawdle, or night might come on, and then it would be hard to find the old squaw, who was perhaps at this moment cutting glittering stars out of the old moons. The difficulty of hanging them up did not once occur to her. Possibly the moon and the stars were not like tinsel, but she had no doubt of the squaw. She had heard that squaws made baskets; would it not be a nice thing to buy a little one for Quillie, and a great big one for nurse!—she would pick out the very prettiest. And so she scrambled on, getting very much heated and soiled, catching her clothes on the briers, getting bits of stone in her shoes, but neither frightened nor concerned about those from whom she had wandered.

STABLE TALK.—Drawn by Frank Beard, Jr.

Meanwhile Quillie, from her high perch on the hay, began wondering why her little companion was so silent. She supposed Julie was behind her, but, fearful of tumbling, she had been still as a mouse. She twisted about now, a little nervously, and called Julie, but there was no response. Then Mr. Brown helped her to dismount, and still no Julie was to be seen. So she went into the house, procured a book, and sat on the piazza. Presently nurse came in.

"Where's Julie?" cried Quillie.

"Where?—was she not with you?"

"No, she was not on the hay-cart."

"Then she must be with the boys."

"No; they are in the barn."

"Then she is hiding. Go and look for her. I must get your rooms in order now." So nurse went in.

Quillie tried to read, but her thoughts were like thistle-down. Where could Julie be? She sought her all about the house; peeped into all sorts of corners. Then she went to the barn. Had the boys seen Julie? No; and they were whittling, making a boat, and couldn't be bothered.

"I wish, Fred, that you had not been so rude to Julie."

Fred looked up, surprised. "Rude! when was I rude?"

"You called her 'little Frenchy,' and imitated her."

"Did I? Oh yes, I remember something of that sort. But she isn't huffy, you know; she's a bright little chick."

Quillie thought so too, and was getting very lonely.

As the afternoon shadows lengthened, and the great conch shell was blown for the men to come in to their early supper, nurse came down to summon the children in to tidy themselves; and when she found Quillie crying in a corner, and no Julie yet to be seen, she too became uneasy. Where could the child have gone? She questioned everybody. No one had seen her. All remembered the little brown hat with its wreath of daisies. Fortunately the farm was a safe place; there was no water to fear. Perhaps she had fallen asleep somewhere. All would hunt for her after supper. And all did hunt, but no one found her.

The moon, like a silver sickle, hung in the sky; the frogs croaked; the soft sweet air puffed out the muslin curtains, and brought in the fragrance of the new-mown hay. The children, too tired to be much alarmed, went to their beds without their usual gambols. Mr. Brown hitched his weary horses, and declared his intention of remaining out all night unless he found Julie. Poor nurse was in a fever of anxiety. She reproached herself in many quite unnecessary ways. She had talked the matter over with Mrs. Brown until both were exhausted, and now she was pacing the piazza in weary restlessness.

Quillie, unable to sleep, came trotting out in her night-gown, and seeing poor nurse's sad face, went up to her, and whispered something about "God being able to take care of little Julie wherever she might be," when far away came the sound of wheels.

"Hark!" said nurse, "is that wagon coming here?"

"Yes," said Quillie, listening, "it is coming here."

[to be continued.]

OUR POST-OFFICE BOX.

[illegible] pigeons and chickens. I was out with my [illegible] the other day, and we found some three feet high.

I have a collection of birds' eggs, and would like to exchange with any of the readers of YOUNG PEOPLE. [illegible]

[illegible], Illinois.

We have some of the handsomest white water-lilies [illegible]. [illegible] on the Fox River, and [illegible] a boat. [illegible]

I would be very much obliged if Harry M. M., of Windsor, Connecticut, [illegible] [illegible] [illegible].

[illegible], Illinois.

I am twelve years old, but people think I am older, because I am so tall. We have a great many pets. We have a white horse, a black and white [illegible], a Maltese cat, and [illegible] [illegible].

My sister and I tried Nellie H.'s recipe for candy.

I would like to exchange pressed flowers with [illegible] of California. [illegible]

HATTIE D. [illegible]

P. O. Box [illegible], Ipswich, Massachusetts.

E. G. KARR.—The best thing for you to do is to go to Prospect Park Lake, Brooklyn, any pleasant Saturday afternoon, when you can witness the regatta, and learn full particulars concerning the yacht club.

W. R. A. B.—The loon is found in all the Northern States. It is a very awkward bird on land, but a graceful and rapid swimmer. It is a remarkable diver, and it is thought that no other feathered creature can dive so far beneath the surface or remain so long a time under water. A specimen was once found attached to the hook of a fisherman's set line in Seneca Lake, it having dived nearly one hundred feet to reach the bait. It feeds on insects, fish, frogs, all kinds of aquatic insects, and the roots of fresh-water plants, usually swallowing its food under water. It is a very large bird, about three feet in length, and spreads its wings fully five feet. It builds its nest in marshes, near water, of rushes and grass, which it twists together in a huge heap on the ground, usually among tall reeds. The eggs, usually three in number, are a little over three inches long, and in color of a dull greenish ochre, with indistinct spots of dark umber, most numerous toward the broad end. During the winter this bird lives near the sea-shore, especially in the salt-marshes on the Long Island coast, and along the shores of the Chesapeake; but in the summer it goes as far north as Maine, and breeds there in great quantities.

RALPH H.—The peculiar spots often found on lemons and oranges are only a natural appearance of the skin of certain varieties. Havana oranges and the best Floridas are more marked in this way than other kinds.

A. R. A.—Your Wiggles are remarkably pretty, but they came too late to be engraved.

A. U. Y.—Japanese wire-flowers can be obtained in New York at nearly every store where toys, novelties, and apparatus for parlor magic are sold. They are also called Surprises, or Japanese Curiosas.

Favors are acknowledged from Carrie E. Lucas, John T., Charles and Fred W., Harry L. Chase, [illegible] Frederick, Aggie M. Mason, Louis Munroe, Edmund L. Sheppard, [illegible], [illegible], [illegible], M. [illegible], J. R. T., [illegible], W. Lloyd Clark, [illegible], Hugh D.

Correct answers to puzzles are received from Alexander Mc[illegible], Charles E. [illegible], Charlie D. [illegible], [illegible], Allie R. [illegible], J. F. S., William L. [illegible], [illegible], A. M. [illegible], [illegible], "Palestine," [illegible], [illegible] Price, [illegible], Fred Pardy.

PUZZLES FROM YOUNG CONTRIBUTORS.

No. 1.

WORD SQUARE.

First, a native of a certain country. Second, an adder. Third, a flower. Fourth, the imperfect form of a verb.

ROBIN.

No. 2.

[illegible].

A component. A title. A [illegible] tribe of Indians. An [illegible] figure. A compound.

S. F. W.

No. 3.

[illegible].

To flourish. One [illegible]. A [illegible]. In District. A species of tree. Arizona. Department. [illegible] and downward spell the name of an early English poet.

"[illegible]."

No. 4.

ENIGMA.

[illegible]

N. A.

No. 5.

[illegible].

The name of a royal house. A Danish [illegible]. A celebrated Russian King. An early King of England. An early King of Spain. A modern English poet. Answer—Primals form the first name and finals the second name of a celebrated American novelist.

E. N. H.

No. 6.

[illegible].

[illegible]

PETER.

ANSWERS TO PUZZLES IN NO. [illegible].

No. 1. Ferragut.

No. 2. Better late than never.

No. 3. 1. Love, lave, late, lath.
2. [illegible], [illegible], [illegible], [illegible], [illegible].
3. [illegible], [illegible], [illegible], [illegible], [illegible].
4. Bead, bend, [illegible], [illegible], [illegible], [illegible].
5. [illegible], [illegible], [illegible], [illegible].
6. [illegible], [illegible], [illegible], [illegible], [illegible], [illegible], [illegible], [illegible].
7. [illegible], [illegible], [illegible], [illegible], [illegible], [illegible], [illegible], [illegible], [illegible], [illegible], [illegible].

No. 4. Nashville.

No. 5. [illegible].

No. 6. [illegible]

ADVERTISEMENTS.

TOO MUCH BIRTHDAY.

Sick poor little Jamie in mamma's low chair,
With the roses all gone from his cheeks so fair.
Too languid to look
At the picture-book;
Too tired even, I think, to care
For the wonderful story kind nurse would tell
To the dear little boy who has not been well.

Why did the roses so suddenly go,
And leave those cheeks as white as the snow?
Ah, Jamie knows of a little boy
Who had far too much of frolic and joy
On a certain day,
So merry and gay;
A birthday party it was, they say.

But Jamie will soon be well again,
Free from weakness, and free from pain.
The dimples will gather in chin and cheek,
And mischief again in his eyes will speak;
No more he'll care
To sit in a chair,
But all over the house for fun will seek.

THE BOTTLED SHOWER-BATH.

PROCURE a small vial of thin glass; such as homœopathic medicines come in are used. In the bottom of this file with a fine file four holes, as represented in our cut; then fill it with water, and hand it to a friend, requesting him to smell it. As soon as he removes the cork, the water will pour out of the holes at the bottom.

Würtemberg.—The house of Würtemberg, it is said, derives its name from the following legend: A poor burgher fell in love with the daughter of the Emperor of Austria, and as the two young people saw no prospect of obtaining the Imperial consent to their union, they fled together into Suabia, where they bought a small piece of land, and established an inn. It stood at the foot of a mountain, and its possessor therefore went by the name of the "Wirt am Berg," or the "Landlord at the Mountain." One day the Emperor was travelling to Frankfort, and stopped on his way at his daughter's house without recognizing her. She knew him directly, and persuaded her husband to make himself known to the Emperor, and to beg his forgiveness. Accordingly, taking their little son, they all fell at his feet, entreating his pardon, which he willingly granted. Moreover, the Emperor created his son-in-law a duke; but in memory of this occurrence he was to keep his name of "Wirt am Berg," which subsequently became Würtemberg.

WAITING FOR THE CIRCUS.

Vol. I.—No. 36. Published by HARPER & BROTHERS, New York. Price Four Cents.
Tuesday, July 6, [illegible]. Copyright, [illegible], by Harper & Brothers. [illegible] per Year, in Advance.

THE MOHAWK BOWMEN.

BY J. O. DAVIDSON.

"HELLO, Foster, what's that you're doing?—shooting with a bow and arrows?"

"Yes, Stuart made 'em for me. Come in and try 'em."

Harry came into the yard, where Foster was shooting at a collar box placed on a grassy bank, and made a few unsuccessful shots at twenty yards, when Foster took the bow, and hit the box frequently, to Harry's wonder and envy.

"Stuart made 'em for me, and taught me how to handle 'em. He has a bow taller than himself, over six feet long; and up in the mountains he killed a deer a week ago—killed a deer with an arrow."

"Do arrows go hard enough to *kill?* Say, Foster, will Stuart make a bow for me? Won't you ask him?"

"We've got a better thing than that. Stuart wants us to get up an archery club, and he will show us how to make our own bows and arrows, just as the Indians do. Henry, Fred, Will, and Ned will join, I know, and then we will have six—just enough to go off hunting on Saturdays, and have a jolly time. And we'll have a name for the club, and make a regular camp somewhere near the Glen, and have our dinners there, and our meetings, just as Robin Hood and his men did in England. How's that, Harry?"

"Best thing out, Foster. But how are we to make our bows, and what shall we make them of?"

"Oh, Stuart has told me all about it. You must pick out the straightest, cleanest sassafras pole in the hen-house, and get Preston to saw it up into sticks one inch square and five and a quarter feet long. Then bring them over here, and Stuart will show you how to make a bow. Stuart will have a lot of pine and spruce sawed up for arrows, and you must get all the goose and turkey feathers you can, and bring them over too, and he will tell us about arrow-making. Now go and tell the rest of the boys, and get your sassafras to Preston's as soon as you can. Perhaps we can get ready to go out Saturday."

After school the next day six eager boys stood around Stuart as he took a sassafras stick, and showed them how to make a hunting bow, talking as he worked.

"Now look close, youngsters. First plane one side of the stick straight and smooth. This is to be the 'back' of the bow, and mustn't be touched again. Next mark the middle of the stick, and lay off four and a half inches to one side for a handle. Then turn the stick on its back, and plane away the 'belly' of the bow, tapering it truly from handle to 'tip.' Do the same to the sides, leaving each tip about three-eighths of an inch square. Now take a file or a spokeshave, and round off the 'sides' and 'belly' carefully, taking care not to touch the 'back' of the bow. There, the bow is in good shape, but it may not bend truly; so file a notch with a small round file in each tip half an inch from each extremity, running the groove straight across the 'back,' and slanting it across the sides away from the tips toward the middle or handle of the bow. Make a strong string of slack-twisted shoe-maker's thread, with a loop in each end, so that when the string is put on the bow by slipping the loops into the nocks, it will bend the bow so much that the middle of the string is five inches from the handle. If the bow when thus bent is too stiff in any spot, file it a little there till it bends right; and when it finally bends truly from tip to tip, put on a piece of plush for a handle, and smooth and polish your bow ready for exhibition. There, Harry, that is your bow. Now one of you may go to work at another stick, while I go and feather some arrows."

At it Henry went, eager and enthusiastic; but it was a bothersome job for young and inexperienced hands. The stick would slip, and the plane would stick, in spite of him, and his face grew very red and his eyes very bright. With Stuart's aid, however, he finally completed a very fair bow before dark, and when he had actually shot an arrow from it, his worry all vanished, and he felt very proud of his new weapon.

The following afternoon they all came together, and more bows were made. Under Stuart's direction arrow shafts were rounded and smoothed, the vanes were cut from the quills, and several fair arrows completed before separating for their homes, where all, even the staid old grandpas and grandmas, were infected by the enthusiasm of the boy archers, and Indian stories were told by the kitchen fire.

By Friday night all the six were armed with sassafras bows, and nicely feathered spruce arrows, with pewter heads, blunt, that they might not stick into and be lost in the trees. Their quivers were of pasteboard rolled in glue, upon a tapering form, and their arm-guards of hard thick leather, securely fastened to their left fore-arms by small straps and buckles. And when, early Saturday morning, they came together at Foster's house, never was a more gallant squad of young archers seen. Stumps, trees, late apples, and one or two wandering mice served as marks for their ready arrows while waiting for the start.

"Here, you boys! shoot them arrers t'other way. They'll spile more'n they're wuth," called out the good-natured hired man; and Foster raised grandma's ire by driving a shaft up to the feathers in a golden pumpkin she had selected for seed, and placed on the well curb to "sun."

By the time their haversacks were filled with potatoes, bread, doughnuts, meat, etc., and they had started for the Glen across lots, shouting as they went, all the family were relieved for the moment, only to worry the rest of the day lest some unlucky arrow, glancing, should hurt one of them; and mother's anxiety wasn't relieved when Stuart wickedly told her how Walter Tyrrel killed King William Rufus with a glancing arrow from his bow while hunting.

The birds and the squirrels that our boys met that day were treated to many a close hissing arrow, though not many of them suffered, because of the boys' lack of skill with the long-bow.

"Sh-h-h! boys," suddenly whispered Foster, as the little band paused for a moment in a clump of spruces; and springing noiselessly up, his bow was braced, his arrow fitted, and a stricken bird was fluttering at their feet in a few seconds. The flutterings of the fallen bird were more than equalled by those of Foster's heart, as he held the still quivering crow-blackbird which his arrow had brought from the highest twig of a tall spruce. Proud and exultant, yet tears glistened in his eyes as he silently gazed upon the soiled plumage of the bird's beautiful neck and breast, and felt its last faint gaspings as its reproachful eyes became glassy in death.

"The beautiful bird! Oh, I won't shoot another bird," he declared, with quivering lips. "How pretty it is, and how warm! I'll ask Stuart to stuff it, so that I can keep it forever."

By this time Will's hunger was too much for his archery enthusiasm, and he began to grumble.

"Say, boys, isn't it about time to get to the Glen, and make our camp? I'm getting hungry. It's hard work drawing this bow of mine, and my arms are tired."

"Yes, let's go to the Glen," said their captain, Foster, and half an hour's silent tramping in the underbrush and up the rising ground—for they were now pretty tired—brought them to the spot known as the Glen.

The Glen was a lovely place. A sparkling spring, rising at the base of a giant hemlock at the head of a long deep gully, had in the course of ages filled in the hollow till a broad level floor was made, surrounded by close-growing hemlocks, pines, and spruces, and carpeted with fine turf and pine needles. The water from the spring, flowing in a shallow brook through the middle of the door, lost itself in the dark recesses of the gully further down. At the very top of the great hemlock by the spring was a rude eyrie, built by the boys, called the Crow's Nest, and from its swaying, breezy height they had a magnificent view of the country for miles around. Here, rocking gently and safely, seventy-five feet above the spring, they picked out their homes, the pretty white villages nestling among the forest masses of green, and the slender streams glistening among the cultivated fields and neat mowings.

Near the spring was a rude hut that Stuart and his mates had built a few years before. Taking possession of this, they took off their haversacks, hung their bows and quivers about on projecting limbs, gathered dry leaves and sticks, and soon had a fire started in a rude stone fire-place.

"Well, my merry bowmen, how do the twanging bow-string and the hissing arrow suit the greenwood?" asked Stuart, who came up as they lay picturesquely about, waiting for a bed of coals.

"Oh, it is splendid. Isn't it, boys?" answered Will, the oldest of the young archers. "Just see how pretty the bows and quivers look, hanging among the green branches. How nice this all is! But what name shall we give our club?"

"Woodland Archers," suggested Ned.

"Mohawk Foresters," added Henry. "We want our river in the name, and the Mohawks were great warriors."

"Let's call it the Mohawk Bowmen," continued Ned. "That's just the thing." And all agreed to it, and so Mohawk Bowmen was decided upon as the club name.

"Who'll be captain?" asked Stuart.

"Oh, Foster, of course," answered all at once. "He's the best shot, and ought to be."

By this time the coals were ready, so the potatoes and corn and meat were roasted, amid much fun and gay talk, and were eaten by the hungry archers. Then, after a rest, the Mohawk Bowmen ranged the woods and fields till sunset found them at home again, tired, indeed, but enthusiastic over archery and their day's sport. They agreed it was the happiest day they had ever seen, and arranged for a grand woodchuck hunt on the following Saturday.

MORNING SIGHTS AND SOUNDS FROM A WINDOW IN JERUSALEM.

BY LYDIA FINKELSTEIN.

THE first sound I heard at daybreak, through the window, was the Moslem's call to prayer, from the minaret, "La Illahâ illa Allah"—"There is no other God but God"—breaking clear and solemn over the stillness of the early dawn, and waking the echoes of the empty streets. Presently I heard a footstep in the distance; as it approached nearer, it made the arches resound. I looked out, and saw a pious Mohammedan hastening to prayer. As he passed under the window I heard him muttering in a low voice, and caught some sentences of his prayer: "Ya Rahim, ya Allah" ("O God, the merciful!"). Scarcely had his footsteps died out when I heard the soft silvery sound of a bell, whose melodious music seemed to roll out like billows into space, and as the reverberations were carried away to a more distant region, a chime of bells rang out merrily; these were the matin bells calling the Christians to prayers. The streets and arches again re-echoed hurrying footsteps, which were those of the Catholic monks hastening to the Church of the Holy Sepulchre. As they passed the window I could hear the clicking of their rosaries, and distinguish the words "Dominus, Dominus," muttered in a low voice.

Another sound broke the stillness: "Ya Karim, ya Allah" ("O bountiful God!"). This was a cake vender, carrying on his head a large wooden tray containing cakes and baked eggs. He uses this exclamation as an acknowledgment that God is the giver of our daily bread.

"Karim" was still sounding, when I heard a different strain, "Chai chai kirna chi-ee," which was sung in a sonorous nasal voice. This was a tea man. In one hand he carried a bright brass tea-urn of boiling water; in the other, several glasses, which he continually jingled against one another. Fastened round his waist he wore a circular tin case, containing glasses, a tea-pot, sugar, lemons, and tea-spoons. The tea man continues his walk through the streets till the day is far advanced, and he meets with a great many customers, for quite a number of Arabs consider a cup of tea a good remedy for a headache in the morning.

The passers now increased, and they exchanged salutations such as "Nihar said!" ("May your morning be enriched!")

There was a coffee shop opposite the window. This was the earliest opened. The waiters came out of the store carrying low stools, which they placed outside the shop along the sidewalk. Their dress was navy blue baggy trousers, which reached a little below the knee; white shirts, the sleeves of which were rolled over their elbows; crimson girdles, and white skull-caps. A couple were barefoot, and the others had red shoes on. They moved about lightly as they arranged the stools for customers.

A tall young man came toward his store, which was a grocery, and next the coffee shop; but before opening it he sat down on one of the low stools, and was at once served by one of the waiters with an "argilé," or hubble-bubble, and a cup of coffee. He wore a suit of dark green cloth, a crimson satin vest, silk girdle of many colors, and a red tarboosh. Another gentleman came up, dressed in a similar costume, only of a bluish-gray. Before seating himself he saluted the other by a graceful wave of the hand, saying, "Issalaâm aleik," or "Peace be on you."

"Ou aleik Issalaâm" ("And unto you be peace"), responded the other.

These two are Christians, as can be seen by their dress. Two Mohammedans, dressed very much like the others, but each wearing a long loose "Jubé" (which is a cloak) over his suit, and a white turban of fine Swiss muslin wound round his tarboosh, came and took seats, after having saluted the others with the same beautiful salutations. Many others in various costumes seated themselves, and conversation became general as they smoked their pipes and sipped their small cups of coffee.

The sparrows were chirping merrily in the green caper bushes which grew out of the walls of the old gray houses. From this window I had also an excellent view of the Mount of Olives, over which I now observed the rosy tint of the rising sun. I watched it, and gradually the rose deepened into a glowing hue; then the sun rose like a ball of living fire. The towering minarets and mountain-tops caught the golden rays. The magnificent blue hue of the distant mountains of Moab reflected the gorgeous gold. The rays were also reflected in the window-panes of the old gray houses, making them look like molten gold, and the dewy domed roofs like glistening silver; and as the sun rose higher, he brightened up the fine old stone houses. A majestic palm-tree, whose green branches were being waved by the soft morning breeze, glittered as the dew on them was touched by the warm rays.

My notice was now attracted to view the passers. Emerging from under an arch was a grave old turbaned Turk. He had a long white beard, and wore a suit of dark blue cloth, red silk girdle, lemon-colored pointed leather shoes, and a tarboosh wound round by a large green turban. This green turban is a sign that he is a Hajj, or one who has been on a pilgrimage to Mohammed's grave at Mecca.

He moved along slowly and majestically, for in the Orient one never sees an Effendi hurrying along the streets. However busy men may be, they always walk calmly and leisurely, as if quite at their ease. Behind this Effendi his slave carried his master's pipe.

Donkeys, mules, horses, and camels were passing, some of the donkeys laden with wood, others with vegetables, and driven by peasants who were dressed in white shirts reaching below the knee, their waists encircled by broad red leather belts, while on their heads they wore large striped silk turbans of bright colors. Their shoes were made of undressed camel's leather, bound round the edge with yellow leather, and fastened by a latchet made of the same. Probably this was the same kind of shoe that was worn in the days of John, when he said of our Lord, "Whose shoe's latchet I am not worthy to unloose."

The mules had small brass bells hung round their necks, which, as they moved along, rung quite merrily. They were laden with tents and canteens belonging to camp life. Probably some travellers had arrived from a trip up the country. The camels roared and bellowed, as if they did not approve coming into the city; they were laden with charcoal, which was in long black sacks.

The gentlemen, after sipping their coffee and smoking their pipes, proceeded to open their stores, and while doing so, they uttered this prayer, "Bismillah ir rahman ir raheem" ("In the name of God, the most merciful").

Peasant women came up, carrying on their heads large brown circular baskets, made of twigs, about eight inches deep, filled with tempting fruits and salads. It was wonderful how well they balanced them, for they were walking erect, and very briskly, without holding them. Stopping under the window, they took the baskets off their heads, and placed them on the ground, sat down with their backs against the wall, and put them in front of them for sale. They looked picturesque in their long dark blue gowns, red silk girdles, wide open sleeves displaying their arms, adorned with bracelets and armlets.

Another young peasant woman came up, not only with a basket of fruit on her head, but a baby dangling in a hammock down her back. This hammock is an oblong piece of red and white striped coarse cloth, made out of camel's hair. She placed her basket alongside of the others, and took out her baby. Soon the baskets were surrounded by eager customers, who had to stoop down in order to pick out what they wanted. The baby meanwhile fell asleep, and the mother, finding it an incumbrance while serving her customers, placed it again in its hammock, on which she had been sitting, and hung it up on the door of one of the neighboring stores.

People passed to and fro, jostling each other as the passers increased; the street looked lively and gay with such a variety of costumes. Among them were several figures walking slowly along; they were enveloped in white sheets from head to foot, their faces covered with thick colored veils, so that it is impossible to distinguish the person. They were Oriental city women. An Oriental city woman never hurries through the streets, as that would be considered an impropriety.

THE WONDERFUL NEST.

BY MARGARET EYTINGE.

Oh! the beautiful bright summer,
Ev'rywhere wild flowers springing;
Honeysuckles to the roses
All day long sweet kisses flinging;
Brooklets sparkling through the meadows,
Humming-birds their glad way winging
With gold-brown bees and butterflies
Where lily-bells are ringing,
Ringing, ringing
Where lily-bells are ringing.

Sunbeams on the greenwood dancing,
Gentle breezes perfume bringing,
In the cedar tree five birdies
To their wee nest closely clinging;
Peeping over at the children,
(Five of them too) laughing, singing,
In nest most wonderful to see,
Between the branches swinging,
Swinging, swinging
Between the branches swinging.

[Begun in Young People No. 31, June 1.]

THE MORAL PIRATES.

BY W. L. ALDEN.

Chapter VI.

THE wave receded as suddenly as it came. The boys sprang up in a terrible fright, and indeed there are few men who in their place would not have been frightened. The shock of the cold water was enough to startle the strongest nerves, and as the boys rushed to the door of the tent in a blind race for life, they fully believed that their last hour had come. Before they could get out of the tent, a second wave swept up and rose above their knees. With wild cries of terror, the two younger boys caught hold of Tom, and losing their footing, dragged him down. Harry caught at Tom impulsively, with a vague idea of saving him from drowning, but the only result of his effort was that he went down with the rest. Fortunately the wave receded before the boys had time to drown, and left them struggling in a heap on the wet sand. There was no return of the water, and in a few moments the boys were outside of the tent, and on the top of the bluff above the river.

"It must have been a tidal wave," said Jim. "Oh, I'd give anything if I was home! The water will come up again, and we'll all be drowned!"

"It was the swell of a steamboat," said Tom. "There's the boat now, just going around that point."

"You're right," said Harry. "It was nothing but the swell of the night boat. What precious fools we were not to think of it before! To-morrow night we'll pitch the tent about a thousand feet above the water."

"Then there'll be a water-spout or something," said Jim. "We're bound to get wet whatever we do. We only started yesterday, and here we've been wet through three times."

"And Harry has been wet four times, counting the time he jumped into the Harlem for me," added Joe.

"It won't do to stand here and talk about it," said Tom. "We've got to have a fire, or we'll freeze. Look at the way Joe's teeth are chattering. The blankets and clothes are all wet, and the sooner we dry them, the better."

There happened to be a dead tree near by, and it was soon converted into fire-wood. The boys built a roaring fire on a large flat rock, and after it had burned for a little while, they pushed it about six feet from the place where they had started it, and after piling fresh fuel on it, lay down on the hot rock with their feet to the flames. The fire had heated the rock so that they could hardly bear to touch it; but the heat dried their wet clothes rapidly, and kept them from taking severe colds. Meanwhile their blankets had been spread out near the fire, and in half an hour were very nearly dry, and pretty severely scorched. Two large logs were then rolled on the fire, and when they were in a blaze the boys wrapped themselves in their blankets, and lying as near to the fire as they could without actually burning, resumed their interrupted sleep. They found the rock rather a hard bed, and it offered no temptation to laziness; so it happened that they were all broad awake at half past four; and though somewhat stiff from lying on a rocky bed, were none the worse for their night's adventure.

"There's one thing I'm going to do this very day," said Harry, as they were dressing themselves after their morning swim. "I'm going to write to the Department to send us a big rubber bag that we can put our spare clothes in and keep them dry. There's no fun in being wet and having nothing dry to put on."

TRYING TO KEEP WARM.

"If we have the bag sent to Albany, it will get there by the time we do," said Tom. "You write the letter while we are getting breakfast."

So Harry wrote to the Department as follows:

"Dear Uncle John,—We've been wet through with a steamboat once, and the tide wet us the first night, and we got rained on, and I jumped in to get Joe out, and we've had a gorgeous time. Please send us a big water-proof bag to put our spare clothes in, so that we can have something dry. Please send it to Albany, and we will stop there at the Post-office for it. Please send it right away. You said the Department furnished everything. We've been dry twice since we started, but it didn't last long. There never was such fun. All the boys send their love to you. Please don't forget the bag. From your affectionate nephew,

Harry."

"This was the morning that you were going to sleep till eight o'clock without waking up, Harry," said Tom, as they were eating their breakfast.

"There's nothing that will wake a fellow up so quick as the Hudson River rolling in on him. I hadn't expected to wake up in that way," answered Harry.

"So far we have done nothing but find out how stupid we are," said Tom. "Seems to me we must have found it pretty near all out by this time. There can't be many more stupid things that we haven't done."

"There won't any accident happen to-night," replied Harry; "for I'll make sure that the tent is pitched so far from the water that we can't be wet again. I wonder if every fellow learns to camp out by getting into scrapes as we do. It is very certain that we won't forget what we learn on this cruise."

"I'm beginning to get tired of ham," exclaimed Joe. "We've been eating ham ever since we started. Let's get some eggs to-day."

"And some raspberries," suggested Jim. "It's the season for them."

"And let's catch some fish," said Tom.

"That's what we'll do," said Harry. "We'll sail till eleven o'clock, and then we'll go fishing, and catch our dinner."

This suggestion pleased everybody; and when, at about six o'clock, they set sail, with a nice breeze from the south, everybody kept a look-out for a good fishing ground, and wondered why they had not thought of fishing before.

[TO BE CONTINUED.]

THE ROVERINGS' FOURTH.

BY MATTHEW WHITE, JUN.

IT had been arranged for weeks beforehand, and the whole family were delighted with the novelty of the proposition. Mrs. Rovering suggested it on the evening of Decoration-day, as she and Mr. Rovering and Edward and Edgar sat at the supper table, with patriotic appetites after their long tramp to and from the soldiers' graves.

"I think," Mrs. Rovering began, as she buttered a biscuit for Edgar—"I think we had better commemorate the Fourth in a manner that will not so weary us as to-day has done."

The good lady always made use of those words which it seemed she must have gone to the dictionary and picked out before she began to speak.

"Oh, pa, how many crackers will you give us this year?" burst out Edward.

Mr. Rovering was in the fire-works business, which fact had always been a source of the greatest satisfaction to his sons, and an awful trial to his wife, who every night expected to see him brought home in a scattered condition on a stretcher.

"What do you say to our not participating in the annual picnic, as it always rains, and the silver-plated ware's mislaid, the ants get into the sugar, and the boys into the pond?—what do you say to foregoing the enjoyment of these sylvan delights, and spending the day in town? We should thus have an opportunity of observing to how great an extent explosives are used here, and you could then gauge your manufacture of the articles accordingly. Aha! I have it!" added the inventive lady, after a moment's reflection. "We'll take the line of cars running entirely around the city, and so we'll be sure of viewing all sides of the question."

"The very thing!" exclaimed her husband.

In due course the famous national holiday arrived, and at about nine o'clock in the morning the family sallied forth on their memorable expedition. The two Eds went first, hurling torpedoes as if they were trade-marks, and now and then touching off a cracker, after having assured themselves that there was no policeman near. Then came the father and mother, arm in arm, under a great cotton umbrella, which Mrs. Rovering always insisted should be carried during their excursions, for fear rain might come on and spoil the silk one.

On reaching the corner where they were to take the car, a discussion arose as to which direction they should go.

"It doesn't make a particle of difference, so long as we get off," affirmed Mr. Rovering.

"Well, then," rejoined the originator of the expedition, "let's take whichever car comes first." And this decision would certainly have finally disposed of the matter if at that instant Edward had not shouted, "Oh, ma, here's a car coming up!" and Edgar, "Oh, pa, here's a car coming down!" and if, moreover, these two cars had not arrived at that identical corner at one and the same moment.

They both stopped, and Mr. Rovering cried, "Dear me, Dolly, which shall we take?—which shall we take?" while Edward hopped up and down on the step of one, and Edgar practiced jumping on and off the platform of the other.

"Take the one that isn't a 'bobtail,'" returned Mrs. Rovering, composedly.

"But they're both 'bobtails!'" exclaimed her poor husband, in an agony of apprehension lest the cars should start off, and cause his sons to fall on their pocketfuls of torpedoes.

Finally Mrs. Rovering said, quietly, "We shall ride in the empty one," and this proving to be the up-bound conveyance, they got in and were off.

"Now, Robert," Mrs. Rovering began, as soon as they had recovered from the shock of starting, which had sent them all down on the seat like a row of bricks, "don't make a mistake in putting our fares in the box. Let me see, five, five—yes, both the boys are over five. Have you got it right?"

But sad to relate, Mr. Rovering had not got it right, for, owing to his wife's constant repetition of the word five, he had become so confused as to drop twenty-five cents into the box, thinking there were five in the party.

"Make the driver extricate it for us," suggested Mrs. Rovering; but that individual promptly replied that he couldn't do it, and coolly proceeded to let the money down into the safe before their very eyes. But upon this his passengers raised such an outcry of indignation that the knight of the brake was forced to open the door again, and pacify them by saying they might take the fare from the next passenger. This appeared to be such a brilliant idea that Mrs. Rovering was almost inclined to envy the driver's genius.

These cars, although "bobtails," were drawn by two horses, and therefore went along at quite a respectable rate, but this did not prevent evil-minded youth from hanging on behind in all the blissful enjoyment of a free ride, and the efforts of the driver to dislodge these highway boys amused the two Eds not a little. One of his stratagems was to suddenly brake up the car as though he were going to stop and personally chastise the offenders, while another was to ring the bell and pretend one of his passengers was about to alight.

But on this occasion there were two boys who persisted in sticking on in spite of everything, and at last they so exasperated the poor driver that he threw down his reins, and rushed around to the rear platform with his whip raised.

Now it so happened that the two Eds had been long waiting for this opportunity, and as the man cut the air with his lash—and the air only, for the young rascals were already half a block away—Edward and Edgar simultaneously threw down six torpedoes apiece on the front platform, the effects of which were to send the horses off at a gallop, with the lines about their feet, and the driver tearing after them in vain.

"Whoa!" shouted Mr. Rovering and the boys.

"Which—where—what shall we do?" groaned Mrs.

Rovering, sinking back on the seat, and covering her face with her hands.

"Stop 'em, somebody. And oh, boys, why did you start 'em?" and Mr. Rovering remained standing motionless on the platform, casting longing looks at the reins trailing in the street.

"Remember," exclaimed Mrs. Rovering, "we're on the continuous line, and so we'll keep on going round and round, and never stop! Oh, why did you ever force me to set out upon this unhappy expedition?"

At this Mr. Rovering grew almost beside himself with despair; and determined on doing something, he seized the two Eds, and extracting from their pockets every torpedo he could find, flung the latter, in the heat of his passion, out of the window, which naturally resulted in a report much louder than the first one, and thus materially quickened the pace of the poor, bewildered animals.

And now a new danger arose. What if they should catch up to the car ahead?

But, luckily for all concerned, the stables of the company were not far off, and when the horses reached the car-house they slowed up, and the Roverings were rescued.

"But why didn't you put on the brake?" asked the superintendent.

Sure enough, why hadn't they?

HOW TO BUILD A STEAM-YACHT.

MOST of you boys know enough about boats to have built your sloop and schooner yacht, and perhaps a canoe; now why not go a little farther, and build a steam-yacht? Don't worry about your engine, boiler, and propeller; these can be bought complete at a low figure—an engine that will reverse, stop, and send your boat ahead at the rate of two miles an hour.

After taking a good look at the plates, and having made up your mind that you are equal to the task, go and see your friend the carpenter, and tell him you want a piece of white pine, free of knots, grain running lengthwise, well seasoned, thirty inches long, seven wide, and six deep. I speak of white pine, for the reason that it is easy to get, inexpensive, and cuts easily. Plane the four sides smooth; mark a centre line, AB, on both top and bottom.

The centre of your block must now be marked at right angles to the line AB on top and bottom; carry this line down the sides as well. This is the line marked X in Plates I. and II. Now for the first cutting of the block—the sheer line SH on Plate I. The dotted lines marked from 1 to 10 must be drawn, beginning at 1, just one inch from the left-hand end of block, No. 2 three inches from this, and so on, 3, 4, 5, 6, 7, 8, 9, 10; the last number will be just two inches from the right-hand end. These are to be marked on top and on both sides. These lines are very important, as the shape of your boat depends upon them. With a pair of compasses take distances from the line AB, Plate I., at numbers 1 to 10 respectively, to the line marked SH, and join the points with a straight-edge. This is your sheer. Work from the bow to about the centre of the block, and then from the stern; if you attempt to cut from end to end, you will certainly split off too much. Finish this sheer line with a spokeshave. The lines having been cut off the top of the block, draw them again on your new surface, as well as the line X and the centre line AB.

Now for Plate II. This gives the shape on deck. Using your compasses again, take the distances from the line AB on the subdivisions from stem to stern, and join with a curved rule, making the line HL. Before cutting away the sides of the block, look at Plate IV.; this gives the shape of the boat amidships. At the line X on deck it is but six inches wide, but it gradually widens to seven inches. Cut away with a draw-knife from 6 on the line MN to L, Plate II., and from 5 on MN to H, striking the line HL at 8 in the former, and at 8 in the latter case. The other side must be cut in the same way. The block had better be put in a bench vise to do this. You have now your boat in the rough. With a spokeshave round up the sides of the hull to HL. Turn your boat over, and cut with a saw three and three-quarter inches from the left-hand end, to a depth of three inches, and split off with a chisel.

Plate IV. gives the lines of the hull from the centre to bow and stern. Make careful and separate tracings of the curves marked from 1 to 10 and X, paste on thin pieces of wood, cut them out with a knife or jig-saw, and number them. Cut away the sides of the hull, testing with your patterns at the respective subdivisions, and finish with a spokeshave. Be careful near the stern-post of the swell where the shaft comes through. In cutting the bow take the pattern of the curve BK, Plate I., and shape accordingly. Now you may begin to dig out the hull. Fit your boat firmly to a table, or put it in a bench vise; but be careful not to mar the sides. Allow half an inch inside of the deck line for the thickness of the sides. Don't go too deep, but between the numbers 7 and 4 get the right depth or bed for your engine and boiler; place a straight-edge across the boat at these points, and get just the depth; the width necessary you will see in Plate V.

Plate II. For the deck use white pine one-eighth of an inch thick, straight-grained, and free from knots. Follow the line DL in cutting the deck. Allow the deck to project one-eighth of an inch all around; this will serve as a beading around the hull. Section of vessel Plate V. shows this at BD.

Plate III. shows deck finished, planking, top of cabin, bitts, etc. Mark the planking with an awl and straight-edge—not too deep, however, or you will split your deck. The double lines in the opening of the deck, Plate II., represent a coping to fit the cabin on, and at the same time to strengthen it. Make it of pine one-sixteenth of an inch thick, and fasten with good-sized pins having points clipped off diagonally by nippers or scissors: a better nail you will not want; use these wherever it is necessary.

The motive power consists of a single oscillating cylinder, half-inch bore, one-inch stroke; copper boiler, with lamp, shaft, and propeller; which will cost you ten dollars. A double oscillating engine costs fifteen dollars. The engine is controlled from the top of the cabin. The lever, if pressed to the right, will start the engine ahead; if left vertical, will stop, and to the left, will reverse it. What more can you want than that? The lamp holds just so much alcohol, and when that is burned out, the water in the boiler is used too. Never refill the lamp without doing the same to the boiler. The boiler is to be filled through the safety-valve, and provided with three steam-taps; these will show the height of water in the boiler. The coupling or connection between the shaft and engine is made so that you may take engine and boiler out, and use them for anything else.

There are three things we've forgotten, the stem, stern-post, and keel. Use the pattern you made for your bow, and cut out one-eighth inch stuff for your cut-water, or stem; the dotted lines at BK, Plate I., will show the shape; fasten on with cut pins. The stern-post, with the exception of the swell for the shaft, should be about the same thickness, and fitted in as shown in Plate I. The keel should be of lead, tapering from half an inch in the centre to one-eighth at the bow and stern: cut a small hole at Z, and let the rudder-post rest in it. Now fasten in your engine; two screws through the bed-plate will do it. Try the boat in water; if she is down by the stern, tack a piece of sheet lead in the bow inside. Nail your deck in with cut pins. Use one-eighth inch strips one-half inch high for the gunwale as far as the rounding of the stern; this must be cut out of a solid piece. Finish the gunwale with a top piece of Spanish cedar lapping over on either side of it.

Your cabin may be made of Spanish cedar one and a

PLATE I.

PLATE II.

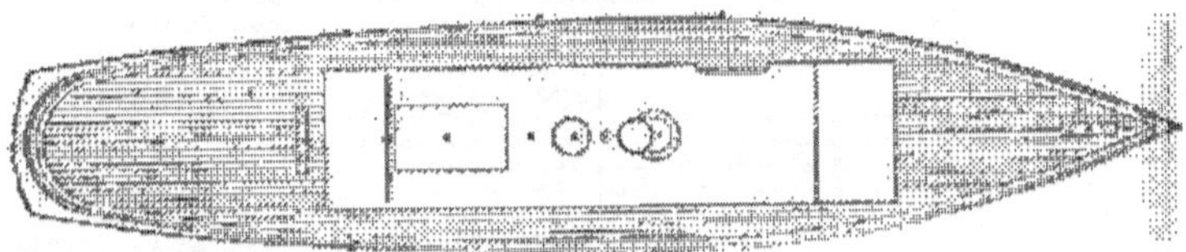

PLATE III.

half inches high, one-eighth thick; make this wide enough to fit outside of the coping; your sheer pattern will give the necessary curve to fit it to the deck. The pilot-house is made separate, two inches high. Before putting the cabin together, cut all openings, windows, etc., and mark with an awl the panellings and plank lines. The doors are simply marked in, not cut out.

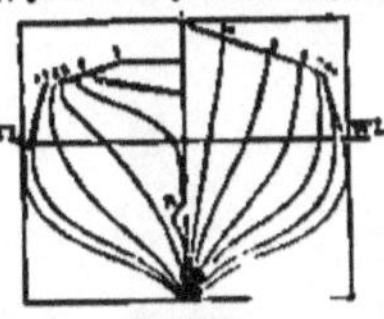

PLATE IV.

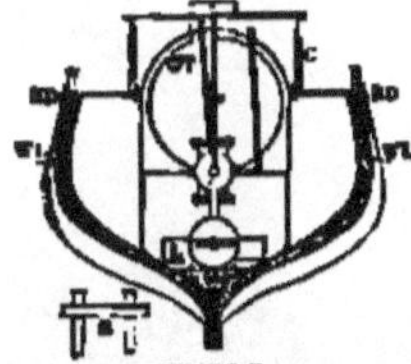

PLATE V.

Leave the front windows in the pilot-house unglazed, so as to serve as ventilator for the lamp. The top of the cabin overlaps the sides one-eighth of an inch all around. Cut a hatch in the cabin roof abaft the steam-drum; this is intended to oil the engine through, and try the steam-taps, without taking off the whole of the cabin. The cabin is kept in place by the funnel, which slips off just above the roof. The slit in the cabin top just back of the hatch is where your engine lever comes through. The bitts, B, fore and aft, are made of Spanish cedar, running through the deck to the hull. Your tiller may be made of steel wire running through the head of the rudder-post, which is made of iron wire; the man who makes your engine will do this for you.

MODEL OF A STEAM-YACHT.

OLD TIMES IN THE COLONIES.

BY CHARLES CARLETON COFFIN.

No. II.

CHAMPLAIN AND THE IROQUOIS.

IT was a long while ago, in 1535, that Jacques Cartier, of France, discovered the St. Lawrence River. He sailed up the mighty stream to the Indian village of Hochelaga—a cluster of wigwams at the foot of a hill which he named Mount Royal, but which time has changed to Montreal. Seventy-four years rolled away before any other white man visited the spot. In 1609, Samuel Champlain, an officer in the French navy, sailed up the great river. He was a brave adventurer, who was ever taking long looks ahead, and dreaming of what might be in the future—how the unexplored wilderness of America might become a New France. He had built houses at Quebec, and was on his way to discover what might be beyond.

He treated the Indians kindly, gave them presents, and made them his friends. There were many tribes, but all the Indians east of the Mississippi, and between Lake Superior and the Ohio, were divided into two great families, the Algonquins and the Iroquois. The Indians along the St. Lawrence, the Ottawa, and Lake Huron were Algonquins. The Iroquois lived in New York. They were the Mohawks, Onondagas, Oneidas, Senecas, and Cayugas. They called themselves the *Five Nations*. They had corn fields, and lived in towns. Their language was different from that of the Algonquins, with whom they were ever at war.

The wild flowers were in bloom in June, 1609, when Samuel Champlain sailed up the St. Lawrence to join a war party against the Iroquois. He had resolved to make the Algonquins his allies, and through them, and with the aid of the Jesuit priests, he would lay the foundations of the empire of New France.

The war party sailed up the Richelieu, or the St. John, carried their canoes past the rapids, launched them once more, and came out into the lake which bears the name of the intrepid explorer. Two Frenchmen accompanied Champlain, and there were twenty-four canoes, carrying sixty warriors, who had put on their feathers, and filled their quivers with arrows.

The woods were full of game, and the lake was swarming with fish, so that there was no lack of provisions. At daybreak they hauled their canoes up on the beach, and secreted themselves, so that no Iroquois might discern them; but when the sun went down they launched their canoes, and stole on in silence over the peaceful waters.

It was ten o'clock in the evening. They were near Crown Point, when they heard the dip of other paddles, and beheld a fleet of Iroquois canoes moving northward. A whoop wilder than the howling of a pack of wolves rent the air, and the Iroquois pulled for the shore to prepare for battle. They hacked down trees with their stone hatchets, and built a barricade.

Both parties danced, sang, howled, and yelled through the night, boasting of what they would do.

"We will fight you at daybreak," came from one side.

"You are cowards, and don't dare to fight," was the answer.

The morning sunlight streamed up the eastern sky, revealing the outline of the Green Mountains, and driving the darkness from the wilderness. The air was calm and peaceful as the Algonquins and Iroquois ranged themselves for battle. Many times had they met, and the great world had been no better—nor perhaps any worse—for their fighting; but this was to be a momentous conflict, affecting the welfare of the people of America through all succeeding ages.

Champlain put on a steel breastplate, and an iron casque to protect his head, with a plume waving from the burnished metal, buckled on his sword, loaded his arquebuse, or gun with a bell-shaped muzzle, putting in four balls.

The other two Frenchmen put on their breastplates and loaded their guns, but all three kept themselves concealed from the Iroquois.

The Iroquois had shields of hide stretched on hoops for defensive armor. Like the Algonquins, they had bows, arrows, and tomahawks.

The Algonquins were only sixty-four, while the Iroquois were more than two hundred. In splendid order, which was the admiration of Champlain, the Iroquois advanced to wipe out the Algonquins at a blow.

The Algonquins opened their ranks, and the Iroquois beheld Champlain—a being in human form, with the sunlight gleaming from his breast. They were transfixed with astonishment at the apparition. They see him pointing something at them. There is a lightning flash—a cloud—a roar. A chief falls dead, and one of the warriors is wounded.

The Iroquois are astounded. For a moment the air is filled with their arrows. Another lightning flash, a third, and they flee in terror, running swifter than the deer, to escape from beings which fight with lightning flashes and hurl invisible thunder-bolts! They were shots which are still echoing down the ages.

The battle has lasted a minute, but the Iroquois never will forget it. More intense their hate of the Algonquins; and it is the beginning of their implacable enmity to the French; an enmity which is to increase as time goes on, and which will make them the allies of the English through the great struggle which is to take place between France and England—between two races, two languages, two religions, and two civilizations—for supremacy upon this continent.

Seven years passed. Champlain had been back to France, and had returned. He was still thinking of the great empire France would one day control in the Western World. He made his way with a dozen Frenchmen up the Ottawa, past Lake Nipissing, to Lake Huron, then turned south to Lake Ontario, sailed along the eastern shore with a great war party of Hurons, to attack their old enemies—the Senecas, tribe of the Iroquois.

It was October. The woods were bright with crimson and magenta hues. The Iroquois had planted corn and pumpkins, and were gathering the harvest when the Hurons burst upon them. They fled to their fortified town on the shore of Lake Canandaigua. It was inclosed by trunks of trees thirty feet high, set in the ground. There was a gallery on which they could stand and fire or throw stones upon their assailants.

The Iroquois were the terror of every tribe east of the Mississippi. If Champlain could but conquer them, he would make the power of France felt to the Gulf of Mexico.

All night long the Hurons worked, building a tower of timber upon which the Frenchmen could stand, and pick off with their guns those inside the walls.

Two hundred warriors, with shouts and yells, amid a volley of arrows, drag the tower into position. The Iroquois swarm upon the walls, and the fight begins—the Frenchmen firing from the top of the tower, the Iroquois sending back arrows.

The Hurons light torches, and run up to the palisade with armfuls of dry sticks, and set them on fire; but the Iroquois run with calabashes of water, mount the gallery, and extinguish the flames. Each warrior yells at the top of his voice. They are crazed with excitement. For every whoop of the Hurons, the Iroquois give an angry yell of defiance. Arrows and stones fly. The Iroquois drop one by one before the unseen thunder-bolts from the men in the tower, but seventeen warriors go down before the arrows of the Iroquois. An arrow wounds Champlain in one knee, another pierces his leg. For three hours the fight goes on, when the Hurons, crest-fallen and disheartened, retreat to their camp. They linger five days, and then retire to their canoes, carrying Champlain on a litter all the way to Lake Ontario. The Iroquois steal upon them in their retreat, letting fly volleys of arrows, and yelling like hyenas over the defeat of the Hurons. They have discovered that the white men with their guns, after all, are not invincible.

HUMPTY DUMPTY AND THE MAGIC FIRECRACKERS.

BY AGNES CARR.

HUMPTY DUMPTY looked very sober one July morning, as he sat on his mother's door-step, his usually good-natured face screwed into a dozen wrinkles, and his button-hole of a mouth drawn down at the corners in the most dismal manner imaginable.

What could be the matter with the merry lad? For he was known far and wide for his fun and jollity.

So thought Mother Goose as she came up the village street.

"Why, Humpty Dumpty, what has happened to you? have you had another fall?" asked Mother Goose.

"No, Mother Goose, it is not a fall this time, but something worse, for I haven't a penny in the world, nor likely to have, and to-morrow is the Fourth of July, when all the boys and girls will have pistols, gunpowder, and fire-works, while I shall not even be able to get one fire-cracker."

"That is a misfortune for a boy, truly," said Mother Goose, "and I wish I could help you, with all my heart, though I don't see how. But stay! I had forgotten;" and diving to the bottom of a capacious pocket, she drew forth a small box, and from it produced three diminutive fire-crackers.

"They are not much," she said, "but such as they are, you are welcome to them, and at least you will not be crackerless. They were given to me, years ago, by the Man in the Moon, when he came down on that trip to Norridge (of which you have learned in your history), and staid overnight at my house, and were part of a pack presented to him by the Man in the South, who dislikes anything that suggests fire. He said they were magic, and you must always make a wish before setting them off."

"Oh, thank you, Mother Goose; they are much better than none at all," said Humpty Dumpty, gratefully; and he looked quite happy once more, as the good old lady nodded "good-by," and proceeded on her way, while the gander waved a yellow webbed foot in farewell.

"I will set off one cracker before breakfast, one at noon, and one to-night," thought Humpty Dumpty, as he tumbled out of bed bright and early next morning; "as I have so few, I must make them go as far as possible."

So as soon as he was dressed he ran into the yard and prepared to salute the "Glorious Fourth."

"Mother Goose said I must make a wish first, so here goes: I wish for a pop-gun, and no end of fire-crackers and torpedoes; now shoot away."

Touching the string with a match, there was a sharp report, and Humpty Dumpty was obliged to dodge, for the air was instantly filled with flying objects. A square package hit him on the nose, a round one landed in his open mouth, while a pop-gun thumped him rudely on the back; and by the time the cracker had burned itself out, he was standing in mute amazement, gazing upon the fulfillment of his wish far beyond his wildest expectations.

"Oh, jolly!" was his first comment, and he soon found courage to stuff his pockets with the crackers and torpedoes until they stood out like balloons, and made him look fatter than ever, when he walked down toward the green, popping at every cat and dog on the way, the envy and admiration of every other boy in Goosetown.

Humpty Dumpty was a generous lad, however, and shared his treasures with all his friends, although he would not tell where he got them; and by noon every cracker and torpedo was a thing of the past, and each boy had had a "pop" with the pop-gun.

Meanwhile Humpty Dumpty had been thinking of his second wish, and at last decided to share it with Bo-peep, of whom he was very fond, and for that purpose asked the little shepherdess to walk with him to the large oak-tree on the edge of the village, and while resting in the shade of its green boughs said,

"If you could have whatever you wished for, what would you choose, Bo-peep?"

"Oh, some blue ribbons, and candy," said Bo-peep, "bolivars, and chocolate drops, and such things."

"Then wish for them, and fire off this," said Humpty Dumpty, handing her a cracker.

Bo-peep looked surprised, but did as she was bid; but to the boy's surprise and disappointment, it only "fizzed," and went out.

"It is a poor one," said Bo-peep.

"We will make a squib of it," said Humpty Dumpty; and he quickly broke it in two, and applied a match; and what a squib it was!—for in place of the usual stream of fire, there issued forth a shower of such sugar-plums and bonbons as neither of the children had ever even dreamed of, and yards and yards of blue ribbon, the very color of the summer sky.

Bo-peep clasped her hands, and sat down suddenly on the grass, but Humpty Dumpty calmly heaped her lap with goodies, and twined the ribbon in her sunny hair, and round the neck of her favorite lamb, which had followed them from the village, and while they regaled themselves with the confections, under the oak-tree, told her of the wonderful gift given him by dear old Mother Goose.

That afternoon the good people of Gooseneck were startled out of their accustomed quiet by an invitation from Humpty Dumpty to an exhibition of fire-works that evening on the village green; and John Stout, Nimble Dick, and a number of other boys were engaged to build a platform for the occasion.

"The boy must have gone out of his mind," said Mrs. Dumpty, when she heard the news. "I'm afraid that last fall has affected his brain;" and all the villagers shook their heads doubtfully.

They were all on hand, however, at the appointed time, Mother Goose occupying a reserved seat in front; and loud was the laugh and many the jokes made on Humpty Dumpty when he appeared on the platform carrying in his chubby hand one small fire-cracker.

"Have we all come here to see a fat boy set off that little squib?" they asked.

"Wait," said Mother Goose.

And in a few moments their ridicule was turned to wonder; for as the cracker went off, a confused medley of rockets, pin-wheels, Roman candles, blue-lights, and other fire-works fell with a loud noise upon the stage.

"Magic!" "magic!" sounded on all sides, but changed to oh! and ah! as a beautiful rocket flew through the air, and burst into a hundred golden balls.

Oh, that was a Fourth of July long to be remembered, for such fire-works had never been seen in Gooseneck before; and when the last piece of all was displayed, showing a figure of Mother Goose herself, surrounded by a rainbow and a shower of silver stars, the delight of the spectators knew no bounds, and cheers for Humpty Dumpty rent the air.

He came forward, his round face all aglow with pleasure, as he bowed and said, "Your thanks, my friends, do not belong to me, but to our beloved Mother Goose, who, to make a poor boy happy, gave him her three magic fire-crackers."

[Begun in Harper's Young People No. 34, June 22.]

MISS VAN WINKLE'S NAP.

BY MRS. W. J. HAYS.

Chapter III.

"Au printemps l'oiseau naît et chante,
N'avez-vous pas ouï sa voix?
Elle est pure, simple, et touchante,
La voix de l'oiseau dans les bois."

So sang Julie Garnier, as she trudged with weary little feet up the mountain-side, listening to the birds, and in search of the squaw in charge of the doors of Day and Night. The pretty Indian legend had bewitched her. Here she was wandering away from all who cared for her, to see an old woman who cut up the old moons into stars; and already twilight was making the woods more dusky. The slanting sunbeams made a golden green in the young underbrush; the birds were seeking their nests; night would soon wrap the world in darkness; then what would become of Julie? The good God would protect her, she felt sure. But she was undoubtedly hungry, and yonder, where the road turned, was a great flat stone; on it she might rest, and eat a little ginger cake she happened to have in her pocket. To it she hastened, and what a world of beauty lay before her! It was at the head of a ravine, one of those deep mountain gorges lined with pines and cedars, through which rushed a rapid stream, but beyond this and over it were the dark defiles of the mountain range sweeping away to the north in purple shadows, while the sun tipped the tops of the nearer forest with gold and crimson. Here Julie paused, overcome with the grandeur and beauty her young eyes beheld. She sat down and listened to the noise of the stream beneath, and she watched the birds skimming over the ravine. Then remembering her cake, she took it from her pocket and nibbled it daintily, for it was all the food she had, and she must make it last until she came to the old squaw's wigwam, where, of course, she would be hospitably regaled. She pushed her daisy-wreathed hat from her head, and leaned against a pine-tree; the soft breeze fanned her hot little head, and played with her brown curls; she drew her knees up and clasped her hands about them, watching the sky change from one bright hue to another. The stream's voice was a lullaby, and slowly, softly fell the fringes of her eyelids; till the bright eyes were closed, and Julie was asleep.

She was so wearied and in so deep a slumber that the approaching stage-coach with its freight of tourists did not disturb her; and so eager was every one to see the famous view, that no one apparently noticed the little sleeping wayfarer, but behind the stage came in a more leisurely manner a private conveyance with only four occupants—a lady and gentleman and two children, all evidently foreigners. The elders were indeed occupied in gazing at the glorious picture Nature here displayed, but the eyes of the children were equally sensitive to smaller objects, and when they beheld a sleeping child, they at once drew the attention of their parents to this interesting incident.

The gentleman bade the driver halt, and assisted his pretty little wife from the carriage. She went hastily forward toward Julie, but as she neared her she stopped, clasped her hands, and turned toward her husband. Her face grew so white that he became alarmed, and asked,

"What is it, ma chère? Are you ill?"

"No, I am not ill; but look at this child—quick! Who is she like?"

The gentleman glanced at Julie, nodded his head, pulled his mustache, and said, briefly, "Yes, I see a resemblance."

"To whom, Max?—say, to whom?"

"To your poor little sister, Marie."

"Yes; is it not strange? Oh, how marvellously like Julie! I must waken her. Is she not lovely, the dear little creature, sleeping so innocently! Oh, Max, perhaps—perhaps—"

"Waken her, Marie. Ask her name."

The lady touched Julie gently, but the tired child slept too soundly for the light touch to arouse her, and it was not until she had kissed her on the cheek—the little red and brown cheek—that Julie opened her eyes. Then the lady gave a hysterical scream, not very loud, but enough to frighten Julie, whose eyes grew bigger and browner every moment.

"Oh, those eyes are Julie's!" said the lady.

"Of course they are, madame," replied Julie. "And are you the squaw?"

"Am I what? Is the child dreaming? What is your name, mon enfant?"

"My name is— But why do you ask, madame? and where am I? Oh, I know: I am on my way to see the old Indian squaw who lives up here in the mountains, and it is getting late. I was very weary, and I fell asleep."

"Your name, my child—tell me your name, that I may know if you are Julie Garnier's child."

"Yes, madame, I am Julie Garnier." With that the little lady embraced her so warmly, and gave her so many kisses, that Julie strove to get away from her.

"Children," said the lady, "come here; this is your cousin, little Julie Garnier, whose mother is my dear sister, from whom I have long been separated. Max, we must take the child home."

"Where are you staying, little one?" asked the gentleman, in a heavy voice, which made Julie shrink toward the lady.

"I am staying with Quillie Coit at Mr. Brown's," was Julie's answer, for she dared not now urge her errand, and was much perplexed by all this agitation. The children were standing beside her, gazing curiously, but not unkindly; the little lady was wiping her eyes; the gentleman was holding a consultation with the driver. It ended by their all getting again into the vehicle, Madame Von Boden taking Julie in her arms, and pouring into her astonished ears sweet caressing words, in her own beloved language, about Julie's own dear mother; their home in France; her marriage to a Prussian; the marriage of Julie's mother to a Frenchman; the dreadful war; a separation; a long silence, in which they had heard nothing about Madame Garnier, who was so proud in her poverty; fears that she was dead; the certain knowledge that her husband, Julie's father, was really dead; and now this happy discovery. It was almost too much for Julie, coming as it did in the midst of her own strange adventure, and she could hardly believe it to be all true; but she submitted with a good grace, stifling her regret at not accomplishing her purpose, since this kind little aunt seemed to be so overjoyed. The driver knew where Mr. Brown lived, and just as Mr. Brown's tired horses were being harnessed, and nurse in woeful anxiety was listening to the comfort which Quillie was trying to whisper to her, this strange vehicle was heard coming down the lane. Every one rushed to the gate—Mr. and Mrs. Brown, the farm hands, the kitchen folk, nurse, and even Quillie in her night-gown; for there was Julie at last—poor tired little Julie—drooping, faint, and tearful.

No one scolded, not even nurse, who had been most sorely tried; and Madame Von Boden, with many mistakes in her use of English, and with much excitement, related her adventure. Of course it was considered wonderful, and the travellers were prevailed upon to remain at Mr. Brown's overnight.

You would not have supposed that following day, when all the children were having a good time in the barn—swinging, feeding the horses, gathering eggs, giving the hens a double supply of corn, and in every way making the most of a barn's generous resources—that one little maiden among them was a heroine of romance, a very tired little heroine, quite contented to watch the swallows and pigeons, and gaze at the far-away mountain-tops. But so it was, and so it often is; for, as the French say, "'tis the unexpected that happens;" and when Madame Garnier heard that her little Julie had found her aunt Marie, and that the little cousins were all housed under one roof, and having much happiness together, her own joy was great.

Julie promised faithfully never to undertake any more expeditions without the consent of her guardians, and she begged Quillie never to say anything more about the squaw; but Fred was allowed, by special grace, to call her Miss Van Winkle; for Fred had a funny way peculiar to himself which seldom excited wrath.

Later in the season, when Madame Garnier was able to join Julie, and Mr. and Mrs. Coit came up from the city, the Von Bodens gave a pretty *fête* to all the children, and at the conclusion of it Quillie was invited to accompany Julie and her cousins, and spend the winter in Paris, which was so nice an opportunity for Quillie to acquire a good French accent that her father and mother felt obliged to accept.

Artie and Will had a great talk about this, and Fred said he wished Miss Van Winkle would just take another nap in the woods, to see what else might happen; possibly next time he would get an invitation from the Prince of Wales to go yachting.

But Miss Van Winkle took her naps at home after that, though she still thinks of the old squaw every time she looks at the moon.

THE END.

A GOOD TIME IN THE BARN.

The following gratifying communication comes from the librarian of a large public library in Illinois:

[illegible]

... I would like to know whether you are going to have a binding for Young People. I read the letters in the Post-office Box over and over, and enjoy them very much. We raise a good many chickens, and I have lots of pet ones, all of which have names. [illegible]

We have already stated in the Post-office Box that an ornamental cover will be ready when the first volume is concluded.

I like Young People very much, especially the story of "The Moral Pirates." I always read it the minute it comes from the post-office. J. W. F.

[illegible]

It is not easy to restore song to a silent canary, and as you will see from a letter in this "Post-office Box," you are not the only one seeking a remedy for this trouble. The companionship of a singing bird will sometimes arouse a canary to display its own musical talent. Your bird may be silent from overfeeding, as too much green food, like lettuce, makes a bird grow fat and stupid, and less likely to sing. Try to place your bird near singing canaries for a few weeks, if you can, and if that does not affect it favorably, we fear nothing will.

Cora S. Price and Mamie E. Evans both send the following legend of the forget-me-not, in answer to the inquiry of "A Constant Reader": Some flower seeds having been cast away by a traveller from a distant country, they fell by the edge of a lake. Some time afterward two lovers were wandering by the lake's side, and the lady, seeing the strange flowers, entreated her companion to gather some. As the gallant knight reached to pluck the blossoms, he fell in a quicksand, and was drawn into the treacherous pool, flinging the flower at the maiden's feet, and crying, "Forget me not," as he disappeared forever.

Here is still another fanciful legend, sent by [illegible]: When Adam and Eve were driven from Eden, the flowers all shrank away from Eve with the exception of a little blue blossom which Eve had named "heaven's flower," as its color was so exactly like the blue sky. As Eve passed, it seemed to murmur, "Forget me not," and she gratefully gathered it, saying, "Henceforth, dear flower, that shall be thy name." It was the only plant transplanted from Paradise, or that survived the flood. It is said to have the power of speaking at midnight, and telling the legend of its name.

[illegible]

The address of "Wee Tot" was given with her letter in Post-office Box No. 28. Walter R. F., who wrote about caterpillars in Post-office Box No. 33, can perhaps tell you the name of the caterpillar, and what kind of butterfly or moth it produces, although you describe only its color. Had you stated its size, length, and other peculiarities, it would be easier to give you its name.

[illegible]

[illegible]

Willie Atkinson.—There are about 225 islands in the Feejee group, of which 140 are inhabited. Viti Levu is the largest and most populous, being 97 miles from east to west, and 64 from north to south. Next to this is Vanua Levu, which is 115 miles long, and about 25 miles wide. The whole group contains, exclusive of coral islets, an area of about 8500 square miles of dry land.

George B.—The stamps you require are somewhat rare, but you may be able to obtain them by means of the exchanges offered by our young correspondents.

Lily B., Mabel C. L., and others.—Your puzzles are very skillfully made, but are rendered unavailable by their solutions, which are precisely the same as those of puzzles published in former numbers of the Young People. Correspondents, by taking special notice of the fact, which we have already stated, that we can not repeat solutions, will save themselves from many disappointments.

[illegible]

PUZZLES FROM YOUNG CONTRIBUTORS.

No. 1.

[illegible]

No. 2.

[illegible]

No. 3.

[illegible]

No. 4.

[illegible]

No. 5.

[illegible]

No. 6.

[illegible]

ANSWERS TO PUZZLES IN No. [illegible]

[illegible]

Pompey, Cæsar.

ADVERTISEMENTS.

ANSWER TO THE STUMP PUZZLE.

HERE is the answer to the Stump Puzzle offered in No. 33. With two straight cuts of the scissors the old dead stump is transformed into a mouse, alive and wide-awake.

MIRTHFUL MAGIC, OR HOW TO TURN A DULL PARTY INTO A MERRY ONE.

BY G. B. BARTLETT.

WHEN young people, and often old ones also, first arrive at a party, they are apt to feel a little stiff and awkward, and to stand about in corners, as if oppressed with the responsibility of their best gloves and clothes, and the giver of the entertainment seeks in vain to enliven and stir them up. For her aid we propose to give a few simple recipes which will answer the purpose, and give them a good laugh, after which they will be ready for the harder games which will follow. First she may ask them to join in the game of "Satisfaction." Every person in the room is invited to stand up, and all join hands in a ring, in the centre of which the leader stands, holding a cane in her hand, with which she points to each one in turn, and asks this question, after requesting silence and careful attention, "Are you satisfied?" Each replies in turn as he or she pleases, many probably saying "No," and others "Yes." The leader then says, "All who are satisfied may sit down, the others may stand up until they are satisfied."

MESMERIC TRICK.

Offer to mesmerize any lady so that she can not get up alone; and when one volunteers, place her in a chair in the centre of the room, and sit facing her, requesting all the company to keep quiet and unite their wills with yours. Ask the lady to fold her arms and lean back comfortably, and proceed to make a variety of passes and motions with your hands with great solemnity. After a few moments say, "Get up," and as she rises from her chair, you rise at the same moment, and say, "I told you you could not get up alone." If she suspects a trick, and does not rise, of course your reply is the same.

THE NEW FIFTEEN PUZZLE.

Draw the squares on a sheet of paper, and say: "I wish to fill these rows of squares, or stalls, full of animals, which you must watch carefully, in order to arrange them according to a formula which I shall give you. I will put down H for horses in the first row, C for cows in the second, and D for donkeys in the third." Put the letters down rapidly as you talk, leaving one square vacant in the third row, as if by accident, and some looker-on will be sure to say words to this effect, "There is one donkey missing," when you reply at once, "Then jump in yourself."

H	H	H	H	H
C	C	C	C	C
D		D	D	D

THE MONDDIA PUZZLE.

WITH one straight cut of the scissors transform this Monddia into a precious stone.

Mosquitoes in China.—Hotel charges in China are not too economical; but the traveller must remember to pay his bill when he leaves any place for a trip that he thinks may be short, but which may exceed his idea of the time required. Happening to be away for four days, I found that the charges for food and bed to a leather bag and a walking-stick which I had left behind were the same as those charged to myself when present in the house. Henceforth, when I went abroad, I took these little things with me, and opened a fresh account on my return. One finds soap and lamp duly charged as extras in all Eastern hotel accounts. The only thing for which no charge is made is the mosquito. This blood-thirsty little creature in China will take no denial. Worried by the heat of the day—the moist heat that so enervates one—a tired traveller will seek mid-day rest, but find it not. The mosquitoes are upon him by day as by night. They care nothing for nettings, and fairly laugh at the efforts of their victim to dislodge them with a long fan they which. They form a very serious drawback to the pleasures of Eastern travel.

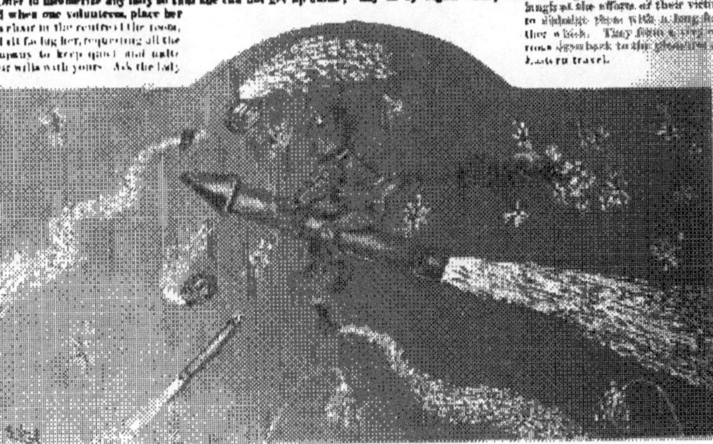

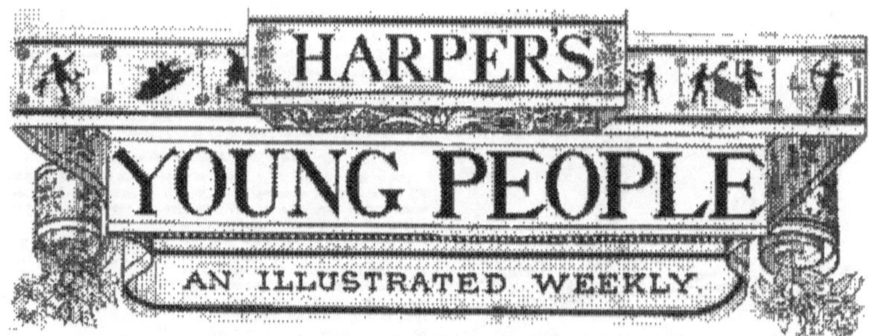

VOL. I.—NO. 37. PUBLISHED BY HARPER & BROTHERS, NEW YORK. PRICE FOUR CENTS.
Tuesday, July 20, 1880. $1.50 per Year, in Advance.

A CRABBING ADVENTURE

BY MATTHEW WHITE, JUN.

THERE were George and Bert, Sarah and the baby.

"And you and I have pretty good appetites, Bert," George would say, whenever the Fieldens' finances were discussed, which, since the father's death, had been pretty often.

"If we could only have staid on in the house in Fayetville! The garden was getting along so nicely, and now to think all the fruit and vegetables will be picked and sold or eaten by somebody else!" and Sarah sighed, as she thought of the spring budding and blossoming in which she had taken such an interest.

"But why can't we live off the river in place of the garden?" asked George. "The boys down at the dock say they can make lots of money selling soft crabs. They get from sixty to seventy-five cents a dozen, and, oh, mother, if Bert and me could only have a net and a boat and a crab car, and roll up our pants like Nat Springer, we'd just bring you so much money that you needn't hardly sew at all!" and in his enthusiasm George's eyes sparkled, and he ruthlessly trampled upon every rule of grammar he had ever learned.

At first Mrs. Fielden was inclined to discourage the young would-be fishermen, she having a perfect terror of their both being swallowed up by the river, as if it were some beast of prey. But she was finally prevailed upon

SETTING THE CRAB NET.—DRAWN BY C. S. REINHART.

to give her consent. A second-hand boat was purchased at a trifling price from Captain Sam, an old sailor, who had taken a great fancy to the boys, and he gave them a net, which he showed them how to use.

Thus fitted out, the boys would anchor near the shore a short distance below the village, roll up their trousers above their knees, and then stepping overboard, each take hold of an end of the net, and, keeping quiet as mice, wait until a crab came sailing up or down with the tide, when they would scoop him up, and shout "Hurrah!" if it proved to be a soft shell, and "Oh, pshaw!" if it was hard. However, in the latter case, it was not thrown away, but shaken off into the boat's locker, to be transferred to the car and left to "shed."

They did not at once make their fortune, for although they might have good "catches," that did not always insure a ready market; but as the warmer weather came on, and the village began to fill up with people from the city, the boys procured two or three regular customers, who did not grudge the fair prices paid for the "little-boy lobsters," as Bert called them.

Captain Sam stood firm friend and adviser to them from the first, and when some of the other crabbers were inclined to find fault with what they termed the injury done their business, he did his best to make peace, saying the river was big enough for all.

But one very hot afternoon, George and Bert came down to the shore looking rather blue, for the day previous some of the other village boys had repaired in a body to where the two were anchored, and made such a splashing about as to frighten all the crabs away.

"I think it's an awful shame," muttered George, as he pushed off. "This is a free country, and I don't see why we haven't as good a right to make money out of the river as Teddy Lee or Nat Springer. They—"

"Hold on a minute, George!" cried Bert, as his brother, with one knee on the bow, was about to send the *Sarah* into deep water with the other foot. "Here comes Captain Sam. Let's tell him about it; maybe he'll know what we ought to do;" and so they waited till the good-natured old man came up.

But there was no need to tell him anything, for he had already heard of the new outbreak on the part of the village boys, and now appeared with a suggestion, by acting on which hostilities might in the future be avoided.

"I'm real sorry, boys," he began, as he took his seat on the side of his own boat, which was drawn up close beside the *Sarah*. "I'm real sorry as how these Yorking youngsters don't treat you no better. They only hurt theirselves by it, they do," and Sam spoke with unusual emphasis, at the same time polishing up the glass of his "jack-light" with an energy that threatened to break the panes. "But now I'll tell you what tack I think you'd better take, an' thet right off, fer the tide's 'most out a'ready. Jist you row across nigh to the other side o' the river, drop yer anchor on the flat right opposite thet little sort o' bay yonder, and then put down yer net to good business. D'ye understand what I mean, lads?" and the Captain pointed with his long, water-shrivelled forefinger, adding, "It seems purty far to go, but it 'll pay when you git thar—it 'll pay;" and leaning forward, Sam gave the *Sarah* a shove that sent her clear of the shore, out into the centre of the cove which served as the harbor for all the fishing-boats in Yorking.

With their hearts considerably lightened by their friend's sympathy and advice, the two Fielden boys lost no time in following his instructions, and each taking an oar, they were soon spinning straight across the river at a speed that in ten minutes or so brought them to the flat. Here the anchor was dropped over the side, and the boys got out in the shallow water.

The net was quickly put in place, and Captain Sam's predictions amply verified, for the outgoing tide brought down quantities of soft shells and "shedders," to say nothing of hard crabs. It was fortunate Bert had the car with him, for he was always seeing "such splendid fellows" just a little further up, that the *Sarah* was soon left quite a distance behind, the lads being not only much interested in their success, but also in the exploration of the flat, which appeared to be long and narrow, with deep channels on every side.

Absorbed in the water at their feet, the boys failed to notice the change that was taking place in the sky overhead, and the first intimation they had of the storm that had been brewing all the afternoon was a terrific squall, which struck them with a suddenness that almost took away their breath.

"Make for the boat, Bert," shouted George, the next instant; and the two splashed their way through the now wave-capped waters with all possible speed.

But what was their horror, when they had almost reached the *Sarah*, to see the latter break away from her anchorage, and drift swiftly down stream with the gale!

The rope had parted, and they were left helpless on the flats.

"Oh, George, what shall we do!" almost sobbed Bert, for he was only ten, and the wind, and rain, and seething floods around him raged most furiously.

George was frightened too, but remembering his twelve years, he tried to look confident and hopeful, as he pointed out the fact that some one would surely come after them.

"But—but won't the tide come in before then?" queried Bert, his voice trembling still, and his cheeks all wet with rain. "I think I feel it a little higher now."

"It's only the waves makes that," returned George, soothingly, although the same horrible possibility had just presented itself to him.

The storm, however, did not last long; but with the going down of the wind, the tide began to come in faster, and Bert stood on his toes, and then sank the crab car, and stood on that. It was a good mile across the river to Yorking—too far to permit of any signals being seen there—and the nearer shore was quite wild, the woods extending down almost to the water's edge.

And still the tide came rushing in; and then the sun went down, and Bert began to cry in earnest, for he was both cold and hungry, besides feeling it a decidedly unpleasant sensation to have the water creep up little by little toward his neck.

"Why don't Captain Sam come after us?" he sobbed, hiding his face on George's coat sleeve.

"Perhaps he will; but, you see, he don't know we've lost our boat; so we'll just have to wait long enough for them to get worried about us at home."

George spoke bravely, but his heart beat very hard and fast, for now the water had reached above where his trousers were rolled, while Bert, who was almost a head shorter, was wet to the waist.

And so the minutes passed by as if they were hours, with the tide creeping up around the lads higher, higher, till just as Bert's shoulders were about to disappear into its cold embrace, George exclaimed:

"A light! a light! Look, Bert, it's coming this way!"

And now both boys strained their eyes to see if they might hope, and then cried out with all their might.

Nearer and nearer came the welcome beacon, casting a shining pathway before it over the waters, and soon answering shouts were echoed back, and a girl's voice rang out, "George! Bertie!" and the next moment Captain Sam's boat shot into view, with the "jack-light" on the bow, and Sarah sitting pale and anxious in the stern.

Tenderly Sam's strong arms lifted the two shivering lads on board, and their sister fell to weeping and laughing over them in the most confusing fashion.

On the way back George told the story of their captivity on the flats, and the Captain explained that soon after they had left him in the afternoon he had gone to Fayetville to see his daughter, not getting back till after supper, when he found Sarah rushing up and down the shore in a most distracted state of mind.

"But we've got lots of crabs," put in Bert, from his seat on the car, which he had guarded safely through it all. "And George was real brave, too. He didn't cry once."

"We've lost our boat, though, I'm afraid," returned his brother, anxious to change the conversation.

"Oh, I guess we'll find her somewheres 'long shore to-morrow," replied Sam; and they did, and afterward took good care not to practice false economy by having an old worn-out rope to their anchor.

The next day the lads' adventure was known all over Yorking, and in future the other crabbers treated them in quite a respectful manner, evidently thinking that now the Fielden boys had really earned the right to follow the business.

EDDIE'S LANTERNS.

BY ALBERT R. HARDY.

Eddie loves to watch the fire-flies
As the summer evenings pass,
Flashing like a shower of diamonds
In and out the meadow-grass.

"What are all the lights?" I ask him;
"Gracious! papa, don't you know?
God has sent these little lanterns,
So the plants can see to grow."

EASY BOTANY.

JULY.

JUNE, with its rounded freshness unsullied by a faded leaf, its wood paths gay with flowers, its glorious sunsets and sunrises, its *perfection* of beauty and sweetness—June has passed along to make room for the fervid July. This midsummer month has its charms, and can show a fair array of bright blossoms, the yellows becoming more prevalent, and all the colors deepening as the heat grows more intense. The delicate spring flowers are succeeded by a stouter and somewhat coarser display. The species of veratrum, or false hellebore, which is now to be seen in New England swamps and pastures, is a very striking plant; it has long leaves, strongly veined and most beautifully plaited, with numerous racemes of green flowers, forming a large terminal pyramid. The Indiana veratrum, found in deep woods at the West and South, is a tall plant, five or six feet high, with very large leaves, and has a kind of unholy look, the flowers almost black, with red stamens.

This is the month for hosts of wild peas and vetches: the purple vetch in New England thickets; the everlasting-pea on Vermont hill-sides; the pink beach-pea and marsh-pea on New Jersey coasts and Western lake shores; the pale purple myrtle-pea climbing over banks by New England road-sides; the blue butterfly-pea, two inches broad, very showy, and found in woods and fields of New York and Pennsylvania. These are all graceful and pretty.

On Western prairies blossoms the deep pink prairie rose, the only native climbing rose of the States, and on rocky banks in Pennsylvania woods may be found the ty, the petals bright reddish purple, with crooked stamens brilliant yellow, and captivating seed-vessels shaped like little antique vases. Several species of the singular orchis tribe are in bloom during this month. As a general thing, these remarkable plants delight in cold, damp, boggy, muddy pastures, and old dark woods and thickets.

The flowers are beautiful, and several are fragrant; the colors white, yellow, and shades of purple, and one, the fragrant purple-fringed orchis, is as perfect and beautiful as can be imagined, and well repays the tramp through damp woods. So also does the superb white lady's-slipper, found in the same localities, and contrasting finely with the dark, shaded places it loves; the large white blossoms, with purple or red lines, two or three on a stalk. In shallow pools and wet places the white arrow-head is plentiful; and the whiter wild calla, really handsomer than its majestic relative the cultivated calla, and the brilliant cardinal-flower gleam out beside the water-courses.

WILD FLOWERS OF JULY.

COMMON NAME.	COLOR.	LOCALITY, ETC.
Aconite, wolf's-bane	Purple, poison	Dry rocky places; Pennsylvania.
Agrimony	Soft yellow	Open woods; New Jersey.
Archangelica	White	Dry open woods; Middle States.
Beach-pea	Purple, large	Sea-coast; New Jersey.
Black snakeroot	White racemes	Deep woods; Maine, West.
Butterfly-pea	Violet, large	Sandy woods; Maryland, Virginia.
Button-bush	White	Wet places. Common.
Callirhoe	Red-purple	Dry fields, prairies; Illinois.
Cardinal-flower	Intense red	Wet places. Common.
Coral-berry	Pink	Dry fields and banks. Middle States.
Deptford pink	Rose-color, white specks	Dry soil; Mass. to Virginia.
Evening primrose	Pale yellow	Sandy soil. Common.
Everlasting-pea	Yellowish white	Hill-sides; Vermont, Mass.
Fringed orchis	Purple	Dark woods; New England.
Fumitory	Rose-color, nodding	Sandy fields; New Jersey.
Ginseng	White	Cool, rich woods. Rare.
Glade mallow	White	Limestone valleys; Pennsylvania.
Grass of Parnassus	Wh., green lines	Damp meadows; Connecticut.
Hardhack	Rose-color	Damp meadows; New England.
Holy-grass	Purple	Vermont, Maine.
Hercules's club	Greenish white	River-banks; Middle States.
Indiana dragon-root	Black and red, poison	Damp woods; West.
Indian physic	White, pink	Rich woods; Pa., New York.
Lady's-slipper	White, red lines	Deep, boggy woods; New England.
Lead-plant	Violet	Crevices of rocks; Michigan.
Marsh-pea	Blue, purple	Moist places; New England.
Meadow-beauty	Bright purple	Borders of ponds; Conn., N. J.
Meadow-sweet	White, pink	Wet, low grounds; New England.
Moss-campion	Purple, white	White Mountains.
Myrtle-pea	Pale purple	Climbing; New England thickets.
New Jersey tea	White clusters	Dry woodlands; Middle States.
Nondo, lovage	Wh., aromatic	Rich woods; Virginia.
Passion-flower	Greenish-yellow	Damp thickets; Pa., Illinois.
Pencil-flower	Yellow	New Jersey; pine-barrens.
Poison-hemlock	White, poison	Waste, wet places. Common.
Prairie rose	Deep pink	Climbing; prairies West.
Prickly poppy	Showy yellow	Open woods; South and West.
Rattle-box	Yellow	Sandy soil; New Jersey.
Royal catchfly	Deep scarlet	Western prairies.
Sea-rocket	Purplish	New England coast and West.
Slender sundew	White	Shores of Western lakes.
Snow-berry	White	Rocky banks; Vermont to Pa.
Spikenard	White	Rich woodlands; New England.
St. Andrew's cross	Yellow, stamens crossing	New Jersey; Illinois.
St. John's-wort	Yellow, large	Stony banks; New England.

FRANKLIN ON HIS WAY TO FRANCE.—Drawn by Howard Pyle.

THE STORY OF THE AMERICAN NAVY.

BY BENSON J. LOSSING.

CHAPTER I.

"YOU have no right to tax us without our consent," said the English-American colonists to the British Parliament more than a hundred years ago. "The Great Charter of England forbids it."

"We have the right to control you in all cases whatsoever," answered the Parliament.

"Taxation without representation is tyranny, and we will not submit to it," the colonists declared. A mighty quarrel then began, which lasted ten years, and ended in blows. The colonists thought with Cromwell that "rebellion to tyrants is obedience to God."

The Parliament levied a stamp tax, but could not enforce it. A tax on tea was laid, when the patriotic women of America ceased drinking tea, while the men resolved that not a pound of the plant should be landed on our shores until the tax should be taken off. Nevertheless, tea ships came to Boston, when the citizens cast their cargoes into the waters of the harbor.

That tea party made the British government very angry. The King called his American subjects "rebels," and proceeded to punish the people of Boston. All the colonists stood by them. British troops were sent to make the Americans obedient vassals instead of loving subjects. The representatives of the colonists all over the land met in a General Congress at Philadelphia. That was in 1774. In that Congress Patrick Henry, of Virginia, said, "We must fight." At the same time Joseph Hawley, of Massachusetts, said in the Provincial Congress, "We must fight." The patriotic people everywhere, with compressed lips and valorous hearts, said, "We must fight."

Faint-hearted men and women shook their heads, and said: "Be prudent. You know Great Britain has scores of ships of war, and we have not one: how can we hope to win in such a contest?"

Stout-hearted men and women replied, "We will buy or build ships, make warriors of them, man them with hardy New England fishermen, and with the faith of lit- of distributed Secretary of the Navy. They ordered more than a dozen war vessels to be built. Officers were appointed, crews were gathered, and Esek Hopkins, a seaman of Rhode Island, then almost sixty years of age, was made Commodore and Commander-in-chief of the Continental Navy. This was the germ of the United States Navy.

Early in 1776 Hopkins sailed from the Delaware to the Bahama Islands, with four ships and three sloops. At New Providence he captured the forts, nearly one hundred cannon, and a large quantity of ammunition and stores. On his return he fought several British vessels, captured two, and took his little squadron safely into the harbor of New London, Connecticut. Not doing so well as the Congress desired, he was soon afterward relieved of command, and no successor was appointed.

John Paul Jones, a little Scotchman less than thirty years of age, was one of the most active officers of this Continental Navy, and became the most conspicuous marine hero of the old war for independence. He was the first who raised an American flag over an American vessel of war, in December, 1775; and in various ships he gained such great renown that after the war he received special honors from the French monarch, became Vice-Admiral in the Russian navy, and when he died, the government of France decreed him a public funeral.

There were other Americans at that time who became naval heroes only a little less famous than Jones. There was John Manly, the veteran sailor of Marblehead, whom Washington appointed Captain when he fitted out some privateers at Boston before a navy was created. While the Congress were talking about a navy, Manly was cruising off the coast of Massachusetts in the armed schooner *Lee*, keenly watching for British vessels laden with military supplies for the army in Boston. He captured three of them laden with arms and munitions of war, then much needed by the patriots who were besieging the New England capital.

There was young Nicholas Biddle, who had served with Nelson in the Royal Navy, and who accompanied Hopkins to the Bahamas. He did gallant service as commander exploits. After fighting British armed vessels, and taking several prizes in the West Indies, he took Dr. Franklin, the representative of the Congress, to France. Then he cruised in the Bay of Biscay, captured a number of English merchantmen, and with the *Reprisal* and two or three other small vessels, sailed entirely around Ireland, sweeping the Channel its whole length, destroying a number of merchant vessels, and creating great alarm in all the British ports. Poor Wickes perished soon afterward with all his crew when his ship was wrecked on the rocks of Newfoundland.

New England privateers were very busy and successful, capturing no less than thirty vessels laden with supplies for the British army in Boston. Among the most active of these was a little Connecticut cruiser of fourteen guns, named the *Defence*. She took prize after prize; and on a starry night in June, 1776, she, with some other small vessels, fought and conquered two British transports near Boston, laden with two hundred soldiers and a large quantity of stores. By midsummer (1776), American cruisers had captured more than five hundred British soldiers.

Captain Whipple, a bold Rhode-Islander, who, when a British naval commander threatened by letter to hang him "to the yard-arm" for an offense against the majesty of Great Britain, replied, "Catch a man before you hang him," was in command of the Continental vessel *Doria*. He was so successful off the coasts of New England, that when he returned to the Delaware his prizes were so numerous, that, after manning them, he had only five of his original crew left on board the *Doria*.

The gallant Jones meanwhile had swept the seas along the coasts of Nova Scotia, and sailed into Newport Harbor with fifteen prizes. After resting on his laurels awhile, he was again on the Acadian coast late in 1776, where he captured a large British transport laden with supplies for Burgoyne's army in Canada. By this time cruisers sent out by Congress and privateers were harrying British shipping in all directions.

Dr. Franklin carried with him to France a number of blank commissions for army and navy officers, signed by the President and Secretary of Congress. These Franklin and the other Commissioners filled and signed, and under this authority cruisers sailed from French ports to attack British vessels. It must be remembered that France at that time, in order to injure her old enemy, England, was giving secret aid to the Americans in revolt.

How active and how harmful to the British marine were some of the cruisers commissioned by Franklin and his associates, and sent out from French ports, we shall observe presently.

[TO BE CONTINUED.]

[Begun in YOUNG PEOPLE No. 31, June 1.]

THE MORAL PIRATES.

BY W. L. ALDEN.

CHAPTER VII.

THE sun was getting to be rather too hot for boating, when the boys saw the half-sunken wreck of a canal-boat close to the west shore, where there was a nice shady grove. They immediately crossed the river, and, landing near the wreck, began to get their fishing tackle in order.

As there were only two poles, one of which belonged to Harry and the other to Tom, the two Sharpe boys were obliged either to cut poles for themselves, or to watch the others while they fished. Jim cut a pole for himself, but Joe preferred to lie on the bank. "I don't care to fish, anyhow," he said. "I'll agree to eat twice as much fish as anybody else, if I can be excused from fishing."

"If you don't want to fish, you'd better hunt bait for us," said Tom.

"I never thought about bait," exclaimed Harry. "How are we going to dig for worms without a spade?"

"Who wants any worms?" replied Tom. "Grasshoppers are the thing; and the field just back of here is full of them. Come, Joe, catch us some grasshoppers, won't you?"

"How many do you want?" asked Joe. "I don't want to waste good grasshoppers on fellows who won't use them. Let's see: suppose I get you ten grasshoppers apiece. Will that do?"

"Are you getting lazy, Joe?" said Tom, "or are you sick? A fellow who don't want to fish must have something wrong in his insides. Harry, you'd better give him some medicine."

AN UNEXPECTED CATCH.—DRAWN BY A. B. FROST.

"Oh, I'm all right," replied Joe. "I'm a little sleepy to-day, but I'll get your grasshoppers."

Joe took an empty tin can and went in search of grasshoppers, while the rest were getting their hooks and lines ready. In a short time he returned, and handed the can to Tom.

"There's just thirty-one grasshoppers in that can," said he. "I threw in one for good measure. Now go ahead and fish, and I'll have a nap." So saying, he stretched himself on the ground, and the other boys began to fish.

There were quantities of perch near the old canal-boat, and they bit ravenously at the grasshoppers. It took only about a quarter of an hour to catch nearly three dozen fish. These were more than the boys could possibly eat; and Tom was just going to remark that they had better stop fishing, when they were startled by a loud cry from Joe. Harry, in swinging his line over his head so as to cast out a long way into the river, had succeeded in hooking Joe in the right ear.

Of course Harry was extremely sorry, and he said so several times; but, as Joe pointed out, "talk won't pull a hook out of a fellow's ear." The barb made it impracticable to draw the hook out, and it was quite impossible that Joe should enjoy the cruise with a fish-hook in his ear. Jim said that the hook must be cut out; but Joe objected to having his ear cut to pieces with a dull jack-knife.

In this emergency, Tom prepared to break off the shank of the hook, and then to push the remainder of it through the ear. It was no easy matter, however, to break the steel. Every time the hook was touched Joe winced with pain; but finally Tom managed to break the shank with the aid of the pair of pliers that formed part of the stores. The hook was then gently and firmly pressed through the ear, and carefully drawn out.

"I knew," said Tom, "that something must be wrong when Joe said he didn't want to fish. This ought to be a warning to him."

"It's a warning to me," said Harry, "not to throw my line all over the State of New York."

"Oh, it's all right now," said Joe. "Only the next time I go cruising with Harry, I'm going to take a pair of cutting pincers to cut off the shanks of fish-hooks after he gets through fishing. We'd better get a pair at Hudson, anyhow, or else we'll all be stuck full of hooks, if Harry does any more fishing."

Harry was so humbled by the result of his carelessness that he offered, by way of penance, to clean and cook the fish. When this was done, and the fish were served up smoking hot, they were so good that Joe forgot his damaged ear, and Harry recovered his spirits. After a course of fish and bread, a can of peaches was opened for dessert, and then followed a good long rest. By three o'clock the heat began to lessen, and the *Whitewing* started on her way with a better breeze than she had yet been favored with.

The boat travelled swiftly, and the breeze gradually freshened. The whitecaps were beginning to make their appearance on the river before it occurred to the boys that they must cross over to the east shore, in order to camp where they could find shade while getting breakfast the next morning. It had been one of Uncle John's most earnest bits of advice that they should always have shade in the morning. "Nothing spoils the temper," he had said, "like cooking under a bright sun; so make sure that you keep in the shade until after breakfast." Harry felt a little nervous about crossing the river in so fresh a breeze, since, as the breeze blew from the south, the boat could not sail directly across the river without bringing the sea on her beam. He did not mention that he was nervous, however, and he showed excellent judgment in crossing the river diagonally, so as to avoid exposing the broadside of the boat to the waves, that by this time were unpleasantly high. The east bank was thus reached without taking a drop of water into the boat, and she was then kept on her course up the river, within a few rods of the shore.

This was a wise precaution in one respect; for if the boat had capsized, the boys could easily have swum ashore; but still it is always risky to keep close to the shore, unless you know that there are no rocks or snags in the way. Harry never thought of the danger of being shipwrecked with the shore so close at hand, and was enjoying the cooling breeze and the speed of the boat, when suddenly the *Whitewing* brought up with a crash that pitched everybody into the bottom of the boat. She had struck a sunken rock, and the speed at which she was going was so great that one of her planks was stove in. Before the boys could pick themselves up, the water had rushed in, and was rising rapidly.

"Jump overboard everybody!" cried Harry. "She won't float with us in her."

There was no time in which to pull off shirts and trousers, and the boys plunged overboard without even taking their hats off. They then took hold of the boat, two on each side of her, and swam toward the shore. With so much water in her, the boat was tremendously heavy; but the boys persevered, and finally reached shallow water, where they could wade and drag her out on the sand.

"Here we are wet again!" exclaimed Jim. "The blankets are wet too this time."

"Never mind," replied Tom; "it's not more than five o'clock, and we can get them dry before night."

"We'll have to work pretty fast, then," said Harry. "Jim and Joe had better build a big fire, and dry the things, while you and I empty the boat; or I'll empty the boat, and you can pitch the tent. We'll have to put off supper till we can make sure of a dry bed."

Harry took the things out of the boat one by one. Everything was wet except the contents of the tin boxes, into which the water luckily had not penetrated. As soon as the fire was built, Jim and Joe gave their whole attention to drying the blankets and the spare clothing; and when the boat was emptied, it was found that a hole nearly six inches long and four inches wide had been made through one of the bottom planks. Harry and Tom set to work to mend it. They took a piece of canvas—which had luckily been kept in one of the tin boxes, and was quite dry—and tacked it neatly over the outside of the hole.

They next covered the canvas with a thin coating of white lead, except at the edges, where the white lead was laid on very thickly. Over the canvas the piece of zinc that had been brought for just such a purpose was carefully tacked, and then thin strips of wood were placed over the edges of the tin, and screwed down tightly with screws that went through the zinc, but not through the canvas. Finally, white lead was put all around the outer edge of the zinc, and the boat was then left bottom-side up on the sand, so that the white lead could harden by exposure to the air.

Nobody cared to go for milk in wet clothes; and so when the boat was mended, the boys all sat around the fire to dry themselves, and made a supper of crackers. What with the heat and the wind, it was not very long before their clothes and blankets were thoroughly dried, and they could look forward to a comfortable night. The tent was pitched where no steamboat swell could possibly touch it, and the boat was apparently out of reach of the tide. It was very early when the boys "turned in," and for the first time in the cruise they slept peacefully all night.

[TO BE CONTINUED.]

THE MANGOSTEEN.

FROM ADVANCE SHEETS OF "THE BOY TRAVELLERS IN THE FAR EAST," PART SECOND. BY THOMAS W. KNOX.

DURING their stay upon the island of Java, Dr. Bronson and his young travelling companions took a trip on a railway from Batavia to Buitenzorg, in order that they might learn something of the interior of the island. While on this trip the boys observed, among other things, that the trees in some instances grew quite close to the track. Doctor Bronson explained to them that in the tropics it was no small matter to keep a railway line clear of trees and vines, and sometimes the vines would grow over the track in a single night. It was necessary to keep men at work along the track to cut away the vegetation where it threatened to interfere with the trains, and in the rainy season the force of men was sometimes doubled. "There is one good effect," said he, "of this luxuriant growth. The roots of the vines and trees become interlaced in the embankment on which the road is built, and prevent its being washed away by heavy rains. So you see there is, after all, a saving in keeping the railway in repair."

At several of the stations the natives offered fruit of different kinds, and nearly all new to our young friends. They had been told that they would probably find the mangosteen for sale along the road; they had inquired for it in Singapore, but it was not in season there, and now their thoughts were bent upon discovering it between Batavia and Buitenzorg. Two or three times they were disappointed when they asked for it; but finally, at one of the stations, when Fred pronounced the word "mangosteen," a native held up a bunch of fruit, and nodded. The Doctor looked at the bunch, and nodded likewise, and Fred speedily paid for the prize.

Perhaps we had best let Fred tell the story of the mangosteen, which he did in his first letter from Buitenzorg:

"We have found the prince of fruits, and its name is mangosteen. It is about the size of a pippin apple, and of a purple color—a very dark purple, too. The husk, or rind, is about half an inch thick, and contains a bitter juice, which is used in the preparation of dye; it stains the fingers like aniline ink, and is not easy to wash off. Nature has wisely provided this protection for the fruit; if it had no more covering than the ordinary skin of an apple, the birds would eat it all up as soon as it was ripe. If I were a bird, and had a bill that would open the mangosteen, I would eat nothing else as long as I could get at it.

"You cut this husk with a sharp knife right across the centre, and then you open it in two parts. Out comes a lump of pulp as white as snow, and about the size of a small peach. It is divided into sections, like the interior of an orange, and there is a sort of star on the outside that tells you, before you cut the husk, exactly how many of these sections there are. Having got at the pulp, you proceed to take the lump into your mouth, and eat it; and you will be too busy for the next quarter of a minute to say anything.

"Hip! hip! hurrah! It melts away in your mouth like an overripe peach or strawberry; it has a taste that is slightly acid—very slightly, too—but you can no more describe all the flavor of it than you can describe how a canary sings, or a violet smells. There is no other fruit I ever tasted that begins to compare with it, though I hesitate to admit that there is anything to surpass our American strawberry in its perfection, or the American peach. If you could get all the flavors of our best fruits in one, and then give that one the 'meltingness' of the mangosteen, perhaps you might equal it; but till you can do so, there is no use denying that the tropics have the prince of fruits.

"Everybody tells us we can eat all the mangosteens we wish to, without the slightest fear of ill results. Perhaps one might get weary of them in time, but at present we are unable to find enough of them. If anything would reconcile me to a permanent residence in the tropics, it would be the hope of always having plenty of mangosteens at my command.

"You may think," Fred added, "that I have taken a good deal of space for describing this fruit, but I assure you I have not occupied half what it deserves. And if you were here, you would agree with me, and be willing to give it all the space at your command—in and beyond your mouth. But be careful and have it fully ripe; green mangosteens are apt to produce colic, as Frank can tell you of his own knowledge."

ROBINSON CRUSOE'S ISLAND.

THE island of Juan Fernandez has always been said to be the island on which Robinson Crusoe was cast away. Nothing can be further from the truth. Crusoe never saw Juan Fernandez, and, so far as we know, never once so much as thought of casting himself away there.

No man has ever charged Robinson Crusoe with not telling the truth. He may have had his faults—and he certainly did show very little judgment when he built his first boat so far from the shore that he could not possibly launch it—but he always told the truth. We ought therefore to believe what he says about the situation of his island. He informs us that, having sailed from Brazil on a voyage to the coast of Guinea, he was driven northward by stormy weather, and was finally wrecked somewhere between the mouth of the river Orinoco and the Caribbean or West India islands. Now the island of Juan Fernandez is in the Pacific Ocean, about three hundred and sixty miles south-west of Valparaiso. To suppose that Crusoe was wrecked on Juan Fernandez, while on his way from Brazil to Guinea, is like saying that a ship on her way from New York to Liverpool was wrecked on one of the Sandwich Islands. Such a story would be perfectly absurd. However, when we have Crusoe's word that he was cast away near the mouth of the Orinoco, there is an end of the matter. He probably could not have told a lie if he had tried to.

In the year 1704 an English vessel called the *Cinque Ports* came to Juan Fernandez. One of her officers, Alexander Selkirk by name, had quarrelled with the Captain, and he said he would much rather stay on this island than sail any longer on board the *Cinque Ports*. The Captain was glad to get rid of him, and therefore sailed away, and left him behind. What Selkirk and the Captain had quarrelled about has never been certainly known, but when we reflect that Selkirk was a Scotchman, we can understand that very likely he was unwilling to practice piracy on Sunday, while the captain insisted that any day was a fit day on which to rob a Spanish ship. This would have led to a quarrel, and very possibly was the precise cause of the quarrel which resulted in Selkirk leaving the ship at Juan Fernandez. It is true that the *Cinque Ports* was called a buccaneer, instead of a pirate, but no man can see the difference between buccaneering and piracy without the help of a large-sized compound microscope.

Selkirk remained all alone on the island for four years and four months, when another English vessel took him off. When he reached home, he wrote an account of his adventures, and very stupid people have since claimed that Daniel Defoe, the author of the story of Crusoe's adventures, had read Selkirk's book, and that it suggested to him the idea of inventing Robinson Crusoe. To suppose that so great a man as Defoe could not write a book without stealing his ideas from Alexander Selkirk is ridiculous. Selkirk and Crusoe were as unlike as two men could well be. The only resemblance between them was that both had lived alone on unfrequented islands, as many other unfortunate men have done before and since.

THE LOOKOUT, ISLAND OF JUAN FERNANDEZ.

We thus see how it came to pass that people have mixed up Selkirk's island with Crusoe's island, and have finally convinced themselves that Crusoe was wrecked on Juan Fernandez. Selkirk's island is firmly believed by nearly everybody to have been Crusoe's island, though we might just as well call it Smith's or Jones's island.

It must be admitted that Juan Fernandez is a beautiful island, with every convenience that Crusoe could have wished for, except cannibals. Selkirk, however, could do nothing with it. He did contrive to catch goats by running after them until they were tired out, but he never thought of taming them and fattening them on tomato cans—as Crusoe did. Of course he never had a Man Friday, and he never built himself a canoe, or periagua. In fact, he did very little that was creditable to him, and there is only too much reason to believe that if he had seen a foot-step on the sand, he would not have known that it was his duty to be terribly frightened.

Juan Fernandez is about sixteen miles long and five and a half miles wide. The shore, especially on the northern side, is steep and rocky. The interior is very picturesque, and contains several beautiful valleys separated by high ridges. On the north side of the island is a very steep mountain of lava, which is eight thousand feet high, the top of which is said to be inaccessible. Part way up this mountain is the place where Selkirk used to watch for passing vessels. In one of the valleys there is a cave where Selkirk lived. It is thirty feet in length and about twenty feet in breadth, with a ceiling of nearly twenty feet in height. While it is a fair substantial cave, it can not be compared for a moment with the cave which Crusoe had on his own island, and which he enlarged with so much perseverance.

The island belongs to Chili, and more than a hundred years ago the Chilian government sent convicts to Juan Fernandez as a punishment. A fort was built, which has now crumbled away, and cells were dug in the solid rock on the side of a hill, and the convicts were locked up in them every night. The convicts, not liking their treatment, rebelled, killed their guards, and seizing on a vessel that had visited the island, escaped to Peru. Since then Juan Fernandez, or Mas-a-tierra, as the Chilians call it, has been inhabited by a few Chilian farmers, who raise, with very little labor, food enough to live on. They also catch fish, which they send to the mainland, and at certain seasons of the year they kill large quantities of seals, which frequent a little rocky island half a mile from Juan Fernandez. At the present time the island is governed by a Mr. Rhode, who rents it from the Chilian government, and proposes to raise quantities of cattle.

In 1868 the British man-of-war *Topaze* touched at Juan Fernandez, and her officers erected an iron tablet in honor of Selkirk. It bears the following inscription:

In memory of Alexander Selkirk,
Mariner,
a native of Largo, in the County of Fife, Scotland,
who lived on this island in complete solitude for four years and four months.
He was landed from the *Cinque Ports* galley, 96 tons, 16 guns, A.D. 1704, and was taken off in the *Duke* privateer, 12th February, 1709.
He died Lieutenant of H. M. S. *Weymouth*, A.D. 1723, aged 47 years.
This tablet is erected near Selkirk's Look-out by Commodore Powell and the officers of H. M. S. *Topaze*, A.D. 1868.

As there is excellent water at Juan Fernandez, vessels occasionally touch there to fill their casks, but it has no regular communication with the rest of the world.

Of course Juan Fernandez will always continue to be called Robinson Crusoe's island, though it is certain that Crusoe was never with-

in three or four thousand miles of it. As for the unbelieving people who pretend that Robinson Crusoe never lived, nobody should listen to them for a moment. There never was anybody more thoroughly real than Robinson Crusoe. Selkirk was not half so real; and in comparison with the shipwrecked mariner of Hull, Julius Cæsar was grossly improbable. Crusoe's island undoubtedly exists somewhere "near the mouth of the great river Orinoco."

PHILEMON'S CIRCUS.

BY MARY DENSEL.

"'—TOGETHER with fifes and drums. The gigantic procession, headed by the stupendous gilded chariot, will move through the town at seven o'clock A. M. precisely,'" ended Tom Tadgers, quoting from the handbills.

"Through *this* town?" asked Philemon, much excited.

Tom Tadgers gave him a withering glance.

"Do you suppose that N. Tirrum and B. Phoolum's 'Great Moral Show,' with 'six tigers, five elephants, a giraffe, hippopotamus, kangaroo, in-nu-mer-a-ble monkeys, wild men of Borneo, living skeleton, educated bull, and a ship of the desert,' would come to a mean little village like this? Skowhegan's the town it's going to move through, and it will pass Tucker's Corner at five o'clock to-morrow morning. So Silas Elder says to me, 'You get into the back of my milk cart, Tadgers'" (Tommy felt deeply the dignity of being "Tadgers"), "'and I'll give you a lift as far as the Corner, Tadgers. Then you can follow the procession, and go to the show at Skowhegan, Tadgers,' says he. Now, Philemon, how would you like to come along too?"

"And Romeo Augustus with me?" questioned Philemon, eagerly.

Tadgers shook his head.

"Come by yourself, or not at all," said he, firmly. "What's more, you must be on hand by four o'clock to-morrow morning."

How could Philemon wake at that early hour? It was his wont not only to "sleep like a top all night," but also to "sleep at noon."

Tom, however, agreed to manage that. So when Philemon went to bed at night, it was with one end of a piece of stout twine tied to his ankle, while the other end hung out at the open window.

Neither Elias, John, nor Romeo Augustus, who shared his chamber, spied the cord. Philemon waited till they were sound asleep before he arranged it.

The sun had not begun to show his face above the horizon when there came a brisk twitch on the twine. Philemon was broad awake in a twinkling, and rolled out of bed to dance a one-footed ballet, by reason of a series of jerks given to the cord by the sprightly Thomas below. It was only after Philemon had knocked over two chairs and a cricket that he managed to hop wildly to the window, and to call out in a hoarse whisper, "You'll wake the whole house if you don't quit," that Tom condescended to desist; and a few minutes later the two comrades were climbing into the back of Silas Elder's cart, all ready to start for "The Great Moral Show."

The cart was not spacious, and its springs were few and far between, as Philemon's bones bore witness. He began, all at once, to wonder if it might not have been *polite* to have mentioned to his parents that he intended to be absent the greater part of the day.

He recollected, with a pang, that it was his mother's custom to be anxious when one of her six precious boys was long out of her sight.

Suddenly, "Look there! there! there!" shouted Tom Tadgers.

Sure enough; there—there—there, in the distance, was a caravan moving slowly toward Tucker's Corner. It must be—it is N. Tirrum and B. Phoolum's show.

Nearer and nearer it came. Tom and Philemon jumped out of the cart, that they might be ready to join the "gigantic procession."

And now they were in its midst. To be sure, the glories of "the stupendous gilded chariot" were shrouded by brown canvas; the monkeys, tigers, and the hippopotamus were shut up in their cages; neither were the giraffe and kangaroo visible as yet. But here were the elephants marching majestically along; here was the educated bull, with a ring through his nose; and so near that Philemon could have touched him was the living skeleton in all his enchanting beauties.

Philemon actually danced up and down in ecstasy. The man who seemed to have charge of affairs caught sight of his beaming face, and broke into a good-natured laugh.

"Hallo, my little chap, would ye like a ride to-day?" said he, and before Philemon knew what was going to happen, he found himself astride of the back of a huge gray elephant.

Was there ever such a morning! It did seem as if the sun fairly outdid itself, such billows of light did it pour forth. The rollicking breeze danced round and about the caravan, and would by no means be left behind. The corn in Farmer Tucker's field waved its silken tassels in a delighted frenzy. All the golden-rod and asters were alert to see the sight.

At last the coverings were taken from the gilded chariot; fifes and drums struck up a tune. All the Skowhegan boys came flocking out of town to meet the caravan. Some one put an American flag into Philemon's hand. What an honor! The lad's heart swelled with pride. He held his head high. He was actually a part of "The Great Moral Show."

So absorbed was he in his new dignity that he did not notice that they were nearing the bridge which stretched across the Kennebec River, just outside of Skowhegan. Neither did he observe that the elephants were separating themselves from the rest of the train, until, just as the gilded chariot passed on the bridge, the animal Philemon rode broke into a trot—and what a trot!—starting down the river-bank, followed by the other four elephants. Philemon clung with both his hands.

Into the stream plunged the beasts, wading clumsily along until the water was breast-high, when they began to swim. Philemon stuck like a little burr to the gray back.

At last the elephants gained a foot-hold once more. But they were by no means ready to give up the cool water. They snorted; they tramped; they plunged; they sucked the water into their trunks, and poured it out again in great streams. Never had Philemon had such a shower-bath. One of the elephants lay down and rolled playfully over and over. Philemon was frightened nearly out of his wits: suppose his elephant should do likewise! Instead of that, he rose to within a few feet of the bank, and, having first treated his rider to a few extra bucketfuls of water, twisted his trunk round one of Philemon's legs.

There was a jerk, a dizzy whirl through the air, and our friend lay "high," but by no means "dry," upon the earth.

The crowd gathered round. He heard Tom Tadgers's voice in a terrified wail: "He's dead! he's dead!"

Then some one else spoke: "Bring water."

That was adding insult to injury. Up as straight as a ramrod sat the afflicted Philemon. "If anybody dares to put another drop of water on me, I'll—I'll—I'll go *home!*" gasped he.

There was a burst of merriment at that tremendous threat, and the young hero was lifted on some one's shoulder, and borne along in triumph. Strange to say, he was not even bruised, and he almost forgot his mishap, when, an hour later, he was permitted to help in spreading tan around the open space where Madame Lucretia Almasilda was to ride the famous horse Pegasus, and perform her "world-renowned feat" of jumping through seventeen hoops and a "barrel wrapped in flames."

That noon Philemon was actually invited to dine with Mons. Duval, the "incomparable gymnast," and a host of other circus celebrities.

"You're a plucky little fellow, and fit to feed along o' us," said Mons. Duval, with a grin.

Philemon was much pleased by the compliment, which, though perchance not expressed in the most refined language, showed a kindly appreciation of his merits.

He entirely forgot Tom Tadgers, who, not having had the luck to meet with an accident, was left outside. In fact, Philemon saw Tom no more that day, and the latter, at the close of the afternoon, met Silas Elder once more, and rode peacefully home, where he went to bed, quite omitting to say a word to anybody about Philemon.

In the mean time that worthy ate his dinner with his new companions. He wondered vaguely what his mother would say if she knew where he was.

He might have wondered more had not one of the men poured a yellow liquid into a cup, and handed it to him.

"Drink this, my man," said he.

Then everybody laughed. The liquid was sweet. Philemon liked it. He drank every drop. Soon he began to feel very bright and merry; and when a new song was sung he joined lustily in the chorus. He had a clear, high, ringing voice.

"Bless us!" exclaimed Mons. Duval. "Tip us a song yourself, boy."

Not a whit abashed, Philemon began to sing.

"Ha! ha! ha!" laughed Mons. Duval. "Tim Loker, what used to do our first tribble, was took sick this morning. What d'ye say, youngster, to bring blacked up, and singing this evening to the circus along o' our minstrel troupe?"

That yellow liquid was in Philemon's blood. His eyes sparkled, his cheeks flamed.

"Yes, I'll sing," cried he, boisterously, "and I'll go to the ends of the earth with you."

After dinner—it was strange—he felt very drowsy. Mons. Duval, for some reason, was extremely amused, and considered it a great joke.

"You lay down here and take a nap," he said, and actually took off his own coat to put over Philemon. The boy slept all that afternoon; indeed, he never opened his eyes till it was nearly time for the evening's entertainment to begin.

The big dingy tent where the performance was to come off was lighted. Philemon followed Mons. Duval into the small tent behind the large one, where those who were to take part awaited their several turns.

He stood meekly silent, while his face, hands, and neck were daubed with some sticky black stuff; and then, as bidden, he arrayed himself in some extraordinary baggy yellow clothes, and a big paper collar.

He caught sight of himself in a bit of glass. He looked like a little black imp. What would his mother say to see him! A feeling of intense shame surged over him. He crouched down in a corner, wishing he could hide himself from the eyes of all men.

Philemon looked around him, and there, close by, was a boy about his own age, with large brown eyes and white cheeks. He was dressed in flesh-colored tights.

"Who are you?" asked Philemon, as the boy stared and half smiled.

"I'm the 'Phenomenal Trapeist,'" announced the lad, solemnly.

"What do you do?"

"Oh, I go up on the trapeze, at the tiptop of the tent, and my father and uncle—they're the crack gymnasts, you know—they toss me about as if I was a ball. By-and-by I'm going to learn to hang by my toes, and take a flying leap, sixty feet, to the slack-rope near the ground."

"Aren't you frightened?" exclaimed Philemon.

"Ye—" began the boy, and then quickly changed his tone, as a man clad in scarlet and gilt came near. "No, I ain't scared. I like it."

"Of course he ain't scared," said the man, roughly. "Come, Bill, it's time for you and me to show ourselves."

They were joined by Bill's uncle, and the three passed into the outer tent. Philemon put his eye against a hole in the canvas to watch them.

Like monkeys the two men and the child swung themselves aloft, and reached the tent roof. Here they twisted, they turned, they made fearful leaps from one trapeze to another, until Philemon trembled to see them. At last both men hung by their knees, head downward, and Bill crept carefully to the end of a long rope, gave a spring, and caught his father's hands. There was an awful pause: then small Bill was sent spinning through the air, sixty-five feet from the ground, to be caught by his uncle, tossed back to his father, now seized by an arm, now by a leg, now almost missed, now twirled round and round like a ball. Philemon caught his breath, and stretched out his hand in an agony of fear. His hand touched another, which was as cold as ice. Glancing up, he found Madame Lucetta Almazida close by, her eye glued to another hole in the canvas, her breath coming short and thick, her face livid and drawn. Not knowing what she did, she clutched Philemon's hand, and he heard her mutter,

"My baby! my baby!"

"Bill" was her own "Phenomenal Trapeist," and under Madame Lucetta Almazida's shabby bodice a mother's heart beat wildly.

Philemon's heart beat too. What if he had been a "Bill," and his own sweet mother had worn short skirts and ridden Pegasus? Horrible!

Poor Lucetta Almazida! Poor little Bill!

But there was time to think of them no more. The band of negro minstrels was ready to sing. A clown seized Philemon's hand, and hurried him into the ring. There was a shout from the spectators. Some one gave him a nudge.

"Pipe up, boy. We're ready for 'Massa's in the cold, cold ground.'"

Philemon opened his mouth, but no sound came. The eyes on every side burned into him. His one desire was to rush away from these blackened men, from the choking odor of tan and kerosene, from the disgrace of standing there, like a little black fiend, to be hooted at and expected to make fun for the crowd. His brain reeled. With a cry he broke from a detaining hand, and ran headlong across the arena, his yellow coat tails flapping about his heels.

Through the back tent he sped, past Madame Lucetta Almazida, who was holding the "Phenomenal Trapeist" in her arms, past Mons. Duval, out into the night. Home—home—home—that was the place toward which, if he had had wings, he would have flown. Being neither an angel nor even a bird, only a little wretched boy, all he could do was to stumble along the dark road. Eight miles away was his home. On and on he went, and at last his weary feet began to flag.

It seemed as if the chirping crickets were hissing at him. The frogs in the ponds croaked disapprovingly. Even the stars winked reproachfully.

He was growing exhausted. He sank down by a fence, and his eyelids closed heavily.

The sun was high when he awoke, and then a colder, hungrier boy you never saw. Six miles from home was he. There was nothing for it but to plod along, for there were no houses on that road. One mile, two miles, he walked. He picked some apples by the road-side, but they were sour and hard. Sometimes he tried to run, but had to give that up.

At five o'clock that afternoon the cook at a certain

farm-house was frying doughnuts in the back kitchen. She was looking very sober, and near her sat a very sober boy, who every now and then drew his hand across his eyes. At last he spoke.

"Cerinthy," said he, "do you cal'late they'll ever find him?"

Cerinthy put another doughnut into the expostulating fat. "Romeo Augustus," said she, "it's my opinion that maybe they may and maybe they mayn't; an' like as not if they do, it 'll only be his body, and— Oh!"

Cerinthy gave a great scream, and dropped her panful of doughnuts on the floor, for on the threshold of the "pump-room" stood a boy as black as the ace of spades, clad in startling yellow clothes, his neck ornamented with a huge paper collar.

This image opened his mouth and spake. "Where's my mother? Give me a doughnut."

Cerinthy shrieked louder than ever. An opposite door opened, and out rushed a lady whose eyes were swollen with crying.

"Mother!" called out the black boy, as he flew into her open arms.

"Philemon! mother's own little boy!" she sobbed; while Romeo Augustus performed a war-dance about the two.

I think Philemon's father was so relieved when he beheld his fifth-born, that he would have *whipped* him soundly. But his mother would by no means allow that. She gave him preserved peach and cream toast instead.

"For you'll never do such a thing again, will you?" demanded she, tenderly.

Philemon gazed lovingly at her, with a mouth full of toast. "*Catch me*," said he.

JAPANESE CHILDREN.

HERE we have a genuine picture of Japanese *kodomo*. They are in every-day dress, with hair and shoes just as one sees them in their own village. There is the baby carried pickapack, and laid on the back of its sister like a slice of meat on a sandwich. Baby's head is shaved as smooth as one's palm, and kept so until it is two years old. Then the next style—a little fringe of hair above the ears and one near the neck—will be proper. The next step will be a tiny top-knot and a circle, in addition to the ear-locks.

All these children live on boiled rice, and they are as round and chubby and rosy-cheeked as it is possible to be without bursting. See their nice loose clothes, with neither a pin to stick nor a button to fly off! They do not wear socks nor stockings, for it is not very cold in Japan. One little tot has on a pair of straw sandals, and the girl and old man wear clogs, held on by a strap passing between the "thumb of the foot," as the Japs call the big toe, and its next-door neighbor.

It would do American boys good, and set them a good example, to notice how kind to animals Japanese children are. There is old daddy telling his children to treat their pet kindly, and doggy knows it will be good for him to have such playmates. See his little straw kennel made like a tent, with a crock of water in it. I'll wager that the children will feed the little *inu* with tidbits from their own chopsticks.

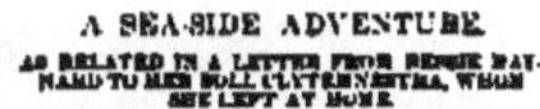

A SEA-SIDE ADVENTURE.

AS RELATED IN A LETTER FROM BESSIE MAYNARD TO HER DOLL CLYTEMNESTRA, WHOM SHE LEFT AT HOME.

Old Orchard Beach, *July*, 1880.

MY DEAREST CLYTEMNESTRA,—Do you miss me? and are you wondering why I do not write? Well, my dear, writing is an impossibility when one is at the sea-shore. You never knew such times as we are having all day long. I must tell you, first of all, of an adventure that befell me yesterday—not *me* exactly, either; it *most* befell Lucille, the beautiful Paris doll that Fanny Bell was so proud of; and well she might be, for a handsomer creature never walked. You remember her, of course; the lovely Mademoiselle Lucille, as she was called, that being the French for Miss, for it would never do to call her plain Lucille, such a fine young lady as she was, just from France, with all the airs and graces that belong to Paris, the politest city in the world. It's no great wonder she was proud—Lucille, I mean—for I'm afraid most of us would be if we looked like her. Such hair as she had, all natural curls down below her waist; and such a *elegant* wardrobe, or "trosso," as Fanny calls it. Perhaps I haven't spelled trosso right, but please excuse it; indeed, you wouldn't know whether it was right or wrong, you are such a poor little ignorant thing. I'm ashamed of myself for neglecting your education as I have done, when I see the dolls here, and realize how much they know. Just as soon as I get home, we'll begin with regular lessons every day. It isn't *your* fault, you sweet lamb, that you don't know anything. *I* am the only one to blame, and I'll try to make up for lost time when I come home.

But, dear me, how I do run on, without telling you a word of the adventure. The "sad sea waves" put all sorts of ideas into my mind, and I get terribly confused. I heard a lady sing last night about the "sad sea waves," and I think it sounds prettier than "the ocean"—don't you? Well, to begin at the beginning: Yesterday morning Fanny Bell, Dora Mason, and I went down to the beach as usual, Mademoiselle Lucille walking along by her mamma, just like a real live beautiful child. We scooped holes in the warm sand, and made caves, and then we built the Pyramids. *They* are in Egypt, you know, curiosities that people go to see; but we make them of sand, so they look just exactly like the pictures, "Sfinks" and all. Perhaps you don't know what the "Sfinks" is, but I will tell you some day, when I begin your education, my poor Clytemnestra.

Well, at last we wanted to go round the point to pick some wild morning-glories, so we sat Lucille up on a kind of throne behind the Pyramids, and left her. We were only gone a little bit of a while, but what do you think? when we came back the tide was in, and the sad sea waves had washed away Pyramids, Sfinks, Lucille, and all! Oh, the despair we were in! Poor Fanny jumped right up and down, and screeched, and then sinking down upon the sand, as the story-books say, "she buried her face in her hands, and wept as if her heart would break." All at once I saw something bobbing around, and if there wasn't Lucille about four feet from the shore, fastened to a cork by the flounce of her pink satin dress! Fanny shrieked aloud, but Dora and I seized a pole, and after working a long, long time, we managed to fish her out of the water. Here is a picture that I have drawn to show you how we looked in our awful excitement.

Lucille is frightfully pale to-day, and her curls are gone forever. She is a bald-headed "faded beauty," as a gentleman truly said when he saw her this morning. When I look at her, and remember how fine she used to think herself, I can't help saying, "Well, my dear, 'pride must have a fall.'" I pity her, though, from the very bottom of my heart, for it must be dreadful to be so changed, and all of a sudden, too. I guess we sha'n't have to be so particular any more about calling her "Mademoiselle."

I can not be thankful enough that I left you at home, my sweet Clytie. The sea-shore is a lovely place for children who know how to take care of themselves, but 'tis dreadful dangerous for *dolls*.

And now good-night, my pet.

Your loving mamma, Bessie Maynard.

P.S.—Dora has just come in to say that Fanny has changed Mademoiselle's name, and hereafter she is to be called "*Jane*." Poor thing!

[illegible]

English sparrows build in little houses, if kind hands provide them, otherwise they seek out any cozy corner wherever there is a shelf upon which to lodge their nest. They never build in trees. You will find an article about them in YOUNG PEOPLE No. 14.

[illegible]

Is this mixture intended as a filling for pie-crust, or an apple jam? In writing out recipes, our young housekeepers must be very careful to omit nothing, and to explain all details, as a slight error may ruin a delicious dish.

[illegible]

I would like to exchange postage stamps with [illegible] if he will send me his full name, and a list of what stamps he would like. I live at No. [illegible] West [illegible] Street, New York city, but during the summer my address is,

[illegible]

Old [illegible] House, Newport, Rhode Island.

[illegible]

H. [illegible].—The engraving of "A Little [illegible]," in YOUNG PEOPLE No. 35, is after an oil-painting by Adrien Marie, a French artist.

I. O.—There is a very good swimming school at the Battery, New York city.

[illegible]

Correspondents will also be interested to know that the ashes of the prison-ship martyrs now rest in a handsome tomb built in the hill-side of Fort Greene, Brooklyn—a pretty grassy spot, now known as Washington Park. As these brave men died, they were taken ashore and buried in the swampy land forming the shore of Wallabout Bay. There they lay until [illegible], when they were removed to a vault near the Brooklyn Navy-yard. In time this vault became very much dilapidated, and was almost [illegible] ... removed in the spring of 1873.

[illegible]

W. D. F.—In the outer wall of St. Mark's Church, Stuyvesant Street, New York, is the original tablet from the tomb of Peter Stuyvesant, [illegible]

[illegible]

PUZZLES FROM YOUNG CONTRIBUTORS.

No. 1.

[illegible]

No. 2.

[illegible]

No. 3.

[illegible]

No. 4.

[illegible]

No. 5.

[illegible]

No. 6.

[illegible]

ANSWERS TO PUZZLES IN No. 24.

[illegible]

OUR LOUIE.

BY M. D. BRINE.

WHAT in the world is our Louie about?
Studying her lessons, I haven't a doubt;
Filling her brain with useful lore,
Thinking and reading o'er and o'er
Ancient history—many a story
Of battle and conquest and warlike glory;
Or maybe 'tis only a difficult rule
Which has followed our student home from school.

Wise little maiden with golden hair,
Brown-eyed, winsome, loving, and fair!
Not even the sunbeams so merry and gay
Can tempt the young scholar from lessons away.
Not even our presence she seems to heed—
An industrious girl is our Louie, indeed.
I'll venture to say such a wonderful lass
Is sure to be always "up head" in her class.

I'll frankly acknowledge I'd like to see
What a lesson so truly absorbing can be;
Over her shoulder I'll take one look,
And—dear me, children, what kind of a book
Do you think she is studying? History?—no.
Much as it grieves me to tell you so,
Little cares she for its ancient glory,
For Louie is deep in—a *fairy story!*

SOLUTION OF THE RUNNING-LINE PUZZLE IN *YOUNG PEOPLE* No. 8.

The Catacombs of Paris.—The vast catacombs by which a large portion of the city of Paris is undermined were only known by popular tradition until the year 1774, when some alarming accidents aroused the attention of the government. The old quarries were then surveyed, and plans of them taken, and the result was the frightful discovery that the churches, palaces, and most of the southern parts of Paris were undermined, and in great danger of sinking into the pit below them. A special commission was appointed, and on the very day it met a house in one of the streets sank ninety-one feet below the level of its court-yard. The pillars which had been left by the quarry-men, in their blind operations, without any regularity, were in many places too weak for the enormous weight above, and in most places had themselves been undermined, or perhaps originally stood upon ground which had previously been hollowed. The aqueduct of Arcueil passed over this treacherous ground; it had already suffered some shocks, and if the quarries had continued to be neglected, an accident must sooner or later have happened to this water-course, which would have cut off its supply from the fountains of Paris, and have filled the excavations with water. Repairs were forthwith commenced, and promptly completed, and a portion of the old quarries was devoted to receive the bones of the dead. This took place in April, 1786; the remains of the dead were removed at night in funeral cars, covered with a pall, and followed by priests chanting the service for the dead. When they reached the catacombs, the bones were shot down a well, and the rattling and echoing which they made in their fall were as impressive as any sound ever heard by human ears. Thus the limestone quarries that had supplied the materials for building the superb monuments, palaces, and houses of Paris became huge charnel-houses, which they now remain! Calculations differ as to the number of bones collected in the catacombs, but it is certain that they contain the remains of at least *three millions* of human beings!

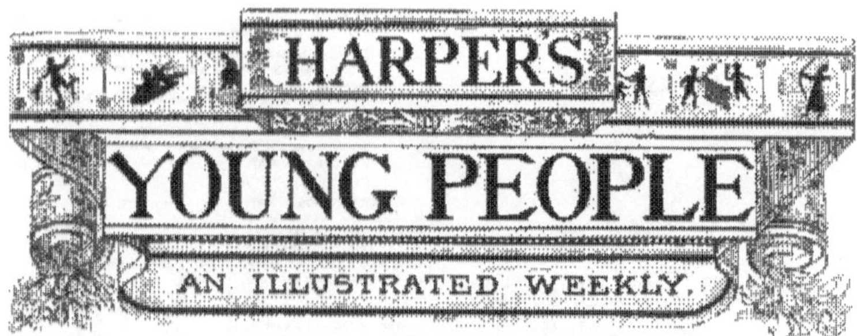

Vol. I.—No. 38. | Published by HARPER & BROTHERS, New York. | Price Four Cents.

Tuesday, July 20, 1880. | $1.50 per Year, in Advance.

THE BIGGEST BLACKBERRY PICKER.

BY W. O. STODDARD.

DOT CALLIPER had come out on the mountain-side, with all the rest of them, after blackberries.

She had picked her little pail full industriously, but she was too fat and too small to climb any further among the rocks and stumps and bushes, so they had left her there, in the shade of the great chestnut-tree, to watch the milk-pails.

Not that there was any milk in them just now, for all three of them were more than half full of great, plump, overgrown berries—blackberries, and the best and largest anybody had ever seen among those mountains. Such a season for berries!

There had been a great fire three years before, and it had burned the woods away, and nobody knew where the blackberry bushes had come from, but they had moved right in as if the country belonged to them, and they had climbed all over everything.

Dot sat by her pails and looked around, and she was half sorry all the berries near her had been picked and put into the big pails.

All the rest, even Johnny Coyne and Pen Burke, had little pails or else baskets, except Dot's big brother Bob, and he was now away up the mountain-side with a pail that would hold almost as much as a milk-pail.

Dot knew where the others were picking, for they didn't keep still a minute. Jessie Mack and Betsy were down

among the rocks at her right, and Molly Calliper was with the boys up there on the left.

Dot was not in the least afraid at being alone, but she did wish she was hungry enough to eat some more berries.

She thought of it, and she tried to, but it was of no use, for all the while she had been picking she had put one berry in her rosy little mouth every time she had put another in her little tin pail.

"Oh, so much berries!" sighed Dot. "They're all our berries, too."

Yes, and Mrs. Calliper meant to dry them all and sell them, and buy some things for Dot and Molly and the baby. Bob had said that he meant to sell his own berries and buy him a new gun.

Want of appetite was the trouble with Dot; but there was somebody else in there, among the thickest of those bushes, picking, picking, picking, and eating every one he picked, and that fellow had never seen an hour in all his life when he could not have eaten some more blackberries.

An enormous fellow he was, and fatter for his size than Dot Calliper was for hers. He did not look at all ill-natured, and there was even a sort of funny twinkle in his little black eyes, as he pulled the branches full of fruit to his mouth with his great clumsy-looking paws.

They were not half so clumsy as they looked, and they were armed with long, sharp, cruel claws that were bent in a curve, like the teeth of the big shell comb Dot's mother bought of the peddler for her back hair. Then, too, when his mouth opened wide, as it did when he made one of his lazy, sleepy yawns, the teeth he showed were something dreadful to look at. Teeth of that size were never needed for eating such things as blackberries. They looked a great deal more as if they were meant for eating Dot Callipers.

He was evidently very fond of berries, and did not seem to have any doubt but what they all belonged to him. It was just as if he had offered a prize that summer for the bush that would bear the most blackberries, and was now going around among them to see which had won it. Every bush he came to just held out its branches for him to look at; but if Dot had been watching him, she would have seen at once that the fat old rascal never seemed to count the berries at all, but just gathered and swallowed them. How would he be able to tell, when he was done, which bush had done the best for him?

But Dot was not watching him. She had not even seen him yet, and she did not know he was there till he made a great crash among the bushes, when his foot slipped, and he rolled down through half a dozen of them.

"Bob," exclaimed Dot, "is that you? Did you tumble down?"

There was no answer, and she asked again, "Bob, did you 'pill your berries?"

Then she thought she heard something like a grunt, such as the pigs made when they were rooting in the garden, and she and Bob went to drive them out, and she said, "Oh, the pigs are come! they'll pick all our berries."

Then there came more rustling and crashing among the bushes, and then Dot jumped up and got behind the three big pails, for it was not anything like a pig that came out and began to walk toward the chestnut-tree.

"Oh dear me!" whispered the frightened Dot. "I daren't 'peak to him."

Neither did he say a word to her. He did not even tell her his name was Bruin, and that he was fond of blackberries, but he walked straight forward, and his little black eyes were twinkling more brightly than ever.

As fast as he came forward Dot stepped back, till she stood right against the tree, and then she slipped around behind it, and began to feel that she was perfectly safe.

Bruin looked into one pail after another, as if he saw at once that all the bushes were beaten, and was trying to decide to which of the pails the prize belonged.

"Bob! Bob!" screamed Dot, at the top of her little voice, "there's a bear come, and he's 'tealing our berries."

He was eating them up very fast, that was a fact—for all the world as if they had been picked for his benefit.

Perhaps he would have liked them better with plenty of milk and sugar, but he did not ask Dot for anything of the kind. He just sat down on the grass, and took a big pail up in his lap with his clumsy fore-paws, and then lifted it high enough to bury half his head in it.

Dot saw that he knew exactly how to eat blackberries out of a milk-pail, and she felt sure they would not last him long.

"Molly! Jessie! Betsy! Johnny Coyne! **Pen Burke!** the bear's 'tealing the berries!"

The other children heard her, and they all began to scream together: "Bear! bear! He's eating up Dot and the berries!"

Bruin had not so much as said a cross word to Dot, although it was true that he had not thanked her for the berries; but he was just lifting the second pail to his mouth, when Dot's big brother Bob heard the screaming, and came hurrying down the hill toward the chestnut-tree.

"Der's one pail left, but he's eat up the odders," said Dot, excitedly, as Bob sprang out of the nearest bushes; but to her surprise he did not pay the least attention to the berries or the bear. He just caught up Dot herself in his strong arms, and ran away with her.

"Bob, did you lose your pail?"

"Boys! Betsy! Molly!" shouted Bob, "run! run!"

They did run; but they were not like Bob, for every one of them kept tight hold of their berry pails. They could not run fast among so many rocks and bushes, but they could scramble, and they had not gone far before they heard a great rough voice near them shouting,

"Hullo! What's arter ye all? Did ye git skeered?"

"Joe—Joe Mix!" exclaimed Bob. "The biggest bear you ever saw in your life. Ain't I glad you've got your gun along!"

"Bar! Whar?"

"Up among the blackberries."

"And I haven't a bullet nor a buckshot; nothin' but small shot. Tell ye what, Bob. Drop that little one. The bar won't foller ye. You just run for the house and git yer gun, and tell yer father, and have him come along, and bring some buckshot and slugs for me. Bars is fat now, and we'll just gather this one."

Bob was putting Dot on the ground, when she said to him,

"Make the bear give back the pails, too."

While Bob was gone, Joe Mix made Dot **tell him all** about it, but he said,

"I guess I won't go ahead and scare him off; **he'll stay** and pick around."

"He'll pick all our berries."

"Now, Dot, there's berries enough. We'll **pick him.** It won't do to have him come and pick some **of your fa**ther's pigs."

"Would he pick me?"

"Not unless the berries were all gone, and the nuts too, and the pigs. But I'm glad Bob got away with ye. He might have mistaken ye for a berry."

"I wasn't in a pail; I got behind a tree."

Dot had been pretty well scared, but Bruin had behaved very well, except about the berries, and she was not half so much frightened as the older children were. Molly and Betsy came and hugged her ever so hard, and Johnny Coyne exclaimed,

"Tell you what, Joe, if I'd had a gun!"

"Oh, don't I wish I'd had a gun!" echoed Pen Burke; and then they both said they'd bring guns with them the next time they came after berries.

Bob Calliper must have been a good runner, and his father too, for it was wonderful how soon the noise they made among the bushes below told that they were coming.

That was not all, either, for a little distance behind them was Mrs. Calliper herself, all out of breath, with the baby in her arms, and she was not nearly so careful as usual in handing the baby to Molly, she was in such a hurry to hug Dot, and kiss her, and exclaim, "Dear! dear! dear! My pet! Bears! Oh, Dot, bears! Berries! My precious!"

"The bear dot the berries, mamma."

"Berries indeed! Who cares for berries!"

Joe Mix asked, the moment Bob came near enough, "Any slugs for me?"

And Bob held out to him a handful of buckshot and rifle-bullets.

Joe had been drawing the old charge out of his gun, and loading it again with more powder, and now he poured in half a dozen big buckshot and three bullets.

"They'll do for slugs. Got yer rifle, Mr. Calliper?"

"No, Bob's brought that. I've got my double-barrelled deer gun, and I've stuck an awful charge into it."

"That 'll do."

"Mary Jane," said her husband to Mrs. Calliper, "you and the children go on down the hill. Pen, you and Johnny see if you can't haul out that old stone-boat. It lies up this way, close to the foot of the mountain. We'll need it to get the bear home."

"Oh, mamma," exclaimed Dot, "is the bear comin' to our house?"

She knew very well that if he did, he would eat up all the berries that were spread out on the roof to dry, but her father and Joe Mix and Bob hurried away in the direction of the big chestnut.

Mrs. Calliper would not let any of the children go, but she put down Dot to carry the baby.

Pen and Johnny were a little sulky at not being allowed to help hunt the bear, but they were glad to have something to do, and went on after the stone-boat.

That was a kind of flat sled, made of a thick piece of plank, and used to haul stones on, and they found it just where Mr. Calliper said.

He and Joe and Bob went on up the mountain-side more and more carefully, but they had not far to go, and [illegible]

mopped his face with his handkerchief, and Pen and Johnny took a useless pull at the stone-boat with the bear on it, and Mrs. Calliper stood behind her husband and hugged the baby.

They had put the three pails of berries down only a few feet from the nose of the bear as he lay on the stone-boat, and Jessie Mack and Betsy went and stood behind the pails, where they were safe, but Dot wasn't a bit afraid of that bear now. She toddled close up to her father, as he stood at the head of the stone-boat, and looked down on the great furry berry picker.

"He didn't pick me, papa."

"No, Dot," remarked Joe Mix; "he couldn't sit up now ef you brung him all the berries you've got."

"He's a poor, dead, dead bear," said Dot, pityingly. "Poor bear!"

"Wa'al, no, Dot," said Joe, "he's the fattest bar I ever hauled on. It's all along of thar being sech heaps and heaps of berries this year."

IN THE SWING.

BY M. M.

Oh, swing me high, and swing me low,
  Under the linden-tree,
Whose fragrant blossoms, like a shower,
  Fall down and cover me.

The sunshine flickers through the leaves
  As to and fro I swing;
Gay butterflies go flashing by;
  Birds in the tree-top sing.

The brook tells stories to the flowers
  The livelong summer day;
And everywhere the earth is bright,
  And all the world is gay.

So swing me high, and swing me low,
  Under the linden-tree,
And let the blossoms, like a shower,
  Fall down and cover me.

PEARLS—REAL AND IMITATION.

FROM ADVANCE SHEETS OF "THE BOY TRAVELLERS IN THE FAR EAST." PART SECOND. BY THOMAS W. KNOX.

carried there, the story does not have much foundation to rest upon."

"If the pearl is so valuable, and so difficult to get, I should think there would be men who would try to imitate it," Frank remarked.

"You are quite right," was the reply; "and men have tried a great many times to make false pearls."

"Have they succeeded?"

"Partially, but not altogether. No counterfeit pearls have yet been made that could pass all the tests of the genuine, but their lustre is quite equal sometimes to the best pearls of Ceylon, and they can be made to deceive anybody but an expert."

"How do they make them?"

"The best of the false pearls," said the Captain, "are made by what is known as Jaquin's process. M. Jaquin was a manufacturer of beads in France, and he spent a great deal of time and money in trying to make his beads better than any other man's. One day he was walking in his garden, and observed a remarkably silvery lustre on some water in a basin. It instantly occurred to him that if he could put that lustre on his beads, he would have something decidedly new.

"So he called his old servant, and asked what had been in the water. She answered that it was nothing but some little fish called *ablettes*, that had been crushed in the basin, and she had neglected to throw the water out.

"M. Jaquin was very glad, for once, that she had neglected her duty. He began experimenting with the scales of the ablette, or bleak—a little fish about the size of a sardine, and very abundant in certain parts of Europe. After several trials he adopted the plan of washing the scales several times in water, and saving the sediment that gathered at the bottom of the basin. This was about the consistency of oil, and had the lustre he desired. Next, he blew some beads of very thin glass, and after coating the inside of a bead with this substance, he filled it up with wax, so as to give it solidity. Thus the fish scales gave the lustre, the glass gave the polish and brilliancy that we find on the genuine pearl, and the wax furnished a solid backing to the thin glass. It is fortunate that the bleak is very abundant, or he would run the risk of extermination."

"Is the manufacture of false pearls so great as that?" Fred inquired.

"It is pretty extensive," was the Captain's response, "but not enormously so. The fact is, it requires more than a thousand of these little fish to make an ounce of the 'essence d'Orient,' as the French call it, or essence of pearl. Other substances have been tried, in the hope of obtaining the same result for a smaller outlay, but none of them have been entirely successful.

"In China and Japan the natives have long followed the practice of putting small beads of porcelain inside the oyster, and then returning him to the water, where he is left undisturbed for three or four years. At the end of that time he is taken up and opened, and the beads are found to be coated with the pearly substance. They also have the trick of putting little images or idols into the oyster, and in course of time these become coated over in the manner I have described."

[Begun in No. 33 of HARPER'S YOUNG PEOPLE, June 15.]

THE MORAL PIRATES.

BY W. L. ALDEN.

CHAPTER VIII.

THE next morning the boys awoke early, having had a thoroughly good night's rest. Tom, whose turn it was to go for milk, found a well-stocked farm-house, where he obtained not only milk, bread, and eggs, but a supply of butter, and a chicken all ready for cooking. After breakfast the boat was put in the water, and, to the delight of all, proved to be almost as tight as she was before running into the rock. A little water came in at first under the edges of the tine, but in a short time the wood swelled, and the leak entirely ceased.

The boat was loaded, and the boys were ready to start soon after six o'clock. There was no wind, but the two long oars, pulled one by Tom and the other by Jim, sent her along at a fine rate. They rowed until ten o'clock, resting occasionally for a few moments, and then, as there were no signs of a breeze, and as it was growing excessively hot, they went ashore, to wait until afternoon before resuming their journey.

The sun became hotter and hotter. The boys tried to fish, but there was no shade near the bank of the river, and it was too hot to stand or sit in the sunshine and wait for fish to bite. They went in swimming, but the sun, beating on their heads, seemed hotter while they were in the water than it did when they were on the land. Jim and Joe tried a game of mumble-to-peg, but they gave it up long before they had reached "ears." It was probably the hottest day of the year; and as it was clearly impossible to row or to do anything else while the heat lasted, the boys brought their blankets from the boat, and going to a grove not far from the shore, lay down and fell asleep.

They were astonished to find, when they awoke, that it was two o'clock. None of them had been accustomed to sleep in the daytime, and they could not understand how it came about that they had all slept for fully two hours. They had yet to learn that one of the results of "camping out," or living in the open air, is an ability to sleep at almost any time. All animals and wild creatures, whether they are beasts or savages, have this happy faculty of sleeping in the daytime. It is one of the habits of our savage ancestors that comes back to us when we abandon civilization, and live as Aryan tribes, from whom we are descended, lived in the far East, before they marched with their wives and children and cattle from India, and made themselves new homes in Europe.

After lunch the boys prepared to start, although there was still no wind; but when they went down to the boat they found that the sun was as hot as ever. So they returned to the shade of the grove, and made up their minds to stay there until the end of the afternoon.

"Harry," said Tom, "we've been on the river three days, and we are only a little way above Hudson. How much longer will it be before we get to Albany?"

"We ought to get there in two days more, even if we have to row all the way," replied Harry.

"And after we get to Albany, what are we to do next?"

"We are going up the Champlain Canal to Fort Edward. There we will have a wagon to carry us and the boat to Warrensburg, on the Schroon River, and will go up the river to Schroon Lake. Uncle John laid out the route for us."

"How many days will it take us to get to the lake?" asked Tom.

Harry thought awhile. "There's two days more on the Hudson, two on the canal, and maybe two on the Schroon River. And then there's a Sunday, which don't count. It 'll be just a week before we get to the lake."

"I've got to be home by two weeks from next Monday," continued Tom, "so I sha'n't have much time on the lake. Can't we get along a little faster? There's a full moon to-night, and suppose we sail all night—or row, if the wind doesn't come up?"

"That's a first-rate idea," exclaimed Harry. "We can take turns sleeping in the bottom of the boat. Why, if the breeze comes up in the night, we might make twenty or thirty miles before morning."

All the boys liked the plan of sailing at night, and they resolved to adopt it. While they were yet discussing it, a light breeze sprang up, from the south as usual, and they hastened to take advantage of it. In the course of an hour more the sun began to lose its power; and when they went ashore at six o'clock to cook their supper, they had sailed about fifteen miles.

As they expected to make so much progress during the night, they were in no hurry about supper, and it was not until after seven o'clock that they again made sail. Harry divided the crew into watches—one consisting of himself and Joe Sharpe, and the other of Tom and Jim. Each watch was to have charge of the boat for three hours, while the other watch slept. At eight o'clock Tom and Jim lay down in the bottom of the boat, and Joe came aft to take Tom's customary place at the sheet. Harry, of course, steered.

All went well. The breeze was light but steady, and Harry kept the boat in the middle of the river to avoid another shipwreck. The watch below did not sleep much, for they had had a long nap at noon, and, besides, the novelty of their position made them wakeful. They had just dropped asleep when eleven o'clock arrived, and they were awakened to relieve the other watch. Tom went sleepily to the helm, and Harry and Joe gladly "turned in," and were soon fast asleep.

Tom always declares that he never closed his eyes while he was at the helm, and Jim also asserts that he was wide-awake during his entire watch, though neither he nor Tom spoke, for fear of waking up the other boys. It was strange that these two wide-awake young Moral Pirates did not notice that a large steamboat—one of the Albany night boats—was in sight, until she was within a mile of them, and it is just possible that, without knowing it, they were a little too drowsy to keep a proper look-out.

JIM AND JOE PLAY MUMBLE-TO-PEG.

As soon as Tom saw the steamboat, he remarked, "Halloo! there's one of the Albany boats," and steered the boat over toward the east shore. The breeze had nearly died away, and the *Whitewing* moved very slowly. The steamboat came rapidly down the river, her paddles throbbing loudly in the night air. Jim began to get a little uneasy, and said, "I hope she won't run us down."

"Oh, there's no danger!" replied Tom; "we shall get out of her way easy enough."

But, to his dismay, the steamboat, instead of keeping in the middle of the river, presently turned toward the east shore, as if she were bent upon running down the *Whitewing*. Tom was now really alarmed; and as he saw that the sail was doing very little good, he hurriedly told Jim to take down the mast and get out the oars as quick as possible. Jim rapidly obeyed the order, dropping the mast on Harry's head, and catching Joe by the nose in his search for the oars. By this time Tom had begun to hail the steamboat at the top of his lungs; but no attention was paid to him by the steamboat men, since the noise of the paddles drowned Tom's voice. Harry and Joe, who were now wide-awake, saw what danger they were in, and they sprang to the oars. The steamboat was frightfully near, and still hugging the shore; but Tom called on the boys to give way with their oars, and steered straight for the shore, knowing that there must be room for the boat between the steamboat and the bank of the river, and fearing that if he steered in the opposite direction the steamboat might change her course and run them down, when they would have little chance of escape by swimming.

It was certainly very doubtful if they could avoid the steamboat, and Tom was well aware of it. He told the other boys that, if they were sure to be run down, they must jump before the steamboat struck them, and dive, so as to escape the paddles. "I'll tell you when to jump, if worst comes to worst," said he; "but don't you look around now, nor do anything but row. Row for your lives, boys."

And the boys did row gallantly. Harry had a pair of sculls, and Jim had a long oar, and between them they made the boat fly through the water. As they neared the shore, it seemed to them that there was not more than three feet of space between the steamboat and the land; and Tom had almost made up his mind that the cruise was coming to a sudden end, when the great steamboat swung her head around, and drew out toward the middle of the river. She did not seem to be more than a rod from them as she changed her course, though in reality she was probably much farther off. At the same moment the *Whitewing* reached what appeared to be the shore, but what was really a long row of piles projecting about a foot above the water. The boys had just ceased rowing, and Tom had given the boat a sheer with the rudder, so as to bring her alongside of the piles, when the steamboat's swell, which the boys, in their excitement over their narrow escape, had totally forgotten, came rushing up, seized the boat, and threw it over the piles into a shallow and muddy lagoon.

It was almost miraculous that the boat was not capsized; but she was actually lifted up and thrown over the piles, without taking more than a few quarts of spray into her. When they saw that they were absolutely safe, the boys began to wonder how in the world they could get the boat back into the river, and Jim proposed to light the lantern and see if anything was missing out of the boat, and if she had been injured.

"Now I see why the steamboat did not notice us," exclaimed Tom.

"Why?" asked all the others together.

"Because," he replied, "we have been such everlasting idiots as to sail at night without showing a light."

[TO BE CONTINUED.]

HOW GIL PLAYED VENTRILOQUIST.

BY JAMES B. MARSHALL.

It was before Dora and Gil Norman came back to the city last fall with their mamma from Farmer Jonathan's, where their papa joined them every Saturday afternoon and staid until Monday morning. If you had asked Dora or Gil what the farmer's full name was, the answer would probably have been, "Why, Farmer Jonathan, of course." Every one called him Farmer Jonathan, but his letters were usually directed, "Mr. Jonathan Wainwright."

One morning he came to the house from his great barn, and told Dora and Gil to go down there and see the largest load of hay that he had ever had on his hay-wagon.

Going to the barn, they saw the huge load of hay waiting for the horses to be put to the wagon tongue, and a long ladder reared against the wagon, by which the farm men had descended from the top of the load after completing it.

"I'm going to the top to see how high it looks," said Gil, beginning to climb.

Dora watched him until he was about half way up the ladder, and then thought that she too would like to see how high it looked. Gil had not thought of Dora following him, nor of the danger she would run, even more than his own small self, climbing to that considerable height, until he had reached the top, and saw that she was half way up. Then he did wisely, encouraging her to continue to climb rather than frightening her by sending her back, and he joyfully caught her in his arms, drawing her to the middle of the broad top of the load of hay. When Farmer Jonathan should come down to the barn to see the horses put to the load, or when Sam should come with the horses, Gil intended to call out, and have Dora carried down the ladder. Gil couldn't see over the sides of the hay, but he knew he would hear Farmer Jonathan or Sam the moment that either of them should come into the barn.

It was so very pleasant to lie half buried on the sweet hay, watching the swallows darting and circling among the barn rafters away above them, that while Gil was wondering why Dora should be taking a nap, his own head nodded in sleep.

When Gil awoke, the whole load was shaking, and he called out, "Are you there, Farmer Jonathan?" Receiving no answer, he rubbed his eyes, and found that he was not in the barn at all. "I've been asleep," said Gil, sitting up, "and Farmer Jonathan is taking us to town on top of his hay, and don't know it. That's jolly. When we get to town, and stop, I can make him hear me, if I can't now, and he will take us down. Then we can see him sell the hay, and afterward, as we ride home, perhaps he will let us take turns driving."

"Oh, won't that be just splendid!" said Dora, having awakened in time to hear nearly all that Gil had been saying to himself.

When they began to pass houses, though they could see nothing of them below the second-story windows, Gil and Dora knew that Farmer Jonathan had reached the town, and was driving along the streets. Directly Dora discovered the steeple of the church that stood just below their aunt Mary's house. Then Gil, looking ahead, saw the very house, and, what was more, Cousin Will eating from a paper of buns while he leaned out of the window to watch the great load of hay coming down the street. Before the wagon came opposite the window it was going on a noisy trot; Will caught sight of Dora and Gil on top, and he was so much surprised that, when Gil made a motion to him to throw them a bun, he threw the whole paperful right on the hay.

While the hay-wagon rolled on, Gil and Dora began eating the buns, and Will disappeared from the window.

He went down stairs four steps at a jump, tumbled into the dining-room, and astonished Aunt Mary, his mother, very much by demanding, "Oh, mamma dear, can I go and take a ride on an awful big load of hay?" Aunt Mary was for some time puzzled to know just what her excited boy meant; but when she did understand, she told him he might go and invite Farmer Jonathan, Gil, and Dora to dinner. The hay-wagon had then disappeared down the street, and Will had to stop every few minutes to inquire which way it had gone, for many persons had noticed how large the load was.

As it was market-day in town, a number of people soon collected around the wagon, when Farmer Jonathan stopped in front of Grocer Bacon's, and went into the store to ask Bacon if he wouldn't buy the hay. Gil didn't like to call to Farmer Jonathan while the people stood around, though by getting as close to the edge of the hay as he dared, Gil could just have a peep at him through the loose hay, as he stood in the store door talking with Dionysius Bacon.

As Dionysius considered himself a pretty smart fellow, and enjoyed cracking jokes with people, particularly when the joke was on his side, he went on chaffing Farmer Jonathan about the hay. He offered to trade brooms, clothes-lines, etc., for it, while those standing around laughed, and those passing along the street paused to see what the fun was.

"Now is this all nice hay?" asked Dionysius, speaking as though he was done joking, and was very much in earnest. At the same time he was slyly working a clothes-peg into the hay, which he intended to find in a moment after, and then go on joking again.

"Every spear of it sweet and dry," was the answer.

"That's so, Grocer Bacon," exclaimed Gil, earnestly, and then lying very quiet, so as not to be discovered, and also cautioning Dora.

Dionysius Bacon jumped away from the hay, dropped the clothes-peg, and looked *foolish*, for the voice seemed to him, as well as to others, to come right out of the middle of the load of hay.

"I didn't know that you pretended to be a ventriloquist, Farmer Jonathan," said he, laughing; "but if you can't imitate a boy's voice better than that, you should take some more lessons in the art."

Farmer Jonathan only smiled, and looked about him to see if he could discover who the ventriloquist was.

"Mr. Dionysius Bacon, don't stand in the sun without your hat," said Gil, in a queer voice. At this every one laughed and shouted, except Dionysius. Gil and Dora laughed, because the people did, and this made the others laugh and shout harder than ever.

"Good for you, Farmer Jonathan!" said half a dozen persons. "You ought to hire the Music Hall, and start a show."

"I don't know anything about ventriloquism," said he, putting his hands into his pockets, and chuckling at the very idea.

"But you can't imitate this," said Dionysius, trying not to appear provoked: "'If Peter Piper picked a peck of pickled peppers.'"

"'If Peter Piper picked a peck of pickled peppers,'" said Gil, imitating the grocer's voice as near as he could. At which you could have heard the people's ha! ha! has! and their shouts of delight a block away.

"Now do you still mean to tell me, Farmer Jonathan, that you are not playing this trick?" asked the grocer.

"Certainly I do. But why don't you suspect some of these gentlemen?"

Then Dionysius appealed to each one separately, not even missing the boys and girls who had been drawn to the spot by the merriment; but all denied being able to ventriloquize, and said that they were sure it had been Farmer Jonathan.

Still, of course, the farmer had to deny it.

"See here," said Dionysius, "I'll buy your hay, and treat every man, girl, and boy present to Smith's best twenty-five-cent oyster stews, if you're not the man; and if you are, you are to pay for the stews."

"One, two, three," said Farmer Jonathan, beginning to number those who stood around.

"It don't matter if there are fifty of them," quickly interposed Dionysius; "will you accept my wager or not?"

"I accept it, of course," said Farmer Jonathan.

Will, having sighted the hay-wagon, just then came running up the street. "Please, Farmer Jonathan," said he, "mother wants you to come to our house to dinner, and bring Gil and Dora. May I too climb up on your hay?"

"Why, my little man, I left Gil and Dora out in the country, at my farm," answered Farmer Jonathan.

"Oh no, you didn't. I saw them on top of your hay-wagon here when you went past our house."

"How are you, Will?" shouted Gil, standing up on the hay.

Then, though the people could see nothing of Gil but his head, they knew at once that Dionysius Bacon had lost his wager. When Farmer Jonathan and some others had lifted Gil and Dora down to the sidewalk, they told how they came to be on the hay. Afterward, Farmer Jonathan, Dionysius, Dora, Gil, and Will headed a procession to Smith's oyster saloon of those who had heard Dionysius make the wager.

It took forty-two oyster stews to supply all, and if it hadn't been a market-day, and just about dinner-time, Smith wouldn't have known how to have served them quickly. Forty-two stews, at a quarter each, you see, would amount to $10 50, and though Smith only charged Dionysius an even ten-dollar bill, the latter seemed to think that he wouldn't make any more wagers that day.

The hay having been unloaded in the mean time, Farmer Jonathan drove around by Will's home, stopping long enough to tell Aunt Mary about the ventriloquist, and then continued on to the farm with Gil and Dora.

But the children hadn't been missed, because mamma thought that they were over at the next farm-house, and she was looking for their return every moment.

BEETLES.

THE great family of beetles is one of the most important in the insect world. In burning sandy plains, in tropical jungles, in fresh green fields, in bogs and swamps—wherever there is a bit of earth or water—there are beetles of one kind or another, following out the instincts assigned to them by nature.

The beetle known as the sacred scarabæus was held in great veneration by the ancient Egyptians, and is carved in great profusion on their tombs. Small gold and porcelain figures of the scarabæus, which were strung on necklaces, and used in other ways for personal ornaments, have also been found in Egyptian sarcophagi.

The way the sacred scarabæus deposits its eggs is a wonderful exhibition of animal instinct. First collecting an ample supply of the material which the young larvæ will need for food, she places her eggs in the middle of it. She then rolls it into a lump, and starts with it on a voyage of discovery. She works backward, pushing the ball containing her eggs behind her, until she finds soil in which she can burrow and conceal her precious burden. It is said to be for this peculiarity that the scarabæus was venerated by the ancient Egyptians. The lump of earth containing the eggs was considered an emblem of fruitfulness, and the devotion of the scarabæus, which would lose its life rather than its precious eggs, was thought to symbolize the exceeding love of the Creator toward men.

The tiger-beetles, of which there are many varieties,

BEETLES—AN EVENING FLIGHT.

are one of the most important branches of the family. They have great hooked jaws, formed to seize the small insects upon which they live. They can not exist in very cold countries, and they are rarely found in cultivated land, as they prefer burrowing in loose, sandy soil, where their little homes are not in danger of being disturbed by the gardener's spade. A remarkable tiger-beetle is the gold-cross of India, which has a deep velvety black body, and a golden mark on its wings in shape like a St. Andrew's cross. The prevailing colors of the tiger-beetle are black, green, and blue; but there is a little Brazilian member of the family of a glistening metallic crimson. It has very long legs, and prefers climbing among the foliage to living on the ground, like most varieties of the tiger-beetle. Its movements are very quick. It will pounce like lightning on a fly, which can rarely escape the grasp of this formidable enemy.

A very curious beetle is the bombardier, a brown creature with green gloss on its wings. It carries a little bomb-shell, which it uses as a weapon of defense when disturbed by an enemy. It is a very sociable little bug, and will gather in a crowd under big flat stones in damp places. If the stone is suddenly overturned, the bombardiers at once begin a cannonade like the explosion of a grain of gunpowder, and throw out a puff of whitish vapor resembling smoke. The bombardiers of South America, China, and other warm countries, are much larger than those found in England, and the fluid they eject, which causes the tiny explosion, is capable of making a black stain, and leaving an unpleasant burning sensation upon the hand of any one trying to capture them.

A large member of the beetle family is found in Nicaragua. It is about five inches long, and is called the big-bodied elephant. It is black in color, but appears of a yellowish-chestnut, as it is entirely covered with a thick, soft fur, something like the down on a butterfly's wing, which rubs off very easily, and shows the scaly black surface beneath. The big-bodied elephant is armed with a formidable black horn, forked at the end, which curves upward like the horn of a white rhinoceros.

Certain species of the elater beetles are familiar to every school-boy. Elater signifies striking or bounding. Boys will know better what is meant by an elater beetle if they are told that it is the same thing as a skip-jack, or snapping-bug. If this beetle is laid on its back, its legs are unable to reach to either side and gain a foot-hold, and it can not roll over. It accordingly goes through a gymnastic movement. Curling its legs closely to its body, it arches itself a little, and suddenly springs into the air, landing on its feet, in which position it is again master of itself.

The most remarkable among the elater beetles is the cucullo, or fire-fly, of the tropics. It is a very common-looking dark brown beetle in the day-time, the two beads, one on each side of its head, which at night are so luminous and beautiful, being dull white. But wait until night comes, and then what countless pairs of tiny yellow-green lanterns are flying over the fields, and creeping about among the foliage! Boys and girls in Cuba make cages of stout reeds, and fill them with cucullos. If the cage is hung in a dark room, the light from the cucullos is strong enough to enable one to read print, if the book is held near the cage. There is also a small place underneath the body from which this singular beetle emits light, but the effect is not so beautiful as that of the two beads on the head. If the cucullo is disturbed by being shaken in its cage, or in any other way, the light it throws out intensifies until it is fairly dazzling.

These beautiful beetles may easily be brought across the ocean in their little cages, and if guarded from cold air, and fed plentifully with sugar-cane, from which they suck the juice, or even with coarse brown sugar moistened a little, they will live a long time.

These varieties of beetles mentioned are only a small handful among thousands, for there are more members of this great family than naturalists have yet been able to count. There are beetles that fly by night, and beetles that fly by day; some that live in the ground, others in the water, and yet others on trees and among the leaves and flowers. They are of all colors, and of varied appetites, some living solely on insects, others on fruits and vegetables and leaves of different kinds.

[Begun in Harper's Young People No. 37, July 13.]

THE STORY OF THE AMERICAN NAVY.

BY BENSON J. LOSSING.

CHAPTER II.

THERE was war on the bosom of Lake Champlain, in Northern New York, in the fall of 1776. The British were about to invade the colonies from Canada by way of that lake. To meet the danger, the Americans built a small flotilla of gun-boats and gondolas in its upper waters. The British constructed a flotilla at its foot. The former sailed from Ticonderoga, under the command of Benedict Arnold, to confront the foe at the foot of the lake.

They met not far from Plattsburg, fought desperately, but not decisively, and during the ensuing dark night Arnold with his vessels escaped up the lake. The British pursued, and gained a complete victory, but did not begin the invasion until the next year.

In May, 1777, Captain Conyngham sailed from Dunkirk, France, in the brig *Surprise*, with one of Franklin's commissions, and soon returned to port with a British brig and packet as prizes. The French were embarrassed. They desired to help the Americans, but did not wish to provoke an open quarrel with the English just then. The English Ambassador at Paris protested, and Conyngham and his crew were imprisoned. They were soon released, and sailed in the *Revenge* for British waters, where they spread havoc among the English shipping. The British were so scared that they were at their wits' end. Insurance rose to twenty per centum; and so unwilling were English merchants to risk their goods in British bottoms that at one time forty French vessels were taking in cargoes in the Thames. The *Revenge* tried to intercept the British transports taking hired German troops to America, but failed.

After the treaty of alliance with France was signed, the French openly assisted the Americans, whose cruisers and privateers became more active than ever. The story of their exploits in detail forms a most romantic chapter of American history.

In the spring of 1778, John Paul Jones first appeared in European waters. With the *Ranger*, of eighteen guns, he went up the western coast of England to Whitehaven; seized the fort, spiked the cannons, set fire to the shipping, and departed as quickly as he came. Then he attempted to make his father's old friend, the Scotch Earl of Selkirk, a prisoner, but failed. His men carried off the family plate, which Jones restored to Lady Selkirk. Sweeping around Ireland, he made several prizes, and sailed for France. This raid greatly frightened the people of the English coasts. To their imagination Jones seemed like a revived old Sea King of the North.

Jones was again in British waters in September, 1779. Dr. Franklin and the French King had jointly fitted out an expedition to cruise in the British Channel and the German Ocean, and placed Jones in command. His flagship was the *Bon Homme Richard*. With his little squadron he went far up the eastern coast of Great Britain; and on a moonlit evening had a desperate battle with the *Serapis*, the larger of two armed vessels just started to convoy the English Baltic fleet across the German Ocean.

Jones ran the *Richard* alongside the *Serapis*, lashed them together; and so, muzzle to muzzle, they poured destructive broadsides into each other for an hour and a half. Sometimes both vessels were on fire. When for a minute the *Richard* ceased firing, the Captain of the *Serapis* called out, "Have you struck your colors?" "I have not yet begun to fight," answered Jones. The struggle was fierce for a few minutes longer, when the colors of the *Serapis* were hauled down. When the vessels were separated, the *Richard* was sinking, and soon went to the bottom of the sea. Her people took refuge on the *Serapis*, and she and her consort were taken into the Texel, in Holland. When, afterward, Jones heard that the King had knighted the commander of the *Serapis*, he said, "He deserves it; and if I fall in with him again, I'll make a lord of him."

The fame of this victory soon spread abroad. The Congress gave Jones a gold medal. European monarchs gave him tokens of high regard. At a grand court banquet the King of France made him a Knight of the "Military Order of Merit," and decorated him with its jewel. He is known in history as the "Chevalier John Paul Jones."

Among the younger naval heroes of the war for independence, who afterward became renowned, was Joshua Barney. At the close of 1780, when he was less than twenty-two years of age, he was made Captain, put in command of the frigate *Alliance*, and conveyed to France John Laurens, a special envoy of the Congress. On his return Barney was attacked by two armed English vessels, and after a severe engagement captured both of them.

In the spring of 1782, Barney, in command of the *Hyder Ali*, a Pennsylvania cruiser keeping the Delaware clear of English marauders, honored the infant American navy by a brilliant exploit. He was convoying some merchant vessels, and while at anchor near Cape May was attacked by an English cruiser with two companions. He sent the merchantmen up the river, and by an expert movement got the *Hyder Ali* entangled with her antagonist in such a way that her great guns swept the decks of the foe with a destructive raking fire. In less than half an hour the British vessel (which proved to be the brig *General Monk*) surrendered. She was badly bruised, and had lost fifty men. This was "one of the most brilliant actions that ever occurred under the American flag," wrote Cooper, fifty years afterward.

The war for independence was now about to close with triumph for the Americans and their cause. The little Continental Navy had fully justified the faith of the stout-hearted people by its grand performances. This little David had fought the Goliath of England most val-

BATTLE BETWEEN THE "BON HOMME RICHARD" AND THE "SERAPIS."—Drawn by Howard Pyle.

tantly for seven years, and in the might of right its "pebbles from the brook" had been equal in efficiency to the huge "spear" of the boastful oppressor. Divine help gave final victory to the patriots.

During the war the Americans had thirty-six public vessels afloat, besides swarms of active and efficient privateers. They had also built a large 74-gun ship (the *America*), but before she was put to sea she was presented to the French government. The veteran Manly, the pioneer of the naval warfare on the part of the Americans, after a long captivity, cruised in the *Hague* among the West India Islands, until the preliminary treaty of peace was signed in the fall of 1782. He there closed the regular maritime operations which he had opened in 1775. The cruisers were recalled, the commissions of the privateers were revoked, and of all the vessels of the remarkable little Continental Navy only the *Alliance* remained in 1783. Nothing but the recollection of the services and sufferings of the navy was left behind. The *Alliance* was reluctantly sold in 1785 to save the expense of repairs. The exhausted Americans craved the enjoyment of peace, and felt no need of a navy.

(TO BE CONTINUED.)

MR. MARTIN'S EYE.

BY JIMMY BROWN.

I'VE made up my mind to one thing, and that is, I'll never have anything to do with Mr. Martin again. He ought to be ashamed of himself, going around and getting boys into scrapes, just because he's put together so miserably. Sue says she believes it's mucilage, and I think she's right. If he couldn't afford to get himself made like other people, why don't he stay at home? His father and mother must have been awfully ashamed of him. Why, he's liable to fall apart at any time, Mr. Travers says, and some of these days he'll have to be swept up off the floor, and carried home in three or four baskets.

There was a ghost one time who used to go around, up stairs and down stairs, in an old castle, carrying his head in his hand, and stopping in front of everybody he met, but never saying a word. This frightened all the people dreadfully, and they couldn't get a servant to stay in the house unless she had the policeman to sit up in the kitchen with her all night. One day a young doctor came to stay at the castle, and said he didn't believe in ghosts, and that nobody ever saw a ghost, unless they had been making beasts of themselves with mince-pie and wedding cake. So the old lord of the castle he smiled very savage, and said, "You'll believe in ghosts before you've been in this castle twenty-four hours, and don't you forget it." Well, that very night the ghost came into the young doctor's room, and woke him up. The doctor looked at him, and said, "Ah, I perceive: painful case of imputation of the neck. Want it cured, old boy?" The ghost nodded, though how he could nod when his head was off I don't know. Then the doctor got up and got a thread and needle, and sewed the ghost's head on, and pushed him gently out of the door, and told him never to show himself again. Nobody ever saw that ghost again, for the doctor had sewed his head on wrong side first, and he couldn't walk without running into the furniture, and of course he felt too much ashamed to show himself. This doctor was Mr. Travers's own grandfather, and Mr. Travers knows the story is true.

But I meant to tell you about the last time Mr. Martin came to our house. It was a week after I had scalped him; but I don't believe he would ever have come if father hadn't gone to see him, and urged him to overlook the rudeness of that unfortunate and thoughtless boy. When he did come, he was as smiling as anything; and he shook hands with me, and said, "Never mind, Bob, only don't do it again."

By-and-by, when Mr. Martin and Sue and Mr. Travers were sitting on the piazza, and I was playing with my new base-ball in the yard, Mr. Martin called out, "Pitch it over here: give us a catch." So I tossed it over gently, and he pitched it back again, and said why didn't I throw it like a man, and not toss it like a girl. So I just sent him a swift ball—a regular daisy-cutter. I knew he couldn't catch it, but I expected he would dodge. He did try to dodge, but it hit him along-side of one eye, and knocked it out. You may think I'm exaggerlying, but I'm not. I saw that eye fly up against the side of the house, and then roll down the front steps to the front walk, where it stopped, and winked at me.

I turned, and ran out of the gate and down the street as hard as ever I could. I made up my mind that Mr. Martin was spoiled forever, and that the only thing for me to do was to make straight for the Spanish Main and be a pirate. I had often thought I would be a pirate, but now there was no help for it; for a boy that had knocked out a gentleman's eye could never be let to live in a Christian country. After a while I stopped to rest, and then I remembered that I wanted to take some provisions in a bundle, and a big knife to kill wolves. So I went back as soon as it was dark, and stole round to the back of the house, so I could get in the window and find the carving knife and some cake. I was just getting in the window, when somebody put their arms around me, and said, "Dear little soul! was he almost frightened to death?" It was Sue, and I told her that I was going to be a pirate and wanted the carving knife and some cake and she mustn't tell father and was Mr. Martin dead yet? So she told me that Mr. Martin's eye wasn't injured at all, and that he had put it in again, and gone home; and nobody would hurt me, and I needn't be a pirate if I didn't want to be.

It's perfectly dreadful for a man to be made like Mr. Martin, and I'll never come near him again. Sue says that he won't come back to the house, and if he does, she'll send him away with something—I forget what it was—in his ear. Father hasn't heard about the eye yet, but if he does hear about it, there will be a dreadful scene, for he bought a new rattan cane yesterday. There ought to be a law to punish men that sell rattan canes to fathers, unless they haven't any children.

POLLY.

BY FIDELIA HESS BOSTON.

"IT'S no use to tell me Polly Clark's only young and flighty, and that she's got a good heart, and she'll be all right when she gets older, and all that kind of thing. That's all stuff and nonsense. I tell you she's the wickedest child I ever laid eyes on, and if she were a boy, I'd know she'd be hung afore she died; as it is, she's sure to get her death in some queer way, with all them outlandish goings on of her'n." Having given vent to her feelings, and settled poor Polly's fate to her own satisfaction, Deacon Jones's wife proceeded to relate the particulars of the latest scandal to Sallie Perkins, the village gossip.

Mrs. Jones—alas that I am forced to say it!—was not alone in her convictions. The majority of the inhabitants of L—— would have assured you, with a solemn shake of the head, that Polly Clark was, without exception, the "most onery youngster" that ever was born, and "such a pity, too, that Squire Clark's only child should be such an everlastin' worrit to him." And yet a look at Polly would disarm suspicion. A more gentle, lovable-looking girl it would be difficult to find; but then we all know that appearances are deceitful. At church on Sunday she looked so fair and innocent, always paying such good attention to the sermon, and gazing so earnestly at the minister with those clear, soft brown eyes of hers, as if so anxious to understand every word he uttered, that the uninitiated would be ready to declare that hers was indeed a heart without guile. But those who knew her best were well aware that behind this calm exterior was a mind in which the love of mischief reigned supreme, and for aught they knew, at the very moment when she seemed most impressed by the minister's arguments, she had unexpectedly thought of some brilliant plan that promised ill for the peace of mind of some intended victim. Indeed, as poor nervous little Mrs. Clark said, "No one ever knows what Polly is going to do next. I never get up in the morning but I dread what may happen before night. I don't even feel safe about her after she goes to bed, since the time she went into the woods in the middle of the night to try some trick or other with a dead cat, thinking, silly child, that in that way she could cure a wart she had on her thumb. But then," Mrs. Clark always adds, "Polly is always so good-tempered when she is scolded for doing wrong, and seems really to be so sorry about it, that I can't help forgiving her, and hoping she will do better next time. But she don't; she keeps on doing the most dreadful things, and—" And here the poor little woman generally broke down completely, and wept bitterly over the unaccountable depravity of her only child.

As her mother said, Polly did indeed do "dreadful things." Many were the sermons the kind-hearted old minister had preached, which, although delivered to the congregation at large, were expressly intended to move Polly's heart, while she would sit calmly unconscious through them all, wondering what old Aunt Casey would say when she found her pet Tabby gayly decorated with red, white, and blue paint in honor of the glorious Fourth; or whether Granny Lukens would enjoy the flavor of Cayenne pepper in her tea.

All the old ladies in the neighborhood stood in wholesome awe of her, and Mrs. Jones's melancholy predictions for her future were called forth by the remembrance of how, a week before, Polly had presented her with a batch of doughnuts of her own making, which, when partaken of by some friends invited to tea, were found to be filled with cotton; and that was not the worst of it, for when Mrs. Jones attempted to pull the cotton from her mouth, her teeth came with it, which unexpected letting of the cat out of the bag, so to speak, was more than a nine days' wonder in L——. It is hardly necessary to add that from that time forth there was open warfare between Mrs. Jones and Polly.

It would be too great a task for me to tell you of all my heroine's adventures. How, for instance, she frightened the servant-girl into convulsions one night by suddenly appearing to her in a dark hall, after having, with the aid of some sulphur matches, succeeded in making her face bear a startling resemblance to a grinning, ghastly-looking skull; and how she tied a bunch of fire-crackers to the tail of her father's best mule, and set them off, in return for which doubtful favor that agile animal bestowed upon her a kick that broke two ribs, and confined her to her bed for many weeks, during which period the old ladies of L—— were allowed to rest in peace.

These are but samples of the dozens of tricks with which Polly busied her active brain, and by means of which she was enabled to keep those around her in a continual state of uncertainty as to what unheard-of thing she would attempt next.

But Polly, like Napoleon, was doomed to meet her Waterloo. Her last and most disastrous exploit ended sadly both for herself and others. It happened in this way. Polly went to the circus. From that time forth her daring acrobatic feats supplied the gossips of L—— with plenty of material for conversation. They would tell how Polly broke her horse's leg by urging him to jump over a stone wall, and how she almost dislocated her collar-bone in turning a double somersault off a hay-rick; and in fact, they argued, "If she was any one else but Polly Clark, she'd 'a been dead long ago; but them that's born to be hanged will never be drowned," though in what way that proverb was appropriate in Polly's case they themselves could not have told you.

One day Polly conceived a brilliant idea. She would get up a circus of her own. The little boys of the town eagerly agreed to Polly's plan of proceedings. They were to meet and rehearse in her father's barn on Wednesday night, while Mr. and Mrs. Clark were attending the Lyceum meeting.

The appointed hour drew near, and so did the boys. With Polly at their head, they marched in grim silence past the house, and when they reached the barn, she informed them that Bridget, thinking she had gone to bed, was entertaining her beau in the front parlor, so they could make all the noise they wanted to, without fear of detection.

After a moment's search Polly unearthed a couple of candles, which Tommy Briggs lighted; and while he and Polly adjusted the trapeze he had constructed in stolen moments, the other actors in the drama rigged up a remarkably insecure tight-rope.

At last all was ready. "Down in front!" shouted Tommy, in an imperative manner, to the imaginary audience. "The performance is a-goin' to begin. First, Mr. Adolphus Popinjay is goin' to do some gymnastics with the trapeze."

Mr. Adolphus Popinjay, otherwise Jack Hybbed, after many attempts, and with much assistance, succeeded in getting into the trapeze, where he went through a number of extraordinary antics, the most difficult of which was that of standing on one foot, the other leg being extended stiffly behind him, while with both hands he clutched convulsively to the sides of the trapeze. Polly felt a keen sense of disappointment over Jack's performance. Somehow or other it lacked the ease and grace that the man in the circus had exhibited. She was impatient for her turn to come, that she might show them her idea of acrobatism. She was delighted when Tommy announced that "Pauline, the great unbeaten tight-rope walker, is now a-goin' to come out."

Polly advanced majestically toward the tight-rope, which was fastened at one end to a big hook in the side of the barn, and at the other end to the loft, against which was placed a ladder, which she proceeded to ascend. There was a beam overhead, which Polly was to hold on to in order to keep herself from falling, and assisted by it, she started out quite bravely; but she had taken but four steps when Tommy shouted, "Hold on fast, Polly! the hook's comin' out." Alas! the warning came too late. Before she could get hold of the beam securely, the hook came out, and with a cry of terror poor Polly fell with a dull thud to the floor. Her dress knocked over the candle as she fell, and in a second the hay that was scattered on the floor was in a blaze. All the boys except Tommy Briggs rushed screaming from the barn, but he, by straining every muscle, succeeded in dragging Polly out of the now blazing building, and then, the necessity for exertion on his part being over, he fell in a dead faint by the side of the unconscious girl.

Help soon arrived, and the doctor being summoned, Polly was found to be severely injured, while Tommy escaped with some slight burns and an attack of brain-fever. Poor Polly! for weeks she suffered the most intense pain, and when at last she was able to leave her bed, she rose up a sadder and a wiser girl.

Polly is a young woman now, but she still bears the mark of her last frolic in the shape of a long scar on her cheek, where she struck on the rake when she fell.

Polly has one peculiarity. She is the confidential friend of every wild tom-boy of a girl in town, because, as she says, she has such unbounded sympathy with them, and also because she is so anxious to keep them from trying any such dangerous experiments as the one to which she fell a victim.

HOW TROTTY GOT HIS JUMPING-JACK

BY AGNES CARR.

TROTTY sat on the nursery floor, gazing sadly at a broken jumping-jack, with only one leg, no arms, and not much of a head to speak of. It was weeks since Christmas, and all the toys Santa Claus had stuffed into Trotty's little striped stocking were cracked and broken, and now this jumping-jack, the last and dearest of all, had gone to pieces too.

"I sink it's time Santa Tlaus [illegible]," remarked Trotty at last.

"Oh no," said nurse, who was holding baby by the window; "he is busy now, making toys to give the good children next Christmas."

"Where does he live?" asked Trotty.

"In a house set in a garden of Christmas trees," began nurse; but just then somebody called her from the room.

"I b'lieve I'll try and find dat house," thought Master Four-year-old, "and ask Santa Tlaus to div me anodder jumping-jack."

To think, with Trotty, was to do, and five minutes later he had on his beloved new rubber boots and was running down the road as fast as his little fat legs would carry him, with a big apple in his hand to eat on the way.

He came first to a pond where a duck was swimming.

"Quack, quack," said the duck; which meant, "What a nice red apple! I wish I had some."

"I will div you a bite," said Trotty, "if you will show me the way to Santa Tlaus's house."

"I don't know the way," said Ducky; "but give me some, and I will take you to the cat, and she will tell you."

So Trotty gave her a bite, and the duck came out of the water, and waddled along in front of Trotty till they came to a barn, where the cat and her five kittens were playing in the door.

"Please, Mrs. Pussy," said Trotty, "show me the way to Santa Tlaus's house, and I will div you a bite of my apple."

"Mew, mew," said the pussy cat; which was, "I don't know the way; but give me some, and I will take you to the dog, and he will tell you."

So Trotty gave her a bite, and she led him to the dog-kennel, where Towser the dog was snapping at flies in the sun.

"Please, doggy," said Trotty, "show me the way to Santa Tlaus's house, and I'll div you a bite of my apple."

"Bow, wow, wow," said Towser; which meant, "I don't know the way; but give me some, and I will take you to the horse, who can tell you."

So Trotty gave him a bite, and together they went on to a green field, where a horse was feeding, and Trotty [illegible] to show him the way.

"Neigh, neigh," said Horse; "I don't know; but give me a piece of your apple, and I will take you to the boy who will surely tell you."

So Trotty gave him a bite, and the horse took him on his back and galloped away, until they came to a little boy sitting on a stone whistling. There was nothing now left of the apple except the core; but Trotty said, "Little boy, show me the way to Santa Tlaus's house, and I'll div you the core of my apple."

"I don't know the road," answered the boy; "but give it to me, and I will take you to the little old woman who lives under the hill, and she will tell you."

So Trotty gave him the core, and the boy took him to a wee bit of a cottage, where an old woman was spinning, and a girl with yellow hair was stirring something in a pot over the fire.

"Please, ma'am, will you show me the way to Santa Tlaus's house?" asked Trotty. But now he had no more apple to offer.

"Yes, my little dear," said the old woman, sweetly. "Come in and rest, and then I will take you there."

But the moment he was inside, she caught hold of him, took off all his pretty clothes, and dressed him in old rags, and would have cut off his curls, but the yellow-haired girl said the scissors were rusty, and she must wait till they were sharpened.

Trotty was dreadfully frightened, and thought he should never get home again; but when it grew dark the old woman went to sleep on a bed in the corner, and then the girl with yellow hair dressed him in his own clothes again, opened the door, and let him run away.

Trotty ran along in the dark until he saw a light, and found it came from a large house, and all around the house grew beautiful evergreen trees.

"Dis must be Santa Tlaus's house," thought Trotty, "for there are the Tismas trees." So he trotted up to the door, and knocked. It was opened by a big man with bushy whiskers.

"Is you Santa Tlaus?" asked Trotty.

"Bless us!" said the man. "And if I am, what do you want?"

"I wants a jumping-jack," sobbed Trotty. "And oh! I's tired, and I wants my supper."

"Bless us!" said the man again. But he caught Trotty up in his arms, carried him in, and set him in a high chair in front of a great bowl of bread and milk.

Trotty went to eating right away, for he was very hungry; but before he came to the bottom of the bowl his head nodded, his eyes closed, and he was fast asleep.

He never knew how long he slept; but when he woke up he was in his own little white bed at home, and papa, mamma, and nurse were hugging and kissing him.

But on the pillow by his side lay a beautiful new jumping-jack; so he knew he had found the house in the garden of Christmas trees, and seen good old Santa Claus himself.

BIRDIE'S VANITY.

BY C. L.

Pussie and Kittie strolled out one day
Into the garden to walk and play;
They rolled on the grass, and jumped so high
That the old drake "quacked" as he passed by.
Said he, "I wish I could hop so light,"
And on he hobbled with all his might.

Above, little Susie's Birdie swung;
His cage from a lofty window hung.
As soon as he heard the drake's lament,
His head on mischief was quickly bent.

"Oho, Mister Drake, you soon shall see
That Mistress Puss can not outjump me;
And although my legs are short and thin,
I'll wager that in a race I'll win."
So saying, he flapped against the door
Till his pretty wings were getting sore.

At last, with a snap, the door came loose,
And Birdie flew out—the little goose!
He flew right down to the very ground
Where Pussie and Kittie played around.
And now there began a lively race,
Which gained excitement at every pace.

Little Birdie chirped, and hopped about,
And Pussie followed him in and out,
Under the rose-tree and through the hedge,
Until they came to the garden's edge;
And then Mister Birdie, full of pride,
Mounted a tree by the water's side;
And there he perched, with a proud delight,
Boasting and singing with all his might,
Until, quite weary and worn, at last
He drooped his head, and soon slept fast.

Then up jumped Puss from her hiding-place,
And mounted the tree with nimble grace;
But so gently did her footsteps fall,
Not a sound the sleeper heard at all.

And now, alas! Pussie crouches low;
Poor Birdie will soon be gone. But no!
A shrill little scream is heard to rise,
And there stands Susie with frightened eyes.
Old Pussie scampers with might and main,
And Birdie opes wide his eyes again.

Now think of his horror when he saw
How near he had been to Pussie's paw!
I really think he deserved the pain,
Because he had been so very vain;
And I'll venture that he did not seek
Another frolic within a week.

"KITTY, WHAT MAKES YOU SO CROSS?"

OUR POST-OFFICE BOX

with "Wee Tot" [illegible], or any other [illegible] girl. I have not a very large collection yet, but I am adding to it fast. [illegible]

[illegible]

My new telescope works a great deal better than my first one. We had to exclude some part of the light by putting a piece of pasteboard with a hole in it in front of the object-glass, which has a diameter of two inches, and a focus of sixty inches. It magnifies the moon about forty times, as near as we can judge. How can I tell exactly how many times it does magnify?

How many of the other boys have tried to make a telescope according to the directions given in YOUNG PEOPLE No. [illegible]?

How can I make a cheap camera obscura?

Is it injurious to the eyes to look at the moon through the telescope without smoked glasses?

[illegible] T.

The dealer from whom you obtained your lenses will tell you their magnifying power.—You do not need smoked glass when looking at the moon.—A simple form of the camera obscura (dark chamber) is a box furnished with a lens whose focal length is equal to the length and height of the box. At the opposite end of the box from the lens a mirror is placed at an angle of forty-five degrees, from which the image received through the lens is reflected upon a piece of glass, the under side of which should be ground, placed flat directly above the mirror. The image will of course be inverted. It will be more distinct if the ground glass be shaded from the light.

GEORGE L. H.—You will see by the letter of [illegible] in this Post-office Box that she did give her right address. Why your letter miscarried we can not explain.

H. SCOTT.—Send your full address, and we will gladly publish your request for exchange.

W. CHAPMAN, MARY L. L., AND OTHERS.—Write directly to the address given by those with whom you desire to exchange.

MAUD W.—Paste your leaves firmly to the paper, and leave them under heavy pressure until they are dry, and you will not be troubled by their curling up. When you take them from the press varnish them, and they will give you more satisfaction.

G. W. DAVIS.—A projectile kaleidoscope may be of any convenient size, varying from six to ten inches in length, fitted with two lenses—one at the object end, to throw light from a lamp through the instrument, and the other at the eye end, through which the image is projected on a screen, placed at the proper focal distance. Any ingenious boy can fit these lenses to an ordinary kaleidoscope, and fit it to a stand, which may be placed on a table.

H. T. WILSON.—The correspondent you inquire about did not desire exchange, and we have no authority to give full address. Any short communication you may wish to make in reference to minerals will be printed in the Post-office Box.

[illegible]

[illegible]

PUZZLES FROM YOUNG CONTRIBUTORS.

No. 1.

[illegible]

No. 2.

[illegible]

No. 3.

[illegible]

No. 4.

[illegible]

No. 5.

[illegible]

ANSWERS TO PUZZLES IN NO. 85.

ADVERTISEMENTS.

HARPER'S YOUNG PEOPLE.

HARPER'S YOUNG PEOPLE will be issued every Tuesday, and may be had at the following rates—payable in advance, postage free:

SINGLE COPIES ....$0 [illegible]

ONE SUBSCRIPTION, one year.... 1 50

FIVE SUBSCRIPTIONS, one year... 7 00

Subscriptions may begin with any Number. When no time is specified, it will be understood that the subscriber desires to commence with the Number issued after the receipt of order.

Remittances should be made by POST-OFFICE MONEY ORDER or DRAFT, to avoid risk of loss.

ADVERTISING.

The extent and character of the circulation of HARPER'S YOUNG PEOPLE will render it a first-class medium for advertising. A limited number of approved advertisements will be inserted on two inside pages at [illegible] cents per line.

Address

HARPER & BROTHERS,

Franklin Square, N. Y.

FISHING OUTFITS.

CATALOGUE FREE.

[illegible], 132 Nassau Street, N. Y.

ELEMENTARY EDUCATION.

Books for the School and Family.

ARITHMETIC.

FRENCH'S FIRST LESSONS IN NUMBERS. [illegible] By JOHN H. FRENCH, LL.D. Illustrated. [illegible], Half Leather, [illegible] cents.

FRENCH'S ELEMENTARY ARITHMETIC FOR THE SLATE. Elementary Arithmetic for the Slate, in which Methods and Rules are based upon Principles established by Induction. By JOHN H. FRENCH, LL.D. [illegible], Half Leather, [illegible] cts.

FRENCH'S MENTAL ARITHMETIC. Mental Arithmetic, in which [illegible] of Problems, and Principles of Arithmetical Analysis are based upon the Laws of Mental Development. By JOHN H. FRENCH, LL.D. Illustrated. [illegible], Half Leather, [illegible] cents.

NATURAL SCIENCE.

FIRST LESSONS IN NATURAL HISTORY AND LANGUAGE. Entertaining and Instructive Lessons in Natural History and Language for Primary and Grammar Schools. [illegible], Cloth, [illegible] cents.

THE CHILD'S BOOK OF NATURE. The Child's Book of Nature, for the Use of Families and Schools: intended to aid Mothers and Teachers in Training Children in the Observation of Nature. In Three Parts. Part I. Plants. Part II. Animals. Part III. Air, Water, Heat, Light, &c. By WORTHINGTON HOOKER, M.D. Illustrated. The Three Parts complete in One Volume, [illegible] [illegible]

HOOKER'S FIRST BOOK IN CHEMISTRY. [illegible]

FARADAY'S CHEMISTRY OF A CANDLE. [illegible] By M. FARADAY. [illegible]

FARADAY'S PHYSICAL FORCES. [illegible] By M. FARADAY. [illegible]

FRENCH AND GERMAN.

FRENCH PRINCIPIA, PART I. A First French Course: containing Grammar, Delectus, and Exercise-Book, with Vocabularies. On the Plan of Dr. Smith's *Principia Latina*. [illegible]

FRENCH PRINCIPIA, PART II. A First French Reading-Book. [illegible] On the Plan of Dr. Smith's *Principia Latina*. [illegible]

GERMAN PRINCIPIA, PART I. A First German Course. Containing Grammar, Delectus, Exercise-Book, and Vocabularies. On the Plan of Dr. Smith's *Principia Latina*. [illegible]

GERMAN PRINCIPIA, PART II. A First German Reading-Book. [illegible] On the Plan of Dr. Smith's *Principia Latina*. [illegible]

COMFORT'S GERMAN PRIMER. [illegible] By GEORGE F. COMFORT, A.M. [illegible]

COMFORT'S FIRST BOOK IN GERMAN. [illegible] By GEORGE F. COMFORT, A.M. [illegible]

COMFORT'S FIRST GERMAN READER. [illegible] By GEORGE F. COMFORT, A.M. [illegible]

OBJECT LESSONS.

WILLSON'S MANUAL OF OBJECT LESSONS. [illegible] By MARCIUS WILLSON. [illegible]

CALKINS'S PRIMARY OBJECT LESSONS. [illegible] By N. A. CALKINS. [illegible]

Published by HARPER & BROTHERS, New York.

Sent by mail, postage prepaid, to any part of the United States, on receipt of the price.

SOME ANSWERS FROM OUR SUBSCRIBERS TO WIGGLE No. 19; OUR ARTIST'S IDEA OF THE SAME; AND NEW WIGGLE, No. 13.

THE following is a list of the names of those who sent us their ideas of Wiggle No. 14, given in YOUNG PEOPLE No. 31:

Lucy Thurber, Sam Hopp, Thomas Allen, Alma Hedtmann, John J. A. Flaherty, Dick, Jack Schroeder, Eugene L. Pratt, F. J. C., C. B. A., P. J. F., Katie Huntington, Clara L. Kellogg, Lucy King, Arthur Pane, Hervie Pane, Sally Gerhard, [illegible], H. B. Tall, George T. [illegible], Allen Curry, Frank [illegible], L. G. S., W. J. S., Dolly Grayson, [illegible] L. George, B. Pratt, M. Pratt, [illegible], W. B. Morris, [illegible], [illegible] Kopp, Bella Levy, Fred Kimberly, Harry [illegible], J. D. [illegible], Jun., [illegible], [illegible], Grace Curry, John A. Brown, Charlie Conklin, [illegible], [illegible], V. [illegible], Frank Ward, Robert Hoyt, [illegible], Emily Tudor, Walter Tudor, Emily [illegible], Grace [illegible], L. R. R., Tom F. [illegible], Albert Wesley, W. H. B., Arthur [illegible], Harry L. S. Watson, Charles F. Park, Jun., Harry B. [illegible], Frank [illegible], A. B. Stoddard, E. P. L., Mary, J. M. F., [illegible], A. G. Thayer, [illegible], William [illegible], W. G. [illegible], Curtis Thompson, George Wesley, A. M. Townsend, [illegible] W. [illegible], Sophie L. Hall, [illegible], [illegible] Moore, W. Cantrell, [illegible], F. A. Conklin, May L. Wight, Charles A. W., B. G. Hicks, S. B. Townsend, Everett C. Fay, Arthur [illegible], G. M., J. M. Ingersoll, [illegible] J. Loening, [illegible], J. R., Walter B. Wyman, J. [illegible], Jun., [illegible], Daisy, E. F., G. B. McLaughlin, William A. Lewis, G. C. [illegible], Nelson Wilson, [illegible], John B. Whitbeck, "North Star" (John B. Blake), Willie [illegible], Edith B. [illegible], Addie [illegible], [illegible] L. James, Willie Fowler, Fred A. W., Maggie Maynard, A. M. J., R. Western, Hattie B. [illegible], [illegible], A. C. [illegible], G. Beck, Louise Hall, [illegible] Sanford, Hattie R. [illegible], F. [illegible], May A. [illegible], Arthur [illegible], William [illegible], Annie [illegible], Harry Morgan, [illegible] Dodge, [illegible], E. W. Little, C. H. Friend, Fanny [illegible], W. B. [illegible], Henry M. Alexander, Jun., W. H. Western, Edith [illegible], [illegible], Katie Hope, [illegible], Carrie [illegible], M. C. [illegible], E. H. [illegible], [illegible], N. F. [illegible], Sarah Q., H. L. Thurber, Henry Robert [illegible], L. V. D., [illegible] and Ida Parsons, Allie [illegible], [illegible], Jennie [illegible], A. D. Gibson, Mabel Warner, A. A. Bell, [illegible], William Levy, Louise D. Hicks, John [illegible], May W. [illegible], B. R., M. B. Wightman, [illegible], Harry B. [illegible], R. E. S., Henry B. Alexander, Annie Oliver, Baby Oliver, John M. [illegible], John B. [illegible], [illegible] York, [illegible], [illegible], Jasper [illegible], [illegible], Dolly [illegible], J. McL., Marion [illegible], [illegible], J. F. S., F. [illegible], W. H. R., Benjamin F. Waterman, Jennie [illegible], C. D. J., G. F. McKinney, Caroline, John R. [illegible], [illegible], [illegible], Louise [illegible], [illegible], Mamie [illegible], Mabel, Lulu S., Frank Schmidt, Gypsy, Elsie H. T., Alice B. Austin, Howard [illegible].

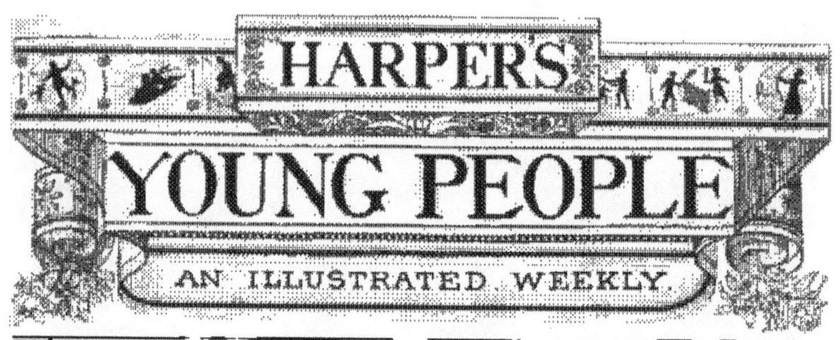

Vol. I.—No. 39. Published by HARPER & BROTHERS, New York. Price Four Cents.

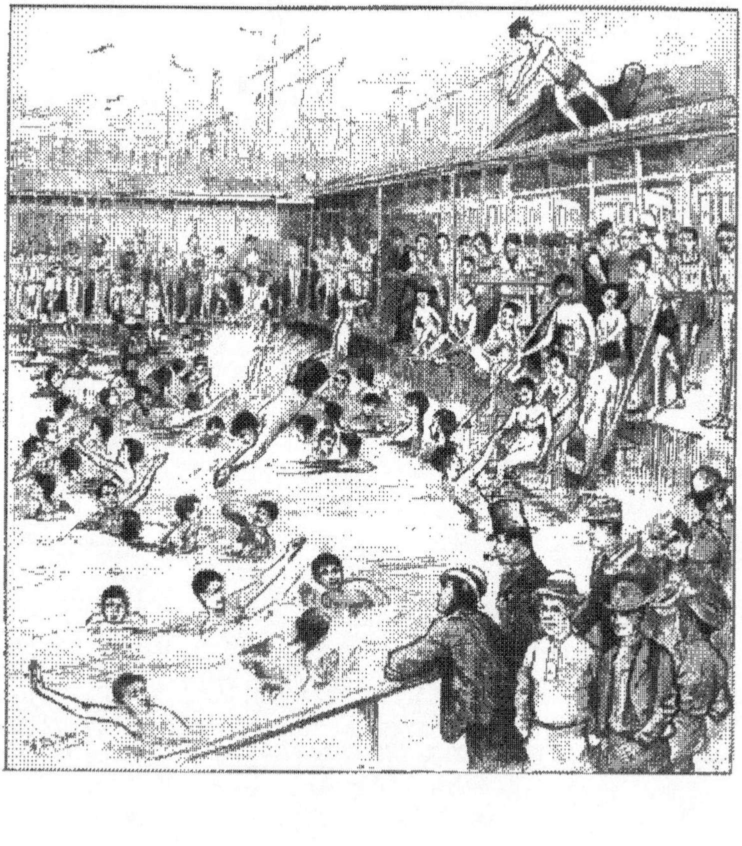

PODDIE AND DICK AT THE FREE BATH.

BY UNCLE FRANK.

"DICK, Uncle Fritz 'll never come!" exclaimed Poddie Monell, with an impatient stamp of his foot, and once more he peered anxiously through the bars of the gate at the South Ferry.

"Hold on; don't be so sure, old fellow; there he comes now," said Dick; "look just beyond the Elevated. Let's go meet him."

"Keep cool, boys, keep cool; don't rush; there's plenty of time," said the gentleman, kindly, giving a hand to each; and crossing the street, they sauntered leisurely along one of the broad walks of the Battery.

"Which of the free baths are we going to, and what are they like?" asked Dick, whose mind was always travelling ahead of time in a curious fashion.

"We are going to the Battery bath, because it is nearest. They are all pretty much alike, however," replied his uncle.

"Do tell us all about them," begged Poddie, earnestly, "for I want to know if they're anything like our bath at Central Park—whether they have hanging rings, a flying trapeze, and places to dive off of."

"Well, no, they don't indulge in the first two luxuries, but they have plenty of space, ropes, diving places, and a fair depth of water. But let me tell you how much good they do.

"There are four free baths stationed on the East River—at One-hundred-and-twelfth Street, Thirty-seventh Street, Fifth Street, and Gouverneur Street; and three on the North River—at the Battery, Bethune Street, and Fifty-first Street; and one floating around without any home at all—that is, it is built, and the authorities have not decided where to anchor it."

"Well?" exclaimed both boys, interestedly.

"Now, boys, in order to understand thoroughly how much these free baths are to the people who use them, you must put yourselves in some other boys' boots, or perhaps I should say jackets, so many of them have no boots at all.

"You and Dick live in a very lovely home. Just imagine yourselves in a dingy tenement-house, shut up for the night, with three or four other boys, to sleep in a dark room where never sunlight or breeze enters through the whole year; the heat is suffocating; you toss uneasily back and forth, more than likely on the floor. You have heard during the day that to-morrow the Gouverneur Street or some other bath will be open. What do you do?

"Before the day breaks you leap from your bed, waken your brothers or comrades, fling on your jackets and trousers, rush down the rickety stairways out into the cooler air of the morning, and scud down to the docks.

"When you arrive there you find already quite a line of boys and men ahead of you. You can not go above them—the policemen won't allow it—so you take your places at the foot of the line, glad that it is no longer. Poddie is number fifty-one, Dick fifty-two. By twos and threes the line grows to be three hundred strong. At five o'clock the doors open, the keepers appear, and one hundred are admitted. But here we are: you shall begin to judge for yourselves."

"Whew!" exclaimed Dick, looking up and down a long line of ragged, grimy urchins, who were tip-toeing in impatience to enter. "How will all those fellows get in? Shall we have to foot the line?"

"Not while I have my 'open, sesame,' with me," replied Uncle Fritz, pointing to a small silver badge on his coat lapel.

The keeper just glanced at it, and Dick was greatly surprised to see how politely they were invited to walk in, "all through a bit of shiny silver," as he expressed it afterward.

"What a crowd of boys!" thought Poddie, as his eye roved from one to another of the hundred ducking, diving, splashing little and big fellows, who were laughing and shouting with delight. "What a jolly time they're having!" said he, turning to his uncle.

"Yes," said that gentleman. "I don't believe you have more fun at the Central Park bath, Poddie."

"Don't know as we do," replied Poddie, dubiously. "But what does that mean?" added he, startled by the brazen clangor of a large bell that rang high above the noises a warning "Ding-dong, ding-dong, ding."

"Time's up!" shouted the keeper, almost as loud as his bell. Silence fell upon the gleeful throng instantly. With downcast faces and slow, reluctant feet the bathers commenced to crawl up the wet steps, tumble over the railings, and trailing little brooks of water behind them, sought the bath-rooms, whence they slowly emerged, some fairly well dressed, but the majority in rags and tatters.

"The boys is putty fair to-day, along o' you visitors, sir," said the keeper; "but we mostly has to hunt 'em out o' the dark corners—where they dart to as soon as the bell rings—with this rattan, or they'd stay in all the day."

"How about the girls—do they enjoy the privileges of these free baths?" inquired Uncle Fritz.

"Yes, sir, they does, on Mondays, Wednesdays, and Fridays, an' a lively lot they is, too; the women keepers has their hands full."

No sooner had the first crowd of boys disappeared than pell-mell in rushed a tumultuous throng, pushing and jostling in spite of the shouting keepers.

Begrimed and perspiring, and panting with impatience to enjoy the blessing of the cooler element, it is the work of but a moment in the bath-rooms; the doors fly open, and down they plunge from steps and railings into the cool green depths.

The water splashes and dashes and foams, lashed by scores of active hands and feet, until the boys are fairly deafened by the roar.

"Gracious! you'd think they hadn't seen water in a year, wouldn't you, Dick?" said Poddie.

"Half o' them's repeaters," said the keeper, overhearing the remark.

"Beg pardon—did you call them repeaters? what's that?" inquired Poddie, politely.

"Repeaters! Why, repeaters is boys who go from bath to bath, only waiting to get their heads dry; then they rubs mud on their faces to make 'em dirty, so we can't know 'em, consequentially they gets in half a dozen times at different baths. How are we to know them? bless your eyes!"

"Have you any fine swimmers among them?" inquired Uncle Fritz, pleasantly.

"Yes, sir," replied the keeper, "some o' these chaps are reg'lar fishes—nat'ral-born eels, you may say. Here, Patsy Miller, 'Rosy,' 'Spider,' come along and show these young gentlemen some o' your tricks."

The three boys, hearing their names shouted by the keeper and their playmates, come forward, looking sheepishly pleased at their momentary importance.

"Go to the roof and dive," commands the keeper.

In a few seconds they appear on the pebbled roof opposite, thin-limbed, brown, and lithe as Arabs.

"Ready—dive!"

One after another the heads are bowed, hands are clasped palm to palm and pointed forward, and away they go, head-first like frogs. Three splashes mark where they go under; three lines of bubbles across the bath tell where the glossy heads will come up.

"Bravo! bravo! well done!" cries Uncle Fritz.

"Dive backward, and swim oar stroke," directs the keeper.

Nothing loath, the boys mount the railings, the swimmers making way for them. One, two, three. Down they go on their backs, come up like corks, throw their arms high in air, bring them down full length behind their heads, draw back their feet, and with an oar-like sweep of their limbs make long darts through the water.

"How splendid!" observes Dick, turning to his uncle.

"Turn somersaults," shouts the keeper.

"Goody gracious! that's what they do up at the Central," says Dick, laughing heartily, as now six heels, then three heads, alternately appear on the surface of the water.

"Make a raft," orders the keeper. Immediately Patsy and "Spider" and "Rosy" are on their backs again; they lock arms, paddle with their feet, and make quite a respectable raft as they cross the bath.

Suddenly the raft goes to pieces, the swimmers dive, and stay under so long that Poddie thinks they are gone for good; but no, they are up again, ready for more fun.

A game of "leap-frog" and "playing porpoise" are both entered into with fine spirit, for the boys all wish to show off.

A boat-race, in which a dozen boys either "sculled" or swam "oar stroke," as they fancied, Dick and Poddie declared "quite the best thing" they had ever seen in the swimming line.

Once more the great bell sounded its notes of doom, and the dripping crowd gave place to a dry one.

"We're obliged to do this in midsummer," remarked the keeper, alluding to the clearing-out process, "to give the largest numbers a chance; we must git through with the boys, for after six the men 'll be comin' along, tired and dusty, from their work."

"What do you think of the free baths, boys?" asked Uncle Fritz, as they crossed the Battery.

"I'm mighty glad that poor boys have as good a chance as we rich fellows," replied Dick, clinking some silver in his pocket, with the air of a banker.

"Then it keeps them from the sharks," remarked Poddie, thoughtfully.

"And makes them clean and healthy, besides giving them any amount of innocent pleasure," added their uncle.

ROSE AND CATERPILLAR.

"Oh, caterpillar," said a rose
  One lovely summer day,
"Your constant eating drives me wild;
  I wish you'd go away.
I really can not see what use
  You and your kind can be;
You naught but mischief do, and are
  Unpleasant things to see."

A moment after that same rose
  Smiled on a butterfly
That stopped to show his rainbowed wings
  As he was passing by.
Oh, if she only could have known—
  The pretty, dainty rose—
He was a caterpillar too,
  Arrayed in splendid clothes!

VISITING A TEA PLANTATION.—PREPARATION OF TEA.

FROM ADVANCE SHEETS OF "THE BOY TRAVELLERS IN THE FAR EAST." PART SECOND. BY THOMAS W. KNOX.

FRANK and Fred had long wished to visit a tea plantation, and while they were in Java this wish was gratified. The following extract from their journal describes what they saw and learned during their visit:

"The first thing the tea-planter has to do after getting possession of his lease is to clear the land and get ready for planting. The outlay for this is considerable, and not much unlike clearing up a farm in New England, or in the backwoods of Canada. Then the young plants are set out; after this has been done, the ground must be kept clear of weeds, just as in raising corn or potatoes. It must be frequently stirred, so that the plant can get as much nourishment as possible from the earth; and when this is done, the planter has the satisfaction of seeing the bushes grow with considerable rapidity.

"We walked through the fields where the plants were growing, and found them of different ages and sizes. If we had not known where we were, we might have thought we were in a field of English myrtle bushes, as the tea-plant is much like the myrtle in general appearance. It grows from two to six feet high, and has white blossoms that resemble small dogroses.

"One of us asked which were the plants that produced green tea, and which the black. The owner of the plantation smiled, and said there was no difference.

"We laughed at our own ignorance, as he explained that the difference of the teas was entirely owing to the manipulation. We asked why it was that some districts in China produced only green teas, while others were reputed to make none but black; and he told us it was because the workmen in those districts had been accustomed to follow only one form of manipulation.

"It takes three years to get a plantation in condition to produce tea. The seeds are sown in a nursery bed, and the young plants are not ready to be set out till they are a year old. They are then about nine inches high, and covered with leaves, and the first crop is taken when they have been growing two years in the field. The leaves are the lungs of the plant, and it would die if all of them were stripped off. Consequently only a part of them are removed at a picking; and if a plant is sickly, it is not disturbed at all. The plants will last from ten to twelve years, and are then renewed; and on all the large plantations it is the custom to make nursery beds every year, so that there will be a constant succession of new plants for setting out in place of the old ones.

"At the first gathering the half-opened buds are taken, and from them the finest teas are made. Then they have another gathering when the leaves are fully opened, and then another and another, till they have five or six gatherings in the course of the year. Each time the leaves are coarser than those of the previous gathering, and consequently the tea is not of so fine a quality. A well-managed plantation produces all kinds of tea; and it was a wise requirement of the Dutch government, when they started the tea-culture in Java, that the planters should produce proportionate quantities of both black and green, and not less than four qualities of each.

"The gathering takes place only in clear weather; and for the best teas the picking is confined to the afternoon, when the leaves are thoroughly dry, and have been warmed by the sun. Only the thumb and forefinger are used in plucking the leaves from the bush; the pickers are generally women and children, who can gather on the average about forty pounds of leaves in a day. It takes nearly four pounds of leaves to make one pound of dry tea; and the usual estimate is that a plantation of one hundred thousand plants can send ten thousand pounds of tea to market in the course of a year.

"Different kinds of tea require different treatment, as we have already seen. For green tea the leaves are roasted as soon as they have been gathered, and are then rolled and dried; but the leaves intended for black teas are spread on bamboo trays five or six inches deep, and placed on frames where they can have plenty of sun and air. They remain here from noon till sunset; and if the weather is damp they are further dried by artificial heat. For this purpose they are placed on frames over shallow pans containing burning charcoal, and are tossed and stirred with the hand until they emit a certain fragrance. The heat should be very slight; and the frames are made so high that it is necessary for a man to mount a small ladder in order to reach the trays.

GATHERING TEA-LEAVES.

"The sense of smell in the skillful workers of tea is very acute, and they can tell, to almost a minute, the exact time when the drying should cease, and the next process begin. The Chinese workmen are better than any others for this branch of the business, and on many plantations most of the manipulation is performed by Chinese, though their labor is more expensive than that of the Malays. Our host showed us through his factory, where the men were busy in the various processes; and as he told us about each step of the business, he took us to the department where that particular work was going on.

"After showing the leaves spread out on the frames, he led the way to a sort of store, where a man was manipulating some tea in a pan over a charcoal fire.

"'This is what we call roasting,' he said, 'and the great object of the roaster is to dry the leaves without burning them. You see he does not allow them to be quiet a single instant, but tosses and turns them in all directions, so that none may stick to the bottom of the pan, which they might easily do, owing to the moisture they contain.'

DRYING TEA IN THE SUN.

"We watched the roasting till we thought we understood it well, and as the place was hot, we did not care to stay there a great while. The leaves lose their fragrance when first thrown into the roasting pan, and give out a rank smell, but they gradually recover their perfume, and are ready for the next process, which is called rolling.

"The tea from the roasting pan was given to a couple of men, who stood in front of a table or bench, with bamboo mats before them. One had a large mustache, the largest we had ever seen on a Chinese face, and the other consoled himself for the absence of that hairy ornament by smoking a pipe.

"The roller takes as much tea as he can cover with both his hands, and places it on the mat in a sort of ball. He keeps the leaves closely together, and rolls them from right to left; this motion gives each leaf a twist on itself, and rolls it so firmly that it retains the shape when dry. This part of the work requires peculiar dexterity, and can only be performed successfully after long practice. When a man becomes skillful in it, he can roll the tea with wonderful rapidity; and when his work is done, every leaf will be found separate from the others, and twisted as though it had been passed through a machine.

"The work of rolling the tea is very tiresome, and so the men sometimes perform it with their feet when they wish to give their hands a rest. We saw one man at his occupation in this way, and he certainly seemed to enjoy it.

"After they have been properly rolled, the leaves are spread on trays, and exposed to the sun and air for several hours, and then they are once more roasted. The second roasting is milder than the first, and is done over a slower fire; and afterward the leaves are rolled again, to

DRYING OVER CHARCOAL.

make sure that none of them have become spread out. For the black tea the roasting is done in a shallow pan, the same as the first; but the green teas are put in a deep pan, and subjected to a very high heat.

"While the green tea is being roasted there must be a great deal of care on the part of everybody concerned.

The pan is nearly red-hot when the tea is put into it, about a pound at a time, and the operator in charge keeps it in rapid motion. One boy tends the fire, while another stands by with a fan to prevent the burning of the tea.

"After their final roasting the teas are put in a long basket, shaped like an hour-glass, and having a sieve in the centre. This basket is placed over a charcoal fire and submitted to the heat for several minutes, when the tea is poured out and receives another rolling. This operation is repeated several times, till the tea is thoroughly tired of it, and also thoroughly dry. Then it is passed through sieves, to separate the different qualities from each other; and finally it is winnowed, to remove all the dust and dirt. Then it is 'fired,' or dried, once more, to drive away the last particle of moisture; and in this condition it is ready to go into the chests in which it is carried to the lands where it is to be used."

[Begun in No. 61 of Harper's Young People, June 1.]

THE MORAL PIRATES.

BY W. L. ALDEN.

CHAPTER IX.

THE boat was in a shallow part of the river, between the shore and a long row of piles that marked the steamboat channel. Harry sounded with an oar, and found that the water was only two feet deep. "We'll have to get overboard and drag the boat over the piles," said he, "and it's going to be a mighty hard job too. That swell threw us over as neat as the bull threw Joe over the fence up at Lenox last summer."

"When I got pitched over that fence I staid there," said Joe. "I didn't try to get back into the field where the bull was, and I don't see what we want to get back where the steamboats are for."

"That's so," exclaimed Harry. "We're safe enough here. Let's get the water out of the boat, and keep on this side of the piles."

When the boat was made dry, and the lighted lantern was hoisted to the top of the mast, Tom resumed his place at the helm, and Harry and Joe prepared to take another nap. "I don't want to grumble," said Joe, "but I wish I didn't have to lie on the coffee-pot and a tin cup. I don't feel comfortable on that kind of bed."

"I'll change with you if you like," replied Harry. "I'm sleeping on a beautiful soft bottle of oil, and some sardine boxes; but I don't want to be selfish and keep the best bed for myself."

"Oh, never mind," returned Joe. "I'll manage to sleep if Jim don't step on my face. I always did hate to have anybody step on my face when I was asleep."

"Well, good-night, everybody," said Harry. "I'm going straight to sleep. Tom, be sure you wake me up if a steamboat tries to climb over these piles."

This time Tom did not fall asleep at the helm, but the wind gradually died away, and the sail hung limp and useless. Jim got out the oars without stepping on anybody, and rowed slowly on. In a little while they came to the end of the shallow lagoon into which the swell had so unexpectedly cast them. A sand-bank stretched from the shore to the line of piles, and it was impossible to go any farther. Tom decided to make the boat fast to the limb of a willow-tree that projected over the water, and to go ashore and sleep on the sand. Neither he nor Jim thought it worth while to wake the other boys; so they gathered up their blankets, crept quietly out of the boat, and were soon asleep on the soft, warm sand. When Harry and Joe awoke at daylight, stiff and cramped, they were disposed to be rather indignant at Tom and Jim, who were sleeping so comfortably on the sand; but Tom soon convinced them that he had acted from the best of motives, and they readily forgave him.

Of course breakfast was the first business of the day, and after that was finished the boat had to be entirely unloaded before she could be lifted over the piles into the channel. For the first time since they had started on the cruise the breeze was ahead, but it was so light that it was of very little consequence. The sky was cloudy, and the day promised to be a cool one; so the boys resolved to take to their oars, and try, if possible, to reach Albany before night. When the boat was loaded, Tom and Jim each took a long oar, and Harry took his usual seat in the stern-sheets. They all felt fresh, in spite of their night's adventure, and started gayly on their intended long day's row.

By this time they had found out that although round

GETTING OUT OF THE TRAP.—Drawn by A. B. Frost.

tin boxes were very well to keep things dry, they are by no means handy to carry in a boat. Their shape made it impossible to stow them compactly. Joe, who sat at the bow, always had to pick his way over these tin boxes in going to or coming from his station; and he was constantly catching his foot in the spaces left between the boxes, and falling down on them. This smashed in the covers, and tried Joe's temper sorely. Once he sat down so violently on the box which held the sugar, that he went completely through the cover, and was fastened in the box as securely as a cork in a bottle. He was only released after a great deal of work, and just in time to enable the boys to have sugar in their coffee at night. Harry resolved that he would never cruise again with round boxes, but would have small rubber bags made, in which to put everything that required to be kept dry.

The boys took turns at the oars every hour, and rowed steadily until noon. They gave themselves an hour for lunch and resting, and then resumed their work. Late in the afternoon they came in sight of Albany, and went ashore, so as to get their dinner before reaching the city. After dinner they again pulled away at the oars, and at about nine o'clock they stopped at a lumber-yard on the outskirts of Albany, and, creeping in among the lumber, wrapped their blankets around them, and dropped asleep, completely worn out, but proud of their long day's row.

Before sunrise the next morning, Tom was awakened by a stick which was thrust into his ribs. Without opening his eyes, he muttered, "You quit that, or I'll get up and pound you," and immediately dropped asleep again. Somebody then kicked him so sharply that he roused himself up, and, opening his eyes, was dazzled by the gleam of a bull's-eye lantern. He could not at first imagine where he was; but as he presently found that a big policeman had him by the collar, and was calling him "an impudent young thief," he began to imagine that something was wrong.

"I've got you this time," said the policeman, "and the whole gang of you. Where did you steal that property in your boat from, you precious young river pirate?"

"We're not river pirates," replied Tom. "We're Moral Pirates, and we brought those things in the boat with us from New York."

"Well, I like your cheek!" said the officer; "owning up that you're pirates. Now just you and your gang take everything out of that boat and let me see what you've got. If any of you try to escape, I'll put a bullet into you. You hear me?"

The other boys had been awakened by the loud voice of the policeman, and were staring at him in utter astonishment.

"He thinks we're river thieves," said Tom. "Harry, we'll have to show him what we've got in the boat, and then he'll see his mistake."

Harry eagerly assured the policeman that they had come from New York on a pleasure cruise, and had nothing in the boat except provisions and stores. "That's a pretty story," said the officer. "You can tell that to the court. Your boat's full of junk that you've stolen from somewhere; and you'd better hand it out mighty quick."

The boys were thus compelled to unload their boat, while the policeman stood over them with his club in one hand and his lantern in the other. He was not a stupid man, and he soon perceived that the boys had told him the truth; they were not the gang of river thieves for whom he had mistaken them. He therefore apologized, in a rough way, and even helped the boys repack the boat.

"What I can't understand," said he, "is why you boys come here and sleep in a lumber-yard, when you might be sleeping at home in your beds. Now if you were thieves, you couldn't get any better lodgings, you know; but you're gentlemen's sons, and you ought to know better. Why don't you go down to the hotel, and live like gentlemen? Where's the fun in being arrested, and taking up my valuable time?"

The boys assured him that they had never enjoyed themselves more than they had while on the cruise, and after a little more talk the officer turned slowly away.

"By-the-bye," he exclaimed, suddenly turning back again, "one of you told me you were pirates. I ought to take you in after all. I believe you're a lot of boys that have been reading dime novels, and have run away from home."

"I didn't say we were pirates," replied Tom. "I said we were Moral Pirates. That's a very different thing."

"Of course it is," said Joe. "A Moral Pirate is a sort of missionary, you know. I'm afraid you don't go to Sunday-school, officer, or you'd know better."

The policeman could not quite make up his mind whether Joe was in joke or in earnest; but as he could find no real reason for arresting the boys, he contented himself with telling them to leave the lumber-yard as soon as the sun rose. "And you'd better look out," he added, "that you don't come across any real river thieves. They'll make no bones of seizing your boat, and knocking you on the head if you make any noise." When he was fairly out of sight, the boys crept back to their shelter among the lumber, and coolly went to sleep again. They were so tired that neither policemen nor river thieves had any terrors for them.

[TO BE CONTINUED.]

A CONFESSION.

BY GEORGE N. LOVEJOY.

"Do you love me?" stammered Benny
To a bright-eyed little maid;
"Do you love me, love me, Jenny?—
I'll not tell; don't be afraid."

"Yes, I love you," answered Jenny;
"But 'twas only yesterday
That I said the same thing, Benny"
(And she blushed), "to Robbie Gray."

POOR BEN!

BY SYDNEY DAYRE.

"HA, Uncle Dud, I've found your lady-love's curl!"

His uncle drew near Hal, as he rummaged in an old desk.

"Ah," he said, "is that there? I haven't seen it for many a year, but now I remember putting it there."

He took the short brown lock of hair in his hand, and looked at it with almost a tender interest.

"He saved my life when I was a boy, Hal."

"Who, uncle?"

"The one who wore this curl."

"Oh, tell me all about it; come, do, Uncle Dud;" and Hal laid his hand coaxingly on his uncle's arm. "Was he one of your playmates?"

"Yes."

"How old was he when he did it?"

"I didn't know exactly his age. Ten or twelve, perhaps, or thereabouts. But there is the tea-bell. I'll tell you about it after tea."

Uncle Dudley found his audience increased by four or five expectant boys and girls, who gathered around him on the broad piazza, attracted by the rumor that "one of Uncle Dud's stories" was in prospect. Little Elsie crept into his lap as he began:

"I don't think I have ever told you anything of my poor friend Ben, but he played a very important part in many of the pranks and sports and joys and sorrows of my earlier boyhood. I think that, outside of my own family, my attachment to him was the strongest I have ever formed. People used to laugh at us, and call him my younger brother, we showed so much affection for each other."

"Was he a son of your neighbor?" asked Hal.

"No, not his son, but his home was with our nearest neighbor. It was never known who his parents were. He came to Mr. Washburn's house one day, nobody knew where from; but he attracted the attention of all by his fine bright, honest face. I shall never forget the look of his great earnest brown eyes; I used to think they expressed more in a minute than some folks could talk in an hour. Then he had soft hair—this you see—brown, with the least tinge of auburn through it, and was most graceful in his movements. He would strike any one as a handsome fellow."

"What did he come for, uncle? Do you mean that he was a beggar? Did he ask for food?"

"He didn't ask for anything, but it was easy to see what he needed, and country hospitality was not likely to wait till he asked. He staid about there a few days, and made friends with every one. Before long he seemed to have quietly grown to be almost one of the family, and I think they would have been as sorry to lose him as he would to go. He and I 'took to' each other at once, and I owe many of the happiest hours of my boy life to his companionship, for I had no brother near my own age."

"And did your parents really allow you to make a companion of such a little tramp?" asked Hal, with a slight sniff, and a toss of the head which he conceived to be rather aristocratic. "How did they know what kind of a fellow he might have been?"

"Well, they never seemed to fear any harm coming to me through him. Ben showed a much better disposition than I ever did. He was very gentle in his manners, always inclined to yield to me in everything, giving me my own way to an extent which unfortunately fostered my tendency to be domineering and overbearing. It was this trait in my character which led to the incident I am about to tell you of.

"In the summer vacations he and I—"

"Excuse me for interrupting you, Uncle Dud; but how did this Ben get along at school?"

"Well, he never went to school—"

"Never went to school! Why, didn't those folks he lived with give him any advantages?"

"—But I don't think any one seemed to consider him neglected. He was naturally very quick of perception, and had a wonderful faculty of gathering information from his surroundings. He seemed so well fitted for whatever duties fell to him, that I don't believe any one thought it necessary to send him to school."

"What was he good for, anyhow?"

"He made himself generally useful and agreeable. He used to drive cows, dig in the garden, etc., and as the family grew fond of him, they used to take him out with them a great deal."

"They must have been a queer set, though, to let him grow to be a man in ignorance."

"Ben never got to be a man. But I agree with you, Hal, that a man without education, or a boy either, is a poor thing."

"Oh, did Ben die young?" said Hal, with a soberer face.

"Yes. I *did* take him to school with me once—what a tricky young rascal I must have been! He walked to the school-house door with me, and I forced him in—much against his will it was, but I always made him mind me. I seated him in the master's chair, and ordered him to stay there, while I went to my seat. Of course the boys all laughed, and poor Ben trembled and looked imploringly at me, but I shook my fist at him to make him sit still. Presently the master came in. He was a quick-tempered man, and when he saw what was going on, how mad he was! He snatched up a rule, but Ben was too smart for him. He sprang from the chair and went out of the half-open window at one bound, with an awful crash of glass and sash, and was off swift as the wind. Then the master tried to find out who was in fault, but could get no further than the truth that he belonged to none of us. No one told of me, so I missed the thrashing which would have been so willingly bestowed."

"I think it was right mean of you to treat Ben so, uncle."

"I think so too, and that wasn't my worst treatment of him, as you shall hear.

"A small river formed the boundary of one side of my father's farm. On its bank, in one spot which was surrounded and sheltered by a thick growth of willows, Ben and I used to spend many an hour. He was an excellent swimmer, and very fond of the water. One morning we were having a merry time; we swam, dived, and rowed in the lovely sunshine. At last I picked up a piece of wood and threw it to the other side of the stream, trying to hit a water-rat. As it left my hand, I saw that it was a piece I had selected for the hull of a miniature boat, just suitable for that purpose, being straight-grained and exactly the right thickness. I told Ben to go and get it for me, but he was probably tired of play, for, for the first time, he refused to do my bidding, and went and lay down under a tree. I was angry, and ordered him loudly and roughly, picking up a stone and threatening him. He looked reproachfully at me, and turned and walked quickly toward his home.

"Now throwing stones was one of my great faults. I can not tell how often my mother had scolded, threatened, and punished me for it. Even at that moment there came vividly before me the remembrance of a time when I had killed a robin, and brought it and showed her what I had done—for I must do myself the justice to say I was always frank in confessing my faults. She took the poor dead bird in her hands, and with tears in her eyes talked to me in a tone of deeper anger and sorrow than I had ever heard from her.

"'They are God's little creatures. They are dumb, except for the sweet songs they bring us. They are helpless, except as their helplessness appeals to human beings for pity and protection. I believe the Lord's blessing will *never* rest on those who are cruel to things weaker than themselves.'

"I was really sorry, and wanted to tell her so, but a spirit of pride tempted me to 'brave it out,' so I said, with a poor attempt at a laugh, 'Oh, I'm sorry, of course, but you know it comes natural to boys to throw stones.'

"If I had been at all decent about it, she would have forgiven me at once; but, ah me! I never saw her move so quickly as when she went out the back door and broke off a supple green apple switch. After making most vigorous use of it she sent me to my room, with the remark, 'It fortunately comes natural to mothers to punish.'

"I spent the rest of the day there, and as I feasted on bread and water, and realized that there was company to tea, and that my whole being craved spring chicken, jelly cake, and quince preserves, I made up my mind that in future there would be one boy to whom it would come less 'natural' to throw stones.

"All this passed through my mind as I stood with the stone in my hand. But my tyrannical temper mastered me, and as Ben turned and looked back, I flung it at him. I did *not* mean to hit his head, but there was where it struck, in the brown hair just above one eye. I saw the blood trickle from a cut, as with a sharp cry of pain he ran away and disappeared. I was shocked at what I had done, but you know there are some conditions of mind in which self-reproach only makes anger hotter. I did not obey my impulse to follow the poor fellow, but threw off my jacket and plunged into the stream to recover the block I wanted. I suppose I had already been too long in

AN UNWELCOME GUEST.—Drawn by H. P. [illegible]

the water, for when about half way over I was seized with a cramp. In a moment I became helpless, and screamed wildly as I felt myself going down—down—down. I arose to the surface again too nearly drowned to scream any more, but with just sense enough left to feel myself seized by something. That was the last I knew.

"But I was afterward told how my father and some of the farm hands came rushing down just in time to see Ben panting, almost exhausted, as he drew me to the shore. There was blood on my face, which added to my mother's great alarm when I was carried to her. Not my blood, as you may guess, but poor Ben's—the result of my cruel blow.

"There is not much more to tell. I was in bed several days after it. The first time Ben came to see me I put my arms around his neck, and begged him to forgive me."

"What did he say?"

"Not a word. He never was a talker. But I knew by his clear, earnest eyes that he had never harbored a hard thought of me. I need not tell you I treated him more kindly after that. We continued, if possible, closer friends than ever, till I was sent away to school."

"And you say Ben did not live to be a man, uncle?" said Hal, whose interest in the "little tramp" had greatly increased. "How old was he when he died? Tell us about it, please."

"His death was a very sad occurrence, taking place the same season I left home. One night a suspicious-looking person came prowling about Mr. Washburn's place. Ben was the first to hear him—he always seemed to have one ear open when the interests of his friends were concerned—and ran toward him, making all the noise he could to arouse the family. The brave fellow seized hold of the marauder, who drew a revolver, and beat him about the head, and as he still held on, shot him."

A murmur of regret and indignation arose from the little audience.

"The man made off, and Ben was found to be not dead, but terribly injured: a leg was broken, and his head fearfully bruised. All that kind care could do for him was done, but it soon appeared that he was beyond all hope of recovery, and to put an end to his sufferings another bullet—this time aimed in sorrowful kindness—did its quick work on the life of poor Ben."

"*What's that?*" cried Hal, starting up. "Do you mean that they *shot* him? Killed a boy because he was badly hurt? I never heard of such—"

"*Boy?*" said his uncle, looking at him in great surprise. Then he went on: "When I heard of it, it almost broke my heart; and the first time I went home after it, and no Ben came bounding to meet me, wagging his tail, and with a face beaming welcome, I felt as though I had—"

"Hey, uncle! Wagging *his tail?* *Whose* tail? What are you talking about? Haven't you been telling us about a *boy* all this time?"

"Yes. *I* was a boy. But Ben was not."

"A—dog?"

Hal threw himself on the grass-plot and shouted with laughter, all his sympathy for Ben lost in his amusement at this unexpected disclosure.

"Oh, Uncle Dud! you're too much for me. 'Never went to school,' 'never grew to be a man'—oh no. 'No talker,' 'didn't ask for anything'—modest fellow! Oh, that's too good!"

Boys and girls had a hearty laugh, and ran away to play hide-and-seek in the summer twilight—all but little Elsie, who tenderly stroked the brown curl, and laid it against her soft cheek, sighing, "Poor Ben! poo-oor doggie!"

(Begun in HARPER'S YOUNG PEOPLE No. 61, July 13.)

THE STORY OF THE AMERICAN NAVY.

BY BENSON J. LOSSING.

CHAPTER III.

"NORTH AFRICAN pirates are out on the Mediterranean Sea; our budding commerce there is in danger; we must have a navy to protect it," wrote a distinguished American in Europe to Alexander Hamilton. President Washington called the attention of Congress to the matter, and in the spring of 1794 he was authorized to have six frigates built, each carrying not less than thirty-two cannon. The keel of the *Constitution* (yet afloat) was soon laid at Boston, and so the creation of the Navy of the United States was begun.

To the heroes of the Continental Navy the people looked for commanders of the new frigates, and Barry, Nicholson, Talbot, Barney, Dale, and Truxton, all of whom had done gallant service in the war for independence, were chosen.

The building of the frigates was unwisely suspended in the fall of 1795. "Pay me so many hundred thousand dollars every year, and I will let your ships alone," said the piratical ruler of Algiers. The terms were agreed to. Congress seemed to think that now all danger to commerce was overpast, and a navy would be an extravagant toy. But when, not long afterward, French cruisers seized American ships, and English cruisers claimed the right (and exercised it) to take seamen from our vessels without leave, Congress perceived the folly of their humiliating action.

War with France was threatened in the spring of 1798. The startled Congress ordered the six frigates to be finished, and more to be built or purchased. A Navy Department was organized, and a Secretary of the Navy appointed. Recruits were called for. The navy became very popular, and the ships were soon filled, with the sons of the best families in the land holding the rank of midshipmen.

The first vessel of the new navy that went to sea was the *Ganges*, twenty-four guns. She was to protect the ports of New York, Philadelphia, and Baltimore against French cruisers. Toward midsummer (1798), Congress authorized the seizure of French armed vessels found prowling along our coasts. For this purpose Truxton, with the *Constellation*, and Decatur the elder, with the *Delaware*, immediately went to sea. Decatur soon returned with the French cruiser *Le Croyable* as a prize. She was added to the navy, named *Retaliation*, and put under the command of Lieutenant Bainbridge. Captain Barry, with the frigate *United States*, soon followed, with many young men who afterward became distinguished in their country's service. Before the end of the year nearly the whole American navy was among the West India Islands, engaged in convoying merchantmen to and from the United States. This sudden appearance on the sea of a new naval power astonished the English and the French, and made both more cautious.

Early in 1799, Truxton, with the *Constellation*, captured the famous French frigate *L'Insurgente*, near the island of Nevis, after a severe battle for an hour. This triumph made Truxton famous. His praises were on every lip. A song called "Truxton's Victory" was sung everywhere in public and private. A year later his fame was increased by his combat with another French frigate, which he had searched for among the islands of the West Indies. Off Guadeloupe he fell in with a large French vessel at twilight, and they fought desperately in the darkness that followed. Suddenly the stranger disappeared in the gloom of night. Some time afterward Truxton learned that the ship was the very one he was searching for—the frigate *La Vengeance*; that he had shattered her terribly; and that she ran away in the darkness to a friendly port to save her life.

These victories made the navy very popular. Truxton was the hero of this war with the French on the ocean. It soon ceased, and the little navy found ample employment in the Mediterranean.

In the year 1800 Bainbridge was sent, in command of the *George Washington*, to pay tribute to the Algerine ruler. The Dey, as he was called, commanded the Captain to take an Ambassador to Constantinople. Bainbridge refused. "You pay me tribute, and are my slave," said the haughty Dey; "you must do as I bid you;" and he pointed to the guns of the castle. The Captain was compelled to obey. The Sultan received him kindly, for the crescent moon on the Turkish banner, and the stars on the American flag, seemed to prophesy good-will between the two nations. He gave Bainbridge an order that made the insolent Dey tremble. With it in his hand, the Captain said to the turbaned ruler, "Release every Christian captive you have, without ransom." The astonished and humbled Dey obeyed, and Bainbridge sailed away with threescore liberated captives under the American flag.

Meanwhile the rulers of Tunis and Tripoli—other North African robbers—had exacted and received tribute from the United States. The treatment of Bainbridge made the latter resolve to pay tribute no longer, but to humble the piratical powers. In the spring of 1801 Commodore Dale was sent with a squadron on that errand. He captured a Tripolitan pirate ship, and appeared before Tunis, where the flag-staff before the house of the American Consul had been cut down. Dale threatened the ruler with chastisement. He was astonished and perplexed. Dale cruised in the Mediterranean until fall, effectually protecting American commerce, for the half-barbarian powers were made timid and cautious.

The following year a relief squadron was sent to the

FIGHT BETWEEN THE "CONSTELLATION" AND "LA VENGEANCE."

Mediterranean under Commodore Morris. The *Constellation* blockaded the harbor of Tripoli. A flotilla of Tripolitan gun-boats tried to drive her away, but failed. At one time the *Constellation* successfully fought seventeen of them, as well as troops of cavalry on shore. The other vessels of the squadron cruised along the northern shores of the Mediterranean, effectually protecting American commerce; and in January, 1803, all the vessels collected at Malta. In the spring they appeared off the ports of the Barbary States, as these African provinces were called, and effectually imprisoned their corsairs, or pirate-ships, in their harbors. In May the *John Adams*, which had been blockading the harbor of Tunis, had a severe combat with Tunisian gun-boats and land batteries, and was much bruised. Very soon Tripolitan and Algerine corsairs appeared, and the whole American squadron was compelled to abandon the blockade of the African ports, after they had destroyed a cruiser from Tripoli. The squadron left the coast, the Africans regained their spirits, and very soon American commerce was again suffering from the depredations of corsairs.

The government of the United States, annoyed by the failure of this naval campaign in the Mediterranean, resolved to act with more vigor in that direction. A squadron of seven vessels was placed under the command of Commodore Preble, and sent to the Mediterranean in 1803.

[TO BE CONTINUED.]

THE STORY OF THE DAISIES.

BY MRS. MARGARET EYTINGE.

DAISIES, golden-hearted, star-like, smiling daisies, all over the fields and meadows, all along the highways and by-ways—bonny wee flowers looking bravely up at the dazzling sun, and giving with child-like generosity their beauty to the loneliest spots and most desolate places. Close up to a fence that surrounded a garden where bloomed hundreds of rare and lovely blossoms they crowded, praising with sweet artlessness the grace and fragrance of their more precious sisters, and wondering every morning when the gardener came out at early dawn and collected many young plants together, and gathered roses, and pansies, and gladioles, and verbenas, and pinks, and other flowers by the basketful, to carry away, where he took them and what became of them.

"I will tell you," said a tall, graceful white lily that grew near the garden gate, one day, as she inclined her fair head toward them. "I have been where they are going—I and the tuberoses over yonder. (We are growing in pots sunk in the ground, and therefore can be taken up and moved from place to place without harm.) Once I helped deck a large, sunshiny room—I was a very young bud then—where a great many little children, looking like flowers themselves in their gay dresses, sang, and played, and laughed, and danced for joy, because a baby friend was three years old that day; and once I stood at the right hand of a gray-haired minister, in a crowded church, and heard him say, 'Solomon in all his glory was not arrayed like one of these.' But, dear, simple, wee things, you don't understand that, do you? I forgot to whom I was talking. They go to a large city, where nothing is seen but brick and stone buildings and hosts of people, and nothing is heard but the sound of voices and footsteps, and the ringing of bells, and the tramping of horses, and rolling of wagons, and where there are no bees, nor butterflies, nor birds, save canaries that live in cages, and sparrows that can live anywhere."

"But the daisies are never taken to the city," said the daisies, after a short pause, "and they are flowers as well as the verbenas and pinks."

"Bless your innocent little hearts! I know they are," said the lily. "But the fact is, no one cares to buy daisies."

"So nobody cares for us in the big city," said the daisies to each other, "and yet the butterflies and birds tell us we are very pretty."

But the lily was mistaken, for the very next morning the gardener came out into the meadow with a trowel in his hand, and digging up some of the largest daisy plants, replanted them in a large flower-pot.

"Somebody wants us after all," they called to the grass, and the dandelions, and the other daisies, as they were carried away, "and we shall see the fine houses, and perhaps live with lilies, roses, and geraniums all the rest of our lives. Good-by, dear friends, good-by."

In a short time the daisies found themselves in a market-place—not among cabbages and tomatoes, but at the end of a row of blooming plants from the garden at which they had so often peeped through the fence. But they had scarcely had time to look about them when they saw a shabbily dressed boy coming slowly toward them—slowly, poor fellow, because one of his feet was sadly misshapen, and in his arms he carried a heavy bundle of newspapers. He looked eagerly at the gardener as he came near.

"I've got your daisies, my boy," the man called, cheerily. "Here they are, still wet with the dew, as handsome daisies as ever I saw. You must keep them in the shade a day or two, giving them a drink now and then, and I don't doubt they'll do finely. Will you take them now?"

"Yes, sir, thank you," said the boy, his whole face lighting up, and his pale cheeks flushing, "if you will let me leave my papers here a few minutes until I can run home with them. But you've brought so many—and they're in a nice pot, too—I'm afraid I haven't money enough to pay for them."

"Five cents was the price agreed on yesterday," said the good-natured gardener, "and I always stick to a bargain. And if there's more than you expected, all the better for you—some of 'em 'll be sure to thrive anyhow. As for the pot, you're welcome to that. A flower-pot more or less won't make me or break me."

The boy threw down his bundle, took the daisies with another "thank you," and hurried away as fast as his poor foot would let him to an old, queer-looking wooden house near the market, where, hugging his treasure closely to his breast, he mounted the shaky stairs until he reached the garret. Pushing open a door here, he entered a small little room with only one window in it, but that a dormer facing the south. The floor of this room was bare, with the exception of two or three round rag mats, and the walls were decorated in the oddest manner with pictures cut from old papers and magazines, bits of colored glass, strips of glittering tin twisted into grotesque shapes, and red and green motto-papers fashioned into some semblance of flowers.

On a bed near the window lay a little pale-faced, brown-haired girl, with wistful gray eyes, and a smile like sunshine breaking through a cloud. In her hands she held a pair of knitting-needles, with which she was knitting with marvellous quickness some coarse thread into wide, strong lace. Beside the bed stood a small table, holding a box of water-colors, a camel's-hair brush or two, a lead-pencil, a cup filled with water, and a piece of paper on which was a rude attempt at a painting of a bunch of daisies.

"See what I've brought you, Phœnie!" cried her brother, joyfully. "To-day's your birthday; thirteen years old—almost as old as I am. Bet you thought I'd forgotten it; but I didn't, dearie; no, indeed."

"Daisies! daisies!" cried the girl, with a sweet glad laugh, dropping her work, and holding out her pretty slender hands. "Oh, brother—dear, good, *darling* brother—will they live and grow?"

"The gardener says they will, and he ought to know," answered her brother. "And now you needn't be aching your poor little head any more trying to think exactly how they look, for you can study them all day long. But, good gracious! I must go and sell my papers, or we'll have no berries for dinner, and that would be dreadful." And giving his sister a kiss, he hurried away again, as happy, I believe, as any boy in that great city on that pleasant summer day.

"I am so glad, so very, very glad that you have come," said Phemie to the daisies as soon as he was gone, as she set them on the table, and gazed at them with tears in her eyes, "and I beg of you to live, dear daisies. I am a poor weak little girl, and I can sit up but a few hours each day. But a long while ago I could run about like other little girls, and I lived in the country, where thousands of daisies grew, and I have never forgotten them. Mamma was alive then, but she's dead now, and father left us here a year after she died, and we have never seen him since. He didn't care for daisies or us. How good of Brother Frank to bring you to me, daisies! I shall knit so much better and faster, and earn so much more money, with your bright faces smiling at me. And some day I shall make a picture of you—I have been trying to paint one from memory—that shall be almost as pretty as your own dear selves." And she leaned back against her pillow, singing softly to herself; and while her fingers plied the knitting-needles, her spirit, led by the spirits of the meadow flowers, wandered to green fields, and listened to the hum of the bees and the song of the birds, and grew lighter and happier every moment. And Frank, coming in quietly at noon, saw her with closed eyes and clasped hands, and heard her say, "Dear God, a helpless child thanks Thee for daisies!"

And the daisies all lived, and increased in numbers until the room overflowed with them. On floor and shelves they bloomed in cracked pitchers, broken jars, old fruit cans, everything that Frank could find to fill with them. And Phemie did paint a beautiful picture of them at last, and through this picture came much good fortune to that garret home. For Frank, showing it, in his brotherly love and pride, to a kind gentleman whom he served with papers, was surprised to learn that it was worth more than his sister knitting lace for three long months could earn.

And now to end the story. The very prettiest New-Year's card that appeared to celebrate the birth of 1880 was one on which the New-Year's greeting was printed on a ribbon encircling the stems of a bunch of daisies. Those daisies are Phemie's daisies. And the young flower painter, growing stronger day by day, is the happy mistress of two pleasant rooms and a mite of a studio.

OLD HANNIBAL.

BY WILLIAM O. STODDARD.

"NO, mother," said Colonel Dunway to his wife, at the breakfast table, "I shall ride the black colt on parade to-day. Hannibal is too fat and too old."

"Too old? He and Barry are just of an age."

"And Barry's only a little colt yet? Well, you may bring him and Prue out to the grand review in the afternoon, but I guess I'll ride the black this morning. You can put Hannibal in the carry-all. Perhaps he'd like to take a look again at a regiment of troops in line."

Barry and Prue listened with all their ears.

They knew there was to be a grand parade of soldiers that day, and they were prouder than they knew how to tell of the fact that their father was to wear a uniform, and ride a horse, and give orders to some of the men.

"Prue," said Barry, "father's going to 'spect them."

"*In*-spect them," whispered Prue, correcting him. "Nobody else knows how."

That might be, for Colonel Dunway had been an officer of the regular army, and he was now Colonel of a regiment of militia; but there was one thing he had said that puzzled Barry and Prue dreadfully.

"Barry," said Prue, after breakfast, "is Nibble old?"

"Father says he is."

"And he said he was fat."

"Dr. Barnes is old, and he's fat."

"But his head's bare."

"Nibble isn't bald, and he isn't gray either."

"He's brown."

Mrs. Dunway had told the exact truth about Hannibal, or Nibble, as the children called him. He and Barry were just of an age, and he had been a mere two-year-old colt when Prue was a baby in her cradle.

It was after that that Colonel Dunway had taken Hannibal with him to the army, and brought him home again.

He had been a war-horse, the Colonel said, and so it would not do to turn him into a plough-horse, and the consequence was that Nibble did not have enough work to do, and he grew fat too fast.

Yet he and Barry were only nine years old apiece. That made eighteen years between them; and if you added seven years for Prue, it would only have made twenty-five, and everybody knows that is not very old, if you had given them all to Hannibal.

Barry and Prue would have given him almost anything they had, for he was a great friend and crony of theirs.

"Prue," said Barry, "let's go out to the barn. I've got an apple."

"He can have my bun."

What there was left of it, that meant, for Prue's little white teeth had been at work on that bun.

That had been a troubled morning for Hannibal. Before he had finished his breakfast a party of men rode by the house, and one of them was playing on a bugle. He had set Hannibal's mind at work upon army matters and war; so when Barry and Prue came to see him, he would not even nibble. He smelled of the apple, and he looked at the bun, but that was all.

"He's getting old," said Barry.

"And fat," added Prue.

"Tell you what, Prue, let's take him out into the lot. I know mother 'd let us."

That was likely, for Mrs. Dunway always felt safer about them if Nibble were keeping them company.

"I'll get on his back."

"And I'll lead him. Wait till I fix the halter."

Prue climbed up on the side of the stall where Nibble was, and he stood perfectly still while she clambered over to her place on his back.

Barry knew exactly what to do, and the old war-horse began to think he did himself. He must have been thinking, for he half closed one eye as he was walking out, and opened the other very wide, with a wonderfully knowing look.

He was looking down the lane, and he saw that the front gate was open, and just at that moment there came up the road, very faint and sweet, the music of the cavalry bugle.

"Nibble! Nibble!" exclaimed Barry, "where are you going?"

Hannibal did not answer a word, but walked on down the lane very fast indeed, and Barry lost hold of the halter.

As for Prue, she was not scared a particle, for she had ridden in that way many a time, and her confidence in herself and old Nibble was unbounded.

"Cluck, cluck, cluck—get-up."

"Stop, Prue, stop. He's going faster."

"Get-up! Come, Barry. Oh, there's mother at the window!"

Mrs. Dunway was not frightened any more than Prue, for she said to herself, "Too old, indeed! Well, they're more like three children, when they're together, than any-

THE "THREE CHILDREN."—DRAWN BY KELL.

thing else. I'm glad he is fat. He won't go too fast for Prue."

He was in the road now, and he seemed disposed to keep Barry from again getting hold of that halter.

"Oh dear," said Barry, "the parade-ground's down there."

Hannibal knew that, by the music, and he was almost trotting now.

In fact, he was looking younger and younger, somehow, every minute, and Barry felt more and more as if he ought to have hold of the halter, instead of merely running alongside and shouting to Prue.

The regiment was drawn up on the great bare field where the review was to be that afternoon, and they looked splendidly.

Colonel Dunway was saying so, as he sat in front of them, on his handsome black colt, and a number of other officers who were riding with him said the same, and so did the ladies who were keeping them company.

Just then the bugle sounded again, from the head of the column, and Prue had to hold on hard, for Hannibal suddenly began to canter, and he answered the music with a loud, clear whinny of delight.

Barry was half out of breath with running, but he kept up with the other two, and in a moment more Hannibal halted, proudly arching his neck, and treading daintily upon the grass, right in front of the regiment.

"I declare," exclaimed Colonel Dunway, "the old fellow has come to review the troops."

"So has Prue," said one of the officers.

Barry hardly knew whether to laugh or to cry, but the soldiers suddenly broke out in a grand "hurrah."

They were cheering Prue and her war-horse, and Colonel Dunway himself was compelled to let the "three children" stay and keep the place Hannibal chose for them at the head of the regiment.

There was plenty of apples for Nibble that day.

SEA BREEZES.

LETTER No. 2 FROM BESSIE MAYNARD TO HER DOLL.

OLD ORCHARD BEACH, *July*, 1880.

THE days must seem very long and lonely to you, my sweet Clytemnestra, and I will send you another letter, to "cheer you up a bit," as nurse used to say when she gave me a lump of sugar, after pulling my curls 'most out of my head, trying to get out the tangles.

How are you getting along all this time? and what do you find to amuse yourself with? Do you sit still in your own corner of the baby-house day after day, or does some kind fairy come in once in a while and wind you up, so that you can run round the room and get a little exercise? We will have lots of walks and talks when I get home, my Clytie. I heard mamma telling Cousin Frank last night that we should probably go next month. If I did not know that you were at home expecting and wanting me, it would be awfully hard to think of leaving this place; for life by the sad sea waves is truly (as I heard a lady say yesterday) "fascinating and entrancing."

There are so many people here it seems like a party all the time. There are not many children, though—at least not at our hotel; only Fanny, Dora, and me for girls; Randolph Peyton, Jack Hunter, Charley Phillips, and Hal Davis for boys; Snip and Moppet for dogs; and the cunningest wee little mite of a pussykin, named Whitetoes, for cats. Not that cats and dogs are exactly *children*, either, but they are just as good, and sometimes better. I'm sure I would rather play any time with Snip and Whitetoes than with that horrid Randolph. He is the very unpolitest boy I ever knew. Let me tell you something he did yesterday, and then I guess you will agree with me. We seven children and the dogs had planned a beautiful picnic down on "the island," as we call it.

You know the geography says (or you *would* know if you had ever been to school, poor child!) that "an island is a portion of land entirely surrounded by water." Well, *this* "portion of land" runs out ever so far into the sea, and has a pretty grove on it; and at high tide the water covers the little strip of land where it really joins the beach, so that for a little while it *is* an island, but the rest of the time it is a *peninsula*. That is a big word, and you don't know a bit what it means, and I can't tell you now; you shall learn about it when we begin our lessons.

But, oh dear, I was going to tell you about the picnic and Randolph Peyton, the great disagreeable boy. Somehow or other, when I begin to write to you, there are so many things to explain that I never seem to "come to the point," as papa says.

We had planned to start at eight o'clock, but what with Moppet's running away, and Snip's taking a nap behind a hay-cock down in the orchard, where we only found him

HOW WE LOOKED JUST BEFORE *IT* HAPPENED.

by accident at the very last minute, we were not fairly on our way till almost nine. The boys carried the lunch baskets. Fan wheeled her baby carriage, with poor invalid Jane lying back on the pillows, looking too forlorn for anything, but really Fan seems to love her even more than she loved Lucille; and I do think, considering what Jane has been through, that she is the very best child in the world.

Sometimes when I look at her woe-begone face, and her poor little head without a single hair on it (she wears a lace cap, but we can see the *bald* right through), and remember her cheeks as they used to be, and her lovely golden curls, and then think how gentle and kind she is, never complaining, nor speaking a single cross word, I can't help saying right out to her, "You poor little dear thing, Solomon was right when he said 'Handsome is, that handsome does.'" Well, Fan wheeled her along, and I carried Moppet curled up in my arms like a white puff-ball, while Dora ran races all along the beach with Snip.

I forgot to tell you that Randolph had been behaving badly all the way, teasing us girls, pinching the dogs and making fun of Jane; but the terrible thing of all did not happen till we were crossing over to the island. We always lay a board across from a rock on the beach side to a rock on the island side, and over that we girls walk, though the boys generally wade right through the water.

Fan and Jane went first on the board, then Dora and Snip, and last Moppet and me.

Now listen, my Clytie, though, without having seen it, you never can quite know how perfectly terrible it was. Just as Dora and Snip were in the very middle of the board, and *all* of us were on it, Randolph, who was standing in the water, gave a most unearthly screech, and at that very minute— But, mercy me! there's the tea-bell, and you *must* excuse me, my lamb, for leaving you right here, for how can I help it when I smell *waffles!*—waffles, and muffins too, I think.

In greatest haste,

Your own mamma, BESSIE.

P.S.—It was waffles I smelled, and I thought of you, dear Clytie, as I ate them. Now I shall have to leave my story of Randolph at its very smilax (or climax, which is it?), and finish it in my next letter, for I have written so much my fingers are all cramped up: so good-night.

THE PITIFUL HARE.

FROM THE JAPANESE, BY W. E. GRIFFIS.

HARES are always treated kindly by the Chinese and Japanese people, who make household pets of them. The Chinese believe that the hare lives to be a thousand years old, and that at the end of five centuries its hair becomes white. Instead of seeing a man in the moon, they imagine they see a hare standing on its hind-legs, and pounding drugs in a mortar. There are great creatures like gigantic men, called genii, who live in the moon, and make "the elixir of life," a draught of which confers very long life. The hare is their steward, and spends his time in pounding the precious roots and bark of the "tree of the king of drugs," from which the elixir is made. In the Japanese fairy tales, whoever smells, touches, or tastes of this tree is immediately healed of all disease.

The country folks in Japan believe a great deal more in the influence of the moon on crops, and good luck, and the weather, than our farmers do, and some of the Japanese almanacs are very funny to read. It is for these reasons that the people do not injure the hare, for fear of hindering the good influence of the moon.

The hare is considered above all others the faithful animal, and in the story which the picture tells he is comforting his master.

It would seem very queer to you, my readers, to see tame hares running about the house instead of your pet dogs and cats! But this is what the little Japanese see.

[illegible]

The ground-squirrel and chipmunk are the same animal, but the gopher, or Canada pouched rat, belongs to a different family.—Feed your minnows by throwing bread-crumbs, and flies and other small insects on the surface of the water.

[illegible]

The word strawberry is from the Anglo-Saxon, and was formerly written streawberie. The reason for applying the name to the delicious little fruit is undecided. Some authorities hold that it should be written strayberry, and that it refers to the creeping or straying habit of the vines.

C. L. R.—Alwar, sometimes written Ulwar or Alvar, is a town of India, eighty-five miles southwest of Delhi.

I have heard that there are a great many towns in the United States named Vicksburg. Can you tell me how many?

My sister tried Helen's recipe for lemon pie, in YOUNG PEOPLE No. 33, and it was very nice.

F. H. G.

There are five towns and cities named Vicksburg, one in each of the following States: Kansas, Michigan, Minnesota, Pennsylvania, Mississippi.

WILLIE M.—Directions for making an ordinary kite were given in Post-office Box No. 17. "Sam Vedder's Kite," in YOUNG PEOPLE No. 25, also contained some valuable suggestions.

WALT.—Common sunfish can not injure the gold-fish and other inhabitants of your aquarium.

[illegible]

[illegible] and now I am reading Charles Dickens's *Child's History of England*. I don't know what to read next. I wish you would tell me the names of some children's histories, for I do not understand very well those written for older people. FANNIE R.

All of Abbott's Illustrated Histories would interest you. Then there are some good histories for young readers by Miss Yonge; and child's histories of the United States, of Greece, and of Rome, by Bonner; an interesting child's history of the United States, by T. W. Higginson; and many other books referring to special periods, like Mr. Coffin's *Story of Liberty* and *Boys of '76*, where you will find much valuable information. The works by Abbott, Bonner, and Coffin are published by Harper & Brothers.

ELLA W.—The date of the invention of gunpowder is unknown. Tradition says that it was used in China as early as A.D. 85, for fireworks and blasting, and that the Arabs employed it at the siege of Mecca in 690. Roger Bacon is supposed to allude to its explosive force, and it is said that Berthold Schwartz, a monk, about 1320, discovered the mode of manufacturing it. It is also said that the knowledge of it was conveyed to Europe by the returning Crusaders.

[illegible] your parrot with English walnuts, bits of apple and pear, and canary and hemp seed, and also give it a red pepper to pick to pieces. Let it out of its cage to climb about an hour or more every morning. A parrot can not be healthy without some exercise.

GEORGE F.—Directions for "Model Yacht Building" were given in YOUNG PEOPLE No. 23.

P. H. L.—Any hardware merchant will send to New York city for a catalogue of toy steam-engines for you, which will give you full information in regard to styles, prices, and how and where the engine you require can be obtained.

[illegible] H. H.—You can purchase turtles at any store where gold-fish and materials for an aquarium are sold. They will cost you very little—ten or fifteen cents apiece, perhaps, for small ones. If you are going to the country, you can catch plenty of them yourself. By reading former numbers of the Post-office Box you will find many directions for the care of turtles. A water turtle needs clean water, and also stones to climb up on.

Favors are acknowledged from [illegible]

Correct answers to puzzles are received from [illegible]

PUZZLES FROM YOUNG CONTRIBUTORS.

No. 1.

[illegible]

I am composed of 14 letters.
My 13, 8, 10, 6 is used in [illegible].
My 1, 14, 8, 3, 5 is [illegible] on the [illegible].
My 2, 9, 14, 8, 10 is a [illegible].
My 7, 2, 9, 12 is a [illegible].
My 1, 12, 10, 4, 5 is [illegible].
My whole was a noted British admiral.

"[illegible]"

No. 2.

[illegible]

First, a division of time. Second, a girl's name. Third, disagreeable. Fourth, [illegible].

M. E. N.

No. 3.

[illegible]

1. I know the girls have [illegible]. 2. Yes, I am going to [illegible] Europe [illegible]. 3. The [illegible]. 4. At the [illegible] many people were [illegible]. 5. The [illegible] was brought home yesterday. 6. When you go to [illegible] do not forget to write often to mother. 7. [illegible] 8. [illegible] 9. [illegible] 10. [illegible]

S. R.

No. 4.

[illegible]

My first is in [illegible], but not in [illegible].
My second is in [illegible], but not in [illegible].
My third is in [illegible], but not in [illegible].
My fourth is in [illegible], but not in [illegible].
My fifth is in garden, but not in [illegible].
My sixth is in [illegible], but not in [illegible].
My whole is a delicious fruit.

W. H. L.

No. 5.

[illegible]

In soprano. A [illegible]. A musical instrument. A verb. In soprano.

[illegible]

No. 6.

[illegible]

A period of time. A [illegible]. An animal. A river in the United States. To signify. Answer—Two of the United States.

[illegible]

ANSWERS TO PUZZLES IN No. 85.

No. 1. [illegible]

No. 2. [illegible]

No. 3. [illegible]

No. 4. A rolling stone gathers no moss.

No. 5. [illegible]

No. 6. Pudding.

ADVERTISEMENTS.

HARPER'S YOUNG PEOPLE.

HARPER'S YOUNG PEOPLE will be issued every Tuesday, and may be had at the following rates—payable in advance, postage free:

SINGLE COPIES $0 04
ONE SUBSCRIPTION, one year 1 50
FIVE SUBSCRIPTIONS, one year 7 00

Subscriptions may begin with any Number. When no time is specified, it will be understood that the subscriber desires to commence with the Number issued after the receipt of order.

Remittances should be made by POST-OFFICE MONEY ORDER or DRAFT, to avoid risk of loss.

ADVERTISING.

The extent and character of the circulation of HARPER'S YOUNG PEOPLE will render it a first-class medium for advertising. A limited number of approved advertisements will be inserted on two inside pages at 75 cents per line.

Address

HARPER & BROTHERS,
Franklin Square, N. Y.

OUR CHILDREN'S SONGS.

Our Children's Songs. Illustrated. 8vo, Ornamental Cover, $1 00.

Songs for the nursery, songs for childhood, for girlhood, boyhood, and sacred songs—the whole melody of childhood and youth bound in one cover. Full of lovely pictures, sweet mother and baby faces, charming bits of scenery, and the dear old Bible story-telling pictures.—*Churchman*, N. Y.

Published by HARPER & BROTHERS, New York.

☞ HARPER & BROTHERS *will send the above work by mail, postage prepaid, to any part of the United States, on receipt of the price.*

ELEMENTARY EDUCATION.

Books for the School and Family.

ARITHMETIC.

FRENCH'S FIRST LESSONS IN NUMBERS. First Lessons in Numbers, in their Natural Order: First, [illegible]; Second, [illegible]; Third, Abstract Numbers. By JOHN H. FRENCH, LL.D. Illustrated. 16mo, Half Leather, [illegible] cents.

FRENCH'S ELEMENTARY ARITHMETIC FOR THE SLATE. Elementary Arithmetic for the Slate, in which Methods and Rules are based upon Principles established by Induction. By JOHN H. FRENCH, LL.D. 16mo, Half Leather, [illegible] cents.

FRENCH'S MENTAL ARITHMETIC. Mental Arithmetic, in which Combinations of Numbers, Solutions of Problems, and Principles of Arithmetical Analysis are based upon the Laws of Mental Development. By JOHN H. FRENCH, LL.D. Illustrated. 16mo, Half Leather, [illegible] cents.

NATURAL SCIENCE.

FIRST LESSONS IN NATURAL HISTORY AND LANGUAGE. Entertaining and Instructive Lessons in Natural History and Language for Primary and Grammar Schools. 16mo, Cloth, [illegible] cents.

THE CHILD'S BOOK OF NATURE. The Child's Book of Nature, for the Use of Families and Schools: intended to aid Mothers and Teachers in Training Children in the Observation of Nature. In Three Parts. Part I. Plants. Part II. Animals. Part III. Air, Water, Heat, Light, &c. By WORTHINGTON HOOKER, M.D. Illustrated. The Three Parts complete in One Volume, Small 4to, Half Leather, $1 [illegible]; or, separately, [illegible]

HOOKER'S FIRST BOOK IN CHEMISTRY. A First Book in Chemistry. By WORTHINGTON HOOKER, M.D. [illegible]

FARADAY'S CHEMISTRY OF A CANDLE. Chemistry of a Candle: A Course of Six Lectures on the Chemical History of a Candle, to which is added a Lecture on Platinum. By M. FARADAY. Edited by W. CROOKES. Illustrated. 16mo, Cloth, $1 00.

FARADAY'S PHYSICAL FORCES. Physical Forces. A Course of Six Lectures on the Various Forces of Matter, and their Relations to Each Other. By M. FARADAY. Edited by W. CROOKES. Illustrated. 16mo, Cloth, $1 00.

FRENCH AND GERMAN.

FRENCH PRINCIPIA, PART I. A First French Course: containing Grammar, Delectus, and Exercise-Book, with Vocabularies. On the Plan of Dr. Smith's *Principia Latina*. 12mo, Cloth, [illegible] cents.

FRENCH PRINCIPIA, PART II. A First French Reading-Book. Containing Fables, Anecdotes, Inventions, Discoveries, Natural History, and French History. With Grammatical Questions, Notes, and a Copious Etymological Dictionary. On the Plan of Dr. Smith's *Principia Latina*. 12mo, Cloth, [illegible] cents.

GERMAN PRINCIPIA, PART I. A First German Course. Containing Grammar, Delectus, Exercise-Book, and Vocabularies. On the Plan of Dr. Smith's *Principia Latina*. 12mo, Cloth, [illegible] cents.

GERMAN PRINCIPIA, PART II. A First German Reading-Book. Containing Fables, Anecdotes, Natural History, German History, and a Comedy. With Grammatical Questions, Notes, and a Dictionary. On the Plan of Dr. Smith's *Principia Latina*. 12mo, Cloth, [illegible] cents.

COMFORT'S GERMAN PRIMER. A German Primer. By GEORGE F. COMFORT, A.M. 16mo, Half Leather, [illegible] cents.

COMFORT'S FIRST BOOK IN GERMAN. A First Book in German. By GEORGE F. COMFORT, A.M. 16mo, Half Leather, [illegible] cents.

COMFORT'S FIRST GERMAN READER. The First German Reader; to succeed the "First Book in German." By GEORGE F. COMFORT, A.M. 12mo, Cloth, [illegible] cents.

OBJECT LESSONS.

WILLSON'S MANUAL OF OBJECT LESSONS. A Manual of Information and Suggestions for Object Lessons, in a Course of Elementary Instruction. By MARCIUS WILLSON. 12mo, Cloth, $1 [illegible].

CALKINS'S PRIMARY OBJECT LESSONS. Primary Object Lessons, for Training the Senses and Developing the Faculties of Children. A Manual of Elementary Instruction for Parents and Teachers. By N. A. CALKINS. [illegible] Edition. Rewritten and Enlarged. 12mo, Cloth, $1 [illegible].

Published by HARPER & BROTHERS, New York.

☞ *Sent by mail, postage prepaid, to any part of the United States, on receipt of the price.*

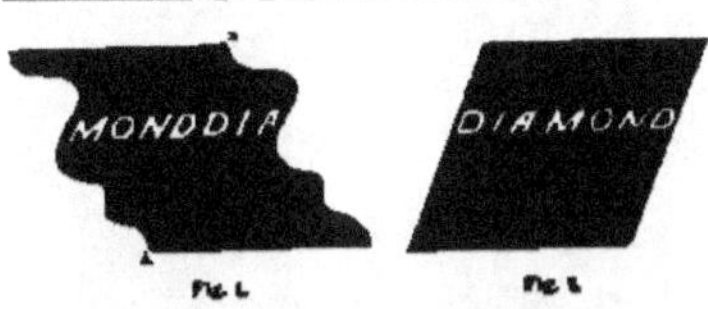

Fig. 1. Fig. 2.

SOLUTION TO MONDDIA PUZZLE.

WITH a pair of scissors cut the straight line from A to B in Fig. 1. Then join the two pieces as in Fig. 2, and you have a Diamond.

FIRE-EATING.

BY F. BELLEW.

YOU have read accounts, no doubt, if you have not seen the actual performance, of men who do wonderful things in the way of swallowing fire. Some of these feats may be executed by amateurs, with very good effect, in parlor entertainments.

I will first describe the feat of swallowing fire. This is very simple. Take a small piece of jeweller's cotton about the size of a walnut, and pour on it a little alcohol; a few drops will do. Then, standing with your face to the audience, you light this with a match. You then take a long breath, and open your mouth wide, holding your breath, mind, all the time; then you put the blazing cotton into your mouth, but just as it passes your lips you blow all the air sharply from your lungs (this extinguishes the fire in the cotton); shut your mouth quickly on the cotton, and press it boldly to the roof of your mouth with your tongue. You then slip the wad of cotton into your cheek, and swallow a draught of water from a tumbler you have ready on the table. As you wipe your mouth with your handkerchief after drinking the water, you remove the bit of cotton, and then you can allow any one of the audience to examine your mouth in order to satisfy himself that you really swallowed the fire.

In these fire-eating tricks, if you wash your mouth out with alum and water, all the better.

The other feat of fire-eating is a very old one, and has been often published, but I have seen so very many people astonished by it that I venture to give it again for the new generation.

THE CANDLE TRICK.

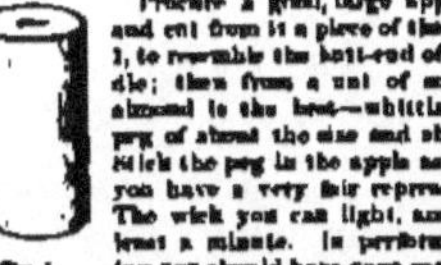

Fig. 1. Fig. 2. Fig. 3.

Procure a good, large apple or turnip, and cut from it a piece of the shape of Fig. 1, to resemble the butt-end of a tallow candle; then from a nut of some kind—an almond is the best—whittle out a small peg of about the size and shape of Fig. 2. Stick the peg in the apple as in Fig. 3, and you have a very fair representation of a candle. The wick you can light, and it will burn for at least a minute. In performing you should have your candle in a clean candlestick, show it plainly to the audience, and then put it into your mouth, taking care to blow it out in the same way as you would the cotton, and munch it up. If you think best, you can blow the candle out and allow the wick to cool, and it will look, with its burned wick, so natural that even the sharpest eyes can not distinguish it from the genuine article.

Once, at a summer resort in Massachusetts, I made use of this candle with considerable effect. While performing a few parlor tricks to amuse some friends, I pretended to need a light. A confederate left the room, and soon returned with a lantern containing one of these apple counterfeits.

"Do you call that a candle?" I said.

"Certainly," he replied.

"Why, there is scarcely a mouthful."

"A mouthful! Rather a disagreeable mouthful, I guess."

"You have never been in Russia, I presume?"

"Never."

"Then you don't know what is good."

"Good?"

"Yes, good. Why, candle ends, with the wick a little burned to give them a flavor, are delicious. They always serve them up before dinner in Russia as a kind of relish. It is considered bad taste in good society there to ask a friend to sit down to dinner without offering him this appetizer."

"The bad taste would be in the relish, I think."

"Not at all. Try a bit."

I took the candle out of the lantern, and extended it toward my confederate, who shrank back with disgust.

"Well," I said, "if you won't have it, I'll eat it myself." And so saying, I put it into my mouth and munched it up, amid the cries of surprise and horror of the assembled party. Two old maids insisted on looking into my mouth to see whether it was not concealed there.

A WARM DAY IN THE COUNTRY—SUDDEN APPEARANCE OF VILLAGE SCHOOL-MISTRESS, AND EQUALLY SUDDEN DISAPPEARANCE OF SCHOLARS.

A RIDDLE IN RHYME.

ON one occasion, while at a dinner party, Dr. O. W. Holmes composed the following riddle:

"My initials show my date to be
The morning of the Christian year;
Though fatherless, as all agree,
I am a father, it is clear:
A mother too, beyond dispute:
And when my son comes,
He's a fruit.
Now, not to puzzle you too much,
'Twas I gave Holland to the Dutch."

VOL. I.—NO. 40. PUBLISHED BY HARPER & BROTHERS, NEW YORK. PRICE FOUR CENTS.

Tuesday, August 3, 1880. $1.50 per Year, in Advance.

(Begun in Young People No. 31, June 1.)

THE MORAL PIRATES.

BY W. L. ALDEN.

CHAPTER X.

THE policeman did not return, and the boys slept until an hour after sunrise. They then rowed down the river to the steamboat landing, where they left their boat in charge of a boatman, and went to a hotel for breakfast. The waiters were rather astonished at the tremendous appetites displayed by the four sunburned boys, and there is no doubt that the landlord lost money that morning. After breakfast, Harry went to the express office, where he found a large water-proof India rubber bag, which the Department had sent in answer to his letter. At the post-office were letters from home for all the boys, and a postal order for ten dollars from Uncle John for the use of the expedition. Harry had no idea that this money would be needed, but it subsequently proved to be very useful.

Quite a quantity of stores were bought at Albany, for the voyage up the Hudson had lasted longer than any one had supposed it would, and the provisions were getting low. No unnecessary time was spent in buying these stores, for a fair wind was blowing, and all the boys were anxious to take advantage of it. By ten o'clock they were again afloat, and soon after noon they reached Troy, and entered the canal.

GOING THROUGH THE LOCK.—DRAWN BY A. B. FROST.

The canal basin was crowded with canal-boats, and to avoid accidents the *Whitewing's* mast was taken down, and the oars were got out. Harry knew that, in order to pass through the locks, it would be necessary to pay toll, and to procure an order from the canal authorities directing the lock-men to permit the *Whitewing* to pass. The canal boatmen, of whom he made inquiries, told him where to find the office, which was some little distance up the canal. When the office was reached, an officer came and inspected the boat, asked a great many questions about the cruise up the Hudson, and seemed to be very much interested in the expedition. He told the boys that the water was low in the Champlain Canal, and that the lock-men might not be willing to open the locks for so small a boat; but that they could avoid all dispute by entering the locks at the same time with some one of the many canal-boats that were on their way north. He charged the *Whitewing* the enormous sum of twenty-five cents for tolls, and gave Harry an important-looking order, by which the lock-men were directed to allow the skiff *Whitewing*, Captain Harry Wilson, to pass through all the locks on the canal.

Thanking the pleasant officer, the boys pushed off. After they had passed the place where the Champlain Canal branches off from the Erie Canal, they were no longer troubled by a crowd of canal-boats, and were able to set the sail again. Unluckily, the mast was just a little too high to pass under the bridges, and at the first bridge which they met they narrowly escaped a capsize—Jim succeeding in getting the mast down only just in time to save it from striking the bridge. They had hardly set sail again when another bridge came in sight, and they could see just beyond it a third bridge. It would never do to stop at every bridge and unship the mast, so Harry went on shore, borrowed a saw from a cooper's shop, and sawed six inches off from the top of the mast, after which the bridges gave them no more trouble.

The boys were very much interested in passing the first lock. They slipped into the lock behind a big canal-boat, which left just room enough between its rudder and the gate for the *Whitewing*. When the lock-men shut the gate behind the boat, and opened the sluices in the upper gate, the water rose slowly and steadily. The sides of the lock were so steep and black that the boys felt very much as if they were at the bottom of a well; but it was not many minutes before the water had risen so high that the upper gates were opened, and the big canal-boat and its little follower were released.

Passing through a lock in a small boat, and in company with a canal-boat, is not a perfectly safe thing to do, for if the ropes which fasten the canal-boat should break—which they sometimes do—the water rushing in through the sluices would force the canal-boat against the lower gate, and crush the small boat like an egg-shell. It is therefore best always to pass through a lock alone, or in company with other small boats. The danger, however, is in reality very slight, and very few accidents occur in canal locks.

The wind died away before sunset; and the boys having had only a light lunch, which they ate on the boat, were glad to go ashore for supper. They bought some corn from a farmer, and roasted it before the fire, while some nice slices of ham were frying, and the coffee-pot was boiling, and so prepared a supper which they greatly enjoyed. The moon came up before they had finished the meal, and they felt strongly tempted to make another attempt at night-work.

"I'll tell you what we can do," exclaimed Harry. "Instead of rowing, let's tow the boat. One fellow can tow while another steers, and the rest can sleep in the boat."

"All right," said Joe. "I'm willing to be a mule. Only I'd like to know where my harness is coming from."

"We've got rope enough for that," replied Harry. "I'll take the first turn, and tow for an hour, while Joe steers; then I'll steer for an hour, while Joe tows. Then the other watch will take charge of the boat for two hours, and Joe and I will sleep."

"If I'm to sleep on the bottom of that boat," said Joe, "I want some nice sharp stones to sleep on. I'm tired of sleeping on coffee-pots, and want a change."

A long tow-line was soon rigged on Harry's shoulders in such a way that it did not chafe him; a space in the bottom of the boat was cleared of coffee-pots and other uncomfortable articles, and a pair of blankets was spread on the bottom board, so as to make a comfortable bed, which Tom and Jim hastened to occupy. Joe took the yoke-lines in his hand, and called to Harry to go ahead. When Harry first tugged at the tow-line, the boat seemed very heavy; but as soon as she was in motion, Harry found that he could tow her as fast as he could walk, and without any difficulty.

Had the locks been open and the canal-boats been out of the way, the experiment of towing the *Whitewing* at night would have been very successful. As it happened, the locks were kept closed during the night, because the water was low; and the canal-boats, not being able to pass the locks, were moored to the tow-path. These boats gave Harry and Joe a great deal of trouble. When one of them was met, Harry had to unharness himself and toss the rope into the boat, and Joe had to get out an oar and scull around the obstacle. This happened so often that Tom and Jim got very little sleep; and long before it was time for them to resume duty, a lock was reached, and Harry had to call all hands to drag the boat around it.

This was a hard piece of work. First, all the heavy things had to be taken out of the boat and carried around the lock. Then the boat had to be dragged out of the canal on to the tow-path, hauled up a steep ascent, and launched above the upper gate. It took a good half-hour to pass the first of these closed locks, and when the boat was again ready to start, it was time to change the watch.

Tom and Jim had managed to get only a few minutes' sleep, but Harry and Joe could not sleep a single wink. They had not "turned in" for more than ten minutes when another lock was reached. This involved a second half-hour of hard work by all hands, and twenty minutes later three more locks close together blocked the way. It was foolish to persevere in dragging the boat around locks all night long; so, after getting her out of the canal on the side opposite to the tow-path, the boys dragged her behind some bushes, where the canal boatmen could not see her at daylight. They then spread their rubber blankets on the ground, and prepared to sleep through the remaining four or five hours of darkness.

"Boys," said Joe, suddenly, "does it hurt a fat woman to jump on her?"

"Don't know," answered Harry. "What do you ask for?"

"Oh, nothing," said Joe. "Only when I was jumping from one canal-boat to another while I was a mule, I landed awfully heavy on a fat woman who was sleeping on deck."

"What did she do?" asked Harry.

"She didn't do anything. She just muttered something that I could not understand, and I got away as quickly as possible."

"Well, if she likes it, that's her business, not yours," suggested Harry. "Go to sleep, do!"

"I am going to sleep; but I don't think we ought to spend our nights in getting run down by steamboats and jumping on strange fat women. I'm sure it isn't right. There, you needn't throw any more shoes at me. I won't say another word."

(TO BE CONTINUED.)

SOME TRUE STORIES ABOUT STEEPLES.

BY C. F. M.

A GREAT many years ago a hurricane occurred in Utica, New York. Just as it began it was noticed that a heavy swing sign in front of a store was held out in a horizontal position for some time.

Before long the force of the wind increased to such a degree that several houses on Genesee Street Hill were unroofed, and the spire of the Second Presbyterian Church was thrown to the ground.

After the storm was over it was discovered that the rod holding the weather-vane on the top of the tall steeple of the First Presbyterian Church was bent so that it became nearly horizontal. It was unsightly; but how to repair the injury was the question. It would be no easy task, as there was a large ball, or globe, on the rod below the vane. After a while a sailor offered his services. He ascended the steeple, and climbed the rod until he came just beneath the globe. Then he threw a rope out a good many times, until, after a while, the end looped around over the rod, above the globe, long enough to reach to him. Twisting the rope together, he let go of the iron rod, and trusting himself to the rope, swung out free. By climbing it he now managed to get on the top of the globe. Standing there, he succeeded in straightening the rod that held the weather-vane.

Now how was he to get down? Again trusting to the rope that was fastened to the rod above the globe, he swung free at a great height from the earth; then lowering himself, and swinging back and forth, he managed to grasp the rod beneath the globe, and soon reaching the spire, descended.

The steeple of Salisbury Cathedral is the highest in England, and next to that of Strasbourg Cathedral, the highest in Europe. Every year a man climbs to the top to grease the weather-vane. This is done by ascending the inside as far as possible, and then going out of a man-hole and climbing the rest of the way by means of the brass staples fastened on the outer wall.

Once on a festal occasion, when the King was present, a reward was offered, as usual, to any person who would ascend and attend to the weather-vane. A sailor agreed to do it, and ascended in the way I have told you, until he came to the capstone, when, to show what he could do, he stood on his head. Then performing the task he was sent to do, that of greasing the vane, he descended, and claimed his reward. But the King was so exasperated at the sailor for needlessly frightening the people by standing on his head at such a great height, that he would not allow him to be paid.

A long time ago, in the town of Northam, England, the steeple of the church was found to be unsteady. It swayed back and forth whenever the great bell struck, and continued to sway thus, until, as it leaned over on one side, it opened large cracks on the opposite.

It was not long before the boys of the town found this out, and the bright idea entered the head of one of them, and was by him told to the others, that it would be a capital place to crack nuts. So, boy-like, they had to try it, and standing at the base of the spire, would fill the cracks as far as they could reach with good English walnuts, and then stand back for the steeple to return to an upright position, cracking the nuts. As the great clock in the tower struck, the jar caused the spire to lean in the opposite direction. The boys now got their nuts, and then put in more, that the operation might be repeated, for they considered it rare sport.

But in the course of time the people of the town who had such matters in charge decided that the steeple was unsafe, and strengthened it with bands of iron; but this not proving satisfactory, after a while each stone was numbered, and the steeple taken down and rebuilt in the old style. And from that day to this, to the regret of the boys, it has never been known to crack nuts.

During a great fire in New York, a few years ago, one of the buildings destroyed was a church having a very tall steeple. The flames ran up inside this steeple, and, bursting out at the top, melted the zinc and copper about the lightning rod, so that they fell in showers of green, gold, and crimson fire, producing a spectacle of most wondrous beauty.

FLOWER QUEENS OF NIGHT.

BY MARGARET EYTINGE.

"Pretty, fragrant four-o'clocks,"
Said the rose one day,
"Pity 'tis your buds unfold
Into blossoms gay
When the west begins to burn
With the sunset light—
Sweetness wondrous rare to waste
On the drowsy night.

"Other blooms have birds to sing,
Bees to hum, their praise,
Butterflies to visit them
Through the summer days.
Bee but seldom hums for you,
Bird but seldom sings,
Butterfly is ne'er your guest,
Pretty, fragrant things."

"Lovely, graceful, crimson rose,"
Said the modest flowers,
"Though the sun we scarcely know,
Happiness is ours.
Moon we have, and sparkling stars
(Each a heavenly gem),
And their light so gentle is,
We can look at them.

"And the flashing fire-flies
Round us gleam and glance,
Like a countless host of fays
In an airy dance.
And the moth king, velvet-winged,
Dainty kiss bestows,
As he whispers, 'You are sweet,
Sweet as any rose.'

"Grieve no more for us, dear friend;
Thrice content we are,
Loved by moth and fire-fly,
Dew-drop, moon, and star.
And while you o'er gardens reign
In the bright daylight,
We are hailed by wand'ring winds,
Flower queens of night."

OLD TIMES IN THE COLONIES.

BY CHARLES CARLETON COFFIN.

No. III.

ISAAC BRADLEY AND JOSEPH WHITTAKER.

TWELVE miles from the sea, on the bank of the Merrimac River, is the busy town of Haverhill. It was a small settlement in 1690. There was a cluster of houses and a meeting-house. The country beyond, all the way to Canada, was a wilderness. The Indians came down the river in their bark canoes, carrying them past the falls where the city of Lowell now stands, past Amoskeag Falls, where the Manchester factories to-day are humming. They caught beaver, bear, and foxes, and sold the furs to the traders.

The Indians were under the influence of the French, and when war broke out between France and England for the restoration of James II. to the throne from which he had fled, the settlers of Haverhill, in common with the people all along the frontier, knew that the Indians, influenced by the French in Canada, might be upon them at any moment.

The settlers had their guns ever at hand. If at work in the field, they placed them where they could seize them quickly. When they went to bed at night, they put a stout bar of wood across the door, and examined the flints and the priming. On Sunday, when they went to meeting, each man carried his gun, and the minister looked down from the pulpit upon men who had powder-horns and bullet-pouches slung across their shoulders, and whose muskets were standing in the corners of their pews. Some of the settlers kept watch outside while the others were in meeting. They went on scouts through the dark woods, peering among the trees to see if the Indians were prowling in the vicinity.

The settlers were obliged to work hard. While the men were at work in the fields, the women were spinning and weaving. Boys and girls had little time for play. There was always something for them to do. When a boy was sixteen years old, he was expected to do the work of a man. They all learned to shoot, and some of them, when they were only twelve, could bring down a squirrel from the highest tree every time, or shoot a deer upon the run.

Two boys—Isaac Bradley, who was fifteen years old, and Joseph Whittaker, who was eleven—were at work one day in Mr. Bradley's field, when suddenly a party of Indians sprang out from the woods and seized them. Isaac was small, but he was bright, cool-headed, and brave-hearted. Joseph, though four years younger, was as large as Isaac, but he was not so stout-hearted nor self-reliant as his companion.

The Indians were from Canada. They did not stop to kill any of the settlers, but hastened away, travelling through the dark woods northward to the beautiful Lake Winnipiseogee, where they remained through the winter. The lake swarmed with trout and pickerel, which they could catch through the ice, and the woods were full of bears and deer.

Isaac made himself at home in the wigwam, and picked up the language of the Indians in a very short time. The squaws made him do their drudgery; but the warriors liked him, and the Indian dogs wagged their tails when he looked at them out of his kindly eyes.

Winter passed and April came.

"We go to Canada now," said one of the Indians.

Isaac had no intention of going to Canada. Day after day he thought over the matter. He knew that the English settlements were far away to the south, but there was no path to them. He had no compass. How could he ever reach them? He would be guided by the sun by day, and the stars by night. He would make the attempt. He might perish, but death was better than captivity.

"I am going to try it to-morrow night, but I am afraid you won't wake," he said to Joseph, who always slept soundly, and snored in his sleep.

EARLY SETTLERS GOING TO MEETING.—Drawn by Howard Pyle.

"Oh yes, I will," Joseph replied.

The Indians had killed a moose, and Isaac had managed to hide a large piece of meat in the bushes near the camp. He filled his pockets with their corn-bread. Night came. All were asleep except Isaac, who was so excited by the thought of escaping that his eyes would not close. Every sense was quickened. He arose softly and touched Joseph, who was sound asleep. He did not stir, and Isaac shook him harder.

"What do you want?" Joseph asked.

In an instant Isaac was stretched out, snoring; but the Indians did not wake, and after a little while the boys arose softly, and crept out of the wigwam, Isaac with an Indian's gun and powder and balls. They made their way to the meat, took it under their arms, and started upon the run, guided on their way by the stars. On through the wilderness, amid the tall trees, over fallen trunks, over stones, through thickets and tangled brushwood, they travelled till morning, and then crept into a hollow log.

Great the consternation in the camp of the Indians. Their captives gone! a gun lost! At daybreak the Indians, with their dogs, were on the trail, and in swift pursuit.

The boys heard the barking of the dogs, which soon came sniffing around the log. What shall they do now? Isaac is quick-witted.

"Good fellow, Bose! good fellow! here is some breakfast for you;" and he tosses the moose meat to them. The dogs know his voice, devour the meat, and are as happy as dogs can be. The boys are their friends. They cease barking, and trot around, with no further concern.

The Indians come up on the run.

The boys hear their voices, as they hasten by, followed by their dogs.

Through the day they lie hidden in the log, and when night comes, strike out in a different direction from that taken by the Indians. All night long they travel, nibbling at their hard corn-bread. Morning comes, and again they conceal themselves. Once more at night they are on the march. On the third day Isaac shoots a pigeon, but does not dare to kindle a fire, and they eat it raw. They find a turtle, smash its shell, and eat the meat. On, day after day, they travel, eating roots, and buds of the trees just ready to burst into leaf. The sixth day comes, and they suddenly find themselves close to an Indian camp. They peep through the underbrush, and see the warriors sitting around their camp fire smoking their pipes. They steal softly away, and then run as fast as their legs can carry them. The morning of the eighth day comes. Joseph's strength is failing; his courage is gone; he cries bitterly. They are in the wilderness, they know not where, with nothing to eat, their clothes in rags, their feet bleeding.

"Cheer up, Joseph; here are some ground-nuts. Here, drink some water," says Isaac.

No brave words, no act of kindness, can quicken the courage of the fainting boy. What shall Isaac do—stay and die with him, or try to find his own way out? Sad the parting, the younger lying down to die upon a mossy bank, the older turning away alone, lost in the wilderness.

With faltering steps, Isaac pushes on, and discerns a house. No one is there, but he knows there must be white men not far away. With quickened pulse, he turns back to the dying boy, awakens him from sleep, rubs his eyes, bathes his temples, cheers him with encouraging words.

ISAAC BRADLEY CARRYING JOSEPH INTO THE SETTLEMENT.

"Come, Joseph, we are saved. There is a house close by."

Joseph's eyes brighten. He stands upon his feet, walks a few steps, and falls. Isaac is stronger than ever. He lifts his fainting comrade, takes him in his arms, staggers on, reaches the empty and desolate house, and discovers a beaten path leading southward. He goes on, resting now and then, but ever speaking words of cheer.

At last they see before them a placid river, and beside it a cluster of houses. They know that in a few moments they will be once more among friends, and brave Isaac Bradley is almost overcome with the joy of this knowledge.

What a sight is that which the soldier on the look-out at the garrison-house on the bank of the Saco beholds, just as the sun is going down—two boys, one carrying the other!

Saved. They are kindly cared for by the soldiers, their wounds are dressed, nourishing food is given them, once more they are clothed in the garments of civilized beings, and there are moist eyes in the garrison as they tell their thrilling story. And what rejoicing when at last they reach their homes!

TOM CHESTER'S SILVER MINE.

BY A. A. HAYES, JUN.

TOM CHESTER'S father lives in a pleasant town in New England, and Tom himself grew up like other boys in that part of the country. In winter he went to the village school, in an old red building with a great stove in one corner, and on his way home "coasted" down the long hill at the foot of which he lived. In summer he helped the hay-makers, and rode on the high-piled cart, and went on picnics to Blue Mountain, and bathed in the clear brook under the willows. He grew to be stout, hardy, and red-cheeked, very unlike his father, who pored over his books, and took no exercise, and grew paler and thinner each year.

One day, as Tom was sitting on the door-step making a whistle out of a slip of willow, he saw old Dr. W—— drive up in his old-fashioned "sulky," tie his horse to a past, and go to his father's library, bidding him good-morning as he passed. He remained some time with Mr. Chester, and as he came out Tom heard him say,

"Very well, then, we will call that settled. And mind, the sooner you start, the sooner you may expect to find yourself better and stronger."

Mr. Chester, who had followed the doctor to the door, saw the inquiring look on Tom's face, and asked him, with a smile, how he would like to go to Colorado.

"What! to dig for silver?" cried Tom.

"No; to seek for what is more valuable than silver—health," said his father. "Dr. W—— says that I must go to the Rocky Mountains, and we shall start in a few days."

It was dark when the train rolled into Denver, and Tom, even if he had not been tired and sleepy, could have seen nothing of the town as they drove to the hotel. But in the morning, when he woke up and looked out of the windows of his room, which was on the western side of the house, he cried aloud with surprise and delight. All along the horizon rose a great range of mountains, with two lofty peaks towering over the others, one at the north and the other at the south. They seemed so near that Tom thought he could walk to them; but when he had dressed himself and gone down to the office, he asked the clerk how long it would take, and the man looked at him, and said, "I wouldn't advise you to try, you little *tender-foot*."

"My feet are *not* tender," replied Tom, sharply.

The people in the room all laughed, and a miner in a blue flannel shirt patted Tom on the back, and said, "That's right, my boy. You remind me of a kid of my own up at Fairplay. The fellow's only chaffing you. When any one's been just a little while in the country, they always call him a 'tender-foot.' You mustn't mind that."

Then he went on to explain to Tom that the foot-hills which looked so near were at least fifteen or twenty miles away. Then he told him about the mining towns, or "camps," as they are called, and how the men who look for mines, called "prospectors," search through the mountains, seeking signs of silver ore; and that when they find them, they put stakes in the ground to mark the "claims" which the law allows, or the right to dig in a space 1500 feet one way and 300 the other. Then he described how they dig down in hopes of finding what they call "pay gravel," or ore which contains enough silver to make it worth sending to the works. He mentioned some men whom he knew who had sold "prospect holes," as he called them (or shafts partly sunk, and not yet proved to be good mines), for large sums. Tom was immensely interested in these narrations, and was eagerly listening when his father came in to find him.

"Guess you'd better let me have that boy of yourn to make a miner of, Colonel," said this new friend to Mr. Chester. "He's got plenty of *sand*."

Mr. Chester knew that people in the West give titles to almost every one, but it was some time before either he or Tom found out that it was a great compliment to say that any one had "sand," which means, in the rough but very expressive language of the mountains, that one possesses bravery and great strength and force of character.

After seeing all the sights of Denver, Tom and his father took the train one morning for a little town called Golden, near the foot-hills. Here they were transferred to a railroad only three feet wide, and found an open or "observation" car, from which they could see very well. The train entered what is called a cañon, or gorge, down which poured the waters of Clear Creek (which, by-the-way, were not clear at all, but very muddy). It wound up this cañon, the walls of which seemed to come together away over the heads of the passengers. No boy who is fortunate enough to make a journey to Colorado should fail to see this remarkable place. The little engine tugged at the train, and dragged it up the steep cañon, and by the side of the winding stream, until it came to a valley surrounded by high hills, where is the town of Idaho Springs. Here Tom and his father left the train, and walked to a neat-looking hotel, where they took up their quarters. Mr. Chester already felt the benefit of the change of climate, and he wanted to spend much time in excursions to different points. He and Tom went up by the railroad to Georgetown, and drove to Central City, and at both places they saw a great many mines. They went down in buckets, lowered by great ropes, six and seven hundred feet into the shafts, and then sometimes came out by tunnels cut from the sides of the hills. They saw mills in which gold ore was crushed by stamps, or great iron bars falling heavily on it, and works where silver ore was put into hot furnaces—in fact, they saw so many things that Tom became rather bewildered. All the time, however, he found himself thinking about what the miner had told him in Denver, and longing to try his own hand at prospecting. When he told his father, one day, that he would like to go up on the hill-sides or in some of the cañons and look for a mine, the latter at first laughed, and then grew rather serious, and began to talk about the danger of being led away by this desire to be suddenly rich without labor.

"You hear, my boy," he said, "about the one, two, or three men who succeed, but not a word about the hundreds, and even thousands, who make failure after failure, and pass their lives in the misery of 'hope deferred.'"

Tom listened respectfully to his father, but could not make up his mind that it would not be a fine thing to find a silver mine. He began to take walks by himself, and look out for the signs about which various miners had told him. At times he would think that he had found something, and he would bring little pieces of rock to show to a friend whose acquaintance he had made in the little town. This was an old miner named Sam, a rough but very kind-hearted man, who did not laugh at all, but told him pleasantly that he had not yet found any mine.

One day, while walking in a cañon near the hotel, and chipping with a hammer at the broken rock, he saw two poorly dressed men carrying bundles, as if on a journey, who stopped and asked what he was doing. They told him that there was no use in searching in that place, but that they had an excellent prospect hole, already showing "pay gravel," which they had been compelled to abandon on account of pressing engagements elsewhere, and which, although it was worth many thousands, they would sell him for ten dollars. Poor little Tom had just that sum, which his father had given him on his birthday, and to which he had proposed to add his savings, for the purpose of buying some fishing-tackle. Perhaps his slight "craze" about a mine made him less cautious than usual. At all events, he accepted the men's offer, and promised to meet them that afternoon near a tree which they pointed out.

He was there on the minute, with his ten dollars in his pocket. The men took him up the hill, and showed him a rather deep hole, into which a rough ladder led. Down this they went, and Tom saw some ore of just the kind that his friend Sam had told him he ought to find. Then the men set two stakes in the ground, on which they rudely marked "T. C.," took his money, and walked hastily away. Tom went down to the hotel full of his purchase. His father had gone to Georgetown, but Sam was there, and to him Tom eagerly narrated what he thought his good fortune. Sam heard him without remark, and then put on his hat, and taking pick and shovel, asked Tom to show him the mine. Arriving there, he shovelled up some of the ore which Tom had seen, and disclosed quite a different rock below. On this lay a piece of board, which he handed to Tom, who read thereon, "u ar sold bad u yung tender-fut this aint no mine."

For a moment he did not understand; then came a shock of disappointment, and then a sense of indignation, not so much against the men who had deceived him as at himself for his delusion and stupidity.

Sam looked kindly at him. "Pretty rough on you, Tom, wasn't it?" he said. "Why, my boy, this is an old claim of mine, which I gave up long ago as no good. They've just gone and salted it—I mean, put some good ore in to deceive you. So they walked off with your ten dollars, the miserable scamps! Tell me what they looked like."

Tom described them.

"Ho! ho!" said Sam. "I saw those same fellows taking the train for Denver. I'm going down there to-morrow, and the Chief of Police is a friend of mine. Perhaps we'll run across them some day."

As they walked home, he tried to cheer Tom up by telling him stories of clever men who had been served in similar ways; but Tom was sober, not on account of his loss, but because it had come to his mind how foolish he had been from the first. He felt easier when he had told his father the whole story.

The latter laughed heartily, and said, "Well, Tom, my boy, considering how badly you had the mining fever, I do not think that ten dollars was a large price to pay for a cure."

Some time after Tom had returned to his home he received a letter from Colorado, which proved to be from his friend Sam, reading partly as follows:

"......I am glad to tell you that we catched them two claim-jumpers [men who steal claims]. They'd spent all your stamps, sure enough, and you won't never see them no more; but it's a comfort that they got two years at Cañon City [where the penitentiary is]. Better luck next time. Come out again next summer, and I'll help you find an A1 mine......"

But Tom says that if he ever has any money at all, it will be earned in some good old-fashioned way; that he is not a "tender-foot," and that he does not want any more interest in prospect holes.

WOLF-CHILDREN.

BY JAMES GREENWOOD.

SOME years ago a soldier stationed at Bondee, in India, while passing near a small stream, saw three wolf cubs and a boy drinking. He managed to seize the boy, who seemed about ten years old, but who was so wild and fierce that he tore the trooper's clothes, and bit him severely in several places. The soldier at first tied him up in the military gun shed, and fed him with raw meat; he was afterward allowed to wander freely about the Bondee bazar. A lad named Tanoo, servant of a Cashmere merchant then at Bondee, took compassion on the poor boy, and prepared a bed for him under the mango-tree where he himself lodged; here he kept him fastened to a tent-pin.

Up to this time he would eat nothing but raw flesh, but Tanoo gradually taught him to eat balls of rice and pulse. In about six weeks after he had been tied up, and after much rubbing of his joints with oil, he was made to stand and walk upright, whereas hitherto he had gone on all fours.

One night, while the boy was lying under the mango-tree, Tanoo saw two wolves creep stealthily toward him, and after smelling him, they touched him, when he got up. Instead, however, of being frightened, the boy put his hand upon their heads, and they began to play with him, capering about while he pelted them with grass and straw. Tanoo tried to drive them off, but could not. At last, however, they left, but the following night three wolves came, and a few nights after four, which returned several times.

The wolf-boy, however, could not be entirely reconciled to civilized life. In being removed from place to place he never lost an opportunity of endeavoring to escape into the jungle. At last Tanoo was sent away on a short journey, and when he returned, his savage charge had disappeared, and was never again heard of.

The story of another wolf-child is even more wonderful than the above.

In March, 1843, a cultivator who lived at Chupra, about twenty miles from Sultanpoor, went to cut his crop of wheat and pulse, taking with him his wife, and a son about three years old. As the father was reaping, a wolf suddenly rushed upon the boy, caught him up, and made off with him toward the ravines. People ran to the aid of the parents, but soon lost sight of the wolf and his prey.

About six years afterward, as two sipahees were watching for hogs on the border of the jungle, they saw three wolf cubs and a boy come out from the jungle and go down to the stream to drink; all four then ran to a den in the ravine. The sipahees followed, but the cubs had already entered, and the boy was half way in, when one of the men caught him by the leg and drew him back. He was very savage, bit at the men, and seizing the barrel of one of their guns in his teeth, shook it fiercely. The sipahees, however, secured him, brought him home, and kept him for twenty days, during which he would eat nothing but raw flesh, and was fed accordingly on hares and birds. His captors soon found it difficult to provide him with sufficient food, and took him to the bazar in the village of Koeleepoor, to be supported by the charitable till he might be recognized and claimed by his parents.

He is unable to speak or to articulate any sound with distinctness. In drinking, he dips his face in the water, but does not lap like a wolf. He still prefers raw flesh; and when a bullock dies, and the skin is removed, he attacks and eats the body in company of the village dogs.

[Begun in Harper's Young People No. 37, July 13.]

THE STORY OF THE AMERICAN NAVY.

BY BENSON J. LOSSING.

Chapter IV.

COMMODORE PREBLE sailed from the United States for the Mediterranean in the frigate *Constitution* late in the spring of 1803. The ships of the squadron did not sail together. Bainbridge, with the frigate *Philadelphia*, first entered the Strait of Gibraltar, and found a Moorish corsair cruising for American prizes. He captured her and took her to Gibraltar. When Preble arrived he proceeded to Tangiers with the squadron, when the Emperor of Morocco declared that he had never authorized any depredations on American commerce. The affair was amicably settled. Soon afterward the *Philadelphia* chased a corsair into the harbor of Tripoli, and in so doing struck upon a sunken rock. She was fast bound. The Tripolitans captured her, made Bainbridge and his officers prisoners of war, and consigned the crew to slavery.

With Preble was Stephen Decatur, a gallant young Lieutenant, son of a veteran naval commander. He was in charge of the brig *Enterprise*, with which, late in December, he captured a Tripolitan ketch laden with girls which the ruler of Tripoli was sending as a present to the Sultan. The maidens were landed at Syracuse, and the ketch (which was renamed *Intrepid*) was used by Decatur in an attempt to recapture or destroy the *Philadelphia*. With seventy daring young men he sailed into the harbor of Tripoli on a bright moon-lit night (February, 1804), the *Intrepid* assuming the character of a vessel in distress. Most of her officers and men were concealed.

The *Intrepid* went alongside the *Philadelphia*, when

Decatur, followed by his men, who sprang from their hiding-places, boarded the frigate, slew many of her defenders and drove the rest into the sea, set her on fire, and escaped with only four men wounded. This daring act produced great commotion in the harbor. The *Philadelphia* was soon in flames; the great guns of the castle and of the corsairs lying near thundered incessantly; and to this roar of artillery was added that of the cannons of the frigate as the flames reached them. The heroes of this exploit were received at Syracuse with demonstrations of great joy, and Decatur was promoted to Captain. The ruler of Tripoli was abashed by this display of American energy and valor.

The harbor of Tripoli was guarded by batteries mounting more than a hundred heavy guns, by numerous gun-boats and other vessels, by twenty-five thousand soldiers, and a sheltering reef. Undismayed by these, Preble entered the harbor in the summer of 1804, with the *Constitution* and several gun-boats, and opened fire on the formidable defenses. In that engagement Decatur again displayed his valor. He captured one gun-boat, and boarded another, on which he had a fierce hand-to-hand fight with its powerful commander, but triumphed. The Americans withdrew, but renewed the struggle a few days afterward, when a hot shot exploded the magazine of one of the American gun-boats, killing two officers and eight of the crew. When the smoke cleared away, Midshipman Spruce and eleven others were seen on the sinking vessel working her great gun. Giving three cheers, and firing it at the enemy, they were picked from the water a few minutes later, for the vessel had gone to the bottom.

In a fourth attack on Tripoli by the gallant Preble a sad accident occurred. It was determined to blow up the cruisers in the harbor by a floating mine or huge torpedo. The *Intrepid* was laden with a hundred barrels of gunpowder, over which were laid shot, shell, and irregular pieces of iron. In charge of Captain Somers, she was towed into the harbor on a very dark night (September 4, 1804), when all eyes were strained to observe the result. Suddenly a fierce and lurid light shot up from the dark bosom of the waters, like a volcanic fire, and was instantly followed by an explosion that shook earth and air for miles around. Flaming fragments rose and fell, and then all was profound darkness again. Somers and his companions were never heard of. They probably perished by the premature explosion of the mine.

DECATUR AND HIS MEN BOARDING THE GUN-BOAT.

Soon after this, Preble, who had done excellent service in the Mediterranean, was relieved by the arrival of Commodore Barron, prepared to carry on the war with Tripoli vigorously, but it was ended by treaty early the next year.

The ruler of Tunis was yet insolent, but the appearance of an American squadron of thirteen vessels before his capital soon so humbled him that he sued for peace and made a treaty. A small American naval force was kept in the Mediterranean, and for several years the Barbary powers kept their hands off American commerce.

At the close of the war of 1812-15, the Dey of Algiers, believing the British navy had utterly destroyed that of the United States, sent out his corsairs to depredate on our commerce. Determined not to pay tribute or longer endure his insolence, the United States accepted the Dey's challenge to war, and sent Commodore Decatur with a small squadron to humble him. Decatur sailed in May, 1815, and as soon as he entered the Mediterranean he found the Algerine pirate fleet cruising in search of American vessels. In June he captured the flag-ship of the Algerine Admiral and another corsair, with six hundred men. With these he entered the harbor of Algiers, and demanded the instant surrender of all American captives in the hands of the Dey, payment in full for all American property destroyed by his forces, and the relinquishment of all claims to tribute from the United States thereafter. The terrified ruler hastened to comply. Obeying the summons of the Commodore, he appeared on the deck of the *Guerrière* (the flag-ship), with his civil officers and the captives. Having complied with all demands, the Dey left the vessel in deep humiliation.

Decatur now sailed for Tunis, and demanded and received of its frightened ruler $46,000, in payment for American vessels which he had allowed the British to capture in his harbor. Then the Commodore went to Tripoli, and summoned the Bashaw, or Governor, before him. He demanded $25,000 of him for similar injuries. The Tripolitan treasury was empty, and Decatur accepted, in place of cash, eight Danish and two Neapolitan captives held by the Bashaw.

This cruise of a little American squadron in the Mediterranean Sea in the summer of 1815, and its results, gave full security to American commerce in those waters, and greatly exalted the character of the government of the United States in the opinion of European nations. A portion of its navy had accomplished, in the way of humbling the rulers of the Barbary States, and weakening their power for mischief, what the combined governments of Europe had not dared to attempt. Decatur was the most conspicuous hero in the war with the Barbary States.

[TO BE CONTINUED.]

WHAT THE BUTTERFLY SAYS.

Throughout all the many summer days
  I wander here and there,
And hardly ever stop to rest
  A moment anywhere.
There are so many things to see,
And time is rather short with me.

I only have a month or two,
  And time soon runs away
When one is seeing something new,
  Or sporting every day,
And how the little people try
To catch me as I flutter by!

But I know what they want me for—
  It's not to use me right;
It's not to give me sunny fields,
  With daisies sprinkled white;
But just to pin me on the wall
To show their friends, and that *is* all.

—

THE SHIP OF THE DESERT.

BY A. E. T.

UNLIKE other ships, this one begins by being a very feeble and helpless little craft indeed. For the first week after its launch on the great sea of life it requires much careful watching on the part of the owners.

Strange as it may sound, in very truth a baby camel is every whit as helpless as a human baby. It can not stand alone; without help it can not so much as take its own food even; while its long neck is at first so flexible and fragile, that unless some one were constantly at hand to watch, the poor little creature would run every risk of dislocating it.

Those who have closely observed camel nature tell us it is never known to play or frolic like lambs or colts, or like most young creatures of the earth, in fact; but that in its babyhood it is as grave and melancholy as in its old age, born apparently with a deep sense of its own ugliness, and a mournful resignation to a long and joyless career.

When it has reached its third year the humpbacked animal is counted old enough to begin its life of labor. The trainers then take it in hand. They teach it to kneel and bear burdens, which gradually they make heavier and heavier, until their charge is supposed to have come to the full strength of camel maturity. This is not until it is about eight years old.

If the camel can rise with the load on its back, this is proof positive that he can carry it throughout the journey, although it sometimes happens, if the journey be only a very short one, the patient beast is loaded so heavily that it must be helped on to its feet by means of bars and levers. In some places camels cry out against this excessive loading in a most piteous and distressing manner—the cry resembling that of a very young child in pain, and being a most dismal sound to hear; but in other parts of the world they will bear their burden, however heavy, without complaining.

An ordinary camel's load is from seven to eight hundred pounds. With this weight on their backs, a train of camels will cross thirty miles of desert during a day. Those used to carry dispatches, having only the light weight of the dispatch-bearer, of course are expected to travel much faster, however, and will easily accomplish two hundred and forty miles in the same length of time.

Ungainly, awkward, repulsive-looking as these creatures are, with their great projecting harelips and their hairy humps, they have the compensation of being most priceless treasures to all those who "dwell in tents" in the vast sandy plains of Egypt, Arabia, and Tartary.

Their stomachs are so formed by nature that they are capable of being converted into a set of water tanks, a number of small cells filled with the purest water being fastened to the sides of each, and when all food fails, it makes little difference to a camel or dromedary—at least for a time.

Their humps are composed of a fatty substance. Day by day the hump diminishes, and the fat is absorbed into the animal's system, furnishing nourishment until food is forth-coming.

Thus, with these stores of water and fuel on board, the "ship" can go on for a fortnight, or even a month, absolutely without eating or drinking, while things that other creatures—unless, perhaps, it be some bird of the ostrich tribe—would never dream of touching, will furnish forth a sumptuous meal for a camel. Off a handful of thorns and briers he can make an excellent breakfast, and I believe he will not disdain anything apparently so untempting as a bit of dry wood.

THE CAMEL AND HIS RIDER.

Provided that at certain periods of the year a short holiday is allowed the camel for pasturing, quite at its leisure, to recruit its strength and fill that store-house on its back with fuel, it will serve its master, on such meagre fare as I have mentioned, for full fifty years. Still, all work and no play is as bad for camels as it is for boys.

Even with plenty of fuel on board, the desert-ship owners are wise enough not to impose too long journeys upon their heavily laden fleets.

A camel's foot is of a peculiar formation. It is wide-spreading, and is provided with fleshy pads or cushions; and if after a certain march rest were not given, the skin would wear off these pads, the flesh become bare, bringing consequences direful indeed. Probably the suffering creature would kneel down, fold its long legs under its body, and stretching out its long neck on the ground, calmly announce in camel language that it would go no further. It is no use whatever to try to make a camel go against his will.

If it once refuses, you have but two ways open to you: you may quietly lie down beside it until it is ready to move, or you may abandon it forever. Other course there is none.

It is a curious fact that, notwithstanding the softness of the camel's foot, it can walk over the sharpest stones, or thorns, or roots of trees without the least danger of wounding itself, and that what this strange beast most dreads is wet and marshy ground.

We read that "the instant it places its feet upon anything like mud, it slips and slides, and generally, after staggering about like a drunken man, falls heavily on its side."

The use of the camel to the various peoples of the East is almost incalculable. Many an Arab finds his chief sustenance in the cheese, butter, and milk of the mother camel. The flesh of young camels is also often eaten.

The Roman Emperor Heliogabalus is said to have reckoned camel's feet one of the daintiest dainties of his sumptuous banquets, and he considered a portion of tender camel roast a thing to be by no means despised. To this day, indeed, camel's hump cut into slices and dissolved in tea is counted a relish by the Tartar tribes.

Camel's skin is made into straps and sandals, while brushes and ropes, cloth and tents, sacks and carpets, are made entirely from camel's hair.

Every year toward the beginning of summer the camel sheds its hair, every bristle of which vanishes before the new hair begins to grow. For three weeks this bare condition lasts. His camelship looks as if he had been shaved without mercy from the tip of his tail to the top of his head, and during this shaven season he is extremely sensitive to the cold or wet, shaking in every limb if a drop of rain falls, shivering painfully in the chilliness of the night air.

By-and-by the new hair begins to grow—fine, soft, curly wool that gradually becomes long, thick, soft fur; and after this, the rain may rain as much as it likes, the night air may be as chilly as it will, the camel will not care a grain. In that armor of nature's providing he will not shiver or shake any more.

The hair of a camel, on an average, will weigh about ten pounds. It is said to be sometimes finer than silk, and longer than the wool of a sheep. In the course of my reading, a short time ago, I met with an account of a camel market in a town of Tartary especially noted for its trade in that species of live stock.

In the centre of Blue Town, it seems, there is a large square, where the animals are ranged in long rows together, their front feet raised upon mud elevations constructed expressly for the purpose, the object of which is to show off the size and height of the ungainly creatures.

The confusion and noise of this market are described as something frightful and "indescribable," with the continual chattering of the buyers and sellers disputing noisily over their bargains, in addition to the wild shrieking of the camels, whose noses are pulled roughly to make them show off their agility in rising and kneeling.

Nature has given the camel, you must remember, no means of defense except its prolonged piercing cry, and a horrible sneeze of its own, whereby the object of its hatred is sometimes covered with a mass of filth from its mouth.

It can not bite its tormentor, and—at least the Tartar camel—seldom kicks, or if it does, as seldom does any harm with that fleshy foot of which I have told you already.

Can you wonder, then, that the air of Blue Town is made hideous with the shrieking of the camels as, to test their strength, they are made to kneel while one thing after another is piled on their backs, and made to rise under each new burden, until they can rise no longer?

"Sometimes while the camel is kneeling a man gets upon its hind-heels, and holds on by the long hair of its hump; if the camel can rise then, it is considered an animal of superior power"—according to the writer above quoted.

"The trade in camels is entirely conducted by proxy; the seller and the buyer never settle the matter between themselves. They select different persons to sell their goods, who propose, discuss, and fix the price, the one looking to the interests of the seller, the other to those of the purchaser. These 'sale-speakers' exercise no other trade. They go from market to market, to promote business, as they say. They have generally a great knowledge of cattle, have much fluency of tongue, and are, above all, endowed with a knavery beyond all shame. They dispute by turns furiously and argumentatively as to the merits and defects of the animal, but as soon as it comes to be a question of price, the tongue is laid aside as a medium, and the conversation proceeds altogether in signs."

A LITTLE GIRL'S ASCENT OF VESUVIUS.

BY KATIE C. YORKE.

ONE beautiful morning we took a carriage and started from Naples on a trip to Mount Vesuvius. We drove along the bay for several miles, and when we reached the foot of the mountain we began to ascend through vast fields of lava, which had flowed there during previous eruptions. I always imagined that lava was white and smooth, but this was of a grayish-black color, and very ragged.

The carriage-road ends at the Observatory, which is a building where a scientific man resides, being appointed by the government to watch the state of the volcano. He can tell when there is going to be an eruption, and always notifies the people.

There we found guides and men with saddled horses waiting to take us to the foot of the cone. After a short ride we reached it, and dismounted, and started up. The cone is so steep, and covered with cinders, that people that are unaccustomed to such walking can't get up it without assistance, because every step you take you slide back several inches. We thought we would be pulled up by the guides, but the rest of the party got tired, and had to be carried on their shoulders. I managed to walk nearly all the way, and when I got tired my guide carried me too.

About half way up we stopped at a cave where some men were waiting to sell us some new Lacrima Christi wine. We drank some, and rested, and went on to the top. When we reached it we were nearly four thousand feet above the level of the sea, and had a beautiful view of Naples, the bay, the islands, the villages, and the surrounding mountains.

We enjoyed the view very much, but every little while the wind would blow a cloud of sulphurous vapor from the crater, and nearly suffocate us. We walked to the edge of the crater and looked down, but we couldn't see much, because of the vapor. One of the guides went down into it a little way, and brought us up some pieces of sulphur. The cinders were so hot they burned our feet, and when we poked sticks into some cavities they caught fire.

The thick vapor annoyed us so that we soon decided to go down. Just as we were starting, the mountain gave a low, deep growl, and trembled under us, so we were very glad to leave. It was great fun going down, because the cinders were so loose that at each step we would slide a long way. Part way down we caught a pale yellow butterfly that was almost stifled by the sulphurous fumes.

When we reached the foot of the cone, we found we had been only twenty minutes coming down, although it took us an hour and a half to go up. No sooner had we arrived at the Observatory than we were surrounded by crowds of ragged, beggarly looking men and boys, who insisted on blacking our shoes, or pretended they had been guides, and tried to make us pay them for things they had never done at all. We ordered them away, but they kept on tormenting us, so we jumped into the carriage, and drove off as fast as we could, leaving them all behind, shouting, screaming, and wildly gesticulating.

Since I was there they have built a railroad up the mountain, but I should not think it would be half so much fun to go up in the cars.

A LETTER FROM INDIA.

Lucknow, India, June 20, 1880.

MY DEAR FRIENDS,—My auntie has sent me several copies of Harper's Young People, and I thought maybe you would like to know a little how we children in India live. I don't know anything about your life except what I read, and my mamma tells me, because I was born here. I am nine years old, and in a little while we are going home. I say home because mamma and papa do, but the only home I know is here, where it is so hot sometimes it seems as if I should die. Last night mamma had to get up and take a towel as wet as it could be, and rub my sheets with it, before I could get to sleep at all, and if the punka stops a single minute, it wakes me right up again. I read my letter to mamma so far, and she says you won't know what a punka is. That is funny to me; but I will tell you. They are very stiff cloth things fixed on frames, and fastened to the ceiling so that they move, and by fanning the air keep a breeze in the room all the time. There are holes in the wall, and ropes put through the holes, and a man outside on the veranda pulls the ropes, and keeps the punka moving. One night I was so hot I got up and went out on the veranda, but the boards of the step burned my feet; so I slipped on my slippers, and tried again. There sat the punka wala nodding, fast asleep, but keeping his arms moving all the time. It looked funny, I can tell you.

We have good times in the winter, though. Christmas-day we always have a picnic. The children of the native Sunday-schools and English schools join together, and have a good time in some grove. And all through the winter we play out under the trees, just as mamma says you do in the summer. But here in summer we can only go out very late in the afternoon or very early in the morning, because if the mid-day sun touches us, it will make us very sick, and perhaps we will die. Theo Carter, a girl I know, when she was real little got away from her nurse, and ran out in the sun without her hat. It was in the morning, too; and now every time she gets warm or tired she has the most dreadful headache, and mamma says she don't believe she will ever be strong, even if she goes to America. But I guess she would, because everybody that gets sick here goes to America, else England, and when they come back they are ever so much better; but sometimes they don't come back, and mamma says people die even in America.

There are lots of thieves in this country. One night last week they got into our house. The servants would keep shutting the bath-room window—the bath-room is between mamma's room and mine—and we wanted it open for air, and mamma told them so; but they said the thieves would climb in from a fig-tree near by. But mamma said if they did, they would be welcome to all they could get. They did get in, and took the clothes Bertie and I had worn through the day. Baby woke, and they were probably frightened, and snatched the first thing they could, which was a box of homœopathic medicine mamma brought from home. We laughed in the morning, because they thought, no doubt, it was something valuable, and it will be worse than nothing to them; but papa says we will cry when we are sick, and have to take bitter medicine instead of little sugar pills.

Last week there was a big procession—something about the government—and one of papa's friends asked us to go to see it, and ride on an elephant. I was real glad, for I never rode on one but once, and then I was so little I don't remember much about it. We had a nice ride. Papa had one elephant to himself, but mamma and I and Mrs. Carter and Theo rode on another. We could see into the up-stairs rooms of people's houses, and it was a delightful view we had of the procession. We had a real good time until our elephant became frightened at a loud noise they called music, and trumpeted dreadful loud. We wanted to get off, but our elephant wouldn't kneel, and the man couldn't make him. Papa came, but mamma said if we tried to get off 'twould only frighten him more. I was real scared, and ready to cry; but mamma took hold of my hand, and spoke just as pleasant as if we were at home, and I didn't think till afterward how white she looked, nor about that man whose elephant ran away with him last winter and killed him; but I guess mamma remembered all the time, for pretty soon the noise passed by, and the men were able to quiet the elephant, so he kneeled, and let papa help us down. And when he took mamma, she fainted, and everybody said it was the fright; but I didn't know she was frightened a bit. I must stop now, because the Home Mail is going very soon; but if you like this, some time I will write you again.

Jennie Anderson.

LITTLE COUSIN RANNA.

BY MRS. LUCY MORSE.

WILL and Almida Handly were rather sorry when they learned that their little cousin Marianne Joy was coming to make them a long visit.

"She won't know a bumble-bee from a butternut," said Will. "City children don't know anything, and she'll be awfully in the way. Won't she tag after you and me, though, Almy?"

"Oh dear!" said Almy, in a complaining tone; "we'll have to keep her every speck of washing and baking days."

"I wish they'd leave her where she belongs," said Will.

The children were silent awhile, and then Almy heaved a sigh, and said: "I s'pose that's just the trouble, Will. If her mother has—has died, where does she belong? Where would you and I—"

"I know it," exclaimed Will, gruffly. "Come on, if you want me to help fix up your old baby-house for her."

The day after Marianne came the children's feelings were altered. Walking down the lane all together, the little cousin was dazzled by buttercups, and ran hither and thither gathering them in such wild delight that she came upon Dowsabell, the cow, unexpectedly. Dowsy only raised her sleepy nose from the grass to sniff at the buttercups, but Marianne dropped the whole bunch, with a cry of ter-

THE FALLEN NEST.—Drawn by S. G. McCutcheon.

ror, and ran like the wind to Will for protection. She flung herself upon him with such a pretty confidence that Will took her right into his big boyish heart, and wished on the spot that Dowsy was a raging lion, or, to say the least, Neighbor Stethaway's cross bull.

"After all," he confided to Almida, "she's only a poor city child: what can you expect? *I* don't mind seeing to her."

"Laws, no," said Almida, with a matronly air. "And if her father's gone to Europe, and every day is baking, or washing, or mending, or something, who is there besides you and me for her to look to, I'd like to know? Only you needn't think you're going to have more than just your own half of the care-taking, Will Handly."

The mother looked on in silence, and understood perfectly the very things which her children thought she had not noticed.

"At first I was troubled lest Will and Almy wouldn't notice the child," she said, one afternoon, to Mrs. Stethaway, as they watched the three children crossing the opposite field. "Next I thought they would tyrannize over her, and that Will would tease her to death."

"And now," said Mrs. Stethaway, "it looks as if they would neglect everything just to follow her bidding. What are you going to do about that?"

"Well," said Mrs. Handly, smiling after the children as they disappeared among the daisies, "it isn't always that old folks know the best turn to take. I'm going to see what the little one's course will be. It seems very much as if my own two children were in the way of getting some lessons in gentleness and self-forgetfulness from the poor little motherless child, which I don't know so well as she does how to teach them."

The children went through the field, the orchard, and over the bars into the lane, through which Ilia Bell was just driving the cows.

"Quick! quick! Oh! oh!" screamed Marianne, as soon as she saw the cows.

"Not that way; you're running right into the face of the enemy, Ranna," said Will, laughing, and taking hold of her as she was trying to climb the bars.

But Ranna struggled, crying, "Get me over! get me over! I ain't 'fraid of cows; it's the birds;" and was so excited that Will on one side and Almida on the other lifted her into the lane as quickly as possible.

"Oh, goodness!" screamed Almy, as Ranna made a dive, right under Dowsabell's very nose, toward a little mound of leaves. Crouching down and spreading her arms over it, she looked up at Dowsy so savagely that Will exclaimed, much amused: "Thunder and lightning! what has poor Dowsy done? I thought you were afraid of her, Ranna, and now you look ready to take her by the horns, and are frightened at two poor little robins flying overhead."

"No, I ain't. Nor I won't mind Towzle even if he is going to bite my—my—my head off," cried Ranna, pale with fright, as the dog ran his nose into her face.

Will called Towzle away, while he and Almy tried very hard not to laugh.

"What have you got under the leaves?" asked Will, while Almy stooped over Ranna, and said, tenderly,

"Show us your treasure, darling, and we won't tell Towzle, nor Dowsy, nor anybody a word about it."

Ranna sat up, brushed away the leaves, and took from under them a pretty little nest full of young robins. "They're my own baby birds, and I thought Dowsy would step on them," she said. "I found them just before I ran to bring you, only the nest was in a great, ugly, dark bush, where the poor little birdies couldn't feel any sun shinin', and I brung them here, and covered them with leaves, so the chickens wouldn't frighten them while I was gone. What are those big birds flying round me for? Cover my birdies up again; they are crying 'cause they are frightened."

"Hi! ho! hum! Harry!" exclaimed Will. "Those two birds are the excited and anxious parents of your baby birdies, Ranna, and they feel just about as comfortable as your father and mother would feel if a great giant—" But Will remembered suddenly that poor little Ranna had no mother, and, blushing fiery red, said: "I'm a good-for-nothing old blunderbuss. You tell her, Almy; it's girl's talk, anyway."

Almy, with her arms around her little cousin, explained the situation. Ranna eagerly pointed out the exact spot from which she had taken the nest, and when Will had carefully restored it, watched with great delight the old birds return to it.

"I'll never touch another nest in my life," she said; and holding one arm tight around Almy's neck, she beckoned to Will with the other. Putting it around him, she drew his head close down to Almy's, and whispered: "*I* don't think you're a *bundlefuss*, Will. I think you and Almy know just as well how to take care of little birds when their papas and mammas can't find them, as you do of little girls when their mammas is—is—is lost. And I'm going to tell all the children in the world that when they lose their mammas, the best thing they can do is to find my cousin Will and my cousin Almy."

"I'S LEARNING TO SWIM, MAMMA."

WE wish to express to our young correspondents our sincere regret that our limited space compels us to simply acknowledge so large a number of the pretty letters which reach us daily from every part of the United States. Do not think, because your letters are not printed, that we do not consider them as well written or as interesting as those that are. We are very sorry not to print all your little histories of your pet dogs, and kittens, and birds, and other little domestic creatures, or the excellent descriptions many of you write of the beautiful natural scenery surrounding your homes; but if there is no more room in the Post-office Box, your letters can not be printed. We thank you heartily for the pleasure you express in "Across the Ocean," "The Moral Pirates," "Miss Van Winkle's Nap," and other stories and poems; and the eagerness with which you "rush to meet papa when he brings home YOUNG PEOPLE" is very gratifying. We trust you will continue your pretty favors to us, and we, in return, will print all of your letters that we can possibly make room for, and will promise to give you more and more pleasure with every new number of YOUNG PEOPLE.

[illegible]

Everything has its uses in the great economy of nature, and although we can not always see why it is necessary for certain things to exist, we may be sure that they were all created for some purpose. The flamingo, however, is useful as an article of food. In certain parts of Egypt and the East roast flamingo is considered very delicate eating, and in ancient Rome a stew of flamingo tongues was a royal dish. It is also a very beautiful bird. Travellers say there is no sight more magnificent than a flock of scarlet flamingos wading in the green waving water grasses, hunting for their breakfast in the morning sunlight. The flamingo, if it could speak, might answer your question in the words of Mr. Emerson, the poet:

"Tell them, dear, that if eyes were made for seeing,
Then beauty is its own excuse for being."

[illegible]

H. P. P.—The quail builds its nest on the ground, among bushes or tall grass. The nesting-time is early in June, and when you find [illegible]

[illegible]

A. S. DAGGETT.—You do not need cards to play the geographical game. [illegible]

[illegible]

PUZZLES FROM YOUNG CONTRIBUTORS.

No. 1.

[illegible]

No. 2.

[illegible]

No. 3.

[illegible]

No. 4.

[illegible]

No. 5.

[illegible]

No. 6.

[illegible]

ANSWERS TO PUZZLES IN NO. 38.

[illegible]

PLEASANT FOR JIM.

LITTLE BOY. "Oh-ow-ow! Look out, Jim—here is a great b-b-b-big Bull-dog coming at us!"

MORE MIRTHFUL MAGIC.

BY W. B. BARTLETT.

THE BOOK PUZZLE.

THE player agrees to let any person in the room turn over as many books, one at a time, as desired, while he is out of the room, and promises to tell you, upon his return, which book was turned over last. He goes out, and comes back when the person who turned the books says, "Come in." When he opens the door, he says, "You must stay outside while I find out, so no one will suspect us of being in league with each other." The one who turned the books is then shut out, and the other selects any thin book, and leans it against the door, and says, "Come in." As the door is opened, of course the book is turned over on the floor, and the victim is told, "That is the last book you turned over."

THE NEWSPAPER TRICK.

Take a common newspaper or handkerchief, and request any one of the company to place it on the floor so that two persons can stand upon it at the same time, and neither be able to see or touch the other.

Answer.—Place it across the door-sill, and let one stand upon it in the entry. Then close the door, and ask the other to step upon the other end in the room, and neither can see nor touch the other, for the door prevents.

THE COW PUZZLE.

Tell the company that seven cows were walking in a straight line into a narrow door, and say to them, "If you should ask the last cow, 'How many pairs of horns are before you?' what would she reply?"

Some will answer, "One pair," and some, "Seven pairs," but after puzzling them for a while, you can reply, "In the opinion of most scientists, she would not say anything, for she could not speak, poor thing!"

ANOTHER COW PUZZLE.

Draw a square with a lead-pencil, and say, "Suppose this field was inclosed with walls fifty feet high, without opening or possibility of digging under, and a cow was in there, how could you get it out?"

Answer.—Rub it out.

CHARADE.

As by the fire the lovers sit,
On rosy wings the moments flit;
One little word confirms their bliss,
And seals it with a loving kiss.

That bliss they never could sustain
Without my second's golden grain;
Yet if it does attend their feet,
Their daily walk is incomplete.

My whole leaps forth from out the flame,
Airy and light, but still the same;
Showing a hard and common thing
Made pure and white through suffering.

THE USEFUL SUNFLOWER.

IN Southwestern Russia, between the Baltic and the Black seas, the sunflower is universally cultivated in fields, gardens, and borders, and every part of the plant is turned to practical account. A hundred pounds of the seeds yield forty pounds of oil, and the pressed residue forms a wholesome food for cattle, as also do the leaves and the green stalks, cut up small, all being eagerly eaten. The fresh flowers, when a little short of full bloom, furnish a dish for the table which bears favorable comparison with the artichoke. They contain a large quantity of honey, and so prove an attraction to bees. The seeds are a valuable food for poultry; ground into flour, pastry and cakes can be made from them; and boiled in alum and water, they yield a blue coloring matter. The carefully dried leaf is used as tobacco. The seed receptacles are made into blotting-paper, and the inner part of the stalk into a fine writing-paper; the woody portions are [illegible] is obtained. Large plantations of them in swampy places are a protection against intermittent fevers.

A NAUGHTY LITTLE DOG.

"You bad dog, you's done gone tore my han'kercher all to pieces. I's a big min' to gib you a whippin' that you'll 'member. Yes, I has."

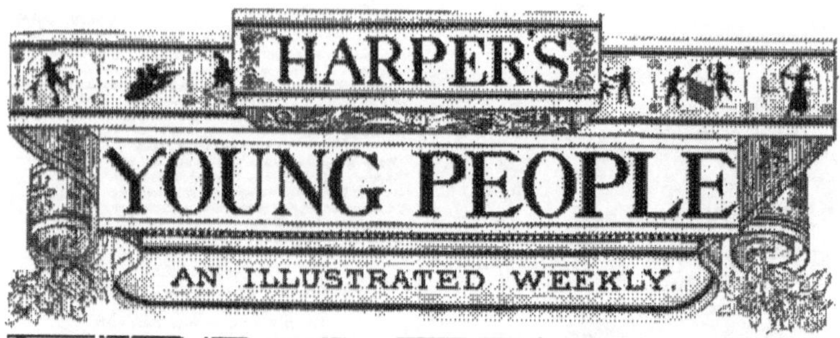

Vol. I.—No. 41. | Published by HARPER & BROTHERS, New York. | Price Four Cents.

Tuesday, August [illegible] | Copyright, [illegible], by Harper & Brothers. | [illegible] per Year, in Advance.

[Begun in No. [illegible] of Harper's Young People, June 1.]

THE MORAL PIRATES.

BY W. L. ALDEN.

Chapter XI.

"BOYS," said Tom, as he was kindling the fire the next morning, "do you know what day it is?"

"Saturday, of course," replied the others.

"You're wrong; it's Sunday."

"It can't be," exclaimed Harry.

"But it is," persisted Tom. "Last night was the sixth night that we've slept out-doors, and we started on a Monday."

Tom was right; but it was some time before his companions could convince themselves that it was actually Sunday. When they finally admitted that it was Sunday morning they gave up the idea of proceeding up the canal, and began to discuss what they had better do.

The boat, which had been drawn out of the water the night before, was concealed by a clump of bushes from the canal boatmen. The boys decided to leave it where it was, and to carry the tent and most of their baggage to a grove a quarter of a mile distant, where they could pass a quiet Sunday. The locks were not yet opened, and no canal-boats were stirring, and the boys made their way to the grove at once while their movements were unobserved. They were afraid that if they attracted the attention of the boatmen to the clump of bushes, some one would steal the *Whitewing* while her crew were absent. They had already seen enough of the "canalers" to know that they were a wild and lawless set of men, and they were not anxious to put the temptation of stealing a nice boat in their way.

The grove was a delightful place; and when they had pitched the tent under the shadow of the great oak-trees, they were glad of the prospect of a good day's rest. Tom and Harry walked nearly a mile to church in the morning, leaving the Sharpe boys to look after the camp, and they all slept most of the afternoon.

About dusk, as the fire for cooking supper was blazing briskly, Joe returned from a foraging expedition quite out of breath, and with his milk-pail half empty. He said that he had met three tramps on the road, which passed through the grove not very far from the camp, and that they had snatched a pie from him that he had bought at a farm-house, and had chased him for some distance.

He had been badly frightened, as he frankly admitted; but the other boys thought that it was a good joke on him. They told him that the tramps would track him by the milk that he had spilled, and would probably attack the camp and scalp him. They soon forgot the adventure, however, with the exception of Tom, who, although he said nothing at the time, poured water on the fire as soon as the supper was cooked—an act which somewhat astonished the rest. Soon afterward he went into the tent for a few moments, and when he returned he was beginning to advise Joe not to laugh quite so loud, when the crackling of branches was heard in the grove, and three very unpleasant-looking men appeared.

It was fast growing dark, but Joe immediately recognized them as the tramps who had stolen his pie. "We've come to supper," said one of them. "Let's see what you've got. Give us the bill of fare, sonny, and look sharp about it."

Tom immediately answered that they had eaten their supper, and that there was nothing left of it but some coffee. "If you want the coffee, take it," said he. "There isn't anything else for you."

"That ain't a perlite way to treat three gen'lemen as come a long ways to call on you," said the tramp. "We'll just have to help ourselves, and we'll begin by looking into your tent. P'r'aps you've got a crust of bread there what 'll save a poor starvin' workin'-man from dyin' on the spot."

Tom hastily stepped before the tent. "You can't go into this tent," he said, very quietly; "and you'd better leave this camp and go about your business."

"Just hear him," said the tramp, addressing his companions. "As if this yere identical camp wasn't our business. Now, boys," he continued, "you've got money with you, and you've got clothes, and one on you's got a watch; and you're goin' to give 'em to three honest hard-workin' men, or else you're goin' to have your nice little throats cut."

"Here, boys, quick!" cried Tom, rushing into the tent, where he was followed by the other boys before the tramps could stop them. "Here, Harry," he continued, "take the boat-hook. There's a hatchet for you, Jim, and a stick for Joe. Now we'll see if they can rob us!" So saying, he stepped outside the tent with the gun in his hand, followed closely by his little army.

The ruffians hesitated when they saw the cool way in which Tom confronted them. So they proposed a compromise, as they called it. "Look a here," said the one who had hitherto been the spokesman; "we ain't unreasonable, and we'll compromise this yere business. You give us your money and that chap's watch, and we'll let you alone. That's what I call a very handsome offer."

"We won't give you a thing," replied Tom; "and I'll shoot the first one of you that lays a hand on us."

The tramps consulted for a moment, and then the leader, with a frightful oath, ordered Tom to drop that gun instantly.

Tom never said a word, but he cocked both barrels and waited, with his eye fixed on the enemy.

Presently the tramps separated a little, the leader remaining where he had been standing, and the others moving one to the right and the other to the left of the boys. They evidently intended to rush on Tom from three directions at once, and so confuse him, and prevent him from shooting.

"I'll take the leader and the man on the right," whispered Tom to Harry. "You lay for the other fellow with your boat-hook. I've given you fair warning," he continued, addressing the ruffians, "and I'll fire the minute you try to attack us."

The boys were standing close together in front of the tent, Tom being a little in advance of the others. Suddenly the leader of the tramps called out, "Now, then!" and all three made a rush toward Tom. He fired at the tramp in front of him, hitting him in the leg, and bringing him to the ground; but before he could fire again, the other two were upon him.

The boys gallantly stood by Tom. Harry attacked one of the tramps with the boat-hook so fiercely that the fellow cried out that he was stabbed, and ran away. Meanwhile Tom was struggling with the third tramp, who had thrown him down, and was trying to wrench the gun from him, while Jim and Joe were hovering around them afraid to strike at the tramp for fear of hitting Tom. But now Harry, having driven off his antagonist, flew to the help of Tom, and seizing the tramp by his hair, and bracing one knee against his back, dragged him backward to the ground, and held him there until Tom regained his feet, and holding the muzzle of the gun at the robber's head, called on him to surrender, which the fellow gladly did.

"Get some rope, Jim, and tie him," cried Tom. "Hold on to his hair, Harry, and I'll blow his brains out if he offers to move."

The tramp was not at all anxious to part with his brains, and he remained perfectly quiet while Jim and Joe tied his feet together, and his hands behind his back.

"Now you stand over him with the boat-hook, Harry," said Tom, "and I'll see to the other fellow."

The other fellow was, of course, the man who had been shot. Tom lighted the lantern, for it was now quite dark, and found that the ruffian had been shot in the lower part of his right leg, and had fainted from loss of blood. Taking a towel, Tom tore it into strips, and bound up the wound, and by the time he had finished the patient became conscious again, and begged Tom not to take him to prison.

Now this was precisely what the boys did not want to do, as it would probably delay them for several days, and perhaps put an end to their cruise. Tom therefore said to the prisoner whom Harry was guarding, that if he would promise to help the wounded man away, and take him to see a doctor, he would be released. The tramp gladly accepted the offer, and Harry unfastened the rope from his legs and arms, while Tom kept his gun in readiness to use it at the first sign of treachery. The tramps, however, had quite enough of fighting, and were only too anxious to get away. The wounded man was helped to his feet by his companion, and the two went slowly off, one half carrying the other, and both cursing the coward who had run away. As they hobbled off, Tom called out, "I'm sorry I had to hurt you, but I couldn't help it, you know; and if any of you come back here to-night, you'll find us ready for you."

It was a long time before the boys fell asleep that night, and Tom was overwhelmed with praise for his coolness and bravery. Though he felt certain that the tramps would not return, he proposed that a sentinel should keep guard outside the tent, offering to share that duty with Harry, since the other boys were not familiar with guns. So all night long Tom and Harry, relieving one another every two hours, marched up and down in front of the tent, keeping a sharp watch for robbers, and prepared for a desperate fight every time they heard the slightest noise.

[TO BE CONTINUED.]

EASY BOTANY.

AUGUST WILD FLOWERS.

THE wild flowers of August have their own distinguishing characteristics. We find the road-sides gleaming and glowing with brilliant colors, and all the tribes of strong-growing and strong-scented plants that prefer the later summer months.

Among others the singular desmodium, or bush trefoil, is interesting from having the leaves and flowers grow on separate plants, quite unconnected apparently, and often some little distance apart.

The large, spreading leaves grow on a stalk as if they had nothing to do with anything else; but the young botanist who may grasp this plume of leaves will find that the root leads along under-ground, till suddenly up comes *another plant*—a tall stem with panicles of purplish flowers. All these freaks or peculiarities become delightful to the observant eye.

The ground-nut, or wild bean, is a very handsome climber, and peculiar in appearance. The clusters of waxy flowers are rich brown and white, growing very thick, and having the scent of violets. The tubers are often eaten.

The wild kidney-bean is found in copses and along road-sides from Connecticut to Illinois. It climbs high from a perennial root, with clusters of small bright purple flowers.

In rich woodlands in the Middle States and west the pea-nut is very interesting to young searchers. The plant bears two kinds of flowers, the upper ones ripening no fruit, but the lower or under-ground ones bearing the well-known pea-nuts.

Try to find a remarkable plant belonging to the convolvulus family, the wild-potato vine, or "man of the earth." It is not very easily overlooked. Several stems spring from the same root, growing and twining seven or eight feet high. The leaves are large, and of various shapes—heart-shaped, pointed, and fiddle-shaped. Three or four large blossoms, several inches broad, grow in clusters; the flowers are white, with purple in the tube. This remarkable vine is found in sandy fields and by road-sides from Connecticut to Illinois and south.

A large plant grows by the end of an old country bridge near Canaan, Connecticut. The stems are long and stout, and grow from a huge root that weighs fifteen or twenty pounds.

The beautiful August lilies make the fields and meadows gay; the stately pale yellow lily spotted with brown or purple, the darker yellow, and the fiery red lily, contrasted with the white spiranthes, or ladies-tresses.

Now the radiant heads of countless *composite* flowers are highest and most showy, and a walk or drive along any country road reveals such masses of color as to arrest and enchant the most unobservant eye.

On one woodland road at Orange, New Jersey, the shades of asters, from the deepest violet-blue and purple to the palest lilac, are bewilderingly beautiful, while the splendid varieties of liatris, or button snakeroot, the rose-purple and white ox-eyed daisies and white asters, golden-rod, and the great open-eyed corn-flowers, or rudbeckias, are certainly beyond description.

Try to find the elegant golden asters, which are more rare. At Cape Cod, Massachusetts, at Nantucket, and on the pine barrens of New Jersey, they may be found.

Look for the compass-plant, if you have the command of prairies. It is not pretty, is rough and coarse-looking, but is immortalized by Longfellow. The peculiarity consists in the arrangement of the leaves, the lower and root leaves, which, being very large, spread out on the open prairies, and are disposed to present their edges pointing north and south, thus sometimes guiding the bewildered traveller.

Another beautiful prairie plant, two or three feet high, is found in dry and sandy soils and in rocky crevices. The flowers are numerous, of a beautiful bright blue or bluish-white, and what makes it interesting is that it is supposed to prefer localities where lead ore prevails, and is called lead-plant.

Now is the time for any so disposed to make a collection of *herbs*, as they are called. In old-fashioned days these herbs were considered great treasures, and cures for many of the ills of humanity. They were tied carefully in bunches, and hung in the garret of the farm-house to dry. The odor of dried herbs comes to me now as I think of a dear old garret—a favorite play-place of early childhood.

No child familiar with the garret of a country home can ever forget its mysterious charm. But I must remember that I am writing of flowers, and leave the captivating subject of garrets. Multitudes of potent herbs may now be found in the woods, by the road-side, *everywhere*: tansy, camomile, wormwood, everlasting, wild basil, lavender, germander, pennyroyal, spearmint, balm, peppermint, horehound, hyssop, thyme, rosemary, sage, wild bergamot, catnip, motherwort, comfrey, boneset, thoroughwort, fennel, and many other life-giving plants. They are generally coarse-looking and rough, with strong stems and strong odors, and no beauty, though in some cases the flowers are a pretty blue or rose-color. All these things, even to the summer gathering of herbs for some dear relative, become interesting to the young student, because it is a real pleasure to become familiar with the *varieties* which are presented in nature's domain, and the homely growths are sometimes of more importance than the ornamental, a consoling thought to such of us as are possessed of but little physical beauty.

DO YOU KNOW HIM?

THE BOY EMIGRANT IN RUSSIA.

A True Story.

BY DAVID KER.

MANY years ago, when Peter the Great was Czar of Russia, and when the improvements that he was making all over the country gave foreign workmen a fine chance of earning high wages, a number of emigrants landed one cold winter morning at one of the Russian ports on the Gulf of Finland, to see if they could find work, as so many others had done.

A curious mixture they were—men, women, and children from every country on either side of the Baltic. Tall, fresh-colored Swedes, in gray frocks and thick blue stockings; stout, light-haired Germans, and ruddy, blue-eyed Danes; big-boned Pomeranians, with low foreheads and shaggy brown beards; and short, squat Finns, whose round puffy faces and thick yellow hair gave them the look of overboiled apple-dumplings.

But their first taste of Russia was not at all a pleasant one. At the port where they had landed it was the rule that all emigrants who came ashore should be kept in one place till the Czar's agents came to examine them; and the place where they were kept was an old ware-house, very bare and dismal-looking, with nothing in it but a few old sails and some heaps of straw. Here they remained for two days, while the snow fell and the wind roared outside, their food being brought them by the soldiers of the port. The men smoked their pipes and played cards, the women knitted stockings or mended the clothes of their husbands and children, while the little people played hide-and-seek in and out of the dark corners, and made the gloomy old place quite merry with their shouts and laughter.

But there was one boy (a bright-eyed little fellow with brown curly hair) who took no part in the fun, but sat in a corner by himself, chalking curious figures on the wall, which he seemed to copy from the book in his other hand. Any one who had looked closely at these figures would have seen that they were *letters*—Russian letters—and that sometimes he would write a whole word at once, and then put the meaning opposite it in German. In fact, he was teaching himself the language of this new country that he had got into, and seemed to be pretty well on with it, for every now and then he would leave off writing, and read a page of his book without meeting a single word that he could not master.

"Look at Karl Osterman yonder, slaving away at that book of his!" said one of the men. "Much good that'll do him! As if one could saw a plank or hammer a rivet any better for knowing that crack-jaw lingo!"

"He's going to teach the Russians their own language—that's what he's at!" grinned another. "A regular professor, ain't he? far too clever for poor fellows like us!"

"Ay, he'll be a great man one of these days," chimed in a third, with a hoarse laugh, "and then perhaps he'll be kind enough to give us a job."

Little Karl's eyes sparkled, and he set his lips firmly, as if making up his mind that he *would* be a great man yet, somehow or other; but he said nothing, and went quietly on with his work.

Suddenly the door flew open, and in came a Russian soldier in a shabby green uniform trimmed with faded gold lace. He was a very tall and powerful man, with a dark, weather-beaten face framed in close-cropped hair, and great black eyes that seemed to pierce right through any one whom they looked at.

"I say, my good fellows," cried he, "here's an order from the Czar, which I'm to paste up in this room; and I want to have it in German and Swedish as well as Russian, that every one who comes in may be able to read it. Perhaps one of you would kindly lend me a hand with the job, for I'm not very glib at foreign languages myself."

The men glanced meaningly at each other, and the two who had been making fun of Osterman looked rather sheepish, as if thinking that they had better have been learning Russian themselves instead of laughing at him.

"I'll do it for you, Mr. Soldier," said little Osterman, stepping boldly forward, "if there aren't any very big words in it. I've only got as far as three-syllable words in Russian yet, you know."

The soldier stared at him for a moment, and then began to laugh.

"Well, my boy, I don't think you'll find many big words on this paper; it's pretty plain sailing so far as it goes. See if you can read it."

Karl took the paper, and read it off easily enough.

"Well done, my fine fellow!" cried the Russian;

"you're a smart lad for your age, I can see that. Now try if you can put it into German."

To work went our hero, with a look as solemn as any professor on his little round face. Once or twice he stopped as if at a loss for a word; but he got through at last, and having finished the German, began upon the Swedish.

"What! do you know Swedish too?" cried his new friend. "Why, man, you're a perfect dictionary!"

"My mother was a Swede," answered Osterman, "and she taught me her own language; and my father was a German, and he taught me his."

"You're a lucky fellow!" said the Russian, with a sigh. "I only wish I'd had some one to teach me when I was your age, I should know a great deal more than I do."

"What! didn't your father teach you, then?"

"He died when I was a mere child," said the Russian, sadly, "and my mother, too."

"Oh dear, I'm so sorry! But had you no brothers or sisters?"

"I had a brother, but he was blind, poor fellow, and couldn't help me; and as for my sister" (here his face darkened fearfully), "instead of being kind to me, she tried to have me killed!"

"What a shame!" cried the boy, indignantly, clinching a fist about the size of a large plum. "I only wish *I'd* been your brother!—I wouldn't have let anybody touch you!"

This valiant promise of protection, made by a tiny boy to a stalwart soldier of six feet three, tickled the other emigrants so much that they burst into a roar of laughter which made the old walls ring. But the soldier did not laugh; he only passed his hand tenderly over the child's curly head, and then stooped to look at the book which Karl had been reading.

"Ah! the story of Ilia the Strong. I used to be very fond of it when I was a boy. How do you like it?"

"Very much indeed. I didn't think I'd have time to finish it, when they said the Czar was coming to look at us; but I suppose he's too busy amusing himself to care about us poor fellows."

The soldier gave such a terrible frown that the men nearest him started back in dismay, and even Osterman himself looked startled. But the next moment the Russian's face cleared again, though it was still very sad.

"You shouldn't talk like that, my boy," said he; "the Czar would have come to you directly you landed, if he hadn't been ill. However, he's well again now, and I shouldn't wonder if you were to see him here to-day."

Just then the door opened again, and in tramped a dozen grand-looking officers in splendid uniforms, the foremost of whom, making a low bow to the shabby soldier, said, very respectfully, "All is ready, your majesty."

At the word "majesty," all the emigrants started as if they had been shot; for they now saw that this shabby-looking fellow, whom they had taken for a common soldier, was no other than the Czar Peter the Great himself. But little Osterman did not seem frightened in the least. He slid his soft little hand into the Emperor's huge brown fist, and cried joyfully:

"I'm so glad you're a good Czar after all, for the Czars that I've read about were all very bad fellows indeed, and I know I shouldn't have liked them."

"Well, well, my boy," said Peter, clapping him on the shoulder, with a hearty laugh, "I hope you'll find me a little better than some of them, even though I *am* an Emperor. Come along with me, and I'll find you something better to do than chalking an old wall."

The boy went with his new friend, and any history of Russia will tell you how high Osterman rose, and what great things he accomplished. Peter the Great made him his secretary; the Empress Catherine I. made him her chamberlain; and the Czar Peter II. gave him a title of honor; and before the Empress Anne had been many years on the throne, the little student whom his comrades had laughed at in the old warehouse thirty years before, had become Count Osterman, Prime Minister of Russia.

(Begun in Harper's Young People No. 37, July 13.)

THE STORY OF THE AMERICAN NAVY.

BY BENSON J. LOSSING.

Chapter V.

"WE have a right to enter any of your vessels without your leave to seek for suspected deserters from our navy, and to take them away when found," said the British government to the Americans again after the war with the Barbary States.

"By so doing you insult our flag. *Beware!*" replied the Americans.

There was no power in that "Beware!" for our little

navy, which had performed such valiant deeds, had, under the pretext of "public economy," been transformed into a swarm of gun-boats—a "mosquito fleet"—that was ridiculed at home and despised abroad. British cruisers patrolled American waters, and insulted our flag whenever they pleased. They became legalized plunderers, and no American merchant vessel leaving port was safe from their depredations.

In 1807 a British squadron lay in a bay on the coast of Virginia. The American frigate *Chesapeake* put to sea from Hampton Roads, when the *Leopard*, one of the English ships, stopped her, and demanded the delivery of three or four alleged deserters on board of her. When the demand was refused, the *Leopard* sent no less than twenty round-shot through the surprised and unprepared *Chesapeake*, and British officers boarded her, and carried away the men. This outrage excited a hot war spirit among the Americans. The government ordered all armed British vessels to leave American waters immediately. Did they do it? No. There was no power back of the order to enforce it. The ridiculous gun-boat fleet was laughed at, and the government was placed in the position of a weak blusterer. British cruisers continued to patrol American waters. The people demanded more war ships. The government heeded the demand. The gun-boats retired, and in 1810 the Americans had four frigates and eight smaller armed vessels afloat.

In the spring of 1811 a British frigate was seen prowling along our coasts. Commodore Rodgers went in search of her in the frigate *President*, and on a pleasant May evening he gave chase to a vessel which he supposed to be the one he was searching for. As he drew near he asked, through his trumpet, "What ship is that?" The stranger repeated the question. Rodgers again asked, "What ship is that?" and was answered by a cannon-ball, which lodged in the main-mast of the *President*. Rodgers opened a broadside upon the surly stranger, and after a short combat silenced her guns. At daylight she was seen several miles away. She was the British sloop-of-war *Little Belt*.

This affair created great excitement, and from that time until the summer of 1812 the American war vessels were kept actively cruising along our coasts. Meanwhile, navy-yards had been built, the moral tone of the navy had been greatly improved, and its discipline was efficient. It was almost unconsciously preparing for a great conflict, in which it was to gain imperishable renown.

Insult after insult caused the Americans to declare war against England in the summer of 1812. Measures were taken to create an efficient army, but, strange as it may seem, when war was to be waged against a powerful maritime nation there was persistent opposition in Congress to a navy. The Southern members, representing a purely agricultural region, could not sympathize with New Englanders in desires for a navy to protect commerce. In vain it was wisely urged that protection to commerce is protection to agriculture. A South Carolina member declared he would "go further to see a navy burned than to extinguish the flames," and a proposition of a Massachusetts member to build thirty frigates was voted down. And yet, so unprepared for maritime war, the Americans went boldly out on the ocean with a few public vessels and active privateers to defy the royal navy of England. The United States had twenty war vessels, exclusive of one hundred and twenty gun-boats. Great Britain had eight hundred efficient cruisers.

The British had nothing but sneers at and ribald jokes about the American Navy. They laughed in derision at our declaration of war. They spoke of the *Constitution* frigate, which had performed such gallant deeds in the Mediterranean, as "a bundle of pine boards sailing under a bit of striped bunting," and they declared that "a few broadsides from England's wooden walls" would "drive the paltry striped bunting from the ocean." They did not heed the injunction, "Let not him that girdeth on his harness boast himself as he that putteth it off."

When war was declared, there was a small American squadron in the harbor of New York under Commodore Rodgers. It immediately went to sea in search of a large fleet of Jamaica merchantmen known to be off the coast. The *President* frigate was Rodgers's flag-ship. She soon encountered the British frigate *Belvidera*, which, after a sharp combat, was lightened, and, outsailing the *President*, escaped. This was the first battle on sea or land of the war of 1812–15, which is properly called the "Second War for Independence." The *Belvidera* carried the news of the declaration of war to the British at Halifax.

Captain Broke was sent from Halifax with a squadron to meet the Americans. His flag-ship was the frigate *Shannon*. He soon captured the little brig *Nautilus*, the *first* vessel taken in that war. She was retaken in the East Indies in 1815, and was the *last* vessel captured in the war.

The frigate *Constitution*, Captain Isaac Hull, had just returned from Europe. She shipped a new crew, and cruised along the New England coasts. In the middle of July she fell in with Broke's squadron. Perceiving his peril, Hull sought safety in flight; and then began one of the most remarkable naval retreats ever recorded, in which skillful seamanship won the race. There was almost a dead calm. Down went the boats of the *Constitution*, with long lines attached to them, and strong sweeps were used with desperate energy in towing her. A long cannon was placed at the stern on her spar-deck, and two others were pointed out of her cabin windows.

A gentle breeze now sprang up, and the *Shannon* approached and attacked the *Constitution* with her bow guns. The breeze died away. The water was shallow, and Hull sent a kedge anchor with ropes attached, in a boat, half a mile ahead. It was cast, and the crew pulled the ship rapidly ahead. For a while Broke was puzzled by her mysterious movement, but discovering the secret he used the same means. Through breezes and calms, and a fierce thunder-storm that swept over the sea, the chase continued sixty-four hours, when Broke gave it up, and the *Constitution* escaped. A rhymer of the day wrote:

> "'Neath Hull's command and a tough band,
> And naught beside to back her,
> Upon a day, as log-books say,
> A fleet bore down to thwack her.
> A fleet, you know, is odds or so
> Against a single ship, sirs;
> So 'cross the tide her legs she tried,
> And gave the rogues the slip, sirs."

[TO BE CONTINUED.]

THE "BOSS" FISH.

BY WILLIAM O. STODDARD.

"NO use, Charley. We might as well go home to breakfast."

"We got here early enough."

"I don't believe there's a trout in the brook."

"If there are any, they don't bite worms early in the morning any more'n they do any other time."

Charley looked mournfully down at his float, as it lopped wearily over on one side. The water of the little pool below the foot-bridge over the trout brook was as smooth as a looking-glass, and the float had not so much as wiggled since he dropped it in.

"I don't care much for trout, Jeff."

"I'd rather have some breakfast."

"And after that we'll take the boat, and go out on the pond. We've dug a pile of worms."

Slowly and grudgingly the line was pulled in, but the faces of both the boys brightened the moment they were turned in the direction of breakfast.

Half an hour later they were stopping for a moment to look at a stout, middle-aged man who was standing on the steps of the little village hotel, talking with the landlord. A strap over one shoulder held up a fishing-basket that swung behind his left hip, and in his right hand he carried, all ready for use, the lightest fishing-rod Charley Morris had ever seen. Even Jeff, who was from the city himself, and had looked at such things in the show windows of the shops, had an idea the stranger must have made a mistake in bringing that plaything into the country.

"It's a trout rod, Charley. If we'd had one like it this morning!"

"'Tisn't much bigger'n a horsewhip."

Just then the landlord was saying, "Thar isn't much in the pond 'cept perch and sunfish, but you may take something in the creek above. Your best show for trout is to work along the trout brook as far as the hill, and then cut across to the creek, and fish down. 'Tain't far to cross. To-morrer you can try the brooks beyond the hill. Some of 'em 'll give you a full baskit."

"Hear that, Jeff," whispered Charley. "Just isn't old Galloway a-fooling him! Sending him to fish in that brook! Why, if our cows got at it all at once, they'd drink it dry."

Jeff was looking at the high boots the stranger wore over his trousers, and was just saying, "They're for wading, so he won't wet his feet," when Charley looked right up into the face of the "fancy fisherman" from the city, and asked,

"Mister, do you want any worms?"

"Angle-worms, my lad?"

"And grubs! I know where you can dig lots of 'em. Where Jeff and I got ours this morning."

"No, thank you, my little man. I don't care for any worms. Would you like to see my bait?"

"Guess I would. Look here, Jeff, he's going to show his bait."

The stout stranger chuckled merrily as he drew from one of his great side pockets a sort of little book, with a leather cover and flap.

"Jeff, he carries his worms in a pocket-book."

"Flies, my little man—flies."

"Our fish won't bite at flies, mister; and they won't hide a hook, neither."

Charley's eyes were opening wide, a moment later, as the little book was opened before them.

"Flies! Why, mister, there's pretty much every kind of bug, except bumblebees. All sorts of hooks, too. If you put them pretty things into the water, you'll get 'em wet, and spoil 'em."

Again the fat man chuckled.

"Will I? Well, now, you and I'll run a race. You two boys go ahead, and see which of us 'll catch the most fish and the biggest."

"Come on, Jeff," shouted Charley; "we'll beat him!"

But then he suddenly turned again to say:

"Now, mister, you've got your scoop-net along. Minners don't count, do they?"

"No, sonny, minnows won't count. Only fish that are big enough to eat."

Charley had never seen a "landing-net" used in his life, but he knew what minnows were good for.

"If we had some, Jeff," he said, as they hurried along toward the pond, "we could try for some pickerel. There's some of them left. Only they've been fished for so much, they know enough to let a hook alone."

"Big ones?"

"Some of 'em. There's one awful big one. Black Dan—he's the best fisherman round here, only he's lame of one leg—he says it's the boss fish, and he's fished for him a whole day at a time."

"Did he ever get him to bite?"

"No; but he says he's seen that pickerel smell of his bait, and then swim up to the top of the water and wink at him."

"Wish we could catch him."

"If I had that feller's scoop-net, and could get some minners."

But he had no such thing; and in a few minutes more they were in their boat on the pond, while the stranger was walking fast, for a fat man, across the meadow toward the trout brook.

This was a very narrow, crooked affair, pretty deep in many places, and almost hidden by high grass, trees, and bushes.

"We know there are no fish there," said Charley, confidently.

"Not even trout?"

"Well, yes, maybe there's trout. But they won't bite. Not even before breakfast. Anyhow, they won't go for a bare hook, with a feather on it."

That seemed sensible, and Charley's own hook now had a worm on it, and so had Jeff's.

"We'll beat him. I know just where to go. We're in the right spot."

Perhaps he did; but before the morning was over he and Jeff had moved their boat into nearly a dozen more that seemed to be just as good.

The "pond" was a sort of miniature lake, and was nearly half a mile long, although it was nowhere very wide. It was supplied by what Mr. Galloway, the landlord, called the "creek"—a pretty stream of water about ten times as large as the trout brook in the meadow.

There were fish in that pond, and it was a pity the man from the city had not known it, and tried for some of them with angle-worms, instead of wasting his time over there in the meadow.

As it was, Jeff and Charley had it all to themselves, and the latter was half glad his city cousin got the first bite.

"Good for you, Jeff!"

"Bull-head! bull-head!"

"Look out for his horns."

"Ain't he a whopper?"

"I say, Jeff, did you ever read about flying-fish?"

"Course I have."

"Well, shouldn't you think their wings 'd get wet under water?"

"Charley! mind your cork; it's gone under."

So it had, and in a moment more he could shout, "I'm even with you. Only mine's a pumpkin-seed."

It looked as if the luck of that morning had settled upon the two boys. It was hard to say which of them came in for the largest share of it. Even before they moved their boat the first time they could count three bull-heads, six perch, twice as many sunfish, or "pumpkin-seed," two shiners, and a sucker. To be sure, none of them were very large fish, but they were all big enough to eat, and would count when they came to compare with the contents of the fat man's basket.

"That was a pretty big fish-basket," said Charley. "Most of 'em are flat little things."

"It's bigger'n he'll need for all the fish he'll find in that brook. Hullo, my bait's off again."

"So's mine. Just a nibble."

"Six prime worms gone hand-running. Jeff, I guess we might as well pull up. The snappin'-turtles have come for us."

"Do they skin a hook that way?"

"That's just what they do. Black Dan says the fish put 'em up to it. Particularly that there boss pickerel."

Charley had more than one story to tell about Black Dan, but he pulled up the big stone that was doing duty as an anchor, and off they went to another "tip-top spot."

It proved so for a while, and there Jeff pulled in his first

JEFF AND CHARLEY FISHING BEFORE BREAKFAST.

eel. Then he had a good time, as Charley said, getting the eel off the hook, and untwisting him from the snarl he had got himself into with the fish-line.

"There he goes," said Charley, "all over the bottom of the boat. Black Dan says an eel just loves to travel round."

"They're mean things to catch."

"I've got one. Now I'll show you."

Charley knew how to take an eel off a hook, but that one bothered him, and when he finally got him loose, he said,

"I say, Jeff, this won't do. I'd as lief fish for turtles. Let's move."

"Wait a bit. Maybe there's something else."

So there was, but not for any great length of time; and as the boys were impatient, they made another move.

They would have given one of their eels to know how the fat man from the city was getting along.

Toward noon their frequent changes brought them away up to the head of the pond, near the mouth of the creek; but they had not been anchored ten minutes before a deep-toned cheery voice from the bank hailed them with,

"Hey, boys! Having good luck?"

"Pretty good," said Charley. "Have you caught anything?—anything bigger'n minnows?"

"Well, a fish or two. Come ashore and I'll show 'em. Besides, I want you to give me a lift with your boat."

The boys were ready enough to have a look into that fish-basket, and the anchor came up in a hurry.

"See," said the fat man, as he lifted the lid of his basket.

"Why, it's more'n half full."

"All trout too, and some of 'em are big ones."

"Mister," said Charley, "did you bring any of them from the city with you?"

"I guess not," chuckled the fat man. "I got most of 'em in the brook, but I did fairly well along the creek. Now do you see those bushes at the foot of the steep bank just below the mouth of the creek?"

"Yes," said Charley; "there's an awful deep hole right there."

"Well, I want to float over, slow and silent, so I can throw a fly right under those bushes."

"You'll get caught in 'em."

"I'll risk that."

He sat down on the front seat, and Charley rowed him over as if he were afraid of making a ripple on the water. He and Jeff were almost holding their breath with excitement over what their fat friend meant to do.

"That's it. Let her float."

The light graceful rod swung back, a remarkable length of very fine line went floating through the air, and the boys could see something like a small dragon-fly at the end of it.

"No sinker, Jeff," whispered Charley.

"It's just lit on the water."

It was a beautiful cast, and the fly fell at the very edge of the bushes, on a dark and shady spot of water with a small eddy in it.

Splash!

What a plunge that was!

"He jumped clean out of the water," exclaimed Jeff.

"You've lost your hook this time, mister, and your bait too. That's a pickerel, and we call him the boss fish."

"It's a bigger fish than I had reckoned on," said the stranger, "or I'd have brought a heavier rod and tackle."

"He'll snap any line you've got."

"We'll see."

The pickerel had felt the sharp point of that small hook, and he was now darting off toward the mouth of the creek.

The fat man took it coolly, holding his rod with one

hand, while the other rested on the large bright brass reel, that was now spinning around as the fish drew the line out.

The tough little rod was bending, but there was no great strain upon it.

"He won't run far. Here he comes back again."

Not far indeed, but there were a hundred yards of fine line out before he could begin to reel it in. Then he cried,

"There he goes, down under the bank. Means to sulk. I'll worry him out of that."

"Why don't you pull him right in?" asked Jeff, excitedly.

"Because he wouldn't come if I did."

It was a good while before there seemed to be any prospect of his coming, and the boys were almost tired of the fun of sitting still to see their stout friend let out his line and reel it in again. But at last the pickerel himself began to get a little tired of pulling and being pulled, and was reeled in closer and closer to the boat, while the trout rod bent nearly double.

"He'll break that line!"

"No, sonny; that's what the landing-net is for."

They saw it darted under the gleaming side of the great fish—a lift, a splash, and the prize was floundering on the bottom of the boat.

"Hurrah, boys! We've got him."

"You've beat us, mister. I'm just going to go home and catch a lot of flies," muttered Charley.

Half an hour later they were all standing on the hotel steps, and Black Dan was holding up the pickerel.

"Dat ar's de boss fish, shuah! And you done catch him wid a fly and dat ar whipstalk! Was you dar, Charley Morris?"

"I saw him do it, and so did Jeff."

"Well, ef I ain't glad he's done got dat ar pickerel out ob my way. Dat fish has been a suah trial to me!"

And Jeff and Charley had had their own fun, and their first lesson in fly-fishing.

WHY PICKLE GAVE THE GERMAN TEACHER A PRESENT.

BY LAURA F. FITCH.

PICKLE had waked in high spirits. That was unlucky, in the first place, for Pickle's high spirits always bubbled over before the day ended into some deed of mischief. Then, Miss Prim had a headache, and could not appear in the school-room. That was unlucky, too, for the new German teacher was to arrive that morning, and she would not be able to introduce him to the girls, and enjoin upon them attention and obedience. To be sure, Miss Meek, the assistant-principal, undertook to perform all necessary ceremonies, but then the girls never minded Miss Meek. In the third place, the new teacher was queer-looking. That was the most unfortunate circumstance of all, and was really to blame for the whole affair.

"What business," Pickle wrathfully demanded of her friend Sally, "has a man, even if he is a German, to come to a girls' boarding-school looking like a guy?"

Sally, who was trying to dispose of two thick slices of bread and butter before recitation, was too much occupied to answer.

But Pickle was not particular about an answer, and continued, nodding her head in the direction of the hall: "Look at him out there, now. Such a great broad-shouldered man. And then see how he blushes. And do just

CAUGHT IN THE ACT.—Drawn by W. T. Smedley.

look at that long curly hair, 'way down to his shoulders. Gracious! I should think he'd be ashamed of it."

Pickle evidently resented the teacher's fine curls, which were too long for a man, as a personal insult to herself, it being one of the sorrows of her life that her own thick hair was kept cropped by her mother's orders.

"I know I sha'n't like him," she added to herself, as the unfortunate possessor of the obnoxious curls entered the room.

He was not naturally a nervous man, he thought, but he had never taught girls before, and he found the calm, cool scrutiny to which he was being subjected by every member of the class something formidable. He would rather teach fifty boys, he said to himself, than these fifteen girls.

Pickle, from her desk, watched the new teacher's every movement. She laughed to see him nervously twist his feet around the leg of the chair, while a smile of scorn played over her lips when he ran his fingers through his waving locks.

"Sal," she whispered, "ain't he too funny for anything, though! I hope he speaks English with an accent; that is, if he ever gets the courage to speak at all."

These disrespectful whispers, though inaudible to Herr Müller, were terminated by his speaking at that moment. In the very mildest possible tones he asked, "Vill some young lady haf se goodness to acquaint me eggsactly how far se class haf read in se book?"

"Oh, he's as meek as Moses, and speaks worse than Professor Schultz used to!" was Pickle's murmured comment upon this speech; while Alice Smith rose to say that the class had read as far as the twenty-fourth page, fifteenth line.

"No, we haven't, either," immediately exclaimed Pickle. Then, as Herr Müller looked inquiringly at her, "We only got to the fourteenth line. I just mentioned it," she added, as the girls tittered, "because you wanted to know eggsactly."

Herr Müller frowned, but judged it best to take no notice of this speech, merely saying to the speaker, "Vill you haf se goodness to read a leetle?"

Pickle knew he was addressing her, but she ignored the request, and gazed blankly before her. Sally nudged her, whispering, "Pickle, he means you."

"He must address me by my name, then."

"Why, how can he, when he doesn't know what it is?"

"That's his look-out," was the reply.

Herr Müller, perceiving that every one else in the room knew whom he was addressing, exclaimed, impatiently, "Vill se young lady wis se *very short hair* please to read!"

Unconscious Herr Müller knew not what mortal offense he had given, as Pickle quickly arose, glibly read as far as desired, and then sat down, boiling with indignation.

"'Very short hair!'" she muttered to Sally. "Maybe it is; but it can grow, I guess; anyway, it's no disgrace. But as for his curls, hair like that is a disgrace to any man."

"Yes, indeed," assented Sally; "his curls are only fit for a girl. They'd look nice, now, on you, Pickle."

Pickle replied to this apparently innocent speech with a withering glance. The next moment, however, her face lighted up with an idea.

The door of the class-room opened, and Miss Meek entered to say that some new German books had arrived, and to request Herr Müller to come and look at them. No sooner had the door closed behind the two teachers than Pickle exclaimed aloud, "I've forgotten my translation book," and also left the room. Sally was suspicious of this errand. Pickle often forgot her books, yet seldom took the trouble to go for them, unless sent. But when she came into the class-room again, with several others who had also seized this opportunity of walking out, she seemed hardly to merit her friend's suspicions. She paused a moment by the teacher's desk, and then took her seat.

In a few minutes Herr Müller's step outside caused all the girls to scramble to their seats, so that when he entered they sat as quiet and demure as though they had not stirred during his absence. He took his seat, and opened his book again at the lesson, when the girls saw him suddenly flush up to the roots of his hair, and run his fingers nervously through his long curls. He next removed a small package that had evidently been lying in his book, and laid it on the side of the desk. In so doing, something fell out of the package on to the floor, and showed itself to the wondering girls to be a *hair-pin*. Thereupon some of the girls giggled, others smiled, and all involuntarily fastened their gaze on the teacher's flowing hair.

Sally turned to Pickle. "How could you do it?" she whispered to her companion, whose face, flushed with the effort to restrain her mirth, was alarmingly red.

"What do you mean?" returned Pickle, with an unconscious air.

The next minute Miss Meek again entered, this time with an inkstand for the teacher's desk. In placing it she evidently saw the bundle of hair-pins, for she looked indignantly around the class before leaving the room, while Herr Müller once more flushed a rosy red.

"She'll tell that to Miss Prim, Pickle—see if she don't," whispered Sally, anxiously, to her friend.

"Do you think so?" queried Pickle, hastily; then, with marked indifference, "Yes, I suppose she will. I wonder if she'll find out who did it?"

"Oh, you needn't try to deceive me, as if I didn't know who did it!" returned the other.

"Do you?" was the only reply she got to her attempt at confidence.

This provoked Sally. "Yes, I do; and Miss Prim 'll find out, too, without much telling—you can be sure of that."

Miss Prim did find out, but not without any telling. Pickle wisely determined to forestall all investigations. She went privately to the grieved Miss Prim, and announced herself as the culprit.

Although Miss Prim punished Pickle at the time for her disrespect, the kind-hearted girl—for she was kind-hearted in spite of her love of mischief—was much more severely punished by her own conscience when, a few days later, she learned why Herr Müller allowed his curly locks to grow down over his shoulders.

A brave young soldier in the German army, he had, during the siege of Metz, left the shelter of the trenches, and in the face of almost certain death rushed across the open ground where shot, shell, and bullets fell thick as hail, to snatch up and bring safely back in his strong arms a little child. It was a blue-eyed four-year-old girl who, terror-stricken and bewildered by the death of her parents and the awful firing, had wandered from one of the crumbling houses outside the walls of the city. When the soldiers in the trenches first saw her she was standing irresolute but unharmed amid the storm of flying death that swept across the plain.

Just as he reached the trenches with his precious burden the young soldier was hurled to the ground badly wounded, and apparently dead. A fragment of a bursting shell had struck him on the back of the neck. Although he lived and finally recovered, a terrible and unsightly scar remained, and was only hidden from sight by the thick curls that Pickle had so despised.

The brave soldier had adopted the child he had saved, and it was to provide means for her support that he now taught German in Miss Prim's school.

You may be sure that after this the little Elsie and her adopted father had no firmer friend nor warmer admirer than Pickle, who through them had learned a lesson that she never forgot.

A GAME FOR A RAINY DAY.

WHILE every hour of a pleasant day by the sea-side or in the country provides its own amusements, on a rainy day young people are apt to find that time hangs heavily on their hands. So it happened, one day last month, that the girls staying at Sandy Beach Hotel visited Miss Walker in her room, and begged her to suggest some new game for them.

After a moment's hesitation she said that she had thought of a game that might be new to them, though she had played it when a child.

"I shall want one assistant," she said, "to whom the secret of the game will be intrusted; the others will have to try to guess it. I shall remain in the room with the rest of you, and my assistant will go out. During her absence I shall place my hand on the shoulder of some girl, or upon the piano, or on my own shoulder, and when she returns she shall tell you who has been touched."

Nobody seemed to know anything about the game, so Miss Walker chose Alice Milne as her assistant.

The girl went out of the room. Miss Walker laid her hand on the girl nearest to her, who happened to be Clara Lane, and on Alice's return asked, "On whom did my hand rest?"

Alice at once replied, "On Clara."

"Right," was the answer.

But the girls, thinking they had found out the game, said, "You touch the girl nearest to you, Miss Walker."

"I certainly did on this occasion; but the position of the girl has nothing to do with the secret."

"I think I know it, but I shall see," said Bertha, and several girls expressed a similar opinion.

Again Alice went out. Miss Walker touched Nellie, and Alice, as promptly as before, named the right person on her return to the room.

The girls were at fault, and again failed to discover any look or gesture that could help them.

"You must have heard, Alice," said one.

But Miss Walker did not speak."

"She placed her hand in a particular position."

"Alice may come in blindfolded if you like," said Miss Walker.

One of the girls went out with Alice, brought her in backward, so that she might not see Miss Walker, held her hands, and did everything but find out the secret.

At last they said: "We give it up, Miss Walker. Do tell us the secret."

"Well," said Miss Walker, "if you really can not guess it, I will tell you. As a rule, I placed my hand on the shoulder of the girl who spoke last before Alice quitted the room. But sometimes there were two or three speakers, and in this case I touched my own shoulders. If no one spoke, I touched the piano. Any article that may be agreed upon will do equally well. With this simple understanding, and an intelligent assistant, a mistake is almost impossible.

SEA-BREEZES.

LETTER No. 1 FROM [illegible] MAYNARD TO HER DOLL.

OLD ORCHARD BEACH, *August*, 1880.

DEAR CHILD,—It is two weeks, I *do declare*, since I have written you one word, and what a state you must be in all this time; for I remember perfectly well how suddenly my letter closed, just at the very *crisis* of that awful adventure. But really, Clytie, so many things have happened since, and every minute is so full of pleasures or catastrophes, that, as I look back, that one seems almost insignificant.

I suppose you are surprised at my using such large words; but here we meet a great many "people of culture," as they are called, and they are all very busy "improving their minds"; and you know Solomon says, "Never do till to-morrow what you can put off to-day," so I am trying to improve mine too, while I am under their confluence.

Papa bought me a little pocket dictionary, and I look out all sorts of words in it, and that is how I get so many big ones that perhaps you don't quite apprehend, but I must use them inasmuch.

Excuse me for scratching out inasmuch, I *should* have said nevertheless. When I am not quite sure of a word, I look it out, for I always have my little dictionary close at hand, and that is a great conveyance, you know. I am trying to get over my babyish way of talking, or at least of writing, and hope I may exceed.

But to go back to my story: where was I? We were crossing over the board to the island, weren't we? Well, Fan was going ahead, wheeling Jane in her carriage, then Dora and Snip, and me on behind with Moppet in my arms. Randolph stood in the water, and watched his chance till we were all fairly on the board, and then he gave a regular Indian war-whoop, and threw himself right across the middle of the board, and shook it with all his might, so that it jiggled awfully right up and down. Before we had time to scream or to paralise our danger, over we all went, pell-mell, helter-skelter, higgledy-piggledy,

HOW WE LOOKED AFTER IT HAPPENED.

down, down, down into the foaming water! What do you think of that, Clytie? Every single one of us—dogs, Jane, carriage, and all! 'Twas worse, a thousand-fold, than when we lost Lucille. Fan sat right down on the pebbles at the bottom of the sea, and gave herself up for lost. I threw Moppet as far as I could on to the beach, while Dora screamed: "You hateful boy! Go at him, Snip! bite him! throw him over! eat him up!" And Snip *did* go at him, as if he would "tear him limb from limb," as the story-books say.

Randolph looked scared out of his wits, and without waiting to help one of us, he turned and ran as fast as he could go, and never stopped till he was safe back at the hotel, the mean coward that he is! We heard afterward how he ran into the house with such a roar as to frighten every one there, crying out at the top of his lungs, "They've set the dog on me, and he'll kill me!" Did you ever know such a horrid boy?

As for the rest of us, we scrambled out as best we could, by the help of the other boys, for, to tell the truth—and you know, my Clytie, I always do that, and never mean even to exaggerate when I am telling a story—the water was not very deep where we fell, not more than half way up to our knees, and we often go in wading there; but it seems a good deal deeper when you are dumped right down into it without any warning. Now wasn't this a tragical end of our picnic on the island?

A few days later Mrs. Peyton and her party left Old Orchard. Where they have gone I do not know, but we children believe they went away on Randolph's account. We *tried* to treat him politely, but how could we? I don't think any one would blame us for turning our backs on him whenever he appeared, and only saying good-morning to him in a lofty way over our shoulders. He

WASHING THE BABIES' FACES.

he evidently didn't like it, and probably coaxed his mother to go away.

Whatever *other* people can do, I am very sure *I* shall never be able to love my enemies. *Love* Randolph Peyton! Just think of it, Clytie. I'd be *ashamed* to love such a mean boy even if I could, enemy or not. I truly hope we may never see him again.

Such heaps and heaps of things as I shall have to tell you, dear Clytemnestra, when I get home! No letter would ever be long enough to get them all in. There will be enough to talk about all next winter.

You don't know anything about the clam-bake we had last week, nor how Dora and I got lost one day in a cave—a real *bona fide* cave, as papa says, dark and dreadful, where smugglers used to hide their things.

I'm saving up lots of things to tell you some day, and if *your* eyes don't open wider than ever before, it will only be because something is the matter with your wires. Such fun as I am having this summer! And, oh, Clytie! what do you think! Mamma is busy packing the trunk, and we are going away from here to-morrow. We are going with some other people to Mount Desert, 'way round the coast of Maine, ever so much farther than this.

It is lovely everywhere here, and I don't believe Maine is half so crooked and queer along the shore as it looks in the geography, and I'm going to tell the girls so when I get back to school.

There's no sense in working so hard on our maps if 'tisn't true, and Maine was the very hardest State of all to draw, for 'twas so awful jiggly along the edge. Really, it isn't so a bit, for I have seen it, and ought to know.

Here come Snip and Moppet, and I hear Fan and Dora rushing up stairs for me, so I will bid you good-by, or "orevo," as I heard Dr. Le Baron say to Miss Farrar when he went away last night—that is, it *sounded* like orevo. I don't know as I spell it right, for I can not find it anywhere in my dictionary.

With ever so much love to the rest of the dolls, as well as to yourself, dear Clytie, good-night.

Your little mamma, BESSIE MAYNARD.

THE GREEDY LITTLE MOUSE.

BY E. C.

TOTTIE and Lillie were twins, with the same wide-open blue eyes, the same rosy dimples, and bright yellow hair. One day, when they were seated at the little table in the nursery eating their dinner—for they were too young yet to dine with mamma—Tottie thought she saw a little black bead shining in a hole by the closet door. No, it could not be a bead, for it popped in and out. Presently out came a little pointed nose, with long stiff whiskers, two little round ears, and two bright black—not beads, but eyes. The children sat very still, and thought they had never seen anything quite so pretty as the little plump body and long graceful tail whisking rapidly and noiselessly, while the little creature peered cautiously about. Lillie threw gently a little piece of bread, but terrified little mousie thought it was surely intended to kill her, and flew back to her stronghold in the closet. Tottie now put a little piece of bread quite close to the hole, and they sat motionless for it to re-appear. They had not long to wait; the bread was too sweet a morsel for mousie to resist, and they soon had the great pleasure of seeing her first nibble a little, and finally drag it into the hole. Lillie said, "Oh, don't you know, Tottie, mousie is the mother, and she has a lot of little children in her house, and that is going to be their dinner: let's give her some every day." And so they did, until mousie grew so tame and so wise she seemed to know the dinner hour as well as they, and would come nearer and nearer, and run in and out under the table picking up the crumbs; but she was ever a little distrustful.

If any one made an effort to catch her, or made ever so little noise, off she flew to her hole, and would wait, and peep out for some time, before she became re-assured. But when every one was fast asleep in bed, then she became more brave; but with all her fine feeding, Mrs. Mouse could not overcome her nature, and, I grieve to add, she was a *thief*. She would rummage in pockets for cake and goodies, and climb to the highest shelf if she smelt any dainty, and so, alas! fell a victim to her greedy propensities.

Nurse had put a bowl of liquid starch on the shelf in the closet, and mousie, thinking she had a fine treat, scaled the side, and reaching over for the dainty, lost her balance, and tumbled in. The fluid was too heavy and the sides too steep and slippery for her to escape; so, after vain endeavors, she sank exhausted to the bottom.

The next day, and the next passed, and no mousie came at the usual hour. Tottie said she "*knew* the old black cat had caught her." Lillie said she "*knew* the children were sick." So she threw little bits down the hole for her. But when nurse went for her forgotten starch, the truth was revealed. Poor mousie was dead. Many tears fell; and although the children had many toys, nothing was equal to that sly, active, bright-eyed, live little play-fellow.

BAD LITTLE MATTY.
THE EARLY BIRD.

[illegible]

[illegible]

[illegible]

Yes, Frank Austin is living, and often comes into the office of YOUNG PEOPLE.

[illegible]

You probably know that many great authors sign a *nom de plume* to their writings, and some little authors like to do the same. Our young correspondents, with but few exceptions, sign their real names, even when they desire the publication of a fictitious one, and it would please us better if they would always do so.

[illegible]

May H. Vinton, Mabel Lowell, Alberta F. Morrill, and E. R. send very nice recipes for candy, but they are so very similar to recipes already published that we can not make room for them. We would request the young housekeepers to avoid repetition as much as possible, for while we thank them all for their favors, we can only print such recipes as are new.

[illegible]

240 Dearborn Avenue, Chicago, Illinois.

[illegible]

Newark, Delaware.

[illegible]

Richmond, Staten Island, New York.

[illegible]

P. O. Box 388, Washington, D. C.

If Paul R. H., of Philadelphia, whose letter was in Post-office Box No. 55, will send his address to Annie M. Wickham, Titusville, Pennsylvania, she will send him some Canton and Hong-Kong postage stamps for his collection.

[illegible]

ALBERT S. RAMSAY.—It is impossible for us to help you. Try some of our exchanges. You might arrange to send them minerals, or some other natural curiosity, in exchange for what you wish.

[illegible]

[illegible] Harper's Bazar, Magazine, and Weekly [illegible] of the same way. I think Young People is the best paper for children that was ever published. I have [illegible] San Francisco, where I was born, a great deal about it.

[illegible]

MARY ANGELICA [illegible].
[illegible], California.

CHARLIE W.—Iris was the daughter of Thaumas, a sea deity who represented the majesty of the sea, and Electra. Originally she personified the rainbow, but came afterward to be the swift messenger of the gods. Homer alludes to her as darting "like hail or snow that falls from the clouds," from one end of the world to the other, and diving into all the hidden depths of the universe to execute the commands of the gods. In ancient art Iris is represented with wings and a herald's staff.

Aurora, or Eos, was the Goddess of Dawn. She was the mother of Boreas, Zephyrus, Eurus, and Notus, the north, west, east, and south winds. Another of her sons was Memnon, King of Ethiopia, who was slain by Achilles. Ever since his death Aurora has wept constantly, and the dew of the early morning is caused by her tears falling to earth. Aurora is pictured as driving a chariot and four horses, or as gliding through the air on wings, hastening to announce the arrival of the God of Day.

JOHN JACOB.—As you do not tell us what style of reading you prefer, it is a little difficult to tell you what books to choose. History is always good reading for a boy of your age. You would find Macaulay's *History of England* both valuable and interesting, and a small volume entitled *A History of Our Own Times*, by Justin McCarthy, might be read in connection with it. The historical writings of Motley and Prescott are also standard works of the greatest value. If you prefer biography, the "English Men of Letters Series" will give you a complete outline of English literature. It would be foolish for you to buy books which would simply amuse you for a short time, and we trust you will select wisely, and lay a solid foundation for a valuable library.

Favors are acknowledged from [illegible]

Correct answers to puzzles are received from [illegible]

PUZZLES FROM YOUNG CONTRIBUTORS.

No. 1.

[illegible]

No. 2.

[illegible]

No. 3.

[illegible]

No. 4.

[illegible]

No. 5.

[illegible]

My [illegible] is a portion of land.
[illegible]
My [illegible] is floating vapor. "TWO TOES."

No. 6.

ENIGMA.

My first is in coat, but not in bag.
[illegible]
A learned [illegible] these letters show. H. L.

ANSWERS TO PUZZLES IN NO. [illegible]

No. 1. [illegible]

No. 2. [illegible]

No. 3. Victoria.

No. 4. [illegible]

No. 5. [illegible]

ADVERTISEMENTS.

EFFIE'S WISH.

BY M. D. BRINE.

Oh, the shine of the laughing ripples,
  Dancing over the silver bay!
Oh, the touch of the frolicsome breezes,
  Outward-bound on this summer's day!
How they rustle and rush and hasten,
  Filling the distant sails so white,
Kissing the cheeks of little Effie
  As she gazes, with blue eyes bright,

Far away, where the waters widen,
  And fade in a mist so soft and blue.
For what are you wishing, pretty watcher?
  That you might sail with the breezes too?
That you might dance with the shining ripples
  Over the waters far away?
Ah, little Effie, your eyes may wander,
  But sacred treasure is your heart to-day.

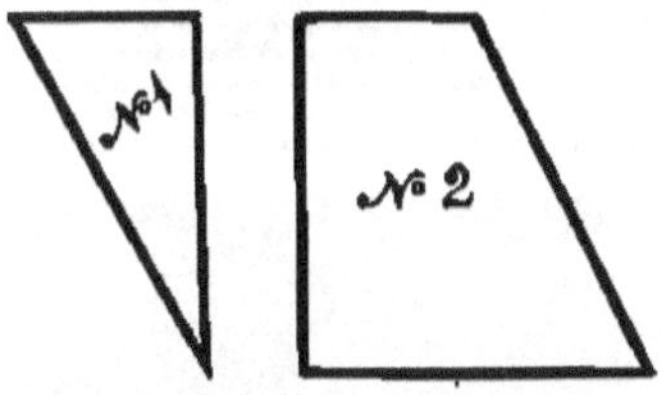

THE SQUARE PUZZLE.

HERE is an old but very good puzzle. Cut five pieces like No. 1, and five like No. 2. Arrange these ten pieces in the form of a square.

"I beg, madam, that you will pardon this almost unwarrantable intrusion, but I am in search of the Coaching Club, and would esteem it a great favor if you could inform me whether they have lately passed the gates of your Park. Whoa, Nero!"

THE RAJAH PUZZLE.

HERE is an old treacherous Hindoo confined in a tower. With one straight cut of the scissors expose his duplicity.

HISTORICAL ANECDOTE.

BY ESPERANZA.

THE captivity of ——— ——— — ———, ——— —, King of ———, son and successor of ——— —, made a solemn vow to lead a ——— to the deliverance of ———. Accordingly, in ———, accompanied by ——— ———, King of ———, he set sail for the ——— ———; but in spite of the bravery of both Kings, a year elapsed, and their object was not yet attained. ——— ——— was compelled to return to his kingdom. His ally, ———, strove to continue the enterprise; but the desertion of ——— of ———, with whom he had quarrelled at the siege of — ——— ———, weakened his army to such an extent that he was forced to abandon the struggle, and return to ———. On the return voyage a terrible storm came up, and after many hours of anxiety, the ship was dashed to pieces against some rocks. All on board perished excepting ———, who, deprived of everything but life, and a few jewels which he wore, was obliged to continue his journey on foot. His route lay through the estates of his enemy ———, and also through those of ——— —, Emperor of ———. Both dignitaries were his sworn enemies, and were very anxious to have him in their power. ——— knew this, and assuming a disguise, proceeded with the utmost caution. He passed safely through a large portion of ———, and would have escaped recognition had he not attempted to sell a valuable ring which he always wore. One of ———'s servants saw the ring, his suspicions were aroused, and he immediately warned his master of his discovery. ——— was seized, delivered into the hands of ——— —, who threw him into prison, and kept him captive for many weary months.

——— ———, Regent of ——— during his brother's absence, instead of freeing him, left him to his sad fate. Indeed, ——— would probably have died in prison had it not been for the devotion of his favorite, ———. This man was a minstrel, and had spent many happy days in close companionship with his beloved master. Hoping to find the King, he journeyed from one castle to another, inquiring everywhere if a distinguished prisoner was detained there, but all in vain. Weary, foot-sore, and disheartened, he arrived near an ancient castle, and seating himself by the road-side, played and sung his master's favorite ballad. Imagine his surprise, his delight, when a well-known voice took up the strain, and sang the remaining verses! In his great joy he hastened back to ———, enlisted the sympathies of the Barons, and gathered together a large ransom, in consideration of which ——— — released his royal captive, after an imprisonment of almost — months.

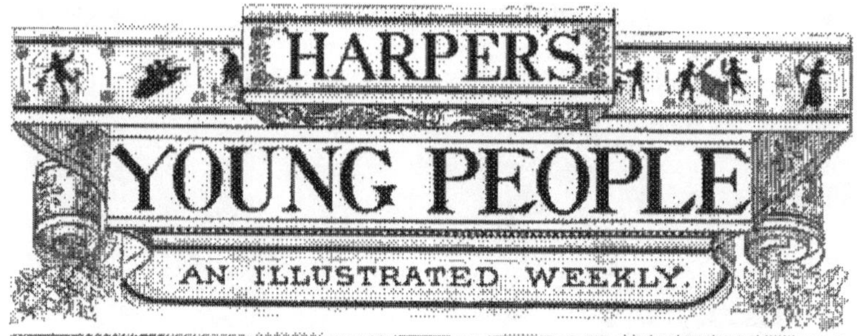

Vol. I.—No. 42. Published by HARPER & BROTHERS, New York. Price Four Cents.

Tuesday, August 17, 1880. Copyright, 1880, by Harper & Brothers. $1.50 per Year, in Advance.

OLD TIMES IN THE COLONIES.

BY CHARLES CARLETON COFFIN.

No. IV.

JOHN KEZAR, HANNAH DUSTIN, AND THE INDIANS.

It was in August, 1692. John Kezar, who lived on the banks of the Merrimac, a few miles from the sea, went out into his meadow with his scythe to cut grass. He took his gun along with him to shoot a bear if he saw one in his corn, or an Indian if one made his appearance. He leaned his gun against a tree, and went on with his mowing, not knowing that an Indian was crawling through the tall grass toward him. The Indian reached the tree, seized the gun, and cocked it.

"Me kill you now," said the Indian.

John Kezar was brave. He was quick to think. He could yell louder than any Indian. No use for him to run; that would be certain death. With a yell like the blast of a trumpet, and uplifted scythe, he rushed upon the Indian, who, instead of firing, dropped the gun and took to his heels. Kezar was upon him in an instant, swinging his scythe, and making such a fearful gash that the Indian fell dead at his feet.

Kezar lived in Haverhill. It was a frontier settlement, and the Indians either had a spite against it, or else it was more convenient for them to attack than other settlements, for they made many attempts to destroy the place.

Thomas Dustin was at work in his field one day, when he saw a large number of Indians coming toward him

THE ESCAPE OF HANNAH DUSTIN.—Drawn by Howard Pyle.

from the woods. He had eight children, the youngest a week old. The mother was in bed with the infant, tended by her nurse Mary Neff. "Run for the garrison," he shouted.

The children started, the oldest boys and girls carrying the youngest. Mr. Dustin rushed to the stable and bridled his horse, intending to take Mrs. Dustin; but the Indians were so close upon him that he could not. He leaped upon the horse with his gun, and galloped away, the bullets flying around him, leaving his wife, baby, and Mary Neff.

The Indians entered the house, dragged Mrs. Dustin from the bed, and seized the nurse. One caught up the infant by the legs, and dashed its head against a rock.

Mr. Dustin overtook his children. It would be impossible, he thought, to save them all; which should he leave? All were equally dear. How could he make a selection? He would not; he would die in defending them, and do what he could to save all.

"Run!" he shouted, urging them on; then leaped from his horse, and fired, sprung upon the animal, again loaded his gun while upon the gallop, overtook his children, dismounted, fired again, and so, keeping the Indians at bay, brought all his children in safety to the garrison.

Not so fortunate his neighbors. In a few minutes the Indians massacred twenty seven men, women, and children, set several houses on fire, and with a number of captives started for Canada.

It was the middle of March. The rivers and streams were swollen. There was snow on the ground. Mrs. Dustin had but one shoe; the other foot was bare; it was torn by the stones, chilled by the cold. Every step was marked with blood. Her fellow-captives fainted and fell one by one, and the tomahawk and scalping-knife finished them. All except Mrs. Dustin and Mary Neff were killed. For four days they travelled through the dark forest toward the northwest. The Indians gave them little to eat. The third day brought them to the rendezvous of the Indians, on a little island where the Contoocook falls into the Merrimac.

"There the old smoked in silence their pipes, and the young
To the pike and the white perch their baited lines flung;
There the boy shaped his arrows, and there the shy maid
Wove her many-hued baskets and bright wampum braid."

There were fertile intervales along the Merrimac where the deer found pasture. The Indians could spear salmon in abundance.

They had captured a little boy named Samuel Leonardson near Worcester, Massachusetts, and he had learned to talk with them.

Having been successful in their raids, all except twelve of the Indians started out to make another attack somewhere upon the English, expecting to return with captives, which they would sell to the French. Upon their return the whole party would go to Canada.

The woman who had seen her infant dashed upon the rock, and who had endured such hardships, had a brave spirit, and preferred death to captivity.

They who would be free, must themselves strike the blow. There was none but God to lean upon. She determined to make the attempt to be free.

"Ask the Indians where they strike with the tomahawk when they want to kill a person quick?" she said to Samuel.

"Strike 'em here," said the Indian, putting his finger on Samuel's temple.

Mrs. Dustin saw where he placed his finger.

"This is the way to take off a scalp," said the Indian, showing the boy how to run a knife around the head, and separate the scalp from the skull.

The strong-hearted woman turns over her plans. They are on an island. There are twelve Indians in all; some are women, some children. Their canoes are drawn up beneath the alders. They are so far from any danger of surprise that no one keeps watch at night. The thought never comes to them that their captives—two *feeble* women and a boy—can escape.

Night comes. The fires burn low. All are asleep, lulled by the music of the falling waters. No—all are not asleep. The woman of brave spirit never before was so wide-awake. Hannah Dustin awakes Mary Neff and Samuel Leonardson, informs them of her purpose, gives each a tomahawk. Each selects a victim.

"Strike hard!"

A signal, and the hatchets crush through the skulls of the sleeping Indians, blow after blow in quick succession. It is the work of a minute, but in that brief time ten of the twelve Indians are killed; two only escape in the darkness.

The prisoners—prisoners no longer—gather the provisions, take the guns of the Indians, and place them in a canoe. The thoughtful women, to prevent pursuit, quickly cut holes in all the other canoes and set them adrift. They take their seats in the remaining canoe, and push out into the stream.

A thought comes. If they are spared to reach their home, will their friends believe their story? They will have evidence that can not be disputed. They paddle back to the island. Mrs. Dustin runs a knife around the scalp-locks of the dead Indians, and takes them from the skulls. They start once more in the darkness. They know that the river will bring them to their homes.

The current bears them on. Soon they are amid the rapids at Pennacook, but the thought of home, of liberty, cools their brains and steadies their nerves. The intrepid women handle the paddles dexterously, steering clear of sunken rocks and dangerous whirlpools.

They come to a space of clear water, and then to falls, around which they must carry the canoe. They are in danger of death by drowning, in danger of prowling savages, whose wigwams are still standing along the bank of the winding stream, but no Indian discovers them. With tireless energy they ply their paddles. Days pass. At last they sweep round a bend, and behold familiar scenes: they are once more at home, coming upon their sorrowing friends like apparitions from the dead. It is a marvellous story they have to tell of endurance, heroism, and victory. No one can doubt their words, for there are the scalps, evidence undoubtable.

By every fireside the story of Hannah Dustin, Mary Neff, and Samuel Leonardson is narrated. Presents come to them—fifty pounds from the General Court of Massachusetts, and a rich present from the Governor of New York.

A monument has been reared upon the spot where they obtained their freedom, commemorative of their endurance, resolution, and heroic action.

THE ROVERINGS AT CONEY ISLAND.

BY MATTHEW WHITE, JUN.

THE two Eds wanted to go very much.

"I can learn to build forts in the sand, and then grow up to be a soldier," urged Edward.

"And I might watch the men steer the boats, and by-and-by be ready to sail off somewheres on a ship, and bring back an India shawl," suggested Edgar, cunningly, and Mrs. Rovering decided at once that they should go.

"By the boat!" cried Edgar.

"No, by the cars," exclaimed Edward; and thereupon arose a discussion on the point, which lasted until Mr. Rovering came home to dinner, and said they could go by both.

So on the next morning, which happened to be Saturday,

the family set out, armed with an immense lunch basket, and shaded by huge straw hats.

"Now, Robert," said Mrs. Rovering, as they hurried down a dirty side street to the river, "are you sure you know where you're going?"

"Why, to Manhattan Beach, to be sure. We decided to begin there, you remember." But they had no sooner reached the end of the long pier than they were set upon by what appeared to be a lot of crazy men, who yelled in such a frightful fashion about bursting boilers and rotten timbers that the Roverings were very glad to find that they were on the wrong dock, and that the Manhattan Beach boats started from a quiet wharf near by, where there were no opposition steamers.

And now a most wonderful thing happened. The crowd on this first pier was a most dreadful one, and yet neither of the Eds got lost in it, nor did Mr. Rovering have his pocket picked; and this fact struck Mrs. Rovering as so extraordinary that she stood still for a full minute in the Battery Park before she could realize it, while an elevated railroad engine overhead dripped grease all over the cherry-colored ribbon on her hat.

After blundering into Castle Garden, and knocking at the door of a free swimming bath, they succeeded in finding the boat they wanted, which, after several very narrow escapes from being run into by ferry-boats, running over tugs, swamping row-boats, and grazing barges, took them safely to the pier where the cars were waiting.

With these latter the two Eds were much delighted, as they were open ones, and consequently offered to them unlimited opportunities for falling out and breaking their necks.

"Here we are!" suddenly announced Edgar, as the train slowed up and then stopped; but after the heavy basket had been carefully lifted out, and Mrs. Rovering had laboriously stepped down, they discovered that there was no station there at all, and they had just time to squeeze back into their places before the engine started again.

The family went through this performance three times, until finally Mr. Rovering found out that these mysterious haltings were only made as a matter of precaution before crossing other railroads.

But at last the cars stopped for good, and after waiting until everybody else had left the train, the Roverings concluded that they had actually arrived at the famous Manhattan Beach.

The two Eds were for at once dashing off to the shore, but Mrs. Rovering declared that they hadn't time for play yet, as they must first walk up as far as the new hotel, so as to be sure they had seen everything. Mr. Rovering, however, had caught sight of the bathing pavilion, and decided that, *for fear they should forget it*, they had better take a dip in the ocean immediately.

So they all went into the Atlantic—and a good deal of it into them; and on coming out, Mrs. Rovering was lost in more wonder than ever when she found that neither of the Eds was drowned.

"And now we must eat our lunch," said Mr. Rovering, when they were once more wandering along the broad plank-walk in the broiling sun.

"And there's a superb place where we may partake of it," added his wife, indicating the invitingly cool-looking piazza of a large hotel, which was plentifully provided with tables and chairs, seemingly on purpose for just such hungry lunch-laden mortals as themselves.

So they all went up the steps, and choosing a table in the shadiest corner, they sat down, and began to unpack the basket.

Mrs. Rovering had just taken a creamcake and a box of sardines from the centre of a lemon pie when a waiter walked up to them with a card-board sign, which read, "Positively no picnic parties allowed in the parlors or on the piazzas of this hotel."

Now this sudden turn of affairs was very humiliating to the Roverings, the more so as they had all grown very hungry after their bath, and the contents of the basket had a most inviting odor.

But there was no help for it; so the sardines and sandwiches and lemon pie and creamcakes and all the silver-plated ware, were thrust hurriedly back in a dreadful heap of confusion, and the four set out for the beach, feeling sure that they would not be molested there.

However, when they sat down on the dry sand, they found it so hot, and it flew about and into everything so easily, that they determined to move down nearer to the water.

They had just established themselves on a cool spot, and Mrs. Rovering was distributing supplies for the third time, while the two Eds were busily engaged in fort-building, when Mr. Rovering suddenly cried out, "Take care!" but before he could say of what, a big wave had dashed up and salted the whole party, and luckily salted them only, yet enough to convince them that the beach was not a convenient lunch table; so the provisions being tumbled into the basket again, Mr. Rovering declared in favor of Brighton, where the four were set down a few minutes later by the Marine Railway.

Here they tried another hotel piazza, but the same dreadful notice stared them in the face, and they began to fear that they would be compelled to go home to eat their lunch, when Mr. Rovering happened to remember having heard something about West Brighton being a resort of "the people"; so they all bundled into a stage, at five cents a head, to ride to the next grand division of the island.

And now the two Eds saw with delight that they were coming to the region of circuses, side shows, and merry-go-rounds, and soon Mrs. Rovering said, "Robert, I observe that we are approaching the Observatory. Let us ascend by the elevator; it may give us an appetite for—"

"But I want to ride round on the lion," broke in Edward.

"And I want to see the Midgets," added Edgar. But Mr. Rovering having noticed that the admission to the Observatory was fifteen cents, children ten cents, thought it would be too bad if he did not take advantage of the reduction to save a dime; so the four got in one of the elevators, and rode to the top, which was several hundred feet above the level of the sea.

The view from this lofty point was certainly very fine, and *for a moment or two* the careful mother forgot all about her sons, while she tried to make out through the telescope, under her husband's guidance, the exact spot of ground on Staten Island where they had once held a Fourth-of-July picnic.

At length she gave up the attempt, and turned around to look after the boys. But neither of the Eds was to be seen.

There were but two persons besides themselves in the cage-like compartment, so the children could not be lost in the crowd. With a cry of horror, Mrs. Rovering rushed to the side, and peering down, down, far below her, saw her two darling boys, stretched on the ground apparently in the positions they had fallen, each leaning on an elbow.

"Let me to my sons!" shrieked the poor mother, tragically; and dragging Mr. Rovering after her, she flew down the stairs only to find that both the elevators were at the bottom of the tower. Then, with the music of the merry-go-round organs ringing in her ears, and the beating of the side-show drums trying to drown it, Mrs. Rovering fainted away.

When she came to herself she was reclining on two chairs on a hotel piazza, staring at the notice, painted on the wall, "No baskets allowed."

This fully restored her to her senses, and turning around, she saw the two Eds calmly drinking milk from the great wooden cow near by.

It seemed that the boys had speedily grown tired of the tower, and quietly slipping down stairs, had taken the elevator back to earth again. Here they had thrown themselves on the ground, and were engaged in counting up their pennies, in order to see, if they both took a ride on the wooden lion, how much would remain for the Midgets, when their mother missed them.

By this time it had grown to be the middle of the afternoon, and Mr. Rovering, becoming desperate, went up to a benevolent-looking gentleman and asked him if he knew of a spot where free American citizens might eat a lunch they had brought with them from home.

"Why, certainly," was the reply; "there is a building especially adapted to that purpose at the other end of the island."

"But we have just come from there," said Mr. Rovering.

"Ah, then, it isn't my fault you didn't see it;" and the gentleman sat down at the very next table, and proceeded to order a mutton-chop and some fried potatoes.

"Dolly, let's go home!" exclaimed Mr. Rovering, in despair; and picking up the basket, which now seemed heavier than ever, he led the way to the Iron Pier.

And now they looked forward to enjoying their lunch on the boat; but the sea was so rough, and they all in consequence became so sick, that they were glad to hide the basket out of sight.

Thus it came to pass that the Roverings ate their lunch and supper all in one, and decided that their day at Coney Island had not been a success.

A SALT-WATER AQUARIUM.

BY A. W. ROBERTS.

HUNDREDS of young people are now spending their vacation on or near the sea-shore, and have a good opportunity to study the wonderful habits of animal and vegetable marine life. Therefore I have undertaken to throw out a few plain hints as to the management of a salt-water aquarium, in which these interesting forms of nature can be observed to greater advantage.

We will start off with one of the small tin frame tanks sold in New York so cheap, or a candy jar, or a small-sized wash-tub—any vessel that will hold water, and is not of iron, tin, or copper, either of which will poison the water.

After washing out the tank carefully, and filling it with clear sea-water, we will place in it twelve silver-shrimps (bait shrimps). At the end of two days they are dead, and you ask why did they die when they had so much water to live in. They died of suffocation, after they had breathed all the air contained in the water. We will take out the dead shrimps, and in the same water place a good handful of ulva (sea-lettuce, sea-salad), one of the most common of all marine plants, and place the aquarium in a strong and direct sunlight, by this means exciting the ulva to work, or, as it is termed, aerify the water. In less than an hour's time a froth will be seen forming on the surface of the water, and adhering to the sides of the aquarium. Now observe the ulva closely, and from its edges and surface very fine threads of silvery bubbles are pouring out and ascending to the surface. In an hour's time the water will be thoroughly charged with air. We will again place twelve more shrimps in the aquarium. This time they will live, and we will have established a *true* aquarium—an aquarium based on the self-sustain-

ULVA.

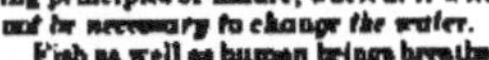

ing principles of nature, wherein *it will not be necessary to change the water.*

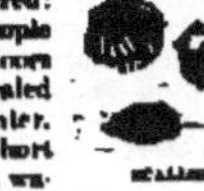

SCALLOPS.

Fish as well as human beings breathe air. Air is contained in all water. After the shrimps had breathed or used the air contained in the water several times over, it became unfit to sustain animal life any longer, and so they smothered: just the same as if a number of people were placed in a room, and all the doors and windows and ventilators were sealed up tight, so that no new air could enter. They, too, would suffocate in a short time and die. All plants living in water are constantly manufacturing new and pure air for their friends and companions the fishes, particularly when under the action of sunlight.

The great secret in establishing a self-supporting aquarium is to establish a natural balance of water, fish, plants, and light, so that none of these agents are wanting in quantity. For instance, a strong light is required to cause a healthy development of the plant life, but not direct sunlight, or the plants will be forced too rapidly, and death will soon follow. Again, direct sunlight will increase the temperature of the water to such an extent that many of the fish will die. If the animal life is in excess of the plant life and the water contained in the aquarium, the animals will perish for want of sufficient air. Again, if the aquarium is overstocked with plants, so that they are crowded so closely that the light fails to reach some of them, decomposition will take place, and everything will become a decaying mass. In fact, it is only by beginning on a very modest scale, with a very few and small fish at first, and by gradually increasing the number, that a beginner can expect to succeed. Overstocking with animal life and overfeeding are the two greatest temptations that beset the path to success for the aquariumist; but patience, perseverance, and critical observation will eventually lead to success.

The greatest care must be taken, and all shells, rock-work, sand, and plants must be washed over several times, so that no injurious substances may be introduced.

SHRIMP.

Ulva, or sea-lettuce, is to be found in abundance in all our small bays and inlets at low tide. For the aquarium, those specimens which are thick in texture, and of a dark green color, only are fit for manufacturing air. Never be tempted to make use of the light green and thin specimens, as they are not sufficiently matured, and will soon decay if placed in the tank.

Scallops when young have a curious way of changing their location by means of opening their shells and then closing them with great force, which sends them off at an angle, and so they go dancing along the bottom till they reach a spot that suits them. This shell-fish forms a beautiful addition to an aquarium.

The silver-shrimp, with figured back (all other varieties must be avoided), I have always considered as constituting a Board of Health in an aquarium; for no sooner does the water become unhealthy than these transparent and grasshopper-like creatures will make desperate attempts to jump out of the tank. These shrimps, and the little hermit-crab, and the buccinum (a small black sea-snail) are Nature's house-cleaners. They are always on the look-out for decaying animal or vegetable matter, which, if not in too large quantities, they speedily devour.

HERMIT-CRAB WITH SHELL.

I have seen these black snails

gather on a dead fish from a distance of half a mile; in less than a day's time nothing was left of the fish but his bones and scales, and these were picked so clean that they had a polished look. These snails are provided with ribbon-like tongues, from which project a great number of minute and beautifully constructed teeth. By passing these tongues backward and forward rapidly they cut their food down much as a mowing-machine cuts grass. These snails are the scavengers of all dead fish and vegetable substances found in our bays and rivers, and to them we owe a great deal of the purity of our waters.

The little hermit-crab lives alone in an empty shell, which he carries about with him wherever he goes. His reason for living in a shell is because the hind part of his body is soft, and not protected with a hard shell, like the fore part of his body. The end of the soft body of the hermit-crab is provided with hooks, or claspers, with which he holds on to the inner chamber of his shell so tightly that it is almost impossible to get him out except by breaking the shell. Very often these crabs are to be found with a colony of living polyps growing on their shells. These polyps are very interesting from the fact of their being the parents of one of our most beautiful jelly-fishes.

HERMIT-CRAB OUT OF SHELL.

When a hermit-crab grows too large, or so fat that his shell pinches him, he hunts up a new one. First he pushes his long claws far into it, just to see that no one is inside, and that it is nice and clean; then he rolls it over and over, often lifting it so as to judge of its weight. If it suits, he drags it close to the entrance of his old home, and in an instant he has whisked into his new house. Hermit-crabs are great house-hunters, often moving just for the fun of it. They are always skylarking with one another like monkeys, and, in truth, they are the monkeys of an aquarium. When the water in an aquarium becomes bad, they are sure to indicate it by leaving their shells, and trying to crawl out of the tank. In all respects they are the most valuable and interesting inhabitants of the aquarium.

PIPE-FISH.

Pipe-fish are apt to be delicate; still, if your aquarium is in perfect health, and the water is teeming with minute animal life, they will get along nicely. Their favorite food consists of the eggs of all small crustaceans, such as shrimps, sand-hoppers, and lady-crabs. Mrs. Pipe-fish does not take care of the children, but Mr. Pipe-fish places them in a long folding pocket that runs along the under side of his body (which I have tried to show in the engraving). When he lets them out of this pocket into the vast ocean world to shift for themselves, they are only a quarter of an inch long, no thicker than a bristle, and almost transparent.

DANDY-CRAB.

Think of a crab decorating himself with bright-colored sea-weed, so that he is called the dandy-crab! Still, he is not so vain, after all, as he covers himself with sea-weed that he may escape the sharp eyes and sharp teeth of hungry fishes. I once had a dandy-crab whose back I had scrubbed clean, after which I placed him in an aquarium containing a plain sand bottom. In this tank I also placed a hungry black-fish, who soon took a nip at him, securing only one of his legs. This so frightened the dandy-crab that he began searching over the aquarium for material to cover himself with. In the tank I placed several sea-flowers (anemones), cut into small pieces. These he immediately seized, and soon had them fastened over his back, using both claws, he being both right and left handed, and sticking them on with a kind of glue that he took from his mouth. In a few days the pieces of sea-flowers began to develop into perfect flowers, causing the crab to look very gorgeous.

SWELL-FISH.

When a crab loses a claw, he does not mind it; in fact, he rather likes it, as it provides him with an extra meal. All he does is to sit right down and bite it off to the next perfect joint, eating the fragments of flesh with much relish. In a week's time a new claw begins to grow. When a spider-crab grows too large for his clothes, he rips them at the back, and out he slides, a helpless soft mass. He is now a "soft crab," and for thirty-six hours he has to hide away, as all fish are hunting for soft-crab dinners. At the end of thirty-six hours he is hard again, and has increased one-third in size.

SEA-ROBIN.

Of all laughable fish a baby swell-fish is the funniest. Beautiful in color, odd in shape, with the power of blowing himself up into a round ball covered on the under side with spines, does he not look wise and important! And he has only two teeth, but can't he bite! Why he swells himself up so is not exactly known; but I imagine that when he finds himself inside of a fish, he makes it so uncomfortable for that fish's general health that the fish is glad to get rid of him.

Next to a young swell-fish comes a young sea-robin, a very interesting fish. He can make a musical grunting noise when he feels good, and will spread his beautiful wings, and sail through the water as proud as a peacock. When he is tired, he likes to bury himself up to his eyes in sand, for which he uses his two curious hooked fingers. He also uses these to dig out the sand-shrimps. Some years ago great numbers of very large sea-robins visited our coast, and were sold in the New York markets under the name of Dolly Vardens, on account of their possessing such bright and showy colors.

OYSTER SHELL.

The shell-fish known as the oyster drill is one of the greatest of all enemies to young oysters, which he destroys by boring minute holes through their shells, and when the oyster opens, after death, eating him up. It is not known how he drills this very minute hole so quickly.

The clinker (*serpula*) is really a vast marine tenement-house for a social community of beautiful sea-worms, who build up houses of shelly tubes twisted and fastened together. Each worm has a stopper, or cork, to his shell, with which he can close up the entrance to his house.

When this sea-worm is feeding he throws out from the entrance of his tube a beautiful double plume. These worms are the favorite food of the sea-horse, who sucks them out with a sharp snapping noise.

SEA-HORSE.

The sea-horse is considered to be one of the greatest prizes that can be obtained for an aquarium. For dignity of carriage, grace of motion, and beauty of form, he excels all other fish. The papa sea-horse takes care of his children the same as the pipe-fish, to which he is closely related; only his pocket is in front of him, and is much larger, and different in shape. This pocket is lined inside with a fatty substance, on which the young sea-horses feed till they are strong enough to be crowded into the world. The sea-horse, when he thinks it time to turn out his children, presses his big pocket (for he has no hands nor claws) against a shell or piece of stone, and out swim the young horses. At first they are apt to form into bundles by locking their tails together, but as they become accustomed to their new surroundings, and are stronger, they separate. The male sea-horse displays much pride over his young, and remains with them several days. Sea-horses can look two ways at once, as each eye moves independently of the other.

TUBE-FLOWER AND MUSSELS.

The tube-flower is very common along our coast. It lives in a long, thin, light-colored tube, composed of a material resembling horn. It has the power of stinging slightly, but, for all that, is so beautiful that no aquarium should be without it. This animal casts off its flower, or head, every few days, after which a new one makes its appearance.

Sea-flowers (anemones) are always to be found in the same locations with tube-flowers. Just to think of taking an animal that moves and eats and breathes, and cutting him up, and that each piece will become a perfect animal again! Yet such is the case with sea-flowers. When they wish to produce young, they tear off pieces from their bodies (the base parts), which soon develop into young sea-flowers. In the illustration I have shown three kinds of sea-flowers, all of which are common on our coast. The inside part of a sea-flower is divided by many partitions, forming a circle of store-rooms; into these rooms he passes his food, where it remains till all the juices are extracted, after which he passes it out again the same way it entered. The colors and forms of all our sea-flowers are wonderfully beautiful. Their thousands of hands (the fringe-like part), which are constantly moving in all directions in search of food, remind one of an animated aster.

SEA-ANEMONE.

Small groups of acorn-barnacles, when attached to stones or wood, are very desirable objects for the aquarium. For a few hours after being placed in their new home they will remain closed, but as soon as they become accustomed to their surroundings, one after another will cautiously throw out his feathery casting-net in search of food. Then the reaching and grasping become so rapid and general that the eye can hardly follow their motions.

BARNACLES.

I feed my fish three times a week with soft or hard shell clams cut fine, taking great care that no food remains uneaten to taint the water. For bottoms for aquariums I use coarse bird-gravel, or pebbles thoroughly washed, with small masses of rock-work.

UNCLE EBENEZER'S UMBRELLA.

BY JAMES B. MARSHALL.

"OH, mamma, we're going to the orchard to play," said Archy. "May we take an umbrella to keep the sun off?"

Mamma Stewardson, being up stairs, called in a low voice over the baluster, "Yes, dears, and take a large one."

So Archy and Gertie took the very largest umbrella in the stand—an enormous one. Its ribs were whalebone, its cover green gingham, and the handle ended in a knob nearly as large as a door-knob. But that umbrella was very highly valued by Uncle Ebenezer Stewardson, its owner, who carried it with him wherever he went, rain or shine. Uncle Ebenezer's grown nieces and nephews thought it very odd in him to carry such a queer-looking umbrella. They often hoped that something would happen to it, so that when they went about with him—he was one of the kindest and happiest of uncles—every one wouldn't be attracted by that great green bundle. How Cousin Adolphus did despise that umbrella!

But Gertie and Archy took the umbrella, only thinking it was a splendid big one; and as Uncle Ebenezer was taking a nap, of course he couldn't know who was carrying off his precious property. As they passed out, Cousin Adolphus was arranging his sketching materials to go down to the pond back of the woods to make a drawing of the mill for a young lady.

Among the daisies in the orchard Gertie started up a rabbit, which ran slowly toward the woods. Gertie and Archy went skimming over the field after it, laughing and flourishing the great green umbrella at such a rate that the rabbit ran into the woods, where it could not be found.

However, they found a cleared space just within the edge of the woods that was covered with soft green moss, and in its midst stood the most inviting smooth-top tree trunk for them to rest on. And while they sat talking about the rabbit, a young man all dressed in green approached them. His face and hands were also green, and he carried a long green bag.

"Children, welcome into my woods," said he, in a queer but pleasant voice.

Archy was about to exclaim, "It's not your woods, but Uncle Eb's," when the man in green went on to say: "I'm the Green Wizard of the Forest, and take great pleasure in exhibiting my tricks to little folks. Would you like to see me perform some of them?"

"Yes, please," said Archy, drawing a long breath, and looking intently at the Wizard.

"My little girl, will you lend me your pocket-handkerchief?" asked the Wizard, in that same queer, pleasant voice. "Now, then," continued he, as he took off his green hat, and placed within it Gertie's handkerchief, "I'll make you some fine candies."

Striking a match, the Wizard seemed to set the handkerchief on fire, as he held the hat in the air. After a few moments he blew out the flame, and then took from the hat four large handfuls of fine bonbons.

"And your handkerchief is just as pretty as ever," said the Wizard, returning it to Gertie. Archy clapped his hands loudly and earnestly, as though he was at a regular show, and Gertie joined in.

"My next trick will be to turn an umbrella into a music-box," said the Wizard, shaking his green bag out to its full length. Even to think of such a trick caused the audience of two to laugh so heartily that it came near rolling off the stump. The Wizard picked up Uncle Ebenezer's umbrella, and holding it in one hand, and the green bag in the other, said "Presto!" three times, and then poked the umbrella inside the bag.

"Now, my little man, what do you see inside?"

Archy peeped, expecting to see the umbrella, but he saw nothing but a neat little music-box.

"Oh, he's done it, Gertie, sure as anything," said Archy, gleefully.

"Let's have some music; it will play three tunes," said the Wizard, lifting the music-box from the bag. It first played "Coming Through the Rye," then "Violets Blue," and next struck up a lively German waltz.

The instant the waltz began, the Green Wizard of the Forest went dancing all over the green moss with the long green bag for a partner, and merrily called for Archy and Gertie to join in. When the music stopped, they did also, but looking around for the Wizard, he was nowhere to be seen. After vainly waiting his return some time, they started home, and as Archy understood how to wind and start the music-box, they had music all the way.

Mamma Stewardson was seated on the veranda as the children came toward the house, and Uncle Ebenezer, in slippers and long linen summer coat, could be seen nervously pacing up and down the wide hall that led to the door.

"My dears," said mamma, as they came near, "you should not have taken Uncle Ebenezer's umbrella; but I hope you have taken good care of it."

Gertie looked at Archy and then at the music-box, and Archy looked at the music-box and then at Gertie.

"Please never take my umbrella again," said Uncle Ebenezer, coming out on the veranda. "I'll buy you as with an ivory handle, and it was so much lighter than the old green gingham one that Uncle Ebenezer was pleased with it at once.

One day, late that summer, while a merry party were out on the mill-pond fishing, Uncle Ebenezer caught something tremendous on his line. It proved to be that old great-handled green gingham umbrella; but then all torn, rusty, and muddied. Mamma said that Cousin Adolphus looked startled when he saw that poor umbrella drawn to the surface, and point its slimy ribs at him like long fingers, and that he seemed glad when the rusty frame was thrown back into the water.

About a month after that Uncle Ebenezer went to a masquerade party, and the following day he saw Gertie and Archy.

"Children, I caught the Green Wizard of the Forest last night," said he, exultantly. "He was dressed all in green, as you said, and his other name is Adolphus Stewardson—the rogue! He wanted to get rid of that umbrella, and now I don't blame him a particle because he did."

[Begun in No. 33 of Harper's Young People, June 15.]

THE MORAL PIRATES.

BY W. L. ALDEN.

A PREDICAMENT.—Drawn by A. B. Frost.

nal. Joe, who was, next to Harry, the best swimmer of the party, followed his example; and a number of the villagers and "canalers" collected on the tow-path to watch the divers.

The canal was not more than eight feet deep, but the bottom was very muddy, and the boys had to feel about in the mud with their feet for the lost articles. They were very fortunate, and before long succeeded in recovering all the shoes, except one of Joe's, and several other things. Meanwhile three women and half a dozen girls, all of whom lived on board the fleet of canal-boats that were lying near by, joined the spectators, and seemed to think that the whole business was a capital joke. Harry and Joe were now anxious to come out of the water; but they could not come ashore while these spectators were there, so they swam some distance up the canal, and crept out behind a barn.

Meanwhile Tom and Jim were busily bailing out the boat, and arranging the wet things so that the sun could dry them. They were so busy that they forgot all about Harry and Joe. Presently Tom said, "Hark! I think I hear somebody calling."

They listened, and presently they heard a voice in the distance calling, "Tom! Jim! boys! somebody! bring us our clothes!"

"It's Harry and Joe," exclaimed Tom. "Where on earth are they?"

They looked up the canal, and finally discovered a naked arm waving frantically from behind a barn that stood near the water. "They must be behind that barn," said Tom. "Why, the mosquitoes will eat 'em alive. I'll take their clothes to them right away." So saying, Tom gathered up the shirts, trousers, and hats of the two unhappy divers, and ran with them to their owners. He found Harry and Joe crouched behind the barn, chattering with cold, and surrounded by clouds of eager mosquitoes. "We've been here half an hour," cried Joe, "and the mosquitoes would have finished us in another half hour. I think my right leg is nearly gone already."

"And I know I must have lost a gallon of blood," said Harry.

The boys hurriedly dressed themselves, and returning to the boat, helped to put it on the wagon; and with the wet shoes hanging from the cart-rungs they started on their ride to Warrensburg. It was a hot and tedious ride, and as the wagon had no springs, the boys were bumped so terribly that they ached all over. They tried to sing, but the words were bumped out of them in the most startling way; and after singing one verse of the "Star-spangled Banner" in this fashion,

"The Sta-a-tar-spangl-led-led ba-a-an-ne-er—"

they gave it up.

About four o'clock they reached Warrensburg, and after getting some dry sugar to replace that which had been mixed with canal water, they launched the boat and rowed up the river. They found it a narrow stream, with a rapid current and a good depth of water. After their tiresome ride the smooth motion of the boat seemed delightful, and they were really sorry when they found it was so late that they must camp for the night.

They chose a pleasant sandy spot between the river and the edge of a thick wood. The opposite bank was also thickly wooded, and they felt as if they were in the depths of a wilderness, though in reality there were houses quite near at hand. They pitched their tent, made a good supper—of which they were in need, for they had eaten very little at noon—and then "turned in."

For some reason—perhaps because the mosquitoes had so cruelly maltreated him—Joe was not sleepy, and after having lain awake a long time while the other boys were sleeping soundly, he began to feel lonesome. He heard a great many mysterious noises, as any one who lies awake in a tent always does. The melancholy call of the loon sounded ghostly, and the sighing of the wind in the trees seemed to him like the breathing of huge animals. After a while he found himself getting nervous as well as lonesome, and imagined that he saw shadows of strange objects passing in front of the tent. By-and-by he distinctly heard the twigs and branches crackling, as somebody or something moved through the woods. The noise came nearer, and suddenly it flashed upon Joe that a bear was approaching. He crept carefully to the opening of the tent, and putting his head out, saw indistinctly a large animal moving slowly in the shadow of the bushes only three or four rods from him.

Joe lost no time in waking up the other boys, cautioning them as he did so not to make the least noise. "There's a bear close by the tent," he whispered. "I've been listening to him for a long while, and just now I saw him."

Harry immediately grasped the gun, both barrels of which he had loaded before going to sleep. Tom wished that he had the hatchet, but as it had been left in the boat, he had no weapon but his penknife. Thus armed, the two crept stealthily out of the tent to fight the bear, leaving Joe and Jim in a very unhappy state of mind, with nothing to defend themselves against the bear, in case he should attack the tent, except a tooth-brush and a lantern.

The outline of the animal could be seen, but Tom and Harry could not make out which end of it was its head. "You must shoot him just behind the shoulder," whispered Tom; "that's the only spot where you can kill a bear." Harry said nothing, but watched carefully to see the animal move. Presently it threw up either its head or tail—the boys could not tell which—and started toward them. Harry forgot all about shooting at the shoulder, but in his excitement fired at the animal generally, without picking out any particular spot in which to plant his shot.

The effect of the shot was surprising. The bear set up a tremendous bellow, and by the flash of the gun the boys saw their dreaded enemy galloping away, with its horns and tail in the air. Tom burst into a loud laugh. "Come out, Joe," he cried. "Your bear's gone home to be milked—that is, if Harry hasn't mortally wounded her."

Fortunately Harry had made a miss; and he found his whole charge of shot the next morning in the trunk of a big white birch-tree. The innocent cow that Joe had mistaken for a bear was, however, so thoroughly frightened that she did not come near the camp again.

"I stick to it that it was a bear," said Joe, as the boys were wrapping themselves in their blankets. "Cows go to roost at sunset. Suppose it did bellow: how do you know that bears don't bellow when they are shot?"

"How about the horns, Joe?" asked Tom.

"There's horned owls—why shouldn't there be horned bears? Anyway, I believe it was a bear, and I shall stick to it." And to this day Joe believes—or thinks he does—that he had a very narrow escape from a ferocious bear on the banks of the Schroon.

[TO BE CONTINUED.]

THE IDLE HOUR.

THE robin sings on the topmost bough of the spreading apple-tree,
Where the cool green leaves to the whispering breeze are nodding merrily;
The sunbeams bright from the azure sky go frolicking here and there,
And the breath of the clover blossom lies sweet on the summer air,
And under the trees so restfully, where the shadows softest lie,
Like a woodland nymph in her netted couch between fair earth and sky,
Behold our dainty darling, safe hidden from friends away,
Content with the merry sunshine, the robin, and breeze to stay.

LITTLE MADGE.

BY MARY D. BRINE.

"OH dear! such fun! Don't I wish just *for* once *I* could be a rich lady's little girl, and wear a white dress and slippers, and a blue sash ever so wide, and curls in my hair! I do wish a fairy could fly right out of the sky this minute, and give me things I want! Oh, dear me!"

Little Madge sat perched on the iron fence surrounding a handsome house, within which a birthday party was going on merrily. It was dark outside, and the street lamps were not bright enough to betray this little watcher to the gaze of the young people who were dancing under the light of brilliant chandeliers, and sending the sweet music of their happy voices out through the open windows into the silent street, where a few moments before little Madge Lee had been trying to sell matches. So she had ceased her cry of "Matches! matches!" which seemed so feeble in comparison to the sounds of merry music that filled the street as she came slowly along, and had clambered like a little monkey to the top of the iron fence, where at last she sat securely, watching the good time going on inside the beautiful rooms.

Madge had never in all the eight years of her life owned such things as a white dress, slippers, or sash. And as for "curls in her hair," her own round head was like a boy's, so closely was the dark hair cut.

Madge, with several others as unfortunate as herself, lived with an old woman who cared for them only according to the pennies they could bring in to her each night. Whether the pennies were begged or stolen or honestly earned made little difference to her. The children were all waifs and strays whom nobody owned or seemed to care for, and, with the exception of little Madge, none of them had ever known a parent's love. Her father died when she was a baby, and after a few years' struggle with poverty, her dear mother had followed him, leaving her child to the tender mercies of Mrs. McLane. For two years Madge had lived with this woman, roaming the streets by day, and sleeping on a handful of straw at night. She was scolded when she failed to bring in her usual amount of pennies, oftener whipped than scolded, and never spoken kindly to except by some kind-hearted stranger in the street.

On this night her little heart had seemed more than ever despondent and weary, for people didn't want her matches, and pushed her aside when she would have offered them. And she was just about ready to cry, when the sound of music fell upon her ear, and drew her toward the house from whence it proceeded.

While she sat upon the railing, intent upon the scene before her, a voice at her side startled her.

"Is it here ye are, Madge Lay? Bad luck to ye, thin, won't ye be afther catchin' the lickin' from Granny McLane for not sellin' yer matches? Sure ye needn't be thryin' the stoyle of yer betthers as kin dance, for lookat!" and seizing what little remained to her of a skirt, Biddy O'Hara commenced a caper on her toes in such a way as made Madge laugh outright. In an instant Biddy dropped flat on the ground under the fence, while Madge, in a vain attempt to follow her example, caught her dress in the railing, and hung helpless, just as a lady, who had been near the window, looked out to see where the laugh came from.

Poor, frightened Madge! She was seen by the lady, who called to her, kindly, "What is the trouble, little girl? can't you get down?"

"Whisht! aisy, Madge; don't spake a wurrid for yer life!" was whispered by Biddy from her hiding-place.

But Madge's fright vanished at the kindly words and tone, and she answered: "Please, lady, I'm caught in the rail; but I wasn't a-doin' any harm, ma'am. I'll go as soon as I can get loose, please, lady."

"Arrah, thin, Madge Lay, if ye bethray me here, I'll have it out wid ye afther—now moind!" came again from the frightened Biddy, who had really nothing to be afraid of, only that her *pocket* held three stolen handkerchiefs, and her *heart* a guilty feeling that weighed like lead.

Meanwhile the lady had sent a servant out to release Madge from her predicament, and bade him also bring the child to the door. There she gave Madge a plate of ice-cream, and told her to sit down on the step and eat it. "It is late for so young a child to be out alone. How happens it so with you, little girl?" she asked.

And Madge replied, simply, "Trying to sell matches, ma'am. And I just stopped to see the fun inside here, that's all; and I happened to laugh, ma'am, and was scared, and stuck on the fence when I was tryin' to get down."

As last Madge finished her ice-cream, gave the plate to the servant, and thanking him (for the lady had returned to the children in the parlor), went down the steps with a bright face.

What she and Biddy talked about after that needn't be told here; but what Biddy *did* is rather important to know, because but for that particular thing I doubt if this story of "Little Madge" would have been told. A few moments more Madge watched the party, climbing the fence again in order to see better, while Biddy, in her rage over Madge's good luck, revenged herself in her own favorite way—a good slap on the little bare foot which hung over the railing.

The front door stood open, and the light from the hall chandelier shone upon something that glittered on the door-mat. The servant was not in sight; the merriment in the parlors was increasing; the way was open to any child who might see and covet the gold locket which lay ready to be picked up either by honest or dishonest hands. And Biddy O'Hara was just the child to creep up the steps as she did, and with just such naughty hands as hers pick up the locket, and, after one instant's examination of it, slip it into the pocket in which were the three stolen handkerchiefs.

But rapid as had been the girl's examination of the locket, she had been noticed by Madge as she sat on her high seat. However, she kept quiet about her discovery as presently she and Biddy went home through the lonely streets; but never had detective sharper eyes to watch than had Madge, who used her blue orbs to the best advantage before she tumbled down upon her share of the straw that night, and prepared to sleep—or rather *appeared* to prepare for sleep; for not one step toward slumber-land would the little girl go until the locket had been removed from the hole in the wall where Biddy had so slyly put it.

And so it happened that when, by-and-by, Biddy and all the others were sleeping, Madge crept over to the hole, and returned with the locket in her own possession. Then she slept too, and the locket remained safely hidden in the little girl's dress until she arose in the early morning.

"Now, thin, Madge Lay," screamed Mrs. McLane, shaking her finger at the child, "here's thim matches av yours, an' moind ye don't come home forninst the eyes av me widout ye've sold the blissed lot, ivery wan av 'em, or it's sorra a taste av supper ye'll git the noight." So Madge was pushed out and up the steps into the glad sunshine so grateful to her. And eagerly she began to search for the house in which the party had been given the night before. It had been a strange street to Madge, and she could not quite locate it again, though she walked until her little *feet* ached, and she finally sat down on the curb-stone of a pleasant shady avenue to rest awhile.

Madge grew discouraged. She looked up at the blue far-off sky, and dimly remembered when people had explained to her that her mamma and papa, poor as they had been in this world, had gone to live there and be happy forevermore. She remembered how she had cried, and how her mother had kissed her the very last thing, and then suddenly turned so pale and cold that the little girl grew frightened, and cried harder than ever in her life before. She hadn't had a kiss since that time from anybody; and how the little motherless heart yearned for just one more warm loving caress from the dear mother who "lived in the sky," as the child expressed it! So when presently she saw a lady and child at the basement window of the house opposite, she went over, and, kneeling at the window, offered a box of matches for sale. The lady noticed the traces of Madge's tears, and kindly inquired the cause as she bought and paid for the matches. Little Madge replied:

"I was wanting to be kissed, ma'am, and wishing for my mother in heaven, and I was so—so tired with looking for a lady who had her locket stole, ma'am, and I watched where the girl hid it, and was goin' to take it back, but I can't find the street, nor house, nor anything, ma'am; and I wish I had a mother to hold me in her lap like you hold your little girl. It must be nice to have a mother."

"Poor little girl!" said the lady, and then she suddenly added: "Come inside, please. I'll let you in, and then I want you to go up stairs with me."

Much astonished, Madge obeyed, and followed the lady up to a pleasant room where a gentleman was at work amid easels, and half-finished pictures, and the pretty confusion of an artist's studio.

"Edward, you wanted a model yesterday," said the lady. "Here's a child who might do for your street picture. See, she carries her matches with her—just the thing."

And so little Madge earned a whole silver dollar for half a day's standing in one position before the artist, who was delighted with his model, and made a charming likeness of her, matches, ragged dress, bare feet, and all. The child left the locket with her new friend to be taken care of until she might find the owner, and then went crying matches through the streets, with a happy heart, little dreaming of what would result from her morning's work.

Only a few days after that a visitor to the artist's studio was admiring his latest picture, called "The Model Match Girl."

"What a strange title!" she said.

And he laughed as he replied: "Yes, I gave it that name to please my wife, who brought me the girl. She was really a model in regard to honesty." And then he told the story of the locket, and of the gratitude of the little girl for the ice-cream the kind owner of the locket had given her; and finally the locket was produced, and recognized by the visitor as her own.

"It must have fallen from my chain while I talked to the child, and yet the dishonest girl got hold of it, after all, before my little match girl had seen it. How I wish I could find her!"

Said the artist in reply: "Well, the girl is coming in a day or two to look at the picture, and I will send her to you. I had no idea that it was you from whom the locket had been stolen. It is strange indeed!"

And thus ere very long Madge met her first kind friend, and was led to tell the whole story of her pitiful life and craving for love. And at last, through the lady's continued kindness, little Madge was transferred with many other little children from the crowded, noisy, and unwholesome street which had so long been her home, to the care of those whose business it is to take just such poor orphaned little ones to new and happy homes far off in the country, where warm, kind hearts are willing and anxious to adopt them, and bring them up to useful womanhood.

Madge wrote a letter to the lady not long ago, and after telling about her happy times in her new home, she added, "And, oh! Mrs. ——, this dear lady here *kisses* me good-night always, and it feels just as if I had a mother *after* all."

(Begun in HARPER'S YOUNG PEOPLE No. 37, July 13.)

THE STORY OF THE AMERICAN NAVY.

BY BENSON J. LOSSING.

CHAPTER VI.

SOON after her exciting chase the *Constitution* sailed from Boston in search of the British frigate *Guerrière*, whose Captain (Dacres) had boastfully enjoined the Americans to remember that she was not the *Little Belt*. On the 19th of August, 1812, the *Constitution* fell in with her, and Hull skillfully managed to lay his vessel alongside the British frigate, to have a battle at close quarters. The *Guerrière* opened fire at once; the *Constitution* kept silent for a while. As the shot from the English frigate began to make havoc on the *Constitution*, Hull's second in command (Lieutenant Morris) asked permission to open fire. "Not yet," quietly said Hull. The request was soon repeated. "Not yet," was the calm reply. A moment afterward, Hull, filled with intense excitement, shouted, "Now, boys, pour it into them!"

This command was obeyed with terrible effect. The guns of the *Constitution* were double-shotted and did fearful work. The frigates were only half-pistol-shot distance from each other. The excitement on both sides was intense. "Hull her! hull her!" shouted Lieutenant Morris. "Hull her! hull her!" shouted the crew in response, for they instantly comprehended the pun. Very soon the *Guerrière* was a shivered, shorn, and helpless wreck, rolling like a log in the trough of the sea. Hull sent an officer on board to inquire of Dacres whether he had struck his flag. Looking up and down, Dacres coolly replied, "Well, I don't know: our mizzenmast is gone, our mainmast is gone, and, upon the whole, you may say we *have* struck our flag."

This victory greatly inspirited the Americans, and astonished the English. Hull was highly honored by the citizens and Congress, from which he received valuable tokens of regard. The London *Times* said, "The new enemy, unaccustomed to such triumphs, is likely to be rendered insolent and confident by them."

At mid-autumn, 1812, Captain Jacob Jones, in the fast-sailing sloop of war *Wasp*, achieved a notable victory over the British war schooner *Frolic*, convoying six merchantmen, four of which were well armed. They fought at close quarters, under very little sail, and soon became entangled, when the crew of the *Wasp* made their way to the deck of the *Frolic* just after it was swept by a raking broadside. They found no one to oppose them. A few surviving officers stood on the quarter-deck, most of them wounded. Lieutenant Biddle, who led the boarding party, hauled down the British flag. When the vessels separated both masts of the *Frolic*, with the tattered rigging, fell upon the deck, which was covered with the dead. Two hours after the victory the British ship of war *Poictiers* appeared, and captured the crippled *Wasp* with the more crippled *Frolic*. Nevertheless, the news of the victory was received with great joy in the United States, and Jones was the recipient of many honors.

Precisely a month after this victory a more important one was achieved by Decatur with the frigate *United States*. On October 25, near the island of Madeira, he gave chase to a British vessel of war, and overtook her. An action was immediately begun at long range, but soon afterward they engaged at close quarters. When the battle had lasted half an hour, the shot of the *United States* carried away her antagonist's mizzenmast. Then her main and foretop masts fell, and she was dreadfully bruised in her hull. The *United States* was yet unhurt. Perceiving longer resistance to be vain, the British commander struck his colors and surrendered.

"What is the name of your ship?" shouted Decatur.

"His Majesty's frigate *Macedonian*," replied her commander.

THE "CONSTITUTION" AND "GUERRIERE."—DRAWN BY J. O. DAVIDSON.

bor. She escaped under cover of darkness, and on the 24th of February, 1813, fell in with, fought, and vanquished the British brig of war *Peacock*. The brig had borne down upon the *Hornet*, and as they passed each other each delivered a broadside. Then, by a quick movement, the *Hornet* closed upon the *Peacock*, and poured round-shot into her for about fifteen minutes. The *Peacock* struck her colors, and at the same time raised a signal of distress. Her mainmast soon fell overboard, and she was in a sinking condition. The removal of the wounded to the *Hornet* was at once begun. At twilight she went down, carrying with her thirteen of her own crew and several of those of the *Hornet*. Nine of the former and three of the latter were drowned. The *Hornet* had only one man killed in the engagement; she lost more in trying to save her enemies than in conquering them.

[TO BE CONTINUED.]

This victory produced a profound sensation in England and the United States. In the former it created astonishment and gloomy forebodings, for it appeared as if the Republic of the West was about to snatch the sceptre from the acknowledged "Mistress of the Seas," and that they might no longer sing, as they had for a century,

"Rule, Britannia! Britannia rules the waves."

Hull generously retired from the *Constitution*, after his victory, to give some brother officer a chance to win fame on the "lucky" vessel. Bainbridge succeeded him in command, and was put in charge of a small squadron. With the *Constitution* and *Hornet* he sailed from Boston late in October, 1812, and at the close of December encountered the British frigate *Java* off the coast of South America, not far from Bahia. They had a most desperate battle, which lasted about two hours, when the *Java*, which had lost her three masts and her bowsprit in the fight, and was leaking badly, was surrendered to Bainbridge. She was one of the finest frigates in the Royal Navy, and was conveying the Governor-General of Bombay and his staff, with more than a hundred officers and soldiers, to the East Indies. Like Hull, Jones, and Decatur, Bainbridge received unstinted honors from his countrymen.

The hulk of the Java was not worth saving; and after transferring the passengers and surviving crew to the *Constitution*, she was fired and blown up. From that time the *Constitution* was called "Old Ironsides."

This fourth brilliant naval victory in the course of a few months caused much exultation in the United States. Meanwhile there had been minor victories, and some defeats. Privateers were numerous, and very active. During six months the American public and private cruisers had captured about three hundred prizes from the British. These successes dispelled the gloom occasioned by misfortunes to the land forces; the friends of the navy were justified and strengthened, and thenceforward no one ventured to speak in disparagement of it. Congress, perceiving the necessity of an increase in the force of the navy, authorized the President to have four 74-gun ships, six frigates, and six sloops of war built.

Bainbridge had left the *Hornet*, Captain Lawrence, blockading the harbor of Bahia, in which was sheltered a British treasure ship. A British 74 came up from the Brazilian capital, and drove the *Hornet* into the har-

BY R. K. MUNKITTRICK.

A QUAGGA stood under a palm
In evening's violet calm,
When a lion passed by,
With a hungerful eye,
The quagga ran off in alarm.

ADRIFT.

BY MRS. M. E. SANGSTER.

Adrift upon a silver tide,
With banks of green on either side,
And, far above, a smiling sky,
A tiny craft goes floating by.

Queer little boat, this woven nest,
Where birdies three had tranquil rest
Until a rough wind shook the tree,
And sent them sailing off to sea.

Oh, father-bird and mother-bird,
In you what trouble will be stirred
When, home returned from weary flight,
You learn your babies' hapless plight!

HYGROMETERS, AND HOW TO MAKE THEM.

Do not let any one who sees this somewhat out-of-the-way name imagine it is anything very dreadful. It is merely that of an instrument for measuring the moisture in the atmosphere.

Nearly every boy and girl has seen the chalet-like "weather-house," where one might suppose the clerk of the unreliable elements to reside, and which is certainly tenanted by a gay old lady, who comes out when the sun shines, and a military gentleman, who, disregarding catarrh, parades in front of the cottage whenever there is a rain-cloud in the sky. In this case the figures are held on a kind of lever sustained by catgut: this, being very sensitive to moisture, twists and shortens on damp days, and untwists and lengthens as the air becomes dry and light.

A simple hygrometer can be made by a piece of catgut and a straw. The catgut, twisted, is put through a hole in a dial, in which a straw is also placed. In dry weather the catgut curls up; in damp, it relaxes; and so the straw is turned either to the one side or the other. Straws do something more than "show which way the wind blows," you see.

Another simple weather-gauge may be made by stretching whip-cord or catgut over five pulleys. To the lower end of the string a small weight is attached, and this rises and falls by the side of a graduated scale as the moisture or dryness of the air shortens or lengthens the string.

Again, whip-cord, well-dried, may be hung against a wainscot, a small plummet affixed to it, and a line drawn at the precise spot it falls to. The plummet will be found to rise before rain, and fall when the prospect brightens.

Another device is to take a clean, unpainted strip of pine—say, twenty inches long, one wide, and a quarter of an inch thick—cut *across the grain*; then have a piece of cedar of the same size, but cut *along the grain*. Let these be glued together and set upright in a stand.

Before a rain-fall the pores of the pine will absorb moisture, and swell until the whole forms a bow; this will gradually straighten on the approach of fine weather.

There are two forms in which a balance is used that are interesting from the natural laws that govern their motions. In one a dry sponge that has been saturated in salt and water is nicely balanced against a small weight at the opposite end. The sponge becomes heavier or lighter according to the presence or absence of moisture, and any variation in this respect may be noted on the gauge above, to which the index finger on a dial points.

The simplest plan of all, and as good as any, is to place in an accurate pair of scales on one side a one-pound weight; on the other, one pound of well-dried salt. This swells and grows heavier on the approach of rain; when brighter skies return, the one-pound weight asserts itself once more.

VACATION DAYS—THE REASON WHY BOB COULD NOT GO A-FISHING.

So many of our correspondents are collecting birds' eggs and nests that we wish to call their attention to some important points. Never take all the eggs in a nest, because if you do you will leave the poor mother bird very desolate. You can always take some from each nest, and still leave enough to make a pretty little brood of young birdlings. In some nests you will find eight or ten eggs, and then you may take three or four. But if there are but three eggs, you must take only one. Always be sure to leave more than half. Be careful to gather them before the mother bird begins to sit, because when her brooding-time has begun she is very jealous of her nest, and is easily frightened away; and then if the eggs have begun to hatch and form young birds, they are useless to you, for you can not blow them, and they will soon change color and become unsightly.

Never take a nest until the mother has flown away with her little ones and left it empty; for to disturb the pretty home the bird has built with so much care for her babies is a wanton cruelty we trust no reader of Young People would be guilty of.

[illegible]

Fannie T. D., of Atlanta, Georgia, sends the following additional directions for the care of full-grown mocking-birds:

[illegible]

Frank K., of Norfolk, Virginia, writes that mocking-birds are fond of the yolk of a hard-boiled egg mixed with Indian meal, made fresh every morning. They will like the food still better if it is moistened with a little milk, and minced raw beef mixed with it now and then. The cage should be hung in a dry, airy place.

[illegible]

So many of our young readers are studying French that we do not give a translation of the following letter:

[illegible]

This curious insect probably belongs to the Phasmidæ, or walking-stick family, of which several varieties are found in America.

[illegible]

When our correspondents request an exchange of delicate and perishable things, like slips of plants, it would be well for them to state a safe way of forwarding them.

[illegible]

Albert H.—We have not yet published any such description.

Harry.—Yes, you may send the history of your doll. If it is interesting and not too long, we will try to print it in the Post-office Box.

G. W. D.—Any number of Harper's Young People can be obtained by sending full address and amount in clean postage stamps, to Harper & Brothers.

Nell R.—By referring to the advertisement of Harper's Young People you will see that one or more copies of the paper will be sent to any address on receipt of the price, postage free.

C. Francis.—Probably the correspondent to whom you wrote for exchange has received so many letters that he has not yet had time to answer you. We know this to be the trouble with some of our correspondents who have ad-

[illegible]

PUZZLES FROM YOUNG CONTRIBUTORS.

No. 1.

[illegible]

No. 2.

[illegible]

No. 3.

[illegible]

No. 4.

[illegible]

No. 5.

[illegible]

ANSWERS TO PUZZLES IN No. 38.

[illegible]

THE MANES LIFE-BOAT.

BY FRANK BELLEW.

A VERY ingenious invention for the preservation of life at sea has recently been patented in Washington, and approved by the United States government. It is called the Manes Life-Boat, and consists of a hollow ball of copper, with a hollow mast for ventilation, a trap-door for ingress and egress, and other contrivances for the convenience of passengers. These hollow balls are to be carried on board ocean vessels, and if a wreck occurs, passengers step inside, and are lowered into the sea, where they can float about, protected from the wind, rain, and waves till they are picked up by some passing vessel. I will not give you a long account of this queer boat, as you can probably form a pretty good idea of what it is by looking at the accompanying picture, which, as you will see, represents the inside, with its cargo of passengers.

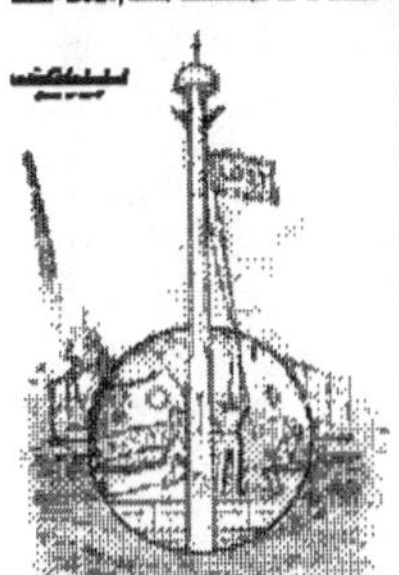

THE MANES LIFE-BOAT.

My present object is to show you how to construct a similar toy boat out of an egg-shell. To do this you require the following materials: one egg, as round as possible, half a tea-spoonful of shot, a piece of bees-wax about as big as a small hickory-nut, some black paint or

Fig. 1.

varnish, some vinegar, a little stick of pine, a cork, and a sharp knife. Now with regard to the knife, let me recommend you to buy one such as is represented in Fig. 1. It is one of a kind that shoe-makers use, and can be bought at most hardware stores for ten or twelve cents. It is a very useful knife for all kinds of fine work.

Take your egg and paint it all over with black paint, leaving only a square white space, and a little white spot on the top, as represented in Fig. 2. When your paint is perfectly dry, which will perhaps take two days, place the egg in a vessel containing vinegar in such a way that the two white spots will be covered with the vinegar (the whole of the egg need not be covered). Let it remain in soak for a day; then change the vinegar. In about three days the white part of the shell may be cut away with the sharp point of your knife; but remember that your knife must be very sharp. Now remove all the inside of the egg, and place the shell to one side until the interior is perfectly dry. Having cut a slender stick of pine for the mast, put some little chips of bees-wax into the egg-shell; then put in about as much shot as you think your boat will require for ballast—probably the third of a tea-spoonful will be sufficient. This done, hold the shell in boiling water (end down) till the wax is melted; then put in your mast through the small hole in the top of the shell; remove the shell from the hot water, and hold it upright in cold water till the wax has perfectly hardened. By looking at Fig. 3 you will see clearly what I mean.

Fig. 2.

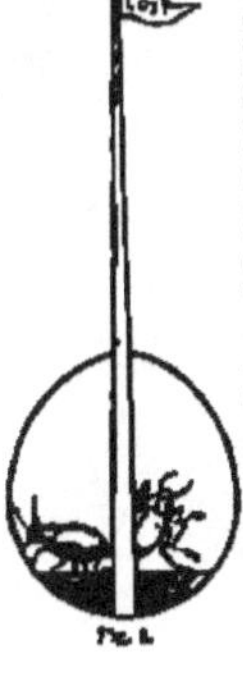

Fig. 3.

I must now stop one minute to tell you that there are two patterns of the Manes Life-Boat made—that of which I have given you a picture is one; another, which is thought to be an improvement, is made with a cork fender round it. This is the kind I propose you shall make.

Get a large, fine cork, and from it cut with your sharp knife two parings, and whittle them neatly into a shape like the pieces forming the band A A, Fig. 4. Now take some white of egg, and stick the pieces of cork round the egg-shell, as represented in the picture of the Toy Life-Boat. You can tie the pieces of cork on, to make them more secure, with thread wrapped round and round them.

You will now cut a piece of thick, tough brown paper to make the door of your life-boat, and fasten one side of it to the shell with white of egg; attach a thread to it to hold it in position when you wish to close it, as you will see represented in the picture of the Toy Life-Boat.

Now take your black paint and paint the whole thing over, hoist your flag, "Lost," and you will have as pretty a little toy as heart could desire.

Put one or two big bugs inside, shut up the trap-door, and set your craft adrift in a tub of water or in a pond, and see how gallantly it will float.

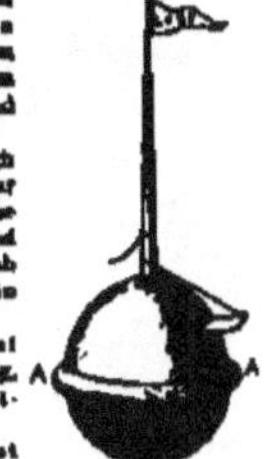

Fig. 4.

THE TOY LIFE-BOAT.

CAPTAIN CORN.

Captain Corn, in the garden,
Straight and strong and tall,
No matter how high his neighbors grow,
He overtops them all.
With silken plume and bright green cloak,
He really cuts a dash;
But when he marries Lima Bean,
He'll lose his rank—I think it's mean—
And be plain Succotash.

A POSSIBILITY.

"Don't say nothink, miss. I'll fetch it for yer."

Vol. I.—No. 43. | Published by HARPER & BROTHERS, New York. | Price Four Cents.
Tuesday, August 24, 1880. | $1.50 per Year, in Advance.

SOME QUEER RACING CRAFT.

from the end of a platform that overhangs the stern of the boat. Out on this is seated a skillful boatman, whose whole attention is given to the main-sheet.

These boats have very large centre-boards, and in races carry crews of from twelve to twenty men, whose duty it is to shift from side to side the many sand-bags that are carried as ballast. Extraordinary speed is made by these boats, and thousands of dollars are often wagered on races between two or more of them.

Some of them have become so famous for speed that their names are seen in the papers almost as often as those of noted race-horses. Among these famous boats are the *Susie S.*, *Brown*, *Nettie*, *Martha M.*, *Dare-Devil*, *Silence*, and many others, the names of which might be mentioned if they could be recalled. The *Susie S.* and *Brown* are now known as the *Albertina* and *Lady Emma*.

Quite a different-looking craft is that shown in the second picture on the same page. It is a catamaran—a style of boat that has only been known in New York waters during the past four years, and which is still so rare as to excite much curiosity. A catamaran consists of two long, narrow, canoe-like hulls, connected by strong wooden cross pieces, which are fastened at the ends with ball-and-socket joints, so that each hull moves up and down with the motion of the waves, independent of the other. These hulls are air-tight as well as water-tight, and so buoyant that they draw but a few inches of water. Upon the cross pieces connecting them is built a light platform, surrounded by a wash-board. This is deck and below-decks all in one, as it affords the only accommodation for the crew that a catamaran can furnish: so you see that it is not a very comfortable cruising boat either, though, to be sure, a small tent might be carried, and raised over the deck when the boat came to anchor for the night.

The speed attained by catamarans, with the wind free, is marvellous, and with a good breeze many of them can beat the fastest steamers. A catamaran has such a breadth of beam, on account of the distance between the hulls, that it is almost impossible for it to capsize as ordinary boats do, but it sometimes—though very rarely—turns a somersault, or "pitch poles"; that is, buries its bows in the water, and upsets head-foremost. This happened once to the first catamaran that was sailed in New York Bay. She was sailing at a tremendous pace right before the wind, when suddenly she buried her nose deep in the water, and turned over so completely that her mast stuck deep in the mud at the bottom of the bay, which was there very shallow. Her astonished crew, who had never heard of such a performance, were thrown into the water far beyond her.

The catamaran of New York Bay is merely a modified form of the famous flying proa of the South-sea Islanders, who build the fastest sailing craft in the world. The hull of the flying proa looks like half a sail-boat that has been split in two, and had one side rebuilt straight up and down. This straight side is always kept to leeward. From the other side project stout bamboo poles, to the outer ends of which is fastened a boat-shaped log of wood. This log, or outrigger, acts the same part in the proa that the second hull does in the catamaran, and practically gives the boat such a breadth of beam that it is impossible to capsize her.

Sailing a catamaran is glorious fun, and the sensations are similar to those felt in sailing an ice-boat; but it is a dangerous craft in unaccustomed hands, and our boy-readers had better not undertake to manage one of them without having been first carefully taught how to do so. This is also a very good rule to apply to all kinds of sailing craft, and, when followed, is the best known preventive of accidents.

A catamaran rarely carries a crew of more than two men, and of course needs no ballast. Three of the most noted of these queer-looking boats are the *Amaryllis*, which was the first one seen in New York waters, the *Tarantella*, and the *John Gilpin*.

THE GOOD KNIGHT.

IN the lovely country of Dauphiné had lived for generations the lords of Terrail, and there in the old castle of Bayard was born, in 1475, Pierre, our "good knight." When a lad of thirteen, his father, finding his health failing, and desirous of providing for his children's future, asked each what he would like to be; and on Pierre's answering that he was determined to be a soldier, told him he would try, through the influence of his uncle, the Bishop of Grenoble, to place him as page in the household of Charles, Duke of Savoy, where he could be properly instructed. The request was granted, and Pierre was made ready to start. His father gave him his blessing, and exhorted him to be valiant; but his mother wept at parting with her young son, and, among other advice, told him there were three things she commanded him always to do. "The first is, you love and serve God, without offending Him in any way, if it be possible to you. The second is, be mild and courteous to all; keep yourself temperate in eating and drinking; avoid envy; be loyal in word and deed; keep your promises; succor poor widows and orphans. The third is, be bountiful of the goods that God shall give you to the poor and needy, for to give for His honor's sake never made any man poor." Pierre promised to remember his mother's advice (and his life shows that he did); and giving him a little purse she had made for him, with some pieces of gold in it, she kissed him, and they parted, never to see each other again.

Charles, Duke of Savoy, was charmed with his page, and would have been glad to keep him; but King Charles of France was so pleased with him, when on a visit to the Duke, that he took him into his own service, and when only seventeen Pierre accompanied the King in his expedition into Italy. Here he gained great fame, and was ever after called "Bayard, the good knight, without fear, and without reproach."

It would be impossible to tell of all his deeds, for "the loyal servant" who wrote his life says of him, "The good knight was a very register of battles, so that on account of his great experience every one deferred to him," and until his death, save times, when laid up with wounds, he was constantly battling for his King and country. Twice was he captured; but so great was his fame both for prowess and goodness that both times his enemies released him without ransom. Once he defended a bridge single-handed against the enemy, and enabled the French army to retreat. So great was his valor at the battle of Marignano that Francis I. of France, after the field was won, craved the accolade at his hand. But never, either in victory or defeat, did he forget the promise he made his dear mother.

"Was he in possession of a crown, all shared it; the first thing he did when he rose was to serve God; he was a great giver of alms; and there was no man during his life who could say he had refused him anything within his power to grant."

Once, when assaulting Brescia, he was severely wounded, and after the town was taken was carried to the house of a nobleman who had fled, leaving his wife and daughters, and Bayard protected them from pillage and insult. When his wound was cured, for his kindness to them the mother besought his acceptance of 2500 ducats, but bidding her ask her daughters to come to him, he said to them: "You must know that military men are not usually furnished with pretty toys to give to ladies. The good lady, your mother, has given me this money, and I present each of you one thousand ducats to aid you in marrying." Then, to the mother, "Madam, I accept these five hundred ducats, to be distributed among the poor nuns of the convents that have been pillaged; I give it to you in charge for me."

When he was ready to mount his horse, the daughters

each gave him a present, one "a pair of bracelets delicately composed of fine gold and silver threads, the other a purse of crimson satin most curiously wrought." He told them the presents came from such good hands, he should value them at ten thousand crowns. "He then put the bracelets on his arms and the purse in his sleeve, declaring he would wear them as long as they lasted for their sakes."

In the year 1524 he was sent to reduce Genoa; but the French were unsuccessful, and were forced to retreat; and while passing the river Sesia (April 30), Bayard was covering the rear of the army, when a stone from an arquebuse shattered his spine. "*Mon Dieu!*" he cried, "I am a dead man," and fell heavily from his horse.

His esquire, by his orders, set him against a tree, with his face to the Spaniards, and taking hold of his sword by the cross-hilt, he kissed it, confessed his sins, and then swooned away. His enemies, when they came up and found him thus, were full of pity, and when he came out of his swoon he found they had erected a pavilion over him, and placed him on a bed. They mourned for him as sincerely as the French, their chief, the Marquis of Pescara, declaring, "Never have I seen or heard tell of any knight who could compare with you in all admirable qualities." He had Bayard's body embalmed, and returned it to his friends, after having solemn service for him two days; and the dead hero was carried home to Grenoble. Half a league from the city the bier was met by all the dignitaries of the place. He was buried in the convent of Minims, and France mourned publicly for him for a month. Of all the vast sums he had obtained from his prisoners by way of ransom he left none behind, having dowered over one hundred orphan maidens, and succored the many widows who appealed to him for aid.

CROCODILE TEARS.

On the banks of the Nile an old crocodile
Lay sunning himself one day,
And he gently did croon an attempt at a tune,
As he watched some small children at play—
At play—
As he watched some small children at play.

He pondered awhile, and a hungering smile
Revealed the extent of his jaw;
He was twenty feet long, was uncommonly strong,
And his teeth were arranged like a saw—
Like a saw—
And his teeth were arranged like a saw.

He used every wile their hearts to beguile,
As toward them he stealthily stole;
He balanced each scale, and waggled his tail,
Then gobbled those children up whole—
Up whole—
Then gobbled those children up whole.

And such is the style of this old crocodile,
He sheds bitter tears o'er his prey;
He was filled with deep gloom when he thought of their doom,
And he wept all the rest of the day—
The day—
And he wept all the rest of the day.

A FRESH WATER AQUARIUM.

BY A. W. ROBERTS.

MANY fresh-water plants have a tendency to grow above the surface. When this takes place, the leaves become so different in shape that they can hardly be recognized as belonging to the same plant. Therefore care must be taken to keep all plants submerged that are intended to supply air for the fish.

One of the most common plants is the mermaid-weed (*Proserpinaca*). I have drawn it submerged and out of water, to show the change in the leaf. It grows along the margins of ponds that partially dry up in summer.

Water-thyme (*Anacharis canadensis*) grows in slow-flowing streams. It requires coaxing to establish it in an aquarium, but when once rooted, is apt to grow too fast, requiring thinning out. Heap plenty of gravel on the root ends. Do not tie the bunch with string, as it will cause it to decay.

Nitella flexis is almost a rootless plant, and will grow without any care. It is found growing in shady parts of cool ponds, streams, and lakes.

Fontinalis antipyretica grows in springs and cool, shady ponds. It resembles a very fine and long moss. In color it is of a beautiful light green. I have often stored up quantities of this plant during summer (it becoming perfectly dry), that I might have it for winter use, and when placed in an aquarium it started out as fresh as ever.

Duck-weed, or duck's-meat, is a small floating plant, covering the surfaces of ponds and lakes in shady places. It is one of the best surface plants for producing shade, or for cutting off light that enters from the top of the water. Its thousands of rootlets afford hiding-places for numerous small aquatic animals, such as the hydra, crimson water-spider, and the brick-maker.

A small stone should be tied to each bunch of plants, to anchor them till they take root.

After your aquarium has been in operation a few days, a green coating will begin to form on the glass. This is a minute plant that is developed by the action of light. It can be removed by means of a swab. In all other parts of your aquarium allow it to grow, as it is the favorite food of gold-fish and snails.

I have given drawings of the two best kinds of snails. One is shown with its broad foot expanded, by which it moves along the surface of the water, or on the glass when eating the green coating spoken of. Snails also eat decaying vegetable matter.

For keeping the water very clear, introduce a small-sized fresh-water mussel. Give him at least two inches of sand, in depth, in a corner of the tank, to burrow in, but watch him well, for if he dies without your knowledge your aquarium will be ruined.

In the illustration are figured three kinds of caddis-worms. These worms are useful for consuming decaying animal matter. When a "cad" has grown too large for his house, he makes a little case of silk, which he covers at each end with pieces of leaves, wood, or straw, biting them to the right length; some fasten on small bits of stone and shells. However rough the outsides of their houses may be, the insides are smooth, and lined with silk. When he changes into a chrysalis, he crawls up a plant, and closes up both ends of his house with a strong net-work of silk, which allows the water to pass through, but prevents the entrance of enemies. As he has taken care to place himself near the surface of the water, he easily escapes when he comes forth a four-winged insect resembling a small moth.

Apple-smellers, or merry-go-rounds, are very interesting. They are of an intense shining black in color, and generally school together, moving in circles, with great rapidity, on the surface of the water. They are called apple-smellers on account of the strong odor they possess, resembling that of apples or quinces, and merry-go-rounds on account of their merry circling motions around one another. Young apple-smellers live on the bottoms of ponds, and look like centipedes. When the time comes for them to change into real apple-smellers, they climb up a plant, and make small bags of gray paper, into which they fasten themselves till they get their swimming legs and shining black new clothes, after which they burst open the paper bags, and swim off to join their friends gliding so merrily on the surface of the pond. When an apple-smeller dives to the bottom of a pond to take a rest or to feed, he attaches a globule of air to his tail (see cut); this he breathes while under water.

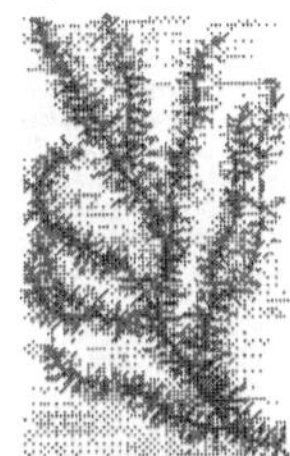

FONTINALIS.

STICKLEBACKS.

The nine and the three spined sticklebacks are, without doubt, the most wonderful fish for their size that are common to our waters. They will live well in either fresh or salt water aquaria, building nests and raising their young under all discouragements. The male builds the nest for the female to lay her eggs in. The nest is composed of plants cemented together with a glue provided by the male, who also carries sand and small stones to the nest in his mouth, with which he anchors it. During the breeding season the male assumes the most brilliant hues of blue, orange, and green; previous to this season he is of a dull silvery color. When an enemy approaches the nest, be he large or small, he will attack him, inflicting wounds with his sharp spines. Nor will he allow the mother of the young sticklebacks to come near, as she is so fond of her babies that she often forgets herself and eats them up. When the young "littlebacks," as they are often called, swim too far from the nest, the male takes them in his mouth and brings them back, throwing them out with such force that they make many somersaults before landing. Sticklebacks are the smallest known fish when first hatched out of the egg, being nearly invisible.

Here is the dragon-fly, as he looks before he gets his wings. He lives on the bottoms of ponds when he is young; but at a certain age he ascends to the surface, and crawling out of his old clothes, comes forth an unmistakable darning-needle. When he lived under the water he had very large and long jaws, folded up on the under side of his head. If a fish came within reach, he would dart out this curious trunk, and seizing it, convey it to his mouth. He also has the power of taking in and squirting out water from his tail; this action forms a current, which draws small insects within his reach. The taking in of the water is also his method of breathing, and the ejecting of it with force propels him through the water.

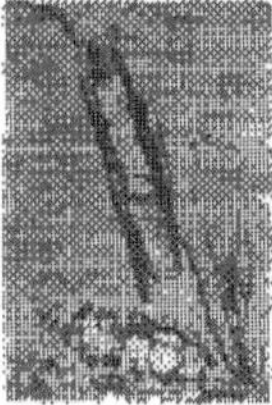

Water-boatmen, or boat-flies, are so named from their resemblance to tiny boats with oars. As they have to swim on their backs, they are provided with large and very observing eyes. When they breathe they come to the surface, and by a quick diving motion, and the assistance of numerous stout hairs on the hind parts of their bodies, they entangle a mass of air, which, as they descend, spreads, giving their bodies a bright silvery color.

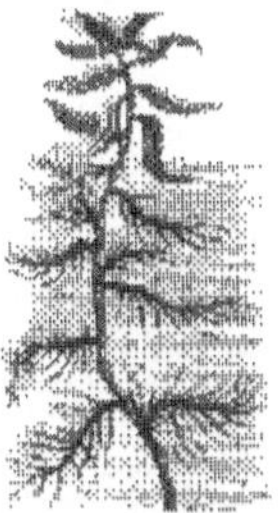

MERMAID-WEED.

It is best to keep these aquatic insects by themselves, as they are all voracious feeders, and fierce in their habits. They are not so beautiful in form, color, and motions as fish, but present a much greater interest as they pass through their many transformations. As most of them can fly, the aquarium should be provided with a close-fitting frame covered with mosquito netting.

BOAT-FLIES. SNAILS.

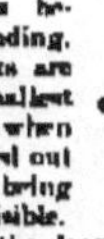

DRAGON-FLY.

DUCK-WEED.

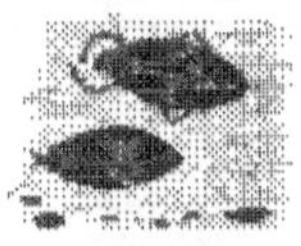

APPLE-SNAILS.

The crimson-spotted newt is one of the most inoffensive of all animals for the aquarium, and is valuable from the fact that he does not breathe water, but rises to the surface to breathe. Every few weeks he casts his skin, which he swallows, seeming to relish it, after which he comes forth more brilliant than ever.

CRIMSON-SPOTTED NEWT.

TADPOLE.

An aquarium without tadpoles, from which to obtain a supply of small frogs, is not much of an aquarium; and as they are also surface breathers, you can use them freely.

The rock-fish is a very safe fish for the aquarium, as it does not breathe the water, but rises to the surface, and stores away a supply of air, with which it descends to the bottom, remaining for half an hour before it rises for a new supply.

All fresh-water fish (excepting the trout family) can be kept in a fresh-water aquarium. Select the very smallest specimens; have all of an equal size, to prevent their quarrelling; feed on shreds of raw beef, or earth-worms that have been freed of all earthy matter by placing them in damp moss or grass overnight. *Look out for food not eaten.*

CADDIS-WORMS.

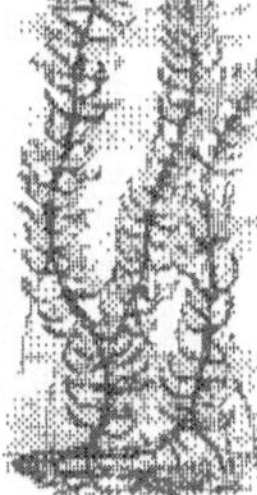

WATER-THYME.

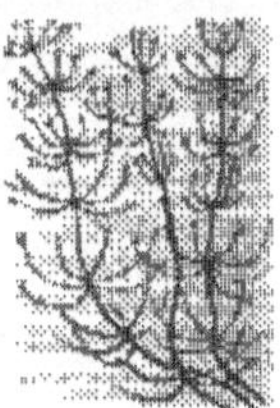

NITELLA.

[Begun in No. 31 of Harper's Young People, June 1.]

THE MORAL PIRATES.

BY W. L. ALDEN.

Chapter XIII.

THE cruise up the Schroon was a delightful one while it lasted. The river was so narrow that the trees on either side frequently met, forming a green and shady arch. Although there was a road not far from the river, and there were houses and small villages at a little distance from its banks, the boys while in their boat saw nothing but the water, the trees, and the sky, and felt as far removed from civilization as if they were sailing on an African river. They saw nothing to shoot, after their adventure with Joe's bear, and there were no signs of fish in the water; but they delighted in the wild and solitary river, and were very much disappointed when, at the close of the day, they reached a dam so high that it seemed hopeless to try to carry the boat around it.

Before camping they walked some distance above the dam, and found that the river was completely blocked up with logs, which had been cut in the forest above, and floated down to the saw-mill. The men at the mill said that the boys would find the river choked with logs for a distance of nearly three miles, and that a little farther up it became a mere brook, too shallow and rapid to be navigated with the *Whitewing*.

It was clear that the cruise on the Schroon had come to an end, and that it would be necessary to hire a wagon to take the boat to the lake. Having reached this decision, the boys made their camp, and being very tired, put off engaging a team until morning.

When morning came, one of the men at the mill came to see them while they were at breakfast, and advised them not to go to Schroon Lake. He said that the lake was full of houses—by which he meant that there were a great many houses along its banks—and that if they were to go there they would find neither shooting nor fishing. He urged them to go to another lake which they had never heard of before—Brandt Lake. It was no farther off than Schroon Lake, and was full of fish. Besides, it was a wild mountain lake, with only two or three houses near it. The boys thanked him, and gladly accepted his advice. They had supposed that Schroon Lake was in the wilderness, and were exceedingly glad to find out their mistake in time to select a more attractive place. The owner of the saw-mill furnished them with a wagon, and soon after breakfast they started for Brandt Lake.

When, after a pleasant ride, they came in sight of the lake, they were overjoyed to find how wild and beautiful it was. Steep and thickly wooded hills surrounded it, except at the extreme southern point, where they launched their boat. It was not more than two miles wide at the widest part, and was about five miles in length, and they could see but two houses—one on the east and the other on the west shore. They eagerly hoisted the sail, and started up the lake to search for a permanent camping ground; and after spending the afternoon in examining almost the entire line of shore, they selected a little rocky island in the upper part of the lake, which seemed made for their purpose.

There was a great deal of work to be done, for they intended to stay at Brandt Lake for a fortnight. They had to clear away the underbrush and cut down several small trees to make room for the tent. A small landing-place had to be built of stones and logs, so that the boat could approach the island without striking on the sharp rocks which surrounded it. Then the stores were all to be taken out of the boat, and placed where they would be dry and easy of access. The provisions had by this time become nearly exhausted; but the boys had been told that they could get milk, eggs, butter, bread, and vegetables at one of the houses, which was not more than a mile from the camp, so they were not troubled to find that of their canned provisions nothing was left except a can of peaches.

Of course all this work was not done in one day. On the afternoon of their arrival at the lake the boys merely pitched the tent, and then went fishing, with a view to supper. Fishing with drop lines from a large rock at one end of their little island, they caught perch as fast as they

HARRY SETS OUT IN PURSUIT OF THE BOAT.

could pull them in, good-sized pickerel, and two or three cat-fish. That night they ate a supper that would have made a boarding-house keeper weep tears of despair, and went to bed rather happier than they had ever felt before.

Tom was to row over to the house for milk and other provisions in the morning; but when morning came, the boat was gone. She had broken loose during the night, not having been properly fastened, and had floated quietly away. A faint speck was visible on the surface of the lake about two miles away, which Harry, who had remarkably good eyes, said was the *Whitewing*. Whether he was right or wrong, it was quite certain that the boys were imprisoned on the island, with nothing to eat but a can of peaches and some coffee and sugar.

The fish, however, were waiting to be caught, and before very long a breakfast of fish and of coffee without milk was ready. The boys then began to discuss the important question of how they were to get back their boat, or to get away from the island.

It was a mile to the shore, and nobody felt able to swim that distance. Joe proposed that they fasten one of their shirts to a tall tree, as a signal of distress, and then fire the gun every minute. The objection to this plan was that the nearest house was out of sight behind a little point of land, and that no one would see the signal, or would understand why the gun was fired. Then Tom proposed to build a raft, on which two boys could paddle after the runaway boat. This was a practicable suggestion, and it was at once put into execution.

It was hard work to cut down timber enough to build a raft, but by perseverance the raft was finished before noon. It consisted of four logs laid side by side, and bound together with handkerchiefs, shoe-strings, green twigs, and a few strips from one of Harry's shirts, which he said was unnecessarily long. It was covered with two or three pieces of flat drift-wood; and when it was finished, a piece of board was found, which was shaped with the hatchet into a rude paddle. Then Tom and Harry proceeded to embark.

The raft floated Harry very well, but promptly sank when Tom also stepped on it. Either more timber must be added to it, or one boy must go alone in search of the boat. Harry insisted upon going at once, and as the lake was perfectly smooth, and he could swim well, there did not seem to be great risk in his making the voyage alone. Bidding the boys good-by, he paddled slowly away, and left his comrades to anxiously wait for his return.

It was ticklish work paddling the raft. The logs were fastened together so insecurely, owing to the fact that all the rope was in the runaway boat, that Harry was in constant fear that they would come apart, and was obliged to paddle very carefully to avoid putting any strain on the raft. With such a craft speed was out of the question; and after an hour of hard work the raft was only half way between the island and the boat. Harry was not easily discouraged, however, and he paddled on, knowing that if nothing happened he must reach the boat in course of time.

Something did happen. When, after paddling for more than two hours, the *Whitewing* was rather less than a quarter of a mile from the raft, Harry missed a stroke with his paddle, and tumbled over. He struck the raft with his shoulder, and went through it as easily as if it had been fastened together with paper. When he came to the surface again he found that the raft had separated into its original logs, and that his voyage on it was ended. Luckily the *Whitewing* was now within swimming distance, so he struck out for her, and finally crept into her over the stern, so much exhausted that he had to lie down and rest before taking to the oars. Had the raft gone to pieces half an hour sooner, he would have been in a dangerous position; for it is doubtful if he could have clung to one of the logs long enough to drift to the shore without becoming totally exhausted.

The boys on the island did not witness the end of Harry's raft, for it was too far away when the accident occurred for them to see anything but a little black dot on the water. They became, however, very anxious about him as the hours went by and he did not come back. Tom was especially uneasy, and blamed himself for permitting Harry to go alone. He thought of making another raft and going in search of Harry; but there were no more strings with which to fasten logs together, and he did not quite like to tear up his clothes and use them for that purpose. He did, however, resolve that, if Harry did not come in sight within another hour, he would take a small log, and, putting it under his arms, try to swim to the mainland and borrow a boat, if one could be found, in which to search for his comrade. He was spared this hazardous experiment; for toward the end of the afternoon Harry and the *Whitewing* came in sight, and were welcomed with a tremendous cheer.

Tom took the boat and went for provisions, and when he returned the *Whitewing* was not only dragged on shore, but fastened to two different trees with two distinct ropes. The boys were determined that she should not escape again; and when Joe proposed that somebody should sit up with her all night, so that she could not cut the ropes and run away, Tom seriously considered the proposal. The next day a snug little dock was built, in which she seemed quite contented, and from which she could not escape without climbing over a stone breakwater—a feat of which there was no reason to believe that she was capable.

[TO BE CONTINUED.]

THE TALL CLOCK.

BY MARY DENSEL.

ONE NIGHT our six tow-headed urchins were sitting round the table chattering like so many magpies. The tall clock in the corner insisted on talking too.

"Tick-tock—tick-tock.
'Tis eight—o'clock;
Come, boys—cease noise,
Quick, tread—to bed;
'Tis eight—o'clock.
Tick-tock—tick-tock."

That is what it said.

Then it rang out eight clear strokes, and the jolly red moon, which for two weeks had been slowly rising in the space above the clock's face to show how the month was passing by, and which was now full and round, like the real moon out-of-doors—this jolly red clock-moon seemed to wink waggishly at the children.

"Hurry! scurry! Here it is eight o'clock, going on nine—next comes ten—eleven—twelve. Half the night gone, and you not in bed yet."

How its eyes twinkled! It nearly burst its fat cheeks laughing at its own joke.

Out the door, up the uncarpeted stairs, clattered the boys—Solomon and Isaac, Elias and John, Philemon and Romeo Augustus.

They all gave a nod to the clock-moon. "Good-night, old fellow," they said. All but Romeo Augustus. He did not like the clock. That is what this story is about.

Solomon and Isaac marched off to their own chamber. They would not condescend to associate with "the babes." Solomon and Isaac were twins. They were, as I have told you before, ancient. They were fourteen years old. Philemon and Romeo Augustus were only eight, and they knew no pleasure equal to that of sitting bolt-upright in their trundle-bed while Elias peered down at them over the foot-board of his bed, and told them stories with gestures.

"Tell us about the clock," said Philemon, on this occasion.

But at this suggestion Romeo Augustus—poor little Romeo Augustus!—quaked in his red flannel night-gown.

Elias always spoke in deep and dreadful tones when he alluded to the clock.

"Persons don't live inside, but THINGS!" said he; and Romeo Augustus quaked afresh. "Two of them hang in air. They haven't a sign of a head, nor feet, nor arms, nor legs. They just dangle. And the other THING"—here Elias's voice was awful—"the other THING writhes in agony. It is never quiet; never, never, nevermore; not when we're asleep, nor when we're eating our porridge. Forever and forever it writhes—anon."

That was a capital word to end with. No one knew what "anon" meant. It was probably some especially horrible way of writhing.

Romeo Augustus shook with terror. He could hear that clock talking still down stairs.

"Tick-tock—tick-tock.
'Tis nine—o'clock.
Ro-meo—be-low,
Come see—in me
THINGS drear—ap-pear.
'Tis nine—o'clock.
Tick-tock—tick-tock."

marched up to the enemy, and then marched back again, vanquished. He dared not breathe a word to Philemon. The big letter C was all ready to cling to his back, and how could he bear such disgrace! No sympathy could he expect from any brother. His work must be done, and done alone.

How loudly the clock called out from below! Could it be actually stalking up stairs?—so sharply did its tones ring in Romeo Augustus's wide-open ears.

"Tick-tock—tick-tock.
'Tis ten—o'clock.
Make haste—don't waste
Minutes—in fits
Of fear.—Come here!
'Tis ten—o'clock.
Tick-tock—tick-tock."

Romeo Augustus put one bare foot out of bed; he drew it back; he half rose, and sank on the pillows again. Then, with a mighty effort, he gave a bound, and stood shivering in the middle of the floor.

The house was still. Elias was sleeping the sleep of the just, never dreaming how he had terrified his small brother.

Out into the entry stole Romeo Augustus. The harvest-moon threw a broad band of light on the stairs. Down

LAKE, NEW YORK.—From Sketches by Frank [illegible].—[See Page 636.]

YOUNG PEOPLE AT CHAUTAUQUA.

A BOY'S LETTER.

DEAR TOM,—I last saw you waving your cap as our train rolled out of the station. That night I slept on a shelf in the sleeping-car, and the next morning we got breakfast at Hornellsville; and it was a good one, I tell you. About noon we got off the cars at Jamestown, and after dinner rode over the hill in a stage, and came to what looked like a narrow river winding among the trees.

This they said was the outlet of Chautauqua Lake. You would suppose that the water runs into Lake Erie, which is only seven miles away from Lake Chautauqua. But instead it goes into the Ohio River, and then down the Mississippi into the Gulf of Mexico.

We went on board a steamboat three stories high, with a big paddle-box fastened on the stern, and steamed up the outlet for about three miles through the wildest swamp I ever saw, until all at once the lake opened before us. I thought that we would be at Chautauqua in a few minutes, but the old stern-wheel kept pushing us on for a couple of hours. At last I began to catch glimpses of cottages among the trees. Then we drew up to a little wharf, and almost everybody went ashore. We followed the crowd through the gate, and so we found ourselves at Chautauqua.

The first thing that I saw was a park, with flowers and fountains and statues under the great trees. Then I came upon the model of a city, with all its houses and churches. This was Jerusalem. A man was explaining it to a crowd of people, and pointing out the places with a long pole. There is an Oriental house, and a park laid out to look like Palestine, with the top of Mount Hermon white-washed, and the Jordan with real water. A frog winked his eye at me, and then jumped into the Dead Sea. (That makes poetry, don't it?)

There are any number of streets laid out in the woods, and lined with all sorts of cottages. We all asked uncle to let us live in a tent, and you don't know how airy and pleasant it is. Cousin Jennie says she can't find any places to hang up "her things"; but I put mine on the floor, which is always handy.

I happened to be awake early the next morning after we came. Everything was quiet and still until the bell rang for six o'clock. Then there was a noise, as if all the boys in our school were hollering at once. I jumped up, wondering if the Fourth of July had come again. But pretty soon I found that it was only the newsboys (which means most of the boys here) selling the morning paper, *The Assembly Herald*. I went out and got a lot of papers, and made ten cents profit on them before breakfast.

There is a big bell on the upper part of the grounds. An old man rang it while I was standing by, and all at once I saw dozens and dozens of boys and girls running from all directions toward the corner where I stood. I asked one fellow what it all meant, and he said, "Why, don't you know?—it's the *children's hour*." So I just dropped into the stream, and went up the street to a large building with a dome and some wings. They call it "The Children's Temple." It was so full of young people that I had hard work to crowd myself into the corner of a seat. There was a platform in front, and a big black-board, and two gentlemen, both with foreheads that went clear over to the back of their heads. There was singing, and then one gentleman talked to us, and got us all to answer and repeat, and we never knew that he was teaching us a lesson until we had learned it. The other gentleman then came forward and drew a picture so fast that it seemed like magic, and so funny that we all laughed and laughed again. It's the jolliest "children's hour" I ever saw, and I'm going every day.

I can't begin to tell you of the good times here for boys. When you read in the papers about the big meetings and the long lectures, you might suppose that young people don't have much chance; but you'd be mistaken. We go boating on the lake, and fishing down at the Point, and bathing in a safe place along the shore. This afternoon all the boys and girls are going pilgriming through Palestine in a procession. Last evening I went out with little Susie for a walk. We came upon an immense telescope. The gentleman let me take a peek through it, and I saw the ring around the planet Saturn. Then he held little Susie up in his arms, and let her see it too.

There is a tent with a lot of microscopes, and two young ladies who show people how to use them. I looked at a drop of water through one, and saw in it an animal fierce enough and almost big enough to bite off your head.

And then there were the fire-works last night. I can't tell you how gorgeous they were: fountains lit up with bright colors; Roman candles flashing, and rockets soaring to the stars; the steamers all hung with Chinese lanterns, and sailing round and round upon the lake; the woods bright with the blazing electric lights overhead. Oh, it was grand!

I can't stop to write about the squirrels that run up and down the trees, nor the big tent where we get our dinners, nor the little tent where we sleep, nor the pictures at evening in the Amphitheatre (that's a great hall where they hold meetings), nor lots of other things. Next year I hope you'll come with us, and have a good time.

Your friend, BOB.

MIMIR'S WELL.

A SCANDINAVIAN MYTH.

BY JULIA CLINTON JONES.

IN the north of Europe there is a rugged land, where the winters are long and dark, with short bright summers. Nine hundred years ago the people there were pagans, believing in gods and giants, and their mythology is full of wonderful stories. As these myths, or sacred fables, tell of strange adventures, I think you will like them quite as well as even the *Arabian Nights*.

Take your maps now, and find this wild north land. It is called Scandinavia, and comprises Norway and Sweden. The home of these Northern gods was a city called Asgard, built above the clouds, in the midst of which stood Valhalla, the hall of the chief god, Odin. Such a marvellous place as this was! It had a golden roof that reflected light over all the earth, just like the sun, and its ceiling was supported by spears, while millions of shields formed its walls, over which were draped coats of mail. A huge wolf stood before its immense gates, through which eight hundred men could march abreast. Around the walls flowed a deep river, through whose waves Odin's guests were forced to wade. But I can not tell you now of Odin's feast, which was always being held in Valhalla, nor of his guests, the heroes, whom the beautiful Battle Maidens brought there on bloody shields from the earth. Asgard was overshadowed by the mighty tree Igdrasil. This tree was more marvellous than any of which you ever heard; no cork, nor India rubber, nor banyan tree could begin to compare with it; for this was the Life-Tree, and had been growing before creation. The horrible dragon, Death, gnawed constantly at its roots, but three sisters, the Norns, watering them daily from the Life-spring, kept the tree flourishing. Seated under its shade, the elder sisters (Past and Present) spun away briskly at the wonderful web of Time, which the youngest (the Future) amused herself by tearing to pieces. Far down in Giant-land, where the roots began to shoot, was an ancient well, guarded by the good giant Mimir (Memory). There the gods always went for a morning draught that should make them wise in their daily tasks, since this was the well of wisdom.

On one occasion there was a disturbance in Asgard.

Loki, a bad spirit, living there in disguise, had been playing tricks on the goddesses, and setting the gods by the ears through his mischief-making pranks, while leading them into many dangerous scrapes, though as yet he had not been found out. His children, too, were just as bad as himself, his son Fenris (Pain), a hideous howling wolf, being the terror of Asgard, while Hela, his daughter (Death), was more horrible than I can describe. Besides these, Loki had brought in other bad spirits, and altogether Asgard was greatly disturbed. Odin himself did not know what to do. He asked the Norns, but they could not answer, although the youngest hinted that if her lips had not been sealed she could have told something. At last he determined to see Mimir, and take a drink from his well. Saddling his eight-footed horse Sleipnir, away he rode in the night, all alone, over the Rainbow Bridge that joins Asgard with Earth, down to dark Giant-land. He had often before been there to consult Mimir; for although Odin was very wise, Mimir was wiser still, since he guarded the source of wisdom.

The giant was sitting deep in thought by the well, his white beard flowing down far below his waist, which was clasped by a girdle graven with curious characters, as old as the world. He heard Odin coming, and rising to meet him, said this was just what he had known must happen; for what else could have been expected with such a set as Loki and his family living in Asgard? The first thing to be done, he said, was to cast them out from among the gods, then bind them fast in some safe place far away.

What do you suppose this advice cost? Giant-land, you know, was very dark, and although the well was full of wisdom, Mimir had not always light enough to read its secrets. Odin's eye was the sun; so Mimir was glad enough to give his horn of water for a daily loan of Odin's glowing eye, while Odin was willing thus to buy the advice that should make Asgard happy again.

[Begun in Harper's Young People No. 37, July 13.]

THE STORY OF THE AMERICAN NAVY.

BY BENSON J. LOSSING.

Chapter VII.

Lieutenant Lawrence had gained great renown by his capture of the *Peacock*. He was promoted to Captain, and when the *Chesapeake* returned to Boston, after a long cruise, in May, 1813, he was offered the command of her. He accepted it with reluctance, for she had the reputation of being an "unlucky" ship. In the cruise just ended she had accomplished nothing, and as she entered Boston Harbor a gale carried away a topmast, and with it several men, who were drowned. This incident confirmed the belief that she was "unlucky," and it was difficult to get a good crew to serve in her.

On the morning of the 1st of June Lawrence received from Captain Broke, of the frigate *Shannon*, a challenge to come out and fight him. It was promptly accepted, and at noon the *Chesapeake* sailed out of Boston Harbor. The hostile frigates met not far at sea. At four o'clock they opened their broadsides within pistol-shot distance, and fought desperately. The loss of life on board the *Chesapeake* was fearful. Lawrence was mortally wounded, and as he was carried below he uttered the famous words, in substance, "Don't give up the ship." The *Chesapeake* was boarded, captured, and taken to Halifax. Lawrence died on the way. Broke was severely wounded, but recovered.

The American sloop of war *Argus*, Lieutenant Allen commander, took Mr. Crawford (American Minister) to France in the summer of 1813, and then cruised in British waters, imitating the exploits of Paul Jones. Allen captured and burned twenty merchantmen in the course of a few weeks (valued, with their cargoes, at full $2,000,000), and spread consternation throughout commercial England. Several cruisers were sent out to capture the *Argus*. This was effected in August by the brig *Pelican*.

The Americans were partially compensated for these misfortunes by the capture of the British brig *Boxer* by the brig *Enterprise*, Lieutenant Burrows. They fought off Portland, at half pistol-shot distance, on the 3d of September, 1813. The commander of the *Boxer* (Lieutenant Blyth) had boastfully nailed his flag to her mast, and after a sharp, short, and destructive engagement, she was compelled to surrender. Her second officer had to announce the fact through his trumpet, for he could not haul down her flag. Burrows and Blyth were both slain, and were buried side by side in a cemetery in Portland.

One of the most remarkable cruises made during the war of 1812-15 was by Commander Porter in the frigate *Essex*. She sailed from the Delaware in October, 1812; went toward the equator to join the *Constitution* and *Hornet*, under Bainbridge; missed them; swept around Cape Horn into the Pacific Ocean, and went into the harbor of Valparaiso, on the western coast of South America. Then she cruised northward in search of British armed whaling vessels, capturing several. Porter converted them into war vessels, and created for himself an active little squadron, with which he sailed for the Marquesas Islands. After remaining there awhile, he returned to Valparaiso, and at that sea-port had a fierce battle with two British vessels which had been sent to oppose his destructive career in the waters of the Pacific. These were the frigates *Phœbe* and *Cherub*.

These vessels cruised off the harbor of Valparaiso, waiting for re-enforcements. The *Essex*, with her consort, *Essex Junior*, in attempting to get to sea, became crippled by a squall, when the *Phœbe* and *Cherub* attacked, in violation of the rights of a neutral port. Then occurred one of the most sanguinary sea-fights of the war, and it was only when her officers and men were nearly all slain or wounded, and she was on fire, that the *Essex* was surrendered. "We have been unfortunate, but not disgraced," wrote Porter to the Secretary of the Navy. That was in February, 1814. Porter had carried the first American flag on a vessel of war ever seen in the Pacific Ocean.

Commodore Rodgers made a memorable cruise of one hundred and forty days on the stormy Atlantic in 1813, sailing from Boston in the frigate *President* in April. He captured eleven British merchant vessels and the armed schooner *Highflyer*, a tender of Admiral Warren's flag-ship. Rodgers had been put in possession of some of the British signals. When he saw the *Highflyer*, he hoisted English colors, and trying his signals, found to his delight that they were answered. He then assumed the character of a British officer. He decoyed the *Highflyer* alongside the *President*, which he pretended was the large British ship *Sea-Horse*, then in American waters. The commander of the *Highflyer* (Lieutenant Hutchinson) was thoroughly deceived. Rodgers ordered him to send him his signal books. He obeyed, and soon followed them in person. He saw the marines of the *President* in British uniform, and mistook them for his own countrymen.

"The *President*," said the unsuspecting Hutchinson, "has spread alarm in British waters, and the main object of the Admiral is to catch her."

"What kind of a man is Rodgers?" asked the Commodore.

"I have never seen him," said Hutchinson, "but have been told that he is an odd fish, and hard to catch."

"Would you like to meet him?"

"Indeed I would, with a vessel of equal size."

"Sir," said Rodgers, in a tone that startled the Lieutenant, "do you know what ship this is?"

"The *Sea-Horse*, of course."

"You are mistaken. You are on board the *President*, and I am Commodore Rodgers."

Then the band struck up "Yankee Doodle," the masts

THE "ESSEX," "PHŒBE," AND "CHERUB."—Drawn by J. O. Davidson.

of the marines were suddenly changed from scarlet to blue, and the American flag was displayed over the quarter-deck. Rodgers took his captive and his prize to Newport. He made another less successful cruise, and about the middle of January, 1814, he dashed through the British blockading squadron at New York, and anchored in the harbor.

The British had carried on a distressing marauding warfare on the coasts during 1813, which kept the smaller vessels of the navy and privateers vigilant and active. During that summer there were only three American frigates at sea, others being either blockaded or undergoing repairs; and yet the Americans, with indomitable will, resolved to carry on the war with vigor. In September, Commodore Perry, in command of a squadron on Lake Erie, won a decisive victory over a British squadron under Commodore Barclay, and thereby secured the absolute control of that lake. Meanwhile Commodore Chauncey, in command on Lake Ontario, was performing gallant services there, standing in the way of British invasions on that frontier, and co-operating efficiently with the land forces on its borders.

[TO BE CONTINUED.]

HOW THE GEESE SAVED THE BABY.

BY MRS. L. G. MORSE.

JOHN EVANS was raking hay in a field on the south side of his cottage, while his wife was in the dairy printing butter for market. Little Elsy, their two-year-old baby, was playing with blocks on the sitting-room floor, and old Robin Hood, the dog, was asleep on the grass close by the door that opened on the lawn.

The sky was almost cloudless, and the sun blazed warm in the fields.

"Just the weather to make the corn grow," said John Evans, resting a quarter of a minute, and looking contentedly over the wall at his flourishing corn blades, already two good inches at least above those of his rich neighbor, Mr. Haverly.

"Elsy is safe," said Barbara, the trim little house-maid. "I might as well knead up the bread." And she whisked through the sitting-room so fast, and with so little noise, that Elsy only looked up to see if a bird had flown in over the low half-door.

Tired of her blocks at last, Elsy went and tugged at the door, and made the latch rattle. Robin opened one eye—the one toward the house—and half-cocked an ear. But Elsy kept up the rattle long enough for him to get used to it, and drawing his tail closer under his nose, he ceased paying any attention to the child. He knew she was behind the door. He had done his full duty by standing on his hind-legs against it, and looking to see what she was about before he settled himself for his nap. She rattled the latch every day, but she had never been able to lift it—he needn't have *that* on his mind. So, by-and-by, when the crown of her little white head showed itself above the door, Robin was dozing away, more sleepy than ever.

She had pushed her block-box close to the sill, and stepped on it to take another view of the latch. For Elsy was enterprising, and had no more idea than have other two-year-old babies of remaining in ignorance of any new and untried danger. Of course she succeeded at last, and so easily that she pushed the door open and let herself backward down the steps without waking the dog.

The oldest mother goose in the barn-yard was as ener-

"KEEP STEP, KEEP STEP; ONE, TWO, THREE—ONE, TWO, THREE."

getic as Elsy. She quacked about among her neighbors until she collected the whole flock, and then matronized them down to the big shallow pond in front of the house. They pottered a good deal on the way among mud-puddles, for there had been a shower the night before.

Dame Evans pottered too in the dairy, but that was because pretty Miss Ruth Haverly called to bespeak some of the butter before it should be sent to market, and was trying her hands at the printing. Very soft white hands they were, and Mrs. Evans enjoyed watching them.

"There," she said, "that one is a beauty!" as Ruth turned one of the yellow balls into a dish. But she never would have allowed anybody else to meddle so with her butter. A spot on the dairy shelf would have been as great a crime as a speck on the snow-white kerchief crossed on her bosom. But no thought would she have taken of the butter, nor even of dainty Miss Ruth, had she known what Elsy was doing. Nor would Barbara have cared so much about the bread. She was singing, and did not hear Elsy fumbling with the door-latch.

But the child had trotted by Robin Hood, down the long path, all the way to the river, and was so pleased at the feat that she laughed aloud. It was the first chance she had ever had to get alone to the river. Somebody had always been on hand to pull her away just in time to save her feet from touching the water. Now they touched it in comfort, and little cool ripples washed over the toes of her stockings—she had pulled her shoes off long ago in the house. She ran up and down the edge of the water a few times, and then began picking up sticks and stray leaves to throw into it. Higher and higher her spirits rose with the sport. If it had not been for Barbara's song, Robin would surely have heard Elsy shout. But Robin was lazy in his old age, and was actually snoring. Elsy spied a pretty goose-feather, and gave it a toss. The breeze carried it farther out on the water than the small maid intended. But she was fearless, and catching at some cat-tails growing on the bank, she waded in after her feather.

She stumbled over the uneven bottom, and the stones hurt her soft little feet. Down she went, head and all under water, just as the geese came, ready at last for their swim. When they saw Elsy splashing about, they thought she was trespassing. Or perhaps they understood perfectly well that the river, although safe for them, was a dangerous place for the innocent baby. Who knows? Certain it was that as Elsy went down under the water, the geese flapped their wings, and made a tremendous racket. They made such a noise as never had been heard in the place before. They wakened old Robin at last, and brought him quick as a flash to his post of duty. Oh, he could make noise enough then, to be sure! He could tear round the house like a hurricane, dash down the path and into the water, seize little Elsy's dress, and hold her head above the surface until her father came to the rescue, plunged into the river, and in another minute had borne his darling safely to land. Her bright eyes were closed, and her form lay quite senseless against her father's bosom, while Robin looked up to be sure she was safe, and Barbara ran terrified from the house, her singing silenced at last.

THE RESCUE.—Drawn by H. P. Share.

But Elsy opened her eyes again before long. Joy greeted the little life saved, and the mother half smothered old Robin with kisses, in spite of his dripping coat, which utterly ruined her kerchief.

John Evans and his good dame would never have cheated a mouse of its due, yet they petted and honored old Robin as long as he lived, and told children and grandchildren hundreds of times how it was *he* saved Elsy, when, as sure as anything, the whole credit was due to the geese.

WE have received a large number of letters from our young readers asking for stamps, leaves, flowers, and other things; but unless they offer some suitable equivalent in exchange, which they must specify in the letter, we can not print such requests.

The cooking club is looking up. We are assured that the disbandment is not on account of any bad feeling among the members, neither for lack of interest, but that the sole reason is the whooping-cough! As we have already given enough recipes to render our young housekeepers skillful bread, cake, and candy makers, if they try them all, we shall not print any after the present number. If any of you wish to give a tea party to your little friends, by using the recipes sent by the little readers of HARPER'S YOUNG PEOPLE you can prepare with your own hands a very inviting supper, for you could wish for nothing nicer than hot pop-overs, little cakes, and candy.

[illegible]

will hold, and after fastening it securely to the cross piece of the hoop, light it, and the balloon will soon expand with the heated air, and rise. If you make the balloon of colored tissue-paper, and it rises while the sponge is still burning, the effect at night is very pretty. A bunch of tow might be used in place of a sponge.

Sarah McB.—We think the address given by the correspondent you wish to exchange with is sufficient. Write, and you will probably receive an answer.

Ed. S. K.—In Young People No. 22 you will find full directions for building a sloop-yacht.

Charles K.—The recipe for butter-scotch was in the Post-office Box of Young People No. 37.

Fred M. G.—The specimen you send is a sphinx moth, of which there are several varieties in the United States.

F. W. H.—You can obtain the numbers of Young People you wish by sending one dollar and fourteen cents to the publishers.

Brownie.—A salt-water turtle feeds upon the tough stems of sea-weeds, and upon crustacea and very small mollusks, but it might eat bits of bread and meat, or insects.

George H. K.—We doubt if you could make a microscope which would be as cheap or as satisfactory as one already manufactured. Microscopes may be bought at all prices.

Favors are acknowledged from Mary C. Hodges, Clara A. [illegible], Amy Fisher, Mabel C. C., Keith W. [illegible], M. C. S., Calvin Taylor, Mary [illegible], [illegible] [illegible] A. Y., Thomas S., H. R. K., [illegible] and W., [illegible], George Paul, Clara S. X., Angie and Anna W., C. Reynolds, [illegible], [illegible] Murphy, Josie Parker, [illegible], [illegible] A. H., K. J. K., Frank [illegible], [illegible], Mary E. [illegible], Victoria Gregory.

Correct answers to puzzles are received from [illegible] Henry, A. H. [illegible], James C. [illegible], [illegible], Hattie Bassett, [illegible], Harry C. and [illegible] H., C. M.; E. A. [illegible], L. M. [illegible], Mary L. [illegible], H. M. Y., Fanny [illegible], Willie Murphy, "Capt. Frank," R. H. King, Marion E. [illegible]; G. [illegible], [illegible], Henry M. [illegible], Frank Henry, Jennie Edwards.

PUZZLES FROM YOUNG CONTRIBUTORS.

No. 1.

ENIGMA.

My first is in black, my second in gold,
My third is in courage, my fourth is in bold,
My fifth is in whimper, my sixth is in scream,
My seventh is in thinking, my eighth is in dream,
My ninth is in [illegible], my tenth is in [illegible],
My eleventh is in hunger, my twelfth is in [illegible],
My thirteenth is in [illegible], my fourteenth in drink,
My fifteenth is in living, my sixteenth in breath,
You may spell out my name, you may [illegible] me by [illegible],
But I'm still an enigma to all but a few. Lottie.

No. 2.

NUMERICAL CHARADE.

I am an ancient historian composed of 8 letters.
My 2, 7, 3, 8 is a [illegible].
My 4, 5, 3, 1 [illegible].
My 1, 6, 5, 2 is a nickname. Frank.

No. 3.

WORD SQUARE.

First, an explosive article. Second, a mixture. Third, [illegible]. Fourth, [illegible].

A. H. E.

No. 4.

DOUBLE ACROSTIC.

[illegible]. [illegible]. A fruit. A form of government. A member of a religious community. [illegible]. Answer—[illegible].

Lone Star.

No. 5.

ENIGMA.

My first is in [illegible], but not in [illegible],
My second is in [illegible], but not in [illegible],
My third is in [illegible], but not in [illegible],
My fourth is in [illegible], but not in [illegible],
My fifth is in [illegible], but not in [illegible],
My sixth is in [illegible], but not in [illegible],
My seventh is in [illegible], but not in [illegible],
My whole is a [illegible];
Are [illegible] English of [illegible]. E. A. L.

ANSWERS TO PUZZLES IN NO. 40.

No. 1. New York

No. 2. [illegible]
Hyena. Tiger.

No. 3. Tierra del Fuego.

No. 4. [illegible]

No. 5. [illegible]

No. 6. Lafayette.

Charade on page 604—Pop-Corn.

A GUNPOWDER PLOT.

A FEW months ago Mr. Two Trees, a Sioux Indian, with his family, visited Fort Benton, where he hoped to dispose of some robes. While bathing in the Missouri the young hopefuls of the family discover a keg of gunpowder that has been washed out from a wrecked steamboat. They rejoice greatly over their prize; and after taking it ashore, hold a long discussion in their own musical language as to what they shall do with it.

All-in-gun-in (the Mouse that Nibbles), the younger of the boys, proposes that they ask their father how they shall dispose of the powder. But his elder brother, the Wise Owl that Hoots, knows of a better plan: it is to dry the powder, and trade it for sugar to the "Man of Many Blankets," as they call the trader.

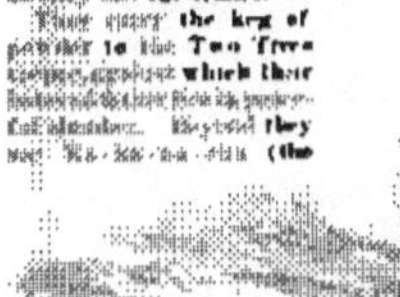

They carry the keg of powder to the Two Trees lodge, against which their [illegible] Beyond they see Wa-ka-na-sha (the Crooked Head), their dear mother, and Chee-chi-cut-sun (the Singing Mud Turtle), their aunt, busily preparing robes for the trader.

Stealing into the lodge unobserved, the boys find a puppy stewing over the fire, but manage to make room beside it for their keg of powder, which they leave to dry.

While it is drying the young Two Trees stroll down to the trader's store, to look over his stock, and try and decide what they shall accept in exchange for their prize. The trader is studying his "medicine," or the paper that talks.

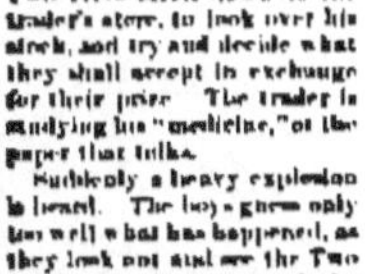

Suddenly a heavy explosion is heard. The boys guess only too well what has happened, as they look out and see the Two Tree lodge sailing through the air, spread open like an umbrella, and followed by the puppy-dog stew. They see their noble father, rudely awakened from his nap, also attempting a short flight, while their mother, the Crooked Head, and their aunt, the Mud Turtle, exhibit every sign of surprise on the foreground.

The boys fly; but after them come the avengers, and they are taught by painful experience the danger of meddling with gunpowder.

Vol. I.—No. 44. | Published by HARPER & BROTHERS, New York. | Price Four Cents.

Tuesday, August [illegible] | [illegible] | [illegible] per Year, in Advance.

CLAUDINE'S DOVES.

BY MRS. E. W. LATIMER.

A FEW days since, as I was driving in the Bois de Boulogne with a friend, a slender, sweet young girl was pointed out to me. She was walking beside her mother, and there was a loving, tender look in her blue eyes, a shrinking modesty in her deportment, which interested me at the first glance. She was apparently about fifteen. I observed to the friend who pointed her out to me that she was fair, modest, and pretty. "Yes," he replied, "and she is the heroine of a very pretty story."

Eight years ago her father and mother occupied an *appartement*, or flat, in the Rue de Rivoli. Part of the Rue de Rivoli has houses only on one side; the other is bordered by a high iron railing with gilt spear-heads, inclosing the Garden of the Tuileries. At one point (which was nearly opposite the house where Claudine lived) one tall pavilion of the palace abutted on the sidewalk. The Rue de Rivoli is the most beautiful street in Paris. The windows of the sitting-room of Claudine's mother looked over the palace and its gardens, its chestnut-trees and its fountains, the Seine and its quays, with a more distant view of the Place de la Concorde and its obelisk, the Chambers of the Legislature, and the gilded dome of the Tuileries. Every procession passed under Claudine's windows. No little girl, I think, who lives in rooms overlooking the Rue de Rivoli would wish to exchange them for any other home.

Claudine's parents, though of good birth and education, were not rich; they lived on the third story. They had only one old servant. Claudine's mother was her daughter's nurse and governess. Till the German army marched on Paris they had a peaceful, refined, and happy home.

At the moment of which I am about to write, the siege had ceased, and the terrible days of the Commune were almost over. The little family began to breathe more freely—only in a certain sense, however, for they were all gathered together in a little close room, which would have looked into the court-yard of their house had not its windows been blocked up by pillows, mattresses, and furniture. They dared not look into the street, they dared not go into their own sitting-room, for the Versailles troops were entering Paris, bomb-shells were bursting in all directions, and volleys of musketry were being fired round every street corner. Paris was like a city expecting to be sacked, with the additional horror that each man's foes might be those of his own household.

Of a sudden they began to feel a stifling heat. Thick smoke rose all around them. There was the sickening and suggestive smell of coal-oil in the air. Claudine's father felt that he must know what was going on. To look out of the windows might be death to all of them; still he ran into the sitting-room, tore down the beds and pillows from a window, and looked out on the Rue de Rivoli.

The palace before him was in flames. As he looked, the fire swept over the venerable gray pile. Forked tongues of flame darted higher than the Mansard roofs of its tall towers, and threatened the stores and dwelling-houses across the way. Claudine's father looked below into the street; there was no safety there. The men and women of the neighborhood, driven from their rooms by falling fiery flakes from the high roofs of the old palace, clustered together under shelter of the great *porte cochères*—entrances by which carriages drive into the court-yards of French houses under the rooms of the first story. Muskets, rifles, and mitrailleuses swept the street. To venture into it seemed sure destruction. To stay beneath their blazing roof would expose them all to perish in the flames. Bomb-shells were falling constantly to right and left, knocking off pieces of the cornices of lofty, stately houses, tearing off their iron balconies, and scattering shattered fragments of wood, window-glass, iron, and plaster on the pavement.

The father of Claudine, aghast with fear and horror, stepped back into the sitting-room. "I see no escape for us," he cried.

At that moment hoarse shouts below them in the court-yard announced that a party of insurgents, accompanied by a band of the fiendish women they called *pétroleuses*, had burst into the house that they inhabited. Already the dangerous fluid from which these women took their name was being poured over the wood-work of the staircase and the two lower *appartements*.

A cry ran through the house of "Save yourselves!" Claudine's father gathered together some important papers, some money, and a few jewels. The mother and her old servant spread a blanket on the floor, and flung into it such objects as they could gather up in haste, tying it by the four corners. As to Claudine, frantic with terror, she ran into her bedroom and brought out what she valued most—a cage containing two young turtle-doves. They were her only pets. She loved them better than anything else in the world, except old Clémence and her father and mother.

The torches of the Communards had already set fire to the wood-work saturated with coal-oil. Flames were breaking out in every direction. The inhabitants of the doomed houses were forced to make their way into the street, or stay to be burned alive. The first to rush down the staircase was Claudine, cage in hand. She ran into the street. A bomb-shell burst as she reached it, and her terrified parents saw her drop upon the sidewalk, while the cage fell at some distance, rolling away out of her hand.

When her father saw her dead, as he supposed, he rushed into the street, undaunted by the bursting of the shell, and picking up her body, retreated with it under shelter of the *porte cochère*.

But Claudine was not dead, nor even wounded. She had fainted with fright, and as her parents hung over her with tender words, she opened her blue eyes and smiled at them. A moment after, she remembered her dear doves. Before any one could stop her or forbid her she ran back into the street through bullets thick as hail, caught up her cage, and ran back with her recovered treasures. A *pétroleuse* who had seen her stopped as she was setting fire to some furniture, and cried out, with a mocking laugh,

"What was the use of running out to pick up those! They will be roast birds anyhow in the next half-hour."

On hearing these cruel words little Claudine began to comprehend for the first time the greatness of the danger. She drew back, darted a look of reproach at the vile woman who stood laughing at her trouble, and then, with the big tears rolling down her cheeks, "God will know how to keep them safe," she said, and opened the cage door. The doves flew out. They poised themselves a moment; then they rose into the air, and flew away to seek a purer sky above the clouds of smoke and sulphur. In spite of what the cruel woman said, the doves were saved.

A few moments later a drum was heard advancing up the street. The drummers marched at the head of a body of troops—the soldiers had come! "*Vive l'armée!*" cried the frightened householders.

In an instant *pétroleuses*, robbers, and insurgents scattered in all directions. It is a queer sight to see a French crowd run when the troops charge. *Now*, however, every soldier "thought on vengeance." The incendiaries dropped fast before the iron hail.

Meantime all hands were busy putting out the flames. The fire was at last got under. The furniture and wood-work of the first and second stories were badly burned and broken, but the rest of the house was saved.

Claudine and her family went back into their rooms, and let in the light of day, the father and mother blessing God for the timely arrival of the troops who had saved all Paris from fire and pillage. By degrees they grew more calm. But one sad heart was inconsolable. Claudine's share in the great catastrophe which had almost laid Paris "even with the ground" was the loss of her dear turtle-doves.

The next morning when she came out early on the balcony to look at the blackened ruins of the noble palace, and to mourn for her lost favorites, she uttered a cry of joy. Her doves sat on the railing of the balcony. They had flown back to their little mistress and their home.

"Mamma! mamma!" she cried, "God has sent me back my doves!" and her little heart recovered the happiness that in her inexperience she fancied had been lost forever.

JOHNNY'S SONG.

BY JOSEPHINE POLLARD.

"Come, now, Johnny, sing me a song—
  Sing me a song," said Mabel.
"I will," said Johnny, whose voice was strong,
  "For I'm the boy that is able."
So he sang, and whistled, and sang again,
  Till all the woods were a-ringing.
And Mabel frowned, and began to complain,
  "Why, Johnny, what's that you're singing?"

"Don't you like it?" said Johnny Stout
  (Mabel her laugh must smother),
As he straightened himself in his roundabout,
  And said, "I'll sing you another."
He sang and whistled with might and main,
  Till Mabel's ears were a-ringing,
And she stopped them up, and exclaimed again
  "Why, Johnny, what are you singing?"

"That's *Pinafore*," said Johnny Stout,
  Who thought himself quite clever;
"You've heard it often enough, no doubt."
  Said Mabel, "N—hardly ever."
And she made up her mind that never again
  Would she ask Minnie Stout's big brother
To sing her a song, when 'twas very plain
  He knew not one tune from another.

VIOLA'S SKETCH.

BY MRS. W. J. HAYS.

WE had been staying at Dinan, a pretty and cheap little summer resting-place in Brittany, and so picturesque were the costumes of the peasantry that Viola, my sister, was fascinated, and her sketch-book was getting crammed, while I, more frivolous, was longing to be in Paris, where I could go to the Bon Marché, see the newest fashions, and hear the latest doings and sayings of the famous actress Sarah Bernhardt. Viola was always more sensible in some things than I, but she was weak on jugs, and mugs, and rugs, and picturesque old rags, and old women, and children; therefore it was no surprise to me, when we were on the road to the railway station, and our trunks already well on the way toward Paris, to have her insist upon stopping to find out what was the matter with a child who was crying bitterly. When, however, Viola discovered that the child was the granddaughter of old Margot, who had been our "maid-of-everything" at the little cottage which aunt had hired for the season, who had cooked for us, and washed for us, and gone to market for us, at some ridiculously low wages, there was no use in arguing with her; stop she would, and alight she would from the queer old conveyance we were in—for it was not the day for the diligence—and aunt had to wait, nolens volens—and that means willingly if you choose, and unwillingly if you don't choose—and I had to wait, and I had to do all the scolding, for aunt is as meek as a turtle-dove. And after a while both aunt and I were just as much interested as was Viola, and there were we three all listening to little Suzette, forgetful of the train and of Paris.

Suzette had ceased crying, and was pulling a flower to pieces as she told us of her trouble. Margot had been obliged to remain away from home on account of our intended departure, and she had left orders, strict orders, for Jacques, Suzette's brother, not to do this, nor that, nor the other—in fact, had forbidden so many things that poor little Suzette knew not what was the thing he could do; nevertheless Jacques insisted upon doing just as he pleased, and Suzette and he had a quarrel. Suzette wished him to obey his grandmother; he called his grandmother an old witch, and said Suzette was her cat, and that as for voice and eyes, their cat had much finer ones. Then they had even worse words, and she had pulled his hair, and he had banged the door, and said he was going to drown himself; and he had come down to the pond, for she had run after him, and she was sure—yes, positively sure—that her brother was dead, and she should never see him again.

"But, Suzette," said Viola, "he may be hiding just to tease you."

"No, ma'm'selle, he has not wit enough for that; he has a tender heart, and I was cruel to him, and of course being desolate from my unkindness, he has effaced himself." And then she burst out sobbing again.

"Oh, come, Viola," said I; "the child believes this to be true; let us prove to her that it is not so. The pond is small; we will hunt high and low for him. You take one bank, I will take the other, and between us Jacques can not escape."

Aunt made a feeble expostulation about the train.

"The train, madame," said I, grandly, "can wait. When humanity demands our time, there should be no thought of personal convenience. You see this weeping girl, you hear what it is that causes her tears; how, then, can you suggest to us the idea of evading responsibility?"

Then aunt feebly again murmured, "Dinner."

"Ah, then, ma chère tante, behold the immense luncheon Margot has provided—good Margot, to whom we wish to render this service!" This was from Viola; and all the while Suzette was sobbing.

"Adieu," I cried, tucking up my skirts, and running to the pond. Viola followed me; but so lost was she in admiration of the water plants and lilies, that had it not been for me she would have sat down and sketched them whether Jacques drowned or not. I hurried her off, telling her the child might be just at the last gasp, and we must hasten.

So Viola took one bank and I the other. Every other moment I shouted, "Have you found him?"

"No-oo," came back to me.

"Neither have I," was my response.

I had a little ivory-handled riding-whip with me, and I began to beat the bushes. Viola was now too far away to hear me, so instead of calling to her I screamed,

"Jacques! Jacques! unless you are drowned, do answer me. Good Jacques, dear Jacques, where are you?"

There was no reply; but the wind sighed in the trees, and the water lapped softly on the margin of the pond. I began to have some fears of my own. What if I should come suddenly upon the boy just as he was sinking, the bubbles perhaps dancing up to the surface of the water? Could I do anything to save him? could I swim? Alas! I could swim in a bathing tank, with some one to hold up my chin. What should I do? would my screams be heard half a mile away?

As I thought thus I again began beating the bushes, which were thick along the edge of the water, and at the same moment a loud something, neither a scream nor a groan, saluted my ears. I stood amazed; I could not scream; and instantly a voice said:

"Ah, what a fine fellow I have lost! that was too bad!" and a scrubby little head appeared above the bushes. "Is it you, ma'm'selle? I beg pardon. I have caused you to be frightened; but you have caused me to lose the finest frog in Brittany."

"Oh, Jacques! naughty Jacques!" I faltered, as well as my beating heart would allow, "how could you serve us all in this way?"

SUZETTE.—Drawn by [illegible]

"In what way, ma'm'selle?" replied the muddy creature, holding up a frog he was in the act of skinning.

"Why, we thought—that is, we feared—or rather Suzette said, you meant to drown yourself."

"I!" exclaimed this gamin, in the most innocent and artless manner.

"Yes, you. Did you not tell her so?"

"In a moment of excitement I may have uttered a careless expression," said the youth, peeling the frog's leg carefully. "Suzette is weak, like all women—begging your pardon, ma'm'selle—she believes all that we men say. She, in truth, irritated me, and I was cross. But I had promised Monsieur le Curé that he should have a fine mess of frogs to-day, and it was a good chance for me to get them; therefore I came to the pond, and left Suzette to recover her composure."

I had recovered mine by this time, but I knew not whether to laugh or to be angry; so I said, "Do you find your conscience tranquil when you utter a falsehood?"

"Oh no, ma'm'selle, never; but this was a jest, done just to make Suzette behave herself. She will not scold me again very soon." And with that he strung his frogs together, slung them over his shoulder, and was marching off.

"Come, come," said I, "you must go with me and show yourself."

"As ma'm'selle pleases," was the cool response, and we trudged back toward the road.

I expected to find Suzette still sobbing, and Viola in hysterics; but what were they doing? Suzette was posing, and Viola making a picture of her—the cap and the sabots had been too tempting. Viola had given up searching for the truant boy, and was trying to secure a correct sketch of his sister. Suzette looked "all smiles" at seeing Jacques, and would have embraced him, but Viola would not let her stir.

It is needless to say that we lost the train, that aunt mildly lectured us, that Jacques and Suzette begged ten thousand pardons, and filled the carriage with water-lilies. We had to stop at the curé's to return some books he had lent us; and when we told him the story, he made us dine with him, and I must confess that I ate some of Jacques's frog legs, and that they were delicious.

[Begun in No. 31 of Harper's Young People, June 1.]

THE MORAL PIRATES.

BY W. L. ALDEN.

Chapter XIV.

THE boys had been on their island for more than a week when they resolved to make an excursion to Schroon, which was the nearest village, in order to get some sugar, coffee, and other necessaries. Schroon Lake, or rather the lower end of it, was not more than five miles from Brandt Lake; but there was a range of high hills between the two, and the village of Schroon was situated at the head of the lake, which was nearly ten miles in length. A long and tiresome journey was, therefore, before them, and they ought to have started early in the morning; but they did not start until nearly eleven o'clock. Harry, Tom, and Joe were to go to Schroon together, and Jim was to stay at the island until six o'clock, when he was to row over to the west shore and bring the others back to the camp.

When they bade good-by to Jim, the three other boys assured him that they would certainly be back as early as six o'clock, and warned him not to fail to meet them with the boat. They then started to cross the hills, following a foot-path that was so little used that it was hardly visible. Unfortunately the path led through a thicket of raspberry bushes, and the fruit was so tempting that the boys lost a good deal of time by stopping to gather it. After a tiresome tramp under the mid-day sun they reached the lower end of Schroon Lake, where they hired a crank little row-boat, and rowed up to Schroon. There was a fresh northerly breeze which delayed them; and the spray from the bow of the boat sprinkled them, so that they were uncomfortably wet when they reached the village. By this time they were very hungry as well as tired, and so they went to the hotel for dinner. It was half past six o'clock when they started to row down the lake, and several men who saw them warned them that they were running a great risk in attempting to return at so late an hour.

The trip down the lake was certainly a rather foolhardy one, for there was a good deal of wind and sea, and long before they reached the landing-place it was quite dark. But the boys were anxious to get back to their camp, and for the first time during the cruise they acted somewhat recklessly. However, they met with no accident; and when they had returned the boat to its owner, they set out to cross the hills.

The path was not easy to find in the daylight, and it was next to impossible to find it in the night. A dozen times the boys lost themselves, and were compelled to depend entirely upon the stars to direct their course. The woods had been all cleared away for a space of a mile or a mile and a half wide between the two lakes, except just along the shore of Brandt Lake; so that it was not absolutely necessary for them to keep in the path, as it would have been had they been passing through a thick forest. Still, it was not pleasant to lose the path, and stumble over stones and stumps, and of course it made the journey longer. They must have walked at least seven or eight miles on their way back before they finally reached their own lake at midnight, at the point where they expected to find Jim waiting for them.

Neither Jim nor the boat was there. He had waited until ten o'clock, and then, making up his mind that they had decided to spend the night at Schroon, he rowed back to the island, and went calmly to bed. An hour later a dense fog settled over the lake; and when the tired boys reached the shore they could see but a few yards in front of their eyes.

It was a terrible disappointment, but Harry tried to be cheerful. "We shall have to stay here to-night, boys," said he; "but we will build a good fire and keep warm." Tom said that he thought that was the best thing to do, for without a fire they would suffer severely from the cold, wet fog, and he asked Harry if he had any matches. Harry had none, Joe had none, and Tom had none; so the plan of building a fire came to nothing.

The cold gradually chilled them as they stood talking over their adventure, and their teeth began to chatter. Joe said he wished he could get hold of Jim for about five minutes, so that he could warm himself up by convincing him that he ought not to have taken the boat back to the island. Harry said nothing; but he was wondering whether he would freeze to death in the fog, and tried to remember how travellers overtaken by the snow on the Alps contrive to fight off the terrible drowsiness that steals over them when they are freezing. Tom was more practical. He did not expect to freeze in July, although he was miserably cold; and he did not want to punish Jim for a mistake of judgment. He knew that the house where they were accustomed to get milk was not far off, and that a boat usually lay on the shore near the house; so he proposed to Harry and Joe to borrow the boat, and make their way into the camp.

"If we go to that house at this time of night, we shall get shot," remarked Harry. "The man is an ugly-tempered chap, and I heard him say the other day that if he ever heard anything prowling around the house at night he always fired at it."

"Then we won't ask him for his boat: we'll borrow it without leave, and Jim can bring it back in the morning," replied Tom.

"This is nice conduct for Moral Pirates," said Joe. "Capturing a vessel at night is real piracy, and when Jim takes the boat back, the man will be sure to shoot him. I'm sorry for Jim, but I hope it will be a warning to him not to leave his friends in such a fix that they've either got to borrow a boat without leave, or freeze."

They made their way stealthily and with great difficulty to the place where the boat lay. It was high and dry on the beach, and though the fog hid the house where the owner of the boat lived, the boys knew that it was very near. They launched the boat with the utmost caution, lest any noise should awaken the bad-tempered man with the shot-gun. They had it almost launched, when Harry's foot slipped on a wet stone, and he fell with a loud crash, clinging to the boat, and dragging Tom and Joe down with him.

It was very certain that if anything could wake the owner of the boat, he must be awake by this time; so the boys sprang up, and shoving the boat into the water, regardless of the noise, seized the oars, and rowed away into the fog. When they had gained what they thought was a safe distance from the shore they ceased rowing, and congratulated themselves that they were all right at last. To be sure, Harry had scraped his ankle badly; Tom had forgotten the coffee, and left it on the shore; and Joe had put the sugar in the bottom of the leaky boat, where it was rapidly dissolving into syrup; but they were once more afloat, and expected to reach their comfortable camp within the next twenty minutes.

There was not a particle of air stirring, and not a star was visible, so they had absolutely nothing to steer by. They could not even hear the sound of the water which ordinarily lapped the shore. Still, they were not discouraged; Harry thought he knew which way the camp lay, and so he and Tom rowed in what they imagined was the right direction.

BIDDING JIM GOOD-BY.—Drawn by A. B. Frost.

They rowed for two hours without finding the island, and without reaching the shore. They could not understand it. The lake seemed to have grown in the night, and to have reached the size of Lake Ontario. They knew that by daylight they could row across it at its widest part in less than an hour, but now it seemed impossible to find any shore. Joe had just suggested that they had made a mistake in coming back from Schroon, and had walked all the way to Lake Champlain, on which they were now rowing, when the bow of the boat struck the shore.

It was some consolation to know that the lake actually had a shore; but they could not tell what part of the shore they had reached. They pushed off again, and resumed their hopeless search for the camp. A new trouble now harassed them. From seeming to have no shore at all, the lake now seemed to have shrunk to a mere mud puddle. No matter in what direction they rowed, they would strike the shore within ten minutes, and always at a different place. Joe said that he had never dreamed that so much shore and so little lake could be put together.

Toward morning Harry and Tom became too tired to row, and they lay down in the bottom of the wet boat, and tried to keep warm by lying close to each other. Joe took the oars, and tried to row without hitting the shore; but he had hardly dipped his oars when the bow grated on the pebbles. He promptly gave up the attempt, and making the boat fast to a tree, joined Tom and Harry, and shared their misery.

They were much too cold and wretched to sleep, but they managed to keep from growing positively stiff with cold. The sun rose, but it did not for a long time make any impression on the fog. All at once, about seven o'clock, the fog vanished, and the boys found themselves in a little bay near the extreme northerly part of the lake. They had been rowing across this little bay, first in one direction and then in another, during all those miserable hours when they found such an unaccountable quantity of shore.

Of course they rowed down to the camp, where they found Jim still sleeping soundly, with a contented, happy look that was awfully exasperating. They woke him up, and scolded him with all the strength they had left, and then, putting on dry clothes, "turned in," and slept all day. Jim towed the borrowed boat back, but was not shot; and the boys afterward said that, on the whole, they were rather glad that he still lived, and that they would mercifully forgive him.

[TO BE CONTINUED.]

JED'S FIRST HALF.

BY WILLIAM O. STODDARD.

JED was thinking.

Anybody who looked at him would have seen that much, for he was standing all alone at the corner, leaning against the big poplar, with both hands in his trousers pockets.

The village was one long "main street," with little short side streets cutting across it, so that it did not have any "middle" to speak of; but the "centre" of it and of everything else was right there before Jed's eyes, on the steps of the grocery. It was in the shape of a stack of boxes of fire-crackers, and Jed was gazing at it.

It had been almost cruel of old Philips, the grocer, to pile them up out there the last week in June, to make Jed and the other boys count their pennies and feel uncomfortable.

Fourth of July was coming, and Jed knew he would not be half ready for it. There were five other little Pullmans, and Jed felt as if he alone could use up "fire-crackers for six."

Think of having one of those boxes—a whole one—with nobody knew how many packs in it!

"I'd treat every boy I know, except Prop Hooker; and mebbe I'd give him some if he'd promise not to throw any more stones at Barlow."

The thought of such riches was a little too much for a boy of nine, and Jed slowly sidled around the trunk of the poplar, as if he were trying to get away, but his eyes did not turn with him. They stuck to the crackers.

"Hullo, my little man, what's your name?"

"Jed, sir."

He had to look up, up, up, to get at the grim, weather-beaten, but not unkindly face of the elderly farmer before him.

"Jed, eh? What's your whole name?"

"Jedediah Rittenhouse Pullman. I live down there in that yellow brick house behind the maple-trees."

"You don't say! Why, if you'd ha' let your name drag after you, the back end of it wouldn't but just be coming out of the front gate now. Can you drive cows?"

"That's what I have to do every night and morning. 'Tain't everybody can drive our brindled heifer neither."

Jed was thinking again. He had made up his mind that the stranger was a head taller than Grandfather Pullman—in fact, that he was taller than any other man in the world, except old Mr. Myer, the maple-sugar man, and he had to stoop to get into his own house.

"You don't say! Well, I'm down here alone, and I've got a loaded team to drive, and I've bought a cow, and I want a smart boy to drive her home for me."

"How far is it?"

"Only to Topham. Little more'n twelve mile. I'll send ye home by somebody. Pay ye well, too. Will you go?"

Jed hesitated a moment, but it was only because he seemed to be listening to a great rattle of fire-crackers to come—a cow-load of them.

"Course I'll go, if mother 'll let me."

"We'll see her about it right away. You're just the boy I want. Give you four shillings."

A York shilling was twelve and a half cents, and four of them made half a dollar. Oh, what fire-works!

Mrs. Pullman met them at the door, and the first word she said was, "Why, is that you, Deacon Giddings?"

Then Jed knew it was all right, and while his mother talked with Deacon Giddings, he went and combed his hair, and put on his Sunday hat and a pair of shoes and stockings.

"Jed's a tough little fellow," said his mother, "and he's used to driving cows."

She might have said more than that for him. Even Deacon Giddings had picked him out as the "toughest-lookin' little chap he'd seen in a long time." The deacon was in a hurry, though, and almost before Jed began to realize it, he was dancing around behind a very reluctant and rebellious cow, right up the main street, with his new friend watching him from the seat of the heavily loaded wagon.

"Ain't I glad I brought Barlow along!" said Jed to himself, again and again. "He's a small dog, but he just knows how to bark the best kind."

Barlow was indeed a small dog, very fat and very yellow, and with less than two inches of stubby tail, but he was keeping up a very steady racket at the heels of the cow. He could hardly have done better if he had been a perpetual pack of fire-crackers, going off one at a time.

Once they were out of the village and into the country road, the work became easier, and Barlow could now and then sit down and pant awhile before opening a fresh bark.

"You're the boy for me," said the Deacon, from the wagon. "But ain't you afraid that dog o' yourn 'll bark himself to death?"

"No, sir, he's used to it. Our brindled heifer always keeps him barking."

"You don't say! Well, I'm glad I know your folks. What do you mean to do with your money?"

"Fourth of July, sir."

"That's it. I declare! Well, now, I might have thought of that. Gingerbread, nuts, candy—"

"No, sir. Fire-crackers."

"You don't say! Look out for that cow; she's heading down the road again. Hear that dog bark! I declare!"

She was quickly headed right again, and Deacon Giddings had by no means got to the end of the questions he wanted to ask.

They were not all about Jed's own affairs. In fact, he seemed willing to know everything there was to be known about the Pullman family, and all their relations, and all their neighbors.

Jed was willing enough to answer, whenever the cow would let him, and it made the long walk in the hot sun go by faster and easier.

It was slow enough even then, and by the time they reached Penniman's Corners, seven miles from the village, Deacon Giddings remarked, "Twelve o'clock, I declare! Jedediah Rittenhouse Pullman, you and I and the horses must have something to eat. The cow too, if she can stand still long enough."

Jed had been thinking of that very thing for the last mile or two, and he was glad enough to drive the cow into the tavern barn-yard.

Barlow stood at the gate for a minute or so after it was shut, and barked his best. Enough to last the cow while they were getting their dinners.

The tavern at Penniman's Corners was not so large as some there are in London and Paris and New York, but it was a wonderful thing to Jed, and so was the long dinner table, nearly three times as long as his mother's biggest table at home. There must have been more than two dozen people at that table.

"Jedediah," said the Deacon, before a great while, "you sit still. Eat all you can. I'm going to see about something."

Jed was busy with a great ear of boiled corn, and all he could do was to nod; but when he at last came out of the dining-room, there was news waiting for him.

A big son of Deacon Giddings had come on horseback to meet him, and Jed would not be needed any more, nor Barlow.

Jed's heart began to trouble him, in spite of the boiled corn.

"Oh, it's all right, Jedediah! You needn't feel bad about it. I've fixed a night's lodgin' for ye with Widder Simmons, right across the road there. She's to have a shillin' for it, and you can keep the other three, and go home in the mornin'. Here they are."

That was liberal, considering that Jed had driven the cow little more than half way to Topham, and Jed's face was bright again instantly.

The Deacon had a good deal more to say to him, but before long he, and his son, and the loaded team, and the cow disappeared in a cloud of dust up the north road.

For the first time in his life Jed felt lonely. The Deacon had taken him over and introduced him to Mrs. Simmons, and nobody could be blamed for feeling lonely in the same room with her. Jed could not remember seeing a smile on the face of Deacon Giddings, but then he had talked, and there was fun in him somewhere, and he had paid him his four shillings like a man. The Widow Simmons did not talk and she did not smile, and she looked at Jed through her silver-rimmed spectacles in a way that made him feel more and more alone in the world every minute.

Barlow had looked in her face just once, and then he had gone out in front of the house, and laid down in the grass.

Nearly an hour went by, or it seemed so to Jed, before he mustered courage to say, "May I go out, ma'am, and walk around a little?"

"Hain't ye walked fur enough for one day? I wonder your mother ever let such a mite of a thing go a-cattle-drovin'. Well, go 'long. Only don't you be late for supper. You won't git a bite if you be."

Jed was out of the house in a twinkling, with his hand on the pocket which contained his four shillings.

"Barlow, come here."

It was no use to say, "Come here," for Barlow was travelling down the home road as fast as his short legs could carry him. When he reached what he may have thought a safe distance, he sat down and barked back. It was his turn to say, "Come here," and Jed understood it.

"It's only seven miles home, and no cow. What's the use of my staying here?"

It was plain enough that Jed was thinking again, and he was counting those four bits of silver coin over and over. There would be only three of them left if he staid all night at Mrs. Simmons's. Two packs of crackers gone, at six and a quarter cents a pack.

"I'd have to walk home, after all, or pay for a ride, or catch on to some wagon. No, sir! I'm going now."

He was afraid to say as much to the widow. He did not even go near the house again.

As for Barlow, that active dog refused to even sit down another time on the grass of Penniman's Corners.

Jed was half afraid he might be headed off and stopped by somebody. Mrs. Simmons might come after him, and insist on his staying overnight and paying her that shilling. Somebody else might take the other three away from him.

It was a great trial to be travelling alone with so much money as that, and Barlow must have felt it more or less, for he did not even bark. He had very few chances to sit down, however, for Jed did not feel really safe until he could see the steeple of the village church, and he walked better than he ever had before.

He was a very tired boy when he reached the corner of his own street, there by Mr. Phillips's grocery, and he leaned up against the big poplar for a long look at the stack of boxes of fire-crackers.

"Ain't I glad I came back! Come here, Barlow."

But Barlow was lying down, with a large job of panting to do, and he did not come.

SOME INHABITANTS OF AFRICA.

BOYS and girls who have visited menageries have probably seen an animal shaped something like a horse, but beautifully adorned with black and tawny stripes, standing silent and sulky in its cage. This is the zebra, the wild horse of the great plains of Southern Africa. There it lives in great herds, and browses on the thin grass and low shrubs of the wilderness. It enjoys the widest liberty, and gallops and gambols merrily with its companions through regions where the foot of man rarely penetrates. It is not strange that when captured it refuses to be tamed, and retains its wild nature to the end. There are, however, exceptions to this rule. There are at present a pair of zebras in the Garden of Plants, at Paris, which, by the constant care and kindness of their young keeper, have gradually come to show a great affection for him, and will even allow him to harness them to a little carriage and drive them about the streets of Paris.

The zebra's chief weapons of defense are its lively little heels, which it uses vigorously when attacked. It is a very wise and cunning beast, and as its sharp ears detect the slightest rustling among the bushes, it is very difficult to approach. The hyenas leave the zebra in peace, and even lions and leopards rarely engage in battle with it. They are quite content to pounce upon the sickly members of

TAKING A DRINK.

the herd which have lagged behind their companions, and are alone and defenseless; for if any enemy attacks a herd, the sagacious animals at once form a circle, their heads facing the centre, and begin such a lively battery with their heels that the attacking party is glad to save himself by flight.

The mane of the zebra is thick, but very short, and forms an upright fringe from its forehead down the back of its neck to its body. Its skin is striped from the tip of its nose to the end of its tail, and down its legs to the hoof. The natives hunt it vigorously, as they prize its beautiful skin for personal adornment, and its meat is favorite food. They kill it with spears, or by pit-falls, in which the poor creatures get entangled, and are easily dispatched.

Large numbers of the zebra are shot by Europeans, who are covetous of its striped skin, while at the same time the meat gives abundant provision to their native followers. Mr. Stanley thus describes the killing of two of these beautiful creatures on the mountainous hunting grounds of Kitangeh, near the east coast of Africa: "It was not until we had walked briskly over a long stretch of tawny grass, crushed by sheer force through a brambly jungle, and trampled down a path through clumps of slender cane stalks, that we came at last in view of a small herd of zebras. These animals are so quick of scent and ear, and so vigilant with their eyes, that across an open space it is most difficult to stalk them. But by dint of tremendous exertion I contrived to approach within two hundred and fifty yards, taking advantage of every thin tussock of grass, and, almost at random, fired. One of the herd leaped from the ground, galloped a few short maddened strides, and then, on a sudden, staggered, kneeled, trembled, and fell over, its legs kicking the air. Its companions whinnied shrilly for their mate, and presently, wheeling in circles with graceful motion, advanced nearer, still whinnying, until I dropped another with a crashing ball through the head—much against my wish, for I think zebras were created for a better purpose than to be eaten."

The quagga and the dauw, both inhabitants of South Africa, resemble the zebra, but are not so regularly striped nor so brilliant in coloring. They are not so vicious in character, and are capable of being tamed. The quagga is made useful by the settlers near the Cape of Good Hope, and is taught to draw and to carry burdens. A settler once captured a zebra when it was a colt. The animal accustomed itself to captivity, and appeared so good-natured that its owner thought to make it as useful as the quagga. As a trial, he bridled it one day and jumped on its back. The animal at once began to rear furiously, and rushed with its rider into a deep river. The man clung desperately to the furious little beast, and was safely carried to the shore. But when he dismounted, the zebra turned in a rage, and suddenly bit his ear off. After that he concluded to remain content with his quagga team.

There are many kinds of large quadrupeds in Africa, some of which are native to no other country. Besides the three members of the zebra family, there is the harmless, shy giraffe, with its beautiful spotted body, its long, slender neck, and its delicate head, which it carries fifteen feet or more from the ground. This graceful animal is also hunted by the natives for its soft skin and its delicate flesh, which is considered a great dainty at a royal African feast.

One can imagine the peaceful life of these herbivorous animals of the great jungles, when not disturbed by the ravages of lions and other blood-thirsty beasts. In our engraving a pretty meeting of these creatures is represented. A company of zebras have gathered by a marshy pool to drink, while a huge two-horned rhinoceros, his great nose resting on a fallen tree, looks wonderingly at these uninvited guests to his particular swamp. Two zebras are in the water, eagerly drinking, while the others look up at the lord of the domain as if saying, "Excuse us, kind sir, and allow us to refresh ourselves a little, after galloping about in the sun; we will not trample the tall reeds half as much as you do yourself."

In the distance a crowd of shy giraffes are watching intently, as if they too were anxious to refresh themselves with a draught of cooling water.

AN ISLAND NEWSBOY.

ON THE WAY TO THE ISLAND.

WEIGHING THE BABY.

THE MERRY-GO-ROUND.

A STUDY OF [illegible].

THE UNINVITED GUEST.

BY ELLA M. BAKER.

"Molly, put the kettle on,
Molly, put the kettle on,
Molly, put the kettle on—
We'll all take tea."

THUS sang the cheerful mother of the Donald family, as she set the kettle of potatoes over the fire to boil for breakfast. The kettle was a tight fit for so many potatoes, and Bonny, looking on with interest from his high chair by the fire, remarked,

"Full, mamma; ain't it?"

"Yes, laddie, full as it can hold—just like our house."

"How it spatters and boils over, mamma!"

"And our house spatters and boils over with us, too, wee one."

Sure enough the Donald dozen did live in such a small tenement that it was a puzzle how they ever could all get packed into it at once.

But then early in the morning the father went out to his work; Alec followed to the shop, Jeanie to the store, Nickie to sell morning papers, some to school and some to do errands, till Bonny and the baby would be left alone with the mother. Then, shutting the door after the last, she would say,

"Do you see how they all boil away, Bonny?" and she would sing merrily as she scrubbed, swept, and cooked.

She did not sing so often after father Donald fell one day and broke a leg. Nor did she fill the kettle of potatoes as full either after that. Mr. Donald lay helpless, and worried about the place he feared he should lose.

"But I've worked for the house till it seems I could not work anywhere else. If they'd only promise to let me back again when I'm able, I'd bear the rest with an easy mind," said the sick man, getting fevered and flushed.

"Lad, I can't have you fret so," spoke his wife at last. She took down her bonnet and shawl. "I'll go and ask the master myself. I don't believe he'll refuse a woman, and you such a faithful hand. Bonny is so good he won't be any trouble to you, and I'll take the baby along."

So Bonny climbed up by the window, and watched his mother and the baby "boil away" like the rest.

Then Bonny played by himself a long while, it seemed to him. He built a church tower with his blocks, like the tower he could see shooting up above the low roofs. He changed the blocks into street cars, and dragged them up and down the window-sill. He thumbed his torn picture-books; he thumped his rag doll. Getting tired of all, he flattened his dear little soft nose against the pane, watching the people tramp, tramping by on the brick sidewalks, and the carts, drays, carriages, that clamp, clamped over the stony street. He liked this, and crooned over to himself, contentedly, tunes that were no tunes, and words that he made up as he went along.

But time went on, and still his mother did not come. Bonny grew hungry, and crept down to ask papa about it. Papa was lying quiet and breathing heavily. Bonny had fairly sung his father to sleep.

It occurred to Bonny, as he tiptoed back, that there could be no good reason why he should not go and find his mother, or else Jeanie, or Nickie, or Ted. Jeanie's old red cape hung in the corner; quickly he threw it over his yellow head, and holding it fast under his chin with one hand, he lifted the latch and stepped forth.

He walked slowly and thoughtfully off in the direction he had seen his mother take, with short, nipping steps, like a meditative chickabiddy's. He had not a doubt that he should come to some member of his numerous family before long, but meanwhile he was thinking less of that than of the sights by the way. Two boys were racing velocipedes. To Bonny that was a splendid sight.

"I wist I had a velohorsipede," he whispered, with a pensive air.

On and on he plodded, blissfully bewildered, absorbed in these enchanting visions, until he found himself before a caterer's show window, tempting with crisp loaves of bread, daintily frosted cakes, and unspeakable cookies, tarts, jellies.

"Oh my! oh my!" cried Bonny, beginning at last to remember that he was nobody but a little hungry boy. "I'm hungry—I'm so hungry!"

While he stared with all his longing eyes, he heard these words spoken loudly right by his side, "Come on, then; we shall be sure of a good dinner."

Bonny turned round. Two men in tall black hats were striding by, and one, as he spoke, clapped the other on the shoulder. The invitation was not meant for Bonny at all. But that did not make any difference to him. He simply received the idea that if he followed these two men he should get to a dinner. So he pressed sturdily after them. He had to walk fast, and sometimes he almost lost sight of them in the throng. But Bonny was so hungry by this time that he was very much in earnest. He did not stop to watch the people, nor to look into any more shop windows.

It was really not long before the two tall hats were seen turning up some low, broad steps. The panting Bonny, tugging after, followed unnoticed through a wide door into a vast hall, all paved with marble. Quite confused and out of breath, Bonny suddenly stood still. Where he had lost sight of the two tall hats and the wearers of them he did not know.

"Seems like another out-doors," the child thought, looking up at the high ceiling; "but where's the dinner? There *is* a dinner; I smell it; it smells good. Seems to me I never did smell so much dinner in my life."

By this time he also became aware of a cheerful clatter of dishes and voices; and following the sound across the wide hall, he pushed open a great door that stood half ajar.

Sure enough, there before him lay table after table, adorned with spotless linen, and spread temptingly not only with flowers and fruit, but with plenty to eat.

How should little Bonny know that this was the day when the grand new Metropolis Hotel first opened to the public? How should he know that here were all the mighty men of the city—merchants, editors, ministers even—with their wives, met together by invitation to celebrate the dedication dinner? You see, they had not invited Bonny: nobody expected him; so at first nobody noticed him as he slipped noiselessly in.

The tables seemed so full of people that Bonny had to walk up the room to find a place. A queer hush fell on the clatter and the chatter. People dropped their forks. They watched this little figure with the sunny hair, the happy face, the shabby shoes, the tumbled check apron, that dragged after it the well-nigh forgotten red cape, and at last mounting into an empty chair, said, with a sigh of satisfaction, and in a very clear voice, "I want dinner, please."

Bonny glanced round him. He thought everybody looked pleased, and catching the eye of a lady who bent toward him, he smiled back a shy, friendly smile.

This lady was the first to speak to him. She crossed eagerly over and said, "May I sit beside you, dear? I knew a little boy once with yellow hair like yours."

Bonny never noticed that she had tears in her soft eyes now.

"I like your hair best," he answered, half timidly, half frankly. The lady's hair was very dark, and she wore in it a splendid yellow flower.

"But, please, I am so hungry! May I have dinner?"

Before the lady could answer, a stout gentleman came hurrying up.

"Well, well, let's see about this," he began, in a rollicking tone. "Shake hands, little stranger. So you came to my dinner, did you?"

Bonny dropped his head. He was rather afraid of the loud-voiced man; but the lady whom he was not afraid of said, re-assuringly, "This is the man who gives the dinner, little one; this is his house; he'll be very good to you, never fear."

So Bonny looked up then, and replied, simply, "I came; I was hungry, and I came."

The host cleared his throat, and said, heartily, while he patted Bonny's curls, "Well, I didn't expect you, that's a fact; but we'll give you just as good a dinner, for all that. A dinner?—I'll warrant you we will; and upon my word, ladies and gentlemen, I rather think the Metropolis Hotel is honored to have the chance."

Never, never had Bonny imagined such a dinner as he ate that day. The lady who sat by his side cut up the chicken, and helped him choose among the lavish dainties that the host kept insisting on having brought for him to taste.

Hungry? It seemed to Bonny that he never in this world could be hungry again.

His innocent heart ran over, and he told his new friend, the lady, all she asked him about his sick father, his tired mother, the little tenement that was like the kettle that all boiled away, and the big family that crammed it so full when gathered together. But one thing neither the lady, nor her husband, who filled Bonny's pocket with pennies, nor the host, could succeed in finding out from him.

This was where the little fellow belonged, and how to return him to his home.

Street and number he knew naught about. What was his name? "Bonny Laddie." His father's name? "Oh, John." What kind of work did his father do? "Oh, nothing; father is sick." He had no clear ideas associated with any calling except with Nickie's, as they found by questioning.

That Nickie peddled papers, and that Bonny would when he was bigger, he was very positive about.

"Well, then," suggested the host, "we'll try the newsboys. We'll just have Laddie standing by the door when they go past, and maybe he can pick out this brother of his from the lot."

The company sat for a long time round the tables. Bonny kept still, listening and wondering, though he understood little of the speeches and the toasts. Once all eyes were again turned toward Bonny.

A gentleman rose and said, "Ladies and gentlemen, I beg to propose the health of the first guest of the Metropolis Hotel, who, though uninvited, has given the patriarch of this palace the privilege of entertaining an angel unawares."

But Bonny answered nothing to the looks bent upon him. With one hand full of nuts and bonbons, the other in his heavy pocket, and a face of perfect peace, the little guest of the Metropolis Hotel lay fast asleep in his chair.

He was really awake again by the time the newsboys were crying their evening papers.

"Come and watch for Nickie," coaxed the host; and with Bonny's small, warm hand in his own he stepped out on the broad granite slab in front of the hotel.

"That isn't Nickie—nor that—nor that," Bonny kept saying at first. "Oh, Nickie!" he shouted, suddenly; and plunging forth into the street, tumbled against a small boy in big trousers and an overgrown cap, whose bundle of papers looked much fatter than he did.

Astonished Nickie, who had not been home since morning, could scarcely believe his senses at first, as he stared at his little brother through the dusk, the fog, and the rain-drops that now began to fall. However, he could answer all the questions that Laddie had been unable to satisfy, and in a very short interval a carriage had been summoned, the host had stowed away in it a capacious basket hastily filled with choice remnants from the feast, and Bonny Laddie was rolling toward his home in charge of the gentle stranger lady and her husband.

Was there ever in the most agitated of kettles such bubbling and boiling over as took place inside the crowded Donald tenement that night? Had not they all been breaking their loving, anxious hearts about Bonny Laddie, and lo! here he was, safe in the old red cape, smiling and shining as usual, and rather mystified at having such a fuss made over him.

The stranger lady, promising Bonny to come again, made haste to go away, but before going she had time to wonder at something she saw. Why did Bonny's tired but blithe-looking mother give the lady's husband such a sad, almost fearful, look? Why did he seem confused, and going over to the sick man, say, "I will reconsider that matter, John. You may rest easy"?

Afterward she understood. When John's master had that afternoon curtly refused Mrs. Donald's petition, and let her go away disappointed and distressed, her patient waiting and her earnest pleading having been in vain, he had considered himself right, from the stand-point of his own interest. But then he had known nothing of the clean, crowded household, and nothing of this yellow-haired laddie who reminded him of another little yellow-haired laddie who had been taken from him.

[Begun in Harper's Young People No. 37, July 13.]

THE STORY OF THE AMERICAN NAVY.

BY BENSON J. LOSSING.

Chapter VIII.

AFTER an almost uneventful cruise, excepting the capture of the British war schooner *Pictou*, and a chase by two British frigates, the gallant and "lucky" *Constitution* remained in Boston eight or nine months. Late in December, 1814, she sailed from Boston for the Bay of Biscay, in command of Captain Charles Stewart, equipped with fifty-two guns and fully manned. She cruised for a while off the port of Lisbon and farther southward; and late in February, 1815, she met, fought, and conquered the English frigate *Cyane* and her consort the *Levant*. The battle occurred in the night—the moon shining brightly. For fifteen minutes the three vessels kept up an incessant cannonade, and the moon was obscured by a dense cloud of smoke. By superior seamanship as well as gunnery, Stewart vanquished both his antagonists, while the *Constitution* was only slightly injured.

Stewart sailed with his prizes to Port Praya, Cape de Verde Islands. The next day three large British vessels were dimly seen in a fog approaching. The *Constitution* slipped out of the harbor under cover of the mist, followed by her prizes. The English vessels gave chase, but Stewart, by expert seamanship, saved his own ship and the *Cyane* from capture, but the *Levant* was overtaken and caught. This was the final cruise of the *Constitution* in the war of 1812–15, for peace had been proclaimed before this victory was achieved. "Old Ironsides" was ever afterward revered by the American people, and she is yet afloat in the service.

In 1814 Lake Champlain as well as Lake Ontario was a theatre of valiant deeds. In September a land and naval force invaded New York from Canada. The Americans had created a little navy on Lake Champlain to oppose the British, and placed it in charge of Commodore Macdonough. The hostile fleets met in Plattsburg Bay, and while a sharp conflict was raging between the land forces, a severe naval battle was fought on the lake. The British Commodore (Downie) was killed, and Macdonough achieved a brilliant victory, for which he was honored by citizens and by Congress. Meanwhile, Chauncey and Sir

COMMODORE PERRY'S SHIPS IN THE BAY OF JEDDO.

James L. Yeo were manœuvring for the control of Lake Ontario without coming to any very serious blows.

In the summer of 1814 some new vessels were added to the navy. In June the frigate *Guerrière* was launched at Philadelphia in the presence of 50,000 people. In August the *Java* was launched at Baltimore before 20,000 spectators. The public and private vessels were very active. Indeed, the story of the cruises of some of the privateers at this time might be made as exciting as any tale of fiction.

The *Wasp*, Captain Blakeley, made a successful cruise southward, vanquishing the *Reindeer*, *Avon*, and *Atlanta*. She was lost at sea in October, 1814, and was never heard of afterward. Captain Warrington cruised in the *Peacock* in the spring of 1814. He captured the *Epervier*, a most valuable prize. In May he crossed the Atlantic to the Bay of Biscay, captured fourteen merchant vessels, and returned to New York. At the same time Barney was very active with a flotilla of gun-boats on the waters of Chesapeake Bay, and in August, having destroyed his vessels to keep them from the British, he and his men assisted in the battle of Bladensburg.

At the beginning of 1815, Decatur was in command of a small squadron at New York. The *President* was his flag-ship. With her alone he sailed out of New York Harbor on a dark night, eluded the blockading fleet, and at dawn the next morning was chased by four British vessels. The *President* was deeply laden for a long cruise. One of her pursuers (the *Endymion*) overtook her, when a sharp action began. The two frigates ran side by side before the wind for two hours in a running fight, during which the *Endymion* was so crippled that she was about to strike her colors. At that moment the other pursuers came up, and the *President* was captured, not by a single vessel, but by a squadron.

The other vessels of Decatur's squadron, ignorant of the fate of the *President*, sailed for an appointed gathering-place in the South Atlantic Ocean. Captain Biddle, in the *Hornet*, captured the *Penguin* in March, after a conflict which called forth the highest praises for the American commander. Afterward, while the *Hornet* and *Peacock* were sailing together, they were chased by the *Cornwallis*, a British 74. They escaped, and the *Peacock*, continuing her cruise eastward, captured the *Nautilus* in the Straits of Sunda, the last vessel captured in the war.

The American privateers made such havoc among English shipping that the mercantile community were dismayed. "One of these sea-devils," said a London newspaper, "is seldom caught; but they impudently defy the English privateers and heavy 74's. Only think—thirteen guineas for one hundred pounds were paid to insure a vessel across the Irish Channel!" They had captured or destroyed during the war about sixteen hundred British merchant vessels of all classes. Our little navy had produced a wonderful change in public opinion in Europe concerning the resources and power of the United States. It had achieved the independence of the Republic.

In time of peace our navy has been employed in the beneficent work of giving aid to commerce; in making explorations of strange seas; in scientific investigations of ocean phenomena; and in the important operations of the Coast Survey, begun in 1817. The most conspicuous of the peaceful performances of our navy were known respectively as the "South Sea Exploring Expedition" and the "Japan Diplomatic Expedition." The former began in 1838, and ended in 1842. It was composed of six government vessels, furnished with a complete corps of scientific men, and was commanded by Lieutenant Charles Wilkes. It went southward until it reached pack ice, in south latitude 66°, and made a voyage of about ninety thousand miles.

The Japan Diplomatic Expedition consisted of a squadron of seven vessels, commanded by Commodore M. C. Perry. Its business was to carry a letter to the Emperor of Japan from the President of the United States, who asked him to open his sea-ports to American commerce. The expedition sailed in the fall of 1852, and reached Japan in 1853. Perry was met on the bosom of the bay of Jeddo, in which his squadron had anchored, by high officials in the Emperor's state barges, and to them the object of the expedition was made known. The Japanese were astonished, for they had never seen a steam-ship. After several months' consideration the Emperor agreed to the President's request, and in 1860 he sent an embassy to the United States. Ever since then there has been free intercourse between the two nations.

[TO BE CONTINUED.]

"I AM THE LAD THAT FOLLOWS THE PLOUGH."

BY MARY A. BARR.

I am the lad that follows the plough—
  Robin and Thrush just whistle for me—
In a hickory suit that's pretty well worn
I go to the field at early morn,
I help to scatter the golden corn—
  Robin and Thrush just whistle for me.

Out in the meadows and woods and leas—
  Robin and Thrush just whistle for me—
I watch the sheep and the lambs at play;
When the grass is high I turn the hay;
There isn't a boy in the world so gay—
  Robin and Thrush just whistle for me.

I go with father to shear the sheep—
  Robin and Thrush just whistle for me—
I fodder the cattle, the mangers fill,
I drive a team, I go to the mill,
I milk the cows with a right good will—
  Robin and Thrush just whistle for me.

I help the preacher and please to serve—
  Robin and Thrush just whistle for me—
For I am the boy can climb a tree;
There isn't an apple too high for me,
There isn't a nut that I can't see—
  Robin and Thrush just whistle for me.

When I am a man I'll own a farm—
  Robin and Thrush just whistle for me—
Horses and sheep and many a cow,
Stacks of wheat, and a barley mow;
I'll be a farmer and follow the plough:
  Robin and Thrush shall whistle for me.

'Tis better to stand in the golden corn—
  Robin and Thrush just whistle for me—
To toss the hay on the breezy lea,
To pluck the fruit on the orchard tree,
Than roam about on the restless sea;
  No, sailor-boy, I'll follow the plough.

'Tis better to hear the wild birds sing,
  Robin and Thrush on the apple bough—
'Tis better to have a farm and a wife,
And lead a busy, peaceable life,
Than march to the noisy drum and fife:
  No, soldier-boy, I'll follow the plough.

MUSIC BY CHAS. F. ROPER.

OUR POST-OFFICE BOX

ed an act to prevent the slave trade, inflicting a heavy fine upon any citizen of the commonwealth who should import, transport, buy, or sell any of the inhabitants of Africa as slaves, or fit out vessels to be employed in the traffic.

Public feeling was for a long time hostile to the negro race, and during the early part of the present century "blacks" were repeatedly warned to depart out of the commonwealth, the pretext being to avoid the increase of a pauper population, "which threatened to become both injurious and burdensome."

C. S. M.—About what animal do you desire to know the habits? You left your sentence unfinished.

Alice P.—Turtles prefer bits of meat and insects to bread-crumbs. If you read former numbers of the Post-office Box carefully, you will find directions for feeding all kinds of turtles.

Camille B.—The poem by your little sick friend is very pretty, but we can not make room for it.

Pearl A. H.—Your story is very pretty, but comes too late for publication.—You must send to the address of the advertiser for the catalogue you wish.

J. L. Towne.—Directions for building a canvas canoe were given in Young People No. [illegible]. There is an interesting paper entitled "The Cruising Canoe and its Outfit" in Harper's Magazine for August, 1880, which will also give you much useful information.

Favors are acknowledged from [illegible]

Correct answers to puzzles are received from [illegible]

PUZZLES FROM YOUNG CONTRIBUTORS.

No. 1.

ENIGMA.

My first is in note, but not in heard.
[illegible]
Where snow lies deep on the frozen ground.
W. D.

No. 2.

WORD SQUARE.

First, a [illegible]. Second, an ancient continent. Third, a river in [illegible]. Fourth, a sign.

No. 3.

[illegible]

A city in New York State. Mountains in Asia. A river in Asia. A city in China. A lake in the United States. Answer—Two rivers in [illegible].

No. 4.

[illegible]

[illegible]

No. 5.

[illegible]

In market. A fruit. An article useful in drawing. A number. In grapes. R. AND M.

No. 6.

[illegible]

1. A beautiful flower composed of [illegible] letters.
[illegible]

ANSWERS TO PUZZLES IN No. 41.

No. 1. Maggie, Parrot.

No. 2. [illegible]

Hellespont, Mignonette.

No. 3. Full fathom five thy father lies.

No. 4. [illegible]

No. 5. Miles Standish.

No. 6. Aristotle.

HISTORICAL ANECDOTE.

If the blanks in the Historical Anecdote published in No. 41 of the Young People are filled by the following words in the order in which they are given, the story will be complete:

Richard Cœur de Lion.	Richard.
Richard I.	Leopold.
England.	Henry VI.
Henry II.	Germany.
[illegible]	Richard.
Palestine.	Austria.
1191.	Leopold's.
Philip Augustus.	Richard.
France.	Henry VI.
Holy Land.	John Lackland.
Philip Augustus.	England.
Richard.	Richard.
Leopold.	Blondel.
Austria.	England.
St. Jean d'Acre.	Henry VI.
England.	Richard.

ADVERTISEMENTS.

THE BIRD-EATING SPIDER.—(See Page 646.)

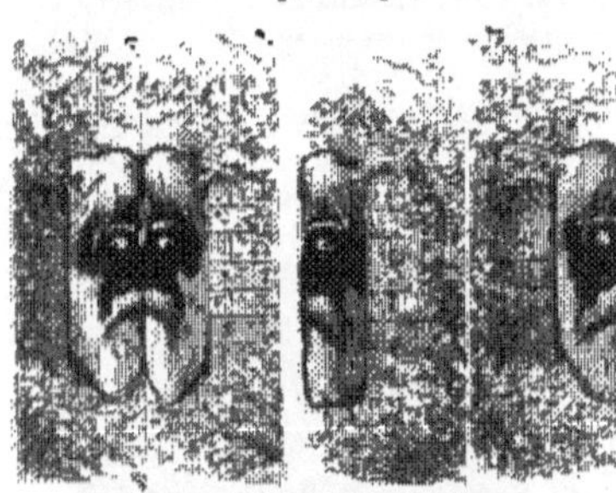

Fig. 1. Fig. 2.

SOLUTION OF RAJAH PUZZLE.

WITH the scissors cut from *A* to *B* in Fig. 1, and arrange the parts as in Fig. 2.

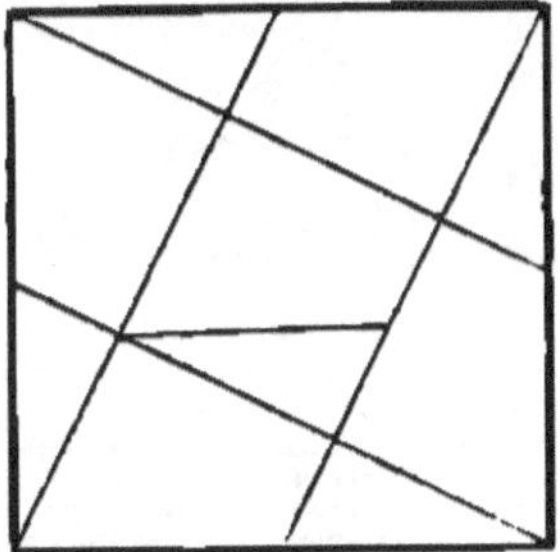

THE SQUARE PUZZLE.

ANSWER to the Square Puzzle given in No. 41 of Harper's Young People.

A MUSICAL ANECDOTE.

ONE very cold morning last winter an old gentleman seized his hat and , and started out for a walk. He had not gone very far before he heard a sound. His first impulse was to around and keep a look-out to ascertain the cause of all this noise. In a few minutes he saw a away horse coming toward him. He immediately sprang to the fence; but in attempting to it he tripped on the first , and fell upon the ground. Shaking with fear, he crept under the fence, and hid behind a of wood just as the horse past. Tired out, breathless, and quite unable to move, he sat down to . A short space of , perhaps a of an hour, elapsed before he continued his walk, but hardly had he travelled a of a mile when he came to a . "What are you doing on my property?" called a voice. "Do you want me to you hand and foot, and send you to prison?" "Why use such strong , friend?" said the old gentleman, with a in his voice. "Because I am quite certain you are the man who stole a of my nice canvas-back ducks yesterday." "I will not allow any one to cast a upon my name," said our hero, in his tone of voice: "I came here to , and for no other purpose." But in spite of all he could say, the angry man led him to the neighboring town, where he was tried, and fully acquitted. His can still be seen in the court register.

Agnes (who has seized a favorable opportunity of trying Aunty's frill on Baby). "There, now, keep still till I see how you'll look when you're older."

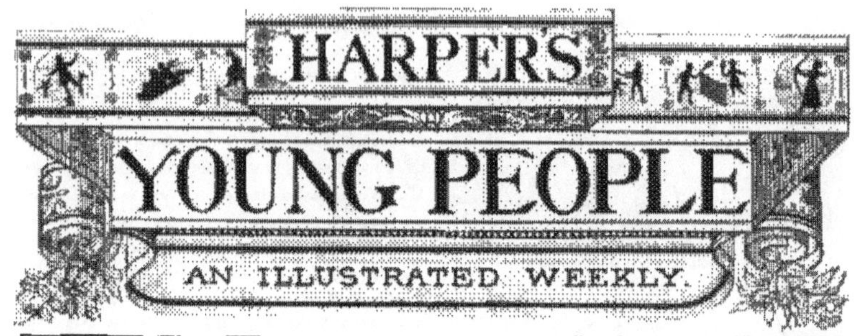
HARPER'S
YOUNG PEOPLE
AN ILLUSTRATED WEEKLY.

Vol. I.—No. 45. | Published by HARPER & BROTHERS, New York. | Price Four Cents.

Tuesday, September 7, 1880. | Copyright, 1880, by Harper & Brothers. | $1.50 per Year, in Advance.

LIGHT-HOUSE SKETCHES.

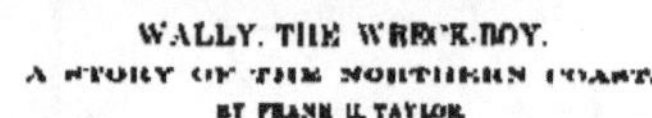

WALLY, THE WRECK-BOY.

A STORY OF THE NORTHERN COAST.

BY FRANK H. TAYLOR.

HIS real name is Wallace, but his mates always called him "Wally," and although he is now a big broad-shouldered young mariner, he is still pointed out as the "wreck-boy." One summer not long ago Wally sailed with me for a week out upon the blue waters across the bar after blue-fish, or among the winding tide-water creeks for sheep's-head, and it was then, by means of many questions, that I heard the following story.

Wally's father was a light-house keeper. The great brick tower stood aloft among the sand-hills, making the little house which nestled at its base look dwarfish and cramped.

Wally was about twelve years old, and seldom had the good fortune to find a playmate. Two miles down the beach, at Three Pine Point, stood a handsome cottage that was occupied by Mr. Burton, a city gentleman and a great ship-owner, during the summer, and sometimes his daughter Elsie, a bright-eyed little girl, would come riding along the sands from the cottage behind a small donkey, and ask Wally to show her his "museum."

It was a matter of great pride with the boy to exhibit the many curious shells, bits of sea-weed, sharks' teeth, fish bones, and the full-rigged ships he had whittled out and completed on winter nights, and Elsie was an earnest listener to all his explanations, showing him in return the pictures she had made in her sketch-book.

Not far from the light-house stood a life-saving station—a strong two-story building, shingled upon its sides to make it warmer. Here, through the winter months, lived a crew of brave fishermen, who were always ready to launch the life-boat, and go out through the stormy waters to help shipwrecked sailors.

Wally was a favorite here, and spent much of his time listening to the tales they told of ocean dangers and escapes; but he liked best of all to trudge along the sands with the guard on dark nights, lantern in hand, watching for ships in distress. The captain of the crew, who was an old seaman, taught him the use of the compass and quadrant, and other matters of navigation, while the rest showed him how to pull an oar, steer, and swim, until he could manage a boat as well as any of them.

Just before sunset each day Wally's father climbed the iron steps of the light tower, and started the lamp, which slowly revolved within the great crystal lens, flashing out four times each minute its beam of warning across the stormy waters. Every few hours it was the watcher's duty to pump oil into a holder above the light, from which it flowed in a steady stream to the round wicks below. If this was neglected, the lamp would cease to burn.

Wally, who was an ingenious boy, had placed a small bit of mirror in his little bedroom in the attic so that as he lay in bed he could see the reflection of the flash across the waters. One wild October evening he had watched it until he fell asleep, and in the night was awakened by the roaring gusts of the gale which swept over the lonely sands, and he missed the faithful flash upon his mirror. *The light had gone out!*

Many ships out upon the sea were sailing to and fro, and there was no light to guide them or warn them of dangerous shoals. Nearer and nearer some of them were drifting to their fate, and still the beacon gave no warning of danger.

The light-keeper, hours before, had gone out upon the narrow gallery about the top of the tower to look at the storm, just as a large wild fowl, bewildered by the glare, had flown with great speed toward it, and striking the keeper's head, had laid him senseless upon the iron grating.

I have seen fractures in the lenses, or glass reflectors, of light-houses as large as your two fists, such as it would require a heavy sledge-hammer to break by human force, caused by the fierce flight of wild fowl; and a netting of iron wire is usually spread upon three sides of the lens as a protection to the light. Sometimes a large number of dead birds will be found at the foot of the light-house in the morning after a stormy autumn night, when wild-geese are flying southward.

Wally sprang from his bed, full of dread lest his father had fallen to the ground; for he knew he would never sleep at his post of duty. But first in his thoughts was the need of starting the lamp again. Calling to his mother, he sped up the spiral stairway, which never seemed so long before, and began to pump the oil. Then he lighted the wick from a small lantern hanging in the watch-room, and pumped again until the oil tank was quite full. His mother in the mean time had found the form of the keeper, and partially restored him. Wally stepped out upon the gallery to find his father's hat, and looking seaward, saw something which for a moment made him sick with terror. In the midst of the breakers lay a large square-rigged vessel, helplessly pounding to pieces upon the outer bar. In the intervals of the wind's moaning Wally could hear the despairing cries of those on board, who seemed to call to him to save them.

The life-saving station was not yet opened for the season. The captain and his men lived upon the mainland, across a wide and swift-flowing channel in the marsh, called the "Thoroughfare." To reach them was of the most vital importance, for their hands only could drag out and man the heavy surf-boat, or fire the mortar, and rig the life-car.

All this passed through Wally's mind in a few seconds, and knowing that his helpless father could do nothing, and that an alarm might make him worse, he sped silently down the stairway, and setting fire to a "Coston torch," such as are used by the coast-guard in cases of wreck, he rushed from the house, swinging the torch, that burned with a bright red flame, above his head as he ran.

Half a mile across the sands there was a small boat landing, where a skiff usually lay moored.

Toward this Wally sped with all his strength; but, alas! the waves had lifted it, the winds had broken it from its moorings, and it was floating miles away down the "Thoroughfare," and now Wally stood upon the landing, in the blackness of the night, full of despair. He might swim, but he had never tried half the width of the channel before. He looked into the blackness beyond, and hesitated; then at the light-house, where his mother still sat in the little watch-room ministering to his injured father; then he thought of the poor men out in the breakers, whose lives depended upon his reaching the crew.

But a moment longer he stood, and then throwing off his coat, he tied a sleeve securely about a post so it would be known, in case he should fail, how he had lost his life. And now he was in the icy water. The wind helped him along; but the incoming tide swept him far out of his course. As he gained the middle of the channel he thought how bitter the consequences might be to his father if the crew of the ship were lost, for who would believe the story of the wild fowl's blow! This nerved his tired arms, but the effort was too much for his strength. He paused, and threw up his arms. As his form sank beneath the waves, his toes touched the muddy bottom, and his hand swept among some weeds. One more effort as he came to the surface, and now he could stand with his mouth out of water. A moment's rest, and he was tearing aside the dense flags that bordered the channel.

The captain, a good mile from the Thoroughfare, had left his warm bed to fasten a loose window-shutter, when he saw a small form tottering toward him, and Wally fell, weak and voiceless, at his feet. Restoratives were brought, and the boy told his story.

Ten minutes later half a dozen of the crew were on their way to the landing, Wally, now fully recovered, foremost among them. He seemed to possess wonderful strength. They crossed the channel, and dragged out the great life-boat from its house. It hardly appeared possible to launch it in such a sea, but each man, in his excitement, had the strength of two, and without waiting to be bid, Wally leaped into the stern and grasped the helm.

"Well done, boy!" cried the captain; "I'll take an oar; we need all help to-night."

Through the night the faithful crew pulled, bringing load after load of men, women, and children from the wreck of the *Argonaut* to the shore, until all were saved. The little house under the light was well filled, and the sailors were crowded into the life-saving station.

"Where is my father?" asked Wally; and as a man came forward with his head bandaged, in reply, the boy sank down, and a blackness came over his eyes.

When he recovered he was in a beautiful room, into which the sun shone, lighting up the bright walls, pictures, and carpets. He was on a pretty bedstead, and a strange lady sat by the window talking to his mother.

He thought it all a dream. The door opened, and Mr. Burton came in, dressed in a fisherman's suit. How queer he looked in such a garb! and Wally laughed at the sight, and thought that when he awoke he would tell his mother about it.

It happened that the ship which had come ashore was one belonging to Mr. Burton, who was on board, returning from a trip to the Mediterranean. So he had opened the cottage at Three Pine Point, and as the little house under the light was full, had insisted upon having Wally, with some others, brought to his summer home, where he could care for them.

Everybody had learned of the boy's brave swim, all had seen him in the life-boat, and they were anxious to have him recover soon.

Wally, too, learned that the ship had become helpless long before she had struck the shore, and that her loss was not caused by his father's mishap.

When Wally had recovered, Mr. Burton and some of the other passengers insisted upon taking him to the city, where they had a full suit of wrecker's clothes made for him—cork jacket, sou'wester, and all. He was also presented with a silver watch and a medal for his bravery. When he was dressed in his new suit, Miss Elsie made a sketch of him, whereupon Wally blushed more than he had done during all the praises lavished upon him.

At the close of the next summer Mr. Burton arranged with the light-keeper to let him send Wally to a city school, and for the next four years the boy lived away from the little house on the sands, making only occasional visits to his home.

Then Mr. Burton took him into his office, where he worked faithfully for two years; but his old life by the sea caused a longing for a sailor's career, and his employer wisely allowed him to go upon a cruise in one of his ships. Upon the following voyage he was made a mate, and this year he is to command a new ship now being built. Captain Wally was asked the other day to suggest a name for the new craft, and promptly gave as his choice the *Elsie*.

And Elsie Burton, who is now an artist, has painted two pictures for the Captain's cabin. One is called "The Loss of the *Argonaut*," and the other, "Wally, the Wreck-Boy."

[Begun in No. [illegible] of Harper's Young People, June 1.]

THE MORAL PIRATES.

BY W. L. ALDEN.

Chapter XV.

THERE was only one fault to be found with Brandt Lake—there was hardly anything to shoot in its vicinity. Occasionally a deer could be found; but at the season of the year when the boys were at the lake it was contrary to law to kill deer. It was known that there were bears in that part of the country as well as lynxes—or catamounts, as they are generally called; but they were so scarce that no one thought of hunting them. Harry did succeed in shooting three pigeons and a quail, and Tom shot a gray squirrel; but the bears, deer, catamounts, and ducks that they had expected to shoot did not show themselves.

On the other hand, they had any quantity of fishing. Perch and cat-fish swarmed all around the island; and large pickerel, some of them weighing six or eight pounds, could be caught by trolling. Two miles farther north was another lake that was full of trout, and the boys visited it several times, and found out how delicious a trout is when it is cooked within half an hour after it is taken from the water. In fact, they lived principally upon fish, and became so dainty that they would not condescend to cook any but the choicest trout and the plumpest cat-fish and pickerel.

It must be confessed that there was a good deal of monotony in their daily life. In the morning somebody went for milk, after which breakfast was cooked and eaten. Then one of the boys would take the gun and tramp through the woods in the hope of finding something to shoot, while the others would either go fishing or lie in the shade. Once they devoted a whole day to sailing entirely around the lake in the boat, and another day a long rainstorm kept them inside of the tent most of the time. With these exceptions, one day was remarkably like another; and at the end of two weeks they began to grow a little tired of camping, and to remember that there were ways of enjoying themselves at home.

Their final departure from their island camp was caused by an accident. They had decided to row to the southern end of the lake, and engage a team to meet them the following week, and to carry them to Glenn's Falls, where they intended to ship the boat on board a canal-boat bound for New York, and to return home by rail. To avoid the heat of the sun, they started down the lake immediately after breakfast, and forgot to put out the fire before they left the island.

After they had rowed at least a mile, Tom, who sat facing the stern, noticed a light wreath of smoke rising from the island, and remarked, "Our fire is burning yet; we ought not to have gone and left it."

Harry looked back, and saw that the cloud of smoke was rapidly increasing.

"It's not the fire that's making all that smoke," he exclaimed.

"What is it, then?" asked Tom.

"Perhaps it's water," said Joe. "I always thought that where there was smoke there must be fire; but Harry says it isn't fire."

"I mean," continued Harry, "that we didn't leave fire enough to make so much smoke. It must have spread and caught something."

"Caught the tent, most likely," said Tom. "Let's row back right away and put it out."

"What's the use?" interrupted Jim. "That tent is as dry as tinder, and will burn up before we can get half way there."

"We must get back as soon as we can," cried Harry. "All our things are in the tent. Row your best, boys, and we may save them yet."

The boat was quickly turned and headed toward the camp.

"There's one reason why I'm not particularly anxious to help put that fire out," Joe remarked, as they approached the island, and could see that a really alarming fire was in progress.

"What's that?" asked Harry.

"As near as I can calculate, there must be about two pounds—"

He was interrupted by a loud report from the island, and a shower of pebbles, sticks, and small articles—among which a shoe and a tin pail were recognized—shot into the air.

"—of powder," Joe continued, "in the flask. I thought it would blow up; and now that it's all gone, I don't mind landing on the island."

"Everything must be ruined," exclaimed Jim.

"Lucky for us that we put on our shoes this morning," Tom remarked, as he rowed steadily on. "That must have been one of my other pair that just went up."

When they reached the island they could not at first land, on account of the heat of the flames; but they could plainly see that the tent and everything in it had been totally destroyed. After waiting for half an hour the fire burned itself out, so that they could approach their dock and land on the smoking ash heap that an hour before had been such a beautiful shady spot. There was hardly anything left that was of any use. A tin pan, a fork, and the hatchet were found uninjured; but all their clothing and other stores were either burned to ashes or so badly scorched as to be useless. Quite overwhelmed by their disaster, the boys sat down and looked at one another.

"We've got to go home now, whether we want to or not," Harry said, as he poked the ashes idly with a stick.

"Well, we meant to go home in a few days anyway," said Tom; "so the fire hasn't got very much the better of us."

"But I hate to have everything spoiled, and to have to go in this sort of way. Our tin pans and fishing-tackle aren't worth much, but all our spare clothes have gone."

"You've got your uncle's gun in the boat, so that's all right," suggested Tom, encouragingly. "As long as the gun and the boat are *safe*, we needn't mind about a few flannel shirts and things."

"But it's such a pity to be driven away, when we were having such a lovely time," continued Harry.

"That's rubbish, Harry," said Joe. "We were all beginning to get tired of camping out. I think it's jolly to have the cruise end this way, with a lot of fire-works. It's like the transformation scene at the theatre. Besides, it saves us the trouble of carrying a whole lot of things back with us."

"The thing to do now," remarked Tom, "is to row right down to the outlet, and get a team to take us to Glenn's Falls this afternoon. We can't sleep here, unless we build a hut, and then we wouldn't have a blanket to cover us. Don't let's waste any more time talking about it."

"That's so. Take your places in the boat, boys, and we'll start for home." So saying, Harry led the way to the boat, and in a few moments the *Whitewing* was homeward bound.

The boys were lucky enough to find a man who engaged to take them to Glenn's Falls in time to catch the afternoon train for Albany. They stopped at the Falls only long enough to see the *Whitewing* safely on board a canal-boat, and they reached Albany in time to go down the river on the night boat.

After a supper that filled the colored waiters with astonishment, the boys selected arm-chairs on the forward deck, and began to talk over the cruise. They all agreed that they had had a splendid time, in spite of hard work and frequent wettings.

"We'll go on another cruise next summer, sure," said Harry. "Where shall we go?"

Tom was the first to reply. Said he, "I've been thinking that we can do better than we did this time."

"How so?" asked the other boys.

"The *Whitewing* is an awfully nice boat," Tom continued, "but she is too small. We ought to have a boat that we can sleep in comfortably, and without getting wet every night."

"But then," Harry suggested, "you couldn't drag a bigger boat round a dam."

"We can't drag the *Whitewing* round much of a dam. She's too big to be handled on land, and too little to be comfortable. Now here's my plan."

"Let's have it," cried the other boys.

"We can hire a cat-boat about twenty feet long, and she'll be big enough, so that we can rig up a canvas cabin at night. We can anchor her, and sleep on board her every night. We can carry mattresses, so we needn't sleep on stones and stumps—"

"And coffee-pots," interrupted Joe.

"—and we can take lots of things, and live comfortably. We can sail instead of rowing; and though I like to row as well as the next fellow, we've had a little too much of that. Now we'll get a cat-boat next summer, and we'll cruise from New York Bay to Montauk Point. We can go all the way through the bays on the south side, and there are only three places where we will have to get a team of horses to drag the boat across a little bit of flat meadow. I know all about it, for I studied it out on the map one day. What do you say to that for a cruise?"

"I'll go," said Harry.

"And I'll go," said Jim.

"Hurrah for the cat-boat!" said Joe. "We can be twice as moral and piratical in a sail-boat as we can in a row-boat, even if it is the dear little *Whitewing*."

THE END.

In Africa wandered a yak;
A jaguar jumped up on his back.
Said the yak, with a frown,
"Prithee quick get thee down;
You're almost too heavy, alack!"

BITS OF ADVICE.

ENTERTAINING FRIENDS.

BY AUNT MARJORIE PRECEPT.

I ONCE overheard a little bit of talk between two school-girls, one of whom said, "Well, the Ames family are coming to our house next week, and for my part I dread it. I don't expect to have a mite of enjoyment while they are with us. I can not entertain people." I have forgotten her companion's reply, but I know that the feeling is common among young people, and when guests arrive they often slip off the responsibility of making them happy upon papa and mamma. This is hardly fair. The art of hospitality is really as easily acquired as a knowledge of geography or grammar.

In the first place, the young girls in a family when expecting friends of their own age should see that their rooms are pleasantly arranged, the beds freshly made, toilet soap provided, and plenty of towels and water at hand. Not *new* towels, dear girls; they are hard and slippery, and nobody likes them. There should be a comb and brush, a button-hook, pins in plenty, and space in the closet to hang dresses and coats, as well as an empty drawer in the bureau at the guest's service. By attending to these little things themselves, girls can take quite a burden from their busy mothers. Then both boys and girls should have in mind some sort of plan by which to carry on operations during the days of their friends' stay. So far as possible it is well to lay aside unnecessary work for the time. As for the morning and evening duties which belong to every day's course, attend to them faithfully, but do not let them drag. Never make apologies if you happen to have some occupation which you fear may seem very humble in the eyes of your guest. All home service is honorable.

If you live in the country there will be fishing, nutting, climbing, riding, driving, and exploring: all of which you can offer to your friends. Be sure that you have fishing-tackle, poles, and baskets, harness in order, and, in short, everything in readiness for your various expeditions. To most out-of-door excursions a nice luncheon is an agreeable addition, and you need not upset the house nor disturb the cook in order to arrange this, for sandwiches, gingerbread, cookies, crackers, and similar simple refreshments, can be obtained in most homes without much difficulty. Every boy, as well as every girl, should know how to make a good cup of coffee by a woodland fire.

In town there are museums, picture-galleries, and concerts, as well as various shows, to delight guests from a distance. In the season you can take them to the beach or the parks. But whether in town or country, do not wear your friends out by too much going about, nor ever let them feel that you are taking trouble for them, nor yet that they are neglected. Forget your own convenience, but remember their comfort. Study their tastes and consult their wishes in a quiet way.

THE HOMES OF THE FARMING ANTS.

BY CHARLES MORRIS.

WOODBINE COTTAGE was just a gem of a place. If any of my readers have ever seen a gem of a place, they will know exactly what that means. For those who have not been so fortunate, I will say that it was the prettiest of cottages, with no end of angles and gables, of shady nooks and sunny corners, and of cunning ins and outs; while to its very roof the fragrant woodbine climbed and clambered, and the bees buzzed about the honeyed blossoms as if they were just wild with delight.

That was Woodbine Cottage itself. But I have said nothing about its surroundings—the neat flower beds, and the prattling brook that ran by just at the foot of the garden, the green lawn as smooth as a table, and the great spreading elm-tree in its centre, against which Uncle Ben Mason was so fond of leaning his chair in the bright summer afternoons, and where Harry and Willie Mason liked nothing better than to lie at his feet on the greensward, and coax him to tell them about the wonderful things he had seen and the marvellous things he had read.

It was only the afternoon succeeding that in which he

A LIVELY TEAM.

had told them the strange story of the honey ants, and they were at him again, anxious to know something more about ant life.

"You know, Uncle Ben," pleaded Harry, coaxingly, "that you said there were ever so many other queer things about them."

"And that they milked cows. And that some of them were just soldiers," broke in Willie, eagerly. "And—and—" The little fellow was quite at a loss for words in his eagerness.

"Now, now, now!" cried Uncle Ben; "you don't want me to tell you all at once, I hope?"

"Tell us sumfin, Uncle Ben—sumfin of just the queerest you knows," pleaded Willie; "cos I wants to know 'bout them ever so much."

"Very well. Suppose I describe the farmer ants."

"The farmer ants?" cried Harry, with interest.

"Yes, there is a species of ants in Texas that have farms of their own, and gather the grain in when it is ripe, and store it away in their granaries; and some people say that they plant the seed in the spring, just like human farmers. But others think that this part of the story is very doubtful."

"You don't believe that, do you, Uncle Ben?" asked Harry, doubtingly. "Why, that would be making them folks at once."

"They are very much like folks without that," said his uncle, settling himself back easily in his chair, and gazing down with his kindly glance on his eager young nephews.

"If you could see one of their clearings," he continued. "But maybe you don't care to hear about them?"

"Yes, we does," cried Willie, eagerly.

"I do, ever so much. I know that," chimed in Harry.

"Well, then, if you will keep just as quiet as two mice, I will tell you the story of our little black farmers. They are, in some ways, the strangest of all ants. You have seen little ant-hills thrown up in the sand about an inch across; but these ants build great solid mounds, surrounded by a level court-yard, sometimes as much as ten or twelve feet in diameter. Here they do not suffer a blade of grass nor a weed to grow, and the whole clearing is as smooth and hard as a barn floor. This is no light labor, I can tell you, for wild plants grow very fast and strong under the hot suns of Texas."

"But how do they do it?" asked Harry.

"You would laugh to see them," continued his uncle. Ben. "Their hard, horny mandibles are good cutting instruments, and are used for teeth, saws, chisels, and pincers all in one. They form a sort of compound tool."

"I'd like to see them ever so much," cried Willie. "But, Uncle Ben, where does they live? Cos they can't be running 'bout all the time out-of-doors. I know that."

"And they must have some place to put their crops in," said Harry.

"Their houses are in the centre of the clearing," continued their uncle. "They are usually rounded mounds of earth, with a depression in the top, of the shape of a basin. In the centre of this basin is a small hole, forming the entrance to the ant city, which is all built under-ground. If you could see one of these mounds cut open, you would be surprised to behold the multitude of galleries not more than a quarter or half an inch high, running in all directions. Some of them lead up and down to the upper and lower stories of the establishment. At the ends of these galleries are many apartments, some of which serve as nurseries where the young ants are kept, and others as granaries where the grain is stored up. The granaries are sometimes one and three-quarter inches high, and two inches wide, neatly roofed over, and filled to the roof with grain. That may not seem much of a barn, but if you had one in the same proportion to your size, it would need no trifle of grain to fill it."

"But you said they were farmer ants," cried Harry, as if he fancied he had now got his uncle in a tight place, "and you haven't said a word about their wheat fields."

"And you tole us they didn't keep cows, too," put in Willie, triumphantly.

"But I am not half through my story yet," replied Uncle Ben, with a quiet smile. "We have only been talking about their homes and their clearings. Now suppose we take a stroll out to the wheat fields by one of the great roads which the ants make."

"Roads!" cried both boys in surprise.

"Just as fine roads as men could make. Our little farmers always have three or four of these roads, and sometimes as many as seven, running straight out from their clearing, often for sixty feet in length. One observer, in fact, says he saw an ant road that was three hundred feet long. The roads are from two to five inches wide at the clearing, but they narrow as they go out until they are quite lost."

"But are they real roads? You ain't funning, Uncle

is no give up in him, however. He is bent on bringing in his share of the crop, and lets nothing hinder him. After he reaches the road, it is all plain sailing. He gets a good hold on his grain, and trots off home like an express messenger, sometimes not stopping to rest once on the long journey."

"Gracious! wouldn't I like to see them!" exclaimed Harry. He had approached his uncle step by step, and was now standing in open-mouthed wonder at his knee.

As for Willie, he was not nearly so eager. He had not yet got over his contempt for farmers who did not keep cows.

"Is there anything else queer about them?" asked Harry.

"There is another sort of grass, called ant rice, of which the seed tastes something like rice. One observer says that this grass is often permitted to grow upon their clearings, all other kinds of grass being cut away, as our farmers clear out the weeds from their grain. When the seeds are ripe and fall, they carry them into their granaries, and afterward clear away the stubble, preparing their wheat field for the next year's crop. It is this writer who says that they plant *the* seeds in the spring, but other writers doubt this statement."

"And you said a while ago that you didn't believe it, either," remarked Harry.

"I think it needs to be pretty thoroughly established before we can accept it as a fact."

"I think so too," said Harry, with great gravity.

"Ain't nuffin more queer 'bout 'em, is there?" asked Willie. "Cos I's getting kind of tired of them."

"You can go 'way, then," retorted Harry. "Uncle

"Then I don't want nuffin at all to do with 'em," cried Willie; "cos I was stinged with a bee once, and I don't like bees."

"I am ever so much obliged, Uncle Ben," said Harry. "Come, Willie, let's go play now, for I know we've been a big bother."

"Maybe you has; I ain't," replied Willie, stolidly, as he followed his brother, leaving Uncle Ben with a very odd smile upon his face.

A ROYAL THIEF.

In the summer weather
 Kindly, gen'rous Night
Flings upon the thirsting grass
 Dew-drops cool and bright.
There they lie and sparkle
 Till return of Day;
Then the Sun—a royal thief—
 Steals them all away.

(Begun in Harper's Young People No. 37, July 13.)

THE STORY OF THE AMERICAN NAVY.

BY BENSON J. LOSSING.

Chapter IX.

BETWEEN the war of 1812-15 and the civil war, 1861-65, our navy had very little to do in actual warfare. It was sometimes called upon to assert the rights and dignity of our government in foreign ports, and during the war with Mexico it assisted in the capture-

FIGHT BETWEEN THE "MONITOR" AND "MERRIMAC."—Drawn by J. O. Davidson.

[illegible], and all through the war they were active and efficient in Western rivers.

Late in October, 1861, a powerful land and naval force left Hampton Roads to take possession of the coasts of South Carolina. The ships were commanded by Commodore S. F. Dupont. The entrance to Port Royal Sound was strongly guarded by Confederate forts. These were reduced, after a sharp engagement with the fleet. The Federals entered, and were soon in complete possession of the sea islands of South Carolina.

At the beginning of 1862 the navy was composed of seven squadrons, each having a distinct field of operation, chiefly in the blockading service. In that service many stirring events occurred. At the very beginning the Confederate cruiser *Petrel* went out of Charleston Harbor and attacked the *St. Lawrence*, supposing her to be a merchant ship. Presently the latter opened her guns, sending a fiery shell that exploded in the *Petrel*, and a heavy solid shot that struck her amidships below water-mark. In an instant she was reduced to a wreck, leaving nothing on the surface of the foaming waters but floating fragments of her hull, and the struggling survivors of her crew. The latter scarcely knew what had happened. A flash of fire, a thunder-peal, and ingulfment had been the events of a moment.

Early in 1862 a land and naval force, the latter commanded by Flag-officer Goldsborough, captured Roanoke Island, which the Confederates had fortified. This was speedily followed by the capture of places on the mainland of North Carolina. A little earlier than this, great excitement was produced by the seizure on board an English mail-steamer, by Captain Wilkes, of our navy, of two Confederate Ambassadors to European courts (Mason and Slidell), and lodging them in Fort Warren, in Boston Harbor. The British government threatened war; but common-sense prevailed, and after a little bluster peace was assured.

After the capture of Forts Henry and Donelson, Commodore Foote's attention was directed to Island Number Ten, in the Mississippi, which the Confederates occupied, and had strongly fortified. It was regarded as the key to the Lower Mississippi. Foote beleaguered it with gun-boats and mortar-boats, and with some assistance of a land force he captured the stronghold. Then the flotilla went down the Mississippi, and captured Fort Pillow and Memphis, terribly crippling the Confederate squadron at the latter place.

The government resolved to repossess New Orleans and Mobile. A land force under General Butler, and a naval force under Commodore Farragut and Commodore D. D. Porter, with a mortar fleet, gathered at Ship Island, off the coast of Mississippi, early in 1862. The ships entered the Mississippi in April. Two forts opposite each other on the Mississippi, some distance from its mouth, had been strongly garrisoned by the Confederates, who considered them a perfect protection to New Orleans. These had to be passed. That perilous feat was performed by the fleet in the dark hours of the morning of April 24, when a terrific scene was witnessed. Farragut, in the wooden ship *Hartford*, led the way. Forts, gun-boats, mortar-boats, and marine monsters called "rams" opened their great guns at the same time. Earth and waters for miles around were shaken. The forts were silenced, the fleet passed, and then met a strong Confederate flotilla in the gloom. After one of the most desperate combats of the war, this flotilla was vanquished, and Farragut pushed on toward New Orleans, which he had virtually captured before the arrival of General Butler. This event gave great joy to the loyal people of the country.

Meanwhile a stirring event had occurred in Hampton Roads. Early in March the Confederates sent down from Norfolk a powerful iron-clad "ram" named *Merrimac* to destroy national vessels near Fortress Monroe. This raid was destructive, and its repetition was expected the next morning. At midnight a strange craft came into the Roads. It seemed to consist of only a huge cylinder floating on a platform. She was under the command of Lieutenant J. L. Worden. That cylinder was a revolving turret of heavy iron, containing two enormous guns. The almost submerged platform was also of iron. It was called the *Monitor*.

The *Merrimac* came down the next morning to attack the frigate *Minnesota*. The little *Monitor* went to her defense—in size a little child defending a giant. Slowly her turret began to revolve. Her cannon sent forth 100-pound shot, and very soon the *Merrimac* was so crippled that she fled with difficulty back to Norfolk, and did not come out again. After that, Monitors were favorites as defenders of land-locked waters.

[TO BE CONTINUED.]

AT THE SEA-SIDE.

IN SEPTEMBER.

BY MARY DENSEL.

IT had been a hot summer, and Cassy Deane, shut up in a close street, had been treated to every atom of heat that the city contained. So at least it seemed to her, for the family had only lately moved into town from the country, and Cassy was like a little wind-flower that had been transplanted from a cool wood into a box of earth near a blazing fire. No wonder that she drooped. She seldom had even a drive to console her.

"Because we are only *middling*," she explained to herself. "If we were poor, we could go on excursions with the charity children; and if we were rich, we'd travel to the mountains or the sea. We're only middling, so we stay at home."

At first Cassy was ready to envy Marion Van Dyck, who started with her mamma and a dozen trunks for Saratoga; and she breathed a sigh over the fortunes of Lillie Downs, whose father had built a cottage on the coast of Maine, where the ocean surged up to the very piazza.

But by-and-by Cassy forgot her woes, such a delightful piece of news came to her ears. Her mother told it to her one evening, and Cassy never went to sleep for two whole hours after she was in bed, so excited was she by the bliss that was to be hers in September.

The truth was that Mr. Deane had come to the city for the express purpose of giving his little daughter the benefit of no less an establishment than Madame McLeod's "Boarding and Day School for Young Ladies." Cassy knew that Marion Van Dyck and Lillie Downs and a host of other damsels were also "to enjoy its advantages." Cassy was overwhelmed with the honor and the joy of it all. She had always been a solitary chick up in her country home, and it seemed almost too good to be true that she was actually to have real live girls to play with, and that she could talk of "*our* games," and "*our* history class."

What matter that the August sun scorched and flamed? What matter if the bricks, baked through and through by day, took their revenge by keeping the air as hot as a furnace all night?

Cassy was as gay as a lark, and sang and chattered by the hour, while she helped her mother run up the breadths of an extraordinary changeable silk gown, which had been cut over from one that had been her grandmother's. This was to be Cassy's school-dress. Think what richness—silk for every-day wear!

"We can't afford to buy anything new," argued Mrs. Deane. Still, it was a solemn moment when the key snapped in the lock of the cedar chest, and that changeable silk was taken from the place where it had lain these thirty years, wrapped in a pillow-case and two towels.

Cassy fairly gasped when the scissors cut into its gorgeousness. She gasped even more when Mrs. Deane also brought from the chest six yards of an ancient bottle-green ribbon to trim the robe withal. To be sure, the ribbon drooped despondingly under the chastening influence of a hot flat-iron, but, "We'll put it on in bands," said Mrs. Deane. "Bows would really be too dressy for you, my daughter."

Stitch, stitch, stitch, Cassy's fingers flew. And all the time she sewed, her busy brain was weaving the most rapturous visions of the new life that was to be hers. In her dreams she made polite little courtesies to Marion Van Dyck, whom she imagined as standing on the threshold of the "Boarding and Day School" to welcome her. To be sure she only knew Marion by sight, but as Marion knew her in the same way, she thought they would instantly become friends. Then Lillie Downs would entreat her to join in all the games, for Lillie Downs was already an acquaintance: at least she had said, "How do you do?" one day when she saw Cassy on the sidewalk. Cassy was sure there were a dozen girls who would stretch out their hands at once, and perhaps she could even think of a secret to tell some of them, and then they would, of course, be friends forever.

"And even if they wear common clothes, I sha'n't be proud in this magnificent dress," thought Cassy. For the changeable silk was finished now, and Cassy stole twenty times a day into the guest-chamber that she might behold its splendor as it lay on the bed.

It did seem as if August would never end. But at last September appeared, and the morning of all mornings dawned.

Cassy rose bright and early. Her mother dressed her with her own hands, and tied up her hair with a narrow pink ribbon.

"Pink goes so well with the green on your gown," said dear, guileless Mrs. Deane; "and, Cassy, here are some new shoes that father bought for you yesterday. He'll go himself with you to the door, so you sha'n't feel strange like."

"Oh, but they'll be so glad to see me I sha'n't feel strange!" cried Cassy, and down the street she skipped.

But for some reason no one was at the door to welcome her. Cassy crept into the big school-room. It was full of girls, and there was Marion Van Dyck among the rest. A wee smile came to Cassy's face. She was about to say "good-morning," but Marion only glanced carelessly at her and turned away.

"Why, she's forgotten that I live round the corner," thought Cassy.

Lillie Downs had evidently "forgotten" too, or else she was too busy to notice.

Cassy turned away, and that just in time to catch a whisper.

"Who, under the sun, is that queer image in a dress that came out of the ark?"

Cassy looked wonderingly about to discover the "image." The girl who had spoken was gazing directly at her with a twinkle in her eyes. Her companion said, "Hush! she'll hear," and the two laughed under their breath, not jeeringly, but only as if they really could not help it.

A "queer image"? Was she "queer"? Cassy asked herself.

All at once it flashed across her that her gown was certainly very unlike the crisp, ruffled dresses around her. Those flimsy satin ribbons did look as if Mrs. Noah might have worn them. A hot flush sprang to Cassy's cheeks. She began to almost wish she had not come, such a sense of loneliness rushed over her.

She was even more forlorn when the school was presently called to order, for every other girl was blessed with a seat-mate, and Cassy sat quite by herself.

When recess-time came she followed the others into a large back yard, and stowed herself meekly away in a corner to watch the fun. She tried to console herself by the thought that she could not have run about even had she been asked to join in the game of "tag," for the new shoes pinched her feet sadly. For all that, she was almost glad when one girl stumbled against her and fairly trod on her toes, for she turned so quickly, and begged her pardon so heartily, that it was worth bearing the pain for the sake of the notice.

Cassy was sure that all the girls were good-natured. They were only busy with their own affairs, and what claim had the stranger upon any one of them?

When noon came, and Cassy went home to dinner, she put a brave face on the matter. She knew it would break her father's heart to know how keen had been her disappointment. So she spoke of the large school-room, and of the classes in which she had been placed; and Mr. Deane nodded approval, while his wife put her head on one side to see if that changeable silk could not bear to be taken in a little in the biases. How could Casey tell her that the gown was "queer"? How could she even mention that her shoes were coarse, and that they hurt her feet?

"Perhaps the girls will speak to me to-morrow," she thought, patiently.

But they did not. Again Casey sat in her corner quite alone. In vain she told herself that it was "no matter," in vain she "played" that she did not care.

"I sha'n't mind it to-morrow."

To-morrow came, and it was just as hard as to-day.

At last one morning at recess it did seem as though she could not bear it any longer. A big lump was in her throat, and two tears sprang to her eyes; but still she tried to say, "Never mind; oh, never mind."

Just at that moment a voice sounded in her ear. She turned and saw a face rosy with blushes.

"I didn't know," began the voice, hesitatingly—"I thought you might like—anyway, I am Bessie Merriam."

Casey looked out shyly from under her lashes. "I am Casey Deane," said she.

"You're a new girl," continued Bessie, more boldly, "so I had to speak first. Would you like to play, 'I spy'?"

Casey sprang up eagerly, then drew back. "I wish I could," she stammered, "but my shoes—and father's only middling, so I don't like to ask for more."

"Of course not," broke in Bessie, who, though puzzled to know what it was to be "middling," was sure there was something wrong about the shoes. "Of course not; but maybe you know 'jack-stones'?"

In a twinkling she brought five marbles from the depth of her pocket, and the two were deep in the mysteries of "horses in the stall," "Johnny over," "peas in the pot," and all the rest of that fascinating game.

One person having spoken to the forlorn stranger, two more appeared on the scene. It is always so. These girls wanted Bessie and her new friend for "hop-scotch," but Bessie interfered before there was any chance for embarrassment.

"We can't leave this game," said she, decidedly.

"How could she think to speak so quickly?" thought Casey. "I should have felt so bad to explain about my shoes?"

It was the very next morning that Bessie Merriam came to school with a mysterious bundle under her arm. She took Casey by the hand, and led her—where? Why, into the coal closet!

"It's so very private here," explained Bessie. "And, do you know, it's no fun to play romping games in these good boots of mine; so I hunted up an old pair. And, do you think, I stumbled on these old ones too. Would you mind using one pair? You won't think me impertinent, will you?"

Bessie was quite out of breath, and gazing at Casey with wide-open, pleading eyes.

Those boots fitted to a T. Casey could jump and run to her heart's content. Jump and run she did, for at recess Bessie drew her into the midst of the other girls, and such a game of "I spy" Casey had never imagined. Nobody said a word about her drab gown. "She is *my* friend," Bessie had announced, and that was enough.

Marion Van Dyck gave her two bites of her pickled lime. Lillie Downs "remembered" her, and did not shrink from partaking of Casey's corn-ball. School was a very different affair to-day.

Casey fairly danced on her way home. She determined to think up a secret that very night that she might confide it to Bessie. In the mean time she bought a bit of card-board and some green, red, and brown worsted. All that afternoon and all that evening she worked. The next day Bessie found in her arithmetic a remarkable book mark, with a red house and a green and brown tree, while underneath were the touching words, "Friendship's Offering."

"Please to keep it for ever and ever," begged Casey, earnestly, "to make you remember how I thank you."

"Thank me for *what*?" asked Bessie, in surprise.

Casey stared at her.

"Don't you know what a beautiful thing it was in you to ask me to play 'jack-stones'? Don't you know you're a—a—an angel?"

"It never says once in the Bible that angels play 'jack-stones,'" cried Bessie, in great glee; "so don't talk nonsense, Casey. But I think the book-mark's lovely."

So the two little girls laughed as if there was a joke somewhere, though neither knew exactly what it was, only Casey Deane was too happy to be sober, and it's my belief Bessie Merriam was just as happy as she. What do you think?

WHAT THE BABIES SAID.

BY MRS. E. T. CORBETT.

LILLIE BENSON and Daisy Brooks sat on the floor in the nursery, and looked at each other, while their delighted mammas looked at them, and each mother thought her own baby the finest. Lillie was ten months old, and Daisy was just twelve. Lillie had great blue eyes, soft flaxen hair curling in little rings all over her head, and pink cheeks. Daisy had brown eyes, golden-brown hair cut straight across her forehead (*banged*, people call it), and two lovely dimples. One wore a white dress all tucks and embroidery, with a blue sash; the other a white dress all ruffles and puffs, with a pink sash.

Daisy looked at Lillie, and said, "Goo-goo!"

"The dear little thing!" said Daisy's mamma. "She's so delighted to see Lillie to-day."

Then Lillie looked at Daisy, and said, "Goo-goo-goo!"

"Oh, the darling!" exclaimed Lillie's mamma. "She's so fond of Daisy, you know, that she is trying to talk."

Presently Daisy turned her back to Lillie, and crept into the corner of the room. "Now just see that! she wants Lillie to follow her. Isn't it cunning?" said Lillie's mamma.

"Of course she does, and see Lillie trying to do it. Isn't she sweet?" answered Daisy's mother, while Lillie crept to the opposite side of the room.

But after a while the two babies were sleepy; so their mammas laid them down side by side in the wide crib, and then went down stairs to lunch.

"We'll leave the door open, so we can hear them if they cry; but I know they won't wake for a couple of hours," said one of the mothers; and the other one said, "Oh no; of course not; they'll sleep soundly, the darlings!"

But in a very few moments something strange happened—something very strange indeed. The babies opened their eyes, looked around the room, and then at each other.

"We're alone at last, and I'm so glad," said Daisy.

"Yes," said Lillie. "Now we can have a nice little chat, I hope. Isn't it dreadful to be a baby, Daisy?"

"Of course it is," sighed Daisy; "yet I suppose it is very ungrateful to say so, when every one loves us so much, and is so kind to us."

"That's the worst of it; I don't want every one to love me, because they will kiss me, and I hate to be kissed so much," objected Lillie. "Ugh! how horrid some people's kisses are!"

"It's enough to make any baby cross, *I* think," added Daisy. "I wish no one but mamma would ever kiss me, and even she does too much of it when I'm sleepy."

"Why, Daisy Brooks! what a thing to say about your own dear mamma!" exclaimed Lillie, looking shocked.

"I don't mean to say anything unkind of mamma.

GETTING ACQUAINTED.—DRAWN BY W. L. SHEPPARD.

for I love her dearly, you know, Lillie; but it is hard to be kissed and kissed when you're hungry or sleepy, or both, and sometimes I have to cry," answered Daisy, quickly.

"Well, I'll tell you something else I hate," continued Lillie, "and that is to have people who don't know anything about it try to amuse me. They have such a dreadful way of rushing at you head-first, and shrieking, 'Chee! *chee!* CHEE!' or 'Choo! *choo!* CHOO!' that you don't know what may be coming next."

"Yes, or else they poke a finger in your neck, and expect you to laugh at the fun. I do laugh sometimes at the absurdity of their behavior," said Daisy, scornfully.

"Yes, and then they always think you're delighted, and go on until you are disgusted, and have to scream, don't they?" asked Lillie.

"Of course. Oh, babies have a great deal to suffer, there's no doubt of *that*," said Daisy.

"And there's another horrid thing," Lillie added, after thinking a moment. "I mean the habit people have of talking to babies about their family affairs in public. My mamma don't do that; but I heard Aunt Sarah talking to her baby in the cars the other day, loud enough for every one to hear, and she said: 'Poor grandpa! grandpa's gone away; don't Minnie feel sorry? She can't play with grandpa's watch now. Grandpa wants Minnie to come and see him, and ride on the pony, and Minnie must have her new sacque made, so she can go. Will Minnie send a kiss to grandpa?' and ever so much more. I know poor Minnie was ashamed, for she fidgeted all the time; but what could she do?"

"Well, mamma would talk to me just the same way this morning, as we came here, and I did my best to stop her, too, but it wasn't any use," said Daisy, looking indignant. "She had to tell everybody that we were going to see 'dear little Lillie Benson,' over and over again."

"But I'll tell you what makes me most angry, after all, Daisy," said her cousin, suddenly. "Does your mamma ever give you a chicken bone to suck?"

"Yes, she does, and oh!— I know what you're going to say," interrupted Daisy. "That's another of our trials. You get a nice bone, and you begin to enjoy yourself, when all at once your nurse or your mother fancies you've found a scrap of meat on the bone, and then one or the other just makes a fish-hook of her finger, and pokes it down your throat before you know where you are!"

"That's it exactly," exclaimed Lillie. "I go through just such an experience nearly every day, and it's too aggravating."

"Hark!" said Daisy, listening; "I hear old Dinah coming up stairs now, and I suppose we'll have to listen to her baby-talk for a half-hour at least. I know what I'll do; I'll make faces and scream."

"And get a dose of medicine, maybe, as I did one day," answered Lillie. "I tried that plan to stop an old lady from saying, 'Itie precious! itie precious! tum ou auntie!' and mamma got so frightened she sent for the doctor, and he gave me a horrid powder. I can taste it yet."

"That was too bad," said Daisy, compassionately; "but hush, dear, for Dinah is at the door."

And when the old nurse came in the room, she found the two babies wide-awake, smiling at each other, and saying, "Goo-goo," as sweetly as if they hadn't a grievance in the world.

ONE MARCH DAY.
THREE LITTLE PRINCESSES.
PEACOCK AND MONKEY.
NOT IN VAIN.

OUR POST-OFFICE BOX.

those given in Paris at the present time are marvels of ingenuity of design and brilliancy and variety of coloring. Filings of copper, zinc, and other metals in combination with certain chemicals are used to produce the brilliant stars which are thrown out by rockets as they explode. Although there is great beauty in many of the combinations of wheels and stars arranged on frames, in the troops of fiery pigeons flying back and forth, and in the wonderful representations of [illegible] buildings, and other devices to be seen at every grand pyrotechnic display, there is nothing so majestic as the rockets and bombs which rush upward to the sky, and, bursting, fill the air with showers of golden serpents, floating stars of brilliant changing hues, and cascades of silver and gold rain.

E. S. A.—The schooner yacht differs from the sloop only in rig, consequently an article on schooner yachts would be but little else than a repetition of that on sloops.

C. A. SAVAGE.—The reason given you as the cause of low water is no doubt correct. If you can take note of the back-water above the mills, you will probably find the increase sufficient to balance the decrease below. The low water is especially noticeable during the present summer, when the long-continued drought of the early part of the season has dried up many of the small streams and springs which usually contribute to the volume of water in the river.

ED.—A descriptive list of the publications of Messrs. Harper & Brothers will be sent, postage free, to any address in the United States, on the receipt of nine cents.

B. B. LEE.—You will find some useful suggestions concerning canoes in *The Canoe and the Flying Proa*, by W. L. Alden, a volume of "Harper's Half-hour Series."

DAISY G.—No article on silk worms has been published in HARPER'S BAZAR, but there was an interesting paper in HARPER'S MAGAZINE on that subject, to which reference was made in Post-office Box No. 41.

ALBERTA N., CARL S. H., HELEN S. F., AND OTHERS.—Write directly to the correspondents with whom you desire to make exchange.

[illegible]

[illegible]

PUZZLES FROM YOUNG CONTRIBUTORS.

No. 1.

[illegible]

No. 4.

[illegible]

No. 5.

WORD SQUARE.

1. First, to beg. Second, a rampart. Third, to salt. Fourth, [illegible]. Fifth, [illegible].

[illegible]

No. 6.

[illegible]

I am the title of a celebrated book composed of 16 letters.

My 4, 10, 6, 7, [illegible].

My 12, 2, 11, 4 is an intoxicating beverage.

My [illegible].

My 13, [illegible].

[illegible]

ANSWERS TO PUZZLES IN No. 43.

No. 2. Napoleon, Waterloo.

No. 3. Geranium.

No. 4. 1. Madrid. 2. Warsaw. 3. Athens. 4. Connecticut.

No. 5. [illegible]

SPECIAL NOTICE.

OUR NEW SERIAL STORY.

In the next Number of HARPER'S YOUNG PEOPLE will be found the opening chapter of a new serial story, entitled

"WHO WAS PAUL GRAYSON?"

written expressly for this paper by JOHN HABBERTON, so widely known as the author of "Helen's Babies." The story is one of school-boy life, and abounds in situations and incidents that will prove familiar to the experience of a large proportion of our readers. Over the life of Paul Grayson, the hero of the story, hangs a mystery that his schoolmates determine to solve, and which is at last cleared up in the most unexpected manner. The story will be fully and beautifully illustrated from original drawings.

SOME ANSWERS TO WIGGLE No. 13, OUR ARTIST'S IDEA, AND NEW WIGGLE No. 14.

The following also sent in answers to Wiggle No. 13:

W. H. Western, C. Fletcher, Philip P. Cooper, Ben S. Darrow, C. W. Lyman, Harry J. P., F. Holton, Harrie Hart, W. H. Hill, Elsie Hopkins, Fred Hougham, Sophie Whitmire, Lulu Craft, Charles N. Rose, Bertha Thompson, Gracie Morton, Sadie Clark, Effie E. Tallman, Pen. Percival, Abby Park, T. K., Henry F., Alexis Merlow, Sam, Frankie Lion, Wieyah Lester, Nella Conover, C. C. McClaughry, Hal, J. M. Bramwell, Jasper Elliott, Theo. P. Jacobs, G. F. B., J. H., Perry F. Jennison, W. Fowler, Johnnie Fletcher, Eddie Cantrell, Frank S. Miller, M. M. Chase, Kyron R. Varry, John Jarvis, Ella C. Reed, Tessie, Theresa Moore, Rebecca Hodges, Josie Parker, Maude T., Ella S., Mamie K., Roy R., G. B. K., Sadie M. L., Annie Lee Bruce, W. T. Benson, Leon Fulton, B. B., C. B. H., Edith

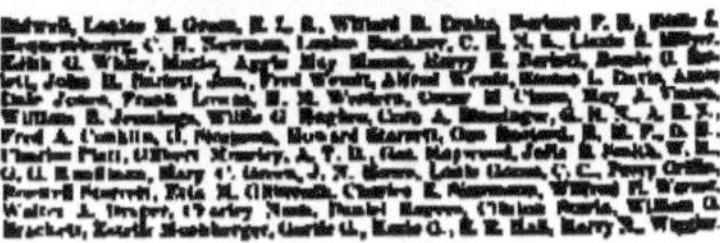

Bidwell, Louise M. Green, E. L. S., Willard B. Drake, Herbert P. B., Eddie J. [illegible], C. H. Newman, Louise Buckley, C. H. N. S., Lizzie & Miller, Edith G. White, Marie, Aggie May Mason, Harry E. Bartlett, Bessie O. [illegible], John H. Hurlbut, Jun., Fred Wendt, Alfred Wendt, Kenneth L. Davis, Annie Dale Jones, Frank Lewis, E. M. Western, Oscar M. Chase, May A. Vinton, William E. Jennings, Willie G. Hughes, Cora A. Hessinger, G. N. K., A. B. Y., Fred A. Conklin, G. Simpson, Howard Starrett, Ona Harland, E. M. F., D. E., Charles Platt, Gilbert Moseley, A. T. D., Geo. Heywood, Jessie E. Smith, W. H. G. G. Rawlinson, Mary C. Green, J. N. Brown, Lottie Green, C. C., Percy Griffin, Roswell Sterrett, Etta M. Gilbreath, Charles E. Simmonds, Wilfred H. Ward, Walter A. Draper, Charley Noon, Daniel Rogers, Claude Searle, William G. Brackett, Eddie Stoneberger, Gertie G., Rosie G., E. E. Hall, Harry S. Wiggle.

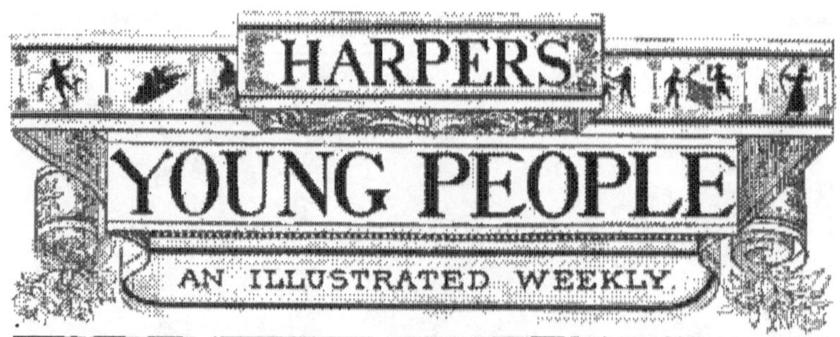
HARPER'S
YOUNG PEOPLE
AN ILLUSTRATED WEEKLY.

Vol. I.—No. 46. Published by HARPER & BROTHERS, New York. Price Four Cents.

Tuesday, September 14, 1880. Copyright, 1880, by Harper & Brothers. $1.50 per Year, in Advance.

WHO WAS PAUL GRAYSON?

BY JOHN HABBERTON,

Author of "Helen's Babies."

Chapter I.

THE NEW PUPIL.

PAUL GRAYSON

THE boys who attended Mr. Morton's Select School in the village of Laketon did not profess to know more than boys of the same age and advantages elsewhere; but of one thing they were absolutely certain, and that was that no teacher ever rang his bell to assemble the school or call the boys in from recess until just that particular instant when the fun in the school-yard was at its highest, and the boys least wanted to come in. A teacher might be very fair about some things; he might help a boy through a hard lesson, or give him fewer bad marks than he had earned; he might even forget to report to a boy's parents all the cases of truancy in which their son had indulged; but when a teacher once laid his hand upon that dreadful bell and stepped to the window, it really seemed as if every particle of human sympathy went out of him.

On one bright May morning, however, the boys who made this regular daily complaint were few; indeed, all of them, except Bert Sharp, who had three consecutive absences to explain, and no written excuse from his father to help him out, were already inside the school-room, and even Bert stood where he could look through the open door while he cudgelled his wits and smothered his conscience in the endeavor to frame an explanation that might seem plausible. The boys already inside lounged near any desks but their own, and conversed in low tones about almost everything except the subject uppermost in their minds, this subject being a handsome but rather sober-looking boy of about fourteen years, who was seated at a desk in the back part of the room, and trying, without any success whatever, to look as if he did not know that all the other boys were looking at him.

It was not at all wonderful that the boys stared, for none of them had ever before seen the new pupil, and Laketon was so small a town that the appearance of a strange boy was almost as unusual an event as the coming of a circus.

"Let's give it up," said Will Palmer, who had for five minutes been discussing with several other boys all sorts of improbabilities about the origin of the new pupil; "let's give it up until roll-call; then we'll learn his name, and that 'll be a little comfort."

"I wish Mr. Morton would hurry, then," said Benny Mallow. "I came early this morning to see if I couldn't win back my striped alley from Ned Johnston, and this business has kept us from playing a single game. Quick, boys, quick! Mr. Morton's getting ready to touch the bell."

The group separated in an instant, and every member was seated before the bell struck; so were most of the other boys, and so many pairs of eyes looked inquiringly at the teacher that Mr. Morton himself had to bite his lower lip very hard to keep from laughing as he formally rang the school to order. As the roll was called, the boys answered to their names in a prompt, sharp, business-like way, quite unusual in school-rooms; and as the call proceeded, the responses became so quick as to sometimes get a little ahead of the names that the boys knew were coming.

Suddenly, as the names beginning with G were reached, and Charlie Gunter had his mouth wide open, ready to say "Here," the teacher called, "Paul Grayson."

"Here!" answered the new boy.

A slight sensation ran through the school; no boy did anything for which he had to be called to order, yet somehow the turning of heads, the catching of breath, and the letting go of breath that had been held in longer than usual made a slight commotion, which reached the ears of the strange pupil, and made his look rather more ill at ease than before. The answers to the roll became at once less spirited; indeed, Benny Mallow was staring so hard, now that he had a name to increase his interest in the stranger, that he forgot entirely to answer to his name, and was compelled to sit on the chair beside the teacher's desk from that moment until recess.

That recess seemed longer in coming than any other that the school had ever known—longer even than that memorable one in which a strolling trio of Italian musicians had been specially contracted with to begin playing in the school-yard the moment the boys came down. Finally, however, the bell rang half past ten, and the whole roomful hurried down stairs, but not before Mr. Morton had called Joe Appleby, the largest boy in school, and formally introduced Paul Grayson, with the expressed wish that he should make his new companion feel at home among the boys.

Appleby went about his work with an air that showed how fully he realized the importance of his position: he introduced Grayson to every boy, beginning with the largest; and it was in vain that Benny Mallow, who was the youngest of the party, made all sorts of excuses to throw himself in the way of the distinguished couple, even to the extent of once getting his feet badly mixed up with those of Grayson. When, however, the ceremony ended, and Appleby was at liberty, so many of the boys crowded around him, that the new pupil was in some danger of being lonely.

"Find out for yourselves," was Appleby's dignified and general reply to his questioners. "I don't consider it gentlemanly to tell everything I know about a man."

At this rebuke the smaller boys considered Appleby a bigger man than ever before, but some of the larger ones hinted that Appleby couldn't very well tell what he didn't know, at which Appleby took offense, and joined the group of boys who were leaning against a fence, in the shade of which Will Palmer had already inveigled the new boy into conversation.

"By-the-way," said Will, "there's time yet for a game or two of ball. Will you play?"

"Yes, I'll be glad to," said Grayson.

"Who else?" asked Will.

"I!" shouted all of the boys, who did not forget their grammar so far as to say "Me!" instead. Really, the eagerness of the boys to play ball had never before been equalled in the memory of any one present, and Will Palmer cooled off some quite warm friends by his inability to choose more than two boys to complete the quartette for a common game of ball. It did the disappointed boys a great deal of good to hear the teacher's bell ring just as Will Palmer "caught himself in" to Grayson's bat.

"You play a splendid game," said Will to Grayson as they went up stairs side by side. "Where did you learn it?"

Joe Appleby, who was on the step in front of the couple, dragged just an instant in order to catch the expected information, but all he got was a bump from Palmer, that nearly tumbled him forward on his dignified nose, as Grayson answered,

"Oh, in several places; nowhere in particular."

Palmer immediately determined that he would follow his new schoolmate home at noon, and discover where he lived. Then he would interview the neighbors, and try to get some information ahead of that stuck-up Joe Appleby, who, considering he was only four months older than Palmer himself, put on too many airs for anything. But when school was dismissed, Palmer was disgusted at noting that at least half of the other boys were distributing themselves for just such an operation as the one he had planned. Besides, Grayson did not come down stairs with the crowd. Could it be possible that he was from the country, and had brought a cold lunch to school with him? Palmer hurried up the stairs to see, but met the teacher and the new boy coming down, and the two walked away, and together entered the house of old Mrs. Bartle, where Mr. Morton boarded.

"He's a boarding scholar," exclaimed Benny Mallow. "I've read of such things in books."

"Then he'll be stuck up," declared Joe Appleby.

This opinion was delivered with a shake of the head that seemed to intimate that Joe had known all the ways of boarding scholars for thousands of years; so most of the boys looked quite sober for a moment or two. Finally Sam Wardwell, whose father kept a store, broke the silence by remarking, "I'll bet he's from Boston; his coat is of just the same stuff as one that a drummer wears who comes to see father sometimes."

"Umph!" grunted Appleby; "do you suppose Boston has some kinds of cloth all to itself? You don't know much."

The smaller boys seemed to side with the senior pupil in this opinion; so Sam felt very uncomfortable, and vowed silently that he would bring a piece of chalk to school that very afternoon, and do some rapid sketching on the back of Appleby's own coat. Then Benny Mallow said: "Say, boys, this old school must be a pretty good one, after all, if people somewhere else send boarders to it. His folks must be rich: did you notice what a splendid knife he cut his finger-nails with?—'twas a four-blader, with a pearl handle. But of course you didn't see it, and I did; he used it in school, and my desk is right beside his."

Will Palmer immediately led Benny aside, and offered him a young fan-tail pigeon, when his long-expected brood was hatched, to change desks, if the teacher's permission could be obtained. Meanwhile Napoleon Nott, who generally was called Notty, and who had more imagination than all the rest of the boys combined, remarked, "I believe he's a foreign prince in disguise."

"He's well-bred, anyhow," said Will Palmer to Benny Mallow. "I hope he'll be man enough to stand no nonsense. He's big enough, and smart enough, if looks go for anything, to run this school, and I'd like to see him do it—anything to get rid of Joe Appleby's airs."

Then the various groups separated, moved by the appetites that boys in good health always have. One boy, however—Joe Appleby—was man enough to deny his palate when greater interests devolved upon him, so he made some excuse to go back to the school-room, so as to be there when the teacher and his new charge returned. Half an hour later Benny Mallow, who had sneaked away from home as soon as the dessert had been brought in, and had vulgarly eaten his pie as he walked along the street—Benny Mallow walked into the school-room, and beheld the teacher, Joe Appleby, and Paul Grayson standing together as if they had been talking. As Benny went to his seat Joe followed him, and bestowed upon him a look of such superiority that Benny determined at once that some marvellous mystery must have been revealed, and that Joe was the custodian of the entire thing. Benny was so full of this fancy that he slipped down stairs and told it as fact to each boy who appeared, the result being to make Joe Appleby a greater man than ever in the eyes of the school, while Grayson became a tormenting yet most invaluable mystery.

[TO BE CONTINUED.]

GOOD-BY.

BY MARY D. BRINE.

Good-by, vacation, you jolly old time—
Good-by to your idle hours;
Good-by to dear fields and mountains and glens,
And the beautiful sweet wild flowers;
Good-by to the hours of frolic and fun,
And to freedom's all-glorious reign;
For vacation is ended, it's season is o'er,
And now for our school life again.

No longer the fences we'll merrily scale,
Nor climb to the tree-tops each day;
But the ladder of learning before us is raised,
And upward we'll wend our way.
Ah, deep in our hearts will the memory lie
Of the happy old days so dear,
And over our books we will wearily sigh,
"Oh, would our vacation were here!"

The bright days yet linger, the grass still is green,
Not yet have the mountains turned gray;
But what are the charms of sweet nature, alas!
Since vacation has vanished away?
But there is one comfort—the seasons roll round,
And all in good time we shall hear
Dame Nature's glad joy-bell ring gayly once more,
"School is out, and vacation is here."

THE 'LONGSHORE YACHT CLUB.

BY WILLIAM O. STODDARD.

"YES, boys, de tide's a-comin' in now. Dat yot ob mine 'll float afore long."

"General," said Bob Fogg, "may we have your skiff for our yacht club a little while to-day?"

"No, sah," replied George Washington, positively, with a wide grin on his wrinkled, old, very black face. "De club can't hab no skiff ob mine. Ef dey wants to borry my yot, dey can, dough."

"Bob," said Tommy Conners, "don't you know a sailin' vessel from a skiff?"

"Look at the mast," said Gus Martin.

"And the sail," said Stuyvesant Rankin, with some dignity.

"Now, Sty," said General George Washington, as he limped a few feet farther from the spot where his rugged-looking old boat lay stuck in the mud, "wot do you know 'bout sails? Youah mudder nebber went to sea. She's a dressmaker."

"We can have the yacht, then, General, mast and sail and all?"

The little old black man evidently liked the members of that club, but he shook his grizzled head doubtfully. "You mought tip ober, and git yerselves drownded."

"No, we won't," exclaimed Pat Varick; "every one of us can swim across the Harlem and back again."

"'Cept wen de tide's runnin' too strong. Well, it's wuff w'ile dat you kin swim. I 'mos' upset her myself dis berry mornin' comin' home. Wouldn't I lost a heap ob crabs! More'n a bushel. Real blue-leg channel crabs, bestest kind."

There was more to be said, but the yacht club carried the day, and the General limped off, turning now and then to chuckle, as he saw his young friends crowding into the wonderful craft on the mud.

"Ef dey hasn't h'isted de sail! Yah! yah! Gwine to sail dat yot ob mine right across de sand-bank!"

There was hardly wind enough for that; but it would be some time before the tide would rise high enough to float the boat, and the club were not in a state of mind to wait.

"Tell you what, boys, we'll have a cruise," said Bob Fogg. "She's a beauty. Let's have a 'lection of officers before we start."

They were all agreed on that, but Joe McGinnis insisted that the grown-up yacht clubs never had any elections.

"They just draw cuts, boys, and they give the longest straw to the man that owns the club, to begin with."

"That's the best way," said Tommy Conners; "but the General's gone home."

"I'll take his cut for him," shouted Bob Fogg. "I'll choose to be Bo's'n, 'cause I know how to steer."

Nobody objected, although every member of the club said he knew how to steer, and Sty Rankin had a lot of straws ready in half a minute.

Tommy Conners drew the longest straw, and said he would be Captain; but when Gus Martin came next, and decided to be a Commodore, Tommy muttered, ruefully, "I'd forgot about that."

Stuyvesant Rankin's memory was still better, for he had hardly compared his straw with the others before he shouted, "I'll be Admiral of this club."

Pat Varick was so stunned by that that he only said, "I'm Cook; there won't be any work for me this trip."

"What am I, then?" asked Joe McGinnis, with the shortest straw in his hand.

"You?" said Bob Fogg: "why, you're the Crew. Take hold of that larboard oar, and pull it out of the mud. There's those three landlubbers up on the bank. They'd pelt us if they dared."

The three landlubbers were there, and they were mak-

THE YACHT CLUB STARTS ON ITS ANNUAL CRUISE.

ing loud remarks about the club, but the yacht was almost ready to float now, and no attention could be paid to them.

Just beyond the little creek where General George Washington kept his boat spread the busy waters of the Harlem River, with the great city of New York on both sides, but not very close to the edge of it. It was a very busy sheet of water indeed. There were small steamboats carrying passengers here and there; little tug-boats tugged and puffed and coughed at the sides of big schooners loaded with lumber from Maine; long race-boats, with gayly dressed oarsmen, darted swiftly over the water, like great wooden pickerel, they were so long and sharp and narrow. There were fishing-boats, pleasure-boats, steam-launches, even canoes that were driven by one man and a paddle. But among them all there was no other craft like General George Washington's "yot."

"Boys," exclaimed Captain Conners, "we've forgotten."

"What?" said Admiral Rankin.

"To name the boat."

"Oh, that's all right!" said Commodore Martin. "The General named her himself. She's the *Hail Columbia*."

"Admiral," shouted Boatswain Bob Fogg, "she's beginning to float. You get away forward there, beyond the mast. Captain, you and the Commodore get in the middle. Now, Cook, you and the Crew pull hard a minute, and we'll be out of the mud."

The Admiral obeyed, although there was hardly room to squeeze into, and the mast crowded his back a little. The Cook and the Crew also obeyed, and the *Hail Columbia* suddenly shot away from the bank, and around the head of the rotten old wooden pier.

"If there ain't those three landlubbers," exclaimed Boatswain Fogg, "out on the pier head. And they've got a lot of half-bricks to spatter us with."

There they were; but at that moment the wind came up with a sudden puff, and filled the sail which the genius of the General had added to the motive power of that "yot." It was just at the wrong moment, for Captain Tommy Conners and Commodore Gus Martin were having an argument over an extra oar they had found in the bottom of the boat, and they were working it badly. The Cook was rowing his best, but the tip of the boat sent his oar deep under water, and the Crew suddenly found his oar lifted out into the air.

"Joe McGinnis, you've caught a crab," exclaimed Boatswain Fogg. But before he could say anything to the Captain and the Commodore, the three landlubbers were at work.

Splash, splash, splatter! how those bricks and sticks did fall around the *Hail Columbia!*

"Oh dear!" said Admiral Stuyvesant Rankin to himself, in the bows. "If the yacht upsets, I'm the only member of the club that's got a new coat on."

The breeze came fresher and fresher, and in a minute more the *Hail Columbia* was out of reach of the "battery" on the pier head. Her sable owner, however, was watching her from the door of his cabin with genuine pride.

"Don't she go! Don't she just slip fru de watah! She does mo'ah sailin' to de squar' foot dan any odder yot on de ribber."

So she did, if he meant that it took her longer to travel that foot, or any other.

It was no joke to be "Bo's'n" of the *Hail Columbia*, as Bob Fogg soon found out.

"Tell you what, boys," he said, "it's 'cause she hasn't any keel on her. I have to keep steering all the while. There's no saying where she won't go to."

"Keep along shore," shouted the Admiral from the bows. "You're heading out into the river."

"Now, Sly, if you think you can steer this yacht better than I can, just you come aft and try."

"Hey, there, you young pirates! Where are you heading for?"

It was the shout of a big-armed young fellow in a shell race-boat, who found himself suddenly compelled to pull to the right desperately to avoid being run down by the *Hail Columbia*.

"Look out! Oh—"

Thump. "I declare!"

The first exclamation was from the tall, slim gentleman in the "out-riggered" wherry, who had been racing with the big-armed young man, and had not been looking out well enough.

He tried to turn to the left, but it was very late to try, and the suddenness of it helped him "catch a crab" with his starboard oar. When he said "Oh," he was just going over into the water.

The "thump" and the other exclamation did no harm to the *Hail Columbia*, but the fat old gentleman in the tub of a pleasure-boat that had bumped against the yacht remarked:

"The river swarms with boys to-day. I'm not sorry that other one got a ducking. I've had to get out of his way twice."

The officers and crew of the *Hail Columbia* were inclined to keep a little quiet, all but their brave Boatswain.

"Don't you know how to steer, you fellows? Don't you know that sailing vessels have the right of way? You ought to have blown your whistle sooner."

"I declare!" again exclaimed the old gentleman. "The child is perfectly right."

"Bo's'n," asked the Commodore, "can't we tack and keep along shore again?"

"We can't tack with the sail up—not in this yacht; but we can let it down and turn her round with the oars." They did that very thing, and in five minutes more the *Hail Columbia* was pointing her Admiral toward the north shore of the Harlem again.

The slim man managed to get back into his "shell," but he had lost his race with the big-armed man.

"Bo's'n," remarked the Commodore, as they sailed along, "you needn't run us into the mud."

"I guess not," said Bob Fogg; "but if I can steer her close enough to land, I'm going up as far as the bridge."

It was a grand cruise, and it lasted a long time; but when the *Hail Columbia* once more ran into the little cove, there was General George Washington ready to say,

"Look a-heah, boys, I didn't say you mought cross de 'Lantic Ocean. I wants dat yot to go for some bass."

OLD TIMES IN THE COLONIES.

BY CHARLES CARLETON COFFIN.

No. V.

HOW THE SETTLERS OF WALPOLE DEFENDED THEMSELVES.

BEAUTIFUL the green meadows, the surrounding hills, and the distant mountains forming the landscape in Walpole, New Hampshire, which Colonel Benjamin Bellows and John Kilburn gazed upon on the banks of the Connecticut River in 1749. They had built

their log-houses with loop-holes in the walls through which they could fire upon the Indians in case they were attacked. Though peace had been agreed upon between France and England, the people who lived along the frontier felt no security, for the French in Canada were continually urging the Indians to commit depredations on the English. It was a short and easy journey from Crown Point, on Lake Champlain, to the valley of the Connecticut, and the Indians who sold their furs to the French were frequent visitors to the settlements along the Connecticut.

One of the Indians who visited John Kilburn was called Captain Philip. He had been baptized and christened by the Jesuit priests at the Indian village of St. Francis, on the banks of the St. Lawrence, half way from Montreal to Quebec. The St. Francis tribe were called Christian Indians. There were rumors that war would break out again between England and France. Before war was declared hostilities began.

It was in the spring of 1755 that Captain Philip made a visit to John Kilburn's house with some beaver-skins for sale. He wanted powder, bullets, and flints for pay. While he was trading, Captain Philip was running his eyes over the house, looking at the thick timbers, the loop-holes in the walls. When he had finished his trade he visited the other houses in the settlement. He was kindly treated. The settlers never mistrusted that he was taking observations for future use.

August came. The settlers heard that war had begun, and knew that the French and Indians might be upon them at any moment. They strengthened their block-houses. No one went into the field to work alone. They always carried their guns with them. They had some faithful watch-dogs which always growled when Indians were about. There were nearly forty men in the settlement. They were stout-hearted, and were determined not to be driven out by the French and Indians. They appointed Colonel Bellows to be their leader. He had a suspicion that Indians were about.

"We must have a supply of meal, so that in case we are attacked we shall have something to eat," he said.

The settlers filled each a bag with corn, shouldered them, and then, in single file, each man carrying his gun, they marched to the grist-mill which they had erected, ground the corn into meal, shouldered the sacks once more, and started homeward, their faithful watch-dogs trotting in advance, paying no attention to squirrels or partridges, or game of that sort.

Suddenly the dogs came back, growling, the hair on their backs in a ruff.

"There are Indians about. Throw down your sacks," said Colonel Bellows.

The men threw their sacks on the ground, dropped into the ferns, and looked to the priming of their guns. The ferns were tall, and completely concealed them. Colonel Bellows suspected that the Indians had laid an ambuscade at a narrow place in the path which they must pass. He crept slowly forward to see what he could discover, careful not to break a twig or make any noise. He crept to the top of a little hill, peeped through the ferns, and discovered a great number of Indians, nearly two hundred, crouching behind trees, or lying on the ground, waiting for the white men to enter the trap. He made his way back to his men, passed his orders in a whisper, and all crawled through the ferns toward the Indians till they were only a few rods from them.

All were ready. Every man sprang to his feet, and yelled as loud as he could, "Hi-ya! hi-ya!" It was a terrific howl.

The next moment not a settler was to be seen; all had dropped upon the ground, and were concealed by the ferns.

In an instant every Indian was on his feet, firing his gun, but hitting nobody.

There was an answering flash from the ferns, each settler taking aim, and the Indians sprang into the air, or fell headlong before the bullets.

The red men outnumbered the settlers five to one, but were so astounded by the surprise that, picking up the wounded, they made a hasty retreat into a swamp, and the settlers made all haste to their block-house, anticipating an attack. Not one of them had been injured.

This body of Indians was a part of a band of more than three hundred, led by Captain Philip, who had come from Canada with the expectation of wiping out the settlements along the Connecticut, and of returning to Canada with many prisoners and no end of scalps. It was at the pleasantest season of the year. The woods were full of game, and with the provisions they would get in the settlements which they intended to destroy they would have an abundance of food.

Captain Philip, with the rest of the Indians, was creeping stealthily through the woods toward John Kilburn's house. Mr. Kilburn and his son John, Mr. Pike and his son, were out in the field reaping wheat, their guns close at hand. Mr. Kilburn had trained his dog to scour the woods, and the faithful animal ever had his eyes and ears open, and was sniffing the wind if a wolf or bear was about. On this afternoon in August the dog came running in with his hair in a ruff, and growling.

"Indians," said Mr. Kilburn. The men and boys seized their guns, ran for the house, and had just time to get inside and bar the door when Captain Philip and nearly two hundred Indians made their appearance.

The Indians staid at a safe distance, and so did **Captain** Philip, though he came near enough to talk.

"Come out, old John! come out, young John! I give you good quarter," he shouted.

There were only the two men, the two boys, Mrs. Kilburn and her daughter and four children, in the house, with three hundred Indians attacking them, but John Kilburn was not in the least frightened—not he. Neither was Mrs. Kilburn, nor her son or daughter. They had several extra guns; Mrs. Kilburn and her daughter knew how to load them. They would rather die than be taken prisoners. The Indians had no cannon, and their bullets would not go through the stout timbers. Only by burning the house would they be able to get in.

"Get you gone, you rascal, or I'll quarter you!" was the defiant answer that John Kilburn shouted through one of the loop-holes to Captain Philip, as the latter went back to the dark crowd of savages, who set up the war-whoop.

"They yell like so many devils," said John Kilburn; but he was not in the least disturbed by the howling.

Then the bullets began to come through the shingles on the roof, and strike against the timbers.

The Indians surrounded the house, but there were loop-holes on each side. Mr. Kilburn and Mr. Pike took two of the sides, and the two boys the others. Bang! bang! went the guns of Mr. Kilburn and Mr. Pike. Bang! bang! went the boys' guns. They could fire at a rest, and take deliberate aim. The Indians could not see the muzzles of the guns, and the moment one of the red men peeped from behind a tree his skull was in danger.

One by one they fell, which enraged them all the more, and they crept nearer, firing rapidly, riddling the shingles, hoping, quite likely, that a bullet might glance down from the roof, and hit those inside.

"The roof looks like a sieve," said **John Kilburn,** as he looked up and saw the holes.

Mrs. Kilburn and her daughter were loading the extra guns the while, and handing them to the men and boys, who kept up such a rapid fire that the Indians came to the conclusion that there were a **large** number of men in the house.

"We shall soon be out of bullets," said Mrs. Kilburn.

A thought came: why not catch the bullets that were

coming through the roof? The balls had nearly spent their force when they came through, and they hung up a blanket, with thick folds, which stopped them entirely; and the girl, gathering them as they fell harmlessly upon the floor, put them into a ladle, melted them, and ran new bullets, which soon were whizzing through the air, and doing damage to the enemy.

All through the afternoon the fight goes on, the Indians aiming at the loop-holes. Their bullets pepper the logs around them. One comes in, and inflicts a ghastly wound in Mr. Pike's thigh, but the Indians do not know it, and the brave defense is kept up till the Indians, foiled in all their efforts, defeated, with several of their number dead and many wounded from the volley fired by Colonel Bellows and his men, and by those in the house, set Mr. Kilburn's wheat on fire, kill his cattle, bury their dead, and slink away, not having taken a scalp or a prisoner. They have only wounded one man.

When everything goes well with the Indian he can be very brave, but when the tide is against him he quickly loses courage and becomes disheartened, and so Captain Philip made his way back to Canada, very much crest-fallen at the repulse received at the hands of two men, a woman, two boys, and a brave-hearted girl.

[TO BE CONTINUED.]

CAMBRIDGE SERIES

OF

INFORMATION CARDS FOR SCHOOLS.

No. 2.

About Combustion.

BY

W. J. ROLFE, A.M.

COMBUSTION is only another name for burning, and burning in all ordinary cases is *oxidation*, or union with oxygen, one of the gases that make up our atmosphere. It is a *chemical* change; that is, one by which we get a new substance entirely unlike any of the substances united. Common salt, for instance, is formed by the chemical union of a yellow, bad-smelling gas and a soft silvery metal. When coal and wood are burned, the chief products of the union with oxygen are carbonic acid and water. The former is a colorless gas, and the latter is in the form of invisible vapor, and both go up the chimney and mix with the outer air. The ashes left behind are only what can not be burned or united with the oxygen. If we collect all the products of the burning, together with the ashes, we find that they weigh more than the coal or wood, the increase being exactly equal to the weight of the oxygen consumed. No kind of matter can be destroyed by any power known to us; it may unite with other matter, and take many new forms, but its weight can be neither increased nor diminished. The amount of matter in the universe is always the same.

Oxygen must be heated before it will unite with coal or wood. The air is at all times in contact with them, but they will not burn unless they are first kindled. The chemical process itself, when once started, generally produces heat enough to raise more oxygen to the proper temperature, and thus the combustion is kept up. The point to which the oxygen must be heated varies much with different substances, as is well shown in kindling a coal fire. The heat produced by rubbing a match on a rough surface suffices to make the oxygen unite with the phosphorus on the end of the match; the burning of this causes heat enough for the union of the oxygen with the sulphur, and the burning of the sulphur enough to set the wood of the match on fire. The shavings, the kindling wood, and the charcoal are in turn ignited, and the burning charcoal develops heat enough to enable the oxygen to combine with the hard coal. Each step in the operation requires more heat than the preceding step. This seems a very simple thing now, but the anthracite beds of Pennsylvania long remained useless because no one had found out how to kindle the fuel, and the discovery was at last made half by accident.

There are some forms of combustion which are very unlike ordinary burning, and yet are essentially the same, being cases of union with oxygen. The only difference is that the process goes on slowly instead of rapidly. We know that vegetable and animal substances decay when exposed to the air; and decay is a slow burning. The oxygen of the air gradually combines with the substances, converting them into carbonic acid and water, and leaving only a small remnant of matter as the ashes of the lingering combustion. The heat produced in this case is found to be precisely the same as in ordinary burning, but it is set free so gradually that it escapes our notice.

We know that green wood decays much sooner than dry wood. Indeed, if wood is kept perfectly dry, it will not decay for ages. In the dry climate of Egypt wooden mummy cases have been preserved for more than three thousand years. On the other hand, dry wood burns much quicker than green wood; it is not easy to set the latter on fire. Why this difference, if decay and burning are similar processes? The decay of the green wood is due to the fact that the presence of moisture causes certain changes in portions of the wood, which enable the oxygen to attack it at a low temperature; and the slow combustion, once started, is self-sustaining. But in ordinary burning the temperature must be raised to a certain point before the oxidation can begin, and this point can not be reached until the moisture is evaporated, which uses up a good deal of heat.

This process of decay is continually going on in our bodies; but during life the matter which is burned up is being constantly renewed from the food we eat. The body is not only decaying, as dead animal matter decays, but it is also wearing out. With every motion a part of the muscles is actually consumed, and must be replaced by fresh material. The heat of the body is likewise due to combustion, and must be kept up by proper fuel, like the fires in our stoves and furnaces. The products of all this burning are carbonic acid and water, which pass out of the body through the lungs.

The rusting of metals is a slow combustion, and scientific men have proved that, like decay, it develops heat. Iron can be easily burned in pure oxygen, with the production of intense light and heat. Zinc and some other metals can be burned in the air if heated very hot, and most metals are rapidly consumed in the flame of the oxyhydrogen blow-pipe. Indeed, every form of matter known to us can be burned, unless it has already been burned. All substances belong to one of these two classes—those that will burn, or unite with oxygen; and those that have been burned, or are products of oxidation. Water belongs to the latter class, and so do nearly all the rocks and solid matter of the earth.

Slow burning sometimes becomes rapid, and then we have what is called *spontaneous combustion*. When cotton or tow which has become soaked with oil is laid aside in heaps, the oxygen of the air begins to unite with it; but the heat developed causes the oxidation to go on faster and faster, until in some cases the mass bursts into a flame. The same thing sometimes takes place in moist hay, the moisture starting the process, as explained above, and the confined heat increasing until it is sufficient to set the heap on fire.

[*By special arrangement with the author, the cards contributed to this useful series, by* W. J. ROLFE, A.M., *formerly Head-Master of the Cambridge High School, will, for the present, first appear in* HARPER'S YOUNG PEOPLE.]

DAVE'S GREAT LUNCH.

BY J. B. MARSHALL.

IT was the great day at the State Fair, and the sidewalks were nearly deserted as Dave Burt went down Main Street toward the post-office. As Dave approached the Town Hall, or the City Hall, as the good people of Rawley were pleased to call that fine building, he glanced up at it, and saw Mr. William Henry Barrington, the great lawyer, standing at one of the large windows of his office. Mr. Barrington was frowning, and looked up the street and down it as if impatiently waiting for some one.

"I'll bet he's mad 'cause he can't go to the fair," thought Dave.

A few days before, Billy Barrington, a nephew, had been telling the boys of that fine office, with its brass-studded revolving chairs, great bookcases of books, and a private room where the great lawyer ate his dinner, which was sent up to him on a dumb-waiter from the restaurant in the basement of the City Hall the moment he touched an electric bell.

Dave was recalling all the delightful possibilities of such

GETTING WEDGED.

a room, when click! went something on the pavement before him.

"A penknife," said he, picking up the article, and then looking in vain among the branches of the tree for its owner. Examining the knife, he noticed a slip of paper shut in under the largest blade, and on which was written:

"Five Dollars Reward! I am on the City Hall roof, and can't get down, as the spring-latch door has blown closed. Please send the janitor to release me. CHARLES M. WILCOX."

"Why, he's our Governor!" said astonished Dave, aloud, and started to look for the janitor. Dave had been on the roof with his father only the day previous, and knew just how the door would act if it was not fastened back.

Stout old Billy Simms, the janitor, in his shirt sleeves, had comfortably propped himself back in an arm-chair to take a nap, when rap-rap-rap sounded on the door. Billy's "office," as he called it, was on the ground-floor of the City Hall.

"Well, boy, what's wanted?" gruffly demanded old Billy, having opened the door and discovered Dave.

"Why, the Governor's shut out on the roof, and can't get down," said Dave, handing Billy the paper. "He must have been looking at the Fair Grounds."

Old Billy lowered his great silver-rimmed glasses from his forehead to his nose, and read the paper. He gazed for a moment in a queer way over his glasses at Dave, and then laying his hand pretty heavily on Dave's shoulder, said, "Come with me."

"I haven't time; and, besides, I don't want any reward," answered Dave.

There was a small room, or closet, back of Billy's "office," toward which he moved, holding fast to Dave.

Remembering that the old janitor was rather deaf, Dave then formed his hands in the shape of a trumpet and shouted in the direction of Billy's right ear, "I say, Billy, I haven't time to go with you."

"Don't you call me Billy, you young rascal!" fiercely exclaimed the old man. "My name's Mr. William Simms."

Before Dave could make reply he felt himself shaken, pushed into the closet, and saw the door nearly closed.

"There, you've played that trick once too often," said old Billy. "It's downright murder in you boys to try and fool me into going up seven long flights of steps on an awful hot day like this."

"I did find that paper," said Dave, indignantly.

"Don't tell me you're innocent; you're a desperate character," said old Billy, slamming to the door, and turning the key. "Now," continued he, shouting through the key-hole, "I'll leave you in there two or three hours to think what a dreadful thing it is to try and trick an old rheumatic veteran."

The closet, Dave saw, was where Billy kept his brooms and brushes; the ceiling was very high, and a small round window far up on the wall furnished the light. At the back of the closet was a small sliding shutter, which, after considerable trouble, Dave managed to push up, hoping he might escape through it into another room. It disclosed a dark, square funnel, that seemed to extend far down below and far up above him, and suspended in which were several wire ropes.

"It must be the funnel where the dumb-waiter slides," thought Dave, and he caught hold of the nearest rope, pulling and shaking it to attract attention, and calling loudly at the same time. At once he heard a tinkle-tinkle of a small bell up the dark funnel; and then a scraping sound from the same direction, seeming to draw nearer him. Directly the dumb-waiter cage was seen descending, and Dave held fast to the wire rope until the cage was within a short distance of his hand.

When the cage ceased to move he climbed into it by aid of a chair, and curled himself up, hoping to go down into the restaurant. There was a wire running through the cage, and supposing it to be the same he had been previously holding, he pulled at it with both hands.

The cage began to move; but in place of going down, it began to move upward. Dave was frightened; but before he could decide what he ought to do, the cage had passed above the open shutter, and went on scraping between four dark wooden walls. Up and up went the cage, until Dave felt that he had traversed a distance far more than enough to have carried him to the very tip of the lightning-rod on the City Hall cupola.

Suddenly he saw a thin streak of light before him, and quickly releasing the wire, the cage moved a little further, and then came to a stop. Dave lost no time in waiting to drum on the door, partition, or whatever it was before him, and loudly called:

"Hello! Let me out! let me out!"

In a moment there was the sound of quick feet, a sliding shutter was pushed aside, and such a flood of light shone into Dave's face that before he could get the dazzle out of his eyes some one carefully lifted him out of the cage, and stood him on his feet.

"What ever possessed you to take a ride in that carriage?" asked a pleasant voice.

Dave shaded his eyes, and saw that he was standing before Mr. Barrington in his private office.

"It's all that old Billy Simms's fault," said Dave, hotly, "and he ought to be arrested. I found a paper on the pavement that said a man was locked out on the City Hall roof, and please somebody come and open the door for him. But when I gave it to Billy, he just locked me up in a room, and said I was playing a trick on him, and the Governor wasn't on the roof. Then I opened a shutter, and—"

"The Governor fastened out on the roof!" said Mr. Barrington. "I've been waiting an hour for him to come and eat lunch with me, but this accounts for his absence. Sit down, my little man." Then Mr. Barrington stepped into another room, where Dave heard him send one of his law clerks to release the Governor.

"I see you are Captain Burt's son David," said Mr. Barrington, returning. "Simms has treated you very badly; but come—you must be hungry, being shut up in that dark hole—sit down here at the table, and eat some lunch. There will be plenty for the Governor."

Dave excused himself, having already dined.

"Then I know what you will eat—a Neapolitan ice."

The door opened, and the Governor entered, looking as though he was nearly roasted; and in a moment Mr. Barrington had explained to him how Dave had tried to have him released.

"I'm many times obliged to you, David," said the Governor, shaking Dave's hand, and making him feel very proud.

The Governor was too near broiled himself to feel like eating lunch, but the ices appearing, he helped Mr. Barrington and Dave to eat them.

When the ices were eaten, the Governor wished to give Dave the five dollars, as promised, but he was very, very sure he ought not to take it. In a few days, however, there came to Captain Burt's house a package of books, marked "Master David Burt," and within was a note with the compliments of the Governor.

[Begun in HARPER'S YOUNG PEOPLE No. 37, July 13.]

THE STORY OF THE AMERICAN NAVY.

BY BENSON J. LOSSING.

CHAPTER X.

THE navy, especially the portion composed of the gun-boat and mortar-boat squadrons, performed most arduous and valuable services in connection with the armies on the inland waters of the great basin of the Mississippi. Soon after the capture of New Orleans, Farragut, with Porter's mortar-boats, and transports with troops, ascended the Mississippi to Vicksburg, and after that national vessels continued to patrol the waters of the great river.

At that time cruisers built in British ports for the use of the Confederates in preying upon American commerce were active on the seas. The most conspicuous of these was the *Alabama*, which for eighteen months illuminated the ocean with burning American vessels which her commander (Semmes) had plundered and set on fire. In the summer of 1864 the *Kearsarge* (Captain Winslow) fought her, off the coast of France, and sent her to the bottom of the sea. Our government held the British responsible for her outrages, and by the decision of an international commission they were compelled to pay the Americans $15,500,000 in gold for damages.

National gun and mortar boats carried on a wonderful amphibious warfare among the bayous and in the tributaries of the Mississippi in 1863. In their exploits Commodore D. D. Porter was most conspicuous. The blockading squadron were very vigilant—so vigilant and active that during the war they captured or destroyed British blockade-runners valued, with their cargoes, at nearly $30,000,000.

In the spring of 1863 it was determined to attempt the capture of Charleston, and Admiral Dupont was sent with a naval force to assist the army in the work. It was a perilous undertaking, for the harbor was guarded by heavy batteries aggregating three hundred great guns, and the channels were strewn with torpedoes. The navy had a terrific battle. "Such a fire, or anything like it, was never seen before," wrote an eye-witness. The little Monitors sustained the battle bravely, while tons of iron were hurled upon them from Fort Sumter and the shore batteries. During the battle of forty minutes the Confederates sent 3500 shots. The attempt to capture the city failed, and the fleet was withdrawn. It was renewed the

following summer, when General Gillmore with troops on Morris Island, and Admiral Dahlgren with a fleet, attacked its most powerful defenses. They jointly attacked Fort Wagner, on Morris Island, and Fort Sumter, not far off. They drove the garrison from the former, and reduced the latter to a heap of ruins. But they did not take Charleston.

Porter, with a fleet of gun-boats, went on a remarkable expedition up the Red River, for the invasion of Texas, in company with a land force under General Banks, in the spring of 1864. Nothing of importance was accomplished. The greatest exploit of that expedition was the passage of Porter's fleet down the rapids at Alexandria. While he was above, the river had fallen. It was now dammed by Michigan troops, and from an opened sluice the gun-boats were passed over the rapids, as logs are borne down a shallow stream by lumbermen.

In the summer of 1864 the government determined to close the two Southern ports yet open to British blockade-runners, namely, Mobile, near the Gulf of Mexico, and Wilmington, on the Cape Fear River. For this purpose Admiral Farragut appeared off the entrance to Mobile Bay, with a strong naval force, in August. He entered the bay on the morning of August 5, four iron-clad vessels leading the way, and immediately followed by the *Hartford* (the flag-ship) and three other wooden vessels bound together in couples.

In order to observe every movement of his fleet, Farragut had himself lashed to the mast in the round-top, and thence gave his orders through a speaking-tube extending to the deck. In that position he endured the terrible tempest of shot and shell while passing the forts guarding the entrance to the bay, also in the subsequent fierce encounters with a huge Confederate "ram" and gun-boats. At the beginning of the latter encounters one of Farragut's best iron-clads (the *Tecumseh*) was sunk in a few seconds by a torpedo exploded under her, when all but seventeen of her one hundred and thirty men perished. Undismayed, Farragut pushed on, won a victory, and permanently closed the port of Mobile. When the *Tecumseh* went to the bottom the Admiral prayed for light and guidance. "It seemed to me," said Farragut, "that a voice commanded me to go on;" and he did.

"The port of Wilmington must now be closed," said the government, when the news of Farragut's victory reached the capital. An immense land and naval force gathered at Hampton Roads, the former under General Butler, the latter under Admiral Porter. They sailed at the middle of December to attack Fort Fisher, a strong work at the mouth of the Cape Fear, and on the anniversary of the birth of the Prince of Peace, 1864, the fleet bombarded that stronghold with very little effect, throwing eighteen thousand shells upon it. A floating mine containing 430,000 pounds of gunpowder had been exploded near the fort, but without effect. Troops landed, but accomplished nothing, and the capture of Fort Fisher was deferred until the middle of January, 1865, when all the defenses at the mouth of the Cape Fear were captured by the same fleet, and a land force under General Terry. The port of Wilmington was effectually closed, and with this victory the most important operations of the navy in the civil war closed.

Here ends our brief story of the navy of the United States. It is only a brief outline; sufficient, perhaps, to indicate what remains in store for you when you come to read its marvellous details in volume at some time in the future. Its record in the past is glorious; it may be made more so in the future, for its capabilities are great. It ought to be cherished as the strong right arm of defense for our government, our commerce, and our free institutions.

Our government is now giving it a fostering care hitherto unknown. It has established training-ships, in which American boys are thoroughly instructed in all the arts of expert seamanship and the military tactics of the sea, while particular attention is given to the training of their minds and morals. There are bright promises that our future navy will be controlled by highly educated officers, and its ships be manned by refined, intelligent, and self-respecting American citizens, the peers of those in any other stations in life.

THE END.

SEA-BREEZES.

LETTER No. 4 FROM [illegible] MAYNARD TO HER DOLL.

Bar Harbor, *August*, 1880.

DO you remember, dear Clytie, a poem I read in school last Forefather's Day, beginning like this,

"The breaking waves dashed high
On a stern and rock-bound coast"?

Well, these two lines I kept saying over and over to myself as the steamer drew near to Mount Desert, on our way from Portland to Bar Harbor, and long before we got here I had changed my mind about the crooked coast. I think I shall *not* tell the girls that the maps are wrong, and that Maine is not as jiggly as they make it out. Between you and me, Clytie, my next winter's maps will be better than they ever were before, and I shouldn't wonder if I were to take the prize, for I have seen with my own eyes the queer ins and outs along here, and I am sure that the more we jiggle our pencils up and down, the more "true to nature," as the artists say, our maps will be.

But I must tell you about our life here. There are mountains around us as well as the ocean, and the waves don't seem sad a bit, but with their pretty white caps on their heads, come rushing along in the sunshine, and splash 'way up over the rocks. There are lovely roads through the woods, and ponds where we go rowing and fishing. A little way from our hotel is an Indian encampment, where *real* Indians and squaws make and sell baskets. I have bought a little beauty, made of sweet-grass, to carry home to you. Yesterday we all went out to Green Mountain on a picnic. "All" means papa and mamma, Cousin Frank and me, with about a dozen of our friends. We had a delightful time, and after dinner, while the others were sitting on the grass telling stories, I wandered off by myself.

Mamma thought I had gone with Cousin Frank, while all the time I was only a few steps from her, searching for blackberries. I could not find any, and at last sat down under a tree to rest, for it was very hot in the sun, and I had walked farther than I knew. I heard voices a little way off, and thought they came from our party; but all at once some one walked round the very tree I was leaning against, and, handing me the prettiest little birch-bark canoe, about six inches long, filled with blackberries, said, "Wouldn't you like some berries?"

I clapped my hands and cried out: "Oh, how cunning! Isn't it lovely! Where—" But not another word did I say, for, on looking up, who should I see standing before me but my enemy from Old Orchard, Randolph Peyton! Yes, there he was; no mistake; and after all that had happened, he *dared* to offer me blackberries! I tossed back my head, and said, proudly, "I scorn your gift: we are enemies."

He made no answer, but walked sadly away. Here is a picture of us. Of course I can not make him look quite as ashamed as he did, nor me quite as scornful.

When he was out of sight I sat down again, and when my surprise and anger had passed off I almost wished he had left the berries, for I was tired and warm and thirsty. But no, he had taken the little canoe with him, and had not dropped a single one.

I was so tired that all at once, before I thought of such a thing, I was sound asleep. When I woke up the sun had set, and it was almost dark. I was alone on Green Mountain, with no idea which way to turn to get home. There wasn't a sound to be heard except the chirping of the crickets, and the queer noises we always hear at night, and never know where they come from. I tried to be brave, but the tears *would* come. I called as loud as I could to papa, and everywhere the cruel echoes called back, "Pa—pa—pa"—but there was no other answer.

At last, after wandering about for what seemed to me *hours*, I sank down, perfectly tired out.

All at once I heard a crackling in the bushes not far away, and started up, expecting to see the fierce eyes of a catamount glaring at me, but instead of that I saw a straw hat waving, and heard some one shouting, "Here she is! I've found her! she's all *right*!" and then happy voices called my name, and in less time than I can write it I was in papa's arms.

As soon as mamma had gone back to the hotel and found that I was *not* with Cousin Frank, papa had started with several of his friends in search of me. But, Clytie dear, the one who waved his hat and shouted, "Here she is!"—the one who *really found* me—was Randolph Peyton!

The little canoe is packed away among my treasures, and I shall never look at it without thinking of the day on Green Mountain when my life was saved by my bitterest enemy, who has become my friend forever!

Don't you think I have had adventures enough for one summer? *I* do, and we shall be home very soon, dear Clytie. Your loving mamma,

Bessie Maynard.

THE ASHES THAT MADE THE TREES BLOOM.

A Japanese Fairy Tale.

BY WILLIAM ELLIOT GRIFFIS.

IN the good old days of the Daimios there lived an old couple whose only pet was a little dog. Having no children, they loved it as though it were the tiny top-knot of a baby. The old dame made him a cushion of blue crape, and at meal-times Inuko—for that was his name—would sit on it as demure as any cat. The kind people would feed him with tidbits of fish from their own chopsticks, and he was allowed to have all the boiled rice he wanted. Whenever the old woman took him out with her on holidays she put a bright red silk crape ribbon around his neck.

Now the old man, being a rice-farmer, went daily with hoe or spade into the fields, working hard from the first croak of the raven until O Tento Sama (as the sun is called) had gone down behind the hills. Every day the dog followed him to work, and kept near by, never once harming the white heron that walked in the footsteps of the old man to pick up worms.

One day doggy came running to him, putting his paws against his straw leggings, and motioning with his head to some spot behind. The old man at first thought his pet was only playing, and did not mind him. But he kept on whining and running to and fro for some minutes. Then the old man followed the dog a few yards, to a place where the animal began a lively scratching. Thinking it only a buried bone or bit of fish, but wishing to humor his pet, the old man struck his iron-shod hoe in the earth, when lo! a pile of gold gleamed before him. He rubbed his old eyes, stooped down, and there was at least a half-peck of kobans (oval gold coins). He gathered them up and hied home at once.

Thus in an hour the old couple were made rich. The good souls bought a piece of land, made a feast to their friends, and gave plentifully to their poor neighbors. As for Inuko, they petted him till they nearly smothered him with kindness.

Now in the same village there lived a wicked old man and his wife, who had always kicked and scolded all dogs whenever any passed their house. Hearing of their neighbors' good luck, they coaxed the dog into their garden, and set before him bits of fish and other dainties, hoping he would find treasure for them. But the dog, being afraid of the cruel pair, would neither eat nor move. Then they dragged him out-of-doors, taking a spade and hoe with them. No sooner had Inuko got near a pine-tree in the garden than he began to paw and scratch the ground as though a mighty treasure lay beneath.

"Quick, wife, hand me the spade and hoe!" cried the greedy old fool, as he danced for joy.

Then the covetous old fellow with a spade, and the old crone with a hoe, began to dig; but there was nothing but a dead kitten, the smell of which made them drop their tools and shut their noses. Furious at the dog, the old man kicked and beat him to death, and the old woman finished the work by nearly chopping off his head with the sharp hoe.

That night the spirit of the dog appeared to his former master in a dream and said, "Cut down the pine-tree which is over my grave, and make from it a mill to grind bean sauce in."

So the old man made the little mill, and filling it with bean sauce, began to grind, while the envious neighbor peeped in at the window. "Goody me!" cried the old woman, as each dripping of sauce turned into yellow gold, until in a few minutes the tub under the mill was full of a shining mass of kobans.

So the old couple were rich again.

The next day the stingy and wicked neighbors, after boiling a mess of beans, came and borrowed the magic mill. They filled it with the boiled beans, and the old man began to grind.

But, at the first turn, the sauce turned into a foul heap of dirt. Angry at this, they chopped the mill in pieces to use as fire-wood.

Not long after that the old man dreamed again, and the spirit of the dog spoke to him, telling him how the wicked people had burned the mill made from the pine-tree.

"Take the ashes of the mill, sprinkle them on withered trees, and they will bloom again," said the dog-spirit.

The old man awoke and went at once to his wicked neighbors' house, where he humbly begged the ashes, and though the covetous couple turned up their noses at him and scolded him as if he were a thief, they let him fill his basket with the ashes.

On coming home the old man took his wife into the garden. It being winter, their favorite cherry-tree was bare. He sprinkled a pinch of ashes on it, and lo! it sprouted blossoms until it became a cloud of pink blooms, which filled the air with perfume.

The kind old man, hearing that his lord the Daimio was to pass along the high-road near the village, set out to see him, taking his basket of ashes. As the train approached he climbed up into an old withered cherry-tree that stood by the way-side.

Now in the days of the Daimios it was the custom, when

their lord passed by, for all the loyal people to shut up their second-story windows, even pasting them shut with slips of paper, so as not to commit the impoliteness of looking down on his lordship. All the people along the road would fall down on their hands and knees until the procession passed by. Hence it seemed very impolite for the old man to climb the tree, and be higher than his master's head.

The train drew near, and the air was full of gay banners, covered spears, state umbrellas, and princes' crests. One tall man marched ahead crying out to the people by the way, "Get down on your knees! get down on your knees!" And every one knelt down while the procession was passing. Suddenly the leader of the van caught sight of the old man up in the tree. He was about to call out to him in an angry tone, but seeing he was such an old fellow he pretended not to notice him, and passed him by.

So when the prince's palanquin drew near, the old man, taking a pinch of ashes from his basket, scattered it over the tree. In a moment it burst into blossom. The delighted Daimio ordered the train to be stopped, and got out to see the wonder. Calling the old man to him, he thanked him, and ordered presents of silk robes, sponge-cake, fans, a *netsuké* (ivory carving), and other rewards to be given him. He even invited him to pay a visit to his castle. So the old daddy went gleefully home to share his joy with his dear wife.

But when the greedy neighbor heard of it he took some of the magic ashes, and went out on the highway. There he waited till a Daimio's train came along, and instead of kneeling down like the crowd, he climbed a withered cherry-tree.

When the Daimio himself was almost directly under him, he threw a handful of ashes over the tree, which did not change a particle. The wind blew the fine dust in the noses and eyes of the Daimio and his nobles.

Such a sneezing and choking!

It spoiled all the pomp and dignity of the procession. The man who cried, "Get down on your knees," seized the old fool by the top-knot, dragged him from the tree, and tumbled him and his ash-basket into the ditch by the road. Then beating him soundly, he left him dead.

Thus the wicked old man died in the mud, but the kind friend of the dog dwelt in peace and plenty, and both he and his wife lived to a green old age.

A BABE IN THE WOOD.—Drawn by F. S. Church.

OUR POST-OFFICE BOX

oyster-drill, a tiny sea creature which does much mischief to all kinds of shell-fish.

ALFRED B. C.—Directions for making a paper balloon were given in the Post-office Box No. 48.

S. B. W.—The numbers of YOUNG PEOPLE you require will be furnished to you, postage paid, by the publishers, on the receipt of one dollar and eight cents.

FOND M. G.—The genuine Bologna sausage is manufactured in the city of Bologna, in Northern Italy. Many imitations of the imported article are sold in the United States under the same name.

DAISY VIOLET.—The first volume of HARPER'S YOUNG PEOPLE will close with No. 52, which will be published on October 26, 1880.

MARY C.—There is no better way to preserve autumn leaves than to press them between the leaves of a book, or sheets of paper, and varnish them when they are thoroughly dry. In the Post-office Box of YOUNG PEOPLE No. 35 there is a letter describing a neat and simple method of varnishing leaves.

PUZZLES FROM YOUNG CONTRIBUTORS.

No. 1.

EASY WORD SQUARE.

First, negative [illegible]. Second, the imperfect form of a verb. Third, the [illegible] form of a noun signifying a portion of the body. Fourth, a bird. [illegible]

No. 2.

ENIGMA.

My first is in [illegible], but not in [illegible].
My second is in [illegible], but not in whip.
My third is in [illegible], but not in [illegible].
My fourth is in [illegible], but not in thread.
My fifth is in [illegible], but not in [illegible].
My sixth is in [illegible], but not in [illegible].
My seventh is in [illegible], but not in [illegible].
My eighth is in [illegible], but not in wrench.
If ever my whole you chance to [illegible],
You would better make a speedy retreat. [illegible]

No. 3.

[illegible]

1. In Labrador. [illegible] all girls should learn to do. To revoke. A [illegible]. In Labrador. 2. In Palermo. Sword. A [illegible]. A [illegible]. In Palermo. [illegible]

No. 4.

DOUBLE ACROSTIC.

A [illegible] animal. One of the United States. A Scottish lake. A [illegible]. A Norman name. A [illegible]. Answer—A city in Europe and a city in the United States. [illegible]

[The following puzzle is from the [illegible] of our young friends who are [illegible].]

No. 5.

[illegible] NUMERICAL CHARADE.

I am a French [illegible], composed of [illegible] letters.
My [illegible] is [illegible].
[illegible]
[illegible]

ANSWERS TO PUZZLES IN NO. 44.

No. 1. [illegible]

No. 2. [illegible]

No. 3. [illegible]

No. 4. [illegible]

No. 5. [illegible]

Puzzles are acknowledged from [illegible]

Correct answers to puzzles are received from Ada [illegible], [illegible], Harry Phillips, [illegible], [illegible], [illegible], Frank T. [illegible], [illegible].

The following poetic answer to "A Riddle in Rhyme" in YOUNG PEOPLE No. [illegible], page [illegible], has been received from a correspondent in Auburn, New York:

From Adam's [illegible] for [illegible] A.D.—
Begins the round of the Christian year;
That Adam was [illegible] all agree;
That he was a father is very clear.
That a [illegible] is a mother who'll [illegible]?
Or that a [illegible] his father's [illegible]?
And [illegible] over it, little or much,
A [illegible] Holland to the Dutch.

THE MUSICAL ANECDOTE.

The Musical Anecdote given in YOUNG PEOPLE No. 44 can be translated by substituting for the musical signs the following words in the order given:

[illegible]	Quarter.
Quick, [illegible].	[illegible].
[illegible].	Full stop.
Sharp.	Very loud.
[illegible].	Bind.
[illegible].	[illegible].
Bar.	Quaver.
[illegible].	[illegible].
Chord.	Slur.
[illegible].	Natural.
[illegible].	[illegible].
[illegible].	Signature.

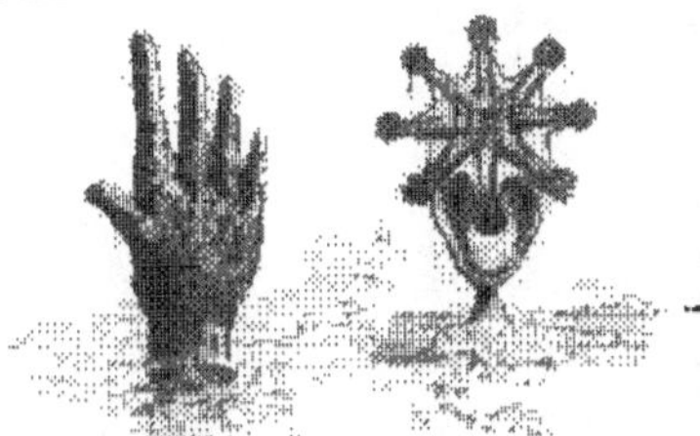

OF these two objects the first is not a hand, and the second is not a windmill. What are they?

ANOTHER SQUARE PUZZLE.

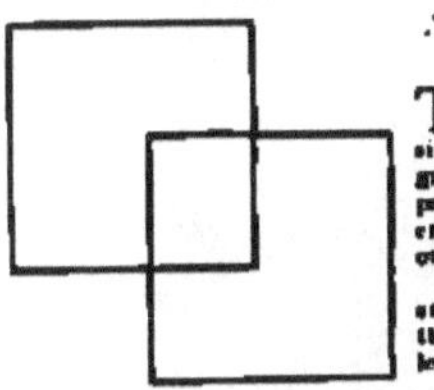

THE puzzle is to draw two squares in the positions shown by the diagram, without lifting the pencil from the paper, or crossing one line with another.

Let our little readers exercise their ingenuity over this apparently simple problem.

HOW TO MAKE A CUCUIUS.

BY FRANK BELLEW.

YOU would like to be able to make a cucuius, would you not? We will tell you. But perhaps you would like to know what, in the name of Memnon, a cucuius is? Well, we will tell you that too.

A cucuius, or cucuij, is a kind of beetle, about three inches long, which emits a very brilliant light from two large protuberances in its head, which look like its eyes. It is called the lantern-fly in English, and lives in South America. The light it gives is so bright that you can read a book by it. The natives employ them in place of candles to illuminate their rooms while performing their domestic work. We have seen one exhibited in a room where eight gas-burners were in full blaze, and yet its two great demoniac-looking eyes (or what appeared to be eyes) shone more brightly than the most brilliant of precious stones—with an intensity, it will be no exaggeration to say, equal to the electric light. The effect was perfectly startling, and rather appalling.

To give light, however, is not the only good quality this wonderful insect possesses: it is a deadly enemy to gnats, by which the natives of the Spanish West Indies are greatly annoyed. When they wish to rid themselves of these pests they procure two or three of the cucuiii, and let them loose in the room, when they soon make short work of the enemy. The method of catching the cucuius adopted by the natives is to repair to some open piece of land with a flaming fire-brand, which they wave vigorously backward and forward, calling out all the time, "Cucuio, cucuio, cucuio." This attracts the insects to them, when they are easily captured with a small net. What a blessing these cucuiii would be to the be-bitten inhabitants of the United States if Mr. Cucuius would only treat our mosquitoes with the vigor that he does the gnats of the tropics!

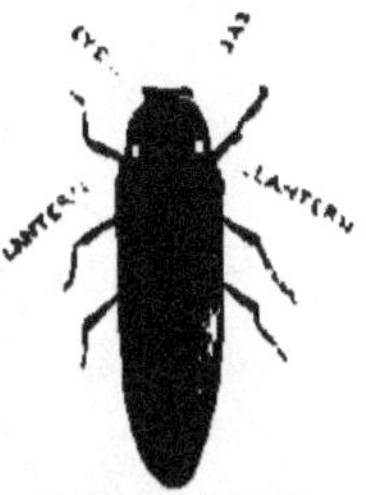

The Cucuius, or Lantern-Fly.

In South America they are used as ornaments for the hair and dresses of the ladies; and on certain festivals young people gallop through the streets on horseback, brilliantly illuminated, horse and rider, with these insects, secured in little nets, or cages made of fine twigs woven together. The effect is marvellous, producing in the dark evening the appearance of a large moving body of light. "Many wanton, wild fellows," as an old writer describes them, rub their faces with the flesh of a killed cucuius, as boys with us sometimes do with phosphorus, to frighten or amuse their friends.

And now we will tell you how to make a very fair—by no means so brilliant—imitation of the cucuius. By looking at our picture you will see the shape of the insect. Cut this out of a piece of cork about three inches long, and make the legs of thin wire (after the manner of the spider we described in a previous number); then get some strips of thin tin-foil, and gum them on the back of the cucuius; then paint over the whole with transparent green color (oil paints if possible). Now gouge out two holes about the size of the head of a common match, and then cut off the heads of two common matches, and insert them into the aforesaid holes, and your cucuius will be complete. To make the eyes shine, rub them with oil or water. If your insect is painted with oil-colors, you can place it in a vessel of water, for it is in that element that the real cucuius shines most brightly.

You can make a still more brilliant imitation of the cucuius by filling the eye-holes with grains of pure phosphorus, easily procured at a druggist's, or with a paste made of tallow and phosphorus, which is less combustible than the pure article. But as both these things are very dangerous to handle, we would not recommend their use except with the consent and in the presence of a grown person. Another point with regard to the handling of phosphorus, which applies also to matches, is that it is apt to destroy the teeth, particularly where any decay has already taken place. For this reason only persons with sound teeth are employed in match factories. Therefore never put the end of a match in your mouth.

A PLEASANT DAY IN THE COUNTRY.

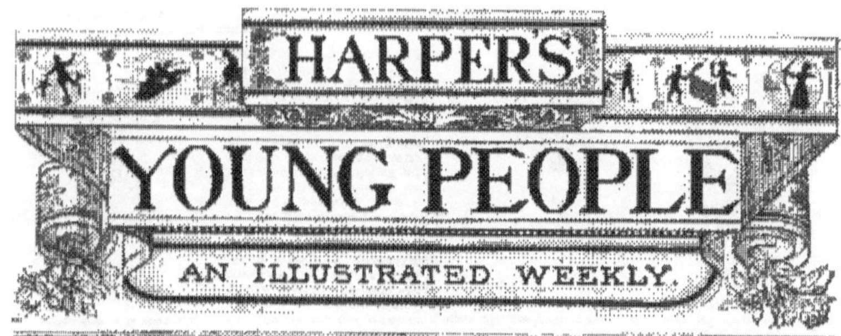

VOL. I.—NO. 47. | PUBLISHED BY HARPER & BROTHERS, NEW YORK. | PRICE FOUR CENTS.

Tuesday, September 21, 1880. | $1.50 per Year, in Advance.

HOW TED AND KITTY CAMPED OUT.

BY EMILY H. LELAND.

KITTY was eight years old, and Ted was seven. They had always lived on a large farm, and knew all about birds and squirrels, and the different kinds of trees, and how to make bonfires and little stone ovens; and they could shoot with bows and arrows, and swim, and climb trees, and split kindlings, and take care of chickens and ducks and turkeys, and do a great many jolly and useful things which city children hardly get even a chance to do. Well, once when they went on a visit with some cousins to an uncle's on

The uncle thought they had gone home, and the father and mother thought they had remained overnight at the uncle's. So nothing was done about it until noon next day, when the uncle came jogging over on horseback to look at a cow he thought of buying, and the mother asked him if Ted and Kitty were not making too long a visit.

Then the uncle said, "Good gracious! they are not at our house; they started for home last night, along with the Elderkins, I think."

Then the mother turned very pale, and said, in a faint voice, "They are lost!"

"Oh no," said the uncle, "not a bit of it. The Elderkins coaxed 'em home with them, of course. I'll ride round their way when I go back and start 'em home."

But the pale look wouldn't leave the mother's face, and in a short time who should come but the Elderkins themselves, to spend the afternoon, they said, with Ted and Kitty. Then there was a fright indeed. The father walked down to the gate, and looked anxiously up the long winding mountain road, as if that would do any good, and the mother followed him, calling out,

"Oh, John! John! where are our children!"

The uncle rode off in one direction, and the father quickly saddled a horse and rode in another, to inquire at all the farm-houses if anything had been seen of Ted and Kitty Curtis. And no one had seen them. All the Elderkins had to say was that Ted and Kitty had told them there was a nearer way to reach home than by following the dusty, roundabout road, and they had run off through the woods to find it. The Elderkins chose to follow the road, because they had on their new lawn dresses trimmed with torchon, and "didn't want to get all scrambled up by the briers."

So while the uncle and the father and all the neighbors were hunting up and down the forest, and the mother was staying in the house, with dear, calm grandma and the little twin babies to keep her from going *quite* crazy, I will tell you what Ted and Kitty were doing in the Big Woods.

After they had run on quite a way, the bushes and brambles began to be so thick they were obliged to drop into a walk, and finally to climb and crawl as best they might, for they never found the "nearer way," and the ground was covered with fallen trees and rocks, while the briers caught them sometimes as if they never meant to let go.

By-and-by the pleasant light of sunset began to fade away, and they sat down to rest on a mossy log, and looked at each other very soberly.

"I don't know which way we ought to go," said Kitty.

"No more don't I," said Ted.

"Well, then, we must stay right where we are, 'stead of trying to go on. 'Cause, don't you know, lost people always go round and round and round and never get anywhere, and just wear their shoes out, and get tired and hungry, and nobody ever can find 'em. You ain't afraid, are you, Teddy?"

"No—o!" answered Ted, with scornful emphasis; "course not! Why, it's only just camping out. We've always wanted to camp out, you know. An' it's warm, an' there's but'nuts, an'—an'—maybe we'll find a pattridge nest," and Ted looked around at the deepening shadows, and bravely winked back the two tears that had gathered in his eyes.

"You know there isn't anything in these woods that can hurt us," said Kitty, cheerfully. "Papa said there was no use for those hunters to come here last year, 'cause there's nothing bigger'n woodchucks anywhere round."

"But somebody killed a bear here the summer I was a baby," said Ted.

"Yes, but he was the last—the very last—and it's just as nice and safe here as if we's camping out in our orchard. And let's fix up a house right away. Let's play we've gone West and got some land of our own."

Then the two children went to work. They were scared a little, in spite of their brave talk, but they were soon so interested in their camp-building that they forgot their fear. First they cleared away the sticks and stones beside the log where they were sitting. Then they pulled large pieces of bark from a partly fallen tree, and leaned them against the log, making a shelter large enough for a very small sleeping-room. Over the bark they laid boughs of butternut and maple, with long sticks placed crossways to keep them in place. Then by the time they had gathered a few armfuls of dry leaves to place underneath, it was quite dusk, and too late for any more work.

"Won't we get bugs in our ears?" asked Ted, peeping into the queer little bedroom.

"Well, we'll tie our handkchiefs over our ears. And we'll only take off our shoes, 'cause we're just emigrants, you know."

"I—I wish it wasn't quite so dark," said Ted, faintly.

"But the moon will be up right away," said brave Kitty; "and maybe we'll hear owls. We won't mind hearing owls, will we?"

"Course not," said Ted.

In a very short time the shoes were off, the handkerchiefs tied on, and the two tired children cuddled up in their wigwam, with Kitty's apron over their shoulders for a blanket.

"The Lord is here just as much as He's—He's in the Methodist church," said Kitty.

"Course He is," said Ted; and with this comforting thought they were soon asleep.

Morning came earlier in the woods than in the quiet bedrooms at home. Birds were twittering around the little camp before sunrise, the breeze blew noisily through the low-hanging branches, and the children were awake before the night shadows were quite gone.

"Papa 'll be sure to find us to-day," said Kitty, after they had crawled out of their nest. "We must have all the emigrant fun we can, for we'll only be Ted and Kitty after we get home."

"What do emigrants have for their breakfast, I wonder?" asked Ted.

"Oh, they—look around for things. Sometimes they have just butternuts, I guess," answered Kitty, while she slipped on her shoes.

"Well, then, let's have but'nuts—and lots of them," said hungry Ted.

So Kitty, who was a nice tidy girl about everything, looked around until she found a clean flat rock for a table; and while they were gathering their breakfast from the nearest butternut-trees, they came across a tiny little spring that bubbled out from under a ledge, and slipped away in a small stream down the mountain-side.

"Oh, isn't it cute!" said Kitty. "We'll build our cabin right here, and we'll play this is our water-power, and build a mill too. I'll be Mr. Brown, and you may be the Co.—Brown & Co., you know."

After a good drink of the clear, cold water from a cup made of a basswood leaf, they washed faces and hands, and went to the flat rock for breakfast. The butternuts were not quite ripe; they stained fingers, and they were hard to crack—with just a stone for a hammer—but there were "lots of them," as Ted had requested.

All the long bright forenoon they worked about their water-power, putting up an extensive mill of stones and sticks, and having no trouble at all, except when Ted got tired of being called "Co.," and insisted on being Mr. Brown a part of the time at least, in spite of Kitty's argument that the youngest ought always to be Co.

So, about one o'clock, when their father and uncle were galloping here and there in search of them, they were sitting at their rock table cracking more nuts, and listening proudly to the mimic roar of the water going over the dam they had just completed.

Sometimes they heard faint echoes and queer hootings off in the distance. "We'll play it's Indians, and we're hiding from them," said Kitty, never dreaming that all the men in the neighborhood of her home were hunting and hallooing through the forest for two very lost children. Once, when the shouts came quite near, the echoes mixed up things, so that Kitty was almost frightened, and drew her brother into the shelter of some thick bushes. "It sounds like a crazy man," she said.

After a while the noise slowly died away down the mountain-side, and the woods seemed more comfortable to Kitty. But sunset drew near, and still there came no cheerful father-voice. The supper of butternuts was not a very jolly one. Ted tried to be brave, but finally he dropped his face into his elbow and wailed forth, "I want some bread and butter," and cried loud and long.

"If we only had matches," sobbed Kitty, after Ted's cries had hushed a little, "we could make a fire, and—and maybe find something to roast."

Ted stopped crying by trying very hard, and began to examine his pockets. The prospect of a bonfire is cheering even to a hungry boy. First a dull jackknife was laid on the rock, then two nails, then a little rusty hinge, then a piece of slate-pencil, then a brass button with an eagle on it, then more slate-pencil, then a piece of string wound into a ball, then half of a match—the end that wouldn't go! Then happily he thought of his inside pocket, and the hole that was in it! Feeling along the lining of his jacket, there in its corner was something which might be—yes, it was a match!

"We won't care very much about it anyway," said experienced Kitty, "and then it will be more apt to burn." Nevertheless, after they had piled up some dry leaves, and laid birch "quirls" and small sticks over the top, she struck the match across the sole of her shoe, shielded it with her hand, and watched it anxiously. The little blue light quivered, paled, almost went out, and then leaped cheerfully upon a dry leaf, and in an instant the pile was alive with snaps and sparkles and dancing flames. The children gave quite a merry shout.

"And now what 'll we roast?" said poor Ted.

"We must fix the fire so it won't spread first," said Kitty; and she carefully scraped away all the leaves and sticks that were near. Then she took her brother's hand, and started to look for she hardly knew what, but trying with all her motherly little heart to think of something likely to be found in such a woods.

"Sour grapes roasted wouldn't be very nice, but maybe they'd be a sort of a relish, you know, Ted;" and she stopped by a tree overgrown with wild grapes, and began looking for the not very tempting clusters.

"Why, here are some that are nearly ripe. See! really purple a little."

Suddenly something alive sprang out of the brambles to roll the eggs in among the glowing ashes. She had just covered them, after a fashion, with the stick she used for a poker, and was saying to Ted they would soon be done, when something came crashing along through the brush, and there was a man with a scratched face and a torn coat, and a gun on his shoulder, standing before them.

"Oh, papa," said Ted, after taking a second look at him, "mayn't we stay until the patridge eggs are done? 'Cause we're so hungry."

"Oh, you—rascals," was all the father could say; and he was either very tired, or else Kitty rushed upon him and hugged his knees too vigorously, for he sank right down on the ground, and commenced wiping his face, and his eyes seemed to need a great deal of wiping.

"We didn't mean to camp out, papa," said Kitty, softly. "We only wanted to go home the nearest way, and we couldn't find it at all; and so when we found we were lost a little bit, we staid right where we were, so's not to get any more lost. Wasn't that right, papa? We knew you'd find us."

"Yes, an' we knew you wouldn't come hollerin' round like crazy Ingins. An' isn't the eggs done, Kit?" said Ted.

"Here's things to eat—things grandma fixed for you;" and the father quickly opened a little bundle that hung at his side. "I was so glad to see you alive, and having a good time, that I almost forgot your lunch, you poor Hottentots."

The lunch was quickly disposed of, and after drinking two swallows apiece of blackberry wine—which grandma sent word they must do—the children "broke camp," and started for home, carrying the eggs in a handkerchief.

"It was a good thing you started your fire, little folks. I was just going to give up the mountain, and follow the others down to the creek, when I saw a smoke curling up, and I remembered your weakness for bonfires, and so—Why, bless me! I've forgotten the signal." And the happy father took his repeating rifle from his shoulder, and fired three shots into the air.

Pop!—pop!—pop! That meant, "Found, and alive, and well." Three or four guns answered from the valley below; and the mother and grandma, waiting and listening by the farm-house gate, thought they had never heard such sweet music in all their lives.

Only a quarter of a mile of very rough ground was travelled before the children found themselves trotting along in the "nearer way" they had tried to find the night before; and in an hour's time, after being much kissed and very tenderly scolded, they were bathed and lying in their clean, sweet beds, and Ted was sleepily saying to himself, "This is nicer'n em'grants, after all."

OLD TIMES IN THE COLONIES.

BY CHARLES CARLETON COFFIN.

No. VI.

"We will go back to our packs," said Lovewell; but when they reached the place they found that the Indians had seized them, and that their retreat was cut off by more than one hundred Pigwackets. The terrible war-whoop rang through the forest, and the fight began, Indians and white men alike sheltering themselves behind the trees and rocks, watching an opportunity to pick each other off without exposing themselves. All day long the contest went on, the Indians howling like tigers. The white men saw that they were outnumbered three to one. It must be victory or death.

Lieutenant Wyman was their commander in place of Lovewell, who was mortally wounded. He was cool and brave.

"Don't expose yourselves. Be careful of your ammunition." So cool and deliberate was the aim of the white men that at nearly every shot an Indian fell. They suffered so severely that they withdrew and held a powwow with their "medicine man," who was going through his incantations, when Lieutenant Wyman, creeping up, put a bullet through him. The Indians, howling vengeance, returned to the fight; but the white men, protected on one side by the pond, held their ground.

All through the afternoon the struggle went on.

"We will give you good quarter," shouted Paugus.

"We want no quarter, except at the muzzle of our guns," shouted Wyman.

Paugus had often been to Dunstable, and was well acquainted with John Chamberlain. They fired at each other many times, till at last Chamberlain sent a bullet through Paugus's head, killing him instantly.

"I am a dead man," said Solomon Keys. "I am wounded in three places." He crawled down to the shore of the pond, found an Indian canoe, and crept into it. The wind blew it out into the lake, and he was wafted to the southern shore. The sun went down, and the Indians stole away. Pitiable the condition of the soldiers. Lovewell was dead, and also their beloved chaplain, Jonathan Frye, who with his dying breath prayed aloud for victory; Jacob Farrar was dying; Lieutenant Rollins and Robert Usher could not last long; eleven others were badly wounded. There were only eighteen left. The Indians had seized their packs; they had nothing to eat; it was twenty miles from the little fort which they had built at Ossipee; but they were victors. They had killed sixty or more Indians, and had inflicted a defeat from which the Pigwackets never recovered.

"Load my gun, so that, when the Indians come to scalp me, I can kill one more," said Lieutenant Rollins.

They must leave him. Sad the parting. In the darkness, guided by the stars, they started. Four were so badly wounded that they could not go on.

"Leave us," they said, "and save yourselves."

Twenty miles! How weary the way! They reach the fort to find it deserted. They had left seven men there, but when the fight began one of their number fled—a coward—and informed the seven that the party had all been cut off, not a man left. Believing that he had told the truth, they abandoned the fort, and returned to their homes.

Nothing to eat. But it was the month of May; the squirrels were out, and they shot two and a partridge; they caught some fish; and so were saved from starvation.

[TO BE CONTINUED.]

(Begun in No. 46 of HARPER'S YOUNG PEOPLE, September 14.)

WHO WAS PAUL GRAYSON?

BY JOHN HABBERTON,

AUTHOR OF "HELEN'S BABIES."

CHAPTER II.

THE FIGHT.

THE afternoon session of Mr. Morton's select school was but little more promising of revelations about the new boy than the morning had been. Most of the boys returned earlier than usual from their respective dinners, and either hung about the school-room, staring at their new companion, or waited at the foot of the stairs for him to come down. The attentions of the first-named division soon became

"JUST IN TIME TO SEE GRAYSON GIVE BENT A BLOW ON THE CHEST."

THE INVENTION OF STEEL PENS.

ACCORDING to the following extract from a manuscript document in the library of Aix-la-Chapelle, entitled "Historical Chronicle of Aix-la-Chapelle, Second Book, year 1748," edited by the writer to the Mayoralty, "Johann Janssen," it would appear that the invention of steel pens is of older date than is commonly supposed. The paper referred to says: "Just at the meeting of the Congress I may without boasting claim the honor of having invented new pens. It is perhaps not an accident that God should have inspired me at the present time with the idea of making steel pens, for all the envoys here assembled have bought the first that have been made, therewith, as may be hoped, to sign a treaty of peace which, with God's blessing, shall be as permanent as the hard steel with which it is written. Of these pens, as I have invented them, no man hath before seen or heard; if kept clean and free from rust and ink, they will continue fit for use for many years. Indeed, a man may write twenty sheets of paper with one, and the last line would be written as well as the first. They are now sent into every corner of the world as a rare thing—to Spain, France, and England. Others will no doubt make imitations of my pens, but I am the man who first invented and made them. I have sold a great number of them, at home and abroad, at one shilling each, and I dispose of them as quickly as I can make them."

OUT IN THE STORM.

BY SYDNEY DAYRE.

"THAT story about the baby in the storm? Oh yes, I'll tell you all about it. See, there's the scar on his dear little forehead yet—he'll carry it all his life, they say—but I shall never get over being thankful he came out of it so much better than I did, the darling."

And Janet glanced at her poor crooked arm as she settled herself more comfortably for a long talk.

"This was the way it came about. Mother said to me one Saturday afternoon, 'Janet, I am going over to the village; I will take the little girls with me, and I want you to take good care of Harry till I come back.'

"This arrangement did not suit me at all. I had other plans for the afternoon, and I said, 'But, mother, I promised Mary Hathaway I would go down there this afternoon. She is going to show me a new stitch for my embroidery.'

"'I don't like to interfere with you, dear,' mother said, 'but it seems to me you have been running there quite often this week, and I must have your help now.'

"This was true, but it made no difference in the fact of my wanting to go again.

"'Can't Bridget take care of him?' I said.

"'No, she has too much else to do.'

"'I hate being tied to babies all the time,' I snarled. 'I think we might keep a nurse as well as the Hathaways. Mary never has to be bothered with the young ones.' Mother looked at me with a look which begged for something better from me, but I kept the scowl on my face till I saw them drive from the gate. She said good-by to me with a loving smile, which faded out, as I would not return it. Even when I saw three hands waved to me as they turned the corner, some ugly thing at my heart kept my hand down, although half a minute later I would have given anything for a chance of answering mother's smile.

"I carried baby out into the grove at the back of the house, and dumped him into the hammock, feeling cross and miserable enough. He sat there cooing and crowing and laughing in a way which would have put a better temper into any one but me. I sat on the ground beside him, fussing away at my embroidery, but I could not get it right, and I got crosser and crosser. At last Harry stretched over toward me, and took rather a rough grasp of one of my ears and a good handful of hair with it. He did it to pull my face around for a kiss, but as his pretty face came against mine with a little bump, I jumped up and spoke sharply to him. I laid him down with a shake, saying, 'Go to sleep now, you little tease.'

"He put up a grieved lip, and sobbed as I swung him. It was about the time of his afternoon nap, and he was asleep in a few minutes.

"Then I tried my embroidery again, but it was no use—I could not get the right stitch without some help from Mary. Then a thought came across my mind—why could I not just run down there? Baby would surely sleep for an hour, and I could easily be back within that time. He could not possibly fall out of the hammock, for there were strings tied to some of the cords which could be fastened above him. I thought of telling Bridget I was going, so she would have 'an eye out' in case he should awake, but I knew she would be crabbed about it, and feel as if I were imposing on her, even if he did not give a single 'peep.' So I tied him in very carefully—he gave another little sob as I kissed him, and I was so sorry I had been cross to him. In ten minutes more I was running in at Mrs. Hathaway's gate.

"I had been going toward the north, so I did not notice that a black, curiously shaped cloud, which lay low in the south as I left home, was rising very fast. Mrs. Hathaway told me Mary was out in an arbor back of the house, so I ran out there, and for a little while we were so deep in the embroidery that I forgot to notice how dark it was getting. Then there came a flash of lightning—oh, how white and terrible that lightning was! It came all about us; we seemed wrapped up in it; and such a burst of thunder as I never heard before or since. It sounded like a cannon-ball falling right at our feet.

"As soon as we could move we flew into the house. I was wild with fright as I saw the awful blackness in the sky. Great drops of rain began to fall, and peal after peal of thunder came, as I snatched my bonnet and rushed to the door. Mary seized my arm and held me back. She cried, 'You must not go; indeed you *shall* not go out in such a storm.'

"Mrs. Hathaway came up to me too, and put her arm around me. 'Why, Janet, you can not go, my child. It might be at the risk of your life.'

"I think they almost meant to keep me by force, but I screamed out, 'I *must* go! I will! I will!' and I broke away from them, and rushed out into that blinding storm. I couldn't think of anything except the poor baby I had left all alone. There was no one there to take care of him, no one knew where he was, and in the noise of the storm nobody could hear him scream.

"The rain poured down in sheets by the time I reached Mrs. Hathaway's gate. It seemed almost to beat me down to the ground, and the water was over my shoes in half a minute. The lightning seemed like one long flash, and the thunder never stopped. I staggered on and floundered on, and slipped down and got up again, all the time just saying to myself, 'The baby! the baby!—if I could only reach him and find him alive!'

"Then it seemed as if night came down all at once. It got dark in one minute, and I heard a horrible roaring sound behind me—louder than all the thunder. I heard a long, rattling crash, and then another. It was Mrs. Hathaway's house and barn going to pieces, but I didn't know it then. I heard people scream; I heard all sorts of things whizzing about me, but it was too dark to see much. Things came striking against me, and soon a heavy thing came banging against me on one side, and just as I was falling down something seemed to pick me up, and I was whirled and twisted round and round, till I didn't know anything more.

"When I opened my eyes the rain was falling on my

face. It was lighter, and I saw boards and timbers, and trees and branches and bushes, lying all about me. I was in a field not far from home. I felt dizzy, and didn't remember anything at first, and then I thought of little Harry, and sprang up to run to him. But, oh, how sick and sore I felt! When I tried to lift a heavy branch which was lying partly over me, I could raise only one of my arms.

"But my feet were all right, and I ran as fast as I could toward home. I saw my father in the road in front of the house, looking up and down, with a white, frightened face. He hurried toward me.

"'Where have you been, child?' he said. 'I must go to see if anything has happened to your mother, but I could not go till I knew you and Harry were safe— Why, dear, you are hurt!'

"But I ran past him, crying, 'The baby, father, he's in the hammock—come quick!'

"When we got round to the grove I screamed at what I saw. The trees lay about as if a scythe had mown them down. I hardly knew the place, or where to look for Harry.

"One of the trees the hammock was tied to was lying exactly where I had left my little brother. Another tree was blown right across it. Father did not stop to look, but called the hired man, and they brought axes and saws. I stooped down and listened, though I felt sure the dear little one must be dead. But I heard a sad little sob, as if he had cried till he was worn out. I was so glad, I got up and danced. But father shook his head and said, 'He's alive, but how do we know how he may be hurt.' They chopped away at the branches, while I held my breath, oh, how long, *long* it seemed to wait! I crouched down and crept as near the baby as I could. I called to him, and he gave a pitiful little cry; he expected me to take him at once, and I was glad he got angry because he had to wait. He tried to free himself from the hammock, and I began to hope he might not be much hurt.

"At last a great branch was taken away, and I got closer to him. I called father, and we looked under, and I heard him say, 'Thank God!'

"There the darling was, in a kind of little bower made by two big branches which came down on each side of him. They had saved him when the other tree fell. His forehead was scratched deeply, but nothing else ailed him. Father reached in and cut away the hammock with his knife, and drew him out with hands that shook as if he had an ague fit. The little fellow held out his arms to me; but as I tried to take him my strength all seemed to go away. I grew dizzy, and fell down. Bridget took the child, and father carried me in and laid me on a bed.

"Then he and Bridget tried to get us into dry clothes. But I cried out every time they touched me, till father was nearly at his wits' end. I called aloud for mother. I knew she would not hurt me so.

"'I will go now and see where she is, dear,' father said at last, wiping his forehead. 'The good Lord only knows where she may be—and the little ones. I'll bring some one to help you, poor child.'

"The sun was shining brightly again by this time, but as I lay there, with a great deal of pain in my arm and head, I seemed to feel that black storm coming after me yet. The roar, roar, roar kept on in my head, and the bed was whirling up in the clouds with me, and Mary Hathaway was holding me, while some one pelted me with the stars; and mother said, 'Oh, my poor darling—look at her head!'

"Then the moon peeped at me, and said, 'Her arm is broken in two places.'

"It was the doctor who said this, and mother had really come to me. After that I seemed to be climbing and climbing through trees—oh, so long! I kept on for years, always hunting for little Harry, hearing him cry for me, and never able to reach him. But at last I saw a light—I had been in the dark all the time—and I struggled toward it, and looked out. Mother was there, but not Harry.

"'Where is he?' I cried.

"'Who, dear?' she said.

"'Why, the baby—little Harry,' I said. 'I was almost up to him.'

"'Here he is.'

"She lifted him up to me, and I tried to take him, but I could not raise myself, and was glad to find that I was in my own bed. I went off into a long sleep, and when I awoke I didn't want anything except to lie quiet and know mother was caring for me, and that Harry sometimes came toddling into my room, for he had learned to walk during the long weeks I had been sick.

"Well, that is about all there is of it. My arm was a long time getting well, and will always be crooked, like this. The doctor said it would have got entirely well if it had not been for the fever.

"But, dear me, how much thinking I did when my head got clear enough to think! When I was out in the storm all I had ever heard about the wrath of God on the children of disobedience seemed to come back to me. How I was punished! If I had been faithful to my duty, I should have been safe at home when the storm came. I shall always feel as if I knew something of that awful wrath, for wasn't I taken up in God's terrible hand?

"When I was getting well I began to wonder why Mary Hathaway never came to see me. Mother put off telling me as long as she could that she and a younger sister had been killed in a moment by the falling of their house, and that Mrs. Hathaway was crippled for life. None of us had been hurt but me. Mother had got beyond the track of the worst part of the storm, but her horse was killed by the lightning. Father lost his barns, most of his stock, and nearly all his crops.

"That's the story of the terrible tornado. Its path was not more than half a mile wide, and it was all over in less than half an hour. Mother says I grew five years older on that day, and I think she is right."

"MOONSHINERS."

BY E. S. MILLER.

CHAPTER I.

CONNY LOSES HIS FATHER.

DR. HUNTER was riding leisurely on his morning rounds among the few people who managed to be sick at Dunsmore in spite of the clear sweet air that carried the balmy scent of the forests into all its pleasant valleys. Under the seat of his sulky was his little old-fashioned box of medicines, and close at his hand a tin box containing what was in the doctor's eyes quite as valuable—a specimen of a rare plant which he had discovered in a cleft of gray rock, and secured at the cost of some pretty hard climbing. The road upon which he was driving wound along the mountain-side, and he could look down upon the tops of the trees below, noting here and there the scattered buildings and stacks of feed that marked some little farm in a clearing, and from the very densest spot of all a faint thread of blue smoke rising above the trees. He had often noticed it, and more than once had asked about it, but no one gave him any satisfactory answer. You would have supposed that of all the men and women in Dunsmore not one had even chanced to see that smoke until the doctor's eyes had spied it.

"Smoke, sor?—so it be," said old Timothy, with a great pretense of straining his eyes to see it. "It's a fire in the woods, belike. Some tramping fellows on a hunt."

"It is always in one spot," said the doctor, "though

sometimes it disappears for weeks. Is there any road that way?"

"Not the track of a squirl, yer honor. There's not a wilder bit in all the State, I'm thinkin'."

"I believe one might find a way on horseback," said the doctor, "and I shall try it some day."

"Ye'd best not do it. I'd be loath to see ye leaving a good trade for a bad one." Timothy grasped his hickory cane, and shook his grizzled head at the doctor. Then, coming a step nearer, he whispered, "*Moonshiners.*"

"To be sure," said the doctor, turning again to look at the smoke.

"It's a bad business," said Timothy, carefully studying the doctor's face.

"Yes, it's a bad business, making whiskey, or selling it, or drinking it; but paying a tax to the government does not make it any better. I believe every dollar that comes to the government from such a source is a curse."

Timothy drew a long breath.

"You're right, sor. I'm not beholden to the stuff myself; but yer honor's done me a good turn, and I couldn't see ye bringin' trouble on yerself by askin' too many questions. It mightn't be—pop'lar, sor."

The doctor asked no more questions, but he watched the blue smoke more curiously than ever, wondering much about the outlaws who carried on their secret trade in the mountain fastnesses. He had been thinking of them that very morning as he rode along, with the reins lying loosely on his knee, when suddenly Prince gave a start that roused his driver. A small figure stepped out from the shadow of a rock, and stood close beside the gig, saying,

"Would you come to my feyther, sir?"

"Who is your father?" asked the doctor.

"He's sick this three days," answered the boy.

"What is his name? Where do you live?"

"It's not far, sir," said the boy, without answering the question.

"Well, jump in here;" and the doctor held down his hand.

"Ye'll not be riding, sir; it's a bit off the road."

The doctor hesitated a moment, then fastened Prince securely in the edge of the woods, and with his box in his hand prepared to follow his guide.

"Now, then, Johnny, go ahead."

"My name is Conny, sir," said the boy.

"Conny, is it? And what else?"

"Just Conny, sir;" and the boy led the way rapidly through what looked like a pathless tangle, until below a sharp ledge of rocks they struck a little stream by whose side they found a narrow but easy passage into the very heart of the wood.

"Surely no human being can live here," thought the doctor; but at that very moment they came upon a small weather-beaten cabin, so low and gray that one might easily have passed it unnoticed among the rocks that hung over it, and the bushes that crowded around and in front of it. The roof, thatched with bark, had fallen in at one end, and the place looked as if it might have been forsaken for years. But the boy led him around to the rear, and they entered quite a comfortable room, with a decent bed in one corner, on which a man was lying with his face to the wall.

"Feyther," said the boy, "I've brought the doctor to ye."

The man neither moved nor answered, and the doctor, going up to the bed, was shocked to see that he was dead. He turned to Conny and asked, "Has your father been long sick?"

"Always sick, sir. He couldn't work at the North, and they told him if he came here the air would cure him, and the smell of the trees, but he coughed just the same."

"Where is your mother?"

"Dead, sir."

"And there is no one but you and your father?"

"Only us two, sir."

"Conny," said the doctor, slowly, "I am afraid your father is dead."

Conny did not answer for a moment, but his thin brown face settled into a look of disappointment.

"He said he should die, sir, and nothing could save him, but I thought maybe if you came— Couldn't you try something? They brought Black Joe round when he'd been long in the water, and was dead and cold—brought him round with rubbing, and stuff they put in his mouth. Isn't there something in your box that 'll do it?"

"Nothing," said the doctor; "he is quite dead, my boy. You had better come with me, and I will send some one to attend to your father."

But no persuasion could induce Conny to leave the cabin, and the doctor was forced to return without him. For a quiet man, the doctor was greatly excited over the

"THEY CAME UPON A SMALL WEATHER-BEATEN CABIN."

mystery of the little cabin, but old Timothy said, coolly, "That would be Sandy McConnell: one o' the moonshiners: varmint, all on 'em."

"But, Timothy, some one must see that he has a decent burial, and if you'll take a couple of men with you, and go down there—"

"Wait till to-morrow morning," said Timothy, significantly. "The birds of the air 'tend to their own funerals."

A terrific storm that swept over the mountains that afternoon compelled the doctor to follow Timothy's advice. The next morning, when they succeeded, with much difficulty, in finding their way through the tangle, the cabin was empty of every trace of human occupancy, and almost seemed as if it might have been undisturbed since the wood-choppers abandoned it. Under a great pine, a few rods away, they found a new-made grave, carefully sodded, and bound over, in old-country fashion, with green withes.

"The moonshiners have buried him," said Timothy. "I told ye, sor, they'd see to their own funerals."

"I wish I knew what had become of the boy," said the doctor, as they slowly picked their way upward; "he seemed such a quaint, old-fashioned little chap."

[TO BE CONTINUED.]

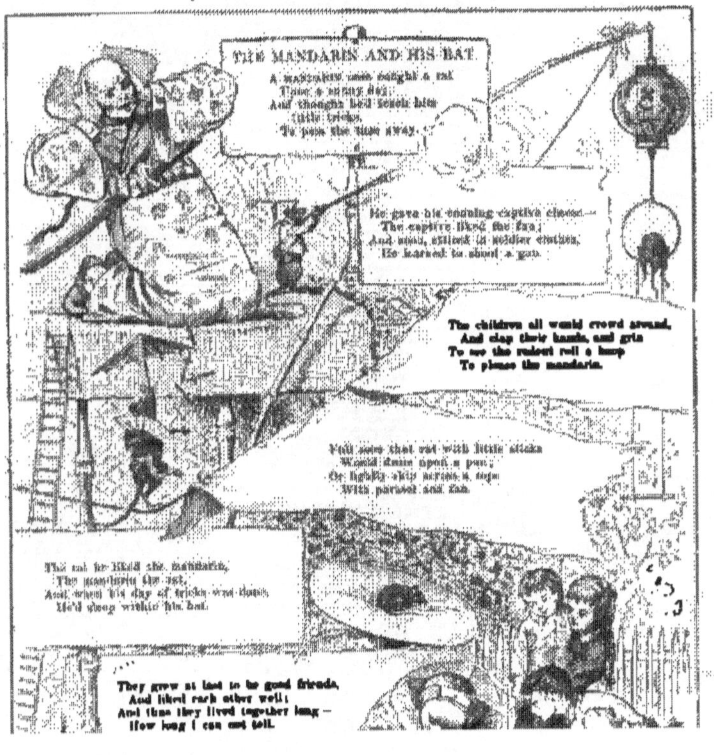

OUR POST-OFFICE BOX

[illegible] or door. Almost any corner is acceptable to these little fellows. A lady who had been absent from the city during the summer, on returning home found one of her chamber windows taken full possession of by the sparrows. The blinds had been closed, and the space between them and the window was stuffed full of rubbish, the birds using an open slat as an entrance to their cosy home. We know of an instance where sparrows have woven an independent nest, and fastened it to the branches of a tree, and for that reason we have not classed them among birds that build their nests in trees.

W., F., and E.—To make a boat swing set two upright posts firmly in the ground about four or five feet apart. Connect them at the top by a strong bar, across which at the centre fasten another bar at right angles. The boat, which should have a seat at each end, is hung by four stout ropes, one to each corner, so as to balance well, to the connecting bar. A rope passing from each end of the cross-bar enables the occupants to swing the boat forward and backward. The upright posts should be well braced. If you can visit some park or picnic ground where one of these swings is in operation, you will understand better how to build one.

WILLIAM F. S.—The coins you describe belong to the class known as Stadtmark tokens. They are issued by private parties, and are valueless.

CLARENCE E. and F. B. W.—You can get the back numbers of YOUNG PEOPLE you require by forwarding the necessary amount to the publishers, with your full address. They will cost four cents for each copy.

BOOK OF LIFE.—The oldest text-book on arithmetic employing the Arabian or Indian figures (those at present in use), and the decimal system, is that of Avicenna, an Arabian physician who lived in Bokhara about A.D. 1000. It was found in manuscript in the library at Cairo, Egypt, and contains, besides the rules for addition, subtraction, multiplication, and division, many peculiar properties of numbers. It was not until the seventeenth century that arithmetic became a regular branch of common education.

CAPTAIN FRANK.—The average price of a boy's bicycle is from twenty-five to fifty dollars. Very small sizes may be obtained at a lower price.

Favors are acknowledged from Lizzie Glassberg, H. N. Thorne, John R. Blake, C. D. Nirenden, Carrie Hard, Lillian McDonald, Nellie Rossman, Henry Coleman, Annie E. Douglas, Aggie E. Mason, Madgie W. H., Sallie E. Ely, Dora Williams, M. W. D., Mary McWhorter.

Correct answers to puzzles are received from Olive Russell, "Chiquita," Blanche H. Ingham, Sidney Abrahams, Emma Shafer, Edward L. Conk, Allie Maxwell, George Vanderhoof.

PUZZLES FROM YOUNG CONTRIBUTORS.

No. 1.

[illegible]

No. 2.

[illegible]

1. I am an ancient Greek astronomer composed of 10 letters. My 1, 2, 3 is a part of the body. My 4, 5, 6, 7, 8 is [illegible]. My 9, 10 is a pronoun. F. W.

2. I am an ancient Greek comedian composed of 10 letters. My 1, 2, 3, 4 is a poetic narrative. My 5, 6, 7, 8 is mighty. My 9, 10 is a pronoun.

3. I am an ancient Greek historian composed of 8 letters. My 1, 2, 3, 4 is a great warrior. My 5, 6, 7 is a small spot. My 8 is a pronoun. R. O. H.

No. 4.

WORD SQUARES.

1. First, [illegible]. Second, one of the United States. Third, designs. Fourth, a vegetable growth.

FRANK.

2. First, a shipping term in ancient legend. Second, to [illegible]. Third, [illegible]. Fourth, a precious stone.

LOUIS.

ANSWERS TO PUZZLES IN No. 44.

No. 1. Napoleon.

No. 2. S T E M / T O N A / E N [illegible] / M A [illegible]

No. 3. [illegible]

No. 4. Chair, hair, air.

No. 5. [illegible]

No. 6. 1. Hyacinth. 2. Antirrhinum.

ADVERTISEMENTS.

HARPER'S YOUNG PEOPLE.

HARPER'S YOUNG PEOPLE will be issued every Tuesday, and may be had at the following rates—payable in advance, postage free:

SINGLE COPIES $0 04
ONE SUBSCRIPTION, one year . . . 1 50
FIVE SUBSCRIPTIONS, one year . . . 7 00

Subscriptions may begin with any Number. When no time is specified, it will be understood that the subscriber desires to commence with the Number issued after the receipt of order.

Remittances should be made by POST-OFFICE MONEY ORDER or DRAFT, to avoid risk of loss.

ADVERTISING.

The extent and character of the circulation of HARPER'S YOUNG PEOPLE will render it a first-class medium for advertising. A limited number of approved advertisements will be inserted on two inside pages at 75 cents per line.

Address

HARPER & BROTHERS,
Franklin Square, N. Y.

OUR CHILDREN'S SONGS.

Our Children's Songs. Illustrated. 8vo, Ornamental Cover, $1 00.

It contains some of the most beautiful thoughts for children that ever found rest in poetry, and beautiful "pictures to match."—Chicago Evening Journal.

This is a large collection of songs for the nursery.

COLUMBIA BICYCLE.

Bicycle riding is the best as well as the healthiest of out-door sports; is easily learned and never forgotten. Send 3c. stamp for 24-page Illustrated Catalogue, containing Price-lists and full information. THE POPE M'F'G CO., 89 Summer St., Boston, Mass.

CHILDREN'S PICTURE-BOOKS.

Square 4to, about 300 pages each, beautifully printed on Tinted Paper, embellished with many Illustrations, bound in Cloth, $1 50 per volume.

The Children's Picture-Book of Sagacity of Animals.

With Sixty Illustrations by HARRISON WEIR.

The Children's Bible Picture-Book.

With Eighty Illustrations, from Designs by STEINLE, OVERBECK, VEIT, SCHNORR, &c.

The Children's Picture Fable-Book.

Containing One Hundred and Sixty Fables. With Sixty Illustrations by HARRISON WEIR.

The Children's Picture-Book of Birds.

With Sixty-one Illustrations by W. HARVEY.

The Children's Picture-Book of Quadrupeds and other Mammalia.

With Sixty-one Illustrations by W. HARVEY.

Published by HARPER & BROTHERS, New York.

☞ Sent by mail, postage prepaid, to any part of the United States, on receipt of the price.

The Child's Book of Nature.

The Child's Book of Nature, for the Use of Families and Schools: intended to aid Mothers and Teachers in Training Children in the Observation of Nature. In Three Parts. Part I. Plants. Part II. Animals. Part III. Air, Water, Heat, Light, &c. By WORTHINGTON HOOKER, M.D. Illustrated. The Three Parts complete in One Volume, Small 4to, Half Leather, $1 12; or, separately, in Cloth, Part I., 45 cents; Part II., 48 cents; Part III., 48 cents.

Fig. 1.

Fig. 2.

WALTZING FAIRY.

A VERY pretty toy, and easily made, is this Waltzing Fairy. It may be familiar to some of our readers, but will be new to a great many more.

Cut a doll out of a good-sized cork—one from a Champagne bottle is best, because broader at the base; into this base insert a number of stout bristles, as in Fig. 1. If you can not procure bristles, fine broom-corn will answer the purpose.

Dress this cork body (Fig. 2), taking care to make the dress just so long that it will not touch the ground. Place this doll on the top or sounding-board of the piano when any one is playing, and it will dance about in a very graceful manner.

If placed on a smooth tea-tray, and the tray tilted a little at one end, the doll will waltz across the tray in lady-like style.

CHARADE.

I.

A GENTLEMAN once, with his children and wife,
Fled away from a town that was burning,
By command of a friend, who added that life
Must depend on their never back turning.
The lady, alas! like her grandmother Eve,
With a longing for knowledge is cursed:
She turns to behold—it is hard to believe—
And is pillared straightway in my *first*.

II.

An elderly female in gorgeous array
Promenades in the streets of Verona;
She is seeking a heart, which has wandered astray,
To the serious loss of its owner.
Her heart is all safe; but her sense of her charms
Is still great—for what woman e'er lost it?—
So my *second* promises her t' allay her alarms,
And to speak in her stead if accosted.

III.

The battle's done; the chieftain's in his tent,
And glories in the victory he has won.
He dreams of plaudits by his sovereign sent—
When, lo! appears a curled perfumed son,
Who claims to be the herald from the King;
Who prates of war, though ne'er a squadron led;
And says but for my *whole*—the villainous thing—
He too had worn a helmet on his head.

How Salt was formerly Made.—The art of making salt was known in very early times to the Gauls and the Germans. The process was very simple, for they did nothing more than throw the salt-water on burning wood, where it evaporated, and left the salt adhering to the ashes or charcoal. The ancient Britons probably extracted the salt by the same method, for in the Cheshire salt-springs pieces of half-burned wood have been frequently dug up. The Romans made salt a source of revenue six hundred and forty years before the birth of Christ. Part of the pay of the Roman soldiers was made in salt, which was thus called *salarium*, whence we derive the word "salary."

THE MARINER'S PUZZLE.

A MARINER at sea discovered, while in a storm, that a [illegible] leak had sprung in his vessel, and he was obliged to stop the inflow of water. The only piece of plank he had on board was in the form of two connected squares, as represented in the annexed diagram.

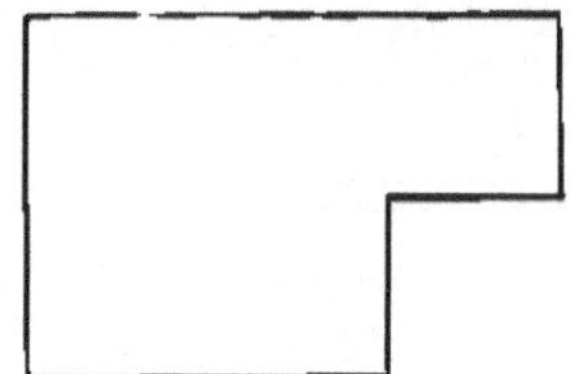

Either of these squares was too small to fill the space, but the two parts, reduced to one single square, would give him a plank of the size required. This he obtained by making two straight cuts with his saw through the plank.

In what direction were the cuts made?

MEADOW-QUAKERS.

IN the early autumn
Come the Meadow-Quakers;
Not the Shakers, not the Shakers—
No, no, no.
These quiet little people
Stand straight as a church steeple,
And no one ever saw them come
Or ever saw them go.

White their hats and broad-brimmed,
Lined with pale pink lining,
On them dew-drops often shining—
Yes, yes, yes.
No butterfly goes near them,
No brown bee hums to cheer them,
And what these Quaker folks are called
I want you all to guess.

VOL. I.—No. 48. PUBLISHED BY HARPER & BROTHERS, NEW YORK. PRICE FOUR CENTS.

Tuesday, September [illegible] [illegible] $1.50 per Year, in Advance.

A CHILDREN'S PARADISE.

IN one corner of the Bois de Boulogne is a pretty zoological garden known as the Jardin d'Acclimatation. The Bois de Boulogne is the pleasure-ground of Paris, and is one of the most beautiful parks in the world. It comprises about twenty-five hundred acres of majestic forests and open grassy meadows, through which flow picturesque streams, tumbling over rocky cliffs in glistening cascades, or spreading out into broad tranquil lakes, upon which float numbers of gay pleasure-boats filled on sunny summer afternoons with crowds of happy children.

But the place where the children are happiest is the Jardin d'Acclimatation. There are no savage beasts here to frighten the little ones with their roaring and growling. The lions and tigers and hyenas are miles away, safe in their strong cages in the Jardin des Plantes, on the other side of the big city of Paris; and in this charming spot are gathered only those members of the great animal kingdom which in one way or another are useful to man.

The Jardin d'Acclimatation has been in existence about twenty-five years. In 1854 a society was formed in Paris for the purpose of bringing to France, from all parts of the world, beasts, birds, fishes, and other living things, which in their native countries were in any way serviceable, and to make every effort to accustom them to the climate and soil of France. The city of Paris ceded to the society a space of about forty acres in a quiet corner of the great park, and the preparation of the ground for the reception of its strange inhabitants was begun at once. The ponds were dug out and enlarged, the meadows were sodded with fresh, rich grass, spacious stalls were built, and a big kennel for dogs, aviaries for birds, aquaria for fish, and a silk-worm nursery, were all made ready. A large greenhouse was also erected for the cultivation of foreign plants. Here the animals were not brought simply to be kept on exhibition, but they were made as comfortable and as much at home as possible.

On pleasant afternoons troops of children with their mammas or nurses crowd the walks and avenues of the Jardin d'Acclimatation. Here, in a comfortable airy kennel, are dogs from all parts of the world, some of them great noble fellows, who allow the little folks to fondle and stroke them. On a miniature mountain of artificial rock-work troops of goats and moufflons—a species of mountain sheep—clamber about, as much at home as if in their far-away native mountains. Under a group of fir-trees a lot of reindeer are taking an afternoon nap, lost in dreams of their home in the distant North. Grazing peacefully on the broad meadows are antelopes, gazelles, and all kinds of deer; and yaks from Tartary, llamas from the great South American plains, Thibet oxen, and cattle of all kinds are browsing in their particular feeding grounds.

In a pretty sunny corner is a neat little chalet inclosed in a yard filled with fresh herbage. A cozy little home indeed, and there, peering inquisitively through the open door, is one of the owners of this mansion—a funny kangaroo, standing as firmly on its haunches as if it scorned the idea of being classed among the quadrupeds.

What is whinnying and galloping about on that meadow? A whole crowd of ponies! Ponies from Siam, from Java, shaggy little Shetlands, quaggas and dauws from Africa, all feeding and frolicking together, and there in the door of his stall, stands a sulky little zebra. He is a very bad-tempered little animal, and evidently something has gone wrong, and he "won't play." In a neighboring paddock is a gnu, the curious horned horse of South Africa. The children are uncertain whether to call it a horse, a buffalo, or a deer, and the creature itself appears a little doubtful as to which character it can rightfully assume.

One of the few animals kept in cages is the guepard, or hunting leopard. The guepard, a graceful, spotted creature, is very useful to hunters in India. It is not a savage animal, and when taken young is very easily trained to work for its master. It is led hooded to the chase, and only when the game is near is the hood removed. The guepard then springs upon the prey, and holds it fast until the hunter comes to dispatch it. The guepard in the Jardin d'Acclimatation is very affectionate toward its keeper, and purrs like a big cat when he strokes its silky head, but it is safer for children to keep their little hands away from it.

In pens provided with little ponds are intelligent seals and families of otters, with their elegant fur coats always clean and in order; and down by the shore of the stream and the large lake a loud chattering is made by the numerous web-footed creatures and long-legged waders. Here are ducks from Barbary and the American tropics, wild-geese from every clime, and swimming gracefully and silently in the clear water are swans—black, gray, and white—that glide up to the summer-houses on the bank, and eat bread and cake from the children's hands.

Among the tall water-grasses at one end of the lake is a group of pelicans, motionless, their long bills resting on their breasts. They look very gloomy, as if refusing to be comforted for the loss of their native fishing grounds in the wild African swamps.

Promenading in a spacious park are whole troops of ostriches, their small heads lifted high in the air, and their beautiful feathers blowing gracefully in the wind. Be careful, or they will dart their long necks through the paling and steal all your luncheon, or perhaps even the pretty locket from your chain, for anything from a piece of plum-cake to a cobble-stone is food for this voracious bird. A poor soldier, whose sole possession was the cross of honor which he wore on the breast of his coat, was once watching the ostriches in the Jardin d'Acclimatation, when a bird suddenly darted at him, seized his cross in its beak, and swallowed it. The soldier went to the superintendent of the garden and entered a bitter complaint; but the feathered thief was not arrested, and the soldier never recovered his treasure.

What a rush and crowd of children on the avenue! No wonder, for there is a pretty barouche, to which is harnessed a large ostrich, which marches up and down, drawing its load as easily as if it were a span of goats or a Shetland pony, instead of a bird.

There are so many beautiful birds in the aviaries, so many odd fowls in the poultry-house, and strange fish in the aquaria, that it is impossible to see them all in one day, and the best thing to do now is to rest on a seat in the cool shade of the vast conservatory, among strange and beautiful plants from all parts of the world. And on every holiday the happy children say, "We will go to the Jardin d'Acclimatation, where there is so much to enjoy, and so much to learn."

FRANK'S WAR WITH THE 'COONS.

BY GEORGE J. VARNEY.

LAST month I spent several weeks at a farm within sight of the White Mountains. One morning the boy Frank came in with a basket of sweet-corn on his arm, and a bad scowl on his countenance.

"What is the matter, Frank?" inquired his mother, coming from the pantry.

Indignation was personified in him, as he answered, "Them pigs has been in my corn."

"I hadn't heard that the pigs had been out. Did they do much harm?"

"Yes, they spoiled a peck of corn, sure; broke the ears half off, and some all off. Rubbed 'em all in the dirt, and only ate half the corn. Left 'most all one side. They didn't know enough to pull the husks clear off."

Just then the hired man came in, and Frank repeated his complaint of the pigs.

"They hain't been out of their yard for a week, I know. I heard some 'coons yellin' over in the woods back of the orchard last night. I guess them's the critters that's been in your corn piece."

"S'pose they'll come again to-night?" inquired the boy, every trace of displeasure vanishing.

"Likely 's not. They 'most always do when they get a good bite, and don't get scared."

"I'll fix 'em to-night," said the boy, with a broad smile at the anticipated sport.

Twilight found Frank sitting patiently on a large pumpkin in the edge of his corn piece, gun in hand, watching for the 'coons. An hour later his patience was gone, and the 'coons hadn't come—at least he had no notice of their coming. As he started from his rolling seat a slight sound in the midst of the corn put him on the alert. He walked softly along beside the outer row, stopping frequently to listen, until he could distinctly hear the rustling of the corn leaves, and even the sound of gnawing corn from the cob. His heart beat fast with excitement as he became assured of the presence of a family of raccoons, and he held his gun ready to pop over the first one that showed itself. There were slight sounds of rustling and gnawing in several places, but they all ceased, one after another, as Frank came near. He listened, but there was nothing to be heard. Then he went to the other side of the piece to cut off their retreat from the woods. He came cautiously up between the corn rows to the midst of the piece, but no 'coon was there.

"'Pity they will eat their suppers in the dark," muttered Frank, to relieve his vexation at the disappointment.

He returned slowly to the house, and went up to his room, where he sat down and read awhile. After an hour or more he became too sleepy to read; so he laid aside his book, put out the light, and popped into bed. Just as he was falling asleep he heard several cries over in the woods. They were half whistle, half scream—a sort of squeal. He sprang up in bed to listen. The cries ceased, and for several minutes all was silence. Then there arose a succession of screams, much nearer, and in a different voice. It was interrupted and broken. It seemed something between the squeal of a pig and the cry of a child.

Frank said to his father the next morning that "it sounded as if it was a young one, and the mother was cuffing it and driving it back. At any rate, the last of the cries sounded as if the little 'coon had turned, and was going away."

"Very likely," said his father; "the little 'coon was probably hungry for the rest of his supper, and was going back to the corn sooner than the old 'coon thought was prudent."

Frank heard no more of the 'coons, and soon went to sleep, but in the morning he found that more corn had been spoiled than in the first night. The 'coons had only run off to come back again, and begun their depredations in a new place. He therefore came to the conclusion that he must watch all night, and every night, if at all.

The hired man told how some boys where he worked once caught a 'coon by setting a trap at the hole in a board fence near the corn piece. There was a wall beside the woods not far from Frank's corn, and there were a plenty of holes in it, but which particular hole the 'coons came through nobody could tell.

"I'll find out," said Frank. He went to a sand-bank with the wheelbarrow, and shovelled in a load of sand. This he spread at the bottom of every large hole, and on the rocks at every low place in the wall. In the morning he walked along there, and the foot-prints in the sand showed where the path of the 'coons crossed the wall. There he set his steel-trap, and another which he borrowed of a neighbor. In the morning he went over to see what had happened. One trap was sprung, and held a few hairs; the other trap had disappeared. It didn't go off alone, Frank thought; but it had a long stick fastened to its chain that would be sure to catch in the bushes before it went far. He sprang over the wall, and peeped round among the knolls and bushes. Suddenly, as he went around a clump of little spruces, a chain rattled, and a brownish-gray creature, "'most as big as a bear," as Frank afterward said, sprang at him, with a sharp, snarling growl, and mouth wide open. The sight was too much for Frank's nerves, and set them in such a tremor that he ran away. When he came in sight of his corn he began to grow angry, and his courage came up again. He now got him a larger stick than he had first carried, and set out for the animal again. He had considered that, after all, it could be only a 'coon, though bears had been heard of in the corn fields further north. Frank and the corn-eater now met again face to face, and for a few seconds there was a lively battle, in which mingled the snarling of the 'coon, the rattling of the chain, and the blows of the stick. At length the 'coon lay still, and Frank stood guard over him with a broken stick. The next day he ate a slice of roast 'coon for dinner with great relish.

The traps were set again for the next night, but never a 'coon was in them in the morning. The cunning fellows evidently considered the place too dangerous, and chose another entrance. Anyway, the corn was still going away fast. Frank feared that he wouldn't have enough to fill his contract with the canning factory unless the family in the house, or the other family in the woods, left off eating. Something must be done. At length Frank bought a dog. He made a nice kennel for him in the middle of the corn field, and tied him there at night. Just after Frank had fallen into a sound sleep the dog woke him up with his barking. Frank went out, but could find nothing. The dog woke him twice more that night, but he didn't trouble himself to leave his bed again. In the morning he found that the 'coons had destroyed as much corn as before, but it was all about the edges. The next night they ventured a little nearer the kennel. The following night the dog was left in the kennel loose. Probably when the 'coons came he made a charge upon them, and they turned upon him and drove him away, for he was only a little young one. He took refuge in the wood-house, where he barked furiously for an hour or more, and then in occasional brief spells all the night—whenever he woke enough to remember the 'coons. After this Frank gave up the defense of the corn, but began to gather it nightly as fast as the ears were sufficiently full. At length he cut the corn and took it into the barn, excepting a single bunch. About this bunch he sunk traps in the ground, and threw hay-seed over them, and placed nice ears of sweet-corn beside them. The next morning he had another 'coon. The other trap was sprung also, but it held nothing but a little tuft of long gray fur. That sly fellow had again sat down on the trencher. From this time the 'coons troubled Frank's corn no more, having found other fields where there was more corn and fewer traps. Frank's final conflict with the 'coons was late in the autumn, when the leaves were nearly gone from the trees, and the ripe beech-nuts were beginning to drop. He had fired all his ammunition away at gray squirrels the day before, except a little powder; but a meeting of crows in the adjoining woods incited his sporting proclivities, and he loaded his gun, putting in peas for shot, and started for the locality of the noisy birds. They cawed a little louder when they discovered the intruder, then began in a straggling manner to fly away. So when Frank arrived at the scene of the meeting it had adjourned. Looking about in the trees to see if by chance a single crow might still be lingering, a slight movement in a tall maple met his eye.

"Biggest gray squirrel ever I saw," muttered the boy, raising his gun. The position was not a good one for a shot, as the head, which had been thrust out over a large branch close to the trunk was now withdrawn, so that

"FOR A FEW SECONDS THERE WAS A LIVELY BATTLE."

only the end of the nose was visible. Close beside this branch was another, and between the two a large surface of gray fur was exposed.

"I'll send him some peas for dinner," thought Frank, and fired. He heard the peas rattle against the hard bark of the tree, but no gray squirrel came down or went up that he could see. When the smoke cleared away, a black nose was thrust out over the branch, and two keen eyes were visible, peering down at the sportsman, as much as to say, "I like peas for dinner, little boy, but don't take 'em that way."

"That's no squirrel," thought Frank. "I believe it's a 'coon—sure as a gun. And I haven't got a thing to shoot him with."

He thought of putting his knife into his gun for a bullet, but it proved too large. Then he looked for some coarse gravel, but did not find any. Feeling in all his pockets, his fingers clutched a board nail.

"Ah, that's the thing! We'll see, Mr. 'Coon, if you care any more for board nails than you do for peas."

Loading his gun again, he dropped in the nail instead of a knife for a bullet. He took careful aim again at the spot of fur between the branches, and fired. The 'coon was more than surprised this time, and he certainly forgot to look before he leaped, or he never would have sprung right out ten feet from the tree, with nothing between him and the ground, thirty or forty feet below. He struck all rounded up in a bunch, like a big ball, bouncing up two or three feet from the ground. Frank started toward the animal, thinking, "Well, that fall's knocked the life out of him."

He never was more mistaken. When he stepped toward him, the 'coon got upon his feet at once, and offered battle. Frank now used his gun in another manner, seizing it by the barrel, and turning it into a war club. There ensued some lively dodging on the part of the 'coon; but at length he was hit slightly, when he turned and ran for the nearest tree. This happened to be a beech, in whose hard, smooth bark his claws would not hold. He slipped down, and as Frank came up, turned and made a dash for the boy's legs. Frank met him with a blow of the gun on the head, at which the 'coon dropped down, apparently lifeless. Another such blow would have finished him; but Frank was unwilling to give it, for the last one had cracked his gun-stock. So he shouldered the gun, took the 'coon up by the hinder legs, and started for home. Before he got there the 'coon had come to his senses again, and made Frank pretty lively work to keep his own legs safe. As soon as he could find a good stake Frank dropped his dangerous burden, and before the 'coon could run away, he was stunned by a blow of the stake.

With this victory the war between Frank and the 'coons ended for the season. He had been obliged to buy some corn of a neighbor in order to fill his contract with the canning factory; but the 'coon-skins sold for enough to make up the money.

"COME ON!"

[Begun in No. 46 of Harper's Young People, September 14.]

WHO WAS PAUL GRAYSON?

BY JOHN HABBERTON,

Author of "Helen's Babies."

Chapter III.

MUSIC AND MANNERS.

THE boys at Mr. Morton's select school were not the only people in Laketon who were curious about Paul Grayson. Although the men and women had daily duties like those of men and women elsewhere, they found a great deal of time in which to think and talk about other people and their affairs. So all the boys who attended the school were interrogated so often about their new comrade, that they finally came to consider themselves as being in some way a part of the mystery.

Mr. Morton, who had opened his school only several weeks before the appearance of Grayson, was himself unknown at Laketon until that spring, when, after an unsuccessful attempt to be made principal of the grammar school, he had hired the upper floor of what once had been a store building, and opened a school on his own account. He had introduced himself by letters that the school trustees, and Mr. Merivale, pastor of one of the village churches, considered very good; but now that Grayson's appearance was explained only by the teacher's statement that the boy was son of an old school friend who now was a widower, some of the trustees wished they were able to remember the names and addresses appended to the letters that the new teacher had presented. Sam Wardwell's father having learned from Mr. Morton where last he had taught, went so far as to write to the wholesale merchants with whom he dealt, in New York, for the name of some customer in Mr. Morton's former town; but even by making the most of this roundabout method of inquiry he only

THE ATTACK ON THE ORGAN-GRINDER.

learned that the teacher had been highly respected, although nothing was known of his antecedents.

With one of the town theories on the subject of Mr. Morton and Paul Grayson the boys entirely disagreed: this was that the teacher and the boy were father and son.

"I don't think grown people are so very smart, after all," said Sam Wardwell, one day, as the boys who were not playing lounged in the shade of the school building and chatted. "They talk about Grayson being Mr. Morton's son. Why, who ever saw Grayson look a bit afraid of the teacher?"

"Nobody," replied Ned Johnston, and no one contradicted him, although Bert Sharp suggested that there were other boys in the world who were not afraid of their fathers—himself, for instance.

"Then you ought to be," said Benny Mallow. Benny looked off at nothing in particular for a moment, and then continued, "I wish I had a father to be afraid of."

There was a short silence after this, for as no other boy in the group had lost a father, no one knew exactly what to say; besides, a big tear began to trickle down Benny's face, and all the boys saw it, although Benny dropped his head as much as possible. Finally, however, Ned Johnston stealthily patted Benny on the back, and then Sam Wardwell, taking a fine winter apple from his pocket, broke it in two, and extended half of it, with the remark, "Halves, Benny."

Benny said, "Thank you," and seemed to take a great deal of comfort out of that piece of apple, while the other boys, who knew how fond Sam was of all things good to eat, were so impressed by his generosity that none of them asked for the core of the half that Sam was stowing away for himself. Indeed, Ned Johnston was so affected that he at once agreed to a barter—often proposed by Sam and as often declined—of his Centennial medal for a rather old bass-line with a choice sinker.

Before the same hour of the next day, however, nearly every boy who attended Mr. Morton's school was wicked enough to wish to be in just exactly Benny Mallow's position, so far as fathers were concerned. This sudden change of feeling was not caused by anything that Lakeston fathers had done, but through fear of what they might do. As no two boys agreed upon a statement of just how this difference of sentiment occurred, the author is obliged to tell the story in his own words.

Usually the boys hurried away from the neighborhood of the school as soon as possible after dismissal in the afternoon, but during the last recess of the day on which the above-recorded conversation occurred Will Palmer and Charley Gunter completed a series of a hundred games of marbles, and had the strange fortune to end exactly even. The match had already attracted a great deal of attention in the school—so much so that boys who took sides without thinking had foolishly made a great many bets on the result, and a deputation of these informed the players that it would be only the fair thing to play the deciding game that afternoon after school, so that boys who had bet part or all of their property might know how they stood. Will and Charley expressed no objection; indeed, each was so anxious to prove himself the best player that in his anxiety he made many blunders during the afternoon recitations.

As soon as the school was dismissed, the boys hurried into the yard, while Grayson, who had lately seen as much of marble-playing as he cared to, strolled off for a walk. The marble ring was quickly scratched on the ground, and the players began work. But the boys did not take as much interest in the game as they had expected to, for a rival attraction had unexpectedly appeared on the ground since recess: two rival attractions, more properly speaking, or perhaps three, for in a shady corner sat an organ-grinder, on the ground in front of him was an organ, and on top of this sat a monkey. Now to city boys more than ten years of age an organ-grinder is almost as uninteresting as a scolding; but Lakeston was not a city, organ-grinders reached it seldom, and monkeys less often; so fully half the boys lounged up to within a few feet of the strangers, and devoured them with their eyes, while the man and the animal devoured some scraps of food that had been begged at a kitchen door.

Nobody can deny that a monkey, even when soberly eating his dinner, is a very comical animal, and no boy ever lived, not excepting that good little boy Abel, who did not naturally wonder what a strange animal would do if some one disturbed him in some way. Which of Mr. Morton's pupils first felt this wonder about the organ-grinder's monkey was never known; the boys soon became too sick of the general subject to care to compare notes about this special phase of it; but the first one who ventured to experiment on the monkey was Bert Sharp, who made so skillful a "plumper" shot with a marble, from the level of his trousers pocket, that the marble struck the monkey fairly in the breast, and rattled down on the organ, while the monkey, who evidently had seen boys before, made a sudden jump to the head of his master, and then scrambled down the Italian's back, and hid himself so that he showed only as much of his head as was necessary to his effort to peer across the organ-grinder's shoulder.

"Maledetta!" growled the Italian, as he looked inquiringly around him. As none of the boys had ever before heard this word, they did not know whether it was a question, a rebuke, or a threat; but they saw plainly enough that the man was angry, and although most of them stepped backward a pace or two, they all joined in the general laugh that a crowd of boys are almost sure to indulge in when they see any one in trouble, that any one of the same boys would be sorry about were he alone when he saw it.

The organ-grinder began munching his food very rapidly, as if in haste to finish his meal, yet he did not forget to pass morsels across his shoulder to his funny little companion, and the manner in which the monkey put up a paw to take the food amused the boys greatly. Benny Mallow thought that monkey was simply delightful, but he could not help wondering what the animal would do if a marble were to strike his paw as he put it up. Animals' paws are soft at bottom, reasoned Benny to himself, and marbles shot through the air can not hurt much if any; the result of this short argument was that Benny tried a "plumper" shot himself; but the marble, instead of striking the monkey's paw, went straight into the mouth of the organ-grinder, who was just about to take a mouthful of bread.

Up sprang the Italian, with an expression of countenance so perfectly dreadful that Benny Mallow dreamed of it, for a month after, whenever he ate too much supper. All the boys ran, and the Italian pursued them with words so strange and numerous that the boys could not have repeated one of them had they tried. Every boy was half a block away before he thought to look around and see whether the footsteps behind him were those of the organ-grinder or of some frightened boy. Sam Wardwell stumbled and fell, at which Ned Johnston, who had been but a step or two behind, fell upon Sam, who instantly screamed, "Oh, don't, mister: I didn't do it—really I didn't."

On hearing this all the other boys thought it safe to stop and look, and when they saw the Italian was not in the street at all, they felt so ashamed that there is no knowing what they would have done if they had not had Sam Wardwell to laugh at. As for Sam, he was so angry about the mistake he had made that he vowed vengeance against the Italian, and hurried back toward the yard. Will Palmer afterward said that he couldn't see how the Italian was to blame, and Ned Johnston said the very same thought had occurred to him; but somehow neither of the two happened to mention the matter, as they, with the other boys, followed Sam Wardwell to see what he would do. Looking through the cracks of the fence, the boys saw the Italian, with his organ and monkey on his back, coming down the yard; at the same time they saw nearly half a brick go up the yard, and barely miss the organ-grinder's head. The man said nothing; perhaps he had been in difficulties with boys before, and had learned that the best way to get out of them was to walk away as fast as possible; besides, there was no one in sight for him to talk to, for Sam had started to run the instant that the piece of brick left his hand. The man came out of the yard, looked around, saw the boys, turned in the opposite direction, and then turned up an alley that passed one side of the school-house.

He could not have done worse; for no one lived on the alley, so any mischievous boy could tease him without fear of detection. He had gone but a few steps when Sam, who had hidden in a garden on the same alley, rose beside a fence, and threw a stick, which struck the organ. The man stopped, turned around, saw the whole crowd of boys slowly following, supposed some one of them was his assailant, threw the stick swiftly at the party, and then started to run. No one was hit, but the mere sight of a frightened man trying to escape seemed to rob the boys of every particle of humanity. Charley Gunter, who was very fond of pets, devoted himself to trying to hit the monkey with stones; Will Palmer, who had once helped nurse a friendless negro who had cut himself badly with an axe, actually shouted "Hurra!" when a stone thrown by himself struck one of the man's legs, and made him limp; Ned Johnston hurriedly broke a soft brick into small pieces, and threw them almost in a shower; and even Benny Mallow, who had always been a most tender-hearted little fellow, threw stones, sticks, and even an old bottle that he found among the rubbish that had been thrown into the alley.

Suddenly a stone—there were so many in the air at a time that no one knew who threw that particular stone—struck the organ-grinder in the back of the head, and the poor fellow fell forward flat, with his organ on top of him, and remained perfectly motionless.

"He's killed!" exclaimed some one, as the pursuers stopped. In an instant all the boys went over the fences on either side of the alley, but not until Paul Grayson, crossing the upper end of the alley, had seen them, and they had seen him.

[TO BE CONTINUED.]

FORDING A RIVER IN CENTRAL ASIA.

BY DAVID KER.

I HAVE heard many complaints made of the impossibility of sleeping in a railway car, and have wondered much how those who made them would have fared if compelled to spend, not one night, but twelve or fourteen in succession, in crossing the roadless plains and hills of Central Asia in a Russian cart, whose whole progress is a series of jolts that might dislocate the spine of a megatherium, flinging one at every turn against the corner of a box, or the broad shoulders of the Tartar driver. The correct way of preparing for a journey in this primitive region is to half fill your cart with hay, lay your baggage upon it as a kind of pavement, and cover the whole with a straw mattress, upon which you recline, walled in with rolled-up wrappers to keep you from being absolutely battered to bits against the sides of the vehicle. You then provide yourself with a hatchet and a coil of rope, as an antidote to the inevitable coming off of a wheel two or three times a day during the whole journey, and thus forearmed, you are, as the Russians significantly say, "ready to *chance it*."

After a night of such travel as this, with all its attendant bumps, bruises, and overturns, among the hills on the frontier of Bokhara, my English comrade and I find ourselves nearing the once famous city of Samarcand, and getting forward much more easily now that the plain is fairly reached at last. But what we gain in comfort we lose in picturesqueness. For several miles our course lies through the wet, miry level of the rice fields, and we leave them only to emerge upon a wide waste of bare gravel, amid which the once formidable current of the "gold-giving Zer-Affshan" has shrunk to a single narrow channel, the only fine feature of the landscape being the dark purple ridge beyond, upon which, in June, 1868, was fought the battle that decided the fate of Bokhara.

But commonplace as it looks, every foot of this region is historic ground. Here stood the centre of a mighty empire, drawing to itself all the pomp and splendor of the East, in days when marsh frogs were croaking upon the site of St. Petersburg, and Indians lighting their camp fires upon that of New York. The very earth seems still shaking with the march of ancient conquerors, and one would hardly wonder to see Alexander's Macedonians coming with measured tramp over the boundless level, or low-browed Attila, with the light of a grim gladness in his deep-set eyes, waving on five hundred thousand horsemen with the sweep of his enchanted sabre. But mingled with these memories comes the thought of one who surpassed them both—a little, swarthy, keen-eyed, limping man, known to history as Timour the Tartar, who crushed into one great whole all the jarring kingdoms of Asia, only that they might melt into chaos again the moment that mighty grasp was relaxed by death.

"We must get out here, David Stepanovitch!"

The shrill call sweeps away my visions, and I look up to find myself in front of a tiny hut—a mere speck in that wilderness of gravel—beside which three or four wild-looking figures are grouped around a huge arba (native cart), conspicuous by its immense breadth of beam, and its gigantic wheals, seven good feet in diameter.

Mourad hastily explains that to attempt fording the river in our little post-cart will be certain destruction to our baggage, and that we must shift to the arba, which, light, strong, and, thanks to its great breadth, almost impossible to overturn, seems made for this roadless region, as the camel is for the desert.

The transfer is soon effected, but it takes some time to secure our packages against the tremendous shaking which awaits them, and our careful henchman goes over his work three times before he can persuade himself to let go. But the reckless Bokhariotes, who care little if we and all our belongings go to the bottom, provided they get their money, cut him short by leaping onto the front of the huge tray, and heading right down upon the river.

We make five or six lesser crossings before coming to the real one, the Zer-Affshan, like Central Asian rivers generally, being given to wasting its strength in minor channels; but even these run with a force and swiftness that show us what we have to expect. At length, after a comparatively long interval of bare gravel, the two Bokhariotes suddenly plant themselves back to back, with their feet against the sides of the cart. The huge vehicle halts for a moment, as if to gather strength for its final leap, and then rushes into the stream.

And now comes the tug of war. The wheels have barely made three turns in the water when the great mass trembles under a shock like the collision of a train, and to our bewildered eyes the river appears to be standing perfectly still, and we ourselves to be flying backward at full speed.

Deeper and deeper grows the water, stronger and stronger presses the current. Already the little post-cart following in our wake is almost submerged, and the water is battering against the bottom of the arba, and splashing over our feet as we sit. More than once the horses stop short, and plant their feet firmly, to save themselves from

THE TUG

being swept bodily away, and the roar of the chafing pebbles comes up to us like the tramp of a charging squadron.

In the midst of the din and hurly-burly, the lashing water, and the blinding spray, a terrible thought suddenly occurs to me. "By Jove! all my sugar's in the bottom of my store chest. It'll be all melted, to a certainty."

"Shouldn't wonder," remarks my friend, with that quiet fortitude wherewith men are wont to bear the misfortunes of other people. "However, you can get some more at Samarcand; and, after all, a trunk lined with sugar will be worth exhibiting at home—if you ever get there."

For the next few minutes it is "touch and go" with us; but even among Asiatics nothing can be spun out forever. Little by little the water grows shallower, the ground firmer, the strain less and less violent, till at length we come out upon dry land once more, decant the contents of the arba back into the cart, reward our pilots, and are off again.

THE TUG OF WAR

THIS is an old English game, which has become a favorite athletic exercise in almost all countries, as a trial of strength and endurance. In England it used to be called "French and English," from the ancient rivalry that existed between the two nationalities. Our picture shows how the game is played. Care should be taken to have a stout rope, and the players should be divided so that each party may as nearly as possible be of equal strength. The party that pulls the other over a line marked on the ground between them is the winner in the game. Sometimes a string is tied on the rope, and when the game begins this string should be directly over the dividing line. It often happens that the parties are so evenly matched that neither can pull the string more than an inch or two over the line; and then it becomes a trial of endurance, and the question is which side can hold out the longer.

Y.A..

mong the Burmese the "tug of war" is a part of the reli-
s ceremonies held when there is a scarcity of rain. Instead
rope, long, slender canes are twisted together, and spokes
thrust through to give a firm hold. The sides are taken
ten from different quarters of a town, or from different vil-
s. Each side is marshalled by two drums and a harsh wind
rument, which make a hideous noise. A few priests are
rally seen squatting on the ground near by, chewing the
l-nut, and reading their laws, which are printed on slips
alm leaf. Every now and then they give a shout of en-
agement. Each side tries to pull the other over the line,
l shouts and cries of the most vigorous description. It makes
ifference which side wins the day, as victory to either party
pposed by the superstitious natives to bring the wished-for
. Continued drought does not discourage them from repeat-
the ceremony time after time; and when the rain comes at
they firmly believe it is in answer to their incantations.

FOUND IN A FROG.

BY MISS VIRGINIA W. JOHNSON,

Author of "The Catskill Fairies."

THE sun had risen when Gita awoke. She lived at the top of a tall old house with her grandmother, and both were poor. When she had put on her thin cotton gown and smoothed her hair with her small brown hands, Gita ran down stairs lightly; and these stairs—some crooked stone steps in a dark passage—would have broken our necks to descend. She came out in a narrow street with the tall houses almost meeting overhead, and steep paths or flights of steps leading down to the shore. The town was Mentone, in the south of France, with the boundary line of Italy not half a mile distant. At one end of the street was visible the blue sky, and two churches, yellow and white, on an open square, with towers, where the bells were ringing.

Gita felt in her pocket for a crust of hard bread, and began to eat. This was her breakfast, and if she had been richer she would have drunk a little black coffee with it. As it was, she paused at the fountain, where the women were gossiping as they drew water in buckets, and placed her mouth under the spout.

Raphael came along, and greeted her. Raphael, a tall young fellow with bright eyes, a face the color of bronze, and a little black mustache, was the son of a merchant who kept goats and donkeys for the visitors who came here every year. The goats furnished rich milk for the invalids to drink, while the ladies and children rode the donkeys. Gita found Raphael very handsome.

He wore a curious straw hat with the brim turned up, a shirt striped with red, blue pantaloons, and a yellow sash about his waist. One could see he esteemed himself rather a dandy. In turn Raphael found Gita the prettiest girl of his acquaintance, with her large black eyes, brown face, and white teeth. Besides, Gita was amiable, and did not mock at him when he walked on the Promenade on Sunday with his hat on one side, and a cigarette in his mouth.

"I have asked the consent of my parents to our marriage," said Raphael. "They refuse, unless you have a dower of at least a hundred francs. We must wait."

Gita sighed and shook her head as she pursued her way down to the shore. In these countries the young people must obtain the consent of their parents to marry, and the bride should have a dowry. Gita had not a penny; Raphael's father might as well have asked him to bring the moon as one hundred francs.

Grandmother was seated under an archway, with her little furnace before her, roasting chestnuts. Grandmother, a wrinkled old woman, with a red handkerchief wound about her head, was a chestnut merchant. The sailors, children, and Italians coming over the border bought her wares, and when she was not employed in serving them she twisted flax on a distaff.

"Raphael's father needs a dowry of one hundred francs," said Gita, as grandmother gave her a few chestnuts.

"Ah, if you were a lemon girl!" said grandmother, beginning to twist the flax.

Gita poised a basket on her head, took a white stocking from her pocket, and began to knit as she walked away. The women of the country carry all burdens on their heads. You may see a mother with a mound of cut grass on her head, dandling a little baby in her arms as she moves along. Grandmother had been a lemon girl in her day, but Gita was not strong enough. The lemon girls bring the fruit on their heads many miles, from the lemon groves down to the ships, when they are sent to America and other distant lands.

When you next taste a lemonade at a Sunday-school picnic, little reader, remember how far the lemon has travelled to furnish you this refreshing drink.

Gita went along the shore knitting, her empty basket tilted on her head. The blue Mediterranean Sea sparkled as far as the eye could reach, and broke on the pebbles of the beach in waves as clear as crystal. Soon she turned back toward the hills, following a narrow path between high garden walls, passed under a railroad bridge, and entered an olive garden. She worked here all day, gathering up the little black olives which fall from the trees, much as children gather nuts in the woods at home. Other women were already at work; their dresses of gay colors, yellow and red, showed against the gray background of the trees. A boy beat the branches with a long pole. Gita began to work with the rest. She did not think much about the olive-tree, although it was a good friend. She was paid twenty sous a day to gather the berries from the ground, which were then taken to the crushing mill up the ravine to be made into oil. Gita ate the green lemons plucked from the trees as a child of the North would eat apples, but she loved the good olive-oil better. When the grandmother made a feast, it was to fry the little silvery sardines in oil, so crisp and brown.

The olive-tree is a native of Asia Minor, and often mentioned in the Bible. Some of the trees in the garden where Gita now worked were so old that the Romans saw them when they conquered the world.

At noon the olive-pickers paused to rest. Gita went away alone, and ate the handful of chestnuts given her by grandmother. When she returned to the town at night she would have another bit of bread and a raw onion. She seated herself on the edge of the ravine, and thought about Raphael as she munched her nuts. Below, this path traversed the ravine, and climbed the opposite slope to the wall of a pretty villa, one of the houses occupied for the winter by rich strangers. Gita looked at the villa, with its window shaded by lace curtains, balconies, and terraces, where orange-trees were covered with little golden balls of fruit.

"If I were rich like that I would have soup every day, sometimes made of pumpkin and sometimes with macaroni in it," she thought.

Then she turned over a stone with her heavy shoe, and it rolled down the hill. Gita uttered a cry. The stone had covered a hole at the root of the olive-tree where she sat, far away from the other workers. In the hole she saw a green frog; she dropped on her knees to look at it more closely. Yes, it was a green frog. How did it come there? She touched it with her fingers; the frog did not move or croak. Then she took it out carefully. The frog was one of those pasteboard boxes which appear each year in the shop windows of Paris for Easter presents, in company with fish, lobsters, and shells.

Gita raised the lid. Inside were bank-bills and a lizard. She knew lizards very well; they were always whisking over the stone walls; but then those were of a sober brown tint, while this one was white until she lifted it, when it sparkled like a dewdrop. The lizard was an ornament made of diamonds. Gita held her breath and closed her eyes. She believed herself asleep. Soon she rose, took the box in her hand, and crossing the ravine, began to climb the path to the villa above.

As she reached the door a pony-carriage drove up. A big servant with many buttons on his coat told her to go away. Gita paused, holding the box. The pale lady in the carriage, who was wrapped in furs, motioned her to approach. Quickly the girl ran forward and held out the frog.

"I found it in a hole at the foot of the olive-tree," she explained. "It must belong to this house."

The lady took the box and opened it, emptying the contents on her lap. There lay the diamond lizard, and the roll of French bank-notes.

"You see that Pierre was a dishonest servant, although nothing was found on him," said the lady to those about her. "He must have hidden this box in the olive grove to return from Nice later and find it."

Gita listened with her mouth and eyes wide open. The lady looked at her and smiled.

"You are a good girl," she said.

Then she selected one of the bills and gave it to Gita. It was a note of one hundred francs.

"Now I can marry Raphael!" she cried.

Raphael was standing beside grandmother's chestnut-roaster when both saw Gita running toward them, her cheeks red, and her eyes flashing like stars. She had to tell all about the frog, not only to them, but to the neighbors. As for grandmother, she could not hear the story often enough. When she had been a lemon girl no such luck had befallen her.

"Who would have thought of finding a wedding dowry in a frog!" laughed Raphael.

Gita and Raphael are soon to be married in the yellow

church on the hill. The olive-pickers in the grove seek for something beside the dark berries; they hope to find a green frog under a stone, containing money and a diamond lizard; but this will never again happen.

JAPANESE LIFE.

THE Japanese is the cleanest of mankind. Cleanliness is, so to speak, more than godliness with him. Though he has no soap, he washes all over at least once a day—he worships but once a week. His candles are made of vegetable wax. He uses a cotton coverlet, well stuffed and padded, for bed-covering and mattress. A sort of stereoscope case—made of wood—makes his pillow. He resorts to that, and so do his wife and daughters, that their carefully arranged hair may not be disarranged during sleep. No head-covering is worn by the Japanese. No nation dresses the hair so tastefully. Usually it is with the men shaved in sections. They are coming now to wear it in European fashion. They are adopting all European customs.

On *levée* day I saw the reception at the Mikado's palace in Yeddo. Every one presented had to come in European full dress. That dress does not become the Japanese figure. He looks awkward in it. His legs are too short. The tails of his claw-hammer coat drag on the ground, and the black dress trousers wrinkle up and get baggy around his feet. His European-fashioned clothes have been sent out ready-made from America or England, and in no case did I notice anything approaching to a good fit. Yet he smiled and looked happy, though he could not get his heels half way down his Wellington boots, and his hat was either too large or too small for his head. He always smiles and looks pleasant. Nothing can make him grumble, and he has not learned to swear. He is satisfied to be paid his due, and never asks for more. As a New York cabman he would be a veritable living curiosity.

WHERE DID POTATOES COME FROM?

NOBODY knows precisely where the potato came from originally. It has been found, apparently indigenous, in many parts of the world. Mr. Darwin, for instance, found it wild in the Chonos Archipelago. Sir W. J. Hooker says that it is common at Valparaiso, where it grows abundantly on the sandy hills near the sea. In Peru and other parts of South America it appears to be at home; and it is a noteworthy fact that Mr. Darwin should have noted it both in the humid forests of the Chonos Archipelago and among the central Chilian mountains, where sometimes rain does not fall for six months at a stretch. It was to the colonists whom Sir Walter Raleigh sent out in Elizabeth's reign that we are indebted for our potatoes.

Herriot, who went out with these colonists, and who wrote an account of his travels, makes what may, perhaps, be regarded as the earliest mention of this vegetable. Under the heading of "Roots," he mentions what he calls the "openawk." "These roots," he says, "are round, some large as a walnut, others much larger. They grow on damp soils, many hanging together as if fixed on ropes. They are good food, either boiled or roasted."

At the beginning of the seventeenth century this root was planted, as a curious exotic, in the gardens of the nobility, but it was long ere it came into general use. Many held them to be poisonous, and it would seem not altogether unreasonably so either. The potato is closely related to the deadly-nightshade and the mandrake, and from its stems and leaves may be extracted a very powerful narcotic. In England prejudice against it was for a long time very strong, especially among the poor.

(Begun in HARPER'S YOUNG PEOPLE No. 47, September 21.)

"MOONSHINERS."

BY S. E. MILLER.

CHAPTER II.

CONNY FINDS A HOME.

TWO days afterward, when the doctor went out for his horse, he found Conny sitting astride the block, his lap filled with sweet white clover, which he was feeding to Prince with one hand, while with the other he stroked the beautiful head that was bent down to him. He dropped to his feet on seeing the doctor, and made a bow, grave and stiff, but not at all bashful.

"I have come to live with you, sir," he said.

"Indeed," laughed the doctor; "and what do you suppose I want of you?"

"I don't know, sir; but my feyther always told me, if he died, I was not to stay on the mountain, but go to some good man who would teach me to work."

"And how do you know I am a good man?" asked the doctor, looking keenly at the boy. "You have never seen me but once."

"I have seen you often. I saw you when you mended the rabbit's leg. Jock Riley broke it with his big cart-whip."

"And where were you, pray?"

"Up in a tree, lying along a limb. And I was in the big tamarack when you climbed up the hill for the little flower. I often wanted to know why you cared to get it. My feyther thought perhaps it was good for medicine; but when I told him you only took one, he said then he couldn't tell; it might be you were crazed."

The doctor laughed heartily. It was by no means the first time his passion for botanizing had been called a craze.

"Well, Conny," said he, "go into the house and get your breakfast, and when I come back we will talk this matter over."

He stopped for a word of explanation with his wife, and drove away, leaving Conny on the door-step, with a substantial slice of bread and meat in his hands, and a bowl of milk beside him, while little Betty peeped shyly at him through the window.

It gave the doctor a curious sensation to think, as he rode through the solitary woods, of the little watcher stretched along a mossy limb, or peering out from a tree-top, like some strange, wild creature.

"He must have been set to keep guard by the moonshiners," he thought. "I wonder if they suspected I meant them mischief?" And then like a flash came another thought: "They have sent him to me now as a spy to find out if I have any secret business for the government. I should rather enjoy giving them a scare, if it were not for my wife and Betty."

The doctor fully made up his mind before he went home to send Conny on his ways, but in the end he did no such thing. Old Timothy made much pretense of finding whether he belonged to Dunmore or Kilbourne, and talked bravely of taking him to the poor-house officers; but Timothy found him a great convenience to his rheumatic old hands and feet, and by the end of the summer Conny was as much at home as if he had been bought, like Betty's ugly little terrier, or born in the house, like blessed little Betty herself. It was Conny who gave the last rub to Prince, and brought him to the door; Conny who, in cold or heat, was ready with such good-natured promptness for any errand far or near; Conny who could mend and make; who oiled rusty hinges, repaired broken locks and latches, sharpened the kitchen knives, filed the old saws, and put new handles to all the cast-away tools on the premises. Best of all, in the doctor's eyes, it was Conny who knew every nook of mountain and forest, and whose swift feet and skillful fingers sought out every plant that grew, and brought it to his master's feet.

Only Bridget held to her deep suspicion of something wrong about Conny.

"The craytur's that shmart wid his two hands ye wudn't belave, mum, but I misthrust he's shly; it's in the blood of 'im."

"You ought not to say such things, Bridget; you have no reason to think Conny is not honest," Mrs. Hunter would say.

"It's not to say that he'd sthale, mum, but he's *shly*. I've coom upon 'im suddent wance or twice, an' seen 'im shlip something intil 'is pocket, an' 'im toornin' red in the face an' confused like. An' says I, 'Conny, is it something fine ye have?' An' the b'y walked away widout a word jist."

Mrs. Hunter laughed. "He is just like every other boy in the world—storing up all sorts of odds and ends, as if they were treasures. I remember when Joe would hardly allow me to mend his pockets for fear I should disturb some of his precious trinkets."

Biddy tossed her head with an air that plainly said her opinion was in no wise changed, as she answered, discreetly, "Ye may be in the rights of it, mum, but it's not meself would be judgin' the craytur by Master Joe, that was born a gintleman, let alone the bringin' up."

Quite by accident Mrs. Hunter herself discovered the mystery in Conny's bosom, for, sitting one day by the window at her sewing, she saw the boy come from the wood-house, and after a quick glance in every direction, dart like a squirrel up one of the great hemlock-trees, where he sat completely screened by the branches, only now and then when a stronger gust of wind swayed the top, and gave her a glimpse of him bending intently over something upon his knees. Mrs. Hunter watched him for some time, and then went quietly under the tree and called, "Conny!"

There was a moment of hesitation, and she fancied she saw him put something into the crotch of the tree before he came sliding down at her feet, looking decidedly confused.

"What were you doing up there, Conny?" she asked, pleasantly.

"No harm at all, ma'am," said Conny, with his eyes on his bare brown feet.

"I suppose not, but I should like to know what it was that you hid up in the tree."

"It's no harm, ma'am," repeated Conny, very red and very earnest.

"Then you can certainly show it to me; I wish to see it," said Mrs. Hunter, decidedly.

Conny disappeared in the tree, and in an instant came down, more slowly than before, carrying something carefully in his hand. He gave it to Mrs. Hunter, and stood before her looking as red and guilty as if he had been found in possession of the doctor's gold watch. It was a miniature sideboard of fragrant red cedar, nearly complete, with drawers, shelves, and exquisite carvings—a lovely little model of the handsome sideboard which was the pride of Mrs. Hunter's heart.

"What a beautiful thing!" said Mrs. Hunter, with such delight in her tone that Conny ventured to look up.

"I was keeping it a secret, ma'am, for little Miss Betty's birthday, to give it her unbeknown."

"It is the very prettiest toy I ever saw," said Mrs. Hunter. "I am sorry I spoiled your secret, Conny, but you don't mind my knowing, do you?"

Conny brightened wonderfully.

"I doubted you might think it was presuming in me, ma'am, to be making little Miss Betty a present. Indeed," he added, with a droll little twinkle of his eyes, "it's trouble enough I've had keeping it. Biddy caught

THE DOCTOR COMING UPON CONNY AND THE MOONSHINER IN HEMLOCK GLEN.

me making a little drawing of the fine chest, and would have it out of me what I was hiding; and once, when I was just using my two eyes at the window, she asked me was I planning to steal the silver. And what with little Miss Betty herself, and Timothy rummaging my bits of things, I was just driven to the tree, ma'am."

"And I pursued you there," laughed Mrs. Hunter, to which Conny only responded with a respectful bow.

"Well, Conny, you shall have a shop. I'll give you the key to the little south attic. That was my boy's play-room, and you may keep your tools there, and lock the door, and nobody shall enter without your leave, not even I."

The evident delight that beamed from Conny's eyes almost brought the tears into Mrs. Hunter's, and made her resolve that this young genius should have a chance to grow. She even felt that it would not be honorable in her to reveal his secret to the doctor, but decided that she would wait a few weeks for Betty's birthday.

But before Betty's birthday another secret came to light. Dr. Hunter had twice noticed a strange, rough-looking man hanging about the premises. He had made a pretense of looking for work, but the doctor distrusted him, and ordered him away.

To his great surprise, a few mornings later, he came suddenly upon the same man in the heart of Hemlock Glen, in earnest conversation with Conny. The man instantly disappeared in the woods, and the doctor reined up his horse, and bade Conny get into the gig. He obeyed silently, crouching, as he often did, at the doctor's feet, and dangling his bare legs over the side of the gig.

"Who was that man, Conny?" asked the doctor, when they were nearly home.

"Jock McCleggan, sir."

"Who is he?"

"Just Jock, sir: a man that lives off and on hereabouts."

"Oh," said the doctor, understanding perfectly well that Jock was a moonshiner; "and what business have you with a rascal like that?"

"He knew my feyther, sir, and he's been saying to me these many days that it was agreed between 'em I was to 'bide with him when my feyther died. It's a lee, sir; my feyther never said it."

"He'd better not show his face to me again," said the doctor. "I'll horsewhip him."

Conny suddenly pulled a crumpled bit of paper from his bosom and showed it to the doctor, saying,

"He brought me that just the morning."

The doctor read:

"To Mr. Jock McCleggin,—I want yu to tak mi sun Cony to du as if he was yure one. I mene wen i am ded."
"Sandy McConel."

"Do you think your father wrote it?" asked the doctor, smiling a little.

Conny looked at him with grave displeasure.

"My feyther was a gentleman, sir, not a blitherin' loon like Jock McCleggan, to stumble at spelling his own name." Then, with a great deal of anxiety, he added,

"Jock says you can be made to give me up; he says it 'll be a case of kidnapping."

"Nonsense, Conny: nobody can touch you, or me either; but I advise you to steer clear of Jock and all his companions."

But after this conversation the doctor thought best to see the authorities of Dunsmore, and have himself duly appointed as guardian for Conny—a proceeding which gave the boy unbounded satisfaction.

"I'm yer servant now, little Miss Betty," he said, with a low bow. "Yer servant to keep and to hold; that was what the magistrate said. 'Deed and you're the first lady that ever had a McConnell for a servant."

Betty's birthday came and went. The wonderful little toy was presented, and it was hard saying who was most delighted, Betty or the doctor.

"You are a genius, Conny—an artist, a poet," he exclaimed; and he made a journey to Kilbourne, bringing back a set of carving tools for Conny, and a furnished doll's house, with which he bribed the little lady to give her dainty sideboard into safe-keeping until her curious fingers should have outgrown their passion for pulling things to pieces.

Day by day the attachment of the family for Conny increased.

"He is a gentleman born," said Mrs. Hunter. "I wish I could know more about his history, but he is as discreet as if he were fifty instead of fifteen."

"I fancy his father was a gentleman with a Scotchman's weakness for whiskey, and that he came up here to keep out of sight. At any rate, the boy is a genius, and I intend he shall have a chance in the world."

[to be continued.]

Many thanks for your pretty drawing. We regret we have no room to give it in the Post-office Box.

We would advise our young chemists to buy some good work on the elements of chemistry, and study it well before they undertake any experiments, as handling reagents, when one is not aware of their true composition and behavior under all conditions, is a very dangerous pastime, by which absolutely nothing can be learned, and a great deal of mischief done to face, eyes, hands, and clothing, to say nothing of mamma's table-cloths and carpets.

[illegible] change for the same. I will give foreign postage-stamps, butterflies, or bugs. [illegible]

[illegible]

Harry K. F.—The letters S. P. Q. R. stand for *Senatus populusque Romanus*, meaning the Senate and people of Rome.

[illegible]—Wild rabbits and hares change their coats with the changing season. This peculiarity is especially marked in the Alpine hares of Switzerland. In Young People No. [illegible], in the paper entitled "Hares, Wild and Tame," is a full description of the summer and winter costumes of these little animals.

Willie H. S.—The army-worm varies considerably in its size and markings according to the locality in which it is found, but its general characteristics are sufficiently marked to distinguish it. Its length varies from one to one and three-quarter inches. Its color is gray, sometimes so dark as to appear nearly black. It usually has narrow yellow stripes along its back and sides, and a few short straggling hairs on its body. The moth of this destructive caterpillar is called *Leucania unipuncta*. It is a small rusty grayish-brown fellow, its wings peppered with black dots. It is a member of the extensive family of owlet moths, and may be seen fluttering about the lamps and gas jets any summer evening.

Pauline M.—If you send eighty-one cents, accompanied by your full address, to the publishers, the numbers of Young People you require will be forwarded to you.

Willie F.—Directions for the construction of an ice-boat will be given in an early number of Young People.

"Pigeon."—The wisest thing you can do is to save your pennies until you can buy a pair of the pets you wish, and give up all idea of snaring wild ones.

Favors are acknowledged from [illegible]

Correct answers to puzzles are received from [illegible]

PUZZLES FROM YOUNG CONTRIBUTORS.

No. 1.

WORD SQUARES.

[illegible]

No. 2.

[illegible]

No. 3.

[illegible]

No. 4.

[illegible]

ANSWERS TO PUZZLES IN No. [illegible]

No. 1. William the Conqueror.

No. 2. [illegible]

No. 3. [illegible]

No. 4. Pilgrim's Progress.

ADVERTISEMENTS.

HOW TO CUT A FIVE-POINTED STAR.

Fig. 1.

TAKE a sheet of paper cut square, and fold it as shown by Fig. 1. Make three divisions at one end with a pencil; fold the paper so that the corner lettered *b* will be at *a*, as shown in Fig. 2. Then turn the corner lettered C so that it will be at D, as shown in Fig. 3. Then fold the paper so that the corner lettered B and the corner lettered *a* will be together, and the edges perfectly even, as shown in Fig. 4. Now divide the space between *e* and *f* into three parts, and with one straight cut with the scissors from the division lettered *g* to the corner lettered B and *a*, of Fig. 4, you have Betsey Griscom's five-pointed star.

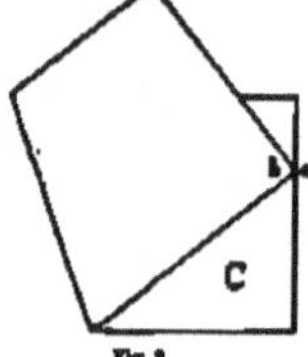

Fig. 2.

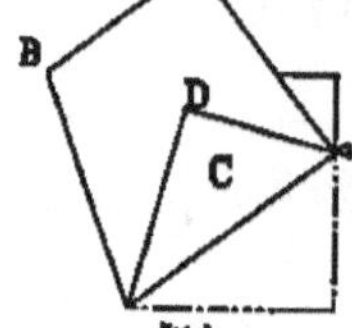

Fig. 3.

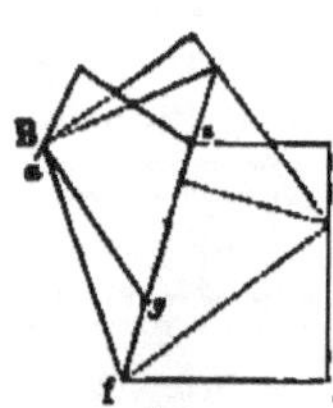

Fig. 4.

GEORGE M. FINCHEL.

The following contributors have also sent in specimens of the five-pointed star so folded as to be cut with one straight clip of the scissors: Emma Schaffer, Samuel R. Lane, W. A. S., Sidney Abenheim, Clyde A. Heller, Pauline Mackay.

OBLIGED TO REFUSE.

BY MADGE ELLIOT.

An agile Gibbon, swinging from
 The top branch of a tree,
Her brown-faced baby in her arms,
 A humming-bird did see
(Upon a lower bough he sat)
 Of Puff-leg family.
"Oh dear!" she cried, "I wish you'd give
 One of your puffs to me;
I hear that they are always used
 In white society.
And though I have no powder, yet
 A pleasure it would be
To dab my face and arms with it,
 Like dames of high degree.
And then I'm sure my darling pet
 Would greatly like it too;
She is the loveliest of babies—"
 "That, ma'am, is very true,"
The humming-bird made haste to say;
 "She much resembles you.
But that small gift you ask is not
 Like stocking nor like shoe:
It won't come off, for it, my friend,
 Grew with me as I grew.
And so I fear I must refuse
 The puff you sweetly beg.
Could I spare *it?* Why, really, now,
 I couldn't spare my leg."

An Odd Combination.—The year 1881 will be a mathematical curiosity. From left to right and from right to left it reads the same; 18 divided by 2 gives 9 as a quotient; 81 divided by 9 gives 9; if divided by 9, the quotient contains a 9; if multiplied by 9, the product contains two 9's; 1 and 8 are 9; 8 and 1 are 9. If the 18 be placed under the 81 and added, the sum is 99. If the figures be added thus, 1, 8, 8, 1, it will give 18. Reading from left to right it is 18, and reading from right to left it is 18, and 18 is two-ninths of 81. By adding, dividing, and multiplying, nineteen 9's are produced, being one 9 for each year required to complete the century.

HARPER'S
YOUNG PEOPLE
AN ILLUSTRATED WEEKLY.

Vol. I.—No. 49. | Published by HARPER & BROTHERS, New York. | Price Four Cents.
Tuesday, October 5, 1880. | Copyright, 1880, by Harper & Brothers. | $1.50 per Year, in Advance.

FRED'S PERILOUS ESCAPE.—Drawn by C. Graham.

HANGING BY A THREAD:

A Canadian Story.

BY DAVID KER.

"WELL, boys, what do you think of *this* for a play-ground? Something like, ain't it?"

And well might Tom Lockyer say so. To be out in the woods on a fine summer morning, with the whole day clear, is a pleasure which any boy can appreciate, more especially such an active one as Master Tom; and he and his two cousins had certainly enjoyed it to the utmost. Ever since breakfast they had been scampering through the woods like wild-cats, climbing trees, tearing through briers, scrambling up and down rocks, chasing each other in and out of the thickets, and making the silent forest ring with their shouts and laughter.

Tom had good reason to remark, with a broad grin, that nothing was left undamaged except their lunch bags; for all three were muddy *from* head to foot, ragged as scarecrows, and so scratched that their hands and faces looked just like railway maps done in red ink. But none the less were they all fully persuaded that they had been enjoying themselves immensely, and were quite ready to begin again as soon as they could find breath to do so.

"Here's the place for us to lunch, my boys!" cried Tom, flinging himself down upon the soft turf that carpeted the summit of the ridge which they had just climbed. "This is one of our best views, and you can feast your eyes and teeth together."

It was, indeed, a splendid "look-out place." The opposite face of the ridge went sheer down to the edge of the river, which, narrowed at this point to less than half its usual width by the huge black cliffs that walled it in, went rushing and foaming through a succession of furious rapids for nearly a quarter of a mile, plunging at length in one great leap over a precipice of nearly a hundred feet—a perfect Niagara in miniature.

"I say, Tom, old fellow, didn't you tell us that you went canoeing along this river every summer? You don't mean to say, surely, that you can take a canoe over that waterfall?"

"Not *exactly*," laughed Tom; "that *would* be a little too much of a good thing. Whenever we come to anything of this sort, we make a portage, as the French boatmen say—carry our canoes round by land, and then launch them again below the fall. There's a snug little path just round the corner, and as soon as we're through with lunch we'll just go down and look about us."

Tom's "snug little path" proved to be very much like the stair of a ruined light-house, and would have seemed to most people almost as bad as going down the precipice itself. But Charlie and Harry Burton, though new to the rocks of the Severn, had had plenty of climbing elsewhere, while as for Tom himself, he could have scaled anything from a church steeple to a telegraph pole.

The view was certainly well worth the trouble. Just at the break of the fall the stream was divided by a small rocky islet crested with half a dozen tall pines, the "Goat Island" of this toy Niagara. In the few rays of sunlight that struggled down into the gloomy gorge the rushing river with its sheets of glittering foam, and the bright green ferns and mosses that clung to the dark cliffs around, and the shining arch of the fall itself, and the rocks starting boldly up in mid-stream, tufted with clustering leaves, made a splendid picture.

Close to the water's edge ran a kind of terrace, formed by the sliding down of the softer parts of the cliff; and along this the three walked till they came right abreast of the fall.

"Hollo!" cried Harry, suddenly, "didn't you say that nobody ever shot these rapids? Why, there's a fellow trying it now!"

There, sure enough, as he pointed up the stream, appeared a canoe with a single figure in it, shooting down the river like an arrow, and already close upon the edge of the rapids.

"Good gracious!" cried Tom, with a look of horror, "it's some fellow being swept down by the stream! See, he's broken his paddle, and can't help himself!"

Instinctively all three sprang forward at once, although the doomed voyager was manifestly beyond the reach of help. But even as they did so, the crisis came. With one leap the boat was in the midst of the rapids, banged to and fro like a shuttlecock by the white leaping waves, amid which it appeared and vanished by turns, till a final plunge sent it right toward the edge of the fall.

The lookers-on turned away their faces; but all was not over yet. By a lucky chance the boat's head had been turned straight toward the island, upon which the current drove it with such force as to dash it in among the sharp rocks, that pierced its sides and held it firm, while its occupant was flung forward on his face among the bushes.

"Phew!" said Tom, drawing a long breath, "what a shave! Ugh! wasn't it horrid, just that last minute? I'm awfully glad he's got off."

"But how's he to get ashore?" asked the practical Charlie. "It seems to me he's in just as bad a fix as ever."

Meanwhile the unlucky voyager had scrambled to his feet, and was staring wildly about him.

"Well, I declare!" exclaimed Tom, "if it isn't my old chum Fred Hope! I'd no idea he was home again."

"I don't think he sees us," said Harry; "let's give him a hail, just to show him there's help at hand. I've heard my father say that if a fellow's left long alone in a place like that he'll go crazy with the fright and the motion of the water."

Tom was not slow to take the hint. He sprang upon the bowlder behind which they were standing, and, putting both hands to his mouth, shouted, above the din of the water-fall, "Hollo, Fred, old boy! how goes it?"

"Who-o's that?" answered a faint voice, tremulous with terror.

"Why, don't you remember Tom Lockyer?"

"Oh, Tom, is that you? Get me out of this somehow, if you can."

"Never fear, old chap; we'll have you out in no time," replied Tom, cheerily.

"But how on earth are you going to do it?" whispered Harry, amazed at his *friend's* confident tone.

"Haven't the least idea, so far," answered the philosophic Tom, coolly; "but it's got to be done *somehow*. If the worst comes to the worst, I can always run home for help, while you two stay here and keep his spirits up."

"If we could only get a rope across," suggested Charlie. "He's got one there, I know, *for* I saw it tumble out of the boat as she swamped; but how are we to get at it?"

"*I* have it!" cried Tom, suddenly. "Fancy my not thinking of this old sling of mine, when I've been using it all morning! I've read lots of yarns about fellows sending messages by arrows: let's see if a stone won't do just as well for once!"

He produced a ball of twine from his pocket as he spoke, and fastened one end of it firmly around a jagged stone which he had picked up.

"See if you've got some more string, boys," said he; "perhaps this bit won't be long enough."

The cord was soon lengthened sufficiently, and Tom, bidding his comrades keep a firm hold of the other end, mounted once more upon the bowlder, and shouted, "Fred, ahoy!"

"Hollo!" responded the islander, whose nerves were being rapidly steadied by the prospect of help, and the sound of Tom's cheery voice.

"We're going to chuck you a line: mind and be ready to catch it."

"All right."

The stone whizzed through the air, and splashed into the water on the other side of the islet, while Fred promptly seized the cord attached to it.

"So far so good, as the hungry boy said when he got half way through the pie," remarked Tom. "Now, old fellow, just knot the string to that rope of yours, and the job's done."

Fred obeyed at once, and the two Burtons hauled in. The rope, once landed, was quickly made fast to the nearest tree, while Fred secured *his* end to one of the pines on the islet. The communication was complete.

"But what next?" asked Harry. "Do you expect the poor fellow to walk ashore on that rope, like Blondin?"

"Not quite," said Tom, laughing. "It's a case of Mohammed and the mountain—if he don't come to me, I must just go to him. Here goes!"

And our hero, swinging himself up on to the rope, began to slide along it, hand over hand, in true gymnastic style.

Taut as the line was, it yielded a little with his weight, and he came perilously near the water midway; but the rope held firm, and in another moment he was safe upon the islet, shaking hands heartily with the expectant Fred.

"Mr. Robinson Crusoe, I presume?" said Tom, with a grin. "I'm the Man Friday, at your service; and a nice little island we've got of it. Now, old boy, there's your road open, and you've just seen the correct way to travel it; so off with you, and show us the latest thing in gymnastics."

"What, along *that rope?*" cried Fred, with a shudder which showed that he had not quite shaken off his panic yet. "Ugh! I couldn't. The bare sight of the fall below me would turn me sick; it looks just as if it was watching for me to tumble in!"

"Oh, if it's only the sight of the water that bothers you, *that's* easily settled," rejoined Tom, struck at that moment with a new and brilliant idea. "I remember hearing a fellow spin a yarn once about how he had escaped being ill at sea, by tying a handkerchief over his eyes so that he couldn't see the jiggle-joggling of the water. If I blindfold you, do you think you can manage it *then?*"

"Ye-es—I should think I might," replied Fred, somewhat doubtfully.

"Here you are, then," said the ever-ready Tom, producing a tattered red handkerchief, with which he bandaged his friend's eyes most scientifically. "Now, old boy, push along—think you're in for an Athletic Cup, with a lot of ladies looking on!"

The device worked wonders. Relieved from the disturbing sight of the precipice and the rushing water, and hearing Tom's hearty voice behind him, cheering him on, Fred went forward manfully; and he was quite surprised to feel his outstretched wrist suddenly seized in a strong grasp, and to hear the shouts of the Burtons proclaiming that he had got safe to land.

"Well done, our side!" shouted Tom, arriving a moment later. "That's what I call blindman's-buff on a new principle, and no mistake!"

A STEAM-ENGINE OUT OF A TIN CAN.

BY THE PROFESSOR.

FEW boys seem to be aware of the entertainment they may obtain with a soldering iron, a pair of shears, and a file. With them it is easy to manufacture working models of machinery, and philosophical apparatus almost without limit. Skill in the use of the iron is readily acquired with a little practice. The quickest way to learn is to observe for a few minutes a tinman at his work. A good-natured one, politely approached, will quickly explain all the mysteries in the process, and take pleasure in filling the office of teacher. For heating the iron, a charcoal fire is generally preferred; a gas stove is also good; and even a common coal fire can be made to answer. The first point is to make a little of the melted solder stick to the point of the iron. For this purpose the iron is filed bright about the point, to remove the oxide and expose the clear metal; then the iron must be quickly applied to the solder. If the heat is sufficient, the iron will get coated, and be ready for use. The oxide has to be removed also from the surface of the material that is to be united; it is the chief obstacle to successful soldering, as the solder refuses to unite with anything but pure metal. Sal ammoniac dissolved in water is good to cleanse off the oxide; better still is muriatic acid, with a little zinc and sal ammoniac added. This is known as the soldering mixture.

One of the most convenient materials for use is common tin, which can be obtained almost everywhere. A tin box can be melted apart, and cut into any desired shape. Pipes to convey liquids, steam, or gas can be made by cutting strips of the tin, and rolling them upon an iron rod. To make a pipe, say, a quarter of an inch in diameter, get an iron rod of that size, cut a strip of the tin about one inch wide, roll it upon the rod, allowing the edges to lap a little. If the tin be not bright, make it so by applying sal ammoniac with a small brush along the seam. Put on a little powdered resin, and then solder neatly by drawing the heated iron, with the solder clinging to it, over the joint. In this way a pipe strong and tight is obtained; and such pipes can be joined to one another indefinitely, in a straight line or at any angle. To unite them in a straight line, pass the end of one into the end of the other before soldering, or else wind an additional piece of tin over the two ends. To make a turn, or elbow, file the ends on a bevel, or slant, bring them together, and apply considerable solder for strength. If the solder be rightly put on, it will hold surprisingly.

A pretty device to illustrate the force of steam is shown in the accompanying picture. The boiler is a simple tin can, which need not be more than six inches high and four in diameter. To make the wheel, cut a circle of tin two inches in diameter, and pieces for the buckets, shaped as in the diagram.

Bend each piece at right angles along the dotted line, and solder them one after another on the circumference of the wheel, which will then appear as in the picture. Bore a hole through the centre, insert a piece of wire for a shaft, and solder it fast at right angles to the wheel. File shoulders on the ends of the shaft, and mount it in uprights fastened to the top of the boiler. Make a small opening through the top of the boiler, and place over it a little spout in such a position as to send a current of steam directly into the buckets of the wheel. Make also a larger opening in or near the top of the boiler, and surround it with a neck to receive a cork. Through this the water is introduced. For this purpose a small funnel will be found convenient.

When all is complete, the boiler may be filled about half full, and set on a hot stove. When the water boils, the steam will emerge through the spout, and propel the wheel. As the steam constantly escapes, no explosion need be apprehended. To remove all possibility of creating too much pressure, place the cork in the neck very lightly, so that it will pop out if more steam is generated than can escape through the spout. Then the miniature steam-engine and boiler may be regarded as harmless as a tea-kettle. As the quantity of steam that can be produced is very limited, care must be taken that there be no leaks, that the mouth of the spout be quite small, and that the current of steam be discharged accurately into the buckets. The bearings of the shaft should be oiled, and everything arranged so that there will be the least possible friction. Then the wheel may be expected to spin very rapidly.

[Begun in No. 46 of Harper's Young People, September 14.]

WHO WAS PAUL GRAYSON?

BY JOHN HABBERTON,

Author of "Helen's Babies."

Chapter IV.

WHO WILL TELL?

AS Benny Mallow hid himself in a barn in the yard into which he had jumped, he had only one distinct thought in his mind: he wished that the Italian had never come to Lakeston at all—never come to the United States, in fact. He wished that the Italians had never heard of such a place as America: if one of the race had to discover it, he need not have gone and let his fellow-countrymen know all about it, so that they should come over with organs and monkeys, and get boys into trouble—boys that weren't doing a thing to that organ-grinder when he threw a stick at them. What made the fellow go into the school yard, anyway? No one asked him to come. Now there would be a fuss made, of course; and if there was anything that Benny hated more than all other things, it was a fuss.

But what if the organ-grinder should really prove to be dead? Oh! that would be too dreadful; all the boys would have to be hanged, to be sure of punishing the murderer, just as the whole class was sometimes kept in for an hour because something wrong had been done, and no one would tell who did it.

Benny could not bear the thought of so dreadful a termination to his life, for he knew of a great deal worth living for; besides, his mother would need his help as soon as he grew old enough to earn anything. What should he do? Wait until dark, and then run away, and tramp off to the West, where other runaway boys went, or should he make for the sea-board, and from there to South America, from which country he had heard that criminals could not be brought back?

BENNY MALLOW IN THE BARN.

But first he ought to learn whether the man was really dead; it might not be necessary to run away at all. But how should he find out? Suddenly he remembered that Mr. Wardwell's barn, in which he was, had a window opening on the alley; so he crept up into the loft, and spent several moments in trying to look up the alley without putting his head out of the window. Finally he partly hid his face by holding a handful of hay in front of it, and peered out. Between the stalks of hay he was delighted to see the organ-grinder on his feet, although two men were helping him. They were not both men, either, Benny saw, after more careful looking, for one of them was Paul Grayson; but the other—horror of horrors!—was Mr Stott, a Justice of the peace. Benny knew that Justice Stott had sent many men to jail for fighting, and if Grayson should tell who took part in the attack, Benny had not the slightest doubt that half of Mr. Morton's pupils would be sent to jail too.

This seemed more dreadful than the prospect of being hanged had done, but it could be done more quickly. Benny determined at once that he must find out the worst, and be ready for it, so he waited until the injured man and his supporters had turned the corner of a street, and were out of sight; then he bounded into the alley again, hurried home, seized a basket that was lying beside the back door, and a moment later was sauntering along the street, whistling, and moving in a direction that seemed to be that in which he might manage to meet the three as if by accident. He did not take much comfort out of his whistling, for in his heart he felt himself to be the most shameful hypocrite that had existed since the days of Judas Iscariot, and the recollection of having been told by his Sunday-school teacher within a week that he was the best boy in his class seemed to make him feel worse instead of better; and his mind was not relieved of this unpleasant burden until at a shady corner he came suddenly upon the organ-grinder and his supporters, when he instantly exchanged his load for a new one.

"Why, what's the matter, Paul?" asked Benny, with as much surprise in his tone and manner as he could affect.

Justice Stott had just gone into an adjacent yard for water for the Italian, when Grayson answered, with a very sober face, "You know as well as I do, Benny, and I saw the whole crowd."

"I don't!" exclaimed Benny, in all the desperation of cowardice. "I didn't do or see—"

"Sh—h!" whispered Grayson, "the Justice is coming back."

Benny turned abruptly and started for home. He felt certain that his face was telling tales, and that Justice Stott would learn the whole story if he saw him. There was one comfort, though: it was evident that Grayson did not want the Justice to know that Benny had taken part in the affair.

There was a great deal of business transacted by the boys of Laketon that night. How it all was managed no one could have explained, but it is certain that before bed-time every boy who had taken part in the assault on the Italian knew that the man was not dead, but had merely been stunned and cut by a stone; that Paul Grayson knew who were of the party that chased the man up the alley. Various plans of getting out of trouble were in turn suggested and abandoned; but several boys for a long time insisted that the only chance of safety lay in calling Grayson out of his boarding-house, and threatening him with the worst whipping that the boys, all working together, could give. Even this idea was finally abandoned when Will Palmer suggested that as Grayson boarded with the teacher, and seemed to be in some sort a friend of his, he probably would already have told all he knew if he was going to tell at all. Some consolation might have been got out of a report of Benny's short interview with Grayson, had Benny thought to give it, but he had, on reaching home, promptly feigned headache, and gone to bed; so such of the boys as did not determine to play truant, and so postpone the evil day, thought bitterly of the morrow as they dispersed to their several homes.

There was not as much playing as usual in the school yard next morning, and when the class was summoned into school the teacher had no difficulty in discovering, by the looks of the various boys, who were innocent and who guilty. Immediately after calling the roll Mr. Morton stood up, and said:

"Boys, a great many of you know what I am going to talk about. Usually your deeds done out of school hours are not for me to notice; but the cowardly, shameful treatment of that organ-grinder began in the school yard, and before you had gone to your homes, so I think it my duty to inquire into the matter. Justice Stott thinks so too. When any one has done a wrong that he can not amend, the only manly course is to confess. I want those boys who followed the organ-grinder up the alley to stand up."

No boy arose. Benny Mallow wished that some one would give the bottom of his seat a hard kick, so that he would have to rise in spite of himself, but no one kicked.

"Be honest, now," said Mr. Morton. "I have been a boy myself; I have taken part in just such tricks. I know how bad you feel, and how hard it is to confess; but I give you my word that you will feel a great deal better after telling the truth. I will give you one minute more before I try another plan."

Mr. Morton took out his watch, and looked at it; the boys who had not been engaged in the mischief looked virtuously around them, and the guilty boys looked at their desks.

"Now," exclaimed Mr. Morton, replacing his watch in his pocket. "Stand up like men. Will none of you do it?"

Benny Mallow whispered, "Yes, sir," but the teacher did not hear him; besides, Benny made no effort to keep his word, so his whispering amounted to nothing.

"Grayson," said Mr. Morton, "come here."

Bert Sharp, who sat near the front of the room, where the teacher could watch him, edged to the end of his seat,

"MR. MORTON, I WAS THERE."

so as to be ready to jump up and run away the moment Grayson told—if he dared to tell. Most of the other boys found their hearts so high in their throats that they could not swallow them again, as Grayson, looking very white and uncomfortable, stepped to the front.

"Grayson," said the teacher, "I have known you for many months: have I ever been unkind to you?"

"No, sir," replied Grayson; then he wiped his eyes; seeing which Bert Sharp thought he might as well run now as later, for boys who began by crying always ended by telling.

"You saw the attack made on the Italian; Justice Stott says you admitted as much to him. Now I want you to tell me who were of the party."

"May I speak first, sir?" asked Grayson.

"Yes," said the teacher.

"Boys," said Grayson, half facing the school, "you all hate a tell-tale, and so do I. Do you think it the fair thing to hold your tongues and make a tell-tale of me?"

Grayson looked at Will Palmer as he spoke, but Will only looked sulky in return; then Grayson looked at Benny Mallow, and Benny was fast making up his mind that he would tell rather than have his friend do it, when up stood Bert Sharp and said,

"Mr. Morton, I was there."

"Bravo, Sharp!" exclaimed the teacher. "Grayson,

you may take your seat. Sharp, step to the front. Now, boys, who is man enough to stand beside Sharp?"

"I am," piped Bunny Mallow, and he almost ran in his eagerness.

"It's no use," whispered Will Palmer to Ned Johnston, and the two boys went to the front together; then there was a general uprising, and a scramble to see who should not be last.

"Good!" exclaimed Mr. Morton, looking at the culprits and then about the school-room; "I believe you're all here. I'm proud of you, boys. You did a shameful thing in attacking a harmless man, but you have done nobly by confessing. I can not let you off without punishment, but you will suffer far less than you would have done by successfully concealing your fault. None of you are to go out at recess next week. Now go to your seats. Sharp, you may take any unoccupied desk you like. After this I think I can trust you to behave yourself without being watched."

The boys had never before seen Sharp look as he did as he walked to a desk in the back of the room and sat down. As soon as the bell was struck for recess Grayson hurried over to Sharp, and said,

"You helped me out of a terrible scrape, do you know it?"

"I'm glad of it," said Sharp. "And that isn't all; I wish I could think of something else to own up to."

[TO BE CONTINUED.]

THREE YOUNG HAWKS.

BY F. M. H.

ONE bright summer afternoon Bob and I slipped away from the other boys as soon as school was out, and went gayly down the road that led to the big bridge.

We were going birdnesting, and were determined to add something handsome this time to the collection of eggs that we had been gathering since spring.

The bobolinks knew us perfectly well; and you would have thought by the way they rose out of the meadows on each side of the road, and sang as if they were too happy for anything, that they were delighted to see us. Not a bit of it. Their singing was meant to attract our attention, and give the Mrs. Bobolinks time to glide through the tall grass, and then rise up so far away from their nests that we would not know where to look for them. We were not after their eggs, however, for we had all the bobolinks' eggs we wanted, carefully blown and laid away in our collection. Sharp as Mr. Bobolink was, we knew all his tricks, and had outwitted him often.

"Where shall we go, Bob?" said I. "We haven't been to see whether that cedar-bird's nest down by the river has any eggs in it yet."

"Oh, bother the cedar-bird! we can attend to his case any day. Let's go through the bushes on the other side of the meadow, and then down to the big bridge. We haven't been to the hill where the old dead tree is for ever so long."

"All right," said I; so we climbed the fence, crossed the meadow, and plunged into the bushes, watching every bush, and listening to every noise. Suddenly we heard a rustling of wings, and then a mournful cry like the wail of a lost kitten.

"Now, Bob, look sharp," I exclaimed; "there's a cat-bird's nest in here, and Fred Sprague asked me to get an egg for him the first time I came across any."

The old bird was fluttering from bush to bush, continually "mewing," and seeming to be in great distress. "There's the nest, Jack," cried Bob, pointing to a mass of twigs on the top of a tall bush. "You stand underneath and hold your hat to catch the eggs if they fall, and I'll bend down the branch."

The cat-bird was now in a terrible state of mind, and flew around our heads scolding at a great rate. We told her that we only meant to take one egg, but she wasn't a bit satisfied with our explanation.

Down came the bush as Bob carefully bent it, and presently we could see into the nest, where four beautiful eggs were lying. We took one of them out, and let the branch slowly up again; but the cat-bird did not seem at all grateful.

"Let's blow the egg now," said I; "'twill be easier to carry. Have you got a pin with you?"

Bob gave me a pin, with which I made a little hole in each end of the egg. Then putting one end to my lips, I blew gently and steadily, until out came the clear white and then the yellow yolk, leaving the empty shell as light as a feather. Wrapping the egg in cotton, and placing it in a little pasteboard box that I took from my pocket, I felt certain that I could carry it home safely.

We found no more nests in the bushes, and after a while Bob said: "Let's make a bee-line for the bridge, and see if there's anything in that dead tree."

So we came back to the road, crossed the bridge, and went to the foot of a great dead elm-tree that stood on the side hill a little way from the river. It must have been struck by lightning, for it was nothing but a shell, and a long blackened crack reached from the top nearly to the bottom of it.

"I don't believe there's as much as a wasp's nest in there," said I.

"We'll see, anyway," replied Bob. "I'll fire a stone at that hole up by the top, and you stand back and watch if anything comes out."

Bob could throw a stone straighter than any other boy in school. He hit the trunk of the tree close by the hole, and in an instant something darted out with a loud whir, and vanished over the tree-tops.

"Bob," cried I, "that was a hawk."

"Hawks don't build in holes," replied Bob. "Perhaps it was an eagle."

"Eagles don't build in holes either," said I; "but I read yesterday that the pigeon-hawk does build in old dead trees."

"Then that's a pigeon-hawk sure enough," exclaimed Bob. "And there she is, sailing round in a circle, and watching us. What won't the boys say when they see us bringing home a lot of hawks' eggs?"

"That's all very well; but who's going to climb the tree?"

"You are," said Bob. "You know you're the best climber. The hole isn't more than thirty feet from the ground."

I was ready enough to climb, and pulled off my jacket at once; but I could not get my arms around the tree, and the lowest branch was a dozen feet from the ground.

"I tell you what we'll do," exclaimed Bob. "Let's get a fence rail, and lean it against the tree. I'll boost you, and when you get on the end of the rail, you can reach that branch."

We selected the longest and knottiest rail we could find, and leaned it up against the tree. Then Bob boosted me, while he kept his foot at the end of the rail to prevent it from slipping. By this means I managed to reach the lower branch, and seat myself on it.

"All right so far," said I; "but, Bob, the next branch is beyond my reach, and I don't see how in the world I'm going to get any higher."

"Jack," replied Bob, in a solemn tone, "you've got to do it. There's a hawk's nest up there, and we're bound to have it."

After making a good many trials, I found that by putting one hand in the big crack of the tree I could get a hold that would support me, and by-and-by I found myself standing on the upper branch, with one arm around the trunk, and the hole within my reach.

"Now," cried Bob, "don't waste any time, but go for those eggs, or we won't get home before dark."

He looked very cool and comfortable on the ground, while I was standing in a very ticklish place, and was afraid that the dead limb might give way at any moment. I didn't very much like to put my hand into the hole, for how did I know but that there might be a big snake in it? However, it had to be done, so in went my hand. Something hit it a vicious dig, and you can be sure that I pulled it out in a hurry. To tell the truth, I was badly frightened for a minute, and nearly lost my balance. Then it flashed on me that the eggs we were in search of were young birds.

"Bob!" I shouted, "there are young ones!"

"Hooray!" cried Bob. "That's better yet. Throw 'em down, and I'll catch 'em in my hat."

Much as I hated to do it, I thrust in my hand again, and out came a young hawk, biting, scratching, and screaming. I didn't hold it long, but in less time than you can say "Jack Robinson," down it went into Bob's hat.

Just as I threw down the third and last bird I heard Bob shout, "Look out! the old one's coming." Then something hit me on all sides of my head at once, just as if half a dozen school-teachers were boxing my ears at the same time. I put up my hands to defend my eyes, lost my balance, and, crash!—I didn't know anything more for the next five minutes.

When I came to myself Bob was dashing water in my face by the hatful. I could just manage to say, "Don't drown me."

"Then you're not dead!" exclaimed Bob. "You gave me an awful scare. Why, I couldn't make you speak a word. Don't ever go and do it again."

"I'm not dead yet, Bob, but it was a pretty ugly fall, wasn't it? Where are the young hawks?"

"Oh, they're all right. I've got 'em tied up in my handkerchief. Try and see if you can stand up."

I did try, but the minute I bore my weight on my right ankle such a sharp pain went through it that down I fell, and fainted away again.

When I came to, the second time, I heard a man say, "Guess we'd better carry him right down to the house, and get the doctor to 'tend to him." Bob had gone to a farm-house near by, and had brought two men to help him take care of me.

"I'm all right now," said I, "except my ankle, and I guess Bob can wheel me home in a wheelbarrow."

"I'll wheel you myself," said one of the men. "You've done a good job breaking up that there hawks' nest, and I owe you something for it."

You'd better believe that the boys stared when they saw Farmer Jones wheeling me home, and Bob carrying three young hawks in his handkerchief. I felt pretty proud, but was laid up for three weeks with my sprained ankle, and I made up my mind that the next time I meddled with a hawk's nest, I'd shoot the old hawk first.

OLD TIMES IN THE COLONIES.

BY CHARLES CARLETON COFFIN.

No. VII.

JOHN STARK AND THE INDIANS.

IN April, 1752, David Stinson, Amos Eastman, William and John Stark, paddled up the Merrimac River in canoes. Just above the junction of the Contoocook River with the Merrimac they passed the last log-cabin. From thence all the way to Canada there was not a white man. They made their way forty miles farther, entered a little stream now known as Baker's River, winding through a beautiful valley, built a camp, and set their traps to catch beaver, which were building their dams along the brooks.

There had been war between France and England, but peace had been agreed upon, and the Indians, who had been on the side of France, came from Canada and traded with the settlers along the frontier; but the settlers were ever on the watch, fearing an outbreak of hostilities at any moment.

The young hunters discovered some tracks in the woods, which had been made by Indians.

"The red-skins are about," they said.

It was agreed that it would be best to take up their traps and leave quietly, for the Indians claimed the whole country as their hunting ground. John Stark went out from the camp to take up his traps, when he found himself confronted by several Indians, who made him their prisoner. They had come from the village of St. Francis, in Canada, to Lake Memphremagog, brought their canoes across the divide between the lake and Connecticut River, and had descended that stream to the present town of Haverhill, in New Hampshire, and were on their way to plunder the settlements on the Merrimac. They did not know that John Stark had any companions near at hand, nor did he inform them.

"Why is John gone so long?" was the question asked by the others.

"Perhaps he is lost. Let us fire a gun."

The report of a gun echoed through the forest.

The Indians' eyes twinkled. There were more prisoners to be had. They stole through the woods with John, and came upon his three companions. Eastman was on shore, his brother William and Stinson in the boat. The Indians seized Eastman.

"Pull to the other shore," shouted John.

Crack! crack! went the guns of the Indians. Stinson fell dead, and a bullet split the paddle in the hands of John's brother, who leaped to the other bank, and escaped. Crack! crack! went the guns again, but he was so far away that they did not harm him. The Indians, enraged at William's escape, gave John a whipping; but instead of whining, he laughed in their faces. They gathered up the hunters' beaver-skins, took their guns and traps, piled them upon John and Eastman, and started for their canoes, greatly pleased with their luck. The Indians divided, one party going over the Green Mountains with the furs which they had captured, going to Albany, where they could get better prices than in Canada, and the other, with John and Eastman, going up the Connecticut to Lake Memphremagog, descending the St. Francis River to their village on the St. Lawrence.

It was a wearisome journey, and John had a heavy pack to carry, but he was young, strong, brave, and was not in the least down-hearted. He did not think that the Indians would harm him; they could do better—sell him to the French.

The Indian town of St. Francis was a collection of miserable cabins and wigwams. The Jesuit fathers had been among the tribe for many years, and had won their confidence; had converted them to Christianity; that is, the Indians had been baptized; they counted their beads, and mumbled a few prayers that the priests had taught them; but they had learned nothing of the justice, mercy, or love pertaining to the Christian religion. They were the same blood-thirsty creatures that they had always been, and were happiest when killing and scalping the defenseless settlers.

The whole population—warriors, squaws, and children—came out to welcome the returning party. True, the French and English were not at war; neither were the English at war with the Indians; but what of that? Had they not made war on their own account? There was no one to rebuke them, for were not the English always considered as their enemies?

The Indians of St. Francis always made their prisoners run the gauntlet. It is not quite certain what the word comes from, but it means running between two files of

"CRACK! CRACK! WENT THE GUNS OF THE INDIANS."

men armed with sticks and clubs, each Indian to give the runner a whack as he passes.

The Indians, squaws, children, and all, paraded in two lines about four feet apart. Eastman was the older, and was the first to run. Whack! whack! went the sticks and clubs, beating him black and blue.

"Your turn now," said an Indian to John.

He is thirty years old, tall, broad-shouldered, his muscles like springs of steel. He has an iron will, and is quick to think and act.

The Indians grasp their cudgels more firmly to give him a good drubbing. What fun it will be to bring them down upon his broad shoulders, and see him cringe!

John comes upon the run. Quick as a flash he seizes the cudgel in the hands of the first Indian, swings it about his head with the strength of a giant. Whack! it goes upon the skull of one, whack! again upon the forehead of the Indian opposite, knocking them right and left. The next two catch it, the third and fourth. They go down as the Philistines fell before Samson. His blows fall so fast that the Indians take to their heels; he breaks up the gauntlet, and marches over the ground like a conqueror. The Indians, instead of punishing him, are greatly pleased.

It is midsummer, and the corn which the Indians have planted needs hoeing. They take him into the field, put a hoe into his hands to work with the squaws.

"You hoe corn," they say. John Stark hoe corn for the Indians! Not he. He cuts up weeds and corn alike, giving a few strokes, doing what damage he can, and then flings the hoe into the river.

"Squaws hoe corn. Braves fight," he says.

Do they beat him? On the contrary, they pat him on the shoulder.

"Bono! bono!" (good! good!) they say.

The Indians look down upon work as degrading. They make their wives do all the drudgery. Women were made to work, men to fight. To humiliate their prisoners they put them to work, degrading them to the condition of women. John Stark understood their character, and acted accordingly, and his captors were so delighted that they wanted him to become an Indian.

"We make you chief," they said.

"You be my son. I give you my daughter," said the chief.

But John Stark had no idea of becoming an Indian. Nevertheless, he kept his eyes and ears open. He studied their ways. They showed him how to follow a trail over the dead leaves of the forest—how the leaves would be rustled here and there, turned up at the edges, or pressed down a little harder where men had set their feet. He saw what cowards they were unless the advantage was all on their side, and how wily they were to steal upon their enemies. He picked up a little of their language. He was ready to go with them upon a deer-hunt; but as for working, he would not.

Little did the Indians think that they were teaching one who would turn all his knowledge to good account against them a few years later; that when they were showing him how to follow a trail they were teaching him to trace their own footsteps; that when the time came he would pay them off roundly for having taken him prisoner.

He was so brave, resolute, stout-hearted, and strong that they set a much higher value upon him than upon his comrade Eastman; for when their friends sent money to Montreal to ransom them, they asked only sixty dollars for Eastman, while John had to pay one hundred. So much for being brave! The money was paid, and the two men were sent to Montreal, and from there to Albany. As they came through Lake Champlain, John Stark looked out upon scenes with which he was to become familiar in after-years, and which we shall read about at another time.

LIL'S FUN.

BY MRS. W. J. HAYS.

"BOYS have the best of it always!" said Lil, flinging herself in the hammock with a sigh, as she saw her two brothers, several cousins, and their comrades, in battered hats, turned-up trousers, and dingiest of jackets, going down through the maples with their fishing-poles over their shoulders.

"I think so too," said Ollie, spreading out her dainty dress, and picking a daring grasshopper off her silk stocking. "It's just too mean that we can't have some fun. They say we are always in the way, that we can't even bait our own hooks—it is horrid to stick those nasty worms on!—but I can catch fish as well as any one, and if boys are around, why shouldn't they make themselves useful? And they say we scream so, and make such a fuss about everything," went on Ollie, in the same injured tone.

"Everything is better for boys than for girls. All the stories are written for them; they can ride, and drive, and play ball, and swim, and skate, and—"

"Lil! Lillie!" called a soft sweet voice, "are you in the sun? Your complexion will be ruined."

"There! didn't I say so?" was the somewhat incoherent reply. "Isn't it always the way? See how we are watched: don't go in the sun, you'll be burned; don't do this, don't do that—all because you're a girl. I'm tired of it.—Aunt Kit, I'm not in the sun.—I wish I was," was added sotto voce.

"Country girls' mothers are not so particular," said Ollie. "Look at those Pokeby girls in their calicoes; they climb trees like monkeys, and they have lots of good times."

"Let's go over and see them; it is not far. Come, Ollie."

"In my new dotted mull and silk stockings?" cried Ollie, in amazement. "Aunt Kit won't let us."

"See if she don't;" and Lil bounced out of the hammock, and into the house, where in the cool darkness of a shaded parlor sat a slender lady, with a pile of flowers in her lap, and a graceful basket in her hands, which she was ornamenting. "Aunt Kit, I have come to ask a favor. We are just bored to death doing nothing."

"Lil, how can you use such an expression? I am shocked. You are really getting very careless in your use of words."

"Well, then, excuse me, but it's the truth all the same. Ollie and I want some fun; the boys wouldn't take us fishing, and now I want you to let us put on some old duds and go over to the Pokebys'. We will promise to come home to tea, we will be as prim as prunes afterward, and I'll play two extra exercises to-morrow, and learn three pages of French. Now you can't say no; there's every reason for saying yes, and you will have a nice quiet time all day, without being bothered. Please—that's a darling!" and she smothered her retreating relative with kisses.

After some hesitation, and after many protestations that they would remember every charge given them, the girls received permission to go to the farm.

"I never was more surprised in my life," said Ollie, as, after donning plainer attire, she and Lil started out. "Now I am going in for a day's fun."

"What are you going to do?"

"Everything. When I get hold of Clara Pokeby—There she is now!"

"Oh, Clara!" broke out both girls at once, "we have come to spend the afternoon, if we may. Is it convenient?"

"I'll ask mother," said the quiet little maid, with a sincerity which somewhat dampened Lil's ardor.

They were joined in a few moments more by two other girls, each a year older and an inch higher; and now Lil, having an audience, began to talk, as they left the orchard where they had met, and from which they were walking to the farm-house, which peered out from its thicket of lilac-bushes, syringas, and overhanging maples. She was waxing eloquent over her dissatisfaction with boarding-house amusements, the boys' neglect, and her aunt's strictness, when they reached the door, and Clara made known her wishes to her mother.

Mrs. Pokeby had heard the conclusion of Lil's speech, and a smile was dancing around the corners of her mouth.

"A little more work and a little less play would be my remedy, Miss Lil." But seeing the girl looked somewhat crest-fallen, she said, kindly: "Come in, come in, all of you, and welcome. If you can wait till my girls have helped me a little, you may have all the fun you can make for yourselves."

The farm kitchen was a very spacious room, and Lil and Ollie thought it ever so much nicer than the one in their city house. The dresser was filled with shining tins, the cupboard with blue china enough to stock two or three cabinets, the floor was white as the fine sand could make it, and the bunches of sweet herbs perfumed the room so pleasantly that bees had evidently mistaken the place for a branch of the flower garden by the way they flitted in and out.

Lil and Ollie sat down to watch Mrs. Pokeby, who was preparing to bake; but in a trice both had on aprons, and were busily assisting Clara and her sisters. It was so nice to be trusted to break and beat eggs, to sift flour, to wash currants, and weigh sugar. They whipped the eggs till they looked like snow, they made the creamy butter dissolve in the sparkling sugar, they tasted and tried the consistency of the cake, they buttered the pans, and watched the oven. Mrs. Pokeby even let them mould some biscuits, and spread the paste over pie plates, and drop in the luscious fruit. So intent were they in their occupation that they hardly noticed the lengthening shadows, and heard Clara Pokeby say it was time to be off if they were going anywhere to play.

"Oh, wouldn't it be nice to give the boys a supper!—a supper all cooked by ourselves?" said Lil, with a sudden inspiration.

"Jolly enough," said Ollie.

"And have it in the woods," said Clara. "Do you know where they have gone?" she asked.

"Yes, they were to fish in Black Creek—down where we gathered pond-lilies last week."

"That is not too far. Mother, may we do it?"

"To be sure. You may have a share of everything we have made. Let me see, there's an apple-pie, a pan of biscuit—I can whip up some corn-bread—"

"Oh, please let me do it," said Lil.

No sooner said than done. Again they went to work. By the time the corn-bread was finished, Mrs. Pokeby had packed the baskets. Lil had looked about fifty times in the oven, and fifty times more at the receipt-book, to see if she had followed the instructions properly, while Clara and Ollie and the other girls had provided glasses and spoons and napkins.

"Now we are all ready—come on, girls," was at last the order issued by Lil, and away they went. Mr. Pokeby gave them a lift on the empty hay-cart, and carried the heaviest basket to the woods. They chose a lovely spot, grassy and smooth, not far from the path where the boys would have to pass. They could hear their voices now, and the occasional splash of an oar. They spread out their table-cloth, made a fire, and Lil said she was going to scramble some eggs; meanwhile Ollie and Clara could be on the watch to secure the guests.

It was a delightful afternoon, and a cool breeze was fluttering the grasses. The water of the creek reflected the overhanging boughs in its dark surface, water-spiders were spinning their little whirls, crickets were singing, and swallows had begun their evening hunt.

The boys, tired and hungry, pushed their boat up on the bank. One or two were elated with their success, and had quite a string of fish to show; the others, disappointed, had been arguing as to their want of luck, and had subsided into silence.

"Whew!" said Lil's brother Charlie; "I smell something good; wish I was home; awful hungry. How is it with you, Ted?"

"Voracious."

"And you, Sam?"

"Tired as that trout I chased and didn't kill."

"My! how gamy you are!"

Here the group came to a sudden halt. Two small maids appeared from the woods, and making a profound courtesy to Charlie as leader, began a speech.

"Those bothersome girls again!" whispered Billy Brittain.

"The Misses Pokeby and the Misses Sinclair have the honor to—to— Oh, Clara, what was I to say?" asked Ollie, blushing tremendously.

"Cut it short, please; we're so hungry," put in Charlie.

"Well, I will. We want you boys to come and get some supper which we have prepared for you—a sort of picnic, you know."

The boys gave a shout, flung down their traps, and made for the water to wash hands and faces, only Ted looked ruefully at his string of fish.

"What is the matter, Ted?" said Lil, coming up, with her face all flushed from being over the fire.

"Why, I was wishing we could have some of these for supper; but it's no matter, after all."

"Oh yes, it is. If you'll scrape and fix them, I can put them in the frying-pan in a jiffy."

So Ted went to work with a will.

Never had the boys tasted anything half so nice as that supper; they ate till they could eat no more. Lil scrambled eggs, and fried fish, and made tea, till Ollie insisted upon it that she should sit down and be served like a princess. Then they sung, and danced, and played games till Mrs. Pokeby and Miss Sinclair came after them, and carried them all home in Mr. Pokeby's big wagon.

"Really I never had more fun in my life," said Lil to Mrs. Pokeby, as they bade her good-by at the farm gate; "and I am so much obliged to you for letting us give that supper, though the getting it ready was the best part."

"That's because you seasoned it."

"What with?" asked Lil, wondering.

"With work—actual work."

"Do you think so? Perhaps that's the reason boys have such good times."

"I dare say."

(Begun in Harper's Young People No. 47, September 21.)

"MOONSHINERS."

BY E. B. MILLER.

Chapter III.

CONNY REPAYS THE DOCTOR'S KINDNESS.

BUT before the mountains were quite bare there came a time when even Conny ceased to interest the family, for Joe was coming home from college. Joe, the handsome young student, whom father, mother, Betty, and the servants all agreed to worship. He was to bring with him a friend, and from garret to cellar the whole house was astir to do them honor.

Conny was in the kitchen, polishing the silver, and listening to Biddy's raptures. "Sure, thin, Conny, and it's a young gintleman ye'll be seein' as there isn't the likes in ahl this miserable country, bad luck till it!"

"Is he like the master?" asked Conny.

"Indade, thin, I couldn't be sayin' whidder it's likest the masther or the misthress he is. Tahl an' straight, an' sooch a look in the two eyes of 'im."

"Conny," said the doctor, coming to the door, "I am obliged to go to Hampton to see a very sick man. You will have to go for Master Joe and the other gentleman to-night."

"Yes, sir," said Conny, well pleased with the commission.

"Be sure you start in season. Put Doll into the sulky, and lead Prince behind. The young gentlemen can drive themselves back, unless Joe chooses to ride Prince. He was always such a boy for a horse!"

The doctor's rugged face softened, as it always did at the thought of his boy, and it was no small self-denial to go away to the bedside of some poor old wreck of humanity, delaying for hours the delight of greeting his prince.

Early in the afternoon Conny started on his long ride of ten miles to meet the young gentlemen at Kilbourne, the nearest railroad station. It was almost November, but the blue haze of the Indian summer hung over the landscape, and the air was warm and mellow with sunshine. Any eye but Conny's would have said that the long mountain gorges, and the thickly wooded glens into which they opened, were deserted of all life save the squirrels and a few wood birds, but Conny heard a hawk's note from above the cliff, and caught sight of a man silently watching him from behind a mossy log. He laughed a little to himself to think how often he had played the spy in that very hollow, watching to see who came or went from Kilbourne, and then with a word started Doll into a quicker pace. He was at Kilbourne in ample time to meet his passengers, and, as the doctor had anticipated, Joe decided that he would ride Prince, as he had so often done before, while Conny should take his friend Douglass in the sulky.

The brief sunshine was already vanishing when they started, and the warmth rapidly leaving the frosty air. Douglass wrapped himself closely in his cloak, and Master Joe was glad to start Prince into a brisk canter. Almost without warning the night shut down, and they found the deeper cuts among the mountains quite dark. Doll was a swift traveller, and old Prince could not keep up his pace, so Master Joe gradually fell back, and kept near the sulky, exchanging words with his friend, and plying Conny with questions about home.

"We shall soon be there now," he said, as they entered a narrow gorge. "We really ought to show you some sort of an adventure, Douglass, to give the proper spice to your first visit to the mountains. If it was summer, now, we could get something terrific in the shape of a storm, and slide a few rods of road down the mountain, or pile up the track with big trees and rocks."

"I should fancy it was just the kind of place for banditti," said his friend; "and I am sure some of those fellows we saw at the station look as if they would take naturally to that sort of life."

They were driving slowly, and at that moment a strange, shrill cry went wavering up from below them.

"That's a murderous voice for a bird," said Douglass.

"It's a hawk, I fancy," said Master Joe; "you often hear it among the mountains, though I've never been able to find the fellow.—What's wrong, Conny?" for Conny had stopped Doll so suddenly that Prince bumped his nose on the sulky.

Alas for Conny! He knew well enough what that cry meant. It was a warning sent up to some one at the rocky pass above, to say that danger was coming up the mountain. He remembered in an instant that old Timothy had said there were stories of government officers in disguise spying about Dunsmore, and that the moonshiners would make it uncomfortable for them if they crossed their tracks.

No dream of fear for himself came to his mind, but how should he save Master Joe? for he knew more than even old Timothy guessed of the lawless and desperate characters among the mountains.

"Master Joe," said he, quickly, "would you mind changing with me a bit? I'm lighter weight to carry, and I'll go on to let old Timothy know. He'd be vexed not to be ready with his lantern."

Joe was quite ready for the exchange. It was many months since he had tried the saddle, and an hour of it was quite enough to satisfy him; so he settled back comfortably in the seat, while Conny went spinning away in the dusk, as if old Prince had suddenly renewed his youth. They heard the hoof-clicks on the hard road grow-

"CONNY WENT SPINNING AWAY IN THE DUSK."

ing fainter in the distance, and then the sharp ring of a rifle that woke a thousand echoes among the hills.

Douglass started, but Joe laughed.

"Your banditti are putting in an appearance."

"Attacking an unfortunate rabbit, I suppose," said Douglass, bravely.

Neither of them guessed what had really happened. When Conny rode at full speed into Hemlock Glen he had hardly a plan as to what he should do, but the next instant a bullet struck him in the shoulder and almost sent him from his horse. He caught the lines in his left hand, and called in a clear but low voice to some invisible foe, "It's I, Conny McConnell, and the lads in the buggy beyond are just Master Joe, the doctor's son, coming home from college with a friend, just a laddie like himsel'."

There was not a sound in response unless a dry twig may have cracked, but Conny paced slowly along until Doll's quick feet brought her into the Glen.

"Hullo, Conny!" called Master Joe, "did you hear a rifle-shot?"

"Yes, sir," said Conny; "there's a deal of game running these nights."

"What sort of game do you folks hunt with rifles up here?" asked Douglass; but Conny did not answer, and in a few moments they came out upon the open road, and saw the lights of Dunsmore about a mile before them.

Old Timothy was on the look-out, and long before they reached the house they saw his lantern moving about the barn.

"Here we are!" called Joe, throwing down the lines and springing out; and in the happy confusion of the greetings no one looked at Conny, until the doctor, taking his hand from the side of Prince, started to see that it was stained with blood.

"What! Why, bless us! Conny, what has happened to you?"

"I think I have a little hurt somewhere in me shoulder, sir," said Conny, sliding from the horse; "it's nothing much, sir, if you'd have the goodness to fix me a little at the barn."

But the doctor would not hear to such a thing, and took Conny to the surgery, where he discovered that the bones of his arm were broken above the elbow; and most unwillingly Conny told the story.

How he had recognized the cry of warning, and understood that the young gentlemen were mistaken for revenue officers, and that mischief would probably be done them unless he could succeed in preventing the attack.

"And so you invited them to empty their rifles on you," said the doctor, gruffly; but as he spoke he wiped his eyes on a roll of bandages.

"It's good luck it was me, sir," said Conny. "Wouldn't it have spited us if Master Joe had been spoiled with a broken arm, and all the fun we've been planning gone for nothing!"

"But the rascals might have killed you."

"I don't think they're that bad, sir; they were meaning a bit of a scare, and maybe a drubbing or the like."

"I'll drub them," said the doctor; "I'll make this county too hot for them," and then, having finished dressing the arm, he threw his own dressing-gown over Conny. "My boy," he said, gently, "I understand perfectly well what a brave thing you have done: you risked your own life to save our Joe. I honor you and love you for it from my heart, but you and I will keep it a secret between us for the present. I think it would kill my wife to know her boy had been in such danger. She shall not know it till that nest of murderers is cleared out."

Conny's part in Master Joe's vacation was not exactly what he had planned, but he scarcely regretted the wound that brought him such gentle and loving care from every member of the family, by whom it was only understood that Conny had been accidentally shot by a careless hunter, and had borne his pain in silence all the long ride home from the Glen.

Months afterward, when the last moonshiner had disappeared, and the old still in the forest had been dismantled, the doctor ventured to tell his wife of Joe's escape.

"And I have never thanked him," she said, her eyes filling with tears, as she went straight to the attic, where Conny was so deeply absorbed in a bit of carving that he did not see or hear her until she put her arms around him and kissed him again and again.

"I know all about it now, Conny—the brave, beautiful thing that you did for my boy."

"Oh, ma'am," said Conny, "it was nothing. I was so glad to do it."

Mrs. Hunter kissed him again, as she repeated, gently, "'Greater love hath no man than this, that a man lay down his life for his friends.'"

And Conny, not understanding, said, earnestly, "Maybe you'll think me presuming to be saying it, but it's that same I'd do for ye, ma'am, or for little Miss Betty, or the master himself, if it's any good it would be bringing ye."

"I believe you, Conny," said Mrs. Hunter, "but I hope you may never have a chance to try."

THE END.

LITTLE MISS TURNER.

BY W. T. PETERS.

"Oh, where have you been to,
  My little Miss Turner—
Oh, where have you been to to-day?
I've brought you my wagon
  To take you a-riding;
So why have I found you away?"

"Oh, I've been to the meadows,"
  Said little Miss Turner,
"With sweet robin-redbreast at play;
And the daisies and daffodils
  Made me a bow,
And said, 'How do you do to-day?'"

EGYPTIAN WONDERS.

IT is said that an Egyptian Prince dreamed one night of an obelisk, and when he awoke ordered his engineers and his workmen to carve in solid stone the strange and useless device. An obelisk resembles nothing so much as the fanciful figures of a dream. It is a tall square pillar of a peculiar form, often carved with hieroglyphics, and commemorating the name and exploits of its founder. These solitary pillars of stone, sometimes more than a hundred feet in height, are formed of one block or piece, and must have been cut in the quarry with incessant labor. They abound in Egypt, and were a common decoration of its immense temples. Later, several of them were transported on great rafts or ships to the city of Rome. There are in all twelve in that city. One of them is one hundred and nine feet high without the base—a solid piece of red granite. Europe has despoiled Egypt of its obelisks. Paris has one; London another, crumbling away on the banks of the Thames; and we have one in New York. The dream of the Egyptian Prince seems to have a strong interest for all ages.

All Egypt, its history, its cities, its buildings, its mummies, gods, cats, hawks, bulls, sphinxes, the Memnonium, resemble the fancies of a dream. The Nile flows through its sandy plain, and covers it with fertility. Late discoveries have shown that it is one of the longest rivers in the world, rising among the high mountains of Africa, and fed by immense lakes. In Egypt it overflows its banks every year, and covers the land with a rich deposit of mud. On its shores are the ruins of the strangest of all architecture, the works of the ancient Egyptians—immense, grand, awful. They are the largest of all buildings. St. Paul's Cathedral, in London, or the Cologne Cathedral, or even St. Peter's, at Rome, would be lost in the vast circuit of the columns of Luxor and Karnak. As one passes them by moonlight on the smooth stream, they seem, it is said, the

palaces of giants. One temple was a mile and a half in circumference. The Pyramids exceed all other buildings in strength, height, and durability. Some of them are

VERY tasteful ornamental covers for the first volume of HARPER'S YOUNG PEOPLE, which will conclude with No. 52, issued October 26, 1880, are now ready, and will be sold for thirty-five cents, or forty-eight cents if sent by mail, postage prepaid. These covers are not self-binding, but any book-binder will put them on for a small charge.

We wish to call the attention of those of our readers engaged in making exchanges to the great importance of careful and clearly written addresses. We receive proofs daily of the neglect of this essential point. In Post-office Box No. 46 we printed a letter from a correspondent anxious to make an acknowledgment of a pretty mineral, but who was unable to do so because she "could not make out the name" of the sender. Another correspondent, whose correct address was printed in full in Our Post-office Box, received a letter on which the only correct portion of the direction was his own name and the city in which he lived, the name and number of the street, and even the State, being entirely wrong. That he ever received it at all is a proof of the great experience and skill of Uncle Sam's Post-office Department. Now such a very careless method of direction might result in the loss of valuable minerals, stamps, or other specimens.

Other correspondents report having received letters without name or address of any kind, and yet the sender expected to be answered, and was no doubt disappointed, as he was probably unaware that he had omitted a very important part of his letter.

We have ourselves received large numbers of correct answers to puzzles, often accompanied by the pretty appeal, "Do, please, print my name in the list of those sending correct answers," and neither initials, name, nor even address attached upon which we could base an acknowledgment. When the answers were published, and these little folks found their solutions were correct, and yet their names didn't appear, no doubt they thought themselves very badly treated; but the fault was not ours.

Now when you direct a letter for purposes of exchange, copy the whole address given in Our Post-office Box very carefully and clearly. And give your own address in full, very plainly written, or else, should your letter reach its destination, you probably will not receive an answer.

Learn to bestow care and attention upon little things now while you are young, and as you grow older you will find it easier to be careful in things of greater importance, and thereby save yourself and others from much unnecessary trouble.

[illegible]

[illegible]. My list of stamps is not large, as I am only beginning a collection. I have no Chinese or West India stamps, and would be glad to exchange for them any of the following, which are all the duplicates I have: [illegible]; one eighty centimes, Empire Français; one [illegible]; two [illegible]; two [illegible]. Corona de [illegible].

Louis [illegible], [illegible], Franklin County, Pennsylvania.

I have about four hundred and twenty-five different kinds of postage stamps, and would like to exchange with any of the readers of Young People. I also have a lot of rare [illegible], which I should like to exchange for stamps. I particularly want the ninety Interior, and the seven, twenty-four, thirty, and ninety of either the War or Treasury Department, or any [illegible] stamps. I have [illegible], [illegible], Canadian, German, English, Swedish, and Interior Department stamps for exchange.

A. [illegible],
P. O. Box [illegible], New Haven, Connecticut.

I would like to exchange with the readers of Young People some rare foreign stamps for other foreign stamps and United States official issues of [illegible].

[illegible],
Hoboken, Bergen County, New Jersey.

I am making a collection of minerals, and I would gladly exchange with any of the readers of Young People.

[illegible],
[illegible] Main Street, Toledo, Ohio.

J. B.—Honey-bees were unknown in America until they were brought here by early European settlers. On this account the honey-bee is called white man's fly by the Indians.

W. A.—From your description your "[illegible] animal" appears to belong to the family of caddis-worms. If he is a member of this family, he is a scavenger, and will feed himself on the bits of decayed matter in the water. After a while he will cling to some weed near the surface, and spin a chrysalis, from which the caddis-fly will break forth.

"Capt. Frank."—The directions you require are in Young People No. 20.

G. F. T.—Experience has shown that canoes [illegible] with two masts are not as serviceable as those with one.

D. C. D.—A very popular Halloween game in Scotland is apple-catching. A large tub of water is placed in the centre of the floor, and a basketful of [illegible], rosy-cheeked apples dumped into it. The young folks then try to pick them from the water with their teeth. As the apples are slippery, and bob around merrily, there are a great many laughable mishaps before the coveted prize is secured. A ten-cent piece may be hidden in one of the apples, which gives more interest to the sport, as the lucky possessor becomes King or Queen of the festival. This game has its disadvantages, as you must play it in the kitchen, where the water may be splashed on the floor without doing mischief. Then, too, you can not wear your pretty new winter frock, but must be contented with a calico dress, which you will get soaked with water, and must change the moment all the apples are captured and the game finished, or you will surely take cold, and remember Halloween with sorrow. We do not advise you to try apple-catching, but give it as one of the few sportive games associated with Halloween. There are many foolish tricks practiced on that night, but they are intended for grown-up young men and maidens. They are most of them innocent, but very silly.

C. B. N.—Nellie H.'s recipe for candy is in Young People No. 24. The recipes for white cake and cream candy are both in No. 28. You will find different recipes for cake and candy in Nos. 19, 27, 28, and 31 to 45 inclusive.

Favors are acknowledged from [illegible], [illegible], Mabel [illegible], [illegible].

Correct answers to puzzles are received from [illegible], [illegible], [illegible], Hugh Lesley, [illegible], Annie Winter, J. N. [illegible], [illegible].

PUZZLES FROM YOUNG CONTRIBUTORS.

No. 1.

[illegible]

1. First, [illegible]. Second, part of a [illegible]. Third, [illegible]. Fourth, a [illegible]. Fifth, [illegible].

[illegible]

2. First, a [illegible]. Second, [illegible]. Third, a [illegible] in mythology. Fourth, a [illegible]. Fifth, rapidity.

[illegible]

No. 2.

DIAMOND.

In Harper's Young People. Backward. [illegible]. A European [illegible]. [illegible]. A boy's [illegible]. In Harper's Young People.

[illegible]

No. 3.

[illegible]

Terrible. One of a wandering race. An [illegible]. In Europe. A domestic animal. Ludicrous. A powerful medicine. Centrals read downward spell the name of an American [illegible].

S. F. W.

No. 4.

ENIGMA.

My first is in symbol, but not in sign.
My second is in [illegible], but not in [illegible].
My third is in [illegible], but not in [illegible].
My fourth is in [illegible], but not in [illegible].
My fifth is in [illegible], not in [illegible].
My sixth is in darkness, but not in night.
My seventh is in [illegible], but not in [illegible].
My whole, a dreadful [illegible] [illegible]. [illegible].

ANSWERS TO PUZZLES IN No. 44.

No. 1. [illegible]

No. 2. Cannibal.

No. 3. [illegible]

No. 4. [illegible]

London, Boston.

No. 5. [illegible]

Answer to Head and Windmill Puzzle in No. 44.—The first is a sponge, and the second is a species of [illegible].

THE WOMBAT.

A gentleman owned a wombat
That grew so excessively fat
That when it would laugh
'Twould most break in half,
And tickle the soul of the cat.

A Dog that could Cipher.—The well-known English astronomer Dr. Huggins had a mastiff that bore the name of Kepler. This dog possessed many rare gifts, and amongst them was one which he was always ready to exercise for the entertainment of visitors. At the close of luncheon or dinner Kepler used to march into the room, and set himself down at his master's feet. Dr. Huggins then asked him a series of arithmetical questions, which the dog invariably solved without a mistake. Square roots were extracted off hand with the utmost readiness and promptness. If asked what was the square root of nine, Kepler replied by three barks; or, if the question were the square root of sixteen, by four. Then various questions followed, in which much more complicated processes were involved—such, for instance, as "Add seven to eight, divide the sum by three, and multiply by two." To such a question as that Kepler gave more consideration, and sometimes hesitated in making up his mind as to where his barks ought finally to stop. Still, in the end, his decision was always right. But how did he do it? may be asked. The solution is easily furnished: the proper answer was unconsciously suggested to the dog by his master. The wonderful fact is that Kepler had acquired the habit of reading in his master's eye or countenance some indication that was not known to Dr. Huggins himself. The case was one of the class which is distinguished by physiologists as that of expectant attention. Dr. Huggins was himself engaged in working out mentally the various stages of his arithmetical processes as he propounded the numbers to Kepler, and being, therefore, aware of what the answer should be, expected the dog to cease barking when that number was reached, and that expectation suggested to his own brain the unconscious signal which was caught by the quick eye of the dog.

SOLUTION TO SQUARE PUZZLE IN No. 46.

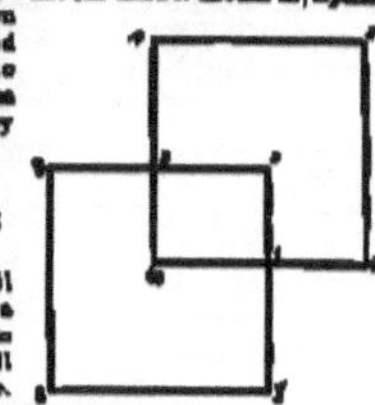

START with your pencil from figure 1 and draw a line to 2, from there to 3, and so on from number to number till you have completed the figure.

CHARADE

BY E.

Up in the air I'm lifted high
Above the worshippers below,
Yet near their hearts I always lie,
As reverently they come and go.

I've many forms, like Proteus old,
But tell forever the same tale;
Men gaze, and see by me foretold
What sometimes makes their cheeks grow pale.

And through my secret winding course
There ebbs and flows a mighty tide;
Alas! what pangs of keen remorse
Are his who turns that stream aside!

Yet in the gay and festive throng
I am what many a maid may be,
While in the pauses of the song
Her lover pleads his cause in me.

Sometimes, a ship, I face the storm;
Sometimes beneath the earth I hide,
And then its beauty men deform
To find the secret that I hide.

But in the air, or in the breast,
Whate'er my form, like beast or bird,
I keep my secret from the rest—
By man my voice is never heard.

THE quicksilver mines of Guancavelica, in Peru, are of a prodigious depth. In their profound abysses are seen streets, squares, and a chapel where religious mysteries are celebrated on all festivals. Thousands of flambeaux are continually burning in it. The miners suffer terribly from the mercurial vapors, which produce convulsions and paralysis. Thousands of workmen were condemned to forced labor in these frightful subterranean regions. These mines were discovered about 1566 by Henry Garces, a Portuguese, who was one day examining a red earth used by the Indians for making paint. He remembered that in Europe quicksilver was extracted from cinnabar, and with this earth he made some experiments which led to the opening of this mine.

HARPER'S
YOUNG PEOPLE
AN ILLUSTRATED WEEKLY.

Vol. I.—No. 50. | Published by HARPER & BROTHERS, New York. | Price Four Cents.
Tuesday, October 12, 1880. | $1.50 per Year, in Advance.

BESSIE RECOVERS THE REMAINS.

COACHY.

BY ELINOR VEY.

THE first time I ever saw Coachy she was scratching about on the garden walk, kicking the dirt out in two ways behind her, and then nimbly hitching back a step or two and staring and pecking at the hole that she had made. Every little while she said something to herself in a comical drawling tone, standing on one foot, and looking up at me with curious eye, as if wondering who I was, and what in the world I was there for. But who was Coachy?—an old yellowish-brown hen, all tousled and sort of round-shouldered. As I was laughing quietly at this old hen scratching, and kicking, and pecking, and crooning about on the garden walk, it occurred to me to toss the least bit of a stone at her. So picking one up, I took aim, when, click! click! upon the porch I heard a pair of slippers. They were down the steps in no time, with their cunning toes pointing straight toward mine. I put that stone into my pocket, and took off my hat to "little slippers." They were blue as the softest blue sky—little slippers—and ever and ever so small. Mine had purple worsted flowers all over them, big flat heels, and were ever and ever so large. Inside those little slippers stood the sweetest mite of a lady the world ever saw; while inside old "flat heels" was the fattest and fondest Uncle John.

Bessie Rathbun's cheeks were about the color of an oleander blossom, her small red mouth was about the color of a cranberry, and her two wide-open eyes about the color of her slippers. Her hair hung in yellow fuzzy curls away down to the strings of her apron; and it always seemed to me there must be a gold dollar rolling off the end of each curl, each end was so round and gold yellow. Dainty Bessie!—and what do you suppose? Why, she was deep in love with that old brown hen. Many and many a time she had sent me scraps of news about her wonderful Coachy, and had wished and wished that I would come and see her for myself. So when, one day, a letter came from Bessie's father, asking me if I would please hurry over to Featherdale to take charge of his house, and his silver spoons, and his little daughter, while he took a journey with his wife to visit a sick friend, I just threw my papers and pens into my valise (I was writing a lecture then), jumped aboard the first train, and went. So here we were together, on a breezy bright June morning—Bessie and Coachy and I.

"There she is, uncle—there's my Coachy!" cried Bessie, as she slipped from my arms. "Come, darling, come;" and Coachy spread out her wings, and rushed toward her little mistress, who eagerly bent down and took her. She kissed her brown back, and from a snowy apron pocket gave her corn, and even while eating, this funny old hen brokenly hummed a tune.

"Let's go on the porch with her," said Bessie at last. So we settled on the porch, with Coachy nestling between us.

"She isn't what you may call a very handsome hen—now is she, Bessie?" laughed I.

But Bessie scarcely smiled. "If you knew something that I know," said she, "you wouldn't make fun of her."

"Why—what?"

"Why, she was a poor orphan chicken—an' a dog killed her mother—an' she had a *dreadful* hard time getting grown up as big as she is now. She's fallen into the well, an' had two of her toes froze off—"

"What! in the well?"

"No; in the winter," said Bessie, gravely. "And she's been so lonesome down here, without any other hens to talk to, that papa says she'll have to go out to the farm, where the other hens are, real soon, or she'll die."

"Is that so?" said I, feeling sorry and a trifle awkward.

The little maid smoothed the rumpled feathers this way and that. "Yes, that's so," she sighed. "Our farm is more'n a mile from here, but I'm going to let her go."

"You can see her very often, can't you?" I asked.

"Yes; but, oh dear!" and there was another kiss put upon the brown back. Perhaps that is what made Coachy look round-shouldered—carrying such a load of sweet kisses on her back.

Just at this moment Bridget came out, and picked up the door-mat. I have never known for certain what Bridget did to the door-mat. Maybe it was taken off somewhere, like a bad child, for a shaking. Anyway, she picked it up quickly, and went back to the kitchen. And right where the mat had lain—so near that we could reach out and take it—was a letter; and the letter was addressed, in big scrawling characters that looked very much indeed like "hen tracks," to

Miss Bessie Rathbun,
Featherdale.

The little lady's eyes and mouth grew perfectly round; she gave a little scream, and Coachy, half scared, went hopping down the steps. I opened the letter, and this is what we found:

"MY DEAR MISTRESS,—You can't guess how sad I am at the thought of leaving you, even for a few short months; but I do believe my general health and spirits would be much improved if you would kindly take me out to the farm to spend the balance of the summer. I miss the Brahmas, and the Shanghais, and the Plymouth Rocks, and even the pert little Bantams, more than I can tell. I get very downhearted somehow, thinking of the merry times they must be having all together in the fields or on the old barn floor. You are very, very good to me, and I love you dearly; but oh! *please* take me back to the farm. I shall be so happy whenever you come out there to see me, and will thank you as long as I live. Answer soon.

"With one peck at your sweet lips, COACHY.

"P. S.—Please don't ever hug me again as you did on the lawn last Sunday. I thought I should choke."

Bessie was smiling; still in the same moment she had to put up her hand and whisk something away from her cheek. I knew what it was—a tear.

"Uncle," she said, putting both hands into her apron pockets, "let's take Coachy to the farm to-morrow;" and we did.

Early next morning we drove out of town, the dear old hen in Bessie's arms, and Bessie and I in the phaeton. Bessie talked softly to her favorite all the way; and when we reached the farm, I have an idea that, in spite of the request in the postscript, Coachy was hugged as hard as she ever was hugged in her life. Down the lane we went toward a group of noisy fowls. The nearer we came to them, the harder was Coachy hugged. I began to be anxious. Her mouth was open, and each particular toe was standing out stiff and straight. Bessie's nose and lips were out of sight in the ruffled back, and Coachy had closed her eyes.

"Darling," said the little girl, steadily, "good-by," and she bravely dropped her pet beside the old companions.

We saw her shake herself, eye the others a moment, and walk quietly into the crowd.

The man who lived on Bessie's papa's farm was named Beck. We hunted all over for Mr. Beck to tell him there was a guest among the poultry; but he was not to be found. So we got into the carriage and started for home.

My little niece was silent during nearly all of our drive back to Featherdale. Her mind was still filled full of Coachy.

By-and-by, though, the cherry lips opened.

"Uncle John," she said, "do you s'pose there'll be room?"

"On the roost?"

"Yes."

"Why, plenty of it—plenty!" said the reckless Uncle John.

I was out of bed an hour before Bessie next morning to take a horseback ride. "Guess I'll go over to the farm," said I to myself, "and see how Coachy is doing." So off to the farm I cantered.

I hitched my horse to a post by the farm-house door, and walked out where the chickens were picking up a breakfast. I looked them all over, and—and—well, Coachy was not there.

Seeing a man coming down the path, and feeling quite

sure it was Mr. Beck, I waited. A narrow-faced, fair-haired, frail-looking man—not at all like a farmer, I thought.

"Good-morning, Mr. Beck," said I.

"Morning," said Mr. Beck, looking puzzled.

"My name is Rathbun. I was just looking around for a hen I brought up from my brother's house yesterday. I don't seem to find her," I said, still peering about.

"Did you bring that hen?" asked the man.

I turned and looked at him then.

"That old yellowish-brown hen?" he went on.

"Yes," said I, sharply. "Why?"

"Why, *I* didn't know where she come from," he drawled. "She was cluckin' round the cows' heels while I was milkin', an' I tuck 'er an' chopped 'er head off."

It seems to me that for one whole minute I never drew a breath. I just stood there, dumb and glaring, till I was conscious the man was shrinking away from my eyes and clinched hands.

"What's the fuss?" said he.

"What's the fuss?" I roared. "Why, you confounded idiot, do you know what you've done? Do you know that you've killed Bessie Rathbun's pet hen?"

"Wa'al," he growled, with his hands in his pockets, "*I* didn't know whose hen it was."

"Well, that's a fine excuse, isn't it?—a fine excuse, Mr. Beck," I went on, hotly.

"Why, I wouldn't have touched 'er 'f I'd known 'er," argued Mr. Beck. "*I* didn't know where she come from."

"And that's your way, I take it—to lay hold and kill a thing when you don't know where it comes from. I wonder if you killed a horse as you came along. I tied one at your door ten minutes ago."

I walked off a few steps to calm myself a little. I thought of poor Bessie. Mr. Beck mumbled something, and started for the barn.

"Mr. Beck," I called after him, "what have you done with her?"

"How say?"

"Where is she—Coachy—the hen?"

He pointed with his thumb toward the barn, and went in. I thought he would be out in a minute. As he did not appear, I followed to the door, and looked in. I could neither see nor hear the man; he had vanished.

It was a hint for me to go, certainly. With a troubled heart I rode slowly back to town, and as I rode I pondered, asking myself what I should say to Bessie. Should I tell her Coachy was lost? "Get on, pony," I said at length; "we must tell her the truth."

Upon entering the driveway I noticed Bessie in the garden picking flowers. She saw me, and beckoned; but I could not go to her then. I unsaddled the horse, led him into his stall, and fed him, and then I stole into the house. A box was standing at one corner of the porch, with a perch, and a nest, and a little trough for corn, and a little cup for water. It was waiting to go to the farm.

I was drinking a cup of coffee when Bessie came skipping into the breakfast-room. When she saw trouble in my face she put away her smile, and crept softly up to me. She told me she had been hunting and hunting for me. She rubbed her pink cheek against my whiskers, declaring that she couldn't make me out at all. She said it was time now to go to the farm.

"Bessie dear," I said, as I took her hand, "I wouldn't go up to the farm to-day."

Surprise came over her face; then trouble with surprise. "Why, uncle?" she said, softly.

"It isn't nice at the farm," I went on, vaguely; "don't go. I just came from there. Don't go, Bessie."

"Why, uncle?" she said again, softly—"why, uncle?" Then all in a breath her fingers bound themselves tight about mine. "Did you see my Coachy?—did you see her?" she hurriedly asked.

I stooped and held the little form just one moment, then said, "No," and then, somehow, I told her.

I did not have a great deal to tell; she guessed over half; and then what a shivering, sobbing little burden it was that I held in my arms!

I don't believe I will try to tell you how she cried, or all she said, as we sat in the parlor that forenoon; it might make me cry to talk it over. Her tiny pocket-handkerchief soon got wet through, and she had to have my great big purple silk one; and more than once did I hear her moan, "Oh, Coachy is dead! my Coachy is dead!" When at last she strove to dry her eyes—poor, swollen eyes—it was truly a difficult matter. At first it seemed of no use to try, for again and again they would fill up, and spill the tears over her cheeks. We had to go and bathe them finally; and then Bessie walked into the kitchen and brokenly told Bridget the news.

A moment later I found her in the hall, tying on her hat. "I must go and bring her home," she said, hurriedly.

She was out of the house, and had called on Dennis to harness the horse, before I had time to consider.

"Dear Bessie, won't you stay here, and let me bring her home alone?" I coaxed.

"No! no! no!" she cried; and so we started together.

"Don't cry, dear," I was saying, as we drove into the farm-yard—her cheeks were all wet again—"don't cry, dear."

When I knocked at Mr. Beck's door, a voice called out, "Come in."

I opened the door, and found Mrs. Beck. I told her we had come to take Coachy home.

Mrs. Beck walked a little toward her hot cook-stove before she spoke:

"Well, we'll give her a live one to take home. I'm certain she can't take the dead one."

"Can't take her?—why?"

"I've got her a-boiling," answered Mrs. Beck.

Boiling?—Coachy boiling! I had been there all this while and hadn't smelled chicken. I felt like talking to Mrs. Beck; but I didn't. I shut my teeth, made her a slight bow, and went out to Bessie.

"I haven't got her, darling."

She was back among the cushions, with her hands over her eyes.

"Haven't got her?"

"No, and I can't get her."

"Why, we must get her!" she cried, straightening up. "Why can't we get her?"

"Why," said I, gently as I could—"why, they are—cooking her."

Bessie's cheeks flamed. In less time than it takes to tell it she sprang from the carriage, burst open the kitchen door, ran against a toddling boy, blindly knocked him over, and faced Mrs. Beck.

"How did you dare do such a thing!" she almost screamed, seizing the astonished woman by her dress skirt. "She's mine! my own Coachy! and I'll carry her home in a pail!"

Jumping on a stool, she reached up to a shelf of tin-ware. Grasping a good-sized pail, she pulled it from its place in such a hurry that half a dozen milk-pans were dragged off with it. Clattering like crazy things they whirled to the floor.

"Put my Coachy in there!—put her in!" she commanded, setting the pail down hard on the stove, and twisting the cover off.

Such a din I never heard. Those tin pans banged and rattled, Bessie's voice piped high, the boy on the floor broke into a hoarse scream, and our horse shied and started for home.

"Whoa! whoa!" I shouted, leaping off the steps, and bringing him round into place again.

Turning to go back to the tragedy in the house, I nearly collided with Bessie. She was running out with the pail in her hand, and with all the Beck children following. Thrusting it upon me, she hurried into the carriage; then reaching after it, she wrapped it in the lap-robe, and leaned back with a sigh of relief.

During the few minutes that it took us to rattle home I wondered what was to be done with poor Coachy. I didn't have long to wait. I led the horse into the stable, and as I was returning I discovered my little girl sitting on the grass by a rose-bush, with what we had brought at her feet.

In a trembling voice she asked me if I would please find a shovel. I found one, and soon stood obedient beside Bessie and the pail.

"Right here, Uncle John," she whispered, flattening the tender grass beneath the rose-bush with her two dimpled hands—"right here where the sun shines."

So we dug a grave, and poured in that hot dinner. In it went, gravy and all—white meat, dark meat, legs, wings, and wish-bone!

Some months went by, and Uncle John came to Featherdale again. As he strolled through the garden in his purple-flowered flat-heeled slippers the morning after his arrival, he came to a little lonely mound. A small white board with scraggly letters on it stood there now. Uncle John stooped down, held aside the grass, and read, "Coachy," and "Forgive us our trespasses as we forgive them that trespass against us."

BAPTIZING COPTIC BABIES.

BY SARA KEABLES HUNT.

YOU have often witnessed the ceremony of infant baptism, when some sweet baby friend of yours has been brought forward to be christened, and have thought it a

beautiful sight, as it indeed is; but the babies that I am going to tell you about now were less fortunate in their birth, for they were born of Egyptian parents—children of the Nile.

Would you like to hear of the strange ceremony?

We had been sailing all day, and at twilight had moored our diabbeh to the bank near a Coptic village. The Copts are said to be the native Egyptians, and pride themselves very much on their antiquity. As we looked out through the brilliant sunset tints that were flushing all the Nile Valley, the walls of an ancient convent rose before us, sharp and well defined in the clear atmosphere, its usual gloom banished by the bright and gorgeous coloring of the Egyptian sunset.

Somebody said, "There is to be a service in the old convent to-night; shall we go?"

It had been a monotonous day, and the walk and change looked attractive; so we were soon scrambling up the steep bank, and walking swiftly toward the old convent walls. The town consisted of a collection of square brown huts, their flat roofs covered with the nests of countless pigeons that are always swarming and cooing around every Egyptian dwelling-place. Quantities of water-jugs lay piled together by the side of the road, waiting to be sent down the river. As we came out into the open field, and on to the narrow beaten path which is raised slightly above the level to keep in the water of the inundation, we threw back our hats, and turned our faces to the glory of the sky and the cool refreshing breeze. All the air was sweet with growing grain. Away in the west the Libyan hills seemed quivering with the flush of the sunset, and the whole plain was wrapped in a glow of light. A short walk brought us to the church, and following the crowd which was rapidly assembling, we mingled with them and obtained seats.

The convent is a lofty inclosure, the roof formed by numerous small domes numbering nearly two hundred. Within is a small open court, an ordinary-sized church surrounded with many small chapels, and the apartments of the monks. Cleanliness is not one of the virtues of the Copts, so we may expect to find everything dirty and in need of repair.

I shall not tire you with a long account of the general services, of the clashing of cymbals and the loud voices of the priests, of the Coptic prayers and long masses, of the blessing of the water when the priest stirred it with a long stick as he prayed, then, dipping a cloth into it, applying it to the wrists, insteps, and foreheads of all the men who came forward to receive it. Time would not permit me to describe this in detail; but the baptism of the children, which immediately followed in another part of the church, was a novel though pitiful sight, and one that will make you realize what a blessing it is to be born in an enlightened land.

The women's department is separated from that of the men; they are never allowed to enter the upper places, and in the ceremony of baptism of children the fathers do not appear.

When all was ready, three little creatures were brought in, their dark eyes looking wonderingly around. Turning to the west, and holding her child, the mother promised to renounce the devil and all his works; then, facing the east, she held it forth to signify her acceptance of Christ for the child, after which it was sprinkled by the priest. But the ceremony did not end here, for the poor babies were taken to a font, and in the midst of long Coptic prayers they were disrobed and immersed three times. Then came the anointing with holy oil, the priest roughly and awkwardly—for he was very old—rubbing it over all the members and joints of the child from its wrist.

It was a cruel sight, for the church was quite cold, and as at last the poor little victims were dressed and handed back to their mothers, we hurried away. I lay for some time in my narrow berth that night unable to sleep and thinking of the ceremony I had just witnessed. At last I fell asleep, but only to see the faces of countless babies calling to me in vain for help, and when I awoke from my troubled dreams it was with a firm determination never again to see a Coptic baptism.

(Begun in No. 46 of HARPER'S YOUNG PEOPLE, September 14.)

WHO WAS PAUL GRAYSON?

BY JOHN HABBERTON,

AUTHOR OF "HELEN'S BABIES."

CHAPTER V.

THOSE JAIL-BIRDS.

ALTHOUGH the people of Laketon could not forgive Mr. Morton and Paul Grayson for not talking more about themselves and their past lives, they could not deny that both the teacher and his pupil were of decided value to the town. All the boys, whether in Mr. Morton's school or the public school, seemed to like Paul Grayson when they became acquainted with him, and the parents of the boys sensibly argued that there could not be anything very bad about a boy who was so popular. Besides, the other boys in talking about Paul declared that he never swore and never lied; and as lying and swearing were the two vices most common among the Laketon boys, and therefore most hated by the parents, they felt that there was, at least, no occasion to regard the new-comer with suspicion.

As for Mr. Morton, he rapidly made his way among the more solid citizens. He was willing to work, whether his services were required by church, Sunday-school, or society, and he did not care to hold office of any sort, so his sincerity was cheerfully admitted by all. When, however, he had one day, soon after his arrival, asked several prominent men why the town had no society or even person to visit the very poor and the persons who might be in prison, he ran some risk of being considered meddlesome.

"We know our own people best," said Sam Wardwell's father. "The only people here who suffer from poverty are those who won't work, while the few people who get into our jail are hard cases; half of them wouldn't listen to you if you talked to them, and the others would listen only to have an excuse to beg tobacco or something. There's a man in the jail now for passing counterfeit money; he's committed for trial when the County Court sits in September; that man is just as smart as you or I. He is as fine a looking fellow as you would wish to see, talks like a straightforward business man, and yet he passed counterfeit bills at four different places in this town. What would talk do for such a fellow?"

THE WINDOW OF THE COUNTERFEITER'S CELL.

"No one knows, until some one tries it," replied the teacher, quietly.

"Well, all I have to say is," remarked Mr. Wardwell, in a tone that was intended to be very sarcastic, "those who have plenty of time to waste must do the trying. If you want such work done, why don't you do it yourself?"

"I would cheerfully do it if it did not seem to be presumptuous on the part of a stranger."

"Don't trouble your mind about that," said the storekeeper, with a laugh; "the counterfeiter is a stranger too, so matters will be even. There's the sheriff, in front of the post-office; do you know him? No? Let us step over, and I'll introduce you. And I'll wish you more luck than you'll have in the jail, if that will be of any consolation."

Mr. Morton found Sheriff Towler quite a pleasant man to talk to, and perfectly willing to have his prisoners improve in body and mind by any method except that of getting out of jail before their respective terms of imprisonment had expired, or before they were by superior authority ordered to some other place of confinement, as he, the sheriff, wished might at once be the case with John Doe, the man who was awaiting trial for passing bad bank-notes. All this the sheriff said as he walked with Mr. Morton from the post-office to the jail. Arrived at the last-named building, the sheriff instructed his deputy, who had charge of the place, to admit Mr. Morton at any time that gentleman might care to converse with any of the prisoners.

The teacher walked first through the upper rooms, where a small but choice assortment of habitual drunkards and petty thieves were confined; these, as Sam Wardwell's father had predicted, either declined to converse or talked stupidly for a moment or two, and then begged either tobacco or money to buy it with. Still, Mr. Morton thought he saw in these wretched fellows some material to work upon, when time allowed. Then he went below, and the deputy took him to the small grated window in the door of the strong cell for desperate offenders, and said to John Doe that a gentleman who was visiting the prisoners would like to speak with him. The deputy went away immediately after saying this, and Mr. Morton quickly put his face to the grated window, a face appeared on the other side of the grating, and then, as Mr. Morton placed his hand between the bars, which were barely wide enough apart to admit it, he felt his fingers grasped most earnestly by the hand of the prisoner. If Mr. Wardwell could have felt that grasp and seen the prisoner's face, he might have greatly changed his opinion of smart prisoners in general.

Somehow John Doe preferred to restrict his remarks to whispers, and for some reason Mr. Morton humored him. The interview lasted but a few moments, and ended with a plea and a promise that another call should be made. Meanwhile, Mr. Wardwell had stood on a corner that commanded the jail, and when the teacher re-appeared the merchant asked, "Well?"

"They are a sad set," Mr. Morton admitted.

"I told you so," said Wardwell, rubbing his hands as if he were glad rather than sorry that the prisoners were as bad as he had thought them. "And how did you find that rascally counterfeiter? I'll warrant he didn't care to see you?"

"On the contrary," replied the teacher, gravely, "he was very glad to see me. He begged me to come again. He was so glad to see some one not a jailer that he cried."

"Well, I never!" exclaimed the merchant. And he told the truth.

It was soon after this first visit of a series that lasted as long as Mr. Morton remained in the village that the boys changed their base-ball ground. They had generally played in some open ground on the edge of the town, but the teacher one day asked why they should go so far, when the entire square on which the court-house and jail stood was vacant, except for those two buildings. The boys spent a whole recess in considering this suggestion; then they reported it favorably to the other boys of the town, and it was adopted almost unanimously that very week; and Canning Forbes could always remember even the day of the month on which the first game was played, for he as a "fielder" caught the ball exactly on the tip of the longest finger of his left hand, and he staid home with that finger, and woke up nights with it, for a full week afterward.

Paul Grayson had not attended Mr. Morton's school a fortnight before every one knew that ball was his favorite game. This preference on the part of the new boy did not entirely please Benny Mallow, who preferred to have his new friend play marbles, and with him alone, because then he could talk to him a great deal, whereas at ball, even "town-ball," which needed but four boys to a game, there was not much opportunity for talking, while at base-ball the chances were less, even were Benny not so generally out of breath when he met Grayson on a "base" that conversation was impossible.

But Grayson clung to ball; he did not seem to care much for it in the school-yard, which, indeed, was rather small for such games, but after school was dismissed in the afternoons he always tried to get up a game on the new grounds, and he generally succeeded. Even boys who did not care particularly for the sport had been told by Mr. Morton that about the only diversion of the wretched men in the jail was to look out the window while ball-playing was going on; and as Mr. Morton had begun to attain special popularity through his work among the prisoners, the boys who liked him, as most of them did, were glad to help him to the small extent they were able.

"I really can't see why Grayson should be so fond of ball," said Canning Forbes one afternoon, as he and several other boys lay under the big elm-tree behind the court-house and criticised the boys who were playing. "He isn't much of a pitcher, he doesn't bat very well, and he often loses splendid chances, while he's catcher, by not seeming to see the ball when it's coming. I wonder if his eyes can be bad?"

"I don't believe they are," said Will Palmer; "he is keen-sighted enough about everything else. Absent-mindedness is his great trouble; every once in a while he gets his eyes fixed on something as if he couldn't move them."

"He gets into a brown-study, you mean," suggested Forbes.

"That's it," assented Will.

"He's thinking about the splendors of the royal home that he is being kept away from," said Napoleon Nott. "You just ought to read what sort of place a royal home is," continued Notty. "I'll bring up the book some day and read it aloud to all of you fellows."

"No you won't, Notty," said Canning Forbes; "not if we have any legs left to run away with."

Some internal hints that supper-time was approaching broke up the game, and the boys moved off the ground, by twos and threes, until only Paul and Benny remained. Paul seemed in no particular hurry to start, and as Benny never seemed to imagine that Paul could see himself safely home from any place, he remained too.

"Benny," said Paul, suddenly, "did you ever see any one in jail?"

"No," said Benny, "I never did."

"Neither did I," said Paul, "but I'm curious to do so now. You needn't go with me; the sight might pain you too much."

"What? Just to go to the jail, and look up at the windows? Oh no; *that* won't hurt me. I've done that lots of times."

"Very well," said Paul, moving toward the jail. He looked up at the windows as he walked; finally he stopped where he could look fairly at the small window of the cell where the counterfeiter was. The sun was not shining upon that side of the jail, so Benny could barely see there was a face behind the window. Evidently the prisoner was standing on a chair, for the little window was quite high. Paul's eyes seemed better than Benny's, however, for he continued looking at that window for some moments. When he finally turned away, it was because he could not see any longer, for his eyes were full of tears.

"Why, you're crying!" exclaimed Benny, in some astonishment. "What is the matter?"

"I'm so sorry for the poor fellow," replied Paul.

"I am too," said Benny, "awfully sorry. I wish I could cry about it, but somehow my eyes don't work right to-day. Some days I can cry real easily. Next time one of those days comes, I'll come over here with you, and let you see what I can do."

[TO BE CONTINUED.]

SANDY HOOK—ITS STORY.

SANDY HOOK is one of the striking features in the scenery of New York. It is a low point of sand projecting from below the Highlands into the sea. Before its extreme end runs the channel of deep water through which passes all the commerce of the port—the most important of all the world's seats of trade. Beyond the deep channel the bar rises, covered with white breakers, and extends to the distant Rockaway shore. Around Sandy Hook all the interest of the scene centres, and its bare point, now marked by the new fortifications, has witnessed some of the most wonderful voyages of the past. It saw Verazzani in his antique craft—the most awkward and dangerous of vessels—make his way slowly, with lead and line, into the wide-spreading harbor, and trace for the first time the unknown shore. What a wild and lonely scene it was!—the home of a few savages and of wild beasts and birds. But Verazzani never came back, and the next ship that sailed by Sandy Hook into the tranquil bay was that of Hendrick Hudson.

His vessel, the *Half-Moon*, was a Dutch galliot, strongly built, as were all the Dutch ships of the time, but so small, heavy, and slow that it seems almost incredible that it should ever outlive a storm or make any headway on the sea. The stern and prow were high and broad, the bow round, the hull unwieldy, the masts and sails too small for such a vessel, and the rudder almost unmanageable. Compared with the modern sailing ship, nothing could seem more inconvenient or unfit for navigating stormy seas than these vessels of the sixteenth and seventeenth centuries. Yet with them Barents broke into the icy ocean of the North, and defied the arctic cold. Great fleets of them, sometimes numbering several hundred, sailed from Amsterdam around the Cape of Good Hope to the East Indies, drove off the Portuguese, and came back laden with the precious products of the East—gems, gold, and spices. The immense quantity of cloves and cinnamon used by our ancestors is startling. But the slow ships sailed safely along the African shore on both sides, and in the midst of pirates, privateers, storms, and cyclones made profitable voyages that gave Holland a wonderful prosperity.

The *Half-Moon* crossed the bar, anchored in the lower bay, and the Dutch navigators proceeded cautiously to survey the hostile shore of Coney Island, where now the countless visitors of Manhattan or Brighton Beach gather on summer evenings, and at length ventured to sail up through the Narrows, drew near to Manhattan Island, and saw some of its early inhabitants. The first New-Yorkers were very indifferently clad; but the young ladies—squaws, as they were called—were well acquainted with paint and powder, and had an inexhaustible appetite for feathers, beads, and other finery. Shells were the money of the country; and fur robes, rich with embroidery, were worn by the chiefs.

After a pleasant voyage in September, 1609, up the Hudson River to Albany, the famous navigator passed through the harbor out to sea, and then sailed away, never to return—unless we accept Irving's legend, and hear with Rip Van Winkle the roar of the balls of the Dutch sailors as they play their weird games amongst the Catskills, while the lightning flashes and the thunder peals in the dismal night. But Sandy Hook now became a well-known scene to the Dutch sailors. Immigrants came over; a few houses were built at first on New York Island; Albany was settled in 1614, and the same year Adrian Block, when his own ship was burned, built a new one on the Manhattan shore. It was the first vessel produced in this centre of the world's trade. It was not quite as broad as it was long; but its length of keel was thirty-eight feet, on deck it was nearly forty-five feet, and its breadth about eleven and a half. On this peculiar craft the gallant explorer set out to survey the great East River. He passed safely the perils of both Hell Gates, coasted the unknown shores to Block Island, and left an imperishable name on that pleasant summer resort. New Amsterdam became a famous seat of trade. Fur and tobacco were its chief commodities. A fine tobacco plantation stretched along the East River at Corlaer's Hook, and at Albany the Van Rensselaers and Schuylers contended for the fur trade of the savages, sometimes coming to blows. Many Dutch galliots now sailed leisurely over from old Amsterdam to the new. New York Island was covered with rich farms. In 1678 peaches were so plenty that they were fed to the swine; strawberries covered the ground in rare profusion. Sheltered within the protecting arm of Sandy Hook, the little city flourished and grew great. It had no idle hands. Its burgomasters all either kept shops, taverns, or worked on farms, and scorned sloth. All was prosperous growth, under the famous Governor Stuyvesant, when suddenly, in August, 1664, for the first time, a hostile English fleet sailed up the great harbor, and anchored in Gravesend Bay. It was composed of two fifty-gun ships and one of forty, with six hundred soldiers. The consternation in the city was great; but Governor Stuyvesant ordered the guns to be run out on the fort at the end of Broadway, called out the militia, and prepared for a desperate contest.

MASTER NOBLE'S LESSON.

BY MRS. ANNIE A. PRESTON.

WHEN Master Noble was appointed to take charge of the Oak Bridge schools, he found, much to his surprise, that in every grade, from the Primary to the High Schools, there were many pupils who had frequently been promoted to higher classes, but, failing to get their lessons during the first term, had, at examination, been sent back to a lower grade again.

This had become such a common occurrence in the schools in Oak Bridge that the spirit of honest and praiseworthy emulation was lost, and the pupils felt it to be no humiliation or disgrace to be dropped from a higher class to a lower one.

"Something must be done to impress upon them the disgrace of such indifference, and to arouse their ambition," thought the new master, and he forthwith invited all the young folks in the community to meet him the next Saturday afternoon at the Town-hall to listen to a story that he would tell.

Of course the promise of a story from the popular new master, and the fact that he had recently returned from extensive travels, called the children and young people all out, and this is what they heard:

"It is said that years ago a beautiful little brown sparrow made her home in the garden of a certain great and renowned magician. She built her nest in the grass, and was content to hop and chirp about in the rose thicket, and to keep very near the ground indeed.

"She might have been happy enough had she not allowed herself to be afraid of the robin-redbreast that had a nest in the golden sweet apple-tree, and was always fluttering down and hop-hop-hopping across the grass-plot, and pecking this way and that at the smaller birds.

"The wise and tender-hearted magician, who had been closely watching proceedings, had so much sympathy for the timid, trembling little sparrow that he said, 'She shall have a chance in the world,' and he forthwith changed her into a robin.

"No sooner had she got over the novelty of her new situation than she began to be afraid of the pigeon-hawk that came sailing down from the wood near by in search of prey. So the magician, still thinking to make something of the timorsome little bird which was his pet, now changed her into a pigeon-hawk.

"'Immediately she cast affrighted glances at the big gray owl that lived in a hollow tree *farther* back toward the edge of the forest, and who came out on a dead branch at night-fall, and hooted until the hill-side rang again with the unearthly screeches, and all the smaller birds tucked their heads under their wings, and put their claws over their ears to shut out the sound.

"'I will persevere,' said the tender-hearted magician; 'I may make something of her yet;' and straightway the pigeon-hawk became an owl, with a voice equal to any of the owls' in all that forest.

"But now, instead of making the most of her opportunity, and *being* a real, vigorous owl, she backed into the old hollow tree, her great staring eyes round with terror, as she tremblingly listened to the terrific screams of a monstrous eagle whose eyrie was on the mountain-side facing the sunrise.

"'You shall be a sparrow again!' angrily cried the magician. 'You have only the life and heart and spirit of a sparrow after all. What is the use of my trying to make anything else of you? Had you asserted and kept your position as an owl, I would soon have made you an eagle, and you could have proudly soared above all the birds of the air. I have done my best to help you along, but you have not made one effort in your own behalf.'

"It is the same with a boy or a girl," continued Master Noble. "If pupils have only the heart and the will and the intellect of a sparrow, they will remain sparrows in spite of all their teachers may do to help them on and to encourage them. *Study* and *will* are the magicians that help them to maintain their promotion, and the public examination is the great magician that assigns them their advanced positions.

"The world over, sparrow-hearted people are getting into eagles' nests, but keen-eyed public opinion is the great magician who says, 'Go back to the thicket and to the grass-plot again! You have only the heart and the brain of a sparrow; there is no use in trying to make eagles of you.'"

That is why to this day the names of those birds are the symbols of the different grades in the Oak Bridge schools, and Master Noble has never once been obliged to say, "*Go back and be a sparrow again.*"

THE STORM-PETREL.

AGES ago this little web-footed fellow was named Petrel, after the Apostle Peter, because he is most often seen walking on the waves—never in them, but just daintily skimming their surface.

To sailors they are "Mother Carey's chickens," and their presence is dreaded, because with them generally

WILLIAM SHAKESPEARE AT THE AGE OF TWELVE.

come storms and bad weather. They revel in storms, and the fiercer the gale and the higher the waves, the more merry are they. This preference of the petrel is explained by the fact that he is more than half nocturnal in his habits, and greatly dislikes the glare of sunshine. But when black clouds and gloomy mists hang low over the ocean, the semi-darkness just suits him, and through it may be be seen skimming the angry billows many leagues from the nearest land.

The inhabitants of some of the outlying Scotch islands make a peculiar use of the young petrels, which are always as fat as butter, and much more easy to catch than the old birds. The young bird is caught, killed, and a wick is passed through his body until it projects from the bill. When this wick is lighted it gradually draws every drop of oil out of the well-supplied little reservoir, and thus a lamp is formed, very cheaply and easily, that lasts and gives a good light for the whole of a long winter's evening.

SHAKESPEARE.

WILLIAM SHAKESPEARE was born at Stratford, on the Avon, April 23, 1564, and was baptized on the 26th. Two months after his birth the plague swept over the pleasant village, carrying off a large part of the inhabitants. The danger that hung over the marvellous infant passed away, and he grew up healthy and strong. His mother, Mary Arden, inherited a large farm at Wilmecote, a mile from Stratford; and his father, John Shakespeare, who held several other pieces of land, was probably an active farmer, raising sheep, and perhaps cattle. The house in which it is said Shakespeare was born is still shown in Henley Street, Stratford—a plain building of timber and plaster, covered with the names of those who have come from every part of the world to visit the dark, narrow room made memorable by the poet's birth.

He had several younger brothers—Gilbert, Richard, Edmund, and a sister Joan—all of whom he aided in his prosperity. The family in Henley Street was a happy one; and the young Shakespeares and their sister probably wandered in the flowery fields around the Avon, or lived on the farm at Wilmecote, saw the cows milked, and the cattle pastured, and all the changes of rural life. Shakespeare lived among the flowers he describes so well; and in the fine park of Fulbroke, not far off, saw the magnificent oaks, the herds of deer, and the gay troops of huntsmen chasing the poor stag along the forest glade. He must have been a precocious boy, seeing everything around him even in childhood. He is described or painted in later life as having a fair, melancholy, sensitive face, his eyes apparently dark, his hair brown and flowing. His disposition was gentle and benevolent; he won the love even of his foes.

As the son of a farmer he probably had little education. He went for several years to the grammar school at Stratford, and was then perhaps employed on his father's farm. Like Virgil, Horace, Burns, and many other poets, he grew up in the country. Nothing is certainly known of his youth. He was fond of rural sports, and amidst his early labors went no doubt to the country fairs, joined in the Christmas games and May-day dances, and probably when the Earl of Leicester gave the magnificent reception to Queen Elizabeth at Kenilworth, described in Scott's novel, Shakespeare was there among the spectators. He was then a boy of twelve. He could enjoy the plays, games, the pomp and glitter, of that famous festival.

He must have read romances and tales early, like Dickens; he may have amused his little brothers and his sister Joan by repeating to them on winter evenings in the low room in Henley Street the story of the wild castle of Elsinore, or of the venerable Lear and the gentle Cordelia. He was all imagination, and precocious in knowledge; he must have studied when his companions played, and read everything that came in his way. At eighteen he fell in love and married Anne Hathaway, a young lady eight years older than himself. Before he was twenty-one he had three children to maintain, and went up to London to find employment. He remained in obscurity for some years; but at last appears, about 1590, the finest poet and dramatist of all ages.

Shakespeare pursued his career in London as author and theatrical manager for nearly twenty-five years. He was very industrious; he was prudent, but generous; he saved money, and grew wealthy. About 1612 or 1613 he returned to Stratford, where he lived in the best house of the little village, called "New Place." Here he gave a home to his father and mother, and provided liberally for his younger brothers. To his sister Joan he gave the house in Henley Street, which remained in the possession of her descendants until 1820. He may have looked forward to a long and honorable old age, but died in 1616, it is said, on the same day of the year on which he was born. His son Hamnet died long before him. He left two daughters.

His writings teach men to be kind and gentle.

MR. MARTIN'S LEO.

BY JIMMY BROWN.

I HAD a dreadful time after that accident with Mr. Martin's eye. He wrote a letter to father and said that "the conduct of that atrocious young ruffian was such," and that he hoped he would never have a son like me. As soon as father said "My son I want to see you up stairs bring me my new rattan cane," I knew what was going to happen. I will draw some veils over the terrible scene, and will only say that for the next week I did not feel able to hold a pen unless I stood up all the time.

Last week I got a beautiful dog. Father had gone away for a few days and I heard mother say that she wished she had a nice little dog to stay in the house and drive robbers away. The very next day a lovely dog that didn't belong to anybody came into our yard and I made a dog-house for him out of a barrel, and got some beefsteak out of the closet for him, and got a cat for him to chase, and made him comfortable. He is part bull-dog, and his ears and tail are gone and he hasn't but one eye and he's lame in one of his hind-legs and the hair has been scalded off part of him, and he's just lovely. If you saw him after a cat you'd say he was a perfect beauty. Mother won't let me bring him into the house, and says she never saw such a horrid brute, but some women haven't any taste about dogs anyway.

His name is Sitting Bull, though most of the time when he isn't chasing cats he's lying down. He knows pretty near everything. Some dogs know more than folks. Mr. Travers had a dog once that knew Chinese. Every time that dog heard a man speak Chinese he would lie down and howl and then he would get up and bite the man. You might talk English or French or Latin or German to him and he wouldn't pay any attention to it, but just say three words in Chinese and he'd take a piece out of you. Mr. Travers says that once when he was a puppy a Chinaman tried to catch him for a stew; so whenever he heard anybody speak Chinese he remembered that time and went and bit the man to let him know that he didn't approve of the way Chinamen treated puppies. The dog never made a mistake but once. A man came to the house who had lost his pilate and couldn't speak plain, and the dog thought he was speaking Chinese and so he had his regular fit and bit the man worse than he had ever bit anybody before.

Sitting Bull don't know Chinese but Mr. Travers says he's a "specialist in cats," which means that he knows the whole science of cats. The very first night I let him loose he chased a cat up the pear-tree and he sat under that tree and danced around it and howled all night. The neighbors next door threw most all their things at him but they couldn't discourage him. I had to tie him up after breakfast and let the cat get down and run away before I let him loose again, or he'd have barked all summer.

The only trouble with him is that he can't see very well and keeps running against things. If he starts to run out of the gate he is just as likely to run head first into the fence, and when he chases a cat round a corner he will sometimes mistake a stick of wood, or the lawn-mower for the cat and try to shake it to death. This was the way he came to get me into trouble with Mr. Martin.

He hadn't been at our house for so long (Mr. Martin, I mean) that we all thought he never would come again. Father sometimes said that his *friend* Martin had been driven out of the house because my conduct was such and he expected I would separate him *from* all his friends. Of course I was sorry that father felt bad about it but if I was his age I would have friends that were made more substantial than Mr. Martin is.

Night before last I was out in the back yard with Sitting Bull looking for a stray cat that sometimes comes around the house after dark and steals the strawberries and takes the apples out of the cellar. At least I suppose it is this particular cat that steals the apples for the cook says a cat does it and we haven't any private cat of our own. After a while I saw the cat coming along by the side of the fence looking wicked enough to steal anything and to tell stories about it afterward. I was sitting on the ground holding Sitting Bull's head in my lap and telling him that I did wish he'd take to rat-hunting like Sam McGinnis's terrier, but no sooner had I seen the cat and whispered to Sitting Bull that she was in sight than he jumped up and went for her.

He chased her along the fence into the front yard where she made a dive under the front piazza. Sitting Bull came round the corner of the house just flying, and I close after him. It happened that Mr. Martin was at that identicular moment going up the steps of the piazza and Sitting Bull mistaking one of his legs for the cat jumped for it and had it in his teeth before I could say a word.

When that dog once gets hold of a thing there is no use in reasoning with him, for he won't listen to anything. Mr. Martin howled and said "Take him off my gracious the dog's mad," and I said "Come here sir. Good dog. Leave him alone" but Sitting Bull hung on to the leg as if he was deaf and Mr. Martin hung on to the railing of the piazza and made twice as much noise as the dog. I didn't know whether I'd better run for the doctor or the police, but after shaking the leg for about a minute Sitting Bull gave it an awful pull and pulled it off just at the knee-joint. When I saw the dog rushing round the yard with the leg in his mouth I ran into the house and told Sue and begged her to cut a hole in the wall and hide me behind the plastering where the police couldn't find me. When she went down to help Mr. Martin she saw him just going out of the yard on a wheelbarrow with a man wheeling him on a broad grin.

If he ever comes to this house again I'm going to run away. It turns out that his leg was made of cork and I suppose the rest of him is either cork or glass. Some day he'll drop apart on our piazza then the whole blame will be put on me.

A MISHAP.

BY JOSEPHINE POLLARD.

A dear little fellow named Noah
Had made up his mind that he'd go a-
Sailing alone
In a boat of his own,
For he was a champion rower.

This dear little fellow named Noah
Hadn't gone very far before—oh! oh!—
His boat was upset,
And he got very wet,
Did this little numskull of a Noah.

CORN-STALK CATTLE.

BY FLORENCE E. TING.

LAST winter my health gave out, and the doctor said I must go South. What a mourning there was among our little boys at the thought of losing Aunt Kate and her "beautiful stories"!

Just before the train started, little Jamie begged to be held up to the car window to give me a good-by kiss. Poor little fellow! his eyes streamed with tears, and not even the promise of a pound of candy could console him.

I was not going to Florida, where fashionable invalids spend their winters, but to the home of an old friend of mine on an Alabama plantation. How glad I was to find that she too had a little boy! He was not much like the nephews I had left behind, but I soon found him to be a good-hearted, brave little lad.

His mamma and I were sitting one rainy morning with our work before a great wood fire, when Frankie and his bosom companion, Abe, a young darky, came in with an armful of long dry corn stalks, a handful of chicken feathers, and two kitchen knives.

"Now, Frankie, you are going to make a mess, so get some papers and put them down on the floor," said Frankie's mamma. Abe ran to get the papers, and very soon the two boys were down on their knees, peeling the stalks.

I noticed that the stalks were old and brittle, and that the boys preserved the hull. After watching them for some minutes, I began to make inquiries as to what the stalks were for.

"Dese is fur cattle," said Abe, grinning.

I then asked how they made cattle. Frankie did not seem communicative, so Abe again answered my question.

"Wa'al, we jest cuts 'em. If yer waits a minute I'll show yer."

He cut off a piece of the peeled stalk about four inches long, then split the hull into four pieces about a quarter of an inch wide and two inches long. He stuck two of these pieces near one end of the stalk for hind-legs, and the two others at a quarter of an inch from the other end for front ones. He then cut a piece of the stalk about an inch long for the head, a niche for the mouth, two pins for eyes, and narrow bits of hull for horns; another little strip of hull was stuck first into the head and then into the body to form the neck, a chicken feather put in for the tail, and the job was finished.

"Now, den," said Abe, triumphantly, holding it up, "don't yer see dat's a cow?"

I smiled, but Abe was too good-natured to notice it. This animal I found, with slight variations, was made to represent horses, cows, mules, sheep, dogs, and pigs, and even chickens, which, of course, were much smaller, and had only two legs. In the course of the morning Frankie and Abe manufactured a sow with seven little pigs, two cows, a mule, and a horse.

It had stopped raining, so the boys asked if I would not like to go out and see their farms. Under a shed in the yard were these two farms, arranged as nearly as possible like Frankie's father's. Barns, stables, wagon-houses, and pig-pens were made of bricks on a very small scale, and inhabited by corn-stalk cattle.

A wagon made of a chip tied to two spools was hitched up with two corn-stalk oxen, their feather tails standing up in the air.

I thought my little friends would like this new breed of cattle. They struck me as being much easier to manage than those of Noah's ark, for there is hardly a boy who has not had all manner of trouble in making Father Noah's cows and horses stand up. Gather together some corn stalks this autumn, let them dry, and stock a farm for yourself.

SEA-BREEZES.

LETTER NO. 5 FROM BESSIE MAYNARD TO HER DOLL.

CAMBRIDGE, *September*, 1880.

MY DEAREST CLYTIE,—When I sent my last letter from Bar Harbor I thought it would be the very last I should write you for a long time, but I shall not see you for two whole weeks more, and I can not wait till then to tell you all the fine things I am precipitating for next winter.

We left Mount Desert last Monday, and have been with grandma and Auntie Belle here in Cambridge ever since, except when we go flying back and forth from Boston. We are very busy, Clytie, and have heaps of shopping to do; for what do you think?—we are all going to Europe, and are to sail one month from to-day. I am awfully glad, of course, but I don't know how I can live all winter long without you. Don't tell the rest of the dolls, Clytie, but I do a little bit believe that you are going too! Now that is a very great secret, so you will keep it close down in your own little heart, and not let the others even suspect a thing about it, because it might make them feel bad that I chose you and left them behind; and one thing I never would do, and that is to let my children think I had a *favorite* among them. You know I love every one of them dearly, but of course I can not take them all to Europe, and as you are the largest, it is more your *place* to go.

Now for another piece of news: Cousin Frank and Miss Carleton are engaged: Yes, Clytie, they really are, and they are going to be married this very month, and go to Europe when we do. If this isn't news enough, here is some more: Randolph Peyton has gone home with his mamma, and they are all coming to our house in New York the week before we sail, and go with our party!

Won't it be lovely? There will be Mr. and Mrs. Peyton, Randolph and his sister Helen, and Miss Rogers, their governess. I have never seen Helen, but Randolph says she is "awfully jolly, considering she is only a girl," so I guess I shall like her. Then there will be papa and mamma and me (and you, if we take you), Cousin Frank and Miss Carleton, only she won't be Miss Carleton then—she will be *Mrs. Howard*, and I am to call her Cousin Carrie: indeed, I call her so now, for Cousin Frank asked me to, and I would do anything to please him. I have forgiven him for sending me away one night when they were talking about little pitchers. When I asked him about it afterward, and if it was really deckerativeart they meant, he tried to exclaim to me, but he laughed so hard all the time, I couldn't make out anything at all except that *I* was the very funniest little pitcher in the whole world! Did you ever know such a comical thing as to call me, a girl ten years old, a *pitcher!* I'm sure he didn't know what he was talking about.

Mamma says I may give them anything I choose for a wedding present, and I have presided on a silver pitcher. I am going to send it with a card tied on the handle marked, "*This is me*," and I guess they will wonder what it means. Don't you?

I have told Cousin Carrie so much about you that she seems to love you already, even though she has never seen you, and she says she shall invite you to her wedding. Won't that be fun? She is going to send you her cards, and you will go with me. I shall get home in time to have your dress made. Mine is to be a kemination dress of white cashmere and silk, and I think yours will be of the same kind in rose-color.

I will tell you one more adventure that befell us at Bar Harbor, and then I shall not write any more letters unless you are left at home when I go to Europe. Of course, if you are, I shall write as often as I possibly can, and I shall have so many new and strange appearances in crossing the ocean and in visiting forran lands that the reading of them will make up in some agree for being left at home.

Randolph and I went down to the beach, the evening before we came away, to launch his ship—a beautiful one, with sails all set, "full-rigged," as the sailors say, that his uncle in Philadelphia had sent him that very day.

The Stars and Stripes waved from the prow or stern—I never know which is which—and on the top of one of the masts he fastened a "pennon," as he called it, with the name of the ship in big blue letters. (He printed it himself with his blue pencil, and it looked real cunning blowing round in the wind, and flapping up and down.) What do you suppose the name was? *Bessie*, to be sure. He says he thinks it is an "awfully jolly" name for a ship, or for a girl either.

Well, the wind blew just the right way for a splendid launch. I held the cord, letting it out as fast as he told me to, and he gave it a push, and off it sailed, straight and lovely as a duck. I was so delighted I couldn't possibly help clapping my hands, and, oh, Clytie! I dropped the cord, and away it went, up and down over the waves as if it was alive. Randolph muttered something that sounded like, "Bother! that's just like a girl!" and scowled awfully at me, and then ran out into the water after it. I screamed as loud as I could, for I was afraid he would drown; and then I remembered how he had saved my life, and I said to myself, He is my friend now, and I will save him, for he saved me when we were enemies. So, as the story-books say, I "dashed into the foaming billows" after him, and just as I caught him by his jacket I thought I heard him say again, "Bother!" and then came a great rushing noise in my ears, my mouth was full of water, and the next thing I knew I was lying in mamma's bed, and she and two or three other people were rubbing me! I was almost drowned, Clytie; and so it was Randolph who saved my life a second time, and I never saved *his* at all.

A MODERN ORPHEUS.

When I pulled him by his jacket, a wave broke over us; but he was stronger and bigger than I, and a *boy* besides (and truly, Clytie, boys do know more than girls about *some* things), and so he caught me, and sort of pulled and rolled and pushed me out of the water; and just then Cousin Frank and Miss Carleton came round the point in their boat, and Cousin Frank took me in his arms, and ran up to the hotel as fast as he could go.

Poor mamma was most subtracted when she saw me, and Randolph was so scared he forgot all about his lovely new ship, that long before that time had gone sailing out to sea all by itself.

Wasn't it awful, Clytie? If I had minded what Solomon says, "Look before you leap," I should have seen that Randolph had his hand on the ship at the very moment I seized him, and he could have got back safe to the shore without any of my help.

Good-by for a little while. I shall see you and the rest of the dolls week after next.

Your loving mamma,

BESSIE MAYNARD.

OUR POST-OFFICE BOX.

their [illegible]. I have twelve hundred stamps, and I am thirteen years old. I would like to know the age of my correspondents. CHARLES S. [illegible],
12 West Thirty-second Street, New York City.

I would like to exchange [illegible] with any boy readers of YOUNG PEOPLE in the West. I am [illegible] years old. [illegible],
[illegible] Third Place, Brooklyn, New York.

I would like to exchange postage stamps with any correspondent. [illegible],
P. O. Box [illegible], Lynchburg, Virginia.

LOUISE.—Your question, "Is the mosquito of any use in the great economy of nature?" has often been asked by many older and wiser than you, but it is not generally known that in their larval state mosquitoes fulfill an important branch of nature's army of [illegible] scavengers. The larvæ live in the water of stagnant pools and marshes, and feed upon particles of decaying matter, and as their number is so very large, the amount they devour is considerable. By thus purifying the water they destroy the miasma which would otherwise arise and pollute the atmosphere to such an extent that no human being could breathe it with safety. The value of the work accomplished in tropical countries by these tiny scavengers is very great. It is estimated that the air of certain [illegible] regions would be so poisonous that no animal higher than a reptile could breathe it and live, were their purifying influence removed. We do not know that mosquitoes in the winged state have any useful mission beyond that of depositing the eggs which produce the larvæ, but that alone saves them from being "nothing but a nuisance."

F. A. [illegible].—The subscription price for HARPER'S YOUNG PEOPLE for 1881 will remain one dollar and fifty cents, the same low figure as for the first volume.

[illegible] R.—The large green worm that feeds on carrot, caraway, parsley, and some other common garden plants is the caterpillar of the *Papilio asterias*, a large black butterfly which is seen in great numbers at midsummer, hovering about the flowers in gardens. It is especially fond of the sweet-scented phlox. This butterfly is very handsomely marked with rows of yellow spots near the margin of its wings, and on the hind wings, which are tailed, there is also a row of blue spots, and near the lower angle an orange-colored eye with a black dot in the centre. The wings of this handsome insect expand from three to four inches.

"[illegible]."—It is not easy to say why such great numbers of potato-bugs are found crawling on the sea beaches. These striped cantharides are so numerous in all parts of the country that they are probably blown seaward by the wind, and naturally wash ashore on the tide.

You will find simple directions for pressing flowers and leaves in the Post-office Boxes of YOUNG PEOPLE Nos. 34 and 40.

F. R. W.—Write again to your correspondent. There are so many possible reasons why he has not answered you that it would not be fair to him to print your notice. Possibly he has misdirected the letter to you.

Favors are acknowledged from Fred P. [illegible], Albert C. B., Jennie R. [illegible], R. N., Richard F. Morgan, Willie C. Chapman, N. R., Frank Davis, S. [illegible], [illegible], Frank [illegible], John R. [illegible], H. E. G.

Correct answers to puzzles are received from Eddie R. [illegible], Mary Tobby, "[illegible]," William H. [illegible], Dora T. [illegible], "[illegible]," Percy McGeorge, "[illegible]," E. D. W., H. [illegible], George [illegible], James H. Beddoe, Howard A. [illegible], "Ivanhoe."

John H. Bartlett, A. G., and J. E. [illegible] have sent [illegible] of the five-pointed star, which were received too late for acknowledgment with the others.

PUZZLES FROM YOUNG CONTRIBUTORS.

No. 1.

[illegible]

1. In strawberry. In [illegible]. A [illegible]. A [illegible]. In [illegible]. A [illegible]. An [illegible]. A [illegible]. A [illegible]. In [illegible]. [illegible] name of a common shrub. OWLET.

No. 2.

WORD SQUARES.

1. First, [illegible]. Second, [illegible] in Asia. Third, a river in Hungary. Fourth, a [illegible] in [illegible] ancient [illegible]. [illegible]

2. First, a part of the body. Second, a disease. Third, [illegible]. Fourth, a hollow. [illegible]

No. 3.

CHARADE.

My first is [illegible] to make my second, and [illegible] always be in my whole. [illegible]

No. 4.

NUMERICAL ENIGMAS.

1. A fanciful character in one of Shakespeare's plays composed of 11 letters.
My 3, 10, 9, 2 is agony to weary fingers.
My 8, 6, 1 is a problem.
My 4, 8, 5, 11 is done by every school-boy.
My 7, 2, 9, 4 is fine powder. LOUISE.
2. An inhabitant of Africa composed of 10 letters.
My 8, 2, 9, 5, 6 is a [illegible].
My 4, 8, 9, 6 is a piece of money.
My 1, 3, 10, 7 is a beautiful flower. FANNIE.

No. 5.

ENIGMA.

My first is in board, but not in plank.
My second is in [illegible], but not in bank.
My third is in skin, but not in [illegible].
My fourth is in tale, but not in [illegible].
My fifth is in sword, but not in [illegible].
My sixth is in [illegible], but not in [illegible].
My whole [illegible] nearly [illegible],
Crowned by two hundred and fifty years.
[illegible]

ANSWERS TO PUZZLES IN No. 47.

No. 1. [illegible]

No. 2. Telephone.

No. 3. 1. [illegible]. 2. [illegible]. 3. [illegible].

No. 4.

```
F O A M    A R C O
O B I G    R E A P
A I M S    G A L A
M G N E    O P A L
```

Charade on page [illegible]—[illegible].

ADVERTISEMENTS.

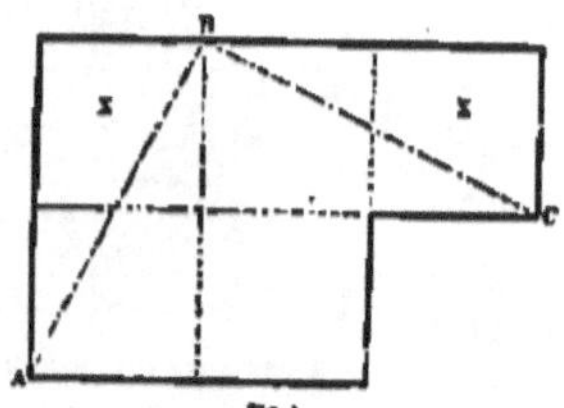

Fig. 1.

SOLUTION TO MARINER'S PUZZLE.

DIVIDE the piece of plank described in the Mariner's Puzzle, published in No. 47, into five squares, as represented in Fig. 1; then draw a line from A to B, and from B to C. Cut off the

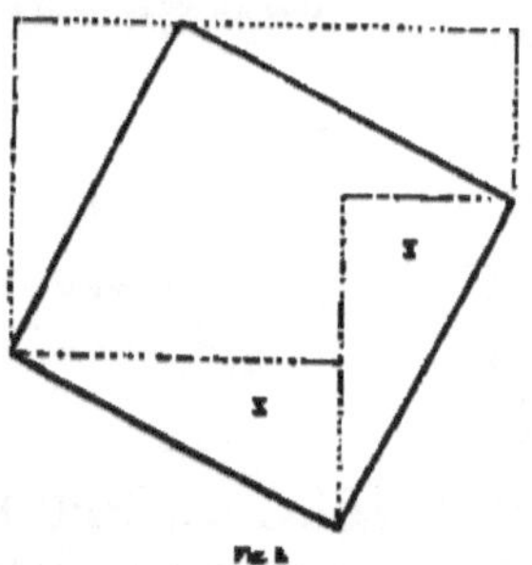

Fig. 2.

two triangular pieces marked X X, and re-arrange them as represented in Fig. 2, and you will have a piece of plank of the shape and size required by the mariner to stop the leak in his ship.

IMITATION SCREW-HEADS.

BY F. BELLEW.

HERE is a simple little thing of my own invention, from which I have derived a good deal of fun from time to time, and from which the readers of YOUNG PEOPLE may extract some amusement. It is an imitation of the common screw-head, and is made in this wise: Take a piece of common tin-foil, and mark on it with a pair of compasses or a small thimble a number of circles; then, with a broad pen or small brush and black ink, rule across each a broad line, as represented in Fig. 1. Then, when your ink is dry, cut out the little circular pieces very neatly with a pair of scissors. They resemble so exactly the head of a real screw as to deceive the most acute observer. Once I made a box for conjuring tricks, with a side swung on hinges, and fixed the sides of the box with these screw-heads in such a way as to impress the spectator with the idea that it was a piece of workmanship that could not be trifled with.

Fig. 1.

On one occasion a much-loved relative of mine had left me alone in her house while she drove over to the station to meet her husband. I did not wish to waste my time while she was away, and having nothing else to do, I cast my eye round for material. At last it lighted on an article of furniture; this was a bureau, highly prized by my much-loved relative. I have attempted, feebly, in the subjoined sketch to convey an idea of it, but am fully conscious that I am far from doing it justice. But this bureau was of solid mahogany, and had belonged to her grandmother—qualities enough to make anything dear to the heart of a true woman. On the side of this solid mahogany bureau I scrawled a ragged line with the sharp corner of a piece of soap, and gummed some of my screw-heads down each side of the mark, as in Fig. 2. Then I waited until my much-loved relative returned.

Fig. 2.

"Aunt," I said, in solemn tones, "look at the end of your mahogany bureau. It is all my fault, and I am as sorry as I can be. I know how you value it, and realize the extent of the disaster; but I've fixed it up as well as I can, and I guess it won't show much."

My aunt rushed to the bureau, and there she saw the patched and botched wreck.

"Oh dear!" cried she, "to think—just to think—how could you be so— I knew something would come of swinging those tool-chests. I'd rather have given a hundred dollars. It's too bad. And such a mess! Why didn't you wait till I could send for a proper man—a cabinet-maker or something—to mend it?"

Then she ran into the garden, and called to her husband: "Oh, George, do come here, and see what that boy has been doing! My dear mahogany grandmother's bureau all knocked to pieces, and patched together with big screws. Such a sight!"

As soon as my aunt left the room I seized a wet towel, and quickly removed all the appearance of damage, so that when she returned with her husband, and with averted face, bade him look upon the wreck, the mild old gentleman, after putting on his specs, and making a careful examination, reported that he could see nothing the matter.

"For pity's sake!—the man must be getting blind and foolish," cried my aunt. "It's as plain as Charley Morker's nose on his face."

A discussion of some length here followed between my aunt and her husband, which was terminated by the lady stepping up to the bureau, with an air of triumph, to point out the broken places. Never before was seen such a perplexed woman. She looked and looked, and felt all over the precious piece of furniture with her finger, and, I believe, would have fairly gone demented had I not broken the spell by a roar of laughter. When I explained the trick I had played, she too laughed heartily, and boxed my ears, saying it was just like me, and that I was always up to some prank or another.

And so ended my first practical joke with the screw-heads.

RE-ENACTING HISTORY—A SKETCH AT TARRYTOWN.

MAJOR ANDRÉ. "Look here, fellers, there ain't a-goin' to be no hanging, yer know."

JOHN PAULDING. "No hangin'! What er yer talkin' 'bout? D' yer s'pose we're a-goin' back on history and Gin'ral Washington? Get out! Course yer've got to be hung'd; and if yer don't like it, we'll get some feller as does. That's all there is to it."

Vol. I.—No. 51. | Published by HARPER & BROTHERS, New York. | Price Four Cents.

Tuesday, October 19, 1880. | Copyright, 1880, by Harper & Brothers. | $1.50 per Year, in Advance.

RABBITS TO FIND.

BY WILLIAM O. STODDARD.

"I SAY, Tad Murray, what's made you so late with your cows this morning?"

"Late! Well, I guess you'd be late if you'd had such a time as I did. It was all old Ben's fault."

"Ben's! Why, there he is now, chasing the brindled heifer. If she'd only turn on him, she could pitch him over the fence like a forkful of hay."

"He's a better cow-dog than that ragged little terrier of yours, Carr Hotchkiss; but he's an awful fellow to let into a corn field, 'specially 'bout this time of year."

"Into a corn field!"

"When there's a lot of rabbits in the shocks."

"Are there rabbits in your corn?"

"It's just alive with 'em. And Ben he gets after 'em, and the corn's all cut and shocked, and he'll tear a shock of corn to pieces in no time; and father says it's too bad, for he hasn't any time to kill rabbits."

"Tell you what, Tad, Whip's the best dog in the world for rabbits."

"Is he?"

"He wouldn't hurt a shock of corn if he scratched clean through it. I'll fetch him along soon's you get your cows in; and we'll get Dan Burrel and Eph McCormick and Frank Perry, and we'll have the biggest rabbit hunt you ever heard of."

"Don't I wish I had a gun!"

"Father's got one, but he won't let me put a finger on it."

IN THE CORN FIELD.

"So's my father got one. It's a splendid good gun, too, but one of the biggest in town, and there's a hole you could stick your finger into in the right barrel, where it got bursted once."

"We don't want any guns. You hurry your cows in. There! the brindled heifer's given Ben an awful dig."

"He won't care."

Old Ben did care, however, for he left the brindled heifer suddenly, and came back toward the boys, with his wise-looking head cocked on one side, as much as to say, "Didn't I hear you two saying something about rabbits?"

It was less than half an hour before they were telling him a good deal about that kind of game. They gathered the rest of their hunting party on their way back to Squire Murray's, only they did not waste any time going to the house. It was a shorter cut through the wheat stubble and the wood lot to the big corn field in the hollow.

Corn, corn, corn. Squire Murray said he had never before raised so good a crop in all his life. And then he had added that the rabbits and squirrels and woodchucks were likely to be his best market, for they were husking it for him, and not charging him a cent. Only they carried off all they husked without paying for it, and he was compelled to charge that part of his crop to "rabbit account."

The old squire loved a bit of fun as well as anybody, and it was a pity he could not have been in his own corn field that morning.

Tad Murray had to catch hold of old Ben the moment they were over the fence, for he half buried himself in the nearest shock of corn the first thing.

"Oh dear! if there was only one of 'em in sight, so he'd have something to run after!"

"Whip! Whip!" shouted Carr Hotchkiss. "Rabbits, Whip—rabbits!"

Whip had been dancing around the shock as if the ground under him were red-hot, and he couldn't keep his feet on any one spot for two seconds; but now he made a sudden dive into the gap from which Tad had pulled out old Ben.

"Find 'em, Whip—find 'em!"

"There's a rabbit in there somewhere," said Dan Burrel, in a loud, earnest whisper.

"Look out you don't scare him," whispered back Eph McCormick; and Frank Perry picked up a long stiff corn stalk, and began to poke it in at every crack he could find.

"Don't, Frank; you'll scare the rabbit."

"Scare him, Eph! Why, that's just what we're up to. If we don't scare him, he won't come out."

There was a loud whine from Whip at that moment, and a sound of very vigorous pawing and scratching away in out of sight.

"Do rabbits ever bite?" said Frank, excitedly.

"Rabbits? bite a dog?" said Carr, scornfully. "I'd back Whip all alone against all the rabbits Squire Murray's got."

Another whine from Whip, and more pawing and rustling in that mysterious place he had scratched into. Every boy of them wished he were in there with a double-barrelled gun or something.

"Tad," said Frank Perry, "maybe it isn't a rabbit. Maybe it's something big."

"Woodchucks?"

"Are there any 'coons around here nowadays?"

"Haven't seen any; but the rabbits are awful big ones, some of 'em."

Yelp, yelp, yelp, from the dog inside, and his voice had a smothered and anxious sound.

"He's got him!" exclaimed Tad. But he had better have kept his hold upon Ben for a moment longer. It had been pretty hard work the last minute or so, for Ben understood every sound Whip had been making. All it had meant really was: "Ben! boys! there's a rabbit here, and he keeps just about a foot ahead of me. He's three sizes smaller than I am, and he can get through the shock faster. One of you be on the look-out for him on that further side."

The instant Tad loosened his arms from around Ben's neck, the sagacious old fellow sprang forward—not at the hole where Whip went in, but straight across, where there was no hole at all, till he came to make one.

There was a big one there before any boy of them all knew what Ben was up to. How the corn stalks did fly as he pawed his way in and tore them aside with his great strong teeth! If he was not much of a hand at setting up a shock, he was a mouth and four paws at pulling one down.

"Ben! Ben!" shouted Tad. "Come here! Rabbits, Ben—rabbits! Come here, sir."

As if Ben needed anybody to say "rabbits" to him, after he had listened to all that anxious whimpering from Whip!

"Shake the shock a little," said Dan Burrel. "He's in there somewhere."

He suited the action to the word, but that was all that was needed, and down it came, flat on the ground, with a big dog and a small one and five excited boys tearing around among the ruins.

There was a rabbit there too when the shock fell over, but he came out of the confusion with a great leap, and would have made his escape entirely if it had not been for the long legs of old Ben.

There was no time given the rabbit to hunt for another hiding-place, for before the boys and Whip had quite made up their minds what had become of their game, Ben was shaking him by the back of the neck half way down the field.

"I say, boys," said Tad, "we must set this shock up again. There comes Josephus, and if we leave such a mess as this is behind us, he won't let us go after another rabbit."

Josephus was Tad's elder brother, and he had been sent down there by his mother to get a pumpkin for some pies. There were plenty of them, that had been planted among the corn, and it was easy enough to pick out a good one and go back to the house; but Joe saw what the boys were about, and he stood for a moment looking at them.

"Set it up carefully," whispered Eph McCormick; "Joe's watching us."

"We've got one rabbit, anyhow."

"I say, what's become of Whip?"

"Never mind, boys. Hurry this thing together again."

So they did, and they were so intent on repairing the mischief they had done that they did not see what Josephus and the two dogs were doing meantime.

"I've got him!"

They were all standing back and looking at their work to see if it was just as good as it had been before it tumbled, when they heard Joe shouting that to them from the other side of the field.

"I've got him! I wouldn't give much for a lot of boys that can't catch rabbits without tearing the corn to pieces. Send in the little dog every time, and wait till the rabbit comes out. The big dog's bound to catch him if you give him a fair chance."

"That's what we'll do," said Tad. "Joe's picking up his pumpkin. He's all right."

No doubt he was, but he would much rather have staid with them in the corn field than have carried that great yellow ball half a mile to the house.

There was plenty of fun after that, for both dogs and boys had learned that there was a right way to work at that kind of hunting. Before noon they had thirteen fine large rabbits hanging on the fence, and nobody could have told by the look of any shock in the field that either a dog or a boy had been through it.

"Boys," said Squire Murray, when he met them coming through the barn-yard gate, "which of you caught the most rabbits?"

"Which of us caught the most?"

"Yes, that's what I'd like to know. Which of you is the one I want to hire to catch my rabbits for me?"

The boys looked at one another for a moment, and then Tad slowly remarked, "Well, father, I guess it's Ben. He got the first bite at every one of 'em."

[Begun in No. 49 of Harper's Young People, September 14.]

WHO WAS PAUL GRAYSON?

BY JOHN HABBERTON,

Author of "Helen's Babies."

Chapter VI.

THE BEANTASSEL BENEFIT.

OF the many boys who were curious about Paul Grayson's antecedents, no one devoted more attention to the subject than Benny Mallow. Benny was short, and Paul was tall; Benny was fat, and Paul was thin; Benny's hair was light, while Paul's was black as jet; Benny had light blue eyes, while those of Paul were of a rich brown; Benny always had something to say about himself, while Paul never seemed to think his affairs of the slightest interest to any one but himself: so, taking all things into account, it is not wonderful that Benny Mallow spent whole half-hours in contemplating his friend with admiration and wonder.

Still more, as Benny had been accepted by every one as Paul's particular friend, he actually was besieged with all sorts of questions, and to answer these without letting himself down in the estimation of the school was no easy matter, when he did not know any more about Paul than any one else did. One question, however, he settled to the entire satisfaction of every one but Napoleon Nott—Grayson was not an exiled prince. Benny was sure of this, because he had asked Paul if he had ever been on the other side of the ocean, and Paul had answered that he had not. Notty endeavored to make light of this evidence by showing how easy it would have been to spirit the mysterious person away from his royal home and to America while he was a baby, and therefore too young to know anything about it, but Will Palmer told Notty that it was about time to stop making a fool of himself, and the other boys present said they thought so too, at which Notty became so angry that he vowed, in the presence of at least a dozen boys, that when the truth came out, and all the boys wanted to borrow his copy of *The Exiled Prince: a Tale of Woe*, he would not lend it to them, even if it were to save them from death; he would not even let them look at the cover, with its picture of the prince and the name of the publisher.

Meanwhile Mr. Morton had continued his visits to the prisoners and to the poor of the town, and out of school hours he had so interested the boys in some of the suffering families of worthless men or widowed women, that it was agreed by the whole school that the teasing of any of the boys of these families about the holes in their trousers, or provoking fights with or between them, should entirely stop; indeed, as this suggestion came from Bert Sharp, who was fonder of fighting than any other boy in the town, the school could not well do otherwise.

The boys went even farther: when one day old Peter Beantassel, whose family was always on the verge of starvation, spent on drink the accidental earnings of a week, and then fell into an abandoned well and was drowned, it was decided by the school to give an exhibition for the benefit of Mrs. Beantassel and her six children. Mr. Morton was delighted, and promised to secure a church or hall without expense to the boys, and to collect enough money from the public to pay for printing the tickets. The boys at once began work in tremendous earnest; they were for a fortnight so busy at determining upon a programme, and studying, rehearsing, selling tickets, and exacting promises from people who would not purchase in advance, that there was but little playing before school and during recess, blackberry hedges were neglected, and the trout in the single brook near the town had not the slightest excuse for apprehension.

Paul Grayson entered into the spirit of the occasion as thoroughly as any one else; he volunteered to recite Longfellow's "Psalm of Life," and when the farce of *Box and Cox* was about to be given up because no boy was willing to dress up in women's clothes, and be laughed at by all the larger girls, for playing the part of Mrs. Bouncer, Paul volunteered for that unpopular character, and saved the play. But this was not all. There were to be some tableaux, and as Mr. Morton had been asked to suggest some scenes, particularly one or two with Indians in them, and was as fond of pointing a moral as teachers usually are, one of his tableaux, to be called "Civilization," was a scene in the interior of an Indian's wigwam. The squaw, who had just been killed, was lying dead on the floor; her husband, with his hands tied, stood bleeding between two soldiers, while between father and mother stood the half-grown son, wondering what it all was about. As all of the boys wanted to see this tragic picture, all of them declined to take part in it; Joe Appleby had been heard to remark with a sneer that only very small and green boys cared to look at Indians, so he was asked to take the part of the wretched son himself; but he said that when any one saw him making a fool of himself by browning his face and dressing up in rags, he hoped some one would tell him about it: so Grayson, as the only other tall boy who had dark hair that was not cut short, was cast for this part also, and offered no objection. As for the bleeding chieftain, Napoleon Nott fought hard to pose in that character, and was quieted only by being allowed to play the dead squaw, which all the boys told him he ought easily to see was the more romantic part, besides being one in which he could by no chance make any mistake.

The place selected for the entertainment was the lecture-room of the Presbyterian church, and the boys had therefore to give up their darling project of devoting half an hour of the evening to amateur negro minstrelsy, for one of the deacons said that while he sometimes doubted that even an organ was a proper musical instrument for use in sacred buildings, he certainly was not going to tolerate banjos and bones. This decision was a great disappointment to Benny Mallow, who had been selected by the managers to perform upon the tambourine, but in the revision of the programme Benny was assigned to duty in a tableau as a little fat goblin, and this so tickled his fancy that he did not suffer long by the disappointment.

At last the eventful night arrived. Some of the boys did not leave the lecture-room at all after the last rehearsal, not even to get their suppers, for fear they should be late, and those who reached the room barely in time to take their parts had all they could do to squeeze through the crowd that blocked the doors and filled the aisles. The spectacle of so crowded a house raised the boys to a high pitch of excitement, which was increased by various peeps from the curtains that served as dressing-rooms at the Beantassel children, who by some thoughtful soul had been provided with free seats in the extreme front bench; there they were, all but the baby; they had been provided with clothing which, though old, was far more sightly than the rags they usually wore, and although they did not seem as much at ease as some others among the spectators, their eyes stood so very open, then and throughout the evening, that even Joe Appleby, who had reluctantly consented to pose, in his best clothes, with gloves, cane, and high hat, as Young America in a tableau of "The Nations," agreed with himself that the exhibition was rather a meritorious idea after all, and that even if the boys did as badly as he knew they would, he was glad it was sure to pay.

But the boys did not do badly: on the contrary, the general performance would have been quite creditable to adults. The opening was somewhat dismal; it was announced to consist of a duet for two flutes by Will Palmer and Ned Johnston. The boys had practiced industriously at several airs in order to discover which would be best, and at last they supposed they had fully agreed; but when

PAUL AS A CHIEF'S SON.

seated Ned began the "Miserere" from *Trovatore*, while Will started "The Old Folks at Home," and each was sure the other was wrong, and would correct himself, which the other in both cases failed to do, and finally both boys retired abruptly, amid considerable laughter, and fought the matter out in the dressing-room.

Paul Grayson soon restored order, however, by his rendering of the "Psalm of Life." He had a fine voice, and he spoke the lines as if he meant them; so gloriously did his voice ring that even the boys in the dressing-room kept silence and listened, though they had heard the same verses a hundred times before.

Most of the performances that followed went very smoothly, although Benny Mallow, who played the Hatter's part in *Box and Cox*, caused some confusion by laughing frequently and unexpectedly, because Paul's disguise as Mrs. Bouncer affected him powerfully in spite of the efforts made by Sam Wardwell, as the Printer, to restrain him. The tableaux pleased the audience greatly; even that of "Prometheus," with Ned Johnston as the sufferer, and Mrs. Battle's big red rooster as the vulture, brought down the house.

But the great tableau of the evening was the teacher's "Civilization." When Paul Grayson had understood fully what the scene was to be, he refused so earnestly to have anything to do with it that the boys were startled. They did not excuse him from taking the part of the young Indian, however; they pleaded so steadily that at last Paul consented, but in worse temper than any one had ever seen him before. No one could complain of the manner in which he acted on the stage, however. When the curtain was drawn he was seen standing beside his dead mother, and shaking a fist at the soldiers; in color, dress, pose, and spirit he seemed to be a real Indian, if the audience was a competent judge; then, when the applause justified a recall, as it soon did, the drawn curtain disclosed Paul clinging to the wounded brave as if nothing should ever tear him away.

Napoleon Nott saw all this, although, as the Indian boy's mother, he was supposed to be dead beyond recall. Suddenly he felt himself to be inspired, and when the curtain was down he flew into the dressing-room and exclaimed, "I've got it!"

"Be careful not to hurt it," said Canning Forbes, sarcastically.

"I've got it!" declared Notty, without noticing Canning's cruel speech. "Grayson is an Indian, a chief's son. You don't suppose he could have made believe so well as all that, do you? That's it. I knew he was a great person of some sort. Sh—h! he's coming."

Somehow the boys who had been able to peep out at the tableau did not laugh at Notty this time. Paul, in his Indian dress, had greatly impressed them all before he left the dressing-room, and certainly his acting had been unlike anything the boys had seen other boys do. The subject was talked over in whispers, so that Paul should not hear, during the remainder of the evening, with the result that that very night at least six boys told other boys or their own parents, in the strictest confidence, of course, that there was more truth than make-believe about Paul Grayson as an Indian. And the parents told the same story to other parents, the boys told it to other boys, and within twenty-four hours Paul Grayson was a far more interesting mystery than before.

[TO BE CONTINUED.]

THE PARASOL ANTS AND THE FORAGING ANTS.

BY CHARLES MORRIS.

WAS there ever such a prattler as the warm-hearted little brook that ran by the foot of the garden of Woodbine Cottage? To be sure, it had good reason to be jolly, for the sunlight buried itself in its bubbles till they sparkled like diamonds; and a hedge of roses overhung it, and dropped crimson leaves that floated away like fairy boats on its bright surface; and broad-winged butterflies floated, like tiny ships of the air, above the happy stream. And away it ran, prattling and chattering, and picking its way through moss-covered stones that lifted above its surface, and tumbling hastily down in little cascades, as though it were in a desperate hurry to get on in the world, and also gether misbehaving itself just as any madcap little stream might when out on a frolic.

Its bank beyond the garden was bordered with the white and gold of daisies and buttercups, and the red and green of blossoming clover, in which Harry Mason was almost buried, only his bright cheeks and curly hair showing out of this verdant nest. As for Uncle Ben, he was gravely seated on the bank of the brook, holding his little friend Willie on his knee. The little chap was quite as grave as his big uncle.

"You neber tole us one word yet 'bout them soldiers an' cows an' tings, 'mong the ants, Uncle Ben," he earnestly remarked, "an' you knows you said you was goin' to tell us all an' all an' all about 'em. An' I don't think it's fair."

"Why, I certainly must have done so," replied Uncle Ben, with affected surprise. "You have surely forgotten. I shall have to leave this affair for Harry to settle."

"Then Willie is right," returned Harry, from his grassy nest. "You told us everything else about them, but you never said one thing about the cows or the soldiers."

"Everything else about them!" exclaimed Uncle Ben, with a sly smile. "Why, I know I did not say a word about the parasol ants, or the foraging ants, or the—"

"The parasol ants!" cried Willie, quite forgetting the cows and the soldiers in his surprise. "You doesn't mean, Uncle Ben, that they carries parasols—jes like mamma, now?"

Harry, too, had lifted himself upon his elbow, the light of curiosity gleaming in his eyes.

"They are the most comical things in the world," replied their uncle. "Just imagine now a great line of ants, marching along like a school of young ladies out on a holiday, each of them holding a piece of green leaf over its head like a parasol. It is not strange that people fancied that this was done to keep the sun off, and called them parasol ants."

"What do they do it for, then?" asked Harry, eagerly.

"Maybe them's the soldiers," suggested Willie; "maybe it's ant guns they's carryin'."

"We have not got to the soldiers yet," said his uncle, smiling. "These leaves are really used in building their nests. But the whole thing is very curious. The ants climb up the bushes, and run out on the leaves. There they cut, with their sharp jaws, a little round piece from the leaf. Then they pick this up, getting a tight hold on it, you may be sure, and away they scamper for the nest. But these ants are not the nest-builders; they are only like the laborers who carry bricks to the bricklayers. They drop their leaves beside the nest, and run back for more, leaving the real builders to finish the work."

"Regular little hod-carriers," suggested Harry. "But they don't build a nest of little bits of leaf, I hope?"

"Not exactly. The leaves are mingled through the earth to sustain the great domes which they erect. The houses which these tropical ants build are wonderfully different from the little ant-hills we see about here. They are not very high, it is true. The dome rises about two feet above the ground. But then it is more than forty

"HAPPY AS THE DAY IS LONG."—FROM AN ETCHING BY W. S. [illegible]

feet across. One of them would reach nearly across our garden, like a great white swelling upon the face of the earth. They certainly need something to hold together the wet clay of their great domes."

"But our ants here live 'way down, 'way under-ground," remarked Willie.

"So do these," replied Uncle Ben. "The dome is only the roof of their house. They are famous diggers—I assure you of that. Talk about our miners, with their tunnels running deep into the mountains: why, their work is nothing in comparison with that of these little creatures. They make wonderful under-ground tunnels, which run out from the nest in all directions, and to incredible distances. No one sees these tunnels, however, unless they may happen to come to the surface in a very disastrous manner, as they sometimes do."

"How do you mean?" asked Harry, curiously. He had now crept out of his lair, and was seated quietly beside his uncle, with his feet hanging just above the stream.

"Why, in one case, in South America, they tunnelled through the bank of a reservoir. The first thing the people knew, the water was rushing out in a torrent. It was never discovered what was the trouble until the reservoir was quite empty, when they found that the parasol ants had caused the mischief."

"Well, I do declare!" cried Willie, laughing so heartily that he nearly tumbled off Uncle Ben's knee. "Wasn't that jes ever so cunning?"

"Why, you don't think they did it just a-purpose, for nothing but mischief, I hope?" asked Harry, with some indignation.

"I s'pose so," replied Willie, laughing to that extent that he dropped his hat into the stream. And then there was a lively scramble until it was rescued again from the merry waters, which were running away with it as fast as they could.

"You're such a comical little fellow," said Harry, as he shook the water from the dripping hat, and pressed it tightly down on Willie's head. "Anybody that can't laugh without shaking his hat overboard!"

"But that was so funny 'bout the ants lettin' the water all run away: don' know how I's to help laughin'," retorted Willie.

"There is another story told," continued Uncle Ben, "about a nest of parasol ants that dug a tunnel into a gold mine. The under-ground streams got turned into this tunnel, and the waters poured in until they flooded the mine. It cost thousands of dollars to pump the water out, and get the mine ready for working again. And the owners had first to send for a professional ant-killer, and destroy the ant nest, before it was safe to go on."

"A professional ant-killer!" repeated Harry, opening his eyes wide in surprise.

"Yes: there are persons who make a regular business of destroying these troublesome ants."

"Guess that can't be much trouble," said Willie, disdainfully. "Jes got to put your foot on 'em, an' smash 'em."

"I hardly think your foot would cover forty square feet of ground," remarked his uncle, lifting up the diminutive foot, and very gravely examining it. "And then there are the tunnels, running eighty or a hundred feet away in all directions. I am afraid this foot would not be quite large enough."

"I don't care," cried Willie, jerking his foot away. "I was thinkin' 'bout ants like what we have here."

"But how do they kill them, then?" asked Harry, looking up inquiringly into his uncle's face.

"They build a sort of oven over the doorway of the nest," was the reply. "In this they make a fire of charcoal and pungent herbs, and some negroes are stationed with bellows, driving the smoke and fumes from the fire down into the nest. When smoke is seen rising from the ground anywhere, they know that a tunnel opens in that spot, and they stop it up with clay. But it is no light task to kill out a nest of ants. The negroes are kept constantly at work with their bellows for four days and nights, driving down the smothering fumes. At the end of that time the oven is taken away and the nest opened, every tunnel being laid bare. If any ants are found to be alive, they are instantly killed, and all the openings are stopped up with clay, which is stamped down hard, until the whole nest is filled with it."

"Who would ever have thought that a nest of ants would be so hard to kill!" remarked Harry, reflectively.

"All that trouble jes to kill some ole ants," said Willie, getting down and walking away disdainfully. "Guess big men with their big boots could smash 'em easier 'an that if they wanted ta."

"Are there other ants that make such tunnels?" asked Harry.

"Oh yes: some of the ants are wonderful diggers. There is a Texan species which on one occasion was found to have run a tunnel under a creek, fifteen or twenty feet deep and thirty feet wide, for the purpose of getting at the vegetables and fruits in a gentleman's garden on the other side of the creek."

"I think *they* should have been smoked out anyhow," said Harry.

"Guess I'd pulled eberyting 'fore the ants got over," suggested Willie.

"And what were those foraging ants you spoke of, Uncle Ben?"

"Jes neber mine them," exclaimed Willie. "You knows you was goin' to tell all 'bout the cows, an' you ain't eber goin' to tell one word. I b'lieves you's jes funnin' with us, Uncle Ben. I jes b'lieves that, now."

"Oh! you want to hear about the cows?" said his uncle, with a look of grave surprise. "Why, of course. The ant cows, you know, are everywhere. There is no trouble to find them."

A stray branch of a grape-vine had grown over the hedge, and stretched itself across the brook. Uncle Ben bent it down and examined it for a minute.

"Why, here they are now!" he exclaimed, pointing to some very small insects on one of the leaves, about which several ants were busying themselves. "These are the ant cows. And here are their keepers looking after them."

"Them little tings cows!" said Willie, with a look of utter disdain.

"You didn't expect to find them as big as our cows, I hope?" asked Harry.

"Their real name is aphis, or plant-louse," said Uncle Ben. "They suck the juices of the leaves. These juices become in their bodies a sort of honey, which they yield from certain pores. The ants are very fond of this honey-dew, and lap it up eagerly. And if you watch close you may see them patting or stroking the aphides to make them yield the honey faster. That is what has been called milking their cows."

"Well, that is very curious, I know," exclaimed Harry. "I am going to watch them after this."

"Each ant seems to claim certain cows as his own property," continued Uncle Ben. "And he will bristle up angrily if any other ant strays into his pasture fields. But that is not the whole story. They not only milk these cows, but they tenderly raise their calves. Some species of the aphis live on the roots of plants. Around these the ants make their nests, so as to have their cows in stables of their own. And they take the greatest care of the eggs and the young of the aphides, raising them as tenderly as they raise their own young. No human farmer could be more careful of his own stock of cows and calves."

"You 'mos' might as well say they's folks right out."

ejaculated Willie, indignantly. "Anyhow, it's ole honey, an' it ain't milk at all."

"I am sure it is not the fault of the ants if their cows give honey instead of milk," replied his uncle, with an odd smile. "And I have certainly seen folks who were not as wise as the ants."

"But never mind the cows, Uncle Ben," persisted Harry. "I want to hear about the foraging ants. Where do they belong, and what queer things do they do?"

"They are a South American ant," was the reply. "They may be seen at certain seasons marching along the ground in a long column, much like an army. They have officers, too. There are large-headed ants that march outside the column, and keep it in order. It is an immense army they command, I can assure you—greater than that with which Xerxes in old times invaded Greece; for there may be millions of ants in the line. There is another species which does not march in column, but in a close mass, often covering from six to ten square yards of ground."

"But what are they after?" asked Harry.

"That's jes what I wants to know," observed Willie, whose curiosity had returned.

"They are after food," replied their uncle. "It is amusing to see the insects scampering off from their line of march. They seem to know the danger that threatens them, for scarcely a living thing escapes the sharp jaws of these fierce foragers. They send out side columns to search the ground and the bushes and low trees. When any insect is found, it is instantly surrounded and covered by these marauders, and torn to pieces, and carried off in fragments. But it is not in the trees and on the ground that they find their chief prey."

"Where, then?" asked Harry, his great blue eyes fixed with speaking interest on his uncle's countenance.

"In the houses. The foraging ants are a perfect blessing to the people of the villages, not a pest, as ants are in our houses. These warm regions, you know, have multitudes of insects that we never see. The houses are infested not only with rats and mice, roaches and fleas, but with snakes and scorpions, with huge spiders and with many other unpleasant things; so the village folks are glad enough to see the approach of the foraging ants. They throw open every door in their houses, unlock their drawers and trunks, and pull the clothes out on the floor. They then vacate the houses, and leave them to the ants, who soon stream in. Those who have seen them say that it is a wonderful spectacle. Nothing living escapes them. They search every hole, nook, and cranny. Here, dozens may be seen surrounding a great spider or scorpion; there, they chase sprawling long-legged creatures across the window-panes; yonder, hundreds of them may be observed dragging out a rat or a mouse which they have killed: even snakes can not escape from the sharp and poisonous bite of these bold foragers. It takes from three to four hours for them to clear out a house. They will not leave it until they are sure that not a living thing remains. Then they stream out again, carrying their prey with them; and the inhabitants gladly return, satisfied that they will have a month or two of comfort after this ants' house-cleaning."

"I do b'lieve you's half funnin' again, Uncle Ben," declared Willie, with an aspect of severe doubt. "How's little tings like ants goin' to pull out snakes an' rats? I'd jes like to know that!"

"But I forgot to tell you that these ants are much larger than any we have here. Some of the tropical ants are an inch long, and as large as a large wasp; so you may imagine that a whole army of them is not to be trifled with."

"Is it them that's the soldiers, Uncle Ben?" asked Willie.

"The soldiers! Oh, you want to hear about the soldiers!—But, I declare, if there isn't the dinner-bell! Who would have thought that we had spent so much time over the ants!"

THE PLUMES OF CRÉCY.*

BY LILLIE E. BARR.

I was reading of kings and nobles,
  Tourney and knightly gage,
Till the summer twilight faded
  From Froissart's ancient page.
Then in the darkened parlor
  I saw a fairer sight—
The brave old King whose valor makes
  The shame of Crécy light.

He stood on the little hill-side,
  Taller than all his peers,
Quite blind, but with eyes uplifted,
  Hoary with many years.
Still wearing his golden armor,
  Crowned with his royal crown,
Leaning upon the sword with which
  He struck the Soldan down.

And high in his gleaming helmet
  Three ostrich plumes, snow white—
From the Paynim's brow he tore them
  In some Jabloma fight.
All scarred with Carpathian arrows,
  His heart with Honor flames;
"Advance!" he cries, "and fight for France,
  Bohemia, and St. James!"

But two of his knights staid by him,
  And little did they say;
The blind old King talked with his heart,
  And that was in the fray.
Alas! alas! He heard too soon
  The sounds of shameful flight;
"Thank God," he sighed, "Bohemia's blind!"—
  He would not see this sight.

"Now, friends, one more good deed I claim,
  Last service for your lord:
I ask a soldier's grave, good knights;
  I'll dig it with my sword.
My horse's reins tie fast to yours—
  A friend on either hand—
Then ride straight on to where you see
  The English archers stand."

They kissed their King most tenderly,
  Then three as one they went
Down to the field of certain death
  With proud and glad content.
They cut a path to where Prince Charles,
  The King's son, stood at bay;
'Twas spirits, and not flesh and blood,
  For honor fought that day.

The three white plumes above the gloom
  Gleamed like a snowy wing;
Victors and vanquished paused to watch
  The blind Bohemian King.
Pierced oft by arrows, stained with blood,
  The Soldan's plumes still wave,
Until Bohemia's sword had cut
  Honor's unsullied grave.

Next day, when English heralds sought
  Over the fatal field
Trampled lilies and flags of France,
  They found upon his shield
The blind old King of Bohemia,
  Son and friends by his side:
But torn and stained the snowy plumes
  That long had been his pride.

Then said the Black Prince over him,
  "O knight, the bravest, best,
Thy plumes are dyed in hero's blood—
  Henceforth they are my crest!"
And still they wave o'er England's crown,
  And teach the young and brave,
When all is lost but honor, then
  Valor digs Honor's grave.

---

* *Froissart's Chronicle*, vol. I., p. 161.

JANUARY.

FEBRUARY.

MARCH.

APRIL.

JULY.

AUGUST.

SEPTEMBER.

OCTOBER.

SUMAC HUNTING.

BY J. ESTEN COOKE.

ANYBODY visiting the valley of Virginia in the autumn will be sure to notice, after sunset, all along the slopes of the Blue Ridge Mountains, little glimmering lights like stars. These are the fires in front of the small tents of the sumac hunters, who, after gathering sumac all day long, are laughing and talking with their wives and children as they eat their suppers before lying down to sleep.

Sumac is a very pretty plant or shrub which grows a few feet high only, and has beautiful blood-red leaves springing from a delicate shoot, or bough. The stalk is smooth, and the leaves are almond-shaped, only more pointed. On the top of the plant and its larger boughs grow bunches of red berries in the shape of grape bunches; and the leaves and berries are of such a deep, rich crimson in the late autumn that they sometimes make the slopes of the hills appear as if they were on fire. If any little girl would like to dress the vases on the parlor mantelpiece prettily, she could not do better than collect a handful of these delicate tendrils with their scarlet leaves, and use them as a background to the lovely little autumn flowers—late primroses, stars-of-Bethlehem, wild honeysuckles, and fringed ferns—which grow in the woods and fields at this time of the year.

But the honest country people who take so much pains about collecting sumac are not thinking about dressing vases with it. They gather it to sell, and are paid from one cent to a cent and a half a pound for it at the sumac mills. This may not seem much, but then the ocean is made up of drops, and with poor people a little money goes a long way. As little children can pull sumac just as well as grown people, a whole family may gather in a day several dollars' worth.

It is used for dyeing, and is said to be better for that purpose than anything else to color fair leather and certain other fabrics. Great quantities of it are employed in printing calicoes in rich patterns, and the dresses worn by ladies and girls often owe their bright colors to the leaves of the sumac. The way in which it is collected and prepared for use is very simple. As soon as the leaves turn red, which is toward the end of summer, the sumac hunters begin their work. They scatter through the fields, or along the sides of the mountain, and break off the twigs on which the leaves are growing; for these twigs do not make the leaves less valuable. Then, when they have collected an armful, they put it in a pile or into bags, and as night comes on the whole is taken to one spot, from which it is hauled home in wagons. Here it is laid on the floor of the barn or any out-house, in the shade, so that it may dry very gradually, and keep the juices which afford the coloring matter. When this process of drying is gone through with, and the leaves are in a proper state, it is loaded on carts or wagons, in bags, and taken to the sumac mills, where it is weighed, and paid for by the owner of the mills at the rate, as I have said, of from one cent to a cent and a half a pound. The largest mills in Virginia, where the finest sumac grows—or at least a very fine article—are at Richmond; but at Winchester, in the lower part of the Shenandoah Valley, toward the Potomac, there is a big mill, where great quantities are purchased, and prepared for the use of the dyers. The leaves and small twigs are pounded and reduced to a fine dust, and then it is ready to be sent away. When it reaches the manufactories where it is to be used as a dye for leather, calico, etc., it is mixed with what are called *mordants*, certain substances that make it *bite in*, as the word means, and take fast hold of the material to be dyed; and then there is the pretty calico with its bright colors, which can not be washed out.

It is only of late years that much attention has been paid to it in Virginia. People thought more about raising corn and wheat than of gathering sumac; but in twenty years they have learned a great deal, and now begin to understand that "every little helps," and that if they can go with their wives and children and pull sumac, and then sell it, they can take their money and buy sugar and coffee, and perhaps some of the very calico for their little girls' dresses which the red leaves of the sumac make so pretty.

The children like the "camping out" on the mountain in the pleasant summer and fall nights very much. It is a sort of frolic, and it is a very good thing to mix up pleasure with work; it makes the work much easier. The tents are very simple little affairs—only a breadth of canvas stretched across a ridge-pole, like the "comb" of a house, held up by forked sticks set in the ground. In this are spread what in Virginia are called "pine tags," that is, the tassels, or needles, of the pine-trees, which are dry and brown, and by spreading a blanket or old comforter on these you have an excellent soft bed. In front of the tent a fire is built to cook by, and by means of forked sticks a pot can be hung above the fire for making soup, boiling meat, etc. By this fire, as I have told you, the sumac hunters gather in the evening, after work, and laugh and talk and sing, and eat their suppers; or perhaps some one of them can play the fiddle, and he strikes up a dancing tune, and the girls and boys dance on the grass, and laugh and enjoy themselves much more than if they were in fine drawing-rooms. After a while the long day's work makes them sleepy, and they lie down on the fresh pine tags in the tent, and go to sleep—to be up at daylight, and once more at work hunting and gathering their sumac.

OLD TIMES IN THE COLONIES.

BY CHARLES CARLETON COFFIN.

No. VIII.

THE BATTLE OF THE RANGERS.

WHEN war broke out between France and England in 1755, the French and Indians came down from Canada and attacked the settlers of New England and New York, as they had done in previous wars, burning their dwellings, killing men and women, or carrying them to Canada as prisoners.

The French had a fort at Crown Point, on Lake Champlain, and another at Ticonderoga; while the English had Fort William Henry, at the southern end of Lake George, and Fort Edward, on the Hudson.

The English officers who had been sent over by the King to command the "Provincials," as the people of England called all who lived in America, thought that soldiers must march in the wilderness with just as much precision as along a hard beaten road, that they must move in platoons and columns, keeping step to the drum-beat. The French officers, on the other hand, adopted the plan of the Indians, marching in single file, each man carrying his provisions. They made quick movements, falling suddenly upon a settlement, with their Indian allies, making all the havoc possible, and before the settlers could gather to resist them, would be far on their way to Crown Point or Canada.

Robert Rogers, of New Hampshire, who was fighting the French, prevailed upon Lord Loudon, the English commander-in-chief, to allow him to form a battalion of troops, who should have the privilege of scouting the woods around Lake George and Lake Champlain, to discover the movements of the French and Indians, to fall upon them just as they were stealing upon the English, strike a blow, and be gone before the French would know what had happened. He would play their own game upon them.

Lord Loudon having given his consent, Major Rogers

and enlisted his men. They were rtic. They had tramped over the that province, hunting bears, and g the streams for beavers. They

Rangers down in the valley fire a volley at the French; holding their ground till all the wounded can make their way back to Stark's position.

Rogers wipes the blood from his face, and issues his

CUTTING OFF A QUEUE TO BIND A WOUND.

The snow had ceased, the air was chill. They must have help. John Stark, leaving them, started for Fort William Henry, reaching it at sunset. Soldiers with horses and sleds started at once, and John Stark with them, stopping not a moment to rest his weary limbs. At sunrise he was back to the Rangers with the re-enforcements and supplies. The French had not followed them, and they made their way safely back to Fort William Henry, having fought one of the most obstinate, unequal, yet victorious battles recorded in history.

THE ANGEL IN THE LILLY FAMILY.

BY SHERWOOD BONNER.

THERE was something rather queer about the Lilly family. In the first place there were so many of them—fourteen precious children. This alone is queer, when it is the fashion of the day to have small families, and "well-springs of pleasure" are as scarce as diamonds in any properly regulated household. But Mrs. Lilly's heart was made on the omnibus plan; and there was no miserable little "Complet" ever scrawled over its door.

Then it was queer how they avoided nicknames in the Lilly family. Each child was called by its full name, which sometimes happened to be a pretty long one.

It was through a sad accident that one of the Lilly children turned into a regular little angel.

The day after Christmas Mrs. Lilly's aunt—grandaunt of the children—carelessly allowed poor Katharine Kirk Lilly to fall on a marble floor. A serious injury to her spine was the result.

Dear! dear! how Mrs. Lilly screamed! She threw herself on the bed, and poured forth tears enough to put out a Christmas bonfire. She was not soothed until the doctor came, and after a careful examination—which the sufferer bore without a word or moan—pronounced that poor Katharine Kirk would live. But, alas! he added that she must always be an invalid. And smiling with the patient sweetness that distinguished her, the dear child sank back on the pillows from which she was never to lift her golden head. All the rest of the Lilly children stood round, showing by a sort of paralyzed expression on their faces how deeply they were moved; but none of them cried.

"Perhaps, dears," said the poor little mother, sobbing, "this affliction will be blessed to you."

"It will," cried the penitent great-aunt, clasping Mrs. Lilly in her arms; "it will teach them lessons of patience, of self-denial, of love, that will be as good as—"

"As the Prince's pricking-conscience ring in the family," suggested Mrs. Lilly's mother, who had a way of turning things into fun, and never gave way to her feelings.

It was surprising what a change from that time dated in the Lilly family. They had been like other children, a little faulty, perhaps, rather apt to stand on their rights—a fierce footing—but merely to look at the darling invalid, her shining hair outspread, her blue eyes ever bright, was to receive a lesson in sweetness and good temper.

Take the case of Phillips Arthur Cliff Lilly. This young gentleman was the youngest of the family, and his mother's favorite. Why, no one knew, except that he was so ugly. He had so many scars on his face, from falls and fights, that somehow he produced the impression of a target. His hair stood out like a halo of straw, and one defiant wisp reared itself above his forehead with the grace of a cat's whisker. Mrs. Lilly could never sleep until he was safe in her arms, and his life knew no cross until after the accident to Katharine Kirk, who became, in her turn, the pivot round which the family revolved. Horrible to relate, his mother one evening, in her hurry to get back to the invalid, forgot her youngest, and left him in the Common. There he lay all night, like a tramp, with the stars twinkling at him, and stray dogs sniffing as they passed him by. Yet when he was found he *did not utter one word*. He opened his blue eyes as he was picked up, and only gave a single plaintive cry as he was pressed to his frantic mother's bosom.

Then there was Myra Miles. She was one of the young ladies of the family, and, as might be forgiven in a beauty, a trifle vain. She was to receive calls on New-Year's Day, and had expected to come out in a fine new dress. Pink tarlatan it was to be, trimmed in the French taste with blue, with a train to thrill you to your finger-tips, which seemed to bear the same relation to Myra Miles as the rest of a snake does to its head. Mrs. Lilly's mamma was making it; but her time was suddenly demanded to do something for the invalid, and the dress was thrown

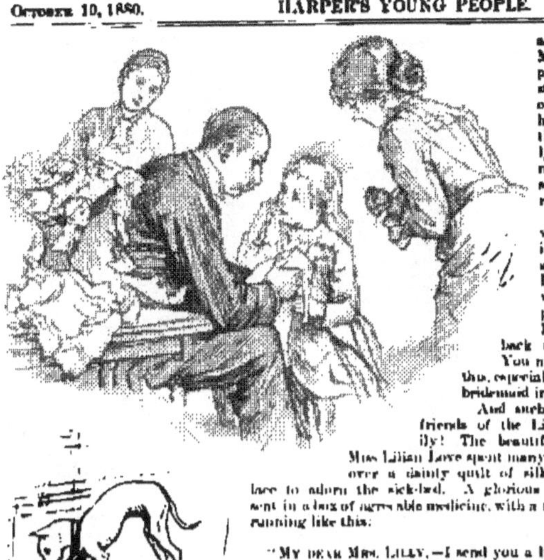

aside. The consequence was that poor Myra Miles appeared in the gorgeous pink dress with a black lace scarf instead of the waist. Still, not one word of complaint did she utter, although her sisters Dorothy Dimple and Martha Bunn—the favorites of Mrs. Lilly's aunt—appeared in exquisite raiment of green and blue. There was something very beautiful about her resignation.

When the lovely Susan Mears Lilly was married, Katharine Kirk was taken in her pretty bed to view the ceremony, and was quite a feature of the occasion. Indeed, she did not begin to look so weak and ill as the bridegroom, who, poor youth, was so tottering that Mrs. Lilly's aunt cruelly suggested that his back should be propped with a hair-pin. You may imagine how the girls laughed at this, especially Teresa Fehmer Lilly, a wicked little bridesmaid in red satin.

And such attentions as the sufferer had from friends of the Lilly family! The beautiful belle Miss Lilian Love spent many hours over a dainty quilt of silk and lace to adorn the sick-bed. A glorious poet sent in a box of agreeable medicine, with a note running like this:

"MY DEAR MRS. LILLY,—I send you a little book for your sick child, and some medicine for her poor broken back. The peculiarity of this medicine is that in order to produce any good effect it must be taken by the nurse. This is rather hard upon the nurse; but if she is a good nurse she will not mind it much."

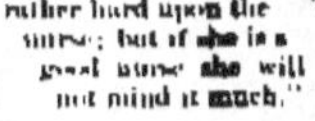

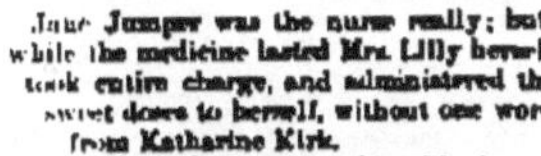

Jane Jumper was the nurse really; but while the medicine lasted Mrs. Lilly herself took entire charge, and administered the sweet doses to herself, without one word from Katharine Kirk.

It may have occurred by this time to some shrewd little reader that under no circumstance was any member of this household apt to give utterance to silver speech. Shall I confess? Or, my dear children, have you guessed that Katharine Kirk and all the cherished fourteen belonged to the beloved, the beautiful, the dumb, family of—Dolls!

Yes, it is too bad to take so many birds' eggs. But if our correspondents are careful to take only one or two from each nest, and to always leave more than half, as we have already begged them to do, the mother-bird will not suffer. If we could believe for a moment that our little friends would be so cruel as to disturb the brooding mother, and rob her nest of all its eggs, we would never publish another letter requesting an exchange of these pretty natural curiosities. The nesting season is now over in all the Northern States, but when it returns, we trust the young egg collectors will never allow their eagerness to secure the coveted treasure to overcome their sense of honor and their kindness of heart.

It is a good plan to fasten the feathers to the arrow with pins until the glue is perfectly dry, when they can be carefully removed.

[illegible] I caught two large pickerel with a [illegible].

JAMES A. B[illegible],
South Norwalk, Connecticut.

I should like to exchange birds' eggs with any correspondent of YOUNG PEOPLE. I have eggs of the following birds: [illegible] pigeon, [illegible], ring-dove, and [illegible].

B. B. [illegible], Wooster, Ohio.

I would like to exchange postage stamps, minerals, [illegible], and Indian arrow-heads for minerals, [illegible] or birds' eggs. The shells are labelled with their scientific names.

R. G. W.,
P. O. Box [illegible], [illegible], New York.

We would request all correspondents not to send us long lists of stamps, eggs, and other things, as they occupy too much space in the Post-office Department. It is much better for them to prepare their lists neatly, and have them ready to send to those who write to them for exchange, after their request has been published in YOUNG PEOPLE.

We are compelled to condense the requests for exchange from the following correspondents:

Postage stamps and birds' eggs for postage stamps.
WILLIAM R. [illegible],
[illegible], Cumberland County, Maine.

Postage stamps, postmarks, and Indian relics for postage stamps.
A. B. [illegible],
Fort Wayne, Allen County, Indiana.

Postage, [illegible], and revenue stamps for others.
HARRY DAVIS,
Fredonia, Chautauqua County, New York.

Postage stamps and [illegible] for postage stamps.
JOHN A. [illegible],
[illegible] Second Street, Albany, New York.

Foreign and United States postage stamps for others.
W. C. T. [illegible],
[illegible] St. George Street, Toronto, Canada.

MABEL.—The recipes you wish are in YOUNG PEOPLE Nos. [illegible] and [illegible].—A good method for [illegible] leaves is described by Edith L. in Post-office Box No. [illegible].

W. DE VEAY.—The different species of the order Chelonia, in which turtles and tortoises belong, are distinguished mainly by the limbs. The common fresh-water turtles have distinct toes, which are webbed and provided with long nails. They are easy and powerful swimmers, but are very helpless on land. They feed upon all kinds of aquatic worms and insects. The tortoises, or land turtles, have short stubbed feet adapted for travelling on the ground, and stout, short claws. They feed upon roots, vegetables, fruit, and small bugs and flies. Their upper shell is more rounded than that of the water turtle. They are capable of swimming, but seldom enter the water.

W. S. B.—Alaric the Goth was proclaimed King of the Visigoths about A.D. 398. He was a bold and artful warrior, and under his leadership the Goths ravaged Greece, and entered Athens. He afterward determined to invade Italy, and after [illegible] he [illegible] in [illegible] Rome in 410, eleven hundred and sixty-three years after the foundation of the city, which for six hundred years previous to the Gothic conquest had remained [illegible] in the presence of any foreign enemy. Alaric, who had already embraced Christianity, showed much moderation in his treatment of the conquered city, and after a short occupation he retired his troops, and proceeded to ravage Southern Italy. He was about to invade Sicily, and from an expedition to Africa, when his death, after a short illness, put an end to his conquests. His army, anxious to conceal his death, and even his burial-place, from the enemy, employed a band of captives to divert the course of the Busento, a small river which washes the walls of Cosenza, an ancient fortified town, and secretly at night a grave was dug in the river-bed, and the body of the dead chieftain was buried. The waters of the Busento were then turned back, and underneath the peaceful river the grave of the warlike Goth was securely concealed. His death occurred in 410, only a few months after his triumphal entry into Rome.

[illegible] C.—Your letter is very gratifying, and we are sorry we can not accede to your request, but the article in question would occupy too large a space in YOUNG PEOPLE.

Favors are acknowledged from [illegible], Willie [illegible], Isabelle Van [illegible], M. L. [illegible], Mary Walcott, C. F. [illegible].

Correct answers to puzzles are received from [illegible], A. H. Elliott, Mary E. De La Mater, [illegible], [illegible], [illegible] J. Washington, W. H. [illegible], May Wells, H. J. [illegible].

PUZZLES FROM YOUNG CONTRIBUTORS.

No. 1.

ACROSTIC.

Place the names of five trees in such order that their initials read downward spell the name of another tree.

DOLLIE.

No. 2.

[illegible]

1. In [illegible]. An [illegible]. A [illegible]. At a distance. In Nevada. 2. In Idaho. A [illegible]. An [illegible] [illegible] for a special purpose. [illegible]. In California. [illegible] read across spell the name of a savage beast.

[illegible].

No. 3.

WORD SQUARES.

1. First, a character in mythology. Second, [illegible]. Third, a body of land. Fourth, [illegible].

A. F. W.

2. First, [illegible]. Second, [illegible]. Third, [illegible]. Fourth, a [illegible].

[illegible].

No. 4.

ENIGMA.

My first is in [illegible], but not in [illegible].
My second is in [illegible], but not in [illegible].
My third is in [illegible], but not in [illegible].
My fourth is in [illegible], but not in [illegible].
My fifth is in [illegible], but not in [illegible].
My whole is a fruit which you [illegible].

[illegible].

No. 5.

[illegible]

An [illegible]. A [illegible]. A [illegible]. In Lexington. [illegible]. One of a [illegible]. A lady's name. [illegible] read downward spell the name of a celebrated battle.

[illegible].

ANSWERS TO PUZZLES IN No. 46.

No. 1. [illegible]

No. 2. [illegible]

No. 3. Cincinnati. Washington.

No. 4. 1. [illegible]. 2. [illegible].

WIGGLES.

For the benefit of those who have not read this [illegible] we would say that the Wiggle is a line [illegible] to be turned into a picture by having other lines added to it. [illegible] is given in this Number. [illegible] and then send your picture to us. [illegible] as promptly as possible.

ADVERTISEMENTS.

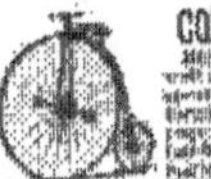

COLUMBIA BICYCLE.

[illegible] THE POPE M'F'G CO., [illegible] Summer St., Boston, Mass.

Notice.

Now is the Time to Subscribe.

Within a year of its first appearance HARPER'S YOUNG PEOPLE has secured a leading place among the periodicals designed for juvenile readers. The object of those who have the paper in charge is to provide for boys and girls from the age of six to sixteen a weekly treat in the way of entertaining stories, poems, historical sketches, and other attractive reading matter, with profuse and beautiful illustrations.

The conductors of **HARPER'S YOUNG PEOPLE** proceed upon the theory that it is not necessary, in order to engage the attention of youthful minds, to fill its pages with exaggerated and sensational stories, to make heroes of criminals, or throw the glamour of romance over bloody deeds. Their design is to make the spirit and influence of the paper harmonize with the moral atmosphere which pervades every cultivated Christian household. The lessons taught are those which all parents who desire the welfare of their children would wish to see inculcated. HARPER'S YOUNG PEOPLE aims to do this by combining the best literary and artistic talent, so that fiction shall appear in bright and innocent colors, sober facts assume such a holiday dress as to be no longer dry or dull, and mental exercise, in the solution of puzzles, problems, and other devices, become a delight.

The cordial approval extended to HARPER'S YOUNG PEOPLE by the intelligent and exacting audience for whose special benefit it was projected shows that its conductors have not miscalculated the requirements of juvenile periodical literature. The paper has attained a wide circulation in the United States, Canada, Europe, the West Indies, and South America. The "Post-office Box," the most complete department of the kind ever attempted, contains letters from almost every quarter of the globe, and not only serves to bring the boys and girls of different states and countries into pleasant acquaintance, but, through its exchanges and answers to questions, to extend their knowledge and quicken their intelligence.

The Bound Volume for 1880 has been got up in the most attractive manner, the cover being embellished with a tasteful and appropriate design. It will be one of the most handsome, entertaining, and useful books for boys and girls published for the coming holidays.

TERMS.

FOUR CENTS A NUMBER. Single Subscriptions for one year, $1 50 each; Five Subscriptions, one year, $7—payable in advance; postage free. Subscriptions will be commenced with the Number issued at the time of receipt of order, except in cases where the subscriber otherwise directs.

The Second Volume will begin with No. 53, to be issued November 2, 1880. Subscriptions should be sent in before that date, or as early as possible thereafter.

The Bound Volume for 1880, containing the first Fifty-two Numbers, will be ready early in November. Price $3, postage prepaid. Cover for YOUNG PEOPLE for 1880 now ready. Price 35 cents; postage 13 cents additional.

Remittances should be made by *Post-office Money Order or Draft*, to avoid risk of loss.

Address HARPER & BROTHERS,
Franklin Square, New York.

SOME ANSWERS TO WIGGLE No. 14, OUR ARTIST'S IDEA, AND NEW WIGGLE No. 15.

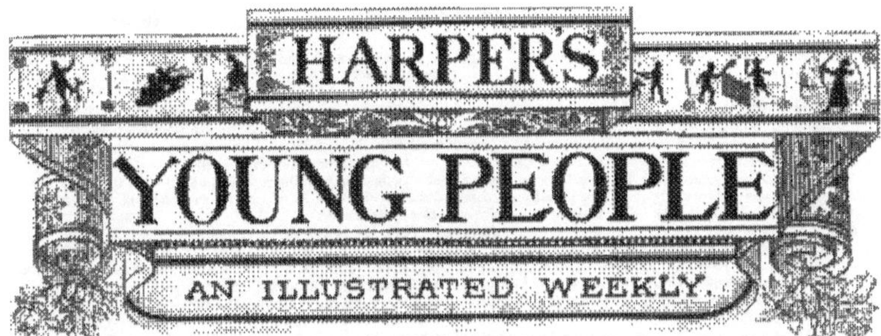
HARPER'S
YOUNG PEOPLE
AN ILLUSTRATED WEEKLY.

Vol. I.—No. 52. | Published by HARPER & BROTHERS, New York. | Price Four Cents.
Tuesday, October 26, 1880. | Copyright, 1880, by Harper & Brothers. | $1.50 per Year, in Advance.

WILBERT'S NOTION

UNDER THE CHESTNUT-TREE.

WORK'S A MINT; OR, WILBERT FAIRLAW'S NOTION

BY FRANK H. TAYLOR.

"WHAT'S your name, boy?"

The question came so suddenly that the boy nearly tumbled from the fence upon which he was perched, as Judge Barton stopped squarely in front of him, and waited for an answer.

"Wilbert Fairlaw, sir," was the timid reply.

"Go to school?"

"No, sir."

"Do any work?"

"Yes, sir; I 'tend marm's cows and fetch wood."

"Well, that's something. But don't you think there's plenty to do in this part of the world that's better than kicking your heels against the fence all the morning? Now just look around, my boy, until you find something that wants fixing up, and take off your coat and go at it. You won't have to look far about here." And the Judge gave a contemptuous glance toward the widow Fairlaw's neglected farm. "Take my word for it, boy," he added, "work's a mint—work's a mint." And then he turned away, walking with dignified pace toward the Willows—the name of his place.

Now I think that most boys would have been tempted to talk back, but Wilbert only sat still and looked after the man as he walked away, and then down at his bare feet.

"It's all true. Somehow our place does look badly, but I can't 'tend to everything," he thought, "like a hired man; an' if I did try to patch things, likely I'd get a lickin' for doin' something I oughtn't. I don't see as it makes any difference whether I work or not. It's all the same about here, but, oh, I would like to have something to do for pay, so I could have a little money—ever so little—and I could feel it in my pocket, and know it was there. I wonder what the Judge meant by saying, 'Work's a mint.' I guess it is something about getting paid. How I wish I had a little money! but I would like to earn it myself."

"Here, bub, get a bucket, will you, and bring my nag some water?"

This time it was a keen-looking young man sitting in a light wagon who addressed him.

"Now stir your pegs, bub, and here's a nickel for you."

Wilbert was already on the way to the well, for he was always quite willing to do a favor, and so he didn't hear the last sentence. Then he unfastened the check-rein by standing upon a horse-block, and gave the tired animal a pail of water.

The driver meanwhile searched his pockets in vain for a nickel.

"Got any change, bub?"

"No, sir."

"Well, then, never mind; here's a quarter to start your fortune. I guess it 'll do you more good than it would me," and away he drove at a lively pace up the road, and Wilbert sat down in the grass by the road-side, too happy even to whistle or dance.

So people sometimes paid for having their horses watered! Why not keep watch for teams, and have a bucket ready? There was plenty of travel over the road. Carriage-loads of excursionists went by to the "Glen"—a resort about six miles distant—almost daily, and the only place to water on the way was always made muddy by the pigs.

But people wouldn't be willing to wait while he went clear to the well every time for water, especially when there were two horses.

Behind the barn lay an unused trough, made for feeding pigs. Wilbert tied a rope around it, and hitching the one old horse his mother owned to this, dragged it to a point in the road where the shadow of a large chestnut-tree rested most of the day. Then he built a stone support about it, out of the plentiful supply of boulders in the fields. Next the water was to be brought. It took a long time to carry enough with one pail to even half fill the trough, and then the very first farmer who drove along the road stopped his horses, and looking with some surprise at Wilbert's "improvement," let his animals drink most of the contents, and was off before Wilbert returned from the pump.

Several teams watered during the morning, and one man tossed the boy ten cents. How pleasantly his two coins jingled, to be sure!

Early the next morning Wilbert was on his way to a ravine which lay back of the big chestnut-tree. He carried a spade, and began to dig where the grass was greenest, and slime was gathered upon the stones. At a depth of two feet he saw the hole fill with water, which speedily became clear, as he sat down to rest, and soon trickled down the slope.

Then he went to that repository of all odds and ends, the shed back of the barn, and selected a number of boards left over when the fence was built; with these and some nails he made a trough to carry the water down the hill, placing them one end upon another in forked stakes, and after two days of hard work was delighted to find that his trough was easily filled with clear cool spring-water.

Upon that day he made twenty cents, and a good-natured peddler gave him a large sponge, and taught him how to rinse out the parched mouths of the horses.

He rode to town with the peddler, and bought a handsome bucket with his money, feeling sure that he would soon get it all back.

Business was now fairly under way, and many were the praises bestowed by passers-by upon his work. Some paid, and others only said "Thank you." The crusty Judge, who had a kind heart in spite of his rough ways, halted his team, and after learning from Wilbert that it was all his own work, told his driver always to stop there when passing, and said he thought he had better pay for the season in advance, and so handed the boy a dollar.

One day Wilbert sat by his trough under the chestnut, looking very thoughtful. He knew that summer would soon be over, and was thinking of the coming winter days, when his occupation would be gone. He had earned quite a nice little sum—ten dollars or more—and had formed and rejected many plans for using it to the best advantage. He became quite unhappy through his uncertain frame of mind. You see, even the possession of money is a cause of sorrow sometimes. There was one thing settled. He had determined to buy a new woollen shawl for his mother with a part of his riches.

Wilbert took his money out of his pocket, and counted it for perhaps the hundredth time. While thus engaged his attention was drawn to a cloud of dust in the road, out of which a pair of black ponies dashed at full speed. They seemed to be running away. Men were shouting to the pale-faced boy who held the reins, and who was presently thrown violently from his seat, and now lay still and senseless by the road-side. There was but a moment in which to form a resolve. Wilbert seized a loose board from the fence and held it squarely across the road, throwing it with all his strength toward the ponies. Thus attacked, they became confused, and turned to the road-side, upsetting the watering-trough, and stopped. Wilbert scrambled up out of the dust into which he had been thrown by the force of his effort, and caught the reins. Two men ran to the horses' heads, while another brought the injured boy to the spot.

"I guess we had better get him home as soon as we can," said one of the men. "He's stopping over to the Judge's, and is his nephew. Here, you, Wilbert, just git in, and hold his head up, while I manage these little scamps. Things ain't much broken, considering how the critters run."

So they drove back to the Willows. Wilbert went in with the man, secretly wondering at the beautiful rooms, the rich carpets, pictures, and easy-chairs. They surpassed anything he had ever seen or dreamed of. Then Wilbert was sent after the doctor, and made himself so handy that it was agreed he should stay and help nurse Clarence, for that was the boy's name.

For six weeks the injured lad lay in bed, and Wilbert remained faithfully by him. As Clarence grew stronger, the boys became very fond of each other, though they had never met before the accident, Clarence having just arrived from Boston on a visit to his uncle.

He told Wilbert that his father was a manufacturer, and that his mother was dead. The young visitor had a great many books, some of which Wilbert found time to read while watching by the bedside. One of these was a story of the life of George Stephenson, who invented the first locomotive. This was such a favorite with Wilbert that the sick boy gave it to him.

All that he read set him to thinking. Why couldn't he too invent something and become famous? Long after everybody else slept Wilbert lay in bed with his eyes wide open, until he had thought out a plan for hitching horses to carriages in such a manner that they couldn't run away.

The very next day he walked to the village and bought a few tools and such material as he thought his device would require, and then set about making a model.

The Judge good-naturedly laughed at his "notion," as he termed it, but allowed him to work at it all of his spare time. "Work's a mint," said he, "and such work ain't mischief, at any rate."

At last Wilbert had his model completed, save a single part, and was obliged to make another trip to the village to get the proper material. When he returned he was alarmed by the discovery that his model was gone. He ran down stairs to the study, but held back as he saw the Judge and a stranger intently examining his missing work.

"I always believe," said the Judge, "in letting boys work out their notions. It don't hurt 'em, and it teaches 'em patience."

"Of course, of course," replied the stranger. "For instance, this 'notion,' as you call it, will never do. It isn't the thing at all; but see here, Judge, examine this hub. There's a 'notion' in that worth something. I tell you what it is, any boy who can stumble on such an idea, even by accident, has got good stuff in him."

Just then the Judge caught sight of Wilbert.

"Here's the lad himself. And so," said he to the boy, with a great show of severity, "this is all that your work for two weeks has brought out. Mr. Congdon here, Clarence's father, says your invention ain't worth anything. What do you say to that? Your work ain't much of a mint, after all, is it?"

Wilbert felt very much like choking with vexation and grief. He couldn't bear to have fun made of his model, especially before a stranger, but he wisely remained silent.

"So your name is Wilbert?" inquired Mr. Congdon. "Well, now, Wilbert, I want you to let me take this toy of yours home with me. I have come after Clarence. We leave this evening for Boston. Trust me with it, and you won't regret doing so."

So Mr. Congdon left with Wilbert's companion and his "notion," after which the boy seemed lost for a few days. He went back to the old farm, and handed his mother the wages the Judge had paid him, and an order for a new suit of clothes kindly added by Mrs. Barton.

Toward the close of the year he sat one night, reading, as usual, by candle-light, and oddly enough it happened to be Christmas-eve, when a rap came at the door, and Judge Barton entered. He held in his hand an important-looking envelope, which he reached toward Wilbert, saying, "Here's a Christmas gift for you, boy. Work's a mint—work's a mint. Yes, indeed, it's better than a gold mine, for it brings its reward already coined."

Now, you see, Wilbert had never had but one letter before in his life, and that was a little boyish scrawl from Clarence, and no wonder he opened the big envelope timidly. The contents began, "Know all men by these presents," and here Wilbert looked again into the envelope to see where the presents it spoke of were hidden.

The Judge explained that this was a paper from the United States Patent-office, granting a patent to Wilbert Fairlaw for an improved carriage hub.

"Now," said the Judge, "that patent was secured for you by Mr. Congdon, who got the hint for the hub from that 'notion' of yours. It will sell for considerable money, but I advise you to hold it. I think, Mrs. Fairlaw"—turning to the widow—"that you had better let your boy go to school for a couple of years. I'll see that the royalty on the manufacture of this hub will pay for his keeping; and when he is old enough, he can do as he thinks best about the patent."

Ten Christmas-eves have come and gone since that visit by the Judge, and many changes have occurred. The old house has been partly rebuilt, and Mrs. Fairlaw still lives there. The Judge, too, is living, and comes down frequently to see the "firm" and the new factory, which stands close by the ravine and the big chestnut-tree. The name of the firm and its purpose is seen upon the large sign:

FAIRLAW & CONGDON,

MANUFACTURERS OF **IMPROVED HUBS** AND SPOKES.

When the Judge came over upon his first visit to the works after business was started, he was conducted to the long work-room, full of whirring machinery, by Wilbert and Clarence, and shown, greatly to his delight, his favorite motto, which was painted across the wall:

"WORK'S A MINT."

POSY PARKER'S HALLOWEEN.

BY MRS. E. W. LATIMER.

POSY and Bob Parker, of Baltimore, went to visit their cousins in England. Posy, who was a little girl, was surprised to see the customs and observances supposed to belong in England to different days. On Michaelmas-day (September 29), for instance, her uncle's family all dined upon roast goose, because Queen Elizabeth, having received at dinner news of the defeat of the Armada on that day, stuck her royal knife into the breast of a fat goose before her, and declared that thenceforward no Englishman should have good luck who did not eat goose upon St. Michael's Day.

When All-hallow Eve came (October 31) the children and their cousins were invited to a beautiful old country place five miles across the Yorkshire moors to keep Halloween.

"But what is Halloween kept for, anyway, uncle?" said little Posy, as they rode over the moors that evening.

"'Really and truly,' Posy, as you would say, the night of October 31 is the vigil of All-saints' Day, one of the four high festivals in the Roman Catholic Church, and a day on which all Christians who hold to ancient forms commemorate the noble doings of the holy dead. But the All-hallow's frolics you will see this evening have nothing whatever to do with Christianity. They are relics of old paganism, of the days when 'millions of spiritual creatures' were supposed to be allowed that night 'to walk the earth'—ghosts, fairy folk, witches, gnomes, and brownies, all creatures of the fancy whose home is fairy-land."

"What is the proper thing to eat on Halloween, uncle?" said Posy.

"To eat, little Posy?"

"Yes, uncle. Every great occasion in England seems to me to have something proper to eat on that day."

"Oh, now I understand you. Apples and nuts, Posy. A vigil was always a fast in the olden time, so those who kept Halloween could have no substantial dainties for their supper."

A NUTTING PARTY—BUMPING THE HICKORY-TREE.

"Nurse Birkenshaw used to call it Nut-crack Day," cried Posy's eldest cousin. "But here we are!"

They were ushered into a low long room on the ground-floor, paved with flag-stones, having an immense hearth at one end. Inside the chimney, and on each side of the blazing fire built of logs and turf, were two oak benches, so that six guests could literally sit in the chimney-corner. This room was made beautiful by blue and white Dutch tiles.

About thirty people soon assembled. From the ceiling hung a stick about two feet long, and five feet from the floor. On one end of this stick was stuck an apple, to the other hung a small bag stuffed loosely with white sand. On one side of the room were three great washing tubs filled with water. Three crocks stood on a side table, and baskets filled with apples, walnuts, chestnuts, and fresh filberts were placed about the room.

The performance began by reading "Tam o' Shanter," accompanied by illustrations, made by a magic lantern. When this was over, and lights were again brought into the room, the tubs of water were drawn forward. Twelve apples were set floating in each tub. Three little boys had their arms pinioned, and water-proof capes were put over their clothes. Then each one was led up to a tub, and told to name one of the girls present; if he could catch an apple in his teeth, she would be his next year's valentine. Fun, splashing, and laughter followed for five minutes; then time was up, and three more boys took their turn. After many such trials Posy's big cousin (an old hand, with a big mouth) brought up a little apple, another fellow caught an apple by its stalk, and Bob (good at a dive), after plunging his face to the bottom of the tub, and holding his apple steady between his nose and chin, rose with it in his teeth, triumphant but dripping.

After this had gone on for some time with varying success, the wet boys were sent off to change their clothes, and the girls' turn came. Many more apples were put into the tubs, and each girl in turn was told to hold a fork as high as she could in her right hand over the tub, and drop it on the apples. If she could spear one, she might choose her valentine. The boys joined in this also, but hardly so many apples were speared as had been caught in the boys' teeth, and the victors in the tub fishery set up a shout of triumph.

Next boys and girls had their hands tied behind them, and took turns to run up to the apple on the stick suspended by a string. This string had been twisted by the master of the revels, and the stick turned round rapidly. The fun was to jump up, and with their teeth to seize the apple. If they missed (which, of course, they did nearly every time), the bag of sand swung round and hit them on the face, to the amusement of the company.

Meantime there were many nuts roasting on the hearth, each named for a boy or girl. If one bearing a boy's name swelled up and popped away, his lady-love would lose him; if it flared up and blazed, he was thinking about her tenderly. If two nuts named for two lovers blazed at once, they would soon be a happy couple.

Some of the older boys and girls of the party were then blindfolded, and hand in hand were conducted to the gate of the walled kitchen-garden, where they were told to find their way into the cabbage patch, where each was to pull up a cabbage stump. When they returned with their prizes to the house, great fun and much dirt were the result. Posy's eldest cousin had brought in a big crooked cabbage stalk, with plenty of mould hanging to its roots; he was to marry a tall, stout, misshapen wife with a large fortune. Miss Clara, the young lady of the house, brought in a tall and slender stalk, with little soil adhering to it; so by-and-by, as some one said, she would marry a tall, straight, penniless bridegroom.

Then the table with the three crocks was brought into the middle of the room. Into one crock was poured fresh water, into another soapy water, and the third was empty. Posy, among the rest, was blindfolded, and led up to the table. She was instructed to dip her fingers into one of the crocks. She felt around, and at last dipped into the one that held the empty water: she was told that she would marry a widower. Miss Clara dipped into clear water, and would marry a bachelor. One of the other girls put her fingers into the empty crock, and would die an old maid.

By this time it was nearly midnight—time for the fairy folk as well as children to be in bed. But Miss Clara first went up stairs to an empty room, and holding a candle in one hand, ate an apple before the looking-glass. Captain Strickland (slender and tall) crept softly up stairs after her, and as she ate her last mouthful, she saw his face over her shoulder. She dropped her candle, with a scream, and they came quietly down after a while in the dark together.

Miss Clara's older sister had meantime gone out into the flower garden, taking with her a ball of blue yarn. This she flung from her as far as possible, keeping hold, however, of one end, and dragging it after her. As she went back to the house she sang,

"Who holds my thread? who holds my clew?
For he loves me, and I him, too."

Suddenly the ball of yarn refused to follow her. She jerked at it in vain. She dared not let her clew break, because if she should lose the lover supposed to be holding its other end, she would die unmarried. "Let me see you! let me see you!" she cried, eagerly, and a figure drew near her in the darkness. An arm covered with dark cloth was almost round her. She drew away with a scream, and began to run, pursued by Bob, the young American, who had stolen away from the other guests to follow her, and whose appearance produced much laughter; for Bob was twelve, and she was seven-and-twenty.

The children had not cared much for these last two trials. They had been popping nuts and eating apples. They were now called to supper. There was at the end of a long table a great tureen of soured oatmeal porridge. The master of the house, who was of Scotch descent, called it "sowens," and declared that every one present must eat some with butter and salt if he

hallow Eve. There were other good things on the table, however, much better, Pussy thought, than sour porridge. And when supper was over the children went off to bed, solemnly assured by their elders that the fairy folk—the witches, ghosts, and so on—had already gone to their beds under the earth, not being permitted, even on such a night as Halloween, to sit up any longer.

(Begun in No. 46 of Harper's Young People, September 14.)

WHO WAS PAUL GRAYSON?

BY JOHN HABBERTON,

Author of "Helen's Babies."

Chapter VII.

A BEAUTIFUL THEORY RUINED.

WHEN Benny Mallow went to bed at night, after the great exhibition, he suddenly remembered that he had forgotten to ask what the grand total of the receipts for the Beantassel family had been. Under ordinary circumstances he would have got out of bed, dressed himself, and scoured the town for full information before he slept. On this particular night, however, he did not give the subject more than a moment of thought, for his mind was full of greater things. Paul Grayson an Indian!

Why, of course; how had he been so stupid as not to think of it before? Paul was only dark, while Indians were red, but then it was easy enough for him to have been a half-breed; Paul was very straight, as Indians always were in books; Paul was a splendid shot with a rifle, as all Indians are; Paul had no parents—well, the tableau made by Paul's own friend Mr. Morton, who knew all about him, explained plainly enough how Indian boys came to be without fathers and mothers.

Even going to sleep did not rid Benny of these thoughts. He saw Paul in all sorts of places all through the night, and always as an Indian. At one time he was on a wild horse, galloping madly at a wilder buffalo; then he was practicing with bow and arrow at a genuine archery target; then he stood in the opening of a tent made of skins; then he lay in the tall grass, rifle in hand, awaiting some deer that were slowly moving toward him. He even saw Paul tomahawk and scalp a white boy of his own size, and although the face of the victim was that of Joe Appleby, the hair somehow was long enough to tie around the belt which Paul, like all Indians in picture-books, wore for the express purpose of providing properly for the scalps he took.

So fully did Benny's dreams take possession of him, that although he had been awake for two hours the next morning before he met Paul, he was rather startled and considerably disappointed to find his friend in ordinary dress, without a sign of belt, scalp, or tomahawk about him. Still, of course Paul was an Indian, and Benny promptly determined that no one should beat him in getting information about the young man's earlier life; so Benny opened conversation abruptly by asking, "Where do you begin to cut when you want to take a man's scalp off?"

"Why, who are you going to scalp, little fellow?" asked Paul.

"Oh, nobody," said Benny, in confusion. "I'd like to know, that's all."

"I'm afraid you'll have to ask some one else, then," said Paul, with a laugh. "Try me on something easier."

"Then how do you ride a wild horse without saddle or bridle?" asked Benny.

"Worse and worse," said Paul. "See here, Benny, have you been reading dime novels, and made up your mind to go West?"

"Not exactly," said Benny; "but," he continued, "I wouldn't mind going West if I had some good safe fellow to go with—some one who has been there and knows all about it."

"Well, I know enough about it to tell you to stay at home," said Paul.

This was proof enough, thought Benny; so although he was aching to ask Paul many other questions about Indian life, he hurried off to assure the other boys that it was all right—that Paul was an Indian, and no mistake. The consequence was that when Paul approached the school-house half of the boys advanced slowly to meet him, and then they clustered about him, and he became conscious of being looked at even more intently than on the day of his first appearance. He did not seem at all pleased by the attention; he looked rather angry, and then turned pale; finally he hurried up stairs into the school-room and whispered something to the teacher, at which Mr. Morton shook his head and patted Paul on the shoulder, after which the boy regained his ease and took his seat.

But at recess he again found himself the centre of a crowd, no member of which seemed to care to begin any sort of game. Paul stopped short, looked around him, frowned, and asked, "Boys, what is the matter with me?"

"Nothing," replied Will Palmer.

"Then what are you all crowding around me for?"

No one answered for a moment, but finally Sam Wardwell said, "We want you to tell us stories."

"Stories about Indians," explained Ned Johnston.

Paul laughed. "You're welcome to all I know," said he; "but I don't think they're very interesting. Really, I can't remember a single one that's worth telling."

This was very discouraging; but Canning Forbes, who was so smart that, although he was only fourteen years of age, he was studying mental philosophy, whispered to Will Palmer that people never saw anything interesting about their own daily lives.

"You can tell us something about birch canoes, can't you?" asked Ned Johnston, by way of encouragement.

"Oh yes," Paul replied; "they're made out of bark, with hoops and strips of wood inside, to give them shape and make them strong."

"How do they fasten up the ends?" asked Ned.

"They first sew or tie them together with strings, and then they put pitch over the seams to make them water-tight."

"Did you ever see the Indians race in birch canoes?" asked Sam.

"Oh yes, often," Paul replied; "and they make fast time too, I can tell you."

"Did you ever race yourself?" asked Benny.

"No," said Paul, "but I learned to paddle a canoe pretty well. I'd rather have a good row-boat, though, than any birch I ever saw. If you run one of them on a sharp stone, it may be cut open, unless it's pretty new."

"How do the Indians kill buffaloes?" asked Will Palmer.

"Why, just as white men do—they shoot them with rifles. Nearly all the Indians have rifles nowadays."

This was very unromantic, most of the boys thought, for an Indian without bows and arrows would not be very different from a white man. Still, something wonderful would undoubtedly come before Paul was done talking.

"Are buffaloes really so terrible-looking as the story-papers say?" asked Bert Sharp.

"Well, they don't look exactly like pets," said Paul. "A bull buffalo, in the winter season, when he has a full coat of hair, looks fiercer than a lion."

"Do the Indians really kill or torture all the white people they catch?" asked Canning Forbes.

"I don't know; I suppose so, but perhaps they're not all as bad as some white people say."

Canning shook his head encouragingly at Will Palmer; evidently this young Indian had a manly spirit, and was not going to have his people abused. There was a moment or two of silence, each boy wondering what next to ask. Finally, Napoleon Nott said,

"You're a chief's son, aren't you?"

"What?" exclaimed Paul, so sharply that Notty dodged behind Will Palmer, and put his hand to his head as if to protect his scalp.

"I meant," said Notty, tremblingly—"I meant to ask what tribe you belonged to."

"I? What tribe? Notty, what are you talking about?"

Notty did not answer, so Paul looked around at the other boys, but they also were silent.

"Notty," said Paul, "what on earth are you thinking about? Do you imagine I'm an Indian?"

"I thought you were," said Notty, very meekly; "and," he continued, "so did all the other boys."

"Well, that's good," said Paul, laughing heartily. "What made you think so, fellows?"

"Benny told us," explained Ned.

"Benny?" exclaimed Paul. "What put that fancy into your head?"

"I—I dreamed it," said Benny, almost ready to cry for shame and disappointment.

"And you told all the other boys?"

"Yes, I believed it; I really did, or I never would have said it."

Then Paul laughed again—a long, hearty laugh it was,

but no one helped him. Most of the boys felt as if in some way Paul had cheated them. As for Ned Johnston, he evidently did not believe Paul, for he began to ask questions.

"If you're not an Indian, how do you know so much about a birch canoe?"

"Why, I've seen dozens of them in Maine, where I used to live; the Indians make them there."

"Wild Indians?" asked Ned, and all the boys listened eagerly for the answer.

"No," said Paul, contemptuously; "they're the tamest kind of tame ones."

This was dreadful, yet Ned thought he would try once more. "How did you come to know so much about buffaloes?" he asked.

"I saw two in Central Park, in New York," Paul replied. "Oh, boys! boys! you're dreadfully sold."

"Say, Paul," said Benny, edging to the front, and looking appealingly at his friend, "you've been away out West anyhow, haven't you?—because you told me you knew about it." Benny awaited the answer with fear and trembling, for he felt he never would hear the end of the affair if he did not get some help from Paul.

"No, I've never been farther West than Laketon," was the disheartening reply. "All I know of the West I've learned from books and newspapers."

"Dear me!" sighed Benny; and for the first time in his life he wished the bell would ring, and give him an excuse to get away. Within a moment his wish was gratified, and he scampered up stairs very briskly, but not before Bert Sharp had caught up with him, and called him "Smarty," and asked him if he hadn't some more dreams that he could go about telling as truth. Poor Benny's only consolation, as he took his seat, was that Notty had been the first to suggest the Indian theory, and he ought therefore to bear a part of whatever abuse might come of the mistake.

At any rate he had learned that Paul had been in Maine and New York: certainly that was more than he had known an hour before.

[TO BE CONTINUED.]

THE SONS OF THE BRAVE.

(See double-page Illustration.)

BOYS and girls now travel so much and so far that no doubt a great number of "Harper's Young People" will have an opportunity to see these fine little fellows, perhaps some pleasant day next summer. Mr. Morris has drawn them just as they are leaving their school for their weekly parade.

This school is in Chelsea, England, and is for the support and education of seven hundred boys and three hundred girls, whose fathers have either been killed in battle or died on foreign stations, or whose mothers have died while their fathers were on duty in foreign lands. The school is a fine building of brick and stone, and the front entrance, out of which you see the boys filing, has a spacious stone portico, supported by four noble pillars of the Doric order, the frieze bearing the following inscription: "The Royal Military Asylum for the Children of Soldiers of the Regular Army."

The Asylum is inclosed by high walls, except before the great front, where there is an iron railing. The grounds connected with this part are beautifully laid out in flower and grass plats, and shaded with fine trees. Attached to each wing are spacious play-grounds, as well as a number of covered arcades. In the latter the children play when the weather is too wet or cold for open-air exercise.

All the domestic affairs are regulated by Commissioners appointed by the Queen's sign-manual, and the officials consist of a commandant, adjutant, and secretary, chaplain, quartermaster, surgeon, matron, and various other persons; for everything about the school is conducted according to military discipline.

The boys are taught reading, writing, and arithmetic, and after they are eleven years of age they are employed on alternate days in works of industry. Five hours daily in summer and four in winter is the time required of them, and in this short period they make every article of clothing they require for their own use. About one hundred boys work as tailors, fifty each day alternately; about one hundred are employed in a similar manner as shoemakers, capmakers, and coverers and repairers of the school's books. Besides, there are two sets or companies of knitters and of shirtmakers, and others who are engaged as porters, gardeners, etc. Everything is done by those who work at the trades, except the cutting out. This branch, requiring experience, is managed by old regimental shoemakers, tailors, etc., who, with aged sergeants and corporals and their wives, manage the affairs of the institution.

The school also furnishes its own drum and fife corps and a very fine military band, the players, of course, devoting a proper proportion of their time to the practice on their instruments. Friday is the best day on which to visit the school, for on that day the entire force is turned out for a dress parade. The boys are then dressed in full uniform—red jackets, blue trousers, and little black caps—and with their flags flying, drums beating, and band playing, they march to the parade-ground, where they give a fine exhibition drill. After the parade they are trained in various difficult and skillful gymnastic exercises.

There is no compulsion on any boy to join the army; but when any regiment is in want of recruits, a notice is placed in the school-rooms, and any boys above fourteen years of age who wish to go into the army are allowed to join that regiment. For those who prefer trades or other occupations situations are provided, and if at the end of a certain number of years they can produce certificates of good conduct from those who employ them, they are publicly rewarded in the chapel of the institution.

The girls, in addition to the usual branches of a good common-school education, are taught needle-work of all kinds, and fitted for lady's-maids, dressmakers, cooks, and the various higher positions of household service. Their dress is uniform, and consists of blue petticoats, red gowns, and straw hats.

The school is supported by an annual grant from Parliament, and by the gift of one day's pay in every year from the whole army.

"MAMMA KNOWS HOW."

THE awful fact is beyond a doubt,
The cage was open, and Dick flew out.
"What shall I do?" cries Pet, half wild,
And Nurse Deb says, "Why, bress you, child,
I knows a plan dat 'll nebber fail:
Jes put some salt on yer birdie's tail."

"Why, you silly old nurse, 'twould never do;
That plan is worthy a goose like you.
What! salt for birds. No, sugar, I say;
I'll coax him back to me right away."
But wicked Dick, with his round black eyes,
He wouldn't be caught in this gentle wise.

Mamma comes in, and she sees the plight;
It will take her wits to set it right:
That big bandana on Deb's black head,
Ere Dick can jump, 'tis over him spread;
Then two soft hands they hold him fast:
The bright little rogue is caught at last.

As into his cage the truant goes
Pet says, "Now, nurse, I do suppose
That salt and sugar, though two nice things,
Are not a match for a birdie's wings;
And, Deb, I think we must just allow,
When a thing's to be done, mamma knows how."

THE KING JACK-O'-LANTERN.

BY WILLIAM O. STODDARD.

"THERE, boys, that's the pumpkin."

"That 'll do, Phil; but what 'll your father say? Doesn't he mean to take that pumpkin to town?"

"Well, no, I guess not. Anyhow, he said I might have it."

"Did you tell him what it's for?"

"Of course I did. Only I guess he guessed near enough that I didn't mean to make any pies."

"What did he say, Phil?"

"Why, he laughed right out—it's easy to get him laughing—and he said if we could invent anything ugly enough to scare the Sewing Society, we might have a cart-load of pumpkins, if we'd see that they were pitched into the big feed kettle after we got done with them, so they could be boiled for the cows."

"Isn't that a whopper, though! Biggest pumpkin I ever saw. Let's go right at it."

Clint Burgess had his knife out, and was opening the big blade, but Prop Corning stopped him.

"Hold on, Clint. Let's practice on some of the little ones first. Besides, we don't want to carry the big one too far after it's done. We might drop it and break it."

"That's so," said Clint. "I say, Phil, where'll we go?"

"Up behind the corn-crib—close to the barn; best place in the world to hide 'em till we want 'em. The Sewing Society don't half get here till pretty near tea-time."

"We'll show 'em something."

"Teach the girls, too, not to laugh at fellows of our age."

"It's too bad. When a man gets to be thirteen, it's time they let him come in to tea."

That was where the rules of the Plumville Sewing Society were pinching the self-esteem of Phil Merritt and his two friends, and Phil's father and his uncle and his two grown-up brothers had gravely expressed their entire sympathy, even to the extent of furnishing unlimited pumpkins.

That was a large pumpkin. It had grown by itself in a corner of the corn field, where it had plenty of room, and, as Clint Burgess remarked when they were rolling it in behind the corn-crib, "it had just sat still and swelled."

Prop Corning was the best hand any of them knew of with a jackknife, and he knew all about jack-o'-lanterns; but they all had learned more by the time they had worked up four of the smaller pumpkins.

"They look more like big apples alongside that other."

"That's the King Pumpkin."

"That's it," shouted Prop. "We'll make the King Jack-o'-lantern. I'll show you! Phil, you run to the house for a big iron spoon."

"To scoop with? I know. The rind 'll be awful thick."

So they found it; and the outer shell was so hard that Phil went to the tool-room after one of his father's small key saws and a gimlet.

"Now we won't break our knives, nor the shell either."

"Nor cut our fingers. But we must keep every piece of shell we cut out," said Prop. "I've got a big idea in my head."

"Big as that pumpkin?"

"Big as the whole Sewing Society. We want a piece out of the top first, about six inches square.

The top piece came out nicely, and it was a wonder what a mass of seeds and pulp was pulled out after it.

Then the spoon was plied till the boys all had a turn at getting tired of scraping, and then Pop Corning went to work with the little saw.

"I'll just cut through the rind," he said, "and we won't make a hole anywhere. We'll cut the pieces out so they'll all stick in again, and then we'll scoop the places thin from the inside—thin as we want 'em, and no thinner. When we come to light it up out here after dark, and try it, we can scrape any spots thinner if they need it."

"That's the way. You never know just how a jack-o'-lantern's going to look till after you've got a candle in it," said Clint Burgess, very seriously. "We must make this one so it would scare a cow if she'd been eating pumpkins all day."

"There," remarked Prop, "that round spot down there'll stand for his chin. Now for his mouth. We must make it turn up at the corners, and have teeth like a mill saw."

That was the hardest kind of a thing to do, and do it right; but Prop was a patient worker, and there was nothing to be said against such a mouth as he sawed for that pumpkin.

"He mustn't have too much nose. Two round holes at the bottom: they're his smellers. Then a long slit away up to above his eyes; that's the bridge of his nose, and they'll have to imagine the rest of it."

"Can we give him any cheeks?" asked Phil, doubtfully.

"Yes, but there mustn't too much light come through 'em. It's to be a Goblin King, and they always have most fire coming out of their mouths and eyes."

Clint and Phil both admitted that Prop was right about that, but they ventured to suggest, "He won't be a King worth a cent if we don't give him some kind of a crown."

"Crown? You wait and see. His teeth won't be anything to the crown we'll put on him. But I mustn't lose a square inch of the rind. He must have ears too—a half-moon on each side—and you can let any amount of blaze shine out there."

It was a long job of sculptor work; but when it was done the three boys could hardly take their eyes away from it. Not until Prop had carefully fitted back to their places all the pieces of rind he had sawed out.

There was nothing to be done after that but for Prop and Clint to go home and attend to their "chores," and for Phil to go after his cows; but the Sewing Society had an experience before it that evening.

It was just as Phil Merritt said it would be about their evening together, and his mother had never before seen him so cheerful and willing about doing all he could, and about not going in to tea with the rest. His father noticed it too, and he whispered to him, once, "Phil, did you take the pumpkin?"

"Don't let 'em know a word about it, father," said Phil, anxiously. "You'll see, by-and-by."

"All right, Phil. I'll wait."

He had to wait until about nine o'clock, and some of the ladies were almost ready to go home, when suddenly there was a great noise out by the front gate.

"What's that?"

"Dear me!"

"Something's happened!"

Whoever made that sound must have been dreadfully unhappy about something; they all felt sure of that—and there was a grand rush to the front door and the windows.

"Sakes alive!"

"What can it be?"

"Mrs. Merritt, there's somethin' awful a-stickin' on the top of one o' your gate posts."

So there was, indeed. Something very large and round, and that looked very dark in spite of strange, mysterious rays of light that crept out of it here and there.

The whole gate post looked like a wooden man without any arms, but with more head than would have answered for half a dozen such men.

Nobody in the house heard Prop Corning whisper at that moment across the front-door walk, "Keep down, Clint, keep under the bushes. We're all ready. Pull out his chin." And then he added, in a lower whisper, "Ain't I glad I brought along my kite-string!—we've used it 'most all up, but we can show 'em that King."

One of the ladies, a second later, gave a little scream, and exclaimed, "Look at it now!—it's on fire."

"Dear me!" added another, "it's got a mouth."

"And a nose."

"And a cheek."

"Oh, Deacon Merrill, eyes too."

There was a subdued chuckle down there among the lilac-bushes, as if somebody were listening to all that was said by the growing crowd on the front-door step, and another whisper went across the walk: "Clint, give him his right ear. The left sticks. I'm afraid I'll pull him off the post."

"There it is."

"Here comes mine too. Now for his crown. Jerk your half."

"Oh!" "Oh!" "Oh!" More than a dozen ladies of all ages said "Oh!" in the same breath, and Deacon Merrill himself exclaimed:

"Capital! capital! The boys have done it. It's by all odds the best jack-o'-lantern I ever saw in my life. It's a King Jack-o'-lantern."

EMBROIDERY FOR GIRLS.

BY S. B. W.

THERE is lying beside me on the table as I write a sampler, worked in pink, green, blue, and dull purple-red silks, on which I read these wise sentences, "Order is the first law of Nature and of Nature's God," "The moon, stars, and tides vary not a moment," and "The sun knoweth the hour of its going down." Below, inclosed in a wreath of tambour-work,* are two words, "Appreciate Time." Under the first four alphabets (there are five in all) comes the date, "September 19, 1823," and in the lower corner another date, "October 24," when the square was completed, with the name of the child who wrought it, long since grown to womanhood, and now nearly forty years dead, but there recorded, in pink silk cross stitch, as "aged eight years."

And these dainty stitches, set so exactly, assure me that the little girls for whom I write are not too young to embroider neatly. Will you let its two mottoes remind you that a few moments carefully used each day will make you as good needle-women as your grandmothers were, and that your work-boxes or baskets should be in such order that you can find your thimbles in the dark, and can tell each several shade of wool by lamp-light? But I leave you to apply the mottoes for yourselves.

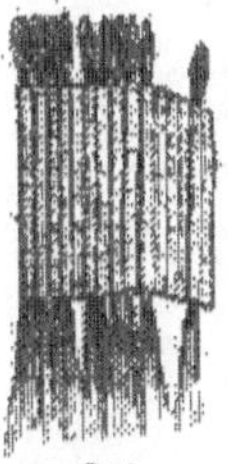

Fig. 1.

If you are to begin work with me, will you buy a few crewel-needles, No. 5 or 6, and two or three shades of crewel of any given color, such as old blue, dull mahogany, or pomegranate reds, or old gold shading into gold browns? These are colors that will always be useful.

First, your wools must be prepared so they can be used in making tidies, or anything that must be washed. The best crewels are not twisted, and will wash; still, as you are never sure of getting the best, it is well to unwind your skeins, pour scalding water on the wools, and rinse them well in it, squeeze out the water, shake the wools thoroughly, and hang them up. When dry, cut the skein across where it is tied double, and with a bodkin and string, or with a long hair-pin, draw the crewel into its case. This case (see Fig. 1) is made by folding together a long piece of thin cotton cloth a foot wide, and running parallel lines across its width half an inch or so apart. When the wools are drawn in in groups—reds, blues, greens, yellows, each by themselves, carefully arranged as to shades—cut the upper end so you need not be tempted to use too long needlefuls, and there your wools are neatly put away, and soon you can distinguish any shade by its position in the case, no matter how deceptive the lamp-light may be. Still, you will not need your case till you have a dozen different colors. If you buy your wools at first by the dozen, which is the cheaper way, be sure that your pinks, blues, greens, etc., have, so far as may be, a yellowish tone. Remember that yellow is the color of sunlight, and that without it your work will look cold and lifeless; and always avoid vivid greens and reds.

First learn the stem stitch, and you can practice on any bit of coarse linen or crash. Draw a line with a pencil (see dotted line Fig. 2); then put your needle in at the back, bringing it out at 1; then put it in at 2, taking up on the needle the threads of cloth from 2 to 3, so making a stitch that is long on the upper but short on the under side of your cloth. The needle points toward you, but your work runs from you, and you put in the needle to the right of your thread. When you wish a wide stem, slant your stitches across the line; if it must be narrow, take up the threads exactly on the line, or you can make two or more rows of stem stitch where you wish the line broadened.

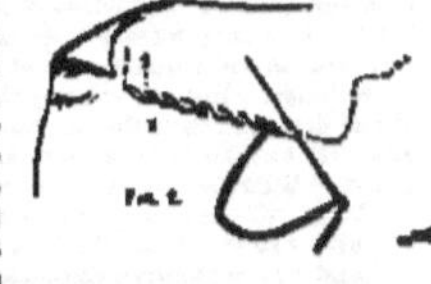

Fig. 2.

Stem stitch can be used by beginners in many ways. Squares of duck, fringed out on the edges, and overcast or hem-stitched, can have simple borders or stripes of any desired width worked in this stitch (see Fig. 3). You can draw the lines yourself with a pencil and ruler; those lines which slant in one direction may be worked in one shade, those slanting in the opposite direction in another shade. The heavier lines can be worked with double crewel, and these squares make very pretty tidies to protect the arms of chairs. Figs. 4, 5, and 6 are set patterns that can be used for borders upon doylies, towels, or table-covers. They should be worked with crewels, outlining crewels—exceedingly fine wools—or fine silks, according to the quality of the linen or other stuffs used. Stem stitch is the foundation of good modern embroidery, and we must not go on with the building until this foundation is laid.

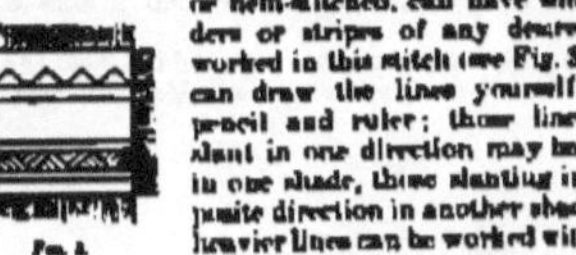

Fig. 3.

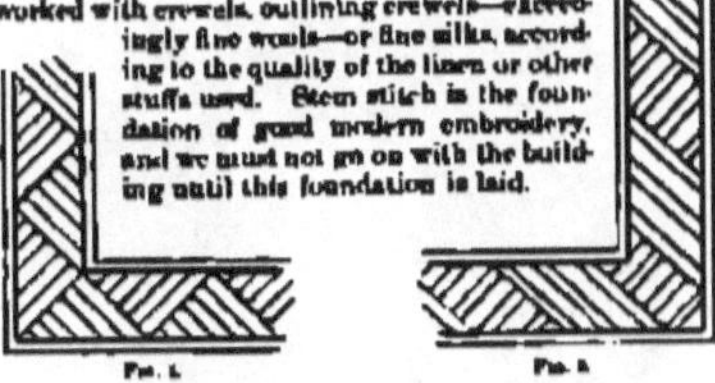

Fig. 4. Fig. 5.

Fig. 6.

* Tambour-work is a chain stitch in which the thread is drawn up through the cloth by a hook. Muslins and thin cloths used to be embroidered in this way.

FILBERT.

BY AGNES CARR.

A PUSSY cat, a parrot, and a monkey once lived together in a funny little red house, with one great round window like a big eye set in the front. And they were a very happy family as long as they had an old woman to cook their dinner and mend their clothes. But one sad day the old woman was taken ill and died, and then the cat, the parrot, and the monkey were left to take care of themselves and the red house, and very little they knew about it.

"Who will cook the porridge now?" asked the cat.

"And who will make the beds?" asked the parrot.

"And who will sweep the floor?" asked the monkey.

But none could answer, and they thought and thought a long time, but could come to no decision, until at last the parrot nodded his head wisely, and said, "We must learn to do them ourselves."

"But who will teach us?" asked Miss Pussy.

"I know," said the monkey. "We will go to town, and watch how the men and women cook their meals and take care of their homes, and then we will be able to do the same."

"So we will," said the other two, and all three immediately put on their scarlet cloaks and blue sun-bonnets,

and set off for the town, but they were in such haste that they forgot to lock the door.

They had not been gone long when a ragged little girl, with bare feet and sunburned face, came up the dusty road, and she was very tired and very hungry. Her real name nobody knew, not even herself, but she was always called Filbert, because her hair, eyes, and skin were all as brown as a nut.

"Oh dear! oh dear!" sighed Filbert, as she dragged her weary feet along. "I wish I had a fairy godmother, like the girl in the fairy book, for then I could wear silk dresses every day, and ride in a golden coach."

Just then she spied the funny little house, and thought, "Well, as I am not so lucky as to have a rich godmother, I will go in here and ask for a drink of milk, and rest awhile on the door-step."

So she went up to the door and knocked, but nobody came. Again rap-tap-tap; still nobody; and at last she lifted the latch and walked in.

"Oh, what a cunning little place!" cried Filbert, "and nobody home: so I will help myself."

In the closet she found meal and milk, which she heated over the fire, and ate with a great relish. Then she went all over the house, exploring the nooks and corners of every room, and wondering what had become of the people who lived there.

She also thought it very queer that in so pretty a house, where almost everything was neat and well kept, the floors should be dirty and the beds not yet made up.

At last the little girl, who had walked far along the dusty road in the hot sun that morning, found herself growing very tired and sleepy; and as the tumbled beds did not look very inviting, she went down stairs and took a nap in a large rocking-chair that had belonged to the old woman. When she was quite rested, she helped herself to a needle and thread out of the work-basket, and went to work to mend her dress, which was badly torn. Just as she had sewed up the last rent she heard steps outside, and glancing out of the round window, saw the pussy cat, the parrot, and the monkey coming in at the gate.

Frightened nearly out of her wits at sight of the queer trio, Filbert jumped up, and ran and hid behind the curtain.

In came the three, as gay as could be, chattering and laughing.

"For I have learned to cook porridge," said the cat.

"And I have learned to make beds," said the parrot.

"And I have learned to sweep the floor," said the monkey.

"Then do let us hurry," cried all three, "for we are hungry and sleepy, and the house is very, very dusty."

The cat set to work first, mixed the meal and milk, and

set it over the fire to boil; and it smelled so good they all felt hungrier than ever; but when they came to taste the porridge they found it was burned, and pussy had forgotten the salt.

"Bah! bah!" cried the parrot and monkey, throwing down their spoons in disgust; "you can't cook, and we shall have to go to bed hungry."

"We can't go to our beds either unless you hurry and make them," said the cat, who was vexed at having failed.

So the parrot set to, and tried to spread the clothes on the bed with her beak; but as fast as she pulled them up one side, they slipped off the other, and at last she gave up in despair.

"Oh dear, we shall have to sleep on the floor," cried the other two.

"Then you had better sweep it first," retorted the parrot.

So the monkey took the broom and began to sweep, but only succeeded in raising such a dust that they were nearly blinded, and had to run out of the house and sit on the door-step until it settled.

And they were so discouraged that they cried, and cried, until their tiny handkerchiefs were wet through, and the tears ran down and formed quite a pool in front of the door.

"It's of no use to try and keep house by ourselves," said the monkey; "we shall have to go to some museum and board."

"What! leave our own pretty little house, where we have lived so long," said the cat.

"I'll stay here and starve before I'll go to the old museum," said the parrot. And overcome with grief at the idea of breaking up their happy home they embraced, and sobbed aloud on each other's necks.

Now Filbert had watched all that was going on, and felt very sorry for the little creatures; so as soon as they left the room she slipped out from behind the curtain, and in a few minutes did all they had tried so hard to accomplish, and returned to her hiding-place just as the three came in, saying sadly to one another, "The dust must have settled, so we will try and sleep on the floor and forget how hungry we are; and to-morrow we will go to town again, and try very much harder than we did to-day to learn how to keep house."

But here they stopped short and stared in surprise, for the floor was as clean and bright as a new penny; the little white beds were tucked smoothly up, and on the table smoked three bowls of nice hot porridge.

"What good fairy has been here?" they all exclaimed.

"A nut-brown maiden, nut-brown maiden," chirped a cricket on the hearth.

"And where has she gone?" they asked.

"Behind the curtain, behind the curtain," sang the cricket.

And in a twinkling Filbert was dragged, blushing and trembling, from her hiding-place.

"Who are you, and how came you here?" asked the cat.

"My name is Filbert, and I came in to rest," said the girl, "for I have no friends and no home."

"And can you cook and sweep and sew?" asked the parrot.

"Yes, indeed, and many other things."

"Oh! will you stay and live with us?" asked the monkey.

"What will you give me?" asked Filbert.

"A good home," said the cat.

"Brand-new clothes," said the parrot.

"And a brass, a silver, and a gold penny every week," said the monkey.

So Filbert staid, and was as happy as a bird in the one-eyed house. She sang so cheerfully as she went about her work that things seemed almost to do themselves for her. The monkey watched in admiration whenever she swept the floor, and wondered why there was no dust. They all learned to love her dearly, and were as good as fairy godmothers to her, giving her everything she wished, and her pile of pennies grew so fast that she became quite rich; and, at last, if she had chosen, could have married a prince.

THE present Number closes the first volume of Young People; and we wish to express our great pleasure at the thought that thousands and thousands of children who one year ago were strangers to us are now our little friends, and, we might say, seem to us like one large family. We have done our best to amuse and instruct them, and to make them happy; and by giving them weekly a rich fund of beautiful pictures, stories, poems, and instructive reading, to awaken in them noble thoughts and impulses, a desire for information, and also to teach them to think for themselves.

Through the letters addressed to our Post-office Box we have become acquainted with large numbers of our readers, and feel as much interest in their little enjoyments, their pets, their studies, and their plans for the future as if they were personally known to us.

Our Post-office Box is the most complete department of its kind in existence. We print all the letters we possibly can, and would be glad to print every one if our space allowed, for each contains some pretty bit of child-life which we are sure would be delightful to other little folks. The letters come to us from all parts of the globe—from every corner of the United States and Canada; from England, Germany, France, and Italy; from the West Indies and South America; and even from distant islands far across the sea. It would seem that wherever there are English-speaking children, even in the most remote localities, Young People has found its way to their hearts; and natural and touching, as little folks are, their expressions of delight in their "little paper" are unmistakable.

Our exchange department has developed a fact that is very gratifying; and that is that boys and girls throughout the country are interested in making collections of minerals, pressed flowers and ferns, ocean curiosities, and other specimens of nature's beautiful and perfect handiwork. It affords us much pleasure to bring them into communication with each other for the exchange of their instructive objects, thus cultivating in them a desire for useful information, which, as they grow older, may develop, in many instances, in ways which will lead to a life-long benefit to themselves and others.

It has also afforded us the greatest satisfaction to answer the questions and varied queries of our inquisitive little readers; and except in instances where the answer, were it given correctly, would occupy too much space in our columns, or be too scientific for the comprehension of the youthful querist, we have left but two or three questions to be noticed.

We thank all of our readers most sincerely for the hearty expressions of approval and delight which we have received; and we promise them that the new volume of Young People shall continue to bring them weekly an entertaining and instructive variety of stories and papers by the most popular writers, good puzzles of all kinds, directions for making various articles useful to boys and girls, and a very full and interesting Post-office Box. We are confident that, before the end of the second volume we shall make friends with thousands of little people whose handwriting is still unknown to us.

[illegible]

There are several varieties of birds that lay white eggs speckled with brown. The king-bird's egg has brown blotches on one end, and is speckled all over; the wood-pewee lays a small white egg speckled with brown, the spots forming a ring around one end; the egg of the meadow-lark is long and white, with brown spots on the large end; swallows' eggs are white, covered with brown spots; and other common varieties of birds lay eggs of a similar appearance.

[illegible]

The stamps in the albums of young collectors, if they are genuine issues, have, with but few exceptions, done service on many letters or packages before they find their way to the collector's hands. Unless they are too much defaced by postal marks they form as valuable specimens as if they were new, and are perhaps more interesting. To obtain full collections of new foreign stamps would be difficult and very expensive.

[illegible]

When mounting certain kinds of sea-weeds on to the paper it will be found necessary to cut away, with a sharp, fine-pointed scissors, many superfluous stems and branches, as otherwise the sea-weed when pressed will present a thick appearance, and much of the delicacy be lost.

[illegible]

PUZZLES FROM YOUNG CONTRIBUTORS.

ANSWERS TO PUZZLES IN NO. 48.

Notice.

Now is the Time to Subscribe.

TERMS.

THE BABY-MOUSE.

Oh, rock-a-by, baby-mouse, rock-a-by, so!
When baby's asleep to the baker's I'll go,
And while he's not looking I'll pop from a hole,
And bring to my baby a fresh penny roll.

IMITATION STAINED GLASS.

BY FRANK BELLEW.

A VERY pretty and cheap imitation of stained glass can be made by any one possessing a little ingenuity, a pair of scissors, a few sheets of colored tissue-paper, and a paste-pot, and the humblest cottage window can be made resplendent as those of a cathedral—more or less.

Take a sheet of white or yellow tissue-paper of the exact size of your window-pane, and with some very fine boiled paste paste it thereon. When this is dry, take two sheets of another color, and fold them; then cut from these folded sheets a form like Fig. 1. You will now, on opening them, have two shields, as in Fig. 2. Now paste one of these shields in the centre of your yellow window-pane. When this is perfectly dry, paste the second shield over the first, only a little to one side and lower down, as represented in Fig. 3, and you will have an effect much resembling stained glass. If you choose you can cut out some design from a fourth sheet to resemble a crest—say, the head of a lion—and paste that in the centre of the shield; that should be of some other colored paper.

Fig. 1.

Or, to produce another effect, you may, after first neatly outlining the design with a pencil, cut and scrape away all the paper

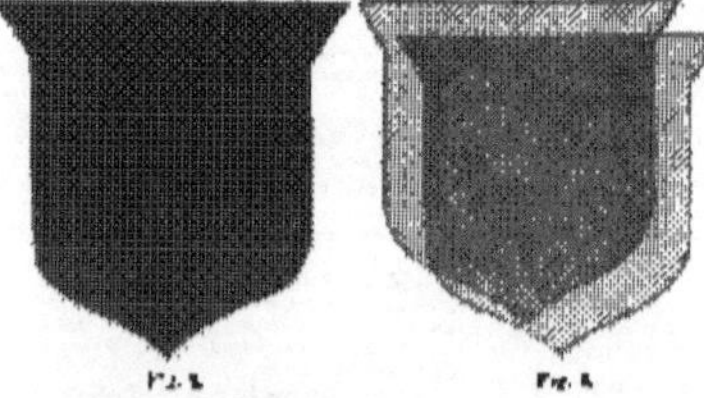

Fig. 2. Fig. 3.

within the limits of the design with a sharp-pointed knife, so as to leave the plain glass, which will have a very pretty effect, particularly if you shade the design on the edges with Indian ink. Or, again, you may fill in this space with some bright contrasting color; say, red on blue, or blue on red.

Fig. 4. Fig. 5.

Of course, in decorating your window, it will be desirable to have a different design on every pane, or at least a great variety. To obtain another and more elaborate form it is only necessary to fold your two sheets of tissue-paper twice, and then cut out, say, a figure like Fig. 4, when, on unfolding it, you will have two patterns like Fig. 5, which will, when pasted over each other, produce a rich effect.

Bravery is of no Nation.—It is admitted on all hands that the Afghans, of whom we are hearing so much just now, fought bravely, and the same as to the Zulus. In Sir Charles James Napier's *History of the Administration in Scinde* there is a story relating to the brave hill-men of Trukker, which is well worth repeating. It was their custom, when their friends fell fighting bravely, face to the foe, to strip them and leave them unburied, but to tie round the right wrist a thread either of green or red. The red thread was the very highest honor that a brave man slain could receive. In the course of one of Sir Charles James Napier's campaigns eleven out of an army of English soldiers lost their way in the mountain gorges, and came "full butt" upon a fort guarded by forty of these formidable mountaineers. The little band of eleven English soldiers at once attacked the fort, and reduced the number of the mountaineers to sixteen. They themselves were all slain, as might be expected. When the English came for the dead bodies of their comrades they found them naked, under the open sky, with a red thread tied round the wrist of every man. The savage hill-men had bestowed upon the corpses of their enemies the highest honor in their code of homage to the brave.

No. 1.—FALL SPORTS.

No. 2.—THE SPORT.

No. 3.—THE FALL.

www.ingramcontent.com/pod-product-compliance
Lightning Source LLC
Chambersburg PA
CBHW020716130726
47899CB00012B/1054
* 9 7 8 3 7 4 2 8 0 2 3 4 7 *